The Works of Mark Twain

VOLUME 10

Pudd'nhead Wilson

T0002728

The Mark Twain Project is an editorial and publishing program of The Bancroft Library, working since 1967 to create a comprehensive critical edition of everything Mark Twain wrote.

This volume is the fourth in that edition to be published simultaneously in print and as an electronic text at http://www.marktwainproject.org.

The following volumes have been published to date by the editors of the Mark Twain Project:

Roughing It
Editors: Harriet Elinor Smith and Edgar Marquess Branch
Associate Editors: Lin Salamo and Robert Pack Browning
1993

Adventures of Huckleberry Finn
Edited by Victor Fischer and Lin Salamo
with the late Walter Blair
2003

Pudd'nhead Wilson: Manuscript and Revised Versions
with "Those Extraordinary Twins"
Edited by Benjamin Griffin
2024

THE MARK TWAIN PAPERS

Letters to His Publishers, 1867–1894
Edited with an introduction by Hamlin Hill
1967

Satires & Burlesques
Edited with an Introduction by Franklin R. Rogers
1967

Which Was the Dream? and Other Symbolic Writings of the Later Years
Edited with an Introduction by John S. Tuckey
1967

Hannibal, Huck & Tom
Edited with an Introduction by Walter Blair
1969

Mysterious Stranger Manuscripts
Edited with an Introduction by William M. Gibson
1969

Correspondence with Henry Huttleston Rogers
Edited with an Introduction by Lewis Leary
1969

Fables of Man
Edited with an Introduction by John S. Tuckey
Text established by Kenneth M. Sanderson and Bernard L. Stein
1972

Notebooks & Journals, Volume I (1855–1873)
Edited by Frederick Anderson, Michael B. Frank, and Kenneth
M. Sanderson
1975

Notebooks & Journals, Volume II (1877–1883)
Edited by Frederick Anderson, Lin Salamo, and Bernard L. Stein
1975

Notebooks & Journals, Volume III (1883–1891)
Edited by Robert Pack Browning, Michael B. Frank, and Lin Salamo
1979

Letters, Volume 1: 1853–1866
Editors: Edgar Marquess Branch, Michael B. Frank, and Kenneth M. Sanderson
Associate Editors: Harriet Elinor Smith, Lin Salamo, and Richard Bucci
1988

Letters, Volume 2: 1867–1868
Editors: Harriet Elinor Smith and Richard Bucci
Associate Editor: Lin Salamo
1990

Letters, Volume 3: 1869
Editors: Victor Fischer and Michael B. Frank
Associate Editor: Dahlia Armon
1992

Letters, Volume 4: 1870–1871
Editors: Victor Fischer and Michael B. Frank
Associate Editor: Lin Salamo
1995

Letters, Volume 5: 1872–1873
Edited by Lin Salamo and Harriet Elinor Smith
1997

Letters, Volume 6: 1874–1875
Editors: Michael B. Frank and Harriet Elinor Smith
2002

Autobiography of Mark Twain, Volume 1
Edited by Harriet Elinor Smith
2010

Autobiography of Mark Twain, Volume 2
Edited by Benjamin Griffin and Harriet Elinor Smith
2013

Autobiography of Mark Twain, Volume 3
Edited by Benjamin Griffin and Harriet Elinor Smith
2015

THE MARK TWAIN LIBRARY

No. 44, The Mysterious Stranger
Edited by John S. Tuckey and William M. Gibson
1982

The Adventures of Tom Sawyer
Edited by John C. Gerber and Paul Baender
1983

Tom Sawyer Abroad • Tom Sawyer, Detective
Foreword and notes by John C. Gerber; text established
by Terry Firkins
1983

The Prince and the Pauper
Edited by Victor Fischer and Michael B. Frank
1983

A Connecticut Yankee in King Arthur's Court
Edited by Bernard L. Stein
1984

Adventures of Huckleberry Finn
Edited by Walter Blair and Victor Fischer
1985

*Huck Finn and Tom Sawyer among the Indians, and Other
Unfinished Stories*
Foreword and Notes by Dahlia Armon and Walter Blair
Texts established by Dahlia Armon, Paul Baender,
Walter Blair, William M. Gibson, and Franklin R. Rogers
1989

Roughing It
Editors: Harriet Elinor Smith and Edgar Marquess Branch
Associate Editors: Lin Salamo and Robert Pack Browning
1996

Adventures of Huckleberry Finn
Edited by Victor Fischer and Lin Salamo,
with Harriet Elinor Smith and the late Walter Blair
2001

OTHER MARK TWAIN PROJECT PUBLICATIONS

Is He Dead? A Comedy in Three Acts
Edited with a foreword, afterword, and notes by Shelley Fisher Fishkin;
Text established by the Mark Twain Project
2003

*Mark Twain's Helpful Hints for Good Living:
A Handbook for the Damned Human Race*
Edited by Lin Salamo, Victor Fischer, and Michael B. Frank
2004

Mark Twain's Book of Animals
Edited with an introduction, afterword, and notes by Shelley Fisher Fishkin
Texts established by the Mark Twain Project
2009

Who Is Mark Twain?
Edited by Robert H. Hirst
2009

Dear Mark Twain: Letters from His Readers
Edited by R. Kent Rasmussen, with foreword by Ron Powers
Texts established by the Mark Twain Project
2013

A Family Sketch and Other Private Writings
by Mark Twain, Livy Clemens, and Susy Clemens
Edited by Benjamin Griffin
2014

Mark Twain's Civil War: The Private History of a Campaign That Failed
Edited by Benjamin Griffin
2019

THE WORKS OF MARK TWAIN

Robert H. Hirst, General Editor

Board of Directors for the Mark Twain Project

Frederick C. Crews
Kate Donovan
Jeffrey MacKie-Mason
Michael Millgate
Eric Schmidt
George A. Starr
G. Thomas Tanselle

Contributing Editors for This Volume

Blake Bronson-Bartlett
Lisa Cardyn
Kerry Driscoll
Harriet Elinor Smith

Mark Twain, about 1891. Photograph taken in Hartford by Normand Smith. Mark Twain House and Museum, Hartford, Connecticut.

Pudd'nhead Wilson

MANUSCRIPT AND REVISED VERSIONS
WITH "THOSE EXTRAORDINARY TWINS"

Mark Twain

Edited by Benjamin Griffin

UNIVERSITY OF CALIFORNIA PRESS

University of California Press
Oakland, California

All texts by Mark Twain in *Pudd'nhead Wilson: Manuscript and Revised Versions, with "Those Extraordinary Twins"* have been published previously, under contract with the Mark Twain Foundation, in the Mark Twain Project's *Microfilm Edition of Mark Twain's Literary Manuscripts Available in the Mark Twain Papers, The Bancroft Library, University of California Berkeley* (Berkeley: The Bancroft Library, 2001). Texts by Mark Twain first published in that microfilm copyright © 2001 by the Mark Twain Foundation. Passages first published in Daniel Morley McKeithan, *The Morgan Manuscript of Mark Twain's Pudd'nhead Wilson* (Cambridge, Mass.: Harvard University Press, 1961) and in *Pudd'nhead Wilson and Those Extraordinary Twins: A Norton Critical Edition,* edited by Sidney E. Berger (New York: W. W. Norton and Co., 1980), copyright © 1961, © 1980 by the Mark Twain Foundation. The Mark Twain Foundation expressly reserves to itself, its successors and assigns, all rights in every medium, including without limitation stage, radio, television, motion picture, and public reading rights, in and to texts in copyright to the Mark Twain Foundation. Transcription, reconstruction, and creation of the texts, introduction, notes, and appendixes copyright © 2024 by The Regents of the University of California.

MARK TWAIN PROJECT® is a registered trademark of The Regents of the University of California in the United States and the European Community.

Library of Congress Cataloging-in-Publication Data

Names: Twain, Mark, 1835-1910, author. | Griffin, Benjamin, 1968- editor. |
 Twain, Mark, 1835-1910. Pudd'nhead Wilson. | Twain, Mark, 1835-1910.
 Those extraordinary twins. | Twain, Mark, 1835-1910. Works. 1972 ; v. 10.
Title: Pudd'nhead Wilson : manuscript and revised versions with Those
 extraordinary twins / Mark Twain ; edited by Benjamin Griffin.
Description: Oakland, California : University of California Press, [2024] | Series:
 The works of Mark Twain ; volume 10 | Includes bibliographical references.
Identifiers: LCCN 2023024873 (print) | ISBN 9780520398092 (cloth) |
 ISBN 9780520398108 (paperback) | ISBN 9780520398115 (pdf)
Subjects: LCSH: Twain, Mark, 1835-1910. Pudd'nhead Wilson—History and
 criticism. | Twain, Mark, 1835-1910. Those extraordinary twins—History
 and criticism. | Infants switched at birth—Fiction. | Passing (Identity)—
 Fiction. | Trials (Murder)—Fiction. | Race relations—Fiction.
Classification: LCC PS1317.A2 .G75 2024 (print) | LCC PS1317.A2 (ebook) |
 DDC 813/.4—dc23/eng/20230720
LC record available at https://lccn.loc.gov/2023024873
LC ebook record available at https://lccn.loc.gov/2023024874

Manufactured in the United States of America

33 32 31 30 29 28 27 26 25 24
10 9 8 7 6 5 4 3 2 1

Editorial work for this volume has been supported
by a generous gift to the Mark Twain Project of
The Bancroft Library from

SHELBY GANS

and by matching and outright grants from

THE NATIONAL ENDOWMENT
FOR THE HUMANITIES:
Democracy demands wisdom.

This volume could not have been produced
without their generous support.

CONTENTS

ABOUT THE TEXTS IN THIS VOLUME

Three critically established texts are published in this edition—two discrete versions of *Pudd'nhead Wilson: A Tale* and one offshoot from it:

- The "Morgan Manuscript" version (PW-MS), transcribed from the holograph manuscript in the Morgan Library and Museum, being the novel as Mark Twain originally completed and intended to publish it in January 1893;
- The "Revised" version of the novel (PW-REV), which Mark Twain revised in July 1893, submitted for magazine serialization, and published in book form in 1894; and
- *Those Extraordinary Twins* (EXT), Mark Twain's selection of passages removed from his text in the course of the 1893 revision, with commentary by him, including his own account of the novel's genesis.

The Introduction to this volume (pages 511–98) collects the historical evidence for the tortuous history of these texts; the Note on the Texts (pages 600–613) sets forth the editor's use of that evidence in constructing the critical editions. This foreword previews that history and briefly explains the rationale for publishing multiple versions.

The Morgan Manuscript, never before published in full, is placed first in the volume, in keeping with the chronology of composition. It may be felt that since Mark Twain did not publish this form of the novel, it ought to be treated as "prepublication" material, perhaps relegated to an appendix or the textual apparatus; is it not (one may reasonably ask) superseded by the published version, which presumably embodied his final intentions? In fact, the case is not so simple, for Mark Twain completed *Pudd'nhead Wilson* to his satisfaction not once but twice.

The first form, completed in January 1892, was the Morgan Manuscript—itself already the product of several major revisions. Its original, farcical theme—a story of aristocratic Italian conjoined twins in pre–Civil War Missouri—had been augmented with murder-mystery and detective elements, and with the character of Roxy, the mixed-race enslaved woman who switches her own infant son with her enslaver's. Mark Twain, then living in Italy, had the finished Morgan Manuscript typed and sent to the office of Charles L. Webster and Co., the publishing house of which he was the principal owner. But doubts were raised (what doubts, and whose, is uncertain), and publication was postponed.

In July 1893, Mark Twain extensively revised his typed copy of the novel for serialization in a magazine. The main object of this revision was to separate the conjoined twins, making them merely identical twins, expatriate aristocrats, and thereby promote the centrality of Roxy and her son Tom. Mark Twain jettisoned the many passages which had depended on the twins' connectedness, greatly shortening the book. The revision was quick and slapdash, introducing glaring narrative flaws which went uncorrected and which cannot be understood without reference to the original manuscript.

Moreover, when Mark Twain submitted his revision for magazine publication, he lost a large measure of control over his novel. The text that appeared in the *Century Magazine* (1893–94) was extensively altered by the magazine editors. Mark Twain opposed these alterations, but could do little to prevent them. He intended to publish *Pudd'nhead Wilson* as a book through Webster and Co.; this would have allowed him to obviate the magazine's changes. But Webster and Co. went bankrupt, and by the time a contract with the American Publishing Company of Hartford had been made, Mark Twain was in Europe, with little power to affect the course of publication. The first editions in book form, published in Hartford and London at the end of 1894, reproduced the *Century Magazine* text, with its many unauthorized changes.

Taking all this into account, we concluded that the most useful course is to provide the text in its two major forms (and one minor form), arranged in the order in which they were created. These texts are still aimed at the author's final intention—with the added proviso that an author may bring his work to "completion" more than once. The Morgan Manuscript is presented in a reading text, such as might have been produced by an uncommonly scrupulous printing house of the period; the manuscript is presented complete, with all its internal revisions, deletions, and irregularities transcribed in its Textual Apparatus. The Revised *Pudd'nhead Wilson* is a critical reconstruction that aims, wherever possible, to undo the *Century Magazine*'s changes and reconstitute the text as it stood in the author's revised typescript, the now lost document that he put before the *Century* printers. Its spelling and punctuation, which were drastically altered by the magazine, are restored from the manuscript, and instances of probable censorship are reversed. Finally, *Those Extraordinary Twins* is presented, again in a version purged, so far as the documentary record will allow, of unauthorized accretions. Each of the three texts has its own set of explanatory notes; this involves the repetition of annotation wherever two texts share an identical passage, but this has been deemed preferable to extensive cross-referencing.

Our flexible application of final authorial intention offers these texts as discrete versions. No aesthetic or cultural priority is asserted for any one of them. Our aim is rather to let today's readers study the successive versions—historical phases of an evolving text—and come to their own conclusions.

ABBREVIATIONS USED IN THIS VOLUME

The edited texts, Explanatory Notes, and Textual Apparatus of the three texts in the present edition are referred to by abbreviations in small capitals:

PW-MS *Pudd'nhead Wilson: A Tale.* The Morgan Manuscript Version. Text on pages 1–201.

PW-REV *Pudd'nhead Wilson: A Tale.* The Revised Version. Text on pages 213–350.

EXT *Those Extraordinary Twins: A Postscript to "Pudd'nhead Wilson."* Text on pages 351–411.

The original documents produced by Mark Twain and his typists and printers have abbreviations in roman type. Extant documents are described more fully in Description of Source Documents (pages 617–21). Nonextant documents, marked below with asterisks, are discussed in the Introduction and the Note on the Texts.

MS Berg The Berg Manuscript. "Those Extraordinary Twins." Henry W. and Albert A. Berg Collection, New York Public Library.

MS Morgan The Morgan Manuscript. "Pudd'nhead Wilson: A Tale." Pierpont Morgan Library and Museum, New York.

MS in CU-MARK This abbreviation is used for various manuscript fragments in the Mark Twain Papers, The Bancroft Library, University of California at Berkeley.

TS1	Typescript 1. Typed transcription of MS Berg, incorporated into MS Morgan.
*TS2	Typescript 2. Typed transcription of MS Morgan (including TS1). Revised by Mark Twain into TS2a and TS2b. Not extant.
*TS2a	Typescript 2a. Pages from TS2, revised by Mark Twain to form printer's copy for *Pudd'nhead Wilson* in the *Century Magazine* (Cent). Not extant.
*TS2b	Typescript 2b. TS2 pages excluded from TS2a, revised by Mark Twain to form printer's copy for *Those Extraordinary Twins* in the American Publishing Company volume (A). Not extant.
Cent	The *Century Magazine* serial *Pudd'nhead Wilson*, published December 1893–June 1894.
A	*The Tragedy of Pudd'nhead Wilson and the Comedy Those Extraordinary Twins* (Hartford: American Publishing Company, 1894).
Apf	Proof copies of A, held at the Library of Congress and the Houghton Library, Harvard University.
E	*Pudd'nhead Wilson: A Tale* (London: Chatto and Windus, 1894).

Expansions of abbreviations for the names of libraries, bibliographical references, and Clemens family members are found in the References (pages 821–36).

OFFENSIVE LANGUAGE IN *PUDD'NHEAD WILSON*

Readers encountering these texts for the first time will find that Mark Twain has his characters invoke racial stereotypes and use racially loaded language which he knew could be offensive and hurtful—including the word that the journalist Farai Chideya has called the "nuclear bomb" of racial epithets.[1] That word occurs 165 times in these texts. Its frequent appearance, however, does not mean that Mark Twain was unaware of, or insensitive to, its depreciatory sense.

His story is set in the border state of Missouri and begins some thirty years before the Emancipation Proclamation, exactly the time and place where the author himself grew up, in a family that sometimes owned or rented enslaved people. "Training is everything," as Pudd'nhead Wilson says; "training is all there is *to* a person," says the Connecticut Yankee. That training for Samuel Clemens was indubitably racist, but long before he wrote this novel, he had rejected its premises, even if he did not entirely overcome its impact. Still, as he wrote in the "Explanatory" to *Huckleberry Finn*, he replicated the speech of that time and place, both Black and white, not "by guesswork; but pains-takingly, and with the trustworthy guidance and support of personal familiarity with these several forms of speech." So it is fair to presume that his characters in *Pudd'nhead Wilson* speak and act the way they do in large part because that is how their real counterparts spoke and acted.

Also, Mark Twain makes very telling discriminations in the *ways* he lets his characters use the N-word. In representing direct speech, his characters use it when referring to Black people or people of mixed racial heritage. They

---

1. Quoted in Randall Kennedy, *Nigger: The Strange Career of a Troublesome Word* (Kennedy 2022), 22.

do so whether they themselves are Black or white, whether their intent is thoughtlessly habitual (Constable Blake and Justice Robinson), openly rancorous (Tom and Roxy), or even, on occasion, playful (Roxy joking with Jasper). The word appears where Mark Twain paraphrases the speech, or reports the unspoken thoughts, of some of the characters; sometimes within quotation marks to reinforce the point that the offensive word is *not* the author's choice but the character's. By contrast, when Mark Twain speaks as the narrator, he uses "negro" or "colored," never the N-word—a small but sure sign that he was aware of, and sought to distance himself from, that word's vulgar, often vicious, connotations.

More generally, the emotional valence of the word, as well as who has permission to say it and/or be offended by it, has changed over time, so that accurately construing its use in a fiction written more than a hundred years ago is challenging. In 1893 the editors of the *Century Magazine* registered no objection to the word in Mark Twain's text, suggesting that they did not regard it as offensive to their (largely white) audience, at least not in the context he gave to it. Decades earlier, in 1837, the minister Hosea Easton, who was of mixed race, had publicly denounced the N-word as "an opprobrious term, employed to impose contempt upon [Black people] as an inferior race."[2] This judgment would be endorsed by a growing number of Americans, Black and white. In 1862, Thomas Wentworth Higginson, the white commander of the first regiment of emancipated Black soldiers in the Union army, was personally offended by it and shocked at the frequency of its use by his Black troops: "This offensive word ... is almost as common with them as at the North, and far more common than with well-bred slaveholders."[3] Around the time Mark Twain was writing *Pudd'nhead Wilson,* the editors of the *Century Dictionary* (1889–91) observed that even though the slur was "formerly and to some extent still is used without opprobrious intent ... its use is now confined to colloquial or illiterate speech, in which it generally conveys more or less of contempt."[4] And a century later, lexicographers of American slang demonstrated, by extensive examples, that "the high degree of offensiveness attached to this term *per se,* particularly in the discourse of

2. Hosea Easton, *A Treatise on the Intellectual Character, and Civil and Political Condition of the Colored People of the U. States: and the Prejudice Exercised Towards Them* (1837), quoted in Kennedy 2022, 5.

3. Thomas Wentworth Higginson, *Army Life in a Black Regiment* (Higginson 1870), 28; entry dated 16 December 1862.

4. *The Century Dictionary* (Whitney and Smith 1889–91), 4:3989.

whites, has increased markedly over time, perhaps especially during the twentieth century."[5] Debate over the slur has only grown more contentious in the present century.

Finally, it is clear that Mark Twain recognized, well ahead of his time, that the very concept of race was socially constructed—"a fiction of law and custom," as he puts it, early in the novel—not based in any meaningful way on "blood." This is at the ethical and moral center of the tale, and it functions as a sort of lens, focusing our attention on the limitations of his characters and their culture. It is also worth noting that there is an added dimension to the pervasive use of racially offensive language, beyond mere historical accuracy. When his characters use the N-word, Mark Twain means to evoke the burden of contempt as it was embedded in the routine language of his time, and to exhibit the racism on which it was based—something today's readers are even more likely to feel, provided they are able to endure utterance of the N-word in the first place. We honor that intention by reproducing the words Mark Twain wrote.

B. G.

5. *Random House Historical Dictionary of American Slang* (*HDAS*), 2:656–57; abbreviations expanded.

ACKNOWLEDGMENTS

Work on this edition of *Pudd'nhead Wilson* has enjoyed truly exceptional support over half a dozen years. Our first thanks must go to the American taxpayers, who have persisted for half a century in funding the National Endowment for the Humanities (NEH). The Endowment has in turn, for its whole existence, generously supported editorial scholarship on Mark Twain and many other American authors, creating in the process a profound body of work but also a deep reservoir of experience and expertise, without which editions like this one could hardly exist. During work on *Pudd'nhead Wilson* the Mark Twain Project has received from NEH multiple grants of outright funds and matching funds, which have in turn elicited a stream of matching gifts from individuals and institutions, only some of which we have space to mention below. For all that vital, indispensable support we are deeply grateful.

We thank the following donors, as well as several who prefer to remain anonymous, for major, sustaining gifts to the Mark Twain Project:

Mr. James Barter
Bob M. Clarke and Carol Kavanagh Clarke
Lester E. and Mary Stephens DeWall
The Renée B. Fisher Foundation
Ann and David Flinn
Robin G. and Peter B. Frazier
Shelby Gans
Drs. Susan K. and William J. Harris
The Estate of Mr. Harold Holbrook
The Mark Twain Foundation
Roger and Jeane Samuelsen

Alison and Thomas Schneider
UC Berkeley Class of 1958
Jeanne Bailard Ware
Sheila Wishek

We also thank all members of the Mark Twain Luncheon Club, whose individual annual contributions together make up another major contribution. The Club was conceived and founded by Robert Middlekauff, Ira Michael Heyman, and Watson M. ("Mac") Laetsch, and it flourished for twenty years while they lived. It remains our constant supporter, now in the hands of their friend and successor, Roger Samuelsen. And we must not fail to mention here that relief from indirect costs on our several NEH grants has been given multiple times by the Berkeley campus, for which we are inexpressibly grateful.

We are fortunate to carry on our work in the library of the University of California, Berkeley. Especially during the closures imposed by the COVID-19 pandemic, the institution's response to the emergency, a model of sane but thorough restrictions, still made essential resources available remotely. Our thanks go to Jeffrey MacKie-Mason, University Librarian; Elaine Tennant, the James D. Hart Director of The Bancroft Library while this work was being done, and her successor, Kate Donovan, as it is being completed; Peter E. Hanff, the longtime Deputy Director of The Bancroft Library, now retired; and Melissa Martin, administrative officer. All gave their unstinting support.

In gathering materials for the texts and annotation we have drawn on an array of libraries and private collections, which we wish to acknowledge and thank here. The Morgan Library and Museum, New York, gave access to the manuscript of *Pudd'nhead Wilson*, and curator Philip S. Palmer gave permission to reproduce several pages in photofacsimile. At the New York Public Library, curator Carolyn Vega made available the manuscript in the Berg Collection, and granted permission to reproduce one page. The Houghton Library, Harvard University, and the Library of Congress supplied scans of the two American Publishing Company proof copies. Samantha Baxter did research in the Chatto and Windus archive at the University of Reading, providing invaluable images of the publisher's ledgers and correspondence. At still other libraries we have had the friendly assistance of David Whitesell, Albert and Shirley Small Special Collections Library, University of Virginia; Kyle R. Triplett, New York Public Library;

Jennifer Miglus, Librarian of the Hartford Medical Society; Mallory Howard, the Mark Twain House and Museum; and the staffs of the Beinecke Rare Book and Manuscript Library at Yale University; and the California Historical Society, San Francisco. Kevin Mac Donnell and Angelo Cifaldi both brought to light rare, previously unknown documents and gave permission to reproduce them in this volume. Ann M. Ryan generously shared invaluable digital images.

Steven Olsen-Smith, of Boise State University, Idaho, examined the volume on behalf of the Center for Scholarly Editions (CSE) of the Modern Language Association. We are grateful to him for the exemplary depth and rigor of his inspection and his many useful suggestions for improving the result, and to the CSE for its help in providing genuine peer review for this edition.

At UC Press we have greatly benefited from the wise guidance of our sponsoring editor, Eric Schmidt; the skill and efficiency of our production editor, Jeff Anderson; the sterling contributions of designer Lia Tjandra; and the comprehensive copy-editing of Amy Smith Bell.

Finally, thanks are due to my colleagues at the Mark Twain Project: Blake Bronson-Bartlett, Lisa Cardyn, Terry Catapano, Kerry Driscoll, and Harriet Elinor Smith. Their ready help and keen insight on matters textual, historical, political, and literary kept me on track when I was straying, and opened new tracks where I was stalled. We have also had invaluable editorial assistance from Takuya Kubo, an honorary member of the Project, who provided us with his digital transcriptions of MS Berg and MS Morgan. A team of student assistants from UC Berkeley—Hyeona Park, Gunnar Rice, and Tulasi Johnson—verified transcriptions and helped to check the collations. Last but far from least, associate editor Michael B. Frank, now retired, will recognize two footnotes in Appendix C, prepared by him sometime in the mid-1970s (on a manual typewriter of uncertain vintage) for an edition of Mark Twain's Notebook 32, still in progress.

B. G.

Pudd'nhead Wilson: A Tale

THE MORGAN MANUSCRIPT VERSION

Pudd'nhead Wilson

A TALE

By Mark Twain

There is no character, howsoever good and fine, but it can be destroyed by ridicule, howsoever poor and witless. Observe the ass, for instance: his character is about perfect, he is the choicest spirit among all the humbler animals, yet see what ridicule has brought him to. Instead of feeling complimented when we are called an ass, we are left in doubt.—*Pudd'nhead Wilson's Calendar.*

Note Concerning the Legal Points

A person who is ignorant of legal matters is always liable to make mistakes when he tries to photograph a court scene with his pen; and so, I was not willing to let the law-chapters in this book go to press without first subjecting them to rigid and exhausting revision and correction by a trained barrister—if that is what they are called. Those chapters are right, now, in every detail, for they were re-written under the immediate eye of William Hicks, who studied law part of a while in south-west Missouri thirty-five years ago and then came over here for his health and is still helping for exercise and board in Maccaroni and Vermicelli's horse-feed shed which is up the back alley as you turn around the corner out of the Piazza del Duomo just beyond the house where that stone that Dante used to sit on six hundred years ago is let into the wall when he let on to be watching them build Giotto's Campanile and yet always got tired looking as soon as Beatrice passed along on her way to get a chunk of chestnut-cake to defend herself with in case of a Ghibelline attack before she got to school, at the same old stand where they sell the same old cake to this day and it is just as light and good as it was then, too, and this is not flattery. He was a little rusty on his law, but he rubbed up for this book, and those two or three legal chapters are right and straight, now, he told me so himself.

Given under my hand this second day of January, 1893, at the Villa Viviani, village of Settignano, two miles back of Florence, on the hills—the same certainly affording the most charming view to be found on this planet, and with it the most dream-like and enchanting sunsets to be found in any planet or even in any solar system—and given, too in the swell room of the house, with the busts of Cerretani senators and other grandees of this line looking approvingly down upon me as they used to look down upon Dante, and mutely asking me to adopt them into my family, which I do with pleasure, for my remotest ancestors are but spring chickens compared with these robed and stately antiques, and it will be a great and satisfying lift for me, that six hundred years will.

Mark Twain.

Chapter 1

The scene of this chronicle is the town of Dawson's Landing, on the Missouri side of the Mississippi, half a day's journey, per steamboat, below St. Louis.

In 1830 it was a snug little collection of modest one and two-story "frame" dwellings whose whitewashed exteriors were almost concealed from sight by climbing tangles of rose vines, honeysuckles and morning-glories. Each of these pretty homes had a garden in front fenced with white palings and opulently stocked with hollyhocks, marigolds, touch-me-nots, prince's feathers and other old-fashioned flowers; while on the window-sills of the houses stood wooden boxes containing moss-rose plants, and terra cotta pots in which grew a breed of geranium whose spread of intensely red blossoms accented the prevailing pink tint of the rose-clad house-front like an explosion of flame. When there was room on the ledge outside of the pots and boxes for a cat, the cat was there—in sunny weather—stretched at full length, asleep and blissful, with her furry belly to the sun and a paw curved over her nose. Then that home was complete, and its contentment and peace made manifest to the world by this symbol, whose testimony is infallible. A home without a cat—and a well fed, well petted, and properly revered cat—may be a perfect home, perhaps, but how can it prove title?

All along the streets, on both sides, at the outer edge of the brick sidewalks, stood locust trees, with trunks protected by wooden boxing, and these furnished shade for summer and a sweet fragrance in spring when the clusters of buds came forth. The main street, one block back from the river, and running parallel with it, was the sole business street. It was six blocks long, and in each block two or three brick stores three stories high towered above interjected bunches of little frame shops. Swinging signs creaked in the wind, the street's whole length. The candy-striped pole which indicates nobility proud and ancient, along the palace-bordered canals of Venice, indicated merely the humble barber shop along the main street of Dawson's Landing. On a chief corner stood a lofty unpainted pole wreathed from top to bottom with tin pots and pans and cups, the chief tin-monger's noisy notice to the world (when the wind blew), that his shop was on hand for business at that corner.

The hamlet's front was washed by the clear waters of the great river; its body stretched itself rearward up a gentle incline; its most rearward border fringed itself out and scattered its houses about the base line of the hills; the hills rose high, enclosing the town in a half-moon curve, clothed with forests from foot to summit.

Steamboats passed up and down every hour or so. Those belonging to the little Cairo line and the little Memphis line always stopped; the big New Orleans and Cincinnati and Louisville liners stopped for hails only, or to land passengers or freight; and this was the case also with the great flotilla of "transients." These latter came out of a dozen rivers—the Illinois, the Missouri, the Upper Mississippi, the Ohio, the Monongahela, the Tennessee, the Red river, the White river, and so on; and were bound everywhither and stocked with every imaginable comfort or necessity which the Mississippi's communities could want, from the frosty Falls of St. Anthony down through nine climates to torrid New Orleans.

Dawson's Landing was a slave-holding town, with a rich slave-worked grain and pork country back of it. The town was sleepy, and comfortable, and contented. It was fifty years old, and was growing slowly—very slowly, in fact, but still it was growing.

The chief citizen was York Leicester Driscoll, about forty years old, Judge of the county court. He was very proud of his old Virginian ancestry, and in his hospitalities and his rather formal and stately manners he kept up its traditions. He was fine, and just, and generous. To be a gentleman—a gentleman without stain or blemish—was his only religion, and to it he was always faithful. He was respected, esteemed, and beloved by all the community. He was well off, and was gradually adding to his store. He and his wife were very nearly happy, but not quite, for they had no children. The longing for the treasure of a child had grown stronger and stronger as the years slipped away, but the blessing never came—and was never to come.

With this pair lived the Judge's widowed sister, Mrs. Rachel Pratt, and she also was childless—childless, and sorrowful for that reason, and not to be comforted. The women were good and commonplace people, and did their duty and had their reward in clear consciences and the community's approbation. They were Presbyterians, the Judge was a freethinker.

Pembroke Howard, lawyer and bachelor, aged about forty, was another old Virginian grandee with proved descent from the First Families. He was a fine, brave, majestic creature, a gentleman according to the nicest require-ments of the Virginian rule, a devoted Presbyterian, an authority on the "code," and a man always courteously ready to stand up before you in the field if any act or word of his had seemed doubtful or suspicious to you, and explain it with any weapon you might prefer, from brad-awls to artillery. He was very popular with the people, and was the Judge's dearest friend.

Then there was Colonel Cecil Burleigh Essex, another F.F.V. of formidable calibre—however, with him we have no concern.

Percy Northumberland Driscoll, brother to the Judge, and younger than he by five years, was a married man, and had had children around his hearth-stone; but they were attacked in detail by measles, croup and scarlet fever, and this had given the doctor a chance with his effective antediluvian methods; so the cradles were empty. He was a prosperous man, with a good head for speculations, and his fortune was growing. On the first of February, 1830, two boy babes were born in his house: one to him, the other to one of his slave girls, Roxana by name. Roxana was twenty years old. She was up and around the same day, with her hands full, for she was tending both babies.

Mrs. Percy Driscoll died within the week. Roxy remained in charge of the children. She had her own way, for Mr. Driscoll soon absorbed himself in his speculations and left her to her own devices.

In that same month of February Dawson's Landing gained a new citizen. This was Mr. David Wilson, a young fellow of Scotch parentage. He had wandered to this remote region from his birth-place in the interior of the State of New York, to seek his fortune. He was twenty-five years old, college-bred, and had finished a post-college course in an eastern law school a couple of years before.

He was a homely, freckled, sandy-haired young fellow, with an intelligent blue eye that had frankness and comradeship in it and a covert twinkle of a pleasant sort. But for an unfortunate remark of his, he would no doubt have entered at once upon a successful career at Dawson's Landing. But he made his fatal remark the first day he spent in the village, and it "gauged" him. He had just made the acquaintance of a group of citizens when an invisible dog began to yelp and snarl and howl and make himself very comprehensively disagreeable; whereupon he said, much as one who is think-ing aloud—

"I wish I owned half of that dog."

"Why?" somebody asked.

"Because, I would kill my half."

The group searched his face with curiosity, with anxiety even, but found no light there, no expression that they could read. They fell away from him as from something uncanny, and went into privacy to discuss him. One said—

"'Pears to be a fool."

"'*Pears*," said another, "*is*, I reckon you better say."

"Said he wished he owned *half* of the dog, the idiot," said a third. "What did he reckon would become of the other half if he killed his half? Do you reckon he thought it would live?"

"Why, he must have thought it, unless he *is* the downrightest fool in the world; because if he hadn't thought that, he would have wanted to own the whole dog, knowing that if he killed his half and the other half died, he would be responsible for that half just the same as if he had killed that half instead of his own. Don't it look that way to you, gents?"

"Yes, it does. If he owned one half of the general dog, it would be so; if he owned one end of the dog and another person owned the other end, it would be so, just the same; particularly in the first case, because if you kill one half of a general dog, there ain't any man that can tell whose half it was, but if he owned one end of the dog, maybe he could kill his end of it and—"

"No, he couldn't, either; he couldn't and not be responsible if the other end died, which it would. In my opinion the man ain't in his right mind."

"In my opinion he hain't *got* any mind."

No. 3 said—

"Well, he's a lummux, anyway."

"That's what he is," said No. 4, "he's a labrick—just a simon-pure labrick, if ever there was one."

"Yes, sir, he's a dam fool, that's the way *I* put him up," said No. 5. "Anybody can think different that wants to, but those are my sentiments."

"I'm with you, gentlemen," said No. 6. "Perfect jackass—yes, and it ain't going too far to say he is a pudd'nhead. If he ain't a pudd'nhead, I ain't no judge, that's all."

Mr. Wilson stood elected. The incident was told all over the town, and gravely discussed by everybody. Within a week he had lost his first name; Pudd'nhead took its place. In time he came to be liked, and well liked, too; but by that time the nickname had got well stuck on, and it stayed. That first day's verdict made him a fool, and he was not able to get it set aside, or even modified. The nickname soon ceased to carry any harsh or unfriendly feeling with it, but it held its place, and was to continue to hold its place for twenty long years.

Chapter 2

Adam was but human—this explains it all. He did not want the apple for the apple's sake, he only wanted it because it was forbidden. The mistake was in not forbidding the serpent; then he would have eaten the serpent.—Pudd'nhead Wilson's Calendar.

Pudd'nhead Wilson had a trifle of money, and he bought a small house on the extreme western verge of the town. Between it and Judge Driscoll's house there was only a grassy yard, with a paling fence dividing the properties in the middle. He hired a small office down in the town and hung out a tin sign with these words on it:

DAVID WILSON
Attorney and Counselor at Law.
Surveying, Conveyancing, etc.

But his deadly remark had ruined his chance—at least in the law. No clients came. He took down his sign, after a while, and put it up on his own house with the law features knocked out of it. It offered his services now in the humble capacities of land surveyor and expert accountant. Now and then he got a job of surveying to do, and now and then a merchant got him to straighten out his books. With Scotch patience and pluck he resolved to live down his reputation and work his way into the legal field yet. Poor fellow, he could not foresee that it was going to take him twenty years to do it.

He had a rich abundance of idle time, but it never hung heavy on his hands, for he interested himself in every new thing that was born in the universe of ideas, and studied it and experimented upon it at his house. One of his pet fads was palmistry. To another one he gave no name, neither would he explain to anybody what its purpose was, but merely said it was an amusement. In fact he had found that his fads added to his reputation as a pudd'nhead; therefore he was growing chary of being too communicative about them. The fad without a name, was one which dealt with people's finger-marks. He carried in his coat pocket a shallow box with grooves in it, and in the grooves strips of glass five inches long and three inches wide. Along the lower edge of each strip was pasted a slip of white paper. He asked people to pass their hands through their hair, (thus collecting upon them a thin coating of the natural oil,) and then make a thumb-mark on a glass strip, following it with the mark of the ball of each finger in succession. Under this row of faint grease-prints he would write a record on the strip of white paper—thus:

"JOHN SMITH, *right hand*"—

and add the day of the month and the year, then take Smith's left hand on another glass strip, and add name and date and the words "left hand." The strips were now returned to the grooved box, and took their place among what Wilson called his "records."

He often studied his records, examining and poring over them with absorbing interest until far into the night; but what he found there—if he found anything—he revealed to no one. Sometimes he copied on paper the involved and delicate pattern left by the ball of a finger, and then vastly enlarged it with a pantagraph so that he could examine its web of curving lines with ease and convenience.

One sweltering afternoon—it was the first day of July, 1830—he was at work over a set of tangled account books in his work-room, which looked westward over a stretch of vacant lots, when a conversation outside disturbed him. It was carried on in yells, which showed that the people engaged in it were not close together:

"Say, Roxy, how does yo' baby come on?" This from the distant voice.

"Fust rate; how does *you* come on, Jasper?" This yell was from close by.

"Oh, I's middlin'; hain't got noth'n to complain of. I'm gwyne to come a court'n you bimeby, Roxy."

"*You* is, you black mud-cat! Yah-yah-yah! I got sump'n better to do den 'sociat'n wid niggers as black as you is. Has ole Miss Cooper's Nancy done give you de mitten?" Roxy followed this sally with another discharge of care-free laughter.

"You's jealous, Roxy, dat's what's de matter wid *you*, you huzzy—yah-yah-yah! Dat's de time I got you!"

"Oh, yes, *you* got me, hain't you! 'Clah to goodness if dat conceit o' yo'n strikes in, Jasper, it gwyne to kill you, sho'. If you b'longed to me I'd sell you down de river 'fo' you git too fur gone. Fust time I runs acrost yo' marster, I's gwyne to tell him so."

This idle and aimless jabber went on and on, both parties enjoying the good-natured duel and each well satisfied with his own share of the wit exchanged—for wit they considered it.

Wilson stepped to the window to observe the combatants; he could not work while their chatter continued. Over in the vacant lots was Jasper, young, coal-black and of magnificent build, sitting on a wheelbarrow in the pelting sun—at work, supposably, whereas he was in fact only preparing for it by taking an hour's rest before beginning. In front of Wilson's porch stood Roxy, with a local hand-made baby-wagon, in which sat her two charges—one at each end and facing each other. From Roxy's manner of speech, a stranger would have expected her to be black, but she was not. Only one-sixteenth of her was black, and that sixteenth did not show. She was of majestic form and stature, her attitudes were imposing and statuesque, and her gestures and movements distinguished by a noble and stately grace. Her complexion was very fair, with the rosy glow of vigorous health in the cheeks, her face was full of character and expression, her eyes were brown and liquid, and she had a heavy suit of fine soft hair which was also brown, but the fact was not apparent because her head was bound about with a checkered handkerchief and the hair was concealed under it. Her face was shapely, intelligent, and comely—perhaps even beautiful. She had an easy, independent carriage—when she was among her own caste—and a high and "sassy" way, withal; but of course she was meek and humble enough where white folks were.

To all intents and purposes Roxy was as white as anybody, but the one-sixteenth of her which was black out-voted the other fifteen parts and made her a negro. She was a slave, and salable as such. Her child was thirty-one parts white, and he, too, was a slave, and by a fiction of law and custom a negro. He had blue eyes and flaxen curls, like his white comrade, but even the father of the white child was able to tell the children apart—little as he had commerce with them—by their clothes: for the white babe wore ruffled soft muslin and a coral necklace, while the other kid wore merely a coarse tow-linen shirt which barely reached to its knees, and no jewelry.

The white child's name was Thomas à Becket Driscoll, the other's name was Valet de Chambre: no surname—slaves hadn't the privilege. Roxana had heard that phrase somewhere, the fine sound of it had pleased her ear, and as she had supposed it was a name, she loaded it onto her darling. It soon got shortened to "Chambers," of course.

Wilson knew Roxy by sight, and when the duel of wit began to play out, he stepped outside to gather-in a record or two. Jasper went to work energetically, at once—perceiving that his leisure was observed. Wilson inspected the children and asked—

"How old are they, Roxy?"

"Bofe de same age, sir—five months. Bawn de fust o' Febuary."

"They're handsome little chaps. One's just as handsome as the other, too."

A delighted smile exposed the girl's white teeth, and she said:

"Bless yo' soul, Misto Wilson, it's pow'ful nice o' you to say dat, caze one of 'em ain't on'y a nigger. Mighty prime little nigger, *I* allays says, but dat's caze it's mine, o' course."

"How do you tell them apart, Roxy, when they haven't any clothes on?"

Roxy laughed a laugh proportioned to her size, and said:

"Oh, *I* kin tell 'em 'part, Misto Wilson, but I bet Marse Percy couldn't, not to save his life."

Wilson chatted along for a while, and presently got Roxy's finger-prints for his collection—right hand and left—on a couple of his glass strips; then labeled and dated them, and took the "records" of both children, and labeled and dated them also.

Two months later, on the third of September, he took this trio of finger-marks again. He liked to have a "series"—two or three "takings" at intervals during the period of childhood, these to be followed by others at intervals of several years.

The next day—that is to say, on the fourth of September,—something occurred which profoundly impressed Roxana. Mr. Driscoll missed another small sum of money—which is a way of saying that this was not a new thing, but had happened before. In truth it had happened three times before. Driscoll's patience was exhausted. He was a fairly humane man, toward slaves and other animals; he was an exceedingly humane man toward the erring of his own race. Theft he could not abide, and plainly there was a thief in his house. Necessarily the thief must be one of his negroes. Sharp measures must be taken. He called his servants before him. There were three of these, besides Roxy: a man, a woman, and a boy twelve years old. They were not related. Mr. Driscoll said:

"You have all been warned before. It has done no good. This time I will teach you a lesson. I will sell the thief! Which of you is the guilty one?"

They all shuddered at the threat, for here they had a good home, and a new one was likely to be a change for the worse. The denial was general. None had stolen anything—not money, anyway—a little sugar, or cake, or honey, or something like that, that "Marse Percy wouldn't mind or miss," but not money—never a cent of money. They were eloquent in their protestations, but Mr. Driscoll was not moved by them. He answered each in turn with a stern "Name the thief!"

The truth was, all were guilty but Roxana; she suspected that the others were guilty, but she did not know them to be so. She was horrified to think how near she had come to being guilty herself; she was saved in the nick of time by a revival in the colored Methodist church a fortnight before, at which time and place she "got religion." The very next day after that gracious experience, while her change of style was fresh upon her and she was vain of her purified condition, her master left a couple of dollars lying unprotected on his desk, and she happened upon that temptation when she was polishing around with a dust-rag. She looked at the money a while with a steadily rising resentment, then she burst out with—

"Dad blame dat revival, I wisht it had a ben put off till tomorrow!"

Then she covered the tempter with a book, and another member of the kitchen cabinet got it. She made this sacrifice as a matter of religious etiquette; as a thing necessary just now, but by no means to be wrested into a precedent; no, a week or two would limber up her piety, then she would be rational again, and the next two dollars that got left out in the cold would find a comforter—and she could name the comforter.

Was she bad? Was she worse than the general run of her race? No. They had an unfair show in the battle of life, and they held it no sin to take military advantage of the enemy—in a small way; in a small way, but not in a large one. They would smouch provisions from the pantry whenever they got a chance; or a brass thimble, or a cake of wax, or an emery-bag, or a paper of needles, or a silver spoon, or a dollar bill, or small articles of clothing, or any other property of light value; and so far were they from considering such reprisals sinful, that they would go to church and shout and pray their loudest and sincerest with their plunder in their pockets. A farm smoke-house had to be kept heavily padlocked, for even the colored deacon himself could not resist a ham when Providence showed him in a dream, or otherwise, where such a thing hung lonesome and longed for some one to love. But with a hundred hanging before him the deacon would not take two—that is, on the same night. On frosty nights the humane negro prowler would warm the end of a plank and put it up under the cold claws of chickens roosting in a tree; a drowsy hen would step onto the comfortable board, softly clucking her gratitude, and the prowler would dump her into his bag, and later into his stomach, perfectly sure that in taking this trifle from the man who daily robbed him of an inestimable treasure—his liberty—he was not committing any sin that God would remember against him in the Last Great Day.

"Name the thief!"

For the fourth time Mr. Driscoll had said it, and always in the same hard tone. And now he added these words of awful import:

"I give you one minute"—he took out his watch—"if at the end of that time you have not confessed, I will not only sell all four of you, *but*—I will sell you *down the river!*"

It was equivalent to condemning them to hell! No Missouri negro doubted this. Roxy reeled in her tracks and the color vanished out of her face; the others dropped to their knees as if they had been shot; tears gushed from their eyes, their supplicating hands went up, and three answers came in the one instant:

"I done it!"

"I done it!"

"I done it—have mercy, marster—Lord have mercy on us po' niggers!"

"Very good," said the master, putting up his watch, "I will sell you here, though you don't deserve it. You ought to be sold down the river."

The culprits flung themselves prone, in an ecstasy of gratitude, and kissed his feet, declaring they would never forget his goodness and never cease to pray for him as long as they lived. They were sincere, for like a god he had stretched forth his mighty hand and closed the gates of hell against them. He knew, himself, that he had done a noble and gracious thing, and he was privately well pleased with his magnanimity; and that night he set the incident down in his diary, so that his son might read it in after years and be thereby moved to deeds of gentleness and humanity himself.

Chapter 3

Whoever has lived long enough to find out what life is, knows how deep a debt of gratitude we owe to Adam, the first great benefactor of our race. He brought death into the world.
—*Pudd'nhead Wilson's Calendar.*

Percy Driscoll slept well the night he saved his house-minions from going down the river, but no wink of sleep visited Roxy's eyes. A profound terror had taken possession of her. Her child could grow up and be sold down the river! The thought crazed her with horror. If she dozed, and lost herself for a moment, the next moment she was on her feet and flying to her child's cradle to see if it was still there. Then she would gather it to her heart and pour out her love upon it in a frenzy of kisses, moaning and crying, and saying "Dey shan't, oh, dey *shan't!*—yo' po' mammy will kill you fust!"

Once, when she was tucking it back in its cradle again, the other child nestled in its sleep and attracted her attention. She went and stood over it a long time, communing with herself:

"What has my po' baby done, dat he couldn't have yo' luck? He hain't done noth'n. God was good to you; why warn't He good to him? Dey can't sell you down de river. I hates yo' pappy; he ain't got no heart—for niggers he hain't, anyways. I hates him, en I could kill him!" She paused a while, thinking; then she burst into wild sobbings again, and turned away, saying, "Oh, I got to kill my chile, dey ain't no yuther way!—killin' *him* wouldn't save de chile fum goin' down de river. Oh, I got to do it, yo' po' mammy's *got* to kill you to save you, honey"—she gathered her baby to her bosom, now, and began to smother it with caresses—"mammy's got to kill you,—how *kin* I do it! But yo' mammy ain't gwyne to desert you!—no, no; *dah*, don't cry—she gwyne *wid* you, she gwyne to kill herself, too. Come along, honey, come along wid mammy; we gwyne to jump in de river, den de troubles o' dis worl' is all over—dey don't sell po' niggers down de river over *yonder!*"

She started toward the door, crooning to the child and hushing it. She caught sight of her new Sunday gown—a cheap curtain-calico thing, a conflagration of gaudy colors and fantastic figures. She surveyed it wistfully, longingly.

"Hain't ever wore it yit," she said, "en it's jist lovely. . . ." Then she nodded her head in response to a pleasant idea, and added, "No, I ain't gwyne to be fished out, wid everybody lookin' at me, in dis misable ole linsey-woolsey."

She put down the child and made the change. She looked in the glass and was astonished at her beauty. She resolved to make her death-toilet perfect. She took off her handkerchief-turban and dressed her glossy wealth of hair "like white folks;" she added some odds and ends of pretty loud ribbon and a spray of atrocious artificial flowers; finally, she threw over her shoulders a fluffy thing called a "cloud" in that day, which was of a blazing red complexion, then she was ready for the tomb.

She gathered up her baby once more; but when her eye fell upon its miserably short little gray tow-linen shirt and noted the contrast between its pauper shabbiness and her own volcanic irruption of infernal splendors, her mother-heart was touched, and she was ashamed.

"No, dolling, mammy ain't gwyne to treat you so. De angels is gwyne to 'mire you jist as much as dey does yo' mammy. Ain't gwyne to have 'em putt'n dey han's up 'fo' dey eyes en sayin' to David en Goliah en dem yuther prophets, Dat chile is dress' too indelicate for dis place."

By this time she had stripped off the shirt. Now she clothed the naked little creature in one of Thomas à Becket's snowy long baby-gowns, with its bright blue bows and dainty flummery of ruffles.

"Dah—now you's fixed." She propped the child in a chair and stood off to inspect it. Her eyes began to widen with astonishment and admiration, and she clapped her hands and cried out, "Why, it do beat all—I *never* knowed you was so lovely! Marse Tommy ain't a bit puttier—not a single bit!"

She stepped over and glanced at the other infant; she flung a glance back at her own; then one more at the heir of the house. Now a strange light dawned in her eyes, and in a moment she was lost in thought. She seemed in a trance; when she came out of it she muttered, "When I 'uz a washin' 'em in de tub, yistiddy, his own pappy asked me which of 'em was his'n!"

She began to move about like one in a dream. She undressed Thomas à Becket, stripping him of everything, and put the tow-linen shirt on him. She put his coral necklace on her own child's neck. Then she placed the children side by side, and after earnest inspection she muttered—

"Now who would b'lieve clo'es could do de like o' dat? Dog my cats if it ain't all *I* kin do to tell t'other fum which, let alone his pappy."

She put her cub in Tommy's elegant cradle and said—

"You's young Marse *Tom* fum dis out, en I got to practice and git used to 'memberin' to call you dat, honey, or I's gwyne to make a mistake some time en git us bofe into trouble. Dah—now you lay still en don't fret no mo', Marse Tom—oh, thank de good Lord in heaven, you's saved, you's saved!—dey ain't no man kin ever sell mammy's po' little honey down de river now!"

She put the heir of the house in her own child's unpainted pine cradle, and said, contemplating its slumbering form uneasily—

"I's sorry for you, honey; I's sorry, God knows I is!—but what *kin* I do, what *could* I do? Yo' pappy would sell him to somebody, some time, en den he'd go down de river, sho', en I couldn't, couldn't, *couldn't* stan' it!"

She flung herself on her bed, and began to think and toss, toss and think. By and by she sat suddenly upright, for a comforting thought had flown through her worried mind—

"'Tain't no sin—*white* folks has done it! It ain't no sin, glory to goodness it ain't no sin! *Dey's* done it—yes, en dey was de biggest quality in de whole bilin', too—*kings!*"

She began to muse; she was trying to gather out of her memory the dim particulars of some tale she had heard some time or other. At last she said—

"Now I's got it; now I 'member. It was dat ole nigger preacher dat tole it, de time he come over here fum Illinois en preached in de nigger church. He said dey ain't nobody kin save his own self—can't do it by faith, can't do it by works, can't do it no way at all. Free grace is de *on'y* way, en dat don't come fum nobody but jis' de Lord; en *He* kin give it to anybody He please, saint or sinner—*He* don't k'yer. He do jis' as He's a mineter. He s'lect out anybody dat suit Him, en put another one in his place, en make de fust one happy forever en leave t'other one to suffer. De preacher said it was jist like dey done in Englan' one time, long time ago. De queen she lef' her baby layin' aroun' one day, en went out callin'; en one o' de niggers roun' 'bout de place dat was mos' white, she come in en see de chile layin' aroun', en tuck en put her own chile's clo'es on de queen's chile, en put de queen's chile's clo'es on her own chile, en den lef' her own chile layin' aroun' en tuck en toted de queen's chile home to de nigger quarter, en nobody ever foun' it out, en her chile was de king, bimeby, en sole de queen's chile down de river one time when dey had a auction to settle up de estate. Dah, now—de preacher said it his own self, en it ain't no sin, caze white folks done it. *Dey* done it—yes, *dey* done it; en not on'y jis' common white folks, nuther, but de biggest quality dey is in de whole bilin'! Oh, I's *so* glad I 'member 'bout dat!"

She got up light-hearted and happy, and went to the cradles and spent what was left of the night "practicing." She would give her own child a light pat and say, humbly, "Lay still, Marse Tom," then give the real Tom a pat and say with severity, "Lay *still*, Chambers!—does you want me to take sump'n *to* you?"

As she progressed with her practice, she was surprised to see how steadily and surely the awe which had kept her tongue reverent and her manner humble toward her young master was transferring itself to her speech and manner toward the usurper, and how similarly handy she was becoming in transferring her motherly curtness of speech and peremptoriness of manner to the unlucky heir of the ancient house of Driscoll.

She took occasional rests from practicing, and absorbed herself in calculating her chances.

"Dey'll sell dese niggers to-day for stealin' de money, den dey'll buy some mo' dat don't know de chillen—so *dat's* all right. When I takes de chillen out to git de air, de minute I's roun' de corner I's gwyne to gaum dey mouths all aroun' wid jam, den dey can't *nobody* notice dey's changed. Yes, I gwineter do dat till I's safe, if it takes a year.

"Dey ain't but one man dat I's afeard of, en dat's dat Pudd'nhead Wilson. Dey calls him a pudd'nhead, en says he's a fool. My lan', dat man ain't no mo' fool den I is! He's de smartes' man in dis town, less'n it's Jedge Driscoll, or maybe Pem. Howard. Blame dat man, he worries me wid dem ornery glasses o' his'n; *I* b'lieve he's a witch. But nemmine, I's gwyne to happen aroun' dah one o' dese days en let on dat I reckon he wants to print de chillen's fingers agin; en if *he* don't notice dey's changed, I boun' dey ain't nobody gwyne to notice it, en den I's safe, *sho'*. But I reckon I'll tote along a hoss-shoe to keep off de witch-work."

The new negroes gave Roxy no trouble, of course. The master gave her none, for one of his speculations was in jeopardy, and his mind was so occupied that he hardly saw the children when he looked at them, and all Roxy had to do was to get them both into a gale of laughter when he came about; then their faces were mainly cavities exposing gums, and he was gone again before the spasm passed and the little creatures resumed a human aspect.

Within a few days the fate of the speculation became so dubious that Mr. Percy went away with his brother the Judge to see what could be done with it. It was a land speculation, as usual, and it had gotten complicated with a lawsuit. The men were gone seven weeks. Before they got back Roxy had paid her visit to Wilson, and was satisfied. Wilson took the finger-prints, labeled them with the names and with the date—October the first—put them carefully away, and continued his chat with Roxy, who seemed very anxious that he should admire the great advance in flesh and beauty which the babies had made since he took their finger-prints a month before. He complimented their improvement to her contentment; and as they were without any disguise of jam or other stain, she trembled all the while and was miserably frightened lest at any moment he—

But he didn't. He discovered nothing; and she went home jubilant, and dropped all concern about this matter permanently out of her mind.

Chapter 4

Adam and Eve had many advantages, but the principal one was, that they escaped teething.—*Pudd'nhead Wilson's Calendar.*

There is this trouble about special providences, that there is so often a doubt as to which party was intended to be the beneficiary. In the case of the children, the bears and the prophet, the bears got more real satisfaction out of the episode than the prophet did, because they got the children.—*Pudd'nhead Wilson's Calendar.*

This history must henceforth accommodate itself to the change which Roxana has consummated, and call the real heir "Chambers" and the usurping little slave "Thomas à Becket"—shortening this latter name to "Tom," for daily use, as the people about him did.

"Tom" was a bad baby, from the very beginning of his usurpation. He would cry for nothing; he would burst into storms of devilish temper without notice, and let go scream after scream and squall after squall, then climax the thing with "holding his breath"—that frightful specialty of the teething nursling, in the throes of which the creature exhausts its lungs, then is convulsed with noiseless squirmings and twistings and kickings in the effort to get its breath, while the lips turn blue and the mouth stands wide and rigid, offering for inspection one wee tooth set in the lower rim of a hoop of red gums; and when the appalling stillness has endured until one is sure the lost breath will never return, a nurse comes flying and dashes water in the child's face, and—presto! the lungs fill, and instantly discharge a shriek, or a yell, or a howl which bursts the listening ear and surprises the owner of it into saying words which would not go well with a halo if he had one. The baby Tom would claw anybody who came within reach of his nails, and pound anybody he could reach with his rattle. He would scream for water until he got it, and then throw cup and all on the floor and scream for more. He was indulged in all his caprices, howsoever troublesome and exasperating they might be; he was allowed to eat anything he wanted, particularly things that would give him the stomach ache; consequently he was hiccuppy beyond reason and a singularly flatulent child.

When he got to be old enough to begin to toddle about, and say broken words, and get an idea of what his hands were for, he was a more consummate pest than ever. Roxy got no rest while he was awake. He would call for anything and everything he saw, simply saying "Awnt it" (want it), which was a command. When it was brought, he said, in a frenzy, and motioning it away with his hands, "Don't awnt it! don't awnt it!" and the moment it was gone he set up frantic yells of "Awnt it! awnt it! awnt it!" and Roxy had to give wings to her heels to get that thing back to him again before he could get time to carry out his intention of going into convulsions about it.

What he preferred above all other things was the tongs. This was because his father had forbidden him to have them lest he break windows and furniture with them. The moment Roxy's back was turned he would toddle to the presence of the tongs and say, "*Like* it!" and cock his eye to one side to see if Roxy was observing; then, "*Awnt* it!" and cock his eye again; then, "*Hab* it!" with another furtive glance; and finally, "*Take* it!"—and the prize was his. The next moment the heavy implement was raised aloft; the next, there was a crash and a squall, and the cat was off, on three legs, to meet an engagement; Roxy was flying, by now, and would arrive just as the lamp or a window went to irremediable smash.

Tom got all the petting, Chambers got none. Tom got all the delicacies going, Chambers got mush and milk, and clabber without sugar. By consequence, Tom was a sickly child and Chambers wasn't. Tom was "fractious," as Roxy called it, and overbearing, Chambers was meek and docile.

With all her splendid common sense and practical every-day ability, Roxy was a doting fool of a mother. She was this toward her child—and she was also more than this: by the fiction created by herself, he was become her master; the necessity of recognizing this relation outwardly and of perfecting herself in the forms required to express the recognition, had moved her to such diligence and faithfulness in practicing these forms that this exercise soon concreted itself into habit; it became automatic and unconscious; then a natural result followed: deceptions intended solely for others gradually grew practically into self-deceptions as well; the mock reverence became real reverence, the mock obsequiousness real obsequiousness, the mock homage real homage; the little counterfeit rift of separation between imitation-slave and imitation-master widened and widened, and became an abyss, and a very real one—and on one side of it stood Roxy, the dupe of her own deceptions, and on the other stood her child, no longer a usurper to her, but her accepted and recognized master.

He was her darling, her master, and her deity, all in one, and in her worship of him she forgot who she was and what he had been.

In babyhood Tom cuffed and banged and scratched Chambers unrebuked, and Chambers early learned that as between meekly bearing it and resenting it the advantage all lay with the former policy. The few times that his persecutions had moved him beyond control and made him fight back had cost him very dear at headquarters; not at the hands of Roxy, for if she ever went beyond scolding him sharply for "fogitt'n who his young marster was," she at least never extended her punishment beyond a box on the ear. No, Percy Driscoll was the party. He told Chambers that under no provocation whatever was he privileged to lift his hand against his little master. Chambers overstepped the line three times, and got three such convincing canings from the man who was his father and didn't know it, that he took Tom's cruelties in all humility after that, and made no more experiments.

Outside of the house the two boys were together, all through their boyhood. Chambers was strong beyond his years, and a good fighter; strong because he was coarsely fed and hard worked about the house, and a good fighter because Tom furnished him plenty of practice—on white boys whom he hated and was afraid of. Chambers was his constant body-guard, to and from school; he was present on the play-ground at recess to protect his charge. He fought himself into such a formidable reputation, by and by, that Tom could have put on his clothes and "ridden in peace," like Sir Kay in Launcelot's armor.

He was good at games of skill, too. Tom staked him with marbles to play "keeps" with, and then took all the winnings away from him. In the winter season Chambers was on hand, in Tom's worn-out clothes, with "holy" red mittens, and "holy" shoes, and pants "holy" at the knees, to drag a sled up the hill for Tom, warmly clad, to ride down on; but he never got a ride himself. He built snow men and snow fortifications under Tom's direction. He was Tom's patient target when Tom wanted to do some snow-balling, but the target couldn't fire back. Chambers carried Tom's skates to the river and strapped them on him, then trotted around after him on the ice, so as to be on hand when wanted; but he wasn't ever asked to try the skates himself.

In summer the pet pastime of the boys of Dawson's Landing was to steal apples, peaches and melons from the farmers' fruit wagons,—mainly on account of the risk they ran of getting their heads laid open with the butt of the farmer's whip. Tom was a distinguished adept at these thefts—by proxy. Chambers did his stealing, and got the peach stones, apple cores and melon rinds for his share.

Tom always made Chambers go in swimming with him, and stay by him as a protection. When Tom had had enough, he would slip out and tie knots in Chambers's shirt, dip the knots in the water to make them hard to undo, then dress himself and sit by and laugh while the naked shiverer tugged at the stubborn knots with his teeth.

Tom did his humble comrade these various ill turns partly out of native viciousness, and partly because he hated him for his superiorities of physique and pluck, and for his manifold clevernesses. Tom couldn't dive, for it gave him splitting headaches. Chambers could dive without inconvenience, and was fond of doing it. He excited so much admiration, one day, among the crowd of white boys, by throwing back-summersaults from the stern of a canoe that it wearied Tom's spirit, and at last he shoved the canoe underneath Chambers while he was in the air—so he came down on his head in the canoe's bottom; and while he lay unconscious several of Tom's ancient adversaries saw that their long-desired opportunity was come, and they gave the false heir such a drubbing that with Chambers's best help he was hardly able to drag himself home afterward.

When the boys were fifteen and upwards, Tom was "showing off" in the river one day, when he was taken with a cramp, and shouted for help. It was a common trick with the boys—particularly if a stranger was present—to pretend a cramp and yell for help; then when the stranger came tearing hand-over-hand to the rescue, the howler would go on struggling and howling till he was close at hand, then replace the howl with a sarcastic smile and swim blandly away, while the town-boys assailed the dupe with a volley of jeers and laughter. Tom had never tried this joke as yet, but was supposed to be trying it now, so the boys held warily back; but Chambers believed his master was in earnest, therefore he swam out and arrived in time, unfortunately, and saved his life.

This was the last feather. Tom had managed to endure everything else, but to have to remain publicly and permanently under such an obligation as this to a nigger, and to *this* nigger of all niggers—this was too much. He heaped insults upon Chambers for "pretending" to think he was in earnest in calling for help, and said that anybody but a blockheaded nigger would have known he was funning and left him alone.

Tom's enemies were in strong force here, so they came out with their opinions quite freely. They laughed at him, and called him coward, liar, sneak, and other sorts of pet names, and told him they meant to always call Chambers by a new name after this, and make it common in the town—"Tom Driscoll's Nigger-pappy"—to signify that he had had a second birth into this life, and that Chambers was the author of his new being. Tom grew frantic under these taunts, and shouted—

"Knock their heads off, Chambers, knock their heads off!—what do you stand there with your hands in your pockets, for?"

Chambers expostulated, and said—

"But Marse Tom, dey's too many of 'em—dey's—"

"Do you *hear* me?"

"Please, Marse Tom, don't make me. Dey's so many of 'em dat—"

Tom sprang at him and drove his pocket knife into him two or three times before the boys could snatch him away and give the wounded lad a chance to escape. He was considerably hurt, but not seriously. If the blade had been a little longer his career would have ended there.

Tom had long ago taught Roxy "her place." It had been many a day, now, since she had ventured a caress or a fondling epithet in his quarter. Such things, from a "nigger," were repulsive to him, and she had been warned to keep her distance and remember who she was. She saw her darling gradually cease from being her son, she saw that detail perish utterly; all that was left was master—master, pure and simple, and it was not a gentle mastership, either. She saw herself sink from the sublime height of motherhood to the sombre deeps of unmodified slavery. The abyss of separation between her and her boy was complete. She was merely his chattel, now, his convenience, his dog, his cringing and helpless slave, the humble and unresisting victim of his capricious temper and vicious nature.

Sometimes she could not go to sleep, even when worn out with fatigue, because her rage boiled so high over the day's experiences with her boy. She would mumble and mutter to herself—

"He struck me, en I warn't no way to blame—struck me in de face, right before folks. En he's allays callin' me nigger wench, en hussy, en all dem mean names, when I's doin' de very bes' I kin. O, Lord, I done so much for him—I lift' him away up to whar he is—en dis is what I git for it!"

Sometimes when some outrage of peculiar offensiveness stung her to the heart, she would plan schemes of vengeance, and revel in the fancied spectacle of his exposure to the world as an impostor and a slave; but in the midst of these joys fear would strike her: she had made him too strong; she could prove nothing, and—heavens, she might get sold down the river for her pains! So her schemes always went for nothing, and she laid them aside in impotent rage against the fates, and against herself for playing the fool on that fatal September day in not providing herself with a witness for use in the day when such a thing might be needed for the appeasing of her vengeance-hungry heart.

And yet the moment Tom happened to be good to her, and kind—and this occurred every now and then—all her sore places were healed and she was happy; happy and proud, for this was her son, her nigger son, lording it among the whites and securely avenging their crimes against her race.

There were two grand funerals in Dawson's Landing that fall—the fall of 1845. One was Colonel Cecil Burleigh Essex's, the other was Percy Driscoll's.

On his death-bed Driscoll set Roxy free and delivered his idolized ostensible son solemnly into the keeping of his brother the Judge and his wife. Those childless people were glad to get him. Childless people are not difficult to please.

Judge Driscoll had gone privately to his brother, a month before, and bought Chambers. He had heard that Tom had been trying to get his father to sell the boy down the river, and he wanted to prevent the scandal—for public sentiment did not approve of that way of treating family servants for light cause or for no cause.

Percy Driscoll had worn himself out in trying to save his great speculative landed estate, and had died without succeeding. He was hardly in his grave before the boom collapsed and left his hitherto envied young devil of an heir a pauper. But that was nothing; his uncle told him he should be his heir and have all his fortune when he died; so Tom was comforted.

Roxy had no home, now; so she resolved to go around and say good-bye to her friends and then clear out and see the world—that is to say, she would go chambermaid on a steamboat, the darling ambition of her race and sex.

Her last call was on the black giant, Jasper. She found him chopping Pudd'nhead Wilson's winter provision of wood. She had remained a Methodist ever since she first "got religion" and lost two dollars by it; she was a most capable hymn-singer, for she had the rich and sweet and pathetic voice so common to the race which she accepted as hers; she was the best shouter in the "amen corner," and if she wasn't a tough customer in a theological argument, she at least thought she was. Jasper was a Dunker Baptist. He had a pretty robust opinion of his own powers in argument, and was fond of meeting Roxy in that field; consequently the theological fur was quite sure to fly whenever they came together. A chief bone of contention between them was the matter of special providences; they had gnawed it till there was no vestige of meat left on it, but that was no matter, they found it as toothsome without meat as with it. Jasper believed in special providences, Roxy didn't. She believed that whatever happened in this world happened in obedience to a body of well regulated general laws, and that these laws were never set aside by sudden caprice to wet some saint's wilting crop or drown some sinner who went a fishing on the Sabbath.

Three days before Roxy's visit, Jasper was tramping up the "Bluff road," among the hills back of the town. It was a heavy pull, and when he reached what was called Precipice Corner he sat down and hung his heels over the abyss and prepared himself for a rest and a smoke. At his right was a stretch of road as straight as a lance and pretty steep; where he sat, this road made an exceedingly abrupt elbow; between the sheer precipice on the one side and the cut wall of the hill on the other there was not room for two wagons to pass. Whoever drove down the stretch of straight road must turn that elbow cautiously if he would turn it safely.

Presently Jasper heard a noise above him, and glanced up and saw a cloud of gray dust flying down the straight road toward him. It was moving so swiftly that he thought it must be a whirlwind. He jumped up to observe it. But it wasn't a whirlwind.

"By gracious it's somebody's hoss runnin' away wid him! If he whirls round dis corner at dat gait, somebody got to climb down in de valley en gether him up in a basket."

He took a position, spat in his hands and gave himself a shake as a kind of notice to his vast strength to get ready for business. He was not able to furnish the particulars of what happened after that. He only knew that the next instant the flying horse was upon him and that he grabbed him and stood him upon his hind heels in the air!

Then the dust settled and he had a great and glad surprise, for he saw his young mistress, with her nurse and baby, sitting in the buggy. Jasper led the horse around the elbow and went to examining the harness to see if it was all right. The occupants of the buggy got out, and thought they would walk back to their summer home on the hill for a change of sensations. When the lady turned the elbow she saw her father and mother and the house servants grouped on the precipice and trying to look over; and all were moaning and wailing and ejaculating. The family, standing on the porch, had seen the horse begin to run when he left the gate, and they and the negroes had followed on foot, in the wake of a flight which none imagined could end otherwise than in destruction at the precipice.

"Father, we are not hurt!" The father turned dreamily and incredulously about, at the sound of this voice which he had supposed would never comfort his ear again in this life, and saw his daughter standing unharmed before him, delivered, he knew not by what miracle, from the very grave itself.

There was nothing but wild embracings and incoherent exclamations of gratitude for a little while, then the father said—

"But how was it done? What is the explanation of it?"

"Jasper happened to be here, and he seized the horse and stopped him."

"That is not possible. No man could do it; ten couldn't. The town will never believe it."

"But Jasper did it, and I saw him."

Jasper was called, and came humbly, with his hat in his hand. His master said—

"Jasper, there is nothing that I can say now—I am too much moved, too much broken up to put rational speech together; but another time—another time I will try to thank you. Put on your hat. Freemen stand covered in each other's presence in the open air; and you are free, from this hour."

For three days Jasper had been a freedman, a hero, and the talk of the town. He was "laying for" Roxy, all loaded and primed and ready with an argument which he judged would silence her guns for one while, anyway.

Wilson was chatting with him when Roxy arrived. He asked her how she could bear to go off chambermaiding and leave her boys; and chaffingly offered to copy off a series of their finger-prints, reaching down to their twelfth year, for her to remember them by; but she sobered in a moment, wondering if he suspected anything; then she said she believed she didn't want them. Wilson said to himself, "The drop of black blood in her is superstitious; she thinks there's some deviltry, some witch-business, about my glass mystery somewhere; she used to come here with an old horseshoe in her hand; it could have been an accident, but I doubt it." He wished her prosperity and a safe return, and turned away, saying—

"You want to modify that highflyer attitude of yours, Roxy, and take your knuckles out of your hips: Jasper's a free citizen and a hero, now, and you must stop putting on airs around him."

The theologians answered with a laugh apiece, and the arguments began to fly. As the fencing went on, Jasper began to lead warily up to his heroic episode; then he set forth the situation: he had to be on that hill, and at that exact spot, at that precise moment of time to the fraction of a minute, or those people's death was an absolutely unpreventable thing. Then he shook a victorious finger in Roxy's face and shouted:

"Dah, now! Dey ain't no special providences, hain't dey? *Who put me dah?*—aha, you answer me dat!"

Roxy's return-blast was instant and disabling:

"Who sent de *hoss* dah in dat shape, you chucklehead? Answer me *dat!*"

Chapter 5

Training is everything. The peach was once a bitter almond, cauliflower is nothing but cabbage with a college education. —*Pudd'nhead Wilson's Calendar.*

Remark of Dr. Baldwin concerning upstarts: We don't care to eat toadstools that think they are truffles.—*Pudd'nhead Wilson's Calendar.*

Mrs. York Driscoll enjoyed two years of bliss with that prize, Tom; bliss that was troubled a little at times, it is true, but bliss nevertheless; then she died, and her husband and his childless sister, Mrs. Pratt, continued the bliss-business at the old stand. Tom was petted and indulged and spoiled to his entire content—or nearly that. This went on till he was nineteen, then he was sent to Yale. He went handsomely equipped with "conditions," but otherwise he was not an object of distinction there. He remained at Yale two years, and then threw up the struggle. He came home with his manners a good deal improved; he had lost his surliness and brusqueness, and was rather pleasantly soft and smooth, now; he was furtively, and sometimes openly, ironical of speech, and given to gently touching people on the raw, but he did it with a good-natured semi-conscious air that carried it off safely and kept him from getting into trouble. He was as indolent as ever, and showed no very strenuous desire to hunt up an occupation. People argued from this that he preferred to be supported by his uncle until his uncle's shoes should become vacant. He brought back one or two new habits with him, one of which he practiced—tippling—but concealed another, which was gambling. It would not do to gamble where his uncle could hear of it; he knew that quite well.

Tom's eastern polish was not popular among the young people. They could have endured it, perhaps, if Tom had stopped there; but he wore gloves, and that they *couldn't* stand, and wouldn't; so he was mainly without society. He brought home with him a suit of clothes of such exquisite style and cut and fashion—eastern fashion, city fashion—that it filled everybody with anguish and was regarded as a peculiarly wanton affront. He enjoyed the feeling which he was exciting, and paraded the town serene and happy all day; but the young fellows set a tailor to work that night, and when he started out on his parade next morning he found the old deformed negro bell-ringer straddling along in his wake tricked out in a flamboyant curtain-calico exaggeration of his finery, and imitating his fancy eastern graces as well as he could.

Tom surrendered, and clothed himself after the local fashion after that. But the dull country town was tiresome to him, since his acquaintanceship with livelier regions, and it grew daily more and more so. He began to make little trips to St. Louis for refreshment. There he found companionship to suit him, and pleasures to his taste, along with more freedom, in some particulars, than he could have at home. So, during the next two years his visits to the city grew in frequency and his tarryings there grew steadily longer in duration.

He was getting into deep waters. He was taking chances, privately, which might get him into trouble some day—in fact, did.

Judge Driscoll had retired from the Bench and from all business activities in 1850, and had now been comfortably idle three years. He was President of the Freethinkers' Society, and Pudd'nhead Wilson was the other member. The Society's weekly discussions were the old lawyer's main interest in life, now. Pudd'nhead was still toiling in obscurity at the bottom of the ladder, under the blight of that unlucky remark which he had let fall twenty-three years before.

Judge Driscoll was his friend, and claimed that he had a mind above the average, but that was regarded as one of the Judge's whims, and it failed to modify the public opinion. Or, rather, that was one of the reasons why it failed, but there was another and better one. If the Judge had stopped with bare assertion, it would have had a good deal of effect; but he made the mistake of trying to prove his position. For some years Wilson had been privately at work on a whimsical almanac, for his amusement—a calendar, with a little dab of ostensible philosophy, usually in ironical form, appended to each date; and the Judge thought that these quips and fancies of Wilson's were neatly turned and cute; so he carried a handful of them around, one day, and read them to some of the chief citizens. But irony was not for those people; their mental vision was not focussed for it. They read those playful trifles in the solidest earnest, and decided without hesitancy that if there had ever been any doubt that Dave Wilson was a pudd'nhead—which there hadn't— this revelation removed that doubt for good and all. That is just the way, in this world; an enemy can partly ruin a man, but it takes a good-natured injudicious friend to complete the thing and make it perfect. After this the Judge felt tenderer than ever toward Wilson, and surer than ever that his calendar had merit.

Judge Driscoll could be a freethinker and still hold his place in society because he was the person of most consequence in the community, and therefore could venture to go his own way and follow out his own notions. The other member of his pet organization was allowed the like liberty because he was a cipher in the estimation of the public, and nobody attached any importance to what he thought or did. He was liked, he was welcome enough all around, but he simply didn't count for anything.

Chapter 6

Observation made by Constable Blake: He speaks English with some kind of a foreign accent, I don't know what, but I think it's hellish.—*Pudd'nhead Wilson's Calendar.*

When an elderly person in Missouri, as elsewhere in the South, has a character that wins the reverent and petting love and esteem of everybody, big and little, in a community, then by the common voice that person is raised to the peerage, so to speak, and is called Uncle or Aunt by all the populace. It is the highest title of honor and affection, and the most gracious, that is known to the South. Negroes get it by mere age, and then it does not mean a great deal; but with the white it is the assayer's stamp upon the golden ingot of character, and stands for a thousand carats fine.

Aunt Patsy Cooper and Aunt Betsy Hale, near neighbors and fast friends, were of this nobility. Aunt Patsy had the sweet face and the spun-glass gray hair that make age beautiful, and the all-embracing sympathies and affections and cordialities and self-immolating activities in everybody's interest and for everybody's benefit that win the homage of men and the unbribed confidence of the other animals. In years she was past fifty, but in spirit, and feeling, and catholicity of interests she was only eighteen or twenty or along there. Nothing nor nobody was too high or too humble to be above or below the reach of her interest. She was always ready to nurse anybody through any sort of sickness, contagious or otherwise; she was active in all church affairs and all charities; she liked to look on at dances, and help at picnics and boat excursions, and be around wherever there were young folks and a good time to the fore; she never had a divided mind except when there was a funeral and a circus at the same hour.

Her daughter Maria, aged nineteen, was confessedly the prettiest girl in the town. But she did not go by the name Maria. She was a creature of dreams and romance, and did not like that name after she had reached fifteen and had begun to live among the upper classes in Scott's novels. She had a middle

34

initial, R, which had been lying idle and paralyzed all the years of her life, and nobody now knew what it stood for except the family; so she thought it would be a good idea to set it to work and let it earn its living. That is what she did. In its paralyzed state it had stood for Riggs; but when she started it in business she suppressed the Riggs and made it stand for Rowena. She gradually worked it into currency, and at last, when all the town had accepted and adopted it, her mother yielded, too, albeit reluctantly, and the detested name of Maria ceased from offending her ears. At least it did except upon occasions when "the boys" were not satisfied with her; then they fretted her with it. The boys were her brothers Joe and Henry, and were younger than she.

The widow Cooper had a spare room which she let to a lodger, with board, when she could find one, but this room had been empty for a year now, to her sorrow. Her income was only sufficient for the family support, and she needed the lodging-money for trifling luxuries. But now, at last, on a flaming June day, she finds herself happy; her tedious long wait is ended; her year-worn advertisement has been answered; and not by a village applicant, oh, no—this letter is from away off yonder in the dim great world to the North: it is from St. Louis! She sits on her porch gazing out with unseeing eyes upon the shining reaches of the mighty Mississippi, her thoughts steeped in her good fortune. Indeed it is especially good fortune, for she is to have two lodgers instead of one.

She has read the letter to the family, and Rowena has danced away to see to the cleaning and airing of the room by the slave woman Nancy, and the boys have rushed abroad in the town to spread the great news, for it is matter of public interest, and the public would wonder and not be pleased if not informed. Presently Rowena returns, all aflush with joyous excitement, and says—

"Do read it again, ma—it's just too lovely for anything! Oh, dear, I *am* so glad!"

"Well, set down then, and be quiet a minute and don't fly around so; it fairly makes me tired to see you. It starts off so: 'Honored Madam'—"

"I like that, ma, don't you? It shows they're high-bred."

"Yes, I noticed that when I first read it. 'My brother and I have seen your advertisement, by chance, in a copy of your local journal—'"

"It's so beautiful and smooth, ma—don't you think so?"

"Yes, seems so to me—'and beg leave to take the room you offer. We are twenty-four years of age, and twins—'"

"I do hope they are handsome, and I just know they are. Don't you hope they are, ma?"

"Land, I ain't particular. 'We are Italians by birth—'"

"It's *so* romantic! Just think—there's never been one in this town, and everybody will want to see them, and they're all *ours!* Think of that."

—"'but have lived long in the various countries of Europe, and several years in the United States.'"

"Oh, just think what wonders they've seen, ma. Won't it be good to hear them talk?"

"I reckon so; yes, I reckon so. 'Our names are Luigi and Angelo Cappello—'"

"Beautiful, perfectly beautiful! Not like Jones and Robinson and those horrible names!"

"'You desire but one guest, but dear madam, if you will allow us to pay for two we will not discommode you, for we will sleep together in the same bed. We have always been used to this, and prefer it.' And then he goes on to say they will be down Thursday."

"And this is Tuesday—I don't know how I'm ever going to wait, ma. The time does drag along so, and I'm so dying to see them. Which of them do you reckon is the tallest, ma?"

"How do you s'pose I can tell, child? Mostly they are the same size—twins are."

"Well, then, which do you reckon is the best looking?"

"Goodness knows—*I* don't."

"*I* think Angelo is; it's the prettiest name, anyway. Don't you think it's a sweet name, ma?"

"Yes, it's well enough. I'd like both of them better if I knew the way to pronounce them—the Eyetalian way, I mean. The Missouri way and the Eyetalian way is different, I judge."

"Maybe—yes. It's Luigi that writes the letter. What do you reckon is the reason Angelo didn't write it?"

"Why, how can *I* tell? What's the difference who writes it, so long as it's done?"

"Oh, I *hope* it wasn't because he is sick! You don't think he is sick, do you, ma?"

"Sick your granny; what's to make him sick?"

"Oh, there's never any telling. Those foreigners with that kind of names are so delicate, and of course that kind of names are not suited to our climate—you wouldn't expect them to be, yourself, ma."

"Oh, go 'long with such nonsense. If a person's name made him sick, couldn't he rake up another one? You done it yourself."

"Well, if I really thought he *was* sick, I—here comes Judge Driscoll in at the gate. He's heard about it. I'll go and open the door."

The Judge was full of congratulations and curiosity. The letter was read and discussed. Soon Justice Robinson arrived with more congratulations, and there was a new reading and a new discussion. This was the beginning. Neighbor after neighbor, of both sexes, followed, and the procession drifted in and out all day and evening and all Wednesday and Thursday. The letter was read and re-read until it was nearly worn out; everybody admired it, everybody was sympathetic and excited, and the Coopers swam in seas of glory all the while.

The boats were very uncertain, in low water, in those primitive times. This time the Thursday boat had not arrived at ten at night—so the people had waited at the landing all day for nothing; they were driven to their homes by a heavy storm without having had a view of the illustrious foreigners.

Eleven o'clock came; then twelve, and the Cooper house was the only one in the town that still had lights burning. The rain and thunder were booming yet, and the anxious family were still waiting, still hoping. At last there was a knock on the door and the family jumped to open it. Two negro men entered, each carrying a trunk, and proceeded up stairs toward the guest room. Then entered a human creature that had two heads, two necks, four arms, and one body, with a single pair of legs attached.

Chapter 7

Nothing is so injurious as other people's habits.—Pudd'nhead Wilson's Calendar.

It—or they, as you please—bowed with elaborate foreign formality, but the Coopers could not respond, immediately; they were paralyzed. At this moment there came from the rear of the group a fervent ejaculation—"My lan'!"—followed by a crash of crockery, and the slave wench Nancy stood petrified and staring, with a tray of wrecked tea things at her feet. The incident broke the spell, and brought the family to consciousness. The beautiful heads of the new-comer bowed again, and one of them said with easy grace and dignity—

"I crave the honor, Madam and Miss, to introduce to you my brother, Luigi Cappello," (the other head bowed,) "and myself—Angelo, and at the same time offer sincere apologies for the lateness of our coming, which was unavoidable;" and both heads bowed again.

The poor old lady was in a whirl of amazement and confusion, but she managed to stammer out—

"I'm sure I'm glad to make your acquaintance, sir—I mean, gentlemen. As for the delay, it is nothing, don't mention it. This is my daughter Rowena, sir—gentlemen. Please step in the parlor and sit down and have a bite and a sup; you are dreadful wet and must be uncomfortable—both of you, I mean."

But to the old lady's relief they courteously excused themselves, saying it would be wrong to keep the family out of their beds longer; then each head bowed in turn and uttered a friendly good-night, and the singular figure moved away in the wake of the boys, who bore candles, and disappeared up the stairs.

The widow tottered into the parlor and sank into a chair with a gasp, and Rowena followed, tongue-tied and dazed. The two sat silent in the throbbing summer heat, unconscious of the million-voiced music of the mosquitoes, unconscious of the roaring gale, the lashing and thrashing of the rain along the windows and the roof, the white glare of the lightnings, the tumultuous booming and bellowing of the thunder, conscious of nothing but that prodigy, that uncanny apparition that had come and gone so suddenly—that weird strange thing that was so soft spoken and so gentle of manner, and yet had shaken them up like an earthquake with the shock of its grewsome aspect. At last a cold little shudder quivered along down the widow's meagre frame and she said in a weak voice—

"Ugh, it was awful—just the mere *look* of that phillipene!"

Rowena did not answer. Her faculties were still caked, she had not yet found her voice. Presently the widow said, a little resentfully—

"Always been *used* to sleeping together—in fact, *prefer* it. And *I* was thinking it was to accommodate me. I thought it was very good of them, whereas a person situated as that young man is—"

"Ma, you oughtn't to begin by getting up a prejudice against him. I'm sure he is good-hearted and means well. Both of his faces show it."

"I'm not so certain about that. The one on the left—I mean the one on *its* left—hasn't near as good a face, in my opinion, as its brother."

"That's Luigi."

"Yes, Luigi; anyway it's the dark-skinned one. Up to all kinds of mischief and disobedience when he was a boy, I'll be bound. I lay his mother had trouble enough to lay her hand on him when she wanted him. But the one on the right is as good as gold, I can see that."

"That's Angelo."

"Yes, Angelo, I reckon, though I can't tell t'other from which by their names, yet awhile. But it's the right-hand one—the blonde one. He has such kind blue eyes, and curly copper hair and fresh complexion—"

"And such a noble face!—oh, it *is* a noble face, ma, just royal, you may say. And beautiful—deary me, how beautiful! But both are that; the dark one's as beautiful as a picture. There's no such wonderful faces and handsome heads in *this* town—none that even begin! And such hands!—especially Angelo's—so shapely and—"

"Stuff, how could *you* tell which they belonged to?—they had gloves on."

"Why, didn't I see them take off their hats?"

"That don't signify. They might have taken off each other's hats. Nobody could tell. There was just a wormy squirming of arms in the air—seemed to be a couple of dozen of them, all writhing at once, and it just made me dizzy to see them go."

"Why, ma, *I* hadn't any difficulty. There's two arms on each shoulder—"

"There, now! One arm on each shoulder belongs to each of the creatures, don't it? For a person to have two arms on one shoulder wouldn't do him any good, would it? Of course not. Each has an arm on each shoulder. Now then, you tell me which of them belongs to which, if you can. They don't know, themselves—they just work whichever arm comes handy. Of course they do; especially if they are in a hurry and can't stop to think which belongs to which."

The mother seemed to have the rights of the argument, so the daughter abandoned the struggle. Presently the widow rose with a yawn and said—

"Poor thing, I hope it won't catch cold; it was powerful wet, just drenched, you may say. I hope it has left its boots outside, so they can be dried." Then she gave a little start, and looked perplexed. "Now I remember I heard one of them ask Joe to call him at half after seven,—I think it was the left-hand one—but I didn't hear the other one say anything. I wonder if he wants to be called, too. Do you reckon it's too late to ask?"

"Why, ma, it's not necessary. Calling one is calling both. If one gets up, the other's *got* to."

"Sho', of course; I never thought of that. Well, come along, maybe we can get some sleep, but I don't know, I'm so shook up with what we've been through."

The stranger had made an impression on the boys, too. They had a word of talk as they were getting to bed. Henry, the gentle, the humane, said—

"I feel ever so sorry for it, don't you, Joe?"

But Joe was a boy of this world, active, enterprising, and had a theatrical side to him.

"Sorry? Why how you talk! It can't stir a step without attracting attention. It's just grand."

Henry said, reproachfully—

"Instead of pitying it, Joe, you talk as if—"

"Talk as if *what*? I know one thing mighty certain: if you can fix me so *I* can eat for two and only have to stub toes for one, I ain't going to fool away no such chance just for sentiment."

The Twins were wet and tired, and they proceeded to undress without any preliminary remarks. The abundance of sleeves made the partnership coat hard to get off, for it was like skinning a tarantula, but it came at last, after much tugging and perspiring. The mutual vest followed. Then the brothers stood up before the glass, and each took off his own cravat and collar. The collars were of the standing kind, and came high up under the ears, like the sides of a wheelbarrow, as required by the fashion of the day. The cravats were as broad as a bank bill, with fringed ends which stood far out to right and left like the wings of a dragon-fly, and this also was strictly in accordance with the fashion of the time. Each cravat, as to color, was in perfect taste, as far as its owner's complexion was concerned—a delicate pink, in the case of the blonde brother, a violent scarlet in the case of the brunette—but as a combination they broke all the laws of taste known to civilization. Nothing more fiendish and irreconcilable than those shrieking and blaspheming colors could have been contrived. The wet boots gave no end of trouble—to Luigi. When they were off at last, Angelo said, with bitterness—

"I wish you wouldn't wear such tight boots, they hurt my feet."

Luigi answered with indifference—

"My friend, when *I* am in command of our body, I choose my apparel according to my own convenience, as I have remarked more than several times already. When you are in command, I beg you will do as *you* please."

Angelo was hurt, and the tears came into his eyes. There was gentle reproach in his voice, but not anger, when he replied:

"Luigi, I often consult your wishes, but you never consult mine. When I am in command I treat you as a guest; I try to make you feel at home; when you are in command you treat me as an intruder, you make me feel unwelcome. It embarrasses me bitterly in company, for I can see that people notice it and comment on it."

"Oh, damn the people," responded the brother languidly, and with the air of one who is tired of the subject.

A slight shudder shook the frame of Angelo, but he said nothing and the conversation ceased. Each buttoned his own share of the night shirt in silence; then Luigi, with Paine's "Age of Reason" in his hand, sat down in one chair and put his feet in another and lit his pipe, while Angelo took his "Whole Duty of Man," and both began to read. Angelo presently began to cough; his coughing increased and became mixed with gaspings for breath, and he was finally obliged to make an appeal to his brother's humanity:

"Luigi, if you would only smoke a little milder tobacco I am sure I could learn not to mind it in time, but this is *so* strong, and the pipe is so rank that—"

"Angelo, I wouldn't be such a baby! I have learned to smoke in a week, and the trouble is already over with me; if you would try, *you* could learn, too, and then you would stop spoiling my comfort with your everlasting complaints."

"Ah, brother, that is a strong word—everlasting—and isn't quite fair. I only complain when I suffocate; you know I don't complain when we are in the open air."

"Well, anyway, you could learn to smoke, yourself."

"But my principles, Luigi, you forget my principles. You would not have me do a thing which I regard as a sin?"

"Oh, d— bosh!"

The conversation ceased again, for Angelo was sick and discouraged and strangling; but after some time he closed his book and asked Luigi to sing with him, but he would not, and when he tried to sing by himself Luigi did his best to drown his plaintive tenor with a rude and rollicking song delivered in a thundering bass.

After the singing there was silence, and neither brother was happy. Before blowing the light out Luigi swallowed half a tumbler of whisky, and Angelo, whose sensitive organization could not endure intoxicants of any kind, took a pill to keep it from giving him the headache.

Chapter 8

Tell the truth or trump—but get the trick.—*Pudd'nhead Wilson's Calendar.*

The family sat in the breakfast room waiting for the Twins to come down. The widow was quiet, the daughter was all alive with happy excitement. She said—

"Ah, they're a boon, ma, just a boon! don't you think so?"

"Laws, I hope so, *I* don't know."

"Why, ma, yes you do. They're so fine, and handsome, and high-bred, and polite, so *every* way superior to our gawks here in this village—why, they'll make life different from what it was—so humdrum and commonplace, you know—oh, you may be sure they're full of accomplishments, and knowledge of the world, and all that, that will be an immense advantage to society here. Don't you think so, ma?"

"Mercy on me, how should *I* know, and I've hardly set eyes on them, yet." After a pause, she added, "They made considerable noise after they went up."

"Noise? Why, ma, they were singing. And it was beautiful, too."

"Oh, it was well enough, but too mixed-up, seemed to me."

"Now, ma, honor bright, did you *ever* hear 'Greenland's Icy Mountains' sung sweeter—now did you?"

"If it had been sung by itself, it would have been uncommon sweet, I don't deny it; but what they wanted to mix it up with 'Old Bob Ridley' for, I can't make out. Why, they don't go together, at all. They are not of the same nature. 'Bob Ridley' is a common rackety slam-bang secular song, one of the rippingest and rantingest and noisiest there is. I am no judge of music, and I don't claim it, but in my opinion nobody can make those two songs go together right."

"Why, ma, I thought—"

"It don't make any difference what you thought, it can't be done. *They* tried it, and to my mind it was a failure. I never heard such a crazy uproar;

seemed to me, sometimes, the roof would come off; and as for the cats—well, I've lived a many a year, and seen cats aggravated in more ways than one, but I've never seen cats take on the way they took on last night."

"Well, I don't think that that goes for anything, ma, because it is the nature of cats that any sound that is unusual—"

"Unusual! You may well call it so. Now if they are going to sing duets every night, I do hope they will both sing the same tune at the same time, for in my opinion a duet that is made up of two different tunes is a mistake; especially when the tunes ain't any kin to one another, that way."

"But ma, *I* think it must be a foreign custom; and it must be right, too, and the best way, because they have had every opportunity to know what *is* right, and it don't stand to reason that with their education they would do anything but what the highest musical authorities have sanctioned. You can't help but admit that, ma."

The argument was formidably strong; the old lady could not find any way around it; so, after thinking it over a while she gave in with a sigh of discontent, and admitted that the daughter's position was probably correct. Being vanquished, she had no mind to continue the topic at that disadvantage, and was about to seek a change when a change came of itself. A footstep was heard on the stairs, and she said—

"There—he's coming."

"*They*, ma—you ought to say *they*—it's nearer right."

The new lodger, rather shoutingly dressed but looking superbly handsome, stepped with courtly carriage into the trim little breakfast room and put out all his cordial arms at once, like one of those pocket knives with a multiplicity of blades, and shook hands with the whole family simultaneously. He was so easy and pleasant and hearty that all embarrassment presently thawed away and disappeared, and a cheery feeling of friendliness and comradeship took its place. He—or preferably they—were asked to occupy the seat of honor at the foot of the table. They consented with thanks, and carved the beef steak with one set of their arms while they distributed it at the same time with the other set.

"Will you have coffee, gentlemen, or tea?"

"Coffee for Luigi, if you please, madam, tea for me."

"Cream and sugar?"

"For me, yes, madam; Luigi takes his coffee black. Our natures differ a good deal from each other, and our tastes also."

The first time the negro girl Nancy appeared in the door and saw the two heads turning in opposite directions and both talking at once, then saw the commingling arms feed potatoes into one mouth and coffee into the other at the same time, she had to pause and pull herself out of a faintness that came over her; but after that she held her grip and was able to wait on the table with fair courage.

Conversation fell naturally into the customary grooves. It was a little jerky, at first, because none of the family could get smoothly through a sentence without a wobble in it here and a break in it there, caused by some new surprise in the way of attitude or gesture on the part of the Twins. The weather suffered the most. The weather was all finished up and disposed of, as a subject, before the simple Missourians had gotten sufficiently wonted to the spectacle of one body feeding two heads to feel composed and reconciled in the presence of so bizarre a miracle. And even after everybody's mind had become tranquilized there was still one slight distraction left: the hand that picked up a biscuit carried it to the wrong head, as often as any other way, and the wrong mouth devoured it. This was a puzzling thing, and marred the talk a little. It bothered the widow to such a degree that she presently dropped out of the conversation without knowing it, and fell to watching, and guessing, and talking to herself: "Now *that* hand is going to take that coffee to—no, it's gone to the other mouth; I can't understand it; and now, here is the dark-complected hand with a potato on its fork, I'll see what goes with *it*—there, the light-complected head's got it, as sure's I live!" Finally Rowena said—

"Ma, what is the matter with you? Are you dreaming about something?"

The old lady came to herself, and blushed; then she explained with the first random thing that came into her mind:

"I saw Mr. Angelo take up Mr. Luigi's coffee, and I thought maybe he— shan't I give *you* a cup, Mr. Angelo?"

"Oh, no, madam, I am very much obliged, but I never drink coffee, much as I would like to. You did see me take up Luigi's cup, it is true, but if you noticed, I did not carry it to my mouth, but to his."

"Y-es, I thought you did. Did you mean to?"

"How?"

The widow was a little embarrassed again. She said:

"I don't know but what I'm foolish, and you mustn't mind; but you see, *he* got the coffee I was expecting to see you drink, and you got a potato that I thought *he* was going to get. So, I thought it might be a mistake all around, and everybody getting what wasn't intended for him."

Both Twins laughed, and Luigi said—

"Dear madam, there wasn't any mistake. We are always helping each other that way. It is a great economy for us both; it saves time and labor. We have a system of signs which nobody can notice or understand but ourselves. If I am using both of my hands and want some coffee, I make the sign and Angelo furnishes it to me; and you saw that when he needed a potato I delivered it."

"How convenient!"

"Yes, and often of the extremest value. Take these Mississippi boats, for instance. They are always overcrowded. There is table-room for only half, therefore they have to set a second table for the second half. The stewards rush both parties, they give them no time to eat a satisfying meal, both divisions leave the table hungry. It isn't so with us. Angelo books himself for the one table, I book myself for the other. Neither of us eats anything at the other's table, but just simply works—works. Thus, you see, there are four hands to feed Angelo, and the same four to feed me. Each of us eats two meals."

The old lady was dazed with admiration, and kept saying "It's *perfectly* wonderful, perfectly wonderful!" and the boy Joe licked his chops enviously but said nothing—at least aloud.

"Yes," continued Luigi, "our construction may have its disadvantages—in fact it *has*—but it also has its compensations, of one sort and another. Take travel, for instance. Travel is enormously expensive, in all countries; we have been obliged to do a vast deal of it—come, Angelo, don't put any more sugar in your tea, I'm just over one indigestion and don't want another right away— been obliged to do a deal of it, as I was saying. Well, we always travel as one person, since we occupy but one seat, so we save half the fare."

"How romantic!" interjected Rowena, with effusion.

"Yes, my dear young lady, and how practical, too, and economical. In Europe, beds in the hotels are not charged with the board, but separately— another saving, for we stood to our rights and paid for the one bed only. The landlords often insisted that as both of us occupied the bed we ought—"

"No, they didn't!" said Angelo. "They did it only twice, and in both cases it was a double bed—a rare thing in Europe—and the double bed gave them some excuse. Be fair to the landlords; twice doesn't constitute 'often.'"

"Well, that depends—that depends. I knew a man who fell down a well twice. He said he didn't mind the first time, but he thought the second time was once too often. Have I misused that word, Mrs. Cooper?"

"To tell the truth, I was afraid you had, but it seems to look, now, like you hadn't." She stopped, and was evidently struggling with the difficult problem a moment, then she added in the tone of one who is convicted without being convinced, "It seems so, but I can't somehow tell why."

Rowena thought Luigi's retort was wonderfully quick and bright, and she remarked to herself with satisfaction that there wasn't any young native of Dawson's Landing that could have risen to the occasion like that. Luigi detected the applause in her face, and expressed his pleasure and his thanks with his eyes, and so eloquently withal, that the girl was proud and pleased, and hung out the delicate sign of it on her cheeks.

Luigi went on, with animation:

"Both of us get a bath for one ticket, theatre seat for one ticket, pew-rent is on the same basis, but at peep-shows we pay double."

"We have much to be thankful for," said Angelo, impressively, with a reverent light in his eye and a reminiscent tone in his voice, "we have been greatly blessed. As a rule, what one of us has lacked, the other, by the bounty of Providence, has been able to supply. My brother is hardy, I am not; he is very masculine, assertive, aggressive, I am less so. I am subject to illnesses, he is never ill. I cannot abide medicines, and cannot take them, but he has no prejudice against them, and—"

"Why, goodness gracious," interrupted the widow, "when you are sick, does he take the medicine for you?"

"Always, madam."

"Well, I *never* heard such a thing in my life. I think it's beautiful of you!"

"Oh, madam, it's nothing, don't mention it, it's really nothing at all."

"But I say it's beautiful, and I stick to it!" cried the widow, with a speaking moisture in her eye. "A well brother to take the medicine for his poor sick brother—I wish I had such a son," and she glanced reproachfully at her boys. "I declare I'll never rest till I've shook you by the hand!" and she scrambled out of her chair in a fever of generous enthusiasm, and made for the Twins, blind with her tears, and began to shake. The boy Joe corrected her, and said—

"You're shaking the wrong one, ma."

This flurried her, but she made a swift change and went on shaking.

"Got the wrong one again, ma," said the boy.

"Oh, shut up, can't you!" said the widow, embarrassed and irritated. "Give me *all* your hands, I want to shake them all; for I know you are both just as good as you can be."

It was a victorious thought, a master-stroke of diplomacy, though that never occurred to her and she cared nothing for diplomacy. She shook the four hands in turn with cordial effusion, and went back to her place in a state of high and fine exaltation that made her look young and handsome.

"Indeed I owe everything to Luigi," said Angelo, affectionately. "But for him I could not have survived our boyhood days, when we were friendless and poor—ah, so poor! We lived from hand to mouth—lived on the coarse fare of unwilling charity, and for weeks and weeks together not a morsel of food passed my lips, for its character revolted me and I could not eat it. But for Luigi I should have died. He ate for us both."

"How noble!" sighed Rowena.

"Do you hear that?" said the widow, severely, to her boys. "Let it be an example to you—I mean you, Joe."

Joe gave his head a barely perceptible disparaging toss and said—

"Et for both. It ain't anything—I'd a done it."

"Hush, if you haven't got any better manners than that. You don't see the point at all. It wasn't *good* food."

"I don't care—it was *food*, and I'd a et it if it was rotten."

"Shame! Such language! Can't you understand? They were starving—actually starving—and he ate for both, and saved his brother's life."

"It ain't anything. If I was starving, you gimme the chance and I'd save a whole family."

"Now you've said enough, Joe, and you can keep still. I never saw such an aggravating boy; the plainer a thing is made to you the more you can't see it."

"Well, anyways, I can see—"

"There!—that'll do. If it ain't asking what I oughtn't to ask, Mr. Angelo, how did you come to be so friendless and in such trouble when you were little? Do you mind telling? But don't, if you do."

"Oh, we don't mind it at all, madam; in our case it was merely misfortune, and nobody's fault. Our parents were well-to-do, there in Italy, and we were their only child. We were of the old Florentine nobility"—Rowena's heart gave a great bound, her nostrils expanded, and a fine light played in her eyes—"and when the war broke out my father was on the losing side and had to fly for his life. His estates were confiscated, his personal property seized, and there we were, in Germany, strangers, friendless, and in fact paupers. My brother and I were ten years old, and well educated for that age, very studious, very fond of our books, and well grounded in the German, French, Spanish and English languages.

"Our father survived his misfortunes only a month, our mother soon followed him, and we were alone in the world. Our parents could have made themselves comfortable by exhibiting us as a show, and they had many and large offers; but the thought revolted their pride, and they said they would starve and die first. But what they wouldn't consent to do we had to do without the formality of consent. We were seized for the debts occasioned by their illness and their funerals, and placed among the 'freaks' of a cheap museum in Berlin to earn the liquidation money. It took us two years to get out of that slavery. We traveled all about Germany, receiving no wages, and not even our keep. We had to exhibit for nothing, and beg our bread. That hateful black bread! but I seldom ate anything during that time, that was poor Luigi's affair—"

"I'll never Mister him again!" cried the widow, with strong emotion, "he's *Luigi* to me, from this out!"

"Thank you a thousand times, madam, a thousand times! though in truth I don't deserve it."

"Ah, Luigi is always the fortunate one when honors are showering," said Angelo, plaintively, "now what have I done, Mrs. Cooper, that you leave me out? Come, you must strain a point in my favor."

"Call you Angelo? Why, *certainly* I will; what are you *thinking* of! In the case of twins, why—"

"But ma, you're breaking up the story—do let him go on."

"You keep still, Rowena Cooper, and he can go on all the better, I reckon. One interruption don't hurt, it's two that makes the trouble."

"But you've added one, now, and that is three."

"And you've made it four, and you think *that's* a good argument against a person that's made it three. There, Joe—close your head; when there's any help wanted out of you, I'll let you know. Go on, Angelo, never mind these people; if you wait for *them* to get quiet, you'll never get anywhere."

"Well, madam, the rest is not of much consequence. When we escaped from that slavery at twelve years of age, we were in some respects men. Experience had taught us some valuable things; among others, how to take care of ourselves, how to avoid and defeat sharks and sharpers, and how to conduct our own business for our own profit and without other people's help. We traveled everywhere—years and years—picking up smatterings of strange tongues, familiarizing ourselves with strange sights and strange customs, accumulating an education of a wide and varied and curious sort. It was a pleasant life. We went to Venice—"

"Venice—oh, think of it!" cried Rowena, with beaming admiration. "You saw the Bridge of Sighs!"

"Yes."

"How lovely! And the Rialto!"

"Yes."

"*Oh!* And the Doge's Palace!"

"Yes."

"It takes a body's breath away! And you've seen St. Mark's—and the Winged Lion on the column—and the Great Square, and the Campanile, and the gondolas, oh, the dear gondolas! You've seen them all—every one!"

"Oh, yes, indeed, all."

"It's heavenly, it's just heavenly!"

"Oh, we are quite familiar with Venice."

"Familiar with Venice! How wonderful, how enchanting, to be able to say that! And you've ridden in a gondola?"

"A thousand times, yes."

"Ah, it's *too* lovely, too lovely for anything! Oh, to hear the gondoliers sing, once!—if I could only hear them sing just once! *You* have—*haven't* you!"

"Well, y-es, I've had that ill luck."

"Ill luck! Why, how can you talk so? Byron and everybody has spoken in raptures of their singing. Can't you say *one* good word for it?"

"Well, to be honest, it would be difficult."

"How strange! Does your brother feel the same way about it?"

"No, not exactly the same. I can tell all I feel about it without swearing."

"And can't he? Dear me, does he swear? You *don't* swear, Mr. Luigi, now *do* you?"

"Well, no—at least not sinfully."

"Not sinfully? How can a person swear and not swear sinfully?"

"Why, when he swears about the gondoliers' singing. *That* isn't any sin."

"O, my," said the widow, aghast at such reasoning, "what makes you think such a thing as that, Luigi?"

"Oh, it isn't I that think it, madam; both the British Parliament and the College of Cardinals at Rome have decided by an almost unanimous vote that it is not sinful to swear at the squawking of the gondoliers—especially when they gather in front of the hotels on the Grand Canal at night and make the cats commit suicide."

"Goodness, is that true, Angelo?" asked the widow, distressed and astonished.

"Not a word of it, madam."

"It *is* true, too," retorted Luigi. "I *know* it to be true; I am not guessing, I *know* it to be true, and I defy *anybody* to disprove it!"

The old lady looked from one face to the other over her glasses and was plainly in great doubt as to which she should believe; but finally she said:

"Of course if he knows it, and knows it for certain, why—and anyway it does look reasonable, if they sing like that. Nothing is made in vain, we all know that; and so swearing ain't. It wouldn't have been made if it hadn't been made for a purpose, and I think this is as likely a one as I know of, because last night—"

"'Sh! *ma!*" cried Rowena, a crimson flush mounting to her temples. The modified mate to it appeared in Angelo's face, but Luigi was not troubled. He said—

"You heard us, madam? We were not in good voice, owing to fatigue and exposure, but—you—I trust you liked it."

"Well—I must say—"

"Of *course* she liked it—ma, you *did* like it, you know you did. Please don't pay any attention to her, Mr. Luigi, she—why, it was beautiful, perfectly beautiful. I *said* so!"

"Certainly, who's denying it; who said you didn't? *You* said so, but I—"

"Now, *ma!* Oh, if you would only—"

"Ole Missus, de house is plum jam full o' people, en dey's jes' a spilin' to see—to see—*him—dem!*" The slave girl indicated the Twins with a nod of her head, and tucked it back out of sight again.

It was a proud occasion for the widow, and she promised herself high satisfaction in showing off her fine foreign birds before her neighbors and friends—simple folk who had hardly ever seen a foreigner of any kind, and never one of any distinction or style. Yet her feeling was moderate indeed, when contrasted with Rowena's. Rowena was in the clouds, she walked on air; this was to be the greatest day, the most romantic episode in the colorless history of that dull country town. She was to be familiarly near the source of its glory and feel the full flood of it pour over her and about her, the other girls could only gaze and envy, not partake.

The widow was ready, Rowena was ready, so also was Luigi; but Angelo said he would like to go and dress first, and he should think Luigi would prefer that, too. He shot a covert, imploring glance at his brother which said, "Be humane, be generous—don't carry me in there before all those people in this heart-breaking costume, which offends against every canon of harmony in color and will make everybody think we have been brought up among African savages;" but the answering glance said, "We will go just as we are, or we will have a scene here—take your choice." So Angelo sighed, and said he was ready.

The party moved along the hall, the Twins in advance, toward the open parlor door, whence issued a low hum of conversation. When they appeared suddenly before the crowd, every eye flew wide and froze to a glassy stare, there was a universal gasp that chorded itself into a single note, and two or three boys skipped out of the open window like frogs. The Twins took a position near the door, the widow stood at Luigi's side, Rowena stood beside Angelo, and the march-past and the introductions began. The widow was all smiles and contentment. She received the procession and passed it on to Rowena.

"Good-mornin' Sister Cooper"—handshake.

"Good-morning, Brother Higgins—Count Luigi Cappello, Mr. Higgins"—handshake, followed by a devouring stare and "I'm glad to see ye," on the part of Higgins, and a courteous inclination of the head and a pleasant "Most happy!" on the part of Count Luigi.

"Good-mornin', Roweny"—handshake.

"Good-morning, Mr. Higgins—present you to Count Angelo Cappello."

Handshake, devouring stare, "Glad to see ye!"—courteous nod, smily "Most happy!" and Higgins passes on.

None of these visitors were at ease, but being honest people, they didn't pretend to be. None of them had ever seen a person bearing a title of nobility before, and none had been expecting to see one now, consequently the title came upon them as a kind of pile-driving surprise and caught them unprepared. A few tried to rise to the emergency, and got out an awkward My Lord, or Your Lordship, or something of the sort, but the great majority were knocked cold by the unaccustomed word and its dim and awful associations with gilded courts and stately ceremony and anointed kingship, so they only fumbled through the handshake, and passed on, speechless. Now and then, as happens at all receptions, everywhere, a more than ordinarily friendly soul blocked the procession and kept it waiting while he inquired how the brothers liked the village, and how long they were going to stay, and inquired if their families were well, and dragged in the weather, and hoped it would get cooler soon, and all that sort of thing, so as to be able to say, when they got home, "I had quite a long talk with them;" but nobody did or said anything of a regretable kind, and so the great affair went through to the end in a creditable and satisfactory fashion.

General conversation followed, and the Twins drifted about from group to group, talking easily and fluently, and winning approval, compelling admiration, and achieving popularity right along. The widow followed their conquering march with a proud eye, and every now and then Rowena said to herself with deep satisfaction, "And to think, they are *ours*—all ours."

There were no idle moments for mother or daughter. Eager inquiries concerning the Twins were pouring into their enchanted ears all the time; each was the constant centre of a group of breathless listeners; each recognized that she knew now for the first time the real meaning of that great word Glory, and perceived the stupendous value of it, and understood why men in all ages had been willing to throw away meaner happinesses, treasure, life itself, to get a taste of its sublime and supreme joy. Napoleon and all his kind stood accounted for—and justified.

When Rowena had at last done all her duty by the young people in the parlor, she went up stairs to satisfy the longings of an overflow meeting up there, for the parlor was not big enough to hold all the comers. Again she was besieged by eager questioners and again she swam in sunset seas of glory. When the forenoon was nearly gone, she recognized with a pang that this most splendid episode of her life was almost over, that nothing could prolong it, that nothing quite its equal could ever fall to her fortune again. But never mind, it was sufficient unto itself, the grand occasion had moved on an ascending scale from the start, and was a noble and memorable success. If the Twins could but do some crowning act, now, to climax it, something unusual, something startling, something to concentrate upon themselves the company's loftiest admiration, something in the nature of an electric surprise—

Here a prodigious slam-banging broke out below, and everybody rushed down to see. It was the duplicates knocking out a classic four-handed piece on the piano, in great style. Rowena was satisfied; satisfied down to the bottom of her heart.

Chapter 9

The Creator admired His glittering array of far-stretching solar systems, the work of His hands, but merely pronounced it "good." Considering the modesty of the word, one might think He was describing a village, whereas when you hear a villager describing his village, you think he is describing the solar systems.—*Pudd'nhead Wilson's Calendar.*

The company broke up reluctantly, and drifted toward their several homes, chatting with vivacity, and all agreeing that it would be many a long day before Dawson's Landing would see the equal of this one again. The Twins had accepted several invitations while the reception was in progress, and had also volunteered to do the balcony scene in Romeo and Juliet at an amateur entertainment for the benefit of a local charity. Society was eager to receive them to its bosom. Judge Driscoll had the good fortune to secure them for an immediate drive, and be the first to display them in public. They entered his buggy with him and were paraded down the main street, everybody flocking to the windows and sidewalks to see, and a herd of little boys chasing behind, wild with excitement, and grateful to the marrow for the benefaction of a free show.

At first the dogs were indifferent, thinking it was merely three men riding in a buggy, and therefore a matter of no consequence; but when they found out the facts of the case, they altered their opinion pretty radically, and joined the boys, expressing their minds as they came. Other dogs got interested; indeed all the dogs. It was a spirited sight to see them come leaping fences, tearing around corners, swarming out of every by-street and alley. The noise they made was something beyond belief—or praise. They did not seem to be moved by malice, but only by prejudice, the common human prejudice against lack of conformity. If the Twins turned their heads, they broke and fled in every direction, but stopped at a safe distance and faced about, and then formed and came on again as soon as the strangers showed them their back. Negroes and farmers' wives took to the woods when the buggy came upon them suddenly, and altogether the drive was pleasant and animated, and a refreshment all around.

The Judge showed the strangers the new graveyard, and the jail, and where the richest man lived, and the Freemasons' hall, and the Methodist church, and the Presbyterian church, and where the Baptist church was going to be when they got some of the money to build it with, and showed them the town hall and the slaughter-house, and got out the independent fire company in uniform and had them squirt out an imaginary fire, and let them inspect the muskets of the militia company, and poured out an exhaustless stream of enthusiasm over all these splendors, and seemed very well satisfied with the responses he got, for the Twins admired his admiration and paid him back the best they could, though they could have done better if some fifteen or sixteen hundred thousand previous experiences of this sort in various countries had not already rubbed off a considerable part of the novelty from it.

The Judge laid himself hospitably out to make them have a good time, and if there was a defect anywhere it was not his fault. He told them a good many humorous anecdotes, and always forgot the nub, but they were always able to furnish it, for these yarns were of a pretty early vintage, and they had had many a rejuvenating pull at them before. And he told them all about his several dignities, and how he had held this and that and the other place of honor or profit, and had once been to the legislature, and was now president of the Society of Freethinkers.

This latter fact interested Luigi as much as it discomforted Angelo. The Judge said the Society had been in existence four years and already had two members, and was firmly established. Luigi wanted to join it. The Judge was delighted, and would call the membership together right away, suspend the rules and make the election immediate. He said that the addition of so distinguished a personage would give the Society a fine lift and a fresh start. He hinted that if Count Angelo also—

But Luigi interrupted, and said, "My brother will attend the meetings, but that will be as far as he can go. He will not be able to join, or take any active part in the proceedings, because he is a member of the Methodist church, and the prejudices of that sect are such that even his passive presence is more than likely to provoke criticism and make talk."

"Ah, I see, I see how the case stands, I see the delicacies and difficulties of the situation. But we shall be very glad to have you present with us unofficially, dear sir—informally, sir, purely informally—and although it has been our rule to exclude all who were not members, I assure you we shall be glad to make an exception in your case; and I may add with confidence that no effort will be spared to make these occasions enjoyable to you, sir."

Angelo concealed his bitter annoyance as well as he could, and answered courteously—

"I thank you sincerely, sir, for your kind welcome, and for the great and undeserved concessions which the Society proposes to make in my favor. I shall attend the meetings, but it would not be honorable in me to conceal the fact that I shall go because I must, not because I wish to. I believe you when you say that the Society will spare no effort to make the meetings enjoyable to me, but I know too well, alas, but too well, sir, that when it has done its best my enjoyment will be of but a doubtful sort. All the positions and arguments of the freethinkers—you will pardon my speaking so frankly—are a horror to me, and so the prospect of sitting out one of these discussions and seeming to countenance it, and be in it and of it, fills me with the keenest suffering. I assure you I do not overstate the case, sir."

"I see your side of the matter, sir, and I wish I could think of some way to—to—can either of you suggest a way out of this really most painful and embarrassing difficulty, gentlemen? The more I look at it the more—the more—er—"

The benevolent Judge came to a stop. The case was too new and complex for him. Nobody suggested anything, and so after a pause, he said:

"Why, there must be some—er—way—some—er—how do you *generally* do?"

"Well," said Luigi, with a touch of resentment in his voice, "I have allowed my brother the opportunity to state that very thing, but apparently he sees that to do it would place him in no very generous attitude after what he has been saying; so I will state it myself: *We always go together.* Ask him if I go to church with him. Just ask him. If he wants to deny it—"

"I don't deny it," said Angelo in a low voice, and coloring.

The Judge bent a pained and reproachful gaze upon him. There was a wordless silence, for many moments, during which each of these erring and yet well-intentioned men was busy with his own sad thoughts; then Angelo spoke:

"You should not be too hard upon me—either of you. My conduct has not been without example. I am merely human. Who is more? Luigi, when you have been in command of our body, have you ever invited me to go to church?"

"Well—no."

"Have you yielded and taken me when I begged you?"

"I—well, I believe I never have."

"When it was my week of command, did you ever go with me except upon compulsion?"

Luigi was silent.

"Judge Driscoll, you see he does not answer. It is because his answer would be a confession. Am I justified? Am I worse than he?"

"Give me your hands, both of you. There—let bygones be bygones. We are all poor erring creatures, quick to judge, prompt to see the wrong in others and be blind to it in ourselves. I see the whole case, now, and find no fault with either of you. You have merely done as I would have done, as anybody would have done, situated as you are. Go on, gentlemen, just as before, and no right-minded man can pick a flaw in your conduct. There is no harm in going to church when one cannot help it; I see, now, and see clearly, that this is perfectly true. It follows that there can be no harm in your coming to our freethinking meetings, sir, upon the same terms and conditions. As I said before, you will be most welcome, and I wish sincerely that you might be correspondingly happy; but it may not be, I suppose, it may not be; we cannot have everything as we would like it in this world, filled as it is, one knows not why, with conflicting opinions and warring desires."

Angelo replied, with much feeling—

"Indeed, sir, I could almost wish I might be happy there, for your sake; for I appreciate and am grateful for the generous sympathy and solicitude which you exhibit for me"—then added with a sigh—"but my beliefs and principles being what they are, it would make me deeply unhappy to be happy in such circumstances. I could not abide it, I could not endure it. Happy there? I shudder to think of it; it would be sacrilege." His voice trembled with emotion; he was not able to go on for some moments; then he added, with touching earnestness: "No, I shall be unhappy; and I shall be far happier in being unhappy than I could be in being happy."

"A noble spirit spoke there!" cried the Judge. "I could embrace you for those words. I would we had a thousand like you in our Society. But they do not exist, sir; the world cannot furnish them. I am proud to know you, sir, proud to know such a man."

"You do me too much honor, sir, indeed you do; but I am thankful for what you have said; I could not be more so if I truly deserved it."

The Judge insisted that he did deserve it, and more. They had now arrived at the widow's gate, and the excursion was ended. The Twins politely expressed their obligations for the pleasant outing which had been afforded them; to which the Judge bowed his thanks, and then said he would now go and arrange for the Freethinkers' meeting, and would call for Count Luigi in the evening.

"For you, also, dear sir," he added, hastily, turning to Angelo and bowing. "In addressing myself particularly to your brother, I was not meaning to leave you out. It was an unintentional rudeness, I assure you, and due wholly to accident—accident and preoccupation. I beg you to forgive me."

His quick eye had seen the sensitive blood mount into Angelo's face, betraying the wound that had been inflicted. The sting of the slight had gone deep, but the apology was so prompt, and so evidently sincere, that the hurt was almost immediately healed, and a forgiving smile testified to the kindly Judge that all was well again.

Concealed behind Angelo's modest and unassuming exterior, and unsuspected by any but his intimates, was a lofty pride, a pride of almost abnormal proportions, indeed, and this rendered him ever the prey of slights; and although they were almost always imaginary ones, they hurt none the less on that account. By ill fortune Judge Driscoll had happened to touch his sorest point: his conviction that his brother's presence was welcomer everywhere than his own; that he was often invited, out of mere courtesy, where only his brother was wanted, and that in the majority of cases he would not be included in an invitation if he could be left out without offence. A sensitive nature like this is necessarily subject to moods; moods which traverse the whole gamut of feeling; moods which know all the climes of emotion, from the sunny heights of joy to the black abysses of despair. At times, in his seasons of deepest depression, Angelo almost wished that he and his brother might become segregated from each other and be separate individuals, like other men. But of course as soon as his mind cleared and these diseased imaginings passed away, he shuddered at the repulsive thought, and earnestly prayed that it might visit him no more. To be separate, and as other men are! How awkward it would seem; how unendurable. What would he do with his hands, his arms? How would his legs feel? How odd, and strange, and grotesque every action, attitude, movement, gesture would be. To sleep by himself, eat by himself, walk by himself—how lonely, how unspeakably lonely! No, no, any fate but that! In every way and from every point of view, the idea was revolting.

This was of course natural; to have felt otherwise would have been unnatural. He had known no life but the combined one; he had been familiar with it from his birth; he was not able to conceive of any other as being agreeable, or even bearable. To him, in the privacy of his secret thoughts, all other men were monsters, deformities; and during three-fourths of his life their aspect had filled him with what promised to be an unconquerable aversion. But at eighteen his eye began to take note of female beauty, and, little by little, undefined longings grew up in his heart, under whose softening influence the old stubborn aversion gradually diminished, and finally disappeared. Men were still monstrosities to him, still deformities, and in his sober moments he had no desire to be like them, but their strange and unsocial and uncanny construction was no longer offensive to him.

This had been a hard day for him, physically and mentally. He had been called in the morning before he had quite slept off the effects of the liquor which Luigi had drank; and so, for the first half hour had had the seedy feeling, the languor, the brooding depression, the cobwebby mouth and druggy taste that come of dissipation, and are so ill a preparation for bodily or intellectual activities; the long and violent strain of the reception had followed; and this had been followed, in turn, by the dreary sight-seeing, the wearying explanations and laudations of the sights, and the stupefying clamor of the dogs. As a congruous conclusion, a fitting end, his feelings had been hurt, a slight had been put upon him. He would have been glad to forego dinner, and betake himself to rest and sleep, but he held his peace and said no word, for he knew his brother. Luigi was fresh, unweary, full of life, spirit, energy, he would have scoffed at the idea of wasting valuable time on a bed or a sofa, and would have refused permission.

Chapter 10

It is a mistake to inflate the truth. Dress a fact in tights, not in an ulster.—*Pudd'nhead Wilson's Calendar.*

Rowena was dining out, the brothers were belated at play, there were but three chairs and four persons that noon, at the home dinner table—the Twins, the widow, and her chum, Aunt Betsy Hale. The widow soon perceived that Angelo's spirits were as low as Luigi's were high, and also that he had a jaded look. Her motherly solicitude was aroused, and she tried to get him interested in the talk and win him to a happier frame of mind, but the cloud of sadness remained on his countenance. Luigi lent his help, too. He used a form and a phrase which he was always accustomed to employ in these circumstances. He gave his brother an affectionate slap on the shoulder and said, encouragingly—

"Cheer up, the worst is yet to come!"

But this did no good. It never did. If anything, it made the matter worse, as a rule, because it irritated Angelo. This made it a favorite with Luigi. By and by the widow said—

"Angelo, you are tired, you've overdone yourself. You go right to bed, after dinner, and get a good nap and a rest, then you'll be all right."

"Indeed I would give anything if I could do that, madam."

"And what's to hender, I'd like to know? Land, the room's yours, to do what you please with. The idea that you can't do what you like with your own!"

"But, you see, there's one prime essential—an essential of the very first importance—which *isn't* my own."

"What is that?"

"My body."

The old ladies looked puzzled, and Aunt Betsy Hale said—

"Why, bless your heart, how is that?"

"It's my brother's."

"Your brother's. I don't quite understand. I supposed it belonged to both of you."

"So it does. But not to both at the same time."

"That is mighty curious; I don't see how it can be. I shouldn't think it could be managed that way."

"Oh, it's a good enough arrangement, and goes very well—in fact it wouldn't do to have it otherwise. I find that the Teetotalers and the Anti-Teetotalers, hire the use of the same hall for their meetings. Both parties don't use it at the same time, do they?"

"You bet they don't!" said both old ladies in a breath. "And moreover," said Aunt Betsy, "the Freethinkers and the Babtist Bible class use the same room over the market house, but you can take my word for it *they* don't mush-up together and use it at the same time."

"Very well," said Angelo, "you understand it now. And it stands to reason that the arrangement couldn't be improved. I'll prove it to you. If our legs tried to obey two wills, how could we ever get anywhere? I would start one way, Luigi would start another, at the same moment—the result would be a standstill, wouldn't it?"

"As sure as you are born! Now ain't that wonderful! A body would never have thought of it."

"We should always be arguing and fussing and disputing over the merest trifles. We should lose worlds of time, for we couldn't go down stairs or up, couldn't go to bed, couldn't rise, couldn't wash, couldn't dress, couldn't stand up, couldn't sit down, couldn't even cross our legs without calling a meeting first, and explaining the case, and passing resolutions, and getting consent. It wouldn't ever do—now would it?"

"Do? Why, it would wear a person out in a week. Did you ever hear anything like it, Patsy Cooper?"

"Oh, you'll find there's more than one thing about them that ain't commonplace," said the widow, with the complacent air of a person with a property right in a novelty that is under admiring scrutiny.

"Well, now, how ever *do* you manage it? I don't mind saying I'm suffering to know."

"He who made us," said Angelo, reverently, "and with us this difficulty, also provided a way out of it. By a mysterious law of our being, each of us has utter and indisputable command of our body a week at a time, turn and turn about."

"Well, I never. Now ain't that beautiful!"

"Yes, it is beautiful and infinitely wise and just. The week ends every Saturday at midnight to the minute, to the second, to the last shade and fraction of a second, infallibly, unerringly, and in that instant the one brother's power over the body vanishes and the other brother takes possession, asleep or awake."

"How marvelous are His ways, and past finding out!"

Luigi said—

"So exactly to the instant does the change come, that during our stay in many of the great cities of the world, the public clocks were regulated weekly by it; and as the hundreds of thousands of private clocks and watches were set and corrected in accordance with the public clocks, we really furnished the standard time for the entire city."

"Don't tell *me* that He don't do miracles any more! Blowing down the walls of Jericho with rams' horns warn't as difficult, in my opinion."

"And that is not all," said Angelo. "A thing that is even more marvelous, perhaps, is the fact that the change takes note of longitude and fits itself to the meridian we are on. Luigi is in command this week. Now, if on Saturday night at a moment before midnight we could fly in an instant to a point fifteen degrees west of here, he would hold possession of the power another hour, for the change observes *local* time and no other."

Betsy Hale was deeply impressed, and said with solemnity—

"Patsy Cooper, for *de*tail it lays over the Passage of the Red Sea."

"No, I shouldn't go as far as that," said Aunt Patsy, "but if you're a mind to say Sodom and Gomorrah, I am with you, Betsy Hale."

"I am agreeable, then, though I do think I was right, and I believe parson Maltby will say the same. Well, now, there's another thing. Suppose one of you wants to *borrow* the legs a minute from the one that's got them, could he let him?"

"Yes, but we hardly ever do that. There were disagreeable results, several times, and so we very seldom ask or grant the privilege, now-a-days, and we never even think of such a thing unless the case is extremely urgent. Besides, a week's possession at a time seems so little that we can't bear to spare a minute of it. People who have the use of their legs *all* the time never think of what a blessing it is, of course. It never occurs to them; it's just their natural ordinary condition, and so it doesn't excite them at all. But when I wake up, on a Sunday morning, and it's my week and I feel the power all through me, oh, *such* a wave of exultation and thanksgiving goes surging over me, and I want to shout 'I can walk! I can walk!' Madam, do you ever, at your uprising, want to shout 'I can walk! I can walk!'"

"No, you poor unfortunate cretur, but I'll never get out of my bed again without *doing* it! Laws, to think I've had this unspeakable blessing all my long life and never had the grace to thank the good God that gave it to me!"

Tears stood in the eyes of both the old ladies, and the widow said, softly—

"Betsy Hale, we have learnt something, you and me."

The conversation now drifted wide, but by and by floated back once more to that admired detail, the rigid and beautiful impartiality with which the possession of power had been distributed between the Twins. Aunt Betsy saw in it a far finer justice than human law exhibits in related cases. She said—

"In my opinion it ain't right now, and never has been right, the way a twin born a quarter of a minute sooner than the other one gets all the land and grandeurs and nobilities in the old countries and his brother has to go bare and be a nobody. Which of you was born first?"

Angelo's head was resting against Luigi's; weariness had overcome him, and for the past five minutes he had been peacefully sleeping. The old ladies had dropped their voices to a lulling drone, to help him steal the rest his brother wouldn't take him up stairs to get. Luigi listened a moment to Angelo's regular breathing, then said in a voice barely audible:

"We were both born at the same time, but I am six months older than he is."

"For the land's sake!—"

"'Sh! don't wake him up; he wouldn't like my telling this. It has always been kept secret till now."

"But how in the world can it *be?* If you were both born at the same time, how can one of you be older than the other?"

"It is very simple, and I assure you it is true. I was born with a full crop of hair, he was as bald as an egg for six months. I could walk six months before he could make a step. I finished teething six months ahead of him. I began to take solids six months before he left the breast. I began to talk six months before he could say a word. Last, and absolutely unassailable proof, *the sutures in my skull closed six months ahead of his.* Always just that six months difference to a day. Was that accident? Nobody is going to claim *that*, I'm sure. It was ordained—it was law—it had its meaning, and we know what that meaning was. Now what does this overwhelming body of evidence establish? It establishes just one thing, and that thing it establishes beyond any peradventure whatever. Friends, we would not have it known for the world, and I must beg you to keep it strictly to yourselves, but the truth is, we are no more twins than you are."

The two old people were stunned, paralyzed, petrified, one may almost say, and could only sit and gaze vacantly at each other for some moments; then Aunt Betsy Hale said, impressively—

"There's no getting around proofs like that. I do believe it's the most amazing thing I ever heard of." She sat silent a moment or two, and breathing hard with excitement, then she looked up and surveyed the strangers steadfastly a little while, and added, "Well, it does beat me, but I would have took you for twins *anywhere.*"

"So would I, so would I," said Aunt Patsy with the emphasis of a certainty that is not impaired by any shade of doubt.

"*Anybody* would—anybody in the world, I don't care who he is," said Aunt Betsy with decision.

"You won't tell," said Luigi, appealingly.

"O, *dear* no!" answered both ladies promptly, "you can trust us, don't you be afraid."

"That is good of you, and kind. Never let on; treat us always just as if we were twins."

"You can depend on us," said Aunt Betsy, "but it won't be easy, because now that I know you ain't, you don't *seem* so."

"*That* swindle has gone through without change of cars," Luigi muttered to himself with satisfaction.

It was not very kind of him to load the poor old things up with a secret like that, which would be always flying to their tongues' ends every time they heard any one speak of the strangers as twins, and would become harder and harder to hang on to with every recurrence of the temptation to tell it, while the torture of retaining it would increase with every new strain that was applied, but he never thought of that, and probably would not have worried much about it if he had.

Chapter 11

Whenever you find out you have been in error, don't change. This is Consistency.—*Pudd'nhead Wilson's Calendar.*

When I reflect upon the number of disagreeable people who I know have gone to a better world, I am moved to lead a different life.—*Pudd'nhead Wilson's Calendar.*

A visitor was announced—some one to see the Twins. They withdrew to the parlor, and the two old ladies began to discuss with interest the strange things which they had been listening to. When they had finished the matter to their satisfaction, and Aunt Betsy rose to go, she stopped to ask a question—

"How does things come on between Roweny and Tom Driscoll?"

"Well, about the same. He writes tolerable often, and she answers tolerable seldom."

"Where is he?"

"In St. Louis, I believe, though he's such a gad-about that a body can't be very certain of him, I reckon."

"Don't Roweny know?"

"Oh, yes, like enough. I haven't asked her lately."

"Do you know how him and the Judge are getting along now?"

"First rate, I believe. Mrs. Pratt says so; and being right in the house, and sister to the one and aunt to t'other, of course she ought to know. She says the Judge is real fond of him when he's away, but frets when he's around and is vexed with his ways, and not sorry to have him go again. He has been gone three weeks this time—a pleasant thing for both of them, I reckon."

"Tom's ruther harum-scarum, but there ain't anything bad in him, I guess."

"Oh, no, he's just young, that's all. Still, twenty-three is old, in one way. A young man ought to be earning his living by that time. If Tom was doing that, or was even trying to do it, the Judge would be a heap better satisfied with him. Tom's always going to begin, but somehow he can't seem to find just the opening he likes."

"Well, now, it's partly the Judge's own fault. Promising the boy his property wasn't the way to set him to earning a fortune of his own. But what do you think—is Roweny beginning to lean any towards him, or ain't she?"

Aunt Patsy had a secret in her bosom; she wanted to keep it there, but nature was too strong for her. She drew Aunt Betsy aside, and said in her most confidential and mysterious manner—

"Don't you breathe a syllable to a soul—I'm going to tell you something. In my opinion Tom Driscoll's chances were considerable better yesterday than they are to-day."

"Patsy Cooper, what *do* you mean?"

"It's so, as sure as you're born. I wish you could a been at breakfast, and seen for yourself."

"You don't mean it!"

"Well, if I'm any judge, there's a leaning—there's a leaning, sure."

"My land! Which one of 'em is it?"

"I can't say for certain, but I think it's the youngest one—Anjy."

Then there were handshakings, and congratulations, and hopes, and so on, and the old ladies parted, perfectly happy—the one in knowing something which the rest of the town didn't, and the other in having been the sole person able to furnish that knowledge.

The visitor who had called to see the Twins was the Rev. Mr. Hotchkiss, pastor of the Baptist church. At the reception Angelo had told him he had lately experienced a change in his religious views, and was now desirous of becoming a Baptist, and would immediately join Mr. Hotchkiss's church. There was no time to say more, and the brief talk ended at that point. The minister was much gratified, and had dropped in for a moment, now, on a special errand. He said—

"I have come to extend a cordial invitation to you, gentlemen, to attend our Bible class, which meets at eight this evening, in room No. 16 over the market house, and I assure you in advance that you may count upon a pleasing and profitable hour there."

Angelo said—

"I cannot express, dear sir, how sorry I am to be obliged to decline your most kind invitation, but my brother has an engagement which—"

"Oh, I have no engagement that can interfere," said Luigi, promptly, "and we accept with pleasure, and shall be there."

Angelo was astonished; and also suspicious. When the minister was gone, he said:

"I was not expecting this grace at your hands, Luigi. How did you come to accept that invitation?"

Luigi answered in a tone of placid indifference—

"I had two reasons. I overheard you, to-day, when you arranged to haul down your Methodist flag day after tomorrow and hoist the Baptist—"

"Ah!"—

—"and as I have to take a prominent part whenever you change your fire insurance and take out a policy in a new company, I thought it might be well enough to get a little coaching on the fresh conditions—examine the prospectus, so to speak. That is one reason why I wanted to exploit the Bible class."

"Something warned me," said Angelo bitterly, "that your impulse was not a generous one. But let it go, it is no matter; it is your disposition to be hard, and I must still bear it, as I have always had to do. And you had another reason?"

"Yes, but it has no importance. The Freethinkers meet at seven, for only an hour, the Bible class at eight. It is no inconvenience to attend the Bible class, as we are already there."

"Already where? How do you mean?"

"They both meet in the same room."

Angelo turned red with anger and mortification, and he said sharply—

"It was like you! Yes, it was like you, to prepare this humiliation for me. I see it all. You propose to keep me there until the minister and his class come and discover me in such company. This is to be my recommendation to the confidence and respect of the congregation whose holy hospitalities I am to seek day after tomorrow, and who, ignorant of the circumstances, will receive me with cold welcome, and say privately, one to another, 'he thinks it courtesy to prepare himself for our companionship by assisting at a freethinker orgy.' Luigi, how can you have the heart to treat me so?"

"Look here!" retorted Luigi, his southern blood suddenly rising, "as usual, blinded and stupefied by your bigotry, you see and appreciate but one side of the case. Nothing ever has two sides for you, but only one. Morally, you are one-eyed; intellectually, when the interests of that precious baggage which you regard as your soul are concerned, you are a bat, just simply a bat. It seems a heartless thing to you that I should prepare this humiliating exposure for you, but you are not able to perceive that you have prepared a bitterer one for me."

"I? Impossible. Out with it; name it, if you can."

"There! It is just as I said. And it simply passes belief! You can easily anticipate the shame *you* are to feel under the accusing eyes of those Baptists when they say to one another, 'there he is, making his hypocrite vows, and he fresh from a freethinker's meeting;' yet you are dully unable to put yourself in my place and feel what I must feel when my freethinking friends, whom I honor and esteem and believe to be as upright and good and honest and respectworthy as anybody in any church, shall wither me with their pitying eyes Sunday afternoon and say in their hearts, 'he came to our meeting only to laugh at us, we never suspecting; he beguiled us of our confidence, merely that he might spit upon it; he tricked us into confessing, with schoolboy enthusiasm, how proud we were going to be to show him off as our brother— and now, here he stands, breast deep in the river, before all this multitude, and will get himself baptised: treachery and insult can no farther go; he is not a man, he is a cur!'"

Angelo was profoundly hurt. He would have left the room instantly, if he could have done it. He said—and his voice showed how deeply he was agitated—

"I beg that you will now cease. For my own dignity's sake I must decline to continue a discussion with one who so far forgets himself as to place Baptists and Freethinkers upon the same level."

"I don't do it," retorted Luigi hotly. "I don't classify the bifurcated creatures of God by their religious politics; I classify them as men or fools, only. I place a Freethinking fool and a Baptist fool on the same level; and a Baptist who is not a fool, and a Freethinker who is not a fool belong on a common and honorable level, and there I place them. When you started out as a Roman Catholic, where did *you* place the Baptist, since you are suddenly become so sensitive about him?"

No reply.

"And when you were a Mohammedan, where did you place the Catholic *and* the Baptist?"

No reply.

"And when you ceased to be a Turk and became a Scotch Presbyterian, how did you regard all the other rag patches in the ecclesiastical quilt?"

Indignant silence.

"You do well to keep still. You change your road to heaven every time you come to a new finger-board, and then the first thing you do is to depreciate all the roads that brought you that far. If you had stuck to one road you might be in heaven, now, but the way you travel you are never going to get anywhere, in my opinion. Not that *I* care how many roads you travel—wouldn't care, I mean, if I didn't have to go along; but as it is, I get dog-tired of these everlasting excursions, for *I* get nothing out of them, not even scenery, for it's all alike—the same old paradise on one side of the track, the same old perdition on the other, and never anything fresh: a monotony of angels and a monotony of devils, and I never know which I prefer, except that it is not the angels. Now what kind of an angel do you think *you* are going to make?"

"Luigi, your cruelty forces me to speak, though I would you could have granted me peace—it would have cost you very little. You are blaming me, criticising me, upbraiding me, for the one merit I have, the sole thing in me that I might be pardoned for taking pride in—the facility and courage with which I discard a religious error when I find myself in one."

"Yes, and the facility and chuckleheadedness with which you take up with the next one that comes along. You are just a theological goat, that is what you are: first you munch a dishrag, and you'll drop that for a last year's newspaper, and that for a pile of pine shavings, and that for a paper of tacks; and you are vain of the facility and courage with which you can sample thirty kinds of refuse in succession and come out with a belly full of nothing at the end, and just as hungry and idiotically enterprising as you were when you started in. You've got the appetite of an ostrich, with the judgment of a kangaroo, and you've got no more shame than to confess that you are proud of it. I wish, for your own sake, you would reform."

"Luigi, you are brutal! It should occur to you, and it should be a reproach to you, that I make this weary and sometimes almost despairing search for salvation, unaided, unencouraged, yes, even reviled, obstructed, harassed, by you, when if you had the sort of heart you ought to have, you would help me."

"*I* help you—the idea! As if I don't get excursions enough the way it is. No, I will do nothing of the kind. I look back upon my past with horror. When you were a Catholic I had to get up before daylight and go with you to early mass; once, when you had command of our legs, you took me to the Convent and had our mutual back scourged for your individual sins—once you did, but you didn't play that again. When you were a Mohammedan I had to starve the Ramadan through, or you would have told on me and got me into trouble; and I had to seem to pray five times a day, like the rest of that detestable sect. When you were this, that and the other experimental ecclesiastical tramp, I had all the privations of the situation and none of the hopes of reward. When you were a Presbyterian—but I will be silent there; I cannot think of those dismal Sabbaths and keep any rag of my patience. And *now* what are you proposing to do day after tomorrow? You are going to risk drowning me, that is what. And after all, what was to be the reward of this lagging dull lifetime of sorrows and sufferings and aggravations that I have been obliged to endure? The salvation of that tedious soul of yours. Oh, there is a long account to be settled between you and me, and I will see that you square it up, to the last farthing."

So ended the controversy.

Chapter 12

Judge Driscoll called for the Twins in the evening, and took them over to No. 16, and on the way told them all about Pudd'nhead Wilson, in order that they might get a favorable impression of him in advance and be prepared to like him. This scheme succeeded with Luigi—the favorable impression was achieved; but with Angelo the favorable impression was not quite perfect, it being marred by the fact that Wilson was a freethinker. The meeting was called to order, a ballot was taken, and Luigi elected to membership. Then the Judge proposed to discuss the six days of the creation from a strictly scientific standpoint; but Wilson made a little speech in which he said he had learned, during the day, that the guest of the evening was a church member, therefore the courtesy due him as a guest forbade that any subject be touched upon which could in any way wound his feelings. He moved that the hour be devoted to conversation upon ordinary topics and the cultivation of friendly relations and good-fellowship, and then sat down.

The Judge cast a proud glance at the Twins which said, "There—what did I tell you?—that is the kind of man he is." Angelo's eyes sent back a glance of surprised and grateful approval, but Luigi remained impassive. Still, he said to himself, I don't like Wilson the less for this; I would do such things myself if I could get the best of my nature. This thought pushed him to an effort, and when the motion was put he made it unanimous by voting aye. Angelo could have embraced him, he was so pleased, but he kept his impulse to himself, knowing that with Luigi it was generally best to let well enough alone.

The hour passed quickly away in lively talk, and when it was ended the lonesome and neglected Wilson was richer by two friends than he had been when it began. He invited the Twins to look in at his lodgings when the Bible class should be over, and Luigi promptly accepted. Angelo said—

"I ought not to go, much as I desire it, since mixing socially with free-thinkers must make talk and be a detriment to me, situated as I am, but I cannot decline any invitation this week which my brother accepts, therefore I shall come—yes, and eagerly, in spirit, although reluctantly in principle."

The freethinkers left, now, and as they went out at the door the Bible class began to file in, the Rev. Mr. Hotchkiss in the lead. It made him gasp to see the Twins there, but the young ladies and gentlemen did not gasp; no, the situation was larks for them, so to speak, as one could see by their arch glances and the way they privately nudged each other and indulged in smothered gigglings. Mr. Hotchkiss had been spreading the fact around that his church had made a capture of one of the distinguished foreigners, and that both were going to visit his Bible class, and the class was not slow, now, to perceive how much the size of these triumphs had been cut down by the precedence given the freethinking crew. They were too young to grieve over Mr. Hotchkiss's misfortune, they only enjoyed it.

However, Mr. Hotchkiss did the best he could, in the circumstances. He threw as much cordiality as he could into his welcome of the Twins, though his embarrassment showed through, rather plainly. He introduced everybody in turn to the strangers, and then the session opened. The Bible class was in effect a debating class, with casting vote and veto lodged in its president, the minister. They now proceeded to discuss the question of whether men would rise from the dead as spirits or clothed on with flesh. The minister closed the discussion, and was gratified to see, he said, that the class was with him in believing that we should enter heaven in the flesh, and differing in no wise from what we are here.

Then he offered the Twins the privilege of speaking, whereupon Angelo took the minister's view, and after talking a while, apologized for Luigi, who was not now a believer but must in time become one; of this Angelo felt sure.

The minister most heartily hoped that this would prove true, and asked Luigi if he was not able to believe that men would be raised in the flesh.

Luigi said yes, he was able to believe it, and did believe it.

The minister was gratified, and asked him why, then, he did not come into the fold and take measures to save himself.

Luigi answered, with simplicity, that he was not fitted by nature and disposition for the religious vocation, and was satisfied to leave it to his brother to save him.

"Your brother! Ah, my dear friend, we cannot delegate these things. Each must enter heaven on his own merits; your brother cannot take you there."

"How will he avoid it?"

There was a sufficiently awkward silence, which endured for some moments; then the minister rallied, and said:

"There—er—well, there is—er—there is certainly reason in the position which you have taken. It is indeed logical—in fact, formidably so; that I must confess. But, on the other hand, consider, my dear friend, that a place is appointed for those who die in sin, and to it they must infallibly go; and surely you would not desire to drag down with you thither your innocent brother?"

Luigi reflected, then said:

"Do you ever teach that an innocent person can be sent to that place because somebody else has led a guilty life and died in sin?"

"Why—n-no. Certainly not—of course not."

"Shall you ever teach that?"

"Well, no, I could not teach that, I am free to say."

"Very well, I believe as you do: the innocent need not be afraid of being punished for the guilty. You have confirmed and solidified in me this belief. I have always depended upon my brother to save me, and I know he will. I shall go on depending on him."

The clock on the wall struck nine, and the minister seemed relieved by the interruption and at once dismissed the class. Luigi had worked him into an awkward dilemma and was gratified; he saw that the class was tickled, and that pleased him; Angelo was ashamed of him, and that completed his happiness and he was glad he had come. Mr. Hotchkiss did not tarry for an effusive leave-taking, but cut it as short as decency would permit and got away; and as he trudged homeward he said to himself with an irritated spirit, "these Twins are in every way an awkward and embarrassing anomaly, and in my opinion the more this community sees of them the more it is going to have that fact borne in upon them." Presently he added, with bitterness—

"These giddy young scamps will carry to-night's performance all over the town tomorrow; from the town it will spread all around the back country, and every sorrowing creature in the land that is suffering for something to laugh at will come to see me baptise that abandoned infidel, Sunday!"

Angelo smarted under the events of the evening, but kept his feelings to himself, making no remark on the way to Pudd'nhead Wilson's.

Pudd'nhead was at home waiting for them and putting in his time puzzling over a thing which had come under his notice that morning. The matter was this. He happened to be up very early—at dawn, in fact; and he crossed the hall which divided his cottage through the centre, and entered a room to get something there. The window of the room had no curtains, for that side of the house had long been unoccupied, and through this window he caught sight of something which surprised and interested him. It was a young woman—a young woman where properly no young woman belonged; for she was in Judge Driscoll's house, and in the bedroom over the Judge's private study or sitting room. This was young Tom Driscoll's bedroom. He and the Judge, the Judge's widowed sister Mrs. Pratt, and three negro servants were the only people who belonged in the house. Who, then, might this young lady be? The two houses were separated by an ordinary yard, with a low fence running back through its middle from the street in front to the lane in the rear. The distance was not great, Wilson was able to see the girl very well, the window shades of the room she was in being up, and the window also. The girl had on a neat and trim summer dress patterned in alternating broad stripes of pink and white, and her bonnet was equipped with a pink veil. She was practicing steps, gaits and attitudes, apparently; she was doing the thing gracefully, and was very much absorbed in her work. Who could she be, and how came she to be in young Driscoll's room?

Wilson had quickly chosen a position from which he could watch the girl without running much risk of being seen by her, and he remained there hoping she would raise her veil and betray her face. But she disappointed him. After a matter of twenty minutes she disappeared, and although he stayed at his post half an hour longer, she came no more.

Toward noon he dropped in at the Judge's and talked with Mrs. Pratt about the great event of the day, the levée of the distinguished foreigners at Aunt Patsy Cooper's. He asked after her nephew Tom, and she said he was on his way home, and that she was expecting him to arrive before night; and added that she and the Judge were gratified to gather from his letters that he was conducting himself very nicely and creditably—at which Wilson winked to himself privately. Wilson did not ask if there was a new-comer in the house, but he asked questions that would have brought light-throwing answers as to that matter if Mrs. Pratt had had any light to throw; so he went away satisfied that he knew of things that were going on in her house which she was not aware of, herself.

He was now waiting for the Twins, and still puzzling over the problem of who that girl might be, and how she happened to be in that young fellow's room at day-break in the morning.

Chapter 13

The holy passion of Friendship is of so sweet and steady and loyal and enduring a nature that it will last through a whole lifetime if not asked to lend money.—*Pudd'nhead Wilson's Calendar.*

It is necessary, now, to hunt up Roxy.

She went away chambermaiding the year she was set free, when she was thirty-five. She got a berth as second chambermaid on a Cincinnati boat in the New Orleans trade, the "Grand Mogul." It was a big steamer for the time—two hundred and fifty feet long. Roxy had never been in a steamer's cabin before—cabin was the western name for the grand salons into which the berth-rooms opened, not the berth-rooms themselves. The cabin was like a long, brilliantly lighted tunnel. It was of pine, covered with a highly polished skin of white paint. On every berth-room door of the two far-stretching sides was an oil picture—Mississippi scenery, the subject—with all the known colors in it and some of the unknown, and all the different kinds of drawing in it except good drawing—dreadful pictures, in fact, but very showy and effective. Separating these crimes were fluted white-painted pine pilasters with gilded Corinthian capitals. Overhead, the receding stretch of ivory-like ceiling fairly bristled with down-pointing wonders of ornamentation done with the jig-saw and the turning-lathe. At fifty-foot intervals there were great pyramidal chandeliers, whose sumptuous fringes of cut-glass prisms, flaming and flashing in the sun, shook out showers of dancing rainbow-flecks upon the white walls and doors in response to the slightest joggle. Tables covered with figured crimson cloths formed a fiery platform down the middle of the tunnel from end to end. Against each wall was backed a stiff rank of windsor chairs, from the bar on the port side and the clerk's office on the starboard clear aft to the piano and the big mirror in the ladies' cabin. And the carpet—the carpet was a revel; not a dream, but a revel, just a revel of bounding and careering great whorls of inflamed scroll-work out on a drunk.

Roxy was entranced. She had often heard of these "floating palaces"—which was the common and quite sincerely-applied name of these museums—but had never been on the inside of one of them before. She moved through it in an ecstasy of bliss. The wilderness of noble furniture amazed her by its magnitude, and its possible cost made all her former notions of wealth seem poor and shabby imaginings; the profusion and richness of the decorations steeped her barbaric soul in delight, and in the glorious insurrection of color she saw her dearest dreams of the splendors of heaven realized. Ah, why hadn't she run away and entered into the joys of this earthly paradise earlier? It grieved her to think she had lost so much time.

Presently passengers began to stream aboard and flock hither and thither in search of their staterooms, inquiring, commanding, exclaiming, and they filled the whole place with inspiriting life and racket and commotion. Ah, it was a thousand times better to be here than in that sleepy dull town.

Soon, a swarm of white-aproned and white-jacketed colored boys burst in from somewhere, and in an instant the red covers were gone and the tables clothed in white! It made Roxy dizzy, the thing was done so suddenly. And she wondered how one mere human establishment could support such a horde of servants. When she came to herself after a couple of seconds, there was another surprise—they had vanished; whither, she didn't know.

Then came a musical kling-kling from a little bell, and they appeared again; they marched in, in a couple of snowy files, and moved down the long cabin, depositing plates and cruets and things as they went, and in a minute the tables stood completely arrayed and ready for the provisions. The last boys in the ranks placed the chairs.

The bell struck again, and again the files entered, some bearing great platters and chafing-dishes of fish, meats and so forth, aloft, and others superb sugar-clad miniature temples, supposed to be made of cake, whereas in truth the finest of them were decorated cheese-boxes, though neither Roxy nor the passengers suspected that.

Then the first gong let go a horrible crash and kept it up two minutes, although there was a passenger behind every chair by the time that the fiend with the gong had hit it the second blow.

At the end of ten minutes the gong broke loose again, the double file of passengers plunged into their seats, and the havoc began.

To Roxy the prodigious noise and confusion about the stage-planks during the final moments before the boat's departure was a most satisfying delight. Every detail had interest for her: the rushing avalanche of barrels thundering down the stages; the belated passengers skipping perilously among them to win to the forecastle; the clarion voices of the mates discharging volume after volume of the most erudite and versatile and magnificent profanity without a tautological blemish in it anywhere; the yelling of news-boys; the slamming of furnace doors; the screaming of gauge-cocks; the deafening banging and clanging of the everlasting "last bell." Every separate detail had a dulcet charm for Roxy, and the combination constituted bliss.

At last the boat did get away, and went plowing down the Ohio, filling all the heavens with sable smoke; and for seven days and nights she piled States and scenery behind her with a celerity which bewildered the second chambermaid and made her realize as she had never realized before that the white man was in very truth a wonder-compelling creature and a creator of marvelous contriv-ances. Then she found herself in New Orleans, and when she saw that the wells (cisterns) and the graves were all on top of the ground instead of under it she was sure her excitements had confused her brain and disordered her eyesight.

A couple of trips made a wonted and easy-going steamboatman of her, and infatuated her with the stir and adventure and independence of steamboat life. She was promoted, then, and became head chambermaid. She was a favorite with the officers, and exceedingly proud of their joking and friendly ways with her.

During eight years she served three parts of the year on that boat, and the winters on a Vicksburg packet. But now for two months she had had rheu-matism in her arms, and was obliged to let the wash-tub alone. So she resigned. But she was well fixed—rich, as she would have described it; for she had lived a steady life, and had saved up and banked four dollars every month as a provision for her old age. She said in the start that she had "put shoes on one bar'footed nigger to tromple on her with," and one mistake like that was enough: she would be independent of the human race thenceforth forever-more if hard work and economy could accomplish it.

She bade good-bye to her comrades on the Grand Mogul and moved her kit ashore when the boat touched the levee at New Orleans.

But she was back in an hour. The bank had gone to smash and carried her four hundred dollars with it. She was a pauper, and homeless. Also disabled bodily, at least for the present. The officers were full of sympathy for her in her trouble, and made up a little purse for her. She resolved to go to her birth-place; she had friends there among the negroes, and the unfortunate always help the unfortunate, she was well aware of that; those lowly comrades of her youth would not let her starve.

She took the little packet at Cairo, and now she was on the homestretch. At once her memory began to travel back over the long ago, and she found that time had worn away her bitterness against her son, and that she was able to think of him with serenity. She put the vile side of him out of her mind, and dwelt only on recollections of his occasional acts of kindness to her. She gilded and otherwise decorated these, and made them very pleasant to contemplate. She began to long to see him. She would go and fawn around him, slave-like—for this would have to be her attitude, of course—and maybe she would find that time had modified him, and that he would be glad to see his long forgotten old nurse and treat her gently. That would be lovely—that would make her forget her woes and her poverty!

Her poverty. That thought inspired her to add another castle to her dream: maybe he would help her; maybe he would give her a trifle now and then— maybe a dollar, once a month, say; any little thing like that would help, oh, ever so much!

By the time she reached Dawson's Landing she was her old self again; her blues were gone, she was in high feather. She would get along, sure; there were many kitchens where the servants would share their meals with her, and also steal sugar and apples and other dainties for her to carry home—or give her a chance to pilfer them herself, which would answer just as well. And there was the church. She was a more rabid and devoted Methodist than ever, and her piety was no sham, but was strong and sincere. Yes, with plenty of creature comforts and her old place in the amen corner in her possession again, she should be perfectly happy and at peace thenceforward to the end.

She went to Judge Driscoll's kitchen first of all. She was received there in great form and with vast enthusiasm. Her wonderful travels, and the strange countries she had seen and the adventures she had had, made her a marvel and a heroine of romance. The negroes hung enchanted upon the great story of her experiences, interrupting her all along with eager questions, with laughter, exclamations of delight and explosions of applause; and she was obliged to confess to herself that if there was anything better in this world than steamboating, it was the glory to be got by telling about it. The audience loaded her stomach with their dinners and then stole the pantry bare to load up her basket.

Tom was in St. Louis. The servants said he had spent the best part of his time there during the previous two years. Roxy came every day, and had many talks about the family and its affairs. Once she asked why Tom was away so much. Chambers said:

"De fac' is, ole marster kin git along better when young marster's away den he kin when he's in de town; yes, en he love him better, too; so he gives him fifty dollahs a month—"

"No, is dat so! Chambers, you's a jokin', ain't you?"

"'Clah to goodness I ain't, mammy; Marse Tom tole me so, his own self. But nemmine, 'tain't enough."

"My lan', what de reason 'tain't enough?"

"Well, I's gwyne to tell you, if you gimme a chanst, mammy. De reason it ain't enough is becase Marse Tom gambles."

Roxy threw up her hands in astonishment, and Chambers went on—

"Ole Marse found it out, becase he had to pay two hunderd dollahs for Marse Tom's gamblin' debts, en dat's true, mammy, jes' as dead certain as you's bawn."

"Two—hund'd—dollahs! Why, what is you talkin' 'bout? Two—hund'd—dollahs! Sakes alive, it's mos' enough to buy a tollable good second-hand nigger wid. En you ain't lyin', honey?—you wouldn't lie to yo' ole mammy?"

"It's Gawd's own truth, jes' as I tell you—two hunderd dollahs—I wisht I may never stir outen my tracks if it ain't so. En, oh, my lan', ole Marse was jes' a hoppin'! he was bilin' mad, I *tell* you! He tuck 'n dissenhurrit him."

He licked his chops with complacent relish after that stately word. Roxy struggled with it a moment, then gave it up and said—

"Dissen*whiched* him?"

"Dissenhurrit him."

"What's dat? What do it mean?"

"Means he busted de will."

"Bus—ted de will! He wouldn't ever treat him so. Take it back, you misable imitation nigger dat I bore in sorrow en tribbilation!"

Roxy's pet castle—an occasional dollar from Tom's pocket—was tumbling to ruin before her eyes. She could not abide such a disaster as that; she couldn't endure the thought of it.

"Yah-yah-yah! jes' listen to dat! If *I's* imitation, what is you? Bofe of us is imitation *white*—dat's what we is—en pow'ful good imitation, too—yah-yah-yah!—we don't 'mount to noth'n as imitation *niggers*; en as for—"

"Shet up yo' foolin', 'fo' I knock you side de head, en tell me 'bout de will. Tell me 'tain't busted—*do*, honey, en I'll never fogit you."

"Well, 'tain't—caze dey's a new one made, en Marse Tom's all right agin. But what is *you* in sich a sweat 'bout it for, mammy, 'tain't none o' your business I don't reckon?"

"'Tain't none o' *my* business? Whose business *is* it den, I'd like to know? Was I his mother tell he was fifteen years old, or wusn't I?—you answer me dat. En you speck I could see him turned out po' en ornery on de worl' en never care noth'n 'bout it? I reckon if you'd ever ben a mother yo'self, Vallet de Chambers, you wouldn't talk sich foolishness as dat."

"Well, den, ole Marse forgive him en fixed up de will agin—do dat satisfy you?"

Yes, she was satisfied, now, and quite happy and sentimental over it. She kept coming daily, and at last she was told that Tom had come home. She began to tremble with emotion, and straightway sent to beg him to let his "po' ole nigger mammy have jes' one sight of him en die for joy."

Tom was stretched at his lazy ease on a sofa when Chambers brought the petition. Time had not modified his ancient detestation of the humble drudge and protector of his boyhood; it was still bitter and uncompromising. He sat up and bent a severe gaze upon the fair face of the young fellow whose name he was using and whose family rights he was enjoying. He maintained the gaze until the victim of it had become satisfactorily pallid with terror, then he said—

"What does the old rip want with me?"

The petition was meekly repeated.

"Who gave you permission to come and disturb me with the social attentions of niggers?"

Tom had risen. The other young man was trembling, now, visibly. He saw what was coming, and bent his head sideways and put up his left arm to shield it. Tom rained cuffs upon the head and its shield, saying no word; the victim received each blow with a beseeching "*Please*, Marse Tom!—oh, *please*, Marse Tom!" Seven blows—then Tom said, "Face the door—march!" He followed behind with one, two, three solid kicks. The last one helped the pure-white slave over the door-sill, and he limped away mopping his eyes with his old ragged sleeve. Tom shouted after him, "Send her in!"

Then he flung himself panting on the sofa again and rasped out the remark, "He arrived just at the right moment; I was full to the brim with bitter thinkings, and nobody to take it out of. How refreshing it was!—I feel better."

Tom's mother entered, now, closing the door behind her, and approached her son with all the wheedling and supplicating servilities that fear and interest can impart to the words and attitudes of the born slave. She stopped a yard from her boy and made two or three admiring exclamations over his manly stature and general handsomeness, and Tom put an arm under his head and hoisted a leg over the sofa-back in order to look properly indifferent.

"My lan', how you is growed, honey! 'Clah to goodness I wouldn't a knowed you, Marse Tom, 'deed I wouldn't. Look at me good; does you 'member ole Roxy?—does you know yo' ole nigger mammy, honey? Well, now, I kin lay down en die in peace, caze I's seed—"

"Cut it short, damn it, cut it short. What is it you want?"

"You heah dat? Jes' de same old Marse Tom, allays so gay and funnin' wid de ole mammy! I 'uz jes' as shore—"

"Cut it short, I tell you, and get along. What do you want?"

This was a bitter disappointment. Roxy had for so many days nourished and fondled and petted her notion that Tom would be glad to see his old nurse and would make her proud and happy to the marrow with a cordial word or two, that it took two rebuffs to convince her that he was not funning and that her beautiful dream was a fond and foolish vanity, a shabby and pitiful mistake. She was hurt to the heart, and so ashamed that for a moment she did not quite know what to do or how to act. Then her breast began to heave, the tears came, and in her forlornness she was moved to try that other dream of hers—an appeal to her boy's charity; and so, upon the impulse, and without reflection, she offered her supplication—

"Oh, Marse Tom, de po' ole mammy is in sich hard luck, dese days; en she's kinder crippled in de arms en can't work, en if you *could* gimme a dollah— on'y jes' one little d—"

Tom was on his feet so suddenly that the supplicant was startled into a jump herself.

"A dollar!—give *you* a dollar! I've a notion to strangle you! Is *that* your errand here? Clear out! and be quick about it."

Roxy backed slowly toward the door. When she was halfway she stopped, and said, mournfully—

"Marse Tom, I nussed you when you was a little baby, en I raised you all by myself tell you was most a young man; en now you is young en rich en I is po' en gitt'n ole, en I come heah b'lievin' dat you would he'p de ole mammy 'long down de little road dat's lef' twix her en de grave, en—"

Tom relished this tune less than any that had preceded it, for it began to wake up a sort of echo in his conscience; so he interrupted and said with decision, though without asperity, that he was not in a situation to help her, and wasn't going to do it.

"Ain't you *ever* gwyne to he'p me, Marse Tom?"

"No! Now go away and don't bother me any more."

Roxy's head was down, in an attitude of humility. But now the fires of her old wrongs flamed up in her breast and began to burn fiercely. She raised her head slowly, till it was well up, and at the same time her great frame unconsciously assumed an erect and masterful attitude, with all the majesty and grace of her vanished youth in it. She raised her finger and punctuated with it:

"You has said de word. You has had yo' chance, en you has trompled it under yo' foot. When you git another one, you'll git down on yo' knees en beg for it!"

A cold chill went to Tom's heart, he didn't know why; for he did not reflect that such words, from such an incongruous source, and so solemnly delivered, could not easily fail of that effect. However, he did the natural thing: he replied with bluster and mockery:

"*You'll* give me a chance—*you!* Perhaps I'd better get down on my knees *now.* But in case I don't—just for argument's sake—what's going to happen, pray?"

"Dis is what is gwyne to happen. I's gwyne as straight to yo' uncle as I kin walk, en tell him every las' thing I knows about you!"

Tom's cheek blenched, and she saw it. Disturbing thoughts began to chase each other through his head. "How can *she* know? And yet she must have found out—she looks it. I've had the will back only three months and am already deep in debt again and moving heaven and earth to save myself from exposure and destruction, with a reasonably fair show of getting the thing covered up if I'm let alone, and now this fiend has gone and found me out somehow or other. I wonder how much she knows? Oh, oh, oh, it's enough to break a body's heart! But I've got to humor her—there's no other way."

Then he worked up a rather sickly sample of a gay laugh and a hollow chipperness of manner, and said—

"Well, well, Roxy dear, old friends like you and me mustn't quarrel. Here's your dollar—now tell me what you know."

He held out the wild-cat bill, she stood as she was, and made no movement. It was her turn to scorn persuasive foolery, now, and she did not waste it. She said, with a grim implacability in voice and manner which made Tom almost realize that even a negro ex-slave can remember for ten minutes insults and injuries returned for compliments and flatteries received, and can also enjoy taking revenge for them when the opportunity offers—

"What does I know? I'll tell you what I knows. I knows enough to bust dat will to flinders—en *more*, mind you, *more!*"

Tom was aghast.

"More?" he said. "What do you call more? Where's there any room for more?"

Roxy laughed a mocking laugh, and said scoffingly, with a toss of her head, and her hands on her hips—

"Yes!—oh, I reckon! 'Cose you'd like to know—wid yo' po' little ole rag dollah! What you reckon I's gwyne to tell *you*, for?—*you* ain't got no money. I's gwyne to tell yo' uncle—en I'll do it dis minute, too—he'll gimme *five* dollahs for de news, en mighty glad, too."

She swung herself around disdainfully, and started away. Tom was in a panic. He seized her skirts and implored her to wait. She turned and said, loftily—

"Look-a-here, what was it I tole you?"

"You—you—I don't remember anything. What was it you told me?"

"I tole you dat de next time I give you a chance you'd git down on yo' knees en beg for it."

Tom was stupefied for a moment. He was panting with excitement. Then he said—

"Oh, Roxy, you wouldn't require your young master to do such a horrible thing. You can't mean it."

"I'll let you know mighty quick whether I means it or not. *You* call *me* names, en as good as spit on me when I comes here po' en ornery en 'umble, to praise you for bein' growed up so fine en handsome, en tell you how I used to nuss you en tend you en watch you when you was sick en you hadn't no mother but me in de whole worl', en beg you to give de po' ole nigger a dollah for to git her sum'n to eat, en you call me names—*names*, dad blame you! Yassir, I gives you jes' one chance mo', and dat's *now*, en it las' on'y a half a second—you *hear*?"

Tom slumped to his knees and began to beg, saying—

"You *see* I'm begging, and it's honest begging, too. Now tell me, Roxy, tell me!"

The heir of two centuries of unatoned insult and outrage looked down on him and seemed to drink in deep draughts of satisfaction. Then she said—

"Fine nice young white gen'lman kneelin' down to a nigger wench! I's wanted to see dat jes' once befo' I's called. Now, Gabrel, blow de hawn, I's ready! . . . . . Git up!"

Tom did it. He said, humbly—

"Now Roxy, don't punish me any more. I deserved what I've got, but be good and let me off with that. Don't go to uncle. Tell me—I'll give you the five dollars."

"Yes, I bet you will; en you won't stop dah, nuther. But I ain't gwyne to tell you here—"

"Good gracious, no!"

"Is you feared o' de ha'nted house?"

"N-no."

"Well, den, you come to de ha'nted house 'bout ten or 'leven to-night, en climb up de ladder, caze de star-steps is broke down, en you'll fine me. I's a roostin' in de ha'nted house becaze I can't 'ford to roos' nowher's else." She started toward the door, but stopped and said "Gimme de dollah bill." He gave it to her. She examined it and said, "Hm—like enough de bank's busted." She started again, but halted again. "Has you got any whisky?"

"Yes, a little."

"Fetch it."

He ran to his room overhead and brought down a bottle which was two-thirds full. She tilted it up and took a drink. Her eyes sparkled with satisfaction, and she tucked the bottle under her shawl, saying,—

"It's prime—I'll take it along."

Tom humbly held the door for her, and she marched out as grim and erect as a grenadier.

Chapter 14

Then Tom flung himself on the sofa, and put his throbbing head in his hands and rested his elbows on his knees. He rocked himself back and forth and moaned.

"I've knelt to a nigger wench!" he muttered. "I thought I had struck the deepest deeps of degradation before, but oh, dear, it was nothing to this. . . . . . . Well, there is one consolation, such as it is—I've struck bottom this time; there's nothing lower than this."

But that was a hasty conclusion.

At ten that night he climbed the ladder in the haunted house, pale, weak, and tolerably sick. Roxy was standing in the door of one of the rooms, waiting, for she had heard him.

This was a two-story log house which had acquired the reputation a few years before of being haunted, and that was the end of its usefulness. Nobody would live in it afterward or go near it by night, and most people even gave it a wide berth in the daytime. As it had no competition, it was called *the* haunted house. It was getting crazy and ruinous, now, from long neglect. It stood three hundred yards beyond Pudd'nhead Wilson's house, with nothing between but vacancy. It was the last house in the town at that end.

Tom followed Roxy into the room. She had a pile of clean straw in the corner for a bed, some cheap but well-kept clothing was hanging on the wall, there was a tin lantern freckling the floor with little spots of light, and there were various soap and candle boxes scattered about, which served for chairs. The two sat down. Roxy said—

"Now, den. I'll tell you straight off, en I'll begin to k'leck de money later on; I ain't in no hurry. What does you reckon I's gwyne to tell you?"

"Well, you—you—oh, Roxy, don't make it too hard for me. Come right out and tell me you've found out somehow what a shape I'm in on account of dissipation and foolishness."

"Disposition en foolishness! *No* sir, *dat* ain't it. Dat jist ain't noth'n at *all*, 'longside o' what *I* knows."

Tom stared at her, and said—

"Why—Roxy, what do you *mean?*"

She rose, and gloomed above him like a fate.

"I means dis—en it's de Lord's truth. *You ain't no more kin to ole Marse Driscoll den I is!*—dat's what I mean!" and her eyes flamed with triumph.

"What!"

"Yassir, en *dat* ain't all. You is a *nigger!*—*bawn* a nigger en a *slave!*—en you's a nigger en a slave dis minute! en if I opens my mouf, ole Marse Driscoll 'll *sell you down de river* befo' you is two days older den what you is now!"

"It's a thundering lie, you miserable old blatherskite!"

"It ain't no lie, nuther. It's jes' de truth, en noth'n *but* de truth, so he'p me! Yassir—*you's my son*—"

"You devil!—"

—"en dat po' boy dat you's ben a kickin' en a cuffin' to-day is Percy Driscoll's son *en yo' marster*—"

"You beast!"

—"en *his* name's Tom Driscoll en *yo'* name's Vallet de Chambers, en you ain't got no surname, becaze niggers don't *have* 'em!"

Tom sprang up and seized a billet of wood and raised it; but his mother only laughed at him and said—

"Set down, you pup! Does you think you kin sk'yer *me?* It ain't in you, nor de likes of you. I reckon you'd shoot me in de back, maybe, if you got a chance, for dat's jist yo' style, *I* knows you, thoo en *thoo*—but *I* don't mind gitt'n killed, becaze all dis is down in writin', en it's in safe hands, too, en de man dat's got it knows whah to look for de right man when I gits killed. Oh, bless yo' soul, if you puts yo' mother up for as big a fool as *you* is, you's pow'ful mistaken, I kin tell you. *Now* den, you set still en behave yo'self; en don't you git up agin till I tell you."

Tom fretted and chafed a while in a whirlwind of doubt, certainty, fear, derision, and all the other emotions, and finally said with something like settled conviction—

"The whole thing is moonshine—now, then, go ahead and do your worst; I'm done with you."

Roxy made no answer. She took the lantern and started toward the door. Tom was in a cold panic in a moment.

"Come back, come back!" he wailed. "I didn't mean it, Roxy, I take it all back, and I'll never say it again. *Please* come back, Roxy."

The woman stood a moment, then she said gravely—

"Dah's one thing you's got to stop, Vallet de Chambers. You can't call *me* Roxy, same as if you was my equal. Chillen don't speak to dey mammies like dat. You'll call me *Ma* or *mammy*, dat's what you'll call me—leastways when dey ain't nobody aroun'. *Say* it!"

It cost Tom a struggle, but he got it out.

"Dat's all right. Don't you ever fogit it agin, if you knows what's good for you. Now, den, you has said you wouldn't ever call it lies en moonshine agin. I'll tell you dis, for a warnin': if you ever does say it agin, it's de *las'* time you'll ever say it to *me*; I'll tramp as straight to de Judge as I kin walk, en tell him who you is en *prove* it! Does you b'lieve me when I says dat?"

"Oh," groaned Tom, "I more than believe it, I *know* it!"

Roxy knew her conquest was complete. She could have proven nothing to anybody, and her threat about the writings was a lie; but she knew the person she was dealing with, and had made both statements without any doubts as to the effect they would produce.

She went and sat down on her candle-box, and the pride and pomp of her victorious attitude made it a throne. She said—

"Now, den, Chambers, we's gwyne to talk cold business, en dey ain't gwyne to be no mo' foolishness. In de fust place, you gits fifty dollahs a month; you's gwyne to han' over half of it to yo' ma. Plank it out!"

But Tom had only six dollars in the world. He gave her that, and promised to start fair on next month's pension.

"Chambers, how much is you in debt?"

Tom shuddered, and said—

"Nearly three hundred dollars."

"How is you gwyne to pay it?"

Tom groaned out—

"Oh, *I* don't know—don't ask me such awful questions!"

But she stuck to her point until she wearied a confession out of him: he had been prowling about in disguise, stealing small valuables from private houses; in fact had made a good deal of a raid on his fellow villagers a fortnight before, when he was supposed to be in St. Louis; but he doubted if he had sent away enough stuff to realize the required amount on, and was afraid to make a further venture in the present excited state of the town. His mother approved of his conduct, and offered to help, but this frightened him. He tremblingly ventured to say that if she would retire from the town he should feel better and safer, and could hold his head higher—and was going on to make an argument, but she interrupted and surprised him pleasantly by saying she was ready, it didn't make any difference to her where she stayed, so that she got her share of the pension regularly. She said she would not go far, and would call at the haunted house once a month for her money. Then she said—

"I don't hate you so much now, but I've hated you a many a year—and anybody would. Didn't I change you off en give you a good fambly en a good name, en made you a white gen'lman en rich, wid store clothes on—en what did I git for it? You despised me all de time; en was allays sayin' mean hard things to me befo' folks, en wouldn't ever let me fogit I's a nigger—en—en—"

She fell to sobbing, and broke down. Tom said—

"But you know, I didn't know you were my mother—and besides—"

"Well, nemmine 'bout dat, now—let it go. I's gwyne to fogit it." Then she added fiercely, "En don't you ever make me remember it agin, or you'll be sorry, *I* tell you!"

When they were parting, Tom said, in the most persuasive way he could command—

"Ma, would you mind telling me who was my father?"

He had supposed he was asking an embarrassing question. He was mistaken. Roxy drew herself up, with a proud toss of her head, and said:

"Does I mine tellin' you? No, dat I don't. You ain't got no 'casion to be shame' o' yo' father, *I* kin tell you. He was de highest quality in dis whole town—Ole Virginny stock, Fust Famblies, he was. Jes' as good stock as de Driscolls en de Howards, de bes' day dey ever seed." She put on a still prouder air, if possible, and added impressively, "Does you 'member Cunnel Cecil Burleigh Essex, dat died de same year yo' young Marse Tom Driscoll's pappy died, en all de Masons en Odd Fellers en churches turned out en give him de bigges' funeral dis town ever seed? Dat's de man!" Under the inspiration of her soaring complacency the departed graces of her earlier days returned to her, and her bearing took to itself a dignity and state that might have passed for queenly if her surroundings had been a little more in keeping with it. "Dey ain't another nigger in dis town dat's as high-bawn as you is. Now, den, go 'long. En jes' you hold yo' head up as high as you want to—you has de *right*, en dat I kin swah!"

Chapter 15

All say "How hard it is that we have to die"—a strange complaint to come from the mouths of people who have had to live.—Pudd'nhead Wilson's Calendar.

Why is it that we rejoice at a birth and weep at a funeral? It is because we are not the person involved.—Pudd'nhead Wilson's Calendar.

Every now and then, after Tom went to bed, he had sudden wakings out of his sleep, and his first thought was, "O, joy, it was all a dream!" Then he laid himself heavily down again, with a bitter groan and the muttered words, "A nigger!—I am a nigger!—oh, I wish I was dead!"

He woke at dawn with one more repetition of this horror, and then he resolved to meddle no more with that treacherous sleep. He began to think. Sufficiently bitter thinkings they were. They wandered along something after this fashion:

"Why were niggers *and* whites made? What crime did the uncreated first nigger commit that the curse of birth was decreed for him? And why is this awful difference made between white and black? . . . . . . How hard the nigger's fate seems, this morning!—yet until last night such a thought never entered my head . . . . . I am a nigger—a nigger! . . . . . Yesterday I hated nobody very much, but now I hate the whole human race . . . . . If I had the courage, I would kill—somebody—anybody. But she was right—I haven't it. I've only material in me for an assassin . . . . . . Better that than . . . . . . I am so changed, so changed! Yesterday I was ashamed of my thefts—but now, why now, I am not, for I stole from the whites. I will do it again. I will do it whenever I can . . . . . . And that poor lowly and ignorant creature is my mother! . . . . . . Well, she has my respect for one thing—she has never owned a slave. All the white respectability of this town is shabby and mean, beside that one virtue. . . . ."

He sighed and groaned an hour or more away. Then "Chambers" came humbly in to say that breakfast was nearly ready. "Tom" blushed scarlet to see

89

this aristocratic white youth cringe to him, a *nigger*, and call him "young marster." He said, roughly—

"Get out of my sight!" and when the youth was gone, he muttered, "He has done me no harm, poor degraded wretch, but he is white, and for that I could kill him—if I had the courage. Ach! he is an eyesore to me, now, for he is Driscoll the young gentleman, and I am a—oh, I *wish* I was dead!"

A gigantic irruption like that of Krakatoa a few years ago, with the accompanying earthquakes, tidal waves and clouds of volcanic dust, changes the face of the surrounding landscape beyond recognition, bringing down the high lands, elevating the low, making fair lakes where deserts had been, and deserts where green prairies had smiled before. The tremendous catastrophe which had befallen Tom had changed his moral landscape in much the same way. Some of his low places he found lifted to ideals, now, some of his ideals had sunk to the valleys, and lay there with the sackcloth and ashes of pumice stone and sulphur on their ruined heads.

For days he wandered in lonely places thinking, thinking, thinking— trying to get his bearings. It was new work; he had not been used to thinking. And it was not easy; his mind was a whirlwind of spinning spirals of dust with elusive rags and fragments of ideas chasing each other through it. But all whirlwinds settle at last, and so did this one; then he had the opportunity to gather his rags and fragments together and put them in order and study the pattern and make out its meaning.

While the whirlwind continued, it furnished him many surprises. If he met a friend he found that the habit of a lifetime had in some mysterious way vanished—his arm hung limp instead of involuntarily extending the hand for a shake. It was the "nigger" in him asserting its humility, and he blushed and was abashed. And the "nigger" in him was surprised when the white friend put out his hand for a shake with him. He found the "nigger" in him involuntarily giving the road, on the sidewalk, to the white rowdy and loafer. When Rowena, the dearest thing his heart knew, invited him in, the "nigger" in him made an embarrassed excuse and was afraid to enter and sit with the dread white folks on equal terms. The "nigger" in him went shrinking and skulking here and there and yonder, and fancying it saw suspicion and maybe detection in all faces, tones and gestures. So strange and uncharacteristic was Tom's conduct that people noticed it and turned to look after him when he had passed on; and when he glanced back—as he could not help doing, in spite of his best resistance—and caught that puzzled expression in a person's face, it gave him a sick feeling, and he took himself out of view as quickly as he could. He presently came to have a hunted sense and a hunted look, and then he fled away to the hill-tops and the solitudes. The curse of Ham was upon him, he said to himself.

He dreaded his meals; the "nigger" in him was ashamed to sit at the white folks' table, and feared discovery all the time; and once when Judge Driscoll said, "What's the matter with you?—you look as meek as a nigger!" he felt as secret murderers are said to feel when the accuser says "Thou art the man!" Tom said he was not well, and left the table.

His aunt's solicitudes and endearments were become a terror to him, and he avoided them.

And all the time, hatred of his uncle was steadily growing in his heart; for he said to himself, "He is white; and I am his chattel, his property, his goods, and he can sell me, just as he could his dog."

In his broodings in the solitudes, he searched himself for the reasons of certain things, and in toil and pain he worked out the answers:

Why was he a coward? It was the "nigger" in him. The nigger *blood?* Yes, the nigger blood degraded from original courage to cowardice by decades and generations of insult and outrage inflicted in circumstances which forbade reprisals, and made mute and meek endurance the only refuge and defence.

Whence came that in him which was high, and whence that which was base? That which was high came from either blood, and was the monopoly of neither color; but that which was base was the *white* blood in him debased by the brutalizing effects of a long-drawn heredity of slave-owning, with the habit of abuse which the possession of irresponsible power always creates and perpetuates, by a law of human nature. So he argued.

But what a totally new and amazing aspect one or two things, in particular, bore to Tom, now that he found himself looking at them from around on the other side! For instance—nigger illegitimacy, yesterday and to-day. Yesterday, of what consequence could it be to a nigger whether he was a bastard or not? To-day the reflection "I am a bastard" made the hot blood leap to Tom's very eyelids. Yesterday, if any had asked him, "Which is more honorable, more desirable, and more a matter for a nigger to be proud of—to be a nigger born in wedlock, or a white man's bastard?" he would have thought the questioner was jesting. It was of course an honor to be a white man's bastard, and the highest honor a nigger could have. Who could doubt it? The question would astonish the nigger himself—go ask him and you will see. But to-day—to-day! to be a nigger was shame, but compared with this million-fold obscener infamy it was nothing, it was less than nothing. "And I am a nigger *and* that other thing!" It was only thought, he could not have uttered it, for his throat was dry and his tongue impotent with rage.

Chapter 16

For as much as a week after this, Tom imagined that his character had undergone a pretty radical change. But that was because he did not know himself. In several ways his *opinions* were totally changed, and would never go back to what they were before, but the main structure of his *character* was not changed, and could not be changed. One or two very important features of it were altered, and in time effects would result from this, if opportunity offered; effects of a quite serious nature, too. Under the influence of a great mental and moral upheaval his character and habits had taken on the appearance of complete change, but now with the subsidence of the storm both began to settle toward their former places. He dropped gradually back into his old frivolous and easy-going ways, and conditions of feeling, and manner of speech, and no familiar of his could have detected anything in him that differentiated him from the weak and careless Tom of other days.

Yet a change or two *was* present, and remained. He hated the whites, he would steal from them without shame, and even with a vengeful exultation; he loathed the "nigger" in him, but got pleasure out of bringing this secret "filth," as he called it, into familiar and constant contact with the sacred whites; he privately despised and hated his uncle and all his aristocratic pretensions.

The theft-raid which he had made upon the village turned out better than he had ventured to hope. It produced the sum necessary to pay his gaming-debts, and saved him from exposure to his uncle and another smashing of the will.

He and his mother learned to like each other fairly well. She couldn't love him, as yet, because there "warn't nothing *to* him," as she expressed it, but her nature needed something or somebody to rule over, and he was better than nothing. Her strong character and aggressive and commanding ways compelled Tom's admiration in spite of the fact that he got more illustrations of them than he needed for his comfort. However, as a rule, her conversation was made up of racy tattle about the privacies of the chief families of the town, for she went harvesting among their kitchens every time she came to the village, and Tom enjoyed this. It was just in his line. She always collected her half of his pension punctually, and he was always at the haunted house to have a chat with her on these occasions. Every now and then she paid him a visit there on between-days also.

Now and then he would run up to St. Louis for a few weeks, and at last temptation caught him again. He won a lot of money, but lost it, and with it a deal more besides, which he promised to raise as soon as possible.

He projected a new raid on his town in this interest. He never meddled with any other town, for he was afraid to venture into houses whose ins and outs he did not know, and the habits of whose households he was not acquainted with. He arrived at the haunted house in disguise on the Wednesday before the advent of the Twins,—after writing his aunt Pratt that he would not arrive until two days later—and lay in hiding there with his mother until toward daylight Friday morning, when he went to his uncle's house and entered by the back way with his own key and slipped up to his room, where he could have the use of mirror and toilet articles. He had a suit of girl's clothes with him as a disguise for his raid, and was wearing a suit of his mother's clothing, with black gloves and veil. By dawn he was tricked out for his raid, but he caught a glimpse of Pudd'nhead Wilson through the window over the way and knew that Pudd'nhead had caught a glimpse of him. So he entertained Wilson with some airs and graces and attitudes for a while, then he stepped out of sight and resumed the other disguise, and by and by went down and out the back way and started downtown to reconnoitre the scene of his intended labors.

But he was ill at ease. He had changed back to Roxy's dress, with the stoop of age added to the disguise, so that Wilson would not bother himself about a humble old woman leaving a neighbor's house by the back way in the early morning, in case he was still spying. But supposing Wilson had seen him leave, and *had* thought it suspicious, and had also followed him? The thought made Tom cold. He gave up the raid for the day, and hurried back to the haunted house by the obscurest route he knew. His mother was gone; but she came back, by and by, with the news of the grand reception at Patsy Cooper's, and soon persuaded him that the opportunity was like a special providence it was so inviting and perfect. So he went raiding, after all, and made a nice success of it while everybody was gone to Patsy Cooper's. Success gave him nerve, and even actual intrepidity; insomuch, indeed, that after he had conveyed his harvest to his mother in a back alley, he went to the reception himself, and added several of that house's valuables to his takings.

———

After this long digression we have now arrived, once more, at the point where Pudd'nhead Wilson, while waiting for the arrival of the Twins from the Bible Society on that same Friday evening, sat puzzling over the strange apparition of that morning—a girl in young Tom Driscoll's bedroom; fretting, and guessing, and puzzling over it, and wondering who the brazen huzzy might be.

Chapter 17

There are three infallible ways of pleasing an author, and the three form a rising scale of compliment: 1, to tell him you have read one of his books; 2, to tell him you have read all of his books; 3, to ask him to let you read the manuscript of his forthcoming book. No. 1 admits you to his respect; No. 2 admits you to his admiration; but No. 3 carries you clear into his heart with all your clothes on.—*Pudd'nhead Wilson's Calendar.*

The duplicates arrived presently, and talk began. It flowed along chattily and sociably, and under its influence Angelo cheered up and forgot his late vexations. Wilson got out his Calendar, by request, and read a passage or two from it, which the Twins complimented quite cordially. This pleased the author so much that he complied gladly when they asked him to lend them a batch of the work to read at home. In the course of their wide travels they had found out that there are three sure ways of pleasing an author: they were now working the best of the three.

There was an interruption, now. Young Tom Driscoll appeared, and joined the party. He pretended to be startled at the figure the Twins made when they rose to shake hands, but this was only a blind, as he had already had a glimpse of them at the reception while robbing the house. The Twins made mental note that he was smooth-faced and rather handsome, and smooth and undulatory in his movements—graceful, in fact. Angelo thought he had a good eye, Luigi thought there was something veiled and sly about it. Angelo thought he had a pleasant free-and-easy way of talking, Luigi thought it was more so than was agreeable. Angelo thought he was a sufficiently nice young man, Luigi reserved his decision. Tom's first contribution to the conversation was a question which he had put to Wilson a hundred times before. It was always cheerily and good-naturedly put, and always inflicted a little pang, for it touched a secret sore; but this time the pang was sharp, since strangers were present:

"Well, how does the law come on? Had a case yet?"

Wilson bit his lip, but answered, "No—not yet," with as much indiffer-ence as he could assume. Judge Driscoll had generously left this feature out of the Wilson biography which he had furnished to the Twins. Young Tom laughed pleasantly and said—

"Wilson's a lawyer, gentlemen, but he doesn't practice now."

The sarcasm bit, but Wilson kept himself under control, and said, without passion—

"I don't practice, it is true. It is true that I have never had a case, and have had to earn a poor living for twenty years as an expert accountant in a town where I can't get hold of a set of books to untangle as often as I would like. But it is also true that I did fit myself well for the practice of the law. By the time I was your age, Tom, I had chosen a profession and was soon competent to enter upon it." [Tom winced.] "I never got a chance to try my hand at it, and I may never get a chance; and yet if I ever do get it I shall be found ready, for I have kept up my law-studies all these years."

"That's it—that's good grit. I like to see it. I've a notion to throw all my business your way. My business and your law-practice ought to make a pretty gay team, Dave," and the young fellow laughed again.

"If you will throw—" He had thought of the girl in Tom's bedroom, and was going to say, "If you will throw the surreptitious and disreputable part of your business my way, it may amount to something," but thought better of it and said, "However, this matter doesn't fit well in a general conversation."

"All right, we'll change the subject—I guess you were about to give me another dig, anyway, so I'm willing to change. How's the Awful Mystery flourishing these days? Wilson's got a scheme for driving plain window-glass out of the market by decorating it with greasy finger-marks and getting rich by selling it at famine prices to the crowned heads over in Europe to outfit their palaces with. Fetch it out, Dave."

Wilson brought three of his glass strips and said:

"I get the subject to pass the fingers of his right hand through his hair, so as to get a little coating of the natural oil on them, and then press the balls of them on the glass. A fine and delicate print of the lines in the skin results, and is permanent if it doesn't come in contact with something able to rub it off. You begin, Tom."

"Why, I think you took my finger-marks once or twice before."

"Yes, but you were a little boy, the last time, only about twelve years old."

"That's so. Of course I've changed entirely since then, and variety is what the crowned heads want, I guess."

He passed his fingers through his crop of short hair and pressed them one at a time on the glass. Angelo made a print of his fingers on another glass, and Luigi followed with the third. Wilson marked the glasses with names and date and put them away. Tom gave one of his little laughs and said—

"I thought I wouldn't say anything, but if variety is what you are after, you have wasted a piece of glass. The hand-print of one twin is the same as the hand-print of the fellow-twin."

"Well, it's done, now, and I like to have them both, anyway," said Wilson, returning to his place.

"But look here, Dave," said Tom, "you used to tell people's fortunes, too, when you took their finger-marks. Dave's just an all-around genius, a genius of the first water, gentlemen, a great scientist running to seed here in this village, a prophet with the kind of honor that prophets generally get at home—for here they don't give shucks for his scientifics, and they call his skull a maggot-factory—hey, Dave, ain't it so?—but never mind, he'll make his mark some day—finger-mark, you know, he-he! But really, you want to let him take a shy at your palms once, it's worth twice the price of admission or your money's returned at the door. Why, he'll read your wrinkles as easy as a book, and not only tell you fifty or sixty things that's going to happen to you, but fifty or sixty thousand that ain't. Come, Dave, show the gentlemen what an inspired Jack-at-all-science we've got here in this town and don't know it."

Wilson winced under this nagging and not very courteous raillery, and the Twins suffered with him and for him. They rightly judged, now, that the best way to relieve him would be to take the thing in earnest and treat it with respect, ignoring Tom's rather overdone raillery; so Luigi said:

"We have seen something of palmistry in our wanderings, and know very well what astonishing things it can do. If it isn't a science, and one of the greatest of them, too, I don't know what its other name ought to be. In the Orient—"

Tom looked surprised and incredulous. He said—

"That jugglery a science? But really, you ain't serious, are you?"

"Yes, entirely so. Four years ago we had our hands read out to us as if our palms had been covered with print."

"Well, do you mean to say there was actually anything *in* it?" asked Tom, his incredulity beginning to weaken a little.

"There was this much in it," said Angelo; "what was told us of our characters was minutely exact—we could not have bettered it ourselves. Next, two or three memorable things that had happened to us were laid bare—things which no one present but ourselves could have known about."

"Why, it's rank sorcery!" exclaimed Tom, who was now becoming very much interested. "And how did they make out with what was going to happen to you in the future?"

"On the whole, quite fairly," said Luigi. "Two or three of the most striking things foretold have happened since; much the most striking one of all happened within that same year. Some of the minor prophecies have come true; some of the minor and some of the major ones have not been fulfilled yet, and of course may never be—still, I should be more surprised if they failed to arrive than if they didn't."

Tom was entirely sobered, and profoundly impressed. He said, apologetically—

"Dave, I wasn't meaning to belittle that science, I was only chaffing—chattering, I reckon I better say. I wish you *would* look at their palms—come, won't you?"

"Why, certainly, if you want me to, but you know I've had no chance to become an expert, and don't claim to be one. When a past event is somewhat prominently recorded in the palm, I can generally detect that, but minor ones often escape me—not always, of course, but often—but I haven't much confidence in myself when it comes to reading the future. I am talking as if palmistry was a daily study with me, but that is not so. I haven't examined half a dozen hands in the last half a dozen years; you see, the people got to joking about it, and I stopped to let the talk die down. I'll tell you what we'll do, Count Luigi—I'll make a try at your past, and if I have any success there—no, on the whole I'll let the future alone—that's really the affair of an expert."

He took Luigi's hand. Tom said—

"Wait—don't look yet, Dave. Count Luigi, here's paper and pencil. Set down that thing that you said was the most striking one that was foretold to you and happened less than a year afterwards, and give it to me so I can see if Dave finds it in your hand."

Luigi wrote a line privately, and folded up the piece of paper and handed it to Tom, saying—

"I'll tell you when to look at it, if he finds it."

Wilson began to study Luigi's palm, tracing life lines, heart lines, head lines, and so on, and noting carefully their relations with the cobweb of finer and more delicate marks and lines that enmeshed them on all sides; he felt of the fleshy cushion at the base of the thumb, and noted its shape; he felt of the fleshy side of the hand between the wrist and the base of the little finger, and noted its shape also; he pains-takingly examined the fingers, observing their form, proportions and natural manner of disposing themselves when in repose. All this process was watched by the three spectators with absorbing interest, their heads bent together over Luigi's palm and nobody disturbing the stillness with a word. Wilson now entered upon a close survey of the palm again, and his revelations began.

He mapped out Luigi's character and disposition, his tastes, aversions, proclivities, ambitions and eccentricities in a way which sometimes made Luigi wince and the others laugh, but both Twins declared that the chart was artistically drawn and was correct.

Next, Wilson took up Luigi's past. He proceeded cautiously and with hesitation, now, moving his finger slowly along the great lines of the palm, and now and then halting it at a "star" or some such landmark and examining that neighborhood minutely. He proclaimed one or two past events, Luigi confirmed his correctness, and the search went on. Presently Wilson glanced up suddenly with a surprised expression—

"Here is record of an incident which you would perhaps not wish me to—"

"Bring it out," said Luigi, good-naturedly, "I promise you it shan't embarrass me."

But Wilson still hesitated, and did not seem to quite know what to do. Then he said—

"I think it is too delicate a matter to—to—. I believe I would rather write it or whisper it to you, and let you decide for yourself whether you want it talked out or not."

"That will answer," said Luigi; "write it."

Wilson wrote something on a slip of paper and handed it to Luigi, who read it and said to Tom—

"Unfold *your* slip and read it, Mr. Driscoll."

Tom read:

"It was prophesied that I would kill a man. It came true before the year was out." Tom added, "Great Scott!"

Luigi handed Wilson's paper to Tom and said—

"Now read this one."

Tom read:

"You have killed some one—but whether man, woman or child, I do not make out." "Caesar's ghost!" commented Tom, with astonishment. "It beats anything that was ever heard of. Why, a man's own hand is his deadliest

enemy. Just think of that—a man's own hand keeps a record of the deepest and fatalest secrets of his life, and is treacherously ready to expose him to any black-magic stranger that comes along! But what do you let a person look at your hand for, with that awful thing printed in it?"

"Oh," said Luigi reposefully, "I don't mind it. I killed the man for good reasons, and I don't regret it."

"What were the reasons?"

"Well, he needed killing."

"*I'll* tell you why he did it, since he won't say himself," said Angelo warmly. "He did it to save my life—that's what he did it for. So it was a noble act, and not a thing to be hid in the dark."

"So it was, so it was," said Wilson; "to do such a thing to save a brother's life is a great and fine action."

"Now come," said Luigi, "it is very pleasant to hear you say these things, but for unselfishness, or heroism, or magnanimity, the circumstance won't stand scrutiny. You overlook one detail: suppose I hadn't saved Angelo's life, what would have become of mine? If I had let the man kill Angelo, how many hours would I have survived? I saved my own life, you see."

"Yes, that is your way of talking," said Angelo, "but I know you, and I don't believe you thought of yourself at all. I keep that weapon yet that Luigi killed the man with, and I'll show it to you some time. That incident makes it interesting, and it had a history before it came into Luigi's hands which adds to its interest. It was given to Luigi by a great Indian prince, the Gaikowar of Baroda, and it had been in his family two or three centuries. It killed a good many disagreeable people who troubled that hearthstone at one time and another. It isn't much to look at, except that it isn't shaped like other knives, or dirks, or whatever it may be called—here, I'll draw it for you." He took a sheet of paper and made a rapid sketch. "There it is—a broad and murderous blade, with edges like a razor for sharpness. The devices engraved on it are the ciphers or names of its long line of possessors—I had Luigi's name added in Roman letters, myself, with our coat of arms, as you see. You notice what a curious handle the thing has. It is solid ivory, polished like a mirror, and is four or five inches long—round, and as thick as a large man's wrist, with the end squared off flat, for your thumb to rest on; for you grasp it, with your thumb resting on the blunt end—so—and lift it aloft and strike downwards. The Gaikowar showed us how the thing was done when he gave it to Luigi, and before that night was ended Luigi had used the knife and the Gaikowar was a man short by reason of it. The sheath is magnificently ornamented with gems of great value. You will find the sheath more worth looking at than the knife itself, of course."

Tom said to himself: "It's lucky I came here; I would have sold that knife for a song; I supposed the jewels were glass."

"But go on—don't stop," said Wilson. "Our curiosity is up, now, to hear about the homicide. Tell us about that."

"Well, briefly, the knife was to blame for that, all around. A native servant slipped into our room in the palace in the night, to kill us and steal that knife on account of the fortune encrusted on its sheath, without a doubt. Luigi had it under our pillow. There was a dim night-light burning. I was asleep, but Luigi was awake, and he thought he detected a dim form nearing the bed. He slipped the knife out of the sheath, and was ready and unembarrassed by hampering bed-clothes, for the weather was hot and we hadn't any. Suddenly that native rose at the bedside and bent over me with his right hand lifted and a dirk in it aimed at my throat, but Luigi grabbed his wrist, pulled him downward and drove his own knife into the man's neck. I think he was dead before his spouting blood struck us. That is the whole story."

Wilson and Tom drew deep breaths, and Tom said—

"I wonder he was so particular. I should have thought he would kill the first one of you that came handy—or jam his dirk into your mutual body and kill you both."

Angelo colored, and said, rather shame-facedly—

"Well, the truth is, he had a reason, and a good one, for preferring me. He could have killed Luigi without much sin, for Luigi was a freethinker and the fact was known; but he could kill me without any sin at all; and not only that, but it would be a very meritorious and praiseworthy deed, because I had just publicly apostatised from the Mohammedan church, and this native was a Mohammedan. If he killed Luigi my death would follow, but *he* wouldn't get any credit for it on high, so the knife's gems would be his only reward. Necessarily, common sense moved him to kill me, and get both rewards."

"Well, I *never* should have thought of that ingenious distinction!" exclaimed Tom, with admiration. "That native was no fool, *I* tell you!"

"Now, Tom," said Wilson, taking Tom's hand, "I've never had a look at your palms, as it happens—perhaps you've got some little questionable privacies that need— Hel-lo!"

Tom had drawn his hand away, and was looking a good deal confused.

"Why, he's blushing!" said Luigi.

Tom darted an ugly look at him and said, sharply—

"Well, if I am, it ain't because I'm a murderer!" Luigi's dark face flushed, but before he could speak or move, Tom added with anxious haste, "Oh, I beg a thousand pardons, I didn't mean that, it was out before I thought, and I'm very, very sorry—you must forgive me."

Wilson came to the rescue, and smoothed things down as well as he could; and in fact was entirely successful as far as the Twins were concerned, for they felt sorrier for the affront put upon him by his guest's outburst of ill manners than for the insult offered to Luigi; but the success was not so pronounced with the offender. Tom tried to seem at his ease, and he went through the motions fairly well, but at bottom he felt resentful toward all the three witnesses of his exhibition—in fact he felt so annoyed at them for having witnessed it and noticed it that he almost forgot to feel annoyed at himself for placing it before them. However, something presently happened which made him almost comfortable, and brought him nearly back to a state of charity and friendliness. This was a little spat between the Twins; not much of a spat, but still a spat; and before they got far with it they were in a decided condition of irritation with each other. Tom was charmed; so pleased, indeed, that he cautiously did what he could to increase the irritation while pretending to be actuated by more respectable motives. By his help the fire got warmed up to the blazing point, and he might have had the happiness of seeing the flames show up, in another moment, but for the interruption of a knock on the door—an interruption which fretted him as much as it gratified Wilson. Wilson opened the door.

The visitor was a good-natured, ignorant, energetic, middle-aged man who spoke English with a slight but noticeable Irish accent. When he first came to the town, a few years before, he gave his name as John Buckstone, and added, "formerly Lord Buckstone, author of the Queen's hounds"—meaning master of the Queen's hounds, probably. He was a great politician in a small way, and always took a large share in public matters of every sort. One of the town's chief excitements, just now, was over the matter of rum. There was a strong rum party and a strong anti-rum party. Buckstone was training with the rum party, and he had been sent to hunt up the Twins and invite them to attend a mass meeting of that faction. He delivered his errand and said the clans were already gathering in the big hall over the market house. Luigi accepted the invitation cordially, Angelo declined it as cordially, and called all present to witness that in going with Luigi he was doing it under protest; that he would not go if he could help it; and that he was totally opposed to the principles of the rum party; he added that he was dying of fatigue, and that it was a shameful cruelty to keep him on his legs any longer.

"*Your* legs!" said Luigi indignantly. "I like your impudence. You will go to the meeting—I will see to that. And don't waste any more pathetic speeches here; save them for the temperance meetings—you will probably carry me to enough of them."

The Twins left with Buckstone, and Tom Driscoll joined company with them uninvited.

In the distance one could see a wavering long line of torches drifting down the main street, and could hear the throbbing of a bass drum, the clash of cymbals, the squeaking of a fife or two, and the faint roar of remote hurrahs. The tail end of this procession was climbing the market house stairs when the Twins arrived in its neighborhood; when they reached the hall it was full of people, torches, smoke, noise and enthusiasm. They were conducted to the platform by Buckstone,—Tom Driscoll still following—and delivered to the chairman in the midst of a prodigious explosion of welcome. When the noise had moderated a little, the chair proposed that "our illustrious guests be at once elected, by complimentary acclamation, to membership in our ever glorious organization, the paradise of the free and the perdition of the slave."

This eloquent discharge opened the flood-gates of enthusiasm again, and the election was carried with thundering unanimity. Then arose a storm of cries,—

"Wet them down! wet them down! give them a drink!"

Glasses of whisky were handed to the Twins. Luigi waved his aloft, then brought it to his lips, but Angelo set his down. There was another storm of cries—

"What's the matter with the other one?"

"What is the blonde one going back on us for?"

"Explain! explain!"

The chairman inquired, and then reported—

"We have made an unfortunate mistake, gentlemen. I find that the Count Angelo Cappello is opposed to our creed—is a pronounced teetotaler, in fact, and was not intending to apply for membership with us. He desires that we reconsider the vote by which he was elected. What is the pleasure of the house?"

There was a general burst of laughter, plentifully accented with whistlings and cat-calls, but the energetic use of the gavel presently restored something like order. Then a man spoke from the crowd and said that while he was very sorry that the mistake had been made, it would not be possible to rectify it at the present meeting. According to the bye-laws it must go over to the next regular meeting for action. He would not offer a motion, as none was required. He desired to apologize to the gentleman in the name of the house, and begged to assure him that as far as it might lie in the power of the Sons of Liberty, his temporary membership in the order would be made pleasant to him.

This speech was received with great applause, mixed with cries of—

"That's the talk!" "He's a good fellow, anyway, if he *is* a teetotaler!" "Drink his health!" "Give him a rouser, and no heel-taps!"

Glasses were handed around, and everybody on the platform drank Angelo's health, while the house bellowed forth in song:

> "For he's a jolly good fel-low,
> For he's a jolly good fel-low.
> For he's a jolly good fe-el-low—
> Which nobody can deny!"

Tom Driscoll drank. It was his second glass, for he had drunk Angelo's the moment that Angelo had set it down. The two drinks made him very merry—almost idiotically so—and he began to take a most lively and prominent part in the proceedings, particularly in the music and cat-calls and side-remarks department of them.

The chairman was still standing at the front, the Twins at his side. The Twins stood with their legs braced slightly apart. Their heads happened to be canted apart, too. Their attitude suggested a witticism to Tom Driscoll, and just as the chairman began a speech he skipped forward and said with an air of tipsy confidence to the audience—

"Boys, I move that he keeps still and lets this human pair of scissors snip you out a speech!"

The descriptive precision of the phrase caught the house, and a mighty burst of laughter followed.

Luigi took a couple of strides and was behind the unsuspecting joker. Then he drew back and delivered a kick of such titanic vigor in the joker's rear that it lifted him clear over the footlights and landed him on the heads of the front row of the Sons of Liberty.

Even a sober person does not like to have a human being emptied on him when he is not doing any harm; a person who is not sober cannot endure such an attention at all. The nest of Sons of Liberty that Driscoll landed in had not a sober bird in it; in fact there was probably not an entirely sober one in the auditorium. Driscoll was promptly and indignantly flung onto the heads of Sons in the next row, and these Sons passed him on toward the rear, and then immediately began to pummel the front-row Sons who had passed him to *them*. This course was strictly followed by bench after bench as Driscoll traveled in his tumultuous and airy flight toward the door; so he left behind him an ever lengthening wake of raging and plunging and fighting and swearing humanity. Down went group after group of torches, and presently, above the deafening clatter of the gavel, roar of angry voices and crash of succumbing benches, rose the paralyzing cry of

"FIRE!"

The fighting ceased instantly; the cursings ceased; for one distinctly defined moment there was a dead hush, a motionless calm, where the tempest had been; then with one impulse the multitude awoke to life and energy again, and went surging and struggling and swaying, this way and that, its outer edges melting away through windows and doors and gradually lessening the pressure and relieving the mass.

The fire-boys were never on hand so suddenly before; for there was no distance to go, this time, their quarters being in the rear end of the market house. There was an engine company and a hook and ladder company. Half of each was composed of rummies and the other half of anti-rummies, after the moral and political share-and-share-alike fashion of the frontier town of the period. Enough anti-rummies were loafing in quarters to man the engine and the ladders. In two minutes they had their red shirts and helmets on— they never stirred officially in unofficial costume—and as the mass meeting overhead smashed through the long row of windows and poured out onto the roof of the arcade, the deliverers were ready for them with a powerful stream of water which washed some of them off the roof and nearly drowned the rest. But water was preferable to fire, and still the outpour from the windows continued, and still the pitiless drenchings assailed it until the building was empty; then the fire-boys mounted to the hall and flooded it with water enough to have annihilated forty times as much fire as there was there: for a village fire company does not often get a chance to show off, and so when it does get a chance it makes the most of it. Such citizens of that village as were of a thoughtful and judicious temperament did not insure against fire, they insured against the fire company.

Chapter 18

There are 869 different forms of lying, but only one of them has been forbidden: thou shalt not bear false witness against thy neighbor.—*Pudd'nhead Wilson's Calendar.*

Next morning all the town was a-buzz with great news: Pudd'nhead Wilson had a law-case!

The public astonishment was so great and the public curiosity so intense, that when the justice of the peace opened his court the place was packed with people, and even the windows were full. Everybody was flushed and perspiring, the summer heat was almost unendurable.

Tom Driscoll had brought a charge of assault and battery against the Twins. Robert Allen was retained by Driscoll, David Wilson by the defence. Tom, his native cheerfulness unannihilated by his back-breaking and bone-bruising passage across the massed heads of the Sons of Liberty the previous night, laughed his little customary laugh, and said to Wilson—

"I've kept my promise, you see: I'm throwing my business your way. Sooner than I was expecting, too."

"It's very good of you—particularly if you mean to keep it up."

"Well, I can't tell about that, yet. But we'll see. If I find you deserve it I'll take you under my protection and make your fame and fortune for you."

"I'll try to deserve it, Tom."

A jury was sworn in; then Mr. Allen said:

"We will detain your honor but a moment with this case. It is not one where any doubt of the fact of the assault can enter in. These gentlemen—the accused—kicked my client, at the Market Hall last night; they kicked him with violence; with extraordinary violence; with even unprecedented violence, I may say; insomuch that he was lifted entirely off his feet and discharged into the midst of the audience. We could prove this by four hundred witnesses—we shall call but three. Mr. Harkness will take the stand."

Mr. Harkness, being sworn, testified that he was chairman upon the occasion mentioned; that he was close at hand and saw the defendants in this action kick the plaintiff into the air and saw him descend amongst the audience.

"Take the witness," said Allen.

"Mr. Harkness," said Wilson, "you say you saw these gentlemen, my clients, kick the plaintiff. Are you sure—and please remember that you are on oath—are you perfectly sure that you saw *both* of them kick him, or only one? Now be careful."

A bewildered look began to spread itself over the witness's face. He hesitated, stammered, but got out nothing. His eyes wandered to the Twins and fixed themselves there with a vacant gaze.

"Please answer, Mr. Harkness, you are keeping the court waiting. It is a very simple question."

Counsel for the prosecution broke in with impatience:

"Your honor, the question is an irrelevant triviality. Necessarily they both kicked him, for they have but the one pair of legs, and both are responsible for them."

Wilson said:

"Will your honor permit this new witness to be sworn? He seems to possess knowledge which can be of the utmost value just at this moment—knowledge which would at once dispose of what every one must see is a very difficult question in this case. Brother Allen, will you take the stand?"

"Go on with your case!" said Allen, petulantly. The audience laughed, and got a warning from the court.

"Now, Mr. Harkness," said Wilson, insinuatingly, "we shall have to insist upon an answer to that question."

"I—er—well, of course I do not absolutely *know*, but in my opinion—"

"Never mind your opinion, sir—answer the question!"

"I—why, I *can't* answer it."

"That will do, Mr. Harkness. Stand down."

The audience tittered, and the discomfited witness retired in a state of great embarrassment.

Mr. Wakeman took the stand and swore that he saw the Twins kick the plaintiff off the platform. The defence took the witness.

"Mr. Wakeman, you have sworn that you saw these gentlemen kick the plaintiff. Do I understand you to swear that you saw them *both* do it?"

"Yes, sir"—with decision.

"How do you know that both did it?"

"Because I *saw* them do it." The audience laughed, and got another warning from the court.

"But by what means do you know that both, and not one, did it?"

"Well, in the first place, the insult was given to both of them equally, for they were called a pair of scissors. Of course they would both want to resent it, and so—"

"Wait! You are theorizing, now. Stick to facts—counsel will attend to the arguments. Go on."

"Well, they both went over there—*that* I saw."

"Very good. Go on."

"And they both kicked him—I swear to it!"

"Mr. Wakeman, was Count Luigi, here, willing to join the Sons of Liberty last night?"

"Yes, sir, he was. He did join, too, and drank a glass or two of whisky, like a man."

"Was his brother willing to join?"

"No, sir, he wasn't. He is a teetotaler, and was elected through a mistake."

"Was he given a glass of whisky?"

"Yes, sir, but of course that was another mistake, and not intentional. He wouldn't drink it. He set it down." A slight pause, then he added, casually, and quite simply, "The plaintiff reached for it and hogged it."

There was a fine outburst of laughter, but as the justice was caught out, himself, his reprimand was not very vigorous.

Mr. Allen jumped up and exclaimed:

"I protest against these foolish irrelevancies. What have *they* to do with the case?"

Wilson said:

"Calm yourself, brother; it was only an experiment. Now, Mr. Wakeman, if one of these gentlemen chooses to join an association and the other doesn't; and if one of them enjoys whisky and the other doesn't, but sets it aside and leaves it unprotected," [titter from the audience], "it seems to show that they have independent minds and tastes and preferences, and that one of them is able to approve of a thing at the very moment that the other is heartily disapproving of it. Doesn't it seem so to you?"

"Certainly it does. It's perfectly plain."

"Now, then, it might be—I only say it *might* be—that one of these brothers wanted to kick the plaintiff last night, and that the other one *didn't* want that humiliating punishment inflicted upon him in that public way and before all those people. Isn't that possible?"

"Of course it is. It's more than possible. *I* don't believe the blonde one would kick anybody. It was the other one that—"

"Silence!" shouted the plaintiff's counsel, and went on with an angry sentence which was lost in the wave of laughter that swept the house.

"That will do, Mr. Wakeman," said Wilson, "you may stand down."

The third witness was called. He had seen the Twins kick the plaintiff. Mr. Wilson took the witness.

"Mr. Rogers, you say you saw these accused gentlemen kick the plaintiff."

"Yes, sir."

"Both of them?"

"Yes, sir."

"Which of them kicked him first?"

"Why—they—they both kicked him at the same time."

"Are you perfectly sure of that?"

"Yes, sir."

"What makes you sure of it?"

"Why, I stood right behind them, and saw them do it."

"How many kicks were delivered?"

"Only one."

"If two men kick, the result should be two kicks, shouldn't it?"

"Why—why—yes, as a rule."

"Then what do you think went with the other kick?"

"I—well—the fact is, I wasn't thinking of two being necessary, this time."

"What do you think now?"

"Well, I—I'm sure I don't quite know what to think, but I reckon that one of them did half of the kick and the other one did the other half."

Somebody in the crowd sung out:

"It's the first sane thing that any of them has said!"

The audience applauded. The judge said—

"Silence! or I will clear the court."

Mr. Allen looked pleased, but Wilson did not seem disturbed. He said:

"Mr. Rogers, you have favored us with what you think and what you reckon, but as thinking and reckoning are not evidence, I will now give you a chance to come out with something positive, one way or the other, and shall require you to produce it. I will ask the accused to stand up and repeat the phenomenal kick of last night." The Twins stood up. "Now, Mr. Rogers, please stand behind them."

A Voice. "No, stand in front!" [Laughter. Silenced by the court.]

Another Voice. "No, give Tommy another highst!" [Laughter. Sharply rebuked by the court.]

"Now, then, Mr. Rogers, two kicks shall be delivered, one after the other, and I give you my word that at least one of the two shall be delivered by one of the Twins alone, without the slightest assistance from his brother. Watch sharply, for you have got to render a decision without any ifs or ands in it." Rogers bent himself behind the Twins, with his palms just above his knees, in the modern attitude of the catcher at a base-ball match, and riveted his eyes on the pair of legs in front of him. "Are you ready, Mr. Rogers?"

"Ready, sir."

"Kick!"

The kick was launched.

"Have you got that one classified, Mr. Rogers?"

"Let me study a minute, sir."

"Take as much time as you please. Let me know when you are ready."

For as much as a minute Rogers pondered, with all eyes and a breathless interest fastened upon him. Then he gave the word—

"Ready, sir."

"Kick!"

The kick that followed was an exact duplicate of the first one.

"Now, then, Mr. Rogers, one of those kicks was an individual kick, not a mutual one. You will now state positively which was the mutual one."

The witness said, with a crestfallen look—

"I've got to give it up. There ain't any man that could tell t'other from which, sir."

"Do you still assert that last night's kick was a mutual kick?"

"Indeed I don't, sir."

"That will do, Mr. Rogers. If my brother Allen desires to address the court, your honor, very well; but as far as I am concerned I am ready to let the case be at once delivered into the hands of this intelligent jury without comment."

Mr. Justice Robinson had been in office only two months, and in that short time had not had many cases to try, of course. He had no knowledge of laws and courts except what he had picked up since he came into office. He was a sore trouble to the lawyers, for his rulings were pretty eccentric sometimes, and he stood by them with Roman simplicity and fortitude; but the people were well satisfied with him, for they saw that his intentions were always right, that he was entirely impartial, and that he usually made up in good sense what he lacked in technique, so to speak. He now perceived that there was likely to be a miscarriage of justice here, and he rose to the occasion.

"Wait a moment, gentlemen," he said, "it is plain that an assault has been committed—it is plain to anybody; but the way things are going, the guilty will certainly escape conviction. I cannot allow this. Now—"

"But your honor!" said Wilson, interrupting him, earnestly but respectfully, "you are deciding the case yourself, whereas the jury—"

"Never mind the jury, Mr. Wilson; the jury will have a chance when there is a reasonable doubt for them to take hold of—which there isn't, so far. There is no doubt whatever that an assault has been committed. The attempt to show that both of the accused committed it has failed. Are they both to escape justice on that account? Not in this court, if I can prevent it. It appears to have been a mistake to bring the charge against them as a corporation; each should have been charged in his capacity as an individual, and—"

"But your honor!" said Wilson, "in fairness to my clients I must insist that inasmuch as the prosecution did *not* separate the—"

"No wrong will be done your clients, sir—they will be protected; also the public and the offended law. Mr. Allen, you will amend your pleadings, and put one of the accused on trial at a time."

Wilson broke in—

"But your honor! this is wholly unprecedented. To imperil an accused person by arbitrarily altering and widening the charge against him in order to compass his conviction when the charge as originally brought promises to fail to convict, is a thing unheard of before."

"Unheard of where?"

"In the courts of this or any other State."

The judge said, with dignity—

"I am not acquainted with the customs of other courts, and am not concerned to know what they are. I am responsible for this court, and I cannot conscientiously allow my judgment to be warped and my judicial liberty hampered by trying to conform to the caprices of other courts, be they—"

"But your honor, the oldest and highest courts in Europe—"

"This court is not run on the European plan, Mr. Wilson; it is not run on any plan but its own. It *has* a plan of its own; and that plan is, to find justice for State and accused, no matter what happens to be practice and custom in Europe or anywhere else." [Great applause.] "Silence! It has not been the custom of this court to imitate other courts; it has not been the custom of this court to take shelter behind the decisions of other courts, and we will not begin now. We will do the best we can by the light that God has given us, and while this court continues to have His approval, it will remain indifferent to what other organizations may think of it." [Applause.] "Gentlemen, I *must* have order!—quiet yourselves! Mr. Allen, you will now proceed against the prisoners one at a time. Go on with the case."

Allen was not at his ease. However, after whispering a moment with his client and with one or two other people, he rose and said:

"Your honor, I find it to be reported and believed that the accused are able to act independently in many ways, but that this independence does not extend to their legs, authority over their legs being vested exclusively in the one brother during a specific term of days, and then passing to the other brother for a like term, and so on, by regular alternation. I could call witnesses who would prove that the accused had revealed to them the existence of this extraordinary fact, and had also made known which of them was in possession of the legs yesterday—and this would of course indicate where the guilt of the assault belongs—but as this would be mere hearsay evidence, these revelations not having been made under oath—"

"Never mind about that, Mr. Allen. It may not all be hearsay. We shall see. It may at least help to put us on the right track. Call the witnesses."

"Then I will call Mr. John Buckstone, who is now present; and I beg that Mrs. Patsy Cooper may be sent for. Take the stand, Mr. Buckstone."

Buckstone took the oath, and then testified that on the previous evening the Count Angelo Cappello had protested against going to the hall, and had called all present to witness that he was going by compulsion and would not go if he could help himself. Also, that the Count Luigi had replied sharply that he would *go*, just the same, and that he, Count Luigi, would see to that, himself. Also, that upon Count Angelo's complaining about being kept on his legs so long, Count Luigi retorted with apparent surprise, "*Your* legs!—I like your impudence."

"Now we are getting at the kernel of the thing," observed the judge, with grave and earnest satisfaction. "It looks as if the Count Luigi was in possession of the battery at the time of the assault."

Nothing further was elicited from Mr. Buckstone on direct examination. Mr. Wilson took the witness.

"Mr. Buckstone, about what time was it that that conversation took place?"

"Toward nine yesterday evening, sir."

"Did you then proceed directly to the hall?"

"Yes, sir."

"How long did it take you to go there?"

"Well, we walked; and as it was from the extreme edge of the town, and there was no hurry, I judge it took us about twenty minutes, maybe a trifle more."

"About what hour was the kick delivered?"

"At seventeen minutes and a half to ten."

"Admirable! You are a pattern witness, Mr. Buckstone. How did you happen to look at your watch at that particular moment?"

"I always do it when I see an assault. It's likely I shall be called as a witness, and it's a good point to have."

"It would be well if others were as thoughtful. Was anything said, between the conversation at my house and the assault, upon the detail which we are now examining into?"

"No, sir."

"If power over the mutual legs was in the possession of one brother at nine, and passed into the possession of the other one during the next thirty or forty minutes, do you think you could have detected the change?"

"By no means!"

"That is all, Mr. Buckstone."

Mrs. Patsy Cooper was called. The crowd made way for her, and she came smiling and bowing through the narrow human lane, with Betsy Hale, as escort and support, smiling and bowing in her wake, the audience breaking into welcoming cheers as they filed along. The judge did not check this kindly demonstration of homage and affection, but let it run its course unrebuked.

The old ladies stopped and shook hands with the Twins with effusion, then gave the judge a friendly nod and bustled into the seats provided for them. They immediately began to deliver a volley of eager questions at the friends around them: "What is this thing for?" "What is that thing for?" "Who is that that's writing at the desk?—why, I declare it's Jake Bunce!—I thought he was sick." "Which is the jury?" "Why, is *that* the jury? Billy Price, and Job Turner, and Jack Lounsbury, and—well, I never!" "Now who would ever a thought—"

But they were gently called to order at this point and asked not to talk in court. Their tongues fell silent, but the radiant interest in their faces remained, and their gratitude for the blessing of a new sensation and a novel experience still beamed undimmed from their eyes. Aunt Patsy stood up and took the oath, and Mr. Allen explained the point in issue and asked her to go on, now, in her own way, and throw as much light upon it as she could. She toyed with her reticule a moment or two, as if considering where to begin, then she said:

"Well, the way of it is this. They are Luigi's legs a week at a time, and then they are Angelo's, and he can do what he wants to with them."

"You are making a mistake, Aunt Patsy Cooper," said the judge. "You shouldn't state that as a fact, because you don't know it to be a fact."

"What's the reason I don't?" said Aunt Patsy, bridling a little.

"What is the reason that you *do* know it?"

"The best in the world—because they told me."

"That isn't a reason."

"Well, for the land's sake! Betsy Hale, do you hear that?"

"Hear it?—I should think so," said Aunt Betsy, rising and facing the court. "Why Judge, I was there and heard it myself. Luigi says to Angelo—no, it was Angelo said it to—"

"Come-come, Mrs. Hale, pray sit down, and—"

"Certainly, it's all right, I'm going to sit down presently, but not until I've—"

"But you *must* sit down."

"Must! Well, upon my word if things ain't getting to a pretty pass when—"

The house broke into laughter but was promptly brought to order, and meantime Mr. Allen persuaded the old lady to take her seat. Aunt Patsy continued:

"Yes, they told me that, and I know it's true. They're Luigi's legs this week, but—"

"Ah, they told you that, did they?" said the justice, with interest.

"Well, no, I don't know that they *told* me, but that's neither here nor there; I know, without that, that at dinner yesterday, Angelo was as tired as a dog, and yet Luigi wouldn't lend him the legs to go up stairs and take a nap with."

"Did he ask for them?"

"Let me see—it seems to me somehow, that—that—Aunt Betsy, do you remember whether he—"

"Never mind about what Aunt Betsy remembers, she is not a witness; we only want to know what you remember, yourself," said the judge.

"Well, it does seem to me that you are most cantankerously particular about a little thing, Sim Robinson. Why, when I can't remember a thing myself, I always—"

"Ah, please go *on!*"

"Now how *can* she, when you keep fussing at her all the time?" said Aunt Betsy. "Why, with a person pecking at me that way, I should get that fuzzled and fuddled that—"

She was on her feet again, but Allen coaxed her into her seat once more while the court squelched the mirth of the house. Then the judge said:

"Madam, do you know—do you absolutely *know*, independently of anything these gentlemen have told you—that the power over their legs passes from the one to the other regularly every week?"

"Regularly? Bless your heart, regularly ain't any name for the exactness of it. All the big cities in Europe used to set the clocks by it." [Laughter—suppressed by the court.]

"How do you *know?* That is the question. Please answer it plainly and squarely."

"Don't you talk to me like that, Sim Robinson—I won't have it. How do I know, indeed! How do *you* know what you know? Because somebody told you. You didn't invent it out of your own head, did you? Why, these Twins are the truthfulest people in the world; and I don't think it becomes you to sit up there and throw slurs at them when they haven't been doing anything to you. And they are orphans besides,—both of them. All—"

But Aunt Betsy was up again, now, and both old ladies were talking at once and with all their might, but as the house was weltering in a storm of laughter and the judge was hammering his desk with an iron paper-weight, one could only see them talk, not hear them. At last when quiet was restored, the court said—

"Let the ladies retire."

"But your honor, I have the right, in the interest of my clients, to cross-exam—"

"You'll not need to exercise it, Mr. Wilson—the evidence is thrown out."

"Thrown out!" said Aunt Patsy, ruffled; "and what's it thrown out, for, I'd like to know?"

"And so would I, Patsy Cooper. It seems to me that if we can save these poor persecuted strangers, it is our bounden duty to stand up here and talk for them till—"

"There, there, there, *do* sit down!"

It cost some trouble and a good deal of coaxing, but they were got into their seats at last. The trial was soon ended, now. The Twins themselves became witnesses in their own defence. They established the fact, upon oath, that the leg-power passed from the one to the other every Saturday night at twelve o'clock, sharp. But on cross-examination their counsel would not allow them to tell whose week of power the current week was. The judge insisted upon their answering, and proposed to compel them, but even the prosecution took fright and came to the rescue then and helped stay the sturdy jurist's revolutionary hand. So the case had to go to the jury with that important point hanging in the air. They were out an hour, and brought in this verdict:

"We the jury do find: 1, that an assault was committed, as charged; 2, that it was committed by one of the persons accused, he having been seen to do it by several credible witnesses; 3, but that his identity is so merged in his brother's that we have not been able to tell which was him. We cannot convict both, for only one is guilty. We cannot acquit both, for only one is innocent. Our verdict is that justice has been defeated by the dispensation of God, and ask to be discharged from further duty."

This was read aloud in court, and brought out a burst of hearty applause. The old ladies made a spring at the Twins, to shake and congratulate, but were gently disengaged by Mr. Wilson and softly crowded back into their places.

The judge rose in his little tribune, laid aside his silver-bowed spectacles, roached his gray hair up with his fingers, and said, with dignity and solemnity, and even with a certain pathos:

"In all my experience on the bench I have not seen Justice bow her sacred head in shame in this court until this day. You little realize what far-reaching harm has just been wrought here under the fickle forms of law. Imitation is the bane of courts—I thank God that this one is free from the contamination of that vice—and in no long time you will see the fatal work of this hour seized upon by profligate so-called guardians of justice in all the wide circumference of this planet and perpetuated in their pernicious decisions. I wash my hands of this iniquity. I would have compelled these culprits to expose their guilt, but support failed me where I had most right to expect aid and encouragement. And I was confronted by a law made in the interest of crime, which protects the criminal from testifying against himself. Yet I had precedents of my own whereby I had set aside that law on two different occasions and thus succeeded in convicting criminals to whose crimes there were no witnesses *but* themselves. What have you accomplished this day? Do you realize it? You have set adrift, unadmonished, in this community, two men endowed with an awful and mysterious gift—a hidden and grisly power for evil—a power by which each in his turn may commit crime after crime of the most heinous character, and no man be able to tell which is the guilty or which the innocent party in any case of them all. Look to your homes—look to your property— look to your lives—for you have need! Prisoners at the bar, stand up! Through suppression of evidence, a jury of your—our—countrymen have been obliged to deliver a verdict concerning your case which stinks to heaven with the rankness of its unjustness! By its terms you, the guilty one, go free with the innocent. Depart in peace, and come no more. The costs devolve upon the outraged plaintiff—another iniquity. The court stands dissolved."

Almost everybody crowded forward to overwhelm the Twins and their counsel with congratulations; but presently the two old aunties dug the duplicates out and bore them away in triumph through the hurrahing crowds, while lots of new friends carried Pudd'nhead Wilson off tavernwards to feast him and "wet down" his great and victorious entry into the legal arena. To Wilson, so long familiar with neglect and depreciation, this strange new incense of popularity and admiration was as a fragrance wafted from paradise. A happy man was Wilson.

Chapter 19

Courage is resistance to fear, mastery of fear—not *absence* of fear. Except a creature be part coward it is not a compliment to say it is brave, it is merely a loose misapplication of the word. Consider the flea!—incomparably the bravest of all the creatures of God, if ignorance of fear were courage. Whether you are asleep or awake he will attack you, caring nothing for the fact that in bulk and strength you are to him as are the massed armies of the earth to a sucking child; he lives both day and night and all days and nights in the very lap of peril and the immediate presence of death, and yet is no more afraid than is the man who walks the streets of a city that was threatened by an earthquake ten centuries before. When we speak of Clive, Nelson and Putnam as men who "didn't know what fear was," we ought always to add the flea—and put him at the head of the procession.—*Pudd'nhead Wilson's Calendar.*

Judge Driscoll was in bed and asleep by ten o'clock on Friday night, and he was up and gone a fishing before daylight in the morning with his friend Pembroke Howard. These two had been boys together in Virginia when that State still ranked as the chief and most imposing member of the Union, and they still coupled the proud and affectionate adjective "old" with her name when they spoke of her. In Missouri a recognized superiority attached to any person who hailed from Old Virginia; and this superiority was exalted to supremacy when a person of such nativity could also prove descent from the First Families of that great commonwealth. The Howards and Driscolls were of this aristocracy. In their eyes it was a nobility. It had its unwritten laws, and they were as clearly defined and as stringent as any that could be found among the printed statutes of the land. The F.F.V. was born a gentleman; his highest duty in life was to watch over that great inheritance and keep it unsmirched. He must keep his honor spotless. Those laws were his chart; his course was marked out on it; if he swerved from it by so much as half a point of the compass it meant shipwreck to his honor; that is to say, degradation from his rank as a gentleman. These laws required certain things of him which his religion might forbid: then his religion must yield—the laws could not be relaxed to accommodate religion or anything else. Honor stood first; and the laws defined what it was and wherein it differed, in certain details, from honor as defined by church creeds and by the social laws and customs of some of the minor divisions of the globe that had got crowded out when the sacred boundaries of Virginia were staked out.

If Judge Driscoll was the recognized first citizen of Dawson's Landing, Pembroke Howard was easily its recognized second citizen. He was called "the great lawyer"—an earned title. He and Driscoll were of the same age—a year or two past sixty.

Although Driscoll was a freethinker and Howard a strong and determined Presbyterian, their warm intimacy suffered no impairment in consequence. They were men whose opinions were their own property and not subject to revision and amendment, suggestion or criticism, by anybody, even their friends.

The day's fishing finished, they came floating down stream in their skiff, talking national politics and other high matters, and presently met a skiff coming up from town, with a man in it who said:

"I reckon you know the new Twins gave your nephew a kicking last night, Judge?"

"They did *what?*"

"Gave him a kicking."

The old Judge's lips paled and his eyes began to flame. He choked with anger for a moment, then he got out what he was trying to say—

"Well—well—*go* on! Give me the details."

The man did it. At the finish, the Judge was silent a minute, turning over in his mind the shameful picture of Tom's flight over the footlights, then he said, as if musing aloud—

"Hm—I don't understand it. I was asleep at home. He did not wake me. Thought he was competent to manage his affair without my help, I reckon." His face lit up with pride and pleasure at that thought, and he said with a cheery complacency, "I like that!—it's the true old blood—hey, Pembroke?"

Howard smiled an iron smile and nodded his head approvingly. Then the news-bringer spoke again—

"But the trial went against Tom."

The Judge looked at the man wonderingly, and said—

"The trial? What trial?"

"Why, Tom had them up before Judge Robinson for assault and battery."

"Oh, my God!"

Howard sprang for his friend, as he sank forward in a swoon, and took him in his arms and bedded him on his back in the boat. He sprinkled water in his face, and said to the startled visitor—

"Go, now—don't let him come to and find you here. You see what an effect your heedless speech has had; you ought to have been more considerate than to blurt out such a cruel piece of slander as that."

"I'm right down sorry I did it, now, Mr. Howard, and I wouldn't have done it if I had thought; but it ain't a slander, it's perfectly true, just as I told him."

He rowed away. Presently the old Judge came out of his faint and looked up piteously into the sympathetic face that was bent over him.

"Say it isn't true, Pembroke, tell me it isn't true," he said, in a weak voice.

There was nothing weak in the deep organ-tones that responded—

"You know it is a lie as well as I do, old friend. He is of the best blood of the Old Dominion, and from that blood can spring no such misbegotten son."

"God bless you for saying it!" said the old gentleman fervently. "Ah, Pembroke, it was such a blow!"

Howard stayed by his friend, and saw him home, and entered the house with him. It was dark, and past supper time, but the Judge was not thinking of supper, he was eager to hear the slander refuted from headquarters, and as eager to have Howard hear it, too. Tom was sent for, and he came immediately. He was bruised and lame, and not a happy-looking object. His uncle made him sit down, and said—

"We have been hearing about your adventure, Tom, with a handsome lie added to it for embellishment. Now pulverize that lie to dust! What measures have you taken? How does the thing stand?"

Tom answered innocently, with a sheepish little laugh—

"Well, the fact is, it don't stand any way at all. I had them up in court, but they beat me."

Howard and the Judge sprang to their feet—why, neither knew; then they stood gazing vacantly at each other. Howard stood a moment, then sat mournfully down without saying anything. The Judge's wrath began to kindle, and he burst out—

"You cur! you scum! you vermin! Do you mean to tell me that blood of my race has suffered a blow and crawled to a court of law about it? Answer me!"

Tom's head drooped, and he answered with an eloquent silence. His uncle stared at him with a mixed expression of amazement and shame and incredulity that was sorrowful to see. At last he said—

"So your refuge, the jury, discovered—as we have been informed—that only one of the pair kicked you, but could not determine which one it was? Which one do you think it was?"

Tom had already been to call at the widow Cooper's, and had gathered a strong suspicion there that Rowena was warming toward Angelo and cooling toward him. Without much reflection he framed a lie, now, which gave him a good deal of satisfaction for a moment—

"I don't need to think, I already know which one it was. It was the one named Angelo—the pious one—the one that is to be baptised tomorrow. He was so set-up because he had got the best of me in the trial that he couldn't resist the temptation to crow—so he whispered and told me, going out of court, that he was the one that kicked me."

The way in which the news was received surprised the young fellow, and not pleasantly:

"Ah, that is good! that is splendid!" exclaimed the uncle, beaming with joy. "It locates the responsibility. You have challenged him?"

"N-no," hesitated Tom, turning pale.

"All right, no harm is done. You will challenge him to-night. Howard will carry it."

Tom began to turn sick, and to show it. He was bitterly sorry he had been so premature with his lie. He turned his hat round and round in his hand, his uncle glowering blacker and blacker upon him as the heavy seconds drifted by, then at last he began to stammer, and said, piteously—

"Oh, please don't ask me to do it, uncle. I never could. They are murderous devils. I—I'm *afraid* of them."

Old Driscoll's mouth opened and closed three times before he could get it to perform its office; then he stormed out—

"A coward in my family! A Driscoll a coward! Oh, what have I done to deserve this infamy!" He tottered to his secretary in the corner, still repeating, again and again, that lament in heart-breaking tones, and got out of a drawer a paper, which he slowly tore to bits and scattered the bits absently in his track as he walked up and down the room, still grieving and lamenting. At last he said—

"There it is, shreds and fragments once more—my will. Once more you have forced me to disinherit you, you base son of a most noble father. Leave my sight! Go—before I spit on you!"

The young man did not tarry. Then the Judge turned to Howard:

"You will be my second, old friend?"

"Of course."

"There is pen and paper. Draft the cartel, and lose no time."

"He shall have it in his hands in fifteen minutes."

Tom was very heavy-hearted. His appetite was gone with his property and his self-respect. He went out the back way and wandered down the obscure lane, grieving, and wondering if any course of future conduct, however discreet and carefully perfected and watched over, could win back his uncle's favor and persuade him to reconstruct once more that generous will which had just gone to rags and ruin before his eyes. He finally concluded that it could. He said to himself that he had accomplished this sort of triumph once already, and that what had been done once could be done again. He would set about it. He would bend every energy to the task, and he would score that triumph once more, cost what it might to his convenience, limit as it might his frivolous and liberty-loving life.

"To begin," he said to himself, "I'll square up with the proceeds of my raid, and then gambling has got to be stopped—and stopped short off. It's the worst vice I've got—from my standpoint it is, anyway, because it's the one he can easiest find out, through the impatience of my creditors. He thought it expensive to have to pay two hundred dollars to them for me once. Expensive—that! Why, it cost *me* the whole of his fortune—but of course he never thought of that; some people can't think of any but their own side of a case. If he had known how deep I am in, now, the will would have gone to pot without waiting for a duel to help. Three hundred dollars! It's a pile! But he'll never hear of it, I'm thankful to say. The minute I've cleared it off, I'm safe; and I'll never touch a card again. Anyway I won't while he lives, I make oath to that. I'm entering on my last reform—I know it—yes, and I'll win; but after that, if I ever slip again I'm gone!"

Chapter 20

Thus mournfully communing with himself Tom moped along the lane past Pudd'nhead Wilson's house, and still on and on, between fences enclosing vacant country on either hand, till he neared the haunted house, then came moping back again, with many sighs and heavy with trouble. He sorely wanted cheerful company. Rowena! His heart gave a bound at the thought, but the next thought quieted it—the detested Twins would be there.

He was on the inhabited side of Wilson's house, and now as he approached it he noticed that the sitting room was lighted. This would do; others made him feel unwelcome sometimes, but Wilson never failed in courtesy toward him, and a kindly courtesy does at least save one's feelings, even if it is not professing to stand for a welcome. Wilson heard footsteps at his threshold, then the clearing of a throat, ["It's that fickle-tempered, dissipated young goose—poor devil, he finds friends pretty scarce to-day, likely."] A dejected knock. "Come in!"

Tom entered and drooped into a chair, without saying anything. Wilson said, kindly—

"Why, my boy, you look desolate. Don't take it so hard. Better luck next time. It's our first law-suit, and we couldn't both win it, you know. It's your turn next."

"Oh, dear," said Tom, wretchedly, "it's not that, Pudd'nhead—it's not that. It's a thousand times worse than that—oh, yes, a million times worse."

"Why, Tom, what do you mean? Has Rowena—"

"Flung me? No, but the old man has."

Wilson said to himself, "Aha!" and thought of the mysterious girl in the bedroom. "The Driscolls have been making discoveries." Then he said aloud, gravely:

"Tom, there are some kinds of dissipation which—"

"Oh, shucks, this hasn't got anything to do with dissipation! He wanted me to challenge that derned human lemon-squeezer, and I wouldn't do it."

"The Twins—yes, of course he would do that," said Wilson in a meditative matter-of-course way; "but the thing that puzzled me, was, why he didn't look to that last night, for one thing, and why he let you carry such a matter into a court of law at all, either before the duel or after it. It's no place for it. It was not like him. I couldn't understand it. How did it happen?"

"It happened because he didn't know anything about it. He was asleep when I got home last night."

"And you didn't wake him? Tom, is that possible?"

Tom was not getting much comfort here. He fidgeted a moment, then said:

"I didn't choose to tell him—that's all. He was going a fishing before dawn, with Pembroke Howard, and if I got the Twins into the common calaboose,—and I thought sure I could—I never dreamed of there being any doubt about it, such crowds of people saw the assault—never once thought of their slipping out of it the way they did, with their vile double-action and single-action, interchangeable at will when they want to commit crime, and the original Satan himself not able to tell t'other from which when you want to fetch them to book—well, once in the calaboose they would be disgraced, and uncle wouldn't want any duels with that sort of characters, and wouldn't allow any."

"Tom, I am ashamed of you. I don't see how you could treat your good old uncle so. I am a better friend of his than you are; for if I had known the circumstances I would have kept that case out of court until I got word to him and let him have a gentleman's chance."

"You would?" exclaimed Tom, with lively surprise. "And it your first case! and you know perfectly well there never would have *been* any case if he had got that chance, don't you? and you'd have finished your days a pauper nobody, instead of being on the top wave of legal prosperity to-day. And you would really have done that, would you?"

"Certainly."

Tom looked at him a moment or two, then shook his head sorrowfully and said—

"I believe you—upon my word I do. I don't know why I do, but I do. Pudd'nhead Wilson, I think you're the biggest fool I ever saw."

"Thank you."

"Don't mention it."

"Well, he has been requiring you to fight the Twins, and you have refused. You degenerate remnant of an honorable line! I'm thoroughly ashamed of you, Tom."

"Oh, that's nothing. I don't care for anything, now that the will's torn up again."

"Tom, tell me squarely—didn't he find any fault with you for anything but those two things—carrying the case into court and refusing to fight?"

He watched the young fellow's face narrowly, but it was entirely reposeful, and so also was the voice that answered:

"No, he didn't find any other fault with me. If he had had any to find, he would have begun yesterday, for he was just in the humor for it. He drove that jack-pair around town and showed them the sights, and when he came home he couldn't find his father's old silver watch that don't keep time and he thinks so much of, and couldn't remember what he did with it three or four days ago when he saw it last; and so when I arrived he was all in a sweat about it, and when I suggested that it probably wasn't lost but stolen, it put him in a regular passion and he said I was a fool—which convinced me, without any trouble, that that was just what he was afraid had happened, himself, but didn't want to believe it, because lost things stand a better chance of being found again than stolen ones."

"Whe-ew!" whistled Wilson; "score another on the list!"

"Another what?"

"Another theft!"

"Theft?"

"Yes, theft. That watch isn't lost, it's stolen. There's been another raid on the town—and just the same old mysterious sort of thing that has happened once before, as you remember."

"You don't mean it!"

"It's as sure as you are born. Have you missed anything yourself?"

"No. That is, I did miss a silver pencil case that Aunt Mary Pratt gave me last birth-day—"

"You'll find it's stolen—that's what you'll find."

"No, I shan't; for when I suggested theft about the watch and got such a rap, I went and examined my room, and the pencil-case was missing, but it was only mislaid, and I found it again."

"You are sure you missed nothing else?"

"Well, nothing of consequence. I missed a small plain gold ring worth two or three dollars, but that will turn up. I'll look again."

"In my opinion you'll not find it. There's been a raid, I tell you. Come in!"

Mr. Justice Robinson entered, followed by Buckstone and the town constable, Jim Blake. They sat down, and after some wandering and aimless weather-conversation, Wilson said—

"By the way, we've just added another to the list of thefts, maybe two. Judge Driscoll's old silver watch is gone, and Tom here has missed a gold ring."

"Well, it is a bad business," said the justice, "and gets worse the further it goes. The Hankses, the Dobsons, the Pilligrews, the Ortons, the Grangers, the Hales, the Fullers, the Holcombs, in fact everybody that lives around about Patsy Cooper's have been robbed of little things like trinkets and teaspoons and such-like small valuables that are easily carried off. It's perfectly plain that the thief took advantage of the reception at Patsy Cooper's, when all the neighbors were in her house and all their niggers hanging around her fence for a look at the show, to raid the vacant houses undisturbed. Patsy is miserable about it; miserable on account of the neighbors, and particularly miserable on account of her foreigners, of course; so miserable on their account that she hasn't any room to worry about her own little losses."

"It's the same old raider," said Wilson, "I suppose there isn't any doubt about that."

"Constable Blake doesn't think so."

"No, you're wrong there," said Blake, "the other times it was a man; there was plenty of signs of that, as *we* know, in the profession, though we never got hands on him; but this time it's a woman."

Wilson thought of the mysterious girl, straight off. She was always in his mind, now. But she failed him again. Blake continued:

"She's a stoop-shouldered old woman with a covered basket on her arm in a black veil dressed in mourning. I saw her going aboard the ferry-boat yesterday. Lives in Illinois, I reckon; but I don't care where she lives, I'm going to get her—she can make herself sure of that."

"What makes you think she's the thief?"

"Well, there ain't any other, for one thing; and for another, some of the nigger draymen that happened to be driving along saw her coming out or going into houses and told me so—and it just happens that they was robbed houses, every time."

It was granted that this was plenty good enough circumstantial evidence. A pensive silence followed, which lasted for some moments, then Wilson said—

"There's one good thing, anyway. She can't either pawn or sell Count Luigi's costly Indian dagger."

"My!" said Tom; "is that gone?"

"Yes."

"Well, that *was* a haul! But why can't she pawn it or sell it?"

"Because when the Twins went home from the Sons of Liberty meeting last night, news of the raid was sifting in from everywhere and Aunt Patsy was in distress to know if they had lost anything. They found that the dagger was gone, and they notified the police and pawnbrokers everywhere. It was a great haul, yes, but the old woman won't get anything out of it, because she'll get caught."

"Did they offer a reward?" asked Buckstone.

"Yes—five hundred dollars for the knife, and five hundred more for the thief."

"What a leather-headed idea!" exclaimed the constable. "The thief dasn't go near them, nor send anybody. Whoever goes is going to get himself nabbed, for there ain't any pawnbroker that's going to lose the chance to—"

If anybody had noticed Tom's face at that time, the gray-green color of it might have provoked curiosity; but nobody did. He said to himself, "I'm gone! I never can square up; the rest of the plunder won't pawn or sell for half of the bill. Oh, I know it—I'm gone, I'm gone—and this time it's for good! Oh, this is awful—I don't know *what* to do, nor which way to turn!"

"Softly, softly," said Wilson to Blake, "I planned their scheme for them at midnight last night, and it was all finished up shipshape by two this morning. They'll get their dagger back, and then I'll explain to you how the thing was done."

There were strong signs of a general curiosity, and Buckstone said—

"Well, you *have* whetted us up pretty sharp, Wilson, and I'm free to say that if you don't mind telling us in confidence—"

"Oh, I'd as soon tell as not, Buckstone, but as long as the Twins and I agreed to say nothing about it, we must let it stand so. But you can take my word for it you won't be kept waiting three days. Somebody will apply for that reward pretty promptly, and I'll show you the thief and the dagger both very soon afterward."

The constable was disappointed, and also perplexed. He said—

"It may all be—yes, and I hope it will, but I'm blamed if I can see *my* way through it. It's too many for yours truly."

The subject seemed about talked out. Nobody seemed to have anything further to offer. After a weighty silence the justice of the peace began to clear his throat, and Wilson said to himself, "People haven't been in the habit of coming here in flocks, as far back as I can remember—I see I am about to have my curiosity set at rest as to what this flock are here for."

"Mr. Wilson," said the justice, with solemnity, "I do not need to remind you that we are soon to cease from being a town, and put on the dignity of a city."

"No, your honor, I am aware of it."

"And I do not need to remind you, either, that the time for our first charter election approaches."

"No, your honor, I am aware of that, also."

Tom said he believed he was not interested in politics, and thought he would excuse himself. He was allowed to go. He went sighing, and miserable.

"Mr. Wilson, you cannot of course be unaware of the great and gratifying leap which you have made to-day in fame and in the admiration and esteem of your fellow-citizens—a leap which I am free to say, much surpasses anything of the kind which I have ever met with before in all my experience on the bench—I-I mean in all my experience—er—anywhere. It is the general wish of our party—the great Democratic party of which you have always been a faithful member—that your name and talents shall be secured for the service of our new municipal organization. We have come, therefore, as a committee, deputed to invite you to stand for office under the forthcoming city government. May I say that you will oblige us?"

The tumultuous blood rushed to Wilson's very forehead for joy and exultation. He said it was the proudest moment of his life, and for once that moss-backed phrase vibrated with the genuine life of truth. He said he was his party's loyal servant—let it command, he was ready to obey. What office did the party desire that he should go into nomination for?

"Any, sir! Any you please! Choose for yourself, Mr. Wilson—such are our instructions. You make your choice sir—the party will look to the rest."

Wilson was mute—he was entirely overcome. Honors?—here were not only honors, but choice of them. He had never dreamed of a fairy land of that amazing sort before, asleep or awake. He was in such a whirl of happiness and emotion that he could not trust his voice, but had to do his thanks with fervent hand-grasps and the deep eloquence of watery eyes.

It was sufficient. The old justice characterized it afterwards as by a long way the most beautiful speech he had ever heard.

The deputation thanked him through their mouthpiece for his acceptance, and went away, leaving him to make choice at his leisure, and report. Wilson stood some little time like one stupefied, then turned to his work murmuring—

"What a day—*what* a day it has been!"

Chapter 21

The true southern watermelon is a boon apart, and not to be mentioned with commoner things. It is chief of this world's luxuries, king by the grace of God over all the fruits of the earth. When one has tasted it, he knows what the angels eat. It was not a southern watermelon that Eve took: we know it because she repented.—Pudd'nhead Wilson's Calendar.

It was the gracious watermelon season. All hearts should have been gay and happy, but some were not. About the time that Wilson was saying the words which close the last chapter, Pembroke Howard was entering the next house to report. He found the old Judge sitting grim and straight in his chair, waiting. Howard sat down near him with that vague and indefinable something in his manner which warns the alert observer to prepare for ill news, but the Judge was oblivious to it, and spoke up with the briskest confidence and interest—

"Well, what is the hour and where is the place?"

Howard hesitated, as one might who is seeking some way to soften an unavoidable blow, then he said—

"I—well, I may as well blurt it straight out, I see no way to mitigate it." He pulled himself together, looked the Judge piteously in the eyes, and said with a sigh—

"He won't fight."

The old man started violently, then his gaze began to wander vacantly about the room, and his face to turn ashy and his lips to move, sometimes emitting no sound, sometimes emitting broken words, parts of sentences: "Won't—fight . . . . ah-h! . . . . cruel . . . . . serve an old man so . . . . My honor . . . . . . what is to become of that? . . . . . Oh, how . . . . . how could one . . . . . believe . . . . ." And so on, and so on. He was like one whose faculties have been stunned by a physical blow and are groping in confusion and semi-consciousness. It made his friend's heart bleed to see him. He brought whisky and made him drink it, and soothed his hurt spirit with caressing and comforting words; and so presently won him back to life, and to tranquillity and resignation. He hastened to reinforce these efforts with his tale, and his reward followed; he saw his patient's eye begin to lose its haziness and brighten with interest as the story went on; and sooner than he had ventured to hope the restoration was complete.

"I will give you the details, York, and then you will understand the situation. I went there and asked to see the foreign gentlemen privately, and was left in the parlor alone. They entered soon, and were very polite and pleasant, remembering my face and name, and also referring to a detail or two of the moment's talk which we had had at the reception. I then introduced the matter of my errand and handed the cartel to Count Angelo, at the same time saying that I was at his second's immediate service and that if he would name him I would go at once and arrange the details with him. To my astonishment he declined to accept the challenge, and explained that his religious views would not allow him to do such a thing. I was surprised at the pretext, of course, but did not betray it. I urged him, with all courtesy, not to restrict himself to considering the matter as it affected himself alone, but to remember and respect your rights and dues in it as well. I went further and begged him as a brother in the faith not to bring a hurt upon our religion by a hasty and incautious interpretation of its precepts, and reminded him that its loftiest admonition, its golden rule, made it at once our privilege and our imperative duty to do unto others as we would have them do unto us in the same circumstances. To my stupefaction this had no more effect upon him than if he had been reared in the outer darkness of paganism. He still refused to fight, and refused point blank.

"At this point a noble thing happened—a sin, it was, but a manly one, if ever sin may be so named—and if ever sin *may* be so named, this was the manliest one that was ever committed in my sight. The Count Luigi *lied* to save his brother from shame—came out with magnificent audacity and said *he* committed the assault and would fight!"

"By the lord Harry he's a man!—he's a man, every inch of him!" cried the Judge. "Ah, it would be a privilege to stand up before a Roman like that, if it were only permissible." He shook his head once or twice, and added, wistfully, "for it wouldn't be right—no, I suppose it wouldn't be right—to let him chance his life for his brother's fault?"

Plainly, he hoped that Howard would argue him out of that scruple; and he was charmed to see, by the sudden clearing of his friend's countenance, that he was applying in the right quarter. Howard took vigorous hold of the moralities and proprieties of the case, and both men were soon convinced that it was not only permissible to shoot one brother for another brother's offence, if he wanted to be shot, but that it was even a high and righteous duty to grant him that privilege and thus enable him to remove a smirch from his brother's honor which would extend to his own if it were allowed to remain. Then Howard said, cheerfully—

"The matter is simple, now, and we can proceed with untroubled consciences. I am very, very glad you look at it as you do, York. I was determined not to suggest this solution to you, for I couldn't have you do a thing upon any hint of mine which you could regret afterwards. I came away from that place miserable, for I didn't dare to let Luigi accept, of course, since that would have been to go beyond the powers vested in me; but I shall go back there in another frame of mind, I assure you. Ah, it's a fine fellow, York!—you'll like to fight that one; I should like it myself. You should have heard him argue his case. He said his brother's honor was just as dear to him as his own, and that he would gladly put himself in danger at any time, gladly have himself shot at, for its protection and preservation. And he insisted upon being allowed to do this, and said that he had the same high right to take the place of a brother who was disabled by his principles from defending himself as he should unquestionably have if that brother were disabled by physical incapacity."

"Why, Pembroke, that's not only fine and manly and handsome, but it's perfectly sound—absolutely sound. Why, of *course* principles are as legitimate and complete a disability as physical disability, when you come to look at it. That young man has got an admirable head, a most capable head, and a most broad and unusual intelligence. His brother was grateful?"

"Well, n-no, he—in fact he wasn't. He disappointed me. Instead of being grateful, he objected—and strenuously. He said it was all very fine for his brother, with his robust nature, not to mind bullets, but as for himself, he was not built in that way, and he *did* mind them. He didn't *want* to stand so near while his brother was being shot at, and wouldn't ever consent to do it; said he should be perfectly sick when the bullets began to fly; and when his brother tried to comfort him, and said the Westerners were all good marksmen and could be depended on to hit the particular man they were shooting at, so *he* needn't be worrying, he turned as gray as a last-year's cobweb, and said if Luigi's head got bored through, it might just as well be his own, the general result would be the same. However, his labored shufflings and irrelevancies had no effect upon his chivalrous brother, who wanted to fight, was bound to fight, and was bent on having the duel straight off, this very night, before twelve o'clock."

"Why, Pembroke, he's magnificent! I never saw so fine a creature. Go and arrange the thing."

Howard seized his hat and started on his joyful errand, saying—

"I'll have him in the vacant stretch between Wilson's and the haunted house within the hour, and I'll bring my own pistols."

Judge Driscoll began to walk the floor in a state of pleased excitement; but presently he stopped, and began to think. Began to think of Tom. Twice he moved toward the secretary, and twice he turned away again; but finally he said—

"This may be my last night in the world—I must not take the chance. He is worthless and unworthy, but it is largely my fault. He was entrusted to me by my brother on his dying bed, and I have indulged him to his hurt, instead of training him up severely and making a man of him. I have violated my trust, and I must not add the sin of desertion to that. I have forgiven him once, already, and would subject him to a long and hard trial before forgiving him again, if I could live; but I must not run that risk. No, I must restore the will. But if I survive the duel I will hide it away and he will not know, and I will not tell him until he reforms and I see that his reformation is going to be permanent."

He re-drew the will, and his ostensible nephew was heir to a fortune again. As he was finishing his task, Tom, wearied with another brooding tramp, entered the house and went tip-toeing past the sitting-room door. He glanced in, and hurried on, for the sight of his uncle had nothing but terrors for him to-night. But his uncle was writing! That was unusual—at this late hour of the night. It was near eleven—a good hour after his ordinary bedtime. What could he be writing? A chill anxiety settled down upon Tom's heart. Did that writing concern him? He was afraid so. He reflected that when ill luck begins, it does not come in sprinkles, but in showers. He said he would get a glimpse of that document or know the reason why. He heard some one coming, and stepped out of sight. It was Pembroke Howard. What *could* be hatching?

Howard had his pistol case with him. He said, with great satisfaction—

"Everything's right and ready. He's gone to the battle ground with his second and the surgeon—also his brother, of course, who is looking indisposed. I've arranged it all with Wilson—Wilson's his second. We are to have three shots apiece."

"Good. How is the moon?"

"Bright as day, nearly. Perfect for the distance—fifteen yards. No wind—not a breath; hot and still."

"All good; all first-rate. Here, Pembroke, read this, and witness it."

Pembroke read and witnessed the will, then gave the old man's hand a hearty shake and said—

"Now that's right, York—but I knew you would do it. You couldn't leave that poor chap to fight along without means or profession, with certain defeat before him, and I knew you wouldn't, for his father's sake if not for his own."

"For his dead father's sake I couldn't, I know; for poor Percy—but you know what Percy was to me. But mind—Tom is not to know of this unless I fall to-night."

"Ah, I understand. I'll keep the secret."

The Judge put the will away, and the two started for the battle ground. In another minute the will was in Tom's hands. His misery vanished, his feelings underwent a tremendous revulsion. He put the will carefully back in its place and spread his mouth and swung his hat once, twice, three times around his head, in mute imitation of three rousing huzzas, no sound issuing from his lips. He fell to communing with himself excitedly and joyously, but every now and then he let off another volley of dumb hurrahs.

He said to himself: "I've got the fortune again, but I'll not let on that I know about it. And this time I'm going to hang on to it. I take no more risks. I'll gamble no more, I'll drink no more, because—well, because I'll not go where there is any of that sort of thing going on, again. It's the sure way, and the only sure way; I might have thought of that sooner—well, yes, if I had wanted to. But *now*—dear me, I've had a bad scare this time, and I'll take no more chances. Not a single chance more. Land! I persuaded myself this evening that I could fetch him around without any great amount of effort, but I've been getting sicker and sicker straight along, ever since. If he tells me about this thing, all right; but if he doesn't, I shan't let on. I—well, I'd like to tell Pudd'nhead Wilson, but—no, I'll think about that; perhaps I won't." He whirled off another dead huzza, and said, "I'm reformed, and this time I'll stay so, sure."

He was about to close with a final grand silent demonstration, when he suddenly recollected that Wilson had put it out of his power to pawn or sell the Indian knife, and that he was once more in awful peril of exposure by his creditors for that reason. His joy collapsed utterly, and he turned away and moped toward the door moaning and lamenting over the bitterness of his luck.

Chapter 22

Let us endeavor to so live that when we approach death even the undertaker will be sorry.—*Pudd'nhead Wilson's Calendar.*

The Judge and his second found the rest of the war party at the further end of the vacant ground, near the haunted house. Pudd'nhead Wilson advanced to meet them, and said anxiously—

"I must say a word in behalf of my principal's proxy, Count Luigi, to whom you have kindly granted the privilege of fighting my principal's battle for him. It is growing late, and Count Luigi is in great trouble lest midnight shall strike before the finish."

"It is another testimony," said Howard, approvingly. "That young man is fine all through. He wishes to save his brother the sorrow of fighting on the Sabbath, and he is right; it is the right and manly feeling and does him credit. We will make all possible haste."

Wilson said—

"There is also another reason—a consideration, in fact, which deeply concerns Count Luigi himself. These Twins have command of their mutual legs turn about. Count Luigi is in command, now; but at midnight, possession will pass to my principal, Count Angelo, and—well, you can foresee what will happen. He will march straight off the field, and carry Luigi with him."

"Why, sure enough!" cried the Judge, "we have heard something about that extraordinary law of their being, already—nothing very definite, it is true, as regards dates and durations of the power, but I see it is definite enough as regards to-night. Of course we must give Luigi every chance. Omit all the ceremonial possible, gentlemen, and place us in position."

The seconds at once tossed up a coin; Howard won the choice. He placed the Judge sixty feet from the haunted house and facing it; Wilson placed the Twins within fifteen feet of the house and facing the Judge—necessarily. The pistol-case was opened and the long slim tubes taken out; when the moonlight glinted from them a shiver went through Angelo. The doctor was a fool, but a thoroughly well-meaning one, with a kind heart and a sincere disposition to oblige, but along with it an absence of tact which often hurt its effectiveness. He brought his box of lint and bandages, and asked Angelo to feel and see how soft and comfortable they were. Angelo's head fell over against Luigi's in a faint, and precious time was lost in bringing him to; which provoked Luigi into expressing his mind to the doctor with a good deal of vigor and frankness. After Angelo came to he was still so weak that Luigi was obliged to drink a stiff horn of brandy to brace him up.

The seconds now stepped at once to their posts, half way between the combatants, one of them on each side of the line of fire. Wilson was to count, very deliberately, "One——two——three——fire!——stop!" and the duelists could bang away at any time they chose during that recitation, but not after the last word. Angelo grew very nervous when he saw Wilson's hand rising slowly into the air as a sign to make ready, and he leaned his head against Luigi's and said—

"O, please take me away from here, I *can't* stay, I know I can't!"

"What in the world are you doing? Straighten up! What's the matter with you?—you're in no danger—nobody's going to shoot at *you*. Straighten up, I tell you!"

Angelo obeyed, just in time to hear—

"One—!"

"Bang!" Just one report, and a little tuft of white hair floated slowly to the Judge's feet in the moonlight. The Judge did not swerve; he still stood, erect and motionless, like a statue, with his pistol-arm hanging straight down at his side. He was reserving his fire.

"Two—!

"Three—!

"Fire!—"

Up came the pistol-arm instantly—Angelo dodged with the report. He said "Ouch!" and fainted again.

The doctor examined and bandaged the wound. It was of no consequence, he said—bullet through fleshy part of arm—no bones broken—the gentleman was still able to fight—let the duel proceed.

Next time, Angelo jumped just as Luigi fired; which disordered his aim and caused him to cut a chip out of Howard's ear. The Judge took his time again, and when he fired Angelo jumped, and got a knuckle skinned. The doctor inspected and dressed the wounds. Angelo now spoke out and said he was content with the satisfaction he had got, and if the Judge—

but Luigi shut him roughly up, and asked him not to make an ass of himself; adding—

"And I want you to stop dodging. You take a great deal too prominent a part in this thing for a person who has delegated his authority to another. You should remember that you are here only by courtesy, and are without official recognition; officially you are not here at all; officially you do not even exist. To all intents and purposes you are absent from this place, and you ought for your own modesty's sake to reflect that it cannot become a person who is not present here to be taking this sort of public and indecent prominence in a matter in which he is not in the slightest degree concerned. Now don't dodge again; the bullets are not for you, they are for me; if I want them dodged I will attend to it myself. I never saw a person act so."

Angelo saw the reasonableness of what his brother had said, and he did try to reform, but it was of no use; both pistols went off at the same instant, and he jumped once more; he got a sharp scrape along his cheek from the Judge's bullet, and so deflected Luigi's aim that his ball went wide and chipped a flake of skin from Pudd'nhead Wilson's chin. The doctor attended to the wounded.

By the terms, the duel was over. But Luigi was entirely out of patience, and begged for one more exchange of shots, insisting that he had had no fair chance, on account of his brother's indelicate behavior. Howard was opposed to granting so unusual a privilege, but the Judge took Luigi's part, and added that indeed he might fairly be considered entitled to another trial himself, because although the proxy on the other side was in no way to blame for his (the Judge's) humiliatingly resultless work, the gentleman with whom he was fighting this duel *was* to blame for it, since if he had played no advantages and had held his head still, his proxy would have been disposed of early. He added—

"Count Luigi's request for another exchange is another proof that he is a brave and chivalrous gentleman, and I beg that the courtesy he asks may be accorded him."

"I thank you most sincerely for this generosity, Judge Driscoll," said Luigi, with a polite bow, and moving to his place. Then he added—to Angelo, "Now hold your grip, hold your *grip*, I tell you, and I'll land him, sure!"

The men stood erect, their pistol-arms at their sides, the two seconds stood at their official posts, the doctor stood five paces in Wilson's rear with his instruments and bandages in his hands. The deep stillness, the peaceful moonlight, the motionless figures, made an impressive picture, and the impending fatal possibilities augmented this impressiveness to solemnity.

Wilson's hand began to rise—slowly—slowly—higher—still higher—in another moment—

"Boom!"—the first stroke of midnight swung up out of the distance. Angelo was off like a deer!

"Oh, you unspeakable traitor!" wailed his brother, as they went soaring over the fence.

The others stood astonished and gazing; and so stood, watching that strange spectacle until distance dissolved it and swept it from their view. Then they rubbed their eyes like people waking out of a dream.

"Well, I've never seen anything like *that* before," said the Judge. "Wilson, I am going to confess, now, that I wasn't quite able to believe in that leg-business, and had a suspicion that it was a put-up convenience between those Twins; and when Count Angelo fainted I thought I saw the whole scheme—thought it was pretext No. 1, and would be followed by others till twelve o'clock should arrive and Luigi would get off with all the credit of seeming to want to fight and yet not have to fight, after all. But I was mistaken. His pluck proved it. He's a brave fellow and did want to fight."

"There isn't any doubt about that," said Howard, and added in a grieved tone, "but what an unworthy sort of Christian that Angelo is—I hope and believe there are not many like him. It is not right to engage in a duel on the Sabbath—I could not approve of that, myself; but to *finish* one that has been begun—that is a duty, let the day be what it may."

They strolled along, still wondering, still talking.

"It is a curious circumstance," remarked the surgeon, halting Wilson a moment to paste some more court plaster on his chin, which had gone to leaking blood again, "that in this duel neither of the parties who handled the pistols lost blood, while nearly all the persons present in the mere capacity of guests got hit. I have not heard of such a thing before. Don't you think it unusual?"

"Yes," said the Judge, "it has struck me as peculiar. Peculiar and unfortunate. I was annoyed at it, all the time. In the case of Angelo it made no great difference, because he was in a measure concerned, though not officially; but it troubled me to see the seconds compromised, and yet I knew no way to mend the matter."

"There was no way to mend it," said Howard, whose ear was being read-justed now by the doctor; "the code fixes our place, and it would not have been lawful to change it. If we could have stood at your side, or behind you, or in front of you, it—but it would not have been legitimate, and the other parties would have had a just right to complain of our trying to protect ourselves from danger; infractions of the code are certainly not permissible in any case whatsoever."

Wilson offered no remarks. It seemed to him that there was very little place here for so much solemnity, but he judged that if a duel where nobody was in danger or got crippled but the seconds and the outsiders had nothing ridiculous about it for these gentlemen, his pointing out that feature would probably not help them to see it.

He invited them in to take a nightcap, and Howard and the Judge accepted, but the doctor said he would have to go and see how Angelo's principal wound was getting on.

Chapter 23

Meantime Tom had been brooding in his room a long time, disconsolate and forlorn, with Luigi's Indian knife for a text. At last he sighed and said:

"When I supposed these stones were glass and this ivory bone, the thing hadn't any interest for me because it hadn't any value and couldn't help me out of my trouble. But now—why, now it is full of interest; yes, and of a sort to break a body's heart. It's a bag of gold that has turned to dirt and ashes in my hands. It could save me, and save me so easily, and yet I've got to go to ruin. It's like drowning with a life-preserver in my reach. All the hard luck comes to me and all the good luck goes to other people. There's Pudd'nhead Wilson, for instance; his fortune's made, and what has he done to deserve it, I would like to know. Yes, he has made his own fortune, but isn't content with that, but must ruin mine. It's a sordid, selfish world, and I wish I was out of it." He allowed the light of the candle to play upon the jewels of the sheath, but the flashings and sparklings had no charm for his eye, they were only just so many pangs for his heart. "I must not say anything to Roxy about this thing," he said, "she is too daring. She would be for digging these stones out and selling them, and then—why, she would be arrested and the stones traced, and *then!*—" The thought made him quake, and he hid the knife away, trembling all over and glancing furtively about, like a criminal who fancies that the accuser is already at hand.

Should he try to sleep? Oh, no, sleep was not for him; his trouble was too haunting, too afflicting for that. He must have somebody to mourn with. He would carry his despair to Roxy.

He had heard several distant gunshots, but that sort of thing was not uncommon, and they had made no impression upon him. He went out at the back door, and just then the Twins whizzed by, on their way home. He wondered what that might mean. Had they seen a ghost at the haunted house? He passed Wilson's house and proceeded along the lane, and presently saw several figures approaching Wilson's place through the vacant lots. These were the duelists, and he thought he recognized them, but as he had no desire for white people's company he stooped down behind the fence until they were out of his way.

Roxy was feeling fine. She said:

"Whah was you, child? Warn't you in it?"

"In what?"

"In de duel."

"Duel? Has there been a duel?"

"'Cose dey has. De ole Jedge has been havin' a duel wid dat pair o' nut-crackers—dem Twins."

"Great Scott!" He added, to himself, "*That's* what made him re-make the will; he thought he might get killed, and it softened him toward me. And that's what he and Howard were so busy about. . . . . . . Oh, dear, if the Twins had only killed him, I should be out of my—"

"What is you mumblin' 'bout, Chambers? Whah was you? Didn't you know dey was gwyne to be a duel?"

"No, I didn't. The old man tried to get me to fight one with Count Angelo, but he didn't succeed; so I reckon he concluded to patch up the family honor himself."

He laughed at the idea, and went rambling on with a detailed account of his talk with the Judge, and how shocked and ashamed the Judge was to find that he had a coward in his family. He glanced up at last, and got a shock himself. Roxana's bosom was heaving with suppressed passion, and she was glowering down upon him with measureless contempt written in her face.

"En you refuse' to fight a man dat kicked you, 'stid o' jumpin' at de chance! En you ain't got no mo' feelin' den to come en tell *me*, dat fetched sich a po' low-down ornery rabbit into de worl'! Pah! it make me sick! It's de *nigger* in you, dat's what it is. Thirty-one parts o' you is white, en on'y one part nigger, en dat po' little one part is yo' soul! 'Tain't wuth savin'; 'tain't wuth totin' out on a shovel en tho'in' in de gutter. You has disgraced yo' birth. What would yo' pa think o' you? It's enough to make him turn in his grave."

The last three sentences stung Tom into a fury, and he said to himself that if his father were only alive and in reach of assassination his mother would soon find that he had a very clear notion of the size of his indebtedness to that man and was willing to pay it up in full, and would do it, too, even at risk of his life; but he kept his thought to himself; that was safest, in his mother's present state.

"Whatever *has* 'come o' yo' Essex blood? Dat's what *I* can't understan'. En it ain't only jist Essex blood dat's in you, not by a long sight—'deed it ain't! My father en yo' gran'father was ole John Randolph of Roanoke, de highes' blood dat Ole Virginny ever turned out; en his great-great-gran'mother or somers along back dah, was Pocahontas de Injun queen—en yit here you is, a slinkin' outen a duel en disgracin' our whole line like a ornery low-down hound! Yes, it's de *nigger* in you."

She sat down on her candle-box and fell into a reverie. Tom did not disturb her; he sometimes lacked prudence, but it was not in circumstances of this kind. Roxana's storm went gradually down, but it died hard, and even when it seemed to be quite gone it would now and then break out in a distant rumble again, so to speak, in the form of muttered ejaculations. One of these was, "Ain't nigger enough in him to show in his finger-nails, en dat takes mighty little—yit dey's enough to paint his soul." Presently she muttered, "Yassir, enough to paint a whole thimbleful of 'em." At last her rumblings ceased altogether and her countenance began to clear—a welcome sign to Tom, who had learned her moods and knew she was on the threshold of good-humor, now. He noticed that from time to time she unconsciously carried her finger to the end of her nose. He looked closer and said—

"Why, mammy, the end of your nose is peeled—how did that come?"

She sent out the sort of whole-hearted peal of laughter which God has vouchsafed in its perfection to none but the happy angels in heaven and the bruised and broken black slave in the earth, and said:

"Dad fetch dat duel, *I* ben in it myseff!"

"Gracious! did a bullet do that?"

"Yassir, you bet it did."

"Well, I declare! Why, how did that happen?"

"Happen dis-away. I 'uz a sett'n here kinder dozin' in de dark, en che-*bang*! goes a gun, right out dah. I skips along out towards t'other end o' de house to see what's gwyne on, en stops by de ole winder on de side towards Pudd'nhead Wilson's house dat ain't got no sash in it—but dey ain't none of 'em got any sashes, fur as dat's concerned—en I stood dah in de dark en look out, en dah I seed everything as plain as day in de moonlight. Right down under me 'uz de Twins a yowlin'—not much, but jist a yowlin' soft,—it 'uz de *white* one dat was yowlin', caze he 'uz hit in de shoulder—dat is, I *reckon* it 'uz *his* shoulder, dough how *he* could tell it 'uz his'n, de way dey arms is mixed up do beat me—but anyway he judged it 'uz his'n en so he 'uz doin' de yowlin' till he could fine out. En Doctor Claypool he 'uz a workin' at him, en Pudd'nhead Wilson he 'uz a he'pin', en ole Jedge Driscoll en Pem. Howard 'uz a standin' out yonder a little piece waitin' for 'em to git ready agin. En toreckly dey squared off en give de word, en *bang-bang* went de pistols, en de white twin he say 'Ouch!'—hit him on de han' dis time—en I hear dat same bullet go *'spat!'* agin de logs under de winder; en de nex' time dey shoot, de white one say 'Ouch!' agin, en I done it too, caze de bullet glance' on his cheek bone en skip up here en glance' on de side o' de winder en whiz right acrost my face en tuck de hide off'n my nose—why, if I'd a ben jist a inch or a inch en a half furder, 'twould a tuck de whole nose en disfigger' me. Den dey 'uz a gwyne to shoot agin, but de Twins dey lit out. De white one 'uz gitt'n more'n his sheer, en I reckon it 'uz him dat run. But I don't know—caze t'other one went too. Here's de bullet; I hunted her up."

"Did you stand there all the time?"

"Dat's a question to ask, ain't it! What else would I do? Does I git a chance to see a duel every day?"

"Why, you were right in range. Weren't you afraid?"

The woman gave a sniff of scorn.

"*'Fraid!* De Randolphs ain't 'fraid o' *nothin'*, let alone bullets."

"They've got pluck enough, I suppose; what they lack is judgment. I wouldn't have stood there."

"Nobody's accusin' you!"

"Did anybody else get hurt?"

"Yes, we all got hit 'cep' de nigger-twin en de doctor. De Jedge didn't get hurt, but I hear Pudd'nhead say de bullet snip some o' his ha'r off."

"'George!" said Tom to himself, "to come so near being out of my trouble, and miss it by an inch! O, dear, dear, he'll live to find me out and sell me to some nigger-trader yet—yes, and he would do it in a minute!" Then he said aloud, in a grave tone—

"Mother, we are in an awful fix."

Roxana caught her breath with a spasm, and said—

"Chile! What you hit a body so sudden for, like dat? What's ben en gone en happen'?"

"Well, there's one thing I didn't tell you. When I wouldn't fight, he tore up the will again, and—"

Roxana's face turned a dead white, and she said—

"*Now* you's *done!*—done forever! Dat's de *end!* Bofe un us is gwyne to starve to—"

"Wait and hear me through, can't you! I reckon that when he resolved to fight, himself, he thought he might get killed and not have a chance to forgive me any more in this life, so he made the will again, and I've seen it and it's all right. But—"

"Oh, thank goodness, den we's safe agin!—safe! en so what did you want to come here en talk sich dreadful—"

"Hold on, I tell you! and let me finish. The swag I gathered won't half square me up, and the first thing we know my creditors—well, you know what'll happen."

Roxana dropped her chin and told her son to leave her alone—she must think this matter out. Presently she said, impressively:

"You got to go mighty keerful now, *I* tell you. En here's what you got to do. He didn't get killed, en if you gives him de least reason, he'll bust de will agin, en dat's de *las'* time, now you hear *me*. So—you's got to show him what you kin do in de nex' few days. You's got to be pison good, en let him see it; you got to do everything dat'll make him b'lieve in you, en you got to sweeten aroun' ole Aunt Pratt, too—she's pow'ful strong wid de Jedge, en de bes' frien' you got. Nex', you'll go 'long away to Sent Louis, en dat'll *keep* him in yo' favor. Den you go en make a bargain wid dem people. You tell 'em he ain't gwyne to live long—en dat's de fac', too—en tell 'em you'll pay 'em intrust, en *big* intrust, too—ten per—what you call it?"

"Ten per cent a month."

"Dat's it. Den you take en sell yo' truck aroun', a little at a time, en pay de intrust. How long will it las'?"

"I think there's enough to pay the interest five or six months."

"Den you's all right. If he don't die in six months, dat don't make no diffrence—Providence 'll provide. You's gwyne to be safe—if you behaves." She bent an austere eye on him and added, "En you's *gwyne* to behave—does you know dat?"

He laughed and said he was going to try, anyway. She did not unbend. She said gravely—

"Tryin' ain't de thing. You's gwyne to *do* it. You ain't gwyne to steal a pin—caze it ain't safe no mo'; en you ain't gwyne into no bad comp'ny—not even *once*, you understand; en you ain't gwyne to drink a drop—nary single drop; en you ain't gwyne to gamble one single gamble—not one. Dis ain't what you's gwyne to *try* to do, it's what you's gwyne to *do*. En I'll tell you how I knows it. Dis is how. I's gwyne to foller along to Sent Louis my own seff; en you's gwyne to come to me every day o' yo' life, en I'll look you over; en if you fails in one single one o' dem things—jist *once*—I take my oath I'll come straight down to dis town en tell de Jedge you is a nigger en a slave—en *prove* it!" She paused, to let her words sink home. Then she added: "Chambers, does you b'lieve me when I say dat?"

Tom was sober enough now. There was no levity in his voice when he answered:

"Yes, mother. I know, now, that I am reformed—and permanently. Permanently—and beyond the reach of any human temptation."

"Den g'long home en begin!"

Chapter 24

He is as conceited as a proverb.—*Pudd'nhead Wilson's Calendar.*

When the doctor arrived at Aunt Patsy Cooper's house, he found the lights going and everybody up and dressed and in a great state of solicitude and excitement. The Twins were stretched on a sofa in the sitting room, Aunt Patsy was fussing at Angelo's arm, Nancy was flying around under her commands, the two young boys were trying to keep out of the way but always getting in it, in order to see and wonder, Rowena stood apart, helpless with apprehension and emotion, and Luigi was growling in unappeasable fury over Angelo's shameful flight.

As has been reported before, the doctor was a fool—a kind-hearted and well-meaning one, but with no tact; and as he was by long odds the most learned physician in the town, and was quite well aware of it, and could talk his learning with ease and precision, and liked to show off when he had an audience, he was sometimes tempted into revealing more of a case than was good for the patient.

He examined Angelo's wound, and was really minded to say nothing, for once; but Aunt Patsy was so anxious and so pressing that he allowed his caution to be overcome, and proceeded to empty himself as follows, with scientific relish—

"Without going too much into detail, madam—for you would probably not understand it anyway—I concede that great care is going to be necessary here; otherwise exudation of the oesophagus is nearly sure to ensue, and this will be followed by ossification and extradition of the *maxillaris superioris*, which must decompose the granular surfaces of the great infusorial ganglionic system, thus obstructing the action of the posterior varioloid arteries and precipitating compound strangulated sorosis of the valvular tissues, and ending unavoidably in the dispersion and combustion of the marsupial fluxes and the consequent embrocation of the bi-cuspid *populo redax referendum rotulorum*."

A miserable silence followed. Aunt Patsy's heart sank, the pallor of despair invaded her face, she was not able to speak; poor Rowena wrung her hands in privacy and silence, and said to herself in the bitterness of her young grief, "There is no hope—it is plain there is no hope;" the good-hearted negro wench, Nancy, paled to chocolate, then to orange, then to amber, and thought to herself with yearning sympathy and sorrow, "Po' thing, he ain' gwyne to las' thoo de half o' dat;" small Henry choked up, and turned his head away to hide his rising tears, and his brother Joe said to himself, with a sense of loss, "The babtizing's busted, that's sure." Luigi was the only person who had any heart to speak. He said, a little bit sharply, to the doctor—

"Well, well, there's nothing to be gained by wasting precious time: give him a barrel of pills—I'll take them for him."

"You?" asked the doctor.

"Yes. Did you suppose he was going to take them himself?"

"Why, of course."

"Well, it's a mistake. He never took a dose of medicine in his life. He *can't.*"

"Well, upon my word it's the most extraordinary thing I ever heard of!"

"Oh," said Aunt Patsy, as pleased as a mother whose child is being admired and wondered at, "you'll find that there's more about them that's wonderful than their just being made in the image of God like the rest of His creatures, now you can depend on that, *I* tell you," and she wagged her complacent head like one who could reveal marvelous things if she chose.

The boy Joe began—

"Why, ma, they *ain't* made in the im—"

"You shut up, and wait till you're asked, Joe! I'll let you know when I want help. Are you looking for something, doctor?"

The doctor asked for a few sheets of paper and a pen, and said he would write a prescription—which he did. It was one of Galen's; in fact it was Galen's favorite, and had been slaying people for sixteen thousand years. Galen used it for everything, applied it to everything, said it would remove everything, from warts all the way through to congested lungs—and it generally did. Galen was still the only medical authority recognized in Missouri, his practice was the only practice known to the Missouri doctors, and his prescriptions were the only ammunition they carried when they went out for game. By and by Dr. Claypool laid down his pen and read the result of his labors aloud, carefully and deliberately, for this battery must be constructed on the premises by the family, and mistakes could occur; for he wrote a

doctor's hand—the hand which from the beginning of time has been so disastrous to the apothecary and so profitable to the undertaker:

> Take of Asarabacca, Henbane, Carpobalsamum, each two Drams and a
> half; of Cloves, Opium, Myrrh, Cyperus, each two Drams; of Opobalsamum,
> Indian Leaf, Cinamon, Zedoary, Ginger, Costus, Coral, Cassia, Euphorbium,
> Gum Tragacanth, Frankincense, Styrax Calamita, Celtic Nard, Spignel,
> Hartwort, Mustard, Saxifrage, Dill, Anise, each one Dram; of Xylaloes,
> Rheum Ponticum, Alipta Moschata, Castor, Spikenard, Galangals,
> Opoponax, Anacardium, Mastich, Brimstone, Peony, Eringo, Pulp of Dates,
> red and white Hermodactyls, Roses, Thyme, Acorus, Penyroyal, Gentian, the
> Bark of the Root of Mandrake, Germander, Valerian, Bishops Weed, Bay-
> Berries, long and white Pepper, Xylobalsamum, Carnabadium, Macedonian
> Parsley-seeds, Lovage, the Seeds of Rue, and Sinon, of each a Dram and a half;
> of pure Gold, pure Silver, Pearls not perforated, the Blatta Byzantina, the
> Bone of the Stag's Heart, of each the Quantity of fourteen Grains of Wheat;
> of Sapphire, Emerald, and Jasper Stones, each one Dram; of Hasle-nut, two
> Drams; of Pellitory of Spain, Shavings of Ivory, Calamus odoratus, each the
> Quantity of twenty-nine Grains of Wheat; of Honey or Sugar a sufficient
> Quantity.

"There," he said, "that will fix the patient; give his brother a dipperful
every three-quarters of an hour—"

—"While he survives," muttered Luigi—

—"and see that the room is kept wholesomely hot and the doors and windows closed tight. Keep Count Angelo nicely covered up with six or seven
blankets, and when he is thirsty—which will be frequently—moisten a rag
in the vapor of the tea-kettle and let his brother suck it. When he is hungry—
which will also be frequently—he must not be humored oftener than every
seven or eight hours; then toast part of a cracker until it begins to brown, and
give it to his brother."

"That is all very well, as far as Angelo is concerned," said Luigi, "but what
am I to eat?"

"I do not see that there is anything the matter with you," the doctor
answered, "you may of course eat what you please."

"And also drink what I please, I suppose?"

"Oh, certainly—at present. When the violent and continuous perspiring
has reduced your strength, I shall have to reduce your diet, of course, and
also bleed you, but there is no occasion for that yet awhile." He turned
to Aunt Patsy and said: "He must be put to bed, and sat up with, and

tended with the greatest care, and not allowed to stir for several days and nights."

"For one, I'm sacredly thankful for that," said Luigi, "it postpones the funeral—I'm not to be drowned *to-day*, anyhow."

Angelo said quietly to the doctor:

"I will cheerfully submit to all your requirements, sir, up to two o'clock this afternoon, and will resume them after three, but I cannot be confined to the house during that intermediate hour."

"Why, may I ask?"

"Because I have entered the Baptist communion, and by appointment am to be baptised in the river at that hour."

"O, insanity!—it cannot be allowed!"

Angelo answered with placid firmness—

"Nothing shall prevent it, if I am alive."

"Why, consider, my dear sir, in your condition it might prove fatal."

A tender and ecstatic smile beamed from Angelo's eyes and he broke forth in a tone of joyous fervency—

"Ah, how blessed it would be to die for such a cause—it would be martyrdom!"

"But your brother—consider your brother; you would be risking his life, too."

"He risked mine an hour ago," responded Angelo, gloomily; "did he consider me?" A thought swept through his mind that made him shudder. "If I had not run, I might have been killed in a duel on the Sabbath day, and my soul would have been lost—lost!"

"O, don't fret, it wasn't in any danger," said Luigi, irritably; "they wouldn't waste it for a little thing like that; there's a glass case all ready for it in the heavenly museum, and a pin to stick it up with."

Aunt Patsy was shocked, and said—

"Looy, *Looy!*—don't talk so, dear!"

Rowena's soft heart was pierced by Luigi's unfeeling words, and she murmured to herself, "O, if I but had the dear privilege of protecting and defending him with my weak voice!—but alas, this sweet boon is denied me by the cruel conventions of social intercourse."

"Get their bed ready," said Aunt Patsy to Nancy, "and shut up the windows and doors, and light their candles, and see that you drive all the mosquitoes out of their bar, and make up a good fire in their stove, and carry up some bags of hot ashes to lay to his feet—"

—"and a shovel of fire for his head, and a mustard plaster for his neck, and some gum shoes for his ears," Luigi interrupted, with temper; and added, to himself, "damnation, I'm going to be roasted alive, I just know it."

"Why, *Looy!* Do be quiet; I never saw such a cantankerous thing. A body would think you didn't care for your brother."

"I don't—to that extent, Aunt Patsy. I was glad the drowning was postponed, a minute ago; but I'm not, now. No, that is all gone by: I want to be drowned."

"You'll bring a judgment on yourself just as sure as you live, if you go on like that. Why, I never heard the beat of it. Now, there-there! you've said enough. Not another word out of you, Looy—I won't have it."

"But Aunt Patsy—"

"Luigi! Didn't you hear what I told you?"

"But Aunt Patsy, I—why, *I'm* not going to set my heart and lungs afloat in that pail of sewage which this criminal here has been prescri—"

"Yes you are, too. You are going to be good, and do everything I tell you, like a dear," and she tapped his cheek affectionately with her finger; but turning her head to give an order, the finger wandered in reach of Luigi's mouth and he bit it. "Why, you impudent thing!" and she gave him a rap; but she was flattered, nevertheless, perceiving that it was a love-bite. "Rowena, take the prescription and go in the kitchen and hunt up the things and lay them out for me. I'll sit up with my patient the rest of the night, doctor; I can't trust Nancy, she couldn't make Luigi take the medicine. Of course you'll drop in again during the day. Have you got any more directions?"

"No, I believe not, Aunt Patsy. If I don't get in earlier, I'll be along by early candle-light, anyway. Meantime, don't allow him to get out of his bed."

Angelo said, with calm determination—

"I shall be baptised at two o'clock. Nothing but death shall prevent it."

The doctor said nothing aloud, but to himself he said, "Why, this chap's got a manly side, after all. Physically he's a coward, but morally he's a lion! I'll go and tell the others about this; it will raise him a good deal in their estimation—and the public will follow their lead, of course."

Privately, Aunt Patsy applauded, too, and was as proud of Angelo's courage in the moral field as she was of Luigi's in the field of honor.

The boy Henry was troubled, but the boy Joe said, inaudibly, and gratefully, "We're all hunky, after all; and no postponement on account of the weather."

Chapter 25

By nine o'clock the town was humming with the news of the midnight duel, and there were but two opinions about it: one, that Luigi's pluck in the field was most praiseworthy and Angelo's flight most scandalous; the other, that Angelo's courage in flying the field for conscience sake was as fine and creditable as was Luigi's in holding the field in the face of the bullets. The one opinion was held by half of the town, the other one was maintained by the other half. The division was clean and exact, and it made two parties, an Angelo party and a Luigi party. The Twins had suddenly become popular idols along with Pudd'nhead Wilson, and haloed with a glory as intense as his. The children talked the duel all the way to Sunday school, their elders talked it all the way to church, the choir discussed it behind their red curtain, it usurped the place of pious thought in the "nigger gallery."

By noon the doctor had added the news, and spread it, that Count Angelo, in spite of his wound and all warnings and supplications, was resolute in his determination to be baptised at the hour appointed. This swept the town like wildfire, and mightily reinforced the enthusiasm of the Angelo faction, who said, "If any doubted that it was moral courage that took him from the field, what have they to say now!"

Still the excitement grew. All the morning it was traveling countrywards, toward all points of the compass; and so, whereas before only the farmers and their wives were intending to come and witness the remarkable baptism, a general holiday was now proclaimed and the children and negroes admitted to the privileges of the occasion. All the farms for ten miles around were vacated, all the converging roads emptied long processions of wagons, horses and yeomanry into the town. The pack and cram of people vastly exceeded any that had ever been seen in that sleepy region before. The only thing that had ever even approached it was the time, long gone by, but never forgotten nor ever referred to without wonder and pride, when two circuses and a Fourth of July fell together. But the glory of that occasion was extinguished, now, for good. It was but a freshet to this deluge.

The great invasion massed itself on the river bank and waited hungrily for the immense event. Waited, and wondered if it would really happen, or if the twin who was not a "professor" would stand out and prevent it.

But they were not to be disappointed. Angelo was as good as his word. He came attended by an escort of honor composed of several hundred of the best citizens, all of the Angelo party; and when the immersion was finished they escorted him back home; and would even have carried him on their shoulders, but that people might think they were carrying Luigi.

Far into the night the citizens continued to discuss and wonder over the strangely-mated pair of incidents that had distinguished and exalted the past twenty-four hours above any other twenty-four in the history of their town for picturesqueness and splendid interest; and long before the lights were out and the burghers asleep it had been decided on all hands that in capturing these Twins Dawson's Landing had drawn a prize in the great lottery of municipal fortune.

At midnight Angelo was sleeping peacefully. His immersion had not harmed him, it had merely made him wholesomely drowsy, and he had been dead asleep many hours, now. It had made Luigi drowsy, too, but he had got only brief naps, on account of his having to take the medicine every three-quarters of an hour—and Aunt Betsy Hale was there to see that he did it. When he complained and resisted, she was quietly firm with him, and said in a low voice:

"No-no, that won't do; you mustn't talk, and you mustn't retch and gag that way, either—you'll wake up your poor brother."

"Well, what of it, Aunt Betsy, he—"

"'Sh-h! Don't make a noise, dear. You mustn't forget that your poor brother is sick and—"

"Sick, is he? Well, I wish *I*—"

"'Sh-h-h! *Will* you be quiet, Luigi! Here, now, take the rest of it—don't keep me holding the dipper all night. I declare if you haven't left a good fourth of it in the bottom! Come—that's a good boy."

"Aunt Betsy, don't make me! I tell you I feel like I've swallowed a cemetery; I do, indeed. Do let me rest a little—just a little; I *can't* take any more of the devilish stuff, now."

"Luigi! Using such language here, and him just baptised! Do you want the roof to fall on you?"

"I wish to heaven it would!"

"Why, you dreadful thing! I've a good notion to—let that blanket alone; do you want your brother to catch his death?"

"Aunt Betsy, I've *got* to have it off; I'm being roasted alive; nobody could stand it—you couldn't, yourself."

"Now, then, you're sneezing again—I just expected it."

"Because I've caught a thundering cold in my head. I always do, when I go in the water with my clothes on. And it takes me weeks to get over it, too. I think it was a shame to serve me so."

"Luigi, you are unreasonable; you know very well they couldn't baptise him dry. I should think you would be willing to undergo a little inconvenience for your brother's sake."

"Inconvenience! Now how you talk, Aunt Betsy. I came as near as anything to getting drowned—you saw that, yourself; and do you call *this* inconvenience?—the room shut up as tight as a drum, and so hot the mosquitoes are trying to get out; and a cold in the head, and dying for sleep and no chance to get any on account of this infernal medicine that that assassin prescri—"

"Why, I'll take something *to* you if you don't hush up this minute! Bless my heart, I never heard the like. See how quiet and good *he* is—you don't hear *him* carrying on like that."

"I wish I could!"

"Looy, be *quiet!* Why, you're the very old Satan for disobedience and wrongheadedness. Instead of which, you ought to be an example to him."

"To Satan?"

"No! What are you talking about? I never said anything about your being an example to Satan. What I meant was, that you are older than he is, and—"

"Older than Satan?"

"Looy, I declare I'll give you a crack with my thimble if you keep catching me up like that and distorting what I say."

"Well, what *did* you say, Aunt Betsy? And don't lose your temper; it's getting shaky. What was it you said?"

"I said—I said—now you've got me so muddled up that I don't hardly know where I was. I said you ought to be an example to Sa—to—to your brother, because you are older than Sa—*him!*—plague take the numskull, he has got me that mixed up and—"

"Who—Satan?"

"Hush up! You are the most aggravating creature that ever—Luigi, you're sneezing again. I do *wish* I knew something to do! Dear me, I get more and more anxious every time you sneeze. Why, I never *saw* such a cold. Something's got to be *done*, and right away, too. I'm going down stairs and make you a pail of sheep-nanny tea, and—"

"Oh, have some compassion! I'd rather have fifty colds than drink that obscene stuff. Come, sit down, now, and I'll be good—try to be, anyway."

"Yes, it's well you put that in—it ain't *in* you, *I* don't believe. You are the tryingest, and the headstrongest, and the most—"

"Well—it's true—I haven't got many virtues, but—I love *you*, Aunt Betsy!"

"O, you *dear!* I'll forgive you everything for saying that," and she caressed his hair with one hand and wiped her eyes with the back of the other. "You certainly do try a body out of all patience, but I don't mind that or anything, as long as you love me. Now you lie still till I go and get that truck; and don't you disturb your brother. I'll make it boiling hot—"

"Aunt Betsy, it's not a bit of use; I'll die before I'll take it."

But she retorted, as she went out—

"No, you won't die, and you *will* take it. Don't you give yourself any uneasiness about that."

Chapter 26

If you pick up a starving dog and make him prosperous, he will not bite you. This is the principal difference between a dog and a man.—*Pudd'nhead Wilson's Calendar.*

During Monday, Tuesday and Wednesday the Twins grew steadily worse; but then the doctor was summoned south to attend his mother's funeral and they got well in forty-eight hours. They appeared on the street on Friday, and were welcomed with enthusiasm by the new-born parties, the Luigi and Angelo factions. The Luigi faction carried its strength into the Democratic party, the Angelo faction entered into a combination with the Whigs. The Democrats nominated Luigi for alderman under the new city government, and the Whigs put up Angelo against him. The Democrats nominated Pudd'nhead Wilson for mayor, and he was left alone in this glory, for the Whigs had no man who was willing to enter the lists against such a formidable opponent. No politician had scored such a compliment as this before in the history of the Mississippi Valley.

On Saturday, Constable Blake and Pudd'nhead Wilson met on the street, and Tom Driscoll joined them in time to open their conversation for them. He said to Blake—

"You are not looking well, Blake, you seem to be annoyed about something. Has anything gone wrong in the detective business? I believe you fairly and justifiably claim to have a pretty good reputation in that line, isn't it so?"—which made Blake feel good, and look it; but Tom added, "for a country detective"—which made Blake feel the other way, and not only look it but betray it in his voice—

"Yes, sir, I *have* got a reputation, and it's as good as anybody's in the profession, too, country or *no* country."

"Oh, I beg pardon, I didn't mean any offence. What I started out to ask, was, only about the old woman that raided the town—the stoop-shouldered old woman, you know, that you said you were going to catch—and I knew

155

you would, too, because you have the reputation of never boasting, and—well, you—you've caught the old woman?"

"Damn the old woman!"

"Why, sho'! you don't mean to say you haven't caught her?"

"No, I *haven't* caught her. If anybody could have caught her, I could; but nobody couldn't, I don't care who he is."

"I am sorry, real sorry—for your sake; because when it gets around that a detective has expressed himself so confidently, and then—"

"Don't you worry, that's all—don't you worry; and as for the town, let the town keep its shirt on, too. She's my meat—make yourself easy about that. I'm on her track; I've got clews that—"

"That's good. Now if you could get an old veteran detective down from St. Louis to help you find out what the clews mean, and where they lead to, and then—"

"I'm plenty veteran enough myself, and I don't need anybody's help. I'll have her inside of a we— inside of a month. That I'll swear to."

Tom said, carelessly—

"I suppose that will answer—yes, that will answer. But I reckon she is pretty old, and old people don't often outlive the cautious pace of the professional detective when he has got his clews together and is out on his still-hunt." Blake's dull face flushed, under this gibe, but before he could set his retort in order Tom had turned to Wilson and was saying, with placid indifference of manner and voice—

"Who got the reward, Pudd'nhead?"

Wilson winced slightly, and saw that his own turn was come.

"What reward?"

"Why, the reward for the thief, and the other one for the knife."

Wilson answered—and rather uncomfortably, to judge by his hesitating fashion of delivering himself—

"Well, the—well, in fact nobody has claimed it yet."

Tom seemed surprised.

"Why, is *that* so?"

Wilson showed a trifle of irritation when he replied—

"Yes, it's so. And what *of* it?"

"Oh, nothing. Only I thought you had struck out a new idea and invented a scheme that was going to revolutionize the time-worn and ineffectual methods of the—" He stopped, and turned to Blake, who was happy, now that another had taken his place on the gridiron: "Blake, didn't you understand him to intimate that it wouldn't be necessary for you to hunt the old woman down?"

"'George, he said he'd have thief and swag both inside of three days!—he did, by hokey! and that's just about a week ago. Why, I said at the time, that no thief and no thief's pal was going to try to pawn or sell a thing where he knowed the pawnbroker could get both rewards by taking *him* into camp along *with* the swag. It *was* the blessedest idea that ever *I* struck!"

"You'd change your mind," said Wilson, with irritated bluntness, "if you knew the entire scheme instead of only part of it."

"Well," said the constable, pensively, "I had the idea that it wouldn't work, and up to now I'm right, anyway."

"Very well, then, let it stand at that, and give it a further show. It has worked at least as well as your own methods, you perceive."

The constable hadn't anything handy to hit back with, so he discharged a discontented sniff and said nothing.

After the night that Wilson had partly revealed his scheme at his house, Tom had tried for several days to guess out the secret of the rest of it, but had failed. Then it occurred to him to give Roxana's smarter head a chance at it. He made up a supposititious case and laid it before her. She thought it over, and delivered her verdict upon it. Tom said to himself, "She's hit it, sure!" He thought he would test that verdict, now, and watch Wilson's face; so he said, reflectively—

"Wilson, you're not a fool—a fact of recent discovery. Whatever your scheme was, it had sense in it, Blake's opinion to the contrary notwithstanding. I don't ask you to reveal it, but I will suppose a case—a case which will answer as a starting point for the real thing I'm going to come at, and that's all I want. You offered five hundred dollars for the knife, and five hundred for the thief. We will suppose, for argument's sake, that the first reward is *advertised*, and the second offered by *private letter* to pawnbrokers and—"

Blake slapped his thigh and cried out—

"By Jackson he's *got* you, Pudd'nhead! Now why couldn't I or *any* fool have thought of that!"

Wilson said to himself, "Anybody with a reasonably good head would have thought of it. I am not surprised that Blake didn't detect it, I am only surprised that Tom did. There is more to him than I supposed." He said nothing aloud, and Tom went on:

"Very well. The thief would not suspect that there was a trap, and he would bring or send the knife and say he bought it for a song, or found it in the road, or something like that, and try to collect the reward, and be arrested—wouldn't he?"

"Yes," said Wilson.

"I think so," said Tom. "There can't be any doubt of it whatever. Have you ever seen that knife?"

"No."

"Has any friend of yours?"

"Not that I know of."

"Well, I begin to think *I* understand why your scheme failed."

"What do you mean, Tom?—What are you driving at?" asked Wilson with a dawning sense of discomfort.

"Why, that there *isn't any such knife.*"

"Look here, Wilson," said Blake, "Tom Driscoll's right, for a thousand dollars!—if I had it."

Wilson's blood warmed a little, and he wondered if he had been played upon by those strangers—it certainly had something of that look. But what could they gain by it? He threw out that suggestion. Tom replied:

"Gain? Oh, nothing that you would value, maybe. But they are strangers making their way in a new community. Is it nothing to them to appear as pets of an Oriental prince—at no expense? Is it nothing to them to be able to dazzle this poor little town with thousand-dollar rewards—at no expense? Wilson, there isn't any such knife, or your scheme would have fetched it to light. Or if there is any such knife they've got it yet. I believe, myself, that they've *seen* such a knife, for Angelo pictured it out with his pencil too swiftly and handily for him to have been inventing it; and of course I can't swear that they've never had it; but this I'll go bail for—if they had it when they came to this town, they've got it yet."

Blake said,—

"It looks mighty reasonable, the way Tom puts it—it most certainly does."

Tom responded—turning to leave—

"You find the old woman, Blake, and if she can't furnish the knife, go and search the Twins."

Tom sauntered away. Wilson felt a good deal depressed. He hardly knew what to think. He was loth to withdraw his faith from the Twins, and was resolved not to do it on the present indecisive evidence; but—well, he would think—and then decide how to act.

"Blake, what do you think of this matter?"

"Well, Pudd'nhead, I'm bound to say I put it up the way Tom does. They hadn't the knife; or if they had it they've got it yet."

The men parted. Wilson said to himself, "I believe they had it; if it had been stolen, the scheme would have restored it, that is certain. And so I believe they've got it yet."

Tom had had no purpose in his mind when he encountered those two men. When he began his talk he hoped to be able to gall them a little and get a trifle of malicious entertainment out of it. But when he left, he left in great spirits, for he perceived that just by pure luck and no troublesome labor, he had accomplished several delightful things: he had touched both men on a raw spot and seen them squirm; he had modified Wilson's sweetness for the Twins with one small bitter taste that he wouldn't be able to get out of his mouth right away; and—best of all—he had taken the hated Twins down a peg with the community; for Blake would gossip around freely, after the manner of detectives, and within a week the town would be laughing at them in its sleeve for offering a gaudy reward for a bauble which they had either never possessed or hadn't lost. Tom was very well satisfied with himself.

Tom's behavior at home had been perfect. His uncle and aunt had seen nothing like it before. They could find no fault with him anywhere. On Saturday evening he said to the Judge—

"I've had something preying on my mind, uncle, and as I am going away and might never see you again, I can't bear it any longer. I made you believe I was afraid to fight those Twins. I had to get out of it on some pretext or other, and maybe I chose badly, being taken unprepared—but no honorable person could consent to meet them in the field, knowing what I knew about them."

"Indeed! What was that?"

"Count Luigi is a confessed assassin."

"Incredible!"

"It is perfectly true. Wilson detected it in his hand, by palmistry, and charged him with it and cornered him up so close that he had to confess; but both Twins begged us on their knees to keep the secret, and swore they would lead straight lives here; and it was all so pitiful that we gave our word of honor never to expose them while they kept that promise. You would have done it yourself, uncle."

"You are right, my boy, I would. A man's secret is still his own property, and sacred, when it has been surprised out of him like that. You did well, and I am proud of you." Then he added, mournfully, "But I wish I could have been saved the shame of meeting an assassin on the field of honor."

"It couldn't be helped, uncle. If *I* had known you were going to challenge him I should have felt obliged to sacrifice my pledged word in order to stop it, but Wilson couldn't be expected to do otherwise than keep silent."

"Oh, no, Wilson did right, and is in no way to blame. Tom, Tom, you have lifted a heavy load from my heart; I was stung to the very soul when I seemed to have discovered that I had a coward in my family."

"You may imagine what it cost *me* to assume such a part, uncle."

"Oh, I know it, poor boy, I know it! And I can understand how much it has cost you to remain under that unjust stigma to this time. But it is all right, now, and no harm is done. You have restored my comfort of mind, and with it your own; and both of us had suffered enough. I will cut those Twins when I get the opportunity—one of them ran away from the field, anyway: perhaps both."

Another point scored against the detested Twins! Really it was a great day for Tom. He was encouraged to chance a parting shot, now, at the same target, and did it—

"You know that wonderful Indian knife that the Twins have been making such a to-do about? Well, there's no track or trace of it yet; so the town is beginning to sneer and gossip and laugh. Half the people believe they never had any such knife, the other half believe they had it and have got it still. I've heard twenty people talking like that to-day."

Yes, Tom's blemishless week had made him solid with the aunt and uncle. His mother was satisfied with him, too. Privately, she believed she was coming to love him, but she did not say so. She told him to go along to St. Louis, now, and she would get ready and follow. Then she smashed her whisky bottle and said—

"Dah, now. I's a gwyne to make *you* walk as straight as a string, Chambers, en so I's boun' you ain't gwyne to git no bad example out o' yo' mammy. I tole you you couldn't go into no bad comp'ny. Well, you's gwyne into my comp'ny, en I's gwyne to fill de bill. Now, den, trot along, trot along!"

Tom went aboard one of the big transient boats that night with his heavy satchel of miscellaneous plunder, and slept the sleep of the unjust, which is serener and sounder than the other kind, as we know by the hanging-eve history of a million rascals. But when he got up in the morning, luck was against him again. A brother-thief had robbed him while he slept, and gone ashore at some intermediate landing.

When Roxana arrived, she found her son in such despair and misery that her heart was touched and her motherhood rose up strong in her. He was ruined past hope, now; his destruction would be immediate and sure, and he would be an outcast and friendless. That was reason enough for a mother to love a child; so she loved him, and told him so. It made him wince, secretly— for she was a "nigger." That he was one himself was far from reconciling him to that despised race.

Roxana poured out endearments upon him, to which he responded uncomfortably, but as well as he could. And she tried to comfort him, but that was not possible. These intimacies quickly became horrible to him, and within the hour he began to try to get up courage enough to tell her so, and require that they be discontinued or very considerably modified. But he was afraid of her; and besides, there came a lull, now, for she had begun to think. She was trying to invent a saving plan. Finally she started up and said she had found a way out. Tom was almost suffocated by the joy of this so sudden good news. Roxana said—

"Here is de plan, en she'll win, sure. I is a nigger, en nobody ain't gwyne to doubt it dat hears me talk. I's wuth six hund'd dollahs. Take en sell me en pay off dese gamblers."

Tom was dazed. He was not sure he had heard aright. He was speechless for a moment; then he said:

"Do you mean that you would be sold into slavery to save me?"

"Ain't you my chile? En does you know anything dat a mother won't do for her chile? Dey ain't nothin' a white mother won't do for her chile. Who made 'em so? De Lord done it. En who made de niggers? De Lord made 'em. In de inside, mothers is all de same. De good Lord He made 'em so. I's gwyne to be sole into slavery, en in a year you's gwyne to buy yo' ole mammy free agin. I'll show you how. Dat's de plan."

Tom's hopes began to rise, and his spirits along with them. He said—

"It's lovely of you, mammy—it's just—"

"Say it agin! En keep on sayin' it! It's all de pay a body kin want in dis worl', en it's mo' den enough. Laws bless you honey, when I's slavin' aroun' en dey 'buses me, if I knows you's a sayin' dat, 'way off yonder somers, it'll heal up all de sore places, en I kin stan' 'em."

"I do say it again, mammy, and I'll keep on saying it, too. But how am I going to sell you?—you're free, you know."

"Hm! Much diffrence dat make! White folks ain't particklar. De *law* kin sell me *now*, if dey tell me to leave de State in six months en I don't go. You draw up a paper—bill o' sale—en put it 'way off yonder, down in de middle o' Kaintuck somers, en sign some names to it, en say you'll sell me cheap caze you's hard up; you'll fine you ain't gwyne to have no trouble. You take me up de country a piece, en sell me on a farm—*dem* people ain't gwyne to ask no questions, if I's a bargain."

Tom forged a bill of sale and sold his mother to an Arkansas cotton planter for a trifle over six hundred dollars. He did not want to commit this treachery, but luck threw the man in his way, and this saved him the necessity of going up country to hunt up a purchaser, with the added risk of having to answer a lot of questions, whereas this planter was so pleased with Roxy that he asked next to none at all. Besides, the planter insisted that Roxy wouldn't know where she was, at first, and that by the time she found out she would already have become contented. And Tom argued with himself that it was an immense advantage for Roxy to have a master who was so pleased with her as this planter manifestly was. In almost no time his flowing reasonings carried him to the point of even half believing he was doing Roxy a splendid surreptitious service in sending her "down the river." And then he kept diligently saying to himself all the time, "It's for only a year—in a year I buy her free again; she'll keep that in mind, and it'll reconcile her." Yes, the little deception could do no harm, and everything would come out right and pleasant in the end, anyway. By agreement, the conversation in Roxy's presence was all about the man's "up-country" farm, and how pleasant a place it was, and how happy the slaves were, there; so poor Roxy was entirely deceived; and easily, for she was not dreaming that her own son could be guilty of treason to a mother who, in voluntarily going into slavery—slavery of any kind, mild or severe, or of any duration, brief or long—was making a sacrifice for him compared with which death would have been a poor and commonplace one. She lavished tears and loving caresses upon him, privately, and then went away with her owner; went away broken-hearted, and yet proud of what she was doing and glad that it was in her power to do it.

Tom squared his accounts, and resolved to keep to the very letter of his reform, and never put that will in jeopardy again. He had three hundred dollars left. According to his mother's plan, he was to put that safely away, and add her half of his pension to it monthly. In one year this fund would buy her free again.

For a whole week he was not able to sleep well, so much the villainy which he had played upon his trusting mother preyed upon his rag of a conscience; but after that he began to get comfortable again and was presently able to sleep like any other miscreant.

The boat bore Roxy away from St. Louis at four in the afternoon, and she stood on the lower guard abaft the paddle-box and watched Tom through a blur of tears until he melted into the throng of people and disappeared; then she looked no more, but sat there on a coil of cable crying, till far into the night. When she went to her foul steerage bunk at last, between the clashing engines, it was not to sleep, but only to wait for the morning; and waiting, grieve.

It had been imagined that she "would not know," and would think she was traveling up stream. She!—why, she had been steamboating for years. At dawn she got up and went listlessly and sat down on the cable-coil again. She passed many a snag whose "break" could have told her a thing to break her heart, for it showed a current moving in the same direction that the boat was going; but her thoughts were elsewhere, and she did not notice. But at last the roar of a bigger and nearer break than usual brought her out of her torpor, and she looked up and her practiced eye fell upon that tell-tale rush of water. For one moment her petrified gaze fixed itself there, then her head dropped upon her breast and she said—

"Oh, de good Lord God have mercy on po' sinful me—I's sole down de river!"

Chapter 27

July 4. Statistics show that we lose more fools on this day than in all the other days of the year put together. This proves, by the number left in stock, that one Fourth of July per year is now inadequate, the country has grown so.—*Pudd'nhead Wilson's Calendar.*

The political campaign in Dawson's Landing opened in a pretty warm fashion, and waxed hotter and hotter every week. Luigi's whole heart was in it, and even Angelo presently developed a surprising amount of interest in it—which was natural, because he was not merely representing Whigism, which was a matter of no consequence to him, he was representing something immensely finer and greater—to wit, Reform. In him was centred the hopes of the whole reform element of the town; he was the chosen and admired champion of every clique that had a pet reform of any sort or kind at heart. He was president of the great Teetotalers' Union and its chiefest prophet and mouthpiece.

But as the canvass went on, troubles began to spring up all around—troubles for the Twins, and through them for all the parties and segments and fractions of parties. Whenever Luigi had possession of the legs, he carried Angelo to balls, rum shops, Sons of Liberty parades, horse-races, campaign riots, and everywhere else that could damage him with his party and his church; and when it was Angelo's week he carried Luigi diligently to all manner of moral and religious gatherings, and did his best to get back the ground which he had lost before. As a result of these double performances, there was a storm blowing all the time, and it was an ever rising storm, too—a storm of frantic criticism of the Twins, and rage over their extravagant and incomprehensible conduct.

Luigi had the final chance. The legs were his for the closing week of the canvass. He began his work by dancing a breakdown on the street corner Sunday forenoon, and kept it up till all the people and all the dogs had flocked there to see. He danced away with all his might, caring not a rap for

Angelo's distress, who cried bitterly all the time, and whose innocence and grief ought to have touched the hearts of the spectators; and in some cases it did, but in only a few; the mass of the crowd only laughed to see the tears flowing down the front of his violently bobbing head. For this performance Angelo was turned out of the church that very day, and that meant the loss of a great block of votes.

But Luigi saved his greatest card for the very eve of the election. There was to be a grand turn-out of the Teetotalers' Union that day, and Angelo was to march at the head of the procession and deliver a great oration afterward. Luigi drank a couple of glasses of whisky—which did not affect him in the least, but made Angelo drunk. Everybody who saw the march, saw that the Champion of the Teetotalers was half seas over, and noted also that his brother, who made no hypocritical pretensions to extra-temperance virtues, was dignified and sober. This eloquent fact could not be unfruitful at the end of a hot political canvass. At the mass meeting Angelo tried to make his great temperance oration but was so discommoded by hiccups and thickness of tongue that he had to give it up; then drowsiness overtook him and his head drooped against Luigi's and he went to sleep. Luigi apologized for him, and was going on to improve his opportunity with a ringing appeal for a moderation of what he called "the prevailing teetotal madness," but rowdies in the audience began to howl and throw things at him, and then the meeting rose in a general burst of wrath and chased him home.

This episode was a crusher for Angelo in another way. It destroyed his chances with Rowena. Those chances had been growing, right along, for two months. Rowena had even partly confessed that she loved him, but had begged for time to consider. But now the tender dream was ended, and she frankly told him so, the moment he was sober enough to understand. She said she would never marry a man who drank.

"But I don't drink," he pleaded.

"That is nothing to the point," she said, coldly, "you get drunk, and that is worse."

"Why, it is not I that am to blame, Rowena, for I never drink a drop."

"You only make your case worse when you say that," responded the girl sternly. "One *might* respect a person who gets drunk himself, but never one who gets drunk by proxy."

"But I implore you to believe that I don't do it purposely, Rowena; I can't help myself."

"Call me Miss Cooper, please."

"Do have pity on me, Miss Cooper. Indeed it is just as I say—I am not able to help myself."

"This is but shuffling, Count Cappello. No person is obliged to get drunk on another person's liquor unless he wants to. I have never heard of a case."

"But dear Miss Cooper my case is not like any one else's. I assure you that I—"

"Please drop the subject. I could never love a person who gets drunk clandestinely in this way. And in no case whatever could I love a dishonest person."

"Dishonest? Oh, please do not say such cruel words. How am I dishonest?"

"Luigi buys that liquor with his own money; and when you lie in wait for it and rob him of the effects of it—effects which *he* is entitled to, not you—it is larceny; it is more, it is burglary. Would you ask me to give my hand to a burglar?"

He saw that he could not contend with her in argument. Reason was on her side, or seemed to him, in his dazed and but half sober condition, to be. Then the austere severity of her manner cowed him. He could plead no more. He begged piteously that if she could not be more to him, she would at least not cast him out utterly, but would be his friend. This touched her, and she said gently, laying her hand upon his head and turning her eyes reverently aloft—

"I will be your friend—nay, more, I will be your sister. Let that suffice. May heaven temper this disaster to you and give you peace."

And saying these words, she quitted the room in tears, and with a heart sore smitten by the pathetic sobs that fell upon her ear as she closed the door behind her.

On Independence Day Rowena went out back to see the fireworks and fell down the well and got drowned. But it is no matter; these things cannot be helped, in a work of this kind.

The closing speech of the campaign was made by Judge Driscoll, and he made it against both of the Twins. He reviewed in acrimonious detail their extraordinary conduct of the preceding two months, and said it was the most scandalous exhibition that had ever been seen outside of an insane asylum. He wound up with charging cowardice upon them for flying the dueling field, and added as a snapper his belief that the reward offered for the lost knife was buncombe, and that Luigi would be able to find it whenever he should have occasion to assassinate somebody.

This last remark flew far and wide over the town and made a prodigious sensation. Everybody was asking "What could he mean by that?" And everybody went on asking that question, but in vain; for the Judge only said he knew what he was talking about, and stopped there; Tom, who was down on a visit, said he hadn't any idea what his uncle meant, and Wilson, whenever he was asked what he thought it meant, parried the question by asking the questioner what *he* thought it meant.

Wilson got the whole city vote for mayor. The Twins got the poorest vote that was cast for anybody, but as they were running against each other, even this meagre showing had to elect one of them, and did—Luigi was the man.

Tom's conduct had remained letter perfect during two whole months, now, and had set him high in his uncle's confidence; so high, indeed, that he trusted him with money with which to influence vacillating or indifferent people to vote against Luigi. He took it out of a tin box in the safe in his private sitting room, and said he would spend the rest of the box's contents to beat Luigi, if necessary. Tom used a hundred dollars, and used it for the purpose for which it was given him, too, merely retiring ten per cent of it as commission—which was ninety per cent better morals than he had had in stock at any time before, since his childhood.

When the election was over he went back to St. Louis happy—fully half happy, at any rate, for one twin had been defeated.

The new city officers were sworn in on the following Monday—at least all but Luigi. There was a complication in his case. He could not sit in the board of aldermen without his brother, and his brother could not sit there because he was not a member. There seemed to be no way out of the difficulty but to carry the matter into the courts, so this was resolved upon. The case was set for the Monday fortnight. The legs were Angelo's for this first week, and the brothers were not on speaking terms, now, but Luigi made no secret anywhere of the fact that there would be a duel when he got possession—either that, or Judge Driscoll would apologize: he could take his choice.

Chapter 28

Gratitude and treachery are merely the two extremities of the same procession. You have seen all of it that is worth staying for when the band and the gaudy officials have gone by.
—*Pudd'nhead Wilson's Calendar.*

The Friday after the election was a rainy one in St. Louis. It rained all day long, and rained hard, apparently trying its best to wash that soot-blackened town white, but of course not succeeding. Toward midnight Tom Driscoll arrived at his lodgings from the theatre in the heavy downpour, and closed his umbrella and let himself in; but when he would have shut the door, he found that there was another person entering—doubtless another lodger; this person closed the door and tramped up stairs behind Tom. Tom found his door in the dark, and entered it and turned up the gas. When he faced about, lightly whistling, he saw the back of a man. The man was closing and locking his door for him. His whistle faded out and he felt uneasy. The man turned around, a wreck of shabby old clothes sodden with rain and all a-drip, and showed a black face under an old slouch hat. Tom was frightened. He tried to order the man out, but the words refused to come, and the other man got the start. He said, in a low voice—

"Keep still—I's yo' mother!"

Tom sunk in a heap on a chair, and gasped out—

"It was mean of me, and base—I know it; but I meant it for the best, I did indeed—I can swear it."

Roxana stood a while looking mutely down on him while he writhed in shame and went on incoherently babbling self-accusations mixed with pitiful attempts at explanation and palliation of his crime; then she seated herself and took off her hat, and her unkempt masses of long brown hair tumbled down about her shoulders.

"It ain't no fault o' yo'n dat dat ain't gray," she said, sadly, noticing the hair.

"I know it, I know it. I am a scoundrel. But I swear I meant for the best. It was a mistake, of course, but I thought it was for the best, I truly did."

Roxy began to cry softly, and presently words began to find their way out between her sobs. They were uttered lamentingly, rather than angrily—

"Sell a pusson down de river—*down de river!*—for de *bes'!* I wouldn't treat a dog so. I is all broke down en wore out, now, en so I reckon it ain't in me to storm aroun' no mo', like I used to when I 'uz trompled on en 'bused. I don't know—but maybe it's so. Leastways, I's suffered so much dat mournin' seem to come mo' handy to me now den stormin'."

These words should have touched Tom Driscoll, but if they did, that effect was obliterated by a stronger one—one which removed the heavy weight of fear which lay upon him, and gave his crushed spirit a most grateful rebound and filled all his small soul with a deep sense of relief. But he kept prudently still, and ventured no comment. There was a voiceless interval of some duration, now, in which no sounds were heard but the beating of the rain upon the panes, the sighing and complaining of the winds, and now and then a muffled sob from Roxana. The sobs became more and more infrequent, and at last ceased. Then the refugee began to talk again:

"Shet down dat light a little. More. More yit. A pusson dat is hunted don't like de light. Dah—dat'll do. I kin see whah you is, en dat's enough. I's gwyne to tell you de tale, en cut it jes' as short as I kin, en den I'll tell you what you's got to do. Dat man dat bought me ain't a bad man, he's good enough, as planters goes; en if he could a had his way I'd a ben a house servant in his fambly en ben comfortable; but his wife she was a Yank, en not right down good lookin', en she riz up agin me straight off; so den dey sent me out to de quarter 'mongst de common fiel' han's. Dat woman warn't satisfied, even wid dat, but she worked up de overseer agin me, she 'uz dat jealous en hateful; so de overseer he had me out befo' day in de mawnins en worked me de whole long day as long as dey 'uz any light to see by; en many's de lashin' I got becaze I couldn't come up to de work o' de stronges'. Dat overseer 'uz a Yank, too, outen New Englan', en anybody down South kin tell you what dat mean. *Dey* knows how to work a nigger to death, en dey knows how to whale 'em, too—whale 'em till dey backs is welted like a washboard. 'Long at fust my marster say de good word for me to de overseer, but dat 'uz bad for me; for de mistis she fine it out, en arter dat I jist ketched it at every turn—dey warn't *no* mercy for me no mo'!"

Tom's heart was fired—with fury against the planter's wife; and he said to himself, "But for that meddlesome fool, everything would have gone all right." He added a deep and bitter curse against her.

The expression of this sentiment was fiercely written in his face, and stood thus revealed to Roxana by a white glare of lightning which turned the sombre dusk of the room into dazzling day at that moment. She was pleased—pleased and grateful; for did not that expression show that her child *was* capable of grieving for his mother's wrongs and of feeling resentment toward her persecutors?—a thing which she had been doubting. But her flash of happiness was but a flash, and went out again and left her spirit dark; for she said to herself, "He sole me down de river—he can't feel for a body long; dis'll pass en go." Then she took up her tale again:

"'Bout ten days ago I 'uz sayin' to myself dat I couldn't las' many mo' weeks, I 'uz so wore out wid de awful work en de lashin's, en so down-hearted en misable. En I didn't care no mo', nuther—life warn't wuth noth'n to me if I got to go on like dat. Well, when a body is in a frame o' mine like dat, what do a body care what a body do? Dey was a little sickly nigger wench 'bout ten year ole dat 'uz good to me, en hadn't no mammy, po' thing, en I loved her en she loved me; en she come out whah I 'uz workin', en she had a roasted tater, en tried to slip it to me—robbin' herself, you see, caze she knowed de overseer didn't gimme enough to eat—en he ketched her at it, en give her a lick acrost de back wid his stick which 'uz as thick as a broom-han'le, en she drop' screamin' on de groun', en squirmin' en wallerin' aroun' in de dust like a spider dat's got crippled. I couldn't *stan'* it! All de hell-fire dat 'uz ever in my heart flame' up, en I snatch de stick outen his han' en laid him flat! He laid dah moanin' en cussin', en all out of his head, you know, en de niggers 'uz plum sk'yerd to death. Dey gethered roun' him to he'p him, en I jumped on his hoss en took out for de river as tight as I could go. I knowed what dey would do wid *me*. Soon as he got well he would start in en work me to death if marster let him; en if dey didn't do dat dey'd sell me furder down de river, en dat's de same thing. So I 'lowed to drown myself en git out o' my troubles. It 'uz gitt'n towards dark. I 'uz at de river in two minutes. Den I see a canoe, en I says dey ain't no use to drown myself tell I *got* to; so I ties de hoss in de edge o' de timber en shove out down de river, keepin' in under de shelter o' de bluff bank en prayin' for de dark to shet down quick. I had a pow'ful good start, caze de big house 'uz three mile back fum de river en on'y de work mules to ride dah on, en on'y niggers to ride 'em, en *dey* warn't gwyne to hurry—dey'd gimme all de chance dey could. Befo' a body could go to de house en back it would be long pas' dark, en dey couldn't track de hoss en fine out which way I went tell mawnin', en de niggers would tell 'em all de lies dey could 'bout it.

"Well, de dark come, en I went on a spinnin' down de river. I paddled mo'n two hours, den I warn't worried no mo'; so I quit paddlin', en floated down de current, considerin' what I 'uz gwyne to do if I didn't have to drown myself. I made up some plans, en floated along, turnin' 'em over in my mine. Well, when it 'uz a little pas' midnight, as I reckoned, en I had come fifteen or twenty mile, I see de lights o' a steamboat layin' at de bank, whah dey warn't no town en no woodyard, en putty soon I ketched de shape o' de chimbly-tops agin de stars, en den good gracious me, I most jumped out o' my skin for joy! It 'uz de Gran' Mogul—I 'uz head chambermaid on her for eight seasons in de Cincinnati en Orleans trade. I slid 'long pas'—don't see nobody stirrin' nowhah—hear 'em a hammerin' away in de engine room, den I knowed what de matter was—some o' de machinery's broke. I got asho' below de boat en turn' de canoe loose, den I goes 'long up, en dey 'uz jes' one plank out, en I step 'board de boat. It 'uz pow'ful hot; deckhan's en roustabouts 'uz sprawled aroun' asleep on de fo'cas'l, de second mate, Jim Bangs, he sot dah on de bitts wid his head down, asleep—caze dat's de way de second mate stan' de cap'n's watch—en de ole watchman, Billy Hatch, he 'uz a noddin' on de companionway;—en I knowed 'em all; en lan', but dey did look good! I says to myseff, I wisht old marster'd come along *now* en try to take me—bless yo' heart, I's 'mong frien's, *I* is! So I tromped right along 'mongst 'em, en went up on de biler deck en 'way back aft to de ladies' cabin guard, en sot down dah in de same cheer dat I'd sot in mos' a hund'd million times, I reckon; en it 'uz jist *home* agin, I tell you!

"In 'bout an hour I hear de ready-bell jingle, en den de racket begin. Putty soon I hear de gong strike. 'Set her back on de outside,' I says to myself—'I reckon I knows *dat* music!' I hear de gong agin. 'Come ahead on de inside,' I says. Gong agin. 'Stop de outside.' Gong agin. 'Come ahead on de outside—now we's pinted for Sent Louis, en I's outer de woods en ain't got to drown myself, at all.' I knowed de Mogul 'uz in de Sent Louis trade now, you see. It 'uz jes' fair daylight when we passed our plantation, en I seed a gang o' niggers en white folks huntin' up en down de sho', en troublin' deyselves a good deal 'bout me, but I warn't troublin' myself none 'bout *dem*.

"'Bout dat time Sally Jackson, dat used to be my second chambermaid en 'uz head chambermaid now, she come out on de guard en 'uz pow'ful glad to see me, en so 'uz all de officers; en I tole 'em I'd got kidnapped en sole down de river, en dey made me up twenty dollahs en give it to me, en Sally she rigged me out wid good clo'es, en when I got here I went straight to whah you used to was, en I come to dis house en dey say you's away but 'spected back every day; so I didn't dast to go down de river to Dawson's, caze I might miss you.

"Well, las' Monday I 'uz pass'n by one o' dem places in Fourth street whah dey sticks up runaway-nigger bills en he'ps to ketch 'em, en I seed my marster! I mos' flopped down on de groun', I felt so gone. He had his back to me, en 'uz talkin' to de man en givin' him some bills—nigger-bills, I reckon, en I's de nigger. He's offerin' a reward—dat's it. Ain't I right, don't you reckon?"

Tom had been gradually sinking into a state of ghastly terror, and he said to himself, now, "I'm lost, no matter what turn things take. This man has said to me that he thinks there was something suspicious about that sale. He said he had a letter from a passenger on the Grand Mogul saying that Roxy came here on that boat and that everybody on board knew all about the case; so he says that her coming here instead of flying to a free State looks bad for me, and that if I don't find her for him, and that pretty soon, he will make trouble for me. I never believed that story; I *couldn't* believe she would be so dead to all motherly instincts as to come *here*, knowing the risk she would run of getting me into irremediable trouble. And after all, here she is! And I stupidly swore I would help him find her, thinking it was a perfectly safe thing to promise. If I venture to deliver her up, she—she—but how can I *help* myself? I've got to do that or pay the money, and where's the money to come from? I—I—well, I should think that if he would swear to treat her kindly hereafter—and she says, herself, that he is a good man—and if he would swear to never allow her to be overworked, or ill fed, or—"

A flash of lightning exposed Tom's pallid face drawn and rigid with these worrying thoughts. Roxana spoke up sharply, now, and there was apprehension in her voice—

"Turn up dat light! I want to see yo' face better. Dah, now—lemme look at you. Chambers, you's as white as yo' shirt. Has you seen dat man? Has he ben to see you?"

"Ye-s."

"When?"

"Monday noon."

"Monday noon! Was he on my track?"

"He—well, he thought he was. That is, he hoped he was. This is the bill you saw." He took it out of his pocket.

"Read it to me."

She was panting with excitement, and there was a dusky glow in her eyes that Tom could not translate with certainty, but there seemed to be something threatening about it. The handbill had the usual rude wood-cut of a turbaned negro woman running, with the customary bundle on a stick over her shoulder, and the heading, in bold type, "*$100 Reward*." Tom read the bill aloud—at least the part that described Roxana and named the master and his St. Louis address and the address of the Fourth-street agency; but he left out the item that applicants for the reward might also apply to Mr. Thomas Driscoll.

"Gimme de bill."

Tom had folded it and was putting it in his pocket. He felt a chilly streak creeping down his back, but said, as carelessly as he could—

"The bill? Why, it isn't any use to you, you can't read it. What do you want with it?"

"Gimme de bill!" Tom gave it to her, but with a reluctance which he could not entirely disguise. "Did you read it all to me?"

"Certainly I did."

"Hole up yo' han' en swah to it."

Tom did it. Roxana put the bill carefully away in her pocket, with her eyes fixed upon Tom's face all the while, then she said—

"You's lyin'!"

"What would I want to lie about it for?"

"I don't know—but you *is*. Dat's my opinion, anyways. But nemmine 'bout dat. When I seed dat man, I 'uz dat sk'yerd dat I could scasely wobble home. Den I give a nigger man a dollah for dese clo'es, en I ain't ben in a house sence, night ner day, till now. I blacked my face en laid hid in de cellar of a ole house dat's burnt down, daytimes, en robbed de sugar hogsheads en grain sacks on de wharf, nights, to git somethin' to eat, en never dast to try to buy noth'n; en I's mos' starved. En I never dast to come near dis place till dis rainy night, when dey ain't no people roun', scasely. But to-night I ben a stannin' in de dark alley ever sence night come, waitin' for you to go by. En here I is."

She fell to thinking. Presently she said—

"You seed dat man at noon, las' Monday?"

"Yes."

"I seed him de middle o' dat arternoon. He hunted you up, didn't he?"

"Yes."

"Did he give you de bill dat time?"

"No, he hadn't got it printed, yet."

Roxana darted a suspicious glance at him.

"Did you he'p him fix up de bill?"

Tom cursed himself for making that stupid blunder, and tried to rectify it by saying he remembered, now, that it *was* at noon Monday that the man gave him the bill. Roxana said—

"You's lyin' agin, sho'." Then she straightened up and raised her finger:

"Now, den! I's gwyne to ask you a question, en I wants to know how you's gwyne to git aroun' it. You knowed he 'uz arter me; en if you run off, 'stid o' stayin' here to he'p him, he'd know dey 'uz somethin' wrong 'bout dis business, en den he would inquire 'bout you, en dat would take him to yo' uncle, en yo' uncle would read de bill en see dat you ben sellin' a free nigger down de river, en you know *him* I reckon! He'd tar up de will en kick you outen he house. Now, den, you answer me dis question: hain't you tole dat man dat I would be sho' to come here, en den you would fix it so he could set a trap en ketch me?"

Tom recognized that neither lies nor arguments could help him any longer—he was in a vise, with the screw turned on, and out of it there was no budging. His face began to take on an ugly look, and presently he said, with a snarl—

"Well, what could I do? You see, yourself, that I was in his grip and couldn't get out."

Roxy scorched him with a scornful gaze a while, then she said—

"What could *you* do? You could be Judas to yo' own mother to save yo' wuthless hide. *Would* anybody b'lieve it! No!—a *dog* couldn't! You is de lowdownest orneriest hound dat was ever pup'd into dis worl'—en I is 'sponsible for it!"—and she spat on him.

He made no offer to resent this. Roxy reflected a moment, then she said—

"Now I'll tell you what you's gwyne to do. You's gwyne to give dat man de money dat you's got laid up, en make him wait till you kin go to de Jedge en git de res' en buy me free agin."

"Thunder! what are you thinking of? Go and ask him for three hundred dollars and odd? What would I tell him I want with it, pray?"

Roxy's answer was delivered in a serene and level voice—

"You'll tell him you's sole me to pay yo' gamblin' debts, en dat you lied to me en was a villain, en dat I 'quires you to git dat money en buy me back agin."

"Why, you've gone stark mad! He would tear the will to shreds in a minute—don't you know that?"

"Yes, I does."

"Then you don't believe I'm idiot enough to go to him, do you?"

"I don't b'lieve nothin' 'bout it—I *knows* it. I knows it becaze *you* knows dat if you don't raise dat money I'll go to him myself, en den he'll sell *you* down de river en you kin see how you like it."

Tom rose, trembling and excited, and there was an evil light in his eye. He strode to the door and said he must get out of this suffocating place for a moment and clear his brain in the fresh air so that he could determine what to do. The door wouldn't open. Roxy smiled grimly, and said—

"I's got de key, honey. Set down! You needn't cle'r up yo' brain none to fine out what you gwyne to do—*I* knows what you's gwyne to do." Tom sat down and began to pass his hands through his hair with a helpless and desperate air. Roxy said, "Is dat man in dis house?"

Tom glanced up with a surprised expression, and asked—

"What gave you such an idea?"

"You done it. Gwyne out to cle'r yo' brain! In de fust place you ain't got none to cle'r, en in de second place yo' ornery eye *tole* on you. You's de low-downest hound dat ever—but I done tole you dat, befo'. Now den, dis is Friday. You kin fix it up wid dat man, en tell him you's gwyne away to git de res' o' de money, en dat you'll be back wid it nex' Tuesday, or maybe Wednesday. You understan'?"

Tom answered sullenly—

"Yes."

"En when you gits de new bill o' sale dat sells me to my own seff, take en send it in de mail to Mr. Pudd'nhead Wilson, en write on de back dat he's to keep it tell I come. You understan'?"

"Yes."

"Dat's all, den. Take yo' umbereller, en put on yo' hat."

"Why?"

"Becaze you's gwyne to see me home to de wharf. You see dis knife? I's toted it aroun' sence de day I seed dat man en bought dese clo'es en *it*. If he ketched me, I 'uz gwyne to kill myself wid it. Now start along, en go sof', en lead de way; en if you gives a sign in dis house, or if anybody comes up to you in de street, I's gwyne to jam it into you. Chambers, does you b'lieve me when I says dat?"

"It's no use to bother me with that question. *I* know your word's good."

"Yes, it's diffrent fum yo'n. Shet de light out en move along—here's de key."

They were not followed. Tom trembled every time a late straggler brushed by them on the street, and half expected to feel the cold steel in his back. Roxy was right at his heels and always in reach. After tramping a mile they reached a wide vacancy on the deserted wharves, and in that dark and rainy desert they parted.

As Tom trudged home, his mind was full of dreary thoughts and wild plans; but at last he said to himself, wearily—

"There is but the one way out. I must follow *her* plan. But with a variation—I will not ask for the money and ruin myself, I will rob the old skinflint!"

Chapter 29

Dawson's Landing had a week of repose, after the election, and it needed it, for the frantic and variegated nightmare which had tormented it all through the preceding week had left it limp, haggard and exhausted at the end. It got the week of repose because Angelo had the legs, and was in too subdued a condition to want to go out and mingle with an irritated community that had come to distrust and detest him because there was such a lack of harmony between his morals, which were confessedly excellent, and his methods of illustrating them, which were distinctly damnable. He took his exercise after eleven at night, when the streets were empty. Luigi was sick of society too, for the present, so this nocturnal arrangement suited him perfectly, though he did not say so, since he and his brother were still not on speaking terms.

However, the season of reposeful dulness was to end now, for Luigi was once more on deck. On Sunday Pudd'nhead Wilson carried his challenge to Judge Driscoll. The Judge declined to fight with an assassin—"that is," he added, significantly, "in the field of honor."

Elsewhere, of course, he would be ready. Wilson tried to convince him that if he had been present himself when Angelo told about the homicide committed by Luigi, he would not have considered the act discreditable to Luigi; but the obstinate old man was not to be moved.

Wilson went back to his principal and reported the failure of his mission. Luigi was incensed, and asked how it could be that the old gentleman, who was by no means dull-witted, held his trifling nephew's evidence and inferences to be of more value than Wilson's. But Wilson laughed, and said—

"That is quite simple; that is easily explicable. I am not his doll—his baby—his infatuation: his nephew is. The Judge and his late wife never had any children. The Judge and his wife were past middle age when this treasure fell into their lap. One must make allowances for a parental instinct that has been starving for twenty-five or thirty years. It is famished, it is crazed with hunger by that time, and will be entirely satisfied with anything that comes handy; its taste is atrophied, it can't tell mud-cat from shad. A devil born to a young couple is measurably recognizable by them as a devil before long, but a devil adopted by an old couple is an angel to them, and remains so, through thick and thin. Tom is this old man's angel; he is infatuated with him. Tom can persuade him into things which other people can't—not all things, I don't mean that, but a good many—particularly one class of things: the things that create or abolish personal partialities or prejudices in the old man's mind. The old man liked both of you. Tom conceived a hatred of you. That was enough; it turned the old man around at once. The oldest and strongest friendship must go to the ground when one of these late-adopted darlings throws a brick at it."

"It's a curious philosophy," said Luigi.

"It ain't a philosophy at all,—it's a fact. And there is something pathetic and beautiful about it, too. I think there is nothing more pathetic than to see one of these poor old childless couples taking a menagerie of yelping little worthless dogs to their hearts; and then adding some cursing and squawking parrots and a jackass-voiced macaw; and next a couple of hundred screeching song-birds; and presently some fetid guinea-pigs and rabbits, and a harem of cats. It is all a groping and ignorant effort to construct out of base metal and brass filings, so to speak, something to take the place of that golden treasure denied them by Nature, a child. But this is a digression. The unwritten law of this region requires you to kill Judge Driscoll on sight, and he and the community will expect that attention at your hands—though of course your own death by his bullet will answer every purpose. Look out for him. Are you heeled—that is, fixed?"

"Yes; he shall have his opportunity. If he attacks me I shall respond."

As Wilson was leaving, he said—

"The Judge is a little used up by his campaign work, and will not get out for a day or so, but when he does get out you want to be on the alert."

About eleven at night Luigi went out for exercise, and started on a long stroll in the veiled moonlight.

Tom Driscoll had landed at Hackett's Store, two miles below Dawson's, just about half an hour earlier, the only passenger for that lonely spot, and had walked up the shore road and entered Judge Driscoll's house without having encountered any one, either on the road or under the roof.

He pulled down his window shades and lit his candle. He laid off his coat and hat, and began his preparations. He unlocked his trunk and got his suit of girl's clothes out from under the male attire in it. Then he blacked his face with a burnt cork and put the cork in his pocket. His plan was, to slip down to his uncle's private sitting room below, pass into the bedroom, steal the safe-key from the old gentleman's clothes, and then go back and rob the safe. He took up his candle to start. His courage and confidence were high, up to this point, but both began to waver a little, now. Suppose he should make a noise, by some accident, and get caught—say in the act of opening the safe? Perhaps it would be well to go armed. He took the Indian knife from its hiding place, and felt a pleasant return of his waning courage. He slipped stealthily down the narrow stair, his hair rising and his pulses halting at the slightest creak. When he was half way down he was disturbed to perceive that the landing below was touched by a faint glow of light. What could that mean? Was his uncle still up? No, that was not likely; he must have left his night-taper there when he went to bed. Tom crept on down, pausing at every step to listen. He found the door standing open, and glanced in. What he saw pleased him beyond measure. His uncle was asleep on the sofa. On a small table at the head of the sofa a lamp was burning low, and by it stood the small tin cash-box, closed. Near the box was a pile of bank notes and a piece of paper covered with figures in pencil. The safe-door was not open. Evidently the sleeper had wearied himself with work upon his finances, and was taking a rest.

Tom set his candle on the stairs, and began to make his way toward the pile of notes, stooping low as he went. When he was passing his uncle, the old man stirred in his sleep and Tom stopped instantly—stopped, and softly drew the knife from its sheath, with his heart thumping and his eyes fastened upon his benefactor's face. After a moment or two he ventured forward again—one step—reached for his prize, and seized it, dropping the knife-sheath. Then he felt the old man's strong grip upon him, and a wild cry of "Help! help!" rang in his ear. Without hesitation he drove the knife home and was free. Some of his notes escaped from his left hand and fell in the blood on the floor. He dropped the knife and snatched them up and started to fly; transferred them to his left hand and seized the knife again, in his fright and confusion, but remembered himself and flung it from him, as being a dangerous witness to carry away with him. He jumped for the stair-foot, and closed the door behind him; and as he snatched his candle and fled upward, the stillness of the night was broken by the sound of urgent footsteps approaching the house. In another moment he was in his room, and the Twins were standing aghast over the body of the murdered man.

Tom put on his coat, buttoned his hat under it, threw on his suit of girl's clothes, dropped the veil, blew out his light, locked the room-door by which he had just entered, taking the key, passed through his other door into the back hall, locked that door and kept the key, then worked his way along in the dark and descended the back stairs. He was not expecting to meet anybody, for all interest was centred in the other part of the house, now; his calculation proved correct. By the time he was passing through the back yard, Mrs. Pratt, her servants, and a dozen half dressed neighbors were with the Twins and the dead, and accessions were still arriving at the front door.

As Tom, quaking as with a palsy, passed out at the gate three women came flying from the house on the opposite side of the lane. They rushed by him and in at the gate, asking him what the trouble was, there, but not waiting for an answer. Tom said to himself, "Those old maids waited to dress—they did the same thing the night Stevens's house burned down next door." In a few minutes he was in the haunted house. He lit a candle, and took off his girl-clothes. There was blood on him all down his left side, and his right hand was red with the stains of the blood-soaked notes which he had crushed in it; but otherwise he was free from this sort of evidence. He cleansed his hand on the straw, and cleaned the most of the smut from his face. Then he burned his male and female attire to ashes, and put on a disguise proper for a tramp. He blew out his light, went below, and was soon loafing down the river road, with the intent to borrow and use one of Roxy's devices. He found a canoe and paddled off down stream, setting the canoe adrift as dawn approached, and making his way by land to the next village, where he kept out of sight till a transient steamer came along, and then took deck passage for St. Louis. He was ill at ease until Dawson's Landing was behind him; then he said to himself, "All the detectives on earth couldn't trace me now; there's not a vestige of a clew left in the world; that homicide will take its place with the permanent mysteries."

In St. Louis, next morning, he read this brief telegram in the papers—dated at Dawson's Landing:

"Judge Driscoll, an old and respected citizen, was assassinated here about midnight by a profligate ex-freak called the Italian Twins, on account of a quarrel growing out of the recent election. One of them is considered innocent, but the other one will probably be lynched."

"The Twins!" soliloquised Tom; "how lucky! It is the knife that has done them this grace. We never know when fortune is trying to favor us. I actually cursed Pudd'nhead Wilson in my heart for putting it out of my power to sell that knife. I take it back, now."

Tom was now rich and independent. He arranged with the planter, and mailed to Wilson the new bill of sale which sold Roxana to herself; then he telegraphed his aunt Pratt:

"Have seen the awful news in the papers and am almost prostrated with grief. Shall start by packet to-day. Try to bear up till I come."

When Wilson reached the house of mourning and had gathered such details as Mrs. Pratt and the rest of the crowd could tell him, he took command, as mayor, and gave orders that nothing should be touched, but everything left as it was until Justice Robinson should arrive and take the proper measures as coroner. He cleared everybody out of the room but the Twins and himself. The sheriff soon arrived and took the Twins away to jail. Wilson told them to keep heart, and promised to do his best in their defence when the case should come to trial. Justice Robinson came presently, and with him Constable Blake. They examined the room thoroughly. They found the knife and the sheath. Wilson noticed that there were finger-prints on the knife handle. That pleased him, for the Twins had required the earliest comers to make a scrutiny of their hands and clothes, and neither these people nor Wilson himself had found any blood-stains upon them. Could there be a possibility that the Twins had spoken the truth when they said they found the man dead when they ran into the house in answer to the cry for help? He thought of that mysterious girl, at once. But this was not the sort of work for a girl to be engaged in. No matter; Tom Driscoll's room must be examined.

After the coroner's jury had viewed the body and its surroundings, Wilson suggested a search up stairs, and he went along. The jury forced an entrance to Tom's room, but found nothing, of course.

The coroner's jury found that the homicide was committed by Luigi, and that Angelo was accessory to it. The grand jury indicted Luigi for murder in the first degree and Angelo as accessory. The Twins were transferred from the city jail to the county prison to await trial.

The town was bitter against them, and for the first few days after the murder they were in constant danger of being lynched.

Wilson examined the finger-marks on the knife handle, and said to himself, "Neither of the Twins made those marks." Then manifestly there was another person concerned, either in his own interest or as hired assassin.

But who could it be? That, he must try to find out. The safe was not open, the cash-box was closed, and had three thousand dollars in it. Then robbery was not the motive, and revenge was. Where had the murdered man an enemy except Luigi? There was but that one person in the world with a deep grudge against him.

The mysterious girl! The girl was a great trial to Wilson. If the motive had been robbery, the girl might answer, but there *wasn't* any girl that would want to take this old man's life for revenge. He had no quarrels with girls; he was a gentleman.

Wilson had perfect tracings of the finger-marks of the knife handle; and among his glass records he had a great array of the finger-prints of women and girls, collected during the past fifteen or eighteen years, but he scanned them in vain, they successfully withstood every test; among them were no duplicates of the prints on the knife.

The presence of the knife on the stage of the murder was a worrying circumstance for Wilson. A week previously he had as good as admitted to himself that he believed Luigi had possessed such a knife and that he still possessed it notwithstanding his pretence that it had been stolen. And now here was the knife, and with it the Twins. Half the town had said the Twins were humbugging when they claimed that they had lost their knife, and now these people were joyful, and said "I told you so."

If their finger-prints had been on the handle—but it was useless to bother any further about that; the finger-prints on the handle were *not* theirs—that he knew, perfectly.

Wilson refused to suspect Tom; for, firstly, Tom couldn't murder anybody—he hadn't character enough; secondly, if he *could* murder a person he wouldn't select his doting benefactor and nearest relative; thirdly, self-interest was in the way; for while the uncle lived, Tom was sure of a free support and a chance to get the destroyed will revived again, but with the uncle gone, that chance was gone, too. It was true the will *had* been revived, but Tom could not have been aware of it, or he would have spoken of it, in his native talky unsecretive way. Finally, Tom was in St. Louis when the murder was done, and got the news out of the morning journals, as was shown by his telegram to his aunt. These speculations were unemphasized sensations rather than articulated thoughts, for Wilson would have laughed at the idea of seriously connecting Tom with the murder.

Wilson regarded the case of the Twins as desperate—in fact, about hopeless. For he argued that if a confederate was not found, an enlightened

Missouri jury would hang them, sure; if a confederate *was* found, that would not improve the matter, but simply furnish one more person for the sheriff to hang. Nothing could save the Twins but the discovery of a person who did the murder on his sole personal account—an undertaking which had all the aspect of the impossible. Still, the person who made the finger-prints must be sought. The Twins might have no case with him, but they certainly would have none without him.

So Wilson mooned around, thinking, thinking, guessing, guessing, day and night, and arriving nowhere. Whenever he ran across a girl or a woman he was not acquainted with, he got her finger-prints, on one pretext or another; and they always cost him a sigh when he got home, for they never tallied with the finger-marks on the knife handle.

As to the mysterious girl, Tom swore he knew no such girl, and did not remember ever seeing a girl wearing a dress like the one described by Wilson. He admitted that he did not always lock his room, and that sometimes the servants forgot to lock the house doors; still, in his opinion the girl must have made but few visits or she would have been discovered. When Wilson tried to connect her with the stealing-raid, and thought she might have been the old woman's confederate, if not the very thief herself disguised as an old woman, Tom seemed struck, and also much interested, and said he would keep a sharp eye out for this person or persons, although he was afraid that she or they would be too smart to venture again into a town where everybody would now be on the watch for a good while to come.

Everybody was pitying Tom, he looked so quiet and sorrowful, and seemed to feel his great loss so deeply. He was playing a part, but it was not all a part. The picture of his alleged uncle, as he had last seen him, was before him in the dark pretty frequently, when he was awake, and called again in his dreams, when he was asleep. He wouldn't go into the room where the tragedy had happened. This charmed the doting Mrs. Pratt, who "realized now, as she had never done before," she said, what a sensitive and delicate nature her darling had, and how he adored his poor uncle.

Chapter 30

Even the clearest and most perfect circumstantial evidence is likely to be at fault, after all, and therefore ought to be received with great caution. Take the case of *any* pencil, sharpened by *any* woman: if you have witnesses, you will find she did it with a knife; but if you take simply the aspect of the pencil, you will say she did it with her teeth.—*Pudd'nhead Wilson's Calendar.*

The weeks dragged along, no friend visiting the jailed Twins but their counsel and the two old aunties, and the day of trial came at last—the heaviest day in Wilson's life, for with all his tireless diligence he had discovered no sign or trace of the missing confederate. "Confederate" was the term he had long ago privately accepted for that person—not as being unquestionably the right term, but as being at least possibly the right one, though he was never able to understand why the Twins didn't vanish and escape, as the confederate had done, instead of remaining by the murdered man and getting caught there.

The court house was crowded, of course, and would remain so to the finish, for not only in the town itself, but in the country for miles around the trial was the one topic of conversation among the people. Mrs. Pratt, in deep mourning, and Tom with a weed on his hat, had seats near Pembroke Howard the public prosecutor, and back of them sat a great array of friends of the family. The Twins had but two friends present to keep their counsel in countenance. These sat near Wilson, and looked their friendliest. One was Aunt Patsy Cooper, the other was Aunt Betsy Hale. In the "nigger corner" sat Chambers; also Roxy, with good clothes on and her bill of sale in her pocket. It was her most precious possession, and she never parted with it, day or night. Tom had allowed her thirty-five dollars a month ever since he came into his property, and had said that he and she ought to be grateful to the Twins for making them rich; but had roused such a fury in her by this speech that he did not repeat the argument afterward. She said the old Judge had treated her child a thousand times better than he deserved, and had never done *her* an unkindness in his life; so she hated those outlandish devils for killing him and shouldn't ever sleep satisfied till she saw them hanged for it. She was here to watch the trial, now, and was going to lift up just one "hoo-raw" over it if the County Judge put her in jail a year for it. She gave her turbaned head a resolute toss and said, "When dat verdic' comes, I's gwyne to lif' dat *roof*, now, I *tell* you!"

Pembroke Howard briefly sketched the State's case. He said he would show by a chain of circumstantial evidence without break or fault in it anywhere, that the principal prisoner at the bar committed the murder; that the motive was partly revenge, and partly a desire to take his own life out of jeopardy, and that his brother, by his silence, was a consenting accessory to the crime; a crime which was the basest known to the calendar of human misdeeds—assassination; that it was conceived by the blackest of hearts and consummated by the cowardliest of hands; a crime which had broken a loving sister's heart, blighted the happiness of a young nephew who was as dear as a son, brought inconsolable grief to many friends, and sorrow and loss to the whole community. The utmost penalty of the outraged law would be exacted, and upon the accused, now present at the bar, that penalty would unquestionably be executed. He would reserve further remark until his closing speech.

He was strongly moved, and so also was the whole house; Mrs. Pratt and several other women were weeping when he sat down, and many an eye that was full of hate was riveted upon the unhappy prisoners.

Witness after witness was called by the State, and questioned at length; but the cross-questioning was brief: Wilson knew they could furnish nothing valuable for his side. People were sorry for Pudd'nhead; his new reputation would get hurt by this trial.

Several witnesses swore they heard Judge Driscoll say in his public speech that the Twins would be able to find their lost knife again when they needed it to assassinate somebody with. This was not news, but now it was seen to have been sorrowfully prophetic, and a profound sensation quivered through the hushed court room when those dismal words were repeated.

The public prosecutor rose and said that it was within his knowledge, through a conversation held with Judge Driscoll on the last day of his life, that counsel for the defence had brought him a challenge from the person charged at this bar with murder; that he had refused to fight with a confessed assassin—"that is, in the field of honor," but had added, significantly, that he would be ready for him elsewhere. Presumably the person here charged with murder was warned that he must kill or be killed the first time he should meet Judge Driscoll. If counsel for the defence chose to let the statement stand so, he would not call him to the witness stand. Mr. Wilson said he would offer no denial. [Murmurs, in the house—"It is getting worse and worse for Wilson's case."]

Mrs. Pratt testified that she heard no outcry, and did not know what woke her up, unless it was the sound of rapid footsteps approaching the front door. She jumped up and ran out in the hall just as she was, and heard the footsteps flying up the front steps and then following behind her as she ran to the sitting room. There she found the accused standing over her murdered brother— [Here she broke down and sobbed. Sensation in the court.] Resuming, she said the persons entering behind her were Mr. Rogers and Mr. Buckstone.

Cross-examined by Wilson, she said the Twins proclaimed their innocence; declared that they had been taking a walk, and had hurried to the house in response to a cry for help which was so loud and strong that they had heard it at a considerable distance; that they begged her and the gentlemen just mentioned to examine their hands and clothes—which was done, and no blood-stains found.

Confirmatory evidence followed, from Rogers and Buckstone.

The finding of the knife was verified, the advertisement minutely describing it and offering a reward for it was put in evidence, and its exact correspondence with that description proven. Then followed a few minor details, and the case for the State was closed.

Wilson said he had three witnesses, the Misses Clarkson, who would testify that they met a veiled young woman leaving Judge Driscoll's premises by the back gate a few minutes after the cries for help were heard, and that their evidence, taken with certain circumstantial evidence which he would call the court's attention to would in his opinion convince the court that there was still one person concerned in this crime who had not yet been found, and also that a stay of proceedings ought to be granted, in justice to his clients, until that person should be discovered. As it was late, he would ask leave to defer the examination of his three witnesses until the next morning.

The crowd poured out of the place and went flocking away in excited groups and couples, talking the events of the session over with vivacity and consuming interest, and everybody seemed to have had a satisfactory and enjoyable day except the accused, their counsel, and their two old-lady friends. There was no cheer among these, and no substantial hope.

In parting with the Twins the two old aunties did attempt a good-night with a great and noble pretense of hope and cheer in it, but broke down without finishing, and went away crying.

Wilson wanted no supper, he had no appetite. He got out all the finger-prints of girls and women in his collection of records and pored gloomily over them an hour or more, trying to convince himself that that troublesome girl's marks were there somewhere and had been overlooked. But it was not so. He drew back his chair, clasped his hands over his head, and gave himself up to dull and arid musings.

Tom Driscoll dropped in, an hour after dark, and said with a pleasant laugh as he took a seat—

"Hello, we've gone back to the amusements of our days of neglect and obscurity for consolation, haven't we?" and he took up one of the glass strips and held it against the light to inspect it. "Come, cheer up, old man, there's no use in losing your grip and going back to this child's play merely because this big sun-spot is drifting across your shiny new disk. It'll pass, and you'll be all right again"—and he laid the glass down. "Did you think you could win always, just because you won once?"

"Oh, no," said Wilson, with a sigh, "I didn't expect that, but I can't believe Luigi killed your uncle, and I feel very sorry for him. It makes me blue. And you would feel as I do, Tom, if you were not prejudiced against those young fellows."

"I don't know about that," and Tom's countenance darkened, for his memory reverted to his kicking; "I owe them no good will, considering their odious treatment of me that night. Prejudice or no prejudice, Pudd'nhead, I don't like them, and when they get their deserts you're not going to find me sitting on the mourners' bench."

He took up another strip of glass, and exclaimed—

"Why, here's old Roxy's label! Are you going to ornament the royal palaces with nigger paw-marks, too? By the date here, I was seven months old when this was done, and she was nursing me and her little nigger cub. There's a line straight across her thumb-print. How comes that?" and Tom held out the piece of glass to Wilson.

"That is common," said the bored man, wearily. "Scar of a cut or a scratch, usually"—and he took the strip of glass indifferently and raised it toward the lamp.

All the blood sunk suddenly out of his face, his hand quaked, and he gazed at the polished surface before him with the glassy stare of a corpse.

"Great Heavens, what's the matter with you, Wilson? Are you going to faint?"

Tom sprang for a glass of water and offered it, but Wilson shrank shuddering from him and said—

"No, no!—take it away!" His breast was rising and falling, and he moved his head about in a dull and wandering way, like a person who has been stunned. Presently he said, "I shall feel better when I get to bed; I have been overwrought to-day; yes, and overworked for many days."

"Then I'll leave you and let you get to your rest. Good night, old man." But as Tom went out he couldn't deny himself a small parting gibe: "Don't take it so hard; a body can't win every time; you'll hang somebody yet."

Wilson muttered to himself, "It is no lie to say I am sorry I have to begin with you, miserable dog though you are."

He braced himself up with a glass of cold whisky and went to work again. He did not compare the new finger-marks left by Tom a few minutes before on Roxy's glass with the tracings of the marks left on the knife handle, there being no need of that—for his trained eye—but busied himself with another matter, muttering from time to time, "Idiot that I was! nothing but a *girl* would do me—a man in girl's clothes never occurred to me." First, he hunted out the plate containing the finger-prints made by Tom when he was twelve years old, and laid it by itself; then he brought forth the marks made by Tom's baby fingers when he was a suckling of seven months, and placed these two plates with the one containing this subject's newly (and unconsciously) made record. "Now the series is complete," he said with satisfaction, and sat down to inspect these things and enjoy them.

But his enjoyment was brief. He stared a considerable time at the three strips, and seemed stupefied with astonishment. At last he put them down and said, "I can't make it out at all—hang it, the baby's don't tally with the others!"

He walked the floor for half an hour puzzling over his enigma, then he hunted out two other glass plates.

He sat down and puzzled over these things a good while, but kept muttering, "It's no use, I can't understand it. They don't tally right, and yet I'll swear the names and dates are right, and so of course they *ought* to tally. I never labeled one of these things carelessly in my life. There is a most extraordinary mystery here."

He was tired out, now, and his brains were beginning to clog. He said he would sleep himself fresh, and then see what he could do with this riddle. He slept through a troubled and unrestful hour, then unconsciousness began to shred away and presently he rose drowsily to a sitting posture. "Now what was that dream?" he said, trying to recal it; "what *was* that dream?—it seemed to unravel that puz—"

He landed in the middle of the floor at a bound, without finishing the sentence, and ran and turned up his light and seized his "records." He took a single swift glance at them and cried out—

"It's *so!* Great guns, what a revelation! And for twenty-three years no man has ever suspected it."

Chapter 31

He is useless on top of the ground; he ought to be under it,
inspiring the cabbages.—*Pudd'nhead Wilson's Calendar.*

Wilson put on enough clothes for business purposes, and went to work under a tremendous pressure of steam. He was awake all over. All sense of weariness had been swept away by the invigorating refreshment of the great and hopeful discovery which he had made. He made fine and accurate reproductions of a number of his "records," and then enlarged them on a scale of ten to one with his pantagraph. He did these pantagraph enlargements on sheets of white cardboard, and made each individual line of the bewildering maze of sworls or curves or loops which constituted the "pattern" of a "record" stand out bold and black by reinforcing it with ink. To the untrained eye the collection of delicate originals made by the human finger on the glass plates looked about alike; but when enlarged ten times, they resembled the markings of a block of wood that has been sawed across the grain, and the dullest eye could detect at a glance, and at a distance of many feet, that no two of the patterns were alike. When Wilson had at last finished his tedious and difficult work, he arranged its results according to a plan in which a progressive order and sequence was a principal feature, then he added to the batch several pantagraph enlargements which he had made from time to time in bygone years.

The night was spent and the day well advanced, now. By the time he had snatched a trifle of breakfast it was nine o'clock and the court ready to begin its sitting. He was in his place twelve minutes later, with his "records." Tom Driscoll caught a slight glimpse of the records and nudged his nearest friend and said, with a wink, "Pudd'nhead's got a rare eye to business—thinks that as long as he can't win his case, it's at least a noble good chance to advertise his palace-window decorations without any expense." Wilson was informed that his witnesses had been delayed, but would arrive presently; but he rose and said he should probably not have occasion to make use of their testimony.

[An amused murmur ran through the room—"It's a clean back-down! he gives up without hitting a lick."] Wilson continued—

"I have other testimony,—and better." [This roused immediate interest, and also evoked murmurs of surprise that had a detectible ingredient of disappointment in them.] "If I seem to be springing this evidence upon the court, I offer as my justification for this, that I did not discover its existence until late last night, and have been engaged in examining and classifying it ever since until half an hour ago. I shall offer it presently; but first I wish to say a few preliminary words.

"May it please the court, the claim given the front place, the claim most persistently urged, the claim most strenuously and I may even say, aggressively and defiantly insisted upon by the prosecution, is this—*that the person whose hand left the blood-stained finger-prints upon the handle of the Indian knife is the person who committed the murder.*" Wilson paused, during several moments, to give impressiveness to what he was about to say, and then added, tranquilly, "We grant that claim."

It was an electrical surprise. No one was prepared for such an admission as this. A buzz of astonishment rose on all sides, and people were heard to intimate that the overworked lawyer had lost his mind. Even the veteran judge, accustomed as he was to legal ambushes and masked batteries in criminal procedure, was not sure that his ears were not deceiving him, and asked counsel what it was he had said. The two old aunties seemed smitten with a collapse. Howard's impassive face betrayed no sign, but his attitude and bearing lost something of their careless confidence for a moment. Wilson resumed:

"We not only grant that claim, but we welcome it and strongly endorse it. Leaving that matter for the present, we will now proceed to consider other points in the case which we propose to establish by evidence, and shall include that one in the chain, in its proper place."

He had made up his mind to try a few hardy guesses, in mapping out his theory of the origin and motive of the murder—guesses designed to fill up gaps in it—guesses which could help if they hit, and would probably do no harm if they didn't.

"To my mind, certain circumstances of the case before the court seem to suggest a motive for the homicide quite different from the one insisted on by the State. It is my conviction that the motive was not revenge, but robbery. It has been urged that the presence of the accused in that fatal room, just after notification that they must take the life of the late Judge Driscoll or lose their own the moment the parties should meet, clearly signifies that the natural instinct of self-preservation moved my clients to go there by night and take their enemy by surprise and save themselves by destroying him.

"Then why did they stay there, after the deed was done? Mrs. Pratt had time, although she did not hear the cry for help, but woke up some moments later, to run to that room—and there she found these men standing, and making no effort to escape. If they were guilty, they ought to have been running out of the house at the same time that she was running to that room. If they had had such a strong instinct toward self-preservation as to move them to kill that unarmed man, what had become of it now, when it should have been more alert than ever? Would any of us have remained there? Let us not slander our intelligence to that degree.

"Much stress has been laid upon the fact that the accused offered a very large reward for the knife with which this murder was done; that no thief came forward to claim that extraordinary reward; that the latter fact was good circumstantial evidence that the claim that the knife had been stolen was a vanity and a fraud; that these details taken in connection with the memorable and apparently prophetic speech of the deceased concerning that knife and the final discovery of that very knife in the fatal room where no living person was found present with the slaughtered man but the owner of the knife and his brother, form an indestructible chain of evidence which fixes the crime upon those unfortunate strangers.

"But I shall presently ask to be sworn, and shall testify that there was a large reward offered for the *thief*, also; that it was offered *secretly* and not advertised; that this fact was indiscreetly mentioned—or at least tacitly admitted—in what was supposed to be safe circumstances, but may not have been. The thief may have been present himself." [Tom Driscoll had been looking at the speaker, but dropped his eyes at this point.] "In that case he would retain the knife in his possession, not daring to offer it for sale, or for pledge in a pawn shop." [There was a nodding of heads among the audience by way of admission that this was not a bad stroke.] "I shall prove to the satisfaction of the jury that there was a person in Judge Driscoll's room several minutes *before* the accused entered it." [This produced a strong sensation; the last drowsy-head in the court room roused up, now, and made preparation to listen.] "If it shall seem necessary, I will prove by the Misses Clarkson that they met a veiled person—ostensibly a woman—coming out of the back gate a few minutes after the cry for help was heard. This person was not a woman, but a man dressed in woman's clothes." [Another sensation. Wilson had his eye on Tom when he hazarded this guess, to see what effect it would produce. He was satisfied with the result, and said to himself, "It was a success—he's hit."]

"The object of that person in that house was robbery, not murder. It is true that the safe was not open, but there was an ordinary tin cash-box on the table with three thousand dollars in it. It is easily supposable that the thief was concealed in the house; that he knew of this box, and of its owner's habit of counting its contents and arranging his accounts at night—if he had that habit, which I do not assert, of course; that he tried to take the box while its owner slept, but made a noise and was seized, and had to use the knife to save himself from capture; and that he fled without his booty because he heard help coming.

"I have now done with my theory, and will proceed to the evidences by which I propose to try to prove its soundness." Wilson took up several of his strips of glass. When the audience recognized these familiar mementoes of Pudd'nhead's old-time childish "puttering" and folly, the tense and funereal interest vanished out of their faces and the house burst into volleys of relieving and refreshing laughter, and Tom chirked up and joined in the fun himself; but Wilson was apparently not disturbed. He arranged his records on the table before him, and said—

"I beg the indulgence of the court while I make a few remarks in explanation of some evidence which I am about to introduce, and which I shall presently ask to be allowed to verify under oath on the witness stand. Every human being carries with him from his cradle to his grave certain marks which do not change their character, and by which he can always be identified—and that without shade of doubt or question. These marks are his signature, his autograph, so to speak, and this autograph cannot be counterfeited, nor can he disguise it or hide it away, nor can it become illegible by the wear and the mutations of time. This signature is not his face—age can change that beyond recognition; it is not his hair, for that can fall out; it is not his height, for duplicates of that exist; it is not his form, for duplicates of that exist, also, whereas *this* signature is each man's very own—there is no duplicate of it among the swarming populations of the globe." [The audience were interested once more.]

"This autograph consists of the delicate lines or corrugations with which Nature marks the insides of the hands and the soles of the feet. If you will look at the balls of your fingers—you that have very sharp eyesight—you will observe that these dainty, curving lines lie close together, like those that indicate the borders of oceans in maps, and that they form various clearly defined patterns, such as arches, circles, long curves, whorls, etc., and that these patterns differ on the different fingers." [Every man in the room had his hand up to the light, now, and his head canted to one side, and was minutely scrutinizing the balls of his fingers; there were whispered ejaculations of, "Why, it's so—I never noticed *that* before!"] "The patterns on the right hand are not the same as those on the left." [Ejaculations of "Why, that's so, too!"] "Taken finger for finger, your patterns differ from your neighbor's." [Comparisons were made, all over the house—even the judge and jury were absorbed in this curious work.] "The patterns of a twin's right hand are not the same as those on his left. One twin's patterns are never the same as his fellow-twin's patterns—the jury will find that the patterns upon the finger-balls of the accused follow this rule." [An examination of the Twins' hands was begun at once.] "You have often heard of twins who were so exactly alike that when dressed alike their own parents could not tell them apart. Yet there was never a twin born into this world that did not carry from birth to death a sure identifier in this mysterious and marvelous natal autograph! *That* once known to you, his fellow-twin could never personate him and deceive you."

Wilson stopped, and stood silent. Inattention dies a quick and sure death when a speaker does that. The stillness gives warning that something is coming. All palms and finger-balls went down, now, all slouching forms straightened, all heads came up, all eyes were fastened upon Wilson's face. He waited yet one, two, three moments, to let his pause complete and perfect its spell upon the house; then, when through the profound hush he could hear the ticking of the clock on the wall, he put out his hand and took the Indian knife by the blade and held it aloft where all could see the sinister spots upon its ivory handle; then he said, in a level and passionless voice—

"Upon this haft stands the assassin's natal autograph, written in the blood of that helpless and unoffending old man who loved you and whom you all loved. There is but one man in the whole earth whose hand can duplicate that crimson sign"—he paused and raised his eyes to the pendulum swinging back and forth—"and please God we will produce that man in this room before the clock strikes noon!"

Stunned, distraught, unconscious of its own movement, the house half rose, as if expecting to see the murderer appear at the door, and a breeze of muttered ejaculations swept the place. *"Order in the court!—sit down!"* This from the sheriff. He was obeyed, and quiet reigned again. Wilson stole a glance at Tom, and said to himself, "He is flying signals of distress, now; even people who despise him are pitying him; they think this is a hard ordeal for a young fellow who has lost his benefactor by so cruel a stroke—and they are right." He resumed his speech:

"For more than twenty years I have amused my compulsory leisure with collecting these curious physical signatures in this town. At my house I have hundreds upon hundreds of them. Each and every one is labeled with name and date; not labeled the next day or even the next hour, but in the very minute that the impression was taken. When I go upon the witness stand I will repeat under oath the things which I am now saying. I have the finger-prints of the court, the sheriff, and every member of the jury. There is hardly a person in this room, white or black, whose natal signature I cannot produce, and not one of them can so disguise himself that I cannot pick him out from a multitude of his fellow creatures and unerringly identify him by his hands. And if he and I should live to be a hundred I could still do it." [The interest of the audience was steadily deepening, now.]

"I have studied some of these signatures so much that I know them as well as the bank cashier knows the autograph of his oldest customer. While I turn my back, now, I beg that several persons will be so good as to pass their fingers through their hair and then press them upon one of the panes of the window near the jury, and that among them the accused may set their finger-marks. Also, I beg that these experimenters, or others, will set their finger-marks upon another pane, and add again the marks of the accused, but not placing them in the same order or relation to the other signatures as before—for, by one chance in a million, a person might happen upon the right marks by pure guesswork, *once*, therefore I wish to be tested twice."

He turned his back, and the two panes were quickly covered with delicately-lined oval spots, but visible only to such persons as could get a dark background for them,—the foliage of a tree, outside, for instance. Then, upon call, Wilson went to the window, made his examination, and said—

"This is Count Luigi's right hand; this one, three signatures below, is his left. Here is Count Angelo's right; down here is his left. Now for the other pane: here and here are Count Luigi's, here and here are his brother's." He faced about. "Am I right?"

A deafening explosion of applause was the answer. The Bench said—

"This certainly approaches the miraculous!"

Wilson turned to the window again and remarked, pointing with his finger—

"This is the signature of Mr. Justice Robinson." [Applause.] "This, of Constable Blake." [Applause.] "This, of John Mason, juryman." [Applause.] "This, of the sheriff." [Applause.] "I cannot name the others, but I have them all at home, named and dated, and could identify them all by my finger-print records."

He moved to his place through a storm of applause—which the sheriff stopped, and also made the people sit down, for they were all standing, and struggling to see, of course. Court, jury, sheriff and everybody had been too absorbed in observing Wilson's performance to attend to the audience earlier.

"Now then," said Wilson, "I have here the natal autographs of two children—thrown up to ten times the natural size by the pantagraph, so that any one who can see at all can tell the markings apart at a glance. We will call the children A and B. Here are A's finger-marks, taken at the age of five months. Here they are again, taken at seven months." [Tom started.] "They are alike, you see. Here are B's at five months, and also at seven months. They, too, exactly copy each other, but the patterns are quite different from A's, you observe. I shall refer to these again presently, but we will turn them face down, now.

"Here, thrown up ten sizes, are the natal autographs of the two persons who are here before you accused of murdering Judge Driscoll. I made these things last night, and will so swear when I go upon the witness stand. I ask the jury to compare them with the finger-marks of the accused upon the window panes, and tell the court if they are the same." He passed a powerful magnifying glass to the foreman.

One juryman after another took the cardboard and the glass and made the comparison. Then the foreman said to the judge—

"Your honor, we are all agreed that they are identical."

Wilson said to the foreman—

"Please turn that cardboard face down, and take this one and compare it searchingly, by the magnifier, with the fatal signature upon the knife handle, and report your finding to the court."

Again the jury made minute examination, and again reported—

"We find them to be exactly identical, your honor."

Wilson turned toward the counsel for the prosecution, and there was a clearly recognizable note of warning in his voice when he said—

"May it please the court, the State has claimed, strenuously and persistently, that the blood-stained finger-prints upon that knife handle were left there by the assassin of Judge Driscoll. You have heard us grant that claim, and welcome it." He turned to the jury: "Compare the finger-prints of the accused with the finger-prints left by the assassin—and report."

The comparison began. As it proceeded, all movement and all sound ceased, and the deep silence of an absorbed and waiting suspense settled upon the house; and when at last the words came—

"They do not even resemble!" a crash of applause followed, the house sprang to its feet, and the two old ladies flung themselves with hysterical gratitude at the Twins, but were promptly repressed by official force and brought to order along with the rest of the assemblage. Tom was altering his position every few minutes, now, but none of his changes brought repose nor any small trifle of comfort. When the house was become tranquil again, Wilson said gravely, indicating the Twins with a gesture—

"These men are innocent—I have no further concern with them." [Another outbreak of applause began, but was promptly checked.] "We will now proceed to find the guilty." [Tom's eyes were starting from their sockets—yes, it *was* a cruel day for the bereaved youth, everybody thought.] "We will return to the infant autographs of A and B. I will ask the jury to take these large pantagraph facsimiles of A's, marked five months and seven months. Do they tally?"

The foreman responded—

"Perfectly."

"Now examine this pantagraph, taken at eight months, and also marked A. Does it tally with the other two?"

The surprised response was—

"No—they differ widely."

"You are quite right. Now take these two pantagraphs of B's autograph, marked five months and seven months. Do they tally with each other?"

"Yes—perfectly."

"Take this third pantagraph marked 'B, eight months.' Does it tally with B's other two?"

"By no means."

"Do you know how to account for these strange discrepancies? I will tell you. For a purpose unknown to us, but probably a selfish one, somebody *changed those children in the cradle.*"

This produced a vast sensation, naturally; Roxana began to fan herself violently, although the fall weather was pleasant; it certainly was not uncomfortably warm, at least.

"Between the ages of seven months and eight months those children were changed in the cradle"—he made one of his effect-collecting pauses, and added—*"and the person who did it is in this house."*

Roxy collapsed and fell over against her next neighbor, but quickly recovered herself. The house was thrilled as with an electric shock, and the people half rose, as if to seek a glimpse of the person who had made that exchange. Tom was growing limp; the life seemed oozing out of him. Wilson resumed:

"A was put into B's cradle in the nursery; B was transferred to the kitchen, and became a negro and a slave"—[Sensation—confusion of angry ejaculations]—"but within a quarter of an hour he will stand before you white and free!" [Burst of applause, checked by the officers.] "From seven months onward until now, A has still been a usurper, and in my finger-records he bears B's name. Here is his pantagraph, at the age of twelve. Compare it with the assassin's signature upon the knife handle. Do they tally?"

The foreman answered—

"To the minutest detail!"

Wilson said, solemnly—

"The murderer of your friend and mine—York Driscoll, of the generous hand and the kindly spirit—sits in your midst! Valet de Chambre, negro and slave—falsely called Thomas à Becket Driscoll—make upon the window the finger-prints that will hang you!"

Tom turned his ashen face imploringly toward the speaker, made some impotent movements with his white lips, then slid limp and lifeless to the floor.

Wilson broke the awed silence with the words—

"There is no need. He has confessed."

Roxy flung herself upon her knees, covered her face with her hands, and out through her sobs the words struggled—

"De Lord have mercy on me, po' misable sinner dat I is!"

The clock struck twelve.

The court rose; the new prisoner, handcuffed, was removed.

Chapter 32

The town sat up all night to discuss the amazing events of the day and swap guesses as to when Tom's trial would begin. Troop after troop of citizens came to serenade Wilson, and require a speech, and shout themselves hoarse over every sentence that fell from his lips—for all his sentences were golden, now, all were marvelous. He was a made man for good, this time; nothing could ever shake his foundations again.

And as each of these roaring gangs of enthusiasts marched away, some remorseful and shame-faced member of it was quite sure to raise his voice and say—

"And *this* is the man the likes of *us* have called a pudd'nhead for more than twenty years! He has resigned from that position, boys."

"Yes, but it ain't vacant—we're elected!"

———

The Twins were heroes of romance, now, and they came into vast and instant favor again, and Aunt Patsy and Aunt Betsy's cups of happiness were full. But the restored popularity of the strangers did not last long. The city government had been at a standstill ever since election day, because without Luigi there was a tie in the board of aldermen, whereas with him the liquor interest—the richest in the political field—would have one majority. But the court decided that Angelo could not sit in the board with him, either in public or executive sessions, and at the same time forbade the board to deny admission to Luigi, a fairly and legally chosen alderman. The case was carried up and up and up from court to court till it promised to reach the high court of the hereafter, yet still the same old original decision was confirmed every time. As a result, the city government not only stood still, with its hands tied, but everything it was created to protect and care for went a steady gait toward rack and ruin. There was no way to levy a tax, so the minor officials had to resign or starve; therefore they resigned. There being no city money, the enormous legal expenses on both sides had to be defrayed by private subscription. But at last the people came to their senses, and said—

"Pudd'nhead was right, at the start—we ought to have hired the official half of that human phillipene to resign; but it's too late, now; some of us haven't got anything left to hire him with."

"Yes we have," said another citizen, "we've got this"—and he produced a halter.

Many shouted—

"That's the ticket!"

But others said—

"No—Count Angelo is innocent; we mustn't hang him."

"Who said anything about hanging him? We are only going to hang the other one."

"Then that is all right—there is no objection to that."

So the town carried the halter to Luigi, explained its persuasions, and asked him to resign and go to Europe, and not stop anywhere this side.

Luigi accepted the invitation, and took his brother along with him. They never returned. Then a new election was held, and the city got started right, this time.

Roxy's heart was broken. The young fellow upon whom she had inflicted twenty-three years of slavery continued the false heir's pension of thirty-five dollars a month to her, but her hurts were too deep for money to heal; the spirit in her eye was quenched, her martial bearing departed with it, and the voice of her laughter ceased in the land. In her church and its affairs she found her only solace.

Aunt Patsy and Aunt Betsy felt the loss of the Twins deeply, and the scar of that loss remained with them permanently; but their hearts were young and their interests limitless, so they were sufficiently bulwarked against serious unhappiness.

The lads Henry and Joe fell down the well and got drowned. But it is no particular matter, and such things cannot well be provided against in a work of this kind.

The real heir suddenly found himself rich and free, but in a most embarrassing situation. He could neither read nor write, and his speech was the basest dialect of the negro quarter. His gait, his attitudes, his gestures, his bearing, his laugh—all were vulgar and uncouth; his manners were the manners of a slave. Money and fine clothes could not mend these defects or cover them up, they only made them the more glaring and the more pathetic. The poor fellow could not endure the terrors of the white man's parlor, and felt at home and at peace nowhere but in the kitchen. The family pew was a misery to him, yet he could nevermore enter into the solacing refuge of the "nigger gallery"—that was closed to him for good and all. But we cannot follow his curious fate further—that would be a long story.

The false heir made a full confession and was sentenced to imprisonment for life. But now a complication came up. The Percy Driscoll estate was in such a crippled shape when its owner died that it could pay only sixty per cent of its great indebtedness, and was settled at that rate. But the creditors came forward, now, and complained that inasmuch as the false heir was not inventoried at that time with the rest of the property, great wrong and loss had thereby been inflicted upon them. They claimed that "Tom" was lawfully their property and had been so for eight years; that they had already lost sufficiently in being deprived of his services during that long period, and ought not to be required to add anything to that loss; that if he had been delivered up to them in the first place, they would have sold him and he could not have murdered Judge Driscoll, therefore it was not he that had really committed the murder, the guilt lay with the dishonest inventory which had suppressed his name. Everybody saw that there was reason in this. Everybody granted that if "Tom" were white and free it would be unquestionably right to punish him—it would be no loss to anybody; but to shut up a valuable slave for life—that was quite another matter.

As soon as the Governor understood the case, he pardoned Tom at once, and the creditors sold him down the river.

Addenda to the Morgan Manuscript

In these leaves added late in the composition of MS Morgan, Mark Twain created a scheme for denoting weather conditions in the various chapters of the book. He entrusted its implementation to the printer but abandoned the idea in his revision of July 1893. (Clemens's previous novel, *The American Claimant*, had likewise been equipped with a labor-saving "weather" scheme [SLC 1892a, x, 275–77].) Clemens placed the "Key to Signs" among the preliminaries of MS Morgan. The "Conclusion," an aphorism on March weather, was written in January 1893 and falsely dated "March." Here Clemens deploys the weather-signs in chaotic profusion, acting on a notebook entry made in December 1892: "March weather.—with all signs" (Notebook 32, TS p. 51). Starting with a leaf from his accumulated manuscript aphorisms, he deleted one of the two maxims (which became a motto for Chapter 11) and supplemented it with a leaf (633½) giving directions to the printer.

The transcriptions are made using "plain text," as described on page 615; the author's insertions are placed between ˌcarets,ˍ and his deletions are ~~struck through.~~

Key to Signs used in this book.

To save the space usually
devoted to~ explanations of the state
of the weather in books of this
kind, the author, ~~will~~ begs leave to substitutes
a simple system of weather-signs.
The hieroglyph at the head of each chapter
~~which~~ will instantly convey to
the reader's mind a perfect comprehension of the ~~sort~~
kind of weather which is going to
prevail below.

The signs & their meanings here
follow:

Sunny.

Pitch Dark

Starlight.

Rainy.

Moonlight.

SNOW.

Fog.

When two or more signs occur together, the ensuing weather is
going to be more, or more yet, or still more
~~mixed~~ variable, according to number of signs employed.

To Printer. Please make fac-similes of those signs, & use them at chapter-tops—one & sometimes two—SLC.

it is not necessary that they fit the weather of the chapter always.

Key to Signs used in this book.

═══

To save the space usually devoted to ~~tedious~~ explanations of the state of the weather in books of this kind, the author ~~will~~ begs leave to substitute a simple system of weather-signs, ~~which~~ The hieroglyph at the head of each chapter, will instantly convey to the reader's mind a perfect comprehension of the ~~condi~~ kind of weather which is going to prevail below.

The signs & their meanings here follow:

Sunny. Pitch Dark

Starlight.

Rainy. Moonlight.

SNOW. Fog.

When two or more signs occur together, ~~it~~ the ensuing weather is going to be more, or more yet, or still more ~~mixed,~~ variable, according to number of signs employed.

4

(Put this paragraph below the succeeding two.)

When there is no sign, it means that there is not going to be any weather. It is a mistake to suppose that weather is at all times necessary in a novel. As often as not, it is an ~~hindrance~~. inconvenience, & keeps the characters from going out.

When all the signs are used it means Stormy. ~~weather~~ When they are doubled it means ~~[struck out]~~ Extremely Violent & Perilous Weather.

(Put it down here.)

Put this paragraph *below* the succeeding two.

When there is no sign, it means that there is not going to be any weather. It is a mistake to suppose that weather is at all times necessary in a novel. As often as not, it is an ~~hindrance.~~ inconvenience, & keeps the characters from going out.

When all the signs are used it means *Stormy*.

When they are doubled ~~& mixed~~ it means ~~*Indescribably*~~ *Extremely* *Violent & Perilous Weather*.

Put it down *here*.

CONCLUSION.

March. Thought by some to be one of the spring months. But this is an error. March is a season by itself, & has not been classified. It was created for some inscrutable, unwise, inexcusable purpose, which we may conjecture about all we want to, but the best plan is to stop there: many a man has died who has been too handy with his opinions about March. —

Pudd'nhead Wilson's Calendar.

~~When I reflect upon the number of disagreeable people who I know have gone to a better world, I am moved to lead a different life.~~

[This chapter could not be written, on account of the weather.]

Florence, March, 1893. THE END.

CONCLUSION.

———

March. Thought by some to be one of the spring months. But this is an error. March is a season by itself, & has not been classified. It was created for some inscrutable, unwise, inexcusable purpose, which we may conjecture about all we want to, but the best plan is to stop there: many a man has died who has been too handy with his opinions about March.—Pudd'nhead Wilson's Calendar.

~~When I reflect upon the number of disagreeable people who I know have gone to a better world, I am moved to lead a different life.~~

[This chapter could not be written, on account of the weather.]

———

THE END.

———

Florence, March, 1893.

6 33 ½

(Private to "Comp.")

Treble all the weather-
signs above "Conclusion",
+ turn some of them upside
down, + others down on
their sides.

Treble all the weather-signs above "Conclusion," and turn some of them up[s]ide down, and others down on their sides.

Pudd'nhead Wilson: A Tale

THE REVISED VERSION

SAMUEL L. CLEMENS (MARK TWAIN).

Pudd'nhead Wilson

A TALE

By Mark Twain

There is no character, howsoever good and fine, but it can be destroyed by ridicule, howsoever poor and witless. Observe the ass, for instance: his character is about perfect, he is the choicest spirit among all the humbler animals, yet see what ridicule has brought him to. Instead of feeling complimented when we are called an ass, we are left in doubt.—*Pudd'nhead Wilson's Calendar.*

A Whisper to the Reader

A person who is ignorant of legal matters is always liable to make mistakes when he tries to photograph a court scene with his pen; and so, I was not willing to let the law-chapters in this book go to press without first subjecting them to rigid and exhausting revision and correction by a trained barrister—if that is what they are called. Those chapters are right, now, in every detail, for they were re-written under the immediate eye of William Hicks, who studied law part of a while in south-west Missouri thirty-five years ago and then came over here to Florence for his health and is still helping for exercise and board in Maccaroni and Vermicelli's horse-feed shed which is up the back alley as you turn around the corner out of the Piazza del Duomo just beyond the house where that stone that Dante used to sit on six hundred years ago is let into the wall when he let on to be watching them build Giotto's Campanile and yet always got tired looking as soon as Beatrice passed along on her way to get a chunk of chestnut-cake to defend herself with in case of a Ghibelline attack before she got to school, at the same old stand where they sell the same old cake to this day and it is just as light and good as it was then, too, and this is not flattery, far from it. He was a little rusty on his law, but he rubbed up for this book, and those two or three legal chapters are right and straight, now, he told me so himself.

Given under my hand this second day of January, 1893, at the Villa Viviani, village of Settignano, three miles back of Florence, on the hills—the same certainly affording the most charming view to be found on this planet, and with it the most dream-like and enchanting sunsets to be found in any planet or even in any solar system—and given, too in the swell room of the house, with the busts of Cerretani senators and other grandees of this line looking approvingly down upon me as they used to look down upon Dante, and mutely asking me to adopt them into my family, which I do with pleasure, for my remotest ancestors are but spring chickens compared with these robed and stately antiques, and it will be a great and satisfying lift for me, that six hundred years will.

Mark Twain.

Chapter 1

Tell the truth or trump—but get the trick.—*Pudd'nhead Wilson's Calendar.*

The scene of this chronicle is the town of Dawson's Landing, on the Missouri side of the Mississippi, half a day's journey, per steamboat, below St. Louis.

In 1830 it was a snug little collection of modest one and two-story "frame" dwellings whose whitewashed exteriors were almost concealed from sight by climbing tangles of rose vines, honeysuckles and morning-glories. Each of these pretty homes had a garden in front fenced with white palings and opulently stocked with hollyhocks, marigolds, touch-me-nots, prince's feathers and other old-fashioned flowers; while on the window-sills of the houses stood wooden boxes containing moss-rose plants, and terra cotta pots in which grew a breed of geranium whose spread of intensely red blossoms accented the prevailing pink tint of the rose-clad house-front like an explosion of flame. When there was room on the ledge outside of the pots and boxes for a cat, the cat was there—in sunny weather—stretched at full length, asleep and blissful, with her furry belly to the sun and a paw curved over her nose. Then that home was complete, and its contentment and peace made manifest to the world by this symbol, whose testimony is infallible. A home without a cat—and a well fed, well petted, and properly revered cat—may be a perfect home, perhaps, but how can it prove title?

All along the streets, on both sides, at the outer edge of the brick sidewalks, stood locust trees, with trunks protected by wooden boxing, and these furnished shade for summer and a sweet fragrance in spring when the clusters of buds came forth. The main street, one block back from the river, and running parallel with it, was the sole business street. It was six blocks long, and in each block two or three brick stores three stories high towered above interjected bunches of little frame shops. Swinging signs creaked in the wind, the street's whole length. The candy-striped pole which indicates nobility proud and ancient, along the palace-bordered canals of Venice, indicated merely the humble barber shop along the main street of Dawson's Landing. On a chief corner stood a lofty unpainted pole wreathed from top to bottom with tin pots and pans and cups, the chief tin-monger's noisy notice to the world (when the wind blew), that his shop was on hand for business at that corner.

The hamlet's front was washed by the clear waters of the great river; its body stretched itself rearward up a gentle incline; its most rearward border fringed itself out and scattered its houses about the base line of the hills; the hills rose high, enclosing the town in a half-moon curve, clothed with forests from foot to summit.

Steamboats passed up and down every hour or so. Those belonging to the little Cairo line and the little Memphis line always stopped; the big New Orleans and Cincinnati and Louisville liners stopped for hails only, or to land passengers or freight; and this was the case also with the great flotilla of "transients." These latter came out of a dozen rivers—the Illinois, the Missouri, the Upper Mississippi, the Ohio, the Monongahela, the Tennessee, the Red river, the White river, and so on; and were bound everywhither and stocked with every imaginable comfort or necessity which the Mississippi's communities could want, from the frosty Falls of St. Anthony down through nine climates to torrid New Orleans.

Dawson's Landing was a slave-holding town, with a rich slave-worked grain and pork country back of it. The town was sleepy, and comfortable, and contented. It was fifty years old, and was growing slowly—very slowly, in fact, but still it was growing.

The chief citizen was York Leicester Driscoll, about forty years old, Judge of the county court. He was very proud of his old Virginian ancestry, and in his hospitalities and his rather formal and stately manners he kept up its traditions. He was fine, and just, and generous. To be a gentleman—a gentleman without stain or blemish—was his only religion, and to it he was always faithful. He was respected, esteemed, and beloved by all the community. He was well off, and was gradually adding to his store. He and his wife were very nearly happy, but not quite, for they had no children. The longing for the treasure of a child had grown stronger and stronger as the years slipped away, but the blessing never came—and was never to come.

With this pair lived the Judge's widowed sister, Mrs. Rachel Pratt, and she also was childless—childless, and sorrowful for that reason, and not to be comforted. The women were good and commonplace people, and did their duty and had their reward in clear consciences and the community's approbation. They were Presbyterians, the Judge was a freethinker.

Pembroke Howard, lawyer and bachelor, aged about forty, was another old Virginian grandee with proved descent from the First Families. He was a fine, brave, majestic creature, a gentleman according to the nicest requirements of the Virginian rule, a devoted Presbyterian, an authority on the "code," and a man always courteously ready to stand up before you in the field if any act or word of his had seemed doubtful or suspicious to you, and explain it with any weapon you might prefer, from brad-awls to artillery. He was very popular with the people, and was the Judge's dearest friend.

Then there was Colonel Cecil Burleigh Essex, another F.F.V. of formidable calibre—however, with him we have no concern.

Percy Northumberland Driscoll, brother to the Judge, and younger than he by five years, was a married man, and had had children around his hearthstone; but they were attacked in detail by measles, croup and scarlet fever, and this had given the doctor a chance with his effective antediluvian methods; so the cradles were empty. He was a prosperous man, with a good head for speculations, and his fortune was growing. On the first of February, 1830, two boy babes were born in his house: one to him, the other to one of his slave girls, Roxana by name. Roxana was twenty years old. She was up and around the same day, with her hands full, for she was tending both babies.

Mrs. Percy Driscoll died within the week. Roxy remained in charge of the children. She had her own way, for Mr. Driscoll soon absorbed himself in his speculations and left her to her own devices.

In that same month of February Dawson's Landing gained a new citizen. This was Mr. David Wilson, a young fellow of Scotch parentage. He had wandered to this remote region from his birth-place in the interior of the State of New York, to seek his fortune. He was twenty-five years old, college-bred, and had finished a post-college course in an eastern law school a couple of years before.

He was a homely, freckled, sandy-haired young fellow, with an intelligent blue eye that had frankness and comradeship in it and a covert twinkle of a pleasant sort. But for an unfortunate remark of his, he would no doubt have entered at once upon a successful career at Dawson's Landing. But he made his fatal remark the first day he spent in the village, and it "gauged" him. He had just made the acquaintance of a group of citizens when an invisible dog began to yelp and snarl and howl and make himself very comprehensively disagreeable; whereupon he said, much as one who is thinking aloud—

"I wish I owned half of that dog."

"Why?" somebody asked.

"Because, I would kill my half."

The group searched his face with curiosity, with anxiety even, but found no light there, no expression that they could read. They fell away from him as from something uncanny, and went into privacy to discuss him. One said—

"'Pears to be a fool."

" *'Pears*," said another, "*is*, I reckon you better say."

"Said he wished he owned *half* of the dog, the idiot," said a third. "What did he reckon would become of the other half if he killed his half? Do you reckon he thought it would live?"

"Why, he must have thought it, unless he *is* the downrightest fool in the world; because if he hadn't thought that, he would have wanted to own the whole dog, knowing that if he killed his half and the other half died, he would be responsible for that half just the same as if he had killed that half instead of his own. Don't it look that way to you, gents?"

"Yes, it does. If he owned one half of the general dog, it would be so; if he owned one end of the dog and another person owned the other end, it would be so, just the same; particularly in the first case, because if you kill one half of a general dog, there ain't any man that can tell whose half it was, but if he owned one end of the dog, maybe he could kill his end of it and—"

"No, he couldn't, either; he couldn't and not be responsible if the other end died, which it would. In my opinion the man ain't in his right mind."

"In my opinion he hain't *got* any mind."

No. 3 said—

"Well, he's a lummux, anyway."

"That's what he is," said No. 4, "he's a labrick—just a simon-pure labrick, if ever there was one."

"Yes, sir, he's a dam fool, that's the way *I* put him up," said No. 5. "Anybody can think different that wants to, but those are my sentiments."

"I'm with you, gentlemen," said No. 6. "Perfect jackass—yes, and it ain't going too far to say he is a pudd'nhead. If he ain't a pudd'nhead, I ain't no judge, that's all."

Mr. Wilson stood elected. The incident was told all over the town, and gravely discussed by everybody. Within a week he had lost his first name; Pudd'nhead took its place. In time he came to be liked, and well liked, too;

but by that time the nickname had got well stuck on, and it stayed. That first day's verdict made him a fool, and he was not able to get it set aside, or even modified. The nickname soon ceased to carry any harsh or unfriendly feeling with it, but it held its place, and was to continue to hold its place for twenty long years.

Chapter 2

Adam was but human—this explains it all. He did not want the apple for the apple's sake, he only wanted it because it was forbidden. The mistake was in not forbidding the serpent; then he would have eaten the serpent.—*Pudd'nhead Wilson's Calendar.*

Pudd'nhead Wilson had a trifle of money when he arrived, and he bought a small house on the extreme western verge of the town. Between it and Judge Driscoll's house there was only a grassy yard, with a paling fence dividing the properties in the middle. He hired a small office down in the town and hung out a tin sign with these words on it:

D<small>AVID</small> W<small>ILSON</small>
Attorney and Counselor at Law.
Surveying, Conveyancing, etc.

But his deadly remark had ruined his chance—at least in the law. No clients came. He took down his sign, after a while, and put it up on his own house with the law features knocked out of it. It offered his services now in the humble capacities of land surveyor and expert accountant. Now and then he got a job of surveying to do, and now and then a merchant got him to straighten out his books. With Scotch patience and pluck he resolved to live down his reputation and work his way into the legal field yet. Poor fellow, he could not foresee that it was going to take him such a weary long time to do it.

He had a rich abundance of idle time, but it never hung heavy on his hands, for he interested himself in every new thing that was born into the universe of ideas, and studied it and experimented upon it at his house. One of his pet fads was palmistry. To another one he gave no name, neither would he explain to anybody what its purpose was, but merely said it was an amusement. In fact he had found that his fads added to his reputation as a pudd'nhead; therefore he was growing chary of being too communicative about them. The fad without a name, was one which dealt with people's finger-marks. He carried in his coat pocket a shallow box with grooves in it, and in the grooves strips of glass five inches long and three inches wide. Along the lower edge of each strip was pasted a slip of white paper. He asked people to pass their hands through their hair, (thus collecting upon them a thin coating of the natural oil,) and then make a thumb-mark on a glass strip, following it with the mark of the ball of each finger in succession. Under this row of faint grease-prints he would write a record on the strip of white paper—thus:

"JOHN SMITH, *right hand* "—

and add the day of the month and the year, then take Smith's left hand on another glass strip, and add name and date and the words "left hand." The strips were now returned to the grooved box, and took their place among what Wilson called his "records."

He often studied his records, examining and poring over them with absorbing interest until far into the night; but what he found there—if he found anything—he revealed to no one. Sometimes he copied on paper the involved and delicate pattern left by the ball of a finger, and then vastly enlarged it with a pantagraph so that he could examine its web of curving lines with ease and convenience.

One sweltering afternoon—it was the first day of July, 1830—he was at work over a set of tangled account books in his work-room, which looked westward over a stretch of vacant lots, when a conversation outside disturbed him. It was carried on in yells, which showed that the people engaged in it were not close together:

"Say, Roxy, how does yo' baby come on?" This from the distant voice.

"Fust rate; how does *you* come on, Jasper?" This yell was from close by.

"Oh, I's middlin'; hain't got noth'n to complain of. I's gwyne to come a court'n you bimeby, Roxy."

"*You* is, you black mud-cat! Yah-yah-yah! I got sump'n better to do den 'sociat'n wid niggers as black as you is. Is ole Miss Cooper's Nancy done give you de mitten?" Roxy followed this sally with another discharge of care-free laughter.

"You's jealous, Roxy, dat's what's de matter wid *you*, you huzzy—yah-yah-yah! Dat's de time I got you!"

"Oh, yes, *you* got me, hain't you! 'Clah to goodness if dat conceit o' yo'n strikes in, Jasper, it gwyne to kill you, sho'. If you b'longed to me I'd sell you down de river 'fo' you git too fur gone. Fust time I runs acrost yo' marster, I's gwyne to tell him so."

This idle and aimless jabber went on and on, both parties enjoying the friendly duel and each well satisfied with his own share of the wit exchanged—for wit they considered it.

Wilson stepped to the window to observe the combatants; he could not work while their chatter continued. Over in the vacant lots was Jasper, young, coal-black and of magnificent build, sitting on a wheelbarrow in the pelting sun—at work, supposably, whereas he was in fact only preparing for it by taking an hour's rest before beginning. In front of Wilson's porch stood Roxy, with a local hand-made baby-wagon, in which sat her two charges—one at each end and facing each other. From Roxy's manner of speech, a stranger would have expected her to be black, but she was not. Only one-sixteenth of her was black, and that sixteenth did not show. She was of majestic form and stature, her attitudes were imposing and statuesque, and her gestures and movements distinguished by a noble and stately grace. Her complexion was very fair, with the rosy glow of vigorous health in the cheeks, her face was full of character and expression, her eyes were brown and liquid, and she had a heavy suit of fine soft hair which was also brown, but the fact was not apparent because her head was bound about with a checkered handkerchief and the hair was concealed under it. Her face was shapely, intelligent, and comely—even beautiful. She had an easy, independent carriage—when she was among her own caste—and a high and "sassy" way, withal; but of course she was meek and humble enough where white people were.

To all intents and purposes Roxy was as white as anybody, but the one-sixteenth of her which was black out-voted the other fifteen parts and made her a negro. She was a slave, and salable as such. Her child was thirty-one parts white, and he, too, was a slave, and by a fiction of law and custom a negro. He had blue eyes and flaxen curls, like his white comrade, but even the father of the white child was able to tell the children apart—little as he had commerce with them—by their clothes: for the white babe wore ruffled soft muslin and a coral necklace, while the other kid wore merely a coarse tow-linen shirt which barely reached to its knees, and no jewelry.

The white child's name was Thomas à Becket Driscoll, the other's name was Valet de Chambre: no surname—slaves hadn't the privilege. Roxana had heard that phrase somewhere, the fine sound of it had pleased her ear, and as she had supposed it was a name, she loaded it onto her darling. It soon got shortened to "Chambers," of course.

Wilson knew Roxy by sight, and when the duel of wit began to play out, he stepped outside to gather-in a record or two. Jasper went to work energetically, at once—perceiving that his leisure was observed. Wilson inspected the children and asked—

"How old are they, Roxy?"

"Bofe de same age, sir—five months. Bawn de fust o' Febuary."

"They're handsome little chaps. One's just as handsome as the other, too."

A delighted smile exposed the girl's white teeth, and she said:

"Bless yo' soul, Misto Wilson, it's pow'ful nice o' you to say dat, caze one of 'em ain't on'y a nigger. Mighty prime little nigger, *I* allays says, but dat's caze it's mine, o' course."

"How do you tell them apart, Roxy, when they haven't any clothes on?"

Roxy laughed a laugh proportioned to her size, and said:

"Oh, *I* kin tell 'em 'part, Misto Wilson, but I bet Marse Percy couldn't, not to save his life."

Wilson chatted along for a while, and presently got Roxy's finger-prints for his collection—right hand and left—on a couple of his glass strips; then labeled and dated them, and took the "records" of both children, and labeled and dated them also.

Two months later, on the third of September, he took this trio of finger-marks again. He liked to have a "series"—two or three "takings" at intervals during the period of childhood, these to be followed by others at intervals of several years.

The next day—that is to say, on the fourth of September,—something occurred which profoundly impressed Roxana. Mr. Driscoll missed another small sum of money—which is a way of saying that this was not a new thing, but had happened before. In truth it had happened three times before. Driscoll's patience was exhausted. He was a fairly humane man, toward slaves and other animals; he was an exceedingly humane man toward the erring of his own race. Theft he could not abide, and plainly there was a thief in his house. Necessarily the thief must be one of his negroes. Sharp measures must be taken. He called his servants before him. There were three of these, besides Roxy: a man, a woman, and a boy twelve years old. They were not related. Mr. Driscoll said:

"You have all been warned before. It has done no good. This time I will teach you a lesson. I will sell the thief! Which of you is the guilty one?"

They all shuddered at the threat, for here they had a good home, and a new one was likely to be a change for the worse. The denial was general. None had stolen anything—not money, anyway—a little sugar, or cake, or honey, or something like that, that "Marse Percy wouldn't mind or miss," but not money—never a cent of money. They were eloquent in their protestations, but Mr. Driscoll was not moved by them. He answered each in turn with a stern "Name the thief!"

The truth was, all were guilty but Roxana; she suspected that the others were guilty, but she did not know them to be so. She was horrified to think how near she had come to being guilty herself; she had been saved in the nick of time by a revival in the colored Methodist church a fortnight before, at which time and place she "got religion." The very next day after that gracious experience, while her change of style was fresh upon her and she was vain of her purified condition, her master left a couple of dollars lying unprotected on his desk, and she happened upon that temptation when she was polishing around with a dust-rag. She looked at the money a while with a steadily rising resentment, then she burst out with—

"Dad blame dat revival, I wisht it had a ben put off till tomorrow!"

Then she covered the tempter with a book, and another member of the kitchen cabinet got it. She made this sacrifice as a matter of religious etiquette; as a thing necessary just now, but by no means to be wrested into a precedent; no, a week or two would limber up her piety, then she would be rational again, and the next two dollars that got left out in the cold would find a comforter—and she could name the comforter.

Was she bad? Was she worse than the general run of her race? No. They had an unfair show in the battle of life, and they held it no sin to take military advantage of the enemy—in a small way; in a small way, but not in a large one. They would smouch provisions from the pantry whenever they got a chance; or a brass thimble, or a cake of wax, or an emery-bag, or a paper of needles, or a silver spoon, or a dollar bill, or small articles of clothing, or any other property of light value; and so far were they from considering such reprisals sinful, that they would go to church and shout and pray their loudest and sincerest with their plunder in their pockets. A farm smoke-house had to be kept heavily padlocked, for even the colored deacon himself could not resist a ham when Providence showed him in a dream, or otherwise, where such a thing hung lonesome and longed for some one to love. But with a hundred hanging before him the deacon would not take two—that is, on the same night. On frosty nights the humane negro prowler would warm the end of a plank and put it up under the cold claws of chickens roosting in a tree; a drowsy hen would step onto the comfortable board, softly clucking her gratitude, and the prowler would dump her into his bag, and later into his stomach, perfectly sure that in taking this trifle from the man who daily robbed him of an inestimable treasure—his liberty—he was not committing any sin that God would remember against him in the Last Great Day.

"Name the thief!"

For the fourth time Mr. Driscoll had said it, and always in the same hard tone. And now he added these words of awful import:

"I give you one minute"—he took out his watch—"if at the end of that time you have not confessed, I will not only sell all four of you, *but*—I will sell you *down the river!*"

It was equivalent to condemning them to hell! No Missouri negro doubted this. Roxy reeled in her tracks and the color vanished out of her face; the others dropped to their knees as if they had been shot; tears gushed from their eyes, their supplicating hands went up, and three answers came in the one instant:

"I done it!"

"I done it!"

"I done it—have mercy, marster—Lord have mercy on us po' niggers!"

"Very good," said the master, putting up his watch, "I will sell you here, though you don't deserve it. You ought to be sold down the river."

The culprits flung themselves prone, in an ecstasy of gratitude, and kissed his feet, declaring they would never forget his goodness and never cease to pray for him as long as they lived. They were sincere, for like a god he had stretched forth his mighty hand and closed the gates of hell against them. He knew, himself, that he had done a noble and gracious thing, and he was privately well pleased with his magnanimity; and that night he set the incident down in his diary, so that his son might read it in after years and be thereby moved to deeds of gentleness and humanity himself.

Chapter 3

Whoever has lived long enough to find out what life is, knows how deep a debt of gratitude we owe to Adam, the first great benefactor of our race. He brought death into the world.
—*Pudd'nhead Wilson's Calendar.*

Percy Driscoll slept well the night he saved his house-minions from going down the river, but no wink of sleep visited Roxy's eyes. A profound terror had taken possession of her. Her child could grow up and be sold down the river! The thought crazed her with horror. If she dozed, and lost herself for a moment, the next moment she was on her feet and flying to her child's cradle to see if it was still there. Then she would gather it to her heart and pour out her love upon it in a frenzy of kisses, moaning and crying, and saying "Dey shan't, oh, dey *shan't!*—yo' po' mammy will kill you fust!"

Once, when she was tucking it back in its cradle again, the other child nestled in its sleep and attracted her attention. She went and stood over it a long time, communing with herself:

"What has my po' baby done, dat he couldn't have yo' luck? He hain't done noth'n. God was good to you; why warn't He good to him? Dey can't sell you down de river. I hates yo' pappy; he ain't got no heart—for niggers he hain't, anyways. I hates him, en I could kill him!" She paused a while, thinking; then she burst into wild sobbings again, and turned away, saying, "Oh, I got to kill my chile, dey ain't no yuther way!—killin' *him* wouldn't save de chile fum goin' down de river. Oh, I got to do it, yo' po' mammy's *got* to kill you to save you, honey"—she gathered her baby to her bosom, now, and began to smother it with caresses—"mammy's got to kill you,—how *kin* I do it! But yo' mammy ain't gwyne to desert you!—no, no; *dah*, don't cry—she gwyne *wid* you, she gwyne to kill herself, too. Come along, honey, come along wid mammy; we gwyne to jump in de river, den de troubles o' dis worl' is all over—dey don't sell po' niggers down de river over *yonder!*"

She started toward the door, crooning to the child and hushing it; midway she stopped, suddenly. She caught sight of her new Sunday gown—a cheap curtain-calico thing, a conflagration of gaudy colors and fantastic figures. She surveyed it wistfully, longingly.

"Hain't ever wore it yit," she said, "en it's jist lovely . . . ." Then she nodded her head in response to a pleasant idea, and added, "No, I ain't gwyne to be fished out, wid everybody lookin' at me, in dis misable ole linsey-woolsey."

She put down the child and made the change. She looked in the glass and was astonished at her beauty. She resolved to make her death-toilet perfect. She took off her handkerchief-turban and dressed her glossy wealth of hair "like white folks;" she added some odds and ends of rather lurid ribbon and a spray of atrocious artificial flowers; finally, she threw over her shoulders a fluffy thing called a "cloud" in that day, which was of a blazing red complexion. Then she was ready for the tomb.

She gathered up her baby once more; but when her eye fell upon its miserably short little gray tow-linen shirt and noted the contrast between its pauper shabbiness and her own volcanic irruption of infernal splendors, her mother-heart was touched, and she was ashamed.

"No, dolling, mammy ain't gwyne to treat you so. De angels is gwyne to 'mire you jist as much as dey does yo' mammy. Ain't gwyne to have 'em putt'n dey han's up 'fo' dey eyes en sayin' to David en Goliah en dem yuther prophets, Dat chile is dress' too indelicate fo' dis place."

By this time she had stripped off the shirt. Now she clothed the naked little creature in one of Thomas à Becket's snowy long baby-gowns, with its bright blue bows and dainty flummery of ruffles.

"Dah—now you's fixed." She propped the child in a chair and stood off to inspect it. Straightway her eyes began to widen with astonishment and admiration, and she clapped her hands and cried out, "Why, it do beat all— I *never* knowed you was so lovely! Marse Tommy ain't a bit puttier—not a single bit!"

She stepped over and glanced at the other infant; she flung a glance back at her own; then one more at the heir of the house. Now a strange light dawned in her eyes, and in a moment she was lost in thought. She seemed in a trance; when she came out of it she muttered, "When I 'uz a washin' 'em in de tub, yistiddy, his own pappy asked me which of 'em was his'n!"

She began to move about like one in a dream. She undressed Thomas à Becket, stripping him of everything, and put the tow-linen shirt on him. She put his coral necklace on her own child's neck. Then she placed the children side by side, and after earnest inspection she muttered—

"Now who would b'lieve clo'es could do de like o' dat? Dog my cats if it ain't all *I* kin do to tell t'other fum which, let alone his pappy."

She put her cub in Tommy's elegant cradle and said—

"You's young Marse *Tom* fum dis out, en I got to practice and git used to 'memberin' to call you dat, honey, or I's gwyne to make a mistake some time en git us bofe into trouble. Dah—now you lay still en don't fret no mo', Marse Tom—oh, thank de good Lord in heaven, you's saved, you's saved!—dey ain't no man kin ever sell mammy's po' little honey down de river now!"

She put the heir of the house in her own child's unpainted pine cradle, and said, contemplating its slumbering form uneasily—

"I's sorry for you, honey; I's sorry, God knows I is!—but what *kin* I do, what *could* I do? Yo' pappy would sell him to somebody, some time, en den he'd go down de river, sho', en I couldn't, couldn't, *couldn't* stan' it!"

She flung herself on her bed, and began to think and toss, toss and think. By and by she sat suddenly upright, for a comforting thought had flown through her worried mind—

"'Tain't no sin—*white* folks has done it! It ain't no sin, glory to goodness it ain't no sin! *Dey's* done it—yes, en dey was de biggest quality in de whole bilin', too—*kings!*"

She began to muse; she was trying to gather out of her memory the dim particulars of some tale she had heard some time or other. At last she said—

"Now I's got it; now I 'member. It was dat ole nigger preacher dat tole it, de time he come over here fum Illinois en preached in de nigger church. He said dey ain't nobody kin save his own self—can't do it by faith, can't do it by works, can't do it no way at all. Free grace is de *on'y* way, en dat don't come fum nobody but jis' de Lord; en *He* kin give it to anybody He please, saint or sinner—*He* don't k'yer. He do jis' as He's a mineter. He s'lect out anybody dat suit Him, en put another one in his place, en make de fust one happy forever en leave t'other one to burn wid Satan. De preacher said it was jist like dey done in Englan' one time, long time ago. De queen she lef' her baby layin' aroun' one day, en went out callin'; en one o' de niggers roun' 'bout de place dat was mos' white, she come in en see de chile layin' aroun', en tuck en put her own chile's clo'es on de queen's chile, en put de queen's chile's clo'es on her own chile, en den lef' her own chile layin' aroun' en tuck en toted de queen's chile home to de nigger quarter, en nobody ever foun' it out, en her chile was de king, bimeby, en sole de queen's chile down de river one time when dey had to settle up de estate. Dah, now—de preacher said it his own self, en it ain't no sin, caze white folks done it. *Dey* done it—yes, *dey* done it; en not on'y jis' common white folks, nuther, but de biggest quality dey is in de whole bilin'! Oh, I's *so* glad I 'member 'bout dat!"

She got up light-hearted and happy, and went to the cradles and spent what was left of the night "practicing." She would give her own child a light pat and say, humbly, "Lay still, Marse Tom," then give the real Tom a pat and say with severity, "Lay *still*, Chambers!—does you want me to take sump'n *to* you?"

As she progressed with her practice, she was surprised to see how steadily and surely the awe which had kept her tongue reverent and her manner humble toward her young master was transferring itself to her speech and manner toward the usurper, and how similarly handy she was becoming in transferring her motherly curtness of speech and peremptoriness of manner to the unlucky heir of the ancient house of Driscoll.

She took occasional rests from practicing, and absorbed herself in calculating her chances.

"Dey'll sell dese niggers to-day fo' stealin' de money, den dey'll buy some mo' dat don't know de chillen—so *dat's* all right. When I takes de chillen out to git de air, de minute I's roun' de corner I's gwyne to gaum dey mouths all roun' wid jam, den dey can't *nobody* notice dey's changed. Yes, I gwineter do dat till I's safe, if it's a year.

"Dey ain't but one man dat I's afeard of, en dat's dat Pudd'nhead Wilson. Dey calls him a pudd'nhead, en says he's a fool. My lan', dat man ain't no mo' fool den I is! He's de smartes' man in dis town, less'n it's Jedge Driscoll, or maybe Pem. Howard. Blame dat man, he worries me wid dem ornery glasses o' his'n; *I* b'lieve he's a witch. But nemmine, I's gwyne to happen aroun' dah one o' dese days en let on dat I reckon he wants to print de chillen's fingers agin; en if *he* don't notice dey's changed, I boun' dey ain't nobody gwyne to notice it, en den I's safe, *sho'*. But I reckon I'll tote along a hoss-shoe to keep off de witch-work."

The new negroes gave Roxy no trouble, of course. The master gave her none, for one of his speculations was in jeopardy, and his mind was so occupied that he hardly saw the children when he looked at them, and all Roxy had to do was to get them both into a gale of laughter when he came about; then their faces were mainly cavities exposing gums, and he was gone again before the spasm passed and the little creatures resumed a human aspect.

Within a few days the fate of the speculation became so dubious that Mr. Percy went away with his brother the Judge to see what could be done with it. It was a land speculation, as usual, and it had gotten complicated with a lawsuit. The men were gone seven weeks. Before they got back Roxy had paid her visit to Wilson, and was satisfied. Wilson took the finger-prints, labeled them with the names and with the date—October the first—put them carefully away, and continued his chat with Roxy, who seemed very anxious that he should admire the great advance in flesh and beauty which the babies had made since he took their finger-prints a month before. He complimented their improvement to her contentment; and as they were without any disguise of jam or other stain, she trembled all the while and was miserably frightened lest at any moment he—

But he didn't. He discovered nothing; and she went home jubilant, and dropped all concern about this matter permanently out of her mind.

Chapter 4

Adam and Eve had many advantages, but the principal one was, that they escaped teething.—*Pudd'nhead Wilson's Calendar.*

There is this trouble about special providences, that there is so often a doubt as to which party was intended to be the beneficiary. In the case of the children, the bears and the prophet, the bears got more real satisfaction out of the episode than the prophet did, because they got the children.—*Pudd'nhead Wilson's Calendar.*

This history must henceforth accommodate itself to the change which Roxana has consummated, and call the real heir "Chambers" and the usurping little slave "Thomas à Becket"—shortening this latter name to "Tom," for daily use, as the people about him did.

"Tom" was a bad baby, from the very beginning of his usurpation. He would cry for nothing; he would burst into storms of devilish temper without notice, and let go scream after scream and squall after squall, then climax the thing with "holding his breath"—that frightful specialty of the teething nursling, in the throes of which the creature exhausts its lungs, then is convulsed with noiseless squirmings and twistings and kickings in the effort to get its breath, while the lips turn blue and the mouth stands wide and rigid, offering for inspection one wee tooth set in the lower rim of a hoop of red gums; and when the appalling stillness has endured until one is sure the lost breath will never return, a nurse comes flying and dashes water in the child's face, and—presto! the lungs fill, and instantly discharge a shriek, or a yell, or a howl which bursts the listening ear and surprises the owner of it into saying words which would not go well with a halo if he had one. The baby Tom would claw anybody who came within reach of his nails, and pound anybody he could reach with his rattle. He would scream for water until he got it, and then throw cup and all on the floor and scream for more. He was indulged in all his caprices, howsoever troublesome and exasperating they might be; he

ROXY AND THE CHILDREN.

was allowed to eat anything he wanted, particularly things that would give him the stomach ache; consequently he was hiccuppy beyond reason and a singularly flatulent child.

When he got to be old enough to begin to toddle about, and say broken words, and get an idea of what his hands were for, he was a more consummate pest than ever. Roxy got no rest while he was awake. He would call for anything and everything he saw, simply saying "Awnt it" (want it), which was a command. When it was brought, he said, in a frenzy, and motioning it away with his hands, "Don't awnt it! don't awnt it!" and the moment it was gone he set up frantic yells of "Awnt it! awnt it! awnt it!" and Roxy had to give wings to her heels to get that thing back to him again before he could get time to carry out his intention of going into convulsions about it.

What he preferred above all other things was the tongs. This was because his "father" had forbidden him to have them lest he break windows and furniture with them. The moment Roxy's back was turned he would toddle to the presence of the tongs and say, "*Like* it!" and cock his eye to one side to see if Roxy was observing; then, "*Awnt* it!" and cock his eye again; then, "*Hab* it!" with another furtive glance; and finally, "*Take* it!"—and the prize was his. The next moment the heavy implement was raised aloft; the next, there was a crash and a squall, and the cat was off, on three legs, to meet an engagement; Roxy would arrive just as the lamp or a window went to irremediable smash.

Tom got all the petting, Chambers got none. Tom got all the delicacies going, Chambers got mush and milk, and clabber without sugar. By consequence, Tom was a sickly child and Chambers wasn't. Tom was "fractious," as Roxy called it, and overbearing, Chambers was meek and docile.

With all her splendid common sense and practical every-day ability, Roxy was a doting fool of a mother. She was this toward her child—and she was also more than this: by the fiction created by herself, he was become her master; the necessity of recognizing this relation outwardly and of perfecting herself in the forms required to express the recognition, had moved her to such diligence and faithfulness in practicing these forms that this exercise soon concreted itself into habit; it became automatic and unconscious; then a natural result followed: deceptions intended solely for others gradually grew practically into self-deceptions as well; the mock reverence became real reverence, the mock obsequiousness real obsequiousness, the mock homage real homage; the little counterfeit rift of separation between imitation-slave and imitation-master widened and widened, and became an abyss, and a very real one—and on one side of it stood Roxy, the dupe of her own deceptions, and on the other stood her child, no longer a usurper to her, but her accepted and recognized master.

He was her darling, her master, and her deity, all in one, and in her worship of him she forgot who she was and what he had been.

In babyhood Tom cuffed and banged and scratched Chambers unrebuked, and Chambers early learned that as between meekly bearing it and resenting it the advantage all lay with the former policy. The few times that his persecutions had moved him beyond control and made him fight back had cost him very dear at headquarters; not at the hands of Roxy, for if she ever went beyond scolding him sharply for "fogitt'n who his young marster was," she at least never extended her punishment beyond a box on the ear. No, Percy Driscoll was the party. He told Chambers that under no provocation whatever was he privileged to lift his hand against his little master. Chambers overstepped the line three times, and got three such convincing canings from the man who was his father and didn't know it, that he took Tom's cruelties in all humility after that, and made no more experiments.

Outside of the house the two boys were together, all through their boyhood. Chambers was strong beyond his years, and a good fighter; strong because he was coarsely fed and hard worked about the house, and a good fighter because Tom furnished him plenty of practice—on white boys whom he hated and was afraid of. Chambers was his constant body-guard, to and from school; he was present on the play-ground at recess to protect his charge. He fought himself into such a formidable reputation, by and by, that Tom could have changed clothes with him, and "ridden in peace," like Sir Kay in Launcelot's armor.

He was good at games of skill, too. Tom staked him with marbles to play "keeps" with, and then took all the winnings away from him. In the winter season Chambers was on hand, in Tom's worn-out clothes, with "holy" red mittens, and "holy" shoes, and pants "holy" at the knees and seat, to drag a sled up the hill for Tom, warmly clad, to ride down on; but he never got a ride himself. He built snow men and snow fortifications under Tom's direction. He was Tom's patient target when Tom wanted to do some snow-balling, but the target couldn't fire back. Chambers carried Tom's skates to the river and strapped them on him, then trotted around after him on the ice, so as to be on hand when wanted; but he wasn't ever asked to try the skates himself.

In summer the pet pastime of the boys of Dawson's Landing was to steal apples, peaches and melons from the farmers' fruit wagons,—mainly on account of the risk they ran of getting their heads laid open with the butt of the farmer's whip. Tom was a distinguished adept at these thefts—by proxy. Chambers did his stealing, and got the peach stones, apple cores and melon rinds for his share.

Tom always made Chambers go in swimming with him, and stay by him as a protection. When Tom had had enough, he would slip out and tie knots in Chambers's shirt, dip the knots in the water to make them hard to undo, then dress himself and sit by and laugh while the naked shiverer tugged at the stubborn knots with his teeth.

Tom did his humble comrade these various ill turns partly out of native viciousness, and partly because he hated him for his superiorities of physique and pluck, and for his manifold clevernesses. Tom couldn't dive, for it gave him splitting headaches. Chambers could dive without inconvenience, and was fond of doing it. He excited so much admiration, one day, among a crowd of white boys, by throwing back-summersaults from the stern of a canoe that it wearied Tom's spirit, and at last he shoved the canoe underneath Chambers while he was in the air—so he came down on his head in the canoe-bottom; and while he lay unconscious several of Tom's ancient adversaries saw that their long-desired opportunity was come, and they gave the false heir such a drubbing that with Chambers's best help he was hardly able to drag himself home afterward.

When the boys were fifteen and upwards, Tom was "showing off" in the river one day, when he was taken with a cramp, and shouted for help. It was a common trick with the boys—particularly if a stranger was present—to pretend a cramp and howl for help; then when the stranger came tearing hand-over-hand to the rescue, the howler would go on struggling and howling till he was close at hand, then replace the howl with a sarcastic smile and swim blandly away, while the town-boys assailed the dupe with a volley of jeers and laughter. Tom had never tried this joke as yet, but was supposed to be trying it now, so the boys held warily back; but Chambers believed his master was in earnest, therefore he swam out and arrived in time, unfortunately, and saved his life.

This was the last feather. Tom had managed to endure everything else, but to have to remain publicly and permanently under such an obligation as this to a nigger, and to *this* nigger of all niggers—this was too much. He heaped insults upon Chambers for "pretending" to think he was in earnest in calling for help, and said that anybody but a blockheaded nigger would have known he was funning and left him alone.

Tom's enemies were in strong force here, so they came out with their opinions quite freely. They laughed at him, and called him coward, liar, sneak, and other sorts of pet names, and told him they meant to call Chambers by a new name after this, and make it common in the town—"Tom Driscoll's Nigger-pappy"—to signify that he had had a second birth into this life, and that Chambers was the author of his new being. Tom grew frantic under these taunts, and shouted—

"Knock their heads off, Chambers, knock their heads off!—what do you stand there with your hands in your pockets, for?"

Chambers expostulated, and said—

"But Marse Tom, dey's too many of 'em—dey's—"

"Do you *hear* me?"

"Please, Marse Tom, don't make me. Dey's so many of 'em dat—"

Tom sprang at him and drove his pocket knife into him two or three times before the boys could snatch him away and give the wounded lad a chance to escape. He was considerably hurt, but not seriously. If the blade had been a little longer his career would have ended there.

Tom had long ago taught Roxy "her place." It had been many a day, now, since she had ventured a caress or a fondling epithet in his quarter. Such things, from a "nigger," were repulsive to him, and she had been warned to keep her distance and remember who she was. She saw her darling gradually cease from being her son, she saw that detail perish utterly; all that was left was master—master, pure and simple, and it was not a gentle mastership, either. She saw herself sink from the sublime height of motherhood to the sombre deeps of unmodified slavery. The abyss of separation between her and her boy was complete. She was merely his chattel, now, his convenience, his dog, his cringing and helpless slave, the humble and unresisting victim of his capricious temper and vicious nature.

Sometimes she could not go to sleep, even when worn out with fatigue, because her rage boiled so high over the day's experiences with her boy. She would mumble and mutter to herself—

"He struck me, en I warn't no way to blame—struck me in de face, right before folks. En he's allays callin' me nigger wench, en hussy, en all dem mean names, when I's doin' de very bes' I kin. O, Lord, I done so much for him—I lift' him away up to whar he is—en dis is what I git for it!"

Sometimes when some outrage of peculiar offensiveness stung her to the heart, she would plan schemes of vengeance, and revel in the fancied spectacle of his exposure to the world as an impostor and a slave; but in the midst of these joys fear would strike her: she had made him too strong; she could prove nothing, and—heavens, she might get sold down the river for her pains! So her schemes always went for nothing, and she laid them aside in impotent rage against the fates, and against herself for playing the fool on that fatal September day in not providing herself with a witness for use in the day when such a thing might be needed for the appeasing of her vengeance-hungry heart.

And yet the moment Tom happened to be good to her, and kind—and this occurred every now and then—all her sore places were healed and she was happy; happy and proud, for this was her son, her nigger son, lording it among the whites and securely avenging their crimes against her race.

There were two grand funerals in Dawson's Landing that fall—the fall of 1845. One was Colonel Cecil Burleigh Essex's, the other was Percy Driscoll's.

On his death-bed Driscoll set Roxy free and delivered his idolized ostensible son solemnly into the keeping of his brother the Judge and his wife. Those childless people were glad to get him. Childless people are not difficult to please.

Judge Driscoll had gone privately to his brother, a month before, and bought Chambers. He had heard that Tom had been trying to get his father to sell the boy down the river, and he wanted to prevent the scandal—for public sentiment did not approve of that way of treating family servants for light cause or for no cause.

Percy Driscoll had worn himself out in trying to save his great speculative landed estate, and had died without succeeding. He was hardly in his grave before the boom collapsed and left his hitherto envied young devil of an heir a pauper. But that was nothing; his uncle told him he should be his heir and have all his fortune when he died; so Tom was comforted.

Roxy had no home, now; so she resolved to go around and say good-bye to her friends and then clear out and see the world—that is to say, she would go chambermaiding on a steamboat, the darling ambition of her race and sex.

Her last call was on the black giant, Jasper. She found him chopping Pudd'nhead Wilson's winter provision of wood.

Wilson was chatting with him when Roxy arrived. He asked her how she could bear to go off chambermaiding and leave her boys; and chaffingly offered to copy off a series of their finger-prints, reaching down to their twelfth year, for her to remember them by; but she sobered in a moment, wondering if he suspected anything; then she said she believed she didn't want them. Wilson said to himself, "The drop of black blood in her is superstitious; she thinks there's some deviltry, some witch-business, about my glass mystery somewhere; she used to come here with an old horseshoe in her hand; it could have been an accident, but I doubt it."

Chapter 5

Training is everything. The peach was once a bitter almond, cauliflower is nothing but cabbage with a college education.
—*Pudd'nhead Wilson's Calendar.*

Remark of Dr. Baldwin concerning upstarts: We don't care to eat toadstools that think they are truffles.—*Pudd'nhead Wilson's Calendar.*

Mrs. York Driscoll enjoyed two years of bliss with that prize, Tom; bliss that was troubled a little at times, it is true, but bliss nevertheless; then she died, and her husband and his childless sister, Mrs. Pratt, continued the bliss-business at the old stand. Tom was petted and indulged and spoiled to his entire content—or nearly that. This went on till he was nineteen, then he was sent to Yale. He went handsomely equipped with "conditions," but otherwise he was not an object of distinction there. He remained at Yale two years, and then threw up the struggle. He came home with his manners a good deal improved; he had lost his surliness and brusqueness, and was rather pleasantly soft and smooth, now; he was furtively, and sometimes openly, ironical of speech, and given to gently touching people on the raw, but he did it with a good-natured semi-conscious air that carried it off safely and kept him from getting into trouble. He was as indolent as ever, and showed no very strenuous desire to hunt up an occupation. People argued from this that he preferred to be supported by his uncle until his uncle's shoes should become vacant. He brought back one or two new habits with him, one of which he rather openly practiced—tippling—but concealed another, which was gambling. It would not do to gamble where his uncle could hear of it; he knew that quite well.

Tom's eastern polish was not popular among the young people. They could have endured it, perhaps, if Tom had stopped there; but he wore gloves, and that they *couldn't* stand, and wouldn't; so he was mainly without society. He brought home with him a suit of clothes of such exquisite style and cut and fashion—eastern fashion, city fashion—that it filled everybody with anguish and was regarded as a peculiarly wanton affront. He enjoyed the feeling which he was exciting, and paraded the town serene and happy all day; but the young fellows set a tailor to work that night, and when Tom started out on his parade next morning he found the old deformed negro bell-ringer straddling along in his wake tricked out in a flamboyant curtain-calico exaggeration of his finery, and imitating his fancy eastern graces as well as he could.

Tom surrendered, and after that clothed himself in the local fashion. But the dull country town was tiresome to him, since his acquaintanceship with livelier regions, and it grew daily more and more so. He began to make little trips to St. Louis for refreshment. There he found companionship to suit him, and pleasures to his taste, along with more freedom, in some particulars, than he could have at home. So, during the next two years his visits to the city grew in frequency and his tarryings there grew steadily longer in duration.

He was getting into deep waters. He was taking chances, privately, which might get him into trouble some day—in fact, did.

Judge Driscoll had retired from the Bench and from all business activities in 1850, and had now been comfortably idle three years. He was President of the Freethinkers' Society, and Pudd'nhead Wilson was the other member. The Society's weekly discussions were the old lawyer's main interest in life, now. Pudd'nhead was still toiling in obscurity at the bottom of the ladder, under the blight of that unlucky remark which he had let fall twenty-three years before.

Judge Driscoll was his friend, and claimed that he had a mind above the average, but that was regarded as one of the Judge's whims, and it failed to modify the public opinion. Or, rather, that was one of the reasons why it failed, but there was another and better one. If the Judge had stopped with bare assertion, it would have had a good deal of effect; but he made the mistake of trying to prove his position. For some years Wilson had been privately at work on a whimsical almanac, for his amusement—a calendar, with a little dab of ostensible philosophy, usually in ironical form, appended to each date; and the Judge thought that these quips and fancies of Wilson's were neatly turned and cute; so he carried a handful of them around, one day, and read them to some of the chief citizens. But irony was not for those people; their mental vision was not focussed for it. They read those playful trifles in the solidest earnest, and decided without hesitancy that if there had ever been any doubt that Dave Wilson was a pudd'nhead—which there hadn't—this revelation removed that doubt for good and all. That is just the way, in this world;

an enemy can partly ruin a man, but it takes a good-natured injudicious friend to complete the thing and make it perfect. After this the Judge felt tenderer than ever toward Wilson, and surer than ever that his calendar had merit.

Judge Driscoll could be a freethinker and still hold his place in society because he was the person of most consequence in the community, and therefore could venture to go his own way and follow out his own notions. The other member of his pet organization was allowed the like liberty because he was a cipher in the estimation of the public, and nobody attached any importance to what he thought or did. He was liked, he was welcome enough all around, but he simply didn't count for anything.

The widow Cooper—affectionately called "Aunt Patsy" by everybody—lived in a snug and comely cottage with her daughter Rowena, who was nineteen, romantic, amiable, and very pretty, but otherwise of no consequence. Rowena had a couple of young brothers—also of no consequence.

The widow had a large spare room which she let to a lodger, with board, when she could find one, but this room had been empty for a year now, to her sorrow. Her income was only sufficient for the family support, and she needed the lodging-money for trifling luxuries. But now, at last, on a flaming June day, she found herself happy; her tedious long wait was ended; her year-worn advertisement had been answered; and not by a village applicant, oh, no—this letter was from away off yonder in the dim great world to the North: it was from St. Louis! She sat on her porch gazing out with unseeing eyes upon the shining reaches of the mighty Mississippi, her thoughts steeped in her good fortune. Indeed it was especially good fortune, for she was to have two lodgers instead of one.

She had read the letter to the family, and Rowena had danced away to see to the cleaning and airing of the room by the slave woman Nancy, and the boys had rushed abroad in the town to spread the great news, for it was matter of public interest, and the public would wonder and not be pleased if not informed. Presently Rowena returned, all aflush with joyous excitement, and begged for a re-reading of the letter. It was framed thus:

> Honored Madam—My brother and I have seen your advertisement, by chance, and beg leave to take the room you offer. We are twenty-four years of age, and twins. We are Italians by birth, but have lived long in the various countries of Europe, and several years in the United States. Our names are Luigi and Angelo Cappello. You desire but one guest, but dear madam, if you will allow us to pay for two we will not discommode you. We shall be down Thursday.

"Italians! How romantic! Just think, ma—there's never been one in this town, and everybody will be dying to see them, and they're all *ours!* Think of that!"

"Yes, I reckon they'll make a grand stir."

"Oh, indeed they will. The whole town will be on its head! Think—they've been in Europe and everywhere! There's never been a traveler in this town before. Ma, I shouldn't wonder if they've seen kings!"

"Well, a body can't tell; but they'll make stir enough, without that."

"Yes, that's of course. Luigi—Angelo. They're lovely names; and so grand and foreign—not like Jones and Robinson and such. Thursday they are coming, and this is only Tuesday; it's a cruel long time to wait. Here comes Judge Driscoll in at the gate. He's heard about it. I'll go and open the door."

The Judge was full of congratulations and curiosity. The letter was read and discussed. Soon Justice Robinson arrived with more congratulations, and there was a new reading and a new discussion. This was the beginning. Neighbor after neighbor, of both sexes, followed, and the procession drifted in and out all day and evening and all Wednesday and Thursday. The letter was read and re-read until it was nearly worn out; everybody admired its courtly and gracious tone, and smooth and practiced style, everybody was sympathetic and excited, and the Coopers were steeped in happiness all the while.

The boats were very uncertain, in low water, in those primitive times. This time the Thursday boat had not arrived at ten at night—so the people had waited at the landing all day for nothing; they were driven to their homes by a heavy storm without having had a view of the illustrious foreigners.

Eleven o'clock came; then twelve, and the Cooper house was the only one in the town that still had lights burning. The rain and thunder were booming yet, and the anxious family were still waiting, still hoping. At last there was a knock on the door and the family jumped to open it. Two negro men entered, each carrying a trunk, and proceeded up stairs toward the guest room. Then entered the Twins—the handsomest, the best dressed, the most distinguished-looking pair of young fellows the West had ever seen. One was a little fairer than the other, but otherwise they were exact duplicates.

Chapter 6

Let us endeavor to so live that when we come to die even the undertaker will be sorry.—*Pudd'nhead Wilson's Calendar.*

Habit is habit, and not to be flung out of the window by any man, but coaxed down stairs a step at a time.—*Pudd'nhead Wilson's Calendar.*

At breakfast in the morning the Twins' charm of manner and easy and polished bearing made speedy conquest of the family's good graces. All constraint and formality quickly disappeared, and the friendliest feeling succeeded. Aunt Patsy called them by their Christian names almost from the beginning. She was full of the keenest curiosity about them, and showed it; they responded by talking about themselves, which pleased her greatly. It presently appeared that in their early youth they had known poverty and hardship. As the talk wandered along the old lady watched for the right place to drop in a question or two concerning that matter, and when she found it she said to the blonde twin, who was now doing the biographies in his turn while the brunette one rested—

"If it ain't asking what I oughtn't to ask, Mr. Angelo, how did you come to be so friendless and in such trouble when you were little? Do you mind telling? But don't, if you do."

"Oh, we don't mind it at all, madam; in our case it was merely misfortune, and nobody's fault. Our parents were well-to-do, there in Italy, and we were their only child. We were of the old Florentine nobility"—Rowena's heart gave a great bound, her nostrils expanded, and a fine light played in her eyes—"and when the war broke out my father was on the losing side and had to fly for his life. His estates were confiscated, his personal property seized, and there we were, in Germany, strangers, friendless, and in fact paupers. My brother and I were ten years old, and well educated for that age, very studious, very fond of our books, and well grounded in the German, French, Spanish and English languages. Also, we were marvelous musical prodigies—if you will allow me to say it, it being only the truth.

"Our father survived his misfortunes only a month, our mother soon followed him, and we were alone in the world. Our parents could have made themselves comfortable by exhibiting us as a show, and they had many and large offers; but the thought revolted their pride, and they said they would starve and die first. But what they wouldn't consent to do we had to do without the formality of consent. We were seized for the debts occasioned by their illness and their funerals, and placed among the attractions of a cheap museum in Berlin to earn the liquidation money. It took us two years to get out of that slavery. We traveled all about Germany, receiving no wages, and not even our keep. We had to exhibit for nothing, and beg our bread.

"Well, madam, the rest is not of much consequence. When we escaped from that slavery at twelve years of age, we were in some respects men. Experience had taught us some valuable things; among others, how to take care of ourselves, how to avoid and defeat sharks and sharpers, and how to conduct our own business for our own profit and without other people's help. We traveled everywhere—years and years—picking up smatterings of strange tongues, familiarizing ourselves with strange sights and strange customs, accumulating an education of a wide and varied and curious sort. It was a pleasant life. We went to Venice—to London, Paris, Russia, India, China, Japan—"

At this point Nancy the slave woman thrust her head in at the door and exclaimed:

"Ole Missus, de house is plum jam full o' people, en dey's jes' a spilin' to see de gen'lmen!" She indicated the Twins with a nod of her head, and tucked it back out of sight again.

It was a proud occasion for the widow, and she promised herself high satisfaction in showing off her fine foreign birds before her neighbors and friends—simple folk who had hardly ever seen a foreigner of any kind, and never one of any distinction or style. Yet her feeling was moderate indeed, when contrasted with Rowena's. Rowena was in the clouds, she walked on air; this was to be the greatest day, the most romantic episode in the colorless history of that dull country town. She was to be familiarly near the source of its glory and feel the full flood of it pour over her and about her, the other girls could only gaze and envy, not partake.

The widow was ready, Rowena was ready, so also were the foreigners.

The party moved along the hall, the Twins in advance, and entered the open parlor door, whence issued a low hum of conversation. The Twins took a position near the door, the widow stood at Luigi's side, Rowena stood beside Angelo, and the march-past and the introductions began. The widow was all smiles and contentment. She received the procession and passed it on to Rowena.

"Good-mornin' Sister Cooper"—handshake.

"Good-morning, Brother Higgins—Count Luigi Cappello, Mr. Higgins"—handshake, followed by a devouring stare and "I'm glad to see ye," on the part of Higgins, and a courteous inclination of the head and a pleasant "Most happy!" on the part of Count Luigi.

"Good-mornin', Roweny"—handshake.

"Good-morning, Mr. Higgins—present you to Count Angelo Cappello."

Handshake, admiring stare, "Glad to see ye!"—courteous nod, smily "Most happy!" and Higgins passes on.

None of these visitors were at ease, but being honest people, they didn't pretend to be. None of them had ever seen a person bearing a title of nobility before, and none had been expecting to see one now, consequently the title came upon them as a kind of pile-driving surprise and caught them unprepared. A few tried to rise to the emergency, and got out an awkward My Lord, or Your Lordship, or something of the sort, but the great majority were knocked cold by the unaccustomed word and its dim and awful associations with gilded courts and stately ceremony and anointed kingship, so they only fumbled through the handshake, and passed on, speechless. Now and then, as happens at all receptions, everywhere, a more than ordinarily friendly soul blocked the procession and kept it waiting while he inquired how the brothers liked the village, and how long they were going to stay, and if their families were well, and dragged in the weather, and hoped it would get cooler soon, and all that sort of thing, so as to be able to say, when they got home, "I had quite a long talk with them;" but nobody did or said anything of a regretable kind, and so the great affair went through to the end in a creditable and satisfactory fashion.

General conversation followed, and the Twins drifted about from group to group, talking easily and fluently, and winning approval, compelling admiration, and achieving popularity right along. The widow followed their conquering march with a proud eye, and every now and then Rowena said to herself with deep satisfaction, "And to think, they are *ours*—all ours."

There were no idle moments for mother or daughter. Eager inquiries concerning the Twins were pouring into their enchanted ears all the time; each was the constant centre of a group of breathless listeners; each recognized that she knew now for the first time the real meaning of that great word Glory, and perceived the stupendous value of it, and understood why men in all ages had been willing to throw away meaner happinesses, treasure, life itself, to get a taste of its sublime and supreme joy. Napoleon and all his kind stood accounted for—and justified.

When Rowena had at last done all her duty by the people in the parlor, she went up stairs to satisfy the longings of an overflow meeting there, for the parlor was not big enough to hold all the comers. Again she was besieged by eager questioners and again she swam in sunset seas of glory. When the forenoon was nearly gone, she recognized with a pang that this most splendid episode of her life was almost over, that nothing could prolong it, that nothing quite its equal could ever fall to her fortune again. But never mind, it was sufficient unto itself, the grand occasion had moved on an ascending scale from the start, and was a noble and memorable success. If the Twins could but do some crowning act, now, to climax it, something unusual, something startling, something to concentrate upon themselves the company's loftiest admiration, something in the nature of an electric surprise—

Here a prodigious slam-banging broke out below, and everybody rushed down to see. It was the Twins knocking out a classic four-handed piece on the piano, in great style. Rowena was satisfied; satisfied down to the bottom of her heart.

The young strangers were kept long at the piano. The villagers were astonished and enchanted with the magnificence of their performance, and could not bear to have them stop. All the music that they had ever heard before seemed spiritless 'prentice-work and barren of grace or charm when compared with these intoxicating floods of melodious sound. They realized that for once in their lives they were hearing masters.

Chapter 7

One of the most striking differences between a cat and a lie is
that a cat has only nine lives.—*Pudd'nhead Wilson's Calendar.*

The company broke up reluctantly, and drifted toward their several homes, chatting with vivacity, and all agreeing that it would be many a long day before Dawson's Landing would see the equal of this one again. The Twins had accepted several invitations while the reception was in progress, and had also volunteered to play some duets at an amateur entertainment for the benefit of a local charity. Society was eager to receive them to its bosom. Judge Driscoll had the good fortune to secure them for an immediate drive, and be the first to display them in public. They entered his buggy with him and were paraded down the main street, everybody flocking to the windows and sidewalks to see.

The Judge showed the strangers the new graveyard, and the jail, and where the richest man lived, and the Freemasons' hall, and the Methodist church, and the Presbyterian church, and where the Baptist church was going to be when they got some money to build it with, and showed them the town hall and the slaughter-house, and got out the independent fire company in uniform and had them squirt out an imaginary fire; then he let them inspect the muskets of the militia company, and poured out an exhaustless stream of enthusiasm over all these splendors, and seemed very well satisfied with the responses he got, for the Twins admired his admiration and paid him back the best they could, though they could have done better if some fifteen or sixteen hundred thousand previous experiences of this sort in various countries had not already rubbed off a considerable part of the novelty of it.

The Judge laid himself hospitably out to make them have a good time, and if there was a defect anywhere it was not his fault. He told them a good many humorous anecdotes, and always forgot the nub, but they were always able to furnish it, for these yarns were of a pretty early vintage, and they had had many a rejuvenating pull at them before. And he told them all about his several dignities, and how he had held this and that and the other place of honor or profit, and had once been to the legislature, and was now president of the Society of Freethinkers. He said the society had been in existence four years, and already had two members, and was firmly established. He would call for the brothers in the evening if they would like to attend a meeting of it.

Accordingly he called for them, and on the way told them all about Pudd'nhead Wilson, in order that they might get a favorable impression of him in advance and be prepared to like him. This scheme succeeded—the favorable impression was achieved. Later it was confirmed and solidified when Wilson proposed that out of courtesy to the strangers the usual topics be put aside and the hour be devoted to conversation upon ordinary subjects and the cultivation of friendly relations and good-fellowship,—a proposition which was put to vote and carried.

The hour passed quickly away in lively talk, and when it was ended the lonesome and neglected Wilson was richer by two friends than he had been when it began. He invited the Twins to look in at his lodgings, presently, after disposing of an intervening engagement, and they accepted with pleasure.

Toward the middle of the evening they found themselves on the road to his house. Pudd'nhead was at home waiting for them and putting in his time puzzling over a thing which had come under his notice that morning. The matter was this. He happened to be up very early—at dawn, in fact; and he crossed the hall which divided his cottage through the centre, and entered a room to get something there. The window of the room had no curtains, for that side of the house had long been unoccupied, and through this window he caught sight of something which surprised and interested him. It was a young woman—a young woman where properly no young woman belonged; for she was in Judge Driscoll's house, and in the bedroom over the Judge's private study or sitting room. This was young Tom Driscoll's bedroom. He and the Judge, the Judge's widowed sister Mrs. Pratt, and three negro servants were the only people who belonged in the house. Who, then, might this young lady be? The two houses were separated by an ordinary yard, with a low fence running back through its middle from the street in front to the lane in the rear. The distance was not great, and Wilson was able to see the girl very well, the window shades of the room she was in being up, and the window also. The girl had on a neat and trim summer dress patterned in alternating broad stripes of pink and white, and her bonnet was equipped with a pink veil. She was practicing steps, gaits and attitudes, apparently; she was doing the thing gracefully, and was very much absorbed in her work. Who could she be, and how came she to be in young Driscoll's room?

Wilson had quickly chosen a position from which he could watch the girl without running much risk of being seen by her, and he remained there hoping she would raise her veil and betray her face. But she disappointed him. After a matter of twenty minutes she disappeared, and although he stayed at his post half an hour longer, she came no more.

Toward noon he dropped in at the Judge's and talked with Mrs. Pratt about the great event of the day, the levée of the distinguished foreigners at Aunt Patsy Cooper's. He asked after her nephew Tom, and she said he was on his way home, and that she was expecting him to arrive a little before night; and added that she and the Judge were gratified to gather from his letters that he was conducting himself very nicely and creditably—at which Wilson winked to himself privately. Wilson did not ask if there was a new-comer in the house, but he asked questions that would have brought light-throwing answers as to that matter if Mrs. Pratt had had any light to throw; so he went away satisfied that he knew of things that were going on in her house which she was not aware of, herself.

He was now waiting for the Twins, and still puzzling over the problem of who that girl might be, and how she happened to be in that young fellow's room at day-break in the morning.

Chapter 8

The holy passion of Friendship is of so sweet and steady and loyal and enduring a nature that it will last through a whole lifetime if not asked to lend money.—*Pudd'nhead Wilson's Calendar.*

Consider well the proportions of things. It is better to be a young June-bug than an old bird of Paradise.—*Pudd'nhead Wilson's Calendar.*

It is necessary, now, to hunt up Roxy.

She went away chambermaiding the year she was set free, when she was thirty-five. She got a berth as second chambermaid on a Cincinnati boat in the New Orleans trade, the "Grand Mogul." A couple of trips made a wonted and easy-going steamboatman of her, and infatuated her with the stir and adventure and independence of steamboat life. She was promoted, then, and became head chambermaid. She was a favorite with the officers, and exceedingly proud of their joking and friendly ways with her.

During eight years she served three parts of the year on that boat, and the winters on a Vicksburg packet. But now for two months she had had rheumatism in her arms, and was obliged to let the wash-tub alone. So she resigned. But she was well fixed—rich, as she would have described it; for she had lived a steady life, and had banked four dollars every month in New Orleans as a provision for her old age. She said in the start that she had "put shoes on one bar'footed nigger to tromple on her with," and one mistake like that was enough: she would be independent of the human race thenceforth forevermore if hard work and economy could accomplish it.

She bade good-bye to her comrades on the Grand Mogul and moved her kit ashore when the boat touched the levee at New Orleans.

But she was back in an hour. The bank had gone to smash and carried her four hundred dollars with it. She was a pauper, and homeless. Also disabled bodily, at least for the present. The officers were full of sympathy for her in her trouble, and made up a little purse for her. She resolved to go to her birth-place; she had friends there among the negroes, and the unfortunate always help the unfortunate, she was well aware of that; those lowly comrades of her youth would not let her starve.

She took the little local packet at Cairo, and now she was on the homestretch. Time had worn away her bitterness against her son, and she was able to think of him with serenity. She put the vile side of him out of her mind, and dwelt only on recollections of his occasional acts of kindness to her. She gilded and otherwise decorated these, and made them very pleasant to contemplate. She began to long to see him. She would go and fawn upon him, slave-like—for this would have to be her attitude, of course—and maybe she would find that time had modified him, and that he would be glad to see his long forgotten old nurse and treat her gently. That would be lovely—that would make her forget her woes and her poverty!

Her poverty. That thought inspired her to add another castle to her dream: maybe he would help her; maybe he would give her a trifle now and then— maybe a dollar, once a month, say; any little thing like that would help, oh, ever so much!

By the time she reached Dawson's Landing she was her old self again; her blues were gone, she was in high feather. She would get along, sure; there were many kitchens where the servants would share their meals with her, and also steal sugar and apples and other dainties for her to carry home—or give her a chance to pilfer them herself, which would answer just as well. And there was the church. She was a more rabid and devoted Methodist than ever, and her piety was no sham, but was strong and sincere. Yes, with plenty of creature comforts and her old place in the amen corner in her possession again, she should be perfectly happy and at peace thenceforward to the end.

She went to Judge Driscoll's kitchen first of all. She was received there in great form and with vast enthusiasm. Her wonderful travels, and the strange countries she had seen and the adventures she had had, made her a marvel and a heroine of romance. The negroes hung enchanted upon the great story of her experiences, interrupting her all along with eager questions, with laughter, exclamations of delight and explosions of applause; and she was obliged to confess to herself that if there was anything better in this world than steamboating, it was the glory to be got by telling about it. The audience loaded her stomach with their dinners and then stole the pantry bare to load up her basket.

Tom was in St. Louis. The servants said he had spent the best part of his time there during the previous two years. Roxy came every day, and had many talks about the family and its affairs. Once she asked why Tom was away so much. The ostensible "Chambers" said:

"De fac' is, ole marster kin git along better when young marster's away den he kin when he's in de town; yes, en he love him better, too; so he gives him fifty dollahs a month—"

"No, is dat so! Chambers, you's a jokin', ain't you?"

"'Clah to goodness I ain't, mammy; Marse Tom tole me so, his own self. But nemmine, 'tain't enough."

"My lan', what de reason 'tain't enough?"

"Well, I's gwyne to tell you, if you gimme a chanst, mammy. De reason it ain't enough is caze Marse Tom gambles."

Roxy threw up her hands in astonishment, and Chambers went on—

"Ole marster found it out, caze he had to pay two hunderd dollahs for Marse Tom's gamblin' debts, en dat's true, mammy, jes' as dead certain as you's bawn."

"Two—hund'd—dollahs! Why, what is you talkin' 'bout? Two—hund'd—dollahs! Sakes alive, it's mos' enough to buy a tollable good second-hand nigger wid. En you ain't lyin', honey?—you wouldn't lie to yo' ole mammy?"

"It's God's own truth, jes' as I tell you—two hunderd dollahs—I wisht I may never stir outen my tracks if it ain't so. En, oh, my lan', ole Marse was jes' a hoppin'! he was bilin' mad, I *tell* you! He tuck 'n dissenhurrit him."

He licked his chops with relish after that stately word. Roxy struggled with it a moment, then gave it up and said—

"Dissen*whiched* him?"

"Dissenhurrit him."

"What's dat? What do it mean?"

"Means he busted de will."

"Bus—ted de will! He wouldn't ever treat him so. Take it back, you misable imitation nigger dat I bore in sorrow en tribbilation!"

Roxy's pet castle—an occasional dollar from Tom's pocket—was tumbling to ruin before her eyes. She could not abide such a disaster as that; she couldn't endure the thought of it. Her remark amused Chambers:

"Yah-yah-yah! jes' listen to dat! If *I's* imitation, what is you? Bofe of us is imitation *white*—dat's what we is—en pow'ful good imitation, too—yah-yah-yah!—we don't 'mount to noth'n as imitation *niggers*; en as for—"

"Shet up yo' foolin', 'fo' I knock you side de head, en tell me 'bout de will. Tell me 'tain't busted—*do*, honey, en I'll never fogit you."

"Well, *'tain't*—caze dey's a new one made, en Marse Tom's all right agin. But what is *you* in sich a sweat 'bout it for, mammy, 'tain't none o' your business I don't reckon?"

"'Tain't none o' *my* business? Whose business *is* it den, I'd like to know? Wuz I his mother tell he was fifteen years old, or wusn't I?—you answer me dat. En you speck I could see him turned out po' en ornery on de worl' en never care noth'n 'bout it? I reckon if you'd ever ben a mother yo'self, Vallet de Chambers, you wouldn't talk sich foolishness as dat."

"Well, den, ole Marse forgive him en fixed up de will agin—do dat satisfy you?"

Yes, she was satisfied, now, and quite happy and sentimental over it. She kept coming daily, and at last she was told that Tom had come home. She began to tremble with emotion, and straightway sent to beg him to let his "po' ole nigger mammy have jes' one sight of him en die for joy."

Tom was stretched at his lazy ease on a sofa when Chambers brought the petition. Time had not modified his ancient detestation of the humble drudge and protector of his boyhood; it was still bitter and uncompromising. He sat up and bent a severe gaze upon the fair face of the young fellow whose name he was unconsciously using and whose family rights he was enjoying. He maintained the gaze until the victim of it had become satisfactorily pallid with terror, then he said—

"What does the old rip want with me?"

The petition was meekly repeated.

"Who gave you permission to come and disturb me with the social attentions of niggers?"

Tom had risen. The other young man was trembling, now, visibly. He saw what was coming, and bent his head sideways and put up his left arm to shield it. Tom rained cuffs upon the head and its shield, saying no word; the victim received each blow with a beseeching "*Please*, Marse Tom!—oh, *please*, Marse Tom!" Seven blows—then Tom said, "Face the door—march!" He followed behind with one, two, three solid kicks. The last one helped the pure-white slave over the door-sill, and he limped away mopping his eyes with his old ragged sleeve. Tom shouted after him, "Send her in!"

Then he flung himself panting on the sofa again and rasped out the remark, "He arrived just at the right moment; I was full to the brim with bitter thinkings, and nobody to take it out of. How refreshing it was!—I feel better."

Tom's mother entered, now, closing the door behind her, and approached her son with all the wheedling and supplicating servilities that fear and interest can impart to the words and attitudes of the born slave. She stopped a yard from her boy and made two or three admiring exclamations over his manly stature and general handsomeness, and Tom put an arm under his head and hoisted a leg over the sofa-back in order to look properly indifferent.

"My lan', how you is growed, honey! 'Clah to goodness I wouldn't a knowed you, Marse Tom, 'deed I wouldn't. Look at me good; does you 'member ole Roxy?—does you know yo' ole nigger mammy, honey? Well, now, I kin lay down en die in peace, caze I's seed—"

"Cut it short, damn it, cut it short. What is it you want?"

"You heah dat? Jes' de same old Marse Tom, allays so gay and funnin' wid de ole mammy! I 'uz jes' as shore—"

"Cut it short, I tell you, and get along. What do you want?"

This was a bitter disappointment. Roxy had for so many days nourished and fondled and petted her notion that Tom would be glad to see his old nurse and would make her proud and happy to the marrow with a cordial word or two, that it took two rebuffs to convince her that he was not funning and that her beautiful dream was a fond and foolish vanity, a shabby and pitiful mistake. She was hurt to the heart, and so ashamed that for a moment she did not quite know what to do or how to act. Then her breast began to heave, the tears came, and in her forlornness she was moved to try that other dream of hers—an appeal to her boy's charity; and so, upon the impulse, and without reflection, she offered her supplication—

"Oh, Marse Tom, de po' ole mammy is in sich hard luck, dese days; en she's kinder crippled in de arms en can't work, en if you *could* gimme a dollah—on'y jes' one little d—"

Tom was on his feet so suddenly that the supplicant was startled into a jump herself.

"A dollar!—give *you* a dollar! I've a notion to strangle you! Is *that* your errand here? Clear out! and be quick about it."

Roxy backed slowly toward the door. When she was halfway she stopped, and said, mournfully—

"Marse Tom, I nussed you when you was a little baby, en I raised you all by myself tell you was most a young man; en now you is young en rich en I is po' en gitt'n ole, en I come heah b'lievin' dat you would he'p de ole mammy 'long down de little road dat's lef' twix her en de grave, en—"

Tom relished this tune less than any that had preceded it, for it began to wake up a sort of echo in his conscience; so he interrupted and said with decision, though without asperity, that he was not in a situation to help her, and wasn't going to do it.

"Ain't you *ever* gwyne to he'p me, Marse Tom?"

"No! Now go away and don't bother me any more."

Roxy's head was down, in an attitude of humility. But now the fires of her old wrongs flamed up in her breast and began to burn fiercely. She raised her head slowly, till it was well up, and at the same time her great frame unconsciously assumed an erect and masterful attitude, with all the majesty and grace of her vanished youth in it. She raised her finger and punctuated with it:

"You has said de word. You has had yo' chance, en you has trompled it under yo' foot. When you git another one, you'll git down on yo' knees en *beg* for it!"

A cold chill went to Tom's heart, he didn't know why; for he did not reflect that such words, from such an incongruous source, and so solemnly delivered, could not easily fail of that effect. However, he did the natural thing: he replied with bluster and mockery:

"*You'll* give me a chance—*you!* Perhaps I'd better get down on my knees *now*. But in case I don't—just for argument's sake—what's going to happen, pray?"

"Dis is what is gwyne to happen. I's gwyne as straight to yo' uncle as I kin walk, en tell him every las' thing I knows about you!"

Tom's cheek blenched, and she saw it. Disturbing thoughts began to chase each other through his head. "How can *she* know? And yet she must have found out—she looks it. I've had the will back only three months and am already deep in debt again and moving heaven and earth to save myself from exposure and destruction, with a reasonably fair show of getting the thing covered up if I'm let alone, and now this fiend has gone and found me out somehow or other. I wonder how much she knows? Oh, oh, oh, it's enough to break a body's heart! But I've got to humor her—there's no other way."

Then he worked up a rather sickly sample of a gay laugh and a hollow chipperness of manner, and said—

"Well, well, Roxy dear, old friends like you and me mustn't quarrel. Here's your dollar—now tell me what you know."

He held out the wild-cat bill, she stood as she was, and made no movement. It was her turn to scorn persuasive foolery, now, and she did not waste it. She said, with a grim implacability in voice and manner which made Tom almost realize that even a former slave can remember for ten minutes insults and injuries returned for compliments and flatteries received, and can also enjoy taking revenge for them when the opportunity offers—

"What does I know? I'll tell you what I knows. I knows enough to bust dat will to flinders—en *more*, mind you, *more!*"

Tom was aghast.

"More?" he said. "What do you call more? Where's there any room for more?"

Roxy laughed a mocking laugh, and said scoffingly, with a toss of her head, and her hands on her hips—

"Yes!—oh, I reckon! *'Cose* you'd like to know—wid yo' po' little ole rag dollah! What you reckon I's gwyne to tell *you*, for?—*you* ain't got no money. I's gwyne to tell yo' uncle—en I'll do it dis minute, too—he'll gimme *five* dollahs for de news, en mighty glad, too."

She swung herself around disdainfully, and started away. Tom was in a panic. He seized her skirts and implored her to wait. She turned and said, loftily—

"Look-a-heah, what 'uz it I tole you?"

"You—you—I don't remember anything. What was it you told me?"

"I tole you dat de next time I give you a chance you'd git down on yo' knees en beg for it."

Tom was stupefied for a moment. He was panting with excitement. Then he said—

"Oh, Roxy, you wouldn't require your young master to do such a horrible thing. You can't mean it."

"I'll let you know mighty quick whether I means it or not. *You* call *me* names, en as good as spit on me when I comes here po' en ornery en 'umble, to praise you for bein' growed up so fine en handsome, en tell you how I used to nuss you en tend you en watch you when you 'uz sick en hadn't no mother but me in de whole worl', en beg you to give de po' ole nigger a dollah for to git her sum'n to eat, en you call me names—*names*, dad blame you! Yassir, I gives you jes' one chance mo', en dat's *now*, en it las' on'y a half a second— you *hear?*"

Tom slumped to his knees and began to beg, saying—

"You *see* I'm begging, and it's honest begging, too. Now tell me, Roxy, tell me!"

The heir of two centuries of unatoned insult and outrage looked down on him and seemed to drink in deep draughts of satisfaction. Then she said—

"Fine nice young white gen'lman kneelin' down to a nigger wench! I's wanted to see dat jes' once befo' I's called. Now, Gabrel, blow de hawn, I's ready! . . . . . Git up!"

Tom did it. He said, humbly—

"Now Roxy, don't punish me any more. I deserved what I've got, but be good and let me off with that. Don't go to uncle. Tell me—I'll give you the five dollars."

"Yes, I bet you will; en you won't stop dah, nuther. But I ain't gwyne to tell you heah—"

"Good gracious, no!"

"Is you feared o' de ha'nted house?"

"N-no."

"Well, den, you come to de ha'nted house 'bout ten or 'leven to-night, en climb up de ladder, caze de star-steps is broke down, en you'll fine me. I's a roostin' in de ha'nted house caze I can't 'ford to roos' nowher's else." She started toward the door, but stopped and said "Gimme de dollah bill." He gave it to her. She examined it and said, "Hm—like enough de bank's busted." She started again, but halted again. "Has you got any whisky?"

"Yes, a little."

"Fetch it."

He ran to his room overhead and brought down a bottle which was two-thirds full. She tilted it up and took a drink. Her eyes sparkled with satisfaction, and she tucked the bottle under her shawl, saying,—

"It's prime—I'll take it along."

Tom humbly held the door for her, and she marched out as grim and erect as a grenadier.

Chapter 9

Why is it that we rejoice at a birth and grieve at a funeral? It is because we are not the person involved.—*Pudd'nhead Wilson's Calendar.*

It is easy to find fault, if one has that disposition. There was once a man, who, not being able to find any other fault with his coal, complained that there were too many pre-historic toads in it.—*Pudd'nhead Wilson's Calendar.*

Tom flung himself on the sofa, and put his throbbing head in his hands and rested his elbows on his knees. He rocked himself back and forth and moaned.

"I've knelt to a nigger wench!" he muttered. "I thought I had struck the deepest deeps of degradation before, but oh, dear, it was nothing to this. . . . . . . Well, there is one consolation, such as it is—I've struck bottom this time; there's nothing lower."

But that was a hasty conclusion.

At ten that night he climbed the ladder in the haunted house, pale, weak, and wretched. Roxy was standing in the door of one of the rooms, waiting, for she had heard him.

This was a two-story log house which had acquired the reputation a few years before of being haunted, and that was the end of its usefulness. Nobody would live in it afterward or go near it by night, and most people even gave it a wide berth in the daytime. As it had no competition, it was called *the* haunted house. It was getting crazy and ruinous, now, from long neglect. It stood three hundred yards beyond Pudd'nhead Wilson's house, with nothing between but vacancy. It was the last house in the town at that end.

Tom followed Roxy into the room. She had a pile of clean straw in the corner for a bed, some cheap but well-kept clothing was hanging on the wall, there was a tin lantern freckling the floor with little spots of light, and there were various soap and candle boxes scattered about, which served for chairs. The two sat down. Roxy said—

"Now, den. I'll tell you straight off, en I'll begin to k'leck de money later on; I ain't in no hurry. What does you reckon I's gwyne to tell you?"

"Well, you—you—oh, Roxy, don't make it too hard for me. Come right out and tell me you've found out somehow what a shape I'm in on account of dissipation and foolishness."

"Disposition en foolishness! *No* sir, *dat* ain't it. Dat jist ain't noth'n at *all*, 'longside o' what *I* knows."

Tom stared at her, and said—

"Why—Roxy, what do you *mean?*"

She rose, and gloomed above him like a fate.

"I means dis—en it's de Lord's truth. *You ain't no more kin to ole Marse Driscoll den I is!*—dat's what I means!" and her eyes flamed with triumph.

"What!"

"Yassir, en *dat* ain't all. You's a *nigger!*—*bawn* a nigger en a *slave!*—en you's a nigger en a slave dis minute! en if I opens my mouf, ole Marse Driscoll 'll *sell you down de river* befo' you is two days older den what you is now!"

"It's a thundering lie, you miserable old blatherskite!"

"It ain't no lie, nuther. It's jes' de truth, en noth'n *but* de truth, so he'p me! Yassir—*you's my son*—"

"You devil!—"

—"en dat po' boy dat you's ben a kickin' en a cuffin' to-day is Percy Driscoll's son *en yo' marster*—"

"You beast!"

—"en *his* name's Tom Driscoll en *yo'* name's Vallet de Chambers, en you ain't got no fambly name, becaze niggers don't *have* 'em!"

Tom sprang up and seized a billet of wood and raised it; but his mother only laughed at him and said—

"Set down, you pup! Does you think you kin sk'yer *me?* It ain't in you, nor de likes of you. I reckon you'd shoot me in de back, maybe, if you got a chance, for dat's jist yo' style, *I* knows you, thoo en *thoo*—but *I* don't mind gitt'n killed, becaze all dis is down in writin', en it's in safe hands, too, en de man dat's got it knows whah to look for de right man when I gits killed. Oh, bless yo' soul, if you puts yo' mother up for as big a fool as *you* is, you's pow'ful mistaken, I kin tell you. *Now* den, you set still en behave yo'self; en don't you git up agin till I tell you."

Tom fretted and chafed a while in a whirlwind of disorganizing sensations and emotions, and finally said with something like settled conviction—

"The whole thing is moonshine—now, then, go ahead and do your worst; I'm done with you."

Roxy made no answer. She took the lantern and started toward the door. Tom was in a cold panic in a moment.

"Come back, come back!" he wailed. "I didn't mean it, Roxy, I take it all back, and I'll never say it again. *Please* come back, Roxy."

The woman stood a moment, then she said gravely—

"Dah's one thing you's got to stop, Vallet de Chambers. You can't call *me* Roxy, same as if you was my equal. Chillen don't speak to dey mammies like dat. You'll call me *Ma* or *mammy*, dat's what you'll call me—leastways when dey ain't nobody aroun'. *Say* it!"

It cost Tom a struggle, but he got it out.

"Dat's all right. Don't you ever fogit it agin, if you knows what's good for you. Now, den, you has said you wouldn't ever call it lies en moonshine agin. I'll tell you dis, for a warnin': if you ever does say it agin, it's de *las'* time you'll ever say it to *me*; I'll tramp as straight to de Judge as I kin walk, en tell him who you is en *prove* it! Does you b'lieve me when I says dat?"

"Oh," groaned Tom, "I more than believe it, I *know* it!"

Roxy knew her conquest was complete. She could have proven nothing to anybody, and her threat about the writings was a lie; but she knew the person she was dealing with, and had made both statements without any doubts as to the effect they would produce.

She went and sat down on her candle-box, and the pride and pomp of her victorious attitude made it a throne. She said—

"Now, den, Chambers, we's gwyne to talk business, en dey ain't gwyne to be no mo' foolishness. In de fust place, you gits fifty dollahs a month; you's gwyne to han' over half of it to yo' ma. Plank it out!"

But Tom had only six dollars in the world. He gave her that, and promised to start fair on next month's pension.

"Chambers, how much is you in debt?"

Tom shuddered, and said—

"Nearly three hundred dollars."

"How is you gwyne to pay it?"

Tom groaned out—

"Oh, *I* don't know—don't ask me such awful questions!"

"DOES YOU B'LIEVE ME WHEN I SAYS DAT?"

But she stuck to her point until she wearied a confession out of him: he had been prowling about in disguise, stealing small valuables from private houses; in fact had made a good deal of a raid on his fellow villagers a fortnight before, when he was supposed to be in St. Louis; but he doubted if he had sent away enough stuff to realize the required amount, and was afraid to make a further venture in the present excited state of the town. His mother approved of his conduct, and offered to help, but this frightened him. He tremblingly ventured to say that if she would retire from the town he should feel better and safer, and could hold his head higher—and was going on to make an argument, but she interrupted and surprised him pleasantly by saying she was ready, it didn't make any difference to her where she stayed, so that she got her share of the pension regularly. She said she would not go far, and would call at the haunted house once a month for her money. Then she said—

"I don't hate you so much now, but I've hated you a many a year—and anybody would. Didn't I change you off en give you a good fambly en a good name, en made you a white gen'lman en rich, wid store clothes on—en what did I git for it? You despised me all de time; en was allays sayin' mean hard things to me befo' folks, en wouldn't ever let me fogit I's a nigger—en—en—"

She fell to sobbing, and broke down. Tom said—

"But you know, I didn't know you were my mother—and besides—"

"Well, nemmine 'bout dat, now—let it go. I's gwyne to fogit it." Then she added fiercely, "En don't you ever make me remember it agin, or you'll be sorry, *I* tell you!"

When they were parting, Tom said, in the most persuasive way he could command—

"Ma, would you mind telling me who was my father?"

He had supposed he was asking an embarrassing question. He was mistaken. Roxy drew herself up, with a proud toss of her head, and said:

"Does I mine tellin' you? No, dat I don't. You ain't got no 'casion to be shame' o' yo' father, *I* kin tell you. He wuz de highest quality in dis whole town—Ole Virginny stock, Fust Famblies, he wuz. Jes' as good stock as de Driscolls en de Howards, de bes' day dey ever seed." She put on a still prouder air, if possible, and added impressively, "Does you 'member Cunnel Cecil Burleigh Essex, dat died de same year yo' young Marse Tom Driscoll's pappy died, en all de Masons en Odd Fellers en churches turned out en give him de bigges' funeral dis town ever seed? Dat's de man!" Under the inspiration of her soaring complacency the departed graces of her earlier days returned to her, and her bearing took to itself a dignity and state that might have passed for queenly if her surroundings had been a little more in keeping with it. "Dey ain't another nigger in dis town dat's as high-bawn as you is. Now, den, go 'long. En jes' you hold yo' head up as high as you want to—you has de *right*, en dat I kin swah!"

Chapter 10

All say "How hard it is that we have to die"—a strange complaint to come from the mouths of people who have had to live.—*Pudd'nhead Wilson's Calendar.*

When angry, count four; when very angry, swear.—*Pudd'nhead Wilson's Calendar.*

Every now and then, after Tom went to bed, he had sudden wakings out of his sleep, and his first thought was, "O, joy, it was all a dream!" Then he laid himself heavily down again, with a groan and the muttered words, "A nigger!—I am a nigger!—oh, I wish I was dead!"

He woke at dawn with one more repetition of this horror, and then he resolved to meddle no more with that treacherous sleep. He began to think. Sufficiently bitter thinkings they were. They wandered along something after this fashion:

"Why were niggers *and* whites made? What crime did the uncreated first nigger commit that the curse of birth was decreed for him? And why is this awful difference made between white and black? . . . . . . How hard the nigger's fate seems, this morning!—yet until last night such a thought never entered my head."

He sighed and groaned an hour or more away. Then "Chambers" came humbly in to say that breakfast was nearly ready. "Tom" blushed scarlet to see this aristocratic white youth cringe to him, a *nigger*, and call him "young marster." He said, roughly—

"Get out of my sight!" and when the youth was gone, he muttered, "He has done me no harm, poor wretch, but he is white, and for that I could kill him—if I had the courage. Ach! he is an eyesore to me, now, for he is Driscoll the young gentleman, and I am a—oh, I *wish* I was dead!"

A gigantic irruption like that of Krakatoa a few years ago, with the accompanying earthquakes, tidal waves and clouds of volcanic dust, changes the face of the surrounding landscape beyond recognition, bringing down the high lands, elevating the low, making fair lakes where deserts had been, and deserts where green prairies had smiled before. The tremendous catastrophe which had befallen Tom had changed his moral landscape in much the same way. Some of his low places he found lifted to ideals, some of his ideals had sunk to the valleys, and lay there with the sackcloth and ashes of pumice stone and sulphur on their ruined heads.

For days he wandered in lonely places thinking, thinking, thinking—trying to get his bearings. It was new work. If he met a friend he found that the habit of a lifetime had in some mysterious way vanished—his arm hung limp instead of involuntarily extending the hand for a shake. It was the "nigger" in him asserting its humility, and he blushed and was abashed. And the "nigger" in him was surprised when the white friend put out his hand for a shake with him. He found the "nigger" in him involuntarily giving the road, on the sidewalk, to the white rowdy and loafer. When Rowena, the dearest thing his heart knew, the idol of his secret worship, invited him in, the "nigger" in him made an embarrassed excuse and was afraid to enter and sit with the dread white folks on equal terms. The "nigger" in him went shrinking and skulking here and there and yonder, and fancying it saw suspicion and maybe detection in all faces, tones and gestures. So strange and uncharacteristic was Tom's conduct that people noticed it and turned to look after him when he had passed on; and when he glanced back—as he could not help doing, in spite of his best resistance—and caught that puzzled expression in a person's face, it gave him a sick feeling, and he took himself out of view as quickly as he could. He presently came to have a hunted sense and a hunted look, and then he fled away to the hill-tops and the solitudes. The curse of Ham was upon him, he said to himself.

He dreaded his meals; the "nigger" in him was ashamed to sit at the white folks' table, and feared discovery all the time; and once when Judge Driscoll said, "What's the matter with you?—you look as meek as a nigger!" he felt as secret murderers are said to feel when the accuser says "Thou art the man!" Tom said he was not well, and left the table.

His ostensible "aunt's" solicitudes and endearments were become a terror to him, and he avoided them.

And all the time, hatred of his ostensible "uncle" was steadily growing in his heart; for he said to himself, "He is white; and I am his chattel, his property, his goods, and he can sell me, just as he could his dog."

For as much as a week after this, Tom imagined that his character had undergone a pretty radical change. But that was because he did not know himself. In several ways his *opinions* were totally changed, and would never go back to what they were before, but the main structure of his *character* was not changed, and could not be changed. One or two very important features of it were altered, and in time effects would result from this, if opportunity offered; effects of a quite serious nature, too. Under the influence of a great mental and moral upheaval his character and habits had taken on the appearance of complete change, but after a while with the subsidence of the storm both began to settle toward their former places. He dropped gradually back into his old frivolous and easy-going ways, and conditions of feeling, and manner of speech, and no familiar of his could have detected anything in him that differentiated him from the weak and careless Tom of other days.

The theft-raid which he had made upon the village turned out better than he had ventured to hope. It produced the sum necessary to pay his gaming-debts, and saved him from exposure to his uncle and another smashing of the will.

He and his mother learned to like each other fairly well. She couldn't love him, as yet, because there "warn't nothing *to* him," as she expressed it, but her nature needed something or somebody to rule over, and he was better than nothing. Her strong character and aggressive and commanding ways compelled Tom's admiration in spite of the fact that he got more illustrations of them than he needed for his comfort. However, as a rule, her conversation was made up of racy tattle about the privacies of the chief families of the town, for she went harvesting among their kitchens every time she came to the village, and Tom enjoyed this. It was just in his line. She always collected her half of his pension punctually, and he was always at the haunted house to have a chat with her on these occasions. Every now and then she paid him a visit there on between-days also.

Now and then he would run up to St. Louis for a few weeks, and at last temptation caught him again. He won a lot of money, but lost it, and with it a deal more besides, which he promised to raise as soon as possible.

He projected a new raid on his town in this interest. He never meddled with any other town, for he was afraid to venture into houses whose ins and outs he did not know, and the habits of whose households he was not acquainted with. He arrived at the haunted house in disguise on the Wednesday before the advent of the Twins,—after writing his aunt Pratt that he would not arrive until two days later—and lay in hiding there with his mother until toward daylight Friday morning, when he went to his uncle's house and entered by the back way with his own key and slipped up to his room, where he could have the use of mirror and toilet articles. He had a suit of girl's clothes with him in a bundle as a disguise for his raid, and was wearing a suit of his mother's clothing, with black gloves and veil. By dawn he was tricked out for his raid, but he caught a glimpse of Pudd'nhead Wilson through the window over the way and knew that Pudd'nhead had caught a glimpse of him. So he entertained Wilson with some airs and graces and attitudes for a while, then he stepped out of sight and resumed the other disguise, and by and by went down and out the back way and started downtown to reconnoitre the scene of his intended labors.

But he was ill at ease. He had changed back to Roxy's dress, with the stoop of age added to the disguise, so that Wilson would not bother himself about a humble old woman leaving a neighbor's house by the back way in the early morning, in case he was still spying. But supposing Wilson had seen him leave, and had thought it suspicious, and had also followed him? The thought made Tom cold. He gave up the raid for the day, and hurried back to the haunted house by the obscurest route he knew. His mother was gone; but she came back, by and by, with the news of the grand reception at Patsy Cooper's, and soon persuaded him that the opportunity was like a special providence it was so inviting and perfect. So he went raiding, after all, and made a nice success of it while everybody was gone to Patsy Cooper's. Success gave him nerve, and even actual intrepidity; insomuch, indeed, that after he had conveyed his harvest to his mother in a back alley, he went to the reception himself, and added several of that house's valuables to his takings.

———

After this long digression we have now arrived, once more, at the point where Pudd'nhead Wilson, while waiting for the arrival of the Twins on that same Friday evening, sat puzzling over the strange apparition of that morning—a girl in young Tom Driscoll's bedroom; fretting, and guessing, and puzzling over it, and wondering who the brazen huzzy might be.

Chapter 11

There are three infallible ways of pleasing an author, and the three form a rising scale of compliment: 1, to tell him you have read one of his books; 2, to tell him you have read all of his books; 3, to ask him to let you read the manuscript of his forthcoming book. No. 1 admits you to his respect; No. 2 admits you to his admiration; but No. 3 carries you clear into his heart with all your clothes on.—*Pudd'nhead Wilson's Calendar.*

As to the Adjective: when in doubt, strike it out.—*Pudd'nhead Wilson's Calendar.*

The Twins arrived presently, and talk began. It flowed along chattily and sociably, and under its influence the new friendship gathered ease and strength. Wilson got out his Calendar, by request, and read a passage or two from it, which the Twins praised quite cordially. This pleased the author so much that he complied gladly when they asked him to lend them a batch of the work to read at home. In the course of their wide travels they had found out that there are three sure ways of pleasing an author: they were now working the best of the three.

There was an interruption, now. Young Tom Driscoll appeared, and joined the party. He pretended to be seeing the distinguished strangers for the first time when they rose to shake hands, but this was only a blind, as he had already had a glimpse of them at the reception while robbing the house. The Twins made mental note that he was smooth-faced and rather handsome, and smooth and undulatory in his movements—graceful, in fact. Angelo thought he had a good eye, Luigi thought there was something veiled and sly about it. Angelo thought he had a pleasant free-and-easy way of talking, Luigi thought it was more so than was agreeable. Angelo thought he was a sufficiently nice young man, Luigi reserved his decision. Tom's first contribution to the conversation was a question which he had put to Wilson a hundred times before. It was always cheerily and good-naturedly put, and always inflicted a little pang, for it touched a secret sore; but this time the pang was sharp, since strangers were present:

"Well, how does the law come on? Had a case yet?"

Wilson bit his lip, but answered, "No—not yet," with as much indifference as he could assume. Judge Driscoll had generously left the law feature out of the Wilson biography which he had furnished to the Twins. Young Tom laughed pleasantly and said—

"Wilson's a lawyer, gentlemen, but he doesn't practice now."

The sarcasm bit, but Wilson kept himself under control, and said, without passion—

"I don't practice, it is true. It is true that I have never had a case, and have had to earn a poor living for twenty years as an expert accountant in a town where I can't get hold of a set of books to untangle as often as I would like. But it is also true that I did fit myself well for the practice of the law. By the time I was your age, Tom, I had chosen a profession and was soon competent to enter upon it." [Tom winced.] "I never got a chance to try my hand at it, and I may never get a chance; and yet if I ever do get it I shall be found ready, for I have kept up my law-studies all these years."

"That's it—that's good grit. I like to see it. I've a notion to throw all my business your way. My business and your law-practice ought to make a pretty gay team, Dave," and the young fellow laughed again.

"If you will throw—" Wilson had thought of the girl in Tom's bedroom, and was going to say, "If you will throw the surreptitious and disreputable part of your business my way, it may amount to something," but thought better of it and said, "However, this matter doesn't fit well in a general conversation."

"All right, we'll change the subject—I guess you were about to give me another dig, anyway, so I'm willing to change. How's the Awful Mystery flourishing these days? Wilson's got a scheme for driving plain window-glass out of the market by decorating it with greasy finger-marks and getting rich by selling it at famine prices to the crowned heads over in Europe to outfit their palaces with. Fetch it out, Dave."

Wilson brought three of his glass strips and said:

"I get the subject to pass the fingers of his right hand through his hair, so as to get a little coating of the natural oil on them, and then press the balls of them on the glass. A fine and delicate print of the lines in the skin results, and is permanent if it doesn't come in contact with something able to rub it off. You begin, Tom."

"Why, I think you took my finger-marks once or twice before."

"Yes, but you were a little boy, the last time, only about twelve years old."

"That's so. Of course I've changed entirely since then, and variety is what the crowned heads want, I guess."

He passed his fingers through his crop of short hair and pressed them one at a time on the glass. Angelo made a print of his fingers on another glass, and Luigi followed with the third. Wilson marked the glasses with names and date and put them away. Tom gave one of his little laughs and said—

"I thought I wouldn't say anything, but if variety is what you are after, you have wasted a piece of glass. The hand-print of one twin is the same as the hand-print of the fellow-twin."

"Well, it's done, now, and I like to have them both, anyway," said Wilson, returning to his place.

"But look here, Dave," said Tom, "you used to tell people's fortunes, too, when you took their finger-marks. Dave's just an all-around genius, a genius of the first water, gentlemen, a great scientist running to seed here in this village, a prophet with the kind of honor that prophets generally get at home—for here they don't give shucks for his scientifics, and they call his skull a maggot-factory—hey, Dave, ain't it so?—but never mind, he'll make his mark some day—finger-mark, you know, he-he! But really, you want to let him take a shy at your palms once, it's worth twice the price of admission or your money's returned at the door. Why, he'll read your wrinkles as easy as a book, and not only tell you fifty or sixty things that's going to happen to you, but fifty or sixty thousand that ain't. Come, Dave, show the gentlemen what an inspired Jack-at-all-science we've got in this town and don't know it."

Wilson winced under this nagging and not very courteous chaff, and the Twins suffered with him and for him. They rightly judged, now, that the best way to relieve him would be to take the thing in earnest and treat it with respect, ignoring Tom's rather overdone raillery; so Luigi said:

"We have seen something of palmistry in our wanderings, and know very well what astonishing things it can do. If it isn't a science, and one of the greatest of them, too, I don't know what its other name ought to be. In the Orient—"

Tom looked surprised and incredulous. He said—

"That jugglery a science? But really, you ain't serious, are you?"

"Yes, entirely so. Four years ago we had our hands read out to us as if our palms had been covered with print."

"Well, do you mean to say there was actually anything *in* it?" asked Tom, his incredulity beginning to weaken a little.

"There was this much in it," said Angelo; "what was told us of our characters was minutely exact—we could not have bettered it ourselves. Next, two or three memorable things that had happened to us were laid bare—things which no one present but ourselves could have known about."

"Why, it's rank sorcery!" exclaimed Tom, who was now becoming very much interested. "And how did they make out with what was going to happen to you in the future?"

"On the whole, quite fairly," said Luigi. "Two or three of the most striking things foretold have happened since; much the most striking one of all happened within that same year. Some of the minor prophecies have come true; some of the minor and some of the major ones have not been fulfilled yet, and of course may never be—still, I should be more surprised if they failed to arrive than if they didn't."

Tom was entirely sobered, and profoundly impressed. He said, apologetically—

"Dave, I wasn't meaning to belittle that science, I was only chaffing—chattering, I reckon I better say. I wish you *would* look at their palms—come, won't you?"

"Why, certainly, if you want me to, but you know I've had no chance to become an expert, and don't claim to be one. When a past event is somewhat prominently recorded in the palm, I can generally detect that, but minor ones often escape me—not always, of course, but often—but I haven't much confidence in myself when it comes to reading the future. I am talking as if palmistry was a daily study with me, but that is not so. I haven't examined half a dozen hands in the last half a dozen years; you see, the people got to joking about it, and I stopped to let the talk die down. I'll tell you what we'll do, Count Luigi—I'll make a try at your past, and if I have any success there—no, on the whole I'll let the future alone—that's really the affair of an expert."

He took Luigi's hand. Tom said—

"Wait—don't look yet, Dave. Count Luigi, here's paper and pencil. Set down that thing that you said was the most striking one that was foretold to you and happened less than a year afterwards, and give it to me so I can see if Dave finds it in your hand."

Luigi wrote a line privately, and folded up the piece of paper and handed it to Tom, saying—

"I'll tell you when to look at it, if he finds it."

Wilson began to study Luigi's palm, tracing life lines, heart lines, head lines, and so on, and noting carefully their relations with the cobweb of finer and more delicate marks and lines that enmeshed them on all sides; he felt of the fleshy cushion at the base of the thumb, and noted its shape; he felt of the fleshy side of the hand between the wrist and the base of the little finger, and noted its shape also; he pains-takingly examined the fingers, observing their form, proportions and natural manner of disposing themselves when in repose. All this process was watched by the three spectators with absorbing interest, their heads bent together over Luigi's palm and nobody disturbing the stillness with a word. Wilson now entered upon a close survey of the palm again, and his revelations began.

He mapped out Luigi's character and disposition, his tastes, aversions, proclivities, ambitions and eccentricities in a way which sometimes made Luigi wince and the others laugh, but both Twins declared that the chart was artistically drawn and was correct.

Next, Wilson took up Luigi's past. He proceeded cautiously and with hesitation, now, moving his finger slowly along the great lines of the palm, and now and then halting it at a "star" or some such landmark and examining that neighborhood minutely. He proclaimed one or two past events, Luigi confirmed his correctness, and the search went on. Presently Wilson glanced up suddenly with a surprised expression—

"Here is record of an incident which you would perhaps not wish me to—"

"Bring it out," said Luigi, good-naturedly, "I promise you it shan't embarrass me."

But Wilson still hesitated, and did not seem to quite know what to do. Then he said—

"I think it is too delicate a matter to—to—. I believe I would rather write it or whisper it to you, and let you decide for yourself whether you want it talked out or not."

"That will answer," said Luigi; "write it."

Wilson wrote something on a slip of paper and handed it to Luigi, who read it to himself and said to Tom—

"Unfold *your* slip and read it, Mr. Driscoll."

Tom read:

"*It was prophesied that I would kill a man. It came true before the year was out.*" Tom added, "Great Scott!"

Luigi handed Wilson's paper to Tom and said—

"Now read this one."

Tom read:

"*You have killed some one—but whether man, woman or child, I do not make out.*" "Caesar's ghost!" commented Tom, with astonishment. "It beats anything that was ever heard of. Why, a man's own hand is his deadliest enemy. Just think of that—a man's own hand keeps a record of the deepest and fatalest secrets of his life, and is treacherously ready to expose him to any black-magic stranger that comes along! But what do you let a person look at your hand for, with that awful thing printed in it?"

"Oh," said Luigi reposefully, "I don't mind it. I killed the man for good reasons, and I don't regret it."

"What were the reasons?"

"Well, he needed killing."

"*I'll* tell you why he did it, since he won't say himself," said Angelo warmly. "He did it to save my life—that's what he did it for. So it was a noble act, and not a thing to be hid in the dark."

"So it was, so it was," said Wilson; "to do such a thing to save a brother's life is a great and fine action."

"Now come," said Luigi, "it is very pleasant to hear you say these things, but for unselfishness, or heroism, or magnanimity, the circumstance won't stand scrutiny. You overlook one detail: suppose I hadn't saved Angelo's life, what would have become of mine? If I had let the man kill him, wouldn't he have killed me, too? I saved my own life, you see."

"Yes, that is your way of talking," said Angelo, "but I know you, and I don't believe you thought of yourself at all. I keep that weapon yet that Luigi killed the man with, and I'll show it to you some time. That incident makes it interesting, and it had a history before it came into Luigi's hands which adds to its interest. It was given to Luigi by a great Indian prince, the Gaikowar of Baroda, and it had been in his family two or three centuries. It killed a good many disagreeable people who troubled that hearthstone at one time and another. It isn't much to look at, except that it isn't shaped like other knives, or dirks, or whatever it may be called—here, I'll draw it for you." He took a sheet of paper and made a rapid sketch. "There it is—a broad and murderous blade, with edges like a razor for sharpness. The devices engraved on it are the ciphers or names of its long line of possessors—I had Luigi's name added in Roman letters, myself, with our coat of arms, as you see. You notice what a curious handle the thing has. It is solid ivory, polished like a mirror, and is four or five inches long—round, and as thick as a large man's wrist, with the end squared off flat, for your thumb to rest on; for you grasp it, with your thumb resting on the blunt end—so—and lift it aloft and strike downwards. The Gaikowar showed us how the thing was done when he gave it to Luigi, and before that night was ended Luigi had used the knife and the Gaikowar was a man short by reason of it. The sheath is magnificently ornamented with gems of great value. You will find the sheath more worth looking at than the knife itself, of course."

Tom said to himself: "It's lucky I came here; I would have sold that knife for a song; I supposed the jewels were glass."

"But go on—don't stop," said Wilson. "Our curiosity is up, now, to hear about the homicide. Tell us about that."

"Well, briefly, the knife was to blame for that, all around. A native servant slipped into our room in the palace in the night, to kill us and steal that knife on account of the fortune encrusted on its sheath, without a doubt. Luigi had it under his pillow; we were in bed together. There was a dim night-light burning. I was asleep, but Luigi was awake, and he thought he detected a vague form nearing the bed. He slipped the knife out of the sheath, and was ready and unembarrassed by hampering bed-clothes, for the weather was hot and we hadn't any. Suddenly that native rose at the bedside and bent over me with his right hand lifted and a dirk in it aimed at my throat, but Luigi grabbed his wrist, pulled him downward and drove his own knife into the man's neck. I think he was dead before his spouting blood struck us. That is the whole story."

Wilson and Tom drew deep breaths, and after some general chat about the tragedy, Pudd'nhead said, taking Tom's hand—

"Now, Tom, I've never had a look at your palms, as it happens—perhaps you've got some little questionable privacies that need— Hel-lo!"

Tom had snatched away his hand, and was looking a good deal confused.

"Why, he's blushing!" said Luigi.

Tom darted an ugly look at him and said, sharply—

"Well, if I am, it ain't because I'm a murderer!" Luigi's dark face flushed, but before he could speak or move, Tom added with anxious haste, "Oh, I beg a thousand pardons, I didn't mean that, it was out before I thought, and I'm very, very sorry—you must forgive me."

Wilson came to the rescue, and smoothed things down as well as he could; and in fact was entirely successful as far as the Twins were concerned, for they felt sorrier for the affront put upon him by his guest's outburst of ill manners than for the insult offered to Luigi; but the success was not so pronounced with the offender. Tom tried to seem at his ease, and he went through the motions fairly well, but at bottom he felt resentful toward all the three witnesses of his exhibition—in fact he felt so annoyed at them for having witnessed it and noticed it that he almost forgot to feel annoyed at himself for placing it before them. However, something presently happened which made him almost comfortable, and brought him nearly back to a state of charity and friendliness. This was a little spat between the Twins; not much of a spat, but still a spat; and before they got far with it they were in a decided condition of irritation with each other. Tom was charmed; so pleased, indeed, that he cautiously did what he could to increase the irritation while pretending to be actuated by more respectable motives. By his help the fire got warmed up to the blazing point, and he might have had the happiness of seeing the flames show up, in another moment, but for the interruption of a knock on the door—an interruption which fretted him as much as it gratified Wilson. Wilson opened the door.

The visitor was a good-natured, ignorant, energetic, middle-aged Irishman named John Buckstone, who was a great politician in a small way, and always took a large share in public matters of every sort. One of the town's chief excitements, just now, was over the matter of rum. There was a strong rum party and a strong anti-rum party. Buckstone was training with the rum party, and he had been sent to hunt up the Twins and invite them to attend a mass meeting of that faction. He delivered his errand and said the clans were already gathering in the big hall over the market house. Luigi accepted the invitation cordially, Angelo less cordially, since he disliked crowds, and did not drink the powerful intoxicants of America. In fact, he was even a teetotaler sometimes—when it was judicious to be one.

The Twins left with Buckstone, and Tom Driscoll joined company with them uninvited.

In the distance one could see a wavering long line of torches drifting down the main street, and could hear the throbbing of a bass drum, the clash of cymbals, the squeaking of a fife or two, and the faint roar of remote hurrahs. The tail end of this procession was climbing the market house stairs when the Twins arrived in its neighborhood; when they reached the hall it was full of people, torches, smoke, noise and enthusiasm. They were conducted to the platform by Buckstone,—Tom Driscoll still following—and delivered to the chairman in the midst of a prodigious explosion of welcome. When the noise had moderated a little, the chair proposed that "our illustrious guests be at once elected, by complimentary acclamation, to membership in our ever glorious organization, the paradise of the free and the perdition of the slave."

This eloquent discharge opened the flood-gates of enthusiasm again, and the election was carried with thundering unanimity. Then arose a storm of cries,—

"Wet them down! wet them down! give them a drink!"

Glasses of whisky were handed to the Twins. Luigi waved his aloft, then brought it to his lips, but Angelo set his down. There was another storm of cries—

"What's the matter with the other one?"

"What is the blonde one going back on us for?"

"Explain! explain!"

The chairman inquired, and then reported—

"We have made an unfortunate mistake, gentlemen. I find that the Count Angelo Cappello is opposed to our creed—is a teetotaler, in fact, and was not intending to apply for membership with us. He desires that we reconsider the vote by which he was elected. What is the pleasure of the house?"

There was a general burst of laughter, plentifully accented with whistlings and cat-calls, but the energetic use of the gavel presently restored something like order. Then a man spoke from the crowd and said that while he was very sorry that the mistake had been made, it would not be possible to rectify it at the present meeting. According to the bye-laws it must go over to the next regular meeting for action. He would not offer a motion, as none was required. He desired to apologize to the gentleman in the name of the house, and begged to assure him that as far as it might lie in the power of the Sons of Liberty, his temporary membership in the order would be made pleasant to him.

This speech was received with great applause, mixed with cries of—

"That's the talk!" "He's a good fellow, anyway, if he *is* a teetotaler!" "Drink his health!" "Give him a rouser, and no heel-taps!"

Glasses were handed around, and everybody on the platform drank Angelo's health, while the house bellowed forth in song:

> "For he's a jolly good fel-low,
> For he's a jolly good fel-low.
> For he's a jolly good fe-el-low—
> Which nobody can deny!"

Tom Driscoll drank. It was his second glass, for he had drunk Angelo's the moment that Angelo had set it down. The two drinks made him very merry—almost idiotically so—and he began to take a most lively and prominent part in the proceedings, particularly in the music and cat-calls and side-remarks department of them.

The chairman was still standing at the front, the Twins at his side. The extraordinarily close resemblance of the brothers to each other suggested a witticism to Tom Driscoll, and just as the chairman began a speech he skipped forward and said with an air of tipsy confidence to the audience—

"Boys, I move that he keeps still and lets this human phillipene snip you out a speech!"

The descriptive aptness of the phrase caught the house, and a mighty burst of laughter followed.

Luigi's southern blood leaped to the boiling-point in a moment under the sharp humiliation of this insult delivered in the presence of four hundred strangers. It was not in the young man's nature to let the matter pass, or to delay the squaring of the account. He took a couple of strides and halted behind the unsuspecting joker. Then he drew back and delivered a kick of such titanic vigor in the joker's rear that it lifted him clear over the footlights and landed him on the heads of the front row of the Sons of Liberty.

Even a sober person does not like to have a human being emptied on him when he is not doing any harm; a person who is not sober cannot endure such an attention at all. The nest of Sons of Liberty that Driscoll landed in had not a sober bird in it; in fact there was probably not an entirely sober one in the auditorium. Driscoll was promptly and indignantly flung onto the heads of Sons in the next row, and these Sons passed him on toward the rear, and then immediately began to pummel the front-row Sons who had passed him to *them*. This course was strictly followed by bench after bench as Driscoll traveled in his tumultuous and airy flight toward the door; so he left behind him an ever lengthening wake of raging and plunging and fighting and swearing humanity. Down went group after group of torches, and presently, above the deafening clatter of the gavel, roar of angry voices and crash of succumbing benches, rose the paralyzing cry of

"Fire!"

The fighting ceased instantly; the cursings ceased; for one distinctly defined moment there was a dead hush, a motionless calm, where the tempest had been; then with one impulse the multitude awoke to life and energy again, and went surging and struggling and swaying, this way and that, its outer edges melting away through windows and doors and gradually lessening the pressure and relieving the mass.

The fire-boys were never on hand so suddenly before; for there was no distance to go, this time, their quarters being in the rear end of the market house. There was an engine company and a hook and ladder company. Half of each was composed of rummies and the other half of anti-rummies, after the moral and political share-and-share-alike fashion of the frontier town of the period. Enough anti-rummies were loafing in quarters to man the engine and the ladders. In two minutes they had their red shirts and helmets on—they never stirred officially in unofficial costume—and as the mass meeting overhead smashed through the long row of windows and poured out onto the roof of the arcade, the deliverers were ready for them with a powerful stream of water which washed some of them off the roof and nearly drowned the rest. But water was preferable to fire, and still the outpour from the windows continued, and still the pitiless drenchings assailed it until the building was empty; then the fire-boys mounted to the hall and flooded it with water enough to have annihilated forty times as much fire as there was there: for a village fire company does not often get a chance to show off, and so when it does get a chance it makes the most of it. Such citizens of that village as were of a thoughtful and judicious temperament did not insure against fire, they insured against the fire company.

Chapter 12

Courage is resistance to fear, mastery of fear—not *absence* of fear. Except a creature be part coward it is not a compliment to say it is brave, it is merely a loose misapplication of the word. Consider the flea!—incomparably the bravest of all the creatures of God, if ignorance of fear were courage. Whether you are asleep or awake he will attack you, caring nothing for the fact that in bulk and strength you are to him as are the massed armies of the earth to a sucking child; he lives both day and night and all days and nights in the very lap of peril and the immediate presence of death, and yet is no more afraid than is the man who walks the streets of a city that was threatened by an earthquake ten centuries before. When we speak of Clive, Nelson and Putnam as men who "didn't know what fear was," we ought always to add the flea—and put him at the head of the procession.—*Pudd'nhead Wilson's Calendar.*

Judge Driscoll was in bed and asleep by ten o'clock on Friday night, and he was up and gone a fishing before daylight in the morning with his friend Pembroke Howard. These two had been boys together in Virginia when that State still ranked as the chief and most imposing member of the Union, and they still coupled the proud and affectionate adjective "old" with her name when they spoke of her. In Missouri a recognized superiority attached to any person who hailed from Old Virginia; and this superiority was exalted to supremacy when a person of such nativity could also prove descent from the First Families of that great commonwealth. The Howards and Driscolls were of this aristocracy. In their eyes it was a nobility. It had its unwritten laws, and they were as clearly defined and as stringent as any that could be found among the printed statutes of the land. The F.F.V. was born a gentleman; his highest duty in life was to watch over that great inheritance and keep it unsmirched. He must keep his honor spotless. Those laws were his chart; his course was marked out on it; if he swerved from it by so much as half a point of the compass it meant shipwreck to his honor; that is to say, degradation from his rank as a gentleman. These laws required certain things of him which his religion might forbid: then his religion must yield—the laws could not be relaxed to accommodate religion or anything else. Honor stood first; and the laws defined what it was and wherein it differed, in certain details, from honor as defined by church creeds and by the social laws and customs of some of the minor divisions of the globe that had got crowded out when the sacred boundaries of Virginia were staked out.

If Judge Driscoll was the recognized first citizen of Dawson's Landing, Pembroke Howard was easily its recognized second citizen. He was called "the great lawyer"—an earned title. He and Driscoll were of the same age—a year or two past sixty.

Although Driscoll was a freethinker and Howard a strong and determined Presbyterian, their warm intimacy suffered no impairment in consequence. They were men whose opinions were their own property and not subject to revision and amendment, suggestion or criticism, by anybody, even their friends.

The day's fishing finished, they came floating down stream in their skiff, talking national politics and other high matters, and presently met a skiff coming up from town, with a man in it who said:

"I reckon you know one of the new Twins gave your nephew a kicking last night, Judge?"

"Did *what?*"

"Gave him a kicking."

The old Judge's lips paled and his eyes began to flame. He choked with anger for a moment, then he got out what he was trying to say—

"Well—well—*go* on! Give me the details."

The man did it. At the finish, the Judge was silent a minute, turning over in his mind the shameful picture of Tom's flight over the footlights, then he said, as if musing aloud—

"Hm—I don't understand it. I was asleep at home. He didn't wake me. Thought he was competent to manage his affair without my help, I reckon." His face lit up with pride and pleasure at that thought, and he said with a cheery complacency, "I like that!—it's the true old blood—hey, Pembroke?"

Howard smiled an iron smile and nodded his head approvingly. Then the news-bringer spoke again—

"But Tom beat the twin on the trial."

The Judge looked at the man wonderingly, and said—

"The trial? What trial?"

"Why, Tom had him up before Judge Robinson for assault and battery."

The old man shrank suddenly together like one who has received a death-stroke. Howard sprang for him as he sank forward in a swoon, and took him in his arms and bedded him on his back in the boat. He sprinkled water in his face, and said to the startled visitor—

"Go, now—don't let him come to and find you here. You see what an effect your heedless speech has had; you ought to have been more considerate than to blurt out such a cruel piece of slander as that."

"I'm right down sorry I did it, now, Mr. Howard, and I wouldn't have done it if I had thought; but it ain't a slander, it's perfectly true, just as I told him."

He rowed away. Presently the old Judge came out of his faint and looked up piteously into the sympathetic face that was bent over him.

"Say it ain't true, Pembroke, tell me it ain't true," he said, in a weak voice.

There was nothing weak in the deep organ-tones that responded—

"You know it's a lie as well as I do, old friend. He is of the best blood of the Old Dominion."

"God bless you for saying it!" said the old gentleman fervently. "Ah, Pembroke, it was such a blow!"

Howard stayed by his friend, and saw him home, and entered the house with him. It was dark, and past supper time, but the Judge was not thinking of supper, he was eager to hear the slander refuted from headquarters, and as eager to have Howard hear it, too. Tom was sent for, and he came immediately. He was bruised and lame, and not a happy-looking object. His uncle made him sit down, and said—

"We have been hearing about your adventure, Tom, with a handsome lie added to it for embellishment. Now pulverize that lie to dust! What measures have you taken? How does the thing stand?"

Tom answered guilelessly: "It don't stand at all; it's all over. I had him up in court and beat him. Pudd'nhead Wilson defended him—first case he ever had, and lost it. The judge fined the miserable hound five dollars for the assault."

Howard and the Judge sprang to their feet with the opening sentence—why, neither knew; then they stood gazing vacantly at each other. Howard stood a moment, then sat mournfully down without saying anything. The Judge's wrath began to kindle, and he burst out—

"You cur! you scum! you vermin! Do you mean to tell me that blood of my race has suffered a blow and crawled to a court of law about it? Answer me!"

Tom's head drooped, and he answered with an eloquent silence. His uncle stared at him with a mixed expression of amazement and shame and incredulity that was sorrowful to see. At last he said—

"Which of the Twins was it?"

"Count Luigi."

"You have challenged him?"

"N-no," hesitated Tom, turning pale.

"You will challenge him to-night. Howard will carry it."

Tom began to turn sick, and to show it. He turned his hat round and round in his hand, his uncle glowering blacker and blacker upon him as the heavy seconds drifted by, then at last he began to stammer, and said, piteously—

"Oh, please don't ask me to do it, uncle. I never could. He is a murderous devil. I—I'm *afraid* of him."

Old Driscoll's mouth opened and closed three times before he could get it to perform its office; then he stormed out—

"A coward in my family! A Driscoll a coward! Oh, what have I done to deserve this infamy!" He tottered to his secretary in the corner, still repeating, again and again, that lament in heart-breaking tones, and got out of a drawer a paper, which he slowly tore to bits and scattered the bits absently in his track as he walked up and down the room, still grieving and lamenting. At last he said—

"There it is, shreds and fragments once more—my will. Once more you have forced me to disinherit you, you base son of a most noble father. Leave my sight! Go—before I spit on you!"

The young man did not tarry. Then the Judge turned to Howard:

"You will be my second, old friend?"

"Of course."

"There is pen and paper. Draft the cartel, and lose no time."

"The Count shall have it in his hands in fifteen minutes," said Howard.

Tom was very heavy-hearted. His appetite was gone with his property and his self-respect. He went out the back way and wandered down the obscure lane, grieving, and wondering if any course of future conduct, however discreet and carefully perfected and watched over, could win back his uncle's favor and persuade him to reconstruct once more that generous will which had just gone to rags and ruin before his eyes. He finally concluded that it could. He said to himself that he had accomplished this sort of triumph once already, and that what had been done once could be done again. He would set about it. He would bend every energy to the task, and he would score that

"A COWARD IN MY FAMILY!"

triumph once more, cost what it might to his convenience, limit as it might his frivolous and liberty-loving life.

"To begin," he said to himself, "I'll square up with the proceeds of my raid, and then gambling has got to be stopped—and stopped short off. It's the worst vice I've got—from my standpoint it is, anyway, because it's the one he can easiest find out, through the impatience of my creditors. He thought it expensive to have to pay two hundred dollars to them for me once. Expensive—that! Why, it cost *me* the whole of his fortune—but of course he never thought of that; some people can't think of any but their own side of a case. If he had known how deep I am in, now, the will would have gone to pot without waiting for a duel to help. Three hundred dollars! It's a pile! But he'll never hear of it, I'm thankful to say. The minute I've cleared it off, I'm safe; and I'll never touch a card again. Anyway I won't while he lives, I make oath to that. I'm entering on my last reform—I know it—yes, and I'll win; but after that, if I ever slip again I'm gone!"

Chapter 13

When I reflect upon the number of disagreeable people who I know have gone to a better world, I am moved to lead a different life.—*Pudd'nhead Wilson's Calendar.*

October. This is one of the peculiarly dangerous months to speculate in stocks in. The others are July, January, September, April, November, May, March, June, December, August, and February.—*Pudd'nhead Wilson's Calendar.*

Thus mournfully communing with himself Tom moped along the lane past Pudd'nhead Wilson's house, and still on and on, between fences enclosing vacant country on either hand, till he neared the haunted house, then came moping back again, with many sighs and heavy with trouble. He sorely wanted cheerful company. Rowena! His heart gave a bound at the thought, but the next thought quieted it—the detested Twins would be there.

He was on the inhabited side of Wilson's house, and now as he approached it he noticed that the sitting room was lighted. This would do; others made him feel unwelcome sometimes, but Wilson never failed in courtesy toward him, and a kindly courtesy does at least save one's feelings, even if it is not professing to stand for a welcome. Wilson heard footsteps at his threshold, then the clearing of a throat, ["It's that fickle-tempered, dissipated young goose—poor devil, he finds friends pretty scarce to-day, likely, after the disgrace of carrying a personal-assault case into a law-court."] A dejected knock. "Come in!"

Tom entered and drooped into a chair, without saying anything. Wilson said, kindly—

"Why, my boy, you look desolate. Don't take it so hard. Try and forget you have been kicked."

"Oh, dear," said Tom, wretchedly, "it's not that, Pudd'nhead—it's not that. It's a thousand times worse than that—oh, yes, a million times worse."

"Why, Tom, what do you mean? Has Rowena—"

"Flung me? No, but the old man has."

Wilson said to himself, "Aha!" and thought of the mysterious girl in the bedroom. "The Driscolls have been making discoveries." Then he said aloud, gravely:

"Tom, there are some kinds of dissipation which—"

"Oh, shucks, this hasn't got anything to do with dissipation! He wanted me to challenge that derned Italian savage, and I wouldn't do it."

"Yes, of course he would do that," said Wilson in a meditative matter-of-course way; "but the thing that puzzled me, was, why he didn't look to that last night, for one thing, and why he let you carry such a matter into a court of law at all, either before the duel or after it. It's no place for it. It was not like him. I couldn't understand it. How did it happen?"

"It happened because he didn't know anything about it. He was asleep when I got home last night."

"And you didn't wake him? Tom, is that possible?"

Tom was not getting much comfort here. He fidgeted a moment, then said:

"I didn't choose to tell him—that's all. He was going a fishing before dawn, with Pembroke Howard, and if I got the Twins into the common calaboose,—and I thought sure I could—I never dreamed of their slipping out on a paltry fine for such an outrageous offence—well, once in the calaboose they would be disgraced, and uncle wouldn't want any duels with that sort of characters, and wouldn't allow any."

"Tom, I am ashamed of you. I don't see how you could treat your good old uncle so. I am a better friend of his than you are; for if I had known the circumstances I would have kept that case out of court until I got word to him and let him have a gentleman's chance."

"You would?" exclaimed Tom, with lively surprise. "And it your first case! and you know perfectly well there never would have *been* any case if he had got that chance, don't you? and you'd have finished your days a pauper nobody, instead of being an actually launched and recognized lawyer to-day. And you would really have done that, would you?"

"Certainly."

Tom looked at him a moment or two, then shook his head sorrowfully and said—

"I believe you—upon my word I do. I don't know why I do, but I do. Pudd'nhead Wilson, I think you're the biggest fool I ever saw."

"Thank you."

"Don't mention it."

"Well, he has been requiring you to fight the Italian, and you have refused. You degenerate remnant of an honorable line! I'm thoroughly ashamed of you, Tom."

"Oh, that's nothing. I don't care for anything, now that the will's torn up again."

"Tom, tell me squarely—didn't he find any fault with you for anything but those two things—carrying the case into court and refusing to fight?"

He watched the young fellow's face narrowly, but it was entirely reposeful, and so also was the voice that answered:

"No, he didn't find any other fault with me. If he had had any to find, he would have begun yesterday, for he was just in the humor for it. He drove that jack-pair around town and showed them the sights, and when he came home he couldn't find his father's old silver watch that don't keep time and he thinks so much of, and couldn't remember what he did with it three or four days ago when he saw it last; and so when I arrived he was all in a sweat about it, and when I suggested that it probably wasn't lost but stolen, it put him in a regular passion and he said I was a fool—which convinced me, without any trouble, that that was just what he was afraid had happened, himself, but didn't want to believe it, because lost things stand a better chance of being found again than stolen ones."

"Whe-ew!" whistled Wilson; "score another on the list!"

"Another what?"

"Another theft!"

"Theft?"

"Yes, theft. That watch isn't lost, it's stolen. There's been another raid on the town—and just the same old mysterious sort of thing that has happened once before, as you remember."

"You don't mean it!"

"It's as sure as you are born. Have you missed anything yourself?"

"No. That is, I did miss a silver pencil case that aunt Mary Pratt gave me last birth-day—"

"You'll find it's stolen—that's what you'll find."

"No, I shan't; for when I suggested theft about the watch and got such a rap, I went and examined my room, and the pencil-case was missing, but it was only mislaid, and I found it again."

"You are sure you missed nothing else?"

"Well, nothing of consequence. I missed a small plain gold ring worth two or three dollars, but that will turn up. I'll look again."

"In my opinion you'll not find it. There's been a raid, I tell you. Come in!"

Mr. Justice Robinson entered, followed by Buckstone and the town constable, Jim Blake. They sat down, and after some wandering and aimless weather-conversation, Wilson said—

"By the way, we've just added another to the list of thefts, maybe two. Judge Driscoll's old silver watch is gone, and Tom here has missed a gold ring."

"Well, it is a bad business," said the justice, "and gets worse the further it goes. The Hankses, the Dobsons, the Pilligrews, the Ortons, the Grangers, the Hales, the Fullers, the Holcombs, in fact everybody that lives around about Patsy Cooper's have been robbed of little things like trinkets and teaspoons and such-like small valuables that are easily carried off. It's perfectly plain that the thief took advantage of the reception at Patsy Cooper's, when all the neighbors were in her house and all their niggers hanging around her fence for a look at the show, to raid the vacant houses undisturbed. Patsy is miserable about it; miserable on account of the neighbors, and particularly miserable on account of her foreigners, of course; so miserable on their account that she hasn't any room to worry about her own little losses."

"It's the same old raider," said Wilson, "I suppose there isn't any doubt about that."

"Constable Blake doesn't think so."

"No, you're wrong there," said Blake, "the other times it was a man; there was plenty of signs of that, as *we* know, in the profession, though we never got hands on him; but this time it's a woman."

Wilson thought of the mysterious girl, straight off. She was always in his mind, now. But she failed him again. Blake continued:

"She's a stoop-shouldered old woman with a covered basket on her arm in a black veil dressed in mourning. I saw her going aboard the ferry-boat yesterday. Lives in Illinois, I reckon; but I don't care where she lives, I'm going to get her—she can make herself sure of that."

"What makes you think she's the thief?"

"Well, there ain't any other, for one thing; and for another, some of the nigger draymen that happened to be driving along saw her coming out or going into houses and told me so—and it just happens that they was robbed houses, every time."

It was granted that this was plenty good enough circumstantial evidence. A pensive silence followed, which lasted for some moments, then Wilson said—

"There's one good thing, anyway. She can't either pawn or sell Count Luigi's costly Indian dagger."

"My!" said Tom; "is that gone?"

"Yes."

"Well, that *was* a haul! But why can't she pawn it or sell it?"

"Because when the Twins went home from the Sons of Liberty meeting last night, news of the raid was sifting in from everywhere and Aunt Patsy was in distress to know if they had lost anything. They found that the dagger was gone, and they notified the police and pawnbrokers everywhere. It was a great haul, yes, but the old woman won't get anything out of it, because she'll get caught."

"Did they offer a reward?" asked Buckstone.

"Yes—five hundred dollars for the knife, and five hundred more for the thief."

"What a leather-headed idea!" exclaimed the constable. "The thief dasn't go near them, nor send anybody. Whoever goes is going to get himself nabbed, for there ain't any pawnbroker that's going to lose the chance to—"

If anybody had noticed Tom's face at that time, the gray-green color of it might have provoked curiosity; but nobody did. He said to himself, "I'm gone! I never can square up; the rest of the plunder won't pawn or sell for half of the bill. Oh, I know it—I'm gone, I'm gone—and this time it's for good! Oh, this is awful—I don't know *what* to do, nor which way to turn!"

"Softly, softly," said Wilson to Blake, "I planned their scheme for them at midnight last night, and it was all finished up shipshape by two this morning. They'll get their dagger back, and then I'll explain to you how the thing was done."

There were strong signs of a general curiosity, and Buckstone said—

"Well, you *have* whetted us up pretty sharp, Wilson, and I'm free to say that if you don't mind telling us in confidence—"

"Oh, I'd as soon tell as not, Buckstone, but as long as the Twins and I agreed to say nothing about it, we must let it stand so. But you can take my word for it you won't be kept waiting three days. Somebody will apply for that reward pretty promptly, and I'll show you the thief and the dagger both very soon afterward."

The constable was disappointed, and also perplexed. He said—

"It may all be—yes, and I hope it will, but I'm blamed if I can see *my* way through it. It's too many for yours truly."

The subject seemed about talked out. Nobody seemed to have anything further to offer. After a silence the justice of the peace informed Wilson that he and Buckstone and the constable had come as a committee, on the part of the Democratic party, to ask him to run for mayor—for the little town was about to become a city and the first charter election was approaching. It was the first attention which Wilson had ever received at the hands of any party; it was a sufficiently humble one, but it was a recognition of his début into the town's life and activities at last; it was a step upward, and he was deeply gratified. He accepted, and the committee departed, followed by young Tom.

Chapter 14

The true southern watermelon is a boon apart, and not to be mentioned with commoner things. It is chief of this world's luxuries, king by the grace of God over all the fruits of the earth. When one has tasted it, he knows what the angels eat. It was not a southern watermelon that Eve took: we know it because she repented.—Pudd'nhead Wilson's Calendar.

About the time that Wilson was bowing the committee out, Pembroke Howard was entering the next house to report. He found the old Judge sitting grim and straight in his chair, waiting.

"Well, Howard—the news?"

"The best in the world."

"Accepts, does he?" and the light of battle gleamed joyously in the Judge's eye.

"Accepts? Why, he jumped at it."

"Did, did he? Now that's fine—that's very fine. I like that. When is it to be?"

"Now! Straight off! To-night! An admirable fellow—admirable!"

"Admirable? He's a darling! Why, it's an honor as well as a pleasure to stand up before such a man. Come—off with you! Go and arrange everything—and give him my heartiest compliments. A rare fellow, indeed; an admirable fellow, as you have said!"

Howard hurried away, saying—

"I'll have him in the vacant stretch between Wilson's and the haunted house within the hour, and I'll bring my own pistols."

Judge Driscoll began to walk the floor in a state of pleased excitement; but presently he stopped, and began to think. Began to think of Tom. Twice he moved toward the secretary, and twice he turned away again; but finally he said—

"This may be my last night in the world—I must not take the chance. He is worthless and unworthy, but it is largely my fault. He was entrusted to me by my brother on his dying bed, and I have indulged him to his hurt, instead of training him up severely and making a man of him. I have violated my trust, and I must not add the sin of desertion to that. I have forgiven him once, already, and would subject him to a long and hard trial before forgiving him again, if I could live; but I must not run that risk. No, I must restore the will. But if I survive the duel I will hide it away and he will not know, and I will not tell him until he reforms and I see that his reformation is going to be permanent."

He re-drew the will, and his ostensible nephew was heir to a fortune again. As he was finishing his task, Tom, wearied with another brooding tramp, entered the house and went tip-toeing past the sitting-room door. He glanced in, and hurried on, for the sight of his uncle had nothing but terrors for him to-night. But his uncle was writing! That was unusual—at this late hour. What could he be writing? A chill anxiety settled down upon Tom's heart. Did that writing concern him? He was afraid so. He reflected that when ill luck begins, it does not come in sprinkles, but in showers. He said he would get a glimpse of that document or know the reason why. He heard some one coming, and stepped out of sight and hearing. It was Pembroke Howard. What *could* be hatching?

Howard said, with great satisfaction—

"Everything's right and ready. He's gone to the battle ground with his second and the surgeon—also with his brother. I've arranged it all with Wilson—Wilson's his second. We are to have three shots apiece."

"Good. How is the moon?"

"Bright as day, nearly. Perfect for the distance—fifteen yards. No wind—not a breath; hot and still."

"All good; all first-rate. Here, Pembroke, read this, and witness it."

Pembroke read and witnessed the will, then gave the old man's hand a hearty shake and said—

"Now that's right, York—but I knew you would do it. You couldn't leave that poor chap to fight along without means or profession, with certain defeat before him, and I knew you wouldn't, for his father's sake if not for his own."

"For his dead father's sake I couldn't, I know; for poor Percy—but you know what Percy was to me. But mind—Tom is not to know of this unless I fall to-night."

"I understand. I'll keep the secret."

The Judge put the will away, and the two started for the battle ground. In another minute the will was in Tom's hands. His misery vanished, his feelings underwent a tremendous revulsion. He put the will carefully back in its place and spread his mouth and swung his hat once, twice, three times around his head, in imitation of three rousing huzzas, no sound issuing from his lips. He fell to communing with himself excitedly and joyously, but every now and then he let off another volley of dumb hurrahs.

He said to himself: "I've got the fortune again, but I'll not let on that I know about it. And this time I'm going to hang on to it. I take no more risks. I'll gamble no more, I'll drink no more, because—well, because I'll not go where there is any of that sort of thing going on, again. It's the sure way, and the only sure way; I might have thought of that sooner—well, yes, if I had wanted to. But *now*—dear me, I've had a bad scare this time, and I'll take no more chances. Not a single chance more. Land! I persuaded myself this evening that I could fetch him around without any great amount of effort, but I've been getting more and more heavy-hearted and doubtful straight along, ever since. If he tells me about this thing, all right; but if he doesn't, I shan't let on. I—well, I'd like to tell Pudd'nhead Wilson, but—no, I'll think about that; perhaps I won't." He whirled off another dead huzza, and said, "I'm reformed, and this time I'll stay so, sure."

He was about to close with a final grand silent demonstration, when he suddenly recollected that Wilson had put it out of his power to pawn or sell the Indian knife, and that he was once more in awful peril of exposure by his creditors for that reason. His joy collapsed utterly, and he turned away and moped toward the door moaning and lamenting over the bitterness of his luck. He dragged himself upstairs, and brooded in his room a long time, disconsolate and forlorn, with Luigi's Indian knife for a text. At last he sighed and said:

"When I supposed these stones were glass and this ivory bone, the thing hadn't any interest for me because it hadn't any value and couldn't help me out of my trouble. But now—why, now it is full of interest; yes, and of a sort to break a body's heart. It's a bag of gold that has turned to dirt and ashes in my hands. It could save me, and save me so easily, and yet I've got to go to ruin. It's like drowning with a life-preserver in my reach. All the hard luck comes to me and all the good luck goes to other people—Pudd'nhead Wilson, for instance; even his career has got a sort of a little start at last, and what has he done to deserve it, I would like to know. Yes, he has opened his own road, but he isn't content with that, but must block mine. It's a sordid, selfish world, and I wish I was out of it." He allowed the light of the candle to play upon the jewels of the sheath, but the flashings and sparklings had no charm for his eye, they were only just so many pangs for his heart. "I must not say anything to Roxy about this thing," he said, "she is too daring. She would be for digging these stones out and selling them, and then—why, she would be arrested and the stones traced, and *then!*—" The thought made him quake, and he hid the knife away, trembling all over and glancing furtively about, like a criminal who fancies that the accuser is already at hand.

Should he try to sleep? Oh, no, sleep was not for him; his trouble was too haunting, too afflicting for that. He must have somebody to mourn with. He would carry his despair to Roxy.

He had heard several distant gunshots, but that sort of thing was not uncommon, and they had made no impression upon him. He went out at the back door, and turned westward. He passed Wilson's house and proceeded along the lane, and presently saw several figures approaching Wilson's place through the vacant lots. These were the duelists returning from the fight; he thought he recognized them, but as he had no desire for white people's company he stooped down behind the fence until they were out of his way.

Roxy was feeling fine. She said:

"Whah was you, child? Warn't you in it?"

"In what?"

"In de duel."

"Duel? Has there been a duel?"

"'Cose dey has. De ole Jedge has ben havin' a duel wid one o' dem Twins."

"Great Scott!" Then he added, to himself, "*That's* what made him re-make the will; he thought he might get killed, and it softened him toward me. And that's what he and Howard were so busy about. . . . . . . Oh, dear, if the twin had only killed him, I should be out of my—"

"What is you mumblin' 'bout, Chambers? Whah was you? Didn't you know dey was gwyne to be a duel?"

"No, I didn't. The old man tried to get me to fight one with Count Luigi, but he didn't succeed; so I reckon he concluded to patch up the family honor himself."

He laughed at the idea, and went rambling on with a detailed account of his talk with the Judge, and how shocked and ashamed the Judge was to find that he had a coward in his family. He glanced up at last, and got a shock himself. Roxana's bosom was heaving with suppressed passion, and she was glowering down upon him with measureless contempt written in her face.

"En you refuse' to fight a man dat kicked you, 'stid o' jumpin' at de chance! En you ain't got no mo' feelin' den to come en tell *me*, dat fetched sich a po' low-down ornery rabbit into de worl'! Pah! it make me sick! It's de *nigger* in you, dat's what it is. Thirty-one parts o' you is white, en on'y one part nigger, en dat po' little one part is yo' soul! 'Tain't wuth savin'; 'tain't wuth totin' out on a shovel en tho'in' in de gutter. You has disgraced yo' birth. What would yo' pa think o' you? It's enough to make him turn in his grave."

The last three sentences stung Tom into a fury, and he said to himself that if his father were only alive and in reach of assassination his mother would soon find that he had a very clear notion of the size of his indebtedness to that man and was willing to pay it up in full, and would do it, too, even at risk of his life; but he kept his thought to himself; that was safest, in his mother's present state.

"Whatever *has* 'come o' yo' Essex blood? Dat's what *I* can't understan'. En it ain't on'y jist Essex blood dat's in you, not by a long sight—'deed it ain't! My father en yo' gran'father was ole John Randolph of Roanoke, de highes' blood dat Ole Virginny ever turned out; en his great-great-gran'mother or somers along back dah, was Pocahontas de Injun queen—en yit here you is, a slinkin' outen a duel en disgracin' our whole line like a ornery low-down hound! Yes, it's de *nigger* in you."

She sat down on her candle-box and fell into a reverie. Tom did not disturb her; he sometimes lacked prudence, but it was not in circumstances of this kind. Roxana's storm went gradually down, but it died hard, and even when it seemed to be quite gone it would now and then break out in a distant rumble, so to speak, in the form of muttered ejaculations. One of these was, "Ain't nigger enough in him to show in his finger-nails, en dat takes mighty little—yit dey's enough to paint his soul." Presently she muttered, "Yassir, enough to paint a whole thimbleful of 'em." At last her rumblings ceased altogether and her countenance began to clear—a welcome sign to Tom, who had learned her moods and knew she was on the threshold of good-humor, now. He noticed that from time to time she unconsciously carried her finger to the end of her nose. He looked closer and said—

"Why, mammy, the end of your nose is skinned. How did that come?"

She sent out the sort of whole-hearted peal of laughter which God has vouchsafed in its perfection to none but the happy angels in heaven and the bruised and broken black slave in the earth, and said:

"Dad fetch dat duel, *I* ben in it myself!"

"Gracious! did a bullet do that?"

"Yassir, you bet it did."

"Well, I declare! Why, how did that happen?"

"Happen dis-away. I 'uz a sett'n here kinder dozin' in de dark, en che-*bang!* goes a gun, right out dah. I skips along out towards t'other end o' de house to see what's gwyne on, en stops by de ole winder on de side towards Pudd'nhead Wilson's house dat ain't got no sash in it—but dey ain't none of 'em got any sashes, fur as dat's concerned—en I stood dah in de dark en look out, en dah I seed everything as plain as day in de moonlight. Right down under me 'uz one o' de Twins a cussin'—not much, but jist a cussin' soft,—it 'uz de *brown* one dat 'uz cussin', caze he 'uz hit in de shoulder. En Doctor Claypool he 'uz a workin' at him, en Pudd'nhead Wilson he 'uz a he'pin', en ole Jedge Driscoll en Pem. Howard 'uz a standin' out yonder a little piece waitin' for 'em to git ready agin. En toreckly dey squared off en give de word, en *bang-bang* went de pistols, en de twin he say 'Ouch!'—hit him on de han' dis time—en I hear dat same bullet go *'spat!'* agin de logs under de winder; en de nex' time dey shoot, de twin say 'Ouch!' agin, en I done it too, caze de bullet glance' on his cheek bone en skip up here en glance' on de side o' de winder en whiz right acrost my face en tuck de hide off'n my nose—why, if I'd a ben jist a inch or a inch en a half furder, 'twould a tuck de whole nose en disfigger' me. Here's de bullet; I hunted her up."

"Did you stand there all the time?"

"Dat's a question to ask, ain't it! What else would I do? Does I git a chance to see a duel every day?"

"Why, you were right in range. Weren't you afraid?"

The woman gave a sniff of scorn.

"*'Fraid!* De Randolphs ain't 'fraid o' *nothin'*, let alone bullets."

"They've got pluck enough, I suppose; what they lack is judgment. I wouldn't have stood there."

"Nobody's accusin' you!"

"Did anybody else get hurt?"

"Yes, we all got hit 'cep' de blon' twin en de doctor. De Jedge didn't git hurt, but I hear Pudd'nhead say de bullet snip some o' his ha'r off."

"'George!" said Tom to himself, "to come so near being out of my trouble, and miss it by an inch! O, dear, dear, he'll live to find me out and sell me to some nigger-trader yet—yes, and he would do it in a minute!" Then he said aloud, in a grave tone—

"Mother, we are in an awful fix."

Roxana caught her breath with a spasm, and said—

"Chile! What you hit a body so sudden for, like dat? What's ben en gone en happen'?"

"Well, there's one thing I didn't tell you. When I wouldn't fight, he tore up the will again, and—"

Roxana's face turned a dead white, and she said—

"*Now* you's *done!*—done forever! Dat's de *end!* Bofe un us is gwyne to starve to—"

"Wait and hear me through, can't you! I reckon that when he resolved to fight, himself, he thought he might get killed and not have a chance to forgive me any more in this life, so he made the will again, and I've seen it and it's all right. But—"

"Oh, thank goodness, den we's safe agin!—safe! en so what did you want to come here en talk sich dreadful—"

"Hold on, I tell you! and let me finish. The swag I gathered won't half square me up, and the first thing we know my creditors—well, you know what'll happen."

Roxana dropped her chin and told her son to leave her alone—she must think this matter out. Presently she said, impressively:

"You got to go mighty keerful now, *I* tell you. En here's what you got to do. He didn't git killed, en if you gives him de least reason, he'll bust de will agin, en dat's de *las'* time, now you hear *me*. So—you's got to show him what you kin do in de nex' few days. You's got to be pison good, en let him see it; you got to do everything dat'll make him b'lieve in you, en you got to sweeten aroun' ole Aunt Pratt, too—she's pow'ful strong wid de Jedge, en de bes' frien' you got. Nex', you'll go 'long away to Sent Louis, en dat'll *keep* him in yo' favor. Den you go en make a bargain wid dem people. You tell 'em he ain't gwyne to live long—en dat's de fac', too—en tell 'em you'll pay 'em intrust, en *big* intrust, too—ten per—what you call it?"

"Ten per cent a month."

"Dat's it. Den you take en sell yo' truck aroun', a little at a time, en pay de intrust. How long will it las'?"

"I think there's enough to pay the interest five or six months."

"Den you's all right. If he don't die in six months, dat don't make no diffrence—Providence 'll provide. You's gwyne to be safe—if you behaves." She bent an austere eye on him and added, "En you's *gwyne* to behave—does you know dat?"

He laughed and said he was going to try, anyway. She did not unbend. She said gravely—

"Tryin' ain't de thing. You's gwyne to *do* it. You ain't gwyne to steal a pin—caze it ain't safe no mo'; en you ain't gwyne into no bad comp'ny—not even *once*, you understand; en you ain't gwyne to drink a drop—nary single drop; en you ain't gwyne to gamble one single gamble—not one. Dis ain't what you's gwyne to *try* to do, it's what you's gwyne to *do*. En I'll tell you how I knows it. Dis is how. I's gwyne to foller along to Sent Louis my own self; en you's gwyne to come to me every day o' yo' life, en I'll look you over; en if you fails in one single one o' dem things—jist *once*—I take my oath I'll come straight down to dis town en tell de Jedge you is a nigger en a slave—en *prove* it!" She paused, to let her words sink home. Then she added: "Chambers, does you b'lieve me when I says dat?"

Tom was sober enough now. There was no levity in his voice when he answered:

"Yes, mother. I know, now, that I am reformed—and permanently. Permanently—and beyond the reach of any human temptation."

"Den g'long home en begin!"

Chapter 15

Nothing so needs reforming as other people's habits.
—*Pudd'nhead Wilson's Calendar.*

Behold, the fool saith, "Put not all thine eggs in the one basket"—which is but a manner of saying, "Scatter your money and your attention;" but the wise man saith, "Put all your eggs in the one basket and—*watch that basket.*"—*Pudd'nhead Wilson's Calendar.*

What a time of it Dawson's Landing was having! All its life it had been asleep, but now it hardly got a chance for a nod, so swiftly did big events and crashing surprises come along in one another's wake: Friday morning, first glimpse of Real Nobility, also grand reception at Aunt Patsy Cooper's, also great robber-raid; Friday evening, dramatic kicking of the heir of the chief citizen in presence of four hundred people; Saturday morning, emergence as practicing lawyer of the long-submerged Pudd'nhead Wilson; Saturday night, duel between chief citizen and titled stranger.

The people took more pride in the duel than in all the other events put together, perhaps. It was a glory to their town to have such a thing happen there. In their eyes the principals had reached the summit of human honor. Everybody paid homage to their names; their praises were in all mouths. Even the duelists' subordinates came in for a handsome share of the public approbation: wherefore Pudd'nhead Wilson was suddenly become a man of consequence. When asked to run for the mayoralty Saturday night he was risking defeat, but Sunday morning found him a made man and his success assured.

The Twins were prodigiously great, now; the town took them to its bosom with enthusiasm. Day after day, and night after night, they went dining and visiting from house to house, making friends, enlarging and solidifying their popularity, and charming and surprising all with their musical prodigies, and now and then heightening the effects with samples of what they could do in other directions, out of their stock of rare and curious accomplishments.

They were so pleased that they gave the regulation thirty days' notice, the required preparation for citizenship, and resolved to finish their days in this pleasant place. That was the climax. The delighted community rose as one man and applauded; and when the Twins were asked to stand for seats in the forthcoming aldermanic board, and consented, the public contentment was rounded and complete.

Tom Driscoll was not happy over these things; they sunk deep, and hurt all the way down. He hated the one twin for kicking him, and the other one for being the kicker's brother.

Now and then the people wondered why nothing was heard of the raider, or of the stolen knife or the other plunder, but nobody was able to throw any light on that matter. Nearly a week had drifted by, and still the thing remained a vexed mystery.

On Saturday, Constable Blake and Pudd'nhead Wilson met on the street, and Tom Driscoll joined them in time to open their conversation for them. He said to Blake—

"You are not looking well, Blake, you seem to be annoyed about something. Has anything gone wrong in the detective business? I believe you fairly and justifiably claim to have a pretty good reputation in that line, isn't it so?"—which made Blake feel good, and look it; but Tom added, "for a country detective"—which made Blake feel the other way, and not only look it but betray it in his voice—

"Yes, sir, I *have* got a reputation, and it's as good as anybody's in the profession, too, country or *no* country."

"Oh, I beg pardon, I didn't mean any offence. What I started out to ask, was, only about the old woman that raided the town—the stoop-shouldered old woman, you know, that you said you were going to catch—and I knew you would, too, because you have the reputation of never boasting, and—well, you—you've caught the old woman?"

"Damn the old woman!"

"Why, sho'! you don't mean to say you haven't caught her?"

"No, I *haven't* caught her. If anybody could have caught her, I could; but nobody couldn't, I don't care who he is."

"I am sorry, real sorry—for your sake; because when it gets around that a detective has expressed himself so confidently, and then—"

"Don't you worry, that's all—don't you worry; and as for the town, let the town keep its shirt on, too. She's my meat—make yourself easy about that. I'm on her track; I've got clews that—"

"That's good. Now if you could get an old veteran detective down from St. Louis to help you find out what the clews mean, and where they lead to, and then—"

"I'm plenty veteran enough myself, and I don't need anybody's help. I'll have her inside of a we— inside of a month. That I'll swear to."

Tom said, carelessly—

"I suppose that will answer—yes, that will answer. But I reckon she is pretty old, and old people don't often outlive the cautious pace of the professional detective when he has got his clews together and is out on his still-hunt." Blake's dull face flushed, under this gibe, but before he could set his retort in order Tom had turned to Wilson and was saying, with placid indifference of manner and voice—

"Who got the reward, Pudd'nhead?"

Wilson winced slightly, and saw that his own turn was come.

"What reward?"

"Why, the reward for the thief, and the other one for the knife."

Wilson answered—and rather uncomfortably, to judge by his hesitating fashion of delivering himself—

"Well, the—well, in fact nobody has claimed it yet."

Tom seemed surprised.

"Why, is *that* so?"

Wilson showed a trifle of irritation when he replied—

"Yes, it's so. And what *of* it?"

"Oh, nothing. Only I thought you had struck out a new idea and invented a scheme that was going to revolutionize the time-worn and ineffectual methods of the—" He stopped, and turned to Blake, who was happy, now that another had taken his place on the gridiron: "Blake, didn't you understand him to intimate that it wouldn't be necessary for you to hunt the old woman down?"

"B'George, he said he'd have thief and swag both inside of three days!—he did, by hokey! and that's just about a week ago. Why, I said at the time, that no thief and no thief's pal was going to try to pawn or sell a thing where he knowed the pawnbroker could get both rewards by taking *him* into camp *with* the swag. It *was* the blessedest idea that ever *I* struck!"

"You'd change your mind," said Wilson, with irritated bluntness, "if you knew the entire scheme instead of only part of it."

"Well," said the constable, pensively, "I had the idea that it wouldn't work, and up to now I'm right, anyway."

"WHO GOT THE REWARD, PUDD'NHEAD?"

"Very well, then, let it stand at that, and give it a further show. It has worked at least as well as your own methods, you perceive."

The constable hadn't anything handy to hit back with, so he discharged a discontented sniff and said nothing.

After the night that Wilson had partly revealed his scheme at his house, Tom had tried for several days to guess out the secret of the rest of it, but had failed. Then it occurred to him to give Roxana's smarter head a chance at it. He made up a supposititious case and laid it before her. She thought it over, and delivered her verdict upon it. Tom said to himself, "She's hit it, sure!" He thought he would test that verdict, now, and watch Wilson's face; so he said, reflectively—

"Wilson, you're not a fool—a fact of recent discovery. Whatever your scheme was, it had sense in it, Blake's opinion to the contrary notwithstanding. I don't ask you to reveal it, but I will suppose a case—a case which will answer as a starting point for the real thing I'm going to come at, and that's all I want. You offered five hundred dollars for the knife, and five hundred for the thief. We will suppose, for argument's sake, that the first reward is *advertised*, and the second offered by *private letter* to pawnbrokers and—"

Blake slapped his thigh and cried out—

"By Jackson he's *got* you, Pudd'nhead! Now why couldn't I or *any* fool have thought of that!"

Wilson said to himself, "Anybody with a reasonably good head would have thought of it. I am not surprised that Blake didn't detect it, I am only surprised that Tom did. There is more to him than I supposed." He said nothing aloud, and Tom went on:

"Very well. The thief would not suspect that there was a trap, and he would bring or send the knife and say he bought it for a song, or found it in the road, or something like that, and try to collect the reward, and be arrested—wouldn't he?"

"Yes," said Wilson.

"I think so," said Tom. "There can't be any doubt of it. Have you ever seen that knife?"

"No."

"Has any friend of yours?"

"Not that I know of."

"Well, I begin to think *I* understand why your scheme failed."

"What do you mean, Tom?—What are you driving at?" asked Wilson with a dawning sense of discomfort.

"Why, that there *isn't any such knife.*"

"Look here, Wilson," said Blake, "Tom Driscoll's right, for a thousand dollars!—if I had it."

Wilson's blood warmed a little, and he wondered if he had been played upon by those strangers—it certainly had something of that look. But what could they gain by it? He threw out that suggestion. Tom replied:

"Gain? Oh, nothing that you would value, maybe. But they are strangers making their way in a new community. Is it nothing to them to appear as pets of an Oriental prince—at no expense? Is it nothing to them to be able to dazzle this poor little town with thousand-dollar rewards—at no expense? Wilson, there isn't any such knife, or your scheme would have fetched it to light. Or if there is any such knife they've got it yet. I believe, myself, that they've *seen* such a knife, for Angelo pictured it out with his pencil too swiftly and handily for him to have been inventing it; and of course I can't swear that they've never had it; but this I'll go bail for—if they had it when they came to this town, they've got it yet."

Blake said,—

"It looks mighty reasonable, the way Tom puts it—it most certainly does."

Tom responded—turning to leave—

"You find the old woman, Blake, and if she can't furnish the knife, go and search the Twins."

Tom sauntered away. Wilson felt a good deal depressed. He hardly knew what to think. He was loth to withdraw his faith from the Twins, and was resolved not to do it on the present indecisive evidence; *but*—well, he would think—and then decide how to act.

"Blake, what do you think of this matter?"

"Well, Pudd'nhead, I'm bound to say I put it up the way Tom does. They hadn't the knife; or if they had it they've got it yet."

The men parted. Wilson said to himself, "I believe they had it; if it had been stolen, the scheme would have restored it, that is certain. And so I believe they've got it yet."

Tom had had no purpose in his mind when he encountered those two men. When he began his talk he hoped to be able to gall them a little and get a trifle of malicious entertainment out of it. But when he left, he left in great spirits, for he perceived that just by pure luck and no troublesome labor, he had accomplished several delightful things: he had touched both men on a raw spot and seen them squirm; he had modified Wilson's sweetness for the Twins with one small bitter taste that he wouldn't be able to get out of his mouth right away; and—best of all—he had taken the hated Twins down a peg with the community; for Blake would gossip around freely, after the manner of detectives, and within a week the town would be laughing at them in its sleeve for offering a gaudy reward for a bauble which they had either never possessed or hadn't lost. Tom was very well satisfied with himself.

Tom's behavior at home had been perfect during the entire week. His uncle and aunt had seen nothing like it before. They could find no fault with him anywhere. On Saturday evening he said to the Judge—

"I've had something preying on my mind, uncle, and as I am going away and might never see you again, I can't bear it any longer. I made you believe I was afraid to fight that Italian adventurer. I had to get out of it on some pretext or other, and maybe I chose badly, being taken unawares—but no honorable person could consent to meet him in the field, knowing what I knew about him."

"Indeed! What was that?"

"Count Luigi is a confessed assassin."

"Incredible!"

"It is perfectly true. Wilson detected it in his hand, by palmistry, and charged him with it and cornered him up so close that he had to confess; but both Twins begged us on their knees to keep the secret, and swore they would lead straight lives here; and it was all so pitiful that we gave our word of honor never to expose them while they kept that promise. You would have done it yourself, uncle."

"You are right, my boy, I would. A man's secret is still his own property, and sacred, when it has been surprised out of him like that. You did well, and I am proud of you." Then he added, mournfully, "But I wish I could have been saved the shame of meeting an assassin on the field of honor."

"It couldn't be helped, uncle. If *I* had known you were going to challenge him I should have felt obliged to sacrifice my pledged word in order to stop it, but Wilson couldn't be expected to do otherwise than keep silent."

"Oh, no, Wilson did right, and is in no way to blame. Tom, Tom, you have lifted a heavy load from my heart; I was stung to the very soul when I seemed to have discovered that I had a coward in my family."

"You may imagine what it cost *me* to assume such a part, uncle."

"Oh, I know it, poor boy, I know it! And I can understand how much it has cost you to remain under that unjust stigma to this time. But it is all right, now, and no harm is done. You have restored my comfort of mind, and with it your own; and both of us had suffered enough."

The old man sat a while plunged in thought; then he looked up with a satisfied light in his eye, and said: "That this assassin should have put the affront upon me of letting me meet him on the field of honor as if he were a gentleman is a matter which I will presently settle—but not now. I will not shoot him until after the election. I see a way to ruin them both before; I will attend to that first. Neither of them shall be elected, that I promise. You are sure that the fact that he is an assassin has not got abroad?"

"Perfectly certain of it, sir."

"It will be a good card. I will fling a hint at it from the stump on the polling-day. It will sweep the ground from under both of them."

"There's not a doubt of it. It will finish them."

"That and outside work among the voters will, to a certainty. I want you to come down here by and by and work privately among the rag-tag and bob-tail. You shall spend money among them; I will furnish it."

Another point scored against the detested Twins! Really it was a great day for Tom. He was encouraged to chance a parting shot, now, at the same target, and did it—

"You know that wonderful Indian knife that the Twins have been making such a to-do about? Well, there's no track or trace of it yet; so the town is beginning to sneer and gossip and laugh. Half the people believe they never had any such knife, the other half believe they had it and have got it still. I've heard twenty people talking like that to-day."

Yes, Tom's blemishless week had made him solid with the aunt and uncle. His mother was satisfied with him, too. Privately, she believed she was coming to love him, but she did not say so. She told him to go along to St. Louis, now, and she would get ready and follow. Then she smashed her whisky bottle and said—

"Dah, now. I's a gwyne to make *you* walk as straight as a string, Chambers, en so I's boun' you ain't gwyne to git no bad example out o' yo' mammy. I tole you you couldn't go into no bad comp'ny. Well, you's gwyne into my comp'ny, en I's gwyne to fill de bill. Now, den, trot along, trot along!"

Tom went aboard one of the big transient boats that night with his heavy satchel of miscellaneous plunder, and slept the sleep of the unjust, which is serener and sounder than the other kind, as we know by the hanging-eve history of a million rascals. But when he got up in the morning, luck was against him again. A brother-thief had robbed him while he slept, and gone ashore at some intermediate landing.

Chapter 16

If you pick up a starving dog and make him prosperous, he will not bite you. This is the principal difference between a dog and a man.—*Pudd'nhead Wilson's Calendar.*

We know all about the habits of the ant, we know all about the habits of the bee, but we know nothing at all about the habits of the oyster. It seems almost certain that we have been choosing the wrong time for studying the oyster.—*Pudd'nhead Wilson's Calendar.*

When Roxana arrived, she found her son in such despair and misery that her heart was touched and her motherhood rose up strong in her. He was ruined past hope, now; his destruction would be immediate and sure, and he would be an outcast and friendless. That was reason enough for a mother to love a child; so she loved him, and told him so. It made him wince, secretly—for she was a "nigger." That he was one himself was far from reconciling him to that despised race.

Roxana poured out endearments upon him, to which he responded uncomfortably, but as well as he could. And she tried to comfort him, but that was not possible. These intimacies quickly became horrible to him, and within the hour he began to try to get up courage enough to tell her so, and require that they be discontinued or very considerably modified. But he was afraid of her; and besides, there came a lull, now, for she had begun to think. She was trying to invent a saving plan. Finally she started up and said she had found a way out. Tom was almost suffocated by the joy of this sudden good news. Roxana said—

"Here is de plan, en she'll win, sure. I's a nigger, en nobody ain't gwyne to doubt it dat hears me talk. I's wuth six hund'd dollahs. Take en sell me en pay off dese gamblers."

Tom was dazed. He was not sure he had heard aright. He was dumb for a moment; then he said:

"Do you mean that you would be sold into slavery to save me?"

"Ain't you my chile? En does you know anything dat a mother won't do for her chile? Dey ain't nothin' a white mother won't do for her chile. Who made 'em so? De Lord done it. En who made de niggers? De Lord made 'em. In de inside, mothers is all de same. De good Lord He made 'em so. I's gwyne to be sole into slavery, en in a year you's gwyne to buy yo' ole mammy free agin. I'll show you how. Dat's de plan."

Tom's hopes began to rise, and his spirits along with them. He said—

"It's lovely of you, mammy—it's just—"

"Say it agin! En keep on sayin' it! It's all de pay a body kin want in dis worl', en it's mo' den enough. Laws bless you honey, when I's slavin' aroun' en dey 'buses me, if I knows you's a sayin' dat, 'way off yonder somers, it'll heal up all de sore places, en I kin stan' 'em."

"I do say it again, mammy, and I'll keep on saying it, too. But how am I going to sell you?—you're free, you know."

"Much diffrence dat make! White folks ain't particklar. De *law* kin sell me *now,* if dey tell me to leave de State in six months en I don't go. You draw up a paper—bill o' sale—en put it 'way off yonder, down in de middle o' Kaintuck somers, en sign some names to it, en say you'll sell me cheap caze you's hard up; you'll fine you ain't gwyne to have no trouble. You take me up de country a piece, en sell me on a farm—*dem* people ain't gwyne to ask no questions, if I's a bargain."

Tom forged a bill of sale and sold his mother to an Arkansas cotton planter for a trifle over six hundred dollars. He did not want to commit this treachery, but luck threw the man in his way, and this saved him the necessity of going up country to hunt up a purchaser, with the added risk of having to answer a lot of questions, whereas this planter was so pleased with Roxy that he asked next to none at all. Besides, the planter insisted that Roxy wouldn't know where she was, at first, and that by the time she found out she would already have become contented. And Tom argued with himself that it was an immense advantage for Roxy to have a master who was so pleased with her as this planter manifestly was. In almost no time his flowing reasonings carried him to the point of even half believing he was doing Roxy a splendid surreptitious service in sending her "down the river." And then he kept diligently saying to himself all the time, "It's for only a year—in a year I buy her free again; she'll keep that in mind, and it'll reconcile her." Yes, the little deception could do no harm, and everything would come out right and pleasant in the end, anyway. By agreement, the conversation in Roxy's presence was all about the man's "up-country" farm, and how pleasant a place it was, and how happy the slaves were, there; so poor Roxy was entirely deceived; and easily, for she was not dreaming that her own son could be guilty of treason to a mother who, in voluntarily going into slavery—slavery of any kind, mild or severe, or of any duration, brief or long—was making a sacrifice for him compared with which death would have been a poor and commonplace one. She lavished tears and loving caresses upon him, privately, and then went away with her owner; went away broken-hearted, and yet proud of what she was doing and glad that it was in her power to do it.

Tom squared his accounts, and resolved to keep to the very letter of his reform, and never put that will in jeopardy again. He had three hundred dollars left. According to his mother's plan, he was to put that safely away, and add her half of his pension to it monthly. In one year this fund would buy her free again.

For a whole week he was not able to sleep well, so much the villainy which he had played upon his trusting mother preyed upon his rag of a conscience; but after that he began to get comfortable again and was presently able to sleep like any other miscreant.

The boat bore Roxy away from St. Louis at four in the afternoon, and she stood on the lower guard abaft the paddle-box and watched Tom through a blur of tears until he melted into the throng of people and disappeared; then she looked no more, but sat there on a coil of cable crying, till far into the night. When she went to her foul steerage bunk at last, between the clashing engines, it was not to sleep, but only to wait for the morning; and waiting, grieve.

It had been imagined that she "would not know," and would think she was traveling up stream. She!—why, she had been steamboating for years. At dawn she got up and went listlessly and sat down on the cable-coil again. She passed many a snag whose "break" could have told her a thing to break her heart, for it showed a current moving in the same direction that the boat was going; but her thoughts were elsewhere, and she did not notice. But at last the roar of a bigger and nearer break than usual brought her out of her torpor, and she looked up and her practiced eye fell upon that tell-tale rush of water. For one moment her petrified gaze fixed itself there, then her head dropped upon her breast and she said—

"Oh, de good Lord God have mercy on po' sinful me—I's sole down de river!"

Chapter 17

Even popularity can be overdone. In Rome, along at first, you are full of regrets that Michael Angelo died; but by and by you only regret that you didn't *see* him do it.—*Pudd'nhead Wilson's Calendar.*

July 4. Statistics show that we lose more fools on this day than in all the other days of the year put together. This proves, by the number left in stock, that one Fourth of July per year is now inadequate, the country has grown so.—*Pudd'nhead Wilson's Calendar.*

The summer weeks dragged by, and then the political campaign opened— opened in pretty warm fashion, and waxed hotter and hotter daily. The Twins threw themselves into it with their whole heart, for their self-love was engaged. Their popularity, so general at first, had suffered afterward; mainly because they had been *too* popular, and so a natural reaction had followed. Besides, it had been diligently whispered around that it was curious—indeed, *very* curious—that that wonderful knife of theirs did not turn up—*if* it was so valuable, or *if* it had ever existed. And with the whisperings went chucklings and nudgings and winks, and such things have an effect. The Twins considered that success in the election would reinstate them, and that defeat would work them irreparable damage. Therefore they worked hard, but not harder than Judge Driscoll and Tom worked against them in the closing days of the canvass. Tom's conduct had remained so letter-perfect during two whole months, now, that his uncle not only trusted him with money with which to persuade voters, but trusted him to go and get it himself out of the safe in the private sitting room.

The closing speech of the campaign was made by Judge Driscoll, and he made it against both of the foreigners. It was disastrously effective. He poured out rivers of ridicule upon them, and forced the big mass meeting to laugh and applaud. He scoffed at them as adventurers, mountebanks, side-show riff-raff, dime-museum freaks; he assailed their showy titles with measureless derision; he said they were back-alley barbers disguised as nobilities, peanut-pedlars masquerading as gentlemen, organ-grinders bereft of their brother-monkey. At last he stopped and stood still. He waited until the place had become absolutely silent and expectant, then he delivered his deadliest shot; delivered it with ice-cold seriousness and deliberation, with a significant emphasis upon the closing words: he said he believed that the reward offered for the lost knife was humbug and buncombe, and that its owner would know where to find it whenever he should have occasion to assassinate somebody.

Then he stepped from the stand, leaving a startled and impressive hush behind him instead of the customary explosion of cheers and party cries.

The strange remark flew far and wide over the town and made an extraordinary sensation. Everybody was asking "What could he mean by that?" And everybody went on asking that question, but in vain; for the Judge only said he knew what he was talking about, and stopped there; Tom said he hadn't any idea what his uncle meant, and Wilson, whenever he was asked what he thought it meant, parried the question by asking the questioner what *he* thought it meant.

Wilson was elected, the Twins were defeated—crushed, in fact, and left forlorn and substantially friendless. Tom went back to St. Louis happy.

Dawson's Landing had a week of repose, now, and it needed it. But it was in an expectant state, for the air was full of rumors of a new duel. Judge Driscoll's election labors had prostrated him, but it was said that as soon as he was well enough to entertain a challenge he would get one from Count Luigi.

The brothers withdrew entirely from society, and nursed their humiliation in privacy. They avoided the people, and went out for exercise only late at night, when the streets were deserted.

Chapter 18

Gratitude and treachery are merely the two extremities of the same procession. You have seen all of it that is worth staying for when the band and the gaudy officials have gone by. —*Pudd'nhead Wilson's Calendar.*

Thanksgiving Day. Let all give humble, hearty, and sincere thanks, now, but the turkeys. In the island of Fiji they do not use turkeys, they use plumbers. It does not become you and me to sneer at Fiji.—*Pudd'nhead Wilson's Calendar.*

The Friday after the election was a rainy one in St. Louis. It rained all day long, and rained hard, apparently trying its best to wash that soot-blackened town white, but of course not succeeding. Toward midnight Tom Driscoll arrived at his lodgings from the theatre in the heavy downpour, and closed his umbrella and let himself in; but when he would have shut the door, he found that there was another person entering—doubtless another lodger; this person closed the door and tramped up stairs behind Tom. Tom found his door in the dark, and entered it and turned up the gas. When he faced about, lightly whistling, he saw the back of a man. The man was closing and locking his door for him. His whistle faded out and he felt uneasy. The man turned around, a wreck of shabby old clothes sodden with rain and all a-drip, and showed a black face under an old slouch hat. Tom was frightened. He tried to order the man out, but the words refused to come, and the other man got the start. He said, in a low voice—

"Keep still—I's yo' mother!"

Tom sunk in a heap on a chair, and gasped out—

"It was mean of me, and base—I know it; but I meant it for the best, I did indeed—I can swear it."

Roxana stood a while looking mutely down on him while he writhed in shame and went on incoherently babbling self-accusations mixed with pitiful attempts at explanation and palliation of his crime; then she seated herself

"KEEP STILL—I'S YO' MOTHER!"

and took off her hat, and her unkempt masses of long brown hair tumbled down about her shoulders.

"It ain't no fault o' yo'n dat dat ain't gray," she said, sadly, noticing the hair.

"I know it, I know it. I'm a scoundrel. But I swear I meant for the best. It was a mistake, of course, but I thought it was for the best, I truly did."

Roxy began to cry softly, and presently words began to find their way out between her sobs. They were uttered lamentingly, rather than angrily—

"Sell a pusson down de river—*down de river!*—for de *bes'!* I wouldn't treat a dog so. I is all broke down en wore out, now, en so I reckon it ain't in me to storm aroun' no mo', like I used to when I 'uz trompled on en 'bused. I don't know—but maybe it's so. Leastways, I's suffered so much dat mournin' seem to come mo' handy to me now den stormin'.'"

These words should have touched Tom Driscoll, but if they did, that effect was obliterated by a stronger one—one which removed the heavy weight of fear which lay upon him, and gave his crushed spirit a most grateful rebound, and filled all his small soul with a deep sense of relief. But he kept prudently still, and ventured no comment. There was a voiceless interval of some duration, now, in which no sounds were heard but the beating of the rain upon the panes, the sighing and complaining of the winds, and now and then a muffled sob from Roxana. The sobs became more and more infrequent, and at last ceased. Then the refugee began to talk again:

"Shet down dat light a little. More. More yit. A pusson dat is hunted don't like de light. Dah—dat'll do. I kin see whah you is, en dat's enough. I's gwyne to tell you de tale, en cut it jes' as short as I kin, en den I'll tell you what you's got to do. Dat man dat bought me ain't a bad man, he's good enough, as planters goes; en if he could a had his way I'd a ben a house servant in his fambly en ben comfortable; but his wife she was a Yank, en not right down good lookin', en she riz up agin me straight off; so den dey sent me out to de quarter 'mongst de common fiel' han's. Dat woman warn't satisfied, even wid dat, but she worked up de overseer agin me, she 'uz dat jealous en hateful; so de overseer he had me out befo' day in de mawnins en worked me de whole long day as long as dey 'uz any light to see by; en many's de lashin' I got caze I couldn't come up to de work o' de stronges'. Dat overseer wuz a Yank, too, outen New Englan', en anybody down South kin tell you what dat mean. *Dey* knows how to work a nigger to death, en dey knows how to whale 'em, too—whale 'em till dey backs is welted like a washboard. 'Long at fust my marster say de good word for me to de overseer, but dat 'uz bad for me; for de mistis she fine it out, en arter dat I jist ketched it at every turn—dey warn't *no* mercy for me no mo'!"

Tom's heart was fired—with fury against the planter's wife; and he said to himself, "But for that meddlesome fool, everything would have gone all right." He added a deep and bitter curse against her.

The expression of this sentiment was fiercely written in his face, and stood thus revealed to Roxana by a white glare of lightning which turned the sombre dusk of the room into dazzling day at that moment. She was pleased—pleased and grateful; for did not that expression show that her child *was* capable of grieving for his mother's wrongs and of feeling resentment toward her persecutors?—a thing which she had been doubting. But her flash of happiness was but a flash, and went out again and left her spirit dark; for she said to herself, "He sole me down de river—he can't feel for a body long; dis'll pass en go." Then she took up her tale again.

"'Bout ten days ago I 'uz sayin' to myself dat I couldn't las' many mo' weeks I 'uz so wore out wid de awful work en de lashin's, en so down-hearted en misable. En I didn't care no mo', nuther—life warn't wuth noth'n to me if I got to go on like dat. Well, when a body is in a frame o' mine like dat, what do a body care what a body do? Dey was a little sickly nigger wench 'bout ten year ole dat 'uz good to me, en hadn't no mammy, po' thing, en I loved her en she loved me; en she come out whah I 'uz workin', en she had a roasted tater, en tried to slip it to me—robbin' herself, you see, caze she knowed de overseer didn't gimme enough to eat—en he ketched her at it, en give her a lick acrost de back wid his stick which 'uz as thick as a broom-han'le, en she drop' screamin' on de groun', en squirmin' en wallerin' aroun' in de dust like a spider dat's got crippled. I couldn't *stan'* it! All de hell-fire dat 'uz ever in my heart flame' up, en I snatch de stick outen his han' en laid him flat! He laid dah moanin' en cussin', en all out of his head, you know, en de niggers 'uz plum sk'yerd to death. Dey gathered roun' him to he'p him, en I jumped on his hoss en took out for de river as tight as I could go. I knowed what dey would do wid *me*. Soon as he got well he would start in en work me to death if marster let him; en if dey didn't do dat dey'd sell me furder down de river, en dat's de same thing. So I 'lowed to drown myself en git out o' my troubles. It 'uz gitt'n towards dark. I 'uz at de river in two minutes. Den I see a canoe, en I says dey ain't no use to drown myself tell I *got* to; so I ties de hoss in de edge o' de timber en shove out down de river, keepin' in under de shelter o' de bluff bank en prayin' for de dark to shet down quick. I had a pow'ful good start, caze de big house 'uz three mile back fum de river en on'y de work mules to ride dah on, en on'y niggers to ride 'em, en *dey* warn't gwyne to hurry—dey'd gimme all de chance dey could. Befo' a body could go to de house en back it would be long pas' dark, en dey couldn't track de hoss en fine out which way I went tell mawnin', en de niggers would tell 'em all de lies dey could 'bout it.

"Well, de dark come, en I went on a spinnin' down de river. I paddled mo'n two hours, den I warn't worried no mo'; so I quit paddlin', en floated down de current, considerin' what I 'uz gwyne to do if I didn't have to drown myself. I made up some plans, en floated along, turnin' 'em over in my mine. Well, when it 'uz a little pas' midnight, as I reckoned, en I had come fifteen or twenty mile, I see de lights o' a steamboat layin' at de bank, whah dey warn't no town en no woodyard, en putty soon I ketched de shape o' de chimbly-tops agin de stars, en den good gracious me, I most jumped out o' my skin for joy! It 'uz de Gran' Mogul—I 'uz chambermaid on her for eight seasons in de Cincinnati en Orleans trade. I slid 'long pas'—don't see nobody stirrin' nowhah—hear 'em a hammerin' away in de engine room, den I knowed what de matter was—some o' de machinery's broke. I got asho' below de boat en turn' de canoe loose, den I goes 'long up, en dey 'uz jes' one plank out, en I step 'board de boat. It 'uz pow'ful hot; deckhan's en rousta-bouts 'uz sprawled aroun' asleep on de fo'cas'l, de second mate, Jim Bangs, he sot dah on de bitts wid his head down, asleep—caze dat's de way de second mate stan' de cap'n's watch—en de ole watchman, Billy Hatch, he 'uz a nod-din' on de companionway;—en I knowed 'em all; en lan', but dey did look good! I says to myself, I wisht old marster'd come along *now* en try to take me—bless yo' heart, I's 'mong frien's, *I* is! So I tromped right along 'mongst 'em, en went up on de biler deck en 'way back aft to de ladies' cabin guard, en sot down dah in de same cheer dat I'd sot in mos' a hund'd million times, I reckon; en it 'uz jist *home* agin, *I* tell you!

"In 'bout an hour I hear de ready-bell jingle, en den de racket begin. Putty soon I hear de gong strike. 'Set her back on de outside,' I says to myself—'I reckon I knows *dat* music!' I hear de gong agin. 'Come ahead on de inside,' I says. Gong agin. 'Stop de outside.' Gong agin. 'Come ahead on de outside—now we's pinted for Sent Louis, en I's outer de woods en ain't got to drown myself, at all.' I knowed de Mogul 'uz in de Sent Louis trade now, you see. It 'uz jes' fair daylight when we passed our plantation, en I seed a gang o' niggers en white folks huntin' up en down de sho', en troublin' deyselves a good deal 'bout me, but I warn't troublin' myself none 'bout *dem*.

"'Bout dat time Sally Jackson, dat used to be my second chambermaid en 'uz head chambermaid now, she come out on de guard, en 'uz pow'ful glad to see me, en so 'uz all de officers; en I tole 'em I'd got kidnapped en sole down de river, en dey made me up twenty dollahs en give it to me, en Sally she rigged me out wid good clo'es, en when I got here I went straight to whah you used to wuz, en den I come to dis house en dey say you's away but 'spected back every day; so I didn't dast to go down de river to Dawson's, caze I might miss you.

"Well, las' Monday I 'uz pass'n by one o' dem places in Fourth street whah dey sticks up runaway-nigger bills, en he'ps to ketch 'em, en I seed my marster! I mos' flopped down on de groun', I felt so gone. He had his back to me, en 'uz talkin' to de man en givin' him some bills—nigger-bills, I reckon, en I's de nigger. He's offerin' a reward—dat's it. Ain't I right, don't you reckon?"

Tom had been gradually sinking into a state of ghastly terror, and he said to himself, now, "I'm lost, no matter what turn things take. This man has said to me that he thinks there was something suspicious about that sale. He said he had a letter from a passenger on the Grand Mogul saying that Roxy came here on that boat and that everybody on board knew all about the case; so he says that her coming here instead of flying to a free State looks bad for me, and that if I don't find her for him, and that pretty soon, he will make trouble for me. I never believed that story; I *couldn't* believe she would be so dead to all motherly instincts as to come *here*, knowing the risk she would run of getting me into irremediable trouble. And after all, here she is! And I stupidly swore I would help him find her, thinking it was a perfectly safe thing to promise. If I venture to deliver her up, she—she—but how can I *help* myself? I've got to do that or pay the money, and where's the money to come from? I—I—well, I should think that if he would swear to treat her kindly hereaf-ter—and she says, herself, that he is a good man—and if he would swear to never allow her to be overworked, or ill fed, or—"

A flash of lightning exposed Tom's pallid face, drawn and rigid with these worrying thoughts. Roxana spoke up sharply now, and there was apprehen-sion in her voice—

"Turn up dat light! I want to see yo' face better. Dah now—lemme look at you. Chambers, you's as white as yo' shirt! Has you seen dat man? Has he ben to see you?"

"Ye-s."

"When?"

"Monday noon."

"Monday noon! Was he on my track?"

"He—well, he thought he was. That is, he hoped he was. This is the bill you saw." He took it out of his pocket.

"Read it to me."

She was panting with excitement, and there was a dusky glow in her eyes that Tom could not translate with certainty, but there seemed to be something threatening about it. The handbill had the usual rude wood-cut of a turbaned negro woman running, with the customary bundle on a stick over her shoulder, and the heading, in bold type, "*$100 Reward.*" Tom read the bill aloud—at least the part that described Roxana and named the master and his St. Louis address and the address of the Fourth-street agency; but he left out the item that applicants for the reward might also apply to Mr. Thomas Driscoll.

"Gimme de bill."

Tom had folded it and was putting it in his pocket. He felt a chilly streak creeping down his back, but said, as carelessly as he could—

"The bill? Why, it isn't any use to you, you can't read it. What do you want with it?"

"Gimme de bill!" Tom gave it to her, but with a reluctance which he could not entirely disguise. "Did you read it *all* to me?"

"Certainly I did."

"Hole up yo' han' en swah to it."

Tom did it. Roxana put the bill carefully away in her pocket, with her eyes fixed upon Tom's face all the while, then she said—

"You's lyin'!"

"What would I want to lie about it for?"

"I don't know—but you *is*. Dat's my opinion, anyways. But nemmine 'bout dat. When I seed dat man, I 'uz dat sk'yerd dat I could scasely wobble home. Den I give a nigger man a dollah for dese clo'es, en I ain't ben in a house sence, night ner day, till now. I blacked my face en laid hid in de cellar of a ole house dat's burnt down, daytimes, en robbed de sugar hogsheads en grain sacks on de wharf, nights, to git somethin' to eat, en never dast to try to buy noth'n; en I's mos' starved. En I never dast to come near dis place till dis rainy night, when dey ain't no people roun', scasely. But to-night I ben a stannin' in de dark alley ever sence night come, waitin' for you to go by. En here I is."

She fell to thinking. Presently she said—

"You seed dat man at noon, las' Monday?"

"Yes."

"I seed him de middle o' dat arternoon. He hunted you up, didn't he?"

"Yes."

"Did he give you de bill dat time?"

"No, he hadn't got it printed, yet."

Roxana darted a suspicious glance at him.

"Did you he'p him fix up de bill?"

Tom cursed himself for making that stupid blunder, and tried to rectify it by saying he remembered, now, that it *was* at noon Monday that the man gave him the bill. Roxana said—

"You's lyin' agin, sho'." Then she straightened up and raised her finger:

"Now, den! I's gwyne to ast you a question, en I wants to know how you's gwyne to git aroun' it. You knowed he 'uz arter me; en if you run off, 'stid o' stayin' here to he'p him, he'd know dey 'uz somethin' wrong 'bout dis business, en den he would inquire 'bout you, en dat would take him to yo' uncle, en yo' uncle would read de bill en see dat you ben sellin' a free nigger down de river, en you know *him*, I reckon! He'd tar up de will en kick you outen he house. Now, den, you answer me dis question: hain't you tole dat man dat I would be sho' to come here, en den you would fix it so he could set a trap en ketch me?"

Tom recognized that neither lies nor arguments could help him any longer—he was in a vise, with the screw turned on, and out of it there was no budging. His face began to take on an ugly look, and presently he said, with a snarl—

"Well, what could I do? You see, yourself, that I was in his grip and couldn't get out."

Roxy scorched him with a scornful gaze a while, then she said—

"What could *you* do? You could be Judas to yo' own mother to save yo' wuthless hide. *Would* anybody b'lieve it? No—a *dog* couldn't! You is de low-downest orneriest hound dat was ever pup'd into dis worl'—en I's 'sponsible for it!"—and she spat on him.

He made no offer to resent this. Roxy reflected a moment, then she said—

"Now I'll tell you what you's gwyne to do. You's gwyne to give dat man de money dat you's got laid up, en make him wait till you kin go to de Jedge en git de res' en buy me free agin."

"Thunder! what are you thinking of? Go and ask him for three hundred dollars and odd? What would I tell him I want with it, pray?"

Roxy's answer was delivered in a serene and level voice—

"You'll tell him you's sole me to pay yo' gamblin' debts, en dat you lied to me en was a villain, en dat I 'quires you to git dat money en buy me back agin."

"Why, you've gone stark mad! He would tear the will to shreds in a minute—don't you know that?"

"Yes, I does."

"Then you don't believe I'm idiot enough to go to him, do you?"

"I don't b'lieve nothin' 'bout it—I *knows* it. I knows it caze *you* knows dat if you don't raise dat money I'll go to him myself, en den he'll sell *you* down de river, en you kin see how you like it."

Tom rose, trembling and excited, and there was an evil light in his eye. He strode to the door and said he must get out of this suffocating place for a moment and clear his brain in the fresh air so that he could determine what to do. The door wouldn't open. Roxy smiled grimly, and said—

"I's got de key, honey—set down! You needn't cle'r up yo' brain none to fine out what you gwyne to do—*I* knows what you's gwyne to do." Tom sat down and began to pass his hands through his hair with a helpless and desperate air. Roxy said, "Is dat man in dis house?"

Tom glanced up with a surprised expression, and asked—

"What gave you such an idea?"

"You done it. Gwyne out to cle'r yo' brain! In de fust place you ain't got none to cle'r, en in de second place yo' ornery eye *tole* on you. You's de low-downest hound dat ever—but I done tole you dat befo'. Now den, dis is Friday. You kin fix it up wid dat man, en tell him you's gwyne away to git de res' o' de money, en dat you'll be back wid it nex' Tuesday, or maybe Wednesday. You understan'?"

Tom answered sullenly—

"Yes."

"En when you gits de new bill o' sale dat sells me to my own self, take en send it in de mail to Mr. Pudd'nhead Wilson, en write on de back dat he's to keep it tell I come. You understan'?"

"Yes."

"Dat's all, den. Take yo' umbereller, en put on yo' hat."

"Why?"

"Becaze you's gwyne to see me home to de wharf. You see dis knife? I's toted it aroun' sence de day I seed dat man en bought dese clo'es en *it*. If he ketched me, I 'uz gwyne to kill myself wid it. Now start along, en go sof', en lead de way; en if you gives a sign in dis house, or if anybody comes up to you in de street, I's gwyne to jam it into you. Chambers, does you b'lieve me when I says dat?"

"It's no use to bother me with that question. *I* know your word's good."

"Yes, it's diffrent fum yo'n. Shet de light out en move along—here's de key."

They were not followed. Tom trembled every time a late straggler brushed by them on the street, and half expected to feel the cold steel in his back. Roxy was right at his heels and always in reach. After tramping a mile they reached a wide vacancy on the deserted wharves, and in that dark and rainy desert they parted.

As Tom trudged home his mind was full of dreary thoughts and wild plans; but at last he said to himself, wearily—

"There is but the one way out. I must follow *her* plan. But with a variation—I will not ask for the money and ruin myself, I will rob the old skinflint!"

Chapter 19

Few things are harder to put up with than the annoyance of a good example.—*Pudd'nhead Wilson's Calendar.*

It were not best that we should all think alike; it is difference of opinion that makes horse-races.—*Pudd'nhead Wilson's Calendar.*

Dawson's Landing was comfortably finishing its season of dull repose and waiting patiently for the duel. Count Luigi was waiting too; but not patiently, rumor said. Sunday came, and Luigi insisted on having his challenge conveyed. Wilson carried it. Judge Driscoll declined to fight with an assassin—"that is," he added, significantly, "in the field of honor."

Elsewhere, of course, he would be ready. Wilson tried to convince him that if he had been present himself when Angelo told about the homicide committed by Luigi, he would not have considered the act discreditable to Luigi; but the obstinate old man was not to be moved.

Wilson went back to his principal and reported the failure of his mission. Luigi was incensed, and asked how it could be that the old gentleman, who was by no means dull-witted, held his trifling nephew's evidence and inferences to be of more value than Wilson's. But Wilson laughed, and said—

"That is quite simple; that is easily explicable. I am not his doll—his baby—his infatuation: his nephew is. The Judge and his late wife never had any children. The Judge and his wife were past middle age when this treasure fell into their lap. One must make allowances for a parental instinct that has been starving for twenty-five or thirty years. It is famished, it is crazed with hunger by that time, and will be entirely satisfied with anything that comes handy; its taste is atrophied, it can't tell mud-cat from shad. A devil born to a young couple is measurably recognizable by them as a devil before long, but a devil adopted by an old couple is an angel to them, and remains so, through thick and thin. Tom is this old man's angel; he is infatuated with him. Tom can persuade him into things which other people can't—not all things, I don't mean that, but a good many—particularly one class of things: the things that create or abolish personal partialities or prejudices in the old man's mind. The old man liked both of you. Tom conceived a hatred for you. That was enough; it turned the old man around at once. The oldest and strongest friendship must go to the ground when one of these late-adopted darlings throws a brick at it."

"It's a curious philosophy," said Luigi.

"It ain't a philosophy at all,—it's a fact. And there is something pathetic and beautiful about it, too. I think there is nothing more pathetic than to see one of these poor old childless couples taking a menagerie of yelping little worthless dogs to their hearts; and then adding some cursing and squawking parrots and a jackass-voiced macaw; and next a couple of hundred screeching song-birds; and presently some fetid guinea-pigs and rabbits, and a harem of cats. It is all a groping and ignorant effort to construct out of base metal and brass filings, so to speak, something to take the place of that golden treasure denied them by Nature, a child. But this is a digression. The unwritten law of this region requires you to kill Judge Driscoll on sight, and he and the community will expect that attention at your hands—though of course your own death by his bullet will answer every purpose. Look out for him. Are you heeled—that is, fixed?"

"Yes; he shall have his opportunity. If he attacks me I will respond."

As Wilson was leaving, he said—

"The Judge is still a little used up by his campaign work, and will not get out for a day or so, but when he does get out, you want to be on the alert."

About eleven at night the Twins went out for exercise, and started on a long stroll in the veiled moonlight.

Tom Driscoll had landed at Hackett's Store, two miles below Dawson's, just about half an hour earlier, the only passenger for that lonely spot, and had walked up the shore road and entered Judge Driscoll's house without having encountered any one, either on the road or under the roof.

He pulled down his window-blinds and lit his candle. He laid off his coat and hat and began his preparations. He unlocked his trunk and got his suit of girl's clothes out from under the male attire in it and laid it by. Then he blacked his face with a burnt cork and put the cork in his pocket. His plan was, to slip down to his uncle's private sitting room below, pass into the bedroom, steal the safe-key from the old gentleman's clothes, and then go back and rob the safe. He took up his candle to start. His courage and confidence were high, up to this point, but both began to waver a little, now.

Suppose he should make a noise, by some accident, and get caught—say, in the act of opening the safe? Perhaps it would be well to go armed. He took the Indian knife from its hiding place, and felt a pleasant return of his waning courage. He slipped stealthily down the narrow stair, his hair rising and his pulses halting at the slightest creak. When he was halfway down, he was disturbed to perceive that the landing below was touched by a faint glow of light. What could that mean? Was his uncle still up? No, that was not likely; he must have left his night-taper there when he went to bed. Tom crept on down, pausing at every step to listen. He found the door standing open, and glanced in. What he saw pleased him beyond measure. His uncle was asleep on the sofa; on a small table at the head of the sofa a lamp was burning low, and by it stood the old man's small tin cash-box, closed. Near the box was a pile of bank notes and a piece of paper covered with figures in pencil. The safe-door was not open. Evidently the sleeper had wearied himself with work upon his finances, and was taking a rest.

Tom set his candle on the stairs, and began to make his way toward the pile of notes, stooping low as he went. When he was passing his uncle, the old man stirred in his sleep, and Tom stopped instantly—stopped, and softly drew the knife from its sheath, with his heart thumping and his eyes fastened upon his benefactor's face. After a moment or two he ventured forward again—one step—reached for his prize and seized it, dropping the knife-sheath. Then he felt the old man's strong grip upon him, and a wild cry of "Help! help!" rang in his ear. Without hesitation he drove the knife home—and was free. Some of his notes escaped from his left hand and fell in the blood on the floor. He dropped the knife and snatched them up and started to fly; transferred them to his left hand and seized the knife again, in his fright and confusion, but remembered himself and flung it from him, as being a dangerous witness to carry away with him. He jumped for the stair-foot, and closed the door behind him; and as he snatched his candle and fled upward, the stillness of the night was broken by the sound of urgent footsteps approaching the house. In another moment he was in his room and the Twins were standing aghast over the body of the murdered man.

Tom put on his coat, buttoned his hat under it, threw on his suit of girl's clothes, dropped the veil, blew out his light, locked the room-door by which he had just entered, taking the key, passed through his other door into the back hall, locked that door and kept the key, then worked his way along in the dark and descended the back stairs. He was not expecting to meet anybody, for all interest was centred in the other part of the house, now; his calculation proved correct. By the time he was passing through the back yard, Mrs. Pratt, her servants, and a dozen half-dressed neighbors had joined the Twins and the dead, and accessions were still arriving at the front door.

As Tom, quaking as with a palsy, passed out at the gate, three women came flying from the house on the opposite side of the lane. They rushed by him and in at the gate, asking him what the trouble was there, but not waiting for an answer. Tom said to himself, "Those old maids waited to dress— they did the same thing the night Stevens's house burned down next door." In a few minutes he was in the haunted house. He lit a candle and took off his girl-clothes. There was blood on him all down his left side, and his right hand was red with the stains of the blood-soaked notes which he had crushed in it; but otherwise he was free from this sort of evidence. He cleansed his hand on the straw, and cleaned the most of the smut from his face. Then he burned his male and female attire to ashes, scattered the ashes, and put on a disguise proper for a tramp. He blew out his light, went below, and was soon loafing down the river road with the intent to borrow and use one of Roxy's devices. He found a canoe and paddled off down stream, setting the canoe adrift as dawn approached, and making his way by land to the next village, where he kept out of sight till a transient steamer came along, and then took deck passage for St. Louis. He was ill at ease until Dawson's Landing was behind him; then he said to himself, "All the detectives on earth couldn't trace me now; there's not a vestige of a clew left in the world; that homicide will take its place with the permanent mysteries, and people won't get done trying to guess out the secret of it for fifty years."

In St. Louis, next morning, he read this brief telegram in the papers— dated at Dawson's Landing:

"Judge Driscoll, an old and respected citizen, was assassinated here about midnight by a profligate Italian nobleman or barber, on account of a quarrel growing out of the recent election. The assassin will probably be lynched."

"One of the Twins!" soliloquised Tom; "how lucky! It is the knife that has done him this grace. We never know when fortune is trying to favor us. I actually cursed Pudd'nhead Wilson in my heart for putting it out of my power to sell that knife. I take it back, now."

Tom was now rich and independent. He arranged with the planter, and mailed to Wilson the new bill of sale which sold Roxana to herself; then he telegraphed his aunt Pratt:

"Have seen the awful news in the papers and am almost prostrated with grief. Shall start by packet to-day. Try to bear up till I come."

When Wilson reached the house of mourning and had gathered such details as Mrs. Pratt and the rest of the crowd could tell him, he took command as mayor, and gave orders that nothing should be touched, but everything left as it was until Justice Robinson should arrive and take the proper measures as coroner. He cleared everybody out of the room but the Twins and himself. The sheriff soon arrived and took the Twins away to jail. Wilson told them to keep heart, and promised to do his best in their defence when the case should come to trial. Justice Robinson came presently, and with him Constable Blake. They examined the room thoroughly. They found the knife and the sheath. Wilson noticed that there were finger-prints on the knife handle. That pleased him, for the Twins had required the earliest comers to make a scrutiny of their hands and clothes, and neither these people nor Wilson himself had found any blood-stains upon them. Could there be a possibility that the Twins had spoken the truth when they said they found the man dead when they ran into the house in answer to the cry for help? He thought of that mysterious girl at once. But this was not the sort of work for a girl to be engaged in. No matter; Tom Driscoll's room must be examined.

After the coroner's jury had viewed the body and its surroundings, Wilson suggested a search up stairs, and he went along. The jury forced an entrance to Tom's room, but found nothing, of course.

The coroner's jury found that the homicide was committed by Luigi, and that Angelo was accessory to it.

The town was bitter against the unfortunates, and for the first few days after the murder they were in constant danger of being lynched. The grand jury presently indicted Luigi for murder in the first degree and Angelo as accessory before the fact. The Twins were transferred from the city jail to the county prison to await trial.

Wilson examined the finger-marks on the knife handle, and said to himself, "Neither of the Twins made those marks." Then manifestly there was another person concerned, either in his own interest or as hired assassin.

But who could it be? That, he must try to find out. The safe was not open, the cash-box was closed, and had three thousand dollars in it. Then robbery was not the motive, and revenge was. Where had the murdered man an enemy except Luigi? There was but that one person in the world with a deep grudge against him.

The mysterious girl! The girl was a great trial to Wilson. If the motive had been robbery, the girl might answer, but there *wasn't* any girl that would want to take this old man's life for revenge. He had no quarrels with girls; he was a gentleman.

Wilson had perfect tracings of the finger-marks of the knife handle; and among his glass-records he had a great array of the finger-prints of women and girls, collected during the past fifteen or eighteen years, but he scanned them in vain, they successfully withstood every test; among them were no duplicates of the prints on the knife.

The presence of the knife on the stage of the murder was a worrying circumstance for Wilson. A week previously he had as good as admitted to himself that he believed Luigi had possessed such a knife, and that he still possessed it notwithstanding his pretence that it had been stolen. And now here was the knife, and with it the Twins. Half the town had said the Twins were humbugging when they claimed that they had lost their knife, and now these people were joyful, and said, "I told you so."

If their finger-prints had been on the handle—but it was useless to bother any further about that; the finger-prints on the handle were *not* theirs—that he knew perfectly.

Wilson refused to suspect Tom; for, firstly, Tom couldn't murder anybody—he hadn't character enough; secondly, if he *could* murder a person he wouldn't select his doting benefactor and nearest relative; thirdly, self-interest was in the way; for while the uncle lived, Tom was sure of a free support and a chance to get the destroyed will revived again, but with the uncle gone, that chance was gone, too. It was true the will had really been revived, as was now discovered, but Tom could not have been aware of it, or he would have spoken of it, in his native talky, unsecretive way. Finally, Tom was in St. Louis when the murder was done, and got the news out of the morning journals, as was shown by his telegram to his aunt. These speculations were unemphasized sensations rather than articulated thoughts, for Wilson would have laughed at the idea of seriously connecting Tom with the murder.

Wilson regarded the case of the Twins as desperate—in fact, about hopeless. For he argued that if a confederate was not found, an enlightened Missouri jury would hang them, sure; if a confederate *was* found, that would not improve the matter, but simply furnish one more person for the sheriff to hang. Nothing could save the Twins but the discovery of a person who did the murder on his sole personal account—an undertaking which had all the aspect of the impossible. Still, the person who made the finger-prints must be sought. The Twins might have no case *with* him, but they certainly would have none without him.

So Wilson mooned around, thinking, thinking, guessing, guessing, day and night, and arriving nowhere. Whenever he ran across a girl or a woman he was not acquainted with, he got her finger-prints, on one pretext or another; and they always cost him a sigh when he got home, for they never tallied with the finger-marks on the knife handle.

As to the mysterious girl, Tom swore he knew no such girl, and did not remember ever seeing a girl wearing a dress like the one described by Wilson. He admitted that he did not always lock his room, and that sometimes the servants forgot to lock the house doors; still, in his opinion the girl must have made but few visits or she would have been discovered. When Wilson tried to connect her with the stealing-raid, and thought she might have been the old woman's confederate, if not the very thief herself disguised as an old woman, Tom seemed struck, and also much interested, and said he would keep a sharp eye out for this person or persons, although he was afraid that she or they would be too smart to venture again into a town where everybody would now be on the watch for a good while to come.

Everybody was pitying Tom, he looked so quiet and sorrowful, and seemed to feel his great loss so deeply. He was playing a part, but it was not all a part. The picture of his alleged uncle, as he had last seen him, was before him in the dark pretty frequently, when he was awake, and called again in his dreams, when he was asleep. He wouldn't go into the room where the tragedy had happened. This charmed the doting Mrs. Pratt, who "realized now, as she had never done before," she said, what a sensitive and delicate nature her darling had, and how he adored his poor uncle.

Chapter 20

Even the clearest and most perfect circumstantial evidence is
likely to be at fault, after all, and therefore ought to be received
with great caution. Take the case of *any* pencil, sharpened by
any woman: if you have witnesses, you will find she did it with
a knife; but if you take simply the aspect of the pencil, you will
say she did it with her teeth.—*Pudd'nhead Wilson's Calendar.*

The weeks dragged along, no friend visiting the jailed Twins but their counsel and Aunt Patsy Cooper, and the day of trial came at last—the heaviest day
in Wilson's life; for with all his tireless diligence he had discovered no sign or
trace of the missing confederate. "Confederate" was the term he had long ago
privately accepted for that person—not as being unquestionably the right
term, but as being at least possibly the right one, though he was never able to
understand why the Twins didn't vanish and escape, as the confederate had
done, instead of remaining by the murdered man and getting caught there.

The court house was crowded, of course, and would remain so to the finish, for not only in the town itself, but in the country for miles around the
trial was the one topic of conversation among the people. Mrs. Pratt, in deep
mourning, and Tom with a weed on his hat, had seats near Pembroke
Howard, the public prosecutor, and back of them sat a great array of friends
of the family. The Twins had but one friend present to keep their counsel in
countenance, their poor old sorrowing landlady. She sat near Wilson, and
looked her friendliest. In the "nigger corner" sat Chambers; also Roxy, with
good clothes on, and her bill of sale in her pocket. It was her most precious
possession, and she never parted with it, day or night. Tom had allowed her
thirty-five dollars a month ever since he came into his property, and had said
that he and she ought to be grateful to the Twins for making them rich; but
had roused such a temper in her by this speech that he did not repeat the
argument afterward. She said the old Judge had treated her child a thousand
times better than he deserved, and had never done *her* an unkindness in his
life; so she hated those outlandish devils for killing him, and shouldn't ever

sleep satisfied till she saw them hanged for it. She was here to watch the trial, now, and was going to lift up just one "hooraw" over it if the County Judge put her in jail a year for it. She gave her turbaned head a toss and said, "When dat verdic' comes, I's gwyne to lif' dat *roof*, now, I *tell* you!"

Pembroke Howard briefly sketched the State's case. He said he would show by a chain of circumstantial evidence without break or fault in it any-where, that the principal prisoner at the bar committed the murder; that the motive was partly revenge, and partly a desire to take his own life out of jeopardy, and that his brother, by his presence, was a consenting accessory to the crime; a crime which was the basest known to the calendar of human misdeeds—assassination; that it was conceived by the blackest of hearts and consummated by the cowardliest of hands; a crime which had broken a lov-ing sister's heart, blighted the happiness of a young nephew who was as dear as a son, brought inconsolable grief to many friends, and sorrow and loss to the whole community. The utmost penalty of the outraged law would be exacted, and upon the accused, now present at the bar, that penalty would unquestionably be executed. He would reserve further remark until his clos-ing speech.

He was strongly moved, and so also was the whole house; Mrs. Pratt and several other women were weeping when he sat down, and many an eye that was full of hate was riveted upon the unhappy prisoners.

Witness after witness was called by the State, and questioned at length; but the cross-questioning was brief: Wilson knew they could furnish nothing valuable for his side. People were sorry for Pudd'nhead; his budding career would get hurt by this trial.

Several witnesses swore they heard Judge Driscoll say in his public speech that the Twins would be able to find their lost knife again when they needed it to assassinate somebody with. This was not news, but now it was seen to have been sorrowfully prophetic, and a profound sensation quivered through the hushed court room when those dismal words were repeated.

The public prosecutor rose and said that it was within his knowledge, through a conversation held with Judge Driscoll on the last day of his life, that counsel for the defence had brought him a challenge from the person charged at this bar with murder; that he had refused to fight with a confessed assassin—"that is, on the field of honor," but had added, significantly, that he would be ready for him elsewhere. Presumably the person here charged with murder was warned that he must kill or be killed the first time he should meet Judge Driscoll. If counsel for the defence chose to let the statement stand so, he would not call him to the witness stand. Mr. Wilson said he would offer no denial. [Murmurs in the house—"It is getting worse and worse for Wilson's case."]

Mrs. Pratt testified that she heard no outcry, and did not know what woke her up, unless it was the sound of rapid footsteps approaching the front door. She jumped up and ran out in the hall just as she was, and heard the footsteps flying up the front steps and then following behind her as she ran to the sitting room. There she found the accused standing over her murdered brother—[Here she broke down and sobbed. Sensation in the court.] Resuming, she said the persons entering behind her were Mr. Rogers and Mr. Buckstone.

Cross-examined by Wilson, she said the Twins proclaimed their innocence; declared that they had been taking a walk, and had hurried to the house in response to a cry for help which was so loud and strong that they had heard it at a considerable distance; that they begged her and the gentlemen just mentioned to examine their hands and clothes—which was done, and no blood-stains found.

Confirmatory evidence followed, from Rogers and Buckstone.

The finding of the knife was verified, the advertisement minutely describing it and offering a reward for it was put in evidence, and its exact correspondence with that description proven. Then followed a few minor details, and the case for the State was closed.

Wilson said that he had three witnesses, the Misses Clarkson, who would testify that they met a veiled young woman leaving Judge Driscoll's premises by the back gate a few minutes after the cries for help were heard, and that their evidence, taken with certain circumstantial evidence which he would call the court's attention to, would in his opinion convince the court that there was still one person concerned in this crime who had not yet been found, and also that a stay of proceedings ought to be granted, in justice to his clients, until that person should be discovered. As it was late, he would ask leave to defer the examination of his three witnesses until the next morning.

The crowd poured out of the place and went flocking away in excited groups and couples, talking the events of the session over with vivacity and consuming interest, and everybody seemed to have had a satisfactory and enjoyable day except the accused, their counsel, and their old-lady friend. There was no cheer among these, and no substantial hope.

In parting with the Twins Aunt Patsy did attempt a good-night with a gay pretence of hope and cheer in it, but broke down without finishing.

Absolutely secure as Tom considered himself to be, the opening solemnities of the trial had nevertheless oppressed him with a vague uneasiness, his being a nature sensitive to even the smallest alarms; but from the moment that the poverty and weakness of Wilson's case lay exposed to the court, he was comfortable once more, even jubilant. He left the court room sarcastically sorry for Wilson. "The Clarksons met an unknown woman in the back lane," he said to himself—"*that* is his case! I'll give him a century to find her in—a couple of them if he likes. A woman who doesn't exist any longer, and the clothes that gave her her sex burnt up, and the ashes thrown away—oh, certainly, he'll find *her* easy enough!" This reflection set him to admiring, for the hundredth time, the shrewd ingenuities by which he had insured himself against detection—more, against even suspicion.

"Nearly always in cases like this there is some little detail or other overlooked, some wee little track or trace left behind, and detection follows; but here there's not even the faintest suggestion of a trace left. No more than a bird leaves when it flies through the air—yes, through the night, you may say. The man that can track a bird through the air in the dark and find that bird is the man to track me out and find the Judge's assassin—no other need apply. And that is the job that has been laid out for poor Pudd'nhead Wilson, of all people in the world! Lord, it will be pathetically funny to see him grubbing and groping after that woman that don't exist, and the right person sitting under his very nose all the time!" The more he thought the situation over, the more the humor of it struck him. Finally he said, "I'll never let him hear the last of that woman. Every time I catch him in company, to his dying day, I'll ask him in the guileless, affectionate way that used to gravel him so when I inquired how his unborn law-business was coming along, 'Got on her track yet—hey, Pudd'nhead?'" He wanted to laugh, but that would not have answered; there were people about, and he was mourning for his uncle. He made up his mind that it would be good entertainment to look in on Wilson that night and watch him worry over his barren law-case and goad him with an exasperating word or two of sympathy and commiseration now and then.

Wilson wanted no supper, he had no appetite. He got out all the finger-prints of girls and women in his collection of records and pored gloomily over them an hour or more, trying to convince himself that that troublesome girl's marks were there somewhere and had been overlooked. But it was not so. He drew back his chair, clasped his hands over his head, and gave himself up to dull and arid musings.

Tom Driscoll dropped in, an hour after dark, and said with a pleasant laugh as he took a seat—

"Hello, we've gone back to the amusements of our days of neglect and obscurity for consolation, have we?" and he took up one of the glass strips and held it against the light to inspect it. "Come, cheer up, old man, there's no use in losing your grip and going back to this child's-play merely because this big sun-spot is drifting across your shiny new disk. It'll pass, and you'll be all right again"—and he laid the glass down. "Did you think you could win always?"

"Oh, no," said Wilson, with a sigh, "I didn't expect that, but I can't believe Luigi killed your uncle, and I feel very sorry for him. It makes me blue. And you would feel as I do, Tom, if you were not prejudiced against those young fellows."

"I don't know about that," and Tom's countenance darkened, for his memory reverted to his kicking; "I owe them no good will, considering the brunette one's treatment of me that night. Prejudice or no prejudice, Pudd'nhead, I don't like them, and when they get their deserts you're not going to find me sitting on the mourners' bench."

He took up another strip of glass, and exclaimed—

"Why, here's old Roxy's label! Are you going to ornament the royal palaces with nigger paw-marks, too? By the date here, I was seven months old when this was done, and she was nursing me and her little nigger cub. There's a line straight across her thumb-print. How comes that?" and Tom held out the piece of glass to Wilson.

"That is common," said the bored man, wearily. "Scar of a cut or a scratch, usually"—and he took the strip of glass indifferently, and raised it toward the lamp.

All the blood sunk suddenly out of his face, his hand quaked, and he gazed at the polished surface before him with the glassy stare of a corpse.

"Great Heavens, what's the matter with you, Wilson? Are you going to faint?"

Tom sprang for a glass of water and offered it, but Wilson shrank shuddering from him and said—

"No, no!—take it away!" His breast was rising and falling, and he moved his head about in a dull and wandering way, like a person who has been stunned. Presently he said, "I shall feel better when I get to bed; I have been overwrought to-day; yes, and overworked for many days."

"Then I'll leave you and let you get to your rest. Good night, old man." But as Tom went out he couldn't deny himself a small parting gibe: "Don't take it so hard; a body can't win every time; you'll hang somebody yet."

Wilson muttered to himself, "It is no lie to say I am sorry I have to begin with you, miserable dog though you are."

He braced himself up with a glass of cold whisky and went to work again. He did not compare the new finger-marks unintentionally left by Tom a few minutes before on Roxy's glass with the tracings of the marks left on the knife handle, there being no need of that (for his trained eye), but busied himself with another matter, muttering from time to time, "Idiot that I was! nothing but a *girl* would do me—a man in girl's clothes never occurred to me." First, he hunted out the plate containing the finger-prints made by Tom when he was twelve years old, and laid it by itself; then he brought forth the marks made by Tom's baby fingers when he was a suckling of seven months, and placed these two plates with the one containing this subject's newly (and unconsciously) made record. "Now the series is complete," he said with satisfaction, and sat down to inspect these things and enjoy them.

But his enjoyment was brief. He stared a considerable time at the three strips, and seemed stupefied with astonishment. At last he put them down and said, "I can't make it out at all—hang it, the baby's don't tally with the others!"

He walked the floor for half an hour puzzling over his enigma, then he hunted out two other glass plates.

He sat down and puzzled over these things a good while, but kept muttering, "It's no use, I can't understand it. They don't tally right, and yet I'll swear the names and dates are right, and so of course they *ought* to tally. I never labeled one of these things carelessly in my life. There is a most extraordinary mystery here."

He was tired out, now, and his brains were beginning to clog. He said he would sleep himself fresh, and then see what he could do with this riddle. He slept through a troubled and unrestful hour, then unconsciousness began to shred away, and presently he rose drowsily to a sitting posture. "Now what was that dream?" he said, trying to recal it; "what *was* that dream?—it seemed to unravel that puz—"

He landed in the middle of the floor at a bound, without finishing the sentence, and ran and turned up his light and seized his "records." He took a single swift glance at them and cried out—

"It's *so!* Heavens, what a revelation! And for twenty-three years no man has ever suspected it."

Chapter 21

He is useless on top of the ground; he ought to be under it, inspiring the cabbages.—*Pudd'nhead Wilson's Calendar.*

April 1. This is the day upon which we are reminded of what we are on the other three hundred and sixty-four.—*Pudd'nhead Wilson's Calendar.*

Wilson put on enough clothes for business purposes and went to work under a high pressure of steam. He was awake all over. All sense of weariness had been swept away by the invigorating refreshment of the great and hopeful discovery which he had made. He made fine and accurate reproductions of a number of his "records," and then enlarged them on a scale of ten to one with his pantagraph. He did these pantagraph enlargements on sheets of white cardboard, and made each individual line of the bewildering maze of sworls or curves or loops which constituted the "pattern" of a "record" stand out bold and black by reinforcing it with ink. To the untrained eye the collection of delicate originals made by the human finger on the glass plates looked about alike; but when enlarged ten times, they resembled the markings of a block of wood that has been sawed across the grain, and the dullest eye could detect at a glance, and at a distance of many feet, that no two of the patterns were alike. When Wilson had at last finished his tedious and difficult work, he arranged its results according to a plan in which a progressive order and sequence was a principal feature, then he added to the batch several pantagraph enlargements which he had made from time to time in bygone years.

The night was spent and the day well advanced, now. By the time he had snatched a trifle of breakfast it was nine o'clock and the court ready to begin its sitting. He was in his place twelve minutes later, with his "records."

Tom Driscoll caught a slight glimpse of the records and nudged his nearest friend and said, with a wink, "Pudd'nhead's got a rare eye to business—thinks that as long as he can't win his case it's at least a noble good chance to advertise his palace-window decorations without any expense." Wilson was informed that his witnesses had been delayed, but would arrive presently; but he rose and said he should probably not have occasion to make use of their testimony. [An amused murmur ran through the room—"It's a clean backdown! he gives up without hitting a lick."] Wilson continued—"I have other testimony—and better." [This compelled interest, and evoked murmurs of surprise that had a detectible ingredient of disappointment in them.] "If I seem to be springing this evidence upon the court, I offer as my justification for this, that I did not discover its existence until late last night, and have been engaged in examining and classifying it ever since, until half an hour ago. I shall offer it presently; but first I wish to say a few preliminary words.

"May it please the court, the claim given the front place, the claim most persistently urged, the claim most strenuously and I may even say aggressively and defiantly insisted upon by the prosecution, is this—*that the person whose hand left the blood-stained finger-prints upon the handle of the Indian knife is the person who committed the murder.*" Wilson paused, during several moments, to give impressiveness to what he was about to say, and then added, tranquilly, "We grant that claim."

It was an electrical surprise. No one was prepared for such an admission. A buzz of astonishment rose on all sides, and people were heard to intimate that the overworked lawyer had lost his mind. Even the veteran judge, accustomed as he was to legal ambushes and masked batteries in criminal procedure, was not sure that his ears were not deceiving him, and asked counsel what it was he had said. Howard's impassive face betrayed no sign, but his attitude and bearing lost something of their careless confidence for a moment. Wilson resumed:

"We not only grant that claim, but we welcome it and strongly endorse it. Leaving that matter for the present, we will now proceed to consider other points in the case which we propose to establish by evidence, and shall include that one in the chain in its proper place."

He had made up his mind to try a few hardy guesses, in mapping out his theory of the origin and motive of the murder—guesses designed to fill up gaps in it—guesses which could help if they hit, and would probably do no harm if they didn't.

"To my mind, certain circumstances of the case before the court seem to suggest a motive for the homicide quite different from the one insisted on by the State. It is my conviction that the motive was not revenge, but robbery. It has been urged that the presence of the accused brothers in that fatal room, just after notification that one of them must take the life of Judge Driscoll or lose his own the moment the parties should meet, clearly signifies that the natural instinct of self-preservation moved my clients to go there secretly and save Count Luigi by destroying his adversary.

"Then why did they stay there, after the deed was done? Mrs. Pratt had time, although she did not hear the cry for help, but woke up some moments later, to run to that room—and there she found these men standing, and making no effort to escape. If they were guilty, they ought to have been running out of the house at the same time that she was running to that room. If they had had such a strong instinct toward self-preservation as to move them to kill that unarmed man, what had become of it now, when it should have been more alert than ever? Would any of us have remained there? Let us not slander our intelligence to that degree.

"Much stress has been laid upon the fact that the accused offered a very large reward for the knife with which this murder was done; that no thief came forward to claim that extraordinary reward; that the latter fact was good circumstantial evidence that the claim that the knife had been stolen was a vanity and a fraud; that these details taken in connection with the memorable and apparently prophetic speech of the deceased concerning that knife, and the final discovery of that very knife in the fatal room where no living person was found present with the slaughtered man but the owner of the knife and his brother, form an indestructible chain of evidence which fixes the crime upon those unfortunate strangers.

"But I shall presently ask to be sworn, and shall testify that there was a large reward offered for the *thief*, also; that it was offered *secretly* and not advertised; that this fact was indiscreetly mentioned—or at least tacitly admitted—in what was supposed to be safe circumstances, but may not have been. The thief may have been present himself." [Tom Driscoll had been looking at the speaker, but dropped his eyes at this point.] "In that case he would retain the knife in his possession, not daring to offer it for sale, or for pledge in a pawn shop." [There was a nodding of heads among the audience by way of admission that this was not a bad stroke.] "I shall prove to the satisfaction of the jury that there was a person in Judge Driscoll's room several minutes *before* the accused entered it." [This produced a strong sensation; the last drowsy-head in the court room roused up, now, and made preparation to listen.] "If it shall seem necessary, I will prove by the Misses Clarkson that they met a veiled person—ostensibly a woman—coming out of the back gate a few minutes after the cry for help was heard. This person was not a woman, but a man dressed in woman's clothes." [Another sensation. Wilson had his eye on Tom when he hazarded this guess, to see what effect it would produce. He was satisfied with the result, and said to himself, "It was a success—he's hit."]

"The object of that person in that house was robbery, not murder. It is true that the safe was not open, but there was an ordinary tin cash-box on the table, with three thousand dollars in it. It is easily supposable that the thief was concealed in the house; that he knew of this box, and of its owner's habit of counting its contents and arranging his accounts at night—if he had that habit, which I do not assert, of course; that he tried to take the box while its owner slept, but made a noise and was seized, and had to use the knife to save himself from capture; and that he fled without his booty because he heard help coming.

"I have now done with my theory, and will proceed to the evidences by which I propose to try to prove its soundness." Wilson took up several of his strips of glass. When the audience recognized these familiar mementoes of Pudd'nhead's old-time childish "puttering" and folly, the tense and funereal interest vanished out of their faces, and the house burst into volleys of relieving and refreshing laughter, and Tom chirked up and joined in the fun himself; but Wilson was apparently not disturbed. He arranged his records on the table before him, and said—

"I beg the indulgence of the court while I make a few remarks in explanation of some evidence which I am about to introduce, and which I shall presently ask to be allowed to verify under oath on the witness stand. Every human being carries with him from his cradle to his grave certain physical marks which do not change their character, and by which he can always be identified—and that without shade of doubt or question. These marks are his signature, his physiological autograph, so to speak, and this autograph cannot be counterfeited, nor can he disguise it or hide it away, nor can it become illegible by the wear and the mutations of time. This signature is not his face—age can change that beyond recognition; it is not his hair, for that can fall out; it is not his height, for duplicates of that exist; it is not his form, for duplicates of that exist also, whereas *this* signature is each man's very own— there is no duplicate of it among the swarming populations of the globe." [The audience were interested once more.]

"This autograph consists of the delicate lines or corrugations with which Nature marks the insides of the hands and the soles of the feet. If you will look at the balls of your fingers—you that have very sharp eyesight—you will observe that these dainty, curving lines lie close together, like those that indicate the borders of oceans in maps, and that they form various clearly defined patterns, such as arches, circles, long curves, whorls, etc., and that these patterns differ on the different fingers." [Every man in the room had his hand up to the light, now, and his head canted to one side, and was minutely scrutinizing the balls of his fingers; there were whispered ejaculations of "Why, it's so—I never noticed *that* before!"] "The patterns on the right hand are not the same as those on the left." [Ejaculations of "Why, that's so, too!"] "Taken finger for finger, your patterns differ from your neighbor's." [Comparisons were made all over the house—even the judge and jury were absorbed in this curious work.] "The patterns of a twin's right hand are not the same as those on his left. One twin's patterns are never the same as his fellow-twin's patterns—the jury will find that the patterns upon the finger-balls of the accused follow this rule." [An examination of the Twins' hands was begun at once.] "You have often heard of twins who were so exactly alike that when dressed alike their own parents could not tell them apart. Yet there was never a twin born into this world that did not carry from birth to death a sure identifier in this mysterious and marvelous natal autograph! *That* once known to you, his fellow-twin could never personate him and deceive you."

Wilson stopped and stood silent. Inattention dies a quick and sure death when a speaker does that. The stillness gives warning that something is coming. All palms and finger-balls went down, now, all slouching forms straightened, all heads came up, all eyes were fastened upon Wilson's face. He waited yet one, two, three moments, to let his pause complete and perfect its spell upon the house; then, when through the profound hush he could hear the ticking of the clock on the wall, he put out his hand and took the Indian knife by the blade and held it aloft where all could see the sinister spots upon its ivory handle; then he said, in a level and passionless voice—

"Upon this haft stands the assassin's natal autograph, written in the blood of that helpless and unoffending old man who loved you and whom you all loved. There is but one man in the whole earth whose hand can duplicate that crimson sign"—he paused and raised his eyes to the pendulum swinging back and forth—"and please God we will produce that man in this room before the clock strikes noon!"

Stunned, distraught, unconscious of its own movement, the house half rose, as if expecting to see the murderer appear at the door, and a breeze of muttered ejaculations swept the place. *"Order in the court!—sit down!"* This from the sheriff. He was obeyed, and quiet reigned again. Wilson stole a glance at Tom, and said to himself, "He is flying signals of distress, now; even people who despise him are pitying him; they think this is a hard ordeal for a young fellow who has lost his benefactor by so cruel a stroke—and they are right." He resumed his speech:

"For more than twenty years I have amused my compulsory leisure with collecting these curious physical signatures in this town. At my house I have hundreds upon hundreds of them. Each and every one is labeled with name and date; not labeled the next day or even the next hour, but in the very minute that the impression was taken. When I go upon the witness stand I will repeat under oath the things which I am now saying. I have the finger-prints of the court, the sheriff, and every member of the jury. There is hardly a person in this room, white or black, whose natal signature I cannot produce, and not one of them can so disguise himself that I cannot pick him out from a multitude of his fellow creatures and unerringly identify him by his hands. And if he and I should live to be a hundred I could still do it." [The interest of the audience was steadily deepening, now.]

"I have studied some of these signatures so much that I know them as well as the bank cashier knows the autograph of his oldest customer. While I turn my back, now, I beg that several persons will be so good as to pass their fingers through their hair, and then press them upon one of the panes of the window near the jury, and that among them the accused may set their finger-marks. Also, I beg that these experimenters, or others, will set their finger-marks upon another pane, and add again the marks of the accused, but not placing them in the same order or relation to the other signatures as before—for, by one chance in a million, a person might happen upon the right marks by pure guesswork, *once*, therefore I wish to be tested twice."

He turned his back, and the two panes were quickly covered with delicately-lined oval spots, but visible only to such persons as could get a dark background for them,—the foliage of a tree, outside, for instance. Then, upon call, Wilson went to the window, made his examination, and said—

"This is Count Luigi's right hand; this one, three signatures below, is his left. Here is Count Angelo's right; down here is his left. Now for the other pane: here and here are Count Luigi's, here and here are his brother's." He faced about. "Am I right?"

A deafening explosion of applause was the answer. The Bench said—

"This certainly approaches the miraculous!"

Wilson turned to the window again and remarked, pointing with his finger—

"AM I RIGHT?"

"This is the signature of Mr. Justice Robinson." [Applause.] "This, of Constable Blake." [Applause.] "This, of John Mason, juryman." [Applause.] "This, of the sheriff." [Applause.] "I cannot name the others, but I have them all at home, named and dated, and could identify them all by my finger-print records."

He moved to his place through a storm of applause—which the sheriff stopped, and also made the people sit down, for they were all standing, and struggling to see, of course. Court, jury, sheriff, and everybody had been too absorbed in observing Wilson's performance to attend to the audience earlier.

"Now then," said Wilson, "I have here the natal autographs of two children—thrown up to ten times the natural size by the pantagraph, so that any one who can see at all can tell the markings apart at a glance. We will call the children A and B. Here are A's finger-marks, taken at the age of five months. Here they are again, taken at seven months." [Tom started.] "They are alike, you see. Here are B's at five months, and also at seven months. They, too, exactly copy each other, but the patterns are quite different from A's, you observe. I shall refer to these again presently, but we will turn them face down, now.

"Here, thrown up ten sizes, are the natal autographs of the two persons who are here before you accused of murdering Judge Driscoll. I made these pantagraph copies last night, and will so swear when I go upon the witness stand. I ask the jury to compare them with the finger-marks of the accused upon the window panes, and tell the court if they are the same." He passed a powerful magnifying glass to the foreman.

One juryman after another took the cardboard and the glass and made the comparison. Then the foreman said to the judge—

"Your honor, we are all agreed that they are identical."

Wilson said to the foreman—

"Please turn that cardboard face down, and take this one and compare it searchingly, by the magnifier, with the fatal signature upon the knife handle, and report your finding to the court."

Again the jury made minute examination, and again reported—

"We find them to be exactly identical, your honor."

Wilson turned toward the counsel for the prosecution, and there was a clearly recognizable note of warning in his voice when he said—

"May it please the court, the State has claimed, strenuously and persistently, that the blood-stained finger-prints upon that knife handle were left there by the assassin of Judge Driscoll. You have heard us grant that claim, and welcome it." He turned to the jury: "Compare the finger-prints of the accused with the finger-prints left by the assassin—and report."

The comparison began. As it proceeded, all movement and all sound ceased, and the deep silence of an absorbed and waiting suspense settled upon the house; and when at last the words came—

"*They do not even resemble!*" a thunder-crash of applause followed and the house sprang to its feet, but was quickly repressed by official force and brought to order again. Tom was altering his position every few minutes, now, but none of his changes brought repose nor any small trifle of comfort. When the house's attention was become fixed once more, Wilson said gravely, indicating the Twins with a gesture—

"These men are innocent—I have no further concern with them." [Another outbreak of applause began, but was promptly checked.] "We will now proceed to find the guilty." [Tom's eyes were starting from their sockets—yes, it *was* a cruel day for the bereaved youth, everybody thought.] "We will return to the infant autographs of A and B. I will ask the jury to take these large pantagraph facsimiles of A's, marked five months and seven months. Do they tally?"

The foreman responded—

"Perfectly."

"Now examine this pantagraph, taken at eight months, and also marked A. Does it tally with the other two?"

The surprised response was—

"No—they differ widely."

"You are quite right. Now take these two pantagraphs of B's autograph, marked five months and seven months. Do they tally with each other?"

"Yes—perfectly."

"Take this third pantagraph marked 'B, eight months.' Does it tally with B's other two?"

"By no means."

"Do you know how to account for these strange discrepancies? I will tell you. For a purpose unknown to us, but probably a selfish one, somebody *changed those children in the cradle.*"

This produced a vast sensation, naturally; Roxana was astonished at this admirable guess, but not disturbed by it. To guess the exchange was one thing, to guess who did it quite another. Pudd'nhead Wilson could do wonderful things, no doubt, but he couldn't do impossible ones. Safe? She was perfectly safe. She smiled privately.

"Between the ages of seven months and eight months those children were changed in the cradle"—he made one of his effect-collecting pauses, and added—"*and the person who did it is in this house.*"

Roxy's pulses stood still! The house was thrilled as with an electric shock, and the people half rose, as if to seek a glimpse of the person who had made that exchange. Tom was growing limp; the life seemed oozing out of him. Wilson resumed:

"A was put into B's cradle in the nursery; B was transferred to the kitchen, and became a negro and a slave"—[Sensation—confusion of angry ejaculations]—"but within a quarter of an hour he will stand before you white and free!" [Burst of applause, checked by the officers.] "From seven months onward until now, A has still been a usurper, and in my finger-records he bears B's name. Here is his pantagraph, at the age of twelve. Compare it with the assassin's signature upon the knife handle. Do they tally?"

The foreman answered—

"To the minutest detail!"

Wilson said, solemnly—

"The murderer of your friend and mine—York Driscoll of the generous hand and the kindly spirit—sits in your midst! Valet de Chambre, negro and slave—falsely called Thomas à Becket Driscoll—make upon the window the finger-prints that will hang you!"

Tom turned his ashen face imploringly toward the speaker, made some impotent movements with his white lips, then slid limp and lifeless to the floor.

Wilson broke the awed silence with the words—

"There is no need. He has confessed."

Roxy flung herself upon her knees, covered her face with her hands, and out through her sobs the words struggled—

"De Lord have mercy on me, po' misable sinner dat I is!"

The clock struck twelve.

The court rose; the new prisoner, handcuffed, was removed.

Conclusion

It is often the case that the man who can't tell a lie thinks he is the best judge of one.—*Pudd'nhead Wilson's Calendar.*

October 12.—The Discovery.—It was wonderful to find America, but it would have been more wonderful to miss it. —*Pudd'nhead Wilson's Calendar.*

The town sat up all night to discuss the amazing events of the day and swap guesses as to when Tom's trial would begin. Troop after troop of citizens came to serenade Wilson, and require a speech, and shout themselves hoarse over every sentence that fell from his lips—for all his sentences were golden, now, all were marvelous. His long fight against hard luck and prejudice was ended; he was a made man for good.

And as each of these roaring gangs of enthusiasts marched away, some remorseful member of it was quite sure to raise his voice and say—

"And *this* is the man the likes of *us* have called a pudd'nhead for more than twenty years! He has resigned from that position, friends."

"Yes, but it isn't vacant—we're elected!"

——

The Twins were heroes of romance, now, and with rehabilitated reputations. But they were weary of Western adventure, and straightway retired to Europe.

Roxy's heart was broken. The young fellow upon whom she had inflicted twenty-three years of slavery continued the false heir's pension of thirty-five dollars a month to her, but her hurts were too deep for money to heal; the spirit in her eye was quenched, her martial bearing departed with it, and the voice of her laughter ceased in the land. In her church and its affairs she found her only solace.

The real heir suddenly found himself rich and free, but in a most embarrassing situation. He could neither read nor write, and his speech was the basest dialect of the negro quarter. His gait, his attitudes, his gestures, his bearing, his laugh—all were vulgar and uncouth; his manners were the manners of a slave. Money and fine clothes could not mend these defects or cover them up, they only made them the more glaring and the more pathetic. The poor fellow could not endure the terrors of the white man's parlor, and felt at home and at peace nowhere but in the kitchen. The family pew was a misery to him, yet he could nevermore enter into the solacing refuge of the "nigger gallery"—that was closed to him for good and all. But we cannot follow his curious fate further—that would be a long story.

The false heir made a full confession and was sentenced to imprisonment for life. But now a complication came up. The Percy Driscoll estate was in such a crippled shape when its owner died that it could pay only sixty per cent of its great indebtedness, and was settled at that rate. But the creditors came forward, now, and complained that inasmuch as through an error for which *they* were in no way to blame the false heir was not inventoried at that time with the rest of the property, great wrong and loss had thereby been inflicted upon them. They rightly claimed that "Tom" was lawfully their property and had been so for eight years; that they had already lost sufficiently in being deprived of his services during that long period, and ought not to be required to add anything to that loss; that if he had been delivered up to them in the first place, they would have sold him and he could not have murdered Judge Driscoll, therefore it was not he that had really committed the murder, the guilt lay with the erroneous inventory. Everybody saw that there was reason in this. Everybody granted that if "Tom" were white and free it would be unquestionably right to punish him—it would be no loss to anybody; but to shut up a valuable slave for life—that was quite another matter.

As soon as the Governor understood the case, he pardoned Tom at once, and the creditors sold him down the river.

Those Extraordinary Twins:

A POSTSCRIPT TO *PUDD'NHEAD WILSON*

Those Extraordinary Twins:
A Postscript to Pudd'nhead Wilson

A man who is not born with the novel-writing gift has a troublesome time of it when he tries to build a novel. I know this from experience. He has no clear idea of his story; in fact he has no story. He merely has some people in his mind, and an incident or two, also a locality. He knows these people, he knows the selected locality, and he trusts that he can plunge those people into those incidents with interesting results. So he goes to work. To write a novel? No—that is a thought which comes later; in the beginning he is only proposing to tell a little tale; a very little tale; a six-page tale. But as it is a tale which he is not acquainted with, and can only find out what it is by listening as it goes along telling itself, it is more than apt to go on and on and on till it spreads itself into a book. I know about this, because it has happened to me so many times.

And I have noticed another thing: that as the short tale grows into the long tale, the original intention (or *motif*) is apt to get abolished and find itself superseded by a quite different one. It was so in the case of a magazine sketch which I once started to write—a funny and fantastic sketch about a prince and a pauper; it presently assumed a grave cast of its own accord, and in that new shape spread itself out into a book. Much the same thing happened with "Pudd'nhead Wilson." I had a sufficiently hard time with that tale, because it changed itself from a farce to a tragedy while I was going along with it,—a most embarrassing circumstance. But what was a great deal worse was, that it was not one story, but two stories tangled together; and they obstructed and interrupted each other at every turn and created no end of confusion and annoyance. I could not offer the book for publication, for I was afraid it would unseat the reader's reason, I did not know what was the matter with it, for I had not noticed, as yet, that it was two stories in one. It took me months to make that discovery. I carried the manuscript back and forth across the Atlantic two or three times, and read it and studied over it on shipboard; and at last I saw where the difficulty lay. I had no further trouble. I pulled one of the stories out by the roots, and left the other one—a kind of literary Caesarean operation.

Would the reader care to know something about the story which I pulled out? He has been told many a time how the born-and-trained novelist works; won't he let me round and complete his knowledge by telling him how the jack-leg does it?

Originally the story was called "Those Extraordinary Twins." I meant to make it very short. I had seen a picture of a youthful Italian "freak"—or "freaks"—which was—or which were—on exhibition in our cities—a combination consisting of two heads and four arms joined to a single body and a single pair of legs—and I thought I would write an extravagantly fantastic little story with this freak of nature for hero— or heroes—a silly young Miss for heroine, and two old ladies and two boys for the minor parts. I lavishly elaborated these people and their doings, of course. But the tale kept spreading along and spreading along, and other people got to intruding themselves and taking up more and more room with their talk and their affairs. Among them came a stranger named Pudd'nhead Wilson, and a woman named Roxana; and presently the doings of these two pushed up into prominence a young fellow named Tom Driscoll, whose proper place was away in the obscure background. Before the book was half finished those three were taking things almost entirely into their own hands and working the whole tale as a private venture of their own—a tale which they had nothing at all to do with, by rights.

When the book was finished and I came to look around to see what had become of the team I had originally started out with—Aunt Patsy Cooper, Aunt Betsy Hale, the two boys, and Rowena the light-weight heroine—they were nowhere to be seen; they had disappeared from the story some time or other. I hunted about and found them— found them stranded, idle, forgotten, and permanently useless. It was very awkward. It was awkward all around, but more particularly in the case of Rowena, because there was a love-match on, between her and one of the twins that constituted the freak, and I had worked it up to a blistering heat and thrown in a quite dramatic love-quarrel, wherein Rowena scathingly denounced her betrothed for getting drunk, and scoffed at his explanation of how it had happened, and wouldn't listen to it, and had driven him from her in the usual "forever" way; and now here she sat crying and broken-hearted; for she had found that he had spoken only the truth; that it was not he, but the other half of the freak that had drunk the liquor that made him drunk; that her half was a prohibitionist and had never drunk a drop in his life, and although tight as a brick three days in the week, was wholly innocent of blame; and indeed, when sober, was constantly doing all he could to reform his brother, the other half, who never got any satisfaction out of drinking, anyway, because liquor never affected him. Yes, here she was, stranded with that deep injustice of hers torturing her poor torn heart.

I didn't know what to do with her. I was as sorry for her as anybody could be, but the campaign was over, the book was finished, she was side-tracked, and there was no possible way of crowding her in, anywhere. I could not leave her there, of course; it would not do. After spreading her out so, and making such a to-do over her affairs, it would be absolutely necessary to account to the reader for her. I thought and thought and studied and studied; but I arrived at nothing. I finally saw plainly that there was really no way but one—I must simply give her the grand bounce. It grieved me to do it, for after associating with her so much I had come to kind of like her after a fashion, notwithstanding she was such an ass and said such stupid, irritating things and was so nauseatingly sentimental. Still it had to be done. So at the top of Chapter 17 I put a "Calendar" remark concerning July the Fourth, and began the chapter with this statistic:

"Rowena went out in the back yard after supper to see the fireworks and fell down the well and got drowned."

It seemed abrupt, but I thought maybe the reader wouldn't notice it, because I changed the subject right away to something else. Anyway it loosened up Rowena from where she was stuck and got her out of the way, and that was the main thing. It seemed a prompt good way of weeding out people that had got stalled, and a plenty good enough way for those others; so I hunted up the two boys and said "they went out back one night to stone the cat and fell down the well and got drowned." Next I searched around and found old Aunt Patsy Cooper and Aunt Betsy Hale where they were aground, and said "they went out back one night to visit the sick and fell down the well and got drowned." I was going to drown some of the others, but I gave up the idea, partly because I believed that if I kept that up it would arouse attention, and perhaps sympathy with those people, and partly because it was not a large well and would not hold any more anyway.

Still the story was unsatisfactory. Here was a set of new characters who were become inordinately prominent and who persisted in remaining so to the end; and back yonder was an older set who made a large noise and a great to-do for a little while and then suddenly played out utterly and fell down the well. There was a radical defect somewhere, and I must search it out and cure it.

The defect turned out to be the one already spoken of—two stories in one, a farce and a tragedy. So I pulled out the farce and left the tragedy. This left the original team in, but only as mere names, not as characters. Their prominence was wholly gone; they were not even worth drowning; so I removed that detail. Also I took those twins apart and made two separate men of them. They had no occasion to have foreign names now, but it was too much trouble to remove them all through, so I left them christened as they were and made no explanation.

Chapter 1

The conglomerate twins were brought on the stage in Chapter 1 of the original extravaganza. Aunt Patsy Cooper has received their letter applying for board and lodging, and Rowena, her daughter, insane with joy, is begging for a hearing of it:

"Well, set down then, and be quiet a minute and don't fly around so; it fairly makes me tired to see you. It starts off so: 'Honored Madam'—"

"I like that, ma, don't you? It shows they're high-bred."

"Yes, I noticed that when I first read it. 'My brother and I have seen your advertisement, by chance, in a copy of your local journal—'"

"It's so beautiful and smooth, ma—don't you think so?"

"Yes, seems so to me—'and beg leave to take the room you offer. We are twenty-four years of age, and twins—'"

"Twins! How sweet! I do hope they are handsome, and I just know they are. Don't you hope they are, ma?"

"Land, I ain't particular. 'We are Italians by birth—'"

"It's *so* romantic! Just think—there's never been one in this town, and everybody will want to see them, and they're all *ours!* Think of that."

—"'but have lived long in the various countries of Europe, and several years in the United States.'"

"Oh, just think what wonders they've seen, ma. Won't it be good to hear them talk?"

"I reckon so; yes, I reckon so. 'Our names are Luigi and Angelo Cappello—'"

"Beautiful, perfectly beautiful! Not like Jones and Robinson and those horrible names!"

"'You desire but one guest, but dear madam, if you will allow us to pay for two we will not discommode you. We will sleep together in the same bed. We have always been used to this, and prefer it.' And then he goes on to say they will be down Thursday."

"And this is Tuesday—I don't know how I'm ever going to wait, ma. The time does drag along so, and I'm so dying to see them. Which of them do you reckon is the tallest, ma?"

"How do you s'pose I can tell, child? Mostly they are the same size—twins are."

"Well, then, which do you reckon is the best looking?"

"Goodness knows—*I* don't."

"*I* think Angelo is; it's the prettiest name, anyway. Don't you think it's a sweet name, ma?"

"Yes, it's well enough. I'd like both of them better if I knew the way to pronounce them—the Eyetalian way, I mean. The Missouri way and the Eyetalian way is different, I judge."

"Maybe—yes. It's Luigi that writes the letter. What do you reckon is the reason Angelo didn't write it?"

"Why, how can *I* tell? What's the difference who writes it, so long as it's done?"

"Oh, I *hope* it wasn't because he is sick! You don't think he is sick, do you, ma?"

"Sick your granny; what's to make him sick?"

"Oh, there's never any telling. Those foreigners with that kind of names are so delicate, and of course that kind of names are not suited to our climate—you wouldn't expect it."

[And so on and so on, no end. The time drags along; Thursday comes; the boat arrives in a pouring storm toward midnight.]

At last there was a knock at the door and the anxious family jumped to open it. Two negro men entered, each carrying a trunk, and proceeded up stairs toward the guest room. Then followed a stupefying apparition— a double-headed human creature with four arms, one body, and a single pair of legs!

It—or they, as you please—bowed with elaborate foreign formality, but the Coopers could not respond, immediately; they were paralyzed. At this moment there came from the rear of the group a fervent ejaculation—"My lan'!"—followed by a crash of crockery, and the slave wench Nancy stood petrified and staring, with a tray of wrecked tea things at her feet. The incident broke the spell, and brought the family to consciousness. The beautiful heads of the new-comer bowed again, and one of them said with easy grace and dignity—

"I crave the honor, Madam and Miss, to introduce to you my brother, Count Luigi Cappello," (the other head bowed,) "and myself—Count Angelo, and at the same time offer sincere apologies for the lateness of our coming, which was unavoidable;" and both heads bowed again.

The poor old lady was in a whirl of amazement and confusion, but she managed to stammer out—

"I'm sure I'm glad to make your acquaintance, sir—I mean, gentlemen. As for the delay, it is nothing, don't mention it. This is my daughter Rowena, sir—gentlemen. Please step in the parlor and sit down and have a bite and a sup; you are dreadful wet and must be uncomfortable—both of you, I mean."

But to the old lady's relief they courteously excused themselves, saying it would be wrong to keep the family out of their beds longer; then each head bowed in turn and uttered a friendly good-night, and the singular figure moved away in the wake of Rowena's small brothers, who bore candles, and disappeared up the stairs.

The widow tottered into the parlor and sank into a chair with a gasp, and Rowena followed, tongue-tied and dazed. The two sat silent in the throbbing summer heat, unconscious of the million-voiced music of the mosquitoes, unconscious of the roaring gale, the lashing and thrashing of the rain along the windows and the roof, the white glare of the lightnings, the tumultuous booming and bellowing of the thunder, conscious of nothing but that prodigy, that uncanny apparition that had come and gone so suddenly—that weird strange thing that was so soft spoken and so gentle of manner, and yet had shaken them up like an earthquake with the shock of its grewsome aspect. At last a cold little shudder quivered along down the widow's meagre frame and she said in a weak voice—

"Ugh, it was awful—just the mere *look* of that phillipene!"

Rowena did not answer. Her faculties were still caked, she had not yet found her voice. Presently the widow said, a little resentfully—

"Always been *used* to sleeping together—in fact, *prefer* it. And *I* was thinking it was to accommodate me. I thought it was very good of them, whereas a person situated as that young man is—"

"Ma, you oughtn't to begin by getting up a prejudice against him. I'm sure he is good-hearted and means well. Both of his faces show it."

"I'm not so certain about that. The one on the left—I mean the one on *its* left—hasn't near as good a face, in my opinion, as its brother."

"That's Luigi."

"Yes, Luigi; anyway it's the dark-skinned one; the one that was west of his brother when they stood in the door. Up to all kinds of mischief and disobedience when he was a boy, I'll be bound. I lay his mother had trouble to lay her hand on him when she wanted him. But the one on the right is as good as gold, I can see that."

"That's Angelo."

"Yes, Angelo, I reckon, though I can't tell t'other from which by their names, yet awhile. But it's the right-hand one—the blonde one. He has such kind blue eyes, and curly copper hair and fresh complexion—"

"And such a noble face!—oh, it *is* a noble face, ma, just royal, you may say. And beautiful—deary me, how beautiful! But both are that; the dark one's as beautiful as a picture. There's no such wonderful faces and handsome heads in *this* town—none that even begin! And such hands!—especially Angelo's—so shapely and—"

"Stuff, how could *you* tell which they belonged to?—they had gloves on."

"Why, didn't I see them take off their hats?"

"That don't signify. They might have taken off each other's hats. Nobody could tell. There was just a wormy squirming of arms in the air—seemed to be a couple of dozen of them, all writhing at once, and it just made me dizzy to see them go."

"Why, ma, *I* hadn't any difficulty. There's two arms on each shoulder—"

"There, now! One arm on each shoulder belongs to each of the creatures, don't it? For a person to have two arms on one shoulder wouldn't do him any good, would it? Of course not. Each has an arm on each shoulder. Now then, you tell me which of them belongs to which, if you can. They don't know, themselves—they just work whichever arm comes handy. Of course they do; especially if they are in a hurry and can't stop to think which belongs to which."

The mother seemed to have the rights of the argument, so the daughter abandoned the struggle. Presently the widow rose with a yawn and said—

"Poor thing, I hope it won't catch cold; it was powerful wet, just drenched, you may say. I hope it has left its boots outside, so they can be dried." Then she gave a little start, and looked perplexed. "Now I remember I heard one of them ask Joe to call him at half after seven,—I think it was the one on the left—no, it was the one to the east of the other one—but I didn't hear the other one say anything. I wonder if he wants to be called, too. Do you reckon it's too late to ask?"

"Why, ma, it's not necessary. Calling one is calling both. If one gets up, the other's *got* to."

"Sho', of course; I never thought of that. Well, come along, maybe we can get some sleep, but I don't know, I'm so shook up with what we've been through."

The stranger had made an impression on the boys, too. They had a word of talk as they were getting to bed. Henry, the gentle, the humane, said—

"I feel ever so sorry for it, don't you, Joe?"

But Joe was a boy of this world, active, enterprising, and had a theatrical side to him.

"Sorry? Why how you talk! It can't stir a step without attracting attention. It's just grand."

Henry said, reproachfully—

"Instead of pitying it, Joe, you talk as if—"

"Talk as if *what?* I know one thing mighty certain: if you can fix me so *I* can eat for two and only have to stub toes for one, I ain't going to fool away no such chance just for sentiment."

The Twins were wet and tired, and they proceeded to undress without any preliminary remarks. The abundance of sleeves made the partnership coat hard to get off, for it was like skinning a tarantula, but it came at last, after much tugging and perspiring. The mutual vest followed. Then the brothers stood up before the glass, and each took off his own cravat and collar. The collars were of the standing kind, and came high up under the ears, like the sides of a wheelbarrow, as required by the fashion of the day. The cravats were as broad as a bank bill, with fringed ends which stood far out to right and left like the wings of a dragon-fly, and this also was strictly in accordance with the fashion of the time. Each cravat, as to color, was in perfect taste, as far as its owner's complexion was concerned—a delicate pink, in the case of the blonde brother, a violent scarlet in the case of the brunette—but as a combination they broke all the laws of taste known to civilization. Nothing more fiendish and irreconcilable than those shrieking and blaspheming colors could have been contrived. The wet boots gave no end of trouble—to Luigi. When they were off at last, Angelo said, with bitterness—

"I wish you wouldn't wear such tight boots, they hurt my feet."

Luigi answered with indifference—

"My friend, when *I* am in command of our body, I choose my apparel according to my own convenience, as I have remarked more than several times already. When you are in command, I beg you will do as *you* please."

Angelo was hurt, and the tears came into his eyes. There was gentle reproach in his voice, but not anger, when he replied:

"Luigi, I often consult your wishes, but you never consult mine. When I am in command I treat you as a guest; I try to make you feel at home; when you are in command you treat me as an intruder, you make me feel unwelcome. It embarrasses me cruelly in company, for I can see that people notice it and comment on it."

"Oh, damn the people," responded the brother languidly, and with the air of one who is tired of the subject.

A slight shudder shook the frame of Angelo, but he said nothing and the conversation ceased. Each buttoned his own share of the night shirt in silence; then Luigi, with Paine's "Age of Reason" in his hand, sat down in one chair and put his feet in another and lit his pipe, while Angelo took his "Whole Duty of Man," and both began to read. Angelo presently began to cough; his coughing increased and became mixed with gaspings for breath, and he was finally obliged to make an appeal to his brother's humanity:

"Luigi, if you would only smoke a little milder tobacco I am sure I could learn not to mind it in time, but this is *so* strong, and the pipe is so rank that—"

"Angelo, I wouldn't be such a baby! I have learned to smoke in a week, and the trouble is already over with me; if you would try, *you* could learn, too, and then you would stop spoiling my comfort with your everlasting complaints."

"Ah, brother, that is a strong word—everlasting—and isn't quite fair. I only complain when I suffocate; you know I don't complain when we are in the open air."

"Well, anyway, you could learn to smoke, yourself."

"But my principles, Luigi, you forget my principles. You would not have me do a thing which I regard as a sin?"

"Oh, bosh!"

The conversation ceased again, for Angelo was sick and discouraged and strangling; but after some time he closed his book and asked Luigi to sing

"From Greenland's Icy Mountains" with him, but he would not, and when he tried to sing by himself Luigi did his best to drown his plaintive tenor with a rude and rollicking song delivered in a thundering bass.

After the singing there was silence, and neither brother was happy. Before blowing the light out Luigi swallowed half a tumbler of whisky, and Angelo, whose sensitive organization could not endure intoxicants of any kind, took a pill to keep it from giving him the headache.

Chapter 2

The family sat in the breakfast room waiting for the Twins to come down. The widow was quiet, the daughter was all alive with happy excitement. She said—

"Ah, they're a boon, ma, just a boon! don't you think so?"

"Laws, I hope so, *I* don't know."

"Why, ma, yes you do. They're so fine, and handsome, and high-bred, and polite, so *every* way superior to our gawks here in this village—why, they'll make life different from what it was—so humdrum and commonplace, you know—oh, you may be sure they're full of accomplishments, and knowledge of the world, and all that, that will be an immense advantage to society here. Don't you think so, ma?"

"Mercy on me, how should *I* know, and I've hardly set eyes on them, yet." After a pause, she added, "They made considerable noise after they went up."

"Noise? Why, ma, they were singing. And it was beautiful, too."

"Oh, it was well enough, but too mixed-up, seemed to me."

"Now, ma, honor bright, did you *ever* hear 'Greenland's Icy Mountains' sung sweeter—now did you?"

"If it had been sung by itself, it would have been uncommon sweet, I don't deny it; but what they wanted to mix it up with 'Old Bob Ridley' for, I can't make out. Why, they don't go together, at all. They are not of the same nature. 'Bob Ridley' is a common rackety slam-bang secular song, one of the rippingest and rantingest and noisiest there is. I am no judge of music, and I don't claim it, but in my opinion nobody can make those two songs go together right."

"Why, ma, I thought—"

"It don't make any difference what you thought, it can't be done. *They* tried it, and to my mind it was a failure. I never heard such a crazy uproar; seemed to me, sometimes, the roof would come off; and as for the cats—well, I've lived a many a year, and seen cats aggravated in more ways than one, but I've never seen cats take on the way they took on last night."

"Well, I don't think that that goes for anything, ma, because it is the nature of cats that any sound that is unusual—"

"Unusual! You may well call it so. Now if they are going to sing duets every night, I do hope they will both sing the same tune at the same time, for in my opinion a duet that is made up of two different tunes is a mistake; especially when the tunes ain't any kin to one another, that way."

"But ma, *I* think it must be a foreign custom; and it must be right, too, and the best way, because they have had every opportunity to know what *is* right, and it don't stand to reason that with their education they would do anything but what the highest musical authorities have sanctioned. You can't help but admit that, ma."

The argument was formidably strong; the old lady could not find any way around it; so, after thinking it over a while she gave in with a sigh of discontent, and admitted that the daughter's position was probably correct. Being vanquished, she had no mind to continue the topic at that disadvantage, and was about to seek a change when a change came of itself. A footstep was heard on the stairs, and she said—

"There—he's coming."

"*They*, ma—you ought to say *they*—it's nearer right."

The new lodger, rather shoutingly dressed but looking superbly handsome, stepped with courtly carriage into the trim little breakfast room and put out all his cordial arms at once, like one of those pocket knives with a multiplicity of blades, and shook hands with the whole family simultaneously. He was so easy and pleasant and hearty that all embarrassment presently thawed away and disappeared, and a cheery feeling of friendliness and comradeship took its place. He—or preferably they—were asked to occupy the seat of honor at the foot of the table. They consented with thanks, and carved the beef steak with one set of their hands while they distributed it at the same time with the other set.

"Will you have coffee, gentlemen, or tea?"

"Coffee for Luigi, if you please, madam, tea for me."

"Cream and sugar?"

"For me, yes, madam; Luigi takes his coffee black. Our natures differ a good deal from each other, and our tastes also."

The first time the negro girl Nancy appeared in the door and saw the two heads turned in opposite directions and both talking at once, then saw the commingling arms feed potatoes into one mouth and coffee into the other at the same time, she had to pause and pull herself out of a faintness that came over her; but after that she held her grip and was able to wait on the table with fair courage.

Conversation fell naturally into the customary grooves. It was a little jerky, at first, because none of the family could get smoothly through a sentence without a wobble in it here and a break there, caused by some new surprise in the way of attitude or gesture on the part of the Twins. The weather suffered the most. The weather was all finished up and disposed of, as a subject, before the simple Missourians had gotten sufficiently wonted to the spectacle of one body feeding two heads to feel composed and reconciled in the presence of so bizarre a miracle. And even after everybody's mind became tranquilized there was still one slight distraction left: the hand that picked up a biscuit carried it to the wrong head, as often as any other way, and the wrong mouth devoured it. This was a puzzling thing, and marred the talk a little. It bothered the widow to such a degree that she presently dropped out of the conversation without knowing it, and fell to watching, and guessing, and talking to herself: "Now *that* hand is going to take that coffee to—no, it's gone to the other mouth; I can't understand it; and now, here is the dark-complected hand with a potato on its fork, I'll see what goes with *it*—there, the light-complected head's got it, as sure's I live!" Finally Rowena said—

"Ma, what is the matter with you? Are you dreaming about something?"

The old lady came to herself, and blushed; then she explained with the first random thing that came into her mind:

"I saw Mr. Angelo take up Mr. Luigi's coffee, and I thought maybe he— shan't I give *you* a cup, Mr. Angelo?"

"Oh, no, madam, I am very much obliged, but I never drink coffee, much as I would like to. You did see me take up Luigi's cup, it is true, but if you noticed, I did not carry it to my mouth, but to his."

"Y-es, I thought you did. Did you mean to?"

"How?"

The widow was a little embarrassed again. She said:

"I don't know but what I'm foolish, and you mustn't mind; but you see, *he* got the coffee I was expecting to see you drink, and you got a potato that I thought *he* was going to get. So, I thought it might be a mistake all around, and everybody getting what wasn't intended for him."

Both Twins laughed, and Luigi said—

"Dear madam, there wasn't any mistake. We are always helping each other that way. It is a great economy for us both; it saves time and labor. We have a system of signs which nobody can notice or understand but ourselves. If I am using both of my hands and want some coffee, I make the sign and Angelo furnishes it to me; and you saw that when he needed a potato I delivered it."

"How convenient!"

"Yes, and often of the extremest value. Take these Mississippi boats, for instance. They are always overcrowded. There is table-room for only half of the passengers, therefore they have to set a second table for the second half. The stewards rush both parties, they give them no time to eat a satisfying meal, both divisions leave the table hungry. It isn't so with us. Angelo books himself for the one table, I book myself for the other. Neither of us eats anything at the other's table, but just simply works—works. Thus, you see, there are four hands to feed Angelo, and the same four to feed me. Each of us eats two meals."

The old lady was dazed with admiration, and kept saying "It's *perfectly* wonderful, perfectly wonderful!" and the boy Joe licked his chops enviously but said nothing—at least aloud.

"Yes," continued Luigi, "our construction may have its disadvantages—in fact, *has*—but it also has its compensations, of one sort and another. Take travel, for instance. Travel is enormously expensive, in all countries; we have been obliged to do a vast deal of it—come, Angelo, don't put any more sugar in your tea, I'm just over one indigestion and don't want another right away—been obliged to do a deal of it, as I was saying. Well, we always travel as one person, since we occupy but one seat, so we save half the fare."

"How romantic!" interjected Rowena, with effusion.

"Yes, my dear young lady, and how practical, too, and economical. In Europe, beds in the hotels are not charged with the board, but separately—another saving, for we stood to our rights and paid for the one bed only. The landlords often insisted that as both of us occupied the bed we ought—"

"No, they didn't!" said Angelo. "They did it only twice, and in both cases it was a double bed—a rare thing in Europe—and the double bed gave them some excuse. Be fair to the landlords; twice doesn't constitute 'often.'"

"Well, that depends—that depends. I knew a man who fell down a well twice. He said he didn't mind the first time, but he thought the second time was once too often. Have I misused that word, Mrs. Cooper?"

"To tell the truth, I was afraid you had, but it seems to look, now, like you hadn't." She stopped, and was evidently struggling with the difficult problem a moment, then she added in the tone of one who is convinced without being converted, "It seems so, but I can't somehow tell why."

Rowena thought Luigi's retort was wonderfully quick and bright, and she remarked to herself with satisfaction that there wasn't any young native of Dawson's Landing that could have risen to the occasion like that. Luigi detected the applause in her face, and expressed his pleasure and his thanks with his eyes, and so eloquently withal, that the girl was proud and pleased, and hung out the delicate sign of it on her cheeks.

Luigi went on, with animation:

"Both of us get a bath for one ticket, theatre seat for one ticket, pew-rent is on the same basis, but at peep-shows we pay double."

"We have much to be thankful for," said Angelo, impressively, with a reverent light in his eye and a reminiscent tone in his voice, "we have been greatly blessed. As a rule, what one of us has lacked, the other, by the bounty of Providence, has been able to supply. My brother is hardy, I am not; he is very masculine, assertive, aggressive, I am much less so. I am subject to illness, he is never ill. I cannot abide medicines, and cannot take them, but he has no prejudice against them, and—"

"Why, goodness gracious," interrupted the widow, "when you are sick, does he take the medicine for you?"

"Always, madam."

"Well, I *never* heard such a thing in my life. I think it's beautiful of you!"

"Oh, madam, it's nothing, don't mention it, it's really nothing at all."

"But I say it's beautiful, and I stick to it!" cried the widow, with a speaking moisture in her eye. "A well brother to take the medicine for his poor sick brother—I wish I had such a son," and she glanced reproachfully at her boys. "I declare I'll never rest till I've shook you by the hand!" and she scrambled out of her chair in a fever of generous enthusiasm, and made for the Twins, blind with her tears, and began to shake. The boy Joe corrected her:

"You're shaking the wrong one, ma."

This flurried her, but she made a swift change and went on shaking.

"Got the wrong one again, ma," said the boy.

"Oh, shut up, can't you!" said the widow, embarrassed and irritated. "Give me *all* your hands, I want to shake them all; for I know you are both just as good as you can be."

It was a victorious thought, a master-stroke of diplomacy, though that never occurred to her and she cared nothing for diplomacy. She shook the four hands in turn cordially, and went back to her place in a state of high and fine exaltation that made her look young and handsome.

"Indeed I owe everything to Luigi," said Angelo, affectionately. "But for him I could not have survived our boyhood days, when we were friendless and poor—ah, so poor! We lived from hand to mouth—lived on the coarse fare of unwilling charity, and for weeks and weeks together not a morsel of food passed my lips, for its character revolted me and I could not eat it. But for Luigi I should have died. He ate for us both."

"How noble!" sighed Rowena.

"Do you hear that?" said the widow, severely, to her boys. "Let it be an example to you—I mean you, Joe."

Joe gave his head a barely perceptible disparaging toss and said—

"Et for both. It ain't anything—I'd a done it."

"Hush, if you haven't got any better manners than that. You don't see the point at all. It wasn't *good* food."

"I don't care—it was *food*, and I'd a et it if it was rotten."

"Shame! Such language! Can't you understand? They were starving—actually starving—and he ate for both, and—"

"Shucks! you gimme a chance and I'll—"

"There, now—close your head! and don't you open it again till you're asked."

[Angelo goes on and tells how his parents the Count and Countess had to fly from Florence for political reasons, and died poor in Berlin bereft of their great property by confiscation; and how he and Luigi had to travel with a freak-show during two years and suffer semi-starvation.]

"That hateful black bread! but I seldom ate anything during that time, that was poor Luigi's affair—"

"I'll never Mister him again!" cried the widow, with strong emotion, "he's *Luigi* to me, from this out!"

"Thank you a thousand times, madam, a thousand times! though in truth I don't deserve it."

"Ah, Luigi is always the fortunate one when honors are showering," said Angelo, plaintively, "now what have I done, Mrs. Cooper, that you leave me out? Come, you must strain a point in my favor."

"Call you Angelo? Why, *certainly* I will; what are you *thinking* of! In the case of twins, why—"

"But ma, you're breaking up the story—do let him go on."

"You keep still, Rowena Cooper, and he can go on all the better, I reckon. One interruption don't hurt, it's two that makes the trouble."

"But you've added one, now, and that is three."

"Rowena! I will not allow you to talk back at me when you have got nothing rational to say."

Chapter 3

[After breakfast the whole village crowded in, and there was a grand reception in honor of the Twins; and at the close of it the gifted "freak" captured everybody's admiration by sitting down at the piano and knocking out a classic four-handed piece in great style. Then the Judge took it—or them—driving in his buggy and showed off his village.]

All along the streets the people crowded the windows and stared at the amazing Twins. Troops of small boys flocked after the buggy, excited and yelling. At first the dogs showed no interest. They thought they merely saw three men in a buggy—a matter of no consequence; but when they found out the facts of the case, they altered their opinion pretty radically, and joined the boys, expressing their minds as they came. Other dogs got interested; indeed all the dogs. It was a spirited sight to see them come leaping fences, tearing around corners, swarming out of every by-street and alley. The noise they made was something beyond belief—or praise. They did not seem to be moved by malice, but only by prejudice, the common human prejudice against lack of conformity. If the Twins turned their heads, they broke and fled in every direction, but stopped at a safe distance and faced about, and then formed and came on again as soon as the strangers showed them their back. Negroes and farmers' wives took to the woods when the buggy came upon them suddenly, and altogether the drive was pleasant and animated, and a refreshment all around.

[It was a long and lively drive. Angelo was a Methodist, Luigi was a freethinker. The Judge was very proud of his Freethinker Society, which was flourishing along in a most prosperous way and already had two members—himself and the obscure and neglected Pudd'nhead Wilson. It was to meet that evening, and he invited Luigi to join; a thing which Luigi was glad to do, partly because it would please himself, and partly because it would gravel Angelo.]

They had now arrived at the widow's gate, and the excursion was ended. The Twins politely expressed their obligations for the pleasant outing which had been afforded them; to which the Judge bowed his thanks, and then said he would now go and arrange for the Freethinkers' meeting, and would call for Count Luigi in the evening.

"For you, also, dear sir," he added, hastily, turning to Angelo and bowing. "In addressing myself particularly to your brother, I was not meaning to leave you out. It was an unintentional rudeness, I assure you, and due wholly to accident—accident and preoccupation. I beg you to forgive me."

His quick eye had seen the sensitive blood mount into Angelo's face, betraying the wound that had been inflicted. The sting of the slight had gone deep, but the apology was so prompt, and so evidently sincere, that the hurt was almost immediately healed, and a forgiving smile testified to the kindly Judge that all was well again.

Concealed behind Angelo's modest and unassuming exterior, and unsuspected by any but his intimates, was a lofty pride, a pride of almost abnormal proportions, indeed, and this rendered him ever the prey of slights; and although they were almost always imaginary ones, they hurt none the less on that account. By ill fortune Judge Driscoll had happened to touch his sorest point, *i.e.*, his conviction that his brother's presence was welcomer everywhere than his own; that he was often invited, out of mere courtesy, where only his brother was wanted, and that in the majority of cases he would not be included in an invitation if he could be left out without offence. A sensitive nature like this is necessarily subject to moods; moods which traverse the whole gamut of feeling; moods which know all the climes of emotion, from the sunny heights of joy to the black abysses of despair. At times, in his seasons of deepest depression, Angelo almost wished that he and his brother might become segregated from each other and be separate individuals, like other men. But of course as soon as his mind cleared and these diseased imaginings passed away, he shuddered at the repulsive thought, and earnestly prayed that it might visit him no more. To be separate, and as other men are! How awkward it would seem; how unendurable. What would he do with his hands, his arms? How would his legs feel? How odd, and strange, and grotesque every action, attitude, movement, gesture would be. To sleep by himself, eat by himself, walk by himself—how lonely, how unspeakably lonely! No, no, any fate but that! In every way and from every point of view, the idea was revolting.

This was of course natural; to have felt otherwise would have been unnatural. He had known no life but the combined one; he had been familiar with it from his birth; he was not able to conceive of any other as being agreeable, or even bearable. To him, in the privacy of his secret thoughts, all other men were monsters, deformities; and during three-fourths of his life their aspect had filled him with what promised to be an unconquerable aversion. But at eighteen his eye began to take note of female beauty, and, little by little, undefined longings grew up in his heart, under whose softening influence the old stubborn aversion gradually diminished, and finally disappeared. Men were still monstrosities to him, still deformities, and in his sober moments he had no desire to be like them, but their strange and unsocial and uncanny construction was no longer offensive to him.

This had been a hard day for him, physically and mentally. He had been called in the morning before he had quite slept off the effects of the liquor which Luigi had drank; and so, for the first half hour had had the seedy feeling, the languor, the brooding depression, the cobwebby mouth and druggy taste that come of dissipation, and are so ill a preparation for bodily or intellectual activities; the long and violent strain of the reception had followed; and this had been followed, in turn, by the dreary sight-seeing, the Judge's wearying explanations and laudations of the sights, and the stupefying clamor of the dogs. As a congruous conclusion, a fitting end, his feelings had been hurt, a slight had been put upon him. He would have been glad to forego dinner, and betake himself to rest and sleep, but he held his peace and said no word, for he knew his brother. Luigi was fresh, unweary, full of life, spirit, energy, he would have scoffed at the idea of wasting valuable time on a bed or a sofa, and would have refused permission.

Chapter 4

Rowena was dining out, Joe and Henry were belated at play, there were but three chairs and four persons that noon at the home dinner table—the Twins, the widow, and her chum, Aunt Betsy Hale. The widow soon perceived that Angelo's spirits were as low as Luigi's were high, and also that he had a jaded look. Her motherly solicitude was aroused, and she tried to get him interested in the talk and win him to a happier frame of mind, but the cloud of sadness remained on his countenance. Luigi lent his help, too. He used a form and a phrase which he was always accustomed to employ in these circumstances. He gave his brother an affectionate slap on the shoulder and said, encouragingly—

"Cheer up, the worst is yet to come!"

But this did no good. It never did. If anything, it made the matter worse, as a rule, because it irritated Angelo. This made it a favorite with Luigi. By and by the widow said—

"Angelo, you are tired, you've overdone yourself. You go right to bed, after dinner, and get a good nap and a rest, then you'll be all right."

"Indeed I would give anything if I could do that, madam."

"And what's to hender, I'd like to know? Land, the room's yours, to do what you please with. The idea that you can't do what you like with your own!"

"But, you see, there's one prime essential—an essential of the very first importance—which *isn't* my own."

"What is that?"

"My body."

The old ladies looked puzzled, and Aunt Betsy Hale said—

"Why, bless your heart, how is that?"

"It's my brother's."

"Your brother's. I don't quite understand. I supposed it belonged to both of you."

"So it does. But not to both at the same time."

"That is mighty curious; I don't see how it can be. I shouldn't think it could be managed that way."

"Oh, it's a good enough arrangement, and goes very well—in fact it wouldn't do to have it otherwise. I find that the Teetotalers and the Anti-Teetotalers, hire the use of the same hall for their meetings. Both parties don't use it at the same time, do they?"

"You bet they don't!" said both old ladies in a breath. "And moreover," said Aunt Betsy, "the Freethinkers and the Babtist Bible class use the same room over the market house, but you can take my word for it *they* don't mush-up together and use it at the same time."

"Very well," said Angelo, "you understand it now. And it stands to reason that the arrangement couldn't be improved. I'll prove it to you. If our legs tried to obey two wills, how could we ever get anywhere? I would start one way, Luigi would start another, at the same moment—the result would be a standstill, wouldn't it?"

"As sure as you are born! Now ain't that wonderful! A body would never have thought of it."

"We should always be arguing and fussing and disputing over the merest trifles. We should lose worlds of time, for we couldn't go down stairs or up, couldn't go to bed, couldn't rise, couldn't wash, couldn't dress, couldn't stand up, couldn't sit down, couldn't even cross our legs without calling a meeting first, and explaining the case, and passing resolutions, and getting consent. It wouldn't ever do—now would it?"

"Do? Why, it would wear a person out in a week. Did you ever hear anything like it, Patsy Cooper?"

"Oh, you'll find there's more than one thing about them that ain't commonplace," said the widow, with the complacent air of a person with a property right in a novelty that is under admiring scrutiny.

"Well, now, how ever *do* you manage it? I don't mind saying I'm suffering to know."

"He who made us," said Angelo, reverently, "and with us this difficulty, also provided a way out of it. By a mysterious law of our being, each of us has utter and indisputable command of our body a week at a time, turn and turn about."

"Well, I never. Now ain't that beautiful!"

"Yes, it is beautiful and infinitely wise and just. The week ends every Saturday at midnight to the minute, to the second, to the last shade and fraction of a second, infallibly, unerringly, and in that instant the one brother's power over the body vanishes and the other brother takes possession, asleep or awake."

"How marvelous are His ways, and past finding out!"

Luigi said—

"So exactly to the instant does the change come, that during our stay in many of the great cities of the world, the public clocks were regulated weekly by it; and as the hundreds of thousands of private clocks and watches were set and corrected in accordance with the public clocks, we really furnished the standard time for the entire city."

"Don't tell *me* that He don't do miracles any more! Blowing down the walls of Jericho with rams' horns warn't as difficult, in my opinion."

"And that is not all," said Angelo. "A thing that is even more marvelous, perhaps, is the fact that the change takes note of longitude and fits itself to the meridian we are on. Luigi is in command this week. Now, if on Saturday night at a moment before midnight we could fly in an instant to a point fifteen degrees west of here, he would hold possession of the power another hour, for the change observes *local* time and no other."

Betsy Hale was deeply impressed, and said with solemnity—

"Patsy Cooper, for *de*tail it lays over the Passage of the Red Sea."

"No, I shouldn't go as far as that," said Aunt Patsy, "but if you're a mind to say Sodom and Gomorrah, I am with you, Betsy Hale."

"I am agreeable, then, though I do think I was right, and I believe parson Maltby will say the same. Well, now, there's another thing. Suppose one of you wants to *borrow* the legs a minute from the one that's got them, could he let him?"

"Yes, but we hardly ever do that. There were disagreeable results, several times, and so we very seldom ask or grant the privilege, now-a-days, and we never even think of such a thing unless the case is extremely urgent. Besides, a week's possession at a time seems so little that we can't bear to spare a minute of it. People who have the use of their legs *all* the time never think of what a blessing it is, of course. It never occurs to them; it's just their natural ordinary condition, and so it doesn't excite them at all. But when I wake up, on a Sunday morning, and it's my week and I feel the power all through me, oh, *such* a wave of exultation and thanksgiving goes surging over me, and I want to shout 'I can walk! I can walk!' Madam, do you ever, at your uprising, want to shout 'I can walk! I can walk!'"

"No, you poor unfortunate cretur, but I'll never get out of my bed again without *doing* it! Laws, to think I've had this unspeakable blessing all my long life and never had the grace to thank the good God that gave it to me!"

Tears stood in the eyes of both the old ladies, and the widow said, softly—

"Betsy Hale, we have learnt something, you and me."

The conversation now drifted wide, but by and by floated back once more to that admired detail, the rigid and beautiful impartiality with which the possession of power had been distributed between the Twins. Aunt Betsy saw in it a far finer justice than human law exhibits in related cases. She said—

"In my opinion it ain't right now, and never has been right, the way a twin born a quarter of a minute sooner than the other one gets all the land and grandeurs and nobilities in the old countries and his brother has to go bare and be a nobody. Which of you was born first?"

Angelo's head was resting against Luigi's; weariness had overcome him, and for the past five minutes he had been peacefully sleeping. The old ladies had dropped their voices to a lulling drone, to help him steal the rest his brother wouldn't take him up stairs to get. Luigi listened a moment to Angelo's regular breathing, then said in a voice barely audible:

"We were both born at the same time, but I am six months older than he is."

"For the land's sake!—"

"'Sh! don't wake him up; he wouldn't like my telling this. It has always been kept secret till now."

"But how in the world can it *be*? If you were both born at the same time, how can one of you be older than the other?"

"It is very simple, and I assure you it is true. I was born with a full crop of hair, he was as bald as an egg for six months. I could walk six months before he could make a step. I finished teething six months ahead of him. I began to take solids six months before he left the breast. I began to talk six months before he could say a word. Last, and absolutely unassailable proof, *the sutures in my skull closed six months ahead of his*. Always just that six months difference to a day. Was that accident? Nobody is going to claim *that*, I'm sure. It was ordained—it was law—it had its meaning, and we know what that meaning was. Now what does this overwhelming body of evidence establish? It establishes just one thing, and that thing it establishes beyond any peradventure whatever. Friends, we would not have it known for the world, and I must beg you to keep it strictly to yourselves, but the truth is, we are no more twins than you are."

The two old people were stunned, paralyzed, petrified, one may almost say, and could only sit and gaze vacantly at each other for some moments; then Aunt Betsy Hale said, impressively—

"There's no getting around proofs like that. I do believe it's the most amazing thing I ever heard of." She sat silent a moment or two, and breathing hard with excitement, then she looked up and surveyed the strangers steadfastly a little while, and added, "Well, it does beat me, but I would have took you for twins *anywhere*."

"So would I, so would I," said Aunt Patsy with the emphasis of a certainty that is not impaired by any shade of doubt.

"*Anybody* would—anybody in the world, I don't care who he is," said Aunt Betsy with decision.

"You won't tell," said Luigi, appealingly.

"O, *dear* no!" answered both ladies promptly, "you can trust us, don't you be afraid."

"That is good of you, and kind. Never let on; treat us always just as if we were twins."

"You can depend on us," said Aunt Betsy, "but it won't be easy, because now that I know you ain't, you don't *seem* so."

"*That* swindle has gone through without change of cars," Luigi muttered to himself with satisfaction.

It was not very kind of him to load the poor old things up with a secret like that, which would be always flying to their tongues' ends every time they heard any one speak of the strangers as twins, and would become harder and harder to hang on to with every recurrence of the temptation to tell it, while the torture of retaining it would increase with every new strain that was applied, but he never thought of that, and probably would not have worried much about it if he had.

A visitor was announced—some one to see the Twins. They withdrew to the parlor, and the two old ladies began to discuss with interest the strange things which they had been listening to. When they had finished the matter to their satisfaction, and Aunt Betsy rose to go, she stopped to ask a question—

"How does things come on between Roweny and Tom Driscoll?"

"Well, about the same. He writes tolerable often, and she answers tolerable seldom."

"Where is he?"

"In St. Louis, I believe, though he's such a gad-about that a body can't be very certain of him, I reckon."

"Don't Roweny know?"

"Oh, yes, like enough. I haven't asked her lately."

"Do you know how him and the Judge are getting along now?"

"First rate, I believe. Mrs. Pratt says so; and being right in the house, and sister to the one and aunt to t'other, of course she ought to know. She says the Judge is real fond of him when he's away, but frets when he's around and is vexed with his ways, and not sorry to have him go again. He has been gone three weeks this time—a pleasant thing for both of them, I reckon."

"Tom's ruther harum-scarum, but there ain't anything bad in him, I guess."

"Oh, no, he's just young, that's all. Still, twenty-three is old, in one way. A young man ought to be earning his living by that time. If Tom was doing that, or was even trying to do it, the Judge would be a heap better satisfied with him. Tom's always going to begin, but somehow he can't seem to find just the opening he likes."

"Well, now, it's partly the Judge's own fault. Promising the boy his property wasn't the way to set him to earning a fortune of his own. But what do you think—is Roweny beginning to lean any towards him, or ain't she?"

Aunt Patsy had a secret in her bosom; she wanted to keep it there, but nature was too strong for her. She drew Aunt Betsy aside, and said in her most confidential and mysterious manner—

"Don't you breathe a syllable to a soul—I'm going to tell you something. In my opinion Tom Driscoll's chances were considerable better yesterday than they are to-day."

"Patsy Cooper, what *do* you mean?"

"It's so, as sure as you're born. I wish you could a been at breakfast, and seen for yourself."

"You don't mean it!"

"Well, if I'm any judge, there's a leaning—there's a leaning, sure."

"My land! Which one of 'em is it?"

"I can't say for certain, but I think it's the youngest one—Anjy."

Then there were handshakings, and congratulations, and hopes, and so on, and the old ladies parted, perfectly happy—the one in knowing something which the rest of the town didn't, and the other in having been the sole person able to furnish that knowledge.

The visitor who had called to see the Twins was the Rev. Mr. Hotchkiss, pastor of the Baptist church. At the reception Angelo had told him he had lately experienced a change in his religious views, and was now desirous of becoming a Baptist, and would immediately join Mr. Hotchkiss's church.

There was no time to say more, and the brief talk ended at that point. The minister was much gratified, and had dropped in for a moment, now, to invite the twins to attend his Bible class at eight that evening. Angelo accepted, and was expecting Luigi to decline, but he did not, because he knew that the Bible class and the Freethinkers met in the same room, and he wanted to treat his brother to the embarrassment of being caught in free-thinking company.

Chapter 5

[A long and vigorous quarrel follows, between the Twins. And there is plenty to quarrel about, for Angelo was always seeking truth, and this obliged him to change and improve his religion with frequency, which wearied Luigi, and annoyed him too; for he had to be present at each new enlistment—which placed him in the false position of seeming to endorse and approve his brother's fickleness; moreover, he had to go to Angelo's prohibition meetings, and he hated them. On the other hand, when it was *his* week to command the legs he gave Angelo just cause of complaint, for he took him to circuses and horse-races and fandangoes, exposing him to all sorts of censure and criticism; and he drank, too; and whatever he drank went to Angelo's head instead of his own and made him act disgracefully. When the evening was come, the two attended the Freethinkers' meeting, where Angelo was sad and silent; then came the Bible class and looked upon him coldly, finding him in such company. Then they went to Wilson's house, and Chapter 11 of "Pudd'nhead Wilson" follows, which tells of the girl seen in Tom Driscoll's room; and closes with the kicking of Tom by Luigi at the anti-temperance mass meeting of the Sons of Liberty; with the addition of some account of Roxy's adventures as a chambermaid on a Mississippi boat. Her exchange of the children had been flippantly and farcically described in an earlier chapter.]

Next morning all the town was a-buzz with great news: Pudd'nhead Wilson had a law-case!

The public astonishment was so great and the public curiosity so intense, that when the justice of the peace opened his court the place was packed with people, and even the windows were full. Everybody was flushed and perspiring, the summer heat was almost unendurable.

Tom Driscoll had brought a charge of assault and battery against the Twins. Robert Allen was retained by Driscoll, David Wilson by the defence. Tom, his native cheerfulness unannihilated by his back-breaking and bone-bruising passage across the massed heads of the Sons of Liberty the previous night, laughed his little customary laugh, and said to Wilson—

"I've kept my promise, you see: I'm throwing my business your way. Sooner than I was expecting, too."

"It's very good of you—particularly if you mean to keep it up."

"Well, I can't tell about that, yet. But we'll see. If I find you deserve it I'll take you under my protection and make your fame and fortune for you."

"I'll try to deserve it, Tom."

A jury was sworn in; then Mr. Allen said:

"We will detain your honor but a moment with this case. It is not one where any doubt of the fact of the assault can enter in. These gentlemen— the accused—kicked my client, at the Market Hall last night; they kicked him with violence; with extraordinary violence; with even unprecedented violence, I may say; insomuch that he was lifted entirely off his feet and discharged into the midst of the audience. We could prove this by four hundred witnesses—we shall call but three. Mr. Harkness will take the stand."

Mr. Harkness, being sworn, testified that he was chairman upon the occasion mentioned; that he was close at hand and saw the defendants in this action kick the plaintiff into the air and saw him descend amongst the audience.

"Take the witness," said Allen.

"Mr. Harkness," said Wilson, "you say you saw these gentlemen, my clients, kick the plaintiff. Are you sure—and please remember that you are on oath—are you perfectly sure that you saw *both* of them kick him, or only one? Now be careful."

A bewildered look began to spread itself over the witness's face. He hesitated, stammered, but got out nothing. His eyes wandered to the Twins and fixed themselves there with a vacant gaze.

"Please answer, Mr. Harkness, you are keeping the court waiting. It is a very simple question."

Counsel for the prosecution broke in with impatience:

"Your honor, the question is an irrelevant triviality. Necessarily they both kicked him, for they have but the one pair of legs, and both are responsible for them."

Wilson said, sarcastically:

"Will your honor permit this new witness to be sworn? He seems to possess knowledge which can be of the utmost value just at this moment— knowledge which would at once dispose of what every one must see is a very difficult question in this case. Brother Allen, will you take the stand?"

"Go on with your case!" said Allen, petulantly. The audience laughed, and got a warning from the court.

"Now, Mr. Harkness," said Wilson, insinuatingly, "we shall have to insist upon an answer to that question."

"I—er—well, of course I do not absolutely *know*, but in my opinion—"

"Never mind your opinion, sir—answer the question!"

"I—why, I *can't* answer it."

"That will do, Mr. Harkness. Stand down."

The audience tittered, and the discomfited witness retired in a state of great embarrassment.

Mr. Wakeman took the stand and swore that he saw the Twins kick the plaintiff off the platform. The defence took the witness.

"Mr. Wakeman, you have sworn that you saw these gentlemen kick the plaintiff. Do I understand you to swear that you saw them *both* do it?"

"Yes, sir"—with decision.

"How do you know that both did it?"

"Because I *saw* them do it." The audience laughed, and got another warning from the court.

"But by what means do you know that both, and not one, did it?"

"Well, in the first place, the insult was given to both of them equally, for they were called a pair of scissors. Of course they would both want to resent it, and so—"

"Wait! You are theorizing, now. Stick to facts—counsel will attend to the arguments. Go on."

"Well, they both went over there—*that* I saw."

"Very good. Go on."

"And they both kicked him—I swear to it!"

"Mr. Wakeman, was Count Luigi, here, willing to join the Sons of Liberty last night?"

"Yes, sir, he was. He did join, too, and drank a glass or two of whisky, like a man."

"Was his brother willing to join?"

"No, sir, he wasn't. He is a teetotaler, and was elected through a mistake."

"Was he given a glass of whisky?"

"Yes, sir, but of course that was another mistake, and not intentional. He wouldn't drink it. He set it down." A slight pause, then he added, casually, and quite simply, "The plaintiff reached for it and hogged it."

There was a fine outburst of laughter, but as the justice was caught out, himself, his reprimand was not very vigorous.

Mr. Allen jumped up and exclaimed:

"I protest against these foolish irrelevancies. What have *they* to do with the case?"

Wilson said:

"Calm yourself, brother; it was only an experiment. Now, Mr. Wakeman, if one of these gentlemen chooses to join an association and the other doesn't; and if one of them enjoys whisky and the other doesn't, but sets it aside and leaves it unprotected," [titter from the audience], "it seems to show that they have independent minds and tastes and preferences, and that one of them is able to approve of a thing at the very moment that the other is heartily disapproving of it. Doesn't it seem so to you?"

"Certainly it does. It's perfectly plain."

"Now, then, it might be—I only say it *might* be—that one of these brothers wanted to kick the plaintiff last night, and that the other one *didn't* want that humiliating punishment inflicted upon him in that public way and before all those people. Isn't that possible?"

"Of course it is. It's more than possible. *I* don't believe the blonde one would kick anybody. It was the other one that—"

"Silence!" shouted the plaintiff's counsel, and went on with an angry sentence which was lost in the wave of laughter that swept the house.

"That will do, Mr. Wakeman," said Wilson, "you may stand down."

The third witness was called. He had seen the Twins kick the plaintiff. Mr. Wilson took the witness.

"Mr. Rogers, you say you saw these accused gentlemen kick the plaintiff."

"Yes, sir."

"Both of them?"

"Yes, sir."

"Which of them kicked him first?"

"Why—they—they both kicked him at the same time."

"Are you perfectly sure of that?"

"Yes, sir."

"What makes you sure of it?"

"Why, I stood right behind them, and saw them do it."

"How many kicks were delivered?"

"Only one."

"If two men kick, the result should be two kicks, shouldn't it?"

"Why—why—yes, as a rule."

"Then what do you think went with the other kick?"

"I—well—the fact is, I wasn't thinking of two being necessary, this time."

"What do you think now?"

"Well, I—I'm sure I don't quite know what to think, but I reckon that one of them did half of the kick and the other one did the other half."

Somebody in the crowd sung out:

"It's the first sane thing that any of them has said!"

The audience applauded. The judge said—

"Silence! or I will clear the court."

Mr. Allen looked pleased, but Wilson did not seem disturbed. He said:

"Mr. Rogers, you have favored us with what you think and what you reckon, but as thinking and reckoning are not evidence, I will now give you a chance to come out with something positive, one way or the other, and shall require you to produce it. I will ask the accused to stand up and repeat the phenomenal kick of last night." The Twins stood up. "Now, Mr. Rogers, please stand behind them."

A Voice. "No, stand in front!" [Laughter. Silenced by the court.]

Another Voice. "No, give Tommy another highst!" [Laughter. Sharply rebuked by the court.]

"Now, then, Mr. Rogers, two kicks shall be delivered, one after the other, and I give you my word that at least one of the two shall be delivered by one of the Twins alone, without the slightest assistance from his brother. Watch sharply, for you have got to render a decision without any ifs or ands in it." Rogers bent himself behind the Twins, with his palms just above his knees, in the modern attitude of the catcher at a base-ball match, and riveted his eyes on the pair of legs in front of him. "Are you ready, Mr. Rogers?"

"Ready, sir."

"Kick!"

The kick was launched.

"Have you got that one classified, Mr. Rogers?"

"Let me study a minute, sir."

"Take as much time as you please. Let me know when you are ready."

For as much as a minute Rogers pondered, with all eyes and a breathless interest fastened upon him. Then he gave the word—

"Ready, sir."

"Kick!"

The kick that followed was an exact duplicate of the first one.

"Now, then, Mr. Rogers, one of those kicks was an individual kick, not a mutual one. You will now state positively which was the mutual one."

The witness said, with a crestfallen look—

"I've got to give it up. There ain't any man in the world that could tell t'other from which, sir."

"Do you still assert that last night's kick was a mutual kick?"

"Indeed I don't, sir."

"That will do, Mr. Rogers. If my brother Allen desires to address the court, your honor, very well; but as far as I am concerned I am ready to let the case be at once delivered into the hands of this intelligent jury without comment."

Mr. Justice Robinson had been in office only two months, and in that short time had not had many cases to try, of course. He had no knowledge of laws and courts except what he had picked up since he came into office. He was a sore trouble to the lawyers, for his rulings were pretty eccentric some-times, and he stood by them with Roman simplicity and fortitude; but the people were well satisfied with him, for they saw that his intentions were always right, that he was entirely impartial, and that he usually made up in good sense what he lacked in technique, so to speak. He now perceived that there was likely to be a miscarriage of justice here, and he rose to the occasion.

"Wait a moment, gentlemen," he said, "it is plain that an assault has been committed—it is plain to anybody; but the way things are going, the guilty will certainly escape conviction. I cannot allow this. Now—"

"But your honor!" said Wilson, interrupting him, earnestly but respect-fully, "you are deciding the case yourself, whereas the jury—"

"Never mind the jury, Mr. Wilson; the jury will have a chance when there is a reasonable doubt for them to take hold of—which there isn't, so far. There is no doubt whatever that an assault has been committed. The attempt to show that both of the accused committed it has failed. Are they both to escape justice on that account? Not in this court, if I can prevent it. It appears to have been a mistake to bring the charge against them as a corporation; each should have been charged in his capacity as an individual, and—"

"But your honor!" said Wilson, "in fairness to my clients I must insist that inasmuch as the prosecution did *not* separate the—"

"No wrong will be done your clients, sir—they will be protected; also the public and the offended law. Mr. Allen, you will amend your pleadings, and put one of the accused on trial at a time."

Wilson broke in—

"But your honor! this is wholly unprecedented. To imperil an accused person by arbitrarily altering and widening the charge against him in order to compass his conviction when the charge as originally brought promises to fail to convict, is a thing unheard of before."

"Unheard of where?"

"In the courts of this or any other State."

The judge said, with dignity—

"I am not acquainted with the customs of other courts, and am not concerned to know what they are. I am responsible for this court, and I cannot conscientiously allow my judgment to be warped and my judicial liberty hampered by trying to conform to the caprices of other courts, be they—"

"But your honor, the oldest and highest courts in Europe—"

"This court is not run on the European plan, Mr. Wilson; it is not run on any plan but its own. It *has* a plan of its own; and that plan is, to find justice for State and accused, no matter what happens to be practice and custom in Europe or anywhere else." [Great applause.] "Silence! It has not been the custom of this court to imitate other courts; it has not been the custom of this court to take shelter behind the decisions of other courts, and we will not begin now. We will do the best we can by the light that God has given us, and while this court continues to have His approval, it will remain indifferent to what other organizations may think of it." [Applause.] "Gentlemen, I *must* have order!—quiet yourselves! Mr. Allen, you will now proceed against the prisoners one at a time. Go on with the case."

Allen was not at his ease. However, after whispering a moment with his client and with one or two other people, he rose and said:

"Your honor, I find it to be reported and believed that the accused are able to act independently in many ways, but that this independence does not extend to their legs, authority over their legs being vested exclusively in the one brother during a specific term of days, and then passing to the other brother for a like term, and so on, by regular alternation. I could call witnesses who would prove that the accused had revealed to them the existence of this extraordinary fact, and had also made known which of them was in possession of the legs yesterday—and this would of course indicate where the guilt of the assault belongs—but as this would be mere hearsay evidence, these revelations not having been made under oath—"

"Never mind about that, Mr. Allen. It may not all be hearsay. We shall see. It may at least help to put us on the right track. Call the witnesses."

"Then I will call Mr. John Buckstone, who is now present; and I beg that Mrs. Patsy Cooper may be sent for. Take the stand, Mr. Buckstone."

Buckstone took the oath, and then testified that on the previous evening the Count Angelo Cappello had protested against going to the hall, and had called all present to witness that he was going by compulsion and would not go if he could help himself. Also, that the Count Luigi had replied sharply that he would *go*, just the same, and that he, Count Luigi, would see to that, himself. Also, that upon Count Angelo's complaining about being kept on his legs so long, Count Luigi retorted with apparent surprise, "*Your* legs!—I like your impudence."

"Now we are getting at the kernel of the thing," observed the judge, with grave and earnest satisfaction. "It looks as if the Count Luigi was in possession of the battery at the time of the assault."

Nothing further was elicited from Mr. Buckstone on direct examination. Mr. Wilson took the witness.

"Mr. Buckstone, about what time was it that that conversation took place?"

"Toward nine yesterday evening, sir."

"Did you then proceed directly to the hall?"

"Yes, sir."

"How long did it take you to go there?"

"Well, we walked; and as it was from the extreme edge of the town, and there was no hurry, I judge it took us about twenty minutes, maybe a trifle more."

"About what hour was the kick delivered?"

"At thirteen minutes and a half to ten."

"Admirable! You are a pattern witness, Mr. Buckstone. How did you happen to look at your watch at that particular moment?"

"I always do it when I see an assault. It's likely I shall be called as a witness, and it's a good point to have."

"It would be well if others were as thoughtful. Was anything said, between the conversation at my house and the assault, upon the detail which we are now examining into?"

"No, sir."

"If power over the mutual legs was in the possession of one brother at nine, and passed into the possession of the other one during the next thirty or forty minutes, do you think you could have detected the change?"

"By no means!"

"That is all, Mr. Buckstone."

Mrs. Patsy Cooper was called. The crowd made way for her, and she came smiling and bowing through the narrow human lane, with Betsy Hale, as escort and support, smiling and bowing in her wake, the audience breaking into welcoming cheers as the old favorites filed along. The judge did not check this kindly demonstration of homage and affection, but let it run its course unrebuked.

The old ladies stopped and shook hands with the Twins with effusion, then gave the judge a friendly nod and bustled into the seats provided for them. They immediately began to deliver a volley of eager questions at the friends around them: "What is this thing for?" "What is that thing for?" "Who is that young man that's writing at the desk?—why, I declare it's Jack Bunce!—I thought he was sick." "Which is the jury?" "Why, is *that* the jury? Billy Price, and Job Turner, and Jack Lounsbury, and—well, I never!" "Now who would ever a thought—"

But they were gently called to order at this point and asked not to talk in court. Their tongues fell silent, but the radiant interest in their faces remained, and their gratitude for the blessing of a new sensation and a novel experience still beamed undimmed from their eyes. Aunt Patsy stood up and took the oath, and Mr. Allen explained the point in issue and asked her to go on, now, in her own way, and throw as much light upon it as she could. She toyed with her reticule a moment or two, as if considering where to begin, then she said:

"Well, the way of it is this. They are Luigi's legs a week at a time, and then they are Angelo's, and he can do what he wants to with them."

"You are making a mistake, Aunt Patsy Cooper," said the judge. "You shouldn't state that as a fact, because you don't know it to be a fact."

"What's the reason I don't?" said Aunt Patsy, bridling a little.

"What is the reason that you *do* know it?"

"The best in the world—because they told me."

"That isn't a reason."

"Well, for the land's sake! Betsy Hale, do you hear that?"

"Hear it?—I should think so," said Aunt Betsy, rising and facing the court. "Why Judge, I was there and heard it myself. Luigi says to Angelo—no, it was Angelo said it to—"

"Come-come, Mrs. Hale, pray sit down, and—"

"Certainly, it's all right, I'm going to sit down presently, but not until I've—"

"But you *must* sit down."

"Must! Well, upon my word if things ain't getting to a pretty pass when—"

The house broke into laughter but was promptly brought to order, and meantime Mr. Allen persuaded the old lady to take her seat. Aunt Patsy continued:

"Yes, they told me that, and I know it's true. They're Luigi's legs this week, but—"

"Ah, they told you that, did they?" said the justice, with interest.

"Well, no, I don't know that they *told* me, but that's neither here nor there; I know, without that, that at dinner yesterday, Angelo was as tired as a dog, and yet Luigi wouldn't lend him the legs to go up stairs and take a nap with."

"Did he ask for them?"

"Let me see—it seems to me somehow, that—that—Aunt Betsy, do you remember whether he—"

"Never mind about what Aunt Betsy remembers, she is not a witness; we only want to know what you remember, yourself," said the judge.

"Well, it does seem to me that you are most cantankerously particular about a little thing, Sim Robinson. Why, when I can't remember a thing myself, I always—"

"Ah, please go *on!*"

"Now how *can* she, when you keep fussing at her all the time?" said Aunt Betsy. "Why, with a person pecking at me that way, I should get that fuzzled and fuddled that—"

She was on her feet again, but Allen coaxed her into her seat once more while the court squelched the mirth of the house. Then the judge said:

"Madam, do you know—do you absolutely *know*, independently of anything these gentlemen have told you—that the power over their legs passes from the one to the other regularly every week?"

"Regularly? Bless your heart, regularly ain't any name for the exactness of it. All the big cities in Europe used to set the clocks by it." [Laughter—suppressed by the court.]

"How do you *know*? That is the question. Please answer it plainly and squarely."

"Don't you talk to me like that, Sim Robinson—I won't have it. How do I know, indeed! How do *you* know what you know? Because somebody told you. You didn't invent it out of your own head, did you? Why, these Twins are the truthfulest people in the world; and I don't think it becomes you to sit up there and throw slurs at them when they haven't been doing anything to you. And they are orphans besides,—both of them. All—"

But Aunt Betsy was up again, now, and both old ladies were talking at once and with all their might, but as the house was weltering in a storm of laughter and the judge was hammering his desk with an iron paper-weight, one could only see them talk, not hear them. At last when quiet was restored, the court said—

"Let the ladies retire."

"But your honor, I have the right, in the interest of my clients, to cross-exam—"

"You'll not need to exercise it, Mr. Wilson—the evidence is thrown out."

"Thrown out!" said Aunt Patsy, ruffled; "and what's it thrown out, for, I'd like to know?"

"And so would I, Patsy Cooper. It seems to me that if we can save these poor persecuted strangers, it is our bounden duty to stand up here and talk for them till—"

"There, there, there, *do* sit down!"

It cost some trouble and a good deal of coaxing, but they were got into their seats at last. The trial was soon ended, now. The Twins themselves became witnesses in their own defence. They established the fact, upon oath, that the leg-power passed from the one to the other every Saturday night at twelve o'clock, sharp. But on cross-examination their counsel would not allow them to tell whose week of power the current week was. The judge insisted upon their answering, and proposed to compel them, but even the prosecution took fright and came to the rescue then and helped stay the sturdy jurist's revolutionary hand. So the case had to go to the jury with that important point hanging in the air. They were out an hour, and brought in this verdict:

"We the jury do find: 1, that an assault was committed, as charged; 2, that it was committed by one of the persons accused, he having been seen to do it by several credible witnesses; 3, but that his identity is so merged in his brother's that we have not been able to tell which was him. We cannot convict both, for only one is guilty. We cannot acquit both, for only one is innocent. Our verdict is that justice has been defeated by the dispensation of God, and ask to be discharged from further duty."

This was read aloud in court, and brought out a burst of hearty applause. The old ladies made a spring at the Twins, to shake and congratulate, but were gently disengaged by Mr. Wilson and softly crowded back into their places.

The judge rose in his little tribune, laid aside his silver-bowed spectacles, roached his gray hair up with his fingers, and said, with dignity and solemnity, and even with a certain pathos:

"In all my experience on the bench I have not seen Justice bow her sacred head in shame in this court until this day. You little realize what far-reaching harm has just been wrought here under the fickle forms of law. Imitation is the bane of courts—I thank God that this one is free from the contamination of that vice—and in no long time you will see the fatal work of this hour seized upon by profligate so-called guardians of justice in all the wide circumference of this planet and perpetuated in their pernicious decisions. I wash my hands of this iniquity. I would have compelled these culprits to expose their guilt, but support failed me where I had most right to expect aid and encouragement. And I was confronted by a law made in the interest of crime, which protects the criminal from testifying against himself. Yet I had precedents of my own whereby I had set aside that law on two different occasions and thus succeeded in convicting criminals to whose crimes there were no witnesses *but* themselves. What have you accomplished this day? Do you realize it? You have set adrift, unadmonished, in this community, two men endowed with an awful and mysterious gift—a hidden and grisly power for evil—a power by which each in his turn may commit crime after crime of the most heinous character, and no man be able to tell which is the guilty or which the innocent party in any case of them all. Look to your homes—look to your property—look to your lives—for you have need!

"Prisoners at the bar, stand up! Through suppression of evidence, a jury of your—our—countrymen have been obliged to deliver a verdict concerning your case which stinks to heaven with the rankness of its injustice! By its terms you, the guilty one, go free with the innocent. Depart in peace, and come no more. The costs devolve upon the outraged plaintiff—another iniquity. The court stands dissolved."

Almost everybody crowded forward to overwhelm the Twins and their counsel with congratulations; but presently the two old aunties dug the duplicates out and bore them away in triumph through the hurrahing crowds, while lots of new friends carried Pudd'nhead Wilson off tavernwards to feast him and "wet down" his great and victorious entry into the legal arena. To Wilson, so long familiar with neglect and depreciation, this strange new incense of popularity and admiration was as a fragrance blown from the fields of paradise. A happy man was Wilson.

Chapter 6

[A deputation came in the evening and conferred upon Wilson the welcome honor of a nomination for mayor; for the village has just been converted into a city by charter. Tom skulks out of challenging the Twins. Judge Driscoll thereupon challenges Angelo, (accused by Tom of doing the kicking;) he declines, but Luigi accepts in his place against Angelo's timid protest.]

It was late Saturday night—nearing eleven.

The Judge and his second found the rest of the war party at the further end of the vacant ground, near the haunted house. Pudd'nhead Wilson advanced to meet them, and said anxiously—

"I must say a word in behalf of my principal's proxy, Count Luigi, to whom you have kindly granted the privilege of fighting my principal's battle for him. It is growing late, and Count Luigi is in great trouble lest midnight shall strike before the finish."

"It is another testimony," said Howard, approvingly. "That young man is fine all through. He wishes to save his brother the sorrow of fighting on the Sabbath, and he is right; it is the right and manly feeling and does him credit. We will make all possible haste."

Wilson said—

"There is also another reason—a consideration, in fact, which deeply concerns Count Luigi himself. These Twins have command of their mutual legs turn about. Count Luigi is in command, now; but at midnight, possession will pass to my principal, Count Angelo, and—well, you can foresee what will happen. He will march straight off the field, and carry Luigi with him."

"Why, sure enough!" cried the Judge, "we have heard something about that extraordinary law of their being, already—nothing very definite, it is true, as regards dates and durations of the power, but I see it is definite enough as regards to-night. Of course we must give Luigi every chance. Omit all the ceremonial possible, gentlemen, and place us in position."

The seconds at once tossed up a coin; Howard won the choice. He placed the Judge sixty feet from the haunted house and facing it; Wilson placed the

Twins within fifteen feet of the house and facing the Judge—necessarily. The pistol-case was opened and the long slim tubes taken out; when the moonlight glinted from them a shiver went through Angelo. The doctor was a fool, but a thoroughly well-meaning one, with a kind heart and a sincere disposition to oblige, but along with it an absence of tact which often hurt its effectiveness. He brought his box of lint and bandages, and asked Angelo to feel and see how soft and comfortable they were. Angelo's head fell over against Luigi's in a faint, and precious time was lost in bringing him to; which provoked Luigi into expressing his mind to the doctor with a good deal of vigor and frankness. After Angelo came to he was still so weak that Luigi was obliged to drink a stiff horn of brandy to brace him up.

The seconds now stepped at once to their posts, half way between the combatants, one of them on each side of the line of fire. Wilson was to count, very deliberately, "One——two——three——fire!——stop!" and the duelists could bang away at any time they chose during that recitation, but not after the last word. Angelo grew very nervous when he saw Wilson's hand rising slowly into the air as a sign to make ready, and he leaned his head against Luigi's and said—

"O, please take me away from here, I *can't* stay, I know I can't!"

"What in the world are you doing? Straighten up! What's the matter with you?—you're in no danger—nobody's going to shoot at *you*. Straighten up, I tell you!"

Angelo obeyed, just in time to hear—

"One—!"

"Bang!" Just one report, and a little tuft of white hair floated slowly to the Judge's feet in the moonlight. The Judge did not swerve; he still stood, erect and motionless, like a statue, with his pistol-arm hanging straight down at his side. He was reserving his fire.

"Two—!"

"Three—!"

"Fire!—"

Up came the pistol-arm instantly—Angelo dodged with the report. He said "Ouch!" and fainted again.

The doctor examined and bandaged the wound. It was of no consequence, he said—bullet through fleshy part of arm—no bones broken—the gentleman was still able to fight—let the duel proceed.

Next time, Angelo jumped just as Luigi fired; which disordered his aim and caused him to cut a chip out of Howard's ear. The Judge took his time again, and when he fired Angelo jumped, and got a knuckle skinned. The doctor inspected and dressed the wounds. Angelo now spoke out and said he was content with the satisfaction he had got, and if the Judge—but Luigi shut him roughly up, and asked him not to make an ass of himself; adding—

"And I want you to stop dodging. You take a great deal too prominent a part in this thing for a person who has got nothing to do with it. You should remember that you are here only by courtesy, and are without official recognition; officially you are not here at all; officially you do not even exist. To all intents and purposes you are absent from this place, and you ought for your own modesty's sake to reflect that it cannot become a person who is not present here to be taking this sort of public and indecent prominence in a matter in which he is not in the slightest degree concerned. Now don't dodge again; the bullets are not for you, they are for me; if I want them dodged I will attend to it myself. I never saw a person act so."

Angelo saw the reasonableness of what his brother had said, and he did try to reform, but it was of no use; both pistols went off at the same instant, and he jumped once more; he got a sharp scrape along his cheek from the Judge's bullet, and so deflected Luigi's aim that his ball went wide and chipped a flake of skin from Pudd'nhead Wilson's chin. The doctor attended to the wounded.

By the terms, the duel was over. But Luigi was entirely out of patience, and begged for one more exchange of shots, insisting that he had had no fair chance, on account of his brother's indelicate behavior. Howard was opposed to granting so unusual a privilege, but the Judge took Luigi's part, and added that indeed he might fairly be considered entitled to another trial himself, because although the proxy on the other side was in no way to blame for his (the Judge's) humiliatingly resultless work, the gentleman with whom he was fighting this duel *was* to blame for it, since if he had played no advantages and had held his head still, his proxy would have been disposed of early. He added—

"Count Luigi's request for another exchange is another proof that he is a brave and chivalrous gentleman, and I beg that the courtesy he asks may be accorded him."

"I thank you most sincerely for this generosity, Judge Driscoll," said Luigi, with a polite bow, and moving to his place. Then he added—to Angelo, "Now hold your grip, hold your *grip*, I tell you, and I'll land him, sure!"

The men stood erect, their pistol-arms at their sides, the two seconds stood at their official posts, the doctor stood five paces in Wilson's rear with his instruments and bandages in his hands. The deep stillness, the peaceful moon-light, the motionless figures, made an impressive picture, and the impending fatal possibilities augmented this impressiveness to solemnity. Wilson's hand began to rise—slowly—slowly—higher—still higher—in another moment—

"Boom!"—the first stroke of midnight swung up out of the distance. Angelo was off like a deer!

"Oh, you unspeakable traitor!" wailed his brother, as they went soaring over the fence.

The others stood astonished and gazing; and so stood, watching that strange spectacle until distance dissolved it and swept it from their view. Then they rubbed their eyes like people waking out of a dream.

"Well, I've never seen anything like *that* before," said the Judge. "Wilson, I am going to confess, now, that I wasn't quite able to believe in that leg-business, and had a suspicion that it was a put-up convenience between those Twins; and when Count Angelo fainted I thought I saw the whole scheme—thought it was pretext No. 1, and would be followed by others till twelve o'clock should arrive and Luigi would get off with all the credit of seeming to want to fight and yet not have to fight, after all. But I was mistaken. His pluck proved it. He's a brave fellow and did want to fight."

"There isn't any doubt about that," said Howard, and added in a grieved tone, "but what an unworthy sort of Christian that Angelo is—I hope and believe there are not many like him. It is not right to engage in a duel on the Sabbath—I could not approve of that, myself; but to *finish* one that has been begun—that is a duty, let the day be what it may."

They strolled along, still wondering, still talking.

"It is a curious circumstance," remarked the surgeon, halting Wilson a moment to paste some more court plaster on his chin, which had gone to leaking blood again, "that in this duel neither of the parties who handled the pistols lost blood, while nearly all the persons present in the mere capacity of guests got hit. I have not heard of such a thing before. Don't you think it unusual?"

"Yes," said the Judge, "it has struck me as peculiar. Peculiar and unfortu-nate. I was annoyed at it, all the time. In the case of Angelo it made no great difference, because he was in a measure concerned, though not officially; but it troubled me to see the seconds compromised, and yet I knew no way to mend the matter."

"There was no way to mend it," said Howard, whose ear was being read-justed now by the doctor; "the code fixes our place, and it would not have been lawful to change it. If we could have stood at your side, or behind you, or in front of you, it—but it would not have been legitimate, and the other parties would have had a just right to complain of our trying to protect ourselves from danger; infractions of the code are certainly not permissible in any case whatsoever."

Wilson offered no remarks. It seemed to him that there was very little place here for so much solemnity, but he judged that if a duel where nobody was in danger or got crippled but the seconds and the outsiders had nothing ridiculous about it for these gentlemen, his pointing out that feature would probably not help them to see it.

He invited them in to take a nightcap, and Howard and the Judge accepted, but the doctor said he would have to go and see how Angelo's principal wound was getting on.

[It was now Sunday, and in the afternoon Angelo was to be received into the Baptist communion by immersion—a doubtful prospect, the doctor feared.]

Chapter 7

When the doctor arrived at Aunt Patsy Cooper's house, he found the lights going and everybody up and dressed and in a great state of solicitude and excitement. The Twins were stretched on a sofa in the sitting room, Aunt Patsy was fussing at Angelo's arm, Nancy was flying around under her commands, the two young boys were trying to keep out of the way but always getting in it, in order to see and wonder, Rowena stood apart, helpless with apprehension and emotion, and Luigi was growling in unappeasable fury over Angelo's shameful flight.

As has been reported before, the doctor was a fool—a kind-hearted and well-meaning one, but with no tact; and as he was by long odds the most learned physician in the town, and was quite well aware of it, and could talk his learning with ease and precision, and liked to show off when he had an audience, he was sometimes tempted into revealing more of a case than was good for the patient.

He examined Angelo's wound, and was really minded to say nothing, for once; but Aunt Patsy was so anxious and so pressing that he allowed his caution to be overcome, and proceeded to empty himself as follows, with scientific relish—

"Without going too much into detail, madam—for you would probably not understand it anyway—I concede that great care is going to be necessary here; otherwise exudation of the oesophagus is nearly sure to ensue, and this will be followed by ossification and extradition of the *maxillaris superioris*, which must decompose the granular surfaces of the great infusorial ganglionic system, thus obstructing the action of the posterior varioloid arteries and precipitating compound strangulated sorosis of the valvular tissues, and ending unavoidably in the dispersion and combustion of the marsupial fluxes and the consequent embrocation of the bi-cuspid *populo redax referendum rotulorum*."

A miserable silence followed. Aunt Patsy's heart sank, the pallor of despair invaded her face, she was not able to speak; poor Rowena wrung her hands in privacy and silence, and said to herself in the bitterness of her young grief, "There is no hope—it is plain there is no hope;" the good-hearted negro wench, Nancy, paled to chocolate, then to orange, then to amber, and thought to herself with yearning sympathy and sorrow, "Po' thing, he ain' gwyne to las' thoo de half o' dat;" small Henry choked up, and turned his head away to hide his rising tears, and his brother Joe said to himself, with a sense of loss, "The babtizing's busted, that's sure." Luigi was the only person who had any heart to speak. He said, a little bit sharply, to the doctor—

"Well, well, there's nothing to be gained by wasting precious time: give him a barrel of pills—I'll take them for him."

"You?" asked the doctor.

"Yes. Did you suppose he was going to take them himself?"

"Why, of course."

"Well, it's a mistake. He never took a dose of medicine in his life. He *can't*."

"Well, upon my word it's the most extraordinary thing I ever heard of!"

"Oh," said Aunt Patsy, as pleased as a mother whose child is being admired and wondered at, "you'll find that there's more about them that's wonderful than their just being made in the image of God like the rest of His creatures, now you can depend on that, *I* tell you," and she wagged her complacent head like one who could reveal marvelous things if she chose.

The boy Joe began—

"Why, ma, they *ain't* made in the im—"

"You shut up, and wait till you're asked, Joe! I'll let you know when I want help. Are you looking for something, doctor?"

The doctor asked for a few sheets of paper and a pen, and said he would write a prescription—which he did. It was one of Galen's; in fact it was Galen's favorite, and had been slaying people for sixteen thousand years. Galen used it for everything, applied it to everything, said it would remove everything, from warts all the way through to congested lungs—and it generally did. Galen was still the only medical authority recognized in Missouri, his practice was the only practice known to the Missouri doctors, and his prescriptions were the only ammunition they carried when they went out for game. By and by Dr. Claypool laid down his pen and read the result of his labors aloud, carefully and deliberately, for this battery must be constructed on the premises by the family, and mistakes could occur; for he wrote a doctor's hand—the hand which from the beginning of time has been so disastrous to the apothecary and so profitable to the undertaker:

Take of Asarabacca, Henbane, Carpobalsamum, each two Drams and a half; of Cloves, Opium, Myrrh, Cyperus, each two Drams; of Opobalsamum, Indian Leaf, Cinamon, Zedoary, Ginger, Costus, Coral, Cassia, Euphorbium, Gum Tragacanth, Frankincense, Styrax Calamita, Celtic Nard, Spignel, Hartwort, Mustard, Saxifrage, Dill, Anise, each one Dram; of Xylaloes, Rheum Ponticum, Alipta Moschata, Castor, Spikenard, Galangals, Opoponax, Anacardium, Mastich, Brimstone, Peony, Eringo, Pulp of Dates, red and white Hermodactyls, Roses, Thyme, Acorus, Penyroyal, Gentian, the Bark of the Root of Mandrake, Germander, Valerian, Bishops Weed, Bay-Berries, long and white Pepper, Xylobalsamum, Carnabadium, Macedonian Parsley-seeds, Lovage, the Seeds of Rue, and Sinon, of each a Dram and a half; of pure Gold, pure Silver, Pearls not perforated, the Blatta Byzantina, the Bone of the Stag's Heart, of each the Quantity of fourteen Grains of Wheat; of Sapphire, Emerald, and Jasper Stones, each one Dram; of Hasle-nut, two Drams; of Pellitory of Spain, Shavings of Ivory, Calamus odoratus, each the Quantity of twenty-nine Grains of Wheat; of Honey or Sugar a sufficient Quantity. Boil down and skim off.

"There," he said, "that will fix the patient; give his brother a dipperful every three-quarters of an hour—"

—"While he survives," muttered Luigi—

—"and see that the room is kept wholesomely hot and the doors and windows closed tight. Keep Count Angelo nicely covered up with six or seven blankets, and when he is thirsty—which will be frequently—moisten a rag in the vapor of the tea-kettle and let his brother suck it. When he is hungry—which will also be frequently—he must not be humored oftener than every seven or eight hours; then toast part of a cracker until it begins to brown, and give it to his brother."

"That is all very well, as far as Angelo is concerned," said Luigi, "but what am I to eat?"

"I do not see that there is anything the matter with you," the doctor answered, "you may of course eat what you please."

"And also drink what I please, I suppose?"

"Oh, certainly—at present. When the violent and continuous perspiring has reduced your strength, I shall have to reduce your diet, of course, and also bleed you, but there is no occasion for that yet awhile." He turned to Aunt Patsy and said: "He must be put to bed, and sat up with, and tended with the greatest care, and not allowed to stir for several days and nights."

"For one, I'm sacredly thankful for that," said Luigi, "it postpones the funeral—I'm not to be drowned *to-day*, anyhow."

Angelo said quietly to the doctor:

"I will cheerfully submit to all your requirements, sir, up to two o'clock this afternoon, and will resume them after three, but I cannot be confined to the house during that intermediate hour."

"Why, may I ask?"

"Because I have entered the Baptist communion, and by appointment am to be baptised in the river at that hour."

"O, insanity!—it cannot be allowed!"

Angelo answered with placid firmness—

"Nothing shall prevent it, if I am alive."

"Why, consider, my dear sir, in your condition it might prove fatal."

A tender and ecstatic smile beamed from Angelo's eyes and he broke forth in a tone of joyous fervency—

"Ah, how blessed it would be to die for such a cause—it would be martyrdom!"

"But your brother—consider your brother; you would be risking his life, too."

"He risked mine an hour ago," responded Angelo, gloomily; "did he consider me?" A thought swept through his mind that made him shudder. "If I had not run, I might have been killed in a duel on the Sabbath day, and my soul would have been lost—lost!"

"O, don't fret, it wasn't in any danger," said Luigi, irritably; "they wouldn't waste it for a little thing like that; there's a glass case all ready for it in the heavenly museum, and a pin to stick it up with."

Aunt Patsy was shocked, and said—

"Looy, *Looy!*—don't talk so, dear!"

Rowena's soft heart was pierced by Luigi's unfeeling words, and she murmured to herself, "O, if I but had the dear privilege of protecting and defending him with my weak voice!—but alas, this sweet boon is denied me by the cruel conventions of social intercourse."

"Get their bed ready," said Aunt Patsy to Nancy, "and shut up the windows and doors, and light their candles, and see that you drive all the mosquitoes out of their bar, and make up a good fire in their stove, and carry up some bags of hot ashes to lay to his feet—"

—"and a shovel of fire for his head, and a mustard plaster for his neck, and some gum shoes for his ears," Luigi interrupted, with temper; and added, to himself, "damnation, I'm going to be roasted alive, I just know it."

"Why, *Looy!* Do be quiet; I never saw such a fractious thing. A body would think you didn't care for your brother."

"I don't—to that extent, Aunt Patsy. I was glad the drowning was postponed, a minute ago; but I'm not, now. No, that is all gone by: I want to be drowned."

"You'll bring a judgment on yourself just as sure as you live, if you go on like that. Why, I never heard the beat of it. Now, there-there! you've said enough. Not another word out of you, Looy—I won't have it."

"But Aunt Patsy—"

"Luigi! Didn't you hear what I told you?"

"But Aunt Patsy, I—why, *I'm* not going to set my heart and lungs afloat in that pail of sewage which this criminal here has been prescri—"

"Yes you are, too. You are going to be good, and do everything I tell you, like a dear," and she tapped his cheek affectionately with her finger. "Rowena, take the prescription and go in the kitchen and hunt up the things and lay them out for me. I'll sit up with my patient the rest of the night, doctor; I can't trust Nancy, she couldn't make Luigi take the medicine. Of course you'll drop in again during the day. Have you got any more directions?"

"No, I believe not, Aunt Patsy. If I don't get in earlier, I'll be along by early candle-light, anyway. Meantime, don't allow him to get out of his bed."

Angelo said, with calm determination—

"I shall be baptised at two o'clock. Nothing but death shall prevent it."

The doctor said nothing aloud, but to himself he said, "Why, this chap's got a manly side, after all. Physically he's a coward, but morally he's a lion! I'll go and tell the others about this; it will raise him a good deal in their estimation—and the public will follow their lead, of course."

Privately, Aunt Patsy applauded, too, and was as proud of Angelo's courage in the moral field as she was of Luigi's in the field of honor.

The boy Henry was troubled, but the boy Joe said, inaudibly, and gratefully, "We're all hunky, after all; and no postponement on account of the weather."

Chapter 8

By nine o'clock the town was humming with the news of the midnight duel, and there were but two opinions about it: one, that Luigi's pluck in the field was most praiseworthy and Angelo's flight most scandalous; the other, that Angelo's courage in flying the field for conscience sake was as fine and creditable as was Luigi's in holding the field in the face of the bullets. The one opinion was held by half of the town, the other one was maintained by the other half. The division was clean and exact, and it made two parties, an Angelo party and a Luigi party. The Twins had suddenly become popular idols along with Pudd'nhead Wilson, and haloed with a glory as intense as his. The children talked the duel all the way to Sunday school, their elders talked it all the way to church, the choir discussed it behind their red curtain, it usurped the place of pious thought in the "nigger gallery."

By noon the doctor had added the news, and spread it, that Count Angelo, in spite of his wound and all warnings and supplications, was resolute in his determination to be baptised at the hour appointed. This swept the town like wildfire, and mightily reinforced the enthusiasm of the Angelo faction, who said, "If any doubted that it was moral courage that took him from the field, what have they to say now!"

Still the excitement grew. All the morning it was traveling countrywards, toward all points of the compass; and so, whereas before only the farmers and their wives were intending to come and witness the remarkable baptism, a general holiday was now proclaimed and the children and negroes admitted to the privileges of the occasion. All the farms for ten miles around were vacated, all the converging roads emptied long processions of wagons, horses and yeomanry into the town. The pack and cram of people vastly exceeded any that had ever been seen in that sleepy region before. The only thing that had ever even approached it was the time, long gone by, but never forgotten nor ever referred to without wonder and pride, when two circuses and a Fourth of July fell together. But the glory of that occasion was extinguished, now, for good. It was but a freshet to this deluge.

The great invasion massed itself on the river bank and waited hungrily for the immense event. Waited, and wondered if it would really happen, or if the twin who was not a "professor" would stand out and prevent it.

But they were not to be disappointed. Angelo was as good as his word. He came attended by an escort of honor composed of several hundred of the best citizens, all of the Angelo party; and when the immersion was finished they escorted him back home; and would even have carried him on their shoulders, but that people might think they were carrying Luigi.

Far into the night the citizens continued to discuss and wonder over the strangely-mated pair of incidents that had distinguished and exalted the past twenty-four hours above any other twenty-four in the history of their town for picturesqueness and splendid interest; and long before the lights were out and the burghers asleep it had been decided on all hands that in capturing these Twins Dawson's Landing had drawn a prize in the great lottery of municipal fortune.

At midnight Angelo was sleeping peacefully. His immersion had not harmed him, it had merely made him wholesomely drowsy, and he had been dead asleep many hours, now. It had made Luigi drowsy, too, but he had got only brief naps, on account of his having to take the medicine every three-quarters of an hour—and Aunt Betsy Hale was there to see that he did it. When he complained and resisted, she was quietly firm with him, and said in a low voice:

"No-no, that won't do; you mustn't talk, and you mustn't retch and gag that way, either—you'll wake up your poor brother."

"Well, what of it, Aunt Betsy, he—"

"'Sh-h! Don't make a noise, dear. You mustn't forget that your poor brother is sick and—"

"Sick, is he? Well, I wish *I*—"

"Sh-h-h! *Will* you be quiet, Luigi! Here, now, take the rest of it—don't keep me holding the dipper all night. I declare if you haven't left a good fourth of it in the bottom! Come—that's a good boy."

"Aunt Betsy, don't make me! I feel like I've swallowed a cemetery; I do, indeed. Do let me rest a little—just a little; I *can't* take any more of the devilish stuff, now."

"Luigi! Using such language here, and him just baptised! Do you want the roof to fall on you?"

"I wish to heaven it would!"

"Why, you dreadful thing! I've a good notion to—let that blanket alone; do you want your brother to catch his death?"

"Aunt Betsy, I've *got* to have it off; I'm being roasted alive; nobody could stand it—you couldn't, yourself."

"Now, then, you're sneezing again—I just expected it."

"Because I've caught a cold in my head. I always do, when I go in the water with my clothes on. And it takes me weeks to get over it, too. I think it was a shame to serve me so."

"Luigi, you are unreasonable; you know very well they couldn't baptise him dry. I should think you would be willing to undergo a little inconvenience for your brother's sake."

"Inconvenience! Now how you talk, Aunt Betsy. I came as near as anything to getting drowned—you saw that, yourself; and do you call *this* inconvenience?—the room shut up as tight as a drum, and so hot the mosquitoes are trying to get out; and a cold in the head, and dying for sleep and no chance to get any on account of this infernal medicine that that assassin prescri—"

"There, you're sneezing again. I'm going down and mix some more of this truck for you, dear."

Chapter 9

During Monday, Tuesday and Wednesday the Twins grew steadily worse; but then the doctor was summoned south to attend his mother's funeral and they got well in forty-eight hours. They appeared on the street on Friday, and were welcomed with enthusiasm by the new-born parties, the Luigi and Angelo factions. The Luigi faction carried its strength into the Democratic party, the Angelo faction entered into a combination with the Whigs. The Democrats nominated Luigi for alderman under the new city government, and the Whigs put up Angelo against him. The Democrats nominated Pudd'nhead Wilson for mayor, and he was left alone in this glory, for the Whigs had no man who was willing to enter the lists against such a formidable opponent. No politician had scored such a compliment as this before in the history of the Mississippi Valley.

The political campaign in Dawson's Landing opened in a pretty warm fashion, and waxed hotter and hotter every week. Luigi's whole heart was in it, and even Angelo presently developed a surprising amount of interest in it—which was natural, because he was not merely representing Whigism, which was a matter of no consequence to him, he was representing something immensely finer and greater—to wit, Reform. In him was centred the hopes of the whole reform element of the town; he was the chosen and admired champion of every clique that had a pet reform of any sort or kind at heart. He was president of the great Teetotalers' Union and its chiefest prophet and mouthpiece.

But as the canvass went on, troubles began to spring up all around—troubles for the Twins, and through them for all the parties and segments and fractions of parties. Whenever Luigi had possession of the legs, he carried Angelo to balls, rum shops, Sons of Liberty parades, horse-races, campaign riots, and everywhere else that could damage him with his party and his church; and when it was Angelo's week he carried Luigi diligently to all manner of moral and religious gatherings, and did his best to get back the ground which he had lost before. As a result of these double performances, there was a storm blowing all the time, and it was an ever rising storm, too—a storm of frantic criticism of the Twins, and rage over their extravagant and incomprehensible conduct.

Luigi had the final chance. The legs were his for the closing week of the canvass. He led his brother a fearful dance.

But he saved his best card for the very eve of the election. There was to be a grand turn-out of the Teetotalers' Union that day, and Angelo was to march at the head of the procession and deliver a great oration afterward. Luigi drank a couple of glasses of whisky—which steadied his nerves and clarified his mind, but made Angelo drunk. Everybody who saw the march, saw that the Champion of the Teetotalers was half seas over, and noted also that his brother, who made no hypocritical pretensions to extra-temperance virtues, was dignified and sober. This eloquent fact could not be unfruitful at the end of a hot political canvass. At the mass meeting Angelo tried to make his great temperance oration but was so discommoded by hiccups and thickness of tongue that he had to give it up; then drowsiness overtook him and his head drooped against Luigi's and he went to sleep. Luigi apologized for him, and was going on to improve his opportunity with a ringing appeal for a moderation of what he called "the prevailing teetotal madness," but persons in the audience began to howl and throw things at him, and then the meeting rose in a general burst of wrath and chased him home.

This episode was a crusher for Angelo in another way. It destroyed his chances with Rowena. Those chances had been growing, right along, for two months. Rowena had even partly confessed that she loved him, but had begged for time to consider. But now the tender dream was ended, and she frankly told him so, the moment he was sober enough to understand. She said she would never marry a man who drank.

"But I don't drink," he pleaded.

"That is nothing to the point," she said, coldly, "you get drunk, and that is worse."

[There was a long and sufficiently idiotic discussion here, which ended as reported in a previous note.]

Chapter 10

Dawson's Landing had a week of repose, after the election, and it needed it, for the frantic and variegated nightmare which had tormented it all through the preceding week had left it limp, haggard and exhausted at the end. It got the week of repose because Angelo had the legs, and was in too subdued a condition to want to go out and mingle with an irritated community that had come to distrust and detest him because there was such a lack of harmony between his morals, which were confessedly excellent, and his methods of illustrating them, which were distinctly damnable.

The new city officers were sworn in on the following Monday—at least all but Luigi. There was a complication in his case. His election was conceded, but he could not sit in the board of aldermen without his brother, and his brother could not sit there because he was not a member. There seemed to be no way out of the difficulty but to carry the matter into the courts, so this was resolved upon. The case was set for the Monday fortnight. In due course the time arrived. In the meantime the city government had been at a standstill, because without Luigi there was a tie in the board of aldermen, whereas with him the liquor interest—the richest in the political field—would have one majority. But the court decided that Angelo could not sit in the board with him, either in public or executive sessions, and at the same time forbade the board to deny admission to Luigi, a fairly and legally chosen alderman. The case was carried up and up and up from court to court, yet still the same old original decision was confirmed every time. As a result, the city government not only stood still, with its hands tied, but everything it was created to protect and care for went a steady gait toward rack and ruin. There was no way to levy a tax, so the minor officials had to resign or starve; therefore they resigned. There being no city money, the enormous legal expenses on both sides had to be defrayed by private subscription. But at last the people came to their senses, and said—

"Pudd'nhead was right, at the start—we ought to have hired the official half of that human phillipene to resign; but it's too late, now; some of us haven't got anything left to hire him with."

"Yes we have," said another citizen, "we've got this"—and he produced a halter.

Many shouted—

"That's the ticket!"

But others said—

"No—Count Angelo is innocent; we mustn't hang him."

"Who said anything about hanging him? We are only going to hang the other one."

"Then that is all right—there is no objection to that."

So they hanged Luigi. And so ends the history of "Those Extraordinary Twins."

Final Remarks

As you see, it was an extravagant sort of a tale, and had no purpose but to exhibit that monstrous "freak" in all sorts of grotesque lights. But when Roxy wandered into the tale she had to be furnished with something to do; so she changed the children in the cradle: this necessitated the invention of a reason for it. This in turn resulted in making the children prominent personages—nothing could prevent it, of course. Their career began to take a tragic aspect, and some one had to be brought in to help work the machinery; so Pudd'nhead Wilson was introduced and taken on trial. By this time the whole show was being run by the new people and in their interest, and the original show was become side-tracked and forgotten; the twin-monster and the heroine and the lads and the old ladies had dwindled to inconsequentialities and were merely in the way. Their story was one story, the new people's story was another story, and there was no connection between them, no interdependence, no kinship. It is not practicable or rational to try to tell two stories at the same time; so I dug out the farce and left the tragedy.

The reader already knew how the expert works; he knows now how the other kind do it.

Mark Twain.

Explanatory Notes

These notes are intended to give information elucidating the text and to document historical, literary, and cultural allusions. As a rule, they do not document the facts of composition, revision, and publication, except where these help to explain difficulties or obscurities in the text; the development of the manuscripts, and the historical models for Clemens's characters, are discussed in the Introduction. Notes are provided for each of the three texts in this volume. Since a given passage may appear in more than one text, many notes will be found in two sections—appearing both in the annotation for the Morgan Manuscript Version and in that for the Revised Version, or else for the notes to *Those Extraordinary Twins*. Complete, independent sets of notes have been deemed more convenient than a system of cross-references between the various sections. Works are cited by the author's last name and date of publication, followed by page number. Quotations follow exactly the wording and punctuation of the original documents, even when a published form is also cited, which may differ to some degree from our transcription of the original. Repositories of unique documents are identified by the standard Library of Congress abbreviations. All abbreviations and names used as citations are defined in the References, pp. 821–36.

Explanatory Notes:
Pudd'nhead Wilson: A Tale
The Morgan Manuscript Version

5.11–12   that stone that Dante used to sit on] The "Stone of Dante" in the Piazza del Duomo in Florence was described by Clemens's friend Laurence Hutton (1843–1904), an authority on literary relics:

> At the side of the Cathedral Square in Florence is still preserved, embedded in the wall of a comparatively modern house, a bit of stone which is highly regarded by those tourists who accept the guide-books as invariable tellers of the truth. This "Stone of Dante" is said to have been a favourite seat of the poet while he watched the building of the Duomo; although why he always occupied the same hard and uninviting resting place and how he could have inspected the erection of a building which at the time of his death had passed nothing but its lower foundation-walls, the guide-books do not explain. (Hutton 1905, 189–90)

5.13   Giotto's Campanile] The bell tower of Florence Cathedral, designed by Giotto di Bondone, was built after Dante's death.

5.15   Ghibelline] The Ghibellines were one of the two political factions that dominated Florence in Dante's time, the other being the Guelphs.

5.20–21   Villa Viviani, village of Settignano] The Villa Viviani is a fourteenth-century, twenty-eight room house, located in Settignano, three miles east of the center of Florence. Clemens's family lived there from September 1892 to June 1893, during which time he composed MS Morgan, the first version of *Pudd'nhead Wilson*, completing the chapters begun in Bad Nauheim in the summer of 1892. While living at the Villa Viviani, he also wrote "Extracts from Adam's Diary" and a large part of *Personal Recollections of Joan of Arc* (Carocci 1906, 42–43; *AutoMT1*, 244–49; Ishihara 2014, 20–26).

5.24–26 in the swell room of the house, with the busts of Cerretani senators . . . as they used to look down upon Dante] The aristocratic Cerretani family of Florence acquired the Villa Viviani in 1577, more than two centuries after the time of Dante. They decorated the walls of its central salon ("the swell room of the house") with medallions of distinguished family members (Carocci 1906, 42–43; *AutoMT1*, 246; Ishihara 2014, 23).

7.2–4 Dawson's Landing . . . St. Louis] Like the St. Petersburg of *Tom Sawyer* and *Huckleberry Finn*, the fictional town of Dawson's Landing is patterned after Hannibal, Missouri, though Clemens has placed it farther south. Evidently it takes its name from John D. Dawson (b. 1812?), who was briefly Clemens's schoolmaster. Dawson, born in Scotland, had fourteen years' teaching experience when he opened his school for boys and young ladies "of good morals, and of ages under 12 years," on Third Street in Hannibal, in April 1847. He ran the school until 1849, when he joined the California gold rush. Dawson's was the last school Clemens attended before being apprenticed to Joseph P. Ament as a typesetter. In *The Adventures of Tom Sawyer*, the schoolteacher Mr. Dobbins is based on Dawson (Wecter 1952, 132–34; *Inds*, 317; *AutoMT1*, 399–400).

8.9 Cairo] The city of Cairo (pronounced *kay-ro*), Illinois, lies at the confluence of the Mississippi and Ohio Rivers, a short steamboat journey from the supposed location of Dawson's Landing.

8.32–34 Mrs. Rachel Pratt, and she also was childless . . . and not to be comforted] The name Rachel associates Mrs. Pratt to a biblical figure proverbial for childlessness: "In Rama was there a voice heard, lamentation, and weeping, and great mourning, Rachel weeping for her children, and would not be comforted, because they are not" (Matthew 2:18, quoting Jeremiah 31:15). Mark Twain gave this name to another mother who has lost her children, Aunt Rachel, in his 1874 sketch "A True Story, Repeated Word for Word as I Heard It" (*FamSk*, 45–50).

8.38 First Families] The phrase "First Families of Virginia," sometimes abbreviated as "F.F.V.," designates those who claim descent from the earliest white settlers of the state.

9.03 the "code,"] The *code duello*, the body of rules governing the conduct of duelists. Dueling was illegal in Missouri from the state's earliest days, but the law did little to curb the practice (Steward 2000, 106–7, 117).

9.15–16 one of his slave girls, Roxana by name] It has been suggested that this character's name alludes to the courtesan heroine of Daniel Defoe's *Roxana, or The Fortunate Mistress* (1724), or else to Roxana, the consort of Alexander the Great. But the name was not uncommon among enslaved women, and perhaps the simplest explanation—that Clemens was drawing on his own memories—is best (*MTHL*, 2:536–37 n. 2; SLC 2015, xvii; McWilliams 1990, 185; Moore 1870, 5; "Sheriff's Sales," Savannah [Ga.] *Georgian*, 6 June 1825, 4; "Ten Dollars Reward," Newbern [N.C.] *Spectator*, 26 Jan 1838, 4; New Orleans *Times-Picayune*: "Creole Slave!," 19 Jan 1842, 3, and "20 Dollars Reward," 27 Jan 1844, 1).

9.38   "Because, I would kill my half."] Compare the anecdote in *The Life of P. T. Barnum, Written by Himself*, in which the co-owner of an elephant, refused the chance to buy out his partner, says: "You may do what you please with your half of that elephant, but I am fully determined *to shoot my half!*" (Barnum 1855, 112–15). Clemens read this book as a young man; he later became a friend of Barnum's and owned a copy inscribed to him by the showman in 1875. Albert Bigelow Paine included Barnum's *Life* among the books Clemens "had read again and again" (*MTB*, 1:410, 3:1536, 3:1540; Gribben 2022, 44–45).

10.24   labrick] In 1906, Benjamin E. Smith, the editor in charge of revising the *Century Dictionary*, asked Clemens for the origins and definition of this word. Clemens replied:

> I am authority for the fact—which is a fact—that the term labrick was in constant use by all grown men except certain of the clergy in the State of Missouri when I was a boy. It had a very definite meaning & occupied in the matter of strength the middle ground between scoundrel & son of a bitch. . . . But I think you are serious about this. If you are, let me brush aside the ornamental & give you the plain & authentic definition of the word. Labrick is substantially ass, a little enlarged & emphasized; let us say, labrick is a little stronger than ass, & not quite as strong as idiot. (6 Aug 1906 to Benjamin E. Smith, collection of Margaret R. Leavy)

According to his secretary, Isabel V. Lyon, "Mr. Clemens did not believe that the gentle editors of the Century Dictionary, whom he called 'side-saddlers,' would accept his pungent definition of the word. And they didn't." The 1911 revision defined *labrick* as "A fool; an ass" (Benjamin E. Smith to SLC, 30 July 1906, NN-BGC; Isabel V. Lyon, MS accompanying Smith's letter, NN-BGC; Whitney and Smith 1911; *CY*, 338.31, and note on 565).

12.18   pantagraph] "An instrument for the mechanical copying of engravings, diagrams, plans, etc., either upon the same scale, or upon a reduced or an enlarged scale" (Whitney and Smith 1889–91). Also spelled *pantograph*. See the illustration on p. 417.

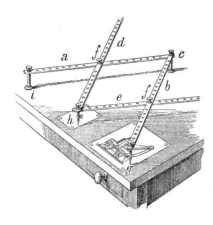

Pantagraph. From Whitney and Smith 1889–91.

12.29   mud-cat] A kind of catfish; hence, a low, disreputable person, a bottom-feeder. Compare Clemens's remark to his brother Orion in 1865: "you would be a scheming, groveling, mud-cat of a lawyer" (19 and 20 Oct 1865 to OC and MEC, *L1*, 323).

12.30   niggers] For comment on Mark Twain's use of this word, see "Offensive Language in *Pudd'nhead Wilson*," pp. xxiii–xxv.

13.28–29   by a fiction of law and custom a negro] Roxy being one-sixteenth and Tom one-thirty-second Black, their legal status in pre–Civil War Missouri is not clearly defined. The relevant statute declared that "every person, other than a negro, any one of whose grand fathers or grand mothers is, or shall have been a negro, although all his or her other progenitors, except those descending from the negro, may have been white persons, shall be deemed a mulatto; and every such person, who shall have one fourth or more negro blood, shall, in like manner, be deemed a mulatto" (*Missouri Statutes* 1845, 392). The statute did not define the racial status of a mulatto's descendants who have less than one-quarter Black ancestry; nor did it specify the difference, if any, between the legal conditions of the negro and the mulatto. It would appear that in such cases custom, rather than law, determined racial status.

13.33   tow-linen] Cloth woven from low-quality flax.

13.34   Thomas à Becket Driscoll] All the grandees of Dawson's Landing are named after the noble families and peerages of England ("York," "Percy," "Howard," etc.), but Percy Driscoll's son is named after a historical individual. Thomas à Becket (1118?–70), the son of a merchant, rose in the reign of Henry II to be chancellor and then archbishop of Canterbury, in which capacity he obstructed the royal will and was assassinated by agents of the king. Canonized soon after, he became one of the most widely venerated saints in Christendom.

13.35   Valet de Chambre] The French phrase means a manservant whose prin-
         cipal duty is to attend to his master's personal needs. Clemens noted
         its comic possibilities (and pronunciation) in an 1880 notebook entry:
         "Valet de chambre Utterback (chief machinist, now, & called VALETT
         D. Utterback" (*N&J2*, 381).

18.5–6   linsey-woolsey] A coarse fabric of linen or cotton woven with wool.

19.19   bilin'] boiling, as in "a mass of material boiled together at one time"—
         laundry, for example (*DARE*, s.v. "boiling," n.).

19.29–30 De preacher said it was jist like dey done in Englan' one time, long time
         ago] The identification of the preacher's story of child-switching as
         happening "in Englan' . . . long time ago" gestures toward the birth of
         King Arthur in Malory's *Le Morte Darthur*. There, the infant Arthur is
         farmed out to be raised in obscurity, and his royal heritage is recognized
         only later. A closer parallel, and one which might more readily occur to
         the preacher, is Exodus 2:1–10, the birth of Moses (Schleiner 1976, 341;
         Gribben 2022, 480–81).

20.17   gaum] To smear with a sticky substance (*OED*).

20.27–28 hoss-shoe to keep off de witch-work] Horseshoes have long been used,
         by both white and Black people, as a charm against witches (Anderson
         2005, 60; Lawrence 1898, 88–103).

22.4   special providences] In Christian theology, acts of direct divine inter-
         vention. In 1886, Clemens wrote in his notebook:

> Special providence! That phrase nauseates me—with its
> implied importance of mankind & triviality of God. In my
> opinion these myriads of globes are merely the blood-corpus-
> cles ebbing & flowing through the arteries of God, & we but
> animalculae that infest them, disease them, pollute them: &
> God does not know we are there, & would not care if he did.
> (*N&J3*, 246–47)

         See also "Three Statements of the 1880s," in *WIM*, 56.

22.6   the case of the children, the bears and the prophet] "And as he [Elisha]
         was going up by the way, there came forth little children out of the city,
         and mocked him, and said unto him, Go up, thou bald head; go up,
         thou bald head. And he turned back, and looked on them, and cursed
         them in the name of the LORD. And there came forth two she bears out
         of the wood, and tare forty and two children of them" (2 Kings 2:23–
         24). The episode of Elisha and the bears was a staple of Enlightenment
         polemic, cited by Matthew Tindal, Voltaire, and Tom Paine as casting
         doubt on the goodness of God as portrayed in the Bible. It was also a
         staple of the lectures of Clemens's friend, the freethinking writer and

lecturer Robert Ingersoll (1833–99), who said that "this miracle, in my judgment, establishes two things: 1. That children should be polite to ministers; and 2. That God is kind to animals—'giving them their meat in due season'" (Ingersoll 1892, 431). Clemens's 1892 notebook shows him working out the final form of the "Calendar" aphorism (see Appendix C, "Mark Twain's Working Notes," pp. 479–80; *CY*, 142; Ingersoll 1878, 38; Ingersoll 1894, 19; Bird 2013; Gribben 2022, 372–74).

23.16–18 *"Like* it!" . . . *"Take* it!"] Tom's behavior here is patterned after the infant Susy Clemens (1872–96). According to her father's 1876 record of the children's doings and sayings, "Susie began to talk a little when she was a year old. If an article pleased her, she said *'Like* it—awnt (want) it—hab (have) it—*take* it'—and took it, unless somebody got in ahead and prevented" ("A Record of the Small Foolishnesses of Susie and 'Bay' Clemens [Infants]," *FamSk*, 53).

24.25–26 "ridden in peace," like Sir Kay in Launcelot's armor] Paraphrasing Malory, *Le Morte Darthur*, book 6, chapter 11. Kay's safety while riding in Launcelot's armor made an enduring impression on Clemens: he alluded to the passage not only here but in his letters, and he reproduced the entire chapter in the "Word of Explanation" prefaced to *A Connecticut Yankee in King Arthur's Court* (14 Aug 1883 to Ellen C. Taft, CtHMTH; *CY*, 1, 50; 22 Aug 1897 to Joseph H. Twichell, transcription in CU-MARK).

27.36 "amen corner,"] "A place in some Methodist churches . . . where formerly sat the deacons who led the responsive 'amens' during the service" (Whitney and Smith 1911); "an area occupied by particularly fervent worshippers" (*OED*).

27.37 Dunker Baptist] A colloquial name for the Church of the Brethren, an anabaptist church with origins in eighteenth-century Germany. Their distinctive theological tenet is baptism of adults by triple immersion (otherwise the faith resembles that of the Mennonites, who sprinkle). Never numerous, American Dunker congregations are found primarily in the mid-Atlantic and midwestern states. Jasper's religious character is based on John T. Lewis, a Black tenant farmer at Quarry Farm outside Elmira, New York, which was owned by Clemens's sister-in-law, Susan Crane. In August 1906, Clemens recalled that Lewis was "a Dunker Baptist. He was born one," and although he sampled other religions, he "finally fetched up in Dunkerdom, whence in his childhood he had started out" (*AutoMT2*, 172–75).

29.11 "Jasper . . . seized the horse and stopped him."] Jasper's exploit is based on the real-life action of John T. Lewis, which occurred at Quarry Farm while Clemens was staying there (see the note at 27.37, above). Clemens memorialized Lewis's feat in a pair of long and nearly identical letters, written two days after the event (25 and 27 Aug 1877 to John Brown,

NN-BGC, and 25 and 27 Aug 1877 to William Dean Howells and Elinor M. Howells, both in *Letters 1876–1880*). The anecdote was dropped from *Pudd'nhead Wilson* in revision. Clemens made two other attempts to fictionalize Lewis's heroic rescue, both in manuscripts he left unfinished: "Simon Wheeler, Detective," and "The Refuge of the Derelicts" (published posthumously in *S&B*, 372–78, and *FM*, 234–38, respectively).

31.2–3   The peach was once a bitter almond, cauliflower is nothing but cabbage with a college education] Clemens could have learned that the peach descends from the bitter almond, and that cauliflower is a kind of cabbage, from Darwin's *Variation of Animals and Plants under Domestication*, of which he owned the 1884 New York edition (Darwin 1884, 1:357–60, 1:341–43; Cummings 1957, 165; Gribben 2022, 182).

31.5   Remark of Dr. Baldwin] William Wilberforce Baldwin (1850–1910) was a renowned American physician specializing in cardiology. In the 1880s he set up a practice in Florence, where he became the favored doctor of the expatriate American community. He treated Olivia during the Clemenses' 1892–93 residence in the city and became friendly with the family. He also treated Olivia on their return to Florence in 1903–1904. Clemens must have meant this quotation from Dr. Baldwin to stand as a semiprivate tribute to him (Kiely 2016; 30 Sept 1892 to Susan L. Crane, CU-MARK; 15 Dec 1892 to Laurence Hutton, NjP; 19 May 1904 to William W. Baldwin, NNPM; Clara L. Clemens to William W. Baldwin, 19 May 1904, NNPM).

31.13   handsomely equipped with "conditions,"] "A student on being examined for admission to college, if found deficient in certain studies, is admitted on *condition* he will make up the deficiency. . . . The branches in which he is deficient are called *conditions*" (B. H. Hall 1856, 123).

32.4–6   the old deformed negro bell-ringer . . . imitating his fancy eastern graces] Clemens transfers to Tom an incident from the life of Cornelius (Neil) Moss (b. 1836). Like Moss, Clemens attended Sunday School at the Old Ship of Zion Methodist Church in Hannibal, and later they were classmates at Dawson's school. In his manuscript "Villagers of 1840–3," Clemens wrote:

> *Neil Moss.* The envied rich boy of the Meth. S. S. Spoiled and of small account. Dawson's. Was sent to Yale—a mighty journey and an incomparable distinction. Came back in swell eastern clothes, and the young men dressed up the warped negro bell ringer in a travesty of him—which made him descend to village fashions. (*Inds*, 94)

35.5   Rowena] Maria fetches her new name from Scott's *Ivanhoe* (1819), a romance of England in the Middle Ages.

39.9 phillipene] A nut with a double kernel, or the double kernel itself. "There is a custom, common in the Northern States at dinner or evening parties when almonds or other nuts are eaten, to reserve such as are double or contain two kernels, which are called *fillipeens*. If found by a lady, she gives one of the kernels to a gentleman, when both eat their respective kernels. When the parties again meet, each strives to be the first to exclaim, *Fillipeen!* for by so doing he or she is entitled to a present from the other" (Bartlett 1859, 148).

41.28 Paine's "Age of Reason"] *The Age of Reason* by Thomas Paine, first published in 1794–95, attacks revealed religion, especially Christianity, and contests the authority of the Bible. In 1908, Albert Bigelow Paine commented to Clemens that "it took a brave man before the Civil War to confess he had read the *Age of Reason*." "So it did," Clemens replied, "and yet that seems a mild book now. I read it first when I was a cub pilot, read it with fear and hesitation, but marveling at its fearlessness and wonderful power. I read it again a year or two ago, for some reason, and was amazed to see how tame it had become" (*MTB*, 3:1445; Gribben 2022, 553).

41.30 "Whole Duty of Man,"] Christian devotional work, first published anonymously in London in 1658, usually attributed to the clergyman Richard Allestree (1621–81). For Clemens, who was familiar with the book from his youth, it represented the trappings of a conventional piety (Gribben 2022, 19).

43.20 'Greenland's Icy Mountains'] "From Greenland's Icy Mountains" is a missionary hymn, written in 1819 by Reginald Heber (1783–1826), an English clergyman who was later bishop of Calcutta. The first verse reads:

> From Greenland's icy mountains,
>   From India's coral strand,
> Where Afric's sunny fountains
>   Roll down their golden sand;
> From many an ancient river,
>   From many a palmy plain,
> They call us to deliver
>   Their land from error's chain.

In *Following the Equator* Clemens wrote: "Those are beautiful verses, and they have remained in my memory all my life. But if the closing lines are true, let us hope that when we come to answer the call and deliver the land from its errors, we shall secrete from it some of our high-civilization ways, and at the same time borrow some of its pagan ways to enrich our high system with" (SLC 1897, 525; Julian 1957, 1:399–400).

43.23 'Old Bob Ridley'] A popular song from the blackface minstrel show, published in 1853 as the composition of W. L. Hargrave (Hargrave 1853; "Musical," Washington [D.C.] *Evening Star*, 7 May 1853, 22).

47.13   peep-shows] At this date, "a sequence of pictures viewed through a magnifying lens or hole set into a box" (*OED*); not yet implicitly indecent.

62.14   walls of Jericho] Joshua 6.

62.22   Passage of the Red Sea] Exodus 13–14.

62.24   Sodom and Gomorrah] Genesis 19.

75.9   the "Grand Mogul."] The name of this fictional steamboat recalls the *Grand Turk*, which plied the Mississippi between St. Louis and New Orleans from 1848 to 1854. Said to be "unsurpassed for magnificence, spaciousness, comfort and *good management*," it burned in 1854, after which a smaller boat of the same name ran the Pittsburgh–St. Louis route until 1862. If Clemens is thinking here of the *Grand Turk*, he is thinking of the first one, which at 241 feet was indeed "a big steamer for the time" (PW-MS, 75.9–10).

The original *Grand Turk*. From Lewis 1857. Library of Congress.

Clemens recalled the *Grand Turk* in *Life on the Mississippi* (chap. 14):

> It was a proud thing to be of the crew of such stately craft as the "Aleck Scott" or the "Grand Turk." Negro firemen, deck hands, and barbers belonging to those boats were distinguished personages in their grade of life, and they were well aware of that fact, too. . . . The barber of the "Grand Turk" was a spruce young negro, who aired his importance with balmy complacency, and was greatly courted by the circle in which he moved. The young colored population of New Orleans were much given to flirting, at twilight, on the banquettes of the

back streets. Somebody saw and heard something like the following, one evening, in one of those localities. A middle-aged negro woman projected her head through a broken pane and shouted (very willing that the neighbors should hear and envy), "You Mary Ann, come in de house dis minute! Stannin' out dah foolin' 'long wid dat low trash, an' heah's de barber offn de 'Gran' Turk' wants to conwerse wid you!" (SLC 1883, 169–71)

When Roxy joins the crew of the *Grand Mogul*, it is in the Cincinnati–New Orleans trade; later, when Clemens needs it to take Roxy from Arkansas up to St. Louis, he has her explain that the boat is "in de Sent Louis trade, now" (PW-MS, 171.27; Way 1983, 197; "Communicated," New Orleans *Times-Picayune*, 28 Feb 1851, 2; St. Louis *Missouri Republican*: "For New Orleans," 13 May 1848, 3; "The Great Fire in New Orleans," 8 Feb 1854, 3; "The steamer Grand Turk . . . ," Sandusky [Ohio] *Commercial Register*, 31 Dec 1852, 2).

82.31–83.7 wild-cat bill . . . rag dollah] Both terms refer to the dubious reputation of paper money in the United States before the National Bank Act of 1863. Banking was regulated only by the individual states, which chartered banks to print their own money. Notes issued by a bank suspected of lacking the capital to redeem them at face value in gold or silver were called "wild-cat." Such failures fed the public's distrust of paper money ("rag dollars").

83.36–37 Now, Gabrel, blow de hawn, I's ready!] The archangel Gabriel's announcement of the Last Judgment by blowing his horn is prominent in African American spirituals. Here Roxy uses it sarcastically to mean that she can die happy (Allen, Ware, and Garrison 1867, 3, 23; Higginson 1870, 212; Fenner 1876, 235–37; Odum and Johnson 1925, 86).

90.7–8 A gigantic irruption like that of Krakatoa . . . clouds of volcanic dust] Krakatoa, a volcano in the Dutch East Indies (now Indonesia), erupted in August 1883. The explosion destroyed the island and triggered a series of destructive tsunamis. Ash was carried on the wind to all parts of the world, causing strange and richly tinted sunsets.

91.4 curse of Ham] In Genesis 9:20–27, Ham, said to be the ancestor of the African peoples, transgresses against his father, Noah, who pronounces a curse upon Ham's son, Canaan: "Cursed be Canaan; a servant of servants shall he be unto his brethren." The text has a long history of being interpreted as a curse against Black people, ordaining them to servitude, and was regularly cited by slavery's apologists. An example of this claim, showing its currency in Clemens's youth, is an article by Dr. Samuel A. Cartwright (1793–1863) which was approvingly excerpted in the Hannibal *Missouri Courier* of 22 May 1851, two years before Clemens left Hannibal:

We learn from the book of Genesis that Noah had three sons, Shem, Ham and Japhet, and that Canaan, the son of Ham, was doomed to be servant of servants to his brethren.—From history we learn that the descendants of Canaan settled in Africa, and are the present Ethiopeans, or black race of men; that Shem occupied Asia, and Japhet the north of Europe. In the 9th chapter and 27th verse of Genesis, one of the most authentic books of the bible, is this remarkable prophecy: "God shall enlarge Japhet, and he shall dwell in the tents of Shem, and Canaan *shall* be his servant." Japhet has been greatly enlarged by the discovery of a new world, the continent of America. He found in it the Indians, whom natural history declares to be of Asiatic origin, in other words the descendants of Shem: he drove out Shem and occupied his tents; and now the remaining part of the prophecy is in process of fulfilment, from the facts everywhere before us, of Canaan having become his servant. . . . The only government under which the negro has made any improvement in mind, morals, religion, and the only government under which he has led a quiet, happy & contented life, is that under which he is subjected to the arbitrary power of Japhet, according to the Divine decree. ("Dr. Cartwright, of Louisiana," 2)

In April 1860, Jefferson Davis (1808–89) argued in the Senate that the Curse of Ham had doomed Black people "to perpetual slavery," drawing this rebuttal from the renowned abolitionist, Massachusetts senator Charles Sumner (1811–74):

To justify the Senator in his application of this ancient curse, he must maintain at least five different propositions, as essential links in the chain of the Afric-American slave: *first*, that, by this malediction, Canaan himself was actually changed into a "chattel," whereas he is simply made the "servant" of his brethren; *secondly*, that not merely Canaan, but all his posterity, to the remotest generation, was so changed, whereas the language has no such extent; *thirdly*, that the Afric-American actually belongs to the posterity of Canaan—an ethnological assumption absurdly difficult to establish; *fourthly*, that each of the descendants of Shem and Japheth has a right to hold an Afric-American fellow-man, as a "chattel"—a proposition which finds no semblance of support; and *fifthly*, that every Slavemaster is truly descended from Shem or Japheth—a pedigree which no anxiety can establish! (*Congressional Globe* 1859–60, 2:1682 [Davis, 12 Apr 1860] and 3:2602 [Sumner, 4 June 1860]; Sollors 1999, 78–111)

91.9   as secret murderers are said to feel when the accuser says "Thou art the man!"] The phrase is the prophet Nathan's denunciation of King David (2 Samuel 12:7). It will also have been familiar to Clemens from Edgar Allan Poe's story "Thou Art the Man" (1844).

101.23–24   the Gaikowar of Baroda] The hereditary ruler of the former Indian state of Baroda. At the time Mark Twain wrote *Pudd'nhead Wilson*, this princely title was familiar to him only from his reading; but in the course of his 1895–96 around-the-world lecture tour, the ruling Gaikowar invited him to Baroda. On 31 January 1896 he lectured in the royal palace before Sayajirao Gaekwad III (1863–1939), whom he called "the stunningest of the Indian Princes," and two hundred guests (SLC 1897, 357–58, 380, 389, 406; Notebook 36, TS pp. 27, 31, in CU-MARK).

103.26–27   "formerly Lord Buckstone, author of the Queen's Hounds"—meaning master of the Queen's hounds, probably] The Master of the Hounds is an officer in the British royal household who oversees the stag-hunting pack; the appointee is always a politically connected aristocrat. In 1892, when Clemens made John Buckstone style himself "author of the Queen's Hounds," the Master was Thomas Lister, fourth Baron Ribblesdale—who almost deserves Buckstone's malformed title: he was later the author of *The Queen's Hounds* (Ribblesdale 1897).

105.1–2   Sons of Liberty] Mark Twain's fictional anti-temperance organization is distinctively of the period just before the Civil War, when temperance agitation was at its height, but its name is borrowed from the Revolutionary period. The Sons of Liberty was an organization, or group of organizations, opposed to British taxation in the American colonies; their most famous exploit was the Boston Tea Party.

105.6   no heel-taps] That is, "drain your glasses"; the *heel-tap* is the last liquor remaining at the bottom of the glass.

111.4   highst] Dialect form of *hoist*. Mark Twain, who also spelled it *hyste*, used it to mean a boost as well as the contrary, a trip or fall. Now in use only as *heist*, a robbery (*ET&S2*, 375, 394; *DARE*, "hoist" *n.*; *HDAS*, "hoist" *n.*).

111.11   the modern attitude of the catcher at a base-ball match] Mark Twain distinguishes the "modern attitude" of the catcher from his stance in earlier times. Originally the catcher stood upright, twenty feet or more behind the plate, and caught the pitch on the bounce. An 1879 rule change required that the ball be caught on the fly, and over the next decade catchers moved closer to the plate and adopted a stooping or crouching posture (Peter Morris 2006, 203–10). See the illustration on p. 426.

112.37   the European plan] The arrangement, typical of European hotels, of charging meals separately from the lodging rate (*OED*).

119.13   Clive, Nelson and Putnam] Military men renowned for personal bravery: Robert, Lord Clive (1725–74), "Clive of India," supreme commander of the

Library of Congress.

British Indian Army; Horatio, Lord Nelson (1758–1805), British naval hero; and Israel Putnam (1718–90), American officer in the Revolutionary War.

126.9   jack-pair] Tom likens the Twins to the conjoined jacks on a playing card; or perhaps simply to a pair of jacks, a minimum hand in many card games.

142.3–5   My father en yo' gran'father was ole John Randolph of Roanoke . . . en his great-great-gran'mother or somers along back dah, was Pocahontas] John Randolph of Roanoke (1773–1833), a scion of a wealthy and powerful Virginia family, served his state as representative and senator. Among the "First Families of Virginia," descent from Pocahontas was considered respectable—an exception to the prevalent stigma of race mixing—and Randolph was proud of his connection with Pocahontas, who was his great-great-great-great-grandmother. Pocahontas (1596?–1617) was a daughter of Powhatan, a Native American chief living in the region of the Virginia Colony settlement at Jamestown. The Virginia colonist John Rolfe married her in 1614, and their only child, Thomas Rolfe, was born the following year; in 1616 the family sailed to England, where Pocahontas died (Robertson and Brock 1887; Randolph 1833). In preparing *Pudd'nhead Wilson* for publication, Clemens altered the manuscript's account of Roxy's paternity, probably at the request of the *Century Magazine*; see PW-REV, Explanatory Note at 299.14–16.

142.13   Ain't nigger enough in him to show in his finger-nails] Roxy alludes to the belief, described by Werner Sollors as "a cultural invention," that

African descent, in a person who presents visually as white, will show in the appearance of the fingernails. The description of the sign has varied "from a dark shade to a bluish tinge and from an opal-tinted onyx to a half-moon" (Sollors 1999, 146, 160–61). Clemens referred to this supposed trait in a sketch for an unwritten story made in 1883 or 1884, known by the unauthorial title "The Man with Negro Blood"; the manuscript is transcribed in Appendix H.

147.29   prescription . . . was one of Galen's] This prescription is not Galen's. Clemens found it in the *Medicinal Dictionary* of Robert James (published 1743–45), where it is ascribed to the Byzantine physician Nicolaus Myrepsus. While writing *A Connecticut Yankee in King Arthur's Court*, Clemens considered using prescriptions from James as examples of medieval medicine: "The leech gives him recipes from James's medical Dictionary. Result bedrids him 2 months" (*N&J3*, 415; also 383). In 1890 he quoted the present remedy in an article exhibiting James's work as "A Majestic Literary Fossil," printed in *Harper's New Monthly Magazine* for February 1890. Clemens revised the prescription, eliminating two parenthetical comments and substituting "brimstone" for the text's "crude Sulphur." On 2 December 1892 he asked his publishing associate, Fred Hall, to send him a copy of his 1890 article for use in the present passage; see the Introduction, p. 532 (SLC 1890; James 1743, s.v. "Alexandri Antidotus Aurea"; Gribben 2022, 381; 17 May 1898 to Edward K. Root, CtHM).

149.35–36   drive all the mosquitoes out of their bar] A mosquito bar is a net canopy placed over a bed to protect the sleeper against bites (Whitney and Smith 1889–91, 4:3868).

153.38   sheep-nanny tea] A folk remedy: sheep's dung boiled in water (Radbill and Hamilton 1960, 435–37; Green 1978, 14 n. 6).

161.35–36   De *law* kin sell me *now*, if dey tell me to leave de State in six months en I don't go] Here, and also in *Huckleberry Finn* (chap. 6), Mark Twain says that free Black people in Missouri could be told to leave the state in six months and sold into slavery if they didn't. The statutes seem not to have made that exact provision, but, as Roxy says, "white folks ain't particklar" (161.35), and Clemens is doubtless remembering how such cases were actually handled. The statutes were, in any case, extremely harsh. A free Black person could enter Missouri only in the service of a white man, or for the purpose of passing through. To gain a license to reside in the state, they had to post a substantial bond (in Hannibal it was $100—about $3,500 today). Roxy, in violating these requirements, would have been fined, and failing payment the court could have ordered her to leave the state immediately or sentenced her to slave labor (*Missouri Statutes* 1845, 392–94; Bellamy 1973; "Free Negro Tax," Hannibal *Journal and Union*, 8 July 1852, 3; McCoy 2017, 206).

163.2   on the lower guard abaft the paddle-box] The guard is the extension of the steamboat's deck beyond the line of the hull, overhanging the water; "abaft the paddle-box": to the stern of the paddle wheel.

163.11   snag . . . "break"] A *snag* is a submerged tree or other obstacle embedded in the river bottom, a navigational hazard; the *break* is its visible disturbance of the water's surface.

164.2   *July 4.* Statistics show that we lose more fools on this day] Deaths and injuries caused by guns and fireworks on the Fourth of July used to be regularly reported in newspapers. On 4 July 1906, Clemens told his audience at a banquet of the American Society in London:

> Two hours from now, on the Atlantic coast when night shuts down, that pandemonium will begin and there will be noise, and noise, and noise, all night long, and there will be more than noise—there will be people crippled, there will be people killed, there will be people who will lose their eyes, and all through that permission which we give to irresponsible boys to play with firearms and fire-crackers and all sorts of dangerous things. We turn that Fourth of July alas! over to rowdies to drink and get drunk and make the night hideous, and we cripple and kill more people than you would imagine. (*AutoMT3*, 118)

Later that year Clemens lent his voice to a campaign to restrain the "bedlam frenzies" of Independence Day, organized by Julia B. Rice (1860–1929) of the Society for the Suppression of Unnecessary Noise. In his draft letter to Rice (the letter sent has not been found) he wrote:

> If I may speak frankly I will say that while I detest the noises & the grotesque insanities of the Day, my main quarrel is with the Day itself.
>
> Why should Americans, of all people in the world, bow down to the Fourth of July & worship it? It is purely an *English* institution, no American had any part in the events which it commemorates. It is as purely, & utterly & comprehensively English as is Guy Fawkes's Day; & that Americans should claim it & celebrate it & magnify it is the largest joke the ages have produced. *There was never a white American in America until the Declaration of Independence was seven years old.*
>
> If we possessed a citizenship of a sturdy & sterling sort, we could rise up & reform Independence Day, but we haven't. We can't reform the Day, but perhaps we can do a better thing— abolish it. (10 Dec 1907 to Julia B. Rice, draft in CU-MARK; Nickerson 2012; "Juvenile Patriotism," *New York Times*, 12 Nov

RANAWAY,

From the residence of A. King, in St. Charles, on Wednesday night, the 2nd instant, my servant girl, named "ANN." She is a bright copper-colored mulatto, medium height, rather slight form, quite likely, and about 20 years of age.

Reward.

I will pay a reward of $25 for the arrest of said girl, if taken in St. Charles county, $50 if taken out of said county, and $100 if taken out of the State and returned to me or said King, in St. Charles county, or placed in confinement so I obtain possession of her. **CATHARINE E. PITTS.**

St. Charles, Mo., August 7th, 1854.

Missouri Historical Society.

$100 REWARD!

☞ **Ranaway on the 27th of September last, from the** Farm of the Hon. Jeremiah Morton, [to whom he was hired,] in the county of Orange, near Raccoon Ford, my negro man

OSBORNE!

He is 33 years of age, very stout and very black, with African features, about 5 feet 9 inches high, with very bad teeth, ruptured with hernia on the right side, and had on when he left a new truss. He sometimes calls himself John.   I will give for the apprehension of said negro so that I get him again, $25, if taken in Culpeper, Orange or Stafford, $50 if taken in any other county, and $100 if taken out of this State.   He was raised in Stafford, on a farm known as Salvington, on Potomac Creek. His mother is owned by Mrs. Rawlings, in that neighborhood.   His wife is owned by Mr. C. C. Beckham, of Culpeper.

Stevensburg, Culpeper Co., Va., Oct. 14, 1854.   **ROBERT O. GRAYSON.**

[ALEXANDRIA GAZETTE, PRINT.]

Missouri Historical Society.

1876, 5; "Fireworks in Politics," *Philadelphia Times*, 17 Feb 1884, 3; "To Amend the Fourth of July," *New York Tribune*, 19 July 1889, 6).

164.29 breakdown] A name used for any dance "in Negro style" (Nathan 1962, 92).

171.14 bitts] Sturdy posts for securing cables on a steamboat. They were fastened in pairs to the deck. About three feet high, the bitts had a crosspiece above the midpoint, forming an H.

172.37–38 usual rude wood-cut of a turbaned negro woman running, with the customary bundle on a stick over her shoulder] Clemens's description appears to combine aspects of the two images commonly used on runaway slave bills—a running man with a bundle, and a seated woman with a bundle by her side. See the illustrations on p. 429.

178.24–25 Are you heeled—that is, fixed?] Both slang terms meaning "armed" (*HDAS*, 2:70, 1:759).

184.24–26 her bill of sale in her pocket . . . she never parted with it, day or night] Roxy carries the bill of sale from her self-purchase because free Black people in Missouri were forbidden by law to keep in their possession a copy of a more important document: the license that certified them as freemen and permitted them to reside in the state (*Missouri Statutes* 1845, 393).

Explanatory Notes:
Pudd'nhead Wilson: A Tale
The Revised Version

217.11–12 that stone that Dante used to sit on] The "Stone of Dante" in the Piazza del Duomo in Florence was described by Clemens's friend Laurence Hutton (1843–1904), an authority on literary relics:

> At the side of the Cathedral Square in Florence is still preserved, embedded in the wall of a comparatively modern house, a bit of stone which is highly regarded by those tourists who accept the guide-books as invariable tellers of the truth. This "Stone of Dante" is said to have been a favourite seat of the poet while he watched the building of the Duomo; although why he always occupied the same hard and uninviting resting place and how he could have inspected the erection of a building which at the time of his death had passed nothing but its lower foundation-walls, the guide-books do not explain. (Hutton 1905, 189–90)

217.13 Giotto's Campanile] The bell tower of Florence Cathedral, designed by Giotto di Bondone, was built after Dante's death.

217.15 Ghibelline] The Ghibellines were one of the two political factions that dominated Florence in Dante's time, the other being the Guelphs.

217.20–21 Villa Viviani, village of Settignano] The Villa Viviani is a fourteenth-century twenty-eight room house, located in Settignano, three miles east of the center of Florence. Clemens's family lived there from September 1892 to June 1893, during which time he composed MS Morgan, the first version of *Pudd'nhead Wilson*, completing the chapters begun in Bad Nauheim in the summer of 1892. While living at the Villa Viviani, he also wrote "Extracts from Adam's Diary" and a large part of *Personal Recollections of Joan of Arc* (Carocci 1906, 42–43; *AutoMT1*, 244–49; Ishihara 2014, 20–26).

217.24–26 in the swell room of the house, with the busts of Cerretani senators . . .
as they used to look down upon Dante] The aristocratic Cerretani
family of Florence acquired the Villa Viviani in 1577, more than two
centuries after the time of Dante. They decorated the walls of its
central salon ("the swell room of the house") with medallions of
distinguished family members (Carocci 1906, 42–43; *AutoMT1*,
246; Ishihara 2014, 23).

219.4–5 Dawson's Landing . . . St. Louis] Like the St. Petersburg of *Tom Sawyer*
and *Huckleberry Finn*, the fictional town of Dawson's Landing is patterned after Hannibal, Missouri, although Clemens has placed it farther south. Evidently it takes its name from John D. Dawson (b. 1812?),
who was briefly Clemens's schoolmaster. Dawson, born in Scotland,
had fourteen years' teaching experience when he opened his school for
boys and young ladies "of good morals, and of ages under 12 years," on
Third Street in Hannibal, in April 1847. He ran the school until 1849,
when he joined the California gold rush. Dawson's was the last school
Clemens attended before being apprenticed to Joseph P. Ament as a
typesetter. In *The Adventures of Tom Sawyer*, the schoolteacher Mr.
Dobbins is based on Dawson (Wecter 1952, 132–34; *Inds*, 317;
AutoMT1, 399–400).

220.12 Cairo] The city of Cairo (pronounced *kay-ro*), Illinois, lies at the confluence of the Mississippi and Ohio Rivers, a short steamboat journey
from the supposed location of Dawson's Landing.

220.35–37 Mrs. Rachel Pratt, and she also was childless . . . and not to be com-
forted] The name Rachel associates Mrs. Pratt to a biblical figure proverbial for childlessness: "In Rama was there a voice heard, lamentation,
and weeping, and great mourning, Rachel weeping for her children,
and would not be comforted, because they are not" (Matthew 2:18,
quoting Jeremiah 31:15). Mark Twain gave this name to another mother
who has lost her children, Aunt Rachel, in his 1874 sketch "A True
Story, Repeated Word for Word as I Heard It" (*FamSk*, 45–50).

221.4 First Families] The phrase "First Families of Virginia," sometimes
abbreviated as "F.F.V.," designates those who claim descent from the
earliest white settlers of the state.

221.7 the "code,"] The *code duello*, the body of rules governing the conduct
of duelists. Dueling was illegal in Missouri from the state's earliest
days, but the law did little to curb the practice (Steward 2000,
106–7, 117).

221.20–21 one of his slave girls, Roxana by name] It has been suggested that this
character's name alludes to the courtesan heroine of Daniel Defoe's
Roxana, or The Fortunate Mistress (1724), or else to Roxana, the consort
of Alexander the Great. But the name was not uncommon among

enslaved women, and perhaps the simplest explanation—that Clemens was drawing on his own memories—is best (*MTHL*, 2:536–37 n. 2; SLC 2015, xvii; McWilliams 1990, 185; Moore 1870, 5; "Sheriff's Sales," Savannah [Ga.] *Georgian*, 6 June 1825, 4; "Ten Dollars Reward," Newbern [N.C.] *Spectator*, 26 Jan 1838, 4; New Orleans *Times-Picayune*: "Creole Slave!," 19 Jan 1842, 3, and "20 Dollars Reward," 27 Jan 1844, 1).

222.5   "Because, I would kill my half."] Compare the anecdote in *The Life of P. T. Barnum, Written by Himself*, in which the co-owner of an elephant, refused the chance to buy out his partner, says: "You may do what you please with your half of that elephant, but I am fully determined *to shoot my half!*" (Barnum 1855, 112–15). Clemens read this book as a young man; he later became a friend of Barnum's, and owned a copy inscribed to him by the showman in 1875. Albert Bigelow Paine included Barnum's *Life* among the books Clemens "had read again and again" (*MTB*, 1:410, 3:1536, 3:1540; Gribben 2022, 44–45).

222.29   labrick] In 1906, Benjamin E. Smith, the editor in charge of revising the *Century Dictionary*, asked Clemens for the origins and definition of this word. Clemens replied:

> I am authority for the fact—which is a fact—that the term labrick was in constant use by all grown men except certain of the clergy in the State of Missouri when I was a boy. It had a very definite meaning & occupied in the matter of strength the middle ground between scoundrel & son of a bitch. . . . But I think you are serious about this. If you are, let me brush aside the ornamental & give you the plain & authentic definition of the word. Labrick is substantially ass, a little enlarged & emphasized; let us say, labrick is a little stronger than ass, & not quite as strong as idiot. (6 Aug 1906 to Benjamin E. Smith, collection of Margaret R. Leavy)

According to his secretary, Isabel V. Lyon, "Mr. Clemens did not believe that the gentle editors of the Century Dictionary, whom he called 'side-saddlers,' would accept his pungent definition of the word. And they didn't." The 1911 revision defined *labrick* as "A fool; an ass" (Benjamin E. Smith to SLC, 30 July 1906, NN-BGC; Isabel V. Lyon, MS accompanying Smith's letter, NN-BGC; Whitney and Smith 1911; *CY*, 338.31, and note on p. 565).

225.18   pantagraph] "An instrument for the mechanical copying of engravings, diagrams, plans, etc., either upon the same scale, or upon a reduced or an enlarged scale" (Whitney and Smith 1889–91). Also spelled *pantograph*. See the illustration on p. 434.

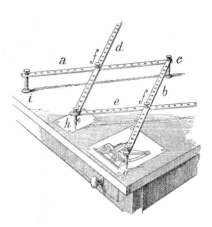

Pantagraph. From Whitney
and Smith 1889–91.

225.29   mud-cat] A kind of catfish; hence, a low, disreputable person, a bottom-feeder. Compare Clemens's remark to his brother Orion in 1865: "you would be a scheming, groveling, mud-cat of a lawyer" (19 and 20 Oct 1865 to OC and MEC, *L1*, 323).

225.30   niggers] For comment on Mark Twain's use of this word, see "Offensive Language in *Pudd'nhead Wilson*," pp. xxiii–xxv.

226.28–29 by a fiction of law and custom a negro] Roxy being one-sixteenth and Tom one-thirty-second Black, their legal status in pre–Civil War Missouri is not clearly defined. The relevant statute declared that "every person, other than a negro, any one of whose grand fathers or grand mothers is, or shall have been a negro, although all his or her other progenitors, except those descending from the negro, may have been white persons, shall be deemed a mulatto; and every such person, who shall have one fourth or more negro blood, shall, in like manner, be deemed a mulatto" (*Missouri Statutes* 1845, 392). The statute did not define the racial status of a mulatto's descendants who have less than one-quarter Black ancestry; nor did it specify the difference, if any, between the legal conditions of the negro and the mulatto. It would appear that in such cases custom, rather than law, determined racial status.

226.32–33 tow-linen] Cloth woven from low-quality flax.

226.34   Thomas à Becket Driscoll] All the grandees of Dawson's Landing are named after the noble families and peerages of England ("York," "Percy," "Howard," etc.), but Percy Driscoll's son is named after a historical individual. Thomas à Becket (1118?–70), the son of a merchant, rose in the reign of Henry II to be chancellor and then archbishop of Canterbury, in which capacity he obstructed the royal will and was assassinated by agents of the king. Canonized soon after, he became one of the most widely venerated saints in Christendom.

226.35   Valet de Chambre] The French phrase means a manservant whose principal duty is to attend to his master's personal needs. Clemens noted
its comic possibilities (and pronunciation) in an 1880 notebook entry:
"Valet de chambre Utterback (chief machinist, now, & called ValLETT
D. Utterback" (*N&J2*, 381).

231.6   linsey-woolsey] A coarse fabric of linen or cotton woven with wool.

232.19   bilin'] boiling, as in "a mass of material boiled together at one time"—
laundry, for example (*DARE*, s.v. "boiling," n.).

232.29–30 De preacher said it was jist like dey done in Englan' one time, long time
ago] The identification of the preacher's story of child-switching as
happening "in Englan' . . . long time ago" gestures toward the birth of
King Arthur in Malory's *Le Morte Darthur*. There, the infant Arthur is
farmed out to be raised in obscurity, and his royal heritage is recognized
only later. A closer parallel, and one which might more readily occur to
the preacher, is Exodus 2:1–10, the birth of Moses (Schleiner 1976, 341;
Gribben 2022, 480–81).

233.18   gaum] To smear with a sticky substance (*OED*).

233.28–29 hoss-shoe to keep off de witch-work] Horseshoes have long been used,
by both white and Black people, as a charm against witches (Anderson
2005, 60; Lawrence 1898, 88–103).

235.4   special providences] In Christian theology, acts of direct divine intervention. In 1886, Clemens wrote in his notebook:

> Special providence! That phrase nauseates me—with its
> implied importance of mankind & triviality of God. In my opin-
> ion these myriads of globes are merely the blood-corpuscles ebb-
> ing & flowing through the arteries of God, & we but animalcu-
> lae that infest them, disease them, pollute them: & God does not
> know we are there, & would not care if he did. (*N&J3*, 246–47)

See also "Three Statements of the 1880s," in *WIM*, 56.

235.6   the case of the children, the bears and the prophet] "And as he [Elisha]
was going up by the way, there came forth little children out of the city,
and mocked him, and said unto him, Go up, thou bald head; go up,
thou bald head. And he turned back, and looked on them, and cursed
them in the name of the LORD. And there came forth two she bears out
of the wood, and tare forty and two children of them" (2 Kings 2:23–
24). The episode of Elisha and the bears was a staple of Enlightenment
polemic, cited by Matthew Tindal, Voltaire, and Tom Paine as casting
doubt on the goodness of God as portrayed in the Bible. It was also a
staple of the lectures of Clemens's friend, the freethinking writer and
lecturer Robert Ingersoll (1833–99), who said that "this miracle, in my

judgment, establishes two things: 1. That children should be polite to ministers; and 2. That God is kind to animals—'giving them their meat in due season'" (Ingersoll 1892, 431). Clemens's 1892 notebook shows him working out the final form of the "Calendar" aphorism (see Appendix C, "Mark Twain's Working Notes," pp. 479–80; *CY*, 142; Ingersoll 1878, 38; Ingersoll 1894, 19; Bird 2013; Gribben 2022, 372–74).

237.16–18 *"Like* it!" . . . *"Take* it!"] Tom's behavior here is patterned after the infant Susy Clemens (1872–96). According to her father's 1876 record of the children's doings and sayings, "Susie began to talk a little when she was a year old. If an article pleased her, she said *'Like* it—awnt (want) it—hab (have) it—*take* it'—and took it, unless somebody got in ahead and prevented" ("A Record of the Small Foolishnesses of Susie and 'Bay' Clemens [Infants]," *FamSk*, 53).

238.25–26 "ridden in peace," like Sir Kay in Launcelot's armor] Paraphrasing Malory, *Le Morte Darthur*, book 6, chapter 11. Kay's safety while riding in Launcelot's armor made an enduring impression on Clemens: he alluded to the passage not only here but in his letters, and he reproduced the entire chapter in the "Word of Explanation" prefaced to *A Connecticut Yankee in King Arthur's Court* (14 Aug 1883 to Ellen C. Taft, CtHMTH; *CY*, 1, 50; 22 Aug 1897 to Joseph H. Twichell, transcription in CU-MARK).

243.2–3 The peach was once a bitter almond, cauliflower is nothing but cabbage with a college education] Clemens could have learned that the peach descends from the bitter almond, and that cauliflower is a kind of cabbage, from Darwin's *Variation of Animals and Plants under Domestication*, of which he owned the 1884 New York edition (Darwin 1884, 1:357–60, 1:341–43; Cummings 1957, 165; Gribben 2022, 182).

243.5 Remark of Dr. Baldwin] William Wilberforce Baldwin (1850–1910) was a renowned American physician specializing in cardiology. In the 1880s he set up a practice in Florence, where he became the favored doctor of the expatriate American community. He treated Olivia during the Clemenses' 1892–93 residence in the city, and became friendly with the family. He also treated Olivia on their return to Florence in 1903–1904. Clemens must have meant this quotation from Dr. Baldwin to stand as a semiprivate tribute to him (Kiely 2016; 30 Sept 1892 to Susan L. Crane, CU-MARK; 15 Dec 1892 to Laurence Hutton, NjP; 19 May 1904 to William W. Baldwin, NNPM; Clara L. Clemens to William W. Baldwin, 19 May 1904, NNPM).

243.13 handsomely equipped with "conditions,"] "A student on being examined for admission to college, if found deficient in certain studies, is admitted on *condition* he will make up the deficiency. . . . The branches in which he is deficient are called *conditions*" (B. H. Hall 1856, 123).

244.5–7   the old deformed negro bell-ringer . . . imitating his fancy eastern graces] Clemens transfers to Tom an incident from the life of Cornelius (Neil) Moss (b. 1836). Like Moss, Clemens attended Sunday School at the Old Ship of Zion Methodist Church in Hannibal, and later they were classmates at Dawson's school. In his manuscript "Villagers of 1840–3," Clemens wrote:

> *Neil Moss.* The envied rich boy of the Meth. S. S. Spoiled and of small account. Dawson's. Was sent to Yale—a mighty journey and an incomparable distinction. Came back in swell eastern clothes, and the young men dressed up the warped negro bell ringer in a travesty of him—which made him descend to village fashions. (*Inds*, 94)

247.4–5   Habit is habit . . . a step at a time] Clemens added this aphorism to the revised *Pudd'nhead Wilson*, even though he had already used it in the manuscript of *Personal Recollections of Joan of Arc*, chapter 6, written in Florence in October 1892. When *Joan of Arc* was published anonymously in *Harper's Monthly*, the shared maxim was recognized as evidence for Clemens's authorship ("'Joan of Arc' and 'Pudd'nhead Wilson,'" Minneapolis *Penny Press*, 28 May 1895).

254.11   the "Grand Mogul."] The name of this fictional steamboat recalls the *Grand Turk*, which plied the Mississippi between St. Louis and New Orleans from 1848 to 1854. Said to be "unsurpassed for magnificence, spaciousness, comfort and *good management*," it burned in 1854, after which a smaller boat of the same name ran the Pittsburgh–St. Louis route until 1862. If Clemens is thinking here of the *Grand Turk*, he is thinking of the first one, which at 241 feet was indeed "a big steamer for the time" (PW-MS, 75.9–10). Clemens also recalled the *Grand Turk* in *Life on the Mississippi* (chap. 14):

> It was a proud thing to be of the crew of such stately craft as the "Aleck Scott" or the "Grand Turk." Negro firemen, deck hands, and barbers belonging to those boats were distinguished personages in their grade of life, and they were well aware of that fact, too. . . . The barber of the "Grand Turk" was a spruce young negro, who aired his importance with balmy complacency, and was greatly courted by the circle in which he moved. The young colored population of New Orleans were much given to flirting, at twilight, on the banquettes of the back streets. Somebody saw and heard something like the following, one evening, in one of those localities. A middle-aged negro woman projected her head through a broken pane and shouted (very willing that the neighbors should hear and envy), "You Mary Ann, come

in de house dis minute! Stannin' out dah foolin' 'long wid dat low trash, an' heah's de barber offn de 'Gran' Turk' wants to conwerse wid you!" (SLC 1883, 169–71)

In revising *Pudd'nhead Wilson* for serial publication, Clemens removed the episode in which Roxy first goes aboard the *Grand Mogul* (PW-MS, chap. 13). When Roxy joins the crew of the *Grand Mogul*, it is in the Cincinnati–New Orleans trade; later, when Clemens needs it to take Roxy from Arkansas up to St. Louis, he has her explain that the boat is "in de Sent Louis trade, now" (PW-REV, 320.32; Way 1983, 197; "Communicated," New Orleans *Times-Picayune*, 28 Feb 1851, 2; St. Louis *Missouri Republican*: "For New Orleans," 13 May 1848, 3; "The Great Fire in New Orleans," 8 Feb 1854, 3; "The steamer Grand Turk . . . ," Sandusky [Ohio] *Commercial Register*, 31 Dec 1852, 2).

The original *Grand Turk*. From Lewis 1857. Library of Congress.

255.25   amen corner] "A place in some Methodist churches . . . where formerly sat the deacons who led the responsive 'amens' during the service" (Whitney and Smith 1911); "an area occupied by particularly fervent worshippers" (*OED*).

259.35–260.11 wild-cat bill . . . rag dollah] Both terms refer to the dubious reputation of paper money in the United States before the National Bank Act of 1863. Banking was regulated only by the individual states, which chartered banks to print their own money. Notes issued by a bank suspected of lacking the capital to redeem them at face value in gold or silver were called "wild-cat." Such failures fed the public's distrust of paper money ("rag dollars").

261.2–3 Now, Gabrel, blow de hawn, I's ready!] The archangel Gabriel's announcement of the Last Judgment by blowing his horn is prominent in African American spirituals. Here Roxy uses it sarcastically to mean that she can die happy (Allen, Ware, and Garrison 1867, 3, 23; Higginson 1870, 212; Fenner 1876, 235–37; Odum and Johnson 1925, 86).

262.7–8 coal . . . too many pre-historic toads in it] Discoveries of "antediluvian toads," found alive in coal or rock beds, were frequently reported in the nineteenth century. An 1889 overview of reports in Great Britain noted:

> A large, fat toad in Derbyshire, found in a compact block of sandstone, which lived for a few seconds only after its release; seven live frogs near Pontefract, in compact rock (sandstone or limestone) free from fissures, the frogs being in separate nodular masses between the strata; a large toad in a cavity in a flint weighing 14 lbs., in which no crack or flaw could be detected; 30 to 40 live young frogs found in a cavity in a block of sandstone 330 feet deep, at Shield Muir Pit, Motherwell, Scotland; a live toad in a solid block of coal in the Forest of Dean, the creature seeming to be firmly embedded in the coal and its form imprinted on the face of the mineral. (Jeffs 1890, 151)

Clemens had substantially composed this aphorism by 1883, when he made notes for a character who "complains too many pre-historic toads in his coal!" (*N&J3*, 12). He alluded to the same phenomenon in *A Connecticut Yankee in King Arthur's Court*, chapter 18, where two prisoners are "kenneled like toads in the same coal" (MS in NN-BGC [all editions wrongly read "kerneled"]); "Have Live Toads and Frogs Ever Been Found in Solid Stone?," *Saturday Evening Post*, 31 Oct 1857, 6; "Scientific Notes," *Appletons' Journal*, 15 Mar 1873, 381; "The Discovery of Live Toads, Frogs, Etc., in Coal, Etc.," *Colliery Engineer* [Scranton, Pa.], 10 [Aug 1889]: 21).

268.29–30 A gigantic irruption like that of Krakatoa . . . clouds of volcanic dust] Krakatoa, a volcano in the Dutch East Indies (now Indonesia), erupted in August 1883. The explosion destroyed the island and triggered a series of destructive tsunamis. Ash was carried on the wind to all parts of the world, causing strange and richly tinted sunsets.

269.26 curse of Ham] In Genesis 9:20–27, Ham, said to be the ancestor of the African peoples, transgresses against his father Noah, who pronounces a curse upon Ham's son, Canaan: "Cursed be Canaan; a servant of servants shall he be unto his brethren." The text has a long history of being interpreted as a curse against Black people, ordaining them to servitude, and was regularly cited by slavery's apologists. An example of this claim, showing its currency in Clemens's youth, is an article by Dr. Samuel A. Cartwright (1793–1863) that was approvingly excerpted in the Hannibal *Missouri Courier* of 22 May 1851, two years before Clemens left Hannibal:

> We learn from the book of Genesis that Noah had three sons, Shem, Ham and Japhet, and that Canaan, the son of Ham, was doomed to be servant of servants to his brethren.—From history we learn that the descendants of Canaan settled in Africa, and are the present Ethiopeans, or black race of men; that Shem occupied Asia, and Japhet the north of Europe. In the 9th chapter and 27th verse of Genesis, one of the most authentic books of the bible, is this remarkable prophecy: "God shall enlarge Japhet, and he shall dwell in the tents of Shem, and Canaan *shall* be his servant." Japhet has been greatly enlarged by the discovery of a new world, the continent of America. He found in it the Indians, whom natural history declares to be of Asiatic origin, in other words the descendants of Shem: he drove out Shem and occupied his tents; and now the remaining part of the prophecy is in process of fulfilment, from the facts everywhere before us, of Canaan having become his servant. . . . The only government under which the negro has made any improvement in mind, morals, religion, and the only government under which he has led a quiet, happy & contented life, is that under which he is subjected to the arbitrary power of Japhet, according to the Divine decree. ("Dr. Cartwright, of Louisiana," 2)

In April 1860, Jefferson Davis (1808–89) argued in the Senate that the Curse of Ham had doomed Black people "to perpetual slavery," drawing this rebuttal from the renowned abolitionist, Massachusetts senator Charles Sumner (1811–74):

> To justify the Senator in his application of this ancient curse, he must maintain at least five different propositions, as essential links in the chain of the Afric-American slave: *first*, that, by this malediction, Canaan himself was actually changed into a "chattel," whereas he is simply made the "servant" of his brethren; *secondly*, that not merely Canaan, but all his posterity, to the remotest generation, was so changed, whereas the language has no such extent; *thirdly*, that the Afric-American actually belongs to the posterity of Canaan—an ethnological assumption absurdly difficult to establish; *fourthly*, that each of the descendants of Shem and Japheth has a right to hold an Afric-American fellow-man, as a "chattel"—a proposition which finds no semblance of support; and *fifthly*, that every Slavemaster is truly descended from Shem or Japheth—a pedigree which no anxiety can establish! (*Congressional Globe* 1859–60, 2:1682 [Davis, 12 Apr 1860] and 3:2602 [Sumner, 4 June 1860]; Sollors 1999, 78–111)

269.29–30 as secret murderers are said to feel when the accuser says "Thou art the man!"] The phrase is the prophet Nathan's denunciation of King David (2 Samuel 12:7). It will also have been familiar to Clemens from Edgar Allan Poe's story "Thou Art the Man" (1844).

272.9 As to the Adjective: when in doubt, strike it out] Clemens's crusade against adjectives was of long standing. In 1880 he answered the letter of a young admirer:

> I notice that you use plain, simple language, short words, & brief sentences. That is the way to write English—it is the modern way, & the best way. Stick to it; don't let fluff & flowers & verbosity creep in. When you catch an adjective, kill it. No, I don't mean that, utterly, but kill the most of them—then the rest will be valuable. They weaken when they are close together, they give strength when they are wide apart. An adjective-habit, or a wordy, diffuse, or flowery habit, once fastened upon a person, is as hard to get rid of as any other vice. (20 Mar 1880 to David Watt Bowser, *Letters 1876–1880*)

A cull of adjectives was a standard part of Clemens's revision process. In 1887 he told his editor at the *Century Magazine* he would "take a day, or maybe two, to knock out adjectives & polish up"; and in 1909 he told the editor of *Harper's Bazaar* he would "wring out the adjectives & forward the pulp to you" (31 Jan 1887 to Richard Watson Gilder, photocopy in CU-MARK; Nov 1909 to Elizabeth G. Jordan, NN).

277.29 the Gaikowar of Baroda] The hereditary ruler of the former Indian state of Baroda. At the time Mark Twain wrote *Pudd'nhead Wilson*, this princely title was familiar to him only from his reading; but in the course of his 1895–96 around-the-world lecture tour, the ruling Gaikowar invited him to Baroda. On 31 January 1896 he lectured in the royal palace before Sayajirao Gaekwad III (1863–1939), whom he called "the stunningest of the Indian Princes," and two hundred guests (SLC 1897, 357–58, 380, 389, 406; Notebook 36, TS pp. 27, 31, in CU-MARK).

280.25 Sons of Liberty] Mark Twain's fictional anti-temperance organization is distinctively of the period just before the Civil War, when temperance agitation was at its height, but its name is borrowed from the Revolutionary period. The Sons of Liberty was an organization, or group of organizations, opposed to British taxation in the American colonies; their most famous exploit was the Boston Tea Party.

280.29 no heel-taps] That is, "drain your glasses"; the *heel-tap* is the last liquor remaining at the bottom of the glass.

281.8–9 lets this human phillipene snip you out a speech] This is one of the places where Mark Twain's 1893 revision separating the Twins results in a genuine botch. In MS Morgan, Tom alludes to the bodily form of the conjoined Twins when he suggests that "this human pair of scissors snip you out a speech." Revising the passage to accommodate the Twins' separation, Clemens deleted "pair of scissors" and—salvaging an image from a canceled manuscript passage—replaced that phrase with "phillipene," meaning a nut with a double kernel; but he failed to carry through the change of metaphor, leaving "snip you out a speech" unrevised.

283.13   Clive, Nelson and Putnam] Military men renowned for personal bravery: Robert, Lord Clive (1725–74), "Clive of India," supreme commander of the British Indian Army; Horatio, Lord Nelson (1758–1805), British naval hero; and Israel Putnam (1718–90), American officer in the Revolutionary War.

291.14   jack-pair] If this image is meant to liken the Twins to the two conjoined jacks on the playing card, it is an unrevised survival from the conjoined Twins of MS Morgan; but it may pass for a reference simply to a pair of jacks, a minimum hand in many card games.

299.14–16   My father en yo' gran'father was ole John Randolph of Roanoke . . . en his great-great-gran'mother or somers along back dah, was Pocahontas] John Randolph of Roanoke (1773–1833), a scion of a wealthy and powerful Virginia family, served his state as representative and senator. Among the "First Families of Virginia," descent from Pocahontas was considered respectable—an exception to the prevalent stigma of race mixing—and Randolph was proud of his connection with Pocahontas, who was his great-great-great-great-grandmother. Pocahontas (1596?–1617) was a daughter of Powhatan, a Native American chief living in the region of the Virginia Colony settlement at Jamestown. The Virginia colonist John Rolfe married her in 1614, and their only child Thomas Rolfe was born the following year; in 1616 the family sailed to England, where Pocahontas died (Robertson and Brock 1887; Randolph 1833). In preparing *Pudd'nhead Wilson* for publication, Clemens altered the manuscript's account of Roxy's paternity. Likely enough the *Century Magazine*'s editors balked at fathering Roxy on John Randolph; in the present edition that revision is considered probable censorship and is not incorporated into the text. The *Century* version reads:

> My great-great-great gran'father en yo' great-great-great-great-granfather was ole Cap'n John Smith, de highest blood dat Ole Virginny ever turned out, en *his* great-great-gran'mother or somers along back dah, was Pocahontas de Injun queen, en her husbun' was a nigger king outen Africa . . .

See PW-REV, Textual Apparatus, entry and textual note at 299.14.

299.24   Ain't nigger enough in him to show in his finger-nails] Roxy alludes to the belief, described by Werner Sollors as "a cultural invention," that African descent, in a person who presents visually as white, will show in the appearance of the fingernails. The description of the sign has varied "from a dark shade to a bluish tinge and from an opal-tinted onyx to a half-moon" (Sollors 1999, 146, 160–61). Clemens referred to this supposed trait in a sketch for an unwritten story made in 1883 or 1884, known by the unauthorial title "The Man with Negro Blood"; the manuscript is transcribed in Appendix H.

303.6–7   "Put all your eggs in the one basket and—*watch that basket.*"] This aphorism was originated by Andrew Carnegie, who published it in his 1890 essay "How to Win Fortune":

> The rule, "Do not put all your eggs in one basket," does not apply to a man's life-work. Put all your eggs in one basket, and then watch that basket, is the true doctrine—the most valuable rule of all. (Carnegie 1890)

Clemens probably heard this from Carnegie's own mouth in April 1893. That month he dined with Carnegie twice and recorded the millionaire's maxim in his notebook. He made it one of Wilson's aphorisms when he revised the novel in July. In 1905, Carnegie laid claim to his contribution, saying, at a dinner for Mark Twain at the Aldine Club: "It has been rumored that I am an author. I am. I will confess it now that I hold Mark Twain's affidavit—his signature—that I am the joint author of 'Pud[d]'nhead Wilson'" ("Joan of Arc Appears to Startle Mark Twain," New York *Times*, 22 Dec 1905, 9; Carnegie 1910; Notebook 33, TS pp. 5, 6, 8, CU-MARK).

310.9   a good card] "An expedient certain to attain its object" (*OED*, "card" *n.* 2, 2b).

312.16–17   De *law* kin sell me *now*, if dey tell me to leave de State in six months en I don't go] Here, and also in *Huckleberry Finn* (chap. 6), Mark Twain says that free Black people in Missouri could be told to leave the state in six months and sold into slavery if they didn't. The statutes seem not to have made that exact provision, but, as Roxy says, "white folks ain't particklar" (312.16), and Clemens is doubtless remembering how such cases were actually handled. The statutes were, in any case, extremely harsh. A free Black person could enter Missouri only in the service of a white man, or for the purpose of passing through. To gain a license to reside in the state, they had to post a substantial bond (in Hannibal it was $100—about $3,500 today). Roxy, in violating these requirements, would have been fined, and failing payment the court could have ordered her to leave the state immediately or sentenced her to slave labor (*Missouri Statutes* 1845, 392–94; Bellamy 1973; "Free Negro Tax," Hannibal *Journal and Union*, 8 July 1852, 3; McCoy 2017, 206).

313.20   on the lower guard abaft the paddle-box] The guard is the extension of the steamboat's deck beyond the line of the hull, overhanging the water; "abaft the paddle-box": to the stern of the paddle wheel.

313.28   snag . . . "break"] A *snag* is a submerged tree or other obstacle embedded in the river bottom, a navigational hazard; the *break* is its visible disturbance of the water's surface.

314.2–4   In Rome, along at first, you are full of regrets that Michael Angelo died; but by and by you only regret that you didn't *see* him do it] In *The Innocents Abroad*, chap. 27, Mark Twain complained of Michelangelo's ubiquity at Rome:

> He designed St. Peter's; he designed the Pope; he designed the Pantheon, the uniform of the Pope's soldiers, the Tiber, the Vatican, the Coliseum, the Capitol, the Tarpeian Rock, the Barberini Palace, St. John Lateran, the Campagna, the Appian Way, the Seven Hills, the Baths of Caracalla, the Claudian Aqueduct, the Cloaca Maxima—the eternal bore designed the Eternal City, and unless all men and books do lie, he painted everything in it! . . . I never felt so fervently thankful, so soothed, so tranquil, so filled with a blessed peace, as I did yesterday when I learned that Michael Angelo was dead.

314.6   *July 4*. Statistics show that we lose more fools on this day] Deaths and injuries caused by guns and fireworks on the Fourth of July used to be regularly reported in newspapers. On 4 July 1906, Clemens told his audience at a banquet of the American Society in London:

> Two hours from now, on the Atlantic coast when night shuts down, that pandemonium will begin and there will be noise, and noise, and noise, all night long, and there will be more than noise—there will be people crippled, there will be people killed, there will be people who will lose their eyes, and all through that permission which we give to irresponsible boys to play with firearms and fire-crackers and all sorts of dangerous things. We turn that Fourth of July alas! over to rowdies to drink and get drunk and make the night hideous, and we cripple and kill more people than you would imagine. (*AutoMT3*, 118)

Later that year Clemens lent his voice to a campaign to restrain the "bedlam frenzies" of Independence Day, organized by Julia B. Rice (1860–1929) of the Society for the Suppression of Unnecessary Noise. In his draft letter to Rice (the letter sent has not been found) he wrote:

If I may speak frankly I will say that while I detest the noises & the grotesque insanities of the Day, my main quarrel is with the Day itself.

Why should Americans, of all people in the world, bow down to the Fourth of July & worship it? It is purely an *English* institution, no American had any part in the events which it commemorates. It is as purely, & utterly & comprehensively English as is Guy Fawkes's Day; & that Americans should claim it & celebrate it & magnify it is the largest joke the ages have produced. *There was never a white American in America until the Declaration of Independence was seven years old.*

If we possessed a citizenship of a sturdy & sterling sort, we could rise up & reform Independence Day, but we haven't. We can't reform the Day, but perhaps we can do a better thing—abolish it. (10 Dec 1907 to Julia B. Rice, draft in CU-MARK; Nickerson 2012; "Juvenile Patriotism," New York *Times*, 12 Nov 1876, 5; "Fireworks in Politics," Philadelphia *Times*, 17 Feb 1884, 3; "To Amend the Fourth of July," New York *Tribune*, 19 July 1889, 6).

315.2–3   barbers . . . peanut-pedlars . . . organ-grinders] Judge Driscoll mentions three trades stereotypically associated with Italian immigrants to America (Hamberlin 2011, 16; "Our Friends the Italians," New York *Sun*, 9 Dec 1891, 6).

320.19   bitts] Sturdy posts for securing cables on a steamboat. They were fastened in pairs to the deck. About three feet high, the bitts had a crosspiece above the midpoint, forming an H.

322.4–6   usual rude wood-cut of a turbaned negro woman running, with the customary bundle on a stick over her shoulder] Clemens's description appears to combine aspects of the two images commonly used on runaway slave bills—a running man with a bundle, and a seated woman with a bundle by her side. See the illustrations on p. 446.

327.19–20   Are you heeled—that is, fixed?] Both slang terms meaning "armed" (*HDAS*, 2:70, 1:759).

333.24–25   her bill of sale in her pocket . . . she never parted with it, day or night] Roxy carries the bill of sale from her self-purchase because free Black people in Missouri were forbidden by law to keep in their possession a copy of a more important document: the license that certified them as freemen and permitted them to reside in the state (*Missouri Statutes* 1845, 393).

349.4–5   *October 12.—The Discovery.* It was wonderful to find America, but it would have been more wonderful to miss it] Changes in the usage of the words *wonderful* and *miss* have caused this aphorism to be interpreted as a mordant comment on the European colonization of

RANAWAY,

From the residence of A. King, in St. Charles, on Wednesday night, the 2nd instant, my servant girl, named "ANN." She is a bright copper-colored mulatto, medium height, rather slight form, quite likely, and about 20 years of age.

Reward.

I will pay a reward of $25 for the arrest of said girl, if taken in St. Charles county, $50 if taken out of said county, and $100 if taken out of the State and returned to me or said King, in St. Charles county, or placed in confinement so I obtain possession of her.　　　　CATHARINE E. PITTS.

St. Charles, Mo., August 7th, 1854,

Missouri Historical Society.

$100 REWARD!

☞Ranaway on the 27th of September last, from the Farm of the Hon. Jeremiah Morton, [to whom he was hired,] in the county of Orange, near Raccoon Ford, my negro man

OSBORNE!

He is 33 years of age, very stout and very black, with African features, about 5 feet 9 inches high, with very bad teeth, ruptured with hernia on the right side, and had on when he left a new truss. He sometimes calls himself John. I will give for the apprehension of said negro so that I get him again, $25, if taken in Culpeper, Orange or Stafford, $50 if taken in any other county, and $100 if taken out of this State. He was raised in Stafford, on a farm known as Salvington, on Potomac Creek. His mother is owned by Mrs. Rawlings, in that neighborhood. His wife is owned by Mr. C. C. Beckham, of Culpeper.

Stevensburg, Culpeper Co., Va., Oct. 14, 1854.　　**ROBERT O. GRAYSON.**

[ALEXANDRIA GAZETTE, PRINT.]

Missouri Historical Society.

America. Clemens's earlier expressions of this idea may be brought to bear upon its interpretation; in an 1886 speech introducing the explorer Henry M. Stanley at a banquet in Hartford, Clemens said:

> Now Columbus started out to discover America. Well, he didn't need to do anything at all but sit in the cabin of his ship and hold his grip and sail straight on, and America would discover itself. (Laughter.) Here it was barring his passage the whole length and breadth of the South American continent, and he couldn't get by it. (Laughter.) He'd got to discover it; he couldn't help it. ("Mark Twain Introduces Stanley," Hartford *Courant*, 11 Dec 1886, 1)

And a manuscript leaf in the Mark Twain Papers shows Clemens trying out "miss it" and "overlook [it]" before settling on "get by it":

350.8   the "nigger gallery"] The section of a church or theater to which Black worshipers were restricted (Craigie and Hulbert 1936–44, s.v. "negro gallery," 3:1590).

Explanatory Notes:
Those Extraordinary Twins: A Postscript to Pudd'nhead Wilson

353.32   jack-leg] One who works in a professional capacity despite lacking skills or training.

359.30   phillipene] A nut with a double kernel, or the double kernel itself. "There is a custom, common in the Northern States at dinner or evening parties when almonds or other nuts are eaten, to reserve such as are double or contain two kernels, which are called *fillipeens*. If found by a lady, she gives one of the kernels to a gentleman, when both eat their respective kernels. When the parties again meet, each strives to be the first to exclaim, *Fillipeen!* for by so doing he or she is entitled to a present from the other" (Bartlett 1859, 148).

362.18   Paine's "Age of Reason"] *The Age of Reason* by Thomas Paine, first published 1794–95, attacks revealed religion, especially Christianity, and contests the authority of the Bible. In 1908, Albert Bigelow Paine commented to Clemens that "it took a brave man before the Civil War to confess he had read the *Age of Reason*." "So it did," Clemens replied, "and yet that seems a mild book now. I read it first when I was a cub pilot, read it with fear and hesitation, but marveling at its fearlessness and wonderful power. I read it again a year or two ago, for some reason, and was amazed to see how tame it had become" (*MTB*, 3:1445; Gribben 2022, 553).

362.20   "Whole Duty of Man,"] Christian devotional work, first published anonymously in London in 1658, usually attributed to the clergyman Richard Allestree (1621–81). For Clemens, who was familiar with the book from his youth, it represented the trappings of a conventional piety (Gribben 2022, 19).

363.1   "From Greenland's Icy Mountains"] A missionary hymn, written in 1819 by Reginald Heber (1783–1826), an English clergyman who was later bishop of Calcutta. The first verse reads:

From Greenland's icy mountains,
 From India's coral strand,
Where Afric's sunny fountains
 Roll down their golden sand;
From many an ancient river,
 From many a palmy plain,
They call us to deliver
 Their land from error's chain.

In *Following the Equator* Clemens wrote: "Those are beautiful verses, and they have remained in my memory all my life. But if the closing lines are true, let us hope that when we come to answer the call and deliver the land from its errors, we shall secrete from it some of our high-civilization ways, and at the same time borrow some of its pagan ways to enrich our high system with" (SLC 1897, 525; Julian 1957, 1:399–400).

364.20   'Old Bob Ridley'] A popular song from the blackface minstrel show, published in 1853 as the composition of W. L. Hargrave (Hargrave 1853; "Musical," Washington [D.C.] *Evening Star*, 7 May 1853, 22).

368.11   peep-shows] At this date, "a sequence of pictures viewed through a magnifying lens or hole set into a box" (*OED*); not yet implicitly indecent.

376.11   walls of Jericho] Joshua 6.

376.19   Passage of the Red Sea] Exodus 13–14.

376.21   Sodom and Gomorrah] Genesis 19.

385.18   highst] Dialect form of *hoist*. Mark Twain, who also spelled it *hyste*, used it to mean a boost as well as the contrary, a trip or fall. Now in use only as *heist*, a robbery (*ET&S2*, 375, 394; *DARE*, "hoist" *n.*; *HDAS*, "hoist" *n.*).

385.25   the modern attitude of the catcher at a base-ball match] Mark Twain distinguishes the "modern attitude" of the catcher from his stance in earlier times. Originally the catcher stood upright, twenty feet or more behind the plate, and caught the pitch on the bounce. An 1879 rule change required that the ball be caught on the fly, and over the course of the next decade catchers moved closer to the plate and adopted a stooping or crouching posture (Peter Morris 2006, 203–10). See the illustration on p. 450.

387.15   the European plan] The arrangement, typical of European hotels, of charging meals separately from the lodging rate (*OED*).

389.15–16   Jack Bunce] In MS Morgan this had been "Jake" Bunce (PW-MS, 114.33). The alteration to "Jack" looks authorial, since Jack Bunce (John L. Bunce, 1868–1907) was a Hartford friend of the Clemens family. Just days before Clemens revised the omitted parts of MS Morgan to create *Those Extraordinary Twins*, he visited the Bunce family in Hartford

Library of Congress.

and wrote to Olivia with news of "Jack Bunce" (3 Aug 1894 to OLC, CU-MARK).

400.27   prescription . . . was one of Galen's] This prescription is not Galen's. Clemens found it in the *Medicinal Dictionary* of Robert James (published 1743–45), where it is ascribed to the Byzantine physician Nicolaus Myrepsus. While writing *A Connecticut Yankee in King Arthur's Court*, Clemens considered using prescriptions from James as examples of medieval medicine: "The leech gives him recipes from James's medical Dictionary. Result bedrids him 2 months" (*N&J3*, 415; also 383). In 1890 he quoted the present remedy in an article exhibiting James's work as "A Majestic Literary Fossil," printed in *Harper's New Monthly Magazine* for February 1890. Clemens revised the prescription, eliminating two parenthetical comments and substituting "brimstone" for the text's "crude Sulphur." On 2 December 1892 he asked his publishing associate, Fred Hall, to send him a copy of his 1890 article for use in the present passage; see the Introduction, p. 532 (SLC 1890; James 1743, s.v. "Alexandri Antidotus Aurea"; Gribben 2022, 381; 17 May 1898 to Edward K. Root, CtHM).

402.32–33 drive all the mosquitoes out of their bar] A mosquito bar is a net canopy placed over a bed to protect the sleeper against bites (Whitney and Smith 1889–91, 4:3868).

Appendixes

MS Berg: Contents and Numbering

MS page sequences	Final page no.	Description	Narrative
[1]–4	[1]–4	**Chapter 1:** 'Those Extraordinary Twins . . . to the rest.'	**Chapter 1:** Dawson's Landing, about 1850. Jake Driscoll, Justice of the Peace. Capt. Tom Baldwin.
	5	**Chapter 1:** 'When an elderly . . . It is the'. A fragment, affixed to a blank leaf using the selvage edge from a sheet of postage stamps, and revised.	"Uncle" and "Aunt" in Missouri.
52–53	6–7	**Chapter 1:** 'highest title of . . . the same hour.'	Patsy Cooper and Betsy Hale. [*Deletion:* Patsy pays a call.]
5–27	8–30	**Chapters 1–2:** 'Her daughter Maria . . . just for sentiment.'"	[*Deletion:* introduction to Patsy Cooper.] Rowena Cooper. Her brothers Joe and Henry. A Tuesday in June: the Twins' letter read and discussed. Thursday night: arrival of the Twins. **Chapter 2:** The Twins retire. The family's first impressions.
27A–27F; 28–33	31–36	**Chapter 2:** 'The Twins were . . . a thundering bass.' An insertion.	The Twins bicker and sing.
27G; 34	37	**Chapter 2:** 'After the singing . . . the headache.' The deleted text is not continuous with p. 27F; it continues from a page no longer extant.	[*Deletion:* part of a superseded account of the Twins' singing.] The Twins go to bed.
A–E; 27J–27N; 27H–27L; 35–39	38–42	**Chapter 3:** 'The family sat . . . '"There—he's coming."' An insertion, forming a new beginning for the chapter.	**Chapter 3:** Friday morning: Patsy and Rowena discuss the Twins.

MS page sequences	Final page no.	Description	Narrative
28–85	43–100	**Chapters 3–4 and unnumbered:** 'The new lodger . . . refused permission.' On p. 79 an inserted heading begins a new chapter, which is left unnumbered.	The Twins at breakfast. Their history, nature, and habits. **Chapter 4:** Levee of the Twins. **Unnumbered chapter:** The Twins drive with Judge Driscoll. The Twins at odds over Freethinkers' Society meeting. Their social and psychological difficulties.
	101–24	**Chapters 5–[6]:** 'Rowena was dining . . . the public opinion.'	**Chapter 5:** The Twins dine with Patsy and Betsy. Details of the Twins' construction. Luigi tells lies. **Chapter [6]:** Judge Driscoll and "Pudd'nhead" Wilson, freethinkers. Story of Wilson's nickname.

MS Morgan: Contents and Numbering

The phases of composition of MS Morgan are set forth in the figure on p. ooo.

TS1 page no.	MS page sequences	Final page nos.	Phase orig. comp.	Description	Narrative
			iii	*Discarded **title page**, with fingerprints clipped from Galton 1892 and directions to printer (in NNPM).*	
1			iii?	**Title and motto.**	
	[1]–2	3–4	v	**Key to Signs Used in This Book.**	
	[1]–4	5–8	v	**Note Concerning the Legal Points.** Dated 2 January 1893 in the text.	
	1½		iv	*Discarded **chapter 1 head and motto** (in CU-MARK).*	
		9	v	Blank except for page number.	
	2–12	10–20	iv	**Chapter 1 text:** 'The scene . . . at Dawson's Landing.' 11 MS leaves replacing the discarded TS1 p. 1.	**Chapter 1:** Dawson's Landing, 1830. Judge Driscoll. Rachel Pratt. Pembroke Howard. Cecil Burleigh Essex. Percy Driscoll. 1 February 1830: births of Thomas à Becket Driscoll and Valet de Chambre. Roxy. February 1830: arrival of David Wilson.

TS1 page no.	MS page sequences	Final page orig. nos.	Phase orig. comp.	Description	Narrative
29–30	44–45; 48–49; 13–14	21–22	iv	**Chapter 1 text:** 'But he made . . . twenty long years.' TS1, revised; p. 22 is the top part of bisected TS1 leaf 30.	Wilson nicknamed "Pudd'nhead."
	14½	23	v	**Chapter 2 head and motto.**	
	15–39	24–48	iv	**Chapter 2 text:** 'Pudd'nhead Wilson had . . . humanity himself.'	**Chapter 2:** Wilson's fads: palmistry and fingerprints. 1 July 1830: Roxy and Jasper; Wilson fingerprints the babies. 3 September 1830: Wilson fingerprints babies again. 4 September 1830: Percy Driscoll's threat to sell Roxy down the river. [*Deletion*: letter illustrating character of Percy Driscoll.]
		48½	v	**Chapter 3 head and motto.**	
	40–57	49–66	iv	**Chapter 3 text:** 'Percy Driscoll slept . . . of her mind.'	[*Deletion*: End of Percy Driscoll letter.] **Chapter 3:** Night of 4 September 1830: Roxy intends to drown herself and her baby, then switches the children. 1 October 1830: Wilson again fingerprints the babies.
		67–68	v	**Chapter 4 head and mottoes.**	
	58–90	69–101	iv	**Chapter 4 text:** 'This history must . . . answer me dat!''	**Chapter 4:** "Tom" a bad baby. Childhood of Tom and "Chambers." Chambers saves Tom, is stabbed by him. Roxy and Tom's relationship. Fall, 1845: Judge Driscoll buys Chambers. Death of Cecil Burleigh Essex. Death of Percy Driscoll. Roxy, set free, will chambermaid on a steamboat. Jasper stops runaway horse and is set free. Jasper and Roxy on Providence.
		102	v	**Chapter 5 head and motto.**	

TS1 page no.	MS page sequences	Final page nos.	Phase orig. comp.	Description	Narrative
	91–96	103–8	iv	**Chapter 5 text:** 'Mrs. York Driscoll ... twenty-three years before.' **Chapter 5 motto** inserted on p. 103.	**Chapter 5:** 1847: Mrs. Driscoll dies. Tom to Yale. 1849: Tom returns. 1853: Judge Driscoll has been retired three years, is friend to the still-underprized Wilson.
unnum.		'follow 108'	i	**Chapter 5 text:** Fragment of TS1, 'Judge Driscoll was ... public opinion.', revised to continue: 'Or, rather ... better one.'	
	46–47; 50–51; 97–98	109–10	ii	**Chapter 5 text:** 'If the Judge ... calendar had merit.' These MS leaves, originally the ending of chapter 11, were moved to this position to establish the Calendar.	Wilson's philosophical Calendar.
28 [foot]		'follow page 110'	i	**Chapter 5 text:** Fragment of TS1, 'Judge Driscoll could ... or did.', revised to continue: 'He was liked ... count for anything.'	Judge Driscoll and Wilson, freethinkers.
	43; 47; 99	111	ii	Author's directive ordering MS leaves: 'Probably runs to Aunts & Twins'. Written on the verso of a leaf discarded from *Personal Recollections of Joan of Arc*.	
		112	v	**Chapter 6 head and motto.**	
2		113	i	**Chapter 6 text:** 'When an elderly ... Younger than she.' TS1, revised.	**Chapter 6:** "Uncle" and "Aunt" in Missouri. Patsy Cooper, Betsy Hale, Rowena Cooper, and her brothers, Joe and Henry.

TS1 page no.	MS page sequences	Final page nos.	Phase orig. comp.	Description	Narrative
3–19		114–29	i	**Chapters 6–8 text:** 'The widow . . . and every now'. TS1, revised. Chapter 7 head and motto inserted on p. 116; **Chapter 8 head and motto** inserted on p. 120.	A Tuesday in June 1853: the Twins' letter read and discussed. Thursday night: arrival of the Twins. **Chapter 7:** The Twins retire. The family's first impressions. The Twins bicker and sing. **Chapter 8:** Friday morning: Patsy and Rowena discuss the Twins. The Twins at breakfast. Their history, nature, and habits. Levee of the Twins.
		130	v	**Chapter 9 motto,** with directive to insert on p. 131.	
19–28		131–40	i	**Chapters 8–10 text:** 'The company broke . . . if he had.' TS1, revised. **Chapter 10 head and motto** inserted on p. 136.	Levee of the Twins. **Chapter 9:** The Twins drive with Judge Driscoll. The Twins at odds over Freethinkers' Society meeting. Their social and psychological difficulties. **Chapter 10:** The Twins dine with Patsy and Betsy. Details of the Twins' construction. Luigi tells lies.
		141	v	**Chapter 11 head and mottoes.**	
	28A–D; 29–32	142–45	ii	**Chapter 11 text:** 'A visitor was . . . furnish that knowledge.'	**Chapter 11:** Aunts gossip about Tom and Rowena.
	29–42; 33–46	146–59	ii	**Chapter 11 text:** 'The visitor who . . . ended the controversy.' Original beginning of chapter 11, revised to dovetail with the inserted pp. 142–45.	Visit of Rev. Hotchkiss to the Twins. Religious controversy.
	43–45; 47–49		ii	*Discarded* **chapter 11** *text. The two leaves that followed, originally numbered 46–47, were moved to become chapter 5 text (final numbering 109–10).*	*[Deletion: unknown.]*

TS1 page no.	MS page sequences	Final page orig. nos.	Phase orig. comp.	Description	Narrative
		160	v	**Chapter 12 head and (canceled) motto.**	
	48–63; 54–69	161–76	ii	**Chapter 12 text:** 'Judge Driscoll called . . . day-break in the morning.' SLC directive at end of this section: 'Here insert 1A & all that batch.', referring to the series originally numbered 1–17 plus H–III.	**Chapter 12:** Friday evening: Freethinkers' Society meeting and Bible class. At home, Wilson waits for the Twins to arrive and ponders what he saw at dawn in the Judge's house: a 'girl' in Tom Driscoll's room. [*Deletion:* Wilson surprised to see the girl is Tom.] Wilson does not recognize the girl; makes inquiries but learns nothing.
		177	v	**Chapter 13 head and motto.**	
	A–G		iii	*7 discarded leaves, not extant: the first leaves written in the addition Clemens calls 'this long digression' (chapters 13–16). They were replaced by pp. 1–17 (next entry).*	[*Deletion: unknown.*]
	1–17	178–94	iv	**Chapter 13 text:** 'It is necessary, now . . . Chambers said:'	**Chapter 13:** 1845, the year Roxy was set free. Her first experience of the steamboat *Grand Mogul*. Eight years as a chambermaid. 1853: disabled, she resigns. Loses her savings in a bank failure. In Dawson's Landing, visits Judge Driscoll's kitchen. Hears that Tom stays in St. Louis, is at odds with his uncle.
	8–10; H–J	195–97	iii	**Chapter 13 text:** 'De fac' is . . . thought of it.' These 3 leaves are salvaged from an earlier layer of composition, and are the earliest extant part of the 'long digression'. In some passages, later revised, Roxy is a 'quadroon'.	Chambers tells Roxy that Tom gets $50 a month and gambles; has been disinherited once and reinstated.

TS1 page no.	MS page sequences	Final page orig. nos.	Phase orig. comp.	Description	Narrative
	K–AA	198–214	iii	**Chapter 13 text:** 'Yah-yah-yah!... her shawl, saying,—'.	Roxy visits Tom, who mistreats her; she threatens him and requires him to come to the haunted house later that night.
	AA½	215	iii	**Chapter 13 text; chapter 14 head, (canceled) motto, and text:** 'It's prime... sofa, and put'. Text replacing that deleted on p. BB.	Roxy leaves, Tom reacts.
	BB–NN	216–28	iii	**Chapter 14 text:** 'his throbbing head... could still command—'.	**Chapter 14:** Tom meets Roxy in the haunted house. She reveals she is his mother, requires half his allowance. Tom admits to thefts.
	OO	229	iii	**Chapter 14 text:** 'Ma, would you... Surroundings had been'. This page and the inserted OOa give the "revised version" of Tom's paternity, replacing canceled text on the page originally numbered OOb (below).	Tom asks who his father was, Roxy says Colonel Essex.
	OOa	230	iii	**Chapter 14 text:** 'a little more... I kin swah!"'	Roxy on Colonel Essex, concluded.
		231	v	**Chapter 15 head and mottoes.**	
	OOb	232	iii	**Chapter 15 text:** 'Every now and... this horror, and'. In the deleted passage beginning this page, Roxy refuses to tell Tom who his father is—text replaced by pages originally numbered OO–OOa (above).	**Chapter 15:** Tom grapples with Roxy's revelations.

TS1 page no.	MS page sequences	Final page orig. nos.	Phase orig. comp.	Description	Narrative
	PP–ZZ	233–43	iii	**Chapter 15 text:** 'then he resolved to . . . impotent with rage.'	Tom rails against his misfortune; hates both white and Black people. [*Deletion*: Tom does not know who his father is, wants to kill him.] The change in Tom's thoughts and behavior.
	AAA	244	iii	**Chapter 16 chapter head and text:** 'For as much . . . not know himself.' SLC deleted the text of p. AAA, flipped the leaf, paginated the verso AAA again, and wrote the chapter 16 head and a little text.	**Chapter 16:** Tom's character not so much changed. [*Deletion*: Tom obsessed with killing his unknown father]
	BBB–III	245–52	iii	**Chapter 16 text:** 'In several ways . . . huzzy might be.'	The change in Tom. [*Deletion*: Tom obsessed with killing his unknown father.] Roxy harvests among the kitchens; she and Tom have a good working relationship. Tom's last raid has saved him from exposure and assured his inheritance, but he has new gambling debts and plans another raid. Dressing in his women's clothes, he sees Wilson observing him. Tom raids the town during Patsy's reception for the Twins; emboldened, he robs the Cooper house. 'After this long digression' we have come again to Friday evening (end of chapter 12), with Wilson awaiting the Twins and puzzling over the girl.
		253	v	**Chapter 17 head and motto.**	

TS1 page no.	MS page sequences	Final page nos.	Phase orig. comp.	Description	Narrative
		254	iii	**Chapter 17 text:** 'The duplicates arrived . . . of the three.' A bridge back to phase ii material, probably a reinscription of earlier-written text.	**Chapter 17:** The Twins arrive at Wilson's.
	64–69; 70–75	255–60	ii	**Chapter 17 text:** 'There was an interruption . . . the fellow-twin.'"	Tom joins the party and is introduced to the Twins. [*Deletion*: Tom is startled by the Twins' appearance.] [*Insertion*: Tom only pretends to be startled, having seen the Twins already while robbing the Cooper house.] Tom baits Wilson. Fingerprints discussed and taken. [*Deletion*: Buckstone arrives.]
	75A–75T	261–80	ii	**Chapter 17 text:** 'Well, it's done . . . English with a'. An insertion, adding the palm reading and the story of Luigi's Indian knife. Realizing that Tom would already have the knife in his possession, SLC made a further insertion to this effect on 274 verso.	Wilson reads Luigi's palm, uncovers his homicide. The Twins describe the Indian knife [*Insertion*: which, although they have not missed it yet, Tom has stolen.] Tom refuses to have his palm read.
	70–80; 76–86	281–91	ii	**Chapter 17 text:** 'slight but noticeable . . . the fire-company.'	Buckstone arrives. The Sons of Liberty meeting. The Twins inducted, Tom kicked. Fire.
		292	v	**Chapter 18 head and motto.**	
	81–94; 87–100	293– 306	ii	**Chapter 18 text:** 'Next morning all . . . If my'.	**Chapter 18:** Saturday: Tom charges the Twins with assault. Wilson will defend them.

TS1 page no.	MS page sequences	Final page nos.	Phase orig. comp.	Description	Narrative
	1–24 (altered in pencil to) 101–24	307–30	ii	**Chapter 18 text:** 'Mr. Justice Robinson . . . man was Wilson.' This 24-page sequence is physically discontinuous from the preceding leaves. The first of these pages, originally numbered 1, is written on the verso of the discarded page 2 of some other work.	Trial of the Twins for assault, continued. Justice Robinson disagrees with the jury's verdict. Wilson victorious.
		331	v	**Chapter 19 head and motto.** The page number 125 is jotted in a corner, showing that this page is to follow the page earlier numbered 124.	
	125–27	332–34	ii	**Chapter 19 text:** 'Judge Driscoll was in bed . . . same age—sixty.' The original introduction to Pembroke Howard. When SLC added chapters 1–5, it came to be a reintroduction, and was trimmed by 3 pages (see next entry).	**Chapter 19:** Saturday morning: Judge and Pembroke Howard go fishing. Code of the Virginia aristocracy. [*Deletion:* beginning of passage on Howard—see next entry.]
	128–30		ii	*Discarded* **chapter 19 text.** *3 leaves, not extant.*	[*Deletion:* anecdote(s) of Pembroke Howard.]
	131–44	335–48	ii	**Chapter 19 text:** 'Although Driscoll was . . . slip again I'm gone!'"	[*Deletion:* end of passage on Howard.] Saturday evening: Judge Driscoll and Howard learn of Tom's kicking. Tom names Angelo as kicker. Tom won't duel; Judge will challenge Angelo. Judge disinherits Tom. Tom vows reform.
		349	v	*Discarded* **chapter 20 head and motto** *(in CU-MARK).*	
		349	v	**Chapter 20 head.** Replaces original 349.	

TS1 page no.	MS page sequences	Final page orig. nos.	Phase orig. comp.	Description	Narrative
	145–65	350–70	ii	**Chapter 20 text:** 'Thus mournfully communing . . . day it has been!"'	**Chapter 20:** Tom goes to Wilson's house. [*Deletion:* allusion to the haunted house.] Wilson informs Tom there has been 'another raid.' A town delegation arrives. An old woman is suspected in the raid. The Twins' Indian knife stolen; reward offered. Wilson and the Twins have a plan to catch thief. Delegation asks Wilson to run for office.
	165½		ii	*Discarded* **chapter 21 head and motto** *(in CU-MARK).*	
		371	v	**Chapter 21 head, motto, and text:** 'It was the . . . Wilson was'. Added leaf, with text made to dovetail with the revised p. 372.	**Chapter 21:** Watermelon season.
	166–83	372–89	ii	**Chapter 21 text:** 'saying the words . . . of his luck.' After deleting the insects passage, SLC inscribed a replacement ending to the chapter on verso of leaf 389.	Howard tells Judge that Angelo won't duel, but Luigi will. Judge redraws the will. Tom eavesdrops and learns of it. [*Deletion:* Tom tortures insects.]
	184–88		ii	*Discarded* **chapter 21 text** *(in CU-MARK).*	[*Discarded:* Tom tortures insects.]
		390	v	**Chapter 22 head and motto.**	
	189–204	391–406	ii	**Chapter 22 text:** 'The Judge and . . . was getting on.'	**Chapter 22:** The duel. Angelo wounded. At midnight the legs become Angelo's and the Twins run away.

TS1 page no.	MS page sequences	Final page nos.	Phase orig. comp.	Description	Narrative
	204A–204S	407–25	iii	**Chapter 23 text:** 'Meantime Tom had . . . home en begin!"'	**Chapter 23:** Early hours of Sunday: Tom needs money but the valuable knife can't be sold. Roxy reports on the duel. She upbraids Tom. He tells her the will has been broken and restored again. He must go to St. Louis and behave; Roxy will go along to see he does.
	204½; 204T	426	ii	**Chapter 24 head, motto, and text:** 'When the doctor . . . he found'.	**Chapter 24:** Early Sunday: Doctor arrives at Cooper house.
	205–18	427–41	ii	**Chapter 24 text:** 'the lights going . . . of the weather.' The prescription, affixed to 432, is a clipping from SLC 1890.	Doctor treats Angelo. An antique prescription. Angelo insists on being baptized.
	219	442	v	**Chapter 25 head.**	
	220–32	443–55	ii	**Chapter 25 text:** 'By nine o'clock . . . uneasiness about that."'	**Chapter 25:** Sunday: town gossips about duel. Angelo baptized. Aunt Betsy calms Luigi. [*Deletion*: Luigi resolves to stay in Dawson's Landing.]
		456	v	**Chapter 26 head and motto.**	
	233–47 and 248 [top]	457–72	ii	**Chapter 26 text:** 'During Monday . . . with him anywhere.'	**Chapter 26:** Monday through Wednesday: the Twins worsen, then recover. Friday: The Twins in politics. Wilson will be mayor of Dawson's Landing, now a city. Wilson, Tom, and Constable Blake discuss the thefts. The old woman and the Indian knife not found. Tom, with Roxy's help, has guessed Wilson's plan and reveals it. Tom opines there never was any knife. Tom's good behavior has won his uncle's trust.

TS1 page no.	MS page sequences	Final page nos.	Phase orig. comp.	Description	Narrative
	248A–248C	473–75	ii	**Chapter 26 text.** 'On Saturday evening… aunt and uncle.' Midway down the page originally numbered 248 (see previous entry), SLC decided to insert a passage of 3 leaves. Subsequently leaf 248 was cut in two so the new material could be physically placed between its halves. In the final numbering, the halves became leaves 472 and 476.	Saturday evening: Tom lies, tells Judge he didn't fight because Luigi is an assassin; casts aspersions on the supposed Indian knife.
	249 [foot], 250–56	476–84	ii	**Chapter 26 text.** 'His mother was … to the very'.	Roxy coming to love her son. Tom robbed of his swag on boat to St. Louis. Roxy offers to be sold to pay his debts. Tom sells her to an Arkansas planter for $600. Tom squares his debts.
	257	485	ii	**Chapter 26 text:** 'letter of his reform … her free again.' This leaf replaces part of the original p. 257, which was renumbered (see next entry).	Tom has saved $300 toward setting Roxy free.
	257; 258	486	ii	**Chapter 26 text:** 'For a whole week … guard abaft'. Original p. 257, partly superseded by another 257 (previous entry). Still another p. 257 was canceled and used to fill out a fragmentary leaf later in the MS (p. 572).	[*Deletion*: Tom has saved $150 of the money and given it to Roxy.] Tom's conscience soon recovers. The boat bears Roxy away.

TS1 page no.	MS page sequences	Final page nos.	Phase orig. comp.	Description	Narrative
	259–60	487–88	ii	**Chapter 26 text:** 'the paddle-box . . . down de river!"'	Roxy discovers she has been sold down the river.
		489	v	**Chapter 27 head, motto, and text:** 'On Independence Day . . . work of this kind.' Rowena's drowning is evidently a misplaced insertion, for she figures in the text that follows.	**Chapter 27:** 4 July 1853: Rowena drowns.
	261–308	490–537	ii	**Chapter 27 and 28 text:** 'The political campaign . . . the old skinflint!"' **Chapter 28 head and motto** squeezed onto p. 504.	The Twins campaign, disgracing each other on alternate weeks. Rowena dumps Angelo. Judge Driscoll slanders the Twins publicly. Tom helps, the Judge giving him campaign funds from a tin cash-box. Wilson elected mayor, Luigi alderman. **Chapter 28:** In St. Louis the escaped Roxy turns up at Tom's, speaks of her enslavement in Arkansas. Her enslaver searching for her. Roxy guesses Tom has agreed to capture her; demands the money he saved to redeem her and requires him to get the rest from Judge Driscoll or she will expose his parentage. Tom decides to rob the Judge.
		538	v	*Discarded* **chapter 29 head and motto** *(in CU-MARK).*	
		538 (bis)	v	**Chapter 29 head.**	

TS1 page no.	MS page sequences	Final page orig. nos. comp.	Phase orig. comp.	Description	Narrative
	309–35	539–65	ii	**Chapter 29 text:** 'Dawson's Landing had ... his poor uncle.'	**Chapter 29:** Luigi challenges the Judge, who refuses to duel with an assassin. Digression on childless people. Tom blacks his face with [*deletion*: candle smut in a saucer] burnt cork. Robbing the Judge's safe, Tom wakes him and kills him. The Twins arrive and find the body. Tom flees to St. Louis. Reads in newspaper that the Twins are accused. Now rich, Tom buys Roxy free and goes to Dawson's Landing. Wilson as mayor takes command of the crime scene. The Twins jailed. Fingerprints on the knife handle. Wilson wonders about the mysterious girl. · [*Deletion*: Wilson takes the blackened saucer, with its fingerprints, into evidence.] The Twins indicted. Wilson ponders the case; finds no match among his records for the knife-handle prints.
		566	v	**Chapter 30 head and motto.**	
	336–38	567–69	ii	**Chapter 30 text:** 'The weeks dragged ... just one "hooraw"'.	**Chapter 30:** Fall, 1853: murder trial of the Twins, first day.
	339 [top]	570	ii	**Chapter 30 text:** 'over it if ... I tell you!'". Leaf 570, originally numbered 339, was bisected to make leaves finally numbered 570 and 572, allowing for the insertion of 339½ (final 571) between them. 570 is filled out (later work) by a graft from part of another leaf, bearing canceled text.	Murder trial of the Twins, first day.

TS1 page no.	MS page sequences	Final page nos.	Phase orig. comp.	Description	Narrative
	339½	571	ii	**Chapter 30 text:** 'Pembroke Howard ... unhappy prisoners.' An insertion, augmenting the account of the prosecution's case against the Twins.	Murder trial of the Twins, first day. Howard opens the case for the prosecution.
[339 foot]		572	ii	**Chapter 30 text:** 'Witness after witness ... been sorrowfully'. This is the lower part of leaf originally numbered 339, filled out to size with part of a discarded attempt at p. 257.	Murder trial of the Twins, first day.
	340–47, 347(bis)– 356	573–90	ii	**Chapters 30–31 text:** 'prophetic, and ... until late last'	Murder trial of the Twins, end of first day. Tom visits Wilson in evening and betrays himself with a fingerprint. Reviewing his fingerprint records Wilson finds Tom and Chambers were switched as babies. **Chapter 31:** Murder trial of the Twins, second day.
	357	591	ii	**Chapter 31 text:** 'night, and have ... say a few'. The top half of leaf originally numbered 357, which was bisected to make two leaves, allowing for the insertion of 592–93 between them.	
	357A– 357B	592–93	ii	**Chapter 31 text:** '"May it please ... its proper place."' An insertion.	Wilson grants prosecution's claim that the bloody fingerprints identify the murderer.
[357 foot]		594	ii	**Chapter 31 text:** 'He had made ... of the accused'. This is the lower part of leaf originally numbered 357.	
		594(bis)	v	Blank p. 594, with a canceled aphorism on the verso.	

TS1 page no.	MS page sequences	Final page nos.	Phase orig. comp.	Description	Narrative
	358–91	595–628	ii	**Chapter 31 text:** 'in that fatal ... right, this time.' **Chapter 31 head and motto** inserted on p. 588.	Fingerprints exonerate the Twins. Tom exposed in court. **Chapter 32:** Tom will be tried for the murder. Wilson celebrated. [*Deletion*: Tom hangs himself.] Trouble seating Luigi as alderman. City government grinds to a standstill. Rash of mortgages. Citizens threaten to hang Luigi. The Twins depart. [*Deletion*: Dawson's Landing nicknamed City of Mortgages; sinks into Mississippi.]
	392		ii	*Discarded* **chapter 32** *original ending of MS Morgan (in CU-MARK).*	[*Deletion*: City of Mortgages, continued. Joe and Henry drown.]
	392–95	629–32	iv?	**Chapter 32 revised ending.** 4-page replacement for the original ending of the novel on (original) p. 392. Original page numbers in an odd part of page. Probably quite late.	Roxy turns to the church. Patsy and Betsy survive. Joe and Henry drown. Chambers is rich and disoriented. Tom confesses, is spared life imprisonment because sold into slavery. [*Deletion*: he sells for $2,500.]
	[1]–2	633–633½	v	**Conclusion:** 'March. Thought ... Florence, March, 1893.' An addendum, with a false date.	The implementation of a notebook entry made before 20 December 1892.
[30 foot]			i	Lower part of a TS1 leaf (presumably 30); no text, only an added and canceled directive about leaf placement.	

Mark Twain's Working Notes

These are working notes for the original (or MS Morgan) version of *Pudd'nhead Wilson*. No notes toward the *revised* version of the novel are extant. The chances are good that Clemens made none, for the revision process consisted mostly of abridgment (see the Introduction, pp. 550–54). His notebook from the period of the revision (July 1893) contains only one relevant entry—not a working note but a draft telegram about placing the serial in a magazine.[1]

GROUP A

Judging by their position in Mark Twain's Notebook 32 (TxU-Hu), these entries were made in November 1892, the earliest being shortly before 16 November and the latest no later than 30 November. They show him at work on MS Morgan, still titled at this point "Those Extraordinary Twins," before the invention of Roxy and the reconception of Tom as her son (the letter "R" in these notes stands for Rowena). This is a continuous run of entries, save for the omission of two notes unrelated to *Pudd'nhead Wilson*, shown by a row of dots.

———

Watermelon for Dysentery—discovered by Wilson.[2]
Explains how he knows the twin-clerks' handwritings apart?
He is engaged for the defence in the assault case.

1. Notebook 33, TS p. 24, CU-MARK.
2. Clemens had great faith in this remedy, which he had been familiar with since childhood (and which, since dysentery leads to dehydration, is not wholly without value). In a notebook entry he mentioned its real "discoverer," Thomas Jefferson Chowning, his family's doctor when they lived in Florida, Missouri: "Dr. Tom—watermelon for dysentery" (Notebook 45, TS p. 17, CU-MARK; Ober 2003, 28; Ober 2011).

Tom Driscoll is a sneak thief. Wilson has lost things. Thinks that *girl* is the thief.

Tom. Stole Luigi's knife & looted other houses during the baptizing.—next day after the assault.

Morganatic compliment (said by Wilson.)

Tom says he arrived at noon (Friday) from St. Louis, but ⱨ was really asleep in his room until about that time. But the girl was there at dawn.

Is often away for weeks in St. L.

Arrives in ˌSundayˌ dress of girl in poor circumstances—gets off at lower landing—walks a mile to the village after waiting in the woods & hills till dark, then goes to old empty house of his uncles out by itself in outskirts & keep costume there in a trunk in garret. Has back door key of this house.

Play Romeo & Juliet.

Twins called Scissors

& Lemon Squeezers

Heads appear above cloak

Formerly Lord Buckstone, author (master) of the Queen's hounds.

. . . .

They play piano, sing duets & do Romeo & Juliet—balcony scene—one lays head on other's shoulder & they do a languishing waltz—sailor's hornpipe, both pulling on imaginary ropes.

Last drink Saturday

Baptising—Luigi catches a bad sneezing cold. ~~Luigi~~ ˌAngelo exposes himˌ & makes it worse—takes hot baths & makes it worse—won't give him hot whisky to cure it.

Luigi will get even.

Love scene A & R during week—gags Luigi.

Scene between Judge & Tom—ˌon Market Hall kick.ˌ the will altered giving the money to a charity or something.

Angelo joins ~~Good Templars~~ Teetotalers. Made Chief. But he can't cease to be a Son of Liberty foˌrˌ a month—at a *business* meeting.[3]

Baptists gossip about his going to that infidel meeting.

Judge requires Tom to challenge ˌAngelo—the kicker.ˌ—he won't. Judge ˌslaps Angelo.ˌ disinherits him & challenges L himself.

3. The Independent Order of Good Templars was a temperance society, founded in 1851. Its structure, rituals, and regalia were modeled on those of the Freemasons. In "Personal Habits of the Siamese Twins," Clemens made Chang a member of the Good Templars (SLC 1869b).

L accepts—Angelo pleads. Pistols. An. wounded.

Second, ~~Buckstone~~ ˌHoward˳ & Wilson.

Judge asks Tom who kicked.

Tom hates Angelo on R's account—& accuses him. Judge doubts, but Tom says Angelo whispered it to him with glee, leaving the court.

Judge slaps, without saying why—& hands his card.

Dreary week for Luigi—prayer meˌeˌtings & so on & no whisky. *Camp meeting* Watermelons.

Picnics.

Luigi jumps in & "saves a nigger worth $900." That wins the friendship of everybody.

Angelo takes tedious walks with R.

Scene between Tom & R

Tom writes anonymous insulting letters to R about Twins. Luigi detects & slaps him & is challenged. Pistols. ˌLuigi fires in air.˳ Angelo wounded.

Recovery. Tried by the church for dueling.

A leaves church, joins Campbellites & is baptised.[4]

Calendar discussed by R & 2 old ladies.

L dances on Sunday. Campbellites turn A out. He talks about joining the Mormons—R dissuades him. Joins the Millerites.[5]

~~Luigi says is glad he hadn't this dagger~~

Wilson admires & brings the dagger away. L explains how it is used. W. shows it to Buckstone & Tom & tells them. "Well he didn't have it that night, Tom."

4. The Campbellites, or Disciples of Christ, were followers of father and son Thomas (1763–1854) and Alexander (1788–1866) Campbell. The Campbells advocated individual interpretation of the Bible and practiced adult baptism. Clemens's father and his sister Pamela reportedly inclined to this sect, and in Hannibal around 1850 he attended a Campbellite revival where Alexander Campbell himself preached: "All converted but me. All sinners again in a week" (*Inds*, 288; *HF 2003*, 549).

5. The Millerites were a religious group led by William Miller (1782–1849), who predicted the Second Coming would occur in 1843 or 1844. The sect lost cohesion after what believers called "the Great Disappointment" (which Clemens, in the first entry on p. 474, blames on Luigi). Clemens's Hannibal friends, the Fuqua family, were Millerites (Notebook 38, TS p. 42, CU-MARK).

Shirted for Resurrection.
˅Reason it failed all over the world was that Luigi a sinner couldn't be admitted.˅[6]

Wilson aswim in the law & in fine social life.

New city gov't. ̶A̶ L̶ elected a member on Whig ticket—A ̶d̶e̶f̶e̶a̶t̶e̶d̶ ˅elected˅ on Dem.

Abolitionist?

That girl seen again on the 9th. Tom away.

Judge murdered on 9th. Letters from Tom on 7th & 9th—that dated 7th arrives 8th—that on 9th on 10th (He had left it with a friend to be mailed 9th.
He ̶i̶s̶ ̶t̶e̶l̶e̶g̶r̶a̶p̶h̶e̶d̶ ˅written˅ ̶f̶o̶r̶ (ostensibly) sees murder by telegraph in ˅evening˅ paper of 11th & arrives 12th. [Been hiding in the old house all the time.
He attends funeral.

Will opened—gives him all the property.

Twins in jail?—not a bailable offence. Opinions asked of Judges everywhere. Meantime L wears handcuffs & is kept under watch by the constable.

Wilson & Tom advertise for that girl & seek her high & low—though Tom insists that it *must* have been L.

W examines all his women finger-prints—can't find that girl's.

He took a foot-print of Tom as a boy. Finds a bloody one in his room on a sheet of paper. They take a new one in court. They tally. Taking footprints not persisted in. He took them in red gummy water color on tissue paper

Wilson draws the new will which restores the prop to Tom?

The trial. L sentenced to death.

6. "Shirted for Resurrection" refers to the garments supposedly worn by Millerites in expectation of their ascent to Heaven. Clemens referred to Millerite "ascension shirts" in an 1867 letter to the San Francisco *Alta California* (SLC 1867; changed to "ascension robes" in *The Innocents Abroad* [SLC 1869a, 415]).

Judge hopes gov will pardon him on A's account.

L's character sobers. He is not so wild, now.

GROUP B

Three leaves of holograph notes in the Mark Twain Papers (Box 36A, No. 9) can be dated approximately to late November and/or early December 1892. They are written on the versos of manuscript leaves discarded by Clemens from *Personal Recollections of Joan of Arc*, on which he had been at work in October. These notes reflect a later stage of composition than the notes in Group A, and assume the narrative alterations which would be made in the "re-casting" of MS Morgan. The ordering of the leaves here is arbitrary.

On page B-1, Tom has received a blackmailing letter from his creditors. Roxy tells him to steal the money to pay them, and blackmails him with the threat to reveal his identity to Judge Driscoll. In a note for a later episode, after Tom has killed Judge Driscoll, Chambers and the Twins discover the body. They are jailed as suspects and Chambers is lynched, despite Roxy's efforts to save him.

On page B-2, Roxy has revealed that Tom is her son, but has refused to say who his father is. Tom bears a fanatical grudge against his unknown father. Tom has a violent encounter with the Judge, who blurts out that he is Tom's father, and Tom kills him. Pardoned for the crime because of his value in enslavement, Tom commits suicide. Aspects of this plotline are foreshadowed in certain passages of MS Morgan, all of them later canceled by Clemens.

On page B-3, Clemens considers having Chambers be identified as the rightful heir by his footprints.

[B-1]

MOTIVE

A QUARREL—then:
If you don't slip down *"dis very night"* & steal the money & pay the debt dey'll go to yo' uncle, jes as dey says in de letter.

What happen *den?*

Old Marse dissenhurrit you *again* ~~en once~~ en for *good*, dis time.

En he'll stop de *pension.*

I can't stand *dat,* en I *won't.*

Take yo' choice—hog de money dis night or I tells de Jedge in de mawnin' who you *is.* You'll be on de oction block in 2 minutes.

~~They are on their way home~~

Chambers enters at one door & drops toddy-glass & stands transfixed at same moment that Twins enter & rush to lift the moribund.

—————

Enter Aunt Pratt & proclaims[7] all three. Rushed off to jail. Town rises, snatch Chambers out & would hang or burn him. Roxy interferes & tries to save him—is heroic, but fails. "Well, twould a ben *my* son if I hadn't changed 'em."

[B-2]

Yesterday, what was illegitimacy of birth to a nigger? I could not conceive of its being unpleasant to him—but to-day! ~~Yesterday~~ And if he had a white father, I supposed it was a thing for him to be proud of—but to-day that doubles, trebles, quadruples the shame of my birth. If I can find my father—
That is my search—
That is my life henceforth—

—————

"Spare me!—I am your father! (He was hesitating—had concluded he couldn't do it)
"Now for *that*, you shall die"
    (Kills him)

Tom (Chambers) is to be pardoned—he is glad—but when he finds it is because he is a valuable slave, he commits suicide.)

—————

Which is it in me that is base & which the high?—~~which the~~
The high is either color, when undegraded by slavery—the base is *slavery*-owning *effects*, not slave *blood*—it is the white blood in me but brutalized by slave-owning heredity

7. Declares them to be outlaws (*OED*, "proclaim" *v.* 6.a).

The coward in me is the negro ~~blood~~ blood debased ~~by~~ & cowed by generations of inhumanities practised by the strong over the weak that must not be resented. A sample-scene which he has witnessed.

[B-3]

Shall we have baby foot-marks of Tom & Chambers taken at 10 months to prove legitimacy of Chambers after Tom's suicide & declaration of what Roxy told him?

.Yes..

GROUP C

After the run of entries reprinted in Group A, Notebook 32 is suddenly given over almost entirely to the creation of aphorisms for "Pudd'nhead Wilson's Calendar." Only selected entries are given here; aphorisms which found their way into either version of *Pudd'nhead Wilson* are not included unless they differ substantially from the versions found there. Clemens occasionally interlined alternative word choices, which are omitted here. A complete edition of the notebook is planned for the Mark Twain Papers series.

———

Some people seem to read it Remember the Sabbath day to break it wholly.

When in doubt, tell the truth.

In our day you hear nothing but praises of Penn's .phenomenal. magnanimity toward the Indians, but before the century is out that feature will have disappeared under the overshadowing admiration of his commercial sagacity in buying the State of Pa. for a ton of glass beads & a bale of ho[r]se-blankets.

The vote is a pistol. You may seldom or never draw it, but [when] your life is in danger you will see that it is a valuable thing to have.

Multiply, & replenish the earth. .~~Not one.~~ Duty has never compelled or even *im*pelled any one to obey this command. No religion is strong enough ~~to persuade coerce any one~~ to force or persuade any one to commit this crime, & none has committed it without at some time repenting ~~of~~ it.[8]

8. Genesis 1:28.

There are ten ~~special~~ ˏmajorˏ ~~ˏor specialˏ~~ commandments & 416 minor ones. Four-fifths of the human ~~regard~~ ˏraceˏ ignoreˏ the bulk of them constantly⸍ˏ while⸍ Only a single one of the 417 has found universal obedience: multiply, &c. To it sinner & saint, scholar & ignoramus, ˏChristian &ˏ savage⸍ ~~& civilized~~ are alike loyal.

Kings clothe a favorite with honors & dignities for a brief time, then cast him forth naked & ashamed. This imitates Nature, who flatters us with youth, to insult us with age.

All things are forgetable but insults. (unatoned)

If you put 500 compliments into one scale & a censure into the other, which will weigh the most? If you send a person a present of 500 birds of Paradise & include a polecat, where is the beneficiary's attention going to be centred?

One should celebrate his birth-days until he is 39. But why afterward?

"Two souls with but a single thought" is ~~a quite common thing~~ not a bad average, for it is half a thought apiece. This village has approached it sometimes, but not often enough to attract attention.[9]

We praise the ˏmanˏ mighty~~iest intellect~~ ˏgeniusˏ & despise the ~~meanest~~ ˏidiot;ˏ ~~yet neither the one nor the other is a personal creation.~~ but neither of ~~them~~ ˏthese menˏ made himself. If credit & blame are due, they are due elsewhere.

Pudd'nhead's Aff~~ee~~ˏeˏyisms

The cat possesses these characteristics. She never cringes, to either friend or enemy; ~~she is no one's slave to no one, & not even servant;~~ she is independent; she ~~has~~ is ~~the only creature who~~ never forgets her dignity & never degrades it; she resents injuries whether offered by friend or enemy, & some ~~thou~~ wise people have called this "treachery;" she is faithful to the friend who is faithful to her; she has never had a master—for she has never been a slave, or even a servant; she will not stay where she is abused; she is the most self-respecting & respect-worthy of all the creatures.

9. Clemens quotes a song from the play *Ingomar, the Barbarian*, adapted from the German by Maria Lovell: "Two souls with but a single thought, / Two hearts that beat as one." Clemens had seen and burlesqued *Ingomar* in 1863, in Virginia City, Nevada (SLC 1863); the song was in any case very popular.

Hers is the finest character that has been created. ~~In a word it is the realization of man's dream.~~ She has no hatreds & no contempts. In character the cat is what man would be if he could.

Wilson's "Affyisms"

He paid him a morganatic compliment.

Nov. 30, 1892—57 yrs old. I wish it were it were either 17 or 97.

If all were hanged who had committed murder in their hearts, there would be one man who would have to hang himself.

The average man would - - - - to win the world's ~~love~~ affection; he would - - - - - to win its applause; ~~but~~ & he would skin himself alive to win its envy. If that would do it; which is doubtful.

People venture to say ˌbraveˌ things in the privacy of the pulpit which they would not have the pluck to say in the publicity of print.

There are 3 things that men desire—admiration, love, envy—& the most precious of these is envy.

At this point in this history Rowena went out in the back yard one day & fell in the well & ~~was~~ ˌgotˌ drowned. But it ˌisˌ no matter; there was nothing to her, & she had outlived her usefulness in this book anyway.

When an election goes with our party we praise the people's intelligence, but when it goes against us we explain by saying the people did not comprehend the issues.

When an election goes with us, we see & feel how intelligent this great nation is; when it goes against us we see & feel how hard it is to make this great nation understand the issues.

Bravery is physical cowardice overcome by moral pluck.

Hell & Russia the same.

The trouble about special providences is that as a rule ~~they most have an element of unfairness in them.~~ it is so hard to tell ~~which~~ what was the particular intention of it. ~~When~~ Some think the eating of the children was intended as a judgment upon them; the bears thought it was merely a reward of their own piety.[10]

Unfairness. It was fair enough to destroy S & G for the wickedness of the community, ˌmaybe,ˌ but what harm had the foreign insurance companies done?[11]

it is so difficult to do ~~the desirable thing by the party they are~~ help or hurt the party they are after without ~~involving~~ ˌaffecting˒ some other party who is not concerned.

It may be that the children were delivered to the bears for insulting the prophet but this is hardly proven. That kind of bears would have eaten good children just the same. *Heading.* Opportunity.

If we say such-&-such a thing is as easy as it is for a cow to go through a stovepipe, it is ~~another wa~~ but a fanciful way of saying that that thing is impossible. The figure of the camel & the needle's eye states in the most unqualified and emphatic way that no rich man can be saved.

The figure of the camel & the needle's eye closes heaven absolutely & irrevocably against the rich man—against all rich men without exception; no rich man can by any possibility be saved. ~~Yet there are very few men, either in the church or out of it, who are not trying their best to acquire this very damnation.~~

~~No man would say he would rather get rich than go to heaven, yet all men are trying to get rich. One would think that this fact would make~~

It seems odd that men should shudder at the thought of staining their souls with the pardonable ~~crime of~~ offences of murder, arson, swindling & drunkenness, & yet ~~commit the unpardonable sin of~~ seek energetically to

GROUP D

These entries are from a single page in Notebook 32, after the aphoristic collection in Group C and preceding by one page an entry dated 20 December 1892. At least

10. Alluding to 2 Kings 2:23–24. Compare the version attached to *Pudd'nhead Wilson* chapter 4 (in both texts).

11. Genesis 19:24–25.

one entry concerns the assignment of mottoes to individual chapters. The chapter and page references do not yet use the final ordering and numbering of MS Morgan.

———

No motto for Roxy's share in the duel.

Ch. 24. ~~180 or 90~~ 204

& 25—~~Luigi sick.~~

The doctor's prescription. ˏ& Angelos courageˏ

& 26—Luigi's illness (Betsy) & Angelo's baptism.

~~& 27—Tom, Blake & W. meet & talk on street.~~

28—on 270 drown Rowena—proceed with 4th July.

GROUP E

Selected entries from Notebook 32, written on and perhaps just after 20 December 1892. After the last entry below, the subject of the notes shifts to everyday reminders and entries about *Personal Recollections of Joan of Arc*, on which Clemens resumed work in January 1893.

———

Dec. 20/92. Finished "Pudd'nhead Wilson" last Wednesday, 14th. Began it 11th or 12th of last month, after the King girls left.[12] Wrote more than 60,000 words between Nov. 12 & Dec. 14. One day, wrote 6,000 words ~~between~~ in 13 hours. Another day wrote 5,000 in 11.

March weather.—with all signs.[13]

If you must, you'd better.

12. Grace King and her sister Nan; see the Introduction, p. 000.
13. See PW-MS, Addenda to the Morgan Manuscript, p. 000.

Pudd'nhead Wilson's Calendar for 1894

This promotional calendar was issued by the Century Company in December 1893, for distribution to *Century Magazine* subscribers and "any one who will inclose them a stamp to pay postage." Jacob Blanck (*BAL* 3439) identified three states, A, B, and C, but B is a "ghost" state: Blanck's unique exemplar, at the New York Public Library, collates as state C. Press corrections made at Clemens's insistence show that C is the uncorrected and A the corrected state. Clemens wrote to Olivia on 30 December 1893:

> Please accept these new Calendars. The idiot proofreader changed my language in two of the maxims, & I went over to the Century & turned the atmosphere purple. So they have made the corrections. I also got them to knock out the first two pages, with the finger-marks. (CU-MARK)

The maxims corrupted in state C were those for March, where "count four" became "count a hundred," and August, where the second sentence was transformed into a question. These are corrected in state A.

There are later printings of *Pudd'nhead Wilson's Calendar* for the years 1897, 1899, 1901–1902, and 1904. It is not known who produced these or why.

Pudd'nhead Wilson's Calendar for 1894 is reproduced here in the corrected state A, from a copy in the collection of Kevin Mac Donnell; following which the "finger-marks" pages from state C, suppressed by Clemens, are reproduced from a copy in the Mark Twain Papers.

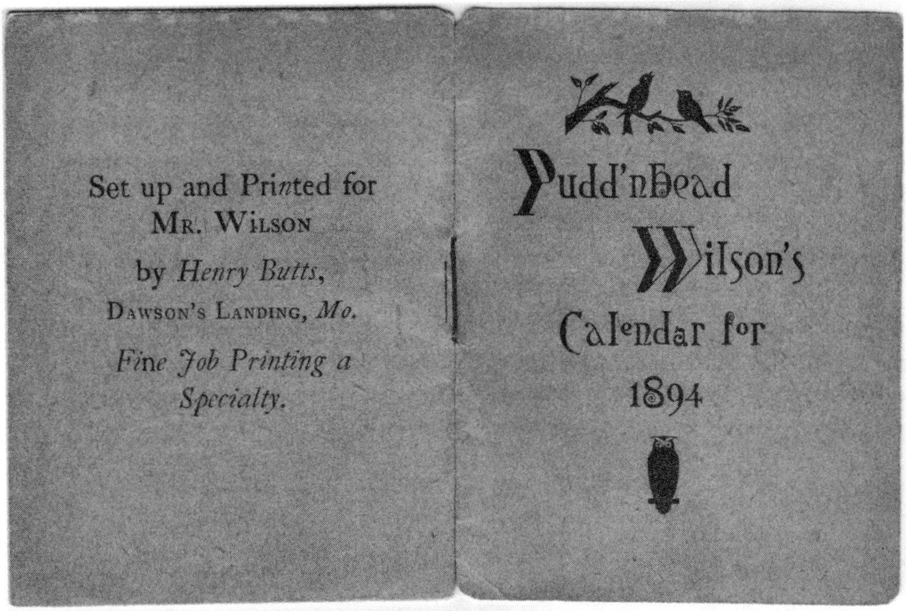

Set up and Printed for
MR. WILSON
by *Henry Butts*,
DAWSON'S LANDING, *Mo.*

*Fine Job Printing a
Specialty.*

Pudd'nhead
Wilson's
Calendar for
1894

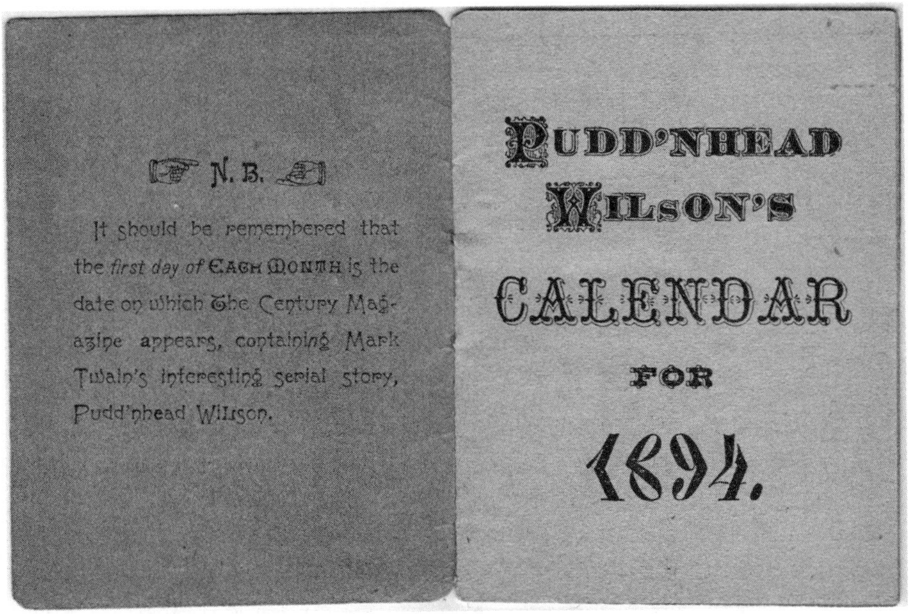

☞ N. B. ☜

It should be remembered that
the *first day of* EACH MONTH is the
date on which The Century Magazine appears, containing Mark
Twain's interesting serial story,
Pudd'nhead Wilson.

PUDD'NHEAD
WILSON'S
CALENDAR
FOR
1894.

Portrait of **MARK TWAIN,**
From an amateur photograph by his friend
"Pudd'nhead Wilson."

2

JANUARY.

S	M	T	W	T	F	S
..	1	2	3	4	5	☉
7	8	9	10	11	12	13
☽	15	16	17	18	19	20
☺	22	23	24	25	26	27
☾	29	30	31	..	..	..

Nothing so needs reform-
ing as other people's habits.

3

FEBRUARY.

S	M	T	W	T	F	S
..	..	..	..	1	2	3
4	☉	6	7	8	9	10
11	12	☽	14	15	16	17
18	☺	20	21	22	23	24
25	26	27	☾	..	..	..
..	..	..	..	..	..	..

Behold the fool saith, "put not all
thine eggs in the one basket," which is
but a manner of saying, "scatter your
money and your attention," but the
wise man saith, put all thine eggs in
the one basket and—*watch that basket.*

4

MARCH.

S	M	T	W	T	F	S
..	..	..	..	1	2	3
4	5	6	☉	8	9	10
11	12	13	☽	15	16	17
18	19	20	☺	22	23	24
25	26	27	28	☾	30	31

When angry, count four; when
bery angry, swear.

5

April.

S	M	T	W	T	F	S
1	2	3	4	☉	6	7
8	9	10	11	☽	13	14
15	16	17	18	☺	20	21
22	23	24	25	26	☾	28
29	30	...	...	...	...	...
...	...					

April 1st: This is the day upon which we are reminded of what we are on the other three hundred and sixty-four.

MAY.

S	M	T	W	T	F	S
...	...	1	2	3	4	☉
6	7	8	9	10	11	☽
13	14	15	16	17	18	☺
20	21	22	23	24	25	26
☾	28	29	30	31	...	...

It were not best that we should all think alike; it is difference of opinion that makes horse-races.

JUNE.

S	M	T	W	T	F	S
...	..	...	...	...	1	2
☉	4	5	6	7	8	9
☽	11	12	13	14	15	16
17	☺	19	20	21	22	23
24	25	☾	27	28	29	30
...	...					

When I reflect upon the number of disagreeable people who I know have gone to a better world, I am moved to lead a different life.

JULY.

S	M	T	W	T	F	S
1	2	☉	4	5	6	7
8	☽	10	11	12	13	14
15	16	☺	18	19	20	21
22	23	24	☾	26	27	28
29	30	31	..	...	...	...

July 4th: Statistics show that we lose more fools on this day than in all the other days of the year put together. This proves, by the number left in stock, that one Fourth of July per year is now inadequate, the country has grown so.

August.

S	M	T	W	T	F	S
..	..	..	☽	2	3	4
5	6	7	☾	9	10	11
12	13	14	15	☺	17	18
19	20	21	22	23	☾	25
26	27	28	29	☽	31	..
..	..	..	..	..	..	..

Why is it that we rejoice at a birth and grieve at a funeral? It is because we are not the person involved.

10

September.

S	M	T	W	T	F	S
—	—	—	—	—	—	—
..	..	..	..	..	..	1
2	3	4	5	☽	7	8
9	10	11	12	13	☺	15
16	17	18	19	20	21	☾
23	24	25	26	27	28	☽
30	..	..	..	..	..	..

If you pick up a starving dog and make him prosperous, he will not bite you. This is the principal difference between a dog and a man.

11

October.

S	M	T	W	T	F	S
..	1	2	3	4	5	☽
7	8	9	10	11	12	13
☺	15	16	17	18	19	20
☾	22	23	24	25	26	27
☽	29	30	31	..	..	..
..	..	..	..	..	..	..

October: This is one of the peculiarly dangerous months to speculate in stocks in. The others are July, January, September, April, November, May, March, June, December, August and February.

12

NOVEMBER.

S	M	T	W	T	F	S
..	..	..	..	..	1	2	3
4	☽	6	7	8	9	10
11	12	☺	☾	14	15	16	17
18	☾	20	21	22	23	24
25	26	☽	28	29	30	..

Few things are harder to put up with than the annoyance of a good example.

13

DECEMBER

S	M	T	W	T	F	S
...	...	...	...	...	...	1
2	3	4	5	6	7	8
9	10	11	☺	13	14	15
16	17	18	☽	20	21	22
23	24	25	☾	27	28	29
30	31	...	...	...	...	...

Even the clearest and most perfect circumstantial evidence is likely to be at fault, after all, and therefore ought to be received with great caution.—Take the case of any pencil sharpened by any woman: if you have witnesses, you will find she did it with a knife; but if you take simply the aspect of the pencil, you will say she did it with her teeth.

14

Persons desirous of knowing more of

PUDD'NHEAD WILSON

are respectfully referred to the pages of THE CENTURY MAGAZINE, where the adventures of Mr. Wilson, as chronicled by

Mark Twain,

are now appearing. This story, like several of Mark Twain's romances, has for its scene a steamboat town on the Mississippi River forty years ago. It is perhaps the most dramatic novel that Mark Twain has ever written. "Pudd'nhead Wilson," a hard-headed country lawyer, furnishes much of the fun that one naturally expects to find in a narrative by the author of "The Innocents Abroad," but he appears in quite another light in the murder trial which forms the thrilling climax of the story. The story introduces a novel and ingenious employment of science in the detection of crime, and is altogether one of the strongest and most interesting that Mark Twain has ever written. THE CENTURY is for sale at all book-stores and news-stands. Price, 35 cents a copy; $4.00 a year.

15

THE CENTURY CO. has bought well nigh the complete literary "output" of Mark Twain during his year of residence abroad, and both *The Century* and *St. Nicholas* will have serial stories by this popular humorist, among the attractions of the new year. "Pudd'nhead Wilson," which is now appearing in *The Century*, was written near Florence, Italy, as is certified in the preface of the story, as follows:

"Given under my hand this second day of January, 1893, at the Villa Viviani, village of Settignano, three miles back of Florence, on the hills—the same certainly affording the most charming view to be found on this planet, and with it the most dream-like and enchanting sunsets to be found in any planet or even in any solar system—and given, too, in the swell room of the house, with the busts of Cerretani senators and other grandees of this line looking approvingly down upon me as they used to look down upon Dante, and mutely asking me to adopt them into my family, which I do with pleasure, for my remotest ancestors are but spring chickens compared with these robed and stately antiques, and it will be a great and satisfying lift for me, that six hundred years will." *Mark Twain.*

16

DO NOT FAIL TO READ
PUDD'NHEAD WILSON.

Read what is said of it:

Gives promise of being Mark Twain's masterpiece in style and plot.—*Union Signal,* Chicago.

Mark Twain begins in THE CENTURY a new novel, "Pudd'nhead Wilson," which promises to be of absorbing interest. The scene is laid in Missouri, and starts out very bravely with the mixing up of two babies by a rebellious slave girl who is nearly white—her child and that of her master. Now, if any one wants any more prospect of excitement than that—he is, indeed, hard to please. One quite trembles at the toils with which he sees the volatile Twain will envelop the children.—*News,* Chicago.

The story opens excellently and promises to rank among the author's best work.—*Examiner,* N. Y.

"Pudd'nhead Wilson" is at once humorous and pathetic.—*Open Court,* Chicago.

Promises to surpass any of the author's previous attempts.—*Review,* Oberlin, O.

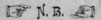 N. B.

It should be remembered that the *first day of* EACH MONTH is the date on which The Century Magazine appears, containing Mark Twain's interesting serial story, Pudd'nhead Wilson.

THUMB PRINTS
From Pudd'nhead Wilson's Collection.
" Every human being carries with him from his cradle to his grave certain physical marks which do not change their character, and by

1

which he can always be identified—and that without shade of doubt or question. These marks are his signature, his physiological autograph, so to speak, and this autograph cannot be counterfeited, nor can he disguise it or hide it away, nor can it become illegible by the wear and the mutations of time. This signature is not his face—age can change that beyond recognition; it is not his hair, for that can fall out; it is not his height, for duplicates of that exist; it is not his form, for duplicates of that exist also, whereas this signature is each man's very own—there is no duplicate of it among the swarming populations of the globe!"—

Pudd'nhead Wilson's Speech
in defense of the Twins

2

JANUARY.

S	M	T	W	T	F	S
..	1	2	3	4	5	☉
7	8	9	10	11	12	13
☽	15	16	17	18	19	20
☺	22	23	24	25	26	27
☾	29	30	31	..	..	..

Nothing so needs reforming as other people's habits.

3

"Finger-marks" pages from state C.

Contract with the American Publishing Company

The contract for the American publication of *Pudd'nhead Wilson* and *Those Extraordinary Twins* is in the Beinecke Rare Book and Manuscript Library at Yale University. It was signed in New York on 24 August 1894 by Henry Huttleston Rogers as attorney for Olivia L. Clemens (as the copyright holder—see the Introduction, p. 555, n. 130); by Bainbridge Colby, the assignee of the bankrupt Charles L. Webster and Company; by Francis E. Bliss; and by a notary, John Flynn. The document is typed, with handwritten additions and corrections.

AGREEMENT made this 24th day of August 1894, between OLIVIA L. CLEMENS, by her attorney, Henry H. Rogers, party of the first part, and the AMERICAN PUBLISHING COMPANY, of Hartford, Connecticut, party of the second part WITNESSETH:

WHEREAS the party of the first part is the owner of a certain work entitled "Pudd'nhead Wilson", written by Samuel L. Clemens and recently published in serial form in the Century Magazine, and is also the owner of a certain unpublished work by the same author entitled "Those Extraordinary Twins—a postscript to Pudd'nhead Wilson", and

WHEREAS the party of the second part is desirous of publishing the said "Pudd'nhead Wilson" and the post-script thereto entitled "Those Extraordinary Twins", in book form,

NOW, THEREFORE, in consideration of the premises and the conditions and covenants hereinafter contained, and of the sum of Fifteen Hundred Dollars ($1500.00) to be paid to the party of the first part by the party of the second part, in instalments as follows:

Two Hundred and Fifty Dollars ($250.00) on September 1st, 1894; Two Hundred and Fifty Dollars ($250.00) on October 1st, 1894, and the balance in monthly instalments of One Hundred Dollars ($100.00) each on the first day of each succeeding month until the said sum of Fifteen Hundred Dollars ($1500.00) is fully paid, IT IS MUTUALLY AGREED by the parties hereto as follows:

I. The party of the first part gives to the party of the second part the exclusive right for the period of three years from the date hereof, to publish said work to be entitled "Pudd'nhead Wilson" with such reference ~~to~~ in the title to the added chapters called "Those Extraordinary Twins" as shall seem advisable to the party of the second part, or to be otherwise entitled as the parties hereto shall mutually agree hereafter;

II: The party of the second part agrees that it will publish in book form the above mentioned literary matter, as soon as practicable after the receipt of the same, assume all cost of publication, copyright the book, place it on the market in good style, and keep the market at all times supplied, and sell the same as a subscription book, with the privilege, however, of also selling the same to the trade or otherwise, should it seem to the party of the second part advisable.

III. IT IS FURTHER AGREED between the parties hereto that said Olivia L. Clemens, party of the first part, shall receive from the party of the second part, one-half (1/2) of the gross profits arising from the publication and sale of said "Pudd'nhead Wilson" and "Those Extraordinary Twins" in addition to the Fifteen Hundred Dollars ($1500.00) hereinabove mentioned, which shall not be a credit to the party of the second part or a charge against the party of the first part in computing the division of the gross profits aforesaid.

Said gross profits to be computed on the final day of each calendar quarter, to wit, September 30th, December 31st, March 31st, and June 30th during the continuation of this contract, and a statement thereof with payment to be given to the party of the first part within two weeks time thereafter.

IV. IT IS FURTHER AGREED that the gross profits shall include the entire difference between the price which the party of the second part shall realize on the sale of said book and the cost of manufacture.

The cost of manufacture is to include only the cost of plates, and repairs thereof, paper, printing, binding and boxes for shipment, together with insurance on the plates, sheets and finished copies of the said book. Any portion of the printing or binding, which may be done by the party of the second part shall be charged for at a fair and reasonable rate for such work, to be approved by the party of the first part; or in case of disagreement as to any charge, the matter shall be referred to an impartial arbitrator to be selected by the parties hereto.

V. The party of the second part AGREES FURTHER to keep an accurate account of the sales and expenses incident to the publication of said book, and to render unto the party of the first part on the final day of every calendar quarter as aforesaid, an account of the number of copies of said book, which shall have been sold during the three months preceding, and shall exhibit on request to the party of the first part or her agent, all books, papers or vouchers relating to the sale and publication of the said book.

VI. The party of the first part agrees that she will do nothing to retard or interfere with the sale of said book.

VII. In the event that the party of the second part fails to perform any of the conditions of this contract, on its part to be performed, the right to publish and sell the said book shall revert to the party of the first part, who shall have the right of purchasing the plates, engravings or finished or unfinished stock in the possession of the party of the second part at a fair valuation, but nothing herein shall be construed as obliging the part of the first part to make such purchase; if for any other reason this contract should be terminated before its expiration, and in any event, at its expiration, the party of the second part shall be allowed to sell the stock remaining on its hands unsold, upon all the conditions hereinabove set forth.

IN WITNESS WHEREOF the parties hereto have hereunto set their hands and seals the day and year first above written.

IN THE PRESENCE OF:

John Flynn   The American Publishing Company
Bainbridge Colby   By Frank E Bliss Prest

                                          Olivia L. Clemens
                                          by Henry H Rogers Atty

American Publishing Company Advertising Flyer

The American Publishing Company printed and distributed this flyer as an advertisement for their edition (1894). The original measures, folded, approximately 6 inches by 9½ inches, with a two-page spread in the center. The first page uses the "frontispiece" for *Those Extraordinary Twins* by Frank M. Senior. The fourth is a sample page from the edition, showing the style of the marginal illustrations. The advertising pages are strewn with verse quotations. Two are from Shakespeare: "We came into the world . . ." (*The Comedy of Errors*, act 5, scene 1), and "So we grew together . . ." (*A Midsummer Night's Dream*, act 3, scene 2). "And make all laugh who never laughed before" was a stock advertising tag; the American Publishing Company had used it to promote *Roughing It* ten years earlier (publisher's advertisement in Miller 1874). The flyer is reproduced from a copy in the collection of Kevin Mac Donnell.

DOUBLE ATTRACTION!
• • • • •

A NEW BOOK
•→ BY ←•
Mark Twain.

THE
Companion Stories.

THE TRAGEDY OF
Pudd'nhead Wilson.

AND THE COMEDY
Those Extraordinary Twins.
With Marginal Illustrations.

"We came into the world, like
brother and brother;
And now, let's go hand in hand,
not one before another."

THE GREAT BOOK OF THE YEAR.

A NOVELTY in both text and illustration, possessing the selling qualities of the author's earlier works — "Innocents Abroad," "A Tramp Abroad," etc. Artistic marginal sketches, vividly portraying each character and scene.

SOLD ONLY BY SUBSCRIPTION.

Octavo volume — size, 6 x 9 inches; nearly 500 pages, over 400 illustrations, and will be delivered at the following prices:

In Finest Quality Cloth with Gold Designs, . $2.50
In Leather (Library Style), ... 3.25
In Half Levant Morocco, Gilt Top, . . . 5.00

AGENTS WANTED   AMERICAN PUBLISHING CO., Hartford, Conn.

"Tragedy, Pathos, and Humor."

PUDD'NHEAD WILSON IS A DRAMATIC NOVEL. Southern life of fifty years or more furnishes the material for the narrative, which is told in Mark Twain's peculiar characteristic way. Nothing for years has so clearly depicted the character of that period in such a realistic manner; the reader lives with the people, absorbing their joys and sorrows, and receives impressions of life in an old-time Mississippi River town that will never be forgotten.

THOSE EXTRAORDINARY TWINS FURNISHES most of the humor; the pent-up fun that was intended for the other story the author had to extract and make another tale of. "There is a time to laugh," and those who read this story will clearly see that the time has arrived.

> "And make all laugh who never laughed before,
> And those who always laugh, make laugh the more."

· · · **The Author** had a difficult time writing this book, planning at first to produce a short, fantastic sketch for magazine use, but once started he could not end it until it assumed its present complete shape. His own characteristic explanation of the matter is as follows:

other at every turn and created no end of confusion and annoyance. I did not know what was the matter with it, for I was afraid it would unseat the reader's reason. It took me months to make that discovery. I carried the manuscript back and forth across the Atlantic two or three times, and read it and studied over it on shipboard; and at last I saw where the difficulty lay. I had no further trouble. I pulled one of the stories out by the roots, and left the other one—a kind of literary Cæsarean operation. . . Originally the story was called "Those Extraordinary Twins." I meant to make it very short. . . . But the tale kept spreading along and spreading along, and other people got to intruding themselves and taking up more and more room with their talk and their affairs. . . . When the book was finished and I came to look around to see what had become of the team I had originally started out with . . they were nowhere to be seen; they had disappeared from the story some time or other. I hunted about and found them—found them stranded, idle, forgotten, and permanently useless. It was very awkward. . . . The story was unsatisfactory. . . . There was a radical defect somewhere, and I must search it out and cure it. . . . The defect turned out to be the one already spoken of—two stories in one, a farce and a tragedy. So I pulled out the farce and left the tragedy. This left the original team in, but only as mere names, not as characters. Their prominence was wholly gone; they were not even worth drowning, so I removed them."

Thus the tragedy was completed and was given a new name — "Pudd'nhead Wilson." The story which was pulled out — the farce — retained the original title —"Those Extraordinary Twins."

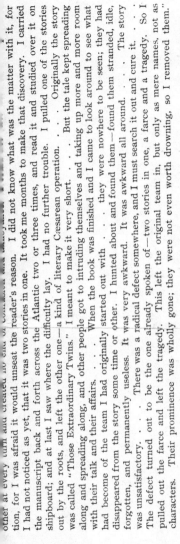

"So we grew together,
Like to a double cherry, seeming parted,
But yet an union in partition."

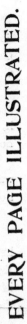

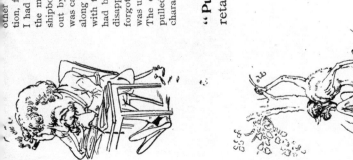

Gazette. — "One of his very best stories."

Ideas. — "Marked not alone by wit but by dramatic promise."

Examiner. — "Promises to rank among the Author's best work."

Presbyterian Banner. — "The Author's humorous vein at its best."

Christian Advocate. — "Bids fair to be one of Mark Twain's best."

Spirit of the Times. — "Mark Twain is a philosopher and great humorist."

Churchman. — "The reader will begin to smile at the very first paragraph."

Ladies' Home Journal. — "How could Mark Twain avoid making his novel humorous."

Am. Woman's Ill. World. — "The irresistible nonsense of P. W. satisfies ones cravings."

EVERY PAGE ILLUSTRATED.

liberty—he was not committing any sin that God would remember against him in the Last Great Day.

" Name the thief ! "

For the fourth time Mr. Driscoll had said it, and always in the same hard tone. And now he added these words of awful import :

" I give you one minute "—he took out his watch. " If at the end of that time you have not confessed, I will not only sell all four of you, *but*— I will sell you DOWN THE RIVER ! "

It was equivalent to condemning them to hell ! No Missouri negro doubted this. Roxy reeled in her tracks and the color vanished out of her face ; the others dropped to their knees as if they had been shot ; tears gushed from their eyes, their supplicating hands went up, and three answers came in the one instant :

" I done it ! "

" I done it ! "

" I done it !—have mercy, marster—Lord have mercy on us po' niggers ! "

" Very good," said the master, putting up his watch, " I will sell you *here* though you don't

Illustrating Pudd'nhead Wilson

This Appendix is meant to give an overview and a sampling of the illustrations in early editions of *Pudd'nhead Wilson* and *Those Extraordinary Twins*. Some information is repeated from the Introduction, where it is more fully documented.

On its original publication in the *Century Magazine* (1893–94), each of the seven installments of *Pudd'nhead Wilson* had a single full-page illustration: a photographic "frontispiece" of Mark Twain for the first installment and six engraved drawings by Louis Loeb; these are reproduced in the present edition of the revised text. Loeb's designs are in the realistic style typical of the best magazines of the era and are closely based on the text; in pursuit of historical authenticity, he consulted his older colleague, illustrator Daniel Beard, for information on the clothing of the antebellum period. According to Beard, Clemens approved the Loeb illustrations and called them "beautiful" but noted that they differed from his own conceptions.

The first *Century* installment also had an engraved title piece, not by Loeb, featuring a vignette of Roxy with the infant Tom and Chambers. Against the explicit indications of the text, it depicts Roxy as visibly darker-skinned than her charges. It is decorated with flowering cotton branches—stock plantation imagery, not representative of the "grain and pork" country around Dawson's Landing, though conceivably connected to the later episode of Roxy's bondage in Arkansas (Freitag 2015, 34–35).

The first American edition (American Publishing Company, 1894) took a totally different approach to illustrating the story, filling the margins of every page with a total of more than four hundred small-scale pictures. The artwork, by Frank M. Senior and Calvin H. Warren, has not been much admired. In particular, the pictures of Black people—Senior's more than Warren's—are crude racist caricatures. A selection of these has been included here: to omit them would be to distort the historical record and to "whitewash" racist attitudes which went into the book's production, marketing, and reception. The American first edition's illustrations

Details from Louis Loeb's illustrations for the *Century Magazine*: left, the young Roxy (chapter 4); right, the older Roxy in blackface and men's clothing (chapter 18).

Pictorial title piece of first installment, *Century Magazine*, December 1893.

are not used in the present editions of the revised *Pudd'nhead Wilson* and *Those Extraordinary Twins*, partly because Clemens seems not to have seen or approved them before publication, and partly because doing so would have required us to adopt the exact format of the first edition.

These selected images from the American first edition have been given captions by the editor—they are not captioned in the original. Senior's illustrations are marked "FMS" and Warren's "CHW."

"A Whisper to the Reader" (FMS).

In the African Methodist Church (FMS).

(FMS).

Tom assaults Chambers (FMS).

Luigi's Indian knife (CHW).

Roxy and her friend on the plantation (FMS).

Roxy, in blackface and men's clothing, confronts Tom (FMS).

Wilson makes his discovery (CHW).

A spectator at the trial (CHW).

"The person who did it is in this house": Roxy in court (CHW).

The Twins, as they appear in
Those Extraordinary Twins (FMS).

Nancy, in *Those Extraordinary Twins* (FMS).

Mark Twain's British publishers, Chatto and Windus, had substantially printed off their edition of *Pudd'nhead Wilson* before the American edition, with its suite of illustrations and its supplement *Those Extraordinary Twins*, was even in the planning stages. The Chatto edition (1894) reproduced the illustrations from the *Century Magazine*. The English-language edition published for Continental Europe (Bernhard Tauchnitz, 1895) was unillustrated, like the rest of the series in which it appeared.

In 1899 the American Publishing Company republished *Pudd'nhead Wilson* in their collected edition of the *Writings of Mark Twain*, commissioning a new set of illustrations for the volume. The decision to retire Senior and Warren's illustrations[1] was not prompted by regret for their insensitivity, as is shown by the choice of Edward W. Kemble (1861–1933) to make their replacements. In 1884, Mark Twain had employed Kemble to illustrate *Adventures of Huckleberry Finn*, which earned the artist a reputation as a specialist in "humorous" caricatures of African Americans; at the time he was hired to illustrate *Pudd'nhead Wilson*, his recent publications included the collections *Kemble's Coons* (1896) and *Comical Coons* (1898). Kemble made six illustrations for the American Publishing Company's 1899 edition, some or all of which continued to decorate their publications, and those of Harper and Brothers, well into the twentieth century.

1. With one exception: Senior's "frontispiece" to *Those Extraordinary Twins* was retained, reworked as a semiphotographic collage.

"Roxy Harvesting among the Kitchens," by E. W. Kemble (from SLC 1899b). Kemble has been reproached for misrepresenting Roxy as a "gross and comic Aunt Jemima" (Fiedler 1955a, 17), but comparison with his other picture of Roxy (see p. 506) confirms that she is the figure glimpsed behind the man, not the woman holding the basket (Sollors 2002, 70–72, 81–83).

"Roxy among the Field Hands," by E. W. Kemble (from SLC 1899b).

Pudd'nhead Wilson, retitled and issued with *A Connecticut Yankee* as a paperback (Royal Books G-28, ca. 1954). The same series included *Savage Mistress* and *Dope Doll*.

["The Man with Negro Blood"]

In 1883 or 1884, Clemens made these notes for a story on themes which would later inform *Pudd'nhead Wilson*. The story remained unwritten. The manuscript (in CU-MARK) is four pages, in pencil, and is untitled; it is not clear who supplied the title by which it has come to be known. For discussion, see Pettit 1974, 142–43, and Fishkin 1991.

Instead of writing out the name of his protagonist (which he had perhaps not yet invented), Clemens writes two crosses or Xs, which a printer would have known to set as asterisks.

Before the War ˏhe is born—ˏ ˏ1850.ˏ
ˏThe Accident,ˏ ——— ˏMch or Apl—1860.ˏ
The Saleˏ, April, 1860.ˏ

The War.

The wanderings.
ˏ(His father his master & mean.)ˏ

ˏDoes not deny but speaks of his n blood.ˏ His struggles—education—advertises & hunts for his mother & sister—at last gives them up. At last, seeing even the best educated negro is at a disadvantage, besides being always insulted, clips his wiry hair close, wears gloves always, (to conceal his telltale nails,) & passes for a white man, in a Northern city.

Makes great success—becomes wealthy.

Falls in love with his ~~sister,~~ ͵cousin,͵ ⸮ 7 years younger than himself.—he used to "nuss"[1] her, on the plantation.

She & her father are very poor; he blows & gasses & talks blood & keeps up the lost cause fires, & she supports him. She is a very fine & every way noble & lovely girl; but of course the moment the revelation comes that he is 1/16 negro, she abhors him. ͵Her father͵ & she wears fictitious names, to indulge his pride, & he makes a mystery of their former history—which enables him to aggrandize it & at the same time prevents either of them from saying anything which would lead * * to recognize them.

He ͵* *͵ keeps his early history a secret, of course—& it is the only secret which he has from *her*. All the towns people try to dig out his secret, but fail.

At the climax when his mother & sister (who is waiting on the table,) expose his origin & his girl throws him & her cousin (proud, poor, & not sweet), voices *her* horror, he is at least able to retort, "Well, rail on; but there is one ~~thing~~ ͵fact͵ which Atlantics of talk cannot wash away; & that is, that this loathsome negro is your *brother*."

———

At time of the climax he is telling the stirring tale of the ͵heroic͵ devotion of a poor negro mother to her son—of course not mentioning that he was ͵the͵ son & that *his* ͵is the͵ mother who bears the scar which he has described. Then she steps forward & shows the scar she got in saving hi~~s~~ ͵m͵ from his own father's brutality. So this gassy man is *his* father, & it is his niece whom * * loves, & who with (perhaps) his daughter, supports him.

1. Nurse.

Introduction

The year 1885 found Mark Twain flourishing. He was America's most famous author, and his newest book, *Adventures of Huckleberry Finn*, was an artistic and commercial triumph. It was the first publication of his own firm, Charles L. Webster and Company (named after his niece's husband, the junior partner); its second publication was the phenomenally successful *Personal Memoirs* of Ulysses S. Grant. With his wife, Olivia, and their three daughters, Susy, Clara, and Jean, he lived in the upscale literary enclave of Nook Farm in Hartford, Connecticut. His fiftieth birthday, on 30 November 1885, brought congratulatory letters and poems from around the world. "I am frightened at the proportions of my prosperity," he told a friend; "it seems to me that whatever I touch turns to gold."[1]

It was not long before Webster and Company seemed to justify his fear. As a publisher, Clemens was guided by his conviction that "nine-tenths of the requisite of success was that there should be a big name back of the good book," and in this belief he directed his company to concentrate on books by or about Great Men.[2] In April 1886 he contracted to publish the authorized biography of Pope Leo XIII, persuading himself, in what William Dean Howells later called "a sort of delirious exultation," that "not only would every Catholic buy it, but every Catholic must, as he was a good Catholic, as he hoped to be saved."[3] In the event, sales of the biography were disappointing. Webster and Company also made a contract with the Rev. Henry Ward Beecher to publish his autobiography, as well as the long-awaited second

1. *MTB*, 2:831, 2:826–29, where the quotation is described as something said to "a friend at his home one night" (2:831).
2. 11 Nov 1885 to Charles L. Webster, NPV, in *MTLP*, 192–95.
3. Howells 1910, 73–74.

Mark Twain, 1892. Photograph by J. C. Schaarwächter, photographer to the court of Kaiser Wilhelm II, Berlin (CU-MARK).

volume of his *Life of Jesus*, but neither book had been completed when Beecher died in March 1887. At the same time, it came to light that a Webster Company bookkeeper had embezzled $25,000 from his employers.[4] In 1888, Webster himself, ill and overworked, was forced by Clemens to take a leave of absence and was soon forced out of the company altogether. Webster's position as manager and part-owner of the firm devolved upon his former assistant, Frederick J. Hall (1860–1926), first hired three years earlier as a stenographer.[5]

4. *N&J3*: 272 n. 156; 338 n. 114; 283 n. 194.
5. *AutoMT1*, 486, note on 79.21–22; *N&J3*, 116 n. 174; 615 n. 151.

The profits from Grant's *Memoirs* seemed to disappear into production expenses for other books. Webster and Company was severely undercapitalized and borrowed heavily to meet such everyday expenses as book-making materials, manufacturing, and royalties. The loans were largely from the Mount Morris Bank of New York (which was itself undercapitalized), but Hall, Olivia Clemens, and Clemens himself, as well as other friends and relations, all lent large sums to the struggling business. Even the healthy sales of *Huckleberry Finn* could not offset the cost of producing and promoting a poorly paying list of books. Particularly burdensome was the eleven-volume *Library of American Literature*. Even after Webster and Company converted itself from a subscription publisher to a trade publisher, the *Library* continued to be sold by subscription. Customers received the entire set upon payment of the first monthly installment of three dollars. Over the next year the company would collect a further thirty dollars—if it could; meanwhile it had already borne the steep costs of printing, binding, and the sales agent's commission. Clemens would later blame the *Library* for "the lingering suicide of Charles L. Webster and Company."[6]

By the spring of 1891, Clemens knew that the company, if it were to become profitable and resume paying dividends, would need larger infusions of capital than he and his friends could provide.[7] Clemens himself could not provide more, because for ten years he had been investing heavily in a typesetting machine invented by James W. Paige (1842–1917). Clemens was certain this machine would revolutionize the printing industry, especially for newspapers publishing vast daily runs. All over the world typesetting was still done the way Gutenberg had done it, with a laborer—a compositor—selecting metal types, character by character, placing them in a "stick," then locking the types into a page forme for printing or stereotyping. Paige's invention was a mechanical compositor powered by electricity: an operator sat at a keyboard and directed the machine as it retrieved and placed the types, automatically justified the line, and sorted and distributed the types for reuse. But the complexity of the Paige compositor, with more than eighteen thousand parts, led to frequent breakdowns and time-consuming repairs. Moreover, Paige was not alone: there were many other inventors trying to devise a machine that would be universally adopted.

6. *AutoMT2*, 78; *N&J3*, 612–13 n. 141; Frederick J. Hall to Albert Bigelow Paine, 14 Jan 1909, in Hall 1947.

7. Unidentified day in April 1891 to Joseph T. Goodman, ViU.

Out of his own pocket Clemens had long paid Paige's salary and expenses, which by 1891 totaled at least $170,000—roughly equivalent to $5 million today. In addition, Clemens, by the terms of his agreement with Paige, was pledged to raise a capital fund of $250,000 by 13 February 1891 or else forfeit his exclusive ownership of the invention.[8] The crisis came two days before that deadline, when the man he had counted on to help raise the money, Senator John P. Jones of Nevada, told Clemens he was unable to interest investors in Paige's machine: they had no confidence in its inventor, and some of them were already backing the rival typesetter developed by the Mergenthaler Linotype Company, which would ultimately prevail.[9] Clemens wrote to Jones: "For a whole year you have breathed the word of promise to my ear to break it to my hope at last. It is stupefying, it is unbelievable."[10]

With a diminished share in the expected profits, and with Paige dismaying investors by his endless tinkering, Clemens resolved to wash his hands of the matter. "I've shook the machine," he wrote to his brother Orion in February 1891, "& never wish to see it or hear it mentioned again. It is superb, it is perfect, it can do 10 men's work. It is worth billions; & when the pigheaded lunatic, its inventor, dies, it will instantly be capitalized & make the Clemens children rich."[11] He spoke too soon; his faith in the machine would not die so easily. But without its imminent bonanza, he could not recapitalize Webster and Company, and he could no longer maintain the Hartford house and the grand lifestyle that went with it. In May 1891, Clemens announced he was taking the family to Europe, intending to stay perhaps two years.[12] He concealed the financial reason for the move, telling his friends it was to treat Olivia's chronic heart disease, and telling the newspapers that it was "to educate my little girls."[13] In Europe, where exchange rates strongly favored the United States dollar, Clemens could support his family by the pen, and Olivia could receive treatment at continental hydropathic spas. Everything

8. On the Paige Compositor see Mark Twain's autobiographical "The Machine Episode" in *AutoMT1*, 101–6, and the notes at 494–98; Legros and Grant 1916, 378–91; and Goble 1997–98.

9. *N&J3*, 572–73.

10. 14–28 Feb 1891 to John P. Jones, draft letter in CU-MARK; letter possibly never sent.

11. 25 Feb 1891 to OC, CU-MARK.

12. Bok 1891.

13. Blathwayt 1891; 20 May 1891 to William Dean Howells, NN-BGC, in *MTHL*, 2:645–46.

was packed up, the Hartford house was shuttered, and new situations were found for the servants. Susy was pulled out of Bryn Mawr College, where she had not yet completed her first year.[14]

The Clemenses, accompanied by Olivia's sister, Susan Crane (1836–1924), sailed from New York on 6 June 1891 aboard the French Line steamship *La Gascogne*. Over the course of the next year, they sampled health spas and medical advice at Aix-les-Bains, Marienbad, Franzensbad, Ouchy, Berlin, and Menton. May 1892 found them in Florence, where they visited with fellow expatriates, including the American scholar Willard Fiske (1831–1904) and the English author Janet Duff Gordon Ross (1842–1927), both of whom lived in magnificent villas outside the city.[15] Charmed with the climate and the lifestyle, the Clemenses decided that they would return to Florence in the fall. Fiske and Ross arranged for them to lease the furnished Villa Viviani, starting on 1 September.[16] Until then the Clemenses would be in Germany: Clara in Berlin, where she was studying piano under Moritz Moszkowski, and the rest of the family at Bad Nauheim, a hydropathic spa that had been recommended for Olivia.[17] They arrived on 6 June 1892, Jean noting in her journal that "Bad Nauheim is situated in a valley surrounded by low hills. It is just twenty-five miles from Frankfurt on-the-Main."[18] It was dull. "The events of the day," wrote Susy, "are the arrival of the Homburg coach, and the garden concert in the afternoon," when "we take our books and sewing out to the terrace and listen to the music till dinner time."[19]

With the family settled, Clemens traveled to Bremen and took ship for America. The purpose of his brief visit—he arrived in New York on 22 June

14. Susy had started at Bryn Mawr in the fall of 1890; Livy retrieved her at the end of April 1891 (*N&J3*, 581 n. 29; 23 Apr 1891 to Sergei M. Stepniak-Kravchinsky, RuM2).

15. 8? May 1892 to Willard Fiske, NIC; OLC to Willard Fiske, 14? May 1892, NIC.

16. OLC to Grace King, 20 May 1892, LaBrUHM, in Pfeffer 2019, 208–9; SLC to Willard Fiske, 12 June 1892, NIC; OLC to Willard Fiske, 21 June 1892, NIC; SLC to Susan L. Crane, 30 Sept 1892, CU-MARK; Notebook 31, TS p. 42.

17. OSC to Louise Brownell, ca. 29 May 1892, NCH; 28 June 1892 to OC, CU-MARK. It is evidently Bad Nauheim to which Clemens refers in his letter to Howells cited in note 13: "The water required seems to be provided at a little obscure & little-visited nook up in the hills back of the Rhine somewhere." Why a whole year passed before the Clemenses proceeded to Bad Nauheim is unclear.

18. JC 1891–94.

19. OSC to Louise Brownell, August 1892, NCH.

1892 and departed on 5 July—was to check up on his several business concerns. These took him to New York, Hartford, Elmira (in Chemung County, New York, where Olivia's family lived), and Chicago, where Paige was building a prototype compositor. It was on this visit that Clemens encountered the picture that inspired his next book: a photograph of Giacomo and Giovanni Tocci, dicephalic twins joined at the sternum, with two heads and four arms but sharing a torso and two legs. They had been born on 4 October 1877 in Locana, Italy, to parents who made their living thereafter by exhibiting the brothers throughout Europe.[20] In September 1891 they came to the United States, where for just over two years they were exhibited in dime museums as the "Two-Headed Boy."[21] Comparison with the so-called "Siamese Twins," Chang and Eng, was inevitable. First exhibited in America in 1829, Chang and Eng (1811–74) settled eventually in North Carolina, where they married a pair of sisters and owned a plantation and enslaved persons. They became firmly imprinted on the popular imagination, their necessary connectedness being exploited by countless speakers, cartoonists, and humorists. Mark Twain's contribution to this literature, "Personal Habits of the Siamese Twins" in *Packard's Monthly* (August 1869), ascribed to Chang and Eng deep incompatibilities of character and placed them in many of the same predicaments he would later inflict upon his "extraordinary twins," including conflicts over drinking, smoking, courtship, and religion.[22]

In an 1895 speech Clemens said he became aware of the Tocci brothers while they were "on exhibition in Philadelphia," and in *Those Extraordinary Twins* (1894) he said he had "seen a picture" of them.[23] Together these clues point to the *Scientific American Supplement* published on 25 June 1892, three days after his arrival in New York; it included photographs of the brothers and an account of their physiology by a doctor who had examined them in

20. See *Scientific American Supplement*, 25 June 1892, 13742–43; "The Twins of Locana," New York *Times*, 10 Sept 1886, 2; "A Short Description of the Twin Brothers Tocci," leaflet in UkLW.

21. Their arrival in America is dated by "Rivals of Shang and Eng," Chicago *Tribune*, 26 Sept 1891, 9; their departure by "Amusements," New York *Evening World*, 22 Dec 1893, 5; their latest advertisement found so far.

22. SLC 1869b.

23. "Twain's Talk on the Twins," New York *Herald*, 23 May 1895, 7; cf. *Those Extraordinary Twins* (EXT), 353.34–35. The abbreviations used for the edited texts in this volume, and for the documents used in their construction, are defined on page xx, and in more detail in the Description of Source Documents, pp. 617–21.

TOCCI BROTHERS.

GIOVANNI, · GIACOMO.

Ronald G. Becker Collection, Syracuse University Libraries.

Philadelphia.[24] Clemens clearly took note of other newspaper items which were making the rounds. They reported that the brothers had very different

24. The *Scientific American Supplement* (25 June 1892, 13742–43) reprints two earlier articles: "The Tocci Twins," from *Scientific American* 65 (12 Dec 1891): 374, and Robert P. Harris, "The Blended Tocci Brothers, and Their Historical Analogues," from the *American Journal of Obstetrics and Diseases of Women and Children*, 25 (April 1892): 460–73. Robert A. Wiggins, who first identified the Tocci brothers as the model for the Twins, was unaware of the June 1892 reprint and proposed that Clemens had seen the article of December 1891 (Wiggins 1951, 356).

Dime museum advertisement. Detroit *Free Press*, 25 December 1892.

dispositions and temperaments; that one was able to eat for both; that they saved on railway fare by booking as a single passenger; and that they differed in complexion, one being fair like "the mother" and the other "of dark complexion, like the father."[25]

MS BERG (BAD NAUHEIM, JULY–SEPTEMBER 1892)

Clemens was back in Bad Nauheim by 18 July, by which time the tale had begun to take shape in his mind. Two years later, in August 1894, he recalled:

> Originally the story was called "Those Extraordinary Twins." I meant to make it very short. I had seen a picture of a youthful Italian "freak"—or "freaks"—which was—or which were—on exhibition in our cities—a combination consisting of two heads and four arms joined to a single body and a single pair of legs—and I thought I would write an extravagantly fantastic little story with this freak of nature for hero—or heroes—a silly young Miss for heroine, and two old ladies and two boys for the minor parts.[26]

Clemens long continued to refer to his story by its first title, "Those Extraordinary Twins," even after his decision to rename it as "Pudd'nhead Wilson." By the time the first American edition of his book was published, at the end of 1894, it contained two separate stories: *Pudd'nhead Wilson*, and a pendant, *Those Extraordinary Twins*. The latter is Clemens's exhibition of passages from an early state of the novel; it is different in extent and content from the manuscript Clemens began to write in Bad Nauheim in the summer of 1892. (That manuscript is here called "MS Berg," from its present location in the Albert A. and Henry W. Berg Collection of the New York Public Library, reserving the title *Those Extraordinary Twins* for the 1894 publication.)

On 28 July 1892, Clemens started writing "Huck Finn in Africa," a children's book to which he soon gave the title *Tom Sawyer Abroad*.[27] Another

---

25. Boston *Globe*: "Two Heads on One Body," 28 Jan 1892, 3; "Two Heads on One Body," 2 Feb 1892, 9, and "Austin & Stone's," 7 Feb 1892, 10; "Another Freak of Old Nature," Philadelphia *Inquirer*, 24 Sept 1891, 5; "Amusements," New York *People*, 13 Mar 1892, 4; "Rivals of Shang and Eng," Chicago *Tribune*, 26 Sept 1891, 9.

26. EXT, 353.33–354.4.

27. 29 July 1892 to Chatto and Windus, in American Art Association 1925, item 31; 5 Aug 1892 to Chatto and Windus, CU-MARK; Notebook 32, TS p. 18. Mark Twain's Notebook 32, cited here and frequently hereafter, is in the collection of the Harry Ransom Center at the University of Texas, Austin (TxU-Hu); all other notebooks cited here are in CU-MARK.

book was begun at this time. Clemens wrote to Orion on 2 September that he was "writing 2 books," both of them begun "5 weeks ago," and that one had grown to the length of seventeen thousand words and the other to twenty-six thousand.[28] When Clemens wrote to Hall two days later, one of the books was finished (this was "Huck Finn in Africa") and the other was progressing:

> By & by I shall have to offer (for grown-folks' magazine,) a novel. Title—
>
> *Those Extraordinary Twins.*
>
> It is the howling farce I told you I had begun a while back. I laid it aside to ferment while I wrote "Tom Sawyer Abroad," but I took it up again on a little different plan lately, & it is swimming along satisfactorily now. I have written about 20,000 words on it, but I can't form any idea of how big a book it is going to make yet. If I keep up my lick it will be a book that will *sell* mighty well, I am sure of that. I think all sorts of folks will read it. It is clear out of the common order—it is a fresh idea—I don't think it resembles anything in literature. *I* believe there's a "boom" in it.[29]

Two weeks later, on 18 September, Clemens wrote to Susan Crane, who had left Bad Nauheim to return to America during the first week of August.[30] His letter gives a broad outline of his work on MS Berg and *Tom Sawyer Abroad:*

> I have been driving this pen hard. I wrote 280 pages on a yarn called "Tom Sawyer Abroad," then took up the "Twins" again, destroyed the last half of the manuscript & re-wrote it in another form, & am going to continue it & finish it in Florence. "Tom Sawyer" seemed rather pale to the family after the extravagances of the Twins, but they came to like it after they got used to it.[31]

The Clemenses had intended to leave Bad Nauheim on 5 September, Clara for Berlin and the rest for Florence, but their departure was delayed by reports of

---

28. 2 Sept 1892 to OC, CU-MARK.

29. 4 and 5 Sept 1892 to Frederick J. Hall, DLC and NN-BGC, in *MTLP*, 318–20. In 2 Dec 1892 to Frederick J. Hall, Clemens dated the first work on MS Berg to "August" (letter in the collection of Angelo Cifaldi). His letter of "a while back," in which he first mentioned the Twins story to Hall, has not been found.

30. 7 Aug 1892 to Charles J. Langdon, CtHMTH; Susan L. Crane to Elizabeth Ford Adams, 5 Dec 1892, photocopy in CU-MARK.

31. 18 Sept 1892 to Susan L. Crane, CU-MARK, in *MTL*, 2:567–69.

Those Extraordinary Twins.

Time – about 1850.

It is a great many years
ago, & so it can do no harm to
tell the story.

    It was long before the advent
of the railroad, & the primitive
little village called Rawson's Landing
had not waked up yet, but was
still slumbering its peaceful
days away in the eventless fashion
which it had so long been used to.
Twice a week the fussy & shabby
little packet that plied between
St. Louis & Cairo stopped there
a moment & received or

The first page of MS Berg. Henry W. and Albert A. Berg Collection, New York Public Library.

cholera, and they did not set out until 10 September.[32] If Clemens, as he told Susan Crane, "destroyed the last half of the manuscript & re-wrote" MS Berg after completing *Tom Sawyer Abroad* on 4 September, then he did so during the five days' delay in Bad Nauheim. At 13,666 words, MS Berg, in the form in which we have it, falls considerably short of Clemens's reports of the work in progress—it had stood at "17,000 words" on 2 September and "20,000" two days later. Unless those estimates were greatly exaggerated, they must have reported the length of the manuscript prior to this reduction by some seven thousand words.

This earliest version of the tale puts the Twins in Dawson's Landing, a fictionalized Hannibal, Missouri, "about 1850."[33] It is a manuscript of 124 leaves comprising six chapters, narrating the arrival in the village of the conjoined twins Luigi and Angelo Cappello, Italians of aristocratic birth, whose warring personalities play out against a backdrop of mild social satire.[34] Only in the very last pages does Clemens introduce the character of David Wilson and explain how he got his nickname. Clemens seems to have completely rewritten the first fifty pages of the original manuscript, for in its present form MS Berg contains two pages, originally numbered 52 and 53, introducing the characters of Patsy Cooper and Betsy Hale. These have been detached from their original context and adapted to a place near the tale's beginning.[35] How Clemens, in the manuscript's original form, brought the Twins through fifty pages without introducing Patsy, who is their landlady in Dawson's Landing and their introduction to society there, is beyond conjecture. The evidence of page numbering shows that two episodes—one in which the Twins argue and another in which Patsy and Rowena discuss the Twins before breakfast—were late insertions; the second of these sequences has had its pages numbered and renumbered five separate times, clearly the result of

32. SLC 1892c; 27 Aug 1892 to Franklin G. Whitmore, CU-MARK; OLC to Grace King, 30 Aug and 2 Sept 1892, LaBrUHM, in Pfeffer 2019, 215–16; JC to MEC, 4 Sept 1892, CU-MARK.

33. MS Berg, first page.

34. MS Berg is the basis of the text published here as chapters 6–10 of the Morgan Manuscript Version. Chapters 1–5 of MS Berg are regularly numbered, except that on page 79 Clemens inserted, between two paragraphs in chapter 4, the heading "CHAPTER," perhaps indicating an alternative starting point for chapter 4. Appendix A, "MS Berg: Contents and Numbering," correlates information about the manuscript's composition and physical makeup with its narrative content.

35. They were renumbered as 6 and 7 in the final page sequence of MS Berg.

numerous deletions, additions, and reshufflings.[36] Starting with the original beginning of the third chapter, where the Twins breakfast with the Cooper family, the page numbering more or less settles down. This uninterrupted stretch of composition presumably represents "the last half of the manuscript," which Clemens said he "destroyed . . . & re-wrote" after completing *Tom Sawyer Abroad*.[37]

TS1 (FRANKFURT, SEPTEMBER 1892)

The day after leaving Bad Nauheim on 10 September, the Clemenses were forced to halt in Frankfurt when Olivia was stricken with a sudden illness, which they feared might be erysipelas. While they "lay idle in Frankfort 4 days doctoring," Clemens called on the help of a highly placed friend.[38] Since *Life on the Mississippi* (1883), it had been his custom to have his book manuscripts typed by a professional copyist and to submit the typed copy to the printer.[39] An English-speaking typist was not easily found in Germany, but Clemens had the help of "an old and valued friend," Frank H. Mason, formerly managing editor of the Cleveland *Leader*, now United States consul general at Frankfurt. It must have been Mason who arranged for the manuscripts of MS Berg and *Tom Sawyer Abroad* to be typed by staffers in the office of his vice consul, Alvesto S. Hogue.[40] Clemens would return the favor in November 1892, when the Democrat Grover Cleveland was elected president, and Mason, a Republican appointee, faced losing his post. Clemens successfully lobbied Cleveland for Mason's retention, addressing his communications to Cleveland's one-year-old daughter, "Baby Ruth."[41]

36. In the final numbering of MS Berg, pages 31–36 and 38–42, respectively.

37. In the final numbering, pages 48 to the end. For a detailed account of the makeup of MS Berg, see Appendix A, "MS Berg: Contents and Numbering."

38. 18 Sept 1892 to Susan L. Crane, CU-MARK, in *MTL*, 2:567–69.

39. *HF 2003*, 687–89.

40. *AutoMT1*, 388–90, 604; 18 Sept 1892 to Susan L. Crane, CU-MARK, in *MTL*, 2:567–69; OSC to Louise Brownell, ca. 19 Sept 1892, NCH. On 4 November 1892, Clemens instructed Hall: "Please send cloth copies of such books of mine as *you* publish (no others) to Vice-Consul-General A. S. Hogue, U.S. Consulate-General, Niedenau F 8, Frankfort-on-the Main, Germany. (He has been having my MS type-written in his office & refuses pay)" (transcript in CU-MARK). The first sixteen thousand words of *Tom Sawyer Abroad* had already been typed when the Clemenses left Frankfurt on 15 September (18 Sept 1892 to Frederick J. Hall, NN-BGC).

41. *MTB*, 2:863–64; *AutoMT1*, 388–90.

The Villa Viviani, ca. 1892. Photograph in CU-MARK.

Leaving his manuscripts in Frankfurt to be typed, Clemens and his family continued their journey toward Florence on 15 September. Their route took them through Basel, Lucerne, Milan, and Bologna, and they reached Florence on 22 September—"the longest trip on record," Clemens wrote to William Walter Phelps, "& Mrs. Clemens's headaches thundered away all the time in the bitterest fashion." After three nights at a hotel in the city, they moved into the Villa Viviani, a twenty-eight-room mansion in Settignano, about three miles east of the center of Florence.[42] Immediately upon arrival

42. 24 Sept 1892 to William Walter Phelps, CSmH; Notebook 32, TS pp. 23–24; JC 1891–94; Ishihara 2014, 21–22.

Clemens got his hair cut close—"*shaved* tight to his head," Susy wrote to her college friend Louise Brownell: "His poor afflicted family wish he would decline all invitations and withdraw to live the life of a hermit till it grows out again."[43] Clemens's admiration for the houseflies who courted danger by buzzing around his shorn head inspired a notebook entry—"He is as brave as a fly"—which would be developed into Pudd'nhead Wilson's maxim about the courage of fleas.[44]

MS MORGAN (FLORENCE, SEPTEMBER–DECEMBER 1892)

Clemens could not resume work on the novel while his manuscript was being typed in Frankfurt. He did not receive the second and last batch of the typescript made from MS Berg (here designated TS1) until mid-October, by which time he was preoccupied with a new project.[45] On 13 October he wrote to Hall: "I am going to begin another long story, now. But now & then I shall work on that farcical novel until I get it done."[46] The new story was *Personal Recollections of Joan of Arc*, which he had been "mulling" for about a year, and which would fully occupy him over the next month or so.[47] Grace King (1851–1932), who with her sister Nan was staying with the Clemenses at this time, remembered Clemens writing *Joan of Arc* and reading his day's work aloud to the company after dinner.[48] But the "farcical novel" lay fallow. Clemens, who was in the habit of pigeonholing a manuscript when it ceased to "write itself," might well have felt uncertain how to continue with this one.[49]

43. OSC to Louise Brownell, 25 Sept 1892, NCH; also CC 1931, 120.

44. Notebook 32, TS pp. 31 and 39–41. This eventually became the motto for chapter 19 in the Morgan Manuscript (PW-MS)—chapter 12 in the revised text.

45. It is not known when Clemens received the first batch of TS1 pages. On 14 October he wrote to Alvesto S. Hogue, thanking him for the consulate staff's work: "The rest of Tom Sawyer Abroad came—& has gone to America. The closing pages of the Twins have also arrived, & for both I am grateful to you" (ViU).

46. 13 Oct 1892 to Frederick J. Hall, NN-BGC, in *MTLP*, 322–23.

47. 2 July 1892 to Mary Mapes Dodge, in Wright 1979, 181. On 13 October, Clemens asked Chatto and Windus to send him books about Joan of Arc (KyLoU).

48. King 1932, 174; OLC to CC, 7 Oct 1892, transcript in CU-MARK; Notebook 32, TS p. 51; Notebook 39, TS p. 49.

49. See *AutoMT2*, 195–96.

In MS Berg he had brought the Cappello twins to Dawson's Landing, displayed their different natures, and shown them interacting with their new American environment; no hint of a plot, however, had emerged. The novel might have remained longer in the pigeonhole had Clemens not received a timely parcel from his London publishers, Chatto and Windus. On 10 November he thanked them for a copy of *Finger Prints*, the newly published book by the English polymath Francis Galton (1822–1911).[50] It suggested new possibilities for his stalled novel: "The Finger-Prints has just arrived, & I don't know how you could have done me a greater favor. I shall devour it."[51] Galton's landmark study, the first scientific monograph ever published on fingerprints, would soon lead to their adoption as a key forensic tool. It is unlikely, however, that it amounted to a revelation, for Clemens had long been aware of Galton's principal contention: that an individual's fingerprints are unique and unchanging, and that finger-marks at a crime scene might be used to identify criminals. He had used this device in chapter 31 of *Life on the Mississippi* (1883), a melodramatic digression entitled "A Thumb-Print and What Came of It," which drew on the journalistic publicity following an 1880 article on the forensic possibilities of fingerprinting. In other words, it seems likely that Galton's treatise served him as a timely reminder.[52]

Clemens would make fingerprinting the hobby of the minor character he had introduced in the last pages of MS Berg, David Wilson; the story, as he now projected it, would show how Wilson's success as a detective redeemed him in the eyes of the community. He now needed a crime for Wilson to solve, and a criminal to commit it. Perhaps at this point Clemens had already conceived the series of thefts that would culminate in the murder of Judge Driscoll; certainly detection by fingerprints would seem to imply theft or murder or both. But much that we are familiar with in the book was still tentative and uncertain at this point. It had been two months and more since

50. Galton 1892; "Messrs. Macmillan & Co.'s New Books," *Bookseller*, 7 Nov 1892, 1151.

51. 10 Sept 1892 to Chatto and Windus, NN-BGC. Almost a year later, on 30 July 1893, Clemens recalled in a letter to Chatto and Windus: "Just then you happened to send me a book which furnished me an idea, & I re-wrote the story" (CtHMTH). Galton was first identified as Clemens's source for fingerprinting in Wigger 1957b.

52. Horst Kruse has shown that the "Thumb-Print" chapter was first written in 1879 and revised in 1881 to incorporate fingerprint identification. The revision shows the influence of press reports of Henry Faulds's October 1880 letter in *Nature*, "On the Skin-Furrows of the Hand" (SLC 1883, 345–46; Kruse 1981, 24–26; Faulds 1880).

Clemens invented Pudd'nhead Wilson and explained his nickname, and in picking up where the typescript left off he several times slipped and called him "Punk'nhead" or "Williams."[53]

This manuscript continuation of TS1, begun on 11 or 12 November 1892,[54] represents the first work done on the typescript and manuscript hybrid, here called MS Morgan from its location in the Morgan Library and Museum, in New York.[55] The first passages added continue the adventures of the Twins in much the same vein as MS Berg. In the first of them, chapter 11,[56] a religious controversy arises between the Twins; in chapter 12 they attend a meeting of the Freethinkers, where they become acquainted with Wilson, and then a Bible class. While Wilson is at home waiting for the Twins to arrive from the Bible class, he ponders what he saw in a window of the Driscoll house that morning: a "girl" in "young Tom Driscoll's bedroom." This was the first mention of any character named Tom Driscoll, so Clemens added, "He was the Judge's nephew" (this sentence would be deleted when the manuscript was later augmented to include the early history of the characters). Wilson is startled to see the girl "removing her bonnet and exposing the face of young Driscoll himself!" At this point Clemens realized he was throwing away a valuable plot contrivance: the discovery that Tom is the girl, and that the girl is the thief, could profitably be deferred to form a later climax, and he immediately revised the passage along these lines. Now Clemens had his criminal; it remained only to connect him with the existing affairs of the Twins and the Cooper family, to which end he wrote a new passage in

53. PW-MS, Textual Apparatus, entries at 73.30, 73.32, 107.5, and 118.15.

54. Clemens wrote on 20 December 1892 that he "began" *Pudd'nhead Wilson* on the "11th or 12th of last month." This reckoning clearly ignores the material written over the summer and can only refer to the beginning of the continuation written in Florence (Notebook 32, TS p. 51).

55. The TS1 chapters numbered 1–5 would become chapters 6–10 of the augmented MS Morgan.

56. The numbering of chapters in TS1 and MS Morgan changed in the course of revision, but all chapters must be referred to here by their *final* numbering. There is really no alternative, despite the unfortunate circumstance that the final chapter numbering does not reflect the order of composition. Detailed information about the writing of the manuscript is summarized in the table "MS Morgan: Phases of Composition" (p. 528), which represents the chronological stints of composition as so many geological strata. Appendix B, "MS Morgan: Contents and Numbering" is a detailed analysis of the manuscript's physical makeup, cataloging its deletions, insertions, revisions, and pagination, and correlating these with the narrative content. Information which might conventionally be placed in footnotes may be found there.

MS Morgan: Phases of Composition.

This diagram represents the compositional strata of MS Morgan, expressed along a vertical time-axis (i–v) from earlier to later. Horizontally, the stints of writing are shown, using the chapter numbers of the finished manuscript, sized by their length in words. The order and dates of composition have been determined using internal and external evidence. The diagram is simplified, and omits lesser, local revisions.

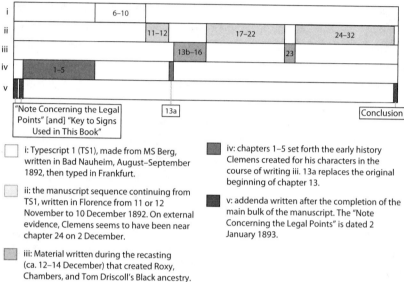

i: Typescript 1 (TS1), made from MS Berg, written in Bad Nauheim, August–September 1892, then typed in Frankfurt.

ii: the manuscript sequence continuing from TS1, written in Florence from 11 or 12 November to 10 December 1892. On external evidence, Clemens seems to have been near chapter 24 on 2 December.

iii: Material written during the recasting (ca. 12–14 December) that created Roxy, Chambers, and Tom Driscoll's Black ancestry.

iv: chapters 1–5 set forth the early history Clemens created for his characters in the course of writing iii. 13a replaces the original beginning of chapter 13.

v: addenda written after the completion of the main bulk of the manuscript. The "Note Concerning the Legal Points" is dated 2 January 1893.

which Patsy and Betsy gossip, establishing Tom and Angelo as rival suitors for Rowena's hand. This passage was inserted to form a new beginning to chapter 11.

At this stage (in early November 1892), chapters 13–16 had not yet been written: the narrative ran directly from the end of chapter 12, where Wilson ponders the enigma of the young woman in the Driscoll house, to chapter 17, which begins with Wilson's conversation with the Twins and Tom. Wilson explains fingerprinting and takes the Twins' prints. Buckstone invites them to a meeting of the Sons of Liberty; Tom tags along to the meeting, where he is kicked by the Twins. Not long after completing chapter 17, Clemens decided on his murder weapon, a "costly Indian dagger" belonging to Luigi. To introduce the dagger, he inserted into the chapter a passage of twenty leaves, adding palm reading to Wilson's hobbies and bringing out the knife and Luigi's act of homicide. If it is jarring to find Clemens, even for the sake of exposition, placing the science of fingerprints on a level with such hokum as palmistry, it should be remembered that all kinds of divination fascinated him, and that he had his palm read on several occasions.[57] Also in this addition, Clemens has Tom refuse to have his palm read. The refusal was meant as Tom's attempt to evade detection as the thief; later revisions would give him something more to hide from the scrutiny of the palmist.

In chapter 18, the trial of the Twins for assault, there is more revision: the last twenty-four leaves are physically discontinuous with the preceding fourteen, though the sense runs smoothly.[58] In chapter 19 the scene is set for Judge Driscoll to learn of Tom's being kicked and his lawsuit against the Twins. So far the Judge had been merely an affable and officious citizen of Dawson's Landing; now Clemens shaded his character with an immense pride in his Virginia background and an inflexible adherence to the "aristocratic" code of the First Families. He also provided him with a like-minded friend in the person of Pembroke Howard and gave anecdotes of him (later deleted). He handled Tom's refusal to duel, the Judge's second disinheriting of Tom, and the discovery of the theft-raid. In chapter 21, where Tom celebrates the redrawing of the will, Clemens treated his villain to a fiendish celebration: Tom tortures two spiders who are themselves torturing a grasshopper, addressing the grasshopper as "unky" (meaning his uncle, Judge Driscoll). Perhaps sensing that in the sadism of this passage he had gone too far, Clemens removed these leaves from the manuscript immediately after writing them.[59] The duel (chapter 22) was originally followed by the

57. Clemens twice had his palm read by "Cheiro" (Louis Hamon, 1866–1936) and years afterward declared himself "persecuted with superstitions . . . born of Cheiro's prophecy of 7 years ago & repeated 4 years ago in the same words: 'In your 68th year you will become—rather suddenly—very rich'" (26 Dec 1902 to Charles J. Langdon, CtHMTH; Clemens recorded Cheiro's reading in 8 Aug 1894 to OSC, collection of Angelo J. Cifaldi). In March 1894, Clemens met W. T. Stead, the journalist and investigator of the paranormal, on an Atlantic crossing; Stead asked for prints of his hand, for analysis by palmists and subsequent publication, and found him enthusiastic. According to Stead, "a controversy . . . had arisen between [Clemens] and some acquaintances, as to whether palmistry was too drivelling a superstition for anyone . . . to allude to its existence, even in a work of fiction" (Baylen 1964, 608). The controversy seems to have followed on the publication, in February's *Century Magazine*, of the palm-reading episode in *Pudd'nhead Wilson* (SLC 1894b). In 1905 Clemens had his palm read by "several New York palmists of the first repute" and evaluated their accuracy for an article commissioned by *Harper's Monthly*, unpublished at that time (*AutoMT2*, 390–400).

58. Pages 293–306 in MS Morgan are followed by a sequence of twenty-four leaves, which are on a different paper and show fewer repaginations; the original numbering of 1–24 is not continuous with anything in the manuscript. Probably these replace deleted matter, but when the change was made remains undetermined.

59. The "grasshopper" passage is on pages originally numbered 183–88. On page 188 Clemens got only so far as writing the page number before he withdrew the five leaves

doctor's visit to the Twins (chapter 24); the intervening chapter was a later addition.

Clemens's Notebook 32 contains a series of working notes pertaining to the early stages of MS Morgan, probably written—to judge from nearby dates—between the middle of November 1892 and the end of the month.[60] Most of them were realized in the narrative as we know it; the few that were not mostly proposed further comic situations for Luigi and Angelo. Resurrecting an idea he had used more than twenty years before, in "Personal Habits of the Siamese Twins," Clemens considered having Angelo join the Good Templars, a temperance organization. He proposed having Angelo take Luigi to a camp meeting, a setting he had used in *Huckleberry Finn*, and having Angelo join the Campbellites and the Millerites, religious sects which flourished in the period of the novel.[61] He considered making some character, presumably Angelo, an "Abolitionist." With some of the rejected ideas it is a puzzle to know how Clemens could have entertained them. One entry places the Indian knife in Wilson's possession on the night of the murder. Another has the court finding Luigi guilty of the murder and sentencing him to death. Still another suggests that Tom should be detected by his bloody footprint, rather than his fingerprints—odd, when fingerprints, as in Galton, are more apt to the purpose, and do not require that the criminal go barefoot.

Chapter 11 had introduced readers to Wilson's "whimsical almanac, for his amusement—a calendar, with a little dab of ostensible philosophy, usually in ironical form, appended to each date."[62] It is not clear when Clemens decided to attribute his own original aphorisms to Wilson and place them as

184–88, which are all now in CU-MARK. He salvaged part of the leaf originally numbered 183 (final numbering 389) and composed a new ending for the chapter on its verso. For the deleted passage, see PW-MS, Textual Apparatus, entry at 134.31–37.

60. This burst of notebook entries (Notebook 32, TS pp. 34–39) shows the influence of Galton's *Finger Prints*, received 10 November, and comes to an end before Clemens's dated entry on his birthday: "Nov. 30, 1892—57 yrs old. I wish it were either 17 or 97" (TS p. 47). The entries are transcribed in Appendix C, "Mark Twain's Working Notes," Group A, pp. 471–75.

61. For Clemens's knowledge of and connections to the Campbellites and Millerites, see Appendix C, "Mark Twain's Working Notes," pp. 473–74 and notes 4 and 5.

62. The history of repagination shows that this description of Wilson's calendar, occupying two pages of MS Morgan (final numbering 109–10), was originally composed as the ending of chapter 11. In revising the manuscript, Clemens moved it to its final position in MS Morgan chapter 5.

mottoes at the chapter heads. The 1880s had seen the rise of the "author's calendar," a printed novelty giving daily quotations from the works of a famous author, often Tennyson or Longfellow but extending occasionally to George Eliot or Schiller.[63] In 1884, Clemens had undertaken to create such a calendar for the Boston stationer L. Prang and Company, to consist of new work as well as excerpts from his books. He had written "special squibs for 10 of the months & all the national holidays" and was just beginning to ransack his books for excerpts when some accident on Prang's end afforded him a way out. "This is the best luck I've had in 7 years," he told Webster: "Get the Prang contract *canceled*, right away; don't let him change his mind. You can't *imagine* what a horrible 3-months' job it would have been."[64] Since that time, Clemens had built up a fine accumulation of unpublished aphorisms, and in David Wilson he had a plausible mouthpiece (more or less; not every reader has been able to accept these mordant and cynical sayings as the utterances of the stolid Wilson). A run of entries in Notebook 32, datable to late November and early December 1892, shows Clemens transcribing his old aphorisms for use in MS Morgan.[65] More than half of the manuscript's twenty-eight mottoes are drawn from his collections; others are newly minted. One—"Dress a fact in tights, not in an ulster"—had already been used in *Life on the Mississippi*, chapter 34. The actual addition of aphorisms to the chapter heads was postponed to a later stage of composition.

Clemens was working rapidly and pleased with his progress. On 16 November he wrote to Clara that the manuscript was "half the size of the Prince & Pauper, now, & going right along."[66] The tale was becoming a full-length book, and publication as a magazine serial was an appealing option. Under ordinary circumstances Clemens preferred not to serialize a novel in its

63. "Literary Notes," Washington (D.C.) *Evening Star*, 13 Dec 1884, 3; "Recent Publications," New Haven *Journal-Courier*, 20 Dec 1888, 1.

64. Letters of 29 Feb, 3 Mar, 5 Mar, and 6 Mar 1884 to Charles L. Webster, all NPV, in *MTBus*, 239–42; 15 July 1886 to Edith Somerville, MH-H; *N&J3*, 71 n. 13. In addition to the Prang manuscript collections, there is in the Mark Twain Papers an undated manuscript in Olivia's hand, headed "Proverbs made by Mr Clemens for Mrs Sayles Callendar." Emma Halsey Sayles (1819–99) was a friend of the Langdon family in Elmira (24 Jan 1869 to Olivia L. Langdon, *L3*, 73–76 n. 4).

65. Notebook 32, TS pp. 43–50; selected entries are reprinted in Appendix C, "Mark Twain's Working Notes," Group C.

66. 16 Nov 1892 to CC, CU-MARK, in *LLMT*, 261–62.

entirety. In the *Century Magazine* he had published three installments of extracts from *Huckleberry Finn* and one installment of extracts from *A Connecticut Yankee*, promoting the novels while protecting sales of the complete book. But in 1891, financial constraints led him to sell *The American Claimant* to a newspaper syndicate to be serialized in full, and he was now arranging for the whole of *Tom Sawyer Abroad* to run in the young people's magazine *St. Nicholas*—reserving, of course, the right to publish the book editions through Charles L. Webster and Company.[67] "If I publish 'Those Extraordinary Twins' serially," he told Hall, "the price must be high. It is going to be a full-sized novel, & longer than the American Claimant. I have now written 43,000 words on it, & I think there will be as much more."[68] His next letter to Hall shows the approximate point he had reached on 2 December:

> Won't you get for me an article which I published in Harper's Monthly several years ago about a Curious Old Book? & tear it out & send it to me. Don't remember the title, but Poole's Index will furnish it. It was about an ancient *Medical Dictionary*. I want a paragraph from it for the extravagant novel I am writing—the one about the Extraordinary Twins which I began in Nauheim last August. I've written about 60,000 words on it, I guess & 20 or 30,000 more will finish it. I shall soon be done.[69]

The article Clemens requested was "A Majestic Literary Fossil," in which he had exhumed an antique remedy from Robert James's *Medicinal Dictionary* (1743–45).[70] The prescription was for Angelo, in chapter 24, which Clemens must therefore have reached around the date of this letter, 2 December. For the time being he left a blank space on the manuscript page where a clipping of the article could later be affixed. The same day, he wrote to his Hartford business manager, Franklin G. Whitmore: "I'm a worker, these days! I wrote 6,000 words on my new novel in 13 hours, yesterday; & I consider 2,000 an honest day's work. The family say yesterday's chapters are the best I've turned out yet."[71]

67. 1–15 Nov 1892 to Frederick J. Hall, NN-BGC; 2 Dec 1892 to Mary Mapes Dodge, transcript in CU-MARK.

68. 24 Nov 1892 to Frederick J. Hall, NN-BGC, in *MTLP*, 326–27.

69. 2 Dec 1892 to Frederick J. Hall, collection of Angelo J. Cifaldi.

70. SLC 1890.

71. 2 Dec 1892 to Franklin G. Whitmore, CU-MARK.

As Clemens neared the conclusion of his story, he decided to revise it along new lines. He was committing himself to a major reconstruction, which in the end would involve writing ten new chapters, supplementing and altering the plot, and introducing two major characters. By chapter 26 the author has begun to assume a backstory, the story of Roxy, which he had conceived but not yet put on paper. An enslaved person in the Driscoll household, Roxy has only a tincture of Black ancestry, and presents physically as white. She had a son born the same day as her enslaver's own son and soon switched them in their cradles. This change in the plot meant that Tom, who up to now has been white and the Judge's genuine nephew, is secretly Roxy's son; the real nephew, and the displaced heir of Percy Driscoll, is Valet de Chambre (Chambers), raised as Roxy's child. Roxy—as Clemens now decided—returns to Dawson's Landing, poor and needy, and revenges herself on the unsympathetic Tom by telling him she is his mother and threatening to expose him. Clemens now saw that, in the denouement, Wilson's fingerprinting hobby could reveal not only the identity of the murderer but also the switching of the children in infancy.

Through this reconception, the most profound in the history of a repeatedly revised text, Clemens would bring into his novel themes of slavery, racism, and race mixing; and he would cast the springs of action far back, twenty-three years before the story he had been narrating. In unfolding this new plot, he was adding material conceived on a completely different order from the farcical story of conjoined twins he had started out with (and which was at this point still there). Clemens would later identify the genre of this new matter as "tragedy."[72] Its immediate model, however, was melodrama, specifically melodrama on the theme of the "tragic mulatto." This genre flourished before the Civil War. Michael Orth has cataloged its typical elements:

> The usual octoroon romance is built around a beautiful girl who is stigmatized in only the faintest degree with Negro blood, but who nevertheless is reduced to slavery and put at the whim of a lecherous master, from whom she is to be rescued by a noble hero. The heroine is always raised by some

---

72. This new matter was first called "tragedy" by Clemens in the introduction to *Those Extraordinary Twins*, written in August 1894 (EXT, 353.19); on "tragedy" in the title of the American Publishing Company edition, see the Note on the Texts, p. 611.

coincidence as a white child, and she is almost always begotten by an illustrious but prejudice-blinded member of the FFV. The death of her protector, who is usually her father, unexpectedly puts her on the market to pay old family debts incurred by the extravagant habits of the Southern Cavalier. A Yankee slave dealer of the lowest and most concupiscently mercenary sort is her purchaser. After various perils and escapes she either dies tragically but nobly or else is helped to escape by the hero and is borne off to Canada or Europe.[73]

It is evident from the recast MS Morgan that Clemens was familiar with Dion Boucicault's play *The Octoroon* (1859), an adaptation of Mayne Reid's novel *The Quadroon; or, A Lover's Adventures in Louisiana* (1856). Boucicault's play, in addition to conforming to the tragic mulatto outline summarized by Orth, features an Uncle who is a Judge; the Judge has an esteemed friend who is a transplanted Yankee; the Yankee friend has a newfangled technological hobby (photography); and his hobby supplies the evidence that secures a conviction in a climactic murder trial. The material of *The Octoroon*, and of tragic mulatto fiction in general, is refracted, rather than replicated, in *Pudd'nhead Wilson*, its characteristic incidents dispersed and assigned to different characters.

In some respects, Roxy is a generic character: the white-appearing woman of fractional Black ancestry who is sold into slavery to settle the gambling debts of a high-living wastrel; structurally, however, it is not Roxy but Tom who is the tragic mulatto of *Pudd'nhead Wilson*. It is *he* who grows up passing for a white Southern aristocrat, it is *his* life that is turned upside down by the secret of his Black ancestry, and in the end it is *he* who is sold into slavery to pay a debt. Of course, where the tragic mulatto heroine is morally unimpeachable, Tom is a monster, and his triumphs and disasters are ironized rather than sentimentalized. Clemens's intention to parody tragic-mulatto melodrama may help to explain the prefabricated, pedestrian tone of certain passages, especially those involving Tom ("Oh, I know it—I'm gone, I'm gone—and this time it's for good! Oh, this is awful—I don't know *what* to do, nor which way to turn," etc.).

Roxy herself is anything but the tragic mulatto of sentimental fiction, and it seems certain that in drawing her character Clemens was, typically, recalling personal acquaintants. Roxy's original has been sought in Mary Ann

73. Orth 1969, 12 (correcting "prejudiced, blinded" to "prejudice-blinded"). See also Brown 1933, Zanger 1966, and Bond 1981.

Cord, a formerly enslaved women whom Clemens knew as a cook in the Elmira household of his in-laws, the Cranes, and whom he memorialized as Aunt Rachel in "A True Story, Repeated Word for Word as I Heard It" (1874).[74] Roxy's membership in the African Methodist Church and her theological disputes with Jasper are certainly modeled on Cord; and Roxy, like Cord, is described by Clemens as a commanding presence, tall, bearing herself like "a grenadier."[75] But this figure of the Black servant woman with the martial air was also realized by Clemens in writing about Maria McLaughlin, Clara Clemens's wet nurse, who in some respects seems more akin to Roxy.[76] Clemens described Maria as a tall woman, of mixed race—"apparently Irish, with a powerful strain of Egyptian in her"—and she too was like a "grenadier."[77] Where "Aunty" Cord was a trusted and loyal family servant, Maria McLaughlin was ungovernable. Clemens described her in a passage from "A Family Sketch," written probably in 1896–97:

> She stood six feet in her stockings, she was perfect in form and contour, raven-haired, dark as an Indian, stately, carrying her head like an empress, she had the martial port and stride of a grenadier, and the pluck and strength of a battalion of them. In professional capacity the cow was a poor thing compared to her, and not even the pump was qualified to take on airs where she was. She was as independent as the flag, she was indifferent to morals and principles, she disdained company, and marched in a procession by herself. She was as healthy as iron, she had the appetite of a crocodile, the stomach of a cellar, and the digestion of a quartz-mill. Scorning the adamantine law that a wet-nurse must partake of delicate things only, she devoured anything and everything she could get her hands on, shoveling into her person fiendish combinations of fresh pork, lemon pie, boiled cabbage, ice cream, green apples, pickled tripe, raw turnips, and washing the cargo down with freshets of coffee, tea, brandy, whisky, turpentine, kerosene—anything that was liquid; she smoked pipes, cigars, cigarettes, she whooped like a Pawnee and swore like a demon; and then she would go up stairs loaded as described and perfectly delight the

74. Cummings 1996. A critical text of "A True Story" is published in *FamSk*, 45–50.
75. Notebook 35, TS p. 8; PW-MS, 84.22.
76. 11 July 1874 to JLC, *L6*, 184–88; 16 Mar 1875 to William Dean Howells, *L6*, 414–16. For Mary Ann Cord, see 25 and 27 Aug 1877 to William Dean and Elinor M. Howells, *Letters 1876–1880*.
77. *FamSk*, 30–31. In addition to the passages already cited, the "grenadier" servant-woman appears as Katrina in the working notes for *No. 44, The Mysterious Stranger* (*MSM*, 456) and as Aunty Phyllis in "The Refuge of the Derelicts" (*FM*, 207).

baby with a banquet which ought to have killed it at thirty yards, but which only made it happy and fat and contented and boozy.[78]

Our last glimpse of Maria McLaughlin comes from 1876. Pregnant, and about to be ejected from a charity hospital for unmarried and indigent mothers, she named Clemens as a character reference, and the superintendent of the institution wrote to him; Clemens's reply, if any, is untraced.[79] Maria had never found favor with Olivia, who described her as "a wet nurse that is tractable and good when I am in the house but who gets drunk when I go away." For Clemens, however, she remained "a delight, a darling, a never failing interest."[80]

Clemens did not turn right away to integrating the story of Roxy's dealings with the Driscoll family into his existing manuscript. As already mentioned, when he reached chapter 26, he alluded to Roxy (on MS page 465) as though she had been there all along. Probably by this time he had imagined her character and planned the plot developments in which she figures, in chapters 13–16; still he deferred the writing of these chapters, continuing the narrative through six more chapters to its ending.[81] In the earliest stratum of chapter 29, Tom prepares to rob his uncle by blacking his face with the "smut" from a saucer darkened with candle smoke; after the murder Wilson has the blackened saucer taken into evidence in case there should be fingerprints on it. Fingerprints on the saucer are superfluous, since there are bloody prints on the knife, and in revision Clemens would dispense with the saucer and have Tom black his face with burnt cork.

In the ending as originally written, Tom hangs himself while awaiting trial as Judge Driscoll's murderer; Dawson's Landing, its government para-

---

78. *FamSk*, 31–32. Clemens also described Maria McLaughlin in his Autobiographical Dictation of 11 April 1907: "Maria was one of the most superb creatures to look at I have ever seen. She was six feet high, and perfectly proportioned; she was erect, straight; she had the soldierly stride and bearing of a grenadier, and she was as finely brave as any grenadier that ever walked. She had a prodigal abundance of black hair; she was of a swarthy complexion, Egyptian in its tone; her features were nobly and impressively Egyptian; there was an Oriental dash about her costume and its colors, and when she moved across a room with her stately stride she was royal to look at—it was as if Cleopatra had come again" (*AutoMT3*, 45).

79. C. C. Ranstead for the New York Infant Asylum to SLC, 13 Jan 1876, CU-MARK; see *AutoMT3*, 460, note on 45.12–14.

80. OLC to Elinor M. Howells, 23 Apr 1875, MH-H; *AutoMT3*, 44.

81. This fact was noted by Arlin Turner (Turner 1968, 510) and developed by Hershel Parker in his important study of the text (Parker 1984, 125–26).

lyzed because Luigi cannot be seated on the city council without also seating the unelected Angelo, goes bankrupt, and in 1870 it sinks into the Mississippi. The Twins flee under a threat of lynching; Roxy's after-history is not mentioned; Joe and Henry drown.[82] In revision, Clemens would retain the matter of the Twins, adding a somber portrait of Roxy, and reserving Tom for a different fate.

On 12 December, Clemens reported on the novel to Hall:

> I finished "Those Extraordinary Twins" night before last—makes 60 or 80,000 words—haven't counted.
>
> The last third of it suits me to a dot. I begin, to-day, to entirely re-cast & re-write the first two-thirds—new plan, with two minor characters made very prominent, one major character dropped out, & the Twins subordinated to a minor but not insignificant place.
>
> *The* minor character will now become the chiefest, & I will name the story after him—"*Pudd'nhead Wilson*."[83]

"The last third" of the manuscript, which suited Clemens "to a dot," was the part he had written with Roxy already in place. Presumably the "two minor characters made very prominent" were Roxy and Wilson; if the "one major character" he meant to eliminate was Rowena, he must have relented, for she remains, although reduced in importance. The first two-thirds now needed rewriting to include Roxy's history, her reunion with Tom, and her revelation of his parentage and race.

Three pages of working notes, written on the versos of discarded leaves from the *Joan of Arc* manuscript, show the roads not taken when Clemens "re-cast" his story.[84] In one of them he makes Tom's resentment at discovering he is Black and a white man's bastard a contributory factor in his murder of Judge Driscoll. Roxy has revealed to Tom that she is his mother but still refuses to name the father. Tom soliloquizes:

> Yesterday, what was illegitimacy of birth to a nigger? I could not conceive of its being unpleasant to him—but to-day! ~~Yesterday~~ And if he had a white

---

82. MS Morgan, canceled passages on 623, 626, 628; and leaf numbered 392 removed from the MS by Clemens, in CU-MARK, Box 40, no. 2; PW-MS, Textual Apparatus, entries at 199.19, 199.37–38, and 200.16–17.

83. 12 Dec 1892 to Frederick J. Hall, NN-BGC, in *MTLP*, 328–29.

84. These pages are transcribed in Appendix C, "Mark Twain's Working Notes," Group B.

MOTIVE

A QUARREL—then:

If you don't slip down "dis very night" & steal the money & pay the debt dey'll go to yo' uncle, jes as dey says in de letter.

What happen den?

Old Morse dissenhurrit you again ~~en do~~ en for good, dis time.

En he'll stop de pension.

I can't stand dat, en I won't.

Take yo' choice—hog de money dis night or I tells de Jedge in de mawnin' who you is. You'll be on de auction block in 2 minutes.

~~They are on their way home~~

Chambers enters at one door & drops toddy-glass & stands transfixed at same moment that twins enter & rush to lift the moribund.

Enter Aunt Pratt & proclaims all three. Rushed off to jail. Town rises, snatch Chambers out & would hang or burn him. Roxy interferes & tries to save him — is heroic, but fails. "Well, 'twould a ben my son if I hadn't changed 'em."

A page from Mark Twain's working notes for the "recasting." All the working notes are transcribed in Appendix C. CU-MARK.

father, I supposed it was a thing for him to be proud of—but to-day that
doubles, trebles, quadruples the shame of my birth. If I can find my father—

That is my search—

That is my life henceforth—

"Spare me!—I am your father! (He was hesitating—had concluded he
couldn't do it)

"Now for *that,* you shall die"

(*Kills him*)

Passages from the earliest stage of the recasting show Clemens preparing
the reader for a plot in which Tom murders his race-mixing father—a father
who, as Henry Nash Smith pointed out in 1962, is implicitly Judge Driscoll.[85]
In the end, this was meat too strong for Clemens and his intended reader-
ship. He deleted the passages in question: Tom would continue being (that
is, *appearing* to be) Judge Driscoll's nephew. His interest in his paternity was
downgraded to a feeble inquiry, and he had to be satisfied with the information that his father was Col. Cecil Burleigh Essex, a cipher of whose former existence the characters are almost never conscious. In yet another of
these working notes, Chambers is present at the scene when the Twins find
Judge Driscoll slain; all three are jailed as suspects and Chambers is lynched,
despite Roxy's efforts to save him. Clemens decided against this line, too,
although the threat of lynching survives into MS Morgan (against the Twins,
however, not Chambers).

The recasting began with the writing of MS Morgan chapters 13–16.[86] As
it now stands in the manuscript, "this long digression" (as Clemens calls it at
the end of chapter 16) begins with Roxy's history after her manumission in
1845, describing her service on the steamboat *Grand Mogul*; but the original
opening of chapter 13 was discarded by Clemens in revision, so it is not clear
how Roxy was first introduced there. Canceled and revised passages show
that as he began writing chapter 13, Roxy was a "quadroon"—meaning that
one of her grandparents was Black. Clemens later decided to reduce Roxy's
Black ancestry to one-sixteenth—that is, one of her *great-great*-grandparents
was Black.[87] In chapters 15 and 16 there survive traces of an early conception,
already mentioned in connection with the working notes, in which Tom

85. MS Morgan, canceled passages on 232, 234–35, and 246–48 (PW-MS, Textual
Apparatus, entries at 89.16, 89.36, and 93.27); Smith 1962, 174.

86. Studies of the recasting include: Wigger 1957a; McKeithan 1961; Parker and Binder
1978; Parker 1981; Cohen 1982; and Parker 1984.

87. PW-MS, Textual Apparatus, entries at 79.20, 83.4, and 85.18.

nurses a murderous rage against his unknown father; when Clemens later revised these pages, he established the deceased Colonel Essex as Tom's father, inserting a passage in which Roxy tells Tom so at the end of chapter 14.[88] At the end of chapter 16, Clemens harmonized the chronology of the "long digression" with the original story by giving an account, as seen by Tom Driscoll, of Friday, the day of Patsy Cooper's reception for the Twins. Tom slips from the haunted house into the Judge's house, dresses in his girl's clothing, sees he is observed by Wilson, and raids Dawson's Landing, including the Cooper house. Roxy and Tom having been elevated to the status of major characters, the older chapters following the newly written matter seemed to go on too long without their participation, and Clemens, to keep them before the reader's eyes (and obviously continuing to revel in Roxy's character and language), wrote chapter 23 for insertion between the duel and the doctoring of Angelo.

Clemens reviewed the old chapters to ensure that they were consistent with the added material, but his review was carelessly done. The most serious inconsistency left unmended in MS Morgan concerns the character of Tom Driscoll. The Tom we meet in the added chapters 15–16 has been deeply affected by Roxy's revelation of his parentage and race; "in toil and pain" he arrives at an utterly revalued vision of life, and his greatest passion, we are told, is a drive to exact vengeance against white people. But reading onward and into the earlier-written material, we find a substantially unrevised Tom, as jaunty and superficial as he began. Clemens was aware of the discrepancy, for in chapter 16 he tried to explain it away: the changes wrought in Tom by the shock, although deep, became suddenly unobtrusive because "the main structure of his *character*" was not changed: "He dropped gradually back into his old frivolous and easy-going ways, and conditions of feeling, and manner of speech, and no familiar of his could have detected anything in him that differentiated him from the weak and careless Tom of other days." Clemens's effort to minimize revisions and retain as much as he could of his existing manuscript created, in the juxtaposition of new and old matter, what Hershel Parker has called "adventitious meanings."[89] Before the recasting, Tom refused to have his palm read by Wilson in order to protect his secret life as a thief; after the recasting, the reader is bound to conclude that he fears palmistry will betray the secret of his birth. The same is true in chapter 20, where

88. See the passages cited in note 85.
89. Parker 1984, 129.

Tom fears exposure as a thief only—exposure as an impostor, a bastard, and a slave does not enter his mind. In chapter 19, Tom's refusal to challenge Luigi to a duel was originally a sign of simple cowardice; but the recasting added these searching reflections by Tom, which allow or invite a different interpretation:

> Why was he a coward? It was the "nigger" in him. The nigger *blood?* Yes, the nigger blood degraded from original courage to cowardice by decades and generations of insult and outrage inflicted in circumstances which forbade reprisals, and made mute and meek endurance the only refuge and defence.
>
> Whence came that in him which was high, and whence that which was base? That which was high came from either blood, and was the monopoly of neither color; but that which was base was the *white* blood in him debased by the brutalizing effects of a long-drawn heredity of slave-owning, with the habit of abuse which the possession of irresponsible power always creates and perpetuates, by a law of human nature. So he argued.[90]

Having composed chapters 13–16 and 23, which tell the story of Roxy's reunion with Tom, Clemens next had to supply a new beginning to the tale, explaining the exchange of babies and its consequences.[91] At this point, MS Morgan still began with TS1, the typescript pages made from MS Berg. The first typescript page was a brief introduction to Dawson's Landing, a transcription of MS Berg pages 1–4; he set about replacing it with manuscript chapters 1–5. The period of the action, which in MS Berg was "about 1850," was set back to 1830, and the events that followed were precisely dated. The new chapters introduced Roxy; the history of Wilson and his nickname, the original and still satisfactory ending of MS Berg chapter 1, was detached and moved forward to form the ending of MS Morgan's *new* chapter 1. In chapters 2–5 Clemens at last set down the series of prior events he had been

---

90. PW-MS, 91.18–28. Parker also considers that Clemens chose to stop developing Tom as a suitor to Rowena after making him "part black." It would be difficult to confidently distinguish this motive from the author's generally declining interest in Rowena, but undoubtedly Clemens failed to remove "the vestiges of that earlier plot" (Parker 1984, 122, 129).

91. The evidence of revision in MS Morgan shows that chapters 1–5 were written later than 13–16 and 23. Plot lines which are clearly being improvised in chapters 13–16 are smoothly assumed in chapters 1–5: the introduction of Colonel Cecil Burleigh Essex in chapter 1, and his death, reported in chapter 4, are meaningful only because he will turn out to be Tom's father—an idea whose development can be traced in the revision history of manuscript chapters 14–15. In chapter 2, Roxy is presented as one-sixteenth Black, whereas in chapter 13 the original conception of her as a "quadroon" shows through in canceled readings.

assuming while writing the manuscript's later chapters: Wilson's hobby of fingerprinting, the switching of the babies, and so forth.

Chapters 1–5 draw intensively on events in Clemens's own personal history. To illuminate Percy Driscoll's character as a man and a slaveowner, he included the text of a letter presented as written by Driscoll, illustrating the double standard that legitimizes his inhumane behavior toward Black people. The text was adapted from a letter written in 1842 by Clemens's father, John Marshall Clemens, who owned and sometimes rented enslaved people.[92] This is one of two passages in MS Morgan where Clemens extenuates a enslaver's brutal behavior as the consequence of the institution of slavery itself (the other is in chapter 13, where Tom beats Chambers); in revising the manuscript Clemens canceled both these passages. The exploit of Jasper in stopping a runaway horse is based on an 1877 event from the life of John T. Lewis, the tenant farmer of Clemens's in-laws, the Cranes; and the theological quarrel of Roxy and Jasper imitates Lewis's disputes with Mary Ann Cord.[93] One of the infant Tom's sayings—"*Like* it . . . *Awnt* it . . . *Hab* it . . . *Take* it!"—comes straight from the infant Susy Clemens; while Tom's education at Yale, and the hostile reception given to his "eastern" affectations, are transferred from the personal experience of Clemens's Hannibal contemporary Neil Moss.[94]

The newly written chapters 1–5 set forth Roxy's character and history, from the birth of the babies to her emancipation and departure to work as a chambermaid on a steamboat; and it seems that this expanded account of her prompted revisions to the beginning of chapter 13, where Clemens had first started to chronicle Roxy's return to Dawson's Landing. Clemens rebuilt the chapter by discarding its first seven leaves, supplanting them with a new composition—the passage in which Roxy has her first sight of the splendors of a Mississippi River steamboat. He also expanded the manuscript's final chapter (32) with a fuller account of the characters' subsequent histories: Roxy turns to the church, while Chambers flounders in his new environment. Tom, who in the original ending committed suicide, confesses the murder and is sentenced to life imprisonment; as a slave, however, he is claimed as property of

92. John Marshall Clemens to JLC and Family, 5 Jan 1842, CU-MARK; MS Morgan, pp. 45–49; PW-MS, Textual Apparatus, entry at 16.28. In his letter John Marshall Clemens speaks of selling "Charley," who has accompanied him on his travels. It has been suggested that this Charley may in fact have been a horse (*Inds*, 90, 277–78), but reading his father' s letter Clemens certainly took him to be an enslaved man, whom he renamed "Jim" in MS Morgan.

93. 25 and 27 Aug 1877 to William Dean and Elinor M. Howells, *Letters 1876–1880*.

94. See PW-MS, Explanatory Notes at 23.16–18 and 32.4–6.

the Percy Driscoll estate and is sold down the river by its creditors. Rowena's role in the novel had long since dwindled to nothingness, and in a notebook entry dating from this time, Clemens decided to drown her, as he had done with Joe and Henry. He effected her death in a brief insertion, which appears, however, to have been incorrectly placed, for she is suddenly alive again in the text that follows.[95]

According to Clemens's own accounting, the recasting—involving the writing of more than twenty-one thousand words—had begun on 12 December and was complete on 14 December—a prodigious feat.[96] Around this time he created a manuscript title page featuring the new title he had announced in his 12 December letter to Hall, making use of facsimile fingerprints clipped from the title page of Galton's book (reproduced on page 544) and adding detailed instructions to the printer about obtaining and processing the fingerprint images. Later—probably before the manuscript was typed—he decided against this title page, canceled his directives to the printer, and marked it "Not to be inserted in the book." This leaf was not part of the manuscript when J. Pierpont Morgan purchased it in 1909; it was acquired by the Morgan Library in 2011.

Clemens now turned to the selection and placement of aphorisms for the chapter heads, many of which—as noted earlier—he had recorded in Notebook 32 in late November and early December.[97] Another addendum, the "Key to Signs used in this book," expounds a plan ostensibly "to save the space usually devoted to explanations of the state of the weather" by

95. In the present edition's Morgan-based text, Rowena's drowning has been relocated, following Clemens's intention as gleaned from the notebook entry; see PW-MS, Textual Apparatus, entry at 164.10.

96. 12 Dec 1892 to Frederick J. Hall, quoted above, p. 537. To Clara (in Berlin) he wrote on 15 December: "I finished the book a week ago, & have been revising & correcting ever since. I finished *that* yesterday evening, & shall take a few days' holiday now" (CU-MARK). In Notebook 32 he wrote: "Dec. 20/92. Finished 'Pudd'nhead Wilson' last Wednesday, 14th. Began it 11th or 12th of last month [i.e., November], after the King girls left. Wrote more than 60,000 words between Nov. 12 & Dec. 14. One day, wrote 6,000 words in 13 hours. Another day wrote 5,000 in 11" (TS p. 51). Clemens gave a similar account in a letter to Orion of 22 December, extant only in Orion's paraphrase of it: "He has just finished a book in 26 days straight work eight hours a day, six days a week, and two days 11 hours, and one day 13 hours, without fatigue or drowsiness. It was six months work in 26 days. He finished and revised and corrected it" (OC to PAM, 15 Jan 1893, CU-MARK).

97. See above, p. 531. A series of entries in Notebook 32, datable before 20 December, either pertain to the assignment of maxims (e.g., "No motto for Roxy's share in the duel") or abstract the content of chapters, perhaps to help in choosing mottoes—e.g., "26 – Luigi's illness (Betsy) & Angelo's baptism" (TS p. 51).

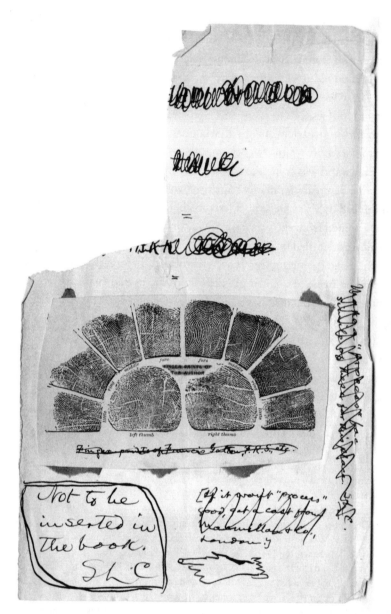

Draft title page removed by Clemens from MS Morgan, making use of fingerprints clipped from the title page of Francis Galton's *Finger Prints* (1892). The manuscript leaf was acquired by the Morgan Library and Museum in 2011. Mark Twain's inscription, which he has mostly canceled, reads: [PUDD'NH]EAD WILSON | A TALE [*short double rule*] | [BY M]ARK TWAIN. [*short double rule*] | Fingerprints of Francis Galton, F.R.S., etc. | Make a "process" fac simile of these for this place. SLC | [If it won't "process" good, get a cast from Macmillan & Co., London.]

substituting a more efficient system of graphic symbols (he had made use of a similar plan in *The American Claimant*). The symbols were meant to be placed at the chapters' beginnings, but Clemens did not add them himself; he sketched them on a separate sheet and delegated their implementation: "*To Printer*. Please make fac-similes of those signs, & use them at chapter-tops—one & sometimes two ... It is not necessary that they fit the weather of the chapter always." The "Conclusion," also added at this time, is an aphorism (left over from the abandoned Prang Calendar) denouncing March weather, with private directions to the printer to "treble all the weather-signs above 'Conclusion,' & turn some of them up[s]ide down, & others down on their sides." The dateline of the "Conclusion," "Florence, March, 1893," is false, made to accord with the aphorism's theme of March weather; it would have been pointless for Clemens to add to the manuscript in March 1893, when the typescript had already been made from it and mailed to Hall in New York.[98] The "weather" addenda may have been written around the same time as the "Note Concerning the Legal Points," which is dated by Clemens "this second day of January, 1893, at the Villa Viviani."

That same day, he wrote to Laurence Hutton: "I've finished that book & revised it. The book didn't cost me any fatigue, but revising it nearly killed me. Revising books is a mistake."[99]

TS2 AND PUBLICATION STRATEGY
(JANUARY–JULY 1893)

On 19 December 1892, Clemens wrote to A. M. Barnes, a typist living in Florence, and asked for a sample of his work.[100] He examined the sample and

98. The "Conclusion" is the realization of a notebook entry, "March weather.—with all signs," which, judging from its position in Notebook 32, was written on or soon after 20 December (TS p. 51).

99. 2 Jan 1893 to Laurence Hutton, NjP. Hutton (1843–1904) was an author and the literary editor of *Harper's Monthly*. A friend of the whole Clemens family, Hutton visited them in Florence in November 1892 (5 Nov 1892 to CC, CU-MARK; OLC to CC, 16 Nov 1892, transcript in CU-MARK).

100. 19 Dec 1892 to A. M. Barnes, Sotheby Parke Bernet 1976, lot 459. The address for Barnes recorded in Clemens's notebook, Via Valfonda 17, was the residence of Lucy E. Baxter (1837–1902; Royal Archaeological Institute 1892, 447). Barnes was her maiden name: she was the daughter of the English poet William Barnes (1801–86). Baxter was

replied on 23 December: "It is carefully done, & that is what I particularly want, as I must do my proof-reading on this side of the ocean. I shall have the MS. ready before many days."[101]

While Barnes was typing MS Morgan, Clemens pondered its publication. He had a long-standing attachment to subscription publishing, which brought the author a much larger share of the profits than the trade could offer. He had founded Charles L. Webster and Company as a subscription publishing house, but the industry was changing, and his company had recently been reorganized to publish mainly in the trade. In January 1893 he asked Hall what he thought about placing *Pudd'nhead Wilson* (referring to it by its original title) with the American Publishing Company, the Hartford subscription house which had brought out his first major books:

> Would it answer for me to publish The Extraordinary Twins through the American Publishing Co.? Mrs. Clemens fears it would damage CL&W [i.e., Charles L. Webster and Co.] to have me publish a new book through another house. Tell me your views—freely.
>
> If the A. P. Co. still have their subscription machinery I should like to try, for there is no money for a book of mine (or anybody else's for that matter) in the "trade."[102]

On 3 February, with Barnes's typed copy (TS2) in hand, and still unsure how to publish it, he wrote again to Hall:

> My book is type-writered & ready for print—"Puddn'head Wilson—a Tale." (Or, "Those Extraordinary Twins," if preferable.)
>
> It makes 82,500 words—12,000 more than Huck Finn. But I don't know what to do with it. Mrs. Clemens thinks it wouldn't do to go to the Am. Pub.

---

an author in her own right (under the pseudonym Leader Scott) and a leading light of Florence's expatriate community; it does not seem likely she was picking up extra money as a typist under the name of "A. M. Barnes," so perhaps the typist was a relative living with Baxter, or receiving mail at her address. Clemens's letters to Barnes are known only from fragmentary quotations in the auction catalog cited for them. Our only guide to whether Barnes was male or female is the Sotheby's cataloger, who saw the letters and who treats Barnes as male. Barnes would also type for Clemens "Extracts from Adam's Diary" (MS in NN-BGC) and several chapters of *Personal Recollections of Joan of Arc* (MS in CU-MARK).

101. 23 Dec 1892 to A. M. Barnes, Sotheby Parke Bernet 1976, lot 459.
102. 24 Jan 1893 to Frederick J. Hall, NN-BGC, in *MTLP*, 332–34.

Co. or anywhere outside of our own house; we have no subscription machinery, & a book in the trade is a book thrown away, as far as money-profit goes. I am in a quandary. Give me a lift out of it.

I will mail the book to you & get you to examine it & see if it is good or if it is bad. I think it is good, & I thought the Claimant bad, when I saw it in print; but as for any real judgment, I think I am destitute of it.[103]

Hall, perplexed by his partner's interest in subscription publishing, tried tactfully to set him straight:

I have received the Ms of "Those Extraordinary Twins" [i.e., TS2] but have not yet looked it over. I wrote you fully the other day regarding the present condition of the small book subscription business. . . . There is a good and profitable sale in the trade for any of your books that strike the public fancy. There is no sale at present by subscription for any book that you could write. . . . As to the American Publishing Company, all the books they sell now are sold through the trade and it is the trade sales of your books that keep them alive, and their subscription sales amount to nothing at all—as I wrote you, the subscription book business is entirely changed and the handling of small books in that way is a thing of the past. . . . While I have not read "Those Extraordinary Twins" I am sure, judging from the condition of the book trade in all its branches, that to get the book up in handsome style, as you suggest, illustrating it fully and putting a high price on it, would merely mean to sink money in it.[104]

On 22 March 1893, Clemens sailed from Genoa for a ten-day visit to America, arriving in New York on 3 April.[105] After visiting Chicago and Elmira, he started back to Italy on 13 May on the *Kaiser Wilhelm II*. He carried TS2 back with him and read it on shipboard.[106] Arrived back in

103. 3 Feb 1893 to Frederick J. Hall, NN-BGC, in *MTLP*, 336–38.

104. Frederick J. Hall to SLC, 10 Mar 1893, CU-MARK. Hall's last sentence shows he had confused Clemens's plans for *Pudd'nhead Wilson* with his plans, outlined in a 3 February letter, for *Personal Recollections of Joan of Arc*: "I am writing a companion to the Prince & Pauper which is half done & will make 200,000 words; & I have had the idea that if it were gotten up in handsome style, with many illustrations & put at a high enough price maybe the L.A.L. [i.e., *Library of American Literature*] canvassers would take it & run it with that book" (3 Feb 1893 to Frederick J. Hall, NN-BGC, in *MTLP*, 336–38).

105. 6 Mar 1893 to Chatto and Windus, KyLoU.

106. On 7 May 1893, Clemens wrote Hall from Elmira, asking him, in preparation for the voyage, to "put 'Puddn'head Wilson' with the shawl-strap of things that are to go on the ship" (transcript in CU-MARK). Hershel Parker (1984, 120) suggests that Clemens began to revise TS2 during this ocean crossing and speaks of "shipboard" revisions "made on the big typescript during the first half of 1893, while it was all one literary work." Although Clemens

Florence, the company's debts preyed on him; the typesetting machine still wasn't finished, and the family were "skimming along like paupers."[107] During the American trip he had been ill and "accomplished nothing that I went home to do."[108]

In mid-June the Clemenses moved from Florence to Munich so that Olivia could be treated by a heart specialist, Professor Max Oertel.[109] Arriving in Munich, Clemens found waiting for him a series of letters from Hall. The Financial Panic of 1893 had begun in earnest: business, the stock market, and banking were devastated. Hall had written on 19 May: "The condition of the money market just at present is something beyond description. You cannot get money even on government bonds or equally good security. . . . and it is difficult to collect for goods that we do sell."[110] On 2 June it was worse:

> You can scarcely conceive of the condition of business generally. If you have kept track of what has been going on since you left you know that there has been failure after failure of banks and prominent business houses. There has been a constant succession of crashes. . . . It is like pulling teeth to get any money at all. . . . In the face of all this our printers and binders, whom we have for years past been in the habit of paying by a two or three months note, so as to give us a chance to turn the stock made into money, find it impossible to use our paper or to use paper of any kind, and we have to carry them along by cash payments. . . . Our noses are right down to the grinding-stone as close as they can be.[111]

Clemens had not received these letters when he wrote Hall on 2 June, announcing his intention to abandon ship: "I am terribly tired of business.

---

later wrote that he had "read it and studied over it on shipboard" (EXT, 353.27), he never says he revised it there, and there is no evidence that he did anything with TS2 until late July 1893. No variant between MS Morgan and its published derivatives can be clearly identified as a revision made on the "big typescript" before its transformation, in July, into the revised TS2a.

107. 30 May and 2 June 1893 to Frederick J. Hall, MS in NN-BGC and transcript in CU-MARK, in *MTLP*, 343–45.

108. 9 June 1893 to Joseph H. Twichell, CtY-BR.

109. 4 June 1893 to William W. Baldwin, NNPM; Notebook 32, TS p. 63; "Max Oertel," *Nature* 135 (16 Mar 1935): 424.

110. Frederick J. Hall to SLC, 19 May 1893, CU-MARK. Clemens's belated receipt of the earlier letters is mentioned in 26 June 1893 to Frederick J. Hall, NN-BGC, in *MTLP*, 346–47.

111. Frederick J. Hall to SLC, 2 June 1893, CU-MARK.

I am by nature & disposition unfitted for it & I want to get out of it. I am standing on the Mount Morris volcano with help from the machine a long ways off. . . . Now here is my idea for getting out." He wanted to sell his two-thirds interest in the firm for $200,000 and pressed Hall to find a buyer. "Wait a little & see if you can't make the deal. . . . Get me out of business!"[112] Hall's reply was remarkably measured. "I hardly know exactly how to write you," he began. While the Panic continued, Clemens's interest could not be sold "for anything like the amount of money you have invested in it nor could you find a purchaser at that price or any other price *just at present*. . . . To go near anyone now, especially rival publishers, with a proposition to sell your interest would merely mean to expose our weakness and precipitate disaster." Hall agreed to attempt the sale "the MOMENT there is the faintest hope of success." If Clemens should leave the business, however, "I will want to do so also. . . . I would not go through another month like the past for ten times what I am making out of it."[113] Clemens and Olivia both replied, apologizing for Clemens's rash letter.[114]

Professor Oertel ordered Olivia to take the waters at Krankenheil, a saltwater spa near the Bavarian town of Tölz. The family arrived on 13 July to stay for "five mortal weeks," as Olivia called them—she thought Krankenheil "the most unattractive spot in Europe."[115] Clemens liked it,[116] but, as he told Hall on 18 July, financial anxiety had now overwhelmed him:

> I have never felt so desperate in my life—& good reason, for I haven't got a penny to my name, & Mrs. Clemens hasn't enough laid up with Langdon to keep us two months. . . . Yet if the firm can be kept alive a while longer no doubt you can save yourself & me too by selling L.A.L.
>
> As no letters arrive I am afraid it means that you have no hopeful news to give me about either our firm or the machine. It is now past the middle of July & no cablegram to say the machine is finished. We are afraid you

112. 30 May and 2 June 1893 to Frederick J. Hall, MS in NN-BGC and transcript in CU-MARK, in *MTLP*, 343–45.

113. Frederick J. Hall to SLC, 16 June 1893, CU-MARK.

114. OLC to Frederick J. Hall, 28 June 1893, photocopy in CU-MARK; 3 July 1893 to Frederick J. Hall, NN-BGC, in *MTLP*, 348–49.

115. OLC to Alice Hooker Day, 5 Sept 1893, CtHSD; OLC to Alice Hooker Day, 8 July 1893, CtHSD; 4 June 1893 to William W. Baldwin, NNPM; 3 July 1893 to Franklin G. Whitmore, CU-MARK; 9 and 10 July 1893 to Susan L. Crane, CU-MARK; Notebook 33, TS p. 23.

116. 9 and 10 July 1893 to Susan L. Crane, CU-MARK.

are having miserable days & worried nights, & we sincerely wish we could relieve you, but it's all black with us & we don't know any helpful thing to say or do.[117]

REVISING *PUDD'NHEAD WILSON*: TS2A (KRANKENHEIL, JULY 1893)

It was in this frantic state of mind that Clemens undertook to make whatever he could out of TS2. He had come to the conclusion (as he explained afterward) "that it was two stories in one & neither had a fair chance": the farce of the Twins needed to be "gutted-out," and the drama of Roxy, Tom, and Wilson made central, "properly finished up & concentrated."[118] It was not as straightforward as it sounded. The Twins, who looked expendable at first, turned out on closer inspection to perform some essential functions. They were the means by which the reader was introduced to the members of the Cooper family; their insult to Tom was the grounds of the assault trial and the duel; it was Wilson's defense of them in that trial that redeemed his reputation; their knife was the murder weapon; and they were the defendants in the climactic murder trial. To eliminate the Twins altogether would have meant a great deal of restructuring and new writing—more than Clemens's current levels of interest and energy permitted. But if they were disjoined and made into "ordinary" twins, they could continue to fulfill their obligations to the plot; only the farcical passages that depended on their physical conjunction required deletion—or so he persuaded himself. On or shortly before 30 July 1893, he went to work on TS2, physically removing from it long stretches of Twins material—"hunks," Hershel Parker has called them, "consisting of many pages which he could remove without taking anything else along."[119] Clemens bridged the gaps with newly written transitional passages, amounting to some twenty-seven hundred words.

Cutting the Twins' longer passages did not impair the narrative, for it had never advanced much while they were around; but there remained several situations, devised for conjoined twins, in which the now-separated Luigi and Angelo continue to participate, with results that some readers of the

117. 18 and 22 July 1893 to Frederick J. Hall, NN-BGC, in *MTLP*, 350–52. "Langdon" was Olivia's brother, Charles J. Langdon, in Elmira.

118. 30 July 1893 to Chatto and Windus, CtHMTH; quoted more fully on p. 554.

119. Parker 1984, 131.

Chapter 8.

so needs reforming

Nothing, ~~is so injurious~~ as other people's habits.
Pudd'nhead Wilson's Calendar.

One of three surviving leaves of TS2 (in CU-MARK). Copying from MS Morgan, the typist failed to reproduce the manuscript's underscoring on 'Pudd'nhead Wilson's Calendar': the underscore seen here was restored by Clemens. Revising the typescript, Clemens altered the motto (from 'is so injurious' to 'so needs reforming'), then canceled it. Adding to the typescript to produce the revised version of the novel, he adapted this page, changing the chapter number and adding a new beginning: 'Toward the middle of the evening they found themselves on the road to his house.' Then he deleted the sentence, which would find a place in chapter 7 of the revised text (PW-REV, 525.19–20).

published text have found disconcerting.[120] They are still together at all times, which, considering their mutual antipathy, is simply implausible: Angelo being his own man, why does he accompany his brother to the Sons of Liberty meeting and the duel, to both of which he has such strong objections? It becomes hard to see why the Twins should have been exhibited in a Berlin museum; and that they should differ in religion, or run for office on opposing tickets, comes to seem less than extraordinary. The trial for assault had to go, for it depended on the impossibility of knowing which of the conjoined twins kicked Tom; now that the kicker was definitely Luigi, such a trial could have no interest, nor could Wilson succeed in defending him. Yet the citizens, as before, invite him to run for office and elect him mayor, on the strength, apparently, of having lost his first and only case. Choosing to explain this away rather than revise it, Clemens attributed it to the glamor of Wilson's service as Luigi's second in the duel. The duel itself was cut, along with the Freethinkers' meeting, the Bible class, the assault trial, the doctoring of the Twins, and several colloquies with the Cooper family. Removing these passages diminished or obliterated several other characters. Rowena, already much pared back in the recasting of December 1892, was still further reduced. Her brothers Henry and Joe (who had never had anything to do except comment on the Twins) vanished, as did Aunt Betsy Hale. The incident of Jasper and the runaway horse, and the theological argument it occasioned, were excised. In a letter of 30 July 1893, Clemens summarized for Hall the result of his labors:

> *This* time "Pudd'nhead Wilson" is a success! Even Mrs. Clemens, the most difficult of critics, confesses it, & without reserves or qualifications. Formerly she would not consent that it be published either before or after my death. I have pulled the Twins apart & made two individuals of them; I have sunk them out of sight, they are mere flitting shadows, now, & of no importance; *their* story has disappeared from the book. Aunt Betsy Hale has vanished wholly, leaving not a trace behind; aunt Patsy Cooper & her daughter Rowena have almost disappeared—they scarcely walk across the stage. The whole story is centred on the murder & the trial; from the first chapter the movement is straight ahead without divergence or side-play to the murder & the trial; everything that is done or said or that happens is a preparation for those events. Therefore, 3 people stand up high, from beginning to end, & only 3—Pudd'nhead, "Tom" Driscoll & his nigger

---

120. The survival of "vestigia" from the original plot is discussed in Feinstein 1942, Wigger 1957a, and Parker 1984.

mother Roxana; none of the others are important, or get in the way of the story or require the reader's attention. Consequently, the scenes & episodes which were the strength of the book formerly are stronger than ever, now.

When I began this final reconstruction the story contained 81,500 words; now it contains only 58,000.[121] I have knocked out everything that delayed the march of the story—even the description of a Mississippi steamboat. There ain't any weather in, & there ain't any scenery—the story is stripped for flight!

Now, then, what is she worth? The amount of matter is but 3,000 words short of the American Claimant, for which the syndicate paid $12,500. There was nothing new in that story, but the finger-prints in this one is virgin ground—absolutely *fresh*, and mighty curious & interesting to everybody.[122]

From this letter one might guess which elements of the original story had been criticized: the conjoined Twins and their humdrum exploits, the Cooper family, the weather-signaling scheme. It may have been Hall who made these points; Clemens had sought his opinion in his letter of 3 February 1893.[123] Hall, however, as an inexperienced junior partner, cannot have "refused" the manuscript or "discouraged" its publication, as has sometimes been claimed.[124] The manuscript version's only known detractor is Olivia, who "would not consent that it be published either before or after my death." It is clear that Clemens regretted the loss of Roxy's first sight of the steamboat *Grand Mogul*, even if it had "delayed the march of the story."

The need for ready money made publication as a magazine serial imperative. In this same letter Clemens told Hall to solicit offers from the *Cosmopolitan* and the *Century*: "Do your best for me, for I do not sleep, these nights, for visions of the poor-house. . . . Everything does look so blue, so dismally blue!"[125] A week later he told Hall he was about to send him the revised typescript (TS2a): "It'll furnish me hash for a while I reckon. I am

121. Clemens's word count of MS Morgan is accurate. His count for the (lost) revised TS2a, however, exceeds by some six thousand words the *Century Magazine* serial eventually set from it. Either TS2a received further cuts after July 1893 (this could include cuts made by the *Century* editors) or Clemens's estimate was simply off.

122. 30 July 1893 to Frederick J. Hall, TxFTC, in *MTLP*, 354–56.

123. 3 Feb 1893 to Frederick J. Hall, NN-BGC, in *MTLP*, 336–38.

124. For Hall's "rejection" of MS Morgan see, e.g., Rowlette 1972, 18; Parker 1978, 139; Parker 1984, 116; Rasmussen 2007, 1:400. The idea may stem from a misunderstanding of Hall's letter to Clemens of 10 March 1893, quoted on p. 547.

125. 30 July 1893 to Frederick J. Hall, TxFTC, in *MTLP*, 354–56.

almost sorry it is finished; it was good entertainment to work at it, & kept my mind away from things."[126]

On 30 July, the same day he summarized the revisions for Hall, he sent Chatto and Windus a letter alerting them to the new book:

> A year ago I wrote a little story—10,000 words—& didn't like it, & threw it aside. Just then you happened to send me a book which furnished me an idea, & I re-wrote the story,—95,000 words, this time, & still unsatisfactory. Last fall I took hold of it again & cut it down to 81,500 words, then threw it aside once more, as still unsatisfactory. A while ago I took hold of it once more—having discovered that the trouble was that it was two stories in one & neither had a fair chance—& this time I have *arrived*. This time it suits me. One story is gutted-out, the other one properly finished up & concentrated, & the bulk reduced to 58,000 words. Now then, whenever a man says to you that industry & perseverance have perished out of this world, you have my authority to tell him he lies, if his size is such as to justify this kind of frankness.[127]

Chatto and Windus replied on 15 August:

> Our expectation is on tip-toe for the new story on which you have been so severe a task master to yourself, and we are all agog to lend a hand in the rewarding of such industry and perseverance. Can we make a start with it? We tremble when we think that even now you may not be satisfied with it. We might arrange for the English serial use of it on your behalf if you could favour us with your views on the subject, and let us have a duplicate typewritten copy.[128]

It is not clear whether, at this point, Clemens and Hall had any "duplicate" copy of TS2a to give them. What is certain is that six months would pass before Chatto and Windus obtained a complete text. Their struggle to publish *Pudd'nhead Wilson* was just beginning.

With the book now out of his hands, Clemens's mind returned to business, and his affairs again required his presence in America. He settled the family in Franzensbad, a health spa in Bohemia, and sailed for New York from Bremen on 29 August, taking Clara along "for company."[129]

126. 6 Aug 1893 to Frederick J. Hall, NN-BGC, mistakenly identified in *MTLP*, 359, as part of a letter dated 14 and 16 Aug 1893.

127. 30 July 1893 to Chatto and Windus, CtHMTH.

128. Chatto and Windus to SLC, 15 Aug 1893, CU-MARK.

129. 14 and 16 Aug 1893 to Frederick J. Hall, NN-BGC and CU-MARK, in *MTLP*, 358–61; 18 Aug 1893 to Chatto and Windus, OC; Notebook 33, TS p. 29.

Arriving in New York on 7 September, Clemens learned that the *Century* had offered to serialize the novel. He wrote Olivia:

> I've sold . . . Pudd'nhead Wilson to the Century for six thousand five hundred, which will go to you by & by—first payment after Nov. 1—for it is even hard for the Century to get money. Story will begin in December number, & be made the "feature."
>
> Gilder and Johnson are vastly pleased with the story, & they say Roxy is a great & dramatic & well-drawn character.[130]

"I like the Century people," he wrote her two weeks later, "& am glad I'm back there again."[131] Clemens had a good working relationship with the editor in chief, Richard Watson Gilder, and he had long favored the magazine as a venue. He was well aware, however, that he could appear in the *Century* only on its own terms. Conscious of its mission as a family magazine, it required Clemens, like its other contributors, to modify his texts in various ways. According to the memoir of *Century* assistant editor L. Frank Tooker— *The Joys and Tribulations of an Editor* (1924)—a contributor's words held sway only "up to the limits of good taste and permissible idiomatic or grammatical construction"—as defined by the editors, of course. Alterations "in the direction of good taste" required the elimination of "affected forms and stereotyped expressions," "solecisms," and "bad literary form." Decency called for the deletion of slang, coarseness, profanity, irreverence, and oaths, as well as "the softening of all expressions or statements likely to offend."[132] "It was really pathetic," wrote associate editor Robert Underwood Johnson, "to see the way authors would plead with us for another 'damn' or for a well-known equivalent of the lower regions."[133]

---

130. 7 Sept 1893 to OLC, CU-MARK, in *LLMT*, 267–68. The *Century* money went to Olivia because Clemens had transferred the copyright of *Pudd'nhead Wilson* to her, "in part pay for her $14,000 which I took out of Halsey's hands & lent to the firm" (14 and 16 Aug 1893 to Frederick J. Hall, NN-BGC and CU-MARK, in *MTLP*, 358–61). Noah Wetmore Halsey was a Wall Street broker (*MTLP*, 301).

131. 21 Sept 1893 to OLC, 2nd of 2, CU-MARK, in *LLMT*, 273–74.

132. Tooker 1924, 69–70, 114. Tooker's chapter 6, "Editor Versus Contributor," explains and defends the *Century*'s way with authors' copy. See also John 1981, 151–58.

133. Robert Underwood Johnson 1923, 142.

Clemens had extensive experience of the *Century*'s requirements. When the magazine published three extracts from the forthcoming *Adventures of Huckleberry Finn* in 1884–85, Gilder sought and obtained Clemens's permission to expunge "some few expressions 'not adapted to our audience.'"[134] This involved censoring references to nakedness, bodily functions, death, and corpses, the removal of vulgarisms and slang such as "rot" and "hogwash," and the suppression of irreverent or profane speeches—even oaths on the order of "dern" and "by jings."[135] The editors also adjusted grammar and syntax and standardized dialect forms. For the *Century*'s 1889 extract from *A Connecticut Yankee in King Arthur's Court*, Clemens himself prepared the text, doing his best to anticipate the magazine's requirements; even so, the editors found that the extract, ten *Century* pages in length, afforded them ample scope for the revision of grammar and syntax, and the removal of slang, irreverence, and double entendres.[136]

Censorship, rewriting, and house styling were the conditions of appearing before a drawing-room public. Clemens knew this, but he did not approve it or entirely accept it. In the fall of 1892, when he was negotiating the serialization of *Tom Sawyer Abroad* in *St. Nicholas*, he had explicitly permitted the editor, Mary Mapes Dodge, to "tame it down or alter it to suit her market."[137] He told Hall: "I tried to leave the improprieties all out; if I didn't, Mrs. Dodge can scissor them out."[138] Dodge, for her part, promised to wield the scissors "very sparingly, and with a reverent hand."[139] When Clemens read proof for the first installment, he tolerated, as promised, the removal of "improprieties" but resisted the magazine's alterations in other areas. "I have been to St. Nicholas," he wrote, "to curse the proof-reader's attempts to improve my spelling and punctuation. He had also written some suggestions in the margin. But Clarke will have the matter set according to copy hereafter and see that the proof-reader retains his suggestions in the mush of his decayed brain."[140] Dan Beard,

---

134. Richard Watson Gilder to SLC, 10 Oct 1884, CU-MARK, quoted in *HF 2003*, 747.

135. *HF 2003*, 748 n. 250; for the examples quoted, see the Emendations and Historical Collations, entries at 157.31–33 and 163.16.

136. *CY*, 604, and Textual Notes on pp. 629 (50.34), 636–37 (129.3–4).

137. 1–15 Nov 1892 to Frederick J. Hall, NN-BGC.

138. 31 Oct 1892 to Frederick J. Hall, transcript in CU-MARK, in *MTLP*, 323–24.

139. Mary Mapes Dodge to SLC, 19 Nov 1892, letter draft, photocopy in CU-MARK; in Wright 1979, 182–84.

140. Sept? 1893 to CC or OLC, in CC 1931, 86. William Fayal Clarke (1855–1937) was associate editor at *St. Nicholas* ("William F. Clarke, Retired Editor, 83," New York *Times*, 24 Aug 1937, 21).

who had illustrated *Connecticut Yankee* and *The American Claimant* and was now illustrating *Tom Sawyer Abroad* for *St. Nicholas*, tells (at second hand) of the scene Clemens made in defiance of the magazine's improvements:

> When Mark Twain sent the manuscript of *Tom Sawyer Abroad* to *St Nicholas*, there was a part of it which the editor thought might be improved, and the wording was consequently changed. Mark Twain was a gentle soul, but if Theodore Roosevelt stood for civic righteousness, Mark stood for the unalienable rights of the author to his own statements. When Mark read the proof he was exceedingly wroth and, entering the sanctum sanctorum, the holy of holies, or the editorial department of *St Nicholas*, he shocked the gentle creatures and terrified the associate editors by exclaiming, "Any editor to whom I submit my manuscripts has an undisputed right to delete anything to which he objects but"—and his brows knit as he cried—"God Almighty Himself has no right to put words in my mouth that I never used!"[141]

In the end, Clemens could fight the magazine only so far before accepting the presence of editorial alterations and substitutions—in the text of the serial; they could be reversed in the book edition. In the event, even this remedy failed him. Although he told Hall to "Use the original—not the St. Nicholas version of 'Tom Sawyer Abroad,'" his directive was ignored or came too late, and the printers set to work using *St. Nicholas* as copy; only after the first two-thirds of the book had been set in type was the error discovered and the compositors supplied with "the original."[142] In consequence, the edition of *Tom Sawyer Abroad* published by Clemens's own firm perpetuated some hundreds of editorial changes which the author, if he approved them at all, had approved solely for use in the magazine.[143]

Discriminating the *Century*'s editing from the TS2 typist's errors and the author's revisions is the greatest of several challenges in editing *Pudd'nhead Wilson*. The problem stems from the loss of a key document: the authorially and editorially revised typescript TS2a. Had this survived, comparison to MS Morgan would have shown where the typist was at fault, while authorial and editorial alterations would be easily distinguished by their handwriting. That TS2a perished is not remarkable. It was usual for printer's copy to be scribbled on and passed from hand to inky hand; each compositor's stint was

141. Beard 1939, 344.

142. Ca. Feb 1894 to Frederick J. Hall, Van Nosdall 1938, item no. 3; *TS 1980*, 624–25.

143. The English edition of *Tom Sawyer Abroad*, published by Chatto and Windus, was set throughout from copy which was free from the changes of the *St. Nicholas* editors (*TS 1980*, 248–49, 622–26; see also Brack 1972).

marked with her name.[144] Once it had rendered its final service as a reference for the proofreader, the soiled and worn copy was generally thrown away.[145] Lacking TS2a, the editor must judge the nature of each textual variant between MS Morgan and the *Century* serial: the source of each *could* be the author, the editors, the typist, or the compositor. These cruxes are described in more detail in the Note on the Texts, and in notes attached to entries in the Textual Apparatus; here we review the historical evidence for the actions of the *Century* editors and proofreaders in preparing TS2a for publication.

The fact that Clemens was in New York—and so able to converse in person with Hall, with the *Century* editors, and with the press of Theodore Low De Vinne, the master printer who designed and oversaw all Century Company publications—has deprived us of a written correspondence that would have shed light on the textual history. Even so, evidence abounds that Clemens was dissatisfied with the *Century*'s editing of *Pudd'nhead Wilson*. On 21 September 1893 he closed his letter to Olivia from his rooms in the Players Club as follows: "Good-bye, Sweetheart, I must go over to the Century & read some proof (for December) on the story which they continually & everlastingly glorify & shout about."[146] Reading those first proofs precipitated a showdown with associate editor Robert Underwood Johnson, as he reported to Olivia in a second letter:

> My darling, I've been in a fine fury since I wrote you from the Players three or four hours ago! I went to the Century, took my Pudd'nhead proofs, & sat down & began my corrections. Presently it began to seem to me that there was

144. "The composition of the magazines is done by young women, whose work is as accurate and acceptable as that done by men. The women are paid the same rates as men" (De Vinne 1890, 88). Among the compositors' names marked in the printer's copy for the *Century Magazine*'s "The £1,000,000 Bank-Note" (CU-MARK) are "Mrs. White," "Miss Heming," "Miss Bazin," "Miss Macarthur," and "Boydie."

145. According to the De Vinne Press manager Frank E. Hopkins (1863–1933), no one at the Press took "the slightest interest in the fate of manuscripts, signed autograph letters, and other documents which now would be considered valuable. . . . Once a month all manuscripts, proofs, and letters of instruction that had fulfilled the purpose for which they had been written, were tied up in a bundle by the composing room and stowed away for a period until all likelihood of their being needed for reference had passed, when they too joined the common pile of refuse. If an author requested the return of his manuscript and proofs, of course he received them; otherwise everything, by whomever written, was taken to the vault below and dumped into huge burlap bags, suspended from the ceiling. Periodically a man lowered himself into the bags, and trampled down the contents solidly. Then the waste-paper merchant hauled them away after paying a cent or two a pound for what may have been worth a dollar or two a pound" (Hopkins 1936, 40–41).

146. 21 Sept 1893 to OLC, 1st of 2, CU-MARK, *LLMT*, 271–73.

something very odd about the punctuation—was it possible that some impertinent puppy had been trying to improve it? Pretty soon I came across a "d—" —a pitiful & sneaking modification which I well knew I *couldn't* have put upon paper, drunk or sober.[147] I asked for the copy—in a most unsteady voice, for I was suffocating with passion. When it came, it was fairly small-poxed with corrections of my punctuation—my punctuation, which I had deeply thought out, & laboriously perfected! Then my volcano turned itself loose, & the exhibition was not suited to any Sunday school. Johnson said that the criminal was De Vinne's peerless imported proof-reader, from Oxford University, & that whatever he did was sacred in De Vinne's eyes—sacred, final, immutable. I said I didn't care if he was an Archangel imported from Heaven, he couldn't puke his ignorant impudence over *my* punctuation, I wouldn't allow it for a moment. I said I couldn't read this proof, I couldn't sit in the *presence* of a proof-sheet where that blatherskite had left his tracks; so Johnson wrote a note to De Vinne telling him the laws of his printing office must be modified, this time; that this stuff must be set up again & my punctuation restored, to the minutest detail, & always be followed hereafter throughout the story. So I'm to return there tomorrow & read the deodorized proof.[148]

The imported proofreader's depredations were still fresh in Clemens's memory a year later, when he wrote to the publisher of *Harper's New Monthly Magazine* about serializing *Joan of Arc*:

> Will you make an order in writing & attach it to my MS., & sign it & back it with your whole authority, requiring the *compositor & proof-reader* to follow my copy exactly, in every minute detail of *punctuation, grammar, construction* and (in the case of proper names) *spelling*. Please do it. I have revised that MS fully five times, & no proofreader is competent to teach me, after one look, how a thing ought to be which I have weighed & studied & examined five times.
>
> I am thus urgent because I know that the Century proof-reader is insane on the subject of his duties, & it makes me afraid of all the guild. That man changed every punctuation point in the Introduction to Pudd'nhead Wilson—*did it in the MS* before it went to the printer, & it came mighty near being set up so. Do you know what that bat was trying to do? He was trying to make *sense* of a lot of stuff which I had taken enormous pains to *deprive* of all semblance of sense.[149]

147. This is true for MS Morgan, in which Clemens wrote three "damns," a "damnation," and a "damnable," but no dashed-out oaths.

148. 21 Sept 1893 to OLC, 2nd of 2, CU-MARK, *LLMT*, 273–74.

149. 11–12 Sept 1894 to J. Henry Harper, ViU. By the "Introduction to Pudd'nhead Wilson" Clemens meant the "Whisper to the Reader." For proofreaders editing in printer's copy, see Jones 1977, 59.

Despite Clemens's "fine fury," *Century* proofreaders continued to repunctuate *Pudd'nhead Wilson* in a way that was quite alien to Clemens's own practice. The punctuation of the serial is logical and analytical, profligate with commas, while that of the manuscript—light, but never inadequate—shows Mark Twain's close attention to the rhythms of speech. On the occasions when Clemens's punctuation suffered in this way, and he had the time and energy to reimpose his own, he did as much as he could and demanded that the printers do the rest. During this distressing season, while he scrambled for survival in New York, restoring his punctuation on his own was impossible. In December, the month the first installment appeared, he wrote in his notebook: "In the first place God made idiots. This was for practice. Then he made proof-readers."[150]

In the matter of censorship, too, Clemens's protestations made little difference in the end. The "d—" he encountered while reading proof of the December 1893 installment was restored to MS Morgan's "dam," but in later installments the manuscript's expletive was rendered as "D—" or "——." Assistant editor L. Frank Tooker remembered that "Mark Twain . . . had been angered by our cutting of certain dubious passages in 'Pudd'nhead Wilson'" and "had not hidden his wrath under a bushel."[151] The omission from the *Century* of references to certain bodily parts or functions is therefore highly suspect. The serial text omits the information that the infant Tom was "a singularly flatulent child"; it omits how Angelo's assailant, struck down by Luigi, died "before his spouting blood struck us"; and it suppresses Tom's kick in the "rear." It cannot have been Clemens who decided the firemen must not "squirt out" a fire and changed it to "put out," or who purged the text of slang, as when Constable Blake is made to say "the town needn't worry" instead of "let the town keep its shirt on." We may be less certain about the omission from the *Century* of strongly worded passages present in MS Morgan chapters 15–16, in which Tom, having learned he is Black and "a white man's bastard," rejoices in his "vengeful exultation," and enjoys bringing "this secret 'filth,' as he called it" among the whites, longing to "kill—somebody—anybody." Some of the omitted passages are plausibly the editors' censorship of material they regarded as violent and lurid; however, it may be that these passages never reached the magazine's offices, having been deleted by Clemens himself on TS2a, in the continuing process, visible in his

150. Notebook 33, TS p. 43. Clemens reworked this as a maxim from "Pudd'nhead Wilson's New Calendar" in chapter 61 of *Following the Equator* (1897), with the object of his scorn changed to "School Boards."

151. Tooker 1924, 126.

revisions on MS Morgan, of eliminating traces of the earlier plot line in which Tom was going to kill Judge Driscoll for fathering him on an enslaved woman.

Clemens justifiably considered himself an expert on the dialects of his characters, and he fought to preserve them as he had written and carefully revised them. In a late September note to *Century* assistant editor William Carey (probably about the first installment), he complained: "Look here! *Now* they've gone to mending my dialect for me—I can't *stand* it. Won't you tell them to follow copy *absolutely*, in *every detail*, even if it goes to hell?"[152] Whatever Carey's answer may have been on this occasion, the *Century* required and—working with the De Vinne Press—achieved an exhaustive renovation of Clemens's dialect spellings. Clemens had to resign himself, if he did not want to lose a major publication and urgently needed money, to hundreds of *Century* alterations, large and small. There is every reason to believe that he accepted these changes for magazine purposes only: he expected his own firm to publish the American book edition, which, as long as a separate copy of TS2a was made and kept, could evade the magazine's and the printers' squeamish alterations.

In the same note Clemens dismissed the publisher's request that he supply individual chapter titles: "Land, I never was able to invent chapter-titles! I'm too old to learn, now." The spurious chapter titles found in many modern editions—"The Twins Thrill Dawson's Landing," "The Shame of Judge Driscoll," and so forth—were introduced into *Pudd'nhead Wilson* in the collected edition of Mark Twain's writings published by Gabriel Wells in 1923 and were adopted the same year into Harper and Brothers printings.[153]

To illustrate the serial, the *Century* hired Louis Loeb (1866–1909), an American artist trained in Paris at the Académie Julian and the École des Beaux-Arts. Loeb, too young to be personally familiar with antebellum America, consulted the older illustrator Dan Beard, who recalled:

> He came to my studio to learn in what sort of clothes he should dress the characters. I looked up the date and showed him a rough sketch of the costume. Then I dove down into my old cedar chest and found the very clothes of that date. The illustrations were made. They were dressed correctly and were a credit to the

152. Ca. 21 Sept 1893 to William Carey, NN-BGC. Carey (1858–1901), an assistant editor at the *Century*, was in charge of magazine proofs, "sending them back and forth between author and printer, and seeing that the forms of The Century went to press on the proper date" (Ellsworth 1919, 31; untitled article, *Current Literature* 2 [Jan 1889], 2–3).

153. The chapter titles are found in some collected editions which have a copyright date of 1899 but are in fact post-1922 printings. Recent editions perpetuating the nonauthorial chapter titles include SLC 2015 and SLC 2016.

artist; but when Mark Twain was asked to come and look them over the great literary commoner carefully inspected all the pictures, murmuring as he did so, "Beautiful! Fine! Excellent!" Then looking up at the editorial group surrounding him, he innocently inquired, "But who are the people in the pictures?"

"Why, Mr Clemens," they hastened to explain, "these are the illustrations for *Pudd'nhead Wilson*."

"They are beautiful," murmured Mr Clemens, "but I don't know them! Dan Beard is the only man who can correctly illustrate my writings, for he not only illustrates the text, but he also illustrates my thoughts."[154]

Setting aside Beard's self-aggrandizement, it is clear that Clemens authorized Loeb's pictures for publication. Hall wrote Chatto and Windus on 9 January 1894: "We saw the 'Century' people yesterday with reference to the illustrations. There are . . . seven very fine full page engravings for 'Pudd'nhead.' . . . We wished to communicate with you and see if you would care to use these illustrations. If so, we can send you electrotypes of them, charging you merely the cost for the electrotyping; and for the privilege of using the illustrations half of what *we* have to pay the 'Century' people for the privilege, viz: $450.00."[155] There were six (not "seven") pictures by Loeb, plus a portrait of Clemens for the first installment; the photograph for this had been selected back in September.[156]

The *Century* serial was scheduled to start in the issue of December 1893 and run for six or seven months, either to June or July 1894.[157] A press release issued in September 1893 announced:

> The Century Company has bought well nigh the complete literary "output" of Mark Twain during his year of residence abroad. . . . For *The Century* he has written a novel which is said to abound with humorous and dramatic incident, and in some chapters to be a revelation of tragic power. Its plot includes a most ingenious employment of science in the detection of crime. It is called "Pudd'n'head Wilson," and like "Huckleberry Finn" and "Tom Sawyer," is a story of a Mississippi steamboat town.[158]

154. Beard 1939, 345.

155. Hall to Chatto and Windus, 9 Jan 1894, UkReU. For Loeb, see "American Illustration: The Story of Louis Loeb," New York *Tribune*, 19 Jan 1896, 30; Armstrong 1900; "Louis Loeb—Illustrator and Painter," *Century Magazine* 79 (Nov 1909): 74.

156. 21 Sept 1893 to OLC, 2nd of 2, CU-MARK, *LLMT*, 273–74. The photograph (reproduced on p. 214) was taken by James Mapes Dodge at Onteora Park, New York, in August 1890. Clemens wrote the photographer: "What I like about that superb one leaning against the tree is that it is almost unendurably charming & beautiful, & yet does not flatter" (18 Sept 1890 to James Mapes Dodge, NjP). James was the son of Mary Mapes Dodge, the editor of *St. Nicholas*.

157. Frederick J. Hall to Chatto and Windus, 3 Jan 1894, UkReU.

158. "Mark Twain's New Stories," St. Joseph (Mo.) *Herald*, 19 Sept 1893, 4.

The *Century*'s advertisements and press releases emphasized the character of Wilson, "a hard-headed country lawyer" who "furnishes much of the fun that one naturally expects to find in a story by the author of 'The Innocents Abroad,'" and promised "graphic scenes from the old slave regime."[159] Newspaper advertisements featured a full-length portrait of Mark Twain, and a publicity poster was produced. The New York *World* noted that this was unprecedented:

> It used to be considered undignified for a publisher to advertise his wares in any but a conservative fashion. No "cuts" and no "display" of any sort; but times have changed. Cuts and ornamental designs have been used by the publishers for several years past. The Century Company is the first of the leading houses to go into advertising by bill posting. It has broken the ice with a life-size poster of Mark Twain, which is to adorn the postings of every town of size in the United States. Mark Twain's disjointed figure was a good one to begin with, and his name is familiar enough to attract attention.... "Business is business," even among authors. Dion Boucicault was a great believer in posters for the theatrical business, and I don't know why they should not serve for books. If the publishers are going into this sort of advertising they should at least set an example in the matter of taste.[160]

Doubtless this poster used the same portrait—from a photograph showing Clemens full-length with rolled umbrella—that the Century Company was using in its newspaper advertisements and on a handbill.[161] At Clemens's request,[162] Olivia, in Paris, had received advance copies of these advertising materials; in letters which have not survived, she wrote to him execrating the portrait. Clemens was delighted with her reaction:

> Your eloquent abuse of that infernal hand-bill portrait caught me unawares at breakfast & made me laugh my teeth loose. You see, I'm not capable of understanding why a body should care what sort of a portrait is published

159. "New Publications," Washington *Post*, 1 Nov 1893, 5; "The Century," Huron (S.D.) *Huronite*, 1 Dec 1893, 2.

160. "Gossip from Bookland," New York *World*, 26 Nov 1893, 26.

161. The photograph was taken by Normand Smith (1835–96), a Hartford acquaintance. Clemens wrote to Olivia: "Don't you remember that photo? It was taken by Normand Smith under the apple tree at Lilly Warner's side door"; it is reproduced as the frontispiece to this volume (4 Dec 1893 to OLC, CU-MARK; *FamSk*, 40, 184; "Obituary. Dr. Normand Smith," New York *Tribune*, 4 Aug 1896, 10).

162. 21 Sept 1893 to OLC, 2nd of 2, CU-MARK.

Century Company newspaper advertisement, with the portrait of Clemens to which Olivia objected. November 1893.

of him. I can't feel any way but indifferent about it. Still, for your sake I must go to Ellsworth & tell him to modify that portrait somehow. However, in defence of the picture I am obliged to admit that many people go into enthusiasms over it & say it is the best portrait of me they have ever seen. And indeed it seemed to me to be very satisfactory.[163]

163. 4 Dec 1893 to OLC, CU-MARK. Clemens mentions William W. Ellsworth, secretary of the Century Company and its advertising director ("The New Officers of the Century Company," *The Bookseller, Newsdealer and Stationer* 38 [15 Mar 1913], 185). From Clemens's letter to Susan Crane of 4 December 1893 we learn that Livy's "latest blast" was her third and "indignantest" letter about the advertising picture (CU-MARK).

Another inventive idea was the Century Company's publication of *Pudd'nhead Wilson's Calendar for 1894*. This tiny paper-covered pamphlet featured twelve of Wilson's aphorisms, drawn from the forthcoming serial numbers. Its typography mimicked the inexpert printing of a rustic almanac, and it bore the bogus imprint of *"Henry Butts,* DAWSON'S LANDING, *Mo."* The *Calendar for 1894* was sent out free to *Century Magazine* subscribers and was available to anyone who provided a postage stamp; in March, Edward Bok wrote in his syndicated column that "nearly a million" of them had been distributed.[164] Newspaper editors around the nation reprinted the aphorisms, charmed by their wit and their usefulness in filling out odd columns.[165]

RECEPTION OF THE *CENTURY* SERIAL

As the novel ran in the *Century Magazine*, Clemens's family and friends were congratulatory. On 18 December he dined with Laurence Hutton, and reported to Olivia: "Mr. Hutton thinks Pudd'nhead opens up in great & fine style. The fact is, I get a great many compliments on that story & the promise [it] holds out to the reader."[166] After publication of the January issue Clemens wrote to Livy: "Not since Innocents Abroad have I heard so much talk about a book of mine as I now hear about Pudd'nhead." He relayed more praise, gathered through Hall:

> In a lecture on "Politics from 1781 to 1815," in New York last night, by Professor Powell of the University of Pennsylvania, where Mr. Hall was present, he had considerable to say about the serious deeps underlying the humor in my several books, & then said that Puddnhead was clearly & powerfully

164. Bok 1894.

165. From Clemens's 30 December 1893 letter to Olivia, it is clear that the *Calendar* was already being distributed in New York: "The President of the Stock Exchange (or maybe it's the Vice) is named Wilson. All Wall Street has got hold of this Calendar, & for a joke they are getting up a complaint, with hundreds of signatures to lay before the Exchange. The Complaint is that their President, partially concealing himself behind a fictitious name—Pudd'nhead—is damaging the very business he is elected to foster [see Maxim for October.]" The maxim was: *"October.* This is one of the peculiarly dangerous months to speculate in stocks in. The others are July, January, September, April, November, May, March, June, December, August and February." The president of the Consolidated Stock Exchange of New York was Charles G. Wilson (Nelson 1907, 18–19). The *Calendar* pamphlet was printed in December and reprinted with corrections in the last days of that month; it is reproduced in photofacsimile in Appendix D.

166. 19 Dec 1893 to OLC, CU-MARK.

drawn & would live & take his place as one of the great creations of American fiction. Isn't that pleasant—& unexpected! For I have never thought of Puddn'head as a *character*, but only as a piece of machinery—a button or a crank or a lever, with a useful function to perform in a machine, but with no dignity above that. I think we all so regarded him at home. Well, oddly enough, other people have spoken of him to me much as Prof. Powell has spoken.[167]

From Keokuk, Iowa, Orion wrote on 16 December 1893: "Your genius flames brilliantly in the Century, the Cosmopolitan and the St. Nicholas. Your name is on all tongues. Among several complimentary editorials in the Gate City, one speaks of your story in the Century" (of which only the first installment had appeared) "as the flower of your autumn."[168]

In reality the acclaim for the serial was nowhere near so general. The aphorisms were generally praised, but few reviewers approved the work as a whole.[169] For the New Orleans *Picayune*, it confirmed Mark Twain was not a "master of humor in that old English sense of the term which comprehends the sources of our tears as well as the springs of our laughter." The character of Wilson had potential for "pathos": as an unappreciated outcast he "might easily have been used to give the narrative an entirely different tone. But here, as elsewhere, the author avoids all the invitations of sentiment. . . . We are not made to care enough for any of the characters."[170] The *Yale Courant* noted that Mark Twain was "writing in a more serious vein than is his wont," and wondered if he was "to turn into a solemn story-teller,"[171] while the Boston *Herald* thought it not serious enough, and denied that it was a novel at all; it was rather "an entertaining dialect story, which takes on the form of fiction in order to give the author the freedom which he desires in the treatment of character."[172] The *Open Court*, edited by the liberal political philoso-

167. 12 Jan 1894 to OLC, 2nd of 2, CU-MARK, in *LLMT*, 289–92. Lyman Pierson Powell (1866–1946) was an extension lecturer at the University of Pennsylvania.

168. CU-MARK. The Keokuk *Gate City* editorials mentioned by Orion have not been found. His letter also refers to Mark Twain's "The Esquimau Maiden's Romance" in *Cosmopolitan*, November 1893.

169. E.g., "Reading for the Month," Chicago *News*, 3 Feb 1894, 4; "Magazine Notes," Poughkeepsie (N.Y.) *Vassar Miscellany* 23 (Mar 1894): 248; "Century Magazine," Rutland (Vt.) *Herald*, 3 Apr 1894, 2.

170. "Frank R. Stockton and Mark Twain," New Orleans *Picayune*, 8 Apr 1894, 24.

171. "Current Magazines," *Yale Courant* 30 (17 Feb 1894): 112.

172. "January Magazines," Boston *Herald*, 3 Jan 1894, 6.

pher Paul Carus, was encouraged by the first installment to hope this would be "the great story of the South, classically describing the conditions and habits of the times before the abolition of slavery."[173] At the other end of the spectrum was Martha McCulloch Williams. The daughter of a Tennessee plantation owner, Williams reviewed the first two installments for the virulently unreconstructed *Southern Magazine*, calling them "tremendously stupid" and a "malicious and misleading" slander on the slaveholders of the old South.[174]

The reviewer for the Chicago *News* wrote in December 1893 that "Mark Twain . . . of late seems to be enjoying an unaccountable boom sprung from nobody knows just where or why," and went on to review the monthly installments of *Pudd'nhead Wilson*. The first installment received cautious praise: "One quite trembles at the toils with which he sees the volatile Twain will envelop the children."[175] In February this critic gave Clemens credit for attempting a "flight at higher ground," but called the result "wearyingly commonplace" and "a failure":

> Mark Twain needs a mental rest or revivification or sharp disapproval to bring back his touch of former days. Steam engines wear out and demand mysterious rests, which are granted. Nobody expects them to go on forever. Neither is it expected of Mr. Twain that he should indefinitely turn out original humor, but he has not yet recognized the fact.[176]

When the "exasperating serial" concluded in June, the *News* gave it a final thrashing. Clemens had made too little of Chambers, "the most interesting character in the whole plot"; the theme was "hackneyed" and the style "execrable." Mark Twain had "ruined his capabilities as a fiction-writer by doing too many pot-boilers. . . . It is to be feared from the abrupt way the novel has ended that Mr. Twain intends to spring a sequel upon us and steps should be taken immediately to restrain him."[177]

Among the serial's defenders was Theodore Roosevelt. Asked by the Buffalo *Commercial* for his views on the future of "the American novel," Roosevelt said: "My answer is that you oughtn't to use the definite article. . . .

173. "Book Notices," *Open Court* 7 (14 Dec 1893): 3910.
174. Williams 1894, 99, 100; MSU Libraries 2003.
175. "Reading for the Month," Chicago *News*, 5 Dec 1893, 4.
176. "Reading for the Month," Chicago *News*, 3 Feb 1894, 4.
177. "Reading for the Month," Chicago *News*, 4 June 1894, 4.

There is room, not for the American novel, but for any distinctively American novel. If you use the term with sufficient elasticity, Mark Twain has written three as good novels as were ever written in 'Tom Sawyer,' 'Huck Finn' and 'Puddinhead Wilson.'"[178]

THE CHATTO AND WINDUS EDITION

Since their initial enthusiastic correspondence with Clemens in August 1893, Chatto and Windus had traveled a hard road with *Pudd'nhead Wilson*. On or about 26 October they had wired Webster and Company requesting "proofs Twains new story to secure European copyright."[179] Chatto wrongly assumed that an American book edition was in the works; such a thing could not be published until the *Century* serial had run its course, and this would not be until July 1894.[180] The Century Company dispatched to Chatto the only part of the story so far made up in "proofs," the first *Century* installment.[181] Hall's cable in reply said that copyright would be secured by British publication of the *Century* installments as they came out but did nothing to discourage the notion that a book edition was in press.[182] On 3 January 1894, Hall answered another plea for complete copy by telling Chatto to "get copy from Unwin," referring to T. Fisher Unwin, the London distributor for the *Century Magazine*.[183] They did so, and found that Unwin could provide them only with "those parts which have appeared . . . in 'The Century' Dec Jan & Feb parts. He says he has no more copy, we shall therefore be glad if you will kindly send us by return mail the further instalments making the complete MS."[184] Two days later they

178. "The Western Wilds," Buffalo (N.Y.) *Commercial*, 6 Nov 1894, 2.

179. Chatto and Windus to Hall, ca. 26 Oct 1893, UkReU.

180. Frederick J. Hall to Chatto and Windus, 3 Jan 1894, UkReU.

181. Chatto did not receive proofs of the first (December 1893) installment until 23 November (Chatto and Windus to Deutsche Verlags-Anstalt, 23 Nov 1893, UkReU). These, being dispatched in mid-November, were presumably page proofs. The proofs of the first installment read by Clemens on 21 September (see above, pp. 558–59) can only have been galleys.

182. Webster and Company to Chatto and Windus, 26 Oct 1893, photocopy in CU-MARK.

183. Frederick J. Hall to Chatto and Windus, 3 Jan 1894, UkReU.

184. Chatto and Windus to Frederick J. Hall, 16 Jan 1894, UkReU.

accepted Hall's offer of the *Century* illustrations, although "the cost seems to us to be very high."[185]

On 28 February, Chatto and Windus were at last able to acknowledge receipt of a complete text: "We thank you for the copy of *Pudd'nhead Wilson*."[186] The exact nature of the document they received is not known; collation of the London edition against MS Morgan and the American edition suggests that it was a copy made from TS2a, prior to the corrections and revisions it would later receive from the *Century Magazine*. TS2 may have been made with a carbon copy, to be retained as a security copy or held in reserve for the production of the book edition; in that case, Clemens, as he made revisions to the ribbon copy, could have made parallel revisions to the carbon. Alternatively, Chatto's copy may have been a complete retyping of TS2a, made before Hall submitted it to the *Century* around August 1893. Chatto wanted the full text for the purpose of securing copyright; they did not at first mean to use it as printer's copy. Having received it, they continued, through April 1894 (i.e., through chapter 17) to set their text from the *Century*. Then, with their book already announced for publication "shortly,"[187] they decided not to wait on the appearance of the May and June installments, and set these last chapters from the copy sent to them in February. The consequences of this change in copy for part of the Chatto and Windus edition are discussed in the Note on the Texts.

HENRY HUTTLESTON ROGERS AND BANKRUPTCY (SEPTEMBER 1893–JUNE 1894)

Clemens had come to the United States from Europe in September 1893, not to oversee the publication of *Pudd'nhead Wilson*, but to try to save his publishing company and his investment in the Paige typesetter. Shortly after his arrival he received an offer of help from "the best new acquaintance I've ever seen."[188] Henry Huttleston Rogers (1840–1909) was a vice president in the Standard Oil Company, a railroad magnate, and a plutocrat of the Gilded Age. Known on Wall Street as "Hell Hound Rogers," he was ruthless in business; but in private he was generous and good company, and a friendship

185. Chatto and Windus to Frederick J. Hall, 18 Jan 1894, UkReU.
186. Chatto and Windus to C. L. Webster and Co., 28 Feb 1894, UkReU.
187. Chatto and Windus publisher's catalog dated April 1894, bound with Zola 1894.
188. 15 Sept 1893 to CC, CU-MARK.

Henry Huttleston Rogers and Mark Twain. Library of Congress.

was rapidly formed. Over the next years Rogers would labor constantly, with "heart & head & pocket," to restore Clemens's fortunes and save him from further missteps.[189] Writing to Olivia in February 1894, Clemens reflected on the good luck that brought Rogers in his way:

> When I arrived in September, lord how black the prospect was—how desperate, how incurably desperate! Webster & Co had to have a small sum of money or go under at once. I flew to Hartford,—to my friends—but they were not moved, not strongly interested, & I was ashamed that I went. It was from Mr. Rogers, a stranger, that I got the money & was by it saved. And then—while still a stranger—he set himself the task of saving my financial life without putting upon me (in his native delicacy) any sense that I was the recipient of a charity, a benevolence—& he has accomplished that task; accomplished it at cost of three months of wearing & difficult labor. He *gave* that time to me—time which could not be bought by any man at a hundred thousand dollars a month—no, nor for three times the money.[190]

189. 29 Jan 1895 to Rogers, NN-BGC, in *HHR*, 123–25.
190. 15 Feb 1894 to OLC, CU-MARK, in *MTL*, 2:611–13.

Rogers made loans to ease the pressure on Webster and Company, and he arranged for his son-in-law to buy the unprofitable *Library of American Literature* for $50,000. He prepared a scheme to fuse the various shareholders in the Paige typesetter into a new, restructured company, to which he would furnish working capital.[191] On 15 January 1894, Clemens received word that Paige had agreed to Rogers's plan. He wrote in his notebook: "This is a great date in my history. . . . Yesterday we were paupers, with but 3 months' rations of cash left & $160,000 in debt, my wife & I, but this telegram makes us wealthy."[192] Writing to his sister Pamela, he gave the credit to Rogers: "By the power & pluck and genius of a better man than I am or than any other man that I am acquainted with, the type-setter *is* on its feet, and permanently. It cost us 3 or 4 months of difficult labor, but the reward will arrive before many months. But Webster & Co.—*that* is another matter!"[193] It was at this time that he revealed to Rogers the full extent of the publishing company's condition: "I did hate to burden his good heart and over-worked head with it, but he took hold with avidity & said it was no burden to work for his friends, but a pleasure."[194] Rogers warned that Clemens himself, as a partner in the company, was liable for its debts if it failed, and advised him to shield his personal assets from the threat of seizure. On 6 March, about to depart on a short visit to his family in Paris, Clemens gave Rogers full power of attorney for the purpose of transferring his assets, including the Hartford house and the copyrights in his books, into Olivia's name.[195]

On 18 April the Mount Morris Bank called in its loans. Clemens and Hall, as partners in the company, acknowledged that they were unable to meet these "maturing obligations" by filing for assignment the same day. The assignee appointed by the court was a Wall Street lawyer, Bainbridge Colby.[196] Clemens was confident that the creditors would permit the business to continue under assignment. "The bank was stupid to crowd us," he wrote to his brother on 23 April: "we haven't been in such good shape for many months. The creditors will doubtless allow us to resume when they see what

191. *HHR*, 11–13; and see Rogers to SLC, 3 Mar 1894, ViU, in *HHR*, 35–37.

192. Notebook 33, TS pp. 47–48.

193. 25 Feb 1894 to PAM, CU-MARK.

194. 15 Feb 1894 to OLC, CU-MARK, in *MTL*, 2:611–13.

195. Power of attorney dated 6 March 1894, ViU. The copyright in *Pudd'nhead Wilson* was already registered in Olivia's name; see note 130.

196. "Mark Twain's Company in Trouble," New York *Times*, 19 Apr 1894, 9; Notebook 33, TS p. 61.

substantial shape we are in."[197] If Webster and Company were to continue business under assignment, the creditors reasoned, its best course might be to publish *Pudd'nhead Wilson*, with the profits going toward settling the firm's debts. Negotiations turned to the royalty to be paid, with Clemens strictly observing the legal dodge that made Olivia the copyright owner. Clemens wrote her that:

> It was confoundedly difficult at first for me to be always saying "Mrs. Clemens's books," "Mrs. Clemens's copyrights," "Mrs. Clemens's type-setter stock," & so on; but it was necessary to do this, & I got the hang of it presently. I was even able to say with gravity, "My wife has two unfinished books, but I am not able to say when they will be completed or where she will elect to publish them when they are done."
> Once Mr. Paine said—
> "Mr. Clemens, if you could let us have Puddn'head Wilson—"
> "So far as I know, she has formed no plans as to that book yet, Mr. Paine"— he took the hint & corrected his phraseology.[198]

For Clemens, in pugnacious mood and supported by Rogers, the collapse of Webster and Company was not entirely unwelcome. In April he had written to Olivia:

> Now & then a good & dear Joe Twichell or Susy Warner condoles with me & says "Cheer up—don't be downhearted," and some other friend says, "I am glad & surprised to see how cheerful you are & how bravely you stand it"—& none of them suspect what a burden has been lifted from me & how blithe I am inside. *Except* when I think of you, dearheart—then I am not blithe; for I seem to see you grieving & ashamed, & dreading to look people in the face.[199]

Olivia did grieve, but stoically. She wrote to Grace King: "Yes we are heavy loosers much heavier than I could wish through Webster & Co. Yet why should I wish it, what right have I? We have been greatly favored in our lives, by being exempt from such anxiety. Why should we not take our turn?"[200] Clemens had transferred his copyrights to Olivia precisely to ensure that his

197. 23 Apr 1894 to OC, quoted in PAM to Samuel E. Moffett, 6 May 1894, CU-MARK; 22 Apr 1894 to OLC, CU-MARK; 1 June 1894 to Frederick J. Hall, ViU; "The Firm's Liabilities Are Small," New York *Times*, 20 Apr 1894, 9; "The Webster Settlement Plan," *Publishers' Weekly* 45 (30 June 1894): 941.

198. 4 May 1894 to OLC, CU-MARK, in *LLMT*, 300–302. William H. Payne was president of the Mount Morris Bank (7 Feb 1898 to Rogers, Salm, in *HHR*, 320).

199. 22 Apr 1894 to OLC, CU-MARK.

200. OLC to Grace King, 16 June? 1894, LaBrUHM, in Pfeffer 2019, 238–39.

family, not the creditors, would benefit from them; Olivia thought of these stratagems as dishonorable, and was frustrated with her husband's boyish glee in foiling the creditors:

> You say that Mr Rogers wanted to ask the creditors 25 cents and that you felt that .20 was enough for Puddin'head Wilson. In that case if I were over there I should probably ask them .10 or .15 What we want is to have those creditors get all their money out of Webster & Co. and surely we want to aid them all that is possible. Oh my darling we want those debts paid and we want to treat them all not only honestly but we want to help them in every possible way. It is money honestly owed and I cannot quite understand the tone which both you & Mr Rogers seem to take—in fact I cannot understand it at all. You say Mr Rogers has said some caustic and telling things to the creditors. (I do not know what your wording was) I should think it was the creditors place to say caustic things to us.[201]

Even while Webster and Company was in business Clemens had inclined to publish *Pudd'nhead Wilson* by subscription with his old publishers, the American Publishing Company.[202] In the first days of May 1894 he met with the president of the company, Francis E. Bliss (1843–1915), whose father, Elisha Bliss, Jr. (1822–80), had published all of Mark Twain's major books from *The Innocents Abroad* (1869) through *A Tramp Abroad* (1880).[203] Clemens proposed that Bliss "should publish Puddnhead Wilson by subscription on a basis of half of the profits above cost of manufacture—same contract, as to all details, that I made with his father on 'A Tramp Abroad.'"[204] Clemens sailed for Europe on 9 May, reaching Paris on 22 May, and passed a month there before conducting his family to La Bourboule-les-Bains, a spa in the Auvergne. Brooding over the question of who was going to publish the American edition, Clemens wrote to Rogers from La Bourboule on 29 June—amid mob violence following the assassination of the prime minister, Sadi Carnot. Rogers, like Hall before him, cautioned against subscription publication,[205] but Clemens was not convinced:

---

201. OLC to SLC, 31 July 1894, CU-MARK.

202. See above, p. 546–47.

203. On 1 May 1894 Clemens wrote Bliss proposing they meet to discuss *Pudd'nhead Wilson* "about next Monday," i.e., 7 May (CStbK).

204. 16 May 1894 to Rogers, CU-MARK, in *HHR*, 53–54.

205. Rogers to SLC, 1 June 1894, CU-MARK, in *HHR*, 59–61.

Don't you think Puddn'head can be put into the hands of some publisher, without waiting longer on the creditors? It will take pretty brisk work to get it ready for the fall Trade, if it is published by "the Trade." If Bliss or some other subscription house should publish it there would not be so much press of time, because such a house could begin taking subscriptions as late as the 1st of October & issue all right by Dec. 1.[206]

THOSE EXTRAORDINARY TWINS
(NEW YORK, AUGUST 1894)

Clemens returned to New York in mid-July, staying at the Players Club. On a "blazing hot" 3 August he wrote to Olivia: "I am going to shut myself up naked by my bath-tub at the Players & write an article for Gilder for the October Century."[207] Briefly sidetracked by an invitation to spend the weekend with J. Henry Harper at his summer residence on Long Island, Clemens was back in the city on 5 August, and an article was duly written.[208] On 9 August he wrote to Olivia: "The other night—did I tell you?—I worked up the refuse matter which I dug out from Puddnhead, & put it together in a way which greatly pleased the Century, & they very much want it. They offer $1500 for it. I am considering; & will answer them to-morrow."[209]

The document created during this solitary night, here called TS2b, is not extant. It was a selection from the TS2 pages excluded in the revision of July 1893—the episodes featuring the original, conjoined Angelo and Luigi. Clemens bridged the gaps in the narrative with summaries of the action of *Pudd'nhead Wilson* and added a prefatory note to explain the relationship of these excerpts to the published novel. The note is a fanciful and inaccurate account of the composition, contrasting the art of "the born-and-trained novelist" with his own, untrained work as a "jack-leg":

> I had a sufficiently hard time with that tale, because it changed itself from a farce to a tragedy while I was going along with it,—a most embarrassing circumstance. But what was a great deal worse was, that it was not one story,

---

206. 29–30 June 1894 to Rogers, CU-MARK, in *HHR*, 68–70.

207. 3 Aug 1894 to Franklin G. Whitmore, CU-MARK; 3 Aug 1894 to OLC, CU-MARK.

208. 3 Aug 1894 to J. Henry Harper, photocopy in CU-MARK; Harper 1912, 571; 5 Aug 1894 to OLC, CU-MARK.

209. 9 Aug 1894 to OLC, CU-MARK.

but two stories tangled together; and they obstructed and interrupted each other at every turn and created no end of confusion and annoyance. I could not offer the book for publication, for I was afraid it would unseat the reader's reason, I did not know what was the matter with it, for I had not noticed, as yet, that it was two stories in one. It took me months to make that discovery. I carried the manuscript back and forth across the Atlantic two or three times, and read it and studied over it on shipboard; and at last I saw where the difficulty lay. I had no further trouble. I pulled one of the stories out by the roots, and left the other one—a kind of literary Caesarean operation.

Although Clemens claims to have withheld the original version from publication because he "was afraid it would unseat the reader's reason," in fact, as we have seen, he had described it as "type-writered and ready for print" in February 1893, at which time he fully expected it to be published. He falsifies the chronology, running different phases of composition together and blurring the distinction between internal revision in MS Morgan and the revisions of July 1893. If this concoction had gone into the *Century Magazine*, it might have had a modest afterlife among Mark Twain's collected sketches; instead it was destined to form part of the American first edition of *Pudd'nhead Wilson*.

PUBLICATION OF THE BOOK EDITIONS
(AUGUST–DECEMBER 1894)

When Clemens left New York on 15 August to rejoin his family (now at Étretat on the Normandy coast), negotiations were under way between Bainbridge Colby, as assignee, and Francis E. Bliss, for the American Publishing Company, to publish *Pudd'nhead Wilson*. The contract signed on 24 August specified that the volume would include "the post-script thereto entitled 'Those Extraordinary Twins.'"[210] The agreement required the company to sell the book by subscription, but allowed it to be sold in the trade as well, with the copyright holder's permission. The copyright holder was to receive $1,500 (matching the Century Company's offer for *Those Extraordinary Twins*) and "one-half (½) of the gross profits" from sales of the volume. The inclusion of *Those Extraordinary Twins* was clearly

---

210. 28 Aug 1894 to Chatto and Windus, MoHM; also 25 Aug 1894 to Rogers, NN-BGC, in *HHR*, 70–72; 2–3 Sept 1894 to Rogers, CU-MARK, in *HHR*, 72–73. For the contract (CtY-BR), see Appendix E.

in the publisher's interest: it was new material, fresh even to readers of the *Century Magazine*, and it helped to bulk out what was shaping up as a skimpy volume. Books sold by subscription were expected to look substantial, and Bliss must have seen that, at some fifty-two thousand words, *Pudd'nhead Wilson* was falling short. Adding *Those Extraordinary Twins* would bring the volume to the size of a short novel, like *The Prince and the Pauper*, and allow them to advertise it as "nearly 500 pages" in length.[211] However arrived at, the decision to bundle the revised novel with extracts from its earlier form significantly affected the book's reception. Inviting the reader to encounter the novel, not just as it was, but also as it had been, the 1894 American first edition drew attention to *Pudd'nhead Wilson*'s troubled gestation, making it part of the reading experience and a factor in how it was judged.

No one had thought to mention the Webster bankruptcy to Chatto and Windus, who continued, with growing anxiety, to write to the defunct firm. On 1 May they had written, hoping to issue their book in July, and again requesting the proofs and electrotypes.[212] On 2 July they noted that their edition was "long since printed off, excepting the illustrations—which we have not received from you."[213] They did not learn of the company's failure until 2 August, when they wrote to Hall: "We were indeed sorry to hear that Messrs Webster & Co were passing under a cloud, but hope the difficulties are only of a temporary nature, & that before long its affairs will go as smoothly as in times gone by." They asked if they might publish "towards the end of September."[214] Receiving no answer, on 27 August they wrote to Clemens in Étretat:

> Can you kindly give us any information respecting the illustrations to "*Pudd'nhead Wilson*," a duplicate set of those used in "The Century" we have been expecting to secure from Messrs Webster & Co of New York? Our English edition of the book has long since been printed off in readiness for the simultaneous issue of it with the New York edition in September, but the electros of the illustrations, which we arranged to take from Mr Hall, have not yet come to hand, and although we have written to Messrs Webster & Co: more than once on the subject, we have not yet received any reply. We apologize for troubling you in the matter; and only do so lest some

211. In the American Publishing Company advertising flyer, reprinted in Appendix F.
212. Chatto and Windus to Charles L. Webster and Co., 1 May 1894, UkReU.
213. Chatto and Windus to Charles L. Webster and Co., 2 July 1894, UkReU.
214. Chatto and Windus to Frederick J. Hall, 2 Aug 1894, UkReU.

communication may have miscarried; and we may go astray by not being ready to publish the volume next month as originally arranged.[215]

Chatto must also have cabled the substance of this letter, for Clemens replied the next day:

> Oh, my God, this *is* a state of things! Mr. Hall, & the Assignee & everybody else knew, away back yonder the last of April that *no* man could name a date for the issue of Puddnhead in America, & you ought of course to have been told that at the time.
>
> In America they *can't* issue before the middle of OCTOBER. I knew that when I sailed from there 2 weeks ago.
>
> I am writing the assignee of CLW & Co to hurry up those illustrations & send them to you.
>
> When I left America a contract was about to be made with the "American Publishing Co.," Hartford for Puddn'head—the firm I first published with. In that case it will be published by subscription, which will delay the issue till mid-October, or first November.
>
> I wish you had written direct to the assignee instead of to the lazy lousy firm of C L Webster & Co.[216]

Chatto wrote to Colby requesting a definite publication date. Colby cabled to Clemens: "Important you see Chatto personally at once arrange postponement of publication until I fix date with Bliss."[217] No personal meeting was necessary; at Clemens's request Chatto promised to withhold their edition "until we both can simultane, as a matter of fact we are still waiting the arrival of the illustrations, but we can issue without them if necessary."[218]

In Hartford the question of illustrations was occupying Bliss as well. For *Pudd'nhead Wilson* there existed the illustrations made by Louis Loeb for the *Century Magazine*, but *Those Extraordinary Twins*, of course, had none. To commission a new artist to illustrate the *Twins*, or to leave it unillustrated, would create an undesirable unevenness. Bliss opted to commission new illustrations throughout the whole volume, and he conceived a way of doing it which would also help to give the book the bulk a subscription volume needed. Every page of the book would have its margins decorated with

215. Chatto and Windus to SLC, 27 Aug 1894, UkReU.

216. 28 Aug 1894 to Chatto and Windus, MoHM.

217. 12 Sept 1894 to Chatto and Windus, MoHM (including paraphrase of SLC letter to Colby, not extant); Colby to SLC, per telegraph operator, 12 Sept 1894, MoHM.

218. Chatto and Windus to SLC, 14 Sept 1894, UkReU.

pictures; accommodating these would call for unusually wide margins, which, in combination with large type, would create a page containing on average 180 words (by comparison, the first edition of *Adventures of Huckleberry Finn* averaged more than 300 words per page). Bliss had evidently made his decision by mid-September, when the company announced that *Pudd'nhead Wilson*, "with other matter not heretofore printed," would be published later in the season with "many new illustrations."[219] The commission for the more than four hundred marginal pictures went to an obscure commercial artist, Frank M. Senior (1849–1903).[220] Since the pictures were meant to illustrate the narrative page by page, they could not be drawn until Senior could have page proofs, so both the printers and Senior worked under intense pressure of time. Senior described his labors in a letter to a friend:

> I got through with my work which had kept me so busy, day and night for the past two months, about a week ago and have plenty of leisure just now to write letters for the next two weeks. * * * I would have gladly complied with your wishes, * * * but had too much to do in getting out a holiday edition of Mark Twain's new story. I got the job of illustrating that book. Every page is illustrated with marginal pictures; on account of the lack of time in making the drawings, they were necessarily hurried and sketchy. I could not do them all on time so had to call in another person to assist, but out of the four hundred illustrations, I made three hundred and forty-one and can say I never was so hard pushed with a job which required that I should make a picture on an average of an hour and half. It was hard to do justice to the pictures in such a short time. The publishers seemed to be pleased with my work and have given me another order.[221]

219. "Literary Notes," New York *Times*, 15 Sept 1894, 3. A puff piece in the Hartford *Courant* promised the book would demonstrate an "advance in the art of illustration" ("Mark Twain's Books," 10 Oct 1894, 4).

220. Frank M. Senior (1849–1903) was born in Hartford. In childhood he became deaf from scarlet fever. He graduated from the New York Institution for the Deaf and Dumb, and, after traveling the country as a newspaper illustrator, settled in Brooklyn. At the time of his death he was a director of the Cox Engraving Company (*U.S. Special Census* 1888–95; Mexico [N.Y.] *Independent and Deaf-Mutes' Journal*, 13 Nov 1873, 2; untitled item, *Deaf-Mutes' Journal* [New York], 5 Jan 1882, 2; "Brooklynites Interested," Brooklyn *Eagle*, 20 June 1898, 7; "Deaths," Brooklyn *Citizen*, 16 Apr 1903, 3).

221. "Industrial Notes," *Silent Worker* 7 (January 1895): 4, reprinting the Malone (N.Y.) *Deaf-Mutes' Advocate*. The *Advocate* did not print the date of Senior's letter. The omissions are either the *Advocate*'s or the *Silent Worker*'s.

The artist called in to assist Senior was Calvin Hills Warren, who was also an occasional writer for the magazines and newspapers, often illustrating his own articles.[222]

On 13 October 1894, Bliss sent a telegram to Clemens, now in Rouen. This telegram, and Clemens's reply, are lost, but his follow-up letter, sent the same day, shows that the publisher had asked about last-minute additions, such as a dedication, introductions to the two parts of the book, and Pudd'nhead Wilson aphorisms for *Those Extraordinary Twins*:

> Dear Frank:
> Your telegraph has just arrived; 1.05 this afternoon. You will receive my answer at 8 this morning:
> "No additions print as it stands."
> I don't want any dedication—I've discarded the custom.
> There *is* an introduction to Pudd'nhead, you know.
> The OPENING PARAGRAPHS of the "Twins" constitute an introduction to that end of the book & explain how the booklet came to be written.
> I can't use calendar-headings in the Twins—they don't belong there. The Puddnhead Wilson of that story didn't construct a calendar, or mention one.
> I intended to send a batch of Calendar-aphorisms to add to the *Puddnhead* end of the book, but I have mislaid them & don't know where they are.[223]

---

222. Warren (1853–1914) was born in New York City and studied drawing at the Cooper Union. From 1907 he worked for the city as a topographical draftsman (Cooper Union 1881, 39, 41; Warren 1886, 1890, 1905; *Borough of Richmond Census* 1900; City of New York 1911, 1051; "Calvin Warren Succumbs," Perth Amboy [N.J.] *Evening News*, 8 Aug 1914, 6). Senior and Warren's original drawings for *Pudd'nhead Wilson* and *Those Extraordinary Twins* are in the Beinecke Library at Yale University (CtY-BR). A selection from their work is in Appendix G, "Illustrating *Pudd'nhead Wilson*."

223. 13 Oct 1894 to Francis E. Bliss, photocopy in CU-MARK. A fragmentary letter by Clemens to an unknown recipient, probably written in August 1894 during the Atlantic crossing, likewise shrugs off a request for additional aphorisms: "I put in some solid hours on those aphorisms before I left, trying to work them into shape to suit me, but it was a failure. I had to give it up, only two or three were satisfactory" (Feldman 1956, no. 275). His letter to Olivia of 11–13 February 1894 shows him continuing to make new aphorisms and praising one of hers:

> My Dear Mrs. Pud'dnhead Wilson Clemens:
> So you've gone into the aphorism-business yourself, it appears! And with distinguished success, too:
> "A thing which has been long expected takes the shape of the unexpected when it comes at last."
> That has gone into my note-book, & will go thence into Puddnhead's mouth. I made half a dozen aphorisms (in the rough) last night. But in the rough an aphorism is valueless; to reduce it to verbal pemmican is the difficult thing. (CU-MARK)

Clemens nearly made good on his promise: in 1896 he added Olivia's maxim to the manuscript of *Following the Equator* but later canceled it (MS p. 696 verso, NN-BGC).

Clearly Bliss was not going to receive any more copy. The main text of *Pudd'nhead Wilson* had already been set in type, using the *Century Magazine* as copy. For *Those Extraordinary Twins* the printer's copy was TS2b—the Twins material removed from the big typescript TS2 and revised in August 1894, supplemented with manuscript leaves containing new introductory and transitional passages.[224]

Late in October 1894, Chatto and Windus received a set of electrotypes but were dismayed to find them of poor quality. They wrote to Colby:

> We thank you for the electros of illustrations to Mark Twain's *Pudd'nhead Wilson*: the blocks are, however, not nearly as good as those in the ["]Century Magazine," and are rather a disappointment: in addition to this, they were so badly packed, that two at least were bent, and have had to be made good.
>
> We are arranging to publish on Thursday November 15: and shall be glad of a telegram from you. . . . It is important that we should hear from you at once in regard of this date.[225]

To secure copyright in both countries, it was necessary that publication be simultaneous, so Chatto had once again to accept a postponement. "We are quite ready to publish the book on Nov: 15th," they wrote, "but in deference to Mr. Colby's imperative cable we shall not issue the book until December 1st, although the chances for its sale would have been better had we been allowed to publish it on the earlier date."[226] Then, in November, it became clear that the American Publishing Company edition would not in fact be ready on 1 December. Fortunately, it was possible to establish *legal* publication in America on that date by depositing two printed copies of the work with the Library of Congress. Two proof copies were accordingly made up

---

224. Bliss's correspondence with Clemens on 13 October, in conjunction with a bibliographical oddity of the American Publishing Company edition, reveals that printing of the main text had already begun. Bliss started printing the text of the first chapter on page 17, reserving an octavo signature of sixteen pages for whatever preliminaries the author might still supply. From Clemens's cable of 13 October ("No additions print as it stands"), Bliss learned that the only preliminary would be the "Whisper to the Reader"; this would make up just two printed pages, so the planned signature became a single leaf (pages 15–16). Merle Johnson, trying to account for fourteen unnumbered pages of preliminary matter, was driven to the "highly irregular" expedient of including the flyleaves, the frontispiece, and even its protective tissue paper in his bibliographic description of the first American edition (Merle Johnson 1935, 59; *BAL* 3442).

225. Chatto and Windus to Colby, 24 Oct 1894, UkReU.

226. Chatto and Windus to SLC, 7 Nov 1894, UkReU.

and sent to the Library, where they were accessioned on 30 November 1894.[227] The proof copies show the book in an unfinished state, the text nearly finalized but the marginal illustrations lacking after a certain point in each of the book's two sections. Comparison of the proof copies to the final publication also reveals a group of verbal alterations in the text of *Those Extraordinary Twins*. In the proof copies the text runs through a final gathering of sixteen pages and onto a final page numbered 433, necessitating an additional tipped-in leaf. In the issued book, this extra leaf has been eliminated, and room found for the "Final Remarks" within the last gathering, through the deletion of fifteen short phrases or single words from the text. The production schedule was much too tight for a set of proofs to be circulated to Clemens in France, even if he had been willing to read them, and so he cannot have approved these space-saving tamperings with his text. Indeed, there is nothing to suggest that Clemens was consulted about any aspect of the book. Frank Bliss seems to have taken full credit for its design and the idea of the marginal illustrations,[228] and it was probably Bliss, not Clemens, who created the title page, with the title *The Tragedy of Pudd'nhead Wilson and The Comedy Those Extraordinary Twins*.[229] Although the American Publishing Company volume achieved its official publication date of 1 December 1894, subscribers did not begin to receive their copies until later in the month.[230]

Chatto and Windus, not best pleased with their delayed publication date of 1 December,[231] were surprised soon after to learn that the American edition contained material that they had not been offered. As we have seen, Chatto had finished printing their edition before Clemens even thought to

227. One of the two proof copies deposited in the Library of Congress was deaccessioned and purchased by Jacob Blanck, who presented it to the Houghton Library at Harvard University in June 1954 (Houghton Library 1953–54).

228. The first edition of Merle Johnson's bibliography quotes Frank Bliss on the illustration and production of the books Mark Twain published with the American Publishing Company; then Johnson states: "Mr. Clemens was not in America in 1894, when *Pudd'nhead Wilson* appeared, or in 1897, when *Following the Equator* was put on the market. Therefore, Mr. Bliss alone determined the form of those books; he originated the idea of the marginal illustrations for *Pudd'nhead*" (Merle Johnson 1910, 164–65). These remarks are omitted from Johnson's second (1935) edition.

229. See the Note on the Texts, p. 611.

230. The Boston Athenaeum received its copy on 21 December 1894 (*BAL* 3442).

231. The Chatto edition was actually published on 28 November ("Chatto & Windus's New Books," *Athenaeum* [London], 24 Nov 1894, 696; "Yesterday's New Books," London *Standard*, 29 Nov 1894, 3).

assemble *Those Extraordinary Twins*; but if they had known about the new matter, it could certainly have been printed and bound into the Chatto book. Andrew Chatto wrote to Clemens: "I have written to Mr. Bliss requesting a copy of the American edition of Puddnhead Wilson, containing the additional story 'The Extraordinary Twins,' which perhaps might be included in the English issue when it is reprinted?"[232] After perusing *Those Extraordinary Twins*, Chatto wrote again: "I am very sorry we did not have it in time to include in our edition but I hope to find a means of using it before long."[233] There was no further correspondence on the subject; *Those Extraordinary Twins* was never added to a Chatto edition, nor did it appear in the English-language edition published on the Continent by Bernhard Tauchnitz.[234]

On 21 December 1894, Clemens, in Paris, received a letter from Rogers. The Paige machine had been given a sixty-day test run at the Chicago *Herald* and had been pronounced a failure.[235] Rogers would not abandon Clemens, but he did withdraw his support from the machine business, and he expected the other investors to do likewise. Clemens, feeling he had "just barely head enough left on my shoulders to protect me from being used as a convenience by the dogs," cabled Rogers, begging him to "delay final action one month."[236] The next morning he wrote to Rogers proposing a series of unfeasible mechanical fixes to the machine; then he put in a full day's work on *Joan of Arc*. The machine's long-awaited triumph was never to be; Webster and Company had debts of nearly $80,000; the Clemenses' European exile was prolonged indefinitely. "We shall try to find a tenant for our Hartford house; not an easy matter, for it costs heavily to live in," Clemens wrote Rogers. "We can never live in it again; though it would break the family's hearts if they could believe it."[237]

232. Andrew Chatto to SLC, 27 Dec 1894, UkReU.

233. Andrew Chatto to SLC, 1 Feb 1895, UkReU.

234. Tauchnitz paid Chatto and Windus £51 on 14 November 1894 for the right to publish their edition, which appeared in March 1895 (Chatto and Windus ledgers, B/1/2, p. 29 [UkReU]; Rodney 1982, 100; catalog of new Tauchnitz publications dated March 1895, bound with Dixon 1895.

235. Rogers's letter is not extant; its purport is inferred from Clemens's letters to Rogers of 21 Dec 1894 (CtHMTH) and 22 Dec 1894 (NN-BGC); in *HHR*, 108–11.

236. 21 Dec 1894 to H.H. Rogers, NN-BGC, in *HHR*, 108–11; 22 Dec 1894 to H.H. Rogers, NN-BGC, in *HHR*, 108–11.

237. 27 Dec 1894 to H.H. Rogers, NN-BGC, in *HHR*, 112–14; Webster and Company debts as summarized in *MTLP*, 365.

RECEPTION OF THE BOOK (DECEMBER 1894–FEBRUARY 1895)

Many reviewers saw *Pudd'nhead Wilson* as departing from Mark Twain's usual style and themes. Some thought it a successful one: the London *Morning Post* called it "a new departure of a highly promising kind.... Even the most devoted lover of Mark Twain's writings could not have anticipated that he would produce a work of such strength and such serious interest as this." The London *Graphic* found it "uncharacteristically powerful and even deeply affecting," "something even finer than humour."[238] Where these reviewers saw innovation, others thought Mark Twain had "recovered much of his old-time spirit."[239] The London *Chronicle* remarked on the novel's unevenness, finding in it "a good deal of Mark Twain at his best, and not a little of Mark Twain at his worst."[240] For Clemens's friend Hjalmar Hjorth Boyesen (1848–95), the melodrama was redeemed by the vividness of the setting:

> If anybody but Mark Twain had undertaken to tell that kind of story, with exchanges of infants in the cradle, a hero with negro taint in his blood substituted for the legitimate white heir, midnight encounters in a haunted house between the false heir and his colored mother, murder by the villain of his supposed uncle and benefactor, accusation of an innocent foreigner, and final sensational acquittal and general unraveling of the tangled skein—if, I say, anybody else had had the hardihood to utilize afresh this venerable stage machinery of fiction, we should have been tempted to class his work with such cheap stuff as that of Wilkie Collins, Hugh Conway, and the dime novelists. But Mark Twain, somehow, has lifted it all into the region of literature.... The Missouri village in which the scene is laid, is so vividly realized in its minutest details; and the people, in all their fatuous prejudice and stolidity, are so credible and authentic, so steeped in the local atmosphere, that the illusion becomes perfect, and we swallow the melodrama without a qualm—exchange of heirs, haunted house, murder, and all.[241]

William Livingston Alden (1837–1908), an American author with a long-standing admiration for Clemens, called it "in point of construction ...

---

238. "Literary Notes," London *Morning Post*, 5 Dec 1894, 6, reprinted in Budd 1999, 359–60; "'Pudd'nhead Wilson,'" London *Graphic*, 29 Dec 1894, 746 (Budd 1999, 361–62).

239. "Mark Twain's New Book," Cincinnati *Commercial Gazette*, 3 Feb 1895, 23 (Budd 1999, 367–68); "Reviews," Manchester *Guardian*, 3 Apr 1895, 510; Zupitza 1895.

240. "More of Mark Twain," London *Chronicle*, 13 Dec 1894, 3 (Budd 1999, 360–61).

241. Boyesen 1895 (Budd 1999, 367).

much the best story that Mark Twain has written."[242] Most appraisals of the novel's construction were more qualified. For the Liverpool *Post*, *Pudd'nhead Wilson*, "with its impossible characters and its equally impossible plot," was "almost everything that a novel ought not to be"; yet pitied the reader "who can peruse it without unalloyed pleasure, or can lay it down without a sigh of regret."[243] The reviewer for *The Critic* (edited by Jeannette and Joseph Gilder, siblings of *Century* editor Richard Watson Gilder) found it too "crude" and "coarse" to be literature, and "so offensive to immemorial canons of taste, that the critic . . . puts it reluctantly down in the category of unclassifiable literary things—only to take it up and enjoy it again!" Mark Twain was a denizen of oral culture, strayed into the written word: "What *is* this? is it literature? is Mr. Clemens a 'writer' at all? must he not after all be described as an admirable after-dinner storyteller—humorous, imaginative, dramatic, like Dickens—who in an evil moment, urged by admiring friends, has put pen to paper and written down his stories?"[244]

The London *Chronicle* said it was "one of the strangest compounds of strength and artificiality we have read for many a day. Pathos and bathos, humour and twaddle, are thrown together in a way that is nothing less than amazing." The "imbecility of much of the incident" was relieved here and there by "a flash of the old wit or a page pregnant with feeling and humanity." Only the aphorisms of the Calendar saved the book from "disaster."[245] The *Westminster Budget* ranked the book alongside *Tom Sawyer* and *Huckleberry Finn* but judged the climactic courtroom drama a failure: "This is not Mark Twain's speciality. Any skilful writer of detective stories could have done it as well, if not better."[246] Many reviewers acclaimed the character of Roxy as a triumph and the best thing in the book, an opinion which would prove durable; "for the rest," said the *Saturday Review* (London), "there is little that

242. Alden 1894, 222–23 (Budd 1999, 359); "Wm. L. Alden, Author, Dead," Boston *Globe*, 16 Jan 1908, 5. In 1885, Alden wrote Clemens about *Huckleberry Finn*: "It is the best book ever written" (Alden to SLC, 15 Mar 1885, CU-MARK). Alden's review of *Pudd'nhead Wilson* appeared in the *Idler*, a magazine published by Chatto and Windus; they must have supplied him with an advance proof copy, for his review appeared in August 1894, four months ahead of publication.

243. "Some Books of the Week," Liverpool *Post*, 9 Jan 1895, 7 (Budd 1999, 363–64).

244. "Literature," *Critic*, 11 May 1895, 338–39 (Budd 1999, 372–73).

245. "More of Mark Twain," London *Chronicle*, 13 Dec 1894, 3 (Budd 1999, 360–61).

246. "Mark Twain's New Book," *Westminster Budget*, 21 Dec 1894, 1147.

can be said to rouse enthusiasm."[247] The characters were called "wooden," Tom Driscoll's speeches "artificial and forced," Wilson a "*deus ex machinâ*," and the Twins deficient in national character: "These two young men are as little like Italians as they are like Apaches."[248] Other critics found Mark Twain's "Whisper to the Reader," with its irreverent handling of Dante and Beatrice, "vulgar," "puerile," and "in bad taste."[249]

Only a few reviews reflected on Mark Twain's treatment of slavery and the antebellum South, and they split, predictably, along Northern and Southern lines. The Richmond, Virginia, *Dispatch* charged that "the author has tried to be fair to the slave-holders of the South, we believe, but has not done them justice."[250] "'Pudd'nhead Wilson' is not funny," wrote the syndicated columnist Joseph Hatton, "nor is it intended to be humorous; it is a powerful and grim story of the worst days of slavery in America."[251] The *Spectator* (London) thought the story a "vigorous indictment of the old social order."[252]

The review in the New York magazine *Public Opinion* was appreciative, but questioned the implications of Mark Twain's handling of nature and nurture, anticipating the theme of much later academic criticism:

> In "Pudd'nhead Wilson," if we reflect upon the career—but lightly sketched—of the rightful heir, it seems to teach the greater force of education and habit than blood or heredity; certainly his pure white blood never taught him to feel his superiority over his surroundings. But the more minutely detailed behavior of his substitute appears to lead to the belief that antecedents and the inherited moral weakness of the slave were too much for training and environment. Perhaps the author would have smiled in his cynical

247. "Our Library Table," *Athenaeum*, 19 Jan 1895, 83–84 (Budd 1999, 364); "Reviews," Manchester *Guardian*, 3 Apr 1895, 510; "Pudd'nhead Wilson," London *Graphic*, 29 Dec 1894, 746 (Budd 1999, 361–62); "New Books and Reprints," *Saturday Review* (London), 29 Dec 1894, 722 (Budd 1999, 362–63).

248. "More of Mark Twain," London *Chronicle*, 13 Dec 1894, 3 (Budd 1999, 360–61); "Our Library Table," *Athenaeum*, 19 Jan 1895, 83–84 (Budd 1999, 364); "New Books and Reprints," *Saturday Review*, 29 Dec 1894, 722 (Budd 1999, 362–63); Alden 1894, 223 (Budd 1999, 359).

249. "Novels and Stories," Glasgow *Herald*, 6 Dec 1894, 10 (Budd 1999, 360); "More of Mark Twain," London *Chronicle*, 13 Dec 1894, 3 (Budd 1999, 360–61); "Our Library Table," *Athenaeum*, 19 Jan 1895, 83–84 (Budd 1999, 364).

250. "Book Notices," Richmond (Va.) *Dispatch*, 10 Mar 1895, 12.

251. Hatton 1894.

252. "Current Literature," London *Spectator* 74 (16 Mar 1895): 367–68. See also "Mark Twain's New Book," Elgin (Scotland) *Courant and Courier*, 25 Dec 1894, 7.

way had he supposed that any attempt would be made at deductions of this nature, when his object, primarily at least, was to entertain.[253]

The unique features of the American Publishing Company edition were not much liked. About *Those Extraordinary Twins*, the reviewer for *Munsey's Magazine* said: "It is almost inconceivable that Mr. Clemens should have permitted such drivel as this to be published in his name, and particularly that he should have allowed it to mar the unity of his really clever 'Pudd'nhead Wilson.'"[254] Elsewhere it was called "extravaganza run mad without sufficient base"[255] and "probably less satisfactory than anything else Mark Twain ever wrote. . . . a labored paraphrase upon the Siamese twins sketch which Twain wrote in his early days."[256] The profusion of marginal pictures was disliked: "this style of illustration . . . is harmful to literary composition by detraction of attention."[257] But even the pictures had their defenders: the *American Hebrew* said they "add much to the pleasure of reading it," and the New York *Times* ran a positive review of the pictures alone, an unusual tribute to "the artist" despite the admission that "he does not draw well."[258]

Clemens was disappointed in the sales of the book both in America and England. The first royalty check from Chatto and Windus was for £196— one-quarter the size of the first check for *More Tramps Abroad*, in 1898—and sales remained weak. It was eleven years before Chatto's first printing of ten thousand copies was sold out.[259] Figures have not been found for the American Publishing Company edition, but Clemens regarded it as a failure. Two months after publication he told Rogers: "The thing has happened which was bound to happen. Bliss got hold of Pudd'nhead so late that he lost the holiday trade; consequently achieved no sale." Clemens shrugged it off; he had now finished *Joan of Arc* and was planning the lecture tour around the world (1895–96) that would yield the material for *Following the Equator* and

253. "Pudd'nhead Wilson," *Public Opinion* 18 (14 Feb 1895): 161 (Budd 1999, 369–70).

254. "Literary Chat," *Munsey's Magazine* 13 (June 1895): 315.

255. "Pudd'nhead Wilson," *Public Opinion* 18 (14 Feb 1895): 161 (Budd 1999, 369–70).

256. "New Publications," Washington (D.C.) *Evening Star*, 27 July 1895, 19.

257. "A Few New Story Books," *Book Buyer* 12 (Mar 1895): 92; "Literary Chat," *Munsey's Magazine* 13 (June 1895): 315; "New Literature," Boston *Globe*, 7 Feb 1895, 8.

258. "Literary," *American Hebrew* (24 May 1895): 66; "Mark Twain's New Volume," New York *Times*, 27 Jan 1895, 27.

259. Chatto and Windus stock books: B/1/3, pp. 63–64, 183; B/2/17, p. 407 (UkReU). A second printing (of one thousand copies) was called for in October 1905. The book's retail price was three shillings and sixpence, the copyright holder earning seven pence royalty per copy.

play a crucial role in bringing him out of bankruptcy.[260] In *Following the Equator* (1897), Clemens continued the device of heading the chapters with the sayings of Pudd'nhead Wilson, which for so many readers had proven the highlight of the earlier book. Clemens and Bliss agreed to publish an actual calendar, with abundant new maxims, though in time Clemens shrank from the task.[261] Perhaps it was with this in mind that he undertook a postpublication review of his *Pudd'nhead Wilson* aphorisms. A letter from Isabel V. Lyon, Clemens's private secretary from 1904 to 1909, to the book collector W. T. H. Howe preserves information from some document no longer extant—apparently a copy of the Chatto and Windus edition which Clemens had marked and annotated:

> He was not satisfied with all the maxims when he saw them in print, & planned a new edition with a revised calendar, & better maxims to take the place of those he struck out, as "unworthy." The maxims which satisfied him were on pp. 1 – 22 – 44 – 52 – 66 – 1st on p. 91 – 2nd on 99 – (121 he would have condensed into the last sentence,) 141 – 156 – 1st on 170 – 2nd on 180 – 197 – 224 – & 243.[262]

THEATRICAL AND CINEMATIC ADAPTATIONS (1894–1916)

In March 1894, Clemens granted his friend, the actor and theatrical manager Frank Mayo, permission to adapt *Pudd'nhead Wilson* as a play, with Mayo to

260. 8–9 Feb 1895 to H. H. Rogers, CU-MARK, in *HHR*, 128–30; 3 Feb 1895 to H. H. Rogers, Salm, in *HHR*, 126–28.

261. Pressed by Bliss in 1898, Clemens replied that in *Pudd'nhead Wilson* and *Following the Equator* "there are only about 60 maxims—not enough for a calendar. And even if there were enough it would not be worth while to waste them on old worn-out idea like a calendar which has a sale for only part of one year [and] then is dead stock" (11 Feb 1898 to Francis E. Bliss, Daley). To a correspondent who wrote asking for permission to compile a calendar herself, he wrote: "Unfortunately I am this long time under promise to make a Puddn'hed Maxim Calendar myself, & have been gradually adding to the original list of Maxims to that end. Maxims are a slow growth, & it will take me a year or two yet" (6 June 1899 to Alice L. Bunner, ViU).

262. Isabel V. Lyon to W. T. H. Howe, ca. 1930s, NN-BGC. The page numbers refer to the Chatto edition. On this evidence Clemens was satisfied with the maxims of the published novel for chapters 1, 3, 5, 6, 8, 10 (first), 11 (second), 12 (in substance), 14, 15, 16 (first), 18 (second), 19, 21, and the "Conclusion"; he was dissatisfied with those for chapters 2, 4, 7, 9, 10 (second), 11 (first), 13, 16 (second), 17, 18 (first), and 20.

Advertising poster for the play, 1895. Frank Mayo as Wilson and Frances Graham as "Rowy." Courtesy of Kevin Mac Donnell.

write the script and star as Wilson.[263] Mayo (1839–96) was already a leading player when Clemens knew him in Nevada and California in the early 1860s; now he was famous nationwide, particularly on account of his perennial appearances in the play of *Davy Crockett*.[264] The *Century* provided Mayo with the text of chapters not yet published, together with an "admonishment" to treat the contents as confidential.[265] The play was soon announced for the next theatrical season.[266] It opened out of town in Hartford on 8 April 1895, then on 15 April at the Herald Square Theatre, New York, where it ran for six weeks before going out on tour.[267] On 22 May, Clemens saw a performance at the Herald Square and made an after-play speech from his box; he complimented the play and Mayo's performance, but mainly he elaborated on the farcical potential of the Twins in their original, unseparated condition.[268]

Mayo's script is, as the New York *Times* remarked, "not a good one."[269] It is a farrago of characters and events from the novel, modified to conform more closely to the stock roles and situations of nineteenth-century melodrama.[270] Key dramatic events are left unstaged and merely alluded to, including the meeting where Tom is kicked, Roxy's kidnapping and sale into slavery, and the whole first day of the trial. Tom's assault on his uncle is not fatal, and it too goes unstaged. Mayo ties Wilson by blood to the Dawson's Landing community, making him Aunt Patsy's brother and Rowena's uncle, although he is still a transplanted Yankee; his spoken part is studded with aphorisms from the Calendar. The role of Rowena (called "Rowy" in the play) is greatly enlarged; there is a romance between her and Chambers, blocked, as they

263. 7 Feb 1894 to OLC, CU-MARK; 2 Mar 1894 to OLC, 1st of 2, CU-MARK, in *LLMT*, 296–97; Mayo 1895b.

264. "Frank Mayo Dead," New York *Tribune*, 9 June 1896, 3.

265. Contract between OLC and Frank Mayo, dated 23 Sept 1894, CtHMTH; Frank Mayo to C. C. Buel, 17 Apr 1894, NN.

266. "Theatrical Notes," Washington *Post*, 6 May 1894, 19.

267. "Entertainments," Hartford *Courant*, 9 Apr 1895, 3; "'Pudd'n-Head Wilson,'" New York *Times*, 16 Apr 1895, 5.

268. "Twain's Talk on the Twins," New York *Herald*, 23 May 1895, 7.

269. "'Pudd'n-Head Wilson,'" New York *Times*, 16 Apr 1895, 5.

270. A facsimile of the script in the collections of the Museum of the City of New York has been used here (Mayo 1895a). The Museum's script belonged to Frances Graham, who was married to Frank Mayo's son Edwin and originated the role of Rowy; she is pictured in the poster reproduced on p. 588 ("Entertainments," Hartford *Courant*, 9 Apr 1895, 3; "Mayo's Death," Cleveland *Plain Dealer*, 25 Feb 1900, 27). Stephen Railton's digital archive, *Mark Twain in His Times* (Railton 2012), reproduces a somewhat cut and adapted script from the New York Public Library for the Performing Arts (NN-L) as well as a large collection of contemporary reviews and a schedule of performances.

Edgar L. Davenport as Chambers and E. J. Henley as Tom, 1895.
Courtesy of Kevin Mac Donnell.

believe, by the color barrier. Judge Driscoll is depicted as paternal and benevolent, with Chambers reconceived as his acknowledged illegitimate son by
Roxy. Roxy is very much reduced in force and agency. In the prologue, set in
1836, Mayo relieves her of responsibility for switching the babies, turning it
into a mere accident. Roxy recognizes Tom on his theft-raid, and when he
later accuses her of the robberies, she allows herself to be convicted rather
than expose him. Mayo contributes an original scene, set in an old mill, in
which Chambers beats Tom for insulting Rowy and makes him "act like a

gentleman." Only after witnessing Tom's humiliation does Roxy threaten him with exposure as the thief (and, almost incidentally, as her son). In the courtroom scene Tom is exposed but not sentenced or sold into slavery. In a final tableau Rowy and Chambers embrace.

Although the theatrical program reprinted, as an "Author's Note," the novel's statement that Roxy and Chambers were "negroes" only "by a fiction of law and custom," Mayo's script retains nothing of the ironic and social-constructivist approach to racial identity that most readers have found to be present, if not necessarily consistent, in the novel. Stephen Railton observes that Mayo's depiction of Tom and Chambers "seems mainly calculated to reassure viewers that 'blood,' like merit, will always eventually tell, that the innate differences between 'white' and 'black' explain the nobility displayed by 'Chambers' and the viciousness of 'Tom.'"[271] The play was certainly so understood by many reviewers. In New Orleans (where it was advertised as a "Beautiful Missouri Idyl"), one critic called it "perhaps the only play that has been presented which in dealing with the question of negro character has not done more or less violence to the traditions and sentiments of southern people." For this critic it was Tom's "taint of negro blood" which caused him to become "a thief, a would-be murderer, and to kidnap and sell his free mother into slavery . . . while his foster brother, of pure white origin, grows up to be a brave, gallant and noble man, despite the fact that he has been brought up as a slave."[272]

Willa Cather, then the drama critic for the Pittsburgh *Leader*, wrote: "Of course the pith and heart of the play is the race question, the struggle between the Negro blood and the white, the demonstration that circumstances and environment could not make a slave a gentleman nor a gentleman a slave. . . . The interest one feels in Pudd'nhead's triumph is secondary."[273] The New York *Times* thought the Chambers–Rowy romance should have been brought more into the open; other critics denied that a romance was even intended, one Boston critic assuring readers that Rowy "likes the boy as a sort of great dog."[274] The drama critic for the New Orleans *Times-Democrat* complained that because Chambers is believed to be Black, the spectacle of Rowy treating

271. Railton 2012.
272. "Amusements," New Orleans *Times-Democrat*, 10 Jan 1898, 3, and advertisement, 5.
273. Pittsburgh *Leader*, 9 Feb 1897, 4, in Cather 1970, 1:477–78.
274. "The Theatrical Week," New York *Times*, 21 Apr 1895, 12; Fletcher 1895.

TOM AND ROXY
IN
Mark Twain's "Pudd'n'head Wilson."

Frank Campau as Tom and Eleanor Moretti as Roxy, 1895 or 1896. Courtesy of Angelo Cifaldi.

him "with a familiarity which nearly borders on love" was "unpleasant to look at."[275]

The play enjoyed the popular and commercial success that had eluded the novel. By common consent, Mayo's performance as Wilson formed the principal attraction. Such tributes as this were plentiful:

> The patience with which he endures poverty and the taunts, almost the persecution, of his neighbors through the best part of his life, his ever-smiling philosophy, his quaint humor with nothing bitter in it . . . his love for Rowey, his consoling and watching over her, his alert eye, that face that one can almost see think—all these things combine to make his Pudd'nhead one of the most, if not the most, interesting characters in the whole range of the American drama.[276]

This kindly, condoling Man of Sorrows was Mayo's creation in script and performance, and a figure quite unknown to Mark Twain, who called Wilson "merely a piece of machinery." After Mayo's early death while touring with the play in 1896, the role of Wilson was taken over first by Theodore Hamilton (1836–1916), and then by Mayo's son Edwin (1854–1900), who played the role in the Northern states while a second company, fronted by Hamilton, toured the South.[277] That the two productions were tailored to appeal to their respective audiences is suggested by the choice of Hamilton, a Southerner and "a gentleman of the old school," once "the most popular actor in the Confederacy," to play in the Southern states; but more direct evidence is lacking.[278] A spokesman for the production denied that Southern sensibilities required any changes from the play as mounted in New York; the South, he said, had progressed a lot in the past thirty years, race and slavery were only "secondary" elements in the play, and Frank Mayo as Wilson diffused "sweetness enough" to neutralize any lingering bitterness.[279] In 1900, Edwin Mayo, like his father before him, died while on tour with the play.[280]

In January 1916 the Jesse L. Lasky Feature Play Company, under the general directorship of Cecil B. DeMille, released a silent motion picture of

275. Sykes 1895.
276. Austin 1896, 18.
277. "*Pudd'nhead Wilson:* Schedule of Performances," in Railton 2012.
278. "Mr. Hamilton Leaves Today," Atlanta *Constitution*, 9 Mar 1898, 9; "Actor of the Olden Time," Indianapolis *Journal*, 10 Jan 1892, 16.
279. "Many Fine Characters," Buffalo *Courier*, 26 Jan 1896, 8.
280. "Mayo's Death," Cleveland *Plain Dealer*, 25 Feb 1900, 27.

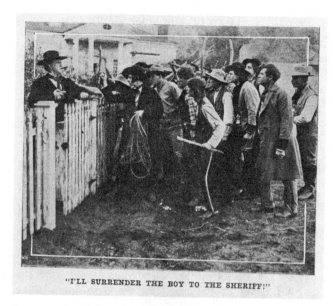

"I'LL SURRENDER THE BOY TO THE SHERIFF!"

Promotional still from the film, with Theodore Roberts as Wilson.
Motion Picture News, 12 February 1916.

Pudd'nhead Wilson. No print is extant today. The studio initially contracted
with Mayo's heir for the dramatic rights, then discovered that they belonged
to the Mark Twain Company, formed by the author in 1908 to manage his
literary assets.[281] The Lasky studio struck a deal with the Company and the
Harpers to film all the author's best-known works, of which *Pudd'nhead
Wilson* was the first to be made.[282] Contemporary reviews allow glimpses of
the scenario, which was written by Margaret Turnbull. Completing a process
begun by Mark Twain and continued by Mayo, the Twins were completely
eliminated. The Mayo play's romance between Rowy and Chambers was
retained, and daredevil action added, with Chambers rescuing Rowena

281. Memorandum of agreement dated 6 Jan 1915, between Eleanor Mayo Elverson,
the Estate of Samuel Clemens, and the Jesse L. Lasky Feature Play Company, NN-BGC;
American Play Company to Jervis Langdon II, 18 May 1915, NN-BGC; "Lasky Obtains
Rights to All Works of Mark Twain," *Motion Picture News*, 13 Nov 1915, 75; Gevinson 1997,
798; *AutoMT3*, 606–7, note on 304.16.
282. Lasky–Famous Players announced plans for six films besides *Pudd'nhead Wilson*,
of which *Tom Sawyer* (1917), *Huck and Tom; or the Further Adventures of Tom Sawyer* (1918),
and *Huckleberry Finn* (1920) were actually made ("Twain's Works in Motion Pictures,"
Hartford *Courant*, 17 Nov 1915, 6).

"from a runaway vehicle onto the back of a runaway horse."[283] A jealous Tom pinned the murder on Chambers. Wilson was shown holding off a mob who threatened to lynch Chambers, and defending him in court.[284]

The contents of the lost film can be glimpsed, to some extent, in reports of the censorship inflicted by state and municipal authorities. In Chicago two title-cards were suppressed because they referred to Judge Driscoll as the father of both Tom and Chambers ("The Father of two sons"; "What you gwine to do for my boy, Marse, he's yours, too, etc."); also censored there were "two closeup views of snake in voodoo's cabin"; and "stealing money."[285] In Ohio the exhibitor was required by the censor to "take out from sub-titles all reference to the word 'nigger,' cut out sub-title about man riding ahead of his master, scene where white man resents affectionate fondling of his mother, and scene where white man forcibly takes girl in his arms."[286] Outdoor scenes, including "slave quarters," were filmed on location "in the small town in Missouri in which Mark Twain laid his immortal story"—apparently a garbled reference to Palmyra, where the trial scene was filmed "in the old court house."[287]

THE CRITICAL HERITAGE

Pudd'nhead Wilson is a remarkable case of the revaluation of a literary work. As we have seen, on its publication critical opinion was deeply mixed, and the book (though not the play) failed to establish itself as a popular favorite. As late as the end of the twentieth century, it could be described as "neglected" and "almost proverbially 'secondary.'"[288] But since the 1950s its place in the canon of Mark Twain's works and in the canon of American literature, as measured in terms of college-level and professional study, has risen continuously, and today *Pudd'nhead Wilson* stands as one of his most read and most studied works.

The novel's early twentieth-century critics, without judging it an artistic success, found a place for it in their very different interpretations of Mark

283. "A Near-Dangerous Accident," Des Moines (Iowa) *Register*, 13 Feb 1916, 77.

284. "Princess," Reading (Pa.) *News-Times*, 17 Feb 1916, 9.

285. "City Hall Sensitiveness," Chicago *Tribune*, 27 Jan 1916, 18.

286. Platz 1916.

287. "'Pudd'nhead Wilson' Now in the Movies," St. Joseph (Mich.) *Herald-Press*, 31 Aug 1916, 1.

288. Gillman and Robinson 1990, introduction, x.

Twain. For Van Wyck Brooks, Clemens had betrayed his gifts and repressed his authentic self in a quest for gentility and acceptance. In *Pudd'nhead Wilson*'s troubled gestation, Brooks saw "the battle of the two Mark Twains," as the repressed "tragedy" overtook the intended "farce," "leav[ing] the reader's mind in tumult and dismay."[289] Bernard DeVoto valued the novel for its "corrosive comment on American life," drawing attention to Roxy and to Mark Twain's honest depiction of sexual relations between enslavers and enslaved women.[290] Sterling A. Brown, in *The Negro in American Fiction* (1937), criticized the ironies in the portrayal of Black people as oversubtle and prone to misconstruction: readers were liable to think Mark Twain endorsed Roxy when she assigned Tom's depravity and cowardice to his Black heritage.[291]

Two essays published in 1955 revived discussion of *Pudd'nhead Wilson* after a period of inactivity. A reprint of the novel carried a new introduction by F. R. Leavis, calling it "an unrecognized classic," "a mature, balanced, and impersonal view of humanity," with Roxy "dominating the book as a triumphant vindication of life."[292] For Leslie Fiedler the published *Pudd'nhead Wilson* was less important than the one we had lost through Mark Twain's revision, which he described as "a rollicking, atrocious melange of bad taste and half-understood intentions and nearly intolerable insights into evil, translated into a nightmare worthy of America." The achievement of the published book was in its transcendence of historical particulars, its characters caught up, not in anything so "parochial" as American slavery, but in "some universal guilt and doom."[293] These essays of 1955 partake of a shift in the critical approach to the book's "failure": from the position that Mark Twain had done something which, on the whole, had best been left undone, to the position that he had attempted something important that had, to some extent, miscarried.

In the 1960s the treatment of race, politics, and history became central to the burgeoning scholarship on *Pudd'nhead Wilson*. As critics searched for thematic connections between the novel's disparate concerns, the question became central whether Mark Twain, in taking on the social construction of race, had bitten off more than he could—or at any rate, did—chew. Had

289. Brooks 1920, 189.
290. DeVoto 1932, 284, 293–94.
291. Brown 1937, 68–69.
292. Introduction in SLC 1955; also published as Leavis 1956.
293. Fiedler 1955a, 1955b.

he failed to do justice to his challenging theme—or was it enough that the theme had been taken up and made available for the work of cultural criticism? The author's treatment of the nature/nurture question in connection with racial vice and virtue was increasingly seen as misleading or objectionable. Since about 1990, however, criticism has increasingly seen *Pudd'nhead Wilson* as opening a field of meaning more complex, and perhaps more valuable, than any clear statement can be, its indirections and ambiguities revalued as positive assets. Interviewed by the *Paris Review*, Toni Morrison singled out *Pudd'nhead Wilson* as an example of how

> Mark Twain talked about racial ideology in the most powerful, eloquent and instructive way I have ever read.... What is exciting about American literature is that business of how writers say things under, beneath and around their stories. Think of *Pudd'nhead Wilson* and all these inversions of what race is, how sometimes nobody can tell, or the thrill of discovery?[294]

As the book has risen in critical esteem, its compositional flaws, and the history of their creation, have taken a central place in the discussion. This line of inquiry had been started by Mark Twain himself, when he published his account of his difficulties in writing the novel; but that was long before research could correct and elaborate his account. The textual scholarship of Hershel Parker has been influential. For Parker, Mark Twain's careless revision created "adventitious meanings," not intended by him either in the original "moment of writing" nor in the later revision; and the resulting fusion of the intentional and the unintentional renders the published *Pudd'nhead Wilson* "patently unreadable."[295] While few have embraced Parker's conclusion, his exposure of textual conditions proved an unexpected godsend to New Historicist literary critics. For the contributors to *Mark Twain's Pudd'nhead Wilson: Race, Conflict, and Culture* (1990), a "readable" text was in no way preferable to a text with tangles and fractures, for these could be read as symptoms of strong and pervasive cultural pressures.[296]

294. Morrison 1993, 101.

295. Parker 1984, ix, x, 136. Parker's other studies of *Pudd'nhead Wilson* include Parker 1978, 1981, 1995, and Parker and Binder 1978.

296. Academic criticism has continued to read *Pudd'nhead Wilson* as illuminating American history and society by disclosing ideological formations. A list of important and influential studies would include: Smith 1962, chap. 8; Butcher 1965; Cox 1966, chap. 10; Turner 1968; Frederick Anderson's introduction to SLC 1968; Chellis 1969; Brodwin 1973; Pettit 1974, chap. 10; Bond 1981; Budd 1987; Thomas 1989; the essays in Gillman and Robinson 1990; Fishkin 1990; David Lionel Smith's afterword in SLC 1996; Moss 1998;

The remarks on reception so far concern the novel in the form in which it has circulated since 1894. Of the first completed version, the Morgan Manuscript, there is no reception history, beyond what readers have been able to glean from the fragments in *Those Extraordinary Twins*. (Fiedler's remarks about the "original," phantasmagoric *Pudd'nhead Wilson* do not refer to the Morgan Manuscript, which he did not consult.) Today there can be no fear (if there ever was any) that the Morgan version will "unseat the reader's reason" with its mixture of melodrama, crime fiction, satire, and grotesquerie that an earlier generation found incongruous. It is far more probable that today's reader—reared on magical realism and postmodernism, accustomed to the theme of the abnormal body, and caring little for older canons of taste and propriety—will accept the manuscript version's mingling of farce with more serious and probing matter. The growing scholarship on *Pudd'nhead Wilson* can only benefit from the availability of the full text, and readers are justifiably interested to read the famous suppressed text. With the present edition, the reception of the Morgan version can begin.

DECEMBER 2022   B.G.

Sollors 2002; Royal 2002; Gair 2005; Linda Morris 2007, chap. 3; Cole 2007; and McCoy 2017. Contemporary reviews in America and Britain are collected in Budd 1999, and the German reception history is summarized in Kinch 1989. Later critical reception is studied in Gooder 1991; Werner Sollors's introduction to SLC 2015; Hsuan Hsu's introduction to SLC 2016; and Goldstein 2017.

Textual Apparatus

NOTE ON THE TEXTS

The Introduction traces the history of composition, revision, transmission, publication, and reception for the three critical texts published here: (1) the original and (2) the revised version of *Pudd'nhead Wilson*, with (3) *Those Extraordinary Twins*. This Note addresses how those texts have been constructed. For the reasons explained in About the Texts in This Volume (p. xvii) it has seemed important to produce a critical text of the first finished version of the story, even though Mark Twain never published it in that form. The second and third texts, both largely derived from the first, he did of course publish, with all the usual distortions involved in that process. In all three cases the critical text aims to preserve the author's textual intentions at the time he finished the work, or submitted it for publication. All three critical texts are constructed by drawing on the full range of documentary evidence. The readings of the final text are drawn from holograph manuscripts, from typewritten or printed texts derived from them, from entries made by the author in his notebook—even, in one case, from a legal document.

The choice between variants does not rely on a default copy-text. Instead, every choice between variants, whether substantive or accidental, is an active editorial judgment based on the available evidence. In his seminal essay "The Rationale of Copy-Text," W. W. Greg recognized that a revising author is generally concerned with the text's "substantives" (meaning, broadly, the actual wording) rather than its "accidentals" (the spelling and punctuation); while amanuenses, compositors, and proofreaders are prone to alter accidentals and respect substantives.[1] In editing the revised *Pudd'nhead Wilson* and *Those Extraordinary Twins*, the accidentals of the Morgan Manuscript are followed; where the manuscript varies substantively from

---

1. Greg 1950–51. Our approach has been modified by the considerations in many subsequent contributions to editorial theory, including, especially, G. Thomas Tanselle's "Editing without a Copy-Text" (Tanselle 1994).

the published texts, the variants are investigated by the editor, who admits or rejects them on a case-by-case basis. We aim to produce authorial versions of each text, purged, so far as possible, of errors and unwanted changes introduced by typists, compositors, proofreaders, and publishers.

• *The Morgan Manuscript Version.* MS Morgan, sometimes wrongly called a "draft," is in fact a finished work, here published as such for the first time. The edited text is a critical transcription of this manuscript, now in the Morgan Library and Museum, rendered as Clemens would have published it before he decided otherwise and before he further revised it.[2] To that end, authorial revisions are reported solely in the Textual Apparatus, leaving the text "clear." Mark Twain's spelling and punctuation are not altered unless one of three conditions applies:

(1) Spelling and punctuation are corrected where they are demonstrably wrong, judged by the standards of his time—as with, for example, the MS Morgan readings 'slaugtered', 'appaling', and 'rhinds'. The grammar of the manuscripts is very seldom defective, but where it is, emendation is uncontroversial—'these gentleman', for example, is corrected to 'these gentlemen'.

(2) Abbreviations such as 'MS' for 'manuscript' are expanded, as Clemens would have expected any printer to do.

(3) Where he has spelled a word in more than one way, the predominating spelling has been used throughout. A complete lexicon of MS Berg and MS Morgan spellings has been compiled and analyzed in order to determine which words show variant spellings and the proportions among them.

Dialect spellings, in the main, have not been standardized. In dialect writing, Clemens aimed at an accurate and discriminating representation of speech, relying on his ear and his memory. As he told William Dean Howells in 1874 while revising "A True Story" for publication in the *Atlantic Monthly*:

> I amend dialect stuff by talking & *talking* it till it sounds right—& I had difficulty with this negro talk because a negro sometimes (rarely) says "goin'" & sometimes "gwyne," & they make just such discrepancies in other words—& when you come to reproduce them on paper they look as if the variation resulted from the writer's carelessness.[3]

Bearing this in mind, dialect forms are generally left alone. 'Nothin'', 'noth'n', and 'nuth'n'' stand in the text wherever they occur in manuscript; so do 'becase' and 'becaze'. As in MS Morgan, characters say both 'jes'' and 'jis'', 'own self' and 'own

---

2. Here, as elsewhere, the manuscript at the Morgan Library and Museum is referred to as MS Morgan; the critical text based upon it is referred to as the Morgan Manuscript Version or with the abbreviation PW-MS.

3. 20 Sept 1874 to William Dean Howells, *L6*, 233–36.

seff'. But where discrepant dialect forms are different spellings of a single word, the spelling is regularized. The criterion for what constitutes a "single word" has been phonetic. If the manuscript's divergent spellings can be interpreted as representing different pronunciations, they have been left alone. But in some cases variation does stem from, as Clemens says, "the writer's carelessness." MS Morgan, for example, has 'gen'lman' and 'genl'man': these are indistinguishable to the ear, and are not the fruit of delicate observation, so the author's predominant spelling ('gen'lman') has been imposed throughout. Dialect gerunds like 'a-fishing' appear in the manuscripts with and without the hyphen and have been adjusted to the predominant form (without).

Clemens's inconsistent use of quotation marks to set off the titles of books has been made uniform, and the bracketed "stage directions" of the courtroom chapters, which he left partly roman and partly italic, have been made consistently roman. All such changes are recorded in the Textual Apparatus.

Although MS Morgan's composition involved frequent insertion, deletion, and relocation of leaves and series of leaves, it received a very careful and thorough revision by Clemens. His numbering and ordering of the final manuscript pages ("final," that is, with regard to *this* phase of the text) is unambiguous.[4] His insertions, deletions, and relocations of very long passages, if reported in the Textual Apparatus, would have strained its tabular format. For this reason the apparatus records all the local insertions and deletions Clemens made to the text—changes to the wording, spelling, and so forth—but *not* the evidence for where any particular passage had previously stood in the manuscript during the various stages prior to the final ordering. Clemens's revisions on a "macro" level, involving whole leaves or groups of leaves, are reported in Appendix B, "MS Morgan: Contents and Numbering," where the manuscript's history is catalogued and described on a leaf-by-leaf basis, in parallel with a summary of narrative content. (Appendix A performs the same service for the shorter and less involved MS Berg.)

The record of variants assumes the final order of the leaves in MS Morgan, as determined by the latest of its many systems of page numbering. For example, in adding mottoes to the chapter heads, Clemens sometimes reached for a leaf from his collection of aphorisms, added to it a chapter heading and some text, and placed it in the midst of an earlier sequence. The Textual Apparatus, in such a case, treats the aphorism as the original text and records his additions to the manuscript leaf. The insertion of *the leaf itself* is accounted for in Appendix B.

MS Morgan was generated as a series of additions to an original typescript, TS1 (the typed copy of MS Berg). The typist of TS1 was obliged, partly by the limitations of his machine, to use handwriting to supply underscores, exclamation points, and

---

4. Only a single inserted passage, reporting the death of Rowena, seems to have been mistakenly placed by Clemens; it has been repositioned on the basis of an entry in his working notes. See PW-MS, Textual Apparatus, entry at 164.10.

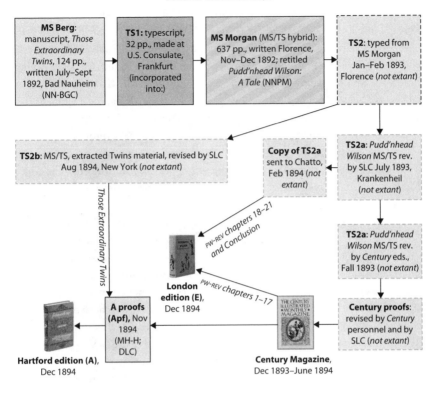

self-corrections. Wherever the typist's handwritten changes were meant to bring his typescript into conformity with the manuscript he was copying, they are not reported; but where TS1 errs in copying MS Berg, the manuscript reading is restored (for example, where MS Berg's 'be blind to it' was miscopied in TS1 as 'be behind it'). In the apparatus the textual sigil used to designate the part of MS Morgan that is actually the typescript is 'MS Morgan/TS1'.

In pages added late in the course of composition, Clemens decided to designate the prevailing weather in each chapter, by means of symbols. In his conception these were to be added by the printer at the heads of the chapters. He wrote a prefatory note explaining the symbols, and in the "Conclusion" he called for all of them to be deployed in a riot of "March weather." But while revising his text for publication in July 1893, he abandoned the weather scheme; we therefore lack any version of it that he approved. No attempt has been made to implement it here. Instead, the relevant texts ("About the Weather in this book" and "Conclusion") have been reproduced in photofacsimile at the end of the Morgan text, with a transcription.[5]

5. See Addenda to the Morgan Manuscript, pp. 203–11.

• *The Revised Version* (PW-REV). As the Introduction reports, the typescript made from MS Morgan underwent both authorial and editorial revision, leading to the 1893–94 publication of *Pudd'nhead Wilson* in three editions: the *Century Magazine* (*Cent*), the Chatto and Windus edition (E), and the American Publishing Company edition (A). Broadly speaking, these three editions share a text, the two books having been set from the magazine serial (an exception to this in the Chatto and Windus edition is discussed below). All three editions derive from TS2a, the document created by Mark Twain in his July 1893 revision; but since they derive by way of *Cent*, which was modified in ways large and small by the magazine's editors and printers, none of these editions necessarily reproduces the author's text. Wherever *Cent* and its descendants vary from MS Morgan, the author of *Cent*'s reading might be either Mark Twain (in his revisions creating TS2a) or the *Century* editors and printers (in the production of the serial text).

In editing the revised text, our policy is to identify and reverse textual changes not initiated or approved by the author, as well as changes he was obliged by practical considerations to accept but would not have made on his own or wanted in the final text. Ideally these changes would be identified by consulting the documents on which the changes were made; as it happens, those two documents have perished: (1) TS2a, the typed copy of MS Morgan, which bore the revisions both of the author and the *Century* editors; and (2) the authorially corrected *Century* proofs set from TS2a.[6] TS2a, bearing Clemens's revisions, was submitted to the *Century Magazine*, where it was marked and revised by the editors. It then went to the De Vinne Press, where it served as printer's copy and afterward was presumably destroyed.[7] Clemens read the proofs and attempted (he said) to restore the spelling and punctuation of his text—in the course of which process he probably continued to make local revisions.[8]

In the absence of these documents, the effort to distinguish authorial from non-authorial changes is certainly challenging; yet the challenge must be accepted. For more than a century since its first publication (with a single exception), *Pudd'nhead Wilson* has been read only in texts that reprint, or which have for their sole authoritative ancestor, the *Century Magazine*. The exception is the Norton Critical Edition, edited by Sidney E. Berger (1980). Rightly basing his text of (the revised) *Pudd'nhead Wilson* on MS Morgan, and correcting where applicable from MS Berg, Berger did much to restore the author's spelling and punctuation. He tended to treat substantive *Century* variants, however, as authorial revisions, accepting a great

---

6. Three leaves of TS2 are in CU-MARK. Removed by Clemens as superfluous and not used in either the revised *Pudd'nhead Wilson* or *Those Extraordinary Twins*, they provide limited but useful information about the characteristics of the typescript.

7. See the Introduction, p. 558, note 145.

8. See the Introduction, pp. 558–60.

many readings which are rejected from the present text as editorial modifications.[9] Editors will differ in their analysis of variants; what is clear is that a critical text must attempt to distinguish the authorial from the nonauthorial among the substantive *Century* variants, and remove spurious readings to which the author gave only a passive or enforced assent.

This edition's goal for the revised *Pudd'nhead Wilson* is to reconstruct the text of the lost typescript TS2a, as revised by Clemens in July 1893, while incorporating any changes he made later on the *Century* proofs. Choices between variants are based on the textual history, supplemented by research into (1) the interrelationship of the source texts, (2) Clemens's composition and revision habits, and (3) the magazine's standards and practices, especially as documented by its handling of other contributions from Clemens, as gathered from comparison of the *Century* with his surviving manuscripts, typescripts, and proofs. The rationale for specific editorial decisions is given in Textual Notes attached to the entries in the PW-REV apparatus.

▪ *The* **Century** *text.* Whenever Clemens collaborated in the adaptation of his books for magazine publication, he tried to ensure that the serial's line of transmission did not contaminate the text issued subsequently as a book. In 1884, when the *Century* published excerpts from *Huckleberry Finn*, the editors' revisions, cuts, and censorship were specific to the magazine series, and were not carried through to the Webster and Company book, then passing through the press.[10] The same is true for the *Century*'s single installment of excerpts from *A Connecticut Yankee* (1889): Clemens had a separate typescript produced to serve as the magazine's setting copy, and its alterations by author and editors were not imported into the book.[11] He tolerated *St. Nicholas*'s bowdlerizing of *Tom Sawyer Abroad*, knowing that the book could be set from "the original—not the St. Nicholas version," even though the plan miscarried.[12] In the case of *Pudd'nhead Wilson*, circumstances once again interfered with orderly process. While Charles L. Webster and Company floundered, Chatto and Windus went to work setting their edition from the magazine text; later, when the American edition was being made up, Clemens was in Europe and unable to contribute to the hasty production process. These circumstances combined to perpetuate the *Century Magazine*'s editorial quirks in all published texts of *Pudd'nhead Wilson* to the present day.

9. Parker 1981 is a thorough review of SLC 1980.

10. *HF 2003*, 744–46.

11. *CY*, 600–607.

12. See the Introduction, pp. 556–57. Information about the *Century*'s editing has been drawn also from Berkelman 1952, Sloane 1971, John 1981, and the Century Company records in the New York Public Library, Manuscripts and Archives Division.

The *Century* prided itself on maintaining decorum and avoiding all indelicacy. Its evident censorship of references to flatulence, a kick in the "rear," "spouting blood," and firemen "squirt[ing]" out a fire were noted in the Introduction.[13] It is practically certain that the *Century* suppressed Roxy's statement that her father was John Randolph of Roanoke. The revised, published version of Roxy's genealogy, which omits reference to her father, was doubtless produced by Mark Twain, but under coercion; so the text of MS Morgan is restored.[14] Likewise, MS Morgan's "harem of cats" was altered in *Cent* to "howling colony of cats."[15] The revised phrase must certainly be Clemens's but, in the belief that the editors censored his original allusion to feline polygamy, the *Cent* reading is rejected.

The *Century* editors also objected to slang, for which they supplied starchy alternatives. Where MS Morgan says that Tom's good behavior had "made him solid with the aunt and uncle," *Cent* reads "restored him to the favor of his aunt and uncle."[16] *Cent* burnishes the manuscript's sometimes informal or nonstandard grammar: it disallows "sure" as an adverb, changing it to "surely," and rearranges sentences.[17] Where MS Morgan elides the verb, *Cent* is prone to supply it.[18] *Cent* also relocates subordinate clauses and adverbial phrases.[19] *Cent* makes typical magazine changes to paragraphing, often to avoid very short paragraphs of one or two words, running them into a neighboring paragraph.[20]

Like other journals, the *Century* had a style sheet, or compendium of in-house editorial rules. No complete copy of this style sheet has been found, but its list of prohibited expressions is reprinted in *English Words and Their Background* by George H. McKnight (1923). Using this list, we have identified six places where the *Century* suppressed figures of speech forbidden by its style sheet.[21] For example, at 171.14, where MS Morgan reads "sits in your midst," *Cent* has "sits in among you." Berger argued that this was an authorial revision bungled by the compositor,

13. See the Introduction, pp. 560–61.

14. PW-REV, Textual Apparatus, entry at 299.14.

15. PW-REV, Textual Apparatus, entry at 327.13–14.

16. See PW-REV, Textual Apparatus, entries at 226.32 ("kid"); 249.20 ("knocked cold"); 249.33 ("right along"); 304.36 ("let the town keep its shirt on").

17. PW-REV, Textual Apparatus, entries at 255.19 and 253.18.

18. E.g. PW-REV, 219.18 ('made' / 'were made'); 285.23 ('not' / 'was not'); 339.26 ('ready' / 'was ready').

19. E.g. PW-REV, 244.20; 251.26; 254.9; 254.24–26; 269.26; 270.31; 286.17–18.

20. We can see alterations of this kind being made by a *Century* editor on the printer's copy for "The £1,000,000 Bank Note." This typescript/manuscript hybrid also shows editorial repunctuation, expurgation, and one rephrasing (CU-MARK).

21. McKnight 1923, 408–9; for the prohibited usages, see PW-REV, Textual Apparatus, entries for *party* (238.13); *proven* (264.22 and 335.21); *onto* (282.9); *past* (256.17 and 331.9); and *in your midst* (348.19).

and emended to "sits among you."[22] The style sheet, however, explicitly forbids the expression "in our midst," making it clear that "sits in among you" was a bungled *editorial* revision, so in our text the manuscript reading is retained.

The standardization of the author's spelling was carried out by the compositors of the De Vinne Press, whose "court of appeal" (as De Vinne termed it) was the massive *Century Dictionary* published by the magazine's parent company.[23] (The copy given to the Press was not, of course, MS Morgan but rather the lost typescript TS2a, which is assumed to have replicated the manuscript's spellings.) Wherever *Cent* agrees substantively with MS Morgan but varies from its spelling, this edition restores the spelling of the manuscript. In passages added by Clemens in his 1893 revision of the text, where *Cent* is necessarily the only substantive witness, inconsistent or doubtfully authorial spellings have been emended to a form attested in manuscript, either in MS Morgan or elsewhere in the collections available to the editor; for example, at 123.12, in an aphorism present only in *Cent*, "Michelangelo" has been emended to "Michael Angelo," the spelling of two holograph inscriptions of the same aphorism in the Mark Twain Papers.

The printing-house staff were also expected to standardize dialect vocabulary.[24] According to De Vinne's 1883 manual, "Dialect must be made uniform in its spelling, even if it is irregular in copy. Different abbreviations or clippings of the same word by the same speaker or writer should not be passed."[25] De Vinne's workers did not, as the present edition does, standardize a word to the form usually found in the copy, as described above; rather, they imposed an entirely new set of dialect spellings. Clemens's complaint to *Century* assistant editor William Carey—"Look here! *Now* they've gone to mending my dialect for me—I can't *stand* it"—was clearly ineffectual: collation shows that, overall, the combined effort of the editors and the printing-house transformed Clemens's representation of dialect.[26] The manuscript (and, we may assume, TS2a) consistently read *gwyne*, which *Cent* changed, mostly, to *gwine*; the manuscript's *caze* became *'ca'se*. The manuscript consistently had *plum*, *Cent* dithered between *plum'* and *plumb*. *Cent* signaled with an apostrophe every elision of one letter or more, causing the text to bristle with stilted contractions: *al'ays, da'sn't, f'om, ag'in'*. Even the manuscript's *fo'cas'l* was judged deficient in

22. SLC 1980, 188.

23. Theodore L. De Vinne to the *Century Magazine*, 10 Mar 1896, NN; Whitney and Smith 1889–91.

24. Compositors were charged with correction and standardization of spelling, punctuation, and capitalization, while proofreaders were responsible for, among other things, standardizing dialect forms and correcting "plain error[s] of statement" (De Vinne 1926, 9, 32, 33).

25. De Vinne 1926, 32. The 1926 edition reprints an 1883 in-house manual of the De Vinne Press. Further information about the Press's operations has been drawn from De Vinne's treatise *Correct Composition* (De Vinne 1901).

26. See the Introduction, p. 561.

apostrophes, and a way was found to add a third one.[27] Clearly the *Century*'s dialect spellings were intended to demonstrate that the editors were not ignorant of the proper spelling.

The ingrained practices of the publishing industry had often thwarted Clemens's persistent attempts to prevent compositors and proofreaders from altering his punctuation. When proofreading, he consistently demanded that their "idiotic punctuating" be "swept away & my own restored."[28] The tedious task of reinstating his punctuation on the proofs, as he told the publisher of *The Prince and the Pauper*, distracted him from reading for style and sense:

> What I want to read proof for is for literary lapses & infelicities (those I'll mark every time); so, in these chapters where I have had to turn my whole attention to restoring my punctuation, I do not consider that I have legitimately read proof at all. I didn't know what those chapters were about when I got through with them.
>
> Let the printers follow my punctuation—it is the one thing I am inflexibly particular about.[29]

Moreover, when Clemens was assured that the printers would restore his punctuation, he lacked the stamina to verify this claim, which collation shows was often false. The punctuation of MS Morgan, except where it is actually defective, is followed here. In passages where *Cent* is the earliest witness, Clemens's manuscript punctuation is beyond conjecture, and the *Cent* punctuation, unless actually defective, is retained.

Some *Cent* additions seem intended to jog the serial reader's memory of what had happened in earlier months—the addition, for example, of the phrase "about the dog" in the second installment (January 1894), which looks back to Wilson's unlucky remark, given in the previous month's installment. Such additions could be either editorial or authorial, but in either case they were devised solely for readers of the serial publication, and have therefore been rejected.

• *The Chatto and Windus edition.* The importance of the copy provided to Chatto and Windus in February 1894, and used by them for the latest chapters of their

---

27. See PW-MS, Textual Apparatus, entry at 320.18.

28. 23 Aug 1881 to James R. Osgood, Sotheby Parke Bernet 1974, lot 89. See also 22 June 1862 to OC, *L1*, 220–22 ("like all d—d fool printers, they can't follow the punctuation as it is in the manuscript"); Frederick J. Hall to SLC, 19 Aug 1889, CU-MARK; 20 Aug 1889 to Frederick J. Hall, ViU ("The proof-reader must follow my punctuation absolutely; I will not allow even the slightest departure from it"); 22–24 July 1897 to Chatto and Windus, photocopy in CU-MARK ("Their commas are too handy; I hate commas"); 25 July 1897 to Chatto and Windus, ViU ("I give it up. These printers pay no attention to my punctuation").

29. 16–22 Aug 1881 to Benjamin H. Ticknor, in Ticknor 1922, 139–41; and see *P&P*, 393.

edition (E), arises from the inference that it stems from the text as it stood in TS2a *before* it was edited by the *Century*. Berger demonstrated that for the text of the serial's final two installments, comprising chapters 18–21 and the "Conclusion," E derives not from *Cent* like the rest of the book, but from a document that frequently agreed with MS Morgan against *Cent*. Berger speculated that, in these chapters, E was set from "uncorrected proofs" of *Cent*, and he therefore treated the *Cent* variants as authorial corrections in proof, accepting all of them into his text.[30] Hershel Parker countered with the suggestion that Chatto had received pages from the *Century*'s setting copy, sent "as soon as the compositor at the *Century* was through setting from them."[31] We can conjecture from Chatto's letter of 28 February 1894, in which they acknowledged receipt of "copy," that they got what they had been asking for since August 1893: "a duplicate typewritten copy" of the whole novel.[32]

It is certain that a complete text was sent to Chatto and Windus in February 1894, at which time the *Century* installments for May and June would not yet have been available in proof; and it seems probable that this document was then used by Chatto as copy for the final chapters. Collation shows that it had escaped the magazine's editorial revision. Berger characterizes the relevant portion of E as lacking the "emendations" of the author, but that is misleading: in these chapters E is not only without the substantive variants found in *Cent* (be they authorial or otherwise), it is also without the whole battery of changes recognizable as *Century* house styling. As the only descendant of TS2a that has not received the editing of the magazine, this portion of E therefore has independent authority, and provides a valuable check on the sophistications of the *Century* editors. For the final chapters, readings in which MS Morgan and E agree are evidence for the readings of TS2a prior to the *Century Magazine*'s attentions; readings in which E and *Cent* agree against MS Morgan are either revisions made by Clemens in July 1893, or errors introduced by the TS2 typist. Any *Cent* reading that is *not* found in E was generated in the course of the *Century Magazine*'s production work. Since Clemens corrected *Century* proofs, such variants—whether substantive or accidental—are possibly authorial and must be considered on their own merits. On the whole, E's derivation, in these chapters, from an earlier ancestor means that our critical text of chapters 18 through the Conclusion is on a marginally sounder basis than the remainder of the text.

• *Textual corruption in TS2.* Some corruptions in *Cent* and E stem from the typist of TS2, A. M. Barnes.[33] Two prominent classes of alteration stand out in this respect:

30. Berger 1978.
31. Parker 1981, 230.
32. Chatto and Windus to SLC, 15 Aug 1893, CU-MARK. See the Introduction, p. 554.
33. For A. M. Barnes, see the Introduction, p. 545, n. 100.

the extensive alteration, between MS Morgan on the one hand and *Cent* and E on the other, in the distribution of emphasis (underscoring, in the manuscript; rendered in print as italic type) and exclamation points. MS Morgan's underscores are seldom replicated in *Cent*, the magazine regularly placing emphasis where it was not found before. If these revised emphases were the result of Clemens's dissatisfaction with his manuscript, they would have a claim to be incorporated in the critical text, and so it becomes important to understand their provenance. The last chapters in E agree with *Cent* in their italicizings, showing that these "revised" emphases are Clemens's (since E, in these chapters, was setting from a copy of TS2a); yet it is surprising that Clemens should so consistently find fault with his original emphases. The mystery is explained by the three surviving leaves of TS2, together with two other typescripts also made by Barnes for Clemens: "Extracts from Adam's Diary" and several chapters of *Personal Recollections of Joan of Arc*.[34]

In these typescripts, Barnes never reproduced the manuscript's underscoring at all: the underscoring visible on them is entirely in Clemens's hand.[35] In restoring his vanished emphases, Clemens, who lacked a passion for the noble work of collating documents, obviously did not consult his manuscript but set about underscoring from scratch. The result varied widely from his original inscription. On the typescript of "Extracts from Adam's Diary" he failed to replicate *any* of the manuscript's original underscorings for emphasis; in the *Joan of Arc* chapters, he restored roughly half of his original underscores and created several new ones. The emphases of *Cent*, being later in point of composition, might be considered as superseding those of the manuscript. The manuscript's emphases, however, are Mark Twain's undoubted work, whereas *Cent*'s, even though some are doubtless authorial, were occasioned by the typist's failure to reproduce the manuscript's underscoring. Therefore the emphases of MS Morgan are retained.

The extant typescripts of "Extracts from Adam's Diary" and *Joan of Arc* suggest that Barnes was also responsible for *Cent*'s variant distribution of exclamation points. Since at least some nineteenth-century typewriters lacked a key for the exclamation point, wherever that mark was called for in his copy Barnes typed a period, intending to complete the character later by adding a handwritten vertical

34. The manuscript and typescript of "Adam's Diary" are in the Berg Collection (NN-BGC). The manuscript of *Joan of Arc* is in the Beinecke Library at Yale (CtY-BR); the typescript of chapters 8–23 is in CU-MARK.

35. This problem was not uncommon. The typist of *Huckleberry Finn* (TS1) apparently failed to reproduce the manuscript's underscores; and the typescript of *The American Claimant*, which was typed by Will Whitmore, had the same defect: "Will, sometimes you follow my italicizings, but as a rule you pay no attention to them. Latterly you left them out entirely" (ca. May 1891 to Will Whitmore, DLC; *HF 2003*, 792). One of the surviving pages of TS2, on which Clemens has repaired the typist's failure to follow his "italicizings," is reproduced in the Introduction, p. 551.

stroke. This latter operation was evidently performed without reference to copy, for the manuscript's exclamation points are very often left as periods and its periods promoted to exclamations. How the process miscarried may be illustrated by page 269 of the *Joan of Arc* typescript: Barnes made vertical strokes over six typed periods, making six exclamation points; four of these misrepresented his copy, having been periods there. Reviewing the work, Clemens repaired only one of them.

▪ *The American Publishing Company edition* (**A**). Although Clemens had little or no involvement in the production of the American Publishing Company volume, it is the earliest and only authoritative witness for the additions and revisions he made in *Those Extraordinary Twins* (for which see below). The authority of its title page must also be considered. When printer's copy was supplied to the Company in August 1894, the works did not bear their now-familiar *Tragedy* and *Comedy* titles. The contract signed in that month between Clemens and Francis Bliss refers to "a certain work entitled 'Pudd'nhead Wilson'" and to "a certain unpublished work . . . entitled 'Those Extraordinary Twins—a postscript to Pudd'nhead Wilson.'"[36] The expanded titles were announced early in November 1894 in a publicity release, and the published title page lists *The Tragedy of Pudd'nhead Wilson and the Comedy Those Extraordinary Twins*.[37] By the terms of the contract, the publisher had the right to change the title, subject to the author's consent; but if Clemens devised or approved the new *Tragedy . . . Comedy* titles, the fact is not mentioned in the extant correspondence. Taken all together, the evidence suggests that the later titles are the publisher's invention, inspired by Clemens's references to "tragedy" and "farce" in his preface to *Those Extraordinary Twins*. In 1899, when Harper and Brothers acquired the rights to these works, the *Tragedy . . . Comedy* titles were retired, never to be revived in any authorized edition.[38] It is not unheard-of for a publisher to retitle a book; in fact it had already happened to Clemens once since he moved to Europe, in the case of the collection *Merry Tales* (1892).[39] The present edition therefore uses the titles that must have stood in TS2a (on the evidence of *Cent*, E, and the contract) and TS2b (on the evidence of the contract).

The hundreds of marginal illustrations in A were the brainchild of Bliss, and are not known to have been reviewed or approved by Clemens.[40] Even if it were desired

36. The contract (CtY-BR) is reproduced in Appendix E, p. 489.

37. The publicity release was reprinted verbatim as an article in many newspapers, the earliest of which found so far is "Mark Twain's New Book," Erie (Pa.) *Times-News*, 5 Nov 1894, 8.

38. SLC 1899a. In that year the revised titles also disappeared from republications by the American Publishing Company (SLC 1899b).

39. When he changed publishers four years later, Clemens said of *Merry Tales*: "If it isn't too late, please squelch that title and call the mess by some other name—almost any other name. Webster and Co. invented that silly title" (5 Dec 1896 to J. Henry Harper, ODaU; SLC 1892b).

40. See the Introduction, p. 581, n. 228.

to reprint them, these pictures, made as they were to surround and illustrate the American edition's particular pages, can be faithfully reproduced only on pages formatted exactly as in that edition.[41] Clemens did, however, see and approve the six full-page illustrations executed by Louis Loeb for the *Century* serial, and they are reproduced here, along with the photographic frontispiece of the author used in the first *Century* installment. The magazine positioned the illustrations according to its house style and its own convenience, usually placing them on the verso facing the first page of each month's installment. Here they have been placed near the incidents they illustrate.

• *Those Extraordinary Twins* (**EXT**). Most of the considerations for editing the revised *Pudd'nhead Wilson* apply also to *Those Extraordinary Twins*, compiled by Mark Twain in August 1894 from the typed pages which he had literally extracted from TS2, and published in the American Publishing Company volume of 1894 alongside its sibling text. The bulk of the text therefore derives from MS Morgan by way of these revised and supplemented TS2 pages, here called TS2b. Throughout *Those Extraordinary Twins*, the American Publishing Company text (A) has potential authority as incorporating Clemens's revisions on TS2b; and for certain passages of the text—that is, the explanatory and "bridging" passages added by Clemens in August 1894—the published book is the sole authoritative source. In a few places the spelling and punctuation of these unique passages (as with the analogous passages of *Cent*/PW-REV) have been emended here to conform to Clemens's typical usage; and the errors of the TS1 typist have again been emended from MS Berg.

The text of A has been collated against the proof copy in the Houghton Library (Apf), revealing sixty-four variants. Clemens did not participate in the production of A, and its variants from the proof copy cannot be authorial. Some of A's departures from Apf correct obvious printer's errors, some correct errors that the printer could have discovered by consulting copy, and some tinker with punctuation. In addition, Berger has drawn attention to a set of fifteen variants in which the reading of the proof was replaced in the published book by a different, shorter reading.[42] In all such cases the proofs agree with the readings of MS Morgan, showing that these changes for the book were a space-saving ploy, devised by the printers to fit the ending of *Those Extraordinary Twins* into a single signature, as described in the Introduction.[43] The goal of this edition is to reconstruct the text of Mark Twain's revised typescript TS2b, as submitted to the publisher in August 1894, with the

---

41. Appendix G, "Illustrating *Pudd'nhead Wilson*," reproduces a sampling from the drawings in A. The volume in *The Oxford Mark Twain*, edited by Shelley Fisher Fishkin, is a photographic facsimile of the American Publishing Company edition (SLC 1996).

42. Berger 1976, 275–76.

43. See the Introduction, p. 581.

errors of typists, editors, and printers rectified. The title in A, as noted above, is rejected here in favor of the title as it is thought to have stood in TS2b, on the evidence of the publication contract.[44]

For the American Publishing Company's "Royal Edition" of 1899, a professional proofreader, Forrest Morgan, read through the *Pudd'nhead Wilson* volume and made corrections. A proofreader's corrections are only authoritative if it is clear the author was consulted and gave them his approval; an examination of Morgan's marked copy (at CtY-BR) revealed no corrections of this kind.

44. See Appendix E, p. 489.

GUIDE TO THE TEXTUAL APPARATUS

The editorial policy of this critical edition is set forth in the Note on the Texts (p. 600). For each of the three critical texts presented here, there is a Textual Apparatus reporting the textual variants among the source texts and recording the editor's emendations.

Apparatus entries. Apparatus entries are cued to the text by page and line number. The word or phrase to the left of the bullet (•) is the lemma, the reading of the edited text. To the right of the bullet stand one or more variant readings: the exact text of each pertinent source at that place. The source of each reading is given in parentheses in an abbreviated form, or sigil. All source documents used in constructing the text are described in the Description of Source Documents (p. 617). All variants among the source documents are reported, with the exception of those listed below as silent emendations. The readings of the source documents are listed in chronological order—that is, a manuscript reading (if any) is given first, followed by each subsequent text in the line of transmission. Textual notes in some entries explain editorial decisions and provide pertinent information about the source documents. Readings supplied by the editor, or which involve even a slight degree of editorial intervention, are marked with the sigil MTP. Wherever a compound word in a source text was divided over a line break, the lemma represents the form—whether a hyphenated or a single word—adopted by the editor on the basis of attested authorial usage.

In the apparatus of the Morgan Manuscript Version (PW-MS), the reading of the edited text—the lemma—is typically the final reading of the Morgan manuscript, and therefore requires no sigil. If the lemma has been adopted from any source *other* than that manuscript, the source is identified by its sigil, and the readings of the other source texts are reported to the right of the bullet. When the lemma is the end product of authorial revision, an exact transcription showing Clemens's alterations will be found to the right of the bullet, as in this example:

168.26   seated herself • ~~sat down~~ ˌseated herselfˌ (MS Morgan)

In the apparatus of the revised versions (PW-REV and EXT), every lemma and every reading has a sigil showing its source. The readings of the manuscripts are given in their "final" state: the end result of Clemens's alterations, omitting all information about the history of inscription—all of which is reported in the PW-MS apparatus. Where, in these revised versions, the author deleted long passages that were present in MS Morgan, the deleted passage is not reproduced in full; instead, the reader is referred to the corresponding passage in the apparatus for PW-MS.

Plain text. In the apparatus of the Morgan Manuscript Version, the author's alterations are shown using the signs developed for "plain text." Plain text is a transcription protocol devised by the editors for the *Mark Twain's Letters* series and only a subset of its conventions is needed here. For a full description, see the Guide to Editorial Practice included in *L6*, 697–726, and online at *MTPO*.

A single inserted character has a caret under it (like so); inserted words and phrases are surrounded with ‚carets‚. Deleted words are represented by horizontal ~~strikethrough lines~~; a single deleted character is struck through with a vertical slash (like soø). The strikethrough represents deletions of all kinds: characters wiped away while the ink is still wet, characters converted into other characters, and so forth. A deletion within a longer deletion is shown with a double strikethrough. Line breaks (|) and page breaks (||) are recorded only where it helps the reader to understand a revision. Paragraph breaks are shown as [¶]. Following normal printing-house rules, underlined words are represented as *italic type*; double-underscored words, as SMALL CAPITALS; and triple-underscored words, as CAPITALS. Plain text conveys how the text of a document was generated and altered, and is not intended as a type facsimile of the original; for example, an insertion made by writing a word in the margin will be shown in the place intended for it, between ‚carets‚. Any manuscript character that the editor has been unable to read is represented by a diamond (◊).

Silent emendations. Certain features of the source documents have been altered by the editors but not reported. In the texts and apparatuses, manuscript ampersands (&) are expanded to "and." The roman numeral chapter headings in the printed sources are silently restored to the manuscript's Arabic numerals. Where the printed sources space out contracted forms like 'should n't', they are silently closed up. Underscoring (single, double, or triple) has been rendered as italics, small capitals, or full capitals, respectively. The *Century Magazine* set the first words of each chapter in capitals and small capitals; this styling is ignored here. The Chatto and Windus edition (E) displays many aspects of house style, of which no account has been taken in text or apparatus, since none can be regarded as authorial. They include the use of British spellings, the form and use of quotation marks, the use of parentheses where MS Morgan and *Cent* have square brackets, and differences in the use of the colon and the dash.

Due to the limitations of either the typewriter or the typist, TS1 has commas where its manuscript copy has apostrophes, and slashes (/) where the copy has brackets or parentheses. The typist routinely supplied certain characters in hand-writing, including the underscore, single quotation marks, and the exclamation point. These aspects of TS1 are not reported. In recording TS1 readings, italics represent the typist's handwritten underscoring unless it is specifically noted as Clemens's. Wherever the typist rectified an error of his own, the correction is not reported; any alterations reported for the witness MS Morgan/TS1 are Clemens's.

DESCRIPTION OF SOURCE DOCUMENTS

Each of the documents described below possesses independent authority for one or more of the three principal texts edited here.

MS Berg   Manuscript of 81 single and double leaves, written at Bad Nauheim, Germany, in August and September 1892, now in the New York Public Library's Henry W. and Albert A. Berg Collection of English and American Literature. STATIONERY: (1) *Monogram*: a cream, laid stationery, measuring approximately 12.3 by 20 centimeters, with vertical chainlines; watermarked 'MONOGRAM LINEN.' (2) a cream, laid stationery, folders torn in two, a single leaf measuring approximately 12.5 by 20 centimeters, with vertical chainlines; watermarked with a crest (helmet within a shield, with halberds and 'S&H HOLYROOD'); with some leaves still double. The manuscript is written in brown ink, and revised in the same ink and in pencil. By 1917, MS Berg was owned by A. S. W. Rosenbach, who sold it, sometime after 1927, to Owen D. Young. In 1941, Henry W. Berg arranged for the New York Public Library to acquire Young's collection as part of the Berg Collection (Rosenbach 1917, 43; Rosenbach 1927, 164; Szladits 1974, 7, 45). The contents of MS Berg are more fully catalogued in Appendix A, "MS Berg: Contents and Numbering."

TS1   Typed copy of MS Berg, of 29 leaves (numbered 2–30, the first leaf having been discarded), made at Frankfurt by staff of the United States Consulate in September and October 1892, then incorporated into MS Morgan. STATIONERY: a cream, laid stationery, measuring approximately 20 by 26.5 centimeters, with vertical chainlines, watermarked 'ORIGINAL' with a crowned shield surmounting a device of three interlinked rings. The ribbon ink used is purple. The typist's handwritten self-corrections are in an ink which has reacted with the paper to give the writing a blurry "halo." Mark Twain's own ink revisions have crisp outlines; he has also revised in pencil. He added new manuscript to TS1 to form a hybrid manuscript/typescript document, MS Morgan (see below).

MS Morgan   Manuscript of 638 leaves, written at Florence, Italy, from November 1892 to January 1893, now in the Morgan Library and Museum, New York. STATIONERY: (1) Paper type 253. A white, laid stationery, folders torn into half-sheets measuring approximately 12.7 by 20.3 centimeters, with vertical chainlines, watermarked '"PEARL" C.G.&L.' (2) A cream laid stationery, measuring approximately 14 by 22 centimeters, with vertical chainlines, no watermark. (3) Paper type 211. A green, heavy laid tablet paper, measuring approximately 14 by 22.5 centimeters, with horizontal chainlines, no watermark. MS Morgan is written in brown ink (perhaps faded from black), and revised by Mark Twain in black ink and pencil. MS Morgan incorporates TS1 (see above). After MS Morgan was typed as TS2, Clemens kept the manuscript; in 1909 he sold it, together with the manuscript of *Life on the Mississippi*, to financier J. Pierpont Morgan (1837–1913), receiving an "honorarium" of $2,500 (J. Pierpont Morgan to SLC, 14 Sept 1909, CU-MARK; 15 Sept 1909 to J. Pierpont Morgan, NNPM). Morgan had the manuscript bound in two volumes, at which time some partial leaves, the result of Clemens's cutting leaves in half to accommodate inserted text, were "filled out" to full size by grafting onto them fragments of other leaves—evidently canceled matter left over from earlier phases of composition. The contents of MS Morgan are more fully described in Appendix B, "MS Morgan: Contents and Numbering."

James 1743	Robert James, *A Medicinal Dictionary; Including Physic, Surgery, Anatomy, Chymistry, and Botany, in All Their Branches Relative to Medicine.* Vol. 1. London: for T. Osborne, 1743. James's work is the source of the doctor's prescription for Luigi (by way of SLC 1890). A facsimile of Clemens's personal copy, in the library of the Hartford Medical Society (CtHM), has been used.
SLC 1890	Mark Twain, "A Majestic Literary Fossil," *Harper's New Monthly Magazine* 80 (February 1890): 439–44. A passage in this article, reprinting a prescription from James 1743, was pasted into MS Morgan by Mark Twain to provide the doctor's prescription for Luigi (PW-MS, 148; EXT, 401).
TS2	Typed copy of MS Morgan, made in Florence, Italy, by A. M. Barnes, in January 1893. Being lost (with the exception of three leaves removed from it by Mark Twain), TS2 is not a source document in the usual sense; it is described here because it is frequently referred to in the Textual Apparatus (as are its revised forms, TS2a and TS2b). The surviving leaves, in the Mark Twain Papers, comprise a copyright page and two pages with chapter headings and aphorisms; one of the latter is reproduced on p. 551. STATIONERY: The surviving leaves were typed on a cream, wove paper, measuring approximately 16.5 centimeters by 20.3 centimeters, watermarked 'SILVERBURN LINEN.' TS2 is discussed in the Introduction, pp. 545–46, and Note on the Texts, 609–11.
MS in CU-MARK	This sigil has been used to designate various manuscripts in the Mark Twain Papers. They are of two principal kinds: (1) leaves from MS Morgan removed but preserved by Mark Twain in the course of revision (Box 40, no. 2); and (2) aphorisms in holograph, from Mark Twain's manuscript collections (Box 40, no. 5).

Cent	Serial publication of *Pudd'nhead Wilson: A Tale* in the *Century Illustrated Monthly Magazine*. Seven installments, December 1893 through June 1894: SLC 1893, 1894a–f.

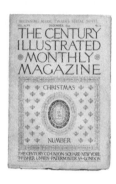

December 1893 issue. Courtesy of Kevin Mac Donnell.

Apf	Two prepublication copies of the first American edition (A), deposited at the Library of Congress on 30 November 1894, with textual differences from the issued edition and many illustrations not yet inserted. One of these copies was later deaccessioned and purchased by Jacob Blanck for the Houghton Library at Harvard University. The Houghton copy lacks four leaves (eight pages) in the *Pudd'nhead Wilson* section, but *Those Extraordinary Twins*, the only part of the book where the American Publishing Company edition has independent textual authority, is complete. For this edition a digital facsimile of the Houghton copy has been collated, and the variants recorded in the Textual Apparatus for EXT.
A	First American edition. *The Tragedy of Pudd'nhead Wilson; And the Comedy Those Extraordinary Twins by Mark Twain (Samuel L. Clemens). With Marginal Illustrations.* Hartford: American Publishing Company, 1894 (*BAL* 3442). A, together with its proof copies (Apf), is an authoritative witness to the text of *Those Extraordinary Twins*; its text of *Pudd'nhead Wilson* is a reprint of *Cent*, and is without textual authority. The salesman's prospectus for the first American edition contains sixty selected

pages of text. The pages from the section *Those Extraordinary Twins* have been collated, using a copy in CU-MARK; since they agree with A throughout, their readings are not reported.

First American edition (A). Mark Twain Papers, The Bancroft Library (CU-MARK).

E First English edition. *Pudd'nhead Wilson: A Tale by Mark Twain (Samuel L. Clemens)*. London: Chatto and Windus, 1894 (*BAL* 3441). Although most of its text was set from *Cent*, E is an authoritative witness for the text of PW-REV, chapters 18 through the Conclusion; see the Note on the Texts, pp. 608–9.

First English edition (E). Mark Twain Papers, The Bancroft Library (CU-MARK).

MS Morgan is emended, where necessary, from MS Berg; and, in one passage, from James 1743 and SLC 1890. For further discussion, see the Guide to the Textual Apparatus; the Description of Source Documents; and the Note on the Texts.

Revisions, variants adopted or rejected, and textual notes.

3.1–3   *Pudd'nhead Wilson* | A TALE | By MARK TWAIN (MTP) • Those Extraordinary Twins. [*short triple rule*] Time—about 1850. [*short double rule*] (MS Berg); Pudd'nhead Wilson [*short double rule*] A TALE [*short double rule*] By MARK TWAIN. [*short double rule*] [*small capitals simulated, not underscored*] (MS Morgan) [TEXTUAL NOTE: *A manuscript title page, removed from MS Morgan by SLC, is reproduced and transcribed on p. 544. The preliminary pages of the manuscript, entitled 'Key to Signs used in this book', are presented in facsimile, with transcription, in a separate section (Addenda to the Morgan Manuscript, pp. 203–11)*]

5.1   *Note Concerning the Legal Points* (MTP) • Note Concerning the Legal Points. [*short single rule*] (MS Morgan)

5.6   Those • T̶h̶e̶ose (MS Morgan)

5.7   William • S̶h̶a̶d̶r̶a̶c̶h̶ ˏWilliamˎ (MS Morgan)

5.8   south-west (MTP) • F̶south- | west (MS Morgan)

5.9–10   Maccaroni and Vermicelli's • I̶l̶ ̶F̶ ̶I̶l̶ ̶F̶r̶a̶t̶e̶l̶l̶o̶ ̶a̶n̶d̶ ̶L̶a̶ ̶S̶o̶r̶e̶l̶l̶a̶'̶s̶ ˏMaccaroni and Vermicelli'sˎ (MS Morgan)

5.10   horse-feed (MTP) • horse- | feed (MS Morgan)

5.12   six hundred years ago • ˏsix hundred years agoˎ (MS Morgan)

5.17   good • g̶o̶o̶d̶ ̶a̶n̶d̶ ̶d̶a̶r̶k̶-̶c̶o̶m̶ good (MS Morgan)

5.17   then, • s̶i̶x̶ ̶h̶u̶n̶d̶r̶e̶d̶ ̶y̶e̶a̶r̶s̶ ̶a̶g̶o̶,̶ ̶ˏthen,ˎ ˏthen,ˎ (MS Morgan)

5.19   he told me • a̶n̶d̶ ̶h̶e̶ ̶s̶a̶y̶s̶ ˏhe told meˎ (MS Morgan)

5.25 the busts • ˌthe˛ ~~Cerretani senators of Dante's~~ busts (MS Morgan)

5.29 be • ~~improve~~ be (MS Morgan)

5.31 *Mark Twain.* (MTP) • Mark Twain. | [*paraph*] (MS Morgan)

7.1 *Chapter 1* (MTP) • CHAPTER I. [*short double rule*] [¶] There be these differences between the dog and the cat. The dog is man's slave, the cat is his friend; the dog worships ~~man,~~ ˌhim,˛ the cat merely loves him; ~~the dog is man~~ ˌhe˛ is the dog's god, but ~~man~~ ˌhe˛ must waive rank and meet the cat on a dead level of equality ˌif he would have her society˛—she will consent to no ~~other~~ ˌmeaner˛ terms. Perfect independence of character is found in not one of God's creatures except the cat. One man in ten millions creates it in himself, and it makes him as conspicuous as the Milky Way; but no cat is born without it.—*Pudd'nhead Wilson's Calendar.* [*notations about other aphorisms, at foot of page, in ink and pencil:*] 102 – 2 souls | 141 – When I reflect | and Consistency | 489 – July 4. (MS in CU-MARK, *discarded from MS Morgan by SLC*); ~~Chapter 1~~ [*short double rule*] ˌChapter 1. [*short triple rule*]˛ [*insertion in pencil*] (MS Morgan) [TEXTUAL NOTE: *MS Morgan's introductory paragraphs (7.1–8.21) supersede the introduction present in MS Berg and deleted from TS1, for which see* PW-MS, *Textual Apparatus, entry at 34.13*]

7.3 journey, per • journey˛ per˛ (MS Morgan)

7.5 collection • ~~place~~ collection (MS Morgan)

7.5 "frame" • ˌ"frame"˛ (MS Morgan)

7.7 vines, honeysuckles • vines˛ ~~and~~ honeysuckles (MS Morgan)

7.9 feathers • feˌathers (MS Morgan)

7.10 on • ~~in~~ ˌon˛ (MS Morgan)

7.12 a breed of • ⱥ ˌa breed of˛ (MS Morgan)

7.12 whose • ~~that~~ ˌwhose˛ (MS Morgan)

7.14 and • and ~~her~~ (MS Morgan)

7.19 may • ⱨ may (MS Morgan)

7.26 two • ~~stood~~ two (MS Morgan)

7.26–27 high . . . shops. • high⟋ ˌtowered above interjected bunches of little frame shops.˛ (MS Morgan)

7.30 Landing • ⱡ Ḷanding ['l' *triple-underscored to capitalize*] (MS Morgan)

7.31 lofty • lofty⟋ (MS Morgan)

7.31 pole • pole⟋ (MS Morgan)

8.6 enclosing • ⱦ ẹnclosing (MS Morgan)

8.6 forests • forests ~~to their summits~~ (MS Morgan)

8.8   belonging • belong͜ing͜ (MS Morgan)

8.9   the big • ~~those~~ ͜the big͜ (MS Morgan)

8.12   latter • ͜latter͜ (MS Morgan)

8.18   slave-holding • slave | ͜ holding (MS Morgan)

8.18   slave-worked • ~~farming~~ ͜slave-worked͜ (MS Morgan)

8.21   still • still, (MS Morgan)

8.22   [¶] The • ~~[¶] The principal~~ [¶] The (MS Morgan)

8.22   about forty years old, • ͜about forty years old,͜ (MS Morgan)

8.30   had grown • ~~grew~~ ͜had grown͜ (MS Morgan)

8.36   freethinker (MTP) • free- | thinker (MS Morgan)

8.37   [¶] Pembroke • ~~[¶] Pemberton~~ [¶] Pembroke (MS Morgan)

8.37   lawyer • lawyer, (MS Morgan)

8.38   Virginian • V~~a~~͜i͜rginian (MS Morgan)

9.3   you • ͜you͜ (MS Morgan)

9.5   prefer, from . . . artillery. • prefer͜,͜, from brad-awls to artillery.͜ (MS Morgan)

9.8   no • ~~little or~~ no (MS Morgan)

9.9   [¶] Percy • ~~[¶] Patsy Cooper and Betsy Hale, both newly widowed, lived together. They were twins in ways, character, and contented confidence in the Westminster Catechism, but no blood relationship existed between them. They were of equal age—about forty-five. We shall speak of them again, by and by.~~ [¶] Percy (MS Morgan)

9.15   to • ~~in~~ to (MS Morgan)

9.25   finished a post-college • ~~lately~~ finished ~~his~~ ͜a post-college͜ (MS Morgan)

9.25–26 school a couple of years before. • school͜,͜ ͜a couple of years before.͜ (MS Morgan)

9.27   with • ~~with~~ | with (MS Morgan)

9.28   comradeship (MTP) • comeradeship (MS Morgan)

9.30   Landing. • Landing. ~~[Here insert from "BUT"—at the mark # on page 48—and correct afterward.]~~ (MS Morgan) [TEXTUAL NOTE: *SLC's* 'mark #' *is inserted on TS1 page 21 (formerly 48)*]

9.30–31 But he made • He was liked, he was welcome enough all around, but he simply didn't count for anything. His was a curious case—the case of a sufficiently promising career killed by a single remark; and killed past resurrection; a case of single-speech Hamilton reversed. He was forty-five years old, and had been a resident twenty years—a homely, freckled, sandy-haired man, with an intelligent blue eye that had frankness and comradeship in it, and a covert twinkle of a pleasant sort. But he made (MS Berg); ~~He was liked, he was welcome enough all around, but he simply didn't count for anything. His was a curious case—the case of a sufficiently promising career killed by a single remark; and killed past resurrection; a case of single-speech Hamilton reversed. He was forty-five years old, and had been a resident twenty years—a homely, freckled, sandy-haired man, with an intelligent blue eye that had frankness and comradeship in it, and a covert twinkle of a pleasant sort.~~ But he made [*in margin:* ⸲#⸲] (MS Morgan/TS1) [TEXTUAL NOTE: *SLC deleted* 'He was liked . . . for anything' *and re-inscribed it on the fragment of TS1 inserted between MS Morgan pages 112 and 113*]

9.34   comprehensively (MTP) • comprehensibly (MS Berg, MS Morgan/ TS1) [TEXTUAL NOTE: *The reading of MS Berg and MS Morgan/TS1,* 'comprehensibly', *is intelligible; but based on SLC's usage it is probable that he intended* 'comprehensively'. *The latter is also the reading of the Century Magazine; it is admitted here as the correction of an unconscious slip in MS Berg*]

9.34   disagreeable; whereupon he • disagreeable. The new-comer, David Wilson, (MS Berg); disagreeable⸲; ~~The new-comer, David Wilson,~~ ⸲whereupon he⸲ (MS Morgan/TS1)

10.1   The • The (MS Berg); ⸮The (MS Morgan/TS1)

10.1   group • grouped (MS Berg); group (MS Morgan/TS1)

10.7   did he • ~~do you~~ did he (MS Berg); did he (MS Morgan/TS1)

10.10   that • that (MS Berg); it (MS Morgan/TS1)

10.12   half • half (MS Berg); half, (MS Morgan/TS1) [TEXTUAL NOTE: *TS1's faint comma appears to be the typist's*]

10.17   whose • ~~which~~ ⸲whose⸲ (MS Berg); whose (MS Morgan/TS1)

10.18   and—" • and—" (MS Berg); and—⸲" (MS Morgan/TS1)

10.22   No. • ⸮No. (MS Berg); No. (MS Morgan/TS1)

10.24   what • ~~wh~~ what (MS Berg); what (MS Morgan/TS1)

10.24   simon-pure (MS Berg) • Simon-pure (MS Morgan/TS1)

10.30   all." • all—I ain't no judge." (MS Berg); all⸲."⸲—~~I ain't no judge."~~ (MS Morgan/TS1)

10.32   week he • week, ~~Wilson~~ ⸲he⸲ (MS Berg); week, he (MS Morgan/TS1)

10.33   its (MS Berg) • it's (MS Morgan/TS1)

10.34   stayed • ~~staid~~ stayed (MS Berg); stayed (MS Morgan/TS1)

10.34   That first • ~~For twenty~~ That first (MS Berg); That first (MS Morgan/TS1)

10.35   him a • ~~Wilson a~~ ⸲him a⸲ (MS Berg); him a (MS Morgan/TS1)

10.35   was not • never was (MS Berg); ~~never~~ was ⸲not⸲ (MS Morgan/TS1)

10.37   its (MS Berg) • it's (MS Morgan/TS1)

10.37–38   was to . . . long years. • Wilson was still Pudd'nhead Wilson to-day, after
            all those twenty years. [¶] He had made many curious remarks during
            that time, and they were held to confirm the original verdict. They had
            long ago ceased to produce comment, they had come to be regarded as
            a thing to be expected, and were allowed to pass in peace. He was at the
            reception, and ~~was~~ when he was asked how the Twins struck him, he said
            they "looked like one of them had swallowed the other, but he couldn't
            tell which." (MS Berg); ˌand was to continue to hold its place for twenty
            long years.ˌ Wilson was still Pudd'nhead Wilson to-day, after all those
            twenty years. (MS Morgan/TS1) [TEXTUAL NOTE: *On MS Morgan/TS1
            SLC made the insertion* 'and was to continue to hold its place for twenty
            long years.' *but neglected to delete the text it was meant to replace:* 'and
            Wilson was still Pudd'nhead Wilson to-day, after all those twenty years.'
            MS Berg's text 'He had made many curious remarks . . . but he couldn't
            tell which."' *was typed as TS1 page 30; in creating MS Morgan, SLC cut
            away that part of the leaf and did not use its text anywhere*]

11.1–6   *Chapter 2 . . . serpent.—Pudd'nhead Wilson's Calendar.* (MTP) •
            ˌCHAPTER 2. [*short double rule*]ˌ [¶] Adam was but human . . . eaten
            the serpent.ˌ—*Pudd'nhead Wilson's Calendar.*ˌ [¶] ~~If you put five hun-
            dred compliments into one scale and a censure into the other, which
            will weigh the most?~~ (MS Morgan)

11.7   [¶] Pudd'nhead • [*centered:*] ~~Chapter 2.~~ [*short double rule*] [¶]
            Pudd'nhead (MS Morgan)

11.10   He hired • ~~He took~~ He hired (MS Morgan)

11.15   had ruined • ˌhadˌ ruined ~~him~~ (MS Morgan)

11.19   and now • ˌandˌ now (MS Morgan)

11.25   upon • ~~with~~ ˌuponˌ (MS Morgan)

11.29   communicative (MTP) • commuicative (MS Morgan)

12.1   finger-marks (MTP) • finger- | marks (MS Morgan)

12.2   shallow • ~~flat box wi~~ shallow (MS Morgan)

12.3   five • ~~three or four~~ ˌfiveˌ (MS Morgan)

12.3   three inches • ~~an~~ ˌtwoˌ ˌthreeˌ inchˌesˌ (MS Morgan)

12.5–6   (thus collecting . . . natural oil,) • ˌ(thus collecting upon them a thin
            coating of the natural oil,)ˌ (MS Morgan)

12.7   the • ~~ea~~ the (MS Morgan)

12.11   and • ˌandˌ (MS Morgan)

12.16   on paper • ˌon paperˌ (MS Morgan)

12.19   lines • ~~lines more conve~~ lines (MS Morgan)

12.20   sweltering • ˌswelteringˌ (MS Morgan)

12.20	July, 1830 • July ˌ, 1830ˌ (MS Morgan)
12.21	set • ~~st~~ set (MS Morgan)
12.21	looked • ~~was~~ looked (MS Morgan)
12.22	stretch • ˌ~~rising~~ˌ stretch (MS Morgan)
12.26	come on, Jasper?" (MTP) • come ~~on, Jim?"~~ ˌon, Sandy?"ˌ ˌon, Jasper?"ˌ ˌJasper?"ˌ (MS Morgan) [TEXTUAL NOTE: *In the course of SLC's revisions, 'on' seems to have been accidentally deleted*]
12.27–28	a court'n (MTP) • a-court'n (MS Morgan)
12.28	bimeby, • ~~by en by,~~ ˌbimeby,ˌ (MS Morgan)
12.30	'sociat'n • 'sociat~~e~~ ˌ'nˌ (MS Morgan)
12.36	Jasper, • ~~Jim,~~ ˌ~~Sandy,~~ˌ ˌJasper,ˌ (MS Morgan)
12.36	sell • ~~send~~ sell (MS Morgan)
13.7	Jasper, • ~~Jim,~~ ˌ~~Sandy,~~ˌ ˌJasper,ˌ (MS Morgan)
13.8	and of magnificent build, • ~~and stalwart,~~ ˌand of magnificent build,ˌ (MS Morgan)
13.8	wheelbarrow • wheebarrow (MS Morgan)
13.14–15	of majestic form and stature, • ~~tall, and beautifully built, ◊~~ ˌof majestic form and stature,ˌ (MS Morgan)
13.16	distinguished by a noble and stately grace. • ~~graceful.~~ ˌdistinguished by a noble and stately grace.ˌ (MS Morgan)
13.22–24	beautiful. She . . . folks were. • beautiful. ˌOVERˌ [*on verso:*] ˌShe had an easy, independent carriage—when she was among her own caste—and a high and "sassy" way, withal; but of course she was meek and humble enough where white folks were. | over againˌ (MS Morgan)
13.29	curls, • curls⸝ ˌ,ˌ (MS Morgan)
13.29	even • ˌevenˌ (MS Morgan)
13.30	apart—little • apart⸝ˌ—ˌlittle (MS Morgan)
13.31	them—by • them⸝ ˌ—ˌˌbyˌ (MS Morgan)
13.35	Chambre: no surname—slaves hadn't the privilege. • Chambre⸝ˌ:ˌ ~~No~~ ˌnoˌ surname—slaves hadn't the privilege.ˌ (MS Morgan)
13.36	the • ~~had~~ the (MS Morgan)
13.37	had • ˌhadˌ (MS Morgan)
13.37	loaded • ~~had~~ loaded (MS Morgan)
14.2	Jasper (MTP) • Jim (MS Morgan) [TEXTUAL NOTE: *Here SLC failed to revise this character's name, which elsewhere he changed from Jim to Sandy to Jasper*]
14.3	once—perceiving that his leisure was observed. • once⸝ˌ—perceiving that his leisure was observed.ˌ. [*original period implicitly deleted*] (MS Morgan)

14.9   Misto • ~~Marse~~ ˌMistoˌ (MS Morgan)

14.12   apart • p̸ apart (MS Morgan)

14.13   laughed a laugh proportioned to her size, and said: • ~~delivered herself of a ringing laugh, and said—~~ ˌlaughed a laugh proportioned to her size, and said:ˌ (MS Morgan)

14.14   Misto • ~~Marse~~ ˌMistoˌ (MS Morgan)

14.20   on • ~~he~~ on (MS Morgan)

14.20   took this • took ~~this the child~~ this (MS Morgan)

14.21   again. • againˌ,ˌ ~~and still once more on the first of October.~~ (MS Morgan)

14.21   at intervals • ˌat intervalsˌ (MS Morgan)

14.22   at intervals • ~~after~~ || ˌatˌ intervals (MS Morgan)

14.24   The • ~~On the fifteenth~~ ˌthirdˌ ~~of this month of Se~~ [¶] The (MS Morgan)

14.27   three • ~~five~~ ˌthreeˌ (MS Morgan)

14.28   fairly • ˌfairlyˌ (MS Morgan)

14.33   Roxy: • Roxy≠ˌ:ˌ (MS Morgan)

14.33   related. • related. ~~The boy's parents and brothers and sisters were on a farm back in the country.~~ (MS Morgan)

14.36   lesson. • ~~lesson that will answer you for all times.~~ || lesson. (MS Morgan)

14.36   thief! • thief!ʳ (MS Morgan)

14.38   one • ~~master~~ ˌoneˌ (MS Morgan)

15.2   that • ~~that~~ | ˌthatˌ (MS Morgan)

15.6   she • ~~and~~ she (MS Morgan)

15.6–7   that the others were guilty, but she did not know them to be so. • ~~that~~ || ~~but~~ ˌthat the others were guilty, but sheˌ did not know ~~it.~~ ˌthem to be so.ˌ (MS Morgan)

15.8   had come • ˌhadˌ ~~came~~ ˌcomeˌ (MS Morgan)

15.9   revival • revival ~~a fortnight before,~~ (MS Morgan)

15.9   church a fortnight before, • ~~church, where~~ churchˌ,ˌ a fortnight before,ˌ (MS Morgan)

15.10–11 day after that gracious experience, • dayˌ,ˌ ˌafter that gracious experience,ˌ (MS Morgan)

15.14   the • ~~that~~ ˌtheˌ (MS Morgan)

15.19   sacrifice • sacrifice ~~unwillingly~~ (MS Morgan)

15.28   small • ~~any~~ small (MS Morgan)

15.35   would not • wouldn̶' not (MS Morgan)

15.36   humane • ~~chari~~ | humane (MS Morgan)

15.38   a • ~~the~~ ˌaˌ (MS Morgan)

15.38   hen • ~~chicken~~ ˌhenˌ (MS Morgan)

15.38–16.1   softly clucking her gratitude, • ~~mumbling its thanks,~~ softly clucking her gratitude, (MS Morgan)

16.1   her • ~~him~~ ˌherˌ (MS Morgan)

16.2   perfectly sure • ~~not doubting~~ ˌperfectly sureˌ (MS Morgan)

16.13   tears • ~~their tears~~ tears (MS Morgan)

16.25   knew • ~~felt~~ knew (MS Morgan)

16.26   his magnanimity; • ~~himself;~~ ˌhis magnanimity;ˌ (MS Morgan)

16.27   thereby • ~~thereby admonished~~ thereby (MS Morgan)

16.28   himself. • himself. ~~[¶] We have been excusing the slave for stealing; it is but fair to excuse the master for what might seem to us a sort of re- rather poor indications of the presence of humanity and softness in his nature. ˌButˌ He *was* a humane man, and most decidedly and unquestionably so. It was totally impossible for him to deal ungently with a *white* person who appealed to him for a grace—even a costly one. But he and his ancestors had always been slave-holders, and habit and heredity had made it impossible for him to realize that a negro was a human being. By name he was that, but it was only a phrase; ˌin realityˌ it meant no more than it would mean to if one should call a horse a human being. [¶] Here is a fact in ~~this man's~~ ˌDriscoll'sˌ history which will illustrate ˌthrow light—electric light—ˌ on ˌhisˌ case. He ˌonceˌ made a journey on horseback through Kentucky; and here and there and yonder over Tennessee; and then down to the near neighborhood of Vicksburg, Mississippi—and that last point was the point which he had originally started for. His object was to collect a debt of four hundred dollars which a planter had been owing him several years,ˌ and which he had vain Then why did he waste three weeks on horseback in the mud and slush of winter, when he could have made the trip in three days by steamboat? Because he wished to pay his expenses with a stroke of business; so he took a negro man along with him to sell—took him from the midst of his humble black family and the friends of his childhood, to exile him forever in a far land; and it never occurred to him that that poor creature had a heart in his bosom to break, and left hearts behind him that could break, also. From the planter's house he wrote like this to his wife: [¶] "I could get no fair offer for Jim anywhere on my tedious and dreary journey. And now the chief and real object of the journey has itself miscarried. Mr. Holcomb says he has not been fortunate, and times are hard; and he appealed to me to be merciful with him. You know the result, without my telling you. I was not made for this kind of business, and I cannot learn it. I had no heart to press him, so I said nothing. It simply amounts to forgiving the debt. I start homeward,~~ ~~tomorrow;~~ ˌsoon,ˌ ~~after looking around here a little, for I cannot be encumbered any longer with~~

Jim. He is valuable, but I will sell him, even if I have to take fifty dollars
for him." [¶] He was a humane and gentle-hearted man—in all cases
where slavery had not blunted his perceptions—and the record of his life
amply proves it. CHAPTER . . . . 3. (MS Morgan)

17.1   *Chapter 3* (MTP) • CHAPTER 3. [*short double rule*]. [Insert this
        under the words "*Chapter 3*" on page 49. ['49' inserted, and the direc-
        tive canceled, in pencil] (MS Morgan)

17.3   deep • to deep (MS Morgan)

17.6   Percy Driscoll • He Percy Driscoll (MS Morgan)

17.6   his • his his (MS Morgan)

17.7   Roxy's • Roxy's (MS Morgan)

17.12   frenzy • passion frenzy (MS Morgan)

17.13   shan't (MTP) • shant (MS Morgan)

17.18   noth'n (MTP) • nuoth'n (MS Morgan)

17.18   He • h He (MS Morgan)

17.19   hain't (MTP) • haint (MS Morgan)

17.20   a • y a (MS Morgan)

17.25   *kin* • *can* kin (MS Morgan)

17.25   it! But • it!—b But (MS Morgan)

17.26   ain't • not ain't (MS Morgan)

17.26   to • to (MS Morgan)

17.27   too. Come • too—□ ¢ Çome [*dash deleted by insertion of a square, the
        printer's symbol for an em quad, indicating a one-em space, the standard
        following a sentence period*] (MS Morgan)

17.30   it • it. Suddenly she stopped | it (MS Morgan)

17.31   cheap • cheap thing (MS Morgan)

18.1–2 She surveyed it wistfully, longingly. • She surveyed it wistfully, long-
        ingly. (MS Morgan)

18.3–4 jist lovely . . . added, "No • jist lovely". . . . OVER "No [*on verso:*]
        Then she nodded her head in response to a pleasant idea, and added, |
        over again (MS Morgan)

18.8   to make • to perfect the make (MS Morgan)

18.9   handkerchief-turban • handkerchief-turban, (MS Morgan)

18.10   she • and she (MS Morgan)

18.11   atrocious • ¢ atrocious (MS Morgan)

18.11   finally, • then finally, (MS Morgan)

18.12   thing • red thing (MS Morgan)

18.13	then • ~~and a fresh glance at the mirror satisfied her that~~ ₌then₌ (MS Morgan)
18.13	tomb. • tomb. ~~She took another glance at the mirror, and was thoroughly resigned.~~ (MS Morgan)
18.15	miserably short (MTP) • miserable₌y short₌ (MS Morgan)
18.15	shirt • shirt₌ (MS Morgan)
18.19	jist as much as dey does yo' • jist ~~de~~ as much as ₌dey does₌ you'. (MS Morgan)
18.20	to David en Goliah en dem • ~~to Noah's Ark en de~~ ₌to David en Goliah en dem₌ (MS Morgan)
18.21	Dat • ₫ Dat (MS Morgan)
18.22	By this time • ₌By this₌ ~~Mean~~time (MS Morgan)
18.23	Becket's • Beckett 's (MS Morgan)
18.26	astonishment and admiration, • astonishment₌ ₌and admiration,₌ (MS Morgan)
18.30	heir • ~~white~~ heir (MS Morgan)
18.31	eyes • eyes₌ (MS Morgan)
18.32	'uz • ~~was~~ ₌'uz₌ (MS Morgan)
18.33	a washin' • a-washin' (MS Morgan)
18.34	his'n • his₌'n₌ (MS Morgan)
18.35	undressed • ~~took~~ undressed (MS Morgan)
18.36	stripping him of everything • ~~and~~ stripping him ₫ of everything (MS Morgan)
19.5	'memberin' • 'member₌in'₌ (MS Morgan)
19.8	ever • ₌ever₌ (MS Morgan)
19.8	honey • ~~dollin'~~ ₌honey₌ (MS Morgan)
19.10	said, • said,⟋ (MS Morgan)
19.22	tole it, • tole it₌, ~~Tole it~~ (MS Morgan)
19.24	his own self—can't • his₌own₌self ~~by works~~—can't (MS Morgan)
19.26	*He* • ⟦ₑ *He* (MS Morgan)
19.30	Englan' • England'₌ (MS Morgan)
19.31	roun' 'bout de place • ₌roun' 'bout de place₌ (MS Morgan)
19.32	she • ₌she₌ (MS Morgan)
19.36	king, bimeby, en • king₌ ~~by en by, en~~ ₌bimeby, en₌ (MS Morgan)
20.1	nuther, • ₌nuther,₌ (MS Morgan)
20.4	a • ⟋ a₌ (MS Morgan)
20.5	humbly, • ₌humbly,₌ (MS Morgan)

20.5   say • say, ~~Lay~~ (MS Morgan)

20.7   practice • ~~lesson~~ practice (MS Morgan)

20.8   reverent • ~~gentl~~ reverent (MS Morgan)

20.11   curtness • ~~sn~~ curtness (MS Morgan)

20.13   and absorbed herself • and absorbed herself˛ (MS Morgan)

20.19   takes • takes ~~me~~ (MS Morgan)

20.20   I's afeard • ~~I's afraid~~ I's afeard (MS Morgan)

20.21   a pudd'nhead • ạ ℙ pudd'nhead (MS Morgan)

20.22   it's • ~~it~~ ˛it's˛ (MS Morgan)

20.23   ornery • ~~dratted~~ ˛ornery˛ (MS Morgan)

20.26   notice • noticeḍ (MS Morgan)

20.27–28 *sho'*. But … witch-work." • *sho'*." OVER˛ [*on verso:*] ˛But I reckon I'll tote
        along a hoss-shoe to keep off de witch-work." | over again˛ (MS Morgan)

20.32   when he • ~~and run~~ when ~~the father~~ ˛he˛ (MS Morgan)

20.33   gone • ₍ gone [*insertion caret made, then canceled*] (MS Morgan)

20.34   the • they̶ (MS Morgan)

21.2   first—put • first—~~and~~ put (MS Morgan)

21.3   carefully • ˛carefully˛ (MS Morgan)

21.3   away, • away, ~~without looking at them,~~ (MS Morgan)

21.5   finger-prints (MTP) • finger- | prints (MS Morgan)

21.8   he— • ˛he˛— (MS Morgan)

21.10   dropped • ḁ dropped (MS Morgan)

21.10   mind • ~~life.~~ ˛mind.˛ (MS Morgan)

22.1   *Chapter 4* (MTP) • ˛CHAPTER 4. [*short double rule*]˛ [*inserted in
        pencil*] (MS Morgan)

22.2   advantages • ∅̸ advantages (MS Morgan)

22.3   *Calendar.* • *Calendar.* ~~Insert the above under the words "Chapter 4,"
        on page ˛69˛˛ and let the paragraph on page 68 follow under it.~~ ['69'
        inserted in pencil] (MS Morgan)

22.4   there • ~~it~~ there (MS Morgan)

22.8   children. • ~~meat.~~ ˛children.˛ (MS Morgan)

22.9   *Calendar.* • *Calendar.* ~~˛This *follows* the paragraph on page 67, and *both*
        come under the words "Chapter 4" on page 69.~~˛ [*alterations in pencil*]
        (MS Morgan)

22.10   [¶] This • [*centered:*] ~~Chapter 4.~~ [*short triple rule*] [¶] This [*deletion in
        pencil*] (MS Morgan)

22.11   and • ~~and the and call~~ ˛and˛ (MS Morgan)

22.14–15   usurpation. He would cry • usurpation.⸲⟋ ⸲He would⸲ cry~~ing~~ (MS Morgan)

22.15   he would burst • ⸲he would⸲ bursting (MS Morgan)

22.16   scream after • ~~shriek~~ scream after (MS Morgan)

22.17   with • with ~~that frightful exhibition~~ ⸲~~which his mother~~⸲ ~~called "holding his breath," in the~~ (MS Morgan)

22.19   noiseless • ~~violent~~ ⸲noiseless⸲ (MS Morgan)

22.22   the • the~~y~~ (MS Morgan)

22.22   appalling (MTP) • appaling (MS Morgan)

22.22   stillness • ~~performance~~ ⸲stillness⸲ (MS Morgan)

22.25   surprises • ~~makes~~ ⸲surprises⸲ (MS Morgan)

22.25   into saying • ⸲into⸲ say⸲ing⸲ (MS Morgan)

23.7   saw, simply • saw⸲ ~~When it~~ | simply (MS Morgan)

23.7   Awnt • ~~a~~ Awnt (MS Morgan)

23.10   up frantic • ~~up crazy~~ ⸲up frantic⸲ (MS Morgan)

23.11   her • ⸲her⸲ (MS Morgan)

23.17   Roxy • ~~anybody~~ Roxy (MS Morgan)

23.24   sugar. • sugar. ~~Tom was~~ (MS Morgan)

23.25   child • child⸲ (MS Morgan)

23.29   he • ~~s~~he (MS Morgan)

23.33–34   then a natural result followed: • ⸲then a natural result followed:⸲ (MS Morgan)

23.35   practically into • ~~into~~ practically into (MS Morgan)

23.36   obsequiousness • ~~h~~ obsequiousness (MS Morgan)

23.37   counterfeit • ~~rift of~~ counterfeit (MS Morgan)

23.38   widened, • wi⸲dened, (MS Morgan)

24.1   and on one • ~~and on on~~ and on one (MS Morgan)

24.8   former • ~~latter~~ ⸲former⸲ (MS Morgan)

24.10   very • ⸲very⸲ (MS Morgan)

24.10   headquarters; not • headquarters⸲; ~~Not~~ not (MS Morgan)

24.11   marster • ma~~s~~rster (MS Morgan)

24.20   and • ⸲and⸲ (MS Morgan)

24.22   hated • ha~~d~~ted (MS Morgan)

24.30   a • ~~Tom's~~ a (MS Morgan)

24.35   so as • ⸲so as⸲ (MS Morgan)

24.37   the pet pastime • ~~it was the grand ambition~~ ⸲the pet pastime⸲ (MS Morgan)

24.37   of • ꝩ of (MS Morgan)

24.37   was • ˏwasˏ (MS Morgan)

25.1   account (MTP) • acount (MS Morgan)

25.2   proxy. • proxy. ˏ□ˏ [*insertion of a square, the printer's symbol for an em quad, indicating a one-em space, the standard following a sentence period*] (MS Morgan)

25.3   apple • ꝏ apple (MS Morgan)

25.4   rinds • rhinds (MS Morgan) [TEXTUAL NOTE: *Although an instance of 'rhind' in the manuscript of* Tom Sawyer *made it into the first American edition (SLC 1876, 259), linguistic data suggests that this spelling has never been anything but an error*]

25.11   superiorities of • superiorities, ~~and~~ of (MS Morgan)

25.14   among • ~~by the~~ among (MS Morgan)

25.16   at last • ˏat lastˏ (MS Morgan)

25.18   canoe's bottom; • canoeˏ's bottom;ˏ (MS Morgan)

25.18–19 several of Tom's ancient adversaries • ˏseveral of Tom's ancient adversariesˏ (MS Morgan)

25.23   It • ~~Tom This~~ ˏItˏ (MS Morgan)

25.24   boys—particularly • boysˏ—particularlyˏ (MS Morgan)

25.24   present—to • present—ˏto (MS Morgan)

25.25   then • ~~and~~ then (MS Morgan)

25.27   the • ƕ the (MS Morgan)

25.28   away, • ˏawayˏ, (MS Morgan)

25.31   therefore • ~~so~~ ˏthereforeˏ (MS Morgan)

25.32   his • ~~Tom's~~ ˏhisˏ (MS Morgan)

25.35   heaped • ~~wished he had had~~ heaped (MS Morgan)

25.37   blockheaded • blockheadˏedˏ (MS Morgan)

26.4   by • Ꝫ by (MS Morgan)

26.5   Nigger-pappy (MTP) • Nigger- | pappy (MS Morgan)

26.5   had had • ˏhadˏ had (MS Morgan)

26.8–9   off! ... pockets, for?" • offˏ!ˏ ~~you block head!"~~ ˏ—what do you stand there with your hands in your pockets, for?"ˏ (MS Morgan)

26.13   me. Dey's • me.ˏ⫟ˏ□ˏᖱ Ɖey's [*dash deleted by insertion of a square, the printer's symbol for an em quad, indicating a one-em space, the standard following a sentence period*] (MS Morgan)

26.14   two or • ˏtwo orˏ (MS Morgan)

26.16   a • ~~an inch~~ a (MS Morgan)

26.18   day, now, • day⌃, now,⌃ (MS Morgan)

26.22   that • ~~him~~ that (MS Morgan)

26.25   unmodified • ⌃unmodified⌃ (MS Morgan)

26.26   now, • ⌃now,⌃ (MS Morgan)

26.30   her boy. • ~~reptile~~ ⌃her boy.⌃ (MS Morgan)

26.30   She • s̸She (MS Morgan)

26.32   en • ~~and~~ en (MS Morgan)

27.9   occurred • ~~hap~~ occurred (MS Morgan)

27.13   1845. • 1845.⟋ (MS Morgan)

27.15   ostensible son • ⟨ostensible⟩ son ~~with the~~ (MS Morgan)

27.17   not difficult to please. • ~~glad to get anything—anything that is made out of meat and bones, no matter about the quality.~~ ⌃not difficult to please.⌃ (MS Morgan)

27.18   privately to his brother, • privately, ⌃to his brother,⌃ (MS Morgan)

27.20   the boy • the⌀ boy (MS Morgan)

27.21   for • ⌃for⌃ (MS Morgan)

27.25   young • ⌃young⌃ (MS Morgan)

27.31   the black giant, Jasper. • ~~Sandy,~~ ⌃the black giant, Jasper.⌃ (MS Morgan)

27.35   the race • ~~her~~ the race (MS Morgan)

27.37   Jasper was a Dunker Baptist. • ~~Sandy~~ ⌃Jasper⌃ ~~had been~~ ⌃was⌃ a Dunker Baptist,⌃. ~~but had examined into things for himself and become a sort of a freethinker in a small way.~~ (MS Morgan)

28.5   Jasper • ~~Sandy~~ ⌃Jasper⌃ (MS Morgan)

28.10   days (MTP) • day's (MS Morgan)

28.10   "Bluff • ~~blu~~ "Bluff (MS Morgan)

28.13   stretch • ~~long~~ stretch (MS Morgan)

28.14   made • ~~wr~~ made (MS Morgan)

28.17   stretch • ~~stra~~ stretch (MS Morgan)

28.23   whirls (MTP) • whirl's (MS Morgan)

28.30   upon • upon [*SLC marked this word to divide it ('up on'), then canceled it*] (MS Morgan)

28.31   had a great and glad surprise, for he • ⌃had a great and glad surprise, for he⌃ (MS Morgan)

28.33   was • ~~had~~ was (MS Morgan)

28.37   grouped • ~~gathered~~ grouped (MS Morgan)

29.4–7   hurt!" … grave itself. • hurt!" ⌃OVER⌃ [*on verso:*] ⌃The father turned … grave itself. | over again⌃ (MS Morgan)

29.9   for a little while, • ~~and amazement and incredulity~~ for a little ~~while;~~ ͵while,͵ (MS Morgan)

29.10   it done • ~~the miracle~~ ͵it͵ done (MS Morgan)

29.11   seized (MTP) • siezed (MS Morgan)

29.12   No • ~~Ten~~ No (MS Morgan)

29.14   him." • him." [¶] ~~"This is the most unbelievable thing that ever—where is Jasper?"~~ [¶] ~~"Around the elbow with the horse and buggy."~~ (MS Morgan)

29.15–16   His master said— • ͵His master said—͵ (MS Morgan)

29.20   air; . . . this hour." • air͵"͵; and you are free, from this hour."͵ (MS Morgan)

29.26   finger-prints, (MTP) • finger- | prints, ~~for~~ (MS Morgan)

29.30   deviltry, some witch-business, • deviltry ͵,͵ some witch-business,͵ (MS Morgan)

30.8   dah in dat shape, • dah͵,͵ in dat shape,͵ (MS Morgan)

31.1   *Chapter 5* (MTP) • ͵Chapter 5. *[short double rule].* [¶] ~~Insert this under the words "Chapter 5," on page͵~~ *[alterations in pencil]* (MS Morgan)

31.4   *Calendar.* • *Calendar.* [¶] ~~"Two souls with but a single thought" is not a bad average, for it is half a thought apiece. This village has approached it sometimes, but not often enough to attract attention.— *Pudd'nhead Wilson's Calendar.*~~ [¶] ~~Remark of Dr. Baldwin concerning upstarts: We don't care to eat toadstools that think they are truffles.— *Pudd'nhead Wilson's Calendar.*͵~~ (MS Morgan)

31.5–7   Remark of Dr. Baldwin . . . *Calendar.* • ͵[¶] Remark of Dr Baldwin concerning upstarts: We don't care to eat toadstools that think they are truffles.—*Pudd'nhead Wilson's Calendar.* | *[centered:]* ~~Chapter~~ *[short double rule]* *[motto inserted at the head of MS page 103, having previously been written (and canceled) on page 102]* (MS Morgan)

31.11   bliss-business • ͵bliss-͵business (MS Morgan)

31.15   manners • ~~matter~~ manners (MS Morgan)

31.17   furtively • ~~furtively, not to say~~ furtively (MS Morgan)

31.19   safely • safely͵ (MS Morgan)

31.23   him, • him͵,͵ (MS Morgan)

32.4   bell-ringer (MTP) • bell- | ringer (MS Morgan)

32.8   tiresome • ~~dull~~ ͵tiresome͵ (MS Morgan)

32.15   day—in fact, did. • day͵,͵—in fact, did.͵ (MS Morgan)

32.17   President • ~~p~~President (MS Morgan)

32.18–20   member. The Society's . . . life, now. • member. ͵OVER͵ *[on verso:]* ͵The Society's weekly discussions were the old lawyer's main interest in life, now. | over again͵ (MS Morgan)

32.21 under • ~~with~~ under (MS Morgan)

32.22 before. • before. [¶] ˌHere insert A, p. 49.ˌ (MS Morgan) [TEXTUAL NOTE: *This directive refers to the single-sentence clipping from TS1 with the text: 'Judge Driscoll . . . public opinion', 32.23–25; the page number was clipped away in revision*]

32.25–26 Or, rather . . . better one. • ˌOr, rather, that was one of the reasons why it failed, but there was another and better one.ˌ (MS Morgan/TS1)

32.26 If • If [*paragraph indented, then marked to begin flush left*] (MS Morgan)

32.28 his position. • ~~that he was right.~~ ˌhis position.ˌ (MS Morgan)

32.29 almanac, • almanac, ~~or calendar,~~ (MS Morgan)

32.29 amusement— • amusement~~,~~—ˌ (MS Morgan)

32.31 thought • ~~held~~ ˌthought.ˌ (MS Morgan)

32.32 a • ~~them~~ a (MS Morgan)

32.35 hesitancy • ~~ℵ~~ hesitancy (MS Morgan)

32.36 pudd'nhead (MTP) • puddn'head (MS Morgan)

33.3 merit. • merit.ˌ ~~so both men got some advantage out of the miscarriage of the Judge's effort, after all.~~ ~~moreover, he now went even so far as to take to nurse another of Wilson's projects.~~ ˌRUN to 47-A &c.ˌ (MS Morgan) [TEXTUAL NOTE: 'RUN to 47-A &c.' *evidently refers to the TS1 fragment which follows, i.e. '[¶] Judge Driscoll . . .', etc.; the directive is canceled in pencil*]

33.4–10 [¶] Judge Driscoll could be a freethinker . . . thought or did. He was liked . . . count for anything. (MTP) • [¶] Judge Driscoll could be a free- | thinker . . . thought or did. . . . count for anything. (MS Berg); [*centered:*] ~~Chapter~~ [¶] Judge Driscoll could be a freethinker . . . thought or did. ˌHe was liked . . . count for anything.ˌ ˌfollow page *110.*ˌ [*placement directive in pencil*] (MS Morgan/TS1) [TEXTUAL NOTE: 'He was liked . . . count for anything' *restored by SLC from the passage he canceled on TS1 page 29*]

34.1 *Chapter 6* (MTP) • ˌ*Chapter 6.* [*short double rule*]ˌ ~~Insert this under the words "Chapter 6" on page~~ [*alterations in pencil*] (MS Morgan) [TEXTUAL NOTE: *This leaf is preceded by another, the recto of which reads, in pencil:* '~~Probably runs to Aunts & Twins~~'; *on verso, there is a discarded passage from* Personal Recollections of Joan of Arc, *which reads:* '~~missed us and said we would drill twice a day thenceforth.~~']

34.2 Constable (MTP) • ~~John Bu~~ ¢ constable (MS Morgan)

34.4 *Calendar.* • ~~Calendar.~~ | *Calendar.* (MS Morgan)

34.5 [¶] When • ˌ[¶] It is a great many years ago, and so it can do no harm to tell the story.ˌ [¶] It was long before the ~~day~~ ˌadvent.ˌ of the railroad, and the primitive little village called Rawson's Langding had not waked up yet, but was still slumbering its peaceful days away in the eventless fashion which ˏitˏ had so long been used to. Twice a week the fussy and shabby little packet that plied between St. Louis and Cairo stopped there a moment and received or discharged a passenger, and left a newspaper, and on the return trips did about the same thing over again. This was the sole excitement known to that little Missouri town. Everybody and his dog swarmed out and made for the landing whenever the boat was reported in sight and remained massed together near the stage-plank, gazing entranced, until she had finished her errand and was off again, then broke apart and drifted homeward refreshed, to wait till next time. Four days in the week they̶ ˏirˏ lives had this five-minute upstirring, the other three the profound stagnation was not disturbed. [¶] P̶o̶l̶i̶t̶i̶c̶s̶ ̶i̶n̶ ̶t̶h̶a̶t̶ ̶t̶o̶w̶n̶ ̶w̶e̶r̶e̶ w̶Whig and d̶Democratic; religion, [¶] Politically, the town was Whig and Democratic; religiously, it was mainly Presbyterianˏ, Methodistˏ and Catholic—it had been settled by the French, away back in the early times; there was a camp of temperance agitators, and a camp of resistants; whatever new thing was started was promptly taken hold of and split in half, in a perfectly fair way, share and share alike, and two camps formed so as to get all the joy and sorrow out of it possible; and whoever could suggest a new thing was a welcome soul, for it was a town that joyed in experiments. ¶ˏEverybody knew everybody, all the community were on the most s̶o̶c̶i̶a̶b̶l̶e̶ familiar terms with each other. G̶i̶v̶e̶n̶ ˏChristianˏ names were oftener used than any others, by c̶o̶n̶ members of contemporaneous generations as toward each other, the surnames being reserved for the generations that were older than the speaker's. Judge Driscoll, the justice of the peace, and seventy years old, was still Jake Driscoll to the old men and women who had been his schoolmates, though he was "Judge" to the rest of the community; the like was the case with old Captain Baldwin, who was still Tom to his contempo | ˏraries, but "Captain to the rest.ˏ [¶] When (MS Berg); o̶f̶ ̶t̶h̶e̶ ̶c̶o̶m̶m̶u̶n̶i̶t̶y̶;̶ ̶t̶h̶e̶ ̶l̶i̶k̶e̶ ̶w̶a̶s̶ ̶t̶h̶e̶ ̶c̶a̶s̶e̶ ̶w̶i̶t̶h̶ ̶o̶l̶d̶ ̶C̶a̶p̶t̶a̶i̶n̶ B̶a̶l̶d̶w̶i̶n̶,̶ ̶w̶h̶o̶ ̶w̶a̶s̶ ̶s̶t̶i̶l̶l̶ ̶T̶o̶m̶ ̶t̶o̶ ̶h̶i̶s̶ ̶c̶o̶n̶t̶e̶m̶p̶o̶r̶a̶r̶i̶e̶s̶,̶ ̶b̶u̶t̶ ̶"̶C̶a̶p̶t̶a̶i̶n̶"̶ ̶t̶o̶ ̶t̶h̶e̶ r̶e̶s̶t̶.̶ [¶] When [*penciled notation in top margin of page 2: 'Chapter 6.'*] (MS Morgan/TS1) [TEXTUAL NOTE: *In MS Morgan,* 'raries . . . rest.' *is recopied from MS Berg page 8. The opening of MS Berg,* '.[¶] It is a great . . . the rest', *was typed as TS1 page 1 and part of page 2; SLC discarded page 1 and deleted (in pencil) that part of the page 2 text, writing in the top margin* 'strike the first two lines']

34.7   the • ˏtheˏ (MS Berg); the (MS Morgan/TS1)

34.13   Betsy Hale . . . fast friends, • B̶e̶t̶s̶y̶ ̶F̶l̶o̶y̶d̶,̶ ˏBetsy Hale,ˏ ˏnear neighbors and fast friends,ˏ (MS Berg); Betsy Hale, near neighbors and fast friends, (MS Morgan/TS1)

34.14   Aunt Patsy • A̶u̶n̶t̶ ̶B̶e̶t̶s̶y̶ ̶w̶a̶s̶ ̶A̶n̶n̶a̶'̶s̶ ̶m̶o̶t̶h̶e̶r̶.̶ ̶S̶h̶e̶ ˏAunt Patsyˏ (MS Berg); Aunt Patsy (MS Morgan/TS1)

34.15   make • ma~~d~~ke (MS Berg); make (MS Morgan/TS1)

34.17   win • wins (MS Berg); win~~s~~ (MS Morgan/TS1)

34.17   men • m~~c~~en (MS Berg); men (MS Morgan/TS1)

34.18   years • ~~ag~~ years (MS Berg); years (MS Morgan/TS1)

34.18   past fifty, • ~~sixty,~~ ˌpast fifty,ˌ (MS Berg); past fifty, (MS Morgan/TS1)

34.20   to be • ~~to be denied entrance at the wide doors of her hospitable heart for a~~ to be (MS Berg); to be (MS Morgan/TS1)

34.23   picnics • pic~~k~~nics (MS Berg); picnics (MS Morgan/TS1)

34.25   she • ~~and~~ she (MS Berg); she (MS Morgan/TS1)

34.26   hour. • hour. [¶] ~~One day, about the time we are treating of, she called~~ (MS Berg); hour. (MS Morgan/TS1)

34.27   [¶] Her • ~~raries but "Captain to the rest. [¶] The widow Cooper was a simple-hearted~~ simple-natured, soft-hearted, ~~dear old body, and well beloved by all the community.~~ ¶ Her (MS Berg); [¶] Her (MS Morgan/TS1)

34.28   town. • village. (MS Berg); ~~village.~~ ˌtown.ˌ (MS Morgan/TS1)

34.30   had begun • ˌhadˌ begun (MS Berg); had (MS Morgan/TS1)

35.3   its (MS Berg) • it's (MS Morgan/TS1)

35.4   its (MS Berg) • it's (MS Morgan/TS1)

35.5   She • ~~She remained Maria to her old mother, whose dead sister,~~ She (MS Berg); She (MS Morgan/TS1)

35.11   she. • ~~herself.~~ ˌshe.ˌ (MS Berg); she. (MS Morgan/TS1)

35.12   Cooper • ~~c~~Cooper (MS Berg); Cooper (MS Morgan/TS1)

35.16   tedious • ~~d~~ tedious (MS Berg); tedious (MS Morgan/TS1)

35.17   and • ~~—and~~ and (MS Berg); and (MS Morgan/TS1)

35.21   Indeed • I~~n~~ndeed (MS Berg); Indeed (MS Morgan/TS1)

35.24   woman • girl (MS Berg); ~~girl~~ ˌwomanˌ (MS Morgan/TS1)

35.25   town • village (MS Berg); ~~village~~ ˌtownˌ (MS Morgan/TS1)

35.27   aflush (MS Berg) • ablush (MS Morgan/TS1)

35.29   too • two (MS Berg); too (MS Morgan/TS1)

35.31   don't • ~~do~~ ˌdon'tˌ (MS Berg); don't (MS Morgan/TS1)

35.34   your • ~~the~~ ˌyourˌ (MS Berg); your (MS Morgan/TS1)

35.35   a • ~~yo~~ a (MS Berg); a (MS Morgan/TS1)

35.37   seems so • seems so (MS Berg); seems ˌsoˌ (MS Morgan/TS1)

36.6   —"but (MTP) • —'but (MS Berg); —'but (MS Morgan/TS1)

36.10   so; (MS Berg) • so: (MS Morgan/TS1)

36.10   so. 'Our • so.⤴ 'Our (MS Berg); so. 'Our (MS Morgan/TS1)

36.10   Cappello • Cappello (MS Berg); Cappello (MS Morgan/TS1)

36.13	madam (MTP) • Madam (MS Berg, MS Morgan/TS1)
36.13	if • ɓ if (MS Berg); if (MS Morgan/TS1)
36.17	I • ~~the~~ I (MS Berg); I (MS Morgan/TS1)
36.29	Maybe (MS Berg) • May be (MS Morgan/TS1)
37.1	nonsense (MS Berg) • nonesense (MS Morgan/TS1)
37.5	Judge (MTP) • judge (MS Berg); Judge (MS Morgan/TS1) [TEXTUAL NOTE: *TS1's form is admitted in line with a regularization policy based (ironically, in this instance) on the typical usage of the manuscripts*]
37.6	Justice Robinson • Captain Baldwin (MS Berg); ~~Captain Baldwin~~ ˯Justice Robinson˯ (MS Morgan/TS1)
37.13	uncertain, in low water, • uncertain (MS Berg); uncertain˯, in low water,˯ (MS Morgan/TS1)
37.13	times. • times. They took life easy, they were never in a hurry, they arrived early or late, according to circumstances, there was no schedule. (MS Berg); times. ~~They took life easy, they were never in a hurry, they arrived early or late, according to circumstances, there was no schedule.~~ (MS Morgan/TS1)
37.15	landing (MS Berg) • landing ˯~~to see the strangers˯~~ (MS Morgan/TS1)
37.16	heavy • ˯heavy˯ (MS Berg); heavy (MS Morgan/TS1)
37.17	then twelve, • then twelve, (MS Berg); [*not in*] (MS Morgan/TS1) [TEXTUAL NOTE: *The TS1 typist inadvertently omitted these two words*]
37.18	town • village (MS Berg); ~~village~~ ˯town˯ (MS Morgan/TS1)
37.20	on (MS Berg) • at (MS Morgan/TS1)
37.21	up • ȼ up (MS Berg); up (MS Morgan/TS1)
38.1	*Chapter 7* (MTP) • Chap. 2. [*short triple rule*] (MS Berg); ~~Chapter 2.~~ ˯Chapter 7. [*short double rule*] Nothing is so injurious as other people's habits.—*Pudd'nhead Wilson's Calendar.*˯ (MS Morgan/TS1)
38.6	came • came (MS Berg); cøame (MS Morgan/TS1)
38.7	crash • ~~fearful~~ crash (MS Berg); crash (MS Morgan/TS1)
38.7	wench • girl (MS Berg); ~~girl~~ ˯wench˯ (MS Morgan/TS1)
38.10	new-comer (MTP) • new comer (MS Berg); new comer (MS Morgan/TS1)
38.10	easy grace • ~~grace~~ easy grace (MS Berg); easy grace (MS Morgan/TS1)
38.13	Cappello," (the other head bowed,) "and (MS Berg) • Cappello,"—/the other head bowed,/—ˬand (MS Morgan/TS1) [TEXTUAL NOTE: *SLC inserted the dashes in TS1, perhaps not realizing that the typist had used slashes as substitutes for the parentheses his typewriter could not produce; the dashes are not adopted because they were prompted by a typist's quirk*]
38.15	unavoidable; (MS Berg) • unavoidable (MS Morgan/TS1)

38.15   both • ~~this~~ both (MS Berg); both (MS Morgan/TS1)

38.16   amazement and • ˏamazement andˏ (MS Berg); amazement and (MS Morgan/TS1)

38.21–22   uncomfortable—both of you, I mean.” • uncomfortableˏ”ˏ—both of you, I mean.”ˏ (MS Berg); uncomfortable—both of you, I mean.” (MS Morgan/TS1)

38.25   good-night (MTP) • good night (MS Berg, MS Morgan/TS1)

38.26   away • away, (MS Berg); away (MS Morgan/TS1)

38.29   and dazed. • ~~for once,~~ and dazed. and dazed. (MS Berg); and dazed. (MS Morgan/TS1)

38.29   sat • ˏsatˏ (MS Berg); sat (MS Morgan/TS1)

39.1   roaring • ~~lashing~~ roaring (MS Berg); roaring (MS Morgan/TS1)

39.5   weird (MTP) • wierd (MS Berg, MS Morgan/TS1)

39.6   them • them them (MS Berg); them (MS Morgan/TS1)

39.6   its (MS Berg) • it's (MS Morgan/TS1)

39.6   grewsome • ˏgrewsomeˏ (MS Berg); grewsome (MS Morgan/TS1)

39.9   phillipene (MS Berg) • phillipena (MS Morgan/TS1)

39.10   Her • ~~She was still~~ Her (MS Berg); Her (MS Morgan/TS1)

39.11   resentfully (MS Berg) • res~~t~~- | ˏentˏfully (MS Morgan/TS1)

39.12   And • ~~Well,~~ And (MS Berg); And (MS Morgan/TS1)

39.16   good-hearted (MTP) • good hearted (MS Berg); good hearted (MS Morgan/TS1)

39.17   *its* (MTP) • *it's* (MS Berg, MS Morgan/TS1)

39.18   its (MS Berg) • it's (MS Morgan/TS1)

39.20   anyway it's • ˏanyway it'sˏ (MS Berg); anyway it's (MS Morgan/TS1)

39.25   t'other (MS Berg) • tother (MS Morgan/TS1)

39.27   and fresh complexion • ˏand fresh complexionˏ (MS Berg); and fresh complexion (MS Morgan/TS1)

39.31–32   hands!—especially Angelo's (MTP) • hands!ˏ—especially Angelo'sˏ (MS Berg); hands—especially Angelo's (MS Morgan/TS1)

39.37   a couple • ˏa couple (MS Berg); a couple (MS Morgan/TS1)

39.37   writhing • ~~going~~ ˏwrithingˏ (MS Berg); writhing (MS Morgan/TS1)

39.37   dizzy • dizz (MS Berg); dizzy (MS Morgan/TS1)

40.12   dried.” • dried.” ~~You take~~ (MS Berg); dried.” (MS Morgan/TS1)

40.14   call him • call~~l~~ him (MS Berg); call him (MS Morgan/TS1)

40.14   I think • ˏI thinkˏ (MS Berg); I think (MS Morgan/TS1)

40.19   Sho' (MTP) • Sho (MS Berg, MS Morgan/TS1)

40.23	getting • ~~und~~ getting (MS Berg); getting (MS Morgan/TS1)
40.24	ever • ever~~y~~ (MS Berg); ever (MS Morgan/TS1)
40.31	can (MS Berg) • can can (MS Morgan/TS1)
40.31	*I* • I (MS Berg); *I* [*underscored, in pencil, to italicize*] (MS Morgan/TS1)
40.33	sentiment." • sentiment."	~~Run to page 27-A B C &c~~ (MS Berg); sentiment." (MS Morgan/TS1)
40.34	Twins (MS Berg) • twins (MS Morgan/TS1)
40.34	without • with͜out͜ (MS Berg); without (MS Morgan/TS1)
40.36	for it was like skinning a tarantula, • ͜for it was like skinning a tarantula,͜ (MS Berg); for it was like skinning a tarantula, (MS Morgan/TS1)
41.1	came (MS Berg) • c~~ø~~a͜me (MS Morgan/TS1)
41.4	strictly • ~~strictly according~~ strictly (MS Berg); strictly (MS Morgan/TS1)
41.6	its • ~~re~~ its (MS Berg); it's (MS Morgan/TS1)
41.14	My friend, • ͜My friend,͜ (MS Berg); My friend, (MS Morgan/TS1)
41.19	never • ~~seld~~ never (MS Berg); never (MS Morgan/TS1)
41.28	Luigi, with Paine's "Age of Reason" in his hand, • Luigi͜, with Paine's "Age of Reason" in his hand,͜ (MS Berg); Luigi, with Paine's "Age of Reason" in his hand, (MS Morgan/TS1)
41.30	"Whole Duty of Man," (MTP) • Testament, (MS Berg); ~~testament,~~ ͜Whole Duty of Man,͜ (MS Morgan/TS1)
41.30	both • ͜both͜ (MS Berg); both (MS Morgan/TS1)
41.31	became (MS Berg) • become (MS Morgan/TS1)
41.34	that—" (MTP) • that— (MS Berg, MS Morgan/TS1)
41.37	too, • ͜too,͜ (MS Berg); too, (MS Morgan/TS1)
42.7	d— bosh! (MTP) • d-bosh! (MS Berg, MS Morgan/TS1) [TEXTUAL NOTE: *Presumably Luigi begins to say "damn your principles," then remembers Angelo has just objected to his profanity (at 41.26)*]
42.9	but • ~~to talk~~ but (MS Berg); but (MS Morgan/TS1)
42.10	when • ~~said he~~ when (MS Berg); when (MS Morgan/TS1)
42.11	plaintive • ~~music~~ plaintive (MS Berg); plaintive (MS Morgan/TS1)
42.13	[¶] After • ~~night, the ruder music of Old Bob Ridley went thundering after it upon the competent vehicle of the~~ ͜in͜ Luigi's brazen basso, ~~and all the dogs and all the cats woke up~~ in Luigi's brazen basso. ~~The household and the neighborhood wondered what might be the reason of so~~ ͜this͜ ~~strange a~~ combination, ~~but there was none to explain.~~ [¶] After (MS Berg); [¶] After (MS Morgan/TS1)
42.14	whisky (MS Berg) • whiskey (MS Morgan/TS1)

42.16	headache. • headache. [¶] ~~Go back to page 27.~~ (MS Berg); headache. (MS Morgan/TS1)
43.1	*Chapter 8* (MTP) • Chapter 3. [*short double rule*] (MS Berg); ~~Chapter 3.~~ ˏChapter 8ˏ [*short double rule*] (MS Morgan/TS1)
43.2–3	[¶] Tell the truth or trump—but get the trick.—*Pudd'nhead Wilson's Calendar.* • [*not in*] (MS Berg); ˏ[¶] Tell the truth or trump—but get the trick.—*Pudd'nhead Wilson's Calendar.*ˏ (MS Morgan/TS1)
43.4	Twins (MS Berg) • twins (MS Morgan/TS1)
43.8	so, • soˏ ˏ (MS Berg); so, (MS Morgan/TS1)
43.9	fine, (MS Berg) • fine (MS Morgan/TS1)
43.13	here. • here.ᵇ (MS Berg); here. (MS Morgan/TS1)
43.16	after • ~~last ni~~ after (MS Berg); after (MS Morgan/TS1)
43.18	singing. • singing.ᵇ (MS Berg); singing. (MS Morgan/TS1)
43.20	'Greenland's Icy Mountains' (MTP) • Greenlandˏ's Icy Mountainsˏ (MS Berg); Greenland's Icy Mountains (MS Morgan/TS1)
43.23	'Old Bob Ridley' (MTP) • ˏOldˏ Bob Ridley (MS Berg); Old Bob Ridley (MS Morgan/TS1)
43.25	'Bob Ridley' (MTP) • Bob Ridley (MS Berg, MS Morgan/TS1)
43.25	rackety slam-bang • ~~low-down~~ ˏrackety slam-bangˏingˏ (MS Berg); rackety slam-bang (MS Morgan/TS1)
43.25–26	rippingest and rantingest and noisiest • ~~low-downest~~ ˏrippingest and rantingest and noisiestˏ (MS Berg); rippingest and rantingest and noisiest (MS Morgan/TS1)
44.6	You • ~~It ain't~~ You (MS Berg); You (MS Morgan/TS1)
44.6	duets • ˏduetsˏ (MS Berg); duets (MS Morgan/TS1)
44.11	opportunity (MS Berg) • oppontunity (MS Morgan/TS1)
44.12	anything • ~~what~~ anything (MS Berg); anything (MS Morgan/TS1)
44.17	admitted • ~~g~~ admitted (MS Berg); admitted (MS Morgan/TS1)
44.18	topic at that disadvantage, • topicˏ ˏat that disadvantage,ˏ (MS Berg); topic at that disadvantage, (MS Morgan/TS1)
44.19	seek • ~~make~~ ˏseekˏ (MS Berg); seek (MS Morgan/TS1)
44.21	coming." • coming."	~~Run to page 28~~ (MS Berg); coming." (MS Morgan/TS1)
44.22	[¶] "*They*, ma—you ought to say *they*—it's nearer right." • [*not in*] (MS Berg); ˏ¶ "*They*, ma—you ought to say *they*—it's nearer right."ˏ [*insertion in pencil*] (MS Morgan/TS1)
44.23	[¶] The • [*centered:*] ~~Chap. 3.~~ [*short triple rule*] [¶] The (MS Berg); [¶] The (MS Morgan/TS1)

44.23   rather shoutingly dressed but (MTP) • ~~beautifully~~ ˏrather shoutinglyˏ
         dressed˒~~and~~ ˏbutˏ (MS Berg); rather shoutingley dressed but (MS
         Morgan/TS1)

44.24   room • room ~~in the morning~~ (MS Berg); room (MS Morgan/TS1)

44.25   his • ~~its~~ ˏhisˏ (MS Berg); his (MS Morgan/TS1)

44.25–26 once, like . . . blades, • onceˏ, like one of those pocket knives with a
         multiplicity of blades,ˏ (MS Berg); once, like one of those pocket knives
         with a multiplicity of blades, (MS Morgan/TS1)

44.28   comradeship (MS Berg) • comeradeship (MS Morgan/TS1)

44.29   its (MS Berg) • it's (MS Morgan/TS1)

44.36   black. • black.⸴ (MS Berg); black. (MS Morgan/TS1)

45.1   The • ~~Conversation flowed smoothly along, broadening its course by~~
         ~~degrees, and eventually taking in, in deeply interesting detail, the his-~~
         ~~tory of the twins and their wide travels in the earth.~~ The (MS Berg);
         The (MS Morgan/TS1)

45.6   courage. • courage. ~~The company sat long at their meal; so long that~~
         ~~when they rose at last, they knew all about each other and were fast~~
         ~~friends. Meantime eager citizens had begun to assemble in the parlor.~~
         ˏOVERˏ [on verso:] ~~When the Twins appeared suddenly before them~~
         ~~every eye flew wide and froze to a glassy stare, there was a universal gasp~~
         ~~that chorded itself into a single note, and two or three boys skipped out~~
         ~~of the open window like frogs. Then the introductions began, the citi-~~
         ~~zens found their breath and their tongues, and soon the hum of eager~~
         ~~talk rose on the air, and~~ ~~soon the~~ ˏtheˏ successfulˏ debut of the strangers
         ~~into Dawson's Landing society was an accomplished fact. From this |~~
         over againˏ [continued on recto:] ~~and from that time forth for several~~
         ~~days, the twins held a reception that hadn't a break in it during~~ (MS
         Berg); courage. (MS Morgan/TS1)

45.10   Twins (MTP) • twins (MS Berg, MS Morgan/TS1)

45.12   the • ~~any~~ ˏtheˏ (MS Berg); the (MS Morgan/TS1)

45.12   gotten • gotˏtenˏ ~~wonted to~~ (MS Berg); gotten (MS Morgan/TS1)

45.13   of one • ~~of one~~ of one (MS Berg); of one (MS Morgan/TS1)

45.14   bizarre • ~~curi~~ bizarre (MS Berg); bizarre (MS Morgan/TS1)

45.17   devoured it. • ~~bit it.~~ ˏdevoured it.ˏ (MS Berg); devoured it. (MS
         Morgan/TS1)

45.21   it; • ~~that;~~ ˏit;ˏ (MS Berg); it; (MS Morgan/TS1)

45.22   dark-complected • ~~light-~~ ˏdark-ˏcomplected (MS Berg); dark complected
         (MS Morgan/TS1)

45.22   potato (MTP) • potatoe (MS Berg, MS Morgan/TS1)

45.22   its (MS Berg) • it's (MS Morgan/TS1)

45.23 light-complected • ~~dark~~ ˌlight-ˌcomplected (MS Berg); light complected (MS Morgan/TS1)

45.26 blushed • ~~blushed~~ | blushed (MS Berg); blushed (MS Morgan/TS1)

45.28 Angelo • ~~Antonio~~ Angelo (MS Berg); Angelo (MS Morgan/TS1)

45.29 *you* • you (MS Berg); *you* [*underscored in pencil, to italicize*] (MS
Morgan/TS1)

45.32 did not (MS Berg) • didn't (MS Morgan/TS1)

45.32 but • ~~but~~ | but (MS Berg); but (MS Morgan/TS1)

45.35 embarrassed again. She said: • ~~confused again; or rather, embarrassed.~~
ˌembarrassed again.ˏ ˌShe said:ˏ (MS Berg); embarrassed again. She
said: (MS Morgan/TS1)

45.36 mustn't (MS Berg) • musn't (MS Morgan/TS1)

45.37 drink • ˌto˴ drink (MS Berg); drink (MS Morgan/TS1)

45.37 you • ~~he~~ you (MS Berg); you (MS Morgan/TS1)

45.37 potato (MTP) • potatoe (MS Berg, MS Morgan/TS1)

46.1 I thought • ˌI thoughtˏ (MS Berg); I thought (MS Morgan/TS1)

46.2 everybody • ~~nob~~ everybody (MS Berg); everybody (MS Morgan/TS1)

46.3 Twins (MTP) • twins (MS Berg, MS Morgan/TS1)

46.8 potato (MTP) • potatoe (MS Berg, MS Morgan/TS1)

46.10 these (MS Berg) • them (MS Morgan/TS1) [TEXTUAL NOTE: *MS
Berg's* 'these' *could be misread as* 'them' *and was so rendered in TS1;
SLC, encountering the typist's error, revised to* 'the'; *his original reading is
restored here*]

46.11 table-room (MS Berg) • table room (MS Morgan/TS1)

46.17 Angelo • ~~us~~ Angelo (MS Berg); Angelo (MS Morgan/TS1)

46.21 its (MS Berg) • it's (MS Morgan/TS1)

46.22 its (MS Berg) • it's (MS Morgan/TS1)

46.24 any more (MS Berg) • anymore (MS Morgan/TS1)

46.25 indigestion (MS Berg) • ˌinˏdigestion [*insertion in pencil*] (MS Morgan/
TS1)

46.35 'often.'" (MTP) • "ˌ'oftenˏ.'ˏ" (MS Berg); 'often'". (MS Morgan/TS1)

47.1 had, • had, ~~and~~ (MS Berg); had, (MS Morgan/TS1)

47.6 herself • herself ~~that~~ (MS Berg); herself (MS Morgan/TS1)

47.18 illnesses (MS Berg) • illness (MS Morgan/TS1)

47.20 them, and—" • them,~~—and I—~~ and—" (MS Berg); them, and—" (MS
Morgan/TS1)

47.21 you • you [*underscore canceled*] (MS Berg); you (MS Morgan/TS1)

47.22   he (MTP) • he [*underscore canceled*] (MS Berg); *he* (MS Morgan/TS1) [TEXTUAL NOTE: *The TS1 typist overlooked SLC's cancellation of his underscoring*]

47.25   it's nothing • ~~don't~~ it's nothing (MS Berg); it's nothing (MS Morgan/TS1)

47.31   Twins (MTP) • twins (MS Berg, MS Morgan/TS1)

47.34   flurried • ~~flu~~ flurried (MS Berg); flurried (MS Morgan/TS1)

48.9   its (MS Berg) • it's (MS Morgan/TS1)

48.18   a et • eat (MS Berg); ~~eat~~ ˏa etˏ (MS Morgan/TS1)

48.26   "There!—that'll do. • "There!ʳ—that'll do.ʳ (MS Berg); "There!—that'll do. (MS Morgan/TS1)

48.27   friendless • friendless ~~when~~ (MS Berg); friendless (MS Morgan/TS1)

48.28   don't, (MS Berg) • don't (MS Morgan/TS1)

48.33   on the • onˣ the (MS Berg); on the (MS Morgan/TS1)

48.34   seized (MS Morgan/TS1) • siezed (MS Berg)

49.1   "Our • ~~My~~ "Our (MS Berg); "Our (MS Morgan/TS1)

49.6   seized (MS Morgan/TS1) • siezed (MS Berg)

49.7   'freaks' (MS Berg) • freaks (MS Morgan/TS1)

49.10   exhibit (MS Berg) • be exhibited (MS Morgan/TS1)

49.15   times! • times!ʳ (MS Berg); times! (MS Morgan/TS1)

49.33   how • ~~and~~ how (MS Berg); how (MS Morgan/TS1)

49.34   help. • help.ʳ (MS Berg); help. (MS Morgan/TS1)

50.9   Winged • ~~w~~Winged (MS Berg); Winged (MS Morgan/TS1)

50.11   all." • all."ˏ W(MS Berg); all." (MS Morgan/TS1)

50.12   it's • ~~oh,~~ it's (MS Berg); it's (MS Morgan/TS1)

50.18   once! • once!ʳ (MS Berg); once! (MS Morgan/TS1)

50.20   has • ~~have~~ has (MS Berg); has (MS Morgan/TS1)

50.21   *one* (MS Berg) • one (MS Morgan/TS1)

50.24   swearing." • swearing,ˏ."ˏ ~~but he can't.~~" (MS Berg); swearing." (MS Morgan/TS1)

50.25   "And can't he? Dear • "ˏAnd can't he?ˏ Dear (MS Berg); "And can't he? Dear (MS Morgan/TS1)

50.30   O (MS Berg) • Oh (MS Morgan/TS1)

50.33   at • ĸ at (MS Berg); at (MS Morgan/TS1)

50.34   squawking • ~~caterwauling~~ ˏsquawkingˏ (MS Berg); squawking (MS Morgan/TS1)

50.37   Goodness, • Goodness, ~~gracious,~~ (MS Berg); Goodness, (MS Morgan/TS1)

51.12   *ma* (MS Berg) • ma (MS Morgan/TS1)

51.17 I • I̶Q̶ I (MS Berg); I (MS Morgan/TS1)

51.18 ma • *ma* ma (MS Berg); ma (MS Morgan/TS1)

51.22 *ma!* (MS Berg) • *ma* (MS Morgan/TS1)

51.23 o' (MS Berg) • o (MS Morgan/TS1)

51.23–24 spilin' to see—to see— • spiling͵ to see—t̶o̶ ̶s̶e̶e̶—̶d̶e̶m̶ ‖ ͵to see—͵ (MS Berg); spilin' to see—to see— (MS Morgan/TS1)

51.24 Twins (MTP) • twins (MS Berg); twins (MS Morgan/TS1)

51.26 [¶] It • [*centered:*] Chapter 4. [*short triple rule*] [¶] It (MS Berg); [*centered:*] C̶h̶a̶p̶t̶e̶r̶ ̶4̶.̶ ̶C̶h̶a̶p̶t̶e̶r̶ ̶9̶.̶ [*short double rule*] [¶] It (MS Morgan/TS1) [TEXTUAL NOTE: *Clemens canceled the typed chapter heading and inserted* 'Chapter 9.', *but canceled it when he decided not to have a chapter break here*]

51.31 the greatest • ͵the͵ greatest (MS Berg); the greatest (MS Morgan/TS1)

51.31 colorless • ȟ colorless (MS Berg); colorless (MS Morgan/TS1)

51.32 country town • village (MS Berg); v̶i̶l̶l̶a̶g̶e̶ ͵country town͵ (MS Morgan/TS1)

51.33 its (MS Berg) • it's (MS Morgan/TS1)

51.34 gaze • l̶o̶o̶k̶ ̶a̶n̶d̶ ̶e̶n̶ gaze (MS Berg); gaze (MS Morgan/TS1)

52.6 the Twins in advance, • ͵the Twins in advance,͵ (MS Berg); the twins in advance, (MS Morgan/TS1)

52.10 Twins • Twins (MS Berg); twins (MS Morgan/TS1)

52.15 handshake (MTP) • hand-shake (MS Berg, MS Morgan/TS1)

52.17 handshake (MTP) • hand-shake (MS Berg, MS Morgan/TS1)

52.17 ye," • y̶o̶u̶ ye," (MS Berg); ye," (MS Morgan/TS1)

52.27 kind of pile-driving • ͵kind of pile-driving͵ (MS Berg); kind of pile-driving (MS Morgan/TS1)

52.30 its (MS Berg) • it's (MS Morgan/TS1)

52.33 soul • sould̶ (MS Berg); soul (MS Morgan/TS1)

52.38 anything • anything t̶o̶ ̶b̶e̶ ̶a̶s̶h̶ (MS Berg); anything (MS Morgan/TS1)

53.3 Twins (MTP) • twins (MS Berg); twins (MS Morgan/TS1)

53.9 Twins (MS Berg) • twins (MS Morgan/TS1)

53.9 enchanted • ͵enchanted͵ (MS Berg); enchanted (MS Morgan/TS1)

53.10 group • groupȼ (MS Berg); group (MS Morgan/TS1)

53.10 recognized (MTP) • reǵcognized (MS Berg); recognizing (MS Morgan/TS1)

53.11 time • time w̶h̶a̶t̶ (MS Berg); time (MS Morgan/TS1)

53.11 great • ͵great͵ (MS Berg); great (MS Morgan/TS1)

53.13 throw • f̶o̶r̶ throw (MS Berg); throw (MS Morgan/TS1)

53.14   its (MS Berg) • it's (MS Morgan/TS1)

53.15   justified. • justified. [¶] ~~The session was long. When it broke up at last, the Twins had accepted several invitations; and were fairly in the swim of~~ (MS Berg); justified. (MS Morgan/TS1)

53.22   its (MS Berg) • it's (MS Morgan/TS1)

53.25   Twins (MTP) • twins (MS Berg, MS Morgan/TS1)

53.26   something to • s̶t̶ something to (MS Berg); something to (MS Morgan/TS1)

54.1   *Chapter 9* (MTP) • ‸CHAPTER‸ (MS Berg); Chapter. ‸9.‸ (MS Morgan/TS1)

54.2–7   [¶] The Creator admired His . . . *Calendar.* • [*not in*] (MS Berg); [¶] [Insert this after the words "Chapter 9" on page. ‸131‸ [¶] The Creator admired ~~the~~ ʰHis . . . *Calendar.* ['h' *triple underscored to capitalize; '131' inserted in pencil*] (MS Morgan) [TEXTUAL NOTE: *This aphorism is on an MS leaf inserted between TS1 leaves originally numbered 18 and 19 and renumbered as 129 and 131*]

54.3   His • [*not in*] (MS Berg); ʰHis ['h' *triple underscored to capitalize*] (MS Morgan)

54.4   "good." • [*not in*] (MS Berg); "good‸,‸." ~~and stopped there:~~ (MS Morgan)

54.5   He • [*not in*] (MS Berg); ʰHe ['h' *triple underscored to capitalize*] (MS Morgan)

54.6   you • [*not in*] (MS Berg); ~~he~~ you (MS Morgan/TS1)

54.10   Twins (MS Berg) • twins (MS Morgan/TS1)

54.11–13   progress, and . . . local charity. • progress. (MS Berg); progress‸,‸ and had also volunteered to do the balcony scene in Romeo and Juliet at an amateur entertainment for the benefit of a local charity.‸ (MS Morgan/TS1)

54.14   its (MS Berg) • it's (MS Morgan/TS1)

54.17   herd of • ~~flock of~~ herd of (MS Berg); herd of (MS Morgan/TS1)

54.23   minds • ~~opinion~~ minds (MS Berg); minds (MS Morgan/TS1)

54.28   Twins (MS Berg) • twins (MS Morgan/TS1)

54.31   farmers' (MS Berg) • farmer's (MS Morgan/TS1)

55.3   strangers • ~~youths~~ ‸strangers‸ (MS Berg); strangers (MS Morgan/TS1)

55.4   Freemasons' (MS Berg) • Freemasons (MS Morgan/TS1)

55.7   hall and the slaughter-house, • hall‸,‸ ‸and the slaughter-house,‸ (MS Berg); hall and the slaughter-house, (MS Morgan/TS1)

55.9   an • s̶ an (MS Berg); an (MS Morgan/TS1)

55.10   splendors, and • ~~glories, and~~ ‸splendors, and‸ (MS Berg); splendors, and (MS Morgan/TS1)

55.11   Twins (MS Berg) • twins (MS Morgan/TS1)

55.12	though they • ~~but~~ ˌthough theyˌ (MS Berg); though they (MS Morgan/TS1)
55.12	if • ~~if they hadn't~~ if (MS Berg); if (MS Morgan/TS1)
55.13	previous • ~~ex~~ previous (MS Berg); previous (MS Morgan/TS1)
55.16	defect • defe~~c~~ct (MS Berg); defect (MS Morgan/TS1)
55.20	held • ~~been~~ ˌheldˌ (MS Berg); held (MS Morgan/TS1)
55.21	president • local agent of the packet line, clerk of the county court, chairman of the debating club and president (MS Berg); ~~local agent of the packet line, clerk of the county court, chairman of the debating club and~~ president (MS Morgan/TS1)
55.24	Society (MTP) • society (MS Berg, MS Morgan/TS1)
55.28	Society (MTP) • society (MS Berg, MS Morgan/TS1)
56.5	welcome • ~~words~~ welcome (MS Berg); welcome (MS Morgan/TS1)
56.6	Society (MTP) • society (MS Berg, MS Morgan/TS1)
56.9	Society (MTP) • society (MS Berg, MS Morgan/TS1)
56.9	effort • effort~~s~~ (MS Berg); effort (MS Morgan/TS1)
56.10	its (MS Berg) • it's (MS Morgan/TS1)
56.16	matter, • ~~case,~~ ˌmatter,ˌ (MS Berg); matter, (MS Morgan/TS1)
56.26	him • hi~~m~~m (MS Berg); him (MS Morgan/TS1)
56.27	so I • ~~there~~ so I (MS Berg); so I (MS Morgan/TS1)
56.29	Angelo • ~~Antonio~~ Angelo (MS Berg); Angelo (MS Morgan/TS1)
56.29–30	coloring. [¶] The • coloring. ~~The~~ ¶ The (MS Berg); coloring. [¶] The (MS Morgan/TS1)
56.31	for • ~~d~~ for (MS Berg); for (MS Morgan/TS1)
56.36	invited • ~~asked~~ ˌinvitedˌ (MS Berg); invited (MS Morgan/TS1)
57.9	be blind to it (MS Berg) • be behind it (MS Morgan/TS1)
57.12	can • can | can (MS Berg); can (MS Morgan/TS1)
57.13	this • ~~that~~ ˌthisˌ (MS Berg); this (MS Morgan/TS1)
57.14	It • ~~Then~~ It (MS Berg); It (MS Morgan/TS1)
57.14	coming (MS Berg) • going (MS Morgan/TS1)
57.15	freethinking (MTP) • free- | thinking (MS Berg); freethinking (MS Morgan/TS1)
57.16	might be • ~~could be~~ ˌmight beˌ (MS Berg); might be (MS Morgan/TS1)
57.20	Angelo • ~~And rel~~ Angelo (MS Berg); Angelo (MS Morgan/TS1)
57.24	it • ~~Is~~ it (MS Berg); it (MS Morgan/TS1)
57.25	Happy • ~~No,~~ Happy (MS Berg); Happy (MS Morgan/TS1)
57.31	would (MS Berg) • wish (MS Morgan/TS1)

57.35	what • ỵwhat (MS Berg); what (MS Morgan/TS1)
57.37	Twins (MS Berg) • twins (MS Morgan/TS1)
58.2	Freethinkers' (MTP) • free- | thinkers' (MS Berg); freethinkers' (MS Morgan/TS1)
58.3	evening. • evening. ~~Turning to Angelo and bowing:~~ (MS Berg); evening. (MS Morgan/TS1)
58.4	added, hastily, • added, ˌhastily,ˌ (MS Berg); added hastily, (MS Morgan/TS1)
58.4	bowing. • bowing. ~~"Permit me to repeat that we shall be proud to have you as our guest—our honored guest."~~ (MS Berg); bowing. (MS Morgan/TS1)
58.8	face • face, ~~and rightly divined that he had felt the slight.~~ face (MS Berg); face (MS Morgan/TS1)
58.9	inflicted. The • inflicted. ~~upon his spirit. The Angelo had~~ ~~fet~~ felt ~~this slight with peculiar sharpness.~~ ˌTheˌ (MS Berg); inflicted. The (MS Morgan/TS1)
58.13	exterior, • ~~nature,~~ ˌexterior,ˌ (MS Berg); exterior, (MS Morgan/TS1)
58.15	slights; and (MTP) • slights;⁄and (MS Berg); slights, and (MS Morgan/TS1)
58.18	everywhere • ˌeverywhereˌ (MS Berg); everywhere (MS Morgan/TS1)
58.21	offence (MS Berg) • offense (MS Morgan/TS1)
58.23	feeling; • feeling; ~~for in the~~ (MS Berg); feeling; (MS Morgan/TS1)
58.30	unendurable • ~~en~~ unendurable (MS Berg); unendurable (MS Morgan/TS1)
58.30	would • ¢would (MS Berg); would (MS Morgan/TS1)
58.37	the (MTP) • ̸the (MS Berg); an (MS Morgan/TS1) [TEXTUAL NOTE: *In MS Berg, SLC mended* 'th' *from* 'a', *producing a misformed word resembling* 'an', *and copied as such in TS1*]
59.3–4	But at eighteen his eye began to take • ~~But his eye began at that time to take~~ ˌBut at eighteen his eye began to take.ˌ (MS Berg); But at eighteen his eye began to take (MS Morgan/TS1)
59.4	little by little, • ˌlittle by little,ˌ (MS Berg); little by little, (MS Morgan/TS1)
59.5	undefined • ~~un-~~ | ˌunˌdefined (MS Berg); undefined (MS Morgan/TS1)
59.5	grew • ~~began to spring~~ ˌgrewˌ (MS Berg); grew (MS Morgan/TS1)
59.5	heart, (MTP) • heart,ˌ [*insertion caret made, then canceled*] (MS Berg); heart (MS Morgan/TS1)
59.5	softening • ~~modifying~~ ˌsofteningˌ (MS Berg); softening (MS Morgan/TS1)
59.6	old • old ~~and~~ (MS Berg); old (MS Morgan/TS1)
59.7	monstrosities to him, • monstrosities, ˌto him,ˌ (MS Berg); monstrosities to him, (MS Morgan/TS1)

59.8   uncanny • ~~inconvenient~~ ˌuncannyˌ (MS Berg); uncanny (MS Morgan/ TS1)

59.10   physically • physically, (MS Berg); physically (MS Morgan/TS1)

59.12   had drank • had drank (MS Berg, MS Morgan/TS1) [TEXTUAL NOTE: 'had drank' *was a legitimate form, which SLC uses elsewhere (cf.* RI 1993, *textual note on 520.9)*]

59.12   had had • ˌhadˌ had (MS Berg); had had (MS Morgan/TS1)

59.13   the languor (MS Berg) • and languor (MS Morgan/TS1)

59.13   cobwebby (MS Berg) • cob-webby (MS Morgan/TS1)

59.14   dissipation, • dissipationˌ (MS Berg); dissipation, (MS Morgan/TS1)

59.15   long and (MTP) • long and (MS Berg); long (MS Morgan/TS1)

59.17   laudations (MS Berg) • landations (MS Morgan/TS1)

60.1–3 *Chapter 10* [¶] It is a mistake ... *Calendar.* (MTP) • Chapter 5 [*short triple rule*] ['Chapter 5' *inserted in pencil*] (MS Berg); ~~Chapter 10.~~ Chapter 10. [*short double rule*] [¶] It is a mistake ... *Calendar.*ˌ (MS Morgan/TS1)

60.4   Rowena • ~~At~~ Rowena (MS Berg); Rowena (MS Morgan/TS1)

60.4   were • ~~was~~ were (MS Berg); were (MS Morgan/TS1)

60.5   persons • person's (MS Berg); persons (MS Morgan/TS1)

60.5   that noon, • [*not in*] (MS Berg); ˌthat noon,ˌ (MS Morgan/TS1)

60.6   Twins (MS Berg) • twins (MS Morgan/TS1)

60.17   by (MS Berg) • bye (MS Morgan/TS1)

60.30   my • ⌀my (MS Berg); my (MS Morgan/TS1)

61.10–13 breath. "And moreover ... same time." • breath. (MS Berg); breath. ˌOVERˌ [*on verso:*] ˌ"And moreover," said Aunt Betsy, "the Freethinkers and the Babtist Bible class use the same room over the market house, ~~and~~ ˌbutˌ you can take my word for it *they* don't mush-up together and use it at the same time." | over againˌ (MS Morgan/TS1)

61.22   worlds • world's (MS Berg); worlds (MS Morgan/TS1)

61.22   go down • ~~cross~~ go down (MS Berg); go down (MS Morgan/TS1)

61.24   legs (MS Berg) • legs, (MS Morgan/TS1)

61.24   without calling • ~~without having~~ without calling (MS Berg); without calling (MS Morgan/TS1)

61.35   also • ~~He~~ also (MS Berg); also (MS Morgan/TS1)

61.35   it. By • it." [¶] ~~"Bless~~ ˌByˌ (MS Berg); it. By (MS Morgan/TS1)

62.3   and fraction (MTP) • and fraction (MS Berg); of a fraction (MS Morgan/TS1)

62.10   set • ~~regulated~~ set (MS Berg); set (MS Morgan/TS1)

62.13   He • ⌀He (MS Berg); He (MS Morgan/TS1)

62.13   any more! • any more!* (MS Berg); anymore! (MS Morgan/TS1)

62.14   Jericho (MS Berg) • Jerico (MS Morgan/TS1)

62.15   Angelo. • Angelo,. (MS Berg); Angelo. (MS Morgan/TS1)

62.15   is • ~~seems~~ is (MS Berg); is (MS Morgan/TS1)

62.17   if • ˌif˳ (MS Berg); if (MS Morgan/TS1)

62.23   you're (MS Berg) • you've (MS Morgan/TS1) [TEXTUAL NOTE: *The TS1 typist did not recognize 'if you're a mind to', a colloquialism which SLC also used in* RI 1993, *chap. 46;* TS 1980, *51;* CY, *202*]

62.34   a blessing • ~~a str~~ a blessing (MS Berg); a blessing (MS Morgan/TS1)

62.34   It never • ~~They nev~~ It never (MS Berg); It never (MS Morgan/TS1)

62.36   Sunday • Monday (MS Berg); ~~Mon~~ Sunˌday (MS Morgan/TS1)

62.37   over • ~~through~~ over (MS Berg); over (MS Morgan/TS1)

63.1   'I • *"ˌI (MS Berg); 'I (MS Morgan/TS1)

63.8–21   The conversation . . . than he is. • The conversation . . . than he is. [*deleted in pencil, then marked* 'STET' *(in ink) in several places; also:* 'Put in this whole page' *(page 111)* and 'Put it all in.' *(page 112)*] (MS Berg); The conversation . . . than he is. (MS Morgan/TS1)

63.8   wide, but by and by floated • ˌwide, but by and by floated˳ (MS Berg); wide, but by and by floated (MS Morgan/TS1)

63.10   Twins (MS Berg) • twins (MS Morgan/TS1)

63.11   law • law ~~and wisdom~~ (MS Berg); law (MS Morgan/TS1)

63.11   related • ~~such~~ related (MS Berg); related (MS Morgan/TS1)

63.14   grandeurs • ~~privileges and~~ grandeurs (MS Berg); grandeurs (MS Morgan/TS1)

63.20   audible: • audible,: ~~the old ladies~~ (MS Berg); audible: (MS Morgan/TS1)

63.22   sake!—" • sake!* —" (MS Berg); sake!—" (MS Morgan/TS1)

63.27   you • ˌyou˳ (MS Berg); you (MS Morgan/TS1)

63.31   and absolutely unassailable proof, • ~~and most~~ ˌand absolutely˳ unassailable proof, ~~of all,~~ (MS Berg); and absolutely unassailable proof, (MS Morgan/TS1)

63.34   its (MS Berg) • it's (MS Morgan/TS1)

64.3–4   petrified, one may almost say, • ~~indeed,~~ ˌpetrified, one may almost say,˳ (MS Berg); petrified, one may almost say, (MS Morgan/TS1)

64.6   proofs (MS Berg) • proof (MS Morgan/TS1)

64.7   silent a moment or two, • silent, ˌa moment or two,˳ (MS Berg); silent a moment or two, (MS Morgan/TS1)

64.8   looked up and • ˌlooked up and˳ (MS Berg); looked up and (MS Morgan/TS1)

64.9	and • ~~then~~ ˌand˳ (MS Berg); and (MS Morgan/TS1)
64.10	*anywhere* (MS Berg) • *any*where (MS Morgan/TS1)
64.11	a • ˌạ (MS Berg); a (MS Morgan/TS1)
64.12	impaired • ~~the prey~~ impaired (MS Berg); impaired (MS Morgan/TS1)
64.16	O (MS Berg) • Oh (MS Morgan/TS1)
64.16	answered • ~~sai~~ answered (MS Berg); answered (MS Morgan/TS1)
64.24	poor • ~~innocent~~ ˌpoorˌ (MS Berg); poor (MS Morgan/TS1)
64.24	old (MS Berg); • [*not in*] (MS Morgan/TS1)
64.25	tongues' (MS Berg) • tongue's (MS Morgan/TS1)
64.26	become harder and • ~~be~~ ˌbecomeˌ harder ~~and~~ and (MS Berg); become harder and (MS Morgan/TS1)
64.27	with • ~~the~~ with (MS Berg); with (MS Morgan/TS1)
64.27	while • ~~and~~ ˌwhileˌ (MS Berg); while (MS Morgan/TS1)
64.28	would increase with • ˌwould increase withˌ ~~augmenting with~~ (MS Berg); would increase with (MS Morgan/TS1)
65.1	*Chapter 11* (MTP) • ~~Insert this under the words "Chapter 11," on page 142.~~ Chapter 11.ˌ [*short double rule*]. [*insertions and deletion in pencil*] (MS Morgan)
65.2	find • ~~have~~ find (MS Morgan)
65.2	in error, • ~~at fault,~~ ˌin error,ˌ (MS Morgan)
65.3	Consistency. • Consistency. ~~As has been remarked of old, consistency is a jewel.~~ ['C' *triple underscored to capitalize*] (MS Morgan)
65.7	[¶] A • [*centered:*] ~~Chapter 11.~~ [*short double rule*] [¶] A [*deletion in pencil*] (MS Morgan)
65.10	she • ~~Aunt Patsy asked—~~ she (MS Morgan)
65.21	aunt • ~~neph~~ aunt (MS Morgan)
65.23	not sorry • ~~is glad~~ ˌnot sorry.ˌ (MS Morgan)
66.2	opening • ~~thing~~ ˌopening.ˌ (MS Morgan)
66.4	own. • own.″ (MS Morgan)
66.20	old • ~~only~~ old (MS Morgan)
66.22	knowledge. • knowledge. ˌ[¶] [~~Strike opening heading and final line of page 29.~~]ˌ (MS Morgan)
66.23	The visitor who had called to see the Twins • [*centered:*] ~~Chapter~~ [*short double rule*] [¶] ~~A visitor was announced. It~~ ˌThe visitor who had called to see the Twinsˌ (MS Morgan)
66.23	Hotchkiss, • ~~Maltby,~~ ˌHotchkiss,ˌ (MS Morgan)
66.24	Baptist • ~~Methodist~~ ˌBaptistˌ (MS Morgan)

66.24   he had • he ~~was a Methodist and should immediately join his church~~ had (MS Morgan)

66.34   Angelo • ~~Angelo was about to explain the difference between his own reli~~ [¶] Angelo (MS Morgan)

67.1   astonished; and also suspicious. • astonished͵;͵ and also suspicious.͵ (MS Morgan)

67.7   day after • ͵day after͵ (MS Morgan)

67.17–18   for only an hour, • ͵for only an hour,͵ (MS Morgan)

67.22   red • ~~pale~~ ͵red͵ (MS Morgan)

67.23   humiliation • ~~mortification~~ ͵humiliation͵ (MS Morgan)

67.27   day after • ͵day after͵ (MS Morgan)

67.29   freethinker • freethinkers̷ (MS Morgan)

67.32   bigotry, • bigotry͵,͵ (MS Morgan)

67.35   It • ~~Why is it that you can't see that *you* began this thing, not I, and by that act *incited* retaliation?" [¶] "*I* began it?" [¶] "Yes, you.~~ | It (MS Morgan)

67.37   have • ~~had~~ ͵have͵ (MS Morgan)

67.38   me." • me͵."͵ ~~before my opportunity came~~ (MS Morgan)

68.4   making • ~~taking~~ making (MS Morgan)

68.4   vows, • vow͵s͵ (MS Morgan)

68.6   freethinking • freething̷king (MS Morgan)

68.7   upright • ~~good~~ upright (MS Morgan)

68.9   Sunday afternoon and • ~~tomorrow and~~ ͵Sunday afternoon and͵ (MS Morgan)

68.9   to our meeting only to • ~~but to~~ ͵to our meeting only to͵ (MS Morgan)

68.10   us, • us, ~~last night,~~ (MS Morgan)

68.14   go; • go̷͵;͵ (MS Morgan)

68.15   cur!'" • cur!͵'"͵ (MS Morgan)

68.24–25   a common and honorable • ~~the same~~ ͵a common and honorable͵ (MS Morgan)

68.36   finger-board (MTP) • finger- | board (MS Morgan)

68.37   If • ~~And right—~~ If (MS Morgan)

69.1   roads • ͵roads͵ (MS Morgan)

69.13   Yes, (MTP) • Yes (MS Morgan)

69.13   chuckleheadedness (MTP) • chuckle- | headedness (MS Morgan)

69.14   a theological (MTP) • ~~an ecclesiastical~~ ͵theological͵ (MS Morgan)

69.18   refuse • ~~rubb~~ refuse (MS Morgan)

69.26	help me." • help ~~and hearten~~ ˌme."ˌ (MS Morgan)
69.28	When • ~~As~~ When (MS Morgan)
69.30	once • ~~you scourged my back for your sins; when you had command of our~~ once (MS Morgan)
69.35	sect. • sect⸌ ˌ (MS Morgan)
70.1	do day after tomorrow • do⸌ ˌday afterˌ tomorrow (MS Morgan)
70.3	lagging dull • ˌlagging dullˌ (MS Morgan)
70.3	sufferings • sufferings ~~that~~ (MS Morgan)
71.1	*Chapter 12* (MTP) • [¶] ~~Insert this under the words "Chapter 12," on page [¶] It would not be best for all to think alike. It is difference of opinion that makes horse-races.~~ ⸍ *Pudd'nhead Wilson's Calendar.* ˌChapter 12 [*short triple rule*]ˌ [*alterations in pencil*] (MS Morgan)
71.2	[¶] Judge • [*centered:*] ~~Chapter 12.~~ [*short double rule*] [¶] Judge [*deletion in pencil*] (MS Morgan)
71.3	Pudd'nhead (MTP) • Puddn'head (MS Morgan)
71.6	favorable • ˌfavorableˌ (MS Morgan)
71.10	learned • ~~been~~ learned (MS Morgan)
71.15	then • ˌthenˌ (MS Morgan)
71.16	Twins • ⸍Twins (MS Morgan)
71.18	surprised and • ˌsurprised andˌ (MS Morgan)
71.22	his • ~~himself~~ his (MS Morgan)
71.24	when • ~~before it~~ when (MS Morgan)
71.25	lonesome • lonsesome (MS Morgan)
71.25	neglected • ~~over~~ neglected (MS Morgan)
71.30	accepts • accep⸍ts (MS Morgan)
72.1	door • door⸍ (MS Morgan)
72.5	the • the⸍ (MS Morgan)
72.8	to perceive • ˌto perceiveˌ (MS Morgan)
72.13	Twins • ⸍Twins (MS Morgan)
72.16	president • ⸌e president (MS Morgan)
72.18	spirits • ⸍spirits (MS Morgan)
72.24	Angelo • ~~he~~ ˌAngeloˌ (MS Morgan)
72.29	why, then, • whyˌ, thenˌ, (MS Morgan)
72.34	brother! Ah • brother!ˌ" ~~exclaimed the astonished minister.~~ "ˌAh (MS Morgan)
73.1	There—er • Thereˌ—erˌ (MS Morgan)
73.2	in fact, • ~~er—~~ ˌin fact,ˌ (MS Morgan)

73.3   that • that ~~if you~~ (MS Morgan)

73.8   that an • tha⌀t an (MS Morgan)

73.13   Very well, • ˏVery well,ˏ (MS Morgan)

73.20   of him • ~~of him: altogether his happiness~~ | of him (MS Morgan)

73.24   an • ~~an~~ | an (MS Morgan)

73.27   carry • ~~spread~~ ˏcarryˏ (MS Morgan)

73.28   from the town • ˏfrom the town,ˏ (MS Morgan)

73.29   sorrowing • ˏsorrowingˏ (MS Morgan)

73.30   Sunday!" • Sunday!" [¶] ~~On the way to Puddn'head Williams's Angelo could not keep from voicing a little of his heart-break: [¶] "I hope you are satisfied, now, with yourself, Luigi. Everybody will know, now, that I attended a freethinker meeting,". then a Bible class as a preparation for the solemnities | the same evening | What will they think of me?" [¶] "There you are—you only think of yourself.~~ (MS Morgan)

73.32   Pudd'nhead Wilson's. • Puddn'head ~~Williams's.~~ ˏWilson's.ˏ (MS Morgan)

73.33   Pudd'nhead (MTP) • Puddn'head (MS Morgan)

73.37   The • ~~Through t~~The ~~unshaded window~~ The (MS Morgan)

74.3   over • ~~next to~~ ˏoverˏ (MS Morgan)

74.3   private • ~~bedroom~~ private (MS Morgan)

74.4   bedroom. • bedroom. ~~He was the Judge's nephew.~~ (MS Morgan)

74.5   Judge, the Judge's widowed sister Mrs. Pratt, • Judgeˏ, the Judge's widowed sister, Mrs. Pratt,ˏ (MS Morgan)

74.6   only people who belonged in • ~~only occupants of~~ ˏonly people who belonged inˏ (MS Morgan)

74.7   low • ~~low~~ ˏlowˏ (MS Morgan)

74.8   running • ~~dividing~~ running (MS Morgan)

74.13   she • ~~and~~ ˏsheˏ (MS Morgan)

74.15   room? • room? ~~Driscoll started to say to him~~ | self that perhaps young Driscoll was adding one more impropriety to a career already sufficiently damaged by them, when the girl took his breath away by removing her bonnet and exposing the face of ~~young Driscoll himself!~~ (MS Morgan)

74.16   [¶] Wilson • ¶ Wilson (MS Morgan)

74.16   from • ˏfromˏ (MS Morgan)

74.17   risk of • riskˏ—as he supposed—ˏof (MS Morgan)

74.17   her, • her,⟋ (MS Morgan)

74.17   there • ~~ab~~ there (MS Morgan)

74.21   with Mrs. Pratt • ˌwith Mrs. Prattˌ (MS Morgan)

74.22   day, • dayˌ ~~with her,~~ (MS Morgan)

74.22   levée (MTP) • levèe (MS Morgan)

74.23–24 he was on his way home, and that • ˌhe was on his way home, and thatˌ (MS Morgan)

74.24   to arrive before night; and • ~~home almost any day, now; and~~ ˌto arrive before night; andˌ (MS Morgan)

74.26–27 creditably—at which Wilson winked to himself privately. • creditably ~~in St. Louis.~~ ˌ—at which Wilson winked to himself privately.ˌ (MS Morgan)

74.28   brought • ~~thr~~ brought (MS Morgan)

74.30   of • ˌofˌ (MS Morgan)

74.34   day-break • ~~dawn~~ day-break (MS Morgan)

74.34   morning. • morning. ˌ*CHAPTER*ˌ ~~Here insert 1A and all that batch.~~ ~~[¶] The young men~~ ˌduplicatesˌ ~~arrived, presently, and talk began. It flowed~~ ˌalongˌ ~~chattily and sociably, and under its influence Angelo cheered up and forgot his late vexations. Wilson got out his Calendar, by request, and read a passage or two from it, which the Twins complimented quite cordially. This pleased the author so much that he complied gladly when they asked him to lend them a batch of the work to read at home.~~ ˌIn the courseˌ ~~((*OVER* [on verso:]~~ ˌof their wide travels they had found out that there are three infallible ways of pleasing an author, and that the three form a rising scale of compliment: 1, to tell him you have read his book; 2, to tell him you have read all his books;~~ ˌ3,ˌ ~~to ask him to let you read the MS of his forthcoming book. No. 1 admits you to his respect; No. 2 admits you to his admiration; but No. 3 carries you~~ ˌclearˌ ~~into his heart with all your clothes on. ◊◊◊◊◊◊ˌ~~ (MS Morgan) [TEXTUAL NOTE: *SLC wrote in the top right corner of this leaf: '[A chapter begins in middle of this page.]' and inserted 'CHAPTER' between two paragraphs, ordering: 'Here insert 1A and all that batch.'— meaning the sequence of 78 leaves taking the text up to '. . . brazen huzzy might be.' (95.8) Later, the chapter head and 'The duplicates . . . at home' were deleted, as was the order to insert '1A', etc. 'The duplicates . . . at home' was recopied as the opening of Chapter 17, while 'In the course . . . clothes on.' would be revised to serve as the motto of that chapter*]

75.1   *Chapter 13* (MTP) • ~~[¶] Insert this under the words "Chapter 13," on page~~ ˌ*CHAPTER* 13.ˌ [*short triple rule*] [*alterations in pencil*] (MS Morgan)

75.2–4   The holy passion . . . to lend money. • [TEXTUAL NOTE: *A manuscript leaf in CU-MARK records the compositional evolution of this aphorism: 'The holy passion of Friendship is of so sweet and steady and loyal and* enduring a nature that it will last through ~~the frowns and smiles, the storms and sunshine, the joys and sorrows, and the manifold vicissitudes of fate and fortune~~ of a whole lifetime if not asked to lend money.']

75.6   [¶] It • [centered:] ~~Chapter 13~~ [short triple rule] [deletion in pencil] [¶] It (MS Morgan)

75.8   Cincinnati • ~~big~~ Cincinnati (MS Morgan)

75.9   It • ~~She stoo~~ It (MS Morgan)

75.13 long, • long⸝ (MS Morgan)

75.14 berth-room • ~~door~~ berth-room (MS Morgan)

75.18–19 white-painted pine pilasters with gilded Corinthian capitals. • ⸝white-painted pine⸝ pilasters with ⸝gilded⸝ Corinthian capitals⸝ ~~showy and gay—white-painted pine, these.~~ (MS Morgan)

75.19–20 Overhead, the receding stretch of ivory-like ceiling • Overhead, ~~the far~~ the receding stretch of ~~ceiling of white-painted pine~~ ⸝ivory-like ceiling⸝ (MS Morgan)

75.22–23 great pyramidal chandeliers, whose sumptuous fringes of cut-glass prisms • ⸝great pyramidal⸝ chandeliers, whose ~~pyramids of pendant pris~~ ⸝sumptuous fringes of cut-glass⸝ prisms (MS Morgan)

75.25 crimson cloths • ~~red~~ ⸝crimson⸝ ~~chot~~ cloths (MS Morgan)

76.1   often • ⸝often⸝ (MS Morgan)

76.1–2 palaces"—which • palaces" ~~before, for this⸝~~—which⸝ (MS Morgan)

76.2   these • ~~this kind of~~ these (MS Morgan)

76.4   an ecstasy • ~~a dream~~ ⸝an ecstasy⸝ (MS Morgan)

76.5   magnitude • ~~extent~~ magnitude (MS Morgan)

76.8   of the splendors • ⸝of the splendors⸝ (MS Morgan)

76.9   the • ~~this fan~~ the (MS Morgan)

76.13 life • ~~life and motion~~ life (MS Morgan)

76.14 to be • ~~to be in this~~ to be (MS Morgan)

76.15 a swarm • ~~files~~ a swarm (MS Morgan)

76.16 and in • ~~and apparently~~ ⸝and⸝ in (MS Morgan)

76.21 appeared • ~~marched in~~ appeared (MS Morgan)

76.24 the provisions. The last boys • ~~business.~~ ⸝the provisions. The last boys⸝ || ~~The last boys~~ (MS Morgan)

76.26 great • ~~gl~~ great (MS Morgan)

76.28–29 whereas in truth the • ~~but the~~ ⸝whereas in truth the⸝ (MS Morgan)

76.29 though • ~~but~~ ⸝though⸝ (MS Morgan)

76.30 suspected • ~~knew~~ ⸝suspected⸝ (MS Morgan)

76.37   before the boat's departure • ˌbefore the boat's departure˳ (MS Morgan)

76.38   delight • ~~delight, with its several details of~~ | delight (MS Morgan)

76.38   avalanche (MTP) • avalanch (MS Morgan)

77.5–6   the deafening • ~~and above all this pow-wow~~ the deafening (MS Morgan)

77.6   Every • ~~It was all~~ ˌEvery˳ (MS Morgan)

77.6   separate • ˌseparate˳ (MS Morgan)

77.7   dulcet • ˌdulcet˳ (MS Morgan)

77.13   that • ~~oranges growing on trees instead of~~ that (MS Morgan)

77.19   proud • ~~proud of the friend~~ proud (MS Morgan)

77.22   now • now, (MS Morgan)

77.25   saved up • ~~laid up~~ saved up (MS Morgan)

77.27–28   one mistake like that was enough: she would • ~~she~~ ˌone mistake like that was enough: she˳ would (MS Morgan)

77.29   thenceforth • ˌthenceforth˳ (MS Morgan)

77.29   economy • ~~ȿ~~ economy (MS Morgan)

78.1   homestretch (MTP) • home- | stretch (MS Morgan)

78.8   this • this~~ℓ~~ (MS Morgan)

78.8   her • ~~the~~ her (MS Morgan)

78.12   thought inspired her to add • ~~awoke ℊ~~ ˌthought inspired her to˳ add~~ed~~ (MS Morgan)

78.12–13   dream: maybe (MTP) • dream͵: M ṃaybe (MS Morgan)

78.19   for her • ˌfor her˳ (MS Morgan)

78.19   home— • home—ˌ ~~with her~~— (MS Morgan)

78.30   laughter, • laughter, ~~with tears,~~ (MS Morgan)

78.32   the • ~~the luxury of~~ the (MS Morgan)

78.33   bare to • ~~dry to~~ ˌbare to˳ (MS Morgan)

78.38   Chambers said: • Chambers said: || ~~the best part of his time there dur- ing the past the previous two or three years. He˳ Chambers˳ and his kitchen mates were naturally quite willing to tell all they knew of family matters to an old family servant like Roxana. Among other things, Chambers said—~~ [*'the best part . . . Chambers said—' is earlier-written text, canceled while adapting the text on MS page 195 to the later-written 194*] (MS Morgan)

79.1   is, • is, ~~Roxy,~~ (MS Morgan)

79.2   love • ~~like~~ love (MS Morgan)

79.3   fifty dollahs • ~~twenty-five dol~~ ˌfifty˳ dollahs (MS Morgan)

79.5   ain't, mammy; • ain't͵, mammy͵; (MS Morgan)

79.6   'tain't (MTP) • t'ain't (MS Morgan)

79.7   'tain't (MTP) • t'ain't (MS Morgan)

79.7   enough?" • enough,?" ~~you black fool?"~~ (MS Morgan)

79.8   mammy. • ~~Roxy.~~ mammy. (MS Morgan)

79.10   astonishment, • ~~holy amazement,~~ astonishment, (MS Morgan)

79.11   Ole • Ol'e (MS Morgan)

79.11   Marse (MTP) • marse (MS Morgan)

79.12   dead • ǝ dead (MS Morgan)

79.14   'bout? • a'bout,? ~~dey ain't dat much money in de worl', en you knows it, chile.~~ (MS Morgan)

79.15   Sakes alive, • ~~Massy sakes~~ Sakes alive, (MS Morgan)

79.15   mos' • mosʒ' (MS Morgan)

79.19   hoppin'! (MTP) • hoppin! (MS Morgan)

79.19   tuck 'n (MTP) • tuck'n (MS Morgan)

79.20   Roxy • ~~The quadroon woman~~ Roxy (MS Morgan)

79.24   dat? What do it mean? • dat?* What do it mean?" (MS Morgan)

79.26   He wouldn't ever treat him so. Take • ~~You lies, you knows you lies!" cried the woman in terror and anger.~~ He wouldn't ever treat him so. " / Take (MS Morgan)

79.27–30   tribbilation!" [¶] Roxy's pet . . . thought of it. • tribbilation!" OVER OVER [on verso:] [¶] Roxy's pet castle—an occasional dollar from Tom's pocket—was . . . thought of it. (MS Morgan)

79.32   pow'ful (MTP) • pow'full (MS Morgan)

79.34   yo' • ~~you~~ o' (MS Morgan)

79.34   knock • knockʒ (MS Morgan)

79.35   'tain't (MTP) • t'ain't (MS Morgan)

79.36   *'tain't* (MTP) • *t'ain't* (MS Morgan)

79.37   'tain't (MTP) • t'ain't (MS Morgan)

80.1   'Tain (MTP) • Tain't (MS Morgan)

80.1   business? • business,? ~~ain't it~~ (MS Morgan)

80.3   ornery • ~~on~~ ornery (MS Morgan)

80.4   yo'self • ~~you~~ yo'self (MS Morgan)

80.8   sentimental • sentimental ~~and snuffly~~ (MS Morgan)

80.9   daily, • ~~every few days,~~ daily, (MS Morgan)

80.10   began to tremble with emotion, and straightway sent to • ~~exhibited a deal of ◊◊◊◊◊◊ ◊◊◊◊ ◊◊◊ emotion, and sent to ask~~ began to tremble with emotion, and straightway sent to (MS Morgan)

80.13–14   petition. Time . . . and uncompromising. • petition. ˏOVERˏ [*on verso:*]
ˏTime had not modified his ˏ~~old~~ ancientˏ detestation of the humble
drudge and protector of his boyhood; it was ~~as~~ still bitter and uncom-
promising. | over againˏ (MS Morgan)

80.15   fair face of • ~~face of~~ fair face of (MS Morgan)

80.20   meekly repeated • ~~humbly re-~~ ˏmeekly re-ˏ | peated (MS Morgan)

80.29   over • ~~out~~ over (MS Morgan)

80.35   [¶] Tom's • ~~[¶] At this distance of time it seems nearly incredible that~~
~~such a performance as the above was~~ ˏeˏ~~w~~ould ˏhaveˏ furnishˏedˏ ~~to a~~
~~stranger~~ˏ ~~no sure indication of Tom's character—for the reason that~~
~~such conduct was not confined to young men of harsh nature. Humane~~
~~young men were quite capable of it, good-| hearted young fellows who~~
~~would protect with their brave lives a dog that was being treated so.~~
~~Slavery was to blame, not innate nature. It placed the slave below the~~
~~brute, without the white man's realizing it.~~ ¶ Tom's (MS Morgan)

80.35   closing • ~~and~~ closing (MS Morgan)

81.1   general • ~~what she~~ general (MS Morgan)

81.3   I • ~~yo' ole~~ I (MS Morgan)

81.5   nigger • ˏniggerˏ (MS Morgan)

81.11–20   This was . . . her supplication— • ~~The~~ ~~old~~ ~~woman realized that her child~~
~~was in a particularly practical mood, and that she must meet him on~~
~~that level and come squarely at her errand—for she had one. So she~~
~~sobered down, her breast began to heave a little, then she got out a sob~~
~~or two and said in a whimpering tone—~~ ˏOVERˏ [*on verso:*] ˏThis was
a bitter disappointment. Roxy had ~~allowed her nursed~~ ˏso longˏ ˏforˏ so
many daysˏ nourished and fondled and petted her notion . . . she offered
her supplication— | over againˏ (MS Morgan)

81.22   kinder crippled in de arms en can't work, • ~~sick en pow'ful weak en~~
~~can't git no work to do,~~ ˏkinder crippled in de arms en can't work,ˏ (MS
Morgan)

81.24   supplicant was • ~~old creature was~~ ˏsupplicant was,ˏ (MS Morgan)

81.28   Roxy • ~~The woman~~ ˏRoxyˏ (MS Morgan)

81.31–32   po' en gitt'n ole, • ~~ole en po',~~ ˏpo' en gitt'n ole,ˏ (MS Morgan)

81.32   he'p (MTP) • h'ep (MS Morgan)

81.33   en de • en*d* de (MS Morgan)

81.38   gwyne • ~~go~~ gwyne (MS Morgan)

82.2   Roxy's • ~~The woman's~~ ˏRoxy'sˏ (MS Morgan)

82.2–3   humility. But . . . burn fiercely. • humility. ˏOVERˏ [*on verso:*] ˏBut
nowˏ The fires of her old wrongs ~~flamed~~ flamed up in her breast and
began to burn fiercely. | over againˏ (MS Morgan)

82.3–4   her head • ~~it~~ ˌher headˌ (MS Morgan)

82.4   slowly, • slowly, ~~now,~~ (MS Morgan)

82.4   her great frame • ~~she~~ ˌher great frameˌ (MS Morgan)

82.5   majesty and • ˌmajesty andˌ (MS Morgan)

82.22   myself • myself, (MS Morgan)

82.24   let • ~~letten let~~ let (MS Morgan)

82.33   implacability • ~~to~~ implacability (MS Morgan)

82.38   en • ˌ~~and~~ˌ ˌenˌ (MS Morgan)

83.4   Roxy • ~~The quadroon~~ ˌwomanˌ ˌRoxyˌ (MS Morgan)

83.4   mocking • ~~scoffing~~ ˌmockingˌ (MS Morgan)

83.11   seized (MTP) • siezed (MS Morgan)

83.14   told • ~~told~~/told (MS Morgan)

83.21   means • meansˌ (MS Morgan)

83.24   en watch • ~~and~~ en watch (MS Morgan)

83.32   heir of . . . and outrage • ~~woman~~ ˌheir of two centuries of unatoned insult and outrageˌ (MS Morgan)

83.35   nigger • ~~ornery old~~ nigger (MS Morgan)

84.4   dah, • ~~there,~~ ˌdah,ˌ (MS Morgan)

84.17   He • "He (MS Morgan)

84.18   drink. • ~~most generous swig.~~ ˌdrink.ˌ (MS Morgan)

85.1   *Chapter 14* (MTP) • [*short double rule*] Chapter . . . . ˌ14.ˌ [*short double rule*] (MS Morgan)

85.2   Then Tom flung himself on the sofa, and put • ~~Then he Kings clothe a favorite with honors and dignities for a brief time, then cast him forth naked and ashamed. This imitates Nature, who flatters us with youth to insult us with age.—*Pudd'nhead Wilson's Calendar.* [¶] Then Tom~~ ˌThen Tom flung himself on the sofa, and putˌ [*directive at foot of page:*] ~~Run to BB~~ [*deleted in pencil*] (MS Morgan)

85.2   his • ~~"It's prime—I'll take it along." [¶] Tom opened the door for her and bowed her out, with deference. He closed it after her and went and flung himself on the sofa, and put~~ his (MS Morgan) [*SLC deletes text which he had recopied, with alterations, on the added MS page 215, where it became:* "'It's prime . . . a grenadier.' (84.20–22)]

85.10   At • ~~Chapter~~ [*short double rule*] [¶] At (MS Morgan)

85.10   he • ~~Tom~~ ˌheˌ (MS Morgan)

85.10   house, (MTP) • house (MS Morgan)

85.11   Roxy • ~~The quadroon~~ ˌ~~The woman.~~ˌ ˌ~~His mother.~~ˌ ˌRoxyˌ (MS Morgan)

85.18	beyond • ~~south of~~ ‸beyond‸ (MS Morgan)
85.19	town at • ~~village at~~ ‸town at‸ (MS Morgan)
85.20	Roxy • ~~the woman~~ ‸Roxy‸ (MS Morgan)
85.20	clean • ‸clean‸ (MS Morgan)
85.21	cheap but well-kept • ~~ragged~~ ‸cheap but well-kept‸ (MS Morgan)
85.22	freckling the floor with little spots of light, • ~~with a tallow candle in it,~~ ‸freckling the floor with little spots of light,‸ (MS Morgan)
85.24	said— • ~~was not perfe not exactly sober, but she was near enough to it to have her wits in fair order. She said—~~ ‸said—‸ (MS Morgan)
85.28	somehow • ‸somehow‸ (MS Morgan)
86.1	Tom • " Tom (MS Morgan)
86.3	She rose, and gloomed above him like a fate. • " She rose, and gloomed above him like a fate.‸ (MS Morgan)
86.4	Lord's • ~~Lawd's~~ ‸Lord's‸ (MS Morgan)
86.8	minute! • minute‸ ! (MS Morgan)
86.11	jes' • ~~jus~~ jes' (MS Morgan)
86.11	noth'n • nu̸othi̸'n (MS Morgan)
86.14	boy dat • boy dat̸s (MS Morgan)
86.14	a cuffin' • a̸ cuffin' (MS Morgan)
86.17	Driscoll en • Driscoll ~~and~~ en (MS Morgan)
86.19	seized (MTP) • siezed (MS Morgan)
86.21	Does • Do‸es‸ (MS Morgan)
86.22	de likes • ~~the~~ ‸de‸ likes (MS Morgan)
86.22	shoot • ‸shoot‸ (MS Morgan)
86.23	yo' • you̸'‸ ‸ (MS Morgan)
86.24	down • ~~in~~ down (MS Morgan)
86.28	agin • ~~again~~in (MS Morgan)
86.30	and all • ~~fe~~ and all (MS Morgan)
86.30	with • ⟋with (MS Morgan)
86.34	took • ~~got up,~~ took (MS Morgan)
86.34	lantern • lantern, (MS Morgan)
86.35	cold • ‸cold‸ (MS Morgan)
86.36	"I • "I' (MS Morgan)
87.3	*Ma* or *mammy,* • *Ma,* or *mammy,*‸ (MS Morgan)
87.5	Tom • ɮ Tom (MS Morgan)
87.8	does • ~~do~~ ‸does‸ (MS Morgan)

87.8   it's (MTP) • its (MS Morgan)

87.10   en • ~~and~~ en (MS Morgan)

87.11   it!" • it͜!", ⹁ ⹁ ⹁ ⹁ ~~ma!"~~ (MS Morgan)

87.13   a • a̹ (MS Morgan)

87.16   pomp • ~~satis~~ pomp (MS Morgan)

87.22   on • ~~and~~ ͜on͜ (MS Morgan)

87.25   dollars." • dollars͵." ͵ ~~ma.͟"͟~~ (MS Morgan)

87.25   "How (MTP) • How (MS Morgan)

87.33   realize the required amount on, • ~~satisfy his creditors,~~ ͵realize the required amount on,͵ (MS Morgan)

88.3   money. • money͵, ~~and she showed him where to put it.~~ (MS Morgan)

88.5   many • many ~~and a many~~ (MS Morgan)

88.7   gen'lman (MTP) • genl'man (MS Morgan)

88.7   wid • ~~with~~ ͵wid͵ (MS Morgan)

88.9   befo' • befo̹r̹'̹ (MS Morgan)

88.15   said • ~~ɑ~~ said (MS Morgan)

88.17   "Ma, • "Ma͵Ȯ͟"͟ (MS Morgan)

88.18–19 He had … mistaken. Roxy • [¶] ~~The woman~~ ͵He had supposed he was asking an embarrassing question. He was mistaken. Roxy͵ (MS Morgan)

88.21   yo' • yo͵~~ur~~ (MS Morgan)

88.22   Fust • ~~Fir~~ Fust (MS Morgan)

88.24   Cecil • ~~S̹~~ Cecil (MS Morgan)

88.25–26 died de same year yo' young Marse Tom Driscoll's pappy died, • ~~died when you was 'leven or twelve year old~~ ͵died de same year yo' young Marse Tom Driscoll's pappy died,͵ (~~MS~~ Morgan)

88.28   earlier • earlie͵r~~st~~ (MS Morgan)

88.30   surroundings • surroundings̹ (MS Morgan)

88.30   been • been | [*inserted in bottom margin:*] ͵~~RUN to OO-A~~͵ (MS Morgan)

88.33   swah!" • swah!" | ~~RUN to OO-B~~ (MS Morgan)

89.1   *Chapter 15* (MTP) • ͵Chapter 15. [*short triple rule*]͵ ~~Insert this after the words "Chapter 15" on page~~ [¶] ~~Why is it that we turn the thing wrong-end-first, and rejoice~~ (MS Morgan) [TEXTUAL NOTE: *The aphorism begun (and deleted) here is revised and completed at 89.5–7*]

89.5–7 [¶] Why is it … *Calendar.* • [¶] ͵Why is it … *Calendar.*͵ (MS Morgan)

89.8   [¶] Every • [¶] ~~"Ma, would you mind telling me who was my father?"~~ [¶] ~~She reflected, then shook her head and said—~~ [¶] ~~"Nemmine, dat'll be~~

soon enough by en by." | [*centered:*] ~~CHAPTER 15~~ [*deletions in pencil*]
[¶] Every (MS Morgan) [TEXTUAL NOTE: *The canceled passage "'Ma, . . .*
by en by.'" was recopied, revised, and inserted earlier, at 88.17–33]

89.14   thinkings • ~~thoughts~~ ͺthinkingsͺ (MS Morgan)

89.16   What • Whyͥat (MS Morgan)

89.16   uncreated • ~~unborn~~ uncreated (MS Morgan)

89.18   black? • black?ͫ (MS Morgan)

89.23   in me • ͺin meͺ (MS Morgan)

89.24   Yesterday • ͺYesterdayͺ (MS Morgan)

89.26   lowly and ignorant • ~~old~~ ͺ~~ragged~~ͺ ͺlowly and ignorantͺ (MS Morgan)

89.27   white • ͺwhiteͺ (MS Morgan)

89.28   virtue. . . ." • virtue.ͺ . . . . ~~Wait till I get this old man's money—I'll show~~
~~them what a nigger can do who has got the~~ ͺ~~a~~ͺ ~~devil in him! . . . . . I will~~
~~have that money—yes, I will have it—I will t~~ͺ~~look to that. . . . . . . I must~~
~~begin a new life to-day—but not outside; no, only inside. I must be the~~
~~same careless, slangy, useless youth as before, outside, but inside I shall~~
~~be a nigger with a grievance—with all that that implies of hate, and~~
~~absence of shame,~~ ͺ~~and~~ͺ ~~absence of mercy where any secret chance shall~~
~~offer. For I~~ *~~am~~* ~~a coward, and that is a disease which is not curable—a~~
~~nigger disease! . . . . . I wish I knew my father . . . . . I will wheedle it out~~
~~of her some day; and if he is alive, then, let him not go out at night!"~~
(MS Morgan) [TEXTUAL NOTE: *SLC decided to delete the latter part of*
Tom's speech and close the quotation after 'virtue.'; but he left four leaders
standing outside the quotation mark. They have been moved within the
quotation marks]

90.4   that • ~~I~~ that (MS Morgan)

90.5   him—if I had the courage. • himͺ—if I had the courageͺ. (MS Morgan)

90.6   a • ąͺ (MS Morgan)

90.8   clouds • ~~globe-encircling~~ clouds (MS Morgan)

90.10   fair • ͺfairͺ (MS Morgan)

90.12   Tom • ~~h~~ Tom (MS Morgan)

90.13   he found • ~~were~~ ͺhe foundͺ (MS Morgan)

90.22   make out • ~~ex~~ make out (MS Morgan)

90.23   While • Whiͥrle (MS Morgan)

90.25   involuntarily • ͺinͺvoluntarily (MS Morgan)

91.1   a • ~~that~~ ąͺ (MS Morgan)

91.4   then he fled away to • ~~it drove him to~~ ͺthen he fled away toͺ (MS Morgan)

91.8   felt • ~~said~~ ͺfeltͺ (MS Morgan)

91.9   are said to • ˏare said toˏ (MS Morgan)

91.18   Yes • ~~No, it~~ Yes (MS Morgan)

91.21   endurance • ~~acceptance~~ ˏenduranceˏ (MS Morgan)

91.25   debased • debased ~~and brutalized~~ (MS Morgan)

91.26   long-drawn • ~~long-descended~~ long-drawn (MS Morgan)

91.26   slave-owning (MTP) • slave- | owning (MS Morgan)

91.28   So he argued. • ˏSo he argued.ˏ (MS Morgan)

91.29   and amazing • ˏand amazingˏ (MS Morgan)

91.29   one or two • ~~certain~~ one or two (MS Morgan)

91.30   looking • lookˏingˏ (MS Morgan)

91.33   hot • ~~boiling~~ ˏhotˏ (MS Morgan)

91.34   more • ~~the~~ more (MS Morgan)

91.35   and • ˏandˏ (MS Morgan)

91.35   for a nigger • ˏfor a niggerˏ (MS Morgan)

91.36   bastard?" he • bastardˏ?".ˏ⟋he (MS Morgan)

92.3   million-fold (MTP) • million- | fold (MS Morgan)

92.5   rage. • rage. [¶] ~~After this he searched the mysteries of human nature and human ways no more for many days; he ceased from philosophizing; his mind centred itself upon one thought a single problem—how to find his father, in case he was alive—and upon a single purpose: to kill him when he should find him. He said he would make this the whole mission of his life, and allow nothing to stay him or divert him until it was accomplished.~~ (MS Morgan)

93.1   *Chapter 16* (MTP) • Chapter 16. [*short double rule*] (MS Morgan)

93.4   In • [*centered:*] ~~Chapter [*short triple rule*]~~ [¶] ~~But Tom did not know himself.~~ In (MS Morgan) [TEXTUAL NOTE: *In the top left corner of page BBB (final numbering, 245), SLC noted:* 'aaa struck out.', *referring to the text deleted at 92.5*]

93.5   main • ˏmainˏ (MS Morgan)

93.8   the influence of a great • ~~great~~ the influence of ˏaˏ great (MS Morgan)

93.10–11 but now . . . settle toward • ~~but when the storm subsided both settled toward~~ ˏbut now with the subsidence of the storm both began to settle towardˏ (MS Morgan)

93.18   constant • ˏconstantˏ (MS Morgan)

93.19   privately • ˏprivatelyˏ (MS Morgan)

93.19   aristocratic • ~~hi~~ aristocratic (MS Morgan)

93.20   pretensions. • pretensions. ~~And there was one thought that sang always in his heart. He called that his father's death-song.~~ (MS Morgan)

93.24–94.6 will. [¶] He . . . as yet . . . between-days also. • will. ~~At first he endured his~~
~~mother, next he liked her, finally he came to love her. She always collected~~
~~her share of his pension punctually, and he was always at the haunted~~
~~house to have a chat with her on these occasions. She became very fond~~
~~of him, and came sometimes to the haunted house on between-days~~
~~to see him. But as to his father—she always postponed that revelation,~~
~~upon one pretext or another.~~ ˌBut he was patient, patient, and tirelessly
~~persistent, and his hope never perished.~~ˌ OVERˌ [*on verso:*] ˌ¶ He and
his mother learned to like each other fairly well. She couldn't love him,
ˌas yet,ˌ because . . . between-days also.ˌ (MS Morgan)

94.7 St. (MTP) • St (MS Morgan)

94.8 it, and • itˌ, ~~and~~ andˌ ~~again, and~~ (MS Morgan)

94.13 arrived at the haunted house in disguise • ~~arrived~~ arrived at ~~the haunted~~
~~house~~ the haunted house ˌin disguiseˌ (MS Morgan)

94.14–15 —after writing . . . two days later— • ˌ—after writing his aunt Pratt
that he would not arrive until two days later—ˌ (MS Morgan)

94.17 entered • ~~wen~~ entered (MS Morgan)

94.18 room, where . . . toilet articles. • roomˌ, where he could have the use of
mirror and toilet articlesˌ. (MS Morgan)

94.20 clothing, with black gloves and veil. • clothing/ˌ, with black gloves and
veil.ˌ (MS Morgan)

94.24 by and by • ~~again presently~~ ˌby and byˌ (MS Morgan)

94.25 started • ~~up toward past Wilson's house to the haunted house~~ started
(MS Morgan)

94.26 intended • inte~~d~~ended (MS Morgan)

94.27 [¶] But he was • ~~[¶] But he had had one plan and now he was attempt-~~
~~ing another. Wilson had~~ He had [¶] But he was (MS Morgan)

94.27–28 dress, with the stoop of age added to the disguise, • dress,ˌ with the
stoop of age added to the disguise,ˌ (MS Morgan)

94.28 not bother • ~~not connect~~ not bother (MS Morgan)

94.29 a humble • ~~an~~ ˌa humbleˌ (MS Morgan)

94.35 persuaded • ~~man~~ persuaded (MS Morgan)

94.36 after all, • ˌafter all,ˌ (MS Morgan)

95.2 and • ~~and mingled with the throng~~ and (MS Morgan)

95.2 valuables • ~~things~~ valuables (MS Morgan)

95.3 [*single rule*] • [*single rule*] (MS Morgan) [TEXTUAL NOTE: *SLC marked
a short rule, using the printer's symbol for a long dash*]

95.9 be. • be. [*centered:*] ~~[*rule*] Chapter [*short double rule*]~~ [*in pencil, canceled
in ink*:] ~~Run back to 69~~ (MS Morgan)

96.1   *Chapter 17* (MTP) • Chapter 17. [*short triple rule*] [¶] ~~Insert this after the words "Chapter" on page~~ [*alterations in pencil*] (MS Morgan)

96.5   manuscript (MTP) • MS (MS Morgan)

96.9   [¶] The • [*centered:*] ~~Chapter 17.~~ [*short double rule*] [¶] The [*chapter heading and alterations in pencil*] (MS Morgan)

96.15   sure • ~~infallible~~ ˌsureˌ (MS Morgan)

96.15   author: • authorˌ; ~~and that the three form~~ (MS Morgan)

96.18   He pretended to be startled • ~~He was visibly startled and also amused, when the~~ ˌHe pretended to be startledˌ (MS Morgan)

96.19–20   hands, but . . . the house. • handsˌ,ˌ but this was only a blind, as he had already had a glimpse of them at the reception while robbing the house.ˌ ~~Talk was resumed, but the young fellow could not help in it for a while, so much was he shaken up by this the curious aspect of this being, or beings— he was not certain whether, to consider it one or a pair.~~ (MS Morgan)

96.20–21   The Twins made mental note that he • ~~He~~ ˌThe Twins made mental note that heˌ (MS Morgan)

96.31   on? • on?* (MS Morgan)

97.2   generously • ˌgenerouslyˌ (MS Morgan)

97.11   fit • ~~not~~ fit (MS Morgan)

97.12   soon • ˌsoonˌ (MS Morgan)

97.14   I ever • ~~it ever~~ I ever (MS Morgan)

97.19   throw— • throw ~~your~~— (MS Morgan)

97.19   had thought of the girl in Tom's bedroom, and • ˌhad thought of the girl in Tom's bedroom, andˌ (MS Morgan)

97.20   the • ~~your~~ the (MS Morgan)

97.29   of his glass strips and said: • ~~sheets of ˌsmall squares ofˌ glass | ordinary glass of uniform size,—about 5 × 8 inches—and said:~~ ˌof his glass strips and said:ˌ (MS Morgan)

97.31   the balls of • ˌthe balls ofˌ (MS Morgan)

97.32   results • resulˌsˌtsˌ (MS Morgan)

97.35   finger-marks (MTP) • finger- | marks (MS Morgan)

97.35   or twice • ˌor twiceˌ (MS Morgan)

97.36   the last time, • the~~n,~~ ˌlast time,ˌ (MS Morgan)

97.38   the crowned heads • ~~you~~ ˌthe crowned headsˌ (MS Morgan)

98.1   his crop • ~~his short~~ his crop (MS Morgan)

98.1–2   one at a time • ˌone at a timeˌ (MS Morgan)

98.6   piece of • ~~sheet of~~ ˌpiece ofˌ (MS Morgan)

98.7   the fellow-twin." • ~~the~~ ˌanˌotherˌ." twin."ˌ ˌthe fellow-twin."ˌ (MS Morgan)

98.8	[¶] "Well • [¶] "Well, it's done, now, and I like to have them both, any-way," said Wilson, and stepped to the door to answer a knock. [¶] The visitor was a good-natured, ignorant, energetic, middle-aged man who spoke English with a ‖ [¶] "Well (MS Morgan) [TEXTUAL NOTE: *At this point SLC, postponing the entrance of Buckstone, made this deletion and inserted new leaves (75A–75T) containing the palm reading and the story of the Indian knife, starting, as before, with 'Well, it's done, now' (98.8)*]
98.8	Wilson, • Wilson,ʳ (MS Morgan)
98.11	Dave's • He used Dave's (MS Morgan)
98.12	scientist (MTP) • scientest (MS Morgan)
98.17	the price • ˏthe priceˏ (MS Morgan)
98.18	your money's • the ˏyourˏ money's (MS Morgan)
98.18	Why, • B'George ˏWhy,ˏ (MS Morgan)
98.19	fifty or sixty things • everything ˏfifty or sixty thingsˏ (MS Morgan)
98.20	you, • you, as you long as you live, but (MS Morgan)
98.24	judged, now, • judgedˏ, now,ˏ (MS Morgan)
98.29	its • it′s (MS Morgan)
98.36	incredulity • incredudʹlity (MS Morgan)
98.36	little. • little.ʳ (MS Morgan)
98.38	minutely • as minutely (MS Morgan)
98.38	Next, two (MTP) • ˏNext,ˏ Two (MS Morgan)
99.4	much • seriously ˏmuchˏ (MS Morgan)
99.7	happened since; • happened ˏsinceˏ; (MS Morgan)
99.8	within that same year. • a year later. ˏwithin that same year.ˏ (MS Morgan)
99.10	still • we can't tell still (MS Morgan)
99.15–16	come, won't you?" • ˏcome,ˏ won't youˏ?ˏ", ˏplease?ˏ" (MS Morgan)
99.17	certainly, • certainly, Tom, (MS Morgan)
99.17	know I've • know, I'm I've (MS Morgan)
99.18	somewhat • very ˏsomewhatˏ (MS Morgan)
99.24	to • and to (MS Morgan)
99.30	less than • ˏless thanˏ (MS Morgan)
99.36	the • outlying the (MS Morgan)
99.38	cushion • pro- ‖ cushion (MS Morgan)
99.38	at • Qt at (MS Morgan)
100.1	little • middle ˏlittleˏ (MS Morgan)
100.2	shape • ha shape (MS Morgan)

100.8	aversions • a̶v̶ aversions (MS Morgan)
100.9	way which • w̶h̶i̶ way which (MS Morgan)
100.15	Luigi • a̶n̶d̶ Luigi (MS Morgan)
100.17	surprised • surprised a̶n̶d̶ t̶r̶o̶u̶b̶l̶e̶d̶ (MS Morgan)
100.30	Tom • "Tom (MS Morgan)
100.31	*prophesied* (MTP) • *prophecied* (MS Morgan)
100.35	read: (MTP) • read. (MS Morgan)
101.1–2	deepest and fatalest secrets of his life, • m̶o̶s̶t̶ s̶e̶c̶r̶e̶t̶ t̶h̶i̶n̶g̶s̶ h̶e̶ d̶o̶e̶s̶— e̶v̶e̶n̶ h̶i̶s̶ c̶r̶i̶m̶e̶s̶— ˏdeepest and fatalest secrets of his life,ˏ (MS Morgan)
101.2	expose • b̶e̶t̶r̶a̶y̶ ˏexposeˏ (MS Morgan)
101.9	Angelo warmly. • Angelo ˏwarmlyˏ. (MS Morgan)
101.10	for. • for.ᵇ (MS Morgan)
101.17	mine? • m̶y̶ o̶w̶n̶?̶ ˏmine?ˏ (MS Morgan)
101.21	time. • time. I̶ c̶a̶l̶l̶ i̶t̶ m̶y̶ l̶i̶f̶e̶-̶p̶r̶e̶s̶e̶r̶v̶e̶r̶ (MS Morgan)
101.22	and it • b̶u̶t̶ i̶t̶ and it (MS Morgan)
101.25	people • f̶a̶m̶i̶ people (MS Morgan)
101.28	a rapid • a̶ r̶a̶p̶i̶d̶ a rapid (MS Morgan)
101.29	with • v̶e̶r̶y̶ with (MS Morgan)
101.30	its long • ˏits longˏ (MS Morgan)
101.30–31	had Luigi's name added • a̶d̶d̶e̶d̶ ˏhadˏ Luigi's name ˏaddedˏ (MS Morgan)
101.31	myself, • ˏmyself,ˏ (MS Morgan)
101.31	arms, as you see. • armsˏ, as you seeˏ. (MS Morgan)
101.32	notice • s̶e̶e̶ ˏnoticeˏ (MS Morgan)
101.33	and • a̶n̶d̶ n̶e̶a̶r̶l̶y̶ ˏandˏ (MS Morgan)
101.33	a large man's wrist, • y̶o̶u̶r̶ w̶r̶i̶s̶t̶,̶ ˏa large man's wrist,ˏ (MS Morgan)
101.35	blunt end • e̶n̶d̶ blunt end (MS Morgan)
101.38	short • short, (MS Morgan)
102.2–4	course." [¶] Tom . . . were glass." • course."ˏOVERˏ [*on verso:*] ˏ[¶] Tom said to himself: "O̶h̶o̶!̶ I̶ h̶a̶d̶ a̶n̶ i̶n̶s̶t̶i̶n̶c̶t̶ t̶h̶a̶t̶ t̶h̶a̶t̶ "It's lucky I came here; I would have sold that knife for a song; I supposed the jewels were glass." | over againˏ (MS Morgan)
102.10	our • h̶i̶s̶ ˏourˏ (MS Morgan)
102.14–15	with his right hand lifted and a dirk in it • a̶n̶d̶ w̶a̶s̶ a̶b̶o̶u̶t̶ t̶o̶ ˏwith his right hand lifted and a dirk in it,ˏ (MS Morgan)
102.15	throat, but • b̶r̶e̶a̶s̶t̶,̶ ˏthroat,ˏ w̶h̶e̶n̶ ˏbutˏ (MS Morgan)
102.16	neck. • t̶h̶r̶o̶a̶t̶.̶ neck. (MS Morgan)

102.24 much • ˌmuchˌ (MS Morgan)

102.24 freethinker • free⁄thinker [*marked to join up*] (MS Morgan)

102.26 but • ˌbutˌ (MS Morgan)

102.27 publicly • ˌpubliclyˌ (MS Morgan)

102.28 If • ~~He did not need to kill Luigi~~ If (MS Morgan)

102.31 ingenious • ~~h◊i◊ s~~ ingenious (MS Morgan)

102.34 at your palms • ˌatˌ your ~~hand~~ palms (MS Morgan)

102.35 need— Hel-lo!" • need—ʳ Hel-lo!" (MS Morgan)

102.36 looking • ~~bl~~ looking (MS Morgan)

102.36 confused. • confused.ʳ (MS Morgan)

102.38 sharply • ⫯sharply (MS Morgan)

103.3 I didn't • ~~A~~ I didn't (MS Morgan)

103.7 outburst of • ~~explosion of~~ outburst of (MS Morgan)

103.10 felt • ~~felt a little~~ ˌfeltˌ (MS Morgan)

103.12 placing • ~~making~~ placing (MS Morgan)

103.14 nearly • ~~al~~ nearly (MS Morgan)

103.16 far • ~~through~~ ˌfarˌ (MS Morgan)

103.19 the blazing • ˌtheˌ blazing (MS Morgan)

103.21 but • ~~wh~~ but (MS Morgan)

103.23–24 [¶] The visitor . . . with a • [¶] The visitor . . . with a [*at foot of page:*] RUN to page 76 (MS Morgan) [TEXTUAL NOTE: *This passage, recopied from the deleted text at 98.8, with SLC's directive, effects a transition out of SLC's added leaves 75A–75T back to the previously written text*]

103.25 gave • ~~pro~~ gave (MS Morgan)

103.29 excitements, (MTP) • excitements (MS Morgan)

103.33 the big • ~~the public~~ ˌthe bigˌ (MS Morgan)

103.35 he was doing • ~~he did~~ he was doing (MS Morgan)

104.3 the temperance meetings • ~~y~~ the temperance ~~gang~~ meetings (MS Morgan)

104.7 one could see • ˌone could seeˌ (MS Morgan)

104.14 welcome. • welcome.ˌ ~~made up~~ (MS Morgan)

104.19–20 cries,— [¶] "Wet • cries,—¶"Wet [*apparently an inserted dash overwritten with a paragraph mark, not obviously meant to cancel it*] (MS Morgan)

104.21 Glasses of whisky were (MTP) • ~~A glass of~~ ˌGˌlasses ofˌ whisky was (MS Morgan) [TEXTUAL NOTE: *SLC failed to alter the number of the verb when he revised 'A glass' to 'Glasses'*]

104.21 waved • ~~raised his with ◊~~ waved (MS Morgan)

104.22	cries • ~~shout~~ cries (MS Morgan)
104.24	blonde • blo‸nde (MS Morgan)
104.28	Cappello • ‸Cappello‸ (MS Morgan)
104.32	accented • acci̸ented (MS Morgan)
105.4	cries • -̸cries (MS Morgan)
105.13	had drunk • had dra̸unk (MS Morgan)
105.14	drinks • ‸drinks‸ (MS Morgan)
105.15	merry—almost idiotically so— • merry;̸ —‸almost idiotically so,̸—‸ (MS Morgan)
105.17	side-remarks department (MTP) • side-remarks-department (MS Morgan)
105.19	slightly • ‸slightly‸ (MS Morgan)
105.19–20	apart. Their . . . apart, too. • apart‸. ~~and the one happened to have his head turned in~~ ‸Their heads happened to be canted apart, too.‸ (MS Morgan)
105.21	a speech he • ~~[*six or more words unrecovered*]~~ ‸a speech he‸ (MS Morgan)
105.22	with an air of tipsy • ~~in an~~ ~~‸with an‸~~ ~~of ◊◊◊◊◊◊◊~~ ~~‸with an air of tipsy‸~~ ‸with an air of tipsy‸ (MS Morgan)
105.23	human • ‸human‸ (MS Morgan)
105.25	phrase • ~~word~~ ‸phrase‸ (MS Morgan)
105.27	couple of strides • ‸couple of‸ strides‸ (MS Morgan)
105.28	Then he drew back and • ~~He~~ ‸Then he drew back and‸ (MS Morgan)
105.28	titanic • ~~astonishing~~ ‸titanic‸ (MS Morgan)
105.33	nest • ne/̸st (MS Morgan)
105.35	auditorium • ~~house~~ ‸auditorium‸ (MS Morgan)
106.5	clatter of the • ~~racket of clattering~~ ‸clatter of the‸ (MS Morgan)
106.5	voices • voices,̸ (MS Morgan)
106.13	lessening • ~~les~~ lessening (MS Morgan)
106.16	company. • company‸.-̸ (MS Morgan)
106.18	moral and political • ‸moral ~~and~~ and political‸ (MS Morgan)
106.18–19	frontier town of the period. • ~~town. A lot of~~ ‸frontier town of the period.‸ (MS Morgan)
106.23	them • them,̸ (MS Morgan)
106.27	flooded • flood‸ed‸ (MS Morgan)
106.28	there: for • there,̸‸: F̸‸for [‘F’ *struck through to make it lowercase*] (MS Morgan)
106.29	often • ‸often‸ (MS Morgan)

106.32	fire company (MTP) • fire-company (MS Morgan)
107.1	*Chapter 18* (MTP) • ˏChapter 18.ˏ [*short triple rule*] [¶] ~~Insert this after the words "Chapter 18" on page~~ ['Chapter 18.' *inserted, and directive canceled, in pencil*] (MS Morgan)
107.5	[¶] Next • ~~Chapter 18.~~ [*short triple rule*] [¶] Next [*deletion in pencil*] (MS Morgan)
107.5	Pudd'nhead (MTP) • Punk'nhead (MS Morgan)
107.13–15	Tom, his . . . previous night, • Tom,ˏ OVERˏ [*on verso:*] ~~with~~ his native cheerfulness unannihilated by his back-breaking and bone-bruising passage across the massed heads of the Sons of Liberty the previous night, | over again. (MS Morgan)
107.26	client, at the Market Hall last night; • clientˏ, at the Market Hall last nightˏ; (MS Morgan)
108.3	audience. • audience. ~~[¶] Mr. Wakeman and Mr. Thornton being sworn, ˏtestifiedˏ that they were on the platform and close at hand; they saw the kick delivered and noted the result of it as already described. Their testimony tallied exactly with that which had already been given. This closed the case for the prosecution.~~ (MS Morgan)
108.6	Are • ~~Did you~~ Are (MS Morgan)
108.9	itself • itself ~~gradually~~ (MS Morgan)
108.10	but • ˏbut. (MS Morgan)
108.14	prosecution • ~~de~~ prosecution (MS Morgan)
108.15	irrelevant • irreˇvelevant (MS Morgan)
108.25	insinuatingly, • ˏinsinuatingly,ˏ (MS Morgan)
108.28	opinion, • opinionsˏ, (MS Morgan)
108.31	discomfited • ˏdiscomfited. (MS Morgan)
108.35	gentlemen (MTP) • gentleman (MS Morgan)
109.1	them do it." • them⸝ˮ ˏdo it."ˏ (MS Morgan)
109.14–15	whisky, like a man." • whisky⸝ˮ ˏ, like a man."ˏ (MS Morgan)
109.22	and quite simply, • ˏand quite simply,ˏ (MS Morgan)
109.22	hogged it." • ~~drank it."~~ ˏhogged it."ˏ (MS Morgan)
109.24	was • ~~lacked~~ was (MS Morgan)
109.33	minds and tastes • minds⸝ and tastes⸝ (MS Morgan)
109.33	one of them • ~~each~~ ˏone of them. (MS Morgan)
109.34	approve • ~~foll~~ approve (MS Morgan)
110.3	It's more than possible. • ˏIt's more than possible.ˏ (MS Morgan)
110.4	anybody • anybody [*underscore canceled*] (MS Morgan)
110.16	[¶] "Why • ~~"Why, they—~~ || [¶] "Why (MS Morgan)

110.16 at the same time." • ~~at once."~~ ˌat the same time."ˌ (MS Morgan)

110.18 [¶] "Yes, sir." • ˌ[¶] "Yes, sir."ˌ (MS Morgan)

110.34 said: • said: [¶] ~~"Both of my clients are charged with this assault. The offence is punishable by fine, or imprisonment for a short term, or both.~~ (MS Morgan)

111.1   Twins • ~~accused~~ ˌTwinsˌ (MS Morgan)

111.3   Laughter. Silenced by the court. (MTP) • *Laughter. Silenced by the court.* (MS Morgan)

111.4–5 Laughter. Sharply rebuked by the court. (MTP) • *Laughter. Sharply rebuked by the court.* (MS Morgan)

111.8   Twins (MTP) • twins (MS Morgan)

111.9   or • ~~and~~ ˌorˌ (MS Morgan)

111.24 kick • ~~one~~ kick (MS Morgan)

111.26 crestfallen (MTP) • crest- | fallen (MS Morgan)

111.31–34 Rogers. If my . . . without comment." • Rogers.ᵇ If my ˌOVERˌ [*on verso:*] ˌbrother Allen desires to address the court, your honor, very well; but as far as I am concerned I am ready to let the case be at once delivered into the hands of this intelligent jury without comment."ˌ (MS Morgan)

111.35 Mr. Justice Robinson • ~~The~~ ˌMr.ˌ ɟJustice ˌRobinsonˌ (MS Morgan)

111.35 two • ~~six~~ ˌtwoˌ (MS Morgan)

112.1   by • ~~to~~ ˌbyˌ (MS Morgan)

112.3   he • ˌheˌ (MS Morgan)

112.7   assault • assault (MS Morgan) [TEXTUAL NOTE: *The text 'Mr. Justice . . . assault' was written on the blank verso of a leaf discarded from an unidentified work by Mark Twain, and has canceled text on the recto:* ~~nursing the sick in some ancient filthy century when the city was desolated by a plague. I knew that Wallenstein had figured hereabouts~~]

112.9   will • ~~must~~ ˌwillˌ (MS Morgan)

112.11 jury—" (MTP) • jury—". (MS Morgan)

112.12 the (MTP) • "the (MS Morgan)

112.14 whatever • ˌwhateverˌ (MS Morgan)

112.15 failed. • failedˌ,ˌ (MS Morgan)

112.19–20 insist that . . . separate the—" • insist⟋ᵇ ˌthat inasmuch as the prosecution did *not* separate the—"ˌ (MS Morgan)

112.21 No • Nₒ̸ (MS Morgan)

112.24 [¶] Wilson broke in— • ˌ[¶] Wilson broke in—ˌ (MS Morgan)

112.25 To • ~~It~~ To (MS Morgan)

112.26	arbitrarily • ˏarbitrarilyˎ (MS Morgan)
112.28	to fail • to fail ~~to fail~~ (MS Morgan)
112.29	Unheard • W̶ Unheard (MS Morgan)
112.33	are. • ~~may be.~~ ˏare.ˎ (MS Morgan)
112.33	and • and ~~for this~~ (MS Morgan)
112.34	my judgment • my~~self~~ judgment (MS Morgan)
113.1	be • ˏbeˎ (MS Morgan)
113.2	Great applause. (MTP) • ˏGreatˎ Applause. (MS Morgan)
113.5	has given • ˏhasˎ giv~~e~~n (MS Morgan)
113.6	approval, it • approval,ˏ ~~of it,~~ it (MS Morgan)
113.10	[¶] Allen • [¶] ~~Allen was not at his ease. However he rose and said—~~ [¶] ~~"Your honor, I have was told yesterday~~ ‖ [¶] Allen (MS Morgan)
113.13	act • ~~th~~ act (MS Morgan)
113.20	hearsay • ~~hearesay~~ ˏhearsayˎ (MS Morgan)
113.25	Cooper • Cooper ~~and Mrs. Betsy Hale~~ (MS Morgan)
113.27	Angelo • ~~Luigi~~ ˏAngelo.ˎ (MS Morgan)
113.31–33	himself. Also . . . your impudence." • himself.* ˏAlso, that upon Count Angelo's OVER.ˎ [on verso:] ˏcomplaining about being kept on his legs so long, Count Luigi retorted with apparent surprise, "*Your* legs!—I like your impudence." ǀ over again.ˎ (MS Morgan)
113.34	at • ~~of~~ ˏatˎ (MS Morgan)
113.35	with grave and earnest • ~~with~~ ˏwithˎ with grave and earnestˎ (MS Morgan)
113.36	of the battery • ˏof the batteryˎ (MS Morgan)
114.3	nine • nineˏ (MS Morgan)
114.9	"About • ~~"At~~ ˏ"Aboutˎ (MS Morgan)
114.13	I • ~~x~~ I (MS Morgan)
114.17	examining into?" • ~~trying to establish?"~~ ˏexamining into?"ˎ (MS Morgan)
114.19	in the • in ˏtheˎ (MS Morgan)
114.26	as escort and support, • ˏas escort and support,ˎ (MS Morgan)
114.26	the audience • ~~and~~ the audience (MS Morgan)
114.27	filed • ~~marche~~ filed (MS Morgan)
114.29	Twins with effusion, • Twins,ˏ with effusion,ˎ (MS Morgan)
114.30	nod • nodˏ (MS Morgan)
114.33	I declare • ˏI declareˎ (MS Morgan)
115.2	undimmed • ˏundimmedˎ (MS Morgan)
115.3	and Mr. • and ~~her friend rose and stood with~~ ǀ Mr. (MS Morgan)

115.30–31 but that's neither here nor there; I know, without that, that • ~~because~~
‸but that's neither here nor there; I know, without that, that‸ (MS
Morgan)

115.34 ask • ~~sa~~ ask (MS Morgan)

115.37 she is not a witness; • ‸she is not a witness;‸ (MS Morgan)

116.2 when • ~~wen~~ when (MS Morgan)

116.5 time?" • time‸;‸" (MS Morgan)

116.12 the • ‸the‸ (MS Morgan)

116.14–15 Laughter—suppressed by the court. • *Laughter—suppressed by the*
~~co◊◊t~~ *court* (MS Morgan)

116.25 but • ~~the~~ but (MS Morgan)

116.32 it, Mr. Wilson • it ‸Mr. Wilson‸ (MS Morgan) [TEXTUAL NOTE: *SLC
forgot to supply the necessary comma when he inserted* 'Mr. Wilson']

116.36 strangers, • ~~Twins,~~ ‸strangers,‸ (MS Morgan)

117.3 became witnesses in their own defence • ~~took the oath and~~ became witnesses ‸in their own defence‸ (MS Morgan)

117.6 current • ~~ꝑ~~ current (MS Morgan)

117.6 The • ~~So the case~~ The (MS Morgan)

117.8 took fright and came • ~~had to come~~ ‸took fright and came‸ (MS
Morgan)

117.8 then • the~~n~~in (MS Morgan)

117.8 helped • help‸ed‸ (MS Morgan)

117.8 sturdy • ~~admira~~ sturdy (MS Morgan)

117.13 several • ~~three~~ ‸several‸ (MS Morgan)

117.14 tell • ~~distinguish him~~ tell (MS Morgan)

117.14 him. • him.″ (MS Morgan)

117.21 places. • places‸ ~~and~~ (MS Morgan)

117.22 judge (MTP) • Judge (MS Morgan)

117.25 Justice • ~~j~~Justice (MS Morgan)

117.26 far-reaching • ‸far-reaching‸ (MS Morgan)

117.28 from the • ~~of the~~ ‸from the‸ (MS Morgan)

117.29 will • ~~shall~~ ‸will‸ (MS Morgan)

117.30 seized (MTP) • siezed (MS Morgan)

117.31 in • ~~and~~ in (MS Morgan)

117.33–34 aid and encouragement. • ~~it.~~ ‸aid and encouragement.‸ (MS Morgan)

118.2 a hidden and grisly • ~~an awful and~~ ‸hidden and grisly‸ (MS Morgan)

118.6 Through • ~~By~~ ‸Through‸ (MS Morgan)

118.7 your—our—countrymen • ~~our~~ ˌyourˌ—ourˌ—countrymen (MS Morgan)

118.8 concerning • ~~in~~ ˌconcerningˌ (MS Morgan)

118.10 The costs • The costs (MS Morgan) [TEXTUAL NOTE: *SLC began here to circle for deletion a passage of unknown intended extent, then decided to let it stand*]

118.13 aunties (MTP) • Aunties (MS Morgan)

118.15 Pudd'nhead • ~~Punk'nhead~~ ˌPudd'nheadˌ (MS Morgan)

118.15 tavernwards (MTP) • tavern- || wards (MS Morgan)

118.16 and victorious • ˌ~~and splendid~~ˌ ˌand victoriousˌ (MS Morgan)

118.16 the • ˌtheˌ (MS Morgan)

118.17 strange • ~~incense~~ strange (MS Morgan)

118.19 Wilson. • Wilson. (MS Morgan) [TEXTUAL NOTE: *In the top margin of page 330, SLC noted:* 'Ch. begins on this p.'; *later he canceled the notation in pencil*]

119.1 *Chapter 19* (MTP) • [*single rule*] ~~Chapter – [short double rule] [¶] [Insert "What is Courage?" from the Calendar.]~~ || Chapter 19. [*short double rule*] (MS Morgan)

119.6 courage. • courageˌ,ˌ (MS Morgan)

119.18 a fishing (MTP) • a-fishing (MS Morgan)

119.22–23 to any person • ~~to anybody~~ ˌ~~to a person~~ˌ ˌto any personˌ (MS Morgan)

119.23 superiority • ~~supremacy~~ ˌsuperiorityˌ (MS Morgan)

119.24 when a • ~~a~~ when ~~the~~ ˌaˌ (MS Morgan)

119.24 also • ~~also show that~~ also (MS Morgan)

119.26 a • ˌaˌ (MS Morgan)

119.27 could • ~~stood upon the printed~~ could (MS Morgan)

119.32 degradation • ~~destruc-~~ | degradation (MS Morgan)

120.4 differed, in certain details, • differedˌ,ˌ in certain detailsˌ,ˌ (MS Morgan)

120.6 some • ~~various~~ some (MS Morgan)

120.8 recognized • ˌrecognizedˌ (MS Morgan)

120.9 its • ~~the~~ ˌitsˌ (MS Morgan)

120.9–10 He was . . . earned title. • ˌHe was called "the great lawyer"—an earned title.ˌ (MS Morgan)

120.11 a year or two past • ˌa year or two pastˌ (MS Morgan)

120.11 sixty. • sixty. ~~But their physical style Driscoll looked his age, he was tall, spare; but Howard did not ˌlook hisˌ. Driscoll was tall, spare, and gray-headed; Howard was as tall, but he was not spare; he was of ˌstately andˌ beautiful build, he was muscled like an athlete, his shoulders~~

were ~~majestically broad and square, he was as straight~~ (MS Morgan)
[TEXTUAL NOTE: *At this point SLC discarded three MS pages numbered 128–30 (not extant), and deleted the first words on page 131 (final numbering, 335):* '~~storm of cheers, and Tisdale always treated him with the deepest respect afterwards.~~']

120.12   freethinker (MTP) • free- | thinker (MS Morgan)

120.15   even • ~~whether friend or~~ even (MS Morgan)

120.17   came • ~~started~~ came (MS Morgan)

120.18   presently • ˌpresentlyˌ ~~met another~~ (MS Morgan)

120.20–21   night, Judge?" • night?"ˌ Judge?" (MS Morgan)

120.26   details (MTP) • delails ['t' *left uncrossed*] (MS Morgan)

120.27   At the finish, the (MTP) • ˌAt the finish,ˌ The (MS Morgan)

120.28   over in his mind the shameful picture of Tom's flight over the footlights, then • ˌover in his mindˌ the shame- | ~~ful scene over in his mind. Then~~ ˌfullˌpicture of Tom's flight over the footlights, thenˌ (MS Morgan)

120.31   Thought • ~~Pro~~ Thought (MS Morgan)

121.3   "Oh, my • ~~"Good~~ ˌ"Oh, myˌ (MS Morgan)

121.4   as • ~~and~~ as (MS Morgan)

121.4   forward • ~~backwards~~ forward (MS Morgan)

121.4   took • ~~eased~~ took (MS Morgan)

121.10   Mr. Howard, • ˌMr. Howard,ˌ (MS Morgan)

121.11   slander, • slander, ~~Mr. Howard,~~ (MS Morgan)

121.36   mournfully • ˌmournfullyˌ (MS Morgan)

122.3   he • ~~his~~ he (MS Morgan)

122.4   a mixed expression of • ~~an~~ ˌa mixed expression ofˌ (MS Morgan)

122.6   discovered—as we have been informed—that (MTP) • ~~could not find out~~ discoveredˌ—as we have been infomed—ˌthat (MS Morgan)

122.11   now • ~~and~~ ˌnowˌ now (MS Morgan)

122.13   the • ~~Angelo.~~ the (MS Morgan)

122.14   pious one • pious one ~~that~~ (MS Morgan)

122.14   tomorrow (MTP) • to-morrow (MS Morgan)

122.21   "It locates the responsibility. You • ˌ"It locates the responsibility.ˌ ⸢You (MS Morgan)

122.23   to-night. • ~~Monday.~~ to-night. (MS Morgan)

122.27   him as the heavy seconds drifted by, • himˌ ˌas the heavy seconds drifted by,ˌ (MS Morgan)

122.28   stammer, • ~~cry,~~ ~~whimper,~~ ˌstammer,ˌ (MS Morgan)

122.29–30 They are murderous devils. • ˏThey are murderous devils.ˏ (MS Morgan)

122.30 I—I'm • ˏI—ˏI'm (MS Morgan)

122.30 *afraid* of them." • *afraid*ˏˮ ˏof them."ˏ (MS Morgan)

122.33–34 what have I done to deserve this infamy!" • ~~my God, my God!"~~ ˏwhat have I done to deserve this infamy!"ˏ (MS Morgan)

122.35 repeating, again and again, that lament • repeating ~~that~~ ˏ, again and again, thatˏ ~~ejaculation~~ ˏlamentˏ (MS Morgan)

122.36 a drawer a • ~~it a~~ ˏa drawer aˏ (MS Morgan)

122.37 still • ˏstillˏ (MS Morgan)

123.3 on • ~~upon~~ ˏonˏ (MS Morgan)

123.9 gone • gone, [*deletion in pencil*] (MS Morgan)

123.14 He finally concluded that it could. • ˏHe finally concluded that it could.ˏ (MS Morgan)

123.15 once • ~~more than~~ once (MS Morgan)

123.16 once could • ~~by a person once or twice or thrice could~~ ˏonce couldˏ (MS Morgan)

123.18 to his • to ~~his ease and~~ ˏhisˏ (MS Morgan)

123.20–21 "I'll square up with the proceeds of my raid, and then gambling • ˏ"I'll square up with the proceeds of my raid, and thenˏ *gambling (MS Morgan)

123.23 can easiest find • ˏcanˏ easiest find~~s~~ (MS Morgan)

123.23 through the impatience of my creditors. • ~~and after that, on account of his having to come up to the rack every now and then and square up my debts of honor to prevent a scandal. It is mainly that sort of episode that has cost me this property three separate and distinct times.~~ ˏthrough the impatience of my creditors.ˏ (MS Morgan)

123.24 to them • ˏto themˏ (MS Morgan)

123.24 once • ~~twice and three hundred~~ once (MS Morgan)

123.25 fortune— • fortune ~~every time~~— (MS Morgan)

123.27 gone • ˏgoneˏ (MS Morgan)

123.28 Three • ~~Five~~ ˏThreeˏ (MS Morgan)

123.31 that. • that. ~~With his protection gone I might relapse—so I'll only promise according to my streng strength; it's best to let the future take care of itself, perhaps. The reform begins right now—straight off. Pretty soon I'll be solid with him once more; he'll begin to soften the minute I'm out of his sight. Yes, sir, I'll have the will back, sure!" He began to feel almost cheerful. But doubts straightway began to gather, and his spirits drooped again. "O, dear, it's easy to *say* I won't gamble, but— there's the rub!—there's no temptation by, now. Blame it all!"~~ ˏ"Hang it!" he broke out fiercely to himself, "it's his own fault! Allows me ~~tw~~ a miserable ~~twenty-five~~ ~~fifty~~ dollars a month to live on,—and I get only half of *that*—. and then makes a great to-do about it because I try to earn a trifle more to scrape through on. *If* I gamble again—oh, dear, I'm bound to do it, I just know it!—I'm horribly afraid ~~it will be the ve, first thing I do will be to dr~~ ,that, the first thing I do ~~wi~~ in the joy of getting the will back will be to celebrate with a thimbleful too much and go and tumble right into the same old snare while my caution's drunk. And then!—oh, oh, oh, *that's* the last! He'll never relent again. Never again in the world. Yes, he is old, and he might die before I could persude him (MS Morgan)

123.31   I know it— • ᵢI know it—ᵢ (MS Morgan)

124.1   *Chapter 20* (MTP) • ~~Insert this under the words "Chapter 20," on page~~ ᵢChapter 20. [*short triple rule*]ᵢ [¶] Sometimes deterrent laws work well, but there is no certainty ᵢabout themᵢ. Fear of ridicule will deter any man from going naked into the street, but ~~it~~ ᵢnothingᵢ will ~~not~~ deter him, or you, ᵢor meᵢ, or anybody we are acquainted with, from trying to get rich; and yet the metaphor of the camel and the needle's eye tells us in the precisest and clearest language that *no* rich man can ~~es~~ enter heaven. It doesn't even deter a millionaire from joining a church, whereas he knows, himself, he hasn't any more chance there than Satan.—*Pudd'nhead Wilson's Calendar.* [*directive deleted, and chapter heading added, in pencil*] (MS in CU-MARK, *removed by SLC from MS Morgan*); Chapter 20. [*short triple rule*] [*in pencil*] (MS Morgan)

124.2   [¶] Thus • [*centered:*] ~~Chapter 20. [short triple rule]~~ [¶] Thus [*deletion in pencil*] (MS Morgan)

124.3   between fences enclosing • ~~with~~ ᵢbetweenᵢ fences ~~and~~ ᵢenclosingᵢ (MS Morgan)

124.4   till he neared the haunted house, then came • ~~for the only house beyond Wilson's on that edge of the village being a decayed and long-ago deserted two-story log house which the villagers forebore to approach at night because it was known to be haunted; and as it had no competition in that line it was always referred to as *the* haunted house. It stood a couple of hundred yards beyond Wilson's, and on the same side of the lane. It has nothing to do with this history at present, but must figure in it further along. [¶] Tom turned, when he found himself in front of that evil building, and came~~ ᵢtill he neared the haunted house, then cameᵢ (MS Morgan)

124.6   cheerful company. • ᵢcheerfulᵢ companyᵢ,ᵢ. ~~but not the company of ghosts and the dead; his mood and theirs would have been too mutual to be pleasant.~~ (MS Morgan)

124.8   and • ~~with~~ and (MS Morgan)

124.9   he noticed that • ~~the~~ he noticed ~~theat~~ lights (MS Morgan)

124.9   sitting room (MTP) • sitting-room (MS Morgan)

124.11   is • ˎisˎ (MS Morgan)

124.13   that • ~~Tom Driscoll," he said to himself~~ | that (MS Morgan)

124.21   Pudd'nhead— • ~~Punk'nhead—~~ ˎPudd'nhead—ˎ (MS Morgan)

124.27   bedroom (MTP) • bed- | room (MS Morgan)

124.28   aloud, gravely: • aloud,⟋ ˎgravely:ˎ (MS Morgan)

124.31   it." • it." [¶] "Goodness!—the Twins?" [¶] "Yes." (MS Morgan)

125.1   meditative • ˎmeditativeˎ (MS Morgan)

125.8   possible?" • ~~true?"~~ possible?" (MS Morgan)

125.11   a fishing (MTP) • a-fishing (MS Morgan)

125.15   did, • did,⟋ (MS Morgan)

125.32   you—upon my word I do. • youˎⱡˎ—upon my word I do.ˎ (MS Morgan)

125.37   remnant • ~~son~~ ˎremnantˎ (MS Morgan)

126.6   that • ~~when it~~ ˎthatˎ (MS Morgan)

126.14   fool— • fool,⸺ˎ (MS Morgan)

126.15   himself, • ˎhimself,ˎ (MS Morgan)

126.23   once • ~~a few times~~ ˎonceˎ (MS Morgan)

126.25   born. • born. ~~There'll be a consultation about it here, this evening.~~ (MS Morgan)

126.26   Aunt (MTP) • aunt (MS Morgan)

126.36   Mr. • *Mr. (MS Morgan)

126.37–38   and after . . . weather-conversation, • ~~and~~ after some wandering and aimless weather-conversation,ˎ [*insertion caret moved by SLC from its first position*] (MS Morgan)

127.1   By the way, we've (MTP) • ˎBy the way,ˎ We've (MS Morgan)

127.1   list of thefts, • list,ˎ ˎof thefts,ˎ (MS Morgan)

127.2   old • ~~father's~~ old (MS Morgan)

127.4   justice (MTP) • ~~Judge,~~ Justice,ˎ (MS Morgan)

127.5   Dobsons • Dobson's (MS Morgan)

127.6   the Hales, • ˎthe Hales,ˎ (MS Morgan)

127.8   such-like (MTP) • such- | like (MS Morgan)

127.8   off. • off.* (MS Morgan)

127.12   undisturbed. • undisturbed.* (MS Morgan)

127.20   though • ~~thog~~ though (MS Morgan)

127.24   woman • ~~thing~~ ˎwomanˎ (MS Morgan)

127.25 in a black veil • ˌin a black veilˌ (MS Morgan)

127.25–26 going aboard the ferry-boat yesterday. • ~~in the Presbyterian church one Sunday, about last Spring, and caught sight of her~~ ˌagainˌ ~~yesterday."~~ going aboard the ferry-boat~~, and recognized her~~ ˌyesterday.ˌ (MS Morgan)

127.31 robbed • ~~robbe~~ ‖ robbed (MS Morgan)

127.34 A • ~~There was a~~ A (MS Morgan)

128.2 Twins • ˌTwinsˌ (MS Morgan)

128.6 haul, • ~~hall,~~ ˌhaul,ˌ (MS Morgan)

128.6–7 because she'll get caught." • ~~unless she wants it for a keepsake."~~ ˌbecause she'll get caught."ˌ (MS Morgan)

128.8 Buckstone. (MTP) • Buckstone?ʳ (MS Morgan)

128.10 thief." • thief." ˌOVERˌ (MS Morgan)

128.13–18 to—" [¶] If anybody . . . turn!" • to—" ˌOVERˌ [*on verso:*] ¶ If anybody had noticed Tom's face at that time, the gray-green color of it might have provoked curiosity; but nobody did. He said to himself, "I'm gone! I never can square up; the rest of the plunder won't pawn or sell for ~~two-thirds~~ half of the bill. Oh, I know it—I'm gone, I'm gone—and this time it's for good!ʳ Oh, this is awful—I don't know *what* to do, nor which way to turn!" | over againˌ (MS Morgan)

128.19 Wilson to Blake, • Wilsonˌ ˌto Blake,ˌ (MS Morgan)

128.27 it, • it, ~~it's~~ (MS Morgan)

128.28 three days. • ~~a week.~~ ˌthree days.ˌ (MS Morgan)

128.29 reward • rewardˌ (MS Morgan)

128.31 constable (MTP) • Constable (MS Morgan)

129.9 miserable. • ~~unrefreshed.~~ ˌmiserable.ˌ (MS Morgan)

129.11 fame • fameˌ (MS Morgan)

129.13 before • ˌbeforeˌ (MS Morgan)

129.16 shall • ˌshallˌ (MS Morgan)

129.20 forehead • ~~eyes~~ ˌforeheadˌ (MS Morgan)

129.22 vibrated • ~~thrill~~ vibrated (MS Morgan)

129.23 servant— • servant | ⚹ — (MS Morgan)

129.27 mute—he was entirely • ~~nearly~~ ˌmute—he wasˌ ˌentirelyˌ (MS Morgan)

129.29 asleep or awake. • ~~even in his sleep.~~ ˌasleep or awake.ˌ (MS Morgan)

129.32 justice (MTP) • ~~Judge~~ ˌJusticeˌ (MS Morgan)

129.32 by • ˌbyˌ (MS Morgan)

129.33 had • ˌhadˌ (MS Morgan)

130.1   *Chapter 21* (MTP) • CHAPTER [*short rule*] [¶] A philosopher chided the animals for being *cruel;* and proposed to teach them, and elevate them nearer toward the ⸗ ˏhighˏ plane ~~of Man,~~ ˏof man,ˏ God's chiefest work. They asked him the meaning of the word. He explained. They could not understand. He explained again, and illustrated by cat and mouse. Still they looked vacantly at each other, and could not understand. The cat said, "I ~~play~~ ˏrompˏ with the mouse, the mouse romps also; we have great pleasure; when the mouse is tired playing, I eat her; what is there objectionable about this?" The philosopher was ~~troubled, and said:~~ ˏashamed, and said to himself,ˏ "I see, now, how it is: they are only ~~cru~~ ignorant; man alone is cruel wittingly. There has been a mistake: it is the beasts that should have been made in the image of God."—~~*From Pudd'nhead Wilson's Calendar.*~~ [*deletion of heading,* "Calendar" *ascription, and alteration of chapter number in pencil*] (MS in CU-MARK, *removed by SLC from MS Morgan, and replaced by the aphorism at 130.27*); Chapter ~~22.~~ ˏ21.ˏ [*short double rule*] [*alteration in pencil*] (MS Morgan)

130.2–7   The true southern watermelon . . . —*Pudd'nhead Wilson's Calendar.* (MS Morgan) • [TEXTUAL NOTE: *A manuscript leaf in CU-MARK bears an earlier version of this aphorism, showing the deletion of a single phrase:* '. . . of the earth. ~~It is to the other fruits of this planet as gold is to brass, as gems are to paste.~~']

130.8–10   [¶] It was . . . last chapter, • [¶] It was the gracious watermelon season. All hearts should have been gay and happy, but some were not. About the time that Wilson was || [*centered:*] ~~Chapter~~ | [*short double rule*] ~~[¶]~~ ~~About the time that Wilson was~~ saying these ~~words,~~ ˏwhich close the last chapter,ˏ (MS Morgan)

130.10   Pembroke • ~~Pem~~ Pembroke (MS Morgan)

130.12   that • ~~that vague and unaccented suggestion~~ that (MS Morgan)

130.16   where • ~~what are the weapons?"~~ where (MS Morgan)

130.24   ashy • ashy, (MS Morgan)

130.24   sometimes • ~~and mow and mutter incoherently.~~ sometimes (MS Morgan)

130.30   made • ma⸌k̸⸍de (MS Morgan)

131.4   as • ~~as his◊~~ as (MS Morgan)

131.9   also • ~~speaking of also recalling a detail~~ also (MS Morgan)

131.11–12   same time • same ~~sa~~ time (MS Morgan)

131.17   as • ~~only~~ as (MS Morgan)

131.19   by • ~~by~~ | by (MS Morgan)

131.21   at • ~~our~~ at (MS Morgan)

131.31   every • ∤ every (MS Morgan)

131.31–32   him!" cried the Judge. "Ah • him!‸" cried the Judge. "‸Ah (MS Morgan)

131.33   were • ∲ were (MS Morgan)

132.7   with • ~~without~~ with (MS Morgan)

132.8   very, • ‸very,‸ (MS Morgan)

132.12   beyond • ~~far~~ beyond (MS Morgan)

132.16   at (MTP) • at at (MS Morgan)

132.21   Pembroke, • ~~York,~~ ‸Pembroke,‸ (MS Morgan)

132.25   intelligence. • intelligence.✸ (MS Morgan)

133.3–4   creature. Go and arrange the thing." • creature.✸ ‸Go and arrange the thing.",‸ (MS Morgan)

133.5   seized (MTP) • siezed (MS Morgan)

133.11   not • ‸not‸ (MS Morgan)

133.12–13   by my brother on his dying bed, • ‸by my brother on his dying bed,‸ (MS Morgan)

133.15   once, already, • ~~three times,~~ ‸once, already,‸ (MS Morgan)

133.16   would • would ~~still~~ (MS Morgan)

133.20   his ostensible nephew • ~~Tom~~ ‸his ‸ostensible‸ nephew‸ (MS Morgan)

133.21   was • ~~finished his task~~ was (MS Morgan)

133.25   near • ~~past~~ ‸near‸ (MS Morgan)

133.29   He • [¶] He [*marked to run into previous paragraph*] (MS Morgan)

133.32   battle ground (MTP) • battle-ground (MS Morgan)

133.35   apiece." (MTP) • apiece. (MS Morgan)

133.37   Perfect • Perfect~~⊦~~ (MS Morgan)

133.38   still." • still.‶ ⌐ (MS Morgan)

134.8   Percy • ~~Dris~~ Percy (MS Morgan)

134.13   His • ~~The~~ His (MS Morgan)

134.15   spread • ~~op~~ spread (MS Morgan)

134.24   I've • ~~but~~ I've (MS Morgan)

134.24   bad scare • ~~narrow escape~~ bad scare (MS Morgan)

134.27   I've • ~~I notice that~~ I've (MS Morgan)

134.27   getting • ~~grow~~ getting (MS Morgan)

134.31–37   sure." [¶] He . . . his luck. • sure." [¶] ~~His notice was called to a large grass-hopper which was resting on~~ ‸on‸ the desk-leaf, in the shadow, ~~toward~~ near where the leaf joined the upright part of the secretary. It was not resting, exactly, either; for it was lifting and lowering its hind elbows and sliding its hind feet forward and aft in an uneasy way. It seemed to be in trouble. Tom

~~stooped, with the candle, to examine. It was in trouble—in pitiful trouble, indeed; for, close against~~ its fat body, on each side, a big gray spider of the springing and hunting sort had clamped itself and was sucking its life away. The ir big prisoner had been unable to shake them off, and was now become too weak to make further effort. Tom took up the grasshopper between his thumb and forefinger and set it down in the middle of the desk-leaf where he could observe better. Then he lit a cigar, drew up ~~his~~ a chair, and made himself comfortable. He watched with strong interest each spasm that was wrung from the tortured captive, and signified his enjoyment of each with a laugh or a chuckle, commenting also with words, now and then: [¶] "Well, what a pair you are, to treat your poor old uncle like that—he-he! . . . . . . Boys, there's three of us; I've just taken my fortune into camp, too—I'd like to shake hands and congratulate, if I could . . . . Good! nip him again, he-he!—that made the old chap squirm! . . . . . . Now ain't you having good times?—oh, no, not you, I reckon!—it fairly makes my mouth water . . . . S'cat, but *that* one made him hoist his elbows!— he-he!—I swear I believe I heard him moan . . . . . Gracious, *you* don't wait for unky to make his will, you set your grip onto the property without any little formality of that sort; now I don't approve of you there; that is really crowding the thing clear away beyond all fairness, you see . . . . . . whe-ew! but you gave him a twister that time—he-he-he! Sock it to him again! Good! do it again . . . . ah, *that* was a hair-raiser!" [¶] At the end of ten or twelve minutes of this sport the novelty of the thing had ~~about~~ spent itself to such a degree that Tom began to tire of it. He was about to go away, and did start, but an idea occurred to him, and he came back. He said, gaily— [¶] "Look here, you fellows are having most *too* good a time, it seems to me; let's see if we can't modify it a little." [¶] He drove a pin down through the centre of the grasshopper's back, lifted him up high above the candle, then brought him gradually down till the heat began to take effect on the undermost spider; when it dropped and landed in the top of the candle and began to squirm and shrivel up, he gave his attention to that, ~~until~~ with happy comments, until the finish, then served the other spider in the same way. He examined the grasshopper, now, but finding, as he said, that there wasn't enough entertainment left in him to make it worth while to sit up with him, he pinned the creature to the window-sash to think out its last dumb reflections upon the sorrow and mystery of its harmless life ungrieved by the presence of God's noblest work; ~~and~~ then he went yawning and stretching to his room, his mind already centred and absorbed in his good fortune again. | Chapter [*on the first leaf of the original passage:*] OVER [*on verso:*] ¶ He was about to close with a final grand silent demonstration, when he suddenly recollected that Wilson had put it out of his power to pawn or sell the Indian knife, and that he was once more in awful peril of exposure by his creditors for that reason. His joy collapsed, utterly, and he turned away and moped toward the door moaning and lamenting over the bitterness of his luck. | ~~Run to 189.~~ ['Run to 189' *written and can-celed in pencil*] (MS Morgan/MS in CU-MARK) [TEXTUAL NOTE: *The original "grasshopper" passage was on MS Morgan leaves numbered 183–88; leaf 183, with '[¶] ~~His notice . . . close against~~' on its recto and SLC's replace-ment passage on its verso, is still part of MS Morgan, while pages 184–88 are in the Mark Twain Papers. SLC deleted the grasshopper passage by removing leaves 184–88 and canceling some surrounding text*]

135.1   *Chapter 22* (MTP) • Chapter ~~23.~~ 22. [*short double rule*] ['23' *altered to '22' in pencil*] (MS Morgan)

135.4   [¶] The • [*centered:*] CHAPTER [*short rule*] [¶] The (MS Morgan)

135.7   of • ~~of the proxy of my~~ of (MS Morgan)

135.7   to • ˌtoˌ (MS Morgan)

135.8   granted • ~~allow~~ granted (MS Morgan)

135.11   "It • ~~"Well," said Howard,~~ [¶] "It (MS Morgan)

135.11   approvingly. "That • approvinglyˌ. "t̶ T̲hat ['t' *triple-underscored to capi-talize*] (MS Morgan)

135.11   young • ˌyoungˌ (MS Morgan)

135.19   —well, • ˌ—well,ˌ (MS Morgan)

135.21   Judge, • Judgeˌ.",ˌ (MS Morgan)

135.26   won • ~~one~~ ˌwonˌ (MS Morgan)

136.3   Angelo • ~~him~~ ˌAngeloˌ (MS Morgan)

136.7   vigor • t̶o̶e̶ vigor (MS Morgan)

136.10   one of them • ~~and~~ one ˌof themˌ (MS Morgan)

136.12   chose • ˌ~~might~~ˌ choose (MS Morgan)

136.12–13 but not • ~~but not~~ but not (MS Morgan)

136.13   Angelo • ~~Angelo saw~~ Angelo (MS Morgan)

136.17   world • ~~nation~~ ˌworldˌ (MS Morgan)

136.20   Angelo obeyed, (MTP) • Angelo, obeyed, (MS Morgan)

136.23   Judge's • Judgeˌ'sˌ ['s' *inserted in pencil*] (MS Morgan)

136.24   pistol-arm • pistol-ˌarm [*hyphen inserted in pencil*] (MS Morgan)

136.29   report. • reportˌ.~~—but dodged toward Luigi by mistake and brought himself into the line of fire.~~ (MS Morgan)

136.31   and bandaged • ˌand bandagedˌ (MS Morgan)

136.32   bones • bok̶nes (MS Morgan)

136.36   jumped, and • jumpedˌ ~~with no better judgment than before,~~ and | ˌandˌ (MS Morgan)

136.37   The doctor inspected and dressed the wounds. • ˌThe doctor inspected and dressed the wounds.ˌ (MS Morgan)

137.5	courtesy • cour*s*tesy (MS Morgan)
137.8	reflect • ~~remember~~ ˏreflectˏ (MS Morgan)
137.9	who is not present • ˏwho is not present ~~here~~ˏ (MS Morgan)
137.10	is • ~~has~~ ˏisˏ (MS Morgan)
137.13	Angelo • *ꞵ* Angelo (MS Morgan)
137.13	had • ˏhadˏ (MS Morgan)
137.14	both pistols . . . instant, and • ˏboth pistols went off at the same instant, andˏ (MS Morgan)
137.15	more; he • moreˏ; ~~and~~ he (MS Morgan)
137.17–18	The doctor attended to the wounded. • ˏThe doctor attended to the wounded.ˏ (MS Morgan)
137.20	exchange • ~~chan~~ exchange (MS Morgan)
137.22	part, and added • partˏ, ~~He said~~ ˏand added⤙ˏ (MS Morgan)
137.26	he • he [*underscore canceled*] (MS Morgan)
137.26–27	and had • and ˏhadˏ (MS Morgan)
137.27	would • ~~h~~ would
137.28	exchange is • exchange ~~shows~~ is (MS Morgan)
137.31	Luigi • ~~Angelo~~ ˏLuigiˏ (MS Morgan)
137.34	sides, • sides⁄ˏ, (MS Morgan)
137.35	at • ~~in~~ ˏatˏ (MS Morgan)
137.36	hands. • hands. ~~All were motionless.~~ (MS Morgan)
137.37	and • ˏandˏ (MS Morgan)
138.1	higher—in (MTP) • higher— ‖ —in (MS Morgan)
138.7	watching • ~~until~~ watching (MS Morgan)
138.8	spectacle • spectacleˏ, (MS Morgan)
138.12	suspicion • ~~vague~~ suspicion (MS Morgan)
138.15	should • ~~w~~ ˏshˏouldˏ (MS Morgan)
138.15	Luigi • ~~they~~ ˏLuigiˏ (MS Morgan)
138.20	him. • him.* (MS Morgan)
138.25	moment • momentˏ, (MS Morgan)
138.25	plaster (MTP) • plaister (MS Morgan) [TEXTUAL NOTE: *Both forms occur in the MSS; SLC's preference is shown by a later instance of 'plaister' which he revised to 'plaster' (PW-MS, Textual Apparatus, entry at 150.1)*]
138.26–27	neither . . . pistols • ~~almost everybody who was not personally interested in it got hit~~ neither of the parties who handled the pistols ~~got hit~~ (MS Morgan)
138.27	present • ~~in~~ present (MS Morgan)

138.36   now by the doctor; • now ˳by the doctor˳; (MS Morgan)

138.37   we • *I* ˳we˳ (MS Morgan)

139.1–2   complain of our trying to protect ourselves from danger; • complain ˳of
          our trying to protect ourselves from danger˳; (MS Morgan)

139.2   certainly • ˳certainly˳ (MS Morgan)

139.5   if • if ~~they a duel with~~ (MS Morgan)

139.7   for these • ~~for them~~ for these (MS Morgan)

139.11   on. • on. [¶] ~~When he arrived there he found~~ | ˳RUN to 204½ A˳. [TEX-
          TUAL NOTE: 'When . . . found' *deleted to accommodate the insertion of
          Chapter 23, then reinscribed and rephrased as the beginning of Chapter
          24;* 'RUN to 204 A.' *deleted in pencil*] (MS Morgan)

140.1   *Chapter 23* (MTP) • CHAPTER [*short rule*] ~~24.~~ ˳23.˳ [*short double rule*]
          [*alterations in pencil*] (MS Morgan)

140.2   Tom • ˳Tom˳ (MS Morgan)

140.10   All • ~~It~~ All (MS Morgan)

140.16   his eye • ~~him~~ his eye (MS Morgan)

140.28   by, • ~~past,~~ ˳by,˳ (MS Morgan)

140.29   Had they . . . haunted house? • ˳Had they seen a ghost at the haunted
          house?˳ (MS Morgan)

141.16   gwyne • ~~gon~~ gwyne (MS Morgan)

141.21   his • ~~the~~ ˳his˳ (MS Morgan)

141.24–25 with measureless contempt written in her face. • ~~in~~ ˳with˳ measureless
          contempt/ ˳written in her face.˳ (MS Morgan)

141.31   You has • You᾽s ˳has˳ (MS Morgan)

141.37   risk of his life • ~~his own life᾽s~~ risk of his life (MS Morgan)

142.1   Whatever (MTP) • What ever (MS Morgan)

142.1   'come • be᾽come (MS Morgan)

142.2   jist • ~~jus~~ jist (MS Morgan)

142.4   dat • dat̸ (MS Morgan)

142.6   duel • duel, (MS Morgan)

142.6   our • ~~owah~~ our (MS Morgan)

142.6   low-down (MTP) • low- | down (MS Morgan)

142.7   hound! Yes, it's de *nigger* in you." • hound!" ˳Yes, it's de *nigger* in you."˳
          (MS Morgan)

142.9   prudence • ~~discr~~ prudence (MS Morgan)

142.11   be • ~~ha~~ be (MS Morgan)

142.11   gone • gone, (MS Morgan)

142.14   soul." • soul̸ .̸.̸".̸ ~~yassir, enough to paint it~~ *yaller.* (MS Morgan)

142.15   muttered • ~~adde~~ muttered (MS Morgan)

142.19   unconsciously • ˏunconsciously˯ (MS Morgan)

142.22   God • ~~is~~ God (MS Morgan)

142.30   end • ~~en en'~~ ˏend˯ (MS Morgan)

142.32   dat • dat' (MS Morgan)

142.35   a yowlin (MTP) • a-yowlin (MS Morgan)

142.35   a yowlin (MTP) • a-yowlin (MS Morgan)

142.38   en • ~~and~~ en (MS Morgan)

143.1   Doctor • d̸ Doctor (MS Morgan)

143.1   'uz • ~~was~~ 'uz (MS Morgan)

143.1   en • ~~and~~ ˏen˯ (MS Morgan)

143.2   he'pin' (MTP) • he'pin (MS Morgan)

143.2   a standin' (MTP) • a-standin' (MS Morgan)

143.4   en de • en̸d̸ de (MS Morgan)

143.5   say • say̸s̸ (MS Morgan)

143.5   'Ouch!' • ˏ'"Ouch!"̸ '̸ (MS Morgan)

143.8   glance' • glance (MS Morgan) [TEXTUAL NOTE: *Emended to the form used in the MS elsewhere in this sentence*]

143.11   'uz • y̸ 'uz (MS Morgan)

143.12   t'other (MTP) • 'tother (MS Morgan)

143.15   question to ask, • question˸ ˏto as̸t̸ˏk˯ˏ (MS Morgan)

143.25   o' his • ~~of his~~ o' his (MS Morgan)

143.25   ha'r • h'a'r (MS Morgan)

143.35   again, and—" • again."̸ˏ and—"̸ (MS Morgan)

144.3   any more in this life, • ~~again,~~ ˏany more in this life˯ (MS Morgan)

144.7   you! • you˸!˯ (MS Morgan)

144.10   told her son to • ~~said~~ ˏtold her son to˯ (MS Morgan)

144.10   alone— • alone˸—˯ (MS Morgan)

144.11   said, • said˸—̸ (MS Morgan)

144.13   agin • ag̸i̸n (MS Morgan)

144.17   wid • wid̸ [*deletion in pencil*] (MS Morgan)

144.26   he • he ~~don't live six m~~ (MS Morgan)

144.27   diffrence (MTP) • diff'rence (MS Morgan)

144.32   "Tryin' • ~~"Tryin's neither here~~ [¶] Tryin' (MS Morgan)

144.37   how. • ~~why.~~ ˏhow.˯ (MS Morgan)

145.1   dem • ~~them~~ ˏdemˏ (MS Morgan)

145.5   in his voice • ˏin his voiceˏ (MS Morgan)

146.1   *Chapter 24* (MTP) • Chapter ~~24.~~ ~~25.~~ ˏ24.ˏ *[short triple rule] [altera-tions in pencil]* (MS Morgan)

146.4   found • found | ~~RUN to 405.~~ (MS Morgan)

146.10   fury • ~~discontent~~ ˏfuryˏ (MS Morgan)

146.13   as • ~~so~~ as (MS Morgan)

146.15   learning • ~~lea~~ | learning (MS Morgan)

146.15   off • off, (MS Morgan)

146.19   for once; • ˏfor once;ˏ (MS Morgan)

146.20   proceeded to empty himself as follows, with • ~~said with~~ ˏproceeded to empty himself as follows, withˏ (MS Morgan)

146.21   relish • ~~rlis~~ relish (MS Morgan)

146.22   probably • pro~~p~~bably (MS Morgan)

146.24   oesophagus (MTP) • aesophagus (MS Morgan)

146.26   infusorial • ~~conchoi~~ infusorial (MS Morgan)

146.26   system, thus • system, ˏthusˏ ~~of course, thus creating~~ (MS Morgan)

146.27   arteries • arteriesˏ (MS Morgan)

146.27–28 precipitating compound • ~~complicated with~~ ˏprecipitating compoundˏ (MS Morgan)

146.29   the dispersion • ˏtheˏ dispersion (MS Morgan)

146.29   marsupial • ~~fluxes and~~ marsupial (MS Morgan)

147.4   hope;" • hope;"ˏ (MS Morgan)

147.5   chocolate, then to orange, then to • ~~purple, then ˏtoˏ brown, then~~ ˏchocolate, then toˏ orange, then ˏtoˏ (MS Morgan)

147.7   turned • ~~he~~ turned (MS Morgan)

147.8   to hide his • to hide ~~to hide his~~ ˏhisˏ (MS Morgan)

147.8   said • ~~said in his~~ said (MS Morgan)

147.12–27 him." . . . something, doctor?" • him." ˏOVER.ˏ *[on verso:]* ˏ"You?" asked . . . something, doctor?" OVER againˏ (MS Morgan)

147.14   them himself?" • them?" ˏhimself?"ˏ (MS Morgan)

147.28   doctor • ˏdoctorˏ (MS Morgan)

147.33   Galen • Galen~~'s book~~ (MS Morgan)

147.33   was • wa~~l~~ș (MS Morgan)

147.33   only • ~~only recognized medical authority~~ | only (MS Morgan)

147.34   practice • ~~book~~ practice (MS Morgan)

147.36   Dr. • Dᴿ (MS Morgan)

148.2 undertaker: • undertaker: | Insert from my Harper article. (MS Morgan) [TEXTUAL NOTE: *Below this directive is affixed a clipping from* Harper's New Monthly Magazine *(SLC 1890). See PW-MS, Explanatory Note at 147.29*]

148.3 Asarabacca (James 1743) • Afarabocca (MS Morgan/SLC 1890) [TEXTUAL NOTE: *Either SLC or the printer of SLC 1890 misread the long 's' of James 1743 as 'f'*]

148.5 Costus (James 1743) • Coftus (MS Morgan/SLC 1890)

148.6 Celtic Nard, (James 1743) • Celtic, Nard, (MS Morgan/SLC 1890)

148.9 Brimstone (MS Morgan/SLC 1890) • crude Sulphur (James 1743)

148.10 Acorus (James 1743) • Acorns (MS Morgan/SLC 1890)

148.12 Carnabadium, (MS Morgan/SLC 1890) • Carnabadium (that is, according to the Commentator, Ethiopian Cummin) (James 1743)

148.12–13 Macedonian Parsley-seeds, (James 1743) • Macodonian, Parsley-seeds, (MS Morgan/SLC 1890)

148.13 Sinon, (MS Morgan/SLC 1890) • Sinon (a sort of wild Parsley, according to the Commentator) (James 1743)

148.13 and a half (MS Morgan/SLC 1890) • and half (James 1743)

148.17 odoratus (James 1743) • Odoratus (MS Morgan/SLC 1890)

148.19 Quantity. • Quantity. (James 1743); Quantity. ~~[¶] Serve with a shovel. No; one might expect such an injunction after such formidable preparation; but it is not so. The dose recommended is "the Quantity of an Haslenut." Only that; it is because there is so much jewelry in it, no doubt.~~ [*deletion in pencil*] (MS Morgan/SLC 1890)

148.20 "that will fix the patient; give his brother a • ~~give him a~~ ‸"that will fix the patient; give his brother a‸ (MS Morgan)

148.24 Count Angelo • ~~him~~ ‸Count Angelo‸ (MS Morgan)

148.30 Angelo • ~~he~~ ‸Angelo‸ (MS Morgan)

149.1 stir • ~~sit up~~ ‸stir‸ (MS Morgan)

149.4 I'm • ~~"~~I'm (MS Morgan)

149.5 said quietly to the doctor: • said~~,~~ quietly~~—~~ ‸to the doctor:‸ (MS Morgan)

149.16 he • ~~he clasped his hands~~ he (MS Morgan)

149.23 had • had | ~~RUN to 214½~~ (MS Morgan)

149.23 might • ~~could~~ might (MS Morgan)

149.30 Luigi's • ~~these~~ ‸Luigi's‸ (MS Morgan)

149.31 but had • ~~might have~~ ‸but had‸ (MS Morgan)

149.34 Patsy • Patsy~~,~~ (MS Morgan)

149.35 drive • ~~get~~ ‸drive‸ (MS Morgan)

149.36   their stove • the˯ir˯ stove (MS Morgan)

150.1   plaster • pla˘ɪster (MS Morgan)

150.7   a minute ago; • ˯a minute ago;˯ (MS Morgan)

150.9   judgment (MTP) • judgement (MS Morgan)

150.11   enough. • enough⸝ ˯ (MS Morgan)

150.11   Looy • ~~you˯ reckless young˯ scamp~~ ˯Looy˯ (MS Morgan)

150.13   "Luigi! • ~~"Looy!~~ "Luigi!˯ (MS Morgan)

150.19   "Why, • "Why,ⁿ (MS Morgan)

150.25   by • ~~toward nightfall,~~ by (MS Morgan)

150.28   baptised (MTP) • baptized (MS Morgan)

151.1   *Chapter 25* (MTP) • Chapter ~~26~~ ˯25.˯ [*short double rule*] [*alteration in pencil*] (MS Morgan)

150.5   for conscience sake • for conscience sake (MS Morgan) [TEXTUAL
          NOTE: *Some grammars (including the text of SLC's school days,
          Kirkham's Grammar) required that* 'conscience' *in this phrase be given
          a possessive apostrophe, but this was not unanimous nineteenth-century
          practice (see, e.g., King James Bibles at Rom. 13:5 and 1 Cor. 27–28;
          Kirkham 1835, 49; Gribben 2022, 414–15)*]

150.8   parties, • ~~par~~ | parties⸝˯ (MS Morgan)

150.8   an • ~~the~~ ˯an˯ (MS Morgan)

150.10   Pudd'nhead (MTP) • Puddn'head (MS Morgan)

150.14   noon the • noon-~~dinner-time, the~~ ˯the˯ (MS Morgan)

150.15   and all warnings and supplications, • ˯and all warnings and supplica-
          tions,˯ (MS Morgan)

150.15   was • ~~and~~ was (MS Morgan)

150.17   wildfire (MTP) • wild- | fire (MS Morgan)

150.21   so • ⟆⟆ so (MS Morgan)

150.22   and witness • ~~to~~ ˯and witness˯ (MS Morgan)

150.26   vastly • ˯vastly˯ (MS Morgan)

150.27   in • ⟆⟆ in (MS Morgan)

150.28   had ever • ˯had ever˯ (MS Morgan)

150.28   by, • by, ~~and~~ (MS Morgan)

150.29   nor • ~~and alw~~ nor (MS Morgan)

152.1   bank • bank~~, with~~ (MS Morgan)

152.5   came attended by • ~~had~~ ˯came attended by˯ (MS Morgan)

152.9   over the • over the ~~two~~ (MS Morgan)

152.10   and exalted • ˯and exalted˯ (MS Morgan)

152.12   long • ˌlongˌ (MS Morgan)

152.14   Dawson's • ℟ Dawson's (MS Morgan)

152.20   Betsy Hale • ~~Patsy was~~ Betsy Hale (MS Morgan)

152.23   up your poor brother." • ˌupˌ your poor brotherˌ."ˌ ~~up."~~ (MS Morgan)

152.27   Well, • ~~Great Scott,~~ ˌWell,ˌ [*alterations in pencil*] (MS Morgan)

152.28   quiet, Luigi! (MTP) • quiet,ˌ,ˌ ~~you troublesome brat!~~ ˌLuigi!ˌ [*alterations in pencil*] (MS Morgan)

152.29   declare if you • declare ~~to goodness~~ if you ~~kee~~ ['to goodness' *deleted in pencil*] (MS Morgan)

152.36   heaven • heaven ˌ [*insertion caret made, then canceled*] (MS Morgan)

152.37   dreadful • ~~owdacious~~ ˌdreadfulˌ (MS Morgan)

153.4   my • ~~the~~ ˌmyˌ (MS Morgan)

153.13   and • and ~~all these~~ (MS Morgan)

153.13   dying • ~~no cha~~ dying (MS Morgan)

153.15   up • up, (MS Morgan)

153.19   disobedience • disobedience∅ (MS Morgan)

153.22   are • are [*underscore canceled*] (MS Morgan)

153.25   declare • declare ~~to goodness~~ (MS Morgan)

153.28   shaky. • ~~pretty far gone, you see.~~ ˌshaky.ˌ (MS Morgan)

153.29   up • up ~~with your impudence and sass~~ (MS Morgan)

153.34   up! • up,!ˌ ~~this minute!~~ [*alterations in ink and in pencil*] (MS Morgan)

154.1   have some compassion! • ~~good land!~~ ˌhave some compassion!ˌ (MS Morgan)

154.1   colds • colds~~, Aunt Betsy,~~ (MS Morgan)

154.8   one • ~~her~~ ˌoneˌ (MS Morgan)

154.13   retorted, • retorted, ~~serenely,~~ [*alterations in pencil*] (MS Morgan)

154.15   that." • that." [*underscore canceled*] [*short rule*] [¶] ~~Luigi dropped into a reverie, in which the lively happenings of the past three days and nights moved through his mind like a huzzahing and pow-wowing torchlight procession, with gaudy explosions of fireworks at intervals along the line, and he closed the review with the remark, "For adventure and plenty of it, these three days break the record. The sheep-nanny tea is a good climax. If I survive it I want to locate here. A brisk We can have but one life, and a brisk one is better than a dull one. I think we have struck the right place."~~ (MS Morgan)

155.1   *Chapter 26* (MTP) • Chapter ~~27.~~ ˌ26.ˌ [*short double rule*] [*alterations in pencil*] (MS Morgan)

155.5   [¶] During • [*centered:*] ~~Chapter 27.~~ [*short triple rule*] [¶] During (MS Morgan)

155.8 welcomed • ~~received with admiring~~ welcomed (MS Morgan)

155.9 into • in͓to͓ ~~th~~ (MS Morgan)

155.26 them in • ~~them just as~~ them in (MS Morgan)

156.4 sho' (MTP) • sho (MS Morgan)

156.9 as for • ͓as for͓ (MS Morgan)

156.10 its (MTP) • it's (MS Morgan)

156.12 St. (MTP) • St (MS Morgan)

156.15 enough • ͓enough͓ (MS Morgan)

156.16 month. • month.⸗ (MS Morgan)

156.20 has • ~~is~~ has (MS Morgan)

156.21 gibe • ~~ȷ~~ gibe (MS Morgan)

156.25 own • ͓own͓ (MS Morgan)

156.28 uncomfortably, • uncomfortably,͓ [*insertion caret made, then canceled*] (MS Morgan)

157.3 three days!— • ~~forty-eight hours!—~~ ͓three days!—͓ (MS Morgan)

157.6 pawnbroker (MTP) • pawn-broker (MS Morgan)

157.7 swag. • swag.⸗ (MS Morgan)

157.14 discharged a • ~~gave~~ ͓discharged a͓ (MS Morgan)

157.16 [¶] After • ~~Tom said, reflectively—~~ | ~~Tom had been puzzling over~~ | ~~Tom~~ | ¶After (MS Morgan)

157.16 at his house, • ͓at his house,͓ (MS Morgan)

157.23 fool—a fact of recent discovery. • fool͓,—a fact of recent discovery.͓ (MS Morgan)

157.28 argument's (MTP) • arguments (MS Morgan)

157.31 you, Pudd'nhead! • you͓, Pudd'nhead͓! (MS Morgan)

157.33 Wilson • ~~Wilson said—~~ [¶] Wilson (MS Morgan)

157.38 bring • ~~come forw~~ bring (MS Morgan)

158.12 "Why, that (MTP) • "͓Why,͓ That (MS Morgan)

158.16 those • those⸗ (MS Morgan)

158.22 little town • ~~village~~ ͓little town͓ (MS Morgan)

158.30 looks • ~~makes~~ looks (MS Morgan)

158.30 the • the͞y (MS Morgan)

158.32 go • ~~you~~ go (MS Morgan)

158.35 from • ~~in~~ ͓from͓ (MS Morgan)

158.36–37 evidence; *but*—well, he would think—and then decide how to act. • evidence͓,͞ ~~still it would~~ ͓but͓—well, he would think—and then decide how to act.͓ (MS Morgan)

159.2   or if they had it (MTP) • or ₍or if they had it₎ (MS Morgan)

159.3   it; • it;⟋ (MS Morgan)

159.11   squirm; • squirm; ~~he had damaged the twins a little~~ (MS Morgan)

159.12   small • small~~er~~ (MS Morgan)

159.13   all— • all—₍ (MS Morgan)

159.19   anywhere. • anywhere. | ~~HERE insert 248-A-B & C.~~ (MS Morgan)
        [TEXTUAL NOTE: *Midway down the page originally numbered 248,*
        SLC's directive calls for the insertion of three leaves of text; this was done by
        bisecting the leaf originally numbered 248 to create two leaves (final num-
        bering 472 and 476), and interposing leaves 248A–248C (final numbering
        473–75). The two stubs of the original leaf 248 have been "filled out" to
        normal leaf size using portions of one or more blank discarded MS leaves]

159.20   On Saturday evening • On~~ce~~ ₍Saturday evening₎ (MS Morgan)

159.21–22   as I am . . . you again, • ₍as I am going away and might never see you
        again,₎ (MS Morgan)

159.25   knowing • know₍ing₎ (MS Morgan)

159.26   was • ~~is~~ ₍was₎ (MS Morgan)

159.33   expose them • ~~tell~~ ₍expose them₎ (MS Morgan)

159.37   But • ~~I~~ But (MS Morgan)

159.37   I could • I could [*underscore canceled*] (MS Morgan)

159.38   on • o~~f~~n (MS Morgan)

160.9   cost • ~~daily~~ cost (MS Morgan)

160.9   to this time. • ~~so long.~~ ₍to this time.₎ (MS Morgan)

160.20   still. • still." (MS Morgan)

160.22   uncle. • uncle. [¶] ~~Return to page 248.~~ (MS Morgan)

160.27–28 Chambers, en so I's boun' • ~~so~~ ₍Chambers, en so I's boun'₎ (MS Morgan)

161.1   sure, • sure,⟋ (MS Morgan)

161.2   friendless. That • friendless.— | That [*end-line dash*] (MS Morgan)

161.6   poured out • ~~lavished~~ ₍poured out₎ (MS Morgan)

161.9   try • ~~meditate flight~~ try (MS Morgan)

161.18   speechless • speechless,⟋ ~~Roxana g◊◊◊◊~~ (MS Morgan)

161.23   Lord • ~~Lawd~~ ₍Lord₎ (MS Morgan)

161.23   De Lord made 'em. • ₍De ~~Lawd~~ ₍Lord₎ made 'em.₎ (MS Morgan)

161.24   De good Lord He made 'em so. • ₍De good ~~Lawd~~ord He made 'em so.₎
        (MS Morgan)

161.25   en in a year • ~~en when you gits yo' propaty~~ ₍en in two years₎ ₍en in a year₎
        (MS Morgan)

161.26	I'll show you how. Dat's • ˌI'll show you how. ˌ T͟h Dat's (MS Morgan)
161.29	it! (MTP) • it (MS Morgan)
161.31	sayin' • saying͐ (MS Morgan)
161.36	months • Q̶Q̶ months (MS Morgan)
162.1	hard up; you'll fine • hard up; e̶n̶ you'll fineˌ (MS Morgan)
162.4	sold • s̶o̶l̶d̶ ̶h̶i̶s̶ ̶m̶o̶t̶h̶e̶r̶,̶ ̶u̶p̶ ̶c̶o̶u̶n̶t̶r̶y̶ ̶f̶o̶r̶ sold (MS Morgan)
162.9–19	all. Besides . . . end, anyway. • all. *OVER.* [*on verso:*] ˌBesides, the planter insisted that Roxy wouldn't know where she was, at first, and that by the time she found out she would already have become contented. And Tom argued with himself that it was an immense advantage for Roxy to have a master who was so m̶a̶n̶i̶f̶e̶s̶t̶l̶y̶ pleased with her as this planter manifestly was. In almost no time his flowing reasonings carried him to the point of even half believing he was doing Roxy a splendid surreptitious service in sending her "down the river." A̶n̶d̶ ̶y̶e̶t̶ ̶i̶n̶ ̶h̶i̶s̶ ̶h̶e̶a̶r̶t̶ ̶h̶e̶ ̶k̶n̶e̶w̶ ̶t̶h̶a̶t̶ ̶i̶n̶ ̶t̶h̶e̶ ̶M̶i̶s̶s̶o̶u̶r̶i̶ ̶s̶l̶a̶v̶e̶'̶s̶ ̶r̶e̶l̶i̶g̶i̶o̶n̶ ̶t̶h̶e̶r̶e̶ ̶w̶e̶r̶e̶ ̶t̶w̶o̶ ̶h̶e̶l̶l̶s̶,̶ ̶a̶n̶d̶ ̶t̶h̶a̶t̶ ̶t̶h̶e̶ ̶o̶n̶e̶ ̶o̶f̶ ̶e̶t̶e̶r̶n̶a̶l̶ ̶f̶i̶r̶e̶ ̶w̶a̶s̶ ̶d̶i̶m̶ ̶a̶n̶d̶ ̶v̶a̶g̶u̶e̶ ̶t̶o̶ ̶h̶i̶m̶,̶ ̶w̶h̶i̶l̶e̶ ̶t̶h̶e̶ ̶t̶h̶r̶e̶a̶t̶ ̶t̶o̶ ̶s̶e̶n̶d̶ ̶h̶i̶m̶ ̶t̶o̶ ̶t̶h̶e̶ ̶o̶t̶h̶e̶r̶—̶t̶h̶a̶t̶ ̶i̶s̶,̶ ̶s̶e̶l̶l̶ ̶h̶i̶m̶ ̶"̶d̶o̶w̶n̶ ̶t̶h̶e̶ ̶r̶i̶v̶e̶r̶,̶"̶—̶c̶o̶u̶l̶d̶ ̶t̶u̶r̶n̶ ̶h̶i̶s̶ ̶b̶l̶a̶c̶k̶ ̶s̶k̶i̶n̶ ̶w̶h̶i̶t̶e̶ ̶w̶i̶t̶h̶ ̶h̶o̶r̶r̶o̶r̶!̶ And then T̶o̶m̶ ˌheˌ kept diligently saying to himself all the time, "It's for only t̶w̶o̶ ˌaˌ years̶—in t̶w̶o̶ ˌaˌ yearş I buy her free again; she'll keep that in mind, and it'll reconcile her." Yes, the little deception could do no harm, and everything would come out right and pleasant in the end, anyway.	over againˌ (MS Morgan)
162.23–24	mother who . . . was making • mother w̶h̶o̶ ̶h̶a̶d̶ ̶m̶a̶d̶e̶ ˌwho, in͐ˌ *OVER*ˌ [*on verso:*] ˌwho, in voluntarily going into slavery—slavery of any kind, mild or severe, or of any duration, brief or long—was making	over againˌ (MS Morgan)
162.25	would • i̶s̶ ̶a̶ would (MS Morgan)
162.26	caresses • e̶n̶d̶e̶a̶r̶m̶e̶n̶t̶s̶ ˌcaressesˌ (MS Morgan)
162.26	privately, and then • a̶n̶d̶ ˌprivately, and thenˌ (MS Morgan)
162.27	owner; went away • ownerˌ; went awayˌ (MS Morgan)
162.32	one year • t̶w̶o̶ ˌoneˌ yearş (MS Morgan)
162.34	[¶] For • l̶e̶t̶t̶e̶r̶ ̶o̶f̶ ̶h̶i̶s̶ ̶r̶e̶f̶o̶r̶m̶ ˌa̶n̶d̶ ̶n̶e̶v̶e̶r̶ ̶p̶u̶t̶ ̶t̶h̶a̶t̶ ̶w̶i̶l̶l̶ ̶i̶n̶ ̶j̶e̶o̶p̶a̶r̶d̶y̶ ̶a̶g̶a̶i̶n̶.̶ˌ H̶e̶ ̶h̶a̶d̶ ̶g̶i̶v̶e̶n̶ ̶R̶o̶x̶y̶ ̶a̶ ̶h̶u̶n̶d̶r̶e̶d̶ ̶a̶n̶d̶ ̶f̶i̶f̶t̶y̶ ̶d̶o̶l̶l̶a̶r̶s̶ ̶o̶f̶ ̶h̶e̶r̶ ̶p̶u̶r̶c̶h̶a̶s̶e̶-̶m̶o̶n̶e̶y̶,̶ a̶n̶d̶ ̶h̶e̶ ̶h̶a̶d̶ ̶a̶s̶ ̶m̶u̶c̶h̶ ̶l̶e̶f̶t̶ ̶t̶o̶ ̶s̶p̶e̶n̶d̶,̶ ̶h̶i̶m̶s̶e̶l̶f̶.̶ ̶A̶n̶d̶ ̶h̶e̶ ̶s̶p̶e̶n̶t̶ ̶i̶t̶,̶ ̶b̶u̶t̶ ̶w̶i̶t̶h̶ g̶o̶o̶d̶ ̶j̶u̶d̶g̶m̶e̶n̶t̶.̶ ̶N̶o̶n̶e̶ ̶o̶f̶ ̶i̶t̶ ̶w̶e̶n̶t̶ ̶t̶h̶e̶ ̶u̶s̶u̶a̶l̶ ̶w̶a̶y̶ ̶o̶f̶ ̶h̶i̶s̶ ̶m̶o̶n̶e̶y̶.̶ [¶] For (MS Morgan) [TEXTUAL NOTE: *The deleted passage, 'letter of . . . his money.', is a superseded form of the text that SLC revised as 162.29–33 ('letter of . . . free again.'). A still earlier, canceled version of this passage is preserved elsewhere in MS Morgan, where it has been used to "fill out" a partial leaf*]
163.2	through • w̶i̶t̶h̶ through (MS Morgan)

163.5   between • ~~between~~ | between (MS Morgan)

163.12   showed • w̸ showed (MS Morgan)

163.14   brought • ~~cau~~ brought (MS Morgan)

163.15   practiced (MTP) • practised (MS Morgan)

163.15   tell-tale (MTP) • tell- | tale (MS Morgan)

163.18   Lord • ~~Lord Gawd~~ ˏLawdˏ ˏLordˏ (MS Morgan)

163.18   I's • I˯'s ₰ (MS Morgan)

164.1   *Chapter 27* (MTP) • ~~Chapter 28.~~ [*short double rule*] | Chapter ~~28.~~ ˏ27.ˏ [*short double rule*] [*alteration of '28' to '27' in pencil*] (MS Morgan)

164.6   *Calendar.* (MTP) • *Calendar.* ˏ[¶] On Independence Day Rowena went out back to see the fireworks and fell down the well and got drowned. But it is no matter; these things cannot be helped˯ˏ₂ in a work of this kind.ˏˏ (MS Morgan) [TEXTUAL NOTE: *This passage has been identified as an insertion on the strength of SLC's notebook entry, made while he was revising MS Morgan:* 'on 270 drown Rowena' (*Notebook 32, TS p. 51, TxU-Hu). But it is clearly inserted in the wrong place—on page 489, bearing the chapter heading and motto about 'July 4,' rather than on the nearby page numbered 270. Rowena cannot plausibly die here, since she is alive in the text that follows (165.23–166.27). In this edition the insertion has been moved to 166.28–30, corresponding to the location specified in the notebook*]

164.7   [¶] The • [*centered:*] ~~Chapter 28.~~ [*short double rule*] [¶] The (MS Morgan)

164.7   Dawson's • ℞ Dawson'sˏ (MS Morgan)

164.9   developed • ~~got~~ developed (MS Morgan)

164.18   for the Twins, (MTP) • for ~~themselves,~~ ˏTwins,ˏ (MS Morgan)

164.18   through • ~~fo~~ through (MS Morgan)

164.20   to balls • ~~to Freethinkers~~ to balls (MS Morgan)

164.20   horse-races (MTP) • horse races (MS Morgan)

164.29   on • ~~of~~ on (MS Morgan)

164.31   all • ˏallˏ (MS Morgan)

164.8   Teetotalers' • ~~Teet~~ Teetotalers' (MS Morgan)

164.12   noted • note∅d (MS Morgan)

164.16   discommoded • discommod~~ate~~ed (MS Morgan)

164.18   Luigi • ~~Then~~ Luigiˏ [*insertion caret made, then canceled*] (MS Morgan)

164.20   rowdies in • ~~rowdies in~~ ˏpersonsˏ ˏrowdies inˏ (MS Morgan)

164.26   ended, and • ended˯ˏ and ~~And~~ (MS Morgan)

164.32   am • ~~get drunk~~ am (MS Morgan)

164.36   I implore you to believe that • ˏI implore you to believe thatˏ (MS Morgan)

166.3   Cappello. (MTP) • Capello,. (MS Morgan) [TEXTUAL NOTE: *In MS Morgan, SLC usually spells 'Cappello' or (at 36.10) alters the one-p to the two-p spelling; he left standing only this one instance of 'Capello'*]

166.3   No person • Noþ person (MS Morgan)

166.11   cruel • ˏcruel˗ (MS Morgan)

166.24   heaven • ~~God~~ ˏheaven˗ (MS Morgan)

166.25   these • the˗se˗ (MS Morgan)

166.26   pathetic • pathetic ~~dumb~~ (MS Morgan)

166.28–30   [¶] On Independence Day . . . of this kind. • [TEXTUAL NOTE: *In MS Morgan this passage occurs at the beginning of Chapter 27; see* PW-MS, *Textual Apparatus, entry and textual note at 164.6*]

167.5   only • ˏonly˗ (MS Morgan)

167.15   vacillating or indifferent (MTP) • ~~purchasable~~ ˏvasilating or indiffer-ent˗ (MS Morgan)

167.17   said • saịd (MS Morgan)

167.20   than • thaɤn (MS Morgan)

167.21   since his • since ~~c~~ his (MS Morgan)

167.22   St. (MTP) • St (MS Morgan)

167.22   happy—fully • happy | ~~—at least half~~ | —fully (MS Morgan)

167.26   board of aldermen • ~~Board of A~~ board of aldermen (MS Morgan)

167.28   carry • ~~get up a supposititious~~ carry (MS Morgan)

168.1–5   *Chapter 28* [¶] Gratitude and treachery . . . *Calendar.* (MTP) • ~~Chapter 29.~~ [*short double rule*] ˏ[*short double rule*] Chapter ~~29~~ ˏ28˗. [*short double rule*] [¶] Gratitude and treachery . . . *Calendar.*ˏ [*chapter renumbered in pencil*] (MS Morgan) [TEXTUAL NOTE: *A manuscript leaf in CU-MARK records the composition of this aphorism:* 'Gratitude and treachery are merely the two ~~ends~~ extremities of the same procession. ~~It is time to retire when one has seen the head of it go by.~~ ˏYou have seen all of it that is worth staying for when˗ the band and the ~~official~~ ˏfancy˗ ~~uniforms go by~~ gaudy officials ˏhave˗ go˗ne˗ by.']

168.6   Friday • ~~Thursday~~ ˏFriday˗ (MS Morgan)

168.6   election • elɤection (MS Morgan)

168.9   from • ~~in the~~ from (MS Morgan)

168.9   downpour (MTP) • down- | pour (MS Morgan)

168.9–10   and closed his umbrella and • ˏand˗ closed his umbrella, ˏand˗ (MS Morgan)

168.16   all a-drip • ~~dripp~~ all a-drip (MS Morgan)

168.26   seated herself • ~~sat down~~ ˏseated herself˗ (MS Morgan)

168.34   and her • ~~fro~~ and her (MS Morgan)

169.5   to • to ~~do~~ (MS Morgan)

169.8   [¶] These • ~~Tom ventured [¶] Tom felt straightway better [¶] These closing words should have touched Tom Driscoll, whereas the only effect they had upon him was to remove ◇◇◇◇ the crushing burden of fear that lay upon him and give him a most grateful sense of relief~~ || [¶] These (MS Morgan)

169.9   heavy • ~~paralyzing~~ heavy (MS Morgan)

169.12   a voiceless • ~~an~~ ‸a voiceless‸ (MS Morgan)

169.14   winds, • wind‸,‸s,‸ (MS Morgan)

169.15   The sobs • ~~At last the sobs~~ The sobs (MS Morgan)

169.16   at • ‸at‸ (MS Morgan)

169.17   dat is • dat's‸ ‸is‸ (MS Morgan)

169.19   en den • ~~so~~ en den (MS Morgan)

169.20   bought me • ~~buy me~~ bought me (MS Morgan)

169.21   I'd • I‸'d‸ ~~a~~ (MS Morgan)

169.23   'mongst (MTP) • mongst (MS Morgan)

169.24   han's. • han's‸,‸ (MS Morgan)

169.25   'uz • ~~was~~ 'uz (MS Morgan)

169.26   me de • ~~me tell~~ me de (MS Morgan)

169.27   'uz • ~~was~~ ‸'uz‸ (MS Morgan)

169.34   and • ~~and~~ and (MS Morgan)

169.34   he (MTP) • [*not in*] (MS Morgan)

169.36   right." • right‸."‸~~, perdition catch her!"~~ (MS Morgan)

169.36   He . . . against her. (MTP) • ‸He added a deep | a deep and bitter curse against her.‸ (MS Morgan)

169.38   to Roxana • ‸to Roxana‸ (MS Morgan)

170.2   did • ~~did~~ did (MS Morgan)

170.3   grieving for • ~~feeling for~~ || ‸grieving for‸ (MS Morgan)

170.3   of feeling • ‸of feeling‸ (MS Morgan)

170.8   myself • myse︊f‸l‸f (MS Morgan) [TEXTUAL NOTE: *In revising MS Morgan, SLC altered nine instances of Roxy's* 'myseff' *to read* 'myself' *(and one* 'herseff' *to* 'herself'*). The two instances of* 'myseff' *he left standing are not emended here*]

170.12   was • ~~wuz~~ ‸was‸ (MS Morgan)

170.12   nigger • ‸nigger‸ (MS Morgan)

170.14   workin', • workin‸'‸,‸ (MS Morgan)

170.15   herself • hersef͜lf (MS Morgan)

170.16   gimme enough • ~~give me~~ ˏgimmeˏ ~~enuff~~ enough (MS Morgan)

170.16   a • ạ (MS Morgan)

170.21   all • ˏallˏ (MS Morgan)

170.21   you know, • ˏyou know,ˏ (MS Morgan)

170.22   sk'yerd • ~~scar~~ sk'yerd (MS Morgan)

170.22   roun' (MTP) • 'roun' (MS Morgan)

170.23   took • ~~went a~~ took (MS Morgan)

170.26   myself • mysef͜lf (MS Morgan)

170.28   myself • mysef͜lf (MS Morgan)

170.28   tell • tɟ́ell (MS Morgan)

170.32   *dey* • ~~day~~ *dey* (MS Morgan)

170.33   a body • ~~dey~~ ˏa bodyˏ (MS Morgan)

170.36   it. • it. ~~Is you lis~~ (MS Morgan)

171.2   myself • mysef͜lf (MS Morgan)

171.3   as • ˏasˏ (MS Morgan)

171.4–5 whah dey warn't no town en no woodyard, • ˏwhah dey warn't no town en no woodyard,ˏ (MS Morgan)

171.6   den (MTP) • de (MS Morgan)

171.8   eight • ~~three~~ ˏeightˏ (MS Morgan)

171.8   en • ~~and~~ ˏenˏ (MS Morgan)

171.16   'em (MTP) • em (MS Morgan)

171.18   yo' • yoᴜ' (MS Morgan)

171.25   outside • outsideʹ (MS Morgan) [TEXTUAL NOTE: *SLC canceled the closing single quotation mark, but did not replace it anywhere else; the only plausible place to end Roxy's self-quotation is the end of the sentence*]

171.27   myself, at all.' (MTP) • mysef͜lf/ˏˏat all.ˏ (MS Morgan)

171.27   see. • seeɟ̣ˏ (MS Morgan)

171.30   myself • mysef͜lf (MS Morgan)

171.33   officers; • officers; ~~caze dey 'u~~ (MS Morgan)

171.37   down de river • ˏdown de riverˏ (MS Morgan)

172.2   ketch • ~~ca~~ ketch (MS Morgan)

172.5   it. • it.ˣ (MS Morgan)

172.8   said to me • ~~broadly hinted to me that there is something~~ ~~that the fact that Roxy ran back here instead of to a free State, means that there was something suspicious about that sale.~~ ˏsaid to meˏ (MS Morgan)

172.10   case; • case ˏ~~and said she was a free woman~~ˏ; (MS Morgan)

172.11	looks • ~~seems to mean~~ looks (MS Morgan)
172.13	that • ~~him~~ that (MS Morgan)
172.15	into • into ~~fa trouble.~~ (MS Morgan)
172.22	exposed • ~~showed~~ exposed (MS Morgan)
172.30	noon." • ~~evening."~~ ˌmorning."ˎ ˌnoon."ˎ (MS Morgan)
172.31	noon! • ~~evenin'!~~ ˌmawnin'!ˎ ˌnoon!ˎ (MS Morgan)
172.33	He took it out of his pocket. • ˌHe took it out of his pocket.ˎ (MS Morgan)
172.36	with • ~~but w~~ with (MS Morgan)
172.37	handbill had • ~~bill had~~ handbill had (MS Morgan)
173.2	and named • and ~~some other particulars~~ named (MS Morgan)
173.19	sk'yerd (MTP) • s'kyerd (MS Morgan)
173.20	dese • ~~b~~ dese (MS Morgan)
173.25	roun', scasely. • roun'ˌ, scaselyˌ. (MS Morgan)
173.26	alley ever • ~~of a do',~~ ˌalleyˎ ~~waiti~~ ˌeverˎ (MS Morgan)
173.30	arternoon. • arternoon.ᶠ (MS Morgan)
173.33	"No • ~~Ro~~ "No (MS Morgan)
173.37	he • ~~that~~ he (MS Morgan)
174.1	"You's lyin' agin, sho'." Then she (MTP) • ~~"I reckon y~~ "You's lyin' aginˌ, sho'ˎ. ~~When~~ *did* ~~he give you de bill? [¶] "Tuesday morning." [¶] Roxana~~ ˌThen sheˎ (MS Morgan)
174.3–4	run off, 'stid o' stayin' here to • ~~didn't stay~~ ˌrun off, 'stid o' stayin'ˎ here ~~en~~ ˌtoˎ (MS Morgan)
174.4	know • ~~suspicion~~ ˌknowˎ (MS Morgan)
174.9	set • ~~lay~~ ˌsetˎ (MS Morgan)
174.11	him • ~~him ˌany longerˎ now,— he~~ him (MS Morgan)
174.19	wuthless • wuthless [*the* 'u' *is dotted as if it were an* 'i'] (MS Morgan)
174.19	hide. *Would* • hide. ˌ□ *Would* [SLC *inserted the square symbol indicating an em quad, the normal space of one em following a sentence period*] (MS Morgan)
174.24	till • tₑ̷ill (MS Morgan)
174.25	agin • agaᵢin (MS Morgan)
174.29	gamblin' (MTP) • gamblin (MS Morgan)
174.35	go to him, • ~~do it,~~ ˌgo to him,ˎ (MS Morgan)
174.36	b'lieve • bₑ̷'lieve (MS Morgan)
174.36	it. • it.ᶠ (MS Morgan)
174.37	myself • myseᶠˌlˎf (MS Morgan)
174.38	it." • it." Ƭ (MS Morgan)

175.3   clear • ~~get~~ clear (MS Morgan)

175.4   Roxy • Ro̸xy (MS Morgan)

175.5   key, honey. • key⌄, honey⌄. (MS Morgan)

175.5   cle'r up • ~~worry~~ clea̸'r up (MS Morgan)

175.11   Gwyne • Ɣ Gwyne (MS Morgan)

175.12   yo' • yo̸u' (MS Morgan)

175.15–16 nex' Tuesday, or maybe Wednesday. • ~~Monday or~~ ⌄nex'⌄ Tuesday/, ⌄or maybe Wednesday.⌄ (MS Morgan)

175.17   Tom • " Tom (MS Morgan)

175.19   "En • ~~"En you tell him I'll be in~~ [¶] "En (MS Morgan)

175.23   den • den ['n' *has an extra minim*] (MS Morgan)

175.27   myself • myse̸⌄l f (MS Morgan)

175.32   Shet • ~~Move along~~ Shet (MS Morgan)

175.34   straggler • straggle̸d'r (MS Morgan)

175.36   mile • mile ~~in~~ (MS Morgan)

177.1   *Chapter 29* (MTP) • Chapter ~~30.~~ ⌄29.⌄ [*short triple rule*] [¶] "Whosoever looketh upon a woman," etc., is a principle which cannot be restricted to one class of offences, but naturally extends itself to the whole list of crimes, murder included. Considered in this way, murder ~~is~~ ⌄nearly,⌄ ~~as common as lying, and fully as~~ ⌄is as⌄ common ⌄as lying⌄. Most people have committed it in their hearts, and would have committed it with their hands if the opportunity had offered itself at the exact moment when the passion of anger was at its supremest. It sounds extravagant, but it is true⌄,. ~~nevertheless.⌄~~ If all were hanged to-day who had ever committed murder in their hearts, the globe would be but a pin-cushion of gallows frames ⌄when the sun went down⌄.—*Pudd'nhead Wilson's Calendar.* (MS in CU-MARK, *removed by SLC from MS Morgan*); Chapter 29. [*short triple rule*] || ~~Chapter 30.~~ [*short double rule*] ['Chapter 29.' *and triple rule in pencil*] (MS Morgan)

177.9–13 He took . . . speaking terms. • ~~The~~ ⌄He took his exercise after eleven at night, when ⌄OVER⌄ [*on verso:*] the streets were empty. Luigi was sick of society too, for the present, so this nocturnal arrangement suited him perfectly, though he did not say so, since he and his brother were still not on speaking terms.⌄ (MS Morgan)

177.14   reposeful • ~~quiet~~ reposeful (MS Morgan)

177.15   Sunday • ~~Monday~~ Sunday (MS Morgan)

177.25   and inferences • ~~to be~~ and inferences (MS Morgan)

177.29   and his wife were past middle age • ~~was fifty-three~~ and his wife ~~forty-eight years old~~ ⌄were past middle age⌄ (MS Morgan)

177.30   a • a̸ (MS Morgan)

177.30 instinct • ~~love~~ instinct (MS Morgan)

178.6 into • into [*SLC deleted a dot over the* 'n'] (MS Morgan)

178.8 personal • ~~the old gentleman's~~ personal (MS Morgan)

178.15 childless • ₍childless₎ (MS Morgan)

178.16 hearts • ~~hearts when death has snatched away their~~ | ~~hearts to appease the~~ hearts (MS Morgan)

178.17 parrots and a jackass-voiced macaw • parrots ₍and₎ a jackass-voiced macaw₍.₎ (MS Morgan)

178.17 hundred • hundr₍e₎d (MS Morgan)

178.18 song-birds (MTP) • song- | birds (MS Morgan)

178.18 fetid • ₍fetid₎ (MS Morgan)

178.20 filings, so to speak, (MTP) • filings,~~◊◊◊◊~~ ₍so to speak,₎ [*the comma after* 'filings' *seems to have been wiped out, but it is necessary;* 'so to speak' *written over a wiped-out interlined word which has not been recovered*] (MS Morgan)

178.24 by • ~~at his~~ by (MS Morgan)

178.24 bullet • bullet~~s~~ (MS Morgan)

178.27–31 [¶] As Wilson . . . veiled moonlight. • ~~[¶] He took an Allen "pepper-box" out of the pocket of his~~ ~~dus~~ ~~linen duster, and Wilson said that that would do; that it was an instrument that always got some~~ || ~~body, ₍game,₎ though not often the person~~ ₍game₎ ~~required.~~ ₍OVER.₎ ₍OVER₎ [*on verso:*] ~~Then he added:~~ ₍[¶] As Wilson was leaving, he said—₎ ₍[¶]₎ "The Judge is a little used up by ~~the~~ his campaign work, and will not get out for a day or so, but when he does get out you want to be on the alert." | ~~over again~~ [¶] About eleven at night Luigi went out for exercise, and started on a long stroll in the veiled moonlight. | ₍over again₎ (MS Morgan)

178.32 Dawson's, (MTP) • Dawson's (MS Morgan)

178.33 just about half an hour earlier, • ~~at two o'clock that morning,~~ ₍just₎ about half an hour earlier,₍ (MS Morgan)

178.35 either • ₍either₎ (MS Morgan)

178.35 roof. • roof. ~~He brought bread and cheese with him for a siege.~~ He (MS Morgan)

178.37 and hat, • ₍and hat,₎ (MS Morgan)

179.1 his face with a burnt cork and put the cork in his pocket. • ~~the white-glazed bottom of a queensware saucer with candle smoke, and disguised his face with~~ ~~a window-sash pattern of smut~~ ~~a coating of this smut, using his finger as a brush.~~ ₍his face with ₍a₎ burnt cork and put the cork in his pocket.₎ (MS Morgan)

179.2 bedroom (MTP) • bed- | room (MS Morgan)

179.4   He • H̶i̶s̶ He (MS Morgan)

179.6   caught • caught i̶n̶ (MS Morgan)

179.7   armed. • armed. B̶u̶t̶ ̶h̶e̶ ̶h̶a̶d̶ ̶n̶o̶ (MS Morgan)

179.9   narrow • s̶t̶a̶i̶r̶ narrow (MS Morgan)

179.9   his hair • a̶t̶ his his hair (MS Morgan)

179.17   cash-box, closed • cash-box̶e̶d̶ˌ closed (MS Morgan)

179.18   The safe-door was not open. • ˌThe safe-door was not open.ˌ (MS Morgan)

179.20   the • h̶i̶s̶ the (MS Morgan)

179.25   reached • a̶n̶d̶ reached (MS Morgan)

179.25   seized (MTP) • siezed (MS Morgan)

179.30   fly; transferred them to his left hand and seized (MTP) • fly,; s̶i̶e̶z̶i̶n̶g̶ ˌtransferred them to his left hand and siezedˌ (MS Morgan)

179.31–32 but remembered . . . with him. • a̶n̶d̶ ̶a̶g̶a̶i̶n̶ ̶d̶r̶o̶p̶p̶i̶n̶g̶ ̶i̶t̶. ˌOVERˌ ̶O̶V̶E̶R̶ˌ [on verso:] but remembered himself and t̶h̶r̶e̶w̶ flung it from him, as being a dangerous witness to carry away with him. (MS Morgan)

179.32   He • A̶s̶ ̶h̶e̶ ̶w̶a̶t̶c̶h̶e̶d̶ ̶h̶i̶s̶ He (MS Morgan)

179.34   by the • by ⱥ the (MS Morgan)

179.35   and the • and h̶i̶s̶ the (MS Morgan)

179.38   the room-door • t̶h̶e̶ ̶d̶o̶o̶r̶ the room-door (MS Morgan)

180.4   his • a̶n̶d̶ ̶h̶ⱥ̶i̶s̶ˌ w̶a̶s̶ ̶n̶o̶t̶ (MS Morgan)

180.6   a dozen • t̶w̶o̶ ̶o̶r̶ ̶h̶a̶l̶f̶ ̶a̶ ̶d̶o̶z̶e̶n̶ a dozen (MS Morgan)

180.6   were • were w̶e̶r̶e̶ (MS Morgan)

180.7   accessions were still • m̶o̶r̶e̶ ̶w̶e̶r̶e̶ ˌaccessions were still ˌ (MS Morgan)

180.8   As Tom, quaking as with a palsy, • T̶o̶m̶ ̶w̶a̶l̶k̶e̶d̶ ̶a̶l̶o̶n̶g̶ ̶t̶h̶e̶ ̶l̶a̶n̶e̶ [¶] As Tomˌ, quaking as with a palsy,ˌ (MS Morgan)

180.12   thing • ˌthingˌ (MS Morgan)

180.13   took off • r̶e̶m̶o̶v̶e̶d̶ took off (MS Morgan)

180.15   it • Ø̶Ø̶ it (MS Morgan)

180.17–18 burned his male and female attire to ashes, • h̶i̶d̶ ̶h̶i̶s̶ ˌburned hisˌ male and female attire i̶n̶ ̶t̶h̶e̶ ̶c̶r̶a̶z̶y̶ ̶a̶t̶t̶i̶c̶,̶ ˌto ashes,ˌ (MS Morgan)

180.23   St. (MTP) • St (MS Morgan)

180.25–26 there's not a vestige of a clew left in the world; • ˌthere's not a vestige of a clew left in the world;ˌ (MS Morgan)

180.28   In • In t̶h̶e̶ (MS Morgan)

180.28   papers— • papers⸝—ˌ(MS Morgan)

180.31   about midnight • l̶a̶s̶t̶ ̶t̶o̶ˌ ˌabout mid-ˌnight (MS Morgan)

180.35 us. • us. ~~If it hadn't been~~ (MS Morgan)

180.37 knife. I take it back, now." • knife." ˌI take it back, now."ˌ (MS Morgan)

181.1 now rich and independent. • ˌnowˌ rich and independentˌ, ~~now.~~ (MS Morgan)

181.2 and mailed to Wilson • ~~and sent~~ and mailed ˌto Wilsonˌ (MS Morgan)

181.2 Roxana • ~~Rowena~~ ˌRoxanaˌ [*alteration in pencil*] (MS Morgan)

181.2 herself • her- | ~~self; but he got the planter to put on the superscription and the "to be kept until she calls for it~~ || self (MS Morgan)

181.3 telegraphed • ~~waited~~ telegraphed (MS Morgan)

181.8 and • ~~and cleared~~ and (MS Morgan)

181.10 but • ~~and charged the sheriff to watch over the Twins and be responsible for~~ || but (MS Morgan)

181.13 trial. • trial. ˌ~~But he took it privately for granted thatˌ~~ (MS Morgan)

181.14 thoroughly. • thoroughlyˌ,ˌ (MS Morgan)

181.15 Wilson • ~~He~~ ˌWilsonˌ (MS Morgan)

181.15 finger-prints (MTP) • finger- | prints (MS Morgan)

181.16 knife handle (MTP) • knife-handle (MS Morgan)

181.18 blood-stains (MTP) • blood- | stains (MS Morgan)

181.21 mysterious • ˌmysteriousˌ (MS Morgan)

181.24 suggested • ~~made~~ suggested (MS Morgan)

181.25 nothing, of course. • nothing, of ~~importance, but Wilson found the blackened saucer on a shelf and asked the coroner to take it into his keeping and not let the finger marks on it get rubbed. They might not be of consequence; still, one~~ nobody could be sure of that. ~~[¶] Before the coroner's jury, and afterwards~~ ˌcourse.ˌ (MS Morgan)

181.32 examined • ~~found that~~ ˌexaminedˌ (MS Morgan)

181.32 finger-marks (MTP) • finger- | marks (MS Morgan)

181.32–33 handle, and said to himself, • handleˌ, ~~and those on the blackened saucer corresponded.~~ ˌand said to himself,ˌ (MS Morgan)

181.33 "Neither • ˌ"Neither (MS Morgan)

181.33 marks." Then manifestly • marks.ˌ."ˌ; ~~his glass records proved that to his satisfaction. Plainly~~ ˌThen manifestlyˌ (MS Morgan)

182.4 There • ~~He~~ There (MS Morgan)

182.6 mysterious • ˌmysteriousˌ (MS Morgan)

182.10 finger-marks of • finger-marks ~~on~~ ˌofˌ (MS Morgan)

182.10 handle; and • handleˌ; and ~~the saucer-bottom; and~~ (MS Morgan)

182.11 finger-prints (MTP) • finger- | prints (MS Morgan)

182.12   during • ~~in~~ during (MS Morgan)

182.13   withstood • ~~de~~ withstood (MS Morgan)

182.14   knife. • knife͜ ~~and the saucer.~~ (MS Morgan)

182.20   claimed that • ~~said~͜ claimed that͜ (MS Morgan)

182.25   Wilson refused • ~~It did not occur to~~ Wilson ͜refused͜ (MS Morgan)

182.26   secondly • secon~l~dly (MS Morgan)

182.27   wouldn't • ¢ wouldn't (MS Morgan)

182.27   doting benefactor • ~~nearest rela-~~ ͜bene͜ doting benefactor (MS Morgan)

182.27–28 self-interest was in the way; for • ͜self-interest was in the way; for͜ (MS Morgan)

182.28   was sure of • ~~had~͜ was sure of͜ (MS Morgan)

182.30   true • true͜, (MS Morgan)

182.31   talky • ͜talky͜ (MS Morgan)

182.32   St. (MTP) • St (MS Morgan)

182.33–34 journals, as was shown by his telegram to his aunt. • journals͜,͜ as was shown by his telegram to his aunt.͜ (MS Morgan)

183.3   the Twins • the~m͜ Twins͜ (MS Morgan)

183.3   discovery • ~~finding~~ discovery (MS Morgan)

183.12   finger-marks (MTP) • finger- | marks (MS Morgan)

183.13   did • ~~never~~ did (MS Morgan)

183.19   an • an ~p~ (MS Morgan)

183.21   a • ~~an~~ a (MS Morgan)

183.21   although • ~~but~~ although (MS Morgan)

184.1   *Chapter 30* (MTP) • Chapter 3~1~Q. [*short triple rule*] [*alteration in pencil*] (MS Morgan)

184.4   pencil, • pencil͜, ['l' *rewritten to eliminate an extra minim*] (MS Morgan)

184.8   [¶] The • [*centered:*] ~~Chapter~~ [*short double rule*] [¶] The (MS Morgan)

184.8–9 no friend . . . aunties, and • ~~and~͜ no friend visiting the ~m~ jailed Twins but their counsel and the two old aunties, and͜ (MS Morgan)

184.12   unquestionably • ¢ unquestionably (MS Morgan)

184.13   at • ~~most prob-~~ | at (MS Morgan)

184.17   only in • ~in~͜ only ͜in͜ (MS Morgan)

184.17   but in • but ͜in͜ (MS Morgan)

184.21   their • ~~his~͜ their͜ (MS Morgan)

184.23   Aunt (MTP) • aunt (MS Morgan)

184.23   Aunt (MTP) • aunt (MS Morgan)

184.24 Chambers; also • ˌChambers; also˛ (MS Morgan)

184.25 and she • ~~and she~~ || and she (MS Morgan)

184.27 grateful to • grateful ~~fo~~ to (MS Morgan)

184.31 so • ~~and~~ ˌso˛ (MS Morgan)

184.31 hated • ~~shouldn't~~ hated (MS Morgan)

185.1 him • ˌhim˛ (MS Morgan)

185.5 you!" • you!" ˌHere insert 339½˛ (MS Morgan) [TEXTUAL NOTE: *SLC's directive calls for the insertion of one new leaf numbered 339½; this was done by cutting the leaf originally numbered 339 (final numbering 570) in half, then interposing a new leaf numbered 339½. Later, the two halves of the original leaf 339 were "filled out" to normal leaf size using portions of one or more discarded leaves from MS Morgan. The one grafted onto the top half of 339 bears the text, canceled in pencil: '[¶] ~~A person who travels by relays, thinking to get to heaven quicker that way~~'. The second half of original 339 was then renumbered 572*]

185.6 sketched • ~~out~~ sketched (MS Morgan)

185.7 circumstantial • ˌcircumstantial˛ (MS Morgan)

185.8 committed • ~~that the mu~~ committed (MS Morgan)

185.9 desire • ~~cowa~~ desire (MS Morgan)

185.17 accused, now • ~~guilty, now~~ accused, now (MS Morgan)

185.22 Witness • Witness (MS Morgan) [TEXTUAL NOTE: *The text beginning at 'Witness' is from the lower part of the bisected leaf originally numbered 339, final numbering 572. The stub has been "filled out" to normal leaf size by grafting onto it portions of one or more discarded leaves from MS Morgan. The one grafted onto the present stub bears the canceled text: '~~letter of his reform. He had three hundred dollars left. It was agreed between him and his mother that he should put that safely away, and add her half of it~~ his pension to it monthly, ~~until~~ In two years this fund ~~would buy her free again~~'*]

185.22 State • ~~p~~ State (MS Morgan)

185.22 and • ˌand˛ (MS Morgan)

185.30 room when those dismal words were repeated. • room. ˌwhen those dismal words were repeated.˛ [*period after 'room' implicitly deleted*] (MS Morgan)

185.31 rose and • ˌrose and˛ (MS Morgan)

185.34 at this bar with murder; • ˌat this bar˛ with murder; ~~at this bar;~~ (MS Morgan)

185.35 significantly, (MTP) • significantly (MS Morgan)

185.36 him • himˌ (MS Morgan)

185.37   that he must • ~~to~~ ˏthat he mustˏ (MS Morgan)

186.2   getting • ~~gro~~ getting (MS Morgan)

186.9   down and sobbed. • down ˏandˏ sobbedˏ. (MS Morgan)

186.16   blood-stains (MTP) • blood stains (MS Morgan)

186.17–20   [¶] Confirmatory evidence . . . a few minor • ~~The finding of the knife was~~ ~~verified,~~ OVERˏ ~~with some other~~ OVERˏ [*on verso:*] [*centered, encircled:*] ⚡ [¶] Confirmatory evidence followed, from Rogers and Buckstone. [¶] The finding of the knife was verified, | ~~over again~~ | [*centered, encircled:*] ⚡ | the advertisement minutely describing it and offering a reward for it was put in evidence, and its exact correspondence with that description proven. Then followed a few minor | run to 343ˏ (MS Morgan)

186.23   Driscoll's • Driscol~~lł~~'s (MS Morgan)

186.24   cries • ~~murder~~ cries (MS Morgan)

186.28   be • b~~ŕ~~e (MS Morgan)

186.33   a • ~~an~~ a (MS Morgan)

187.2   of records and • ~~and~~ ˏof records andˏ (MS Morgan)

187.10   strips • ~~squares~~ ˏstripsˏ (MS Morgan)

187.13   this • ~~your new~~ this (MS Morgan)

187.25   strip • ~~square~~ ˏstripˏ (MS Morgan)

187.27   I • ˏ~~it appears that~~ˏ I (MS Morgan)

187.29   thumb-print (MTP) • thumb- | print (MS Morgan)

187.29–30   and Tom held out the piece of glass to Wilson. • ˏand Tom held out the ~~square to Wilson. Wilson.~~ ˏpiece of glass to Wilson.ˏˏ (MS Morgan)

187.31   cut or a scratch, • cut, ˏor a scratch,ˏ (MS Morgan)

187.32   usually"—and he took the strip of glass indifferently • usuallyˏ"—[¶] ~~Tom was holding it out to him~~ ˏand he tookˏ ~~the piece~~ ˏthe stripˏ of glass ˏindifferentlyˏ (MS Morgan)

187.34   suddenly • ˏsuddenlyˏ (MS Morgan)

187.34   face, • faceˏ,ˏ (MS Morgan)

188.1–2   shuddering from him and • ~~away and~~ ˏshuddering from him andˏ (MS Morgan)

188.3   no! • noˏ,ˏ! (MS Morgan)

188.8   Tom • ~~he~~ ˏTomˏ (MS Morgan)

188.13   a few minutes before • ˏa few minutes beforeˏ (MS Morgan)

188.14–15   handle, there being no need of that—for his trained eye— • ~~handle. He~~ ~~knew they would tally without that~~ | handle, ˏthere being no need of that—for his trained eye—ˏ (MS Morgan)

188.16   was! • wasˏ,ˏ! (MS Morgan)

188.18 the plate containing • ‸the plate containing‸ (MS Morgan)

188.19 marks • ~~one~~ marks (MS Morgan)

188.19 Tom's • ~~his~~ ‸Tom's‸ (MS Morgan)

188.20–22 months, and placed these two plates with the one containing this subject's newly (and unconsciously) made record. • months‸,‸ ‸OVER‸ [*on
verso:*] ‸and placed these two plates with the one containing this sub-
ject's newly ~~made record. (and unin~~ (and unconsciously) made record. |
over again‸ (MS Morgan)

188.22 series is • ~~record is~~ ‸series is‸ (MS Morgan)

188.22 said with satisfaction, • said‸,‸ ‸with satisfaction,‸ (MS Morgan)

188.24 [¶] But • ¶ But (MS Morgan)

188.25 strips, • ‸~~squares,~~‸ ‸strips,‸ (MS Morgan)

188.26 out • out‸,‸ (MS Morgan)

188.29 plates. • plates‸.‸ ~~and two flakes of white tissue paper—these latter had
red markings on them.~~ (MS Morgan)

188.32 tally. I • tally‸,‸ ~~of course. I~~ ‸I‸ (MS Morgan)

188.37 slept through • ~~slept like the dead~~ slept ‸away‸ ‸through‸ (MS Morgan)

188.37 unconsciousness • ‸unconsciousness‸ (MS Morgan)

188.38 away • away‸,‸ (MS Morgan)

189.4 seized (MTP) • siezed (MS Morgan)

189.6 years • years ~~and more~~ (MS Morgan)

190.1 *Chapter 31* [¶] He is useless . . . *Calendar.* (MTP) • ~~Chapter 32.~~ [*short
triple rule*] ‸Chapter ~~32.~~ ‸31.‸ [*short triple rule*] ‸[¶] He is useless on top
of the ground; he ought to be under it, ~~inspiring~~ ‸fertilizing‸ ‸inspir-
ing‸ ‸inspiring‸ the cabbages.—*Pudd'nhead Wilson's Calendar.*‸ ['32.'
altered to '31.' in pencil]* (MS Morgan)

190.8 "records," • ~~finger~~ | "records," (MS Morgan)

190.9 ten • ~~five~~ ‸ten‸ (MS Morgan)

190.9 his • ~~a~~ ‸his‸ (MS Morgan)

190.9 did • ~~made~~ ‸did‸ (MS Morgan)

190.9 enlargements • ~~reproductions~~ ‸enlargements‸ (MS Morgan)

190.10 line • ‸line‸ (MS Morgan)

190.11 or curves or • ~~and~~ ‸or‸ curves ~~and~~ ‸or‸ (MS Morgan)

190.13 collection of • ‸collection of‸ (MS Morgan)

190.14–15 times, they resembled the markings of a block of wood that has been
sawed across the grain, and • times, ‸OVER‸ [*on verso:*] ‸they resembled
the markings of a block of wood that has been sawed across the grain,
and | over again‸ (MS Morgan) [TEXTUAL NOTE: *Before the verso of this*

leaf was used for this insertion, it bore a brief text: '[¶] Such of us as have
lived fifty years'. *This is the beginning of an early form of the aphorism
SLC would revise as the motto for chapter 3; a separate manuscript leaf
in CU-MARK records its evolution, with various uncanceled alternative
phrases:* 'Whosoever has lived ~~forty~~ ˌfiftyˌ years [*written above as alter-
nate:* 'lives long enough to find out what this world is, realizes how'] has ˌfound out.ˌ ~~learned to say, deep down in his secret heart,~~ know and
feel ˌbows his head in gratˌitudeˌeful homageˌ when the name of Adam ~~is
our first benefactor is uttered.ˌ how deep a debt of gratitude we owe our
first benefactor, Adam. He brought death into the world.'*]

190.20 several • ~~a goodly pile of~~ ˌseveralˌ (MS Morgan)

190.23 o'clock • o'clockˌ (MS Morgan)

190.24 twelve • ~~five~~ ˌtwelveˌ (MS Morgan)

190.24–28 later, with . . . expense." Wilson • laterˌ,ˌ with his "records."ˌ HeˌOVERˌ
[*on verso:*] ˌTom Driscoll ˌcaught ~~sight~~ ˌa slight glimpseˌ of the records
andˌ nudged his nearest ~~fam~~ friend and said, with a wink, "Pudd'nhead's
got a rare eye to business—thinks that as long as he can't win his case, it's
at least a noble good chance to advertise his palace-window decorations
without any expense." Wilson | over againˌ (MS Morgan)

190.30 said • saidˌ/ˌ (MS Morgan)

190.30 probably • ˌprobablyˌ (MS Morgan)

191.1 An • Aⱷn (MS Morgan)

191.3 testimony,—and • testimony, ~~and~~ ˌ—andˌ (MS Morgan)

191.4 that • ~~with~~ that (MS Morgan)

191.6 justification • justifica-ˌtion.ˌ | tion (MS Morgan)

191.6 its • ~~that~~ its (MS Morgan)

191.9 preliminary • ˌpreliminaryˌ (MS Morgan)

191.9 words. (MTP) • words." ˌHere insert 357A and B.ˌ (MS Morgan) [TEX-
TUAL NOTE: *SLC's directive calls for the insertion of two pages of text; this
was done by bisecting the leaf originally numbered 357 (final numbering
591) and placing between the two halves the leaves originally numbered
357A–357B. The upper part of original leaf 357 has been joined to part of
a leaf headed '266', which is fragmentary; it happens to preserve several
drafts of the passage in which Rowena dies, all struck through in pencil:*
(Substitute this for closing ¶ on 266: [*rule*] [¶] These were indeed sad
days for Angelo. On the Fourth, ˌamong other things,ˌ Rowena went out
back to see the fireworks and fell down the well and got drowned. [¶] On
Independence day Rowena went out back to see the fireworks and fell
down the well and got drowned. But it is no matter; these things cannot be
helped. ~~She is better off, and we are all better off.~~ | and started out back and
fell down stairs, ~~sustaining injuries which resulted~~ and broke her neck.]

191.11   claim • ~~came~~ ˌclaimˌ (MS Morgan)

191.13   hand • *hand⁄* (MS Morgan)

191.13   *finger-prints* (MTP) • *finger- | prints* (MS Morgan)

191.17   such an • such ~~a startling~~ ˌanˌ (MS Morgan)

191.20   judge (MTP) • Judge (MS Morgan)

191.29   place." • place." | ~~Go back to 357. Run to 358~~ (MS Morgan)

191.30   hardy • ~~chance~~ hardy (MS Morgan)

191.34   certain • ~~all the~~ ˌcertainˌ (MS Morgan)

191.37   accused • accused | ~~Run to 357A and B~~ || [*the recto of the next leaf is blank except for its page number, 594; on verso, all struck through in pencil:* [¶] ~~We approach our Creator nearer in our~~ in the satisfaction which ~~we get out of contemplating the works of our hands than in any other way, perhaps. But we~~ ~~exaggerate;~~ ˌsurpass our modelˌ ~~in one detail; for our works are small and our adjectives large, whereas~~ when ~~h~~He looks abroad over his ~~soaring~~ multitudinous array of solar systems a one-syllable word serves him for a verdict, whereas we exhaust the ~~dictionary~~ vocabulary ~~of epith~~ complimentary epithet when we catch a stranger and show him ~~the village.~~ ['h' *triple-underscored to capitalize*] (MS Morgan)

192.9   had had • ˌhadˌ had (MS Morgan)

192.17   fraud; that • fraud⁄; ~~Th~~ that (MS Morgan)

192.18   memorable and • ˌmemorable andˌ (MS Morgan)

192.19   knife • knife, (MS Morgan)

192.19   that very • th⁄at very (MS Morgan)

192.20   living • ˌlivingˌ (MS Morgan)

192.20   found • ˌfoundˌ (MS Morgan)

192.20   slaughtered (MTP) • slaugtered (MS Morgan)

192.22   which fixes • ~~and fix~~ ˌwhich fixesˌ (MS Morgan)

192.25   mentioned • mentioned ~~where~~ (MS Morgan)

192.36   veiled • ~~p~~ veiled (MS Morgan)

193.2   "It (MTP) • 'It (MS Morgan)

193.3   hit." (MTP) • hit.' (MS Morgan)

193.5   cash-box (MTP) • cash- | box (MS Morgan)

193.8–9 night—if . . . of course; • night⁄ ~~—if~~ ˌ—if he had that habit, which I do not assert⁄ˌ, of course;ˌˌ (MS Morgan)

193.9   while • ~~but made a noise and~~ while (MS Morgan)

193.10   was • ~~had~~ ˌwasˌ (MS Morgan)

193.10   seized (MTP) • siezed (MS Morgan)

193.11   fled • ~~had to fly~~ ˌfledˌ (MS Morgan)

193.13 my • ‸my‸ (MS Morgan)

193.14–15 took up several of his strips of glass • ~~began to take the wrappings from some boxes; from the boxes he began to take squares~~ ‸took up‸ ‸several of‸ his strips‸ of glass (MS Morgan)

193.18 relieving and refreshing • ~~uncontrollable~~ ‸relieving and refreshing‸ (MS Morgan)

193.18 the fun • ~~it~~ ‸the fun‸ (MS Morgan)

193.24 being • ‸being‸ (MS Morgan)

193.26 These • ~~It is~~ These (MS Morgan)

193.27 so to speak, and this autograph • ~~and~~ ‸so to speak, and this autograph‸ (MS Morgan)

193.28 nor can he disguise it or hide it away, • ‸nor can he disguise it or hide it‸ away,‸ (MS Morgan)

193.28 the • ~~w~~ the (MS Morgan)

193.30 fall out; • ~~whiten, or fall out, or be disguised under a wig;~~ ‸fall out;‸ (MS Morgan)

193.31 height, • height, ~~or his form,~~ (MS Morgan)

193.32 also, • ‸also,‸ (MS Morgan)

193.33 swarming • ‸swarming‸ (MS Morgan)

193.35 delicate • ‸delicate‸ (MS Morgan)

193.35 with • ~~whi~~ with (MS Morgan)

193.38 curving • ‸curving‸ (MS Morgan)

194.1–2 clearly defined patterns • ‸clearly defined‸ pat~~t~~erns (MS Morgan)

194.4 hand up • ~~palm~~ ‸hand‸ up, (MS Morgan)

194.5 fingers • ~~fingers.] The patterns on the right hand are not the same~~ fingers (MS Morgan)

194.6 "Why ... before!" • ~~"~~'Why ... before!'‸ (MS Morgan) [TEXTUAL NOTE: *SLC, forgetting that he had already closed Wilson's speech, mistakenly altered these double quotation marks to single; also at 194.7 and 194.13–14*]

194.6 on • ~~of~~ on (MS Morgan)

194.7 "Why • ~~"~~'Why (MS Morgan)

194.7 too!" • too!'‸ (MS Morgan)

194.10 patterns • ~~mar~~ patterns (MS Morgan)

194.11 One • ~~The a◊r◊~~ One (MS Morgan)

194.12 the jury • ~~as~~ the jury (MS Morgan)

194.13 rule." • rule." – (MS Morgan)

194.16 twin • ~~pair of~~ twin~~s~~ (MS Morgan)

194.17   mysterious and • ˏmysterious andˏ (MS Morgan)

194.17   autograph! *That* • autograph!⟋ *t̸That* (MS Morgan)

194.18   personate • ~~impose himself upon you~~ | ~~deceive you.~~ | personate (MS Morgan)

194.21   slouching • ˏslouchingˏ (MS Morgan)

194.23   complete • ~~accumulate~~ complete (MS Morgan)

194.27   said, • said, ~~in grave and level tones~~ (MS Morgan)

194.28   assassin's natal autograph, • ˏassassin'sˏ natal autograph, of (MS Morgan)

194.31   crimson sign"— • ~~sign~~ crimson sign"—ᵖ (MS Morgan)

194.31–32 pendulum swinging back and forth—"and • ~~wall—"and~~ ˏpendulum swinging back and forth—"andˏ (MS Morgan)

194.34   Stunned • ~~The~~ Stunned (MS Morgan)

194.34   unconscious • unconscịous (MS Morgan)

194.37   stole • ~~resumed:~~ stole ∅ (MS Morgan)

195.2   cruel • ~~foul and~~ cruel (MS Morgan)

195.10   finger-prints (MTP) • finger- | prints (MS Morgan)

195.15   [The interest of the audience was steadily deepening, now.] • ˏ[The interest of the audience was steadily deepening, now.]ˏ (MS Morgan)

195.18   back, now, • backˏ, now,ˏ (MS Morgan)

195.19   then • ˏthenˏ (MS Morgan)

195.20   finger-marks (MTP) • finger- | marks (MS Morgan)

195.21   experimenters • experimentø̸ers (MS Morgan)

195.21   will • ~~will shall~~ ˏwillˏ (MS Morgan)

195.23–25 before—for . . . tested twice." • beforeˏ." (OVERˏ [*on verso:*] ˏ—for . . . tested twice." | over againˏ (MS Morgan)

195.28   them,—the • them,— ~~like~~ the (MS Morgan)

195.32   right; • right⟋; (MS Morgan)

195.36   certainly • ˏcertainlyˏ (MS Morgan)

196.1   [Applause.] (MTP) • [*Applause.*] (MS Morgan)

196.2   [Applause.] (MTP) • [*Applause.*] (MS Morgan)

196.2   [Applause.] (MTP) • [*Applause.*] (MS Morgan)

196.3   [Applause.] (MTP) • ˏ[*Applause.*]ˏ (MS Morgan)

196.4   finger-print (MTP) • finger- | print (MS Morgan)

196.8   and struggling to see, • ˏand struggling to see,ˏ (MS Morgan)

196.14   finger-marks (MTP) • finger- | marks (MS Morgan)

196.17   They, too, exactly copy each other, • Theyˏ, ~~are alike,~~ ˏtoo, exactly copy each other,ˏ (MS Morgan)

196.18–19 presently, but . . . now. • presently,/₂ [¶] " ˏbut we will turn them face down, now.ˏ (MS Morgan)

196.20 Here, • Here, ~~now~~ (MS Morgan)

196.20 two persons • ~~pers~~ two persons (MS Morgan)

196.24 tell • tell ~~me~~ (MS Morgan)

196.24 if • ø if (MS Morgan)

196.24–25 He passed . . . the foreman. • ˏHe passed a powerful magnifying glass to the foreman.ˏ (MS Morgan)

196.26 and the glass • ˏand the glassˏ (MS Morgan)

196.27 said • said⫫ (MS Morgan)

196.27 judge (MTP) • Judge (MS Morgan)

196.30–31 one and compare it searchingly, by the magnifier, • one, and compare it searchinglyˏ, by the magnifier,ˏ (MS Morgan)

196.31 knife handle (MTP) • knife-handle (MS Morgan)

196.34 *"We find . . . your honor."* • *"We find . . . your honor."* [*underscore apparently blotted and redrawn*] (MS Morgan)

196.37 court • ⸮ court (MS Morgan)

197.2 finger-prints (MTP) • finger- | prints (MS Morgan)

197.4 all movement • ~~min~~ all movement (MS Morgan)

197.5 ceased, • ceased, ~~in~~ (MS Morgan)

197.5 an • ~~a suspense that was strained~~ an (MS Morgan)

197.7 *even* • *ˏevenˏ* (MS Morgan)

197.7 a • ~~The pent~~ a (MS Morgan)

197.10 along • ~~by~~ along (MS Morgan)

197.10 assemblage • ~~publ~~ assemblage (MS Morgan)

197.11 nor • ̣nor (MS Morgan)

197.12 become • becomeꜱ́ (MS Morgan)

197.13 gravely, • gravely,⫫ (MS Morgan)

197.14–15 them." [Another . . . promptly checked.] "We • them."ˏ *OVER*ˏ [*on verso:*] ˏ[Another outbreak of applause began, but was promptly checked.] | over againˏ [*on recto:*] "We (MS Morgan)

197.23 eight months, • ~~twelve years of age,~~ ˏeight months,ˏ (MS Morgan)

197.25 surprised • ˏsurprisedˏ (MS Morgan)

197.27 pantagraphs • pantagraphs, (MS Morgan)

197.30 eight months • ~~seven mont~~ eight months (MS Morgan)

197.36 vast • ~~great~~ ˏvastˏ (MS Morgan)

197.36 Roxana • ~~and~~ Roxana (MS Morgan)

197.37	violently, • violently, ~~with her straw~~ (MS Morgan)
197.37–38	pleasant; it . . . at least. • pleasant; ~~and not~~ ˏit̠ certainly ˏwas̠ not uncomfortably warm/, ~~OO~~ at least.ˏ (MS Morgan)
198.3	house." • house." [¶] ~~This was another electric shock for the house~~ (MS Morgan)
198.5	the people • ˏthe people̠ (MS Morgan)
198.6	as if • ˏas if̠ (MS Morgan)
198.8	cradle • cradle; ~~B was~~ (MS Morgan)
198.8	kitchen, • kitchen/, ~~[Sensation.] From seven months~~ (MS Morgan)
198.9	a negro and • ˏa negro and̠ (MS Morgan)
198.9–10	Sensation—confusion of angry ejaculations (MTP) • *Sensation—confusion of angry ejaculations* (MS Morgan)
198.10	he • ˏhe̠ (MS Morgan)
198.11	free!" • free!" " [*quotation mark canceled and rewritten*] (MS Morgan)
198.11	Burst of applause, checked by the officers. (MTP) • *Burst of applause, checked by the officers.* (MS Morgan)
198.21	finger-prints (MTP) • finger- | prints (MS Morgan)
198.22	Tom • ~~The~~ Tom (MS Morgan)
198.22	imploringly • ~~app~~ imploringly (MS Morgan)
198.23	slid • slid ~~in~~ (MS Morgan)
198.29	on • ~~'pon~~ ˏon̠ (MS Morgan)
199.1	*Chapter 32* (MTP) • Chapter ~~33.~~ ˏ32.̠ [*short triple rule*] [*alteration in pencil*] (MS Morgan)
199.2	day • day, (MS Morgan)
199.4	Wilson • ~~w~~ Wilson (MS Morgan)
199.6	this time; • ~~now;~~ ˏthis time;̠ (MS Morgan)
199.12	elected!" • elected!" [*short rule*] [¶] ~~There was no occasion to try Tom; he hanged himself with his suspenders in the night.~~ (MS Morgan)
199.15	Aunt Patsy (MTP) • aunt Patsy (MS Morgan)
199.15	Aunt Betsy's (MTP) • aunt Betsy's (MS Morgan)
199.18	aldermen • ~~A~~ ˏa̠ldermen (MS Morgan)
199.26	went • ~~traveled~~ went (MS Morgan)
199.26	toward • ~~town~~ ˏtoward̠ (MS Morgan)
199.27	so • ˏso̠ (MS Morgan)
199.29	on • ~~ha~~ on (MS Morgan)
199.29–30	subscription. But . . . their senses, • sub-ˏscription. But at last the people came to their senses,ˏ || ~~scription. Party rancor ran so high that people~~

who had any money spent it all on the issue and then mortgaged their property to raiisse more. When at last there was no more property to mortgage and the whole community was bankrupt and beggared, the people came to their senses (MS Morgan)

200.1   hired the • hired ~~that~~ the (MS Morgan)

200.2   human • ˏhumanˏ (MS Morgan)

200.2   some of us • ~~we~~ ˏsome of usˏ (MS Morgan)

200.3   left • ˏleftˏ (MS Morgan)

200.9   Count • ₵ Çount (MS Morgan)

200.16–17 started right, this time. • started ˏright, this time.ˏ ~~if galvanizing a corpse may be called by that active epithet. It stood just as still as it was before. It got nicknamed the City of Mortgages, and kept the name until the~~ ˏitsˏ ~~last house caved into the Mississippi twenty-two years ago. Even to this day the transient fisherman of the in the regions along below there now and then gets excited and hauls furiously away on his trot-line in the gray dawn, thinking he has hooked a half-ton bull-cat nine feet long, and when it emerges heis temper goes all to pieces, and he says, with ac-~~ || ~~rimony, "it's another of them hellfired mortgages!" [¶] All the characters in this book which remain to be accounted for lived happy lives and came to a satisfactory end, including aunt Patsy's young boys, Joe and Henry, who fell in the well and got drowned.~~ (MS Morgan/MS in CU-MARK) [TEXTUAL NOTE: *The text up through* 'with ac-' *is deleted in MS Morgan;* 'rimony . . . drowned' *was on the next leaf, which SLC deleted by removing it from the MS and which is in CU-MARK*]

200.20   too deep • ~~two d~~ too deep (MS Morgan)

200.26   interests • ~~activities~~ ˏintˏ | interests (MS Morgan)

200.27   serious • ~~un-~~ | serious (MS Morgan)

200.35   fine • findₑ [*alteration in pencil*] (MS Morgan)

201.2   "nigger gallery" (MTP) • "nigger⁷ gallery (MS Morgan) [TEXTUAL NOTE: *In MS Morgan the closing quotation mark has been smudged out, but no replacement has been inserted anywhere else; emended here to conform to the other instance in the MS*]

201.20   life— • life,—ˏ (MS Morgan)

201.22   once, and the • once,ˏ, andˏ *T* ţhe (MS Morgan)

201.22   river. • river. ~~They got twenty-five hundred dollars for him~~ (MS Morgan)

TEXTUAL APPARATUS:
PUDD'NHEAD WILSON: A TALE
THE REVISED VERSION

Witnesses and extents. This table shows which source documents have been drawn on in constructing the text of each chapter of the revised *Pudd'nhead Wilson*. Mark Twain's local revisions, additions, and excisions are recorded in the entries which follow. The source documents, which are described on pp. 617–21, include MS Berg; MS Morgan (which in some places is TS1); MSS in CU-MARK; *Cent*; and E.

Text	Source documents
Title and epigraph	MS Morgan; *Cent*
A Whisper to the Reader	MS Morgan ('Note Concerning the Legal Points'); *Cent*
Chapter 1	TEXT: MS Morgan chapter 1, derived in part from MS Berg chapter [6]; *Cent*
	MOTTO: MS Morgan chapter 8; *Cent*
Chapters 2–4	TEXT and MOTTOES: MS Morgan chapters 2–4; *Cent*
Chapter 5	TEXT and MOTTOES: MS Morgan chapter 5, derived in part from MS Berg chapters 1 and [6]; *Cent*
Chapter 6	TEXT: MS Morgan chapter 8, derived in part from MS Berg chapters 3–4; *Cent*
	MOTTO 1: MS Morgan chapter 22; *Cent*
	MOTTO 2: MS in CU-MARK; *Cent*
Chapter 7	TEXT: MS Morgan chapter 9 (derived in part from MS Berg chapter 4) and chapter 12; *Cent*
	MOTTO: *Cent*
Chapter 8	TEXT and MOTTO 1: MS Morgan chapter 13; *Cent*
	MOTTO 2: *Cent*
Chapter 9	TEXT: MS Morgan chapter 14; *Cent*
	MOTTO 1: MS Morgan chapter 15; *Cent*
	MOTTO 2: MS in CU-MARK; *Cent*

(continued)

Text	Source documents
Chapter 10	TEXT: MS Morgan chapters 15–16; *Cent*
	MOTTO 1: MS Morgan chapter 15; *Cent*
	MOTTO 2: *Cent*
Chapter 11	TEXT and MOTTO 1: MS Morgan chapter 17; *Cent*
	MOTTO 2: *Cent*
Chapter 12	TEXT and MOTTO: MS Morgan chapter 19; *Cent*
Chapter 13	TEXT: MS Morgan chapter 20; *Cent*
	MOTTO 1: MS Morgan chapter 11; *Cent*
	MOTTO 2: *Cent*
Chapter 14	TEXT: MS Morgan chapters 21 and 23; *Cent*
	MOTTO: MS Morgan chapter 21; *Cent*
Chapter 15	TEXT: MS Morgan chapter 26, 'On Saturday . . . intermediate landing.' (PW-MS, 159.20–160.36); *Cent*
	MOTTO 1: MS Morgan chapter 7; *Cent*
	MOTTO 2: *Cent*
Chapter 16	TEXT: MS Morgan chapter 26, 'When Roxana . . . down de river!"' (PW-MS, 160.37–163.19); *Cent*
	MOTTO 1: MS Morgan chapter 26; *Cent*
	MOTTO 2: *Cent*
Chapter 17	TEXT and MOTTO 2: MS Morgan chapter 27; *Cent*
	MOTTO 1: *Cent*
Chapter 18	TEXT and MOTTO 1: MS Morgan chapter 28; *Cent*; E
	MOTTO 2: MS in CU-MARK; *Cent*; E
Chapter 19	TEXT: MS Morgan chapter 29; *Cent*; E
	MOTTO 1: *Cent*; E
	MOTTO 2: MS Morgan chapter 12 (where it is deleted); *Cent*; E
Chapter 20	TEXT and MOTTO: MS Morgan chapter 30; *Cent*; E
Chapter 21	TEXT and MOTTO 1: MS Morgan chapter 31; *Cent*; E
	MOTTO 2: *Cent*; E
Conclusion	TEXT: MS Morgan chapter 32; *Cent*; E
	MOTTOES: *Cent*; E

Revisions, variants adopted or rejected, and textual notes.

frontis   SAMUEL L. CLEMENS (MARK TWAIN). (*Cent*) • [*not in*] (MS Morgan)

215.1–3   [*centered:*] *Pudd'nhead Wilson* | A TALE | By MARK TWAIN (MTP) • [*centered*: Those Extraordinary Twins. [*short triple rule*] Time—about 1850. [*short double rule*] (MS Berg); [*centered:*] Pudd'nhead Wilson | A TALE | By MARK TWAIN. [*small capitals simulated, not underscored*] (MS Morgan); [*within woodcut title:*] PUDD'NHEAD WILSON. | A TALE BY MARK TWAIN (*Cent*)

217.1   *A Whisper to the Reader* (MTP) • Note Concerning the Legal Points (MS Morgan); A WHISPER TO THE READER (*Cent*)

217.3   so, (MS Morgan) • so (*Cent*)

217.4   law-chapters (MS Morgan) • law chapters (*Cent*)

217.6   Those (MS Morgan) • These (*Cent*) [TEXTUAL NOTE: *The three places where Cent has 'these' in place of MS Morgan's 'those' (here, and at 246.21 and 333.31) suggest misreading by the TS2 typist rather than authorial revision. In this case, the concurrence of Cent and E confirms that the error originated prior to the Century Magazine's editing*]

217.7   re-written (MS Morgan) • rewritten (*Cent*)

217.8   south-west (MS Morgan) • southwest (*Cent*)

217.8–9 here to Florence (*Cent*) • here (MS Morgan)

217.9–10 Maccaroni and Vermicelli's (MS Morgan) • Macaroni Vermicelli's (*Cent*)

217.13   Campanile (MS Morgan) • campanile (*Cent*)

217.15   chestnut-cake (MS Morgan) • chestnut cake (*Cent*)

217.15   attack (MS Morgan) • outbreak (*Cent*) [TEXTUAL NOTE: *Cent's reading probably stems from the TS2 typist's misreading of MS Morgan*]

217.17–18 flattery, far from it (*Cent*) • flattery (MS Morgan)

217.19   now, he (MS Morgan) • now. He (*Cent*)

217.21   three (*Cent*) • two (MS Morgan)

217.24   too (MS Morgan) • too, (*Cent*)

217.31   *Mark Twain.* (MTP) • Mark Twain. | [*paraph*] (MS Morgan); *Mark Twain.* (*Cent*)

219.2–3 [¶] Tell the truth or trump—but get the trick.—*Pudd'nhead Wilson's Calendar.* (*Cent*) • [*not in*] (MS Morgan)

219.6   one and two-story "frame" (MS Morgan) • one- and two-story frame (*Cent*)

219.8   rose vines (MS Morgan) • rose-vines (*Cent*)

219.10   prince's feathers (MS Morgan) • prince's-feathers (*Cent*)

219.12   plants, (MS Morgan) • plants (*Cent*)

219.12   terra cotta (MS Morgan) • terra-cotta (*Cent*)

219.18   home (MS Morgan) • house (*Cent*) [TEXTUAL NOTE: *Elsewhere in this paragraph SLC uses 'home' and 'house' indifferently, so he is unlikely to have altered MS Morgan's reading here; Cent's reading more probably reflects a fussy distinction by an in-house editor, or a compositor's error*]

219.18   made (MS Morgan) • were made (*Cent*) [TEXTUAL NOTE: *Cent tends to supply the verb where Clemens prefers to elide it, as also at, e.g., 285.23 and 339.26*]

219.20   well fed (MS Morgan) • well-fed (*Cent*)

219.20	well petted, (MS Morgan) • well-petted (*Cent*)
219.23	locust trees, (MS Morgan) • locust-trees (*Cent*)
219.30	ancient, (MS Morgan) • ancient (*Cent*)
220.1	barber shop (MS Morgan) • barber-shop (*Cent*)
220.3	tin-monger's (MS Morgan) • tinmonger's (*Cent*)
220.4	blew), (MS Morgan) • blew) (*Cent*)
220.8	base line (MS Morgan) • base-line (*Cent*)
220.9	enclosing (MS Morgan) • inclosing (*Cent*)
220.12–13	big New Orleans and Cincinnati and Louisville liners (MS Morgan) • big Orleans liners (*Cent*) [TEXTUAL NOTE: *The exact purport of Cent's revision is unclear. The change from* 'New Orleans' *to* 'Orleans' *is suspicious: Clemens considered it ignorant, and uses it only in reported speech* (ET&S2, *313;* HF 2003, *532, 118*)]
220.17	Red river (MS Morgan) • Red River (*Cent*)
220.17	White river (MS Morgan) • White River (*Cent*)
220.17	everywhither (MS Morgan) • every whither (*Cent*)
220.21	slave-holding (MTP) • slave | -holding (MS Morgan) • slaveholding (*Cent*)
220.22	sleepy, and comfortable, (MS Morgan) • sleepy and comfortable (*Cent*)
220.25	Judge (MS Morgan) • judge (*Cent*)
220.28	fine, and just, (MS Morgan) • fine and just (*Cent*)
220.30	esteemed, (MS Morgan) • esteemed (*Cent*)
221.2	freethinker (MTP) • free- | thinker (MS Morgan); free-thinker (*Cent*)
221.9	prefer, (MS Morgan) • prefer (*Cent*)
221.13	calibre (MS Morgan) • caliber (*Cent*)
221.19	first (MS Morgan) • 1st (*Cent*)
221.26	February (MS Morgan) • February, (*Cent*)
221.28	birth-place (MS Morgan) • birthplace (*Cent*)
221.30	eastern (MS Morgan) • Eastern (*Cent*)
221.36	"gauged" (MS Berg, MS Morgan/TS1) • "gaged" (*Cent*)
222.1	comprehensively (*Cent*) • comprehensibly (MS Berg, MS Morgan/TS1) [TEXTUAL NOTE: *The reading of MS Morgan/TS1,* 'comprehensibly', *is correctly transcribed from MS Berg and is not impossible; but Cent's reading* 'comprehensively' *is plausibly the author's correction of his earlier slip*]
222.2	disagreeable; (MS Berg, MS Morgan/TS1) • disagreeable, (*Cent*)
222.2	he (MS Berg, MS Morgan/TS1) • young Wilson (*Cent*)

222.5   Because, (MS Berg, MS Morgan/TS1) • Because (*Cent*)

222.8   said— (MS Berg, MS Morgan/TS1) • said: (*Cent*)

222.10   "'Pears," (MS Berg, MS Morgan/TS1) • " 'Pears?" (*Cent*)

222.10   another, "*is* (MS Berg, MS Morgan/TS1) • another. "*Is* (*Cent*)

222.15   that (MS Berg) • it (MS Morgan/TS1, *Cent*)

222.27–28 said— [¶] "Well (MS Berg, MS Morgan/TS1) • said: "Well (*Cent*)
           [TEXTUAL NOTE: *That the Century preferred to eliminate very short
           paragraphs such as this one is clear from the surviving printer's copy for
           "The £1,000,000 Bank Note" where a Century editor has several times
           marked them to run into neighboring paragraphs (CU-MARK)*]

222.28   lummux (MS Berg, MS Morgan/TS1) • lummox (*Cent*)

222.29   simon-pure (MS Berg, *Cent*) • Simon-pure (MS Morgan/TS1)

222.31   *I* (MS Berg, MS Morgan/TS1) • I (*Cent*)

222.38   well liked, (MS Berg, MS Morgan/TS1) • well liked (*Cent*)

224.3   only wanted it (MS Morgan) • wanted it only (*Cent*)

224.6   when he arrived (*Cent*) • [*not in*] (MS Morgan)

224.11–13 DAVID WILSON | *Attorney and Counselor at Law.* | *Surveying,
           Conveyancing, etc.* (MS Morgan) • DAVID WILSON. | ATTORNEY
           AND COUNSELOR-AT-LAW. | SURVEYING, CONVEYANCING, ETC.
           (*Cent*)

224.17   land surveyor (MS Morgan) • land-surveyor (*Cent*)

224.21   such a weary long time (*Cent*) • twenty years (MS Morgan)

224.23   into (*Cent*) • in (MS Morgan)

224.25   name, (MS Morgan) • name (*Cent*)

225.4   hair, (MS Morgan) • hair (*Cent*)

225.5   oil, (MS Morgan) • oil (*Cent*)

225.9   "JOHN SMITH, *right hand*"— (MS Morgan) • JOHN SMITH, *right
           hand*— (*Cent*)

225.18   pantagraph (MS Morgan) • pantograph (*Cent*) [TEXTUAL NOTE:
           *Cent's form is that preferred by the magazine's authority for spelling, the
           Century Dictionary (Whitney and Smith 1889–91), but MS Morgan's
           spelling was not wrong or even unusual*]

225.21   account books (MS Morgan) • account-books (*Cent*)

225.21   work-room (MS Morgan) • workroom (*Cent*)

225.26   Fust rate (MS Morgan) • Fust-rate (*Cent*)

225.26   on (*Cent*) • [*not in*] (MS Morgan) [TEXTUAL NOTE: *In MS Morgan,
           SLC obliterated the word 'on' in the course of revising the name of Roxy's
           interlocutor*]

225.27 noth'n (MS Morgan) • noth'n' (*Cent*)

225.27 I's (*Cent*) • I'm (MS Morgan) [TEXTUAL NOTE: *This is the only place in MS Morgan where a Black speaker says 'I'm', so 'I's' is plausibly SLC's revision on TS2a or in Century proofs*]

225.27 gwyne (MS Morgan) • gwine (*Cent*)

225.28 a court'n (MTP) • a-court'n (MS Morgan); a-court'n' (*Cent*)

225.29 Yah-yah-yah! (MS Morgan) • Yah—yah—yah! (*Cent*)

225.29 sump'n (MS Morgan) • somep'n' (*Cent*)

225.30 'sociat'n (MS Morgan) • 'sociat'n' (*Cent*)

225.30 Is (*Cent*) • Has (MS Morgan)

225.33 huzzy (MS Morgan) • hussy (*Cent*)

225.33–34 yah-yah-yah! (MS Morgan) • yah—yah—yah! (*Cent*)

225.34 you! (MS Morgan) • you. (*Cent*)

225.36 gwyne (MS Morgan) • gwine (*Cent*)

225.36 you, (MS Morgan) • you (*Cent*)

226.2 gwyne (MS Morgan) • gwine (*Cent*)

226.4 friendly (*Cent*) • good-natured (MS Morgan)

226.8 wheelbarrow (*Cent*) • wheebarrow (MS Morgan)

226.13 one-sixteenth (MS Morgan) • one sixteenth (*Cent*)

226.21 intelligent, (MS Morgan) • intelligent (*Cent*)

226.22 even (*Cent*) • perhaps even (MS Morgan)

226.24 people (*Cent*) • folks (MS Morgan)

226.26 one-sixteenth (MS Morgan) • one sixteenth (*Cent*)

226.26 out-voted (MS Morgan) • outvoted (*Cent*)

226.29 curls, (MS Morgan) • curls (*Cent*)

226.32 other kid (MS Morgan) • other (*Cent*)

226.37 onto (MS Morgan) • on to (*Cent*)

227.2 gather-in (MS Morgan) • gather in (*Cent*)

227.2 Jasper (*Cent*) • Jim (MS Morgan) [TEXTUAL NOTE: *In MS Morgan, SLC left this instance of* 'Jim' *standing; elsewhere in the manuscript he revised to* 'Jasper'. *Presumably he caught this in revising TS2*]

227.3 once—perceiving (MS Morgan) • once, perceiving (*Cent*)

227.6 Febuary (MS Morgan) • Feb'uary (*Cent*)

227.9 caze (MS Morgan) • 'ca'se (*Cent*)

227.10 allays (MS Morgan) • al'ays (*Cent*)

227.11 caze (MS Morgan) • 'ca'se (*Cent*)

227.20	third (MS Morgan) • 3d (*Cent*)
227.21	"series"—two (MS Morgan) • "series," two (*Cent*)
227.24	fourth (MS Morgan) • 4th (*Cent*)
227.24	September,— (MS Morgan) • September— (*Cent*)
227.28	man, (MS Morgan) • man (*Cent*)
227.36	thief! (MS Morgan) • thief. (*Cent*)
228.8	had been (*Cent*) • was (MS Morgan) [TEXTUAL NOTE: *Cent's change is accepted as SLC's, on the assumption that he was completing a change to the past perfect tense which he had begun in MS Morgan when he revised 'came' to 'had come' (see* PW-MS, *Textual Apparatus, entry at 15.8)*]
228.9	church (MS Morgan) • Church, (*Cent*) [TEXTUAL NOTE: *Cent's change to an initial capital assumes a religious body is spoken of, but reference to the church building is plausible too, so the original spelling is retained*]
228.14	a while (MS Morgan) • awhile (*Cent*)
228.16	a ben (MS Morgan) • 'a' be'n (*Cent*)
228.16	tomorrow (MS Morgan) • to-morrow (*Cent*)
228.38	onto (MS Morgan) • on to (*Cent*)
229.8	watch—"if (MS Morgan) • watch. "If (*Cent*)
229.10	*down the river!* (MS Morgan) • DOWN THE RIVER! (*Cent*)
229.18	it— (MS Morgan) • it!— (*Cent*)
229.19	here (MS Morgan) • *here* (*Cent*)
229.22	they (MS Morgan) • that they (*Cent*)
229.25	he was (MS Morgan) • was (*Cent*)
229.27	years (MS Morgan) • years, (*Cent*)
230.9	dozed, (MS Morgan) • dozed (*Cent*)
230.12	moaning and crying (MS Morgan) • moaning, crying (*Cent*)
230.13	shan't (MS Morgan) • sha'n't (*Cent*)
230.13	*shan't* (MS Morgan) • *sha'n't* (*Cent*)
230.18	noth'n (MS Morgan) • noth'n' (*Cent*)
230.18	He (MS Morgan) • he (*Cent*) [TEXTUAL NOTE: *In MS Morgan, SLC revises the pronoun from 'he' to 'He', anticipating a common printing convention; but the printer of the Century Magazine, Theodore Low De Vinne, required that "the pronouns he, his, and him, when referring to Deity, will always begin with lower-case h, as is done in the Bible" (De Vinne 1926, 10)*]
230.18	you (MS Morgan) • *you* (*Cent*)
230.20	a while (MS Morgan) • awhile (*Cent*)

230.22   way! (MS Morgan) • way, (*Cent*)

230.23   *got* (MS Morgan) • got (*Cent*)

230.25   you, (MS Morgan) • you (*Cent*)

230.26   gwyne (MS Morgan) • gwine (*Cent*)

230.26   you! (MS Morgan) • you, (*Cent*)

230.26   gwyne (MS Morgan) • gwine (*Cent*)

230.27   gwyne (MS Morgan) • gwine (*Cent*)

230.27   herself, (MS Morgan) • herself (*Cent*)

230.28   gwyne (MS Morgan) • gwine (*Cent*)

230.29   de (MS Morgan) • the (*Cent*)

230.29   *yonder!* (MS Morgan) • *yonder.* (*Cent*)

230.30–31   it; midway she stopped, suddenly (*Cent*) • it (MS Morgan)

230.31   caught (MS Morgan) • had caught (*Cent*)

231.3   yit (MS Morgan) • yet (*Cent*)

231.3   lovely . . . ." (MS Morgan) • lovely." (*Cent*)

231.4   gwyne (MS Morgan) • gwine (*Cent*)

231.5   misable (MS Morgan) • mis'able (*Cent*)

231.10   folks;" (MS Morgan) • folks"; (*Cent*)

231.10   rather lurid (*Cent*) • pretty loud (MS Morgan)

231.11   finally, (MS Morgan) • finally (*Cent*)

231.13   complexion. Then (*Cent*) • complexion, then (MS Morgan)

231.18   ain't gwyne (MS Morgan) • ain't gwine (*Cent*)

231.18   is gwyne (MS Morgan) • is gwine (*Cent*)

231.19   gwyne (MS Morgan) • gwine (*Cent*)

231.19   putt'n (MS Morgan) • putt'n' (*Cent*)

231.21   Dat chile is dress' too indelicate fo' dis place. (MTP) • Dat chile is
         dress' too indelicate for dis place. (MS Morgan); 'Dat chile is dress' too
         indelicate fo' dis place.' (*Cent*) [TEXTUAL NOTE: *The change from 'for'
         to 'fo' may well show SLC revising dialect, in which he did not attempt
         consistency but relied on his ear. In MS Morgan, Roxy says 'for' through-
         out; in Cent she twice says 'fo' (meaning 'for', and not to be confused with
         "fo" meaning 'before'). Cf. SLC's alteration in the MS of* Huckleberry
         Finn *(HF 2003, alterations list entry at 325.30)*]

231.26   Straightway her (*Cent*) • Her (MS Morgan)

231.27   all— (MS Morgan) • all!— (*Cent*)

231.28   lovely! (MS Morgan) • lovely.

231.29   bit! (MS Morgan) • bit. (*Cent*)

231.33	a washin' (MTP) • a-washin' (MS Morgan, *Cent*)
231.34	his'n! (MS Morgan) • his'n. (*Cent*)
232.4	practice (MS Morgan) • practise (*Cent*)
232.5	gwyne (MS Morgan) • gwine (*Cent*)
232.11	is! (MS Morgan) • is, (*Cent*)
232.13	it! (MS Morgan) • it. (*Cent*)
232.14	bed, (MS Morgan) • bed (*Cent*)
232.26	*He* (MS Morgan) • *he* (*Cent*)
232.26	He (MS Morgan) • he (*Cent*)
232.27	*He* (MS Morgan) • *he* (*Cent*)
232.27	k'yer (MS Morgan) • kyer (*Cent*)
232.27	He's (MS Morgan) • he's (*Cent*)
232.28	Him (MS Morgan) • him (*Cent*)
232.29	burn wid Satan (*Cent*) • suffer (MS Morgan)
232.31	roun' 'bout (MS Morgan) • roun'-	'bout (*Cent*)
232.32	mos' (MS Morgan) • 'mos' (*Cent*)
232.35	nigger quarter (MS Morgan) • nigger-quarter (*Cent*)
232.36	king, (MS Morgan) • king (*Cent*)
232.37	had (*Cent*) • had a auction (MS Morgan)
232.38	caze (MS Morgan) • 'ca'se (*Cent*)
233.1	folks, (MS Morgan) • folks (*Cent*)
233.2	bilin'! (MS Morgan) • bilin'. (*Cent*)
233.4	"practicing." (MS Morgan) • "practising." (*Cent*)
233.5	say, (MS Morgan) • say (*Cent*)
233.6	sump'n (MS Morgan) • somep'n' (*Cent*)
233.14	practicing (MS Morgan) • practising (*Cent*)
233.16	fo' (*Cent*) • for (MS Morgan) [TEXTUAL NOTE: *See PW-REV, Textual Apparatus, entry and textual note at 231.21*]
233.18	gwyne (MS Morgan) • gwine (*Cent*)
233.19	roun' (*Cent*) • aroun' (MS Morgan)
233.20	it's (*Cent*) • it takes (MS Morgan)
233.23	Driscoll, (MS Morgan) • Driscoll (*Cent*)
233.24	Pem. (MS Morgan) • Pem (*Cent*)
233.25	his'n (MS Morgan) • hisn (*Cent*)
233.25	gwyne (MS Morgan) • gwine (*Cent*)
233.27	agin (MS Morgan) • ag'in (*Cent*)

233.27   boun' (MS Morgan) • bound (*Cent*)

233.27   gwyne (MS Morgan) • gwine (*Cent*)

233.28   *sho'* (MS Morgan) • sho' (*Cent*)

233.37   Judge (MS Morgan) • Judge, (*Cent*)

233.38   speculation, (MS Morgan) • speculation (*Cent*)

234.4   away, (MS Morgan) • away (*Cent*)

234.11   this (MS Morgan) • the (*Cent*)

235.4   providences, that (MS Morgan) • providences—namely, (*Cent*)

235.22   appalling (*Cent*) • appaling (MS Morgan)

235.23   flying (MS Morgan) • flying, (*Cent*)

236 *illus*   ROXY AND THE CHILDREN. (*Cent*) • [*not in*] (MS Morgan)

237.2–3   stomach ache; consequently he was hiccuppy beyond reason and a sin-
          gularly flatulent child (MS Morgan) • stomach-ache (*Cent*) [TEXTUAL
          NOTE: *This clause was either censored by the Century editors or deleted by
          SLC in the expectation they would do so, and is therefore restored*]

237.4   about, (MS Morgan) • about (*Cent*)

237.5   words, (MS Morgan) • words (*Cent*)

237.7   Awnt it (MS Morgan) • Awnt it! (*Cent*)

237.8   said, (MS Morgan) • said (*Cent*)

237.14   "father" (*Cent*) • father (MS Morgan) [TEXTUAL NOTE: *This revision
          is part of a pattern in Cent in which quotation marks and verbal ampli-
          fications have been added to distinguish between the apparent and the
          actual relationships between the characters. The change at this point looks
          like SLC continuing a practice he began in MS Morgan, where he alters
          'nephew'* to *'ostensible nephew' (133.20) and refers to Judge Driscoll as
          Tom's 'alleged uncle' (183.26)*]

237.16   say, (MS Morgan) • say (*Cent*)

237.16   *Like* (MS Morgan) • Like (*Cent*)

237.17   *Awnt* (MS Morgan) • Awnt (*Cent*)

237.17   *Hab* (MS Morgan) • Hab (*Cent*)

237.18   *Take* (MS Morgan) • Take (*Cent*)

237.20   off, on three legs, (MS Morgan) • off on three legs (*Cent*)

237.21   Roxy (*Cent*) • Roxy was flying, by now, and (MS Morgan)

237.23   delicacies going (MS Morgan) • delicacies (*Cent*) [TEXTUAL NOTE: *This
          use of 'going' was perhaps too slangy for the Century Magazine editors*]

237.24   By consequence, (MS Morgan) • In consequence (*Cent*)

237.26   overbearing, (MS Morgan) • overbearing; (*Cent*)

237.32	practicing (MS Morgan) • practising (*Cent*)
238.3–4	master. [¶] He (MS Morgan) • master. He (*Cent*)
238.4	deity, (MS Morgan) • deity (*Cent*)
238.7	as (MS Morgan) • [*not in*] (*Cent*)
238.8	it (MS Morgan) • it, (*Cent*)
238.11	fogitt'n (MS Morgan) • forgitt'n (*Cent*)
238.13	party (MS Morgan) • person (*Cent*) [TEXTUAL NOTE: *The Century Magazine's style sheet disallowed* 'party' *where* 'person' *was meant (McKnight 1923, 408–9)*]
238.18	together, (MS Morgan) • together (*Cent*)
238.23	play-ground (MS Morgan) • playground (*Cent*)
238.25	Tom could have changed clothes with him, (*Cent*) • Tom could have put on his clothes (MS Morgan)
238.30	and seat (*Cent*) • [*not in*] (MS Morgan)
238.32	direction (MS Morgan) • directions (*Cent*)
238.33	snow-balling (MS Morgan) • snowballing (*Cent*)
238.38	peaches (MS Morgan) • peaches, (*Cent*)
238.38	fruit wagons (MS Morgan) • fruit-wagons (*Cent*)
239.3	peach stones (MS Morgan) • peach-stones (*Cent*)
239.3	apple cores (MS Morgan) • apple-cores, (*Cent*)
239.4	melon rinds (MTP) • melon rhinds (MS Morgan); melon-rinds (*Cent*) [TEXTUAL NOTE: *Although an instance of* 'rhind' *in the manuscript of* Tom Sawyer *made it into the first American edition (SLC 1876, 259), linguistic data suggests that this spelling has never been anything but an error*]
239.14	a (*Cent*) • the (MS Morgan)
239.15	back-summersaults (MS Morgan) • back somersaults (*Cent*)
239.15	canoe (MS Morgan) • canoe, (*Cent*)
239.17	canoe-bottom (*Cent*) • canoe's bottom (MS Morgan)
239.18	unconscious (MS Morgan) • unconscious, (*Cent*)
239.22	upwards (MS Morgan) • upward (*Cent*)
239.25	howl (*Cent*) • yell (MS Morgan)
239.26	hand-over-hand (MS Morgan) • hand over hand (*Cent*)
239.28	town-boys (MS Morgan) • town boys (*Cent*)
239.31	out (MS Morgan) • out, (*Cent*)
239.35	*this* (MS Morgan) • this (*Cent*)
240.3	call (*Cent*) • always call (MS Morgan)

240.5 Nigger-pappy (MTP) • Nigger- | pappy (MS Morgan); niggerpappy (*Cent*)

240.8 Chambers, (MS Morgan) • Chambers! (*Cent*)

240.8 off!—what (MS Morgan) • off! What (*Cent*)

240.9 pockets, for (MS Morgan) • pockets for (*Cent*)

240.10–11 said— [¶] "But (MS Morgan) • said, "But, (*Cent*)

240.12 *hear* (MS Morgan) • hear (*Cent*)

240.13 me. (MS Morgan) • me! (*Cent*)

240.14 pocket knife (MS Morgan) • pocket- | knife (*Cent*)

240.18 day, now, (MS Morgan) • day now (*Cent*)

240.22 that (MS Morgan) • *that* (*Cent*)

240.25 sombre (MS Morgan) • somber (*Cent*)

240.33 allays (MS Morgan) • al'ays (*Cent*)

240.33 nigger wench (MS Morgan) • nigger-wench (*Cent*)

240.34 O (MS Morgan) • Oh (*Cent*)

240.35 whar (MS Morgan) • what (*Cent*)

240.35 it! (MS Morgan) • it. (*Cent*)

240.37 vengeance, (MS Morgan) • vengeance (*Cent*)

241.9 kind— (MS Morgan) • kind,— (*Cent*)

241.10 then— (MS Morgan) • then,— (*Cent*)

241.10 healed (MS Morgan) • healed, (*Cent*)

241.14 Colonel Cecil Burleigh Essex's (MS Morgan) • that of Colonel Cecil Burleigh Essex (*Cent*)

241.14 was Percy Driscoll's (MS Morgan) • that of Percy Driscoll (*Cent*)

241.29 good-bye (MS Morgan) • good-by (*Cent*)

241.31 chambermaiding (*Cent*) • chambermaid (MS Morgan)

241.33 wood. (*Cent*) • wood. She had . . . one while, anyway. (MS Morgan [27.32–29.23])

241.36 down (MS Morgan) • up (*Cent*)

242.3 deviltry (MS Morgan) • devilry (*Cent*)

242.3 witch-business, (MS Morgan) • witch-business (*Cent*)

242.5 it." (*Cent*) • it." He wished . . . Answer me *dat!*" (MS Morgan [29.32–30.8])

243.2 almond, (MS Morgan) • almond; (*Cent*)

243.5 Baldwin (MS Morgan) • Baldwin's, (*Cent*)

243.8 Tom; bliss (MS Morgan) • Tom—bliss (*Cent*)

243.19 semi-conscious (MS Morgan) • semiconscious (*Cent*)

243.19   safely (MS Morgan) • safely, (*Cent*)

243.20   ever, (MS Morgan) • ever (*Cent*)

243.24   rather openly (*Cent*) • [*not in*] (MS Morgan)

243.24   practiced (MS Morgan) • practised (*Cent*)

243.27   eastern (MS Morgan) • Eastern (*Cent*)

243.29   *couldn't* (MS Morgan) • couldn't (*Cent*)

244.1   fashion—eastern (MS Morgan) • fashion,—Eastern (*Cent*)

244.1   fashion—that (MS Morgan) • fashion,—that (*Cent*)

244.4   Tom (*Cent*) • he (MS Morgan)

244.7   eastern (MS Morgan) • Eastern (*Cent*)

244.8   after that clothed himself in the local fashion (*Cent*) • clothed himself after the local fashion after that (MS Morgan)

244.16   did (MS Morgan) • *did* (*Cent*)

244.17   Bench (MS Morgan) • bench (*Cent*)

244.18   President (MS Morgan) • president (*Cent*)

244.19   Freethinkers' (MS Morgan) • Free-thinkers' (*Cent*)

244.20   Society's (MS Morgan) • society's (*Cent*)

244.20   were the old lawyer's main interest in life, now (MS Morgan) • were now the old lawyer's main interest in life (*Cent*)

244.23   before. (MS Morgan) • before about the dog. (*Cent*) [TEXTUAL NOTE: *The addition of* 'about the dog' *is an attempt to jog the memories of readers of the Century Magazine serial: the present passage appeared in the second installment (January 1894), and the story of Wilson's unlucky remark had been told back in the first installment (December 1893)*]

244.26   Or, (MS Berg, MS Morgan/TS1) • Or (*Cent*)

244.38   way, (MS Morgan) • way (*Cent*)

245.4   freethinker (MS Berg, MS Morgan/TS1) • free-thinker (*Cent*)

245.11–14 The widow Cooper . . . of no consequence. (*Cent*) • Observation made by . . . younger than she. (MS Morgan [34.2–35.11])

245.11   Aunt (MTP) • [*not in*] (MS Morgan); aunt (*Cent*)

245.15   widow (*Cent*) • widow Cooper (MS Berg, MS Morgan/TS1)

245.15   large (*Cent*) • [*not in*] (MS Berg, MS Morgan) [TEXTUAL NOTE: *SLC revises to make Patsy's spare room* 'large' *because the Twins, having been separated, now need more room and two beds*]

245.19   found (*Cent*) • finds (MS Berg, MS Morgan/TS1)

245.19   tedious long wait (MS Berg, MS Morgan/TS1) • tedious wait (*Cent*)

245.19   was (*Cent*) • is (MS Berg, MS Morgan/TS1)

245.20   had (*Cent*) • has (MS Berg, MS Morgan/TS1)

245.21   no (MS Berg, MS Morgan/TS1) • no! (*Cent*)

245.21   was (*Cent*) • is (MS Berg, MS Morgan/TS1)

245.22   was (*Cent*) • is (MS Berg, MS Morgan/TS1)

245.22   St. Louis! (MS Berg, MS Morgan/TS1) • St. Louis. (*Cent*)

245.22   sat (*Cent*) • sits (MS Berg, MS Morgan/TS1)

245.24   was (*Cent*) • is (MS Berg, MS Morgan/TS1)

245.24   especially (MS Berg, MS Morgan/TS1) • specially (*Cent*)

245.24   was (*Cent*) • is (MS Berg, MS Morgan/TS1)

245.26   had (*Cent*) • has (MS Berg, MS Morgan/TS1)

245.26   had (*Cent*) • has (MS Berg, MS Morgan/TS1)

245.28   had (*Cent*) • have (MS Berg, MS Morgan/TS1)

245.28   was (*Cent*) • is (MS Berg, MS Morgan/TS1)

245.30   returned (*Cent*) • returns (MS Berg, MS Morgan/TS1)

245.30   aflush (MS Berg) • ablush (MS Morgan/TS1, *Cent*)

245.31–246.11   begged . . . to wait. Here (*Cent*) • says— [¶] "Do . . . sick, I—here (MS Berg, MS Morgan/TS1 [35.28–37.3])

245.32   Honored Madam— (MS Berg, MS Morgan/TS1) • HONORED MADAM: (*Cent*) [TEXTUAL NOTE: *The Cent text of the Twins' letter (245.32–38) was adapted by SLC from the version in MS Morgan, where the letter is read out by Aunt Patsy with interruptions from Rowena. The manuscript text is drawn on here for its authorial spelling and punctuation, and for one substantive reading (245.37)*]

245.34   age, (MS Berg, MS Morgan/TS1) • age (*Cent*)

245.36   Cappello (MS Berg, MS Morgan/TS1) • Capello (*Cent*) [TEXTUAL NOTE: *MS Morgan has the spelling 'Cappello' almost consistently. At the first occurrence of the name (PW-MS, 36.10), Clemens is seen altering the one-p to the two-p spelling; at 166.3 he left a single 'Capello' standing uncorrected. In Cent the spelling has been changed to 'Capello', except for one surviving 'Cappello'. There are two instances of 'Cappello' in the 1894 American Publishing Company book: once where the printers are following Cent, and once where they are setting from TS2b, the revised typescript copy for* Those Extraordinary Twins. *On balance the decision to use the one-p spelling seems to have been the Century Magazine's, and the manuscript spelling has been used here throughout*]

245.36   guest, (MS Berg, MS Morgan/TS1) • guest; (*Cent*)

245.36   madam (MTP) • Madam (MS Berg, MS Morgan/TS1, *Cent*)

245.37   two (MS Berg, MS Morgan/TS1) • two, (*Cent*)

245.37 discommode (MS Berg, MS Morgan/TS1) • incommode (*Cent*) [TEX-TUAL NOTE: 'discommode', *sometimes considered incorrect or uncouth (see Ellis 1895, 72), survived into the revision of this passage in* Those Extraordinary Twins (*EXT, 357.29*). *Therefore* 'discommode' *was the reading of TS2a, and* 'incommode' *is probably the work of the Century Magazine editors*]

246.13 Judge (MTP) • judge (MS Berg); Judge (MS Morgan/TS1, *Cent*)

246.18–19 its courtly and gracious tone, and smooth and practiced style (MTP) • it (MS Berg, MS Morgan/TS1); its courtly and gracious tone, and smooth and practised style (*Cent*)

246.20 were steeped in happiness (*Cent*) • swam in seas of glory (MS Berg, MS Morgan/TS1)

246.21 uncertain, (MS Berg, MS Morgan/TS1) • uncertain (*Cent*)

246.21 those (MS Berg, MS Morgan/TS1) • these (*Cent*)

246.25 then twelve, (MS Berg) • [*not in*] (MS Morgan, *Cent*) [TEXTUAL NOTE: *Phrase inadvertently omitted by the TS1 typist*]

246.28 on (MS Berg) • at (MS Morgan, *Cent*)

246.29 up stairs (MS Berg, MS Morgan/TS1) • up-stairs (*Cent*)

246.30 guest room (MS Berg, MS Morgan/TS1) • guest-room (*Cent*)

246.30–33 the Twins—the handsomest, the best dressed, the most distinguished-looking pair of young fellows the West had ever seen. One was a little fairer than the other, but otherwise they were exact duplicates. (MTP) • a human creature that had two heads, two necks, four arms, and one body, with a single pair of legs attached. (MS Berg, MS Morgan/TS1); the twins—the handsomest, the best dressed, the most distinguished-looking pair of young fellows the West had ever seen. One was a little fairer than the other, but otherwise they were exact duplicates. (*Cent*)

247.2 Let us endeavor . . . rested— [¶] "If (*Cent*) • The family sat . . . that'll do. If (MS Berg); Tell the truth or trump . . . that'll do. If (MS Morgan/TS1 [43.2–48.26])

247.2 to so live (MS Morgan) • [*not in*] (MS Berg); so to live (*Cent*)

247.5 down stairs (MS in CU-MARK) • [*not in*] (MS Berg, MS Morgan); down-stairs (*Cent*)

247.7 Twins' (MTP) • twins' (MS Berg, MS Morgan/TS1, *Cent*)

247.16 blonde (MTP) • [*not in*] (MS Berg, MS Morgan); blond (*Cent*) [TEXTUAL NOTE: *In the MSS Angelo and Luigi, though male, are* 'blonde' *and* 'brunette' *respectively; Cent altered to* 'blond', *but its authority for spelling, the Century Dictionary, did not recognize* 'brunet']

247.18 oughtn't (MS Berg, MS Morgan/TS1) • ought not (*Cent*)

247.20   don't, (MS Berg) • don't (MS Morgan/TS1, *Cent*)

247.22   well-to-do (MS Berg, MS Morgan/TS1) • well to do (*Cent*)

247.29   Spanish (MS Berg, MS Morgan/TS1) • Spanish, (*Cent*)

248.1–2   Also, we were marvelous musical prodigies—if you will allow me to say it, it being only the truth. (*Cent*) • [*not in*] (MS Berg, MS Morgan)

248.9   attractions (*Cent*) • 'freaks' (MS Berg); freaks (MS Morgan/TS1)

248.12   exhibit (MS Berg) • be exhibited (MS Morgan/TS1, *Cent*)

248.12   bread. (*Cent*) • bread. That hateful . . . get anywhere." (MS Berg, MS Morgan/TS1 [49.10–29])

248.21–23   Venice—to London . . . and exclaimed: (*Cent*) • Venice—" [¶] "Venice . . . would only—" (MS Berg, MS Morgan/TS1 [49.38–51.22])

248.24   missus (MS Berg, MS Morgan/TS1) • Missus (*Cent*)

248.24   plum (MS Berg, MS Morgan/TS1) • plum' (*Cent*)

248.24   o' (MS Berg, *Cent*) • o (MS Morgan/TS1)

248.24   jes' (MS Berg, MS Morgan/TS1) • jes (*Cent*)

248.24   a spilin' (MS Berg, MS Morgan/TS1) • a-spi'lin' (*Cent*)

248.25   de gen'lmen!" She (*Cent*) • —to see—*him*—*dem*!" The slave girl (MS Berg, MS Morgan/TS1)

248.25   Twins (MTP) • twins (MS Berg, MS Morgan/TS1, *Cent*)

248.30   indeed, (MS Berg, MS Morgan/TS1) • indeed (*Cent*)

248.32   episode (MS Berg, MS Morgan/TS1) • episode, (*Cent*)

248.34   her, (MS Berg, MS Morgan/TS1) • her; (*Cent*)

248.36   were the foreigners. (*Cent*) • was Luigi . . . was ready. (MS Berg, MS Morgan/TS1 [51.35–52.5])

248.37   Twins (MTP) • twins (MS Berg, MS Morgan/TS1, *Cent*)

248.37   and entered (*Cent*) • toward (MS Berg, MS Morgan/TS1)

248.38   conversation. (*Cent*) • conversation. When . . . like frogs. (MS Berg, MS Morgan/TS1 [52.7–10])

248.38   Twins (MTP) • twins (MS Berg, MS Morgan/TS1, *Cent*)

249.5   Good-mornin' (MS Berg, MS Morgan/TS1) • Good mornin', (*Cent*)

249.5   handshake (MTP) • hand-shake (MS Berg, MS Morgan/TS1); hand- | shake (*Cent*)

249.6   Good-morning (MS Berg, MS Morgan/TS1) • Good morning (*Cent*)

249.6   Cappello (MTP) • Capello (MS Berg, MS Morgan/TS1, *Cent*)

249.7   handshake (MTP) • hand-shake (MS Berg, MS Morgan/TS1, *Cent*)

249.10   Good-mornin' (MS Berg, MS Morgan/TS1) • Good mornin' (*Cent*)

249.10   handshake (MS Berg, MS Morgan/TS1) • hand-shake (*Cent*)

249.11 Good-morning (MS Berg, MS Morgan/TS1) • Good morning (*Cent*)

249.11–12 Cappello." [¶] Handshake (MS Berg, MS Morgan/TS1) • Capello." Hand-shake (*Cent*)

249.12 admiring (*Cent*) • devouring (MS Berg, MS Morgan/TS1)

249.12 ye! (MS Berg, MS Morgan/TS1) • ye, (*Cent*)

249.14 None of these visitors were (MS Berg, MS Morgan/TS1) • None of these visitors was (*Cent*) [TEXTUAL NOTE: *Cent's reading reflects the superstition that 'None' must take a singular verb; MS Morgan's form is frequent in SLC's writing and is approved by grammars of the period*]

249.14 but (MS Berg, MS Morgan/TS1) • but, (*Cent*)

249.19 My Lord, or Your Lordship, (MS Berg, MS Morgan/TS1) • "My lord," or "Your lordship," (*Cent*)

249.19 the (MS Berg, MS Morgan/TS1) • that (*Cent*)

249.20 knocked cold (MS Berg, MS Morgan/TS1) • overwhelmed (*Cent*)

249.20 its (MS Berg, *Cent*) • it's (MS Morgan/TS1)

249.22 handshake, (MS Berg, MS Morgan/TS1) • hand-shake (*Cent*)

249.23 receptions, (MS Berg, MS Morgan/TS1) • receptions (*Cent*)

249.25 and if (*Cent*) • and inquired if (MS Berg, MS Morgan/TS1)

249.28 them;" (MS Berg, MS Morgan/TS1) • them"; (*Cent*)

249.31 Twins (MTP) • twins (MS Berg, MS Morgan/TS1, *Cent*)

249.32 fluently, (MS Berg, MS Morgan/TS1) • fluently (*Cent*)

249.33 admiration, (MS Berg, MS Morgan/TS1) • admiration (*Cent*)

249.33 popularity right along (MS Berg, MS Morgan/TS1) • favor from all (*Cent*) [TEXTUAL NOTE: *The unbuttoned Western form 'right along,' as used by SLC in the authorial voice, may have been marked for alteration by the Century Magazine*]

249.35 think, (MS Berg, MS Morgan/TS1) • think (*Cent*)

249.35 *ours* (MS Berg, MS Morgan/TS1) • ours (*Cent*)

249.35 ours. (MS Berg, MS Morgan/TS1) • ours! (*Cent*)

249.37 Twins (MTP) • twins (MS Berg, MS Morgan/TS1, *Cent*)

249.38 centre (MS Berg, MS Morgan/TS1) • center (*Cent*)

249.38 recognized (MS Berg, *Cent*) • recognizing (MS Morgan/TS1) [TEXTUAL NOTE: *TS1's 'recognizing' is the typist's error. Cent restores MS Berg's original form without having access to the manuscript, suggesting that this was an authorial correction on TS2a or on magazine proofs*]

250.4 its (MS Berg, *Cent*) • it's (MS Morgan/TS1)

250.6 people (*Cent*) • young people (MS Berg, MS Morgan/TS1)

250.7 up stairs (MS Berg, MS Morgan/TS1) • up-stairs (*Cent*)

250.7	overflow meeting (MS Berg, MS Morgan/TS1) • overflow-meeting (*Cent*)
250.7	there (*Cent*) • up there (MS Berg, MS Morgan/TS1)
250.12	its (MS Berg, *Cent*) • it's (MS Morgan/TS1)
250.14	Twins (MTP) • twins (MS Berg, MS Morgan/TS1, *Cent*)
250.19	Twins (MTP) • duplicates (MS Berg, MS Morgan/TS1); twins (*Cent*)
250.20	satisfied; (MS Berg, MS Morgan/TS1) • satisfied— (*Cent*)
250.22–27	[¶] The young strangers . . . hearing masters. (*Cent*) • [*not in*] (MS Berg, MS Morgan)
250.25	'prentice-work (MTP) • [*not in*] (MS Berg, MS Morgan); prentice-work (*Cent*) [TEXTUAL NOTE: *For this passage added in revision, no manuscript source exists; the apostrophe is supplied on the basis of SLC's practice in other manuscripts*]
251.2–3	One of the most striking differences between a cat and a lie is that a cat has only nine lives. (*Cent*) • The Creator admired . . . solar systems. (MS Morgan [54.2–7])
251.6	Twins (MS Berg) • twins (MS Morgan/TS1, *Cent*)
251.7–9	progress, and had also volunteered to play some duets at an amateur entertainment for the benefit of a local charity (*Cent*) • progress (MS Berg); progress, and had also volunteered to do the balcony scene in Romeo and Juliet at an amateur entertainment for the benefit of a local charity (MS Morgan/TS1)
251.9	its (MS Berg, *Cent*) • it's (MS Morgan/TS1)
251.10	be (MS Berg, MS Morgan/TS1) • to be (*Cent*)
251.11	him (MS Berg, MS Morgan/TS1) • him, (*Cent*)
251.13	see. (*Cent*) • see, and . . . all around. (MS Berg, MS Morgan/TS1 [54.17–55.2])
251.15	Freemasons' (MS Berg, *Cent*) • Freemasons (MS Morgan/TS1)
251.17	money (*Cent*) • of the money (MS Berg, MS Morgan/TS1)
251.19	squirt (MS Berg, MS Morgan/TS1) • put (*Cent*)
251.19	fire; then he (*Cent*) • fire, and (MS Berg, MS Morgan/TS1)
251.22	Twins (MTP) • twins (MS Berg, MS Morgan/TS1, *Cent*)
251.22	admiration (MS Berg, MS Morgan/TS1) • admiration, (*Cent*)
251.25	of it (*Cent*) • from it (MS Berg, MS Morgan/TS1)
251.26	hospitably out (MS Berg, MS Morgan/TS1) • out hospitably (*Cent*)
252.3	Freethinkers (MS Berg, MS Morgan/TS1) • Free-thinkers (*Cent*)
252.3–6	He said the society . . . all about (*Cent*) • [¶] This latter fact . . . over to No. 16, (MS Berg, MS Morgan/TS1 [55.23–71.3])

252.7	Pudd'nhead (MS Berg, *Cent*) • Puddn'head (MS Morgan)
252.8–13	succeeded—the favorable impression . . . vote and carried. (*Cent*) • succeeded with Luigi . . . let well enough alone. (MS Morgan [71.5–23])
252.16	Twins (MS Morgan) • twins (*Cent*)
252.16–20	lodgings, presently . . . house. Pudd'nhead (*Cent*) • lodgings when . . . Wilson's. [¶] Puddn'head (MS Morgan [71.26–73.33])
252.22	this. (MS Morgan) • this: (*Cent*)
252.23	centre (MS Morgan) • center (*Cent*)
252.29	sitting room (MS Morgan) • sitting-room (*Cent*)
252.30	Pratt, (MS Morgan) • Pratt (*Cent*)
252.34	and (*Cent*) • [*not in*] (MS Morgan)
252.35	window shades (MS Morgan) • window-shades (*Cent*)
252.36	dress (MS Morgan) • dress, (*Cent*)
252.36–37	alternating broad stripes (MS Morgan) • broad stripes (*Cent*) [TEXTUAL NOTE: *Probably an editor is likelier than an author to see that stripes of two colors are* 'alternating' *by their very nature, and delete the adjective as redundant*]
252.38	practicing (MS Morgan) • practising (*Cent*)
253.2	Driscoll's (MS Morgan) • Tom Driscoll's (*Cent*)
253.9	levée (MS Morgan) • levee (*Cent*)
253.11	a little before (*Cent*) • before (MS Morgan)
253.15	new-comer (MS Morgan) • newcomer (*Cent*)
253.18	which she was not aware of, herself (MS Morgan) • of which she herself was not aware (*Cent*)
253.19	Twins (MS Morgan) • twins (*Cent*)
253.21	day-break (MS Morgan) • daybreak (*Cent*)
254.3	lifetime (MS Morgan) • lifetime, (*Cent*)
254.5–7	[¶] Consider well . . . *Calendar.* (*Cent*) • [*not in*] (MS Morgan)
254.6	Paradise (MS in CU-MARK) • [*not in*] (MS Morgan); paradise (*Cent*)
254.8	necessary, (MS Morgan) • necessary (*Cent*)
254.9	She went away chambermaiding the year she was set free, when (MS Morgan) • At the time she was set free and went away chambermaiding, (*Cent*)
254.11	"Grand Mogul." (MS Morgan) • *Grand Mogul.* (*Cent*)
254.11	A (*Cent*) • It was a . . . her eyesight. [¶] A (MS Morgan [75.9–77.16])
254.11–12	a wonted and easy-going steamboatman of her (MS Morgan) • her wonted and easy-going at the work (*Cent*) [TEXTUAL NOTE: *Cent's*

reading may originate in an editorial objection to Roxy being called, in spite of her sex, a 'steamboatman']

254.13   She was promoted, then, (MS Morgan) • Then she was promoted (*Cent*)

254.20   banked (*Cent*) • saved up and banked (MS Morgan)

254.20–21   in New Orleans (*Cent*) • [*not in*] (MS Morgan)

254.22   and (MS Morgan) • and that (*Cent*)

254.23   enough: (MS Morgan) • enough; (*Cent*)

254.24–26   it. [¶] She bade good-bye to her comrades on the Grand Mogul and moved her kit ashore when the boat touched the levee at New Orleans. (MS Morgan) • it. When the boat touched the levee at New Orleans she bade good-by to her comrades on the *Grand Mogul* and moved her kit ashore. (*Cent*)

255.1   birth-place (MS Morgan) • birthplace (*Cent*)

255.4   local (*Cent*) • [*not in*] (MS Morgan)

255.5   homestretch (MTP) • home- | stretch (MS Morgan); home-stretch (*Cent*)

255.5   Time (*Cent*) • At once her . . . found that time (MS Morgan)

255.5   and (*Cent*) • and that (MS Morgan)

255.9   around (MS Morgan) • upon (*Cent*) [TEXTUAL NOTE: *A typist's or compositor's banalization*]

255.12   long forgotten (MS Morgan) • long-forgotten (*Cent*)

255.12   lovely—that (MS Morgan) • lovely; that (*Cent*)

255.13–14   poverty! [¶] Her poverty. (MS Morgan) • poverty. [¶] Her poverty! (*Cent*)

255.15   maybe he would help her; (MTP) • Maybe he would help her; (MS Morgan); [*not in*] (*Cent*) [TEXTUAL NOTE: *Probable eyeskip by the typist of TS2*]

255.17   much! (MS Morgan) • much. (*Cent*)

255.19   sure (MS Morgan) • surely (*Cent*)

255.25   amen corner (MS Morgan) • amen-corner (*Cent*)

255.26   should (MS Morgan) • would (*Cent*)

255.29   marvel (MS Morgan) • marvel, (*Cent*)

255.32   explosions of applause (MS Morgan) • expressions of applause (*Cent*) [TEXTUAL NOTE: *Probably the TS2 typist misread MS Morgan. SLC's typical metaphors for applause strengthen the case against the bland Cent reading:* 'volcanic eruption of applause', 'burst of applause', 'storm of applause', 'thunders of applause', 'tempests of applause', 'hurricanes of applause', *etc.*]

256.2   The ostensible "Chambers" (*Cent*) • Chambers (MS Morgan)

256.6	so! (MS Morgan) • so? (*Cent*)
256.6	a jokin' (MS Morgan) • a-jokin' (*Cent*)
256.7	so, (MS Morgan) • so (*Cent*)
256.8	'tain't (*Cent*) • t'ain't (MS Morgan)
256.9	'tain't (*Cent*) • t'ain't (MS Morgan)
256.10	gwyne (MS Morgan) • gwine (*Cent*)
256.11	caze (MTP) • becase (MS Morgan); 'ca'se (*Cent*) [TEXTUAL NOTE: *Cent* ''ca'se' *usually occurs where MS Morgan reads* 'caze', *suggesting that here SLC revised his own* 'becase' *to* 'caze' *(his spelling of that form) and that Century restyled it as* ''ca'se']
256.12	astonishment, (MS Morgan) • astonishment (*Cent*)
256.13	marster (*Cent*) • marse (MS Morgan)
256.13	caze (MTP) • becase (MS Morgan); 'ca'se (*Cent*) [TEXTUAL NOTE: *See* PW-REV, *Textual Apparatus, textual note at 256.11*]
256.14	jes' (MS Morgan) • jes (*Cent*)
256.17	dollahs! (MS Morgan) • dollahs. (*Cent*)
256.17	mos' (MS Morgan) • 'mos' (*Cent*)
256.17	tollable (MS Morgan) • tol'able (*Cent*)
256.20	God's (*Cent*) • Gawd's (MS Morgan)
256.20	jes' (MS Morgan) • jes (*Cent*)
256.20	hunderd (MS Morgan) • hund'd (*Cent*)
256.21	jes' (MS Morgan) • jes (*Cent*)
256.22	a hoppin' (MTP) • a hoppin (MS Morgan); a-hoppin' (*Cent*)
256.22	bilin' (MS Morgan) • b'ilin' (*Cent*)
256.22	*tell* (MS Morgan) • tell (*Cent*)
256.22	tuck 'n (MS Morgan) • tuck 'n' (*Cent*)
256.23	relish (*Cent*) • complacent relish (MS Morgan)
256.28	busted (MS Morgan) • bu'sted (*Cent*)
256.29	Bus—ted (MS Morgan) • Bu's—ted (*Cent*)
256.29	ever (MS Morgan) • *ever* (*Cent*)
256.29	so. (MS Morgan) • so! (*Cent*)
256.30	misable (MS Morgan) • mis'able (*Cent*)
256.30	tribbilation! (MS Morgan) • tribbilation. (*Cent*)
256.33	Her remark amused Chambers: (*Cent*) • [*not in*] (MS Morgan)
256.34	jes' (MS Morgan) • jes (*Cent*)
256.34	*I*'s (MS Morgan) • I's (*Cent*)

256.35   pow'ful (*Cent*) • pow'full (MS Morgan)

256.36   noth'n (MS Morgan) • noth'n' (*Cent*)

256.38   'tain't (*Cent*) • t'ain't (MS Morgan)

256.38   busted (MS Morgan) • bu'sted (*Cent*)

256.38   *do* (MS Morgan) • do (*Cent*)

256.38   fogit (MS Morgan) • forgit (*Cent*)

257.1   *'tain't* (*Cent*) • *t'ain't* (MS Morgan)

257.1   caze (MS Morgan) • 'ca'se (*Cent*)

257.1   agin (MS Morgan) • ag'in (*Cent*)

257.2   *you* (MS Morgan) • you (*Cent*)

257.2   mammy, (MS Morgan) • mammy? (*Cent*)

257.2   'tain't (MTP) • t'ain't (MS Morgan); 'Tain't (*Cent*)

257.3   reckon? (MS Morgan) • reckon. (*Cent*)

257.4   'Tain't (*Cent*) • Tain't (MS Morgan)

257.4   *my* (MS Morgan) • my (*Cent*)

257.4   *is* (MS Morgan) • is (*Cent*)

257.5   Wuz (*Cent*) • Was (MS Morgan) [TEXTUAL NOTE: *In the part of the text where E is an authoritative witness, its concurrence with Cent in 'wuz'— never found in MS Morgan—shows this dialect form was introduced by the author in revising TS2a. In the* Huckleberry Finn *manuscript, SLC revised Jim's 'was' to 'wuz' or ''uz' in seven places (HF 2003, Alterations in the Manuscript, at 340.15 (twice), 340.16, 340.36, 340.37, 361.22, 362.2)*]

257.7   noth'n (MS Morgan) • noth'n' (*Cent*)

257.7   ben (MS Morgan) • be'n (*Cent*)

257.7   Vallet (MS Morgan) • Valet (*Cent*)

257.9   agin (MS Morgan) • ag'in (*Cent*)

257.11   satisfied, (MS Morgan) • satisfied (*Cent*)

257.14   jes' (MS Morgan) • jes (*Cent*)

257.19   unconsciously (*Cent*) • [*not in*] (MS Morgan)

257.26   trembling, (MS Morgan) • trembling (*Cent*)

257.27   sideways (MS Morgan) • sideways, (*Cent*)

257.28   word; (MS Morgan) • word: (*Cent*)

257.29   *Please* (MS Morgan) • Please (*Cent*)

257.29   *please* (MS Morgan) • please (*Cent*)

257.34   again (MS Morgan) • again, (*Cent*)

257.36   was!—I (MS Morgan) • was! I (*Cent*)

257.37	entered, (MS Morgan) • entered (*Cent*)
258.6	goodness (MS Morgan) • goodness, (*Cent*)
258.7	a knowed (MS Morgan) • a-knowed (*Cent*)
258.7	Tom, (MS Morgan) • Tom! (*Cent*)
258.7	wouldn't. (MS Morgan) • wouldn't! (*Cent*)
258.8	'member ole (MS Morgan) • 'member old (*Cent*)
258.8	yo' ole (MS Morgan) • yo' old (*Cent*)
258.8	Well, (MS Morgan) • Well (*Cent*)
258.9	caze (MS Morgan) • 'ca'se (*Cent*)
258.10	damn (MS Morgan) • —— (*Cent*)
258.10	short. (MS Morgan) • short! (*Cent*)
258.11	Jes' (MS Morgan) • Jes (*Cent*)
258.11	allays (MS Morgan) • al'ays (*Cent*)
258.12	mammy! (MS Morgan) • mammy. (*Cent*)
258.12	jes' (MS Morgan) • jes (*Cent*)
258.13	along. (MS Morgan) • along! (*Cent*)
258.16	nurse (MS Morgan) • nurse, (*Cent*)
258.17	funning (MS Morgan) • funning, (*Cent*)
258.23	supplication— (MS Morgan) • supplication: (*Cent*)
258.24	luck, (MS Morgan) • luck (*Cent*)
258.25	*could* (MS Morgan) • could (*Cent*)
258.26	jes' (MS Morgan) • jes (*Cent*)
258.26	d— (MS Morgan) • dol— (*Cent*)
258.29	*you* (MS Morgan) • you (*Cent*)
258.30	it. (MS Morgan) • it! (*Cent*)
258.31	halfway (MS Morgan) • half-way (*Cent*)
258.32	said, mournfully— (MS Morgan) • said mournfully: (*Cent*)
258.34	most (MS Morgan) • 'most (*Cent*)
258.34	rich (MS Morgan) • rich, (*Cent*)
258.35	gitt'n (MS Morgan) • gitt'n' (*Cent*)
258.35	he'p (*Cent*) • h'ep (MS Morgan)
258.36	twix (MS Morgan) • 'twix' (*Cent*)
259.3	*ever* (MS Morgan) • ever (*Cent*)
259.3	gwyne (MS Morgan) • gwine (*Cent*)
259.19	*now.* (MS Morgan) • now! (*Cent*)

259.21 gwyne (MS Morgan) • gwine (*Cent*)

259.21 gwyne (MS Morgan) • gwine (*Cent*)

259.22 about (MS Morgan) • 'bout (*Cent*)

259.22 you! (MS Morgan) • you. (*Cent*)

259.24 *she* (MS Morgan) • she (*Cent*)

259.25 months (MS Morgan) • months, (*Cent*)

259.26 again (MS Morgan) • again, (*Cent*)

259.32 said— (MS Morgan) • said: (*Cent*)

259.35 bill, (MS Morgan) • bill; (*Cent*)

259.38 former slave (*Cent*) • negro ex-slave (MS Morgan)

260.2 offers— (MS Morgan) • offers: (*Cent*)

260.3 bust (MS Morgan) • bu'st (*Cent*)

260.4 *more* (MS Morgan) • more (*Cent*)

260.10 'Cose (MS Morgan) • Co'se (*Cent*)

260.11 dollah! (MS Morgan) • dollah. (*Cent*)

260.11 gwyne (MS Morgan) • gwine (*Cent*)

260.11 *you,* (MS Morgan) • *you* (*Cent*)

260.11 *you* (MS Morgan) • you (*Cent*)

260.12 gwyne (MS Morgan) • gwine (*Cent*)

260.15 seized (*Cent*) • siezed (MS Morgan)

260.15 skirts (MS Morgan) • skirts, (*Cent*)

260.17 Look-a-heah (*Cent*) • Look-a-here (MS Morgan) [TEXTUAL NOTE: *In the manuscript of* Huckleberry Finn, *SLC six times revised* 'here' *to* 'heah' *or vice versa (HF 2003, Alterations in the Manuscript, entries at 54.26, 97.18, 103.21, 150.31, 150.33, 201.30)*]

260.17 'uz (*Cent*) • was (MS Morgan)

260.22 said— (MS Morgan) • said: (*Cent*)

260.25 not. (MS Morgan) • not! (*Cent*)

260.25 *You* call *me* (MS Morgan) • You call me (*Cent*)

260.28 'uz (*Cent*) • was (MS Morgan)

260.28 hadn't (*Cent*) • you hadn't (MS Morgan)

260.30 sum'n (MS Morgan) • sum'n' (*Cent*)

260.31 jes' (MS Morgan) • jes (*Cent*)

260.32 *hear* (MS Morgan) • hear (*Cent*)

260.34 *see* (MS Morgan) • see (*Cent*)

260.34 too. (MS Morgan) • too! (*Cent*)

260.35   me! (MS Morgan) • me. (*Cent*)

260.37   drink in (MS Morgan) • drink-in (*Cent*)

261.1   gen'lman (MS Morgan) • gen'l'man (*Cent*)

261.1   nigger wench (MS Morgan) • nigger-wench (*Cent*)

261.2   jes' (MS Morgan) • jes (*Cent*)

261.2   Gabrel (MS Morgan) • Gabr'el (*Cent*)

261.3   ready! . . . . . (MS Morgan) • ready . . . (*Cent*)

261.5   Now (MS Morgan) • Now, (*Cent*)

261.8   gwyne (MS Morgan) • gwine (*Cent*)

261.9   heah (*Cent*) • here (MS Morgan)

261.11   feared (MS Morgan) • 'feared (*Cent*)

261.14   caze (MS Morgan) • 'ca'se (*Cent*)

261.14   star-steps (MS Morgan) • sta'r-steps (*Cent*)

261.15   a roostin' (MS Morgan) • a-roostin' (*Cent*)

261.15   caze (MTP) • becaze (MS Morgan); 'ca'se (*Cent*)

261.16   said (MS Morgan) • said, (*Cent*)

261.16   bill. (MS Morgan) • bill! (*Cent*)

261.17   Hm (MS Morgan) • H'm (*Cent*)

261.17   busted (MS Morgan) • bu'sted (*Cent*)

261.20   it. (MS Morgan) • it! (*Cent*)

261.22   two-thirds (MS Morgan) • two thirds (*Cent*)

261.23–24 saying,— [¶] "It's prime—I'll (MS Morgan) • saying, "It's prime. I'll (*Cent*)

262.2–9   Why is it . . . Tom (*Cent*) • Then Tom (MS Morgan)

262.6   man, (MS in CU-MARK) • [*not in*] (MS Morgan); man (*Cent*)

262.7   pre-historic (MS in CU-MARK) • [*not in*] (MS Morgan); prehistoric (*Cent*)

262.9   hands (MS Morgan) • hands, (*Cent*)

262.12   nigger wench (MS Morgan) • nigger-wench (*Cent*)

262.13   deepest deeps (MS Morgan) • deepest depths (*Cent*)

262.14   this. . . . . . (MS Morgan) • this. . . . (*Cent*)

262.15   lower (*Cent*) • lower than this (MS Morgan)

262.17   house, (*Cent*) • house (MS Morgan)

262.18   wretched (*Cent*) • tolerably sick (MS Morgan)

262.22   afterward (MS Morgan) • afterward, (*Cent*)

263.1   soap and candle boxes (MS Morgan) • soap- and candle-boxes (*Cent*)

263.3   Now, den. (MS Morgan) • Now den, (*Cent*)

263.4	gwyne (MS Morgan) • gwine (*Cent*)
263.5	me. (MS Morgan) • me! (*Cent*)
263.8	*dat* (MS Morgan) • dat (*Cent*)
263.8	noth'n (MS Morgan) • nothin' (*Cent*)
263.8	*all* (MS Morgan) • all (*Cent*)
263.11	Why— (MS Morgan) • Why, (*Cent*)
263.11	*mean* (MS Morgan) • mean (*Cent*)
263.12	fate (MS Morgan) • Fate (*Cent*)
263.13–14	*You ain't no more kin to ole Marse Driscoll den I is!*—dat's (MS Morgan) • You ain't no more kin to ole Marse Driscoll den I is!—*dat's* (*Cent*)
263.14	means (*Cent*) • mean (MS Morgan)
263.16	all. (MS Morgan) • all! (*Cent*)
263.16	You's (*Cent*) • You is (MS Morgan)
263.17	minute! (MS Morgan) • minute; (*Cent*)
263.17	mouf, (MS Morgan) • mouf (*Cent*)
263.18	*sell you down de river* (MS Morgan) • sell you down de river (*Cent*)
263.21	jes' (MS Morgan) • jes (*Cent*)
263.21	noth'n (MS Morgan) • nothin' (*Cent*)
263.21	me! (MS Morgan) • me. (*Cent*)
263.22	*you's my son* (MS Morgan) • you's my *son* (*Cent*)
263.23	devil!—" (MS Morgan) • devil!" (*Cent*)
263.24	—"en (MS Morgan) • "En (*Cent*)
263.24	ben (MS Morgan) • be'n (*Cent*)
263.24	a kickin' en a cuffin' (MS Morgan) • a-kickin' en a-cuffin' (*Cent*)
263.25	*en yo' marster* (MS Morgan) • en yo' *marster* (*Cent*)
263.27	—"en (MS Morgan) • "En (*Cent*)
263.27	Driscoll (MS Morgan) • Driscoll, (*Cent*)
263.27	Vallet (MS Morgan) • Valet (*Cent*)
263.28	got (MS Morgan) • *got* (*Cent*)
263.28	fambly name (*Cent*) • surname (MS Morgan)
263.28	becaze (MS Morgan) • beca'se (*Cent*)
263.29	seized (*Cent*) • siezed (MS Morgan)
263.30	him (MS Morgan) • him, (*Cent*)
263.31	sk'yer (MS Morgan) • skyer (*Cent*)
263.31	*me?* (MS Morgan) • me? (*Cent*)
263.33	style, *I* (MS Morgan) • style—*I* (*Cent*)

263.33	*thoo* (MS Morgan) • thoo (*Cent*)
263.33	*I* (MS Morgan) • I (*Cent*)
263.33	gitt'n (MS Morgan) • gitt'n' (*Cent*)
263.34	becaze (MS Morgan) • beca'se (*Cent*)
263.37	you. (MS Morgan) • you! (*Cent*)
263.37	*Now* (MS Morgan) • Now (*Cent*)
263.38	agin (MS Morgan) • ag'in (*Cent*)
263.38	you. (MS Morgan) • you! (*Cent*)
264.1	a while (MS Morgan) • awhile (*Cent*)
264.1–2	disorganizing sensations and emotions (*Cent*) • doubt, certainty, fear, derision, and all the other emotions (MS Morgan)
264.2	said (MS Morgan) • said, (*Cent*)
264.3	moonshine—now, (MS Morgan) • moonshine; now (*Cent*)
264.7	Roxy, (MS Morgan) • Roxy; (*Cent*)
264.8	again. (MS Morgan) • again! (*Cent*)
264.8	*Please* (MS Morgan) • Please (*Cent*)
264.8	Roxy. (MS Morgan) • Roxy! (*Cent*)
264.9	gravely— (MS Morgan) • gravely: (*Cent*)
264.10	Vallet (MS Morgan) • Valet (*Cent*)
264.11	*me* Roxy (MS Morgan) • me *Roxy* (*Cent*)
264.12	*Ma* or *mammy* (MS Morgan) • ma or mammy (*Cent*)
264.15	fogit (MS Morgan) • forgit (*Cent*)
264.15	agin (MS Morgan) • ag'in (*Cent*)
264.16	Now, (MS Morgan) • Now (*Cent*)
264.17	agin (MS Morgan) • ag'in (*Cent*)
264.17	agin (MS Morgan) • ag'in (*Cent*)
264.18	*me* (MS Morgan) • me (*Cent*)
264.19	is (MS Morgan) • is, (*Cent*)
264.19	it! (MS Morgan) • it. (*Cent*)
264.21	it, (MS Morgan) • it; (*Cent*)
264.21	it! (MS Morgan) • it. (*Cent*)
264.22	proven (MS Morgan) • proved (*Cent*) [TEXTUAL NOTE: *The Century Magazine's style sheet demanded* 'proved' *rather than* 'proven' *(McKnight 1923, 408–9)*]
264.24	doubts (MS Morgan) • doubt (*Cent*)
264.28	Now, (MS Morgan) • Now (*Cent*)

264.28	we's gwyne (MS Morgan) • we's gwine (*Cent*)
264.28	business (*Cent*) • cold business (MS Morgan)
264.28	gwyne (MS Morgan) • gwine (*Cent*)
264.30	gwyne (MS Morgan) • gwine (*Cent*)
264.36	"How (*Cent*) • How (MS Morgan)
264.36	gwyne (MS Morgan) • gwine (*Cent*)
264.38	*I* (MS Morgan) • I (*Cent*)
264.38	know— (MS Morgan) • know; (*Cent*)
264.38	questions! (MS Morgan) • questions. (*Cent*)
265 *illus*	"DOES YOU B'LIEVE ME WHEN I SAYS DAT?" (MTP) • "'DOES YOU B'LIEVE ME WHEN I SAYS DAT?'" (*Cent*); [*not in*] (MS Morgan)
266.3	fact (MS Morgan) • fact, (*Cent*)
266.3	fellow villagers (MS Morgan) • fellow-villagers (*Cent*)
266.5	amount (*Cent*) • amount on (MS Morgan)
266.11	ready, (MS Morgan) • ready; (*Cent*)
266.16	off (MS Morgan) • off, (*Cent*)
266.17	gen'lman (MTP) • genl'man (MS Morgan); gen'l'man (*Cent*)
266.18	time; (MS Morgan) • time, (*Cent*)
266.18	allays (MS Morgan) • al'ays (*Cent*)
266.19	fogit (MS Morgan) • forgit (*Cent*)
266.22	know, (MS Morgan) • know (*Cent*)
266.22	mother— (MS Morgan) • mother; (*Cent*)
266.23	now— (MS Morgan) • now; (*Cent*)
266.23	gwyne (MS Morgan) • gwine (*Cent*)
266.23	fogit (MS Morgan) • fo'git (*Cent*)
266.24	agin (MS Morgan) • ag'in (*Cent*)
266.25	you! (MS Morgan) • you. (*Cent*)
266.30	up, (MS Morgan) • up (*Cent*)
266.30	said: (MS Morgan) • said— (*Cent*)
266.31	don't. (MS Morgan) • don't! (*Cent*)
266.32	wuz (*Cent*) • was (MS Morgan)
266.33	Ole (MS Morgan) • ole (*Cent*)
266.33	stock, (MS Morgan) • stock. (*Cent*)
266.33	Famblies (MS Morgan) • famblies (*Cent*)
266.33	wuz (*Cent*) • was (MS Morgan)

266.33   Jes' (MS Morgan) • Jes (*Cent*)

266.34   still (MS Morgan) • little (*Cent*)

266.35   impressively, (MS Morgan) • impressively: (*Cent*)

266.37   churches (MS Morgan) • Churches (*Cent*)

266.38   man!" Under (MS Morgan) • man." [¶] Under (*Cent*)

267.4   "Dey (MS Morgan) • [¶] "Dey (*Cent*)

267.4   Now, (MS Morgan) • Now (*Cent*)

267.5   'long. (MS Morgan) • 'long! (*Cent*)

267.5   jes' (MS Morgan) • jes (*Cent*)

267.6   *right* (MS Morgan) • right (*Cent*)

267.6   swah! (MS Morgan) • swah. (*Cent*)

268.2   say (MS Morgan) • say, (*Cent*)

268.5   When angry, count four; when very angry, swear. (*Cent*) • Why is it that we rejoice at a birth and weep at a funeral? It is because we are not the person involved. (MS Morgan)

268.8   O (MS Morgan) • Oh (*Cent*)

268.9   groan (*Cent*) • bitter groan (MS Morgan)

268.10   nigger!— (MS Morgan) • nigger! (*Cent*)

268.10   nigger!—oh (MS Morgan) • nigger! Oh (*Cent*)

268.17   black? . . . . . . (MS Morgan) • black? . . . (*Cent*)

268.19   head." (*Cent*) • head . . . virtue. . . . ." (MS Morgan [89.20–28])

268.22   *nigger* (MS Morgan) • nigger (*Cent*)

268.22–23   young marster (MS Morgan) • Young Marster (*Cent*)

268.23   said, (MS Morgan) • said (*Cent*)

268.25   wretch (*Cent*) • degraded wretch (MS Morgan)

268.25–26   he is white, and for that I could kill him—if I had the courage. Ach! he is (MS Morgan) • he is (*Cent*) [TEXTUAL NOTE: *Presumably eyeskip of the TS2 typist from the first* 'he is' *to the second*]

268.26   me, (MS Morgan) • me (*Cent*)

268.27   *wish* (MS Morgan) • wish (*Cent*)

268.29   [*one line skipped*] A gigantic irruption (MS Morgan) • A gigantic irruption, (*Cent*)

268.30   waves (MS Morgan) • waves, (*Cent*)

269.5   ideals, (*Cent*) • ideals, now, (MS Morgan)

269.7   pumice stone (MS Morgan) • pumice-stone (*Cent*)

269.8   places (MS Morgan) • places, (*Cent*)

269.9   work. (*Cent*) • work; he had . . . many surprises. (MS Morgan [90.17–23])

269.9   friend (MS Morgan) • friend, (*Cent*)

269.10   limp (MS Morgan) • limp, (*Cent*)

269.15–16   the idol of his secret worship, (*Cent*) • [*not in*] (MS Morgan) [TEXTUAL NOTE: *A passage deleted from TS2 in SLC's July 1893 revision (PW-MS, 65.7–66.22) had established a budding romance between Tom and Rowena, which is hastily reinforced here*]

269.19   tones (MS Morgan) • tones, (*Cent*)

269.21   it (MS Morgan) • it, (*Cent*)

269.21   had passed (MS Morgan) • passed (*Cent*)

269.26   The curse of Ham was upon him, he said to himself. (MS Morgan) • He said to himself that the curse of Ham was upon him. (*Cent*)

269.29   you?—you (MS Morgan) • you? You (*Cent*)

269.29   nigger! (MS Morgan) • nigger, (*Cent*)

269.30   says (MS Morgan) • says, (*Cent*)

269.32   ostensible "aunt's" (*Cent*) • aunt's (MS Morgan)

269.34   ostensible "uncle" (*Cent*) • uncle (MS Morgan)

269.37   For as (*Cent*) • In his . . . For as (MS Morgan [91.16–92.5])

270.1   In (MS Morgan) • [¶] In (*Cent*)

270.1   *opinions* (MS Morgan) • opinions (*Cent*)

270.2   *character* (MS Morgan) • character (*Cent*)

270.5   offered; (MS Morgan) • offered— (*Cent*)

270.7   after a while (*Cent*) • now (MS Morgan)

270.9   ways, (MS Morgan) • ways (*Cent*)

270.9   feeling, (MS Morgan) • feeling (*Cent*)

270.11   days. (*Cent*) • days. [¶] Yet . . . pretensions. (MS Morgan [93.14–20])

270.15–16   will. [¶] He (MS Morgan) • will. He (*Cent*)

270.21   rule, (MS Morgan) • rule (*Cent*)

270.23   town, for (MS Morgan) • town (for (*Cent*)

270.24   village, (MS Morgan) • village), (*Cent*)

270.28   Now and then (MS Morgan) • Occasionally (*Cent*)

270.28   St. (*Cent*) • St (MS Morgan)

270.31   He projected a new raid on his town in this interest. (MS Morgan) • For this purpose he projected a new raid on his town. (*Cent*)

270.33   know, (MS Morgan) • know (*Cent*)

270.35   Twins,— (MS Morgan) • twins— (*Cent*)

270.36   later (MS Morgan) • after (*Cent*)

270.38   key (MS Morgan) • key, (*Cent*)

271.2   in a bundle (*Cent*) • [*not in*] (MS Morgan)

271.5   way (MS Morgan) • way, (*Cent*)

271.7   he (MS Morgan) • [*not in*] (*Cent*)

271.9   downtown (MS Morgan) • down town (*Cent*)

271.9   reconnoitre (MS Morgan) • reconnoiter (*Cent*)

271.18   providence (MS Morgan) • providence, (*Cent*)

271.21   nerve (MS Morgan) • nerve, (*Cent*)

271.23   that house's valuables (MS Morgan) • the valuables of that house (*Cent*)

271.24   [*centered rule*] (MS Morgan) • [*one extra line-space*] (*Cent*)

271.25   arrived, once more, (MS Morgan) • arrived once more (*Cent*)

271.26   Twins (MTP) • Twins from the Bible Society (MS Morgan); twins (*Cent*)

271.29   brazen huzzy (MS Morgan) • shameless creature (*Cent*) [TEXTUAL NOTE: *The Century allowed* huzzy (*or* hussy) *in dialect speech, but, on the evidence of this variant, barred it in the authorial voice*]

272.5   manuscript (*Cent*) • MS (MS Morgan)

272.7   but (MS Morgan) • [*not in*] (*Cent*)

272.7–8   with all your clothes on (MS Morgan) • [*not in*] (*Cent*)

272.9–10 [¶] As to the Adjective: when in doubt, strike it out.—*Pudd'nhead Wilson's Calendar.* (*Cent*) • [*not in*] (MS Morgan)

272.11   Twins (MTP) • duplicates (MS Morgan); twins (*Cent*)

272.12–13 the new friendship gathered ease and strength (*Cent*) • Angelo cheered up and forgot his late vexations (MS Morgan)

272.14   Twins (MS Morgan) • Twins (*Cent*)

272.14   praised (*Cent*) • complimented (MS Morgan)

272.17   author: (MS Morgan) • author; (*Cent*)

272.20–21 seeing the distinguished strangers for the first time (*Cent*) • startled at the figure the Twins made (MS Morgan)

272.21   hands, (MS Morgan) • hands; (*Cent*)

272.22   reception (MS Morgan) • reception, (*Cent*)

272.23   Twins (MS Morgan) • twins (*Cent*)

272.25   eye, (MS Morgan) • eye; (*Cent*)

272.26   talking, (MS Morgan) • talking; (*Cent*)

272.28   man, (MS Morgan) • man; (*Cent*)

273.2   present: (MS Morgan) • present. (*Cent*)

273.3	yet?" (MS Morgan) • yet? (*Cent*)
273.5	the law feature (*Cent*) • this feature (MS Morgan)
273.6	Twins (MS Morgan) • twins (*Cent*)
273.7	pleasantly (MS Morgan) • pleasantly, (*Cent*)
273.7	said— (MS Morgan) • said: (*Cent*)
273.8	practice (MS Morgan) • practise (*Cent*)
273.9	said, (MS Morgan) • said (*Cent*)
273.10	passion— (MS Morgan) • passion: (*Cent*)
273.11	practice (MS Morgan) • practise (*Cent*)
273.13	would (MS Morgan) • should (*Cent*)
273.15	profession (MS Morgan) • profession, (*Cent*)
273.16	[Tom winced.] (MS Morgan) • Tom winced. (*Cent*)
273.19	it— (MS Morgan) • it; (*Cent*)
273.19	grit. (MS Morgan) • grit! (*Cent*)
273.22	Wilson (*Cent*) • He (MS Morgan)
273.24	something," (MS Morgan) • something"; (*Cent*)
273.27	subject— (MS Morgan) • subject; (*Cent*)
273.30	finger-marks (MS Morgan) • finger-marks, (*Cent*)
273.33	strips (MS Morgan) • strips, (*Cent*)
273.33	said: (MS Morgan) • said— (*Cent*)
273.37	permanent (MS Morgan) • permanent, (*Cent*)
274.2	Yes, (MS Morgan) • Yes; (*Cent*)
274.2	boy, (MS Morgan) • boy (*Cent*)
274.5	hair (MS Morgan) • hair, (*Cent*)
274.8	date (MS Morgan) • date, (*Cent*)
274.8	laughs (MS Morgan) • laughs, (*Cent*)
274.12	done, (MS Morgan) • done (*Cent*)
274.15	all-around genius, (MS Morgan) • all-round genius— (*Cent*)
274.16	gentlemen, (MS Morgan) • gentlemen; (*Cent*)
274.16	scientist (*Cent*) • scientest (MS Morgan)
274.19	maggot-factory (MS Morgan) • notion-factory (*Cent*)
274.19	so?—but (MS Morgan) • so? But (*Cent*)
274.19	mind, (MS Morgan) • mind; (*Cent*)
274.21	once, (MS Morgan) • once; (*Cent*)
274.25	got here (MS Morgan) • got (*Cent*)

274.25	town (MS Morgan) • town, (*Cent*)
274.27	chaff (*Cent*) • raillery (MS Morgan)
274.28	Twins (MS Morgan) • twins (*Cent*)
274.30	said: (MS Morgan) • said— (*Cent*)
274.36	jugglery (MS Morgan) • juggling (*Cent*) [TEXTUAL NOTE: *In SLC's writings* 'jugglery' *is the noun and* 'juggling' *the adjective*]
275.1	*in* (MS Morgan) • in (*Cent*)
275.3	Angelo; (MS Morgan) • Angelo: (*Cent*)
275.7	Tom, (MS Morgan) • Tom. (*Cent*)
275.14	be— (MS Morgan) • be: (*Cent*)
275.18	science, (MS Morgan) • science; (*Cent*)
275.19	I better (MS Morgan) • I'd better (*Cent*)
275.19	*would* (MS Morgan) • would (*Cent*)
275.19	palms—come (MS Morgan) • palms. Come (*Cent*)
275.21	to, (MS Morgan) • to; (*Cent*)
275.23	palm, (MS Morgan) • palm (*Cent*)
275.24	me (MS Morgan) • me, (*Cent*)
275.24	often (MS Morgan) • often, (*Cent*)
275.27	half a dozen (MS Morgan) • half dozen (*Cent*)
275.29	Luigi— (MS Morgan) • Luigi: (*Cent*)
275.30	whole (MS Morgan) • whole, (*Cent*)
275.30	alone— (MS Morgan) • alone; (*Cent*)
275.33	Dave. (MS Morgan) • Dave! (*Cent*)
275.35	you (MS Morgan) • you, (*Cent*)
275.35	afterwards (MS Morgan) • afterward (*Cent*)
275.37	paper (MS Morgan) • paper, (*Cent*)
276.7	pains-takingly (MS Morgan) • painstakingly (*Cent*)
276.8	proportions (MS Morgan) • proportions, (*Cent*)
276.10	palm (MS Morgan) • palm, (*Cent*)
276.14	ambitions (MS Morgan) • ambitions, (*Cent*)
276.15	Twins (MS Morgan) • twins (*Cent*)
276.17	past (MS Morgan) • history (*Cent*) [TEXTUAL NOTE: 'past', *though not in this precise sense, was on the Century Magazine's list of* "words and phrases to be avoided"; *in any case this revision is not likely to be Clemens's* (McKnight 1923, 408)]
276.19	landmark (MS Morgan) • landmark, (*Cent*)

276.24	good-naturedly, (MS Morgan) • good-naturedly; (*Cent*)
276.24	shan't (MS Morgan) • sha'n't (*Cent*)
276.26	to quite know (MS Morgan) • quite to know (*Cent*)
276.28	to—. I (MS Morgan) • to—I (*Cent*)
276.33	to himself (*Cent*) • [*not in*] (MS Morgan)
276.34	*your* (MS Morgan) • your (*Cent*)
276.36	*prophesied* (*Cent*) • *prophecied* (MS Morgan)
276.37	*out.*" Tom (MS Morgan) • *out.*" [¶] Tom (*Cent*)
276.38	Tom (MS Morgan) • Tom, (*Cent*)
277.2	read: (*Cent*) • read. (MS Morgan)
277.3	*some one—but* (MS Morgan) • *some one, but* (*Cent*)
277.4	*out.*" "Caesar's (MS Morgan) • *out.*" [¶] "Caesar's (*Cent*)
277.5	of. (MS Morgan) • of! (*Cent*)
277.6	enemy. (MS Morgan) • enemy! (*Cent*)
277.8	along! (MS Morgan) • along. (*Cent*)
277.10	Luigi (MS Morgan) • Luigi, (*Cent*)
277.14	*I'll* (MS Morgan) • I'll (*Cent*)
277.14	Angelo (MS Morgan) • Angelo, (*Cent*)
277.15	life—that's (MS Morgan) • life, that's (*Cent*)
277.20	circumstance (MS Morgan) • circumstances (*Cent*)
277.22–23	him, wouldn't he have killed me, too (*Cent*) • Angelo, how many hours would I have survived (MS Morgan)
277.24	Yes, (MS Morgan) • Yes; (*Cent*)
277.24	you, and (MS Morgan) • you— (*Cent*)
277.36	letters, myself, (MS Morgan) • letters myself (*Cent*)
278.3	downwards (MS Morgan) • downward (*Cent*)
278.4	knife (MS Morgan) • knife, (*Cent*)
278.8	himself: "It's (MS Morgan) • himself— [¶] "It's (*Cent*)
278.8	here; (MS Morgan) • here. (*Cent*)
278.10	on— (MS Morgan) • on; (*Cent*)
278.10	up, (MS Morgan) • up (*Cent*)
278.13	that (MS Morgan) • the (*Cent*)
278.14	encrusted (MS Morgan) • incrusted (*Cent*)
278.15	his (*Cent*) • our (MS Morgan)
278.15	pillow; we were in bed together (*Cent*) • pillow (MS Morgan)
278.17	vague (*Cent*) • dim (MS Morgan)

278.17–18 sheath, and was ready (MS Morgan) • sheath and was ready, (*Cent*)

278.19 bedside (MS Morgan) • bedside, (*Cent*)

278.20 throat, (MS Morgan) • throat; (*Cent*)

278.21 downward (MS Morgan) • downward, (*Cent*)

278.22 I think he was dead before his spouting blood struck us. (MS Morgan) • [*not in*] (*Cent*)

278.24–26 after some general chat about the tragedy, Pudd'nhead said, taking Tom's hand—[¶] "Now, Tom, I've (*Cent*) • Tom said— [¶] "I . . . Tom's hand, "I've (MS Morgan [102.18–33])

278.26 happens— (MS Morgan) • happens; (*Cent*)

278.27 need— Hel-lo! (MS Morgan) • need—hel-lo! (*Cent*)

278.28 snatched away his hand (*Cent*) • drawn his hand away (MS Morgan)

278.30 him and said, (MS Morgan) • him, and said (*Cent*)

278.32 haste, (MS Morgan) • haste: (*Cent*)

278.33 pardons, (MS Morgan) • pardons. (*Cent*)

278.33 that, (MS Morgan) • that; (*Cent*)

278.34 me. (MS Morgan) • me! (*Cent*)

278.36 Twins (MS Morgan) • twins (*Cent*)

278.38 Luigi; but (MS Morgan) • Luigi. But (*Cent*)

279.3 exhibition—in fact (MS Morgan) • exhibition; in fact, (*Cent*)

279.7 Twins (MS Morgan) • twins (*Cent*)

279.12 blazing point (MS Morgan) • blazing-point (*Cent*)

279.16–17 Irishman named John Buckstone, who (*Cent*) • man who spoke . . . probably. He (MS Morgan [103.23–27])

279.19 excitements, (*Cent*) • excitements (MS Morgan) [TEXTUAL NOTE: *Cent's comma is accepted as grammatically necessary*]

279.21 Twins (MS Morgan) • twins (*Cent*)

279.22 mass meeting (MS Morgan) • mass-meeting (*Cent*)

279.22 errand (MS Morgan) • errand, (*Cent*)

279.23 market house (MS Morgan) • market-house (*Cent*)

279.24–26 less cordially . . . to be one. (*Cent*) • declined it . . . of them." (MS Morgan [103.34–104.4])

279.27 Twins (MS Morgan) • twins (*Cent*)

279.28 uninvited. (MS Morgan) • uninvited (*Cent*)

279.29 wavering long line (MS Morgan) • long wavering line (*Cent*)

279.30 a (MS Morgan) • the (*Cent*)

279.32 tail end (MS Morgan) • tail-end (*Cent*)

279.32	market house (MS Morgan) • market-house (*Cent*)
279.33	Twins (MS Morgan) • twins (*Cent*)
279.34	noise (MS Morgan) • noise, (*Cent*)
279.35	Buckstone,— (MS Morgan) • Buckstone— (*Cent*)
279.35	delivered (MS Morgan) • were delivered (*Cent*)
280.1	ever glorious (MS Morgan) • ever-glorious (*Cent*)
280.5	cries,— (MS Morgan) • cries: (*Cent*)
280.6	wet (MS Morgan) • Wet (*Cent*)
280.6	give (MS Morgan) • Give (*Cent*)
280.7	were (*Cent*) • was (MS Morgan) [TEXTUAL NOTE: *MS Morgan's reading is an error arising from authorial revision*]
280.7	Twins (MS Morgan) • twins (*Cent*)
280.8	lips, (MS Morgan) • lips; (*Cent*)
280.9	cries— (MS Morgan) • cries; (*Cent*)
280.10–11	one?" [¶] "What (MS Morgan) • one?" "What (*Cent*)
280.11	blonde (MS Morgan) • blond (*Cent*)
280.11–12	for?" [¶] "Explain! explain!" (MS Morgan) • for?" "Explain! Explain!" (*Cent*)
280.15	teetotaler (*Cent*) • pronounced teetotaler (MS Morgan)
280.20	crowd (MS Morgan) • crowd, (*Cent*)
280.22	bye-laws (MS Morgan) • by-laws (*Cent*)
280.32	"For (MS Morgan) • For (*Cent*)
280.33	fel-low. (MS Morgan) • fel-low, (*Cent*)
280.34	fe-el-low— (MS Morgan) • fe-el-low,— (*Cent*)
280.35	deny!" (MS Morgan) • deny. (*Cent*)
281.2–3	cat-calls and side-remarks department of them (MTP) • cat-calls and side-remarks-department of them (MS Morgan); cat-call and side-remarks (*Cent*)
281.4	Twins (MS Morgan) • twins (*Cent*)
281.5	extraordinarily close resemblance of the brothers to each other (*Cent*) • Twins stood with their legs braced slightly apart. Their heads happened to be canted apart, too. Their attitude (MS Morgan)
281.8	phillipene (MTP) • pair of scissors (MS Morgan); philopena (*Cent*) [TEXTUAL NOTE: *SLC altered MS Morgan's metaphor 'pair of scissors' when he separated the Twins. Cent's reading 'philopena' is the spelling given by the Century Dictionary; 'phillipene', which occurs twice in MS Morgan, is preferred here*]

281.9	speech! (MS Morgan) • speech. (*Cent*)
281.10	aptness (*Cent*) • precision (MS Morgan)
281.12–15	Luigi's southern . . . account. He (*Cent*) • Luigi (MS Morgan)
281.15	halted (*Cent*) • was (MS Morgan)
281.17	in the joker's rear (MS Morgan) • [*not in*] (*Cent*)
281.17	him (MS Morgan) • Tom (*Cent*)
281.23	onto (MS Morgan) • on to (*Cent*)
281.26	*them* (MS Morgan) • them (*Cent*)
281.29	presently, (MS Morgan) • presently (*Cent*)
281.30	voices (MS Morgan) • voices, (*Cent*)
281.33	cursings (MS Morgan) • cursing (*Cent*)
282.2–3	market house (MS Morgan) • market-house (*Cent*)
282.3	hook and ladder (MS Morgan) • hook-and-ladder (*Cent*)
282.9	onto (MS Morgan) • upon (*Cent*) [TEXTUAL NOTE: *The Century Magazine's style sheet disallowed* 'onto' *where* 'on *or* upon' *might be used (McKnight 1923, 408–9). Elsewhere in Cent* 'onto' *has slipped through, perhaps on the watch of a less vigilant editor*]
282.12	outpour (MS Morgan) • stampede (*Cent*)
282.15	have annihilated (MS Morgan) • annihilate (*Cent*)
282.15	there: (MS Morgan) • there; (*Cent*)
282.16	fire company (MS Morgan) • fire-company (*Cent*)
282.18	fire, (MS Morgan) • fire; (*Cent*)
282.19	fire company (MTP) • fire-company (MS Morgan, *Cent*)
283. 2	*absence* (MS Morgan) • absence (*Cent*)
283.4	brave, (MS Morgan) • brave; (*Cent*)
283.13	Nelson (MS Morgan) • Nelson, (*Cent*)
283.18	a fishing (MTP) • a-fishing (MS Morgan, *Cent*)
283.27	stringent (MS Morgan) • strict (*Cent*)
283.28	F.F.V. (MS Morgan) • F.F V. (*Cent*)
284.3	religion (MS Morgan) • religions (*Cent*)
284.4	differed, (MS Morgan) • differed (*Cent*)
284.4	details, (MS Morgan) • details (*Cent*)
284.12	freethinker (MS Morgan) • free-thinker (*Cent*)
284.20	one of (*Cent*) • [*not in*] (MS Morgan)
284.20	Twins (MS Morgan) • twins (*Cent*)
284.22	Did (*Cent*) • They did (MS Morgan)

284.24   paled (MS Morgan) • paled, (*Cent*)

284.26   *go* (MS Morgan) • go (*Cent*)

284.26   details (*Cent*) • delails ['t' *left uncrossed*] (MS Morgan)

284.27   finish, (MS Morgan) • finish (*Cent*)

284.28   footlights, (MS Morgan) • footlights; (*Cent*)

284.30   Hm (MS Morgan) • H'm (*Cent*)

284.30   didn't (*Cent*) • did not (MS Morgan)

284.33   that!— (MS Morgan) • that— (*Cent*)

284.34   smile (MS Morgan) • smile, (*Cent*)

284.36   Tom beat the Twin on the trial (*Cent*) • the trial went against Tom (MS Morgan)

285.1   him (*Cent*) • them (MS Morgan)

285.2–3   The old man shrank suddenly together like one who has received a death-stroke. Howard (*Cent*) • "Oh, my God!" [¶] Howard (MS Morgan)

285.3   him as (*Cent*) • his friend, as (MS Morgan)

285.4   arms (MS Morgan) • arms, (*Cent*)

285.9   it, (MS Morgan) • it (*Cent*)

285.10   thought; (MS Morgan) • thought: (*Cent*)

285.10   slander, (MS Morgan) • slander; (*Cent*)

285.13   ain't (*Cent*) • isn't (MS Morgan)

285.13   Pembroke, (MS Morgan) • Pembroke; (*Cent*)

285.13   ain't (*Cent*) • isn't (MS Morgan)

285.13   true, (MS Morgan) • true! (*Cent*)

285.13   said, (MS Morgan) • said (*Cent*)

285.15   it's (*Cent*) • it is (MS Morgan)

285.16   Dominion. (*Cent*) • Dominion, and from that blood can spring no such misbegotten son (MS Morgan)

285.17   gentleman (MS Morgan) • gentleman, (*Cent*)

285.20   supper time (MS Morgan) • supper-time (*Cent*)

285.21   supper, (MS Morgan) • supper; (*Cent*)

285.23   not (MS Morgan) • was not (*Cent*)

285.28–31 guilelessly: "It . . . the assault." (*Cent*) • innocently, with a sheepish little laugh— [¶] "Well, the fact is, it don't stand any way at all. I had them up in court, but they beat me." (MS Morgan)

285.32   with the opening sentence (*Cent*) • [*not in*] (MS Morgan)

285.36   you scum! you (MS Morgan) • You scum! You (*Cent*)

286.4–6   "Which of the . . . "You (*Cent*) • "So your refuge . . . responsibility. You (MS Morgan [122.6–21])

286.4   Twins (MTP) • [*not in*] (MS Morgan); twins (*Cent*)

286.7   N-no (MS Morgan) • N—no (*Cent*)

286.8   "You (*Cent*) • "All right, no harm is done. You (MS Morgan)

286.9   it. (*Cent*) • it. He was bitterly sorry he had been so premature with his lie. (MS Morgan)

286.11   by, (MS Morgan) • by; (*Cent*)

286.11   said, (MS Morgan) • said (*Cent*)

286.12   uncle. (MS Morgan) • uncle! (*Cent*)

286.12–13   I never could. He is a murderous devil. I—I'm *afraid* of him. (MTP) • I never could. ˌThey are murderous devils.ˌ I—I'm *afraid* of them. (MS Morgan); He is a murderous devil—I never could—I—I'm afraid of him! (*Cent*) [TEXTUAL NOTE: *In MS Morgan, SLC's insertion of* 'They are murderous devils.' *was typed in the wrong place by the TS2 typist: SLC's insertion caret is after* 'could.' *Consequently the phrase was out of place when SLC came to revise TS2. The present edition preserves the originally intended order of the clauses and the author's change of subject from plural to singular but rejects Cent's punctuation and altered emphasis*]

286.17–18   corner, still repeating, again and again, that lament (MS Morgan) • corner repeating that lament again and again (*Cent*)

286.18   heart-breaking (MS Morgan) • heartbreaking (*Cent*)

286.19   and scattered (MS Morgan) • scattering (*Cent*)

286.23   father. (MS Morgan) • father! (*Cent*)

286.29   The Count (*Cent*) • He (MS Morgan)

286.29   minutes," said Howard. (*Cent*) • minutes." (MS Morgan)

286.32   lane, (MS Morgan) • lane (*Cent*)

286.35   rags and ruin (MS Morgan) • ruin (*Cent*) [TEXTUAL NOTE: *The Century editor may have disallowed MS Morgan's reading as a corruption of* 'rack and ruin']

287 *illus*   "A COWARD IN MY FAMILY!" (*Cent*) • [*not in*] (MS Morgan)

288.5   it is (MS Morgan) • [*not in*] (*Cent*)

288.6   easiest (MS Morgan) • most easily (*Cent*)

288.8   that (MS Morgan) • *that* (*Cent*)

288.8   *me* (MS Morgan) • me (*Cent*)

288.13   Anyway (MS Morgan) • Anyway, (*Cent*)

288.15   gone! (MS Morgan) • gone. (*Cent*)

289.2–4   [¶] When I reflect . . . *Calendar.* (*Cent*) • [*not in*] (MS Morgan) [TEX-
TUAL NOTE: *This aphorism is in fact present in MS Morgan but in a different place, at the head of chapter 11. In CU-MARK (Box 40, no. 5) there
is a draft text showing SLC's alterations:* 'When I reflect upon the ~~great~~
number of ~~people~~ ‸disagreeable‸ ~~acquaintances of mine~~ ‸people‸ whom
I know have gone to a better world, I am moved to lead a different life.']

289.5   *October* (MTP) • [*not in*] (MS Morgan); OCTOBER (*Cent*)

289.10   on, (MS Morgan) • on (*Cent*)

289.11   enclosing (MS Morgan) • inclosing (*Cent*)

289.11   either hand, (MS Morgan) • each hand (*Cent*)

289.12   came (MS Morgan) • he came (*Cent*)

289.14   Twins (MS Morgan) • twins (*Cent*)

289.17   sitting room (MTP) • sitting-room (MS Morgan, *Cent*)

289.21–23 throat, ["It's that . . . into a law-court."] A (MTP) • throat, ["It's that
fickle-tempered, dissipated young goose—poor devil, he finds friends
pretty scarce to-day, likely."] A (MS Morgan); throat. [¶] "It's . . . pretty
scarce to-day, likely, after the disgrace of carrying a personal-assault case
into a law-court." [¶] A (*Cent*) [TEXTUAL NOTE: *The added phrase* 'after
the disgrace . . . law-court.'' *is retained as an authorial revision, but the
changes to the original punctuation and paragraphing are probably a
Century editor's*]

289.25   entered (MS Morgan) • entered, (*Cent*)

289.26   said, (MS Morgan) • said (*Cent*)

289.27–28 Try and forget you have been kicked. (*Cent*) • Better luck next time. It's
our first law-suit, and we couldn't both win it, you know. It's your turn
next. (MS Morgan)

290.4   discoveries." (MS Morgan) • discoveries! (*Cent*)

290.7   dissipation! (MS Morgan) • dissipation. (*Cent*)

290.8   Italian savage (*Cent*) • human lemon-squeezer (MS Morgan)

290.9   Yes (*Cent*) • The Twins—yes (MS Morgan)

290.10   me, (MS Morgan) • me (*Cent*)

290.19   a fishing (MTP) • a-fishing (MS Morgan, *Cent*)

290.20   Twins (MS Morgan) • twins (*Cent*)

290.21   calaboose,— (MS Morgan) • calaboose— (*Cent*)

290.21–22 their slipping out on a paltry fine for such an outrageous offence (*Cent,
spelling* offense) • there being any . . . to book (MS Morgan [125.13–18])

290.25   you. (MS Morgan) • you! (*Cent*)

290.30   and (MS Morgan) • And (*Cent*)

290.31	and (MS Morgan) • And (*Cent*)
290.32	an actually launched and recognized lawyer (*Cent*) • on the top wave of legal prosperity (MS Morgan)
291.3	Italian, (MTP) • Italian (*Cent*); Twins, (MS Morgan) [TEXTUAL NOTE: *The emendation admits SLC's substantive revision but rejects the magazine's punctuation in favor of MS Morgan's*]
291.5	Tom. (MS Morgan) • Tom! (*Cent*)
291.6	nothing. (MS Morgan) • nothing! (*Cent*)
291.20	had (MS Morgan) • *had* (*Cent*)
291.21	didn't (MS Morgan) • did not (*Cent*)
291.23	list! (MS Morgan) • list. (*Cent*)
291.31	born. (MS Morgan) • born! (*Cent*)
291.32	pencil case (MS Morgan) • pencil-	case (*Cent*)
291.32	aunt (MS Morgan) • Aunt (*Cent*)
291.33	birth-day (MS Morgan) • birth-	day (*Cent*)
291.35	shan't (MS Morgan) • sha'n't (*Cent*)
292.3	in (MS Morgan) • *in* (*Cent*)
292.4–5	town constable (MS Morgan) • town-constable (*Cent*)
292.6	weather-conversation, (MS Morgan) • weather-conversation (*Cent*)
292.7	we've (*Cent*) • We've (MS Morgan)
292.10	justice (MTP) • Justice (MS Morgan, *Cent*)
292.13	have (MS Morgan) • has (*Cent*) [TEXTUAL NOTE: *In MS Morgan the long list of neighbors comprises the plural subject of the verb* 'have'; *the grammar is informal, but Cent's alteration is unnecessary*]
292.22	said Wilson, "I (MS Morgan) • said Wilson. "I (*Cent*)
292.25	Blake, (MS Morgan) • Blake; (*Cent*)
292.26	*we* (MS Morgan) • we (*Cent*)
292.28	girl, (MS Morgan) • girl (*Cent*)
292.29	mind, (MS Morgan) • mind (*Cent*)
292.30	arm (MS Morgan) • arm, (*Cent*)
292.31	veil (MS Morgan) • veil, (*Cent*)
292.36	out (MS Morgan) • out of (*Cent*)
292.37	houses (MS Morgan) • houses, (*Cent*)
292.37	robbed (MS Morgan) • *robbed* (*Cent*)
293.2	lasted for (MS Morgan) • lasted (*Cent*)
293.6	Tom; (MS Morgan) • Tom, (*Cent*)

293.6   that (MS Morgan) • *that* (*Cent*)

293.8   *was* (MS Morgan) • was (*Cent*)

293.9   Twins (MS Morgan) • twins (*Cent*)

293.10   everywhere (MS Morgan) • everywhere, (*Cent*)

293.15   Buckstone. (*Cent*) • Buckstone? (MS Morgan)

293.16   Yes— (MS Morgan) • Yes; (*Cent*)

293.19   dasn't (MS Morgan) • da'sn't (*Cent*)

293.23   himself, (MS Morgan) • himself: (*Cent*)

293.25   good! (MS Morgan) • good. (*Cent*)

293.26   *what* (MS Morgan) • what (*Cent*)

293.27   Blake, (MS Morgan) • Blake. (*Cent*)

293.32   *have* (MS Morgan) • have (*Cent*)

293.34   Twins (MS Morgan) • twins (*Cent*)

294.1   constable (*Cent*) • Constable (MS Morgan)

294.2   *my* (MS Morgan) • my (*Cent*)

294.5   silence (*Cent*) • weighty silence (MS Morgan)

294.5–12   informed Wilson . . . young Tom. (*Cent*) • began to clear . . . has been!"
          (MS Morgan [128.34–129.38])

295.2   southern (MS Morgan) • Southern (*Cent*)

295.6   southern (MS Morgan) • Southern (*Cent*)

295.8   About the time that Wilson was bowing the committee out,
          (*Cent*) • It was the gracious watermelon season. All hearts should
          have been gay and happy, but some were not. About the time
          that Wilson was saying the words which close the last chapter,
          (MS Morgan)

295.11–23   [¶] "Well, Howard . . . hurried away, (*Cent*) • [*no* ¶] Howard sat down
          . . . joyful errand, (MS Morgan [130.12–133.5])

295.27   think. Began (MS Morgan) • think—began (*Cent*)

295.31   entrusted (MS Morgan) • intrusted (*Cent*)

296.2   severely (MS Morgan) • severely, (*Cent*)

296.3   once, (MS Morgan) • once (*Cent*)

296.6   duel (MS Morgan) • duel, (*Cent*)

296.6   away (MS Morgan) • away, (*Cent*)

296.10   tip-toeing (MS Morgan) • tiptoeing (*Cent*)

296.12   unusual— (MS Morgan) • unusual (*Cent*)

296.12 hour (*Cent*) • hour of the night. It was near eleven—a good hour after his ordinary bedtime (MS Morgan)

296.13 chill anxiety (MS Morgan) • chill of anxiety (*Cent*) [TEXTUAL NOTE: *SLC elsewhere uses* 'chill' *as an adjective, so the "correction" here was probably editorial*]

296.17 and hearing (*Cent*) • [*not in*] (MS Morgan) [TEXTUAL NOTE: *The addition of* 'and hearing' *may arise because, as we are told later on, Tom does not overhear the conversation between the Judge and Howard*]

296.18 *could* (MS Morgan) • could (*Cent*)

296.19 Howard (*Cent*) • Howard had his pistol case with him. He (MS Morgan)

296.19 satisfaction— (MS Morgan) • satisfaction: (*Cent*)

296.20 battle ground (MS Morgan) • battle-ground (*Cent*)

296.21 also with his brother (*Cent*) • also his brother, of course, who is looking indisposed. (MS Morgan)

296.22 apiece." (*Cent*) • apiece. (MS Morgan)

296.23 Good. (MS Morgan) • Good! (*Cent*)

296.24 Perfect (MS Morgan) • Perfect, (*Cent*)

296.28 said— (MS Morgan) • said: (*Cent*)

296.36 I (*Cent*) • Ah, I (MS Morgan)

296.37 battle ground (MS Morgan) • battle-ground (*Cent*)

297.2 place (MS Morgan) • place, (*Cent*)

297.3 imitation (*Cent*) • mute imitation (MS Morgan)

297.11 *now* (MS Morgan) • now (*Cent*)

297.14 more and more heavy-hearted and doubtful (*Cent*) • sicker and sicker (MS Morgan)

297.16 shan't (MS Morgan) • sha'n't (*Cent*)

297.18 sure. (MS Morgan) • sure! (*Cent*)

297.24 He dragged himself upstairs, and brooded (*Cent*) • [¶] Meantime Tom had been brooding (MS Morgan)

297.24 time, (MS Morgan) • time (*Cent*)

297.28 value (MS Morgan) • value, (*Cent*)

297.33 me (MS Morgan) • me, (*Cent*)

297.33 people— (*Cent*) • people. There's (MS Morgan)

297.34 even his career has got a sort of a little start at last (*Cent*) • his fortune's made (MS Morgan)

297.35	would (MS Morgan) • should (*Cent*)
297.35	know. (MS Morgan) • know? (*Cent*)
297.35	opened (*Cent*) • made (MS Morgan)
297.35	road (*Cent*) • fortune (MS Morgan)
297.36	he (*Cent*) • [*not in*] (MS Morgan)
297.36	block (*Cent*) • ruin (MS Morgan)
298.1	eye, (MS Morgan) • eye; (*Cent*)
298.1	for (MS Morgan) • to (*Cent*)
298.4	*then* (MS Morgan) • then (*Cent*)
298.12	turned westward. (*Cent*) • just then the Twins whizzed by, on their way home. He wondered what that might mean. Had they seen a ghost at the haunted house? (MS Morgan)
298.14	duelists returning from the fight; (*Cent*) • duelists, and (MS Morgan)
298.16	company (MS Morgan) • company, (*Cent*)
298.22	'Cose (MS Morgan) • 'Co'se (*Cent*)
298.22	ben (MTP) • been (MS Morgan); be'n (*Cent*) [TEXTUAL NOTE: *Cent's reading repunctuates what is presumed to be an authorial correction of TS2's reading* 'been' *to* 'ben', *Roxy's usual form*]
298.22	one o' dem (*Cent*) • dat pair o' nutcrackers—dem (MS Morgan)
298.22	Twins (MS Morgan) • twins (*Cent*)
298.23	Then he (*Cent*) • He (MS Morgan)
298.23	added, (MS Morgan) • added (*Cent*)
298.23	himself, (MS Morgan) • himself: (*Cent*)
298.23	*That's* (MS Morgan) • That's (*Cent*)
298.25	about. . . . . . . Oh, (MS Morgan) • about. . . . Oh (*Cent*)
298.25	twin (*Cent*) • Twins (MS Morgan)
298.29	Luigi (*Cent*) • Angelo (MS Morgan)
298.30	succeed; (MS Morgan) • succeed, (*Cent*)
298.38	*me* (MS Morgan) • me (*Cent*)
299.1	*nigger* (MS Morgan) • nigger (*Cent*)
299.3	soul! (MS Morgan) • *soul.* (*Cent*)
299.3	'Tain't (MS Morgan) • Tain't (*Cent*)
299.3	'tain't (MS Morgan) • tain't (*Cent*)
299.4	tho'in' (MS Morgan) • thowin (*Cent*)
299.9	man (MS Morgan) • man, (*Cent*)
299.9	it, (MS Morgan) • it (*Cent*)

299.10   safest, (MS Morgan) • safest (*Cent*)

299.12   Whatever (*Cent*) • What ever (MS Morgan)

299.12   *has* 'come (MS Morgan) • has come (*Cent*)

299.12   *I* (MS Morgan) • I (*Cent*)

299.13   on'y (*Cent*) • only (MS Morgan)

299.14   father (MS Morgan) • great-great-great-gran'father (*Cent*) [TEXTUAL NOTE: *In MS Morgan, Roxy says she is the daughter of John Randolph of Roanoke (1773–1833), whom she correctly calls a descendant of Pocahontas. In the Century text, Roxy's father is not named, and she traces her ancestry to Captain John Smith. Probably the editors of the Century Magazine balked at fathering a fictional child on the historical John Randolph, and required SLC to omit Roxy's paternity and name only distant ancestors. On this conjecture the passage is treated as an instance of censorship, and the readings of MS Morgan are followed here and at 300.24*]

299.14   gran'father (MS Morgan) • great-great-great-great-gran'father (*Cent*)

299.14   John Randolph of Roanoke (MS Morgan) • Cap'n John Smith (*Cent*)

299.14   highes' (MS Morgan) • highest (*Cent*)

299.15   out; (MS Morgan) • out, (*Cent*)

299.15   his (MS Morgan) • *his* (*Cent*)

299.16   queen (MS Morgan) • queen, en her husbun' was a nigger king outen Africa (*Cent*)

299.18   *nigger* in you. (MS Morgan) • nigger in you! (*Cent*)

299.22   gone (MS Morgan) • gone, (*Cent*)

299.23   rumble (*Cent*) • rumble again (MS Morgan)

299.25   soul." Presently (MS Morgan) • soul." [¶] Presently (*Cent*)

299.26   rumblings (MS Morgan) • ramblings (*Cent*)

299.27   altogether (MS Morgan) • altogether, (*Cent*)

299.28   moods (MS Morgan) • moods, (*Cent*)

299.30   said— (MS Morgan) • said: (*Cent*)

299.31   skinned. How (*Cent*) • peeled—how (MS Morgan) [TEXTUAL NOTE: *Perhaps SLC moving to remedy the jingle of 'peeled' and 'peal', twelve words later*]

299.34   in (MS Morgan) • on (*Cent*)

299.35   *I* ben (MS Morgan) • I be'n (*Cent*)

299.35   myself! (MTP) • myself. (*Cent*); myseff! (MS Morgan) [TEXTUAL NOTE: *Cent's form may reflect SLC's continuation of a process, begun in his internal revisions to MS Morgan, of altering '-seff' to '-self'; cf. the entries below at 302.4, 320.22, and 324.26, and PW-MS, textual note at 170.8*]

299.37	did. (MS Morgan) • did! (*Cent*)
300.1	a sett'n (MS Morgan) • a-sett'n' (*Cent*)
300.1	che-*bang* (MS Morgan) • *che-bang* (*Cent*)
300.4	it— (MS Morgan) • it,— (*Cent*)
300.5	concerned— (MS Morgan) • concerned,— (*Cent*)
300.5	dah (MS Morgan) • dar (*Cent*)
300.6	I seed everything as plain as day in de moonlight. Right (MS Morgan) • in de moonlight, right (*Cent*) [TEXTUAL NOTE: *This looks like the TS2 typist's eye skipped from* 'dah' *to* 'day' *seven words after it. Still, it is clear that SLC made other revisions in the neighborhood of this passage, and it is not easy to decide whether* 'I seed . . . moonlight' *was omitted deliberately, and if so by whom*]
300.7	one o' (*Cent*) • [*not in*] (MS Morgan)
300.7	Twins (MS Morgan) • twins (*Cent*)
300.7	a cussin' (MTP) • a-yowlin' (MS Morgan); a-cussin' (*Cent*)
300.7	a cussin' (MTP) • a-yowlin' (MS Morgan); a-cussin' (*Cent*)
300.7	soft,— (MS Morgan) • soft— (*Cent*)
300.7	*brown* (MTP) • *white* (MS Morgan); brown (*Cent*)
300.8	'uz cussin' (*Cent*) • was yowlin' (MS Morgan)
300.8	caze (MS Morgan) • 'ca'se (*Cent*)
300.8	shoulder. (*Cent*) • shoulder—dat is, I *reckon* it 'uz *his* shoulder, dough how *he* could tell it 'uz his'n, de way dey arms is mixed up do beat me—but anyway he judged it 'uz his'n en so he 'uz doin' de yowlin' till he could fine out. (MS Morgan)
300.9	a workin' (MS Morgan) • a-workin' (*Cent*)
300.9	a he'pin' (MTP) • a he'pin (MS Morgan); a-he'pin' (*Cent*)
300.10	Pem. (MS Morgan) • Pem (*Cent*)
300.10	a standin' (MTP) • a-standin' (MS Morgan, *Cent*)
300.11	toreckly (MS Morgan) • treckly (*Cent*)
300.12	twin (*Cent*) • white twin (MS Morgan)
300.12	say (MS Morgan) • say, (*Cent*)
300.12	time— (MS Morgan) • time,— (*Cent*)
300.13	'*spat!*' (MS Morgan) • *spat!* (*Cent*)
300.13	agin (MS Morgan) • ag'in' (*Cent*)
300.14	twin (*Cent*) • white one (MS Morgan)
300.14	say (MS Morgan) • say, (*Cent*)
300.14	agin (MS Morgan) • ag'in (*Cent*)

300.14 caze (MS Morgan) • 'ca'se (*Cent*)

300.15 cheek bone (MS Morgan) • cheek-bone (*Cent*)

300.15 glance' (MTP) • glance (MS Morgan, *Cent*) [TEXTUAL NOTE: *Emended to the form employed ten words above*]

300.16 a ben (MS Morgan) • 'a' be'n (*Cent*)

300.17 'twould a (MS Morgan) • 't would 'a' (*Cent*)

300.17 disfigger' (MS Morgan) • disfigger (*Cent*)

300.17 me. (*Cent*) • me. Den dey 'uz a gwyne to shoot agin, but de Twins dey lit out. De white one 'uz gitt'n more'n his sheer, en I reckon it 'uz him dat run. But I don't know—caze 'tother one went too. (MS Morgan)

300.22 range. (MS Morgan) • range! (*Cent*)

300.24 'Fraid (MS Morgan) • 'Fraid (*Cent*)

300.24 Randolphs (MS Morgan) • Smith-Pocahontases (*Cent*)

300.24 *nothin'* (MS Morgan) • nothin' (*Cent*)

300.25 I wouldn't (MS Morgan) • *I* wouldn't (*Cent*)

300.29 blon' twin (*Cent*) • nigger-twin (MS Morgan)

300.29 doctor (MS Morgan) • doctor en de seconds (*Cent*) [TEXTUAL NOTE: *Cent adds the 'seconds' to the list of those not injured in the duel. This pointless and pedantic addition is unlikely to have been made by SLC, who, in addition, would remember that in the duel as written in MS Morgan the seconds, Wilson and Howard, are in fact injured. It is more readily ascribed to a Century editor, who would not have seen the duel passage (which was removed from TS2a before submission to the magazine) and would think the seconds had escaped unscathed*]

300.32 inch! O, (MS Morgan) • inch. Oh (*Cent*)

300.32 he'll (MS Morgan) • he will (*Cent*)

300.33 minute! (MS Morgan) • minute. (*Cent*)

300.37 ben (MS Morgan) • be'n (*Cent*)

301.4 *Now* (MS Morgan) • Now (*Cent*)

301.4 *end!* (MS Morgan) • end. (*Cent*)

301.8 it (MS Morgan) • it, (*Cent*)

301.12 on (MS Morgan) • *on* (*Cent*)

301.12 you! (MS Morgan) • you, (*Cent*)

301.13 know (MS Morgan) • know, (*Cent*)

301.15 chin (MS Morgan) • chin, (*Cent*)

301.16 said, (MS Morgan) • said (*Cent*)

301.17 *I* (MS Morgan) • I (*Cent*)

301.17	you. (MS Morgan) • you! (*Cent*)
301.18	agin (MS Morgan) • ag'in (*Cent*)
301.19	*me.* (MS Morgan) • *me!* (*Cent*)
301.22	too— (MS Morgan) • too,— (*Cent*)
301.25	too— (MS Morgan) • too,— (*Cent*)
301.26	*big* (MS Morgan) • big (*Cent*)
301.26	too— (MS Morgan) • too,— (*Cent*)
301.27	cent a month. (MS Morgan) • cent. a month? (*Cent*)
301.28	en sell (MS Morgan) • and sell (*Cent*)
301.32	diffrence (MTP) • diff'rence (MS Morgan, *Cent*)
301.33	you's *gwyne* (MS Morgan) • you *is* gwyne (*Cent*) [TEXTUAL NOTE: *This apparently subtle change is explained by the conjecture that TS2's typist failed to replicate the manuscript's underscoring. Confronting* 'you's gwyne' *in TS2, SLC sensed that the emphasis he had given the phrase in MS Morgan was gone; he restored the emphasis by revising to* 'you *is*']
301.36	gravely— (MS Morgan) • gravely: (*Cent*)
301.38	caze (MS Morgan) • 'ca'se (*Cent*)
302.1	*once* (MS Morgan) • once (*Cent*)
302.2	one. (MS Morgan) • one! (*Cent*)
302.4	own self (*Cent*) • own seff (MS Morgan)
302.6	*once* (MS Morgan) • *one* (*Cent*)
302.7	you is (MS Morgan) • you's (*Cent*)
302.8	paused, (MS Morgan) • paused (*Cent*)
302.8	added: (MS Morgan) • added, (*Cent*)
302.9	says (*Cent*) • say (MS Morgan)
303.2	Nothing so needs reforming as other people's habits. (*Cent*) • If you pick up a starving dog and make him prosperous, he will not bite you. This is the principal difference between a dog and a man. (MS Morgan) [TEXTUAL NOTE: *In revising, SLC moved the maxim about* 'other people's habits' *from its place at the head of MS Morgan chapter 7*]
303.4–8	[¶] Behold, the fool saith . . . *Calendar.* (*Cent*) • [*not in*] (MS Morgan)
303.6	attention;" (MTP) • [*not in*] (MS Morgan); attention"; (*Cent*)
303.7	*watch that basket* (MS in CU-MARK) • [*not in*] (MS Morgan); WATCH THAT BASKET (*Cent*) [TEXTUAL NOTE: *Cent's small capitals are typical of the magazine's house style but do not appear in Clemens's manuscripts of this maxim, in which* 'watch that basket' *is usually underscored, but*

never double-underscored (the marking for small capitals); Pudd'nhead Wilson's Calendar for 1894, *printed from some derivative of TS2a, also has italics here (SLC to Unknown, 2 July 1893, photocopy in CU-MARK; Notebook 33, TS p. 8, CU-MARK)*]

303.9–304.13   What a time . . . a vexed mystery. (*Cent*) • During Monday, Tuesday . . . Mississippi Valley. (MS Morgan [155.5–16])

303.15   practicing (MTP) • [*not in*] (MS Morgan); practising (*Cent*)

303.25   Twins (MTP) • [*not in*] (MS Morgan); twins (*Cent*)

304.4   Twins (MTP) • [*not in*] (MS Morgan); twins (*Cent*)

304.14   Saturday, (MS Morgan) • Saturday (*Cent*)

304.17   Blake, (MS Morgan) • Blake; (*Cent*)

304.21   it (MS Morgan) • it, (*Cent*)

304.23   reputation, (MS Morgan) • reputation; (*Cent*)

304.24   *no* (MS Morgan) • no (*Cent*)

304.25   pardon, (MS Morgan) • pardon; (*Cent*)

304.25   offence (MS Morgan) • offense (*Cent*)

304.26   ask, was, (MS Morgan) • ask was (*Cent*)

304.27   catch— (MS Morgan) • catch; (*Cent*)

304.30   Damn (MS Morgan) • D—— (*Cent*)

304.31   sho' (MTP) • sho (MS Morgan, *Cent*)

304.32   No, (MS Morgan) • No; (*Cent*)

304.32   *haven't* (MS Morgan) • haven't (*Cent*)

304.34   because (MS Morgan) • because, (*Cent*)

304.36–37 let the town keep its shirt on, too (MTP) • let the town keep it's shirt on, too (MS Morgan); the town needn't worry, either (*Cent*)

304.38   clews (MS Morgan) • clues (*Cent*)

305.1   good. (MS Morgan) • good! (*Cent*)

305.2   St. Louis (*Cent*) • St Louis (MS Morgan)

305.2   clews (MS Morgan) • clues (*Cent*)

305.5   we— inside (MTP) • we— | inside (MS Morgan); we—inside (*Cent*)

305.5   to. (MS Morgan) • to! (*Cent*)

305.6   said, (MS Morgan) • said (*Cent*)

305.9   clews (MS Morgan) • clues (*Cent*)

305.9–10   still-hunt." Blake's (MS Morgan) • still-hunt." [¶] Blake's (*Cent*)

305.10   flushed, (MS Morgan) • flushed (*Cent*)

305.11   Wilson (MS Morgan) • Wilson, (*Cent*)

305.19   fact (MS Morgan) • fact, (*Cent*)

305.21   *that* (MS Morgan) • that (*Cent*)

305.23   *of* (MS Morgan) • of (*Cent*)

305.24   idea (MS Morgan) • idea, (*Cent*)

305.26   happy, (MS Morgan) • happy (*Cent*)

305.30   B'George (*Cent*) • 'George (MS Morgan)

305.30   days!— (MS Morgan) • days— (*Cent*)

305.31   time, (MS Morgan) • time (*Cent*)

305.33   pawnbroker (*Cent*) • pawn-broker (MS Morgan)

305.34   *with* (*Cent*) • along *with* (MS Morgan)

305.34   *was* (MS Morgan) • was (*Cent*)

306 *illus*   "WHO GOT THE REWARD, PUDD'NHEAD?" (*Cent*) • [*not in*] (MS Morgan)

307.4   sniff (MS Morgan) • sniff, (*Cent*)

307.8   case (MS Morgan) • case, (*Cent*)

307.10   said, (MS Morgan) • said (*Cent*)

307.15   starting point (MS Morgan) • starting-point (*Cent*)

307.15   I'm (MS Morgan) • I am (*Cent*)

307.17   argument's (*Cent*) • arguments (MS Morgan)

307.19   thigh (MS Morgan) • thigh, (*Cent*)

307.20   Jackson (MS Morgan) • Jackson, (*Cent*)

307.20   *got* (MS Morgan) • got (*Cent*)

307.21   that! (MS Morgan) • that? (*Cent*)

307.23   it, (MS Morgan) • it; (*Cent*)

307.27   knife (MS Morgan) • knife, (*Cent*)

307.31   it (*Cent*) • it whatever (MS Morgan)

307.36   *I* (MS Morgan) • I (*Cent*)

307.37   Tom?— (MS Morgan) • Tom? (*Cent*)

307.37   Wilson (MS Morgan) • Wilson, (*Cent*)

308.1   *any such knife* (MS Morgan) • any such knife (*Cent*)

308.3   dollars!— (MS Morgan) • dollars— (*Cent*)

308.5   strangers— (MS Morgan) • strangers; (*Cent*)

308.12   knife (MS Morgan) • knife, (*Cent*)

308.13   *seen* (MS Morgan) • seen (*Cent*)

308.14   it; (MS Morgan) • it, (*Cent*)

308.17   said,— (MS Morgan) • said— (*Cent*)

308.18   it— (MS Morgan) • it; (*Cent*)

308.19   responded— (MS Morgan) • responded, (*Cent*)

308.21   Twins. (MS Morgan) • twins! (*Cent*)

308.23   Twins (MS Morgan) • twins (*Cent*)

308.24   *but* (MS Morgan) • but (*Cent*)

308.25   think— (MS Morgan) • think, (*Cent*)

308.28   or (*Cent*) • or | or (MS Morgan)

308.28   if they had it (MS Morgan) • if they had it, (*Cent*)

308.29   himself, "I (MS Morgan) • himself: [¶] "I (*Cent*)

308.32   had had (MS Morgan) • had (*Cent*)

308.35   labor, (MS Morgan) • labor (*Cent*)

308.38   Twins (MS Morgan) • twins (*Cent*)

309.1   and—best of all— (MS Morgan) • and, best of all, (*Cent*)

309.1   Twins (MS Morgan) • twins (*Cent*)

309.4   had (MS Morgan) • [*not in*] (*Cent*)

309.6   during the entire week (*Cent*) • [*not in*] (MS Morgan)

309.8   [*no* ¶] On Saturday (MS Morgan) • [¶] Saturday (*Cent*)

309.9   away; (MS Morgan) • away, (*Cent*)

309.11   that Italian adventurer (*Cent*) • those Twins (MS Morgan)

309.12   unawares— (MTP) • unprepared— (MS Morgan); unawares, (*Cent*)

309.13   him (*Cent*) • them (MS Morgan)

309.14   him (*Cent*) • them (MS Morgan)

309.15   Indeed! (MS Morgan) • Indeed? (*Cent*)

309.19   it (MS Morgan) • it, (*Cent*)

309.20   Twins (MS Morgan) • twins (*Cent*)

309.24   boy, (MS Morgan) • boy; (*Cent*)

309.26   added, (MS Morgan) • added (*Cent*)

309.28   *I* (MS Morgan) • I (*Cent*)

309.31   Oh, no, (MS Morgan) • Oh no; (*Cent*)

309.35   it! (MS Morgan) • it. (*Cent*)

309.37   right, (MS Morgan) • right (*Cent*)

309.38–310.14   enough." [¶] The . . . furnish it." (*Cent*) • enough. I will cut those
          Twins when I get the opportunity—one of them ran away from the
          field, anyway: perhaps both." (MS Morgan)

310.1   a while (MTP • [*not in*] (MS Morgan); awhile (*Cent*)

310.5   the election (MTP) • [*not in*] (MS Morgan); election (*Cent*)

310.15	Twins (MS Morgan) • twins (*Cent*)
310.17	it— (MS Morgan) • it. (*Cent*)
310.18	Twins (MS Morgan) • twins (*Cent*)
310.23	made him solid with the (MS Morgan) • restored him to the favor of his (*Cent*)
310.24	uncle. His (MS Morgan) • uncle. [¶] His (*Cent*)
310.28	Dah, now. (MS Morgan) • Dah now! (*Cent*)
310.28	a gwyne (MS Morgan) • a-gwyne (*Cent*)
310.28	*you* (MS Morgan) • you (*Cent*)
310.29	boun' (MS Morgan) • bown' (*Cent*)
310.36	again. (MS Morgan) • again: (*Cent*)
311.2–4	[¶] If you pick . . . *Calendar.* (*Cent*) • [*aphorism present at head of chapter 26*] (MS Morgan)
311.5–9	[¶] We know all . . . *Calendar.* (*Cent*) • [*not in*] (MS Morgan)
311.23	up (MS Morgan) • up, (*Cent*)
311.24	sudden (*Cent*) • so sudden (MS Morgan)
311.25	said— (MS Morgan) • said: (*Cent*)
311.26	I's (*Cent*) • I is (MS Morgan)
311.27	sell me (MS Morgan) • sell me, (*Cent*)
311.29	dumb (*Cent*) • speechless (MS Morgan)
312.5	He (MS Morgan) • he (*Cent*)
312.7	agin (MS Morgan) • ag'in (*Cent*)
312.10	agin (MS Morgan) • ag'in (*Cent*)
312.10	it! (*Cent*) • it (MS Morgan)
312.11	you (MS Morgan) • you, (*Cent*)
312.11	aroun' (MS Morgan) • aroun', (*Cent*)
312.12	a sayin' (MS Morgan) • a-sayin' (*Cent*)
312.14	do (MS Morgan) • *do* (*Cent*)
312.15	you?—you're (MS Morgan) • you? You're (*Cent*)
312.16	Much (*Cent*) • Hm! Much (MS Morgan)
312.16	diffrence (MS Morgan) • diff'rence (*Cent*)
312.16	particklar (MS Morgan) • partic'lar (*Cent*)
312.16	*law* (MS Morgan) • law (*Cent*)
312.17	*now,* (MS Morgan) • now (*Cent*)
312.18–19	middle o' (MS Morgan) • middle'o (*Cent*)
312.19	caze (MS Morgan) • 'ca'se (*Cent*)

312.21	farm—*dem* (MS Morgan) • farm; dem (*Cent*)
312.21	questions, (MS Morgan) • questions (*Cent*)
312.23	cotton planter (MS Morgan) • cotton-planter (*Cent*)
312.31	her (MS Morgan) • her, (*Cent*)
312.34	selling (*Cent*) • sending (MS Morgan) [TEXTUAL NOTE: *Only here does MS Morgan have 'send' instead of 'sell' (down the river); Cent's reading is assumed to be an authorial rephrasing*]
312.35	time, (MS Morgan) • time: (*Cent*)
312.35	year—in (MS Morgan) • year. In (*Cent*)
312.36	Yes, (MS Morgan) • Yes; (*Cent*)
312.38	anyway (MS Morgan) • any way (*Cent*)
313.2	were, (MS Morgan) • were (*Cent*)
313.7	him, (MS Morgan) • him (*Cent*)
313.8	owner; (MS Morgan) • owner— (*Cent*)
313.9	doing (MS Morgan) • doing, (*Cent*)
313.11	put (MS Morgan) • to put (*Cent*)
313.17	again (MS Morgan) • again, (*Cent*)
313.18–19	miscreant. [*one line space*] The (MS Morgan) • miscreant. The (*Cent*)
313.22	crying, (MS Morgan) • crying (*Cent*)
313.23	steerage bunk (MS Morgan) • steerage-bunk (*Cent*)
313.24	morning; and (MS Morgan) • morning, and, (*Cent*)
313.26	She!—why (MS Morgan) • She! Why (*Cent*)
313.32	up (MS Morgan) • up, (*Cent*)
313.32	practiced (MS Morgan) • practised (*Cent*)
313.33	there, then (MS Morgan) • there. Then (*Cent*)
313.34	breast (MS Morgan) • breast, (*Cent*)
313.35–36	I's sole down de river! (MS Morgan) • *I's sole down de river!* (*Cent*)
314.2–5	[¶] Even popularity . . . *Calendar.* (*Cent*) • [*not in*] (MS Morgan)
314.3	Michael Angelo (MS in CU-MARK) • [*not in*] (MS Morgan); Michelangelo (*Cent*) [TEXTUAL NOTE: *Two MS leaves and one notebook, all in CU-MARK, record this maxim, spelling the name* 'Michael Angelo' *and* 'Michel Angelo'. *Although SLC did sometimes write* 'Michelangelo', *Cent's reading has been emended to the more usual of his two manuscript forms*]
314.4	*see* him do it • (*Cent*); [*not in*] (MS Morgan) [TEXTUAL NOTE: *Two MS leaves and one notebook, all in CU-MARK, record this maxim; one leaf places emphasis (underscoring) upon* 'see', *one (marked by SLC*

'Pudd'nhead Wilson's Calendar') cancels the underscore on 'see' and dou-
ble-underscores 'do', and the entry in Notebook 36, written in December
1895, after publication of the book, places it upon 'see'. It seems probable
that the Century Magazine has obliterated SLC's original emphasis, and
the more numerous of the two variant emphases has been preferred]

314.10 Calendar. (*Cent*) • *Calendar.* [¶] On Independence Day Rowena went out
back to see the fireworks and fell down the well and got drowned. But it
is no matter; these things cannot be helped, in a work of this kind. (MS
Morgan)

314.11–26 The summer . . . private (*Cent*) • The political campaign . . . behind her.
(MS Morgan [164.7–166.27])

314.13 Twins (MTP) • [*not in*] (MS Morgan); twins (*Cent*)

314.19 Twins (MTP) • [*not in*] (MS Morgan); twins (*Cent*)

314.26 sitting room. (MTP) • [*not in*] (MS Morgan); sitting-room. (*Cent*)

314.28–315.7 foreigners. It . . . he believed (*Cent*) • Twins. He reviewed . . . his
belief (MS Morgan [166.32–36])

314.29 mass meeting (MTP) • [*not in*] (MS Morgan); mass-meeting (*Cent*)
[TEXTUAL NOTE: *Cent's spelling emended on the basis of SLC's manuscript usage; see PW-REV, Textual Apparatus, entry at 279.22*]

315.2–3 peanut-pedlars (MTP) • [*not in*] (MS Morgan); peanut pedlers (*Cent*)
[TEXTUAL NOTE: *In this Cent-only passage spelling is emended on the
basis of SLC's manuscript usage (cf. "Three Thousand Years Among the
Microbes," WWD, 551)*]

315.8 humbug and (*Cent*) • [*not in*] (MS Morgan)

315.8 its owner (*Cent*) • Luigi (MS Morgan)

315.9 know where (*Cent*) • be able (MS Morgan)

315.9–10 to assassinate somebody (MS Morgan) • *to assassinate somebody*
(*Cent*)

315.11–12 [¶] Then he stepped . . . party cries. (*Cent*) • [*not in*] (MS Morgan)

315.13 The strange (*Cent*) • This last (MS Morgan)

315.13–14 an extraordinary (*Cent*) • a prodigious (MS Morgan)

315.14 asking (MS Morgan) • asking, (*Cent*)

315.16 Tom (*Cent*) • Tom, who was down on a visit, (MS Morgan) [TEXTUAL
NOTE: *MS Morgan had last placed Tom in St. Louis, but in revision SLC
added some text (314.11–26) locating him in Dawson's Landing, so that
MS Morgan's 'who was down on a visit' became redundant*]

315.20–28 Wilson was . . . were deserted. (*Cent*) • Wilson got . . . his choice. (MS
Morgan [167.10–32])

315.20 Twins (MTP) • [*not in*] (MS Morgan); twins (*Cent*)

316.6–9   [¶] *Thanksgiving Day . . . at Fiji.—Pudd'nhead Wilson's Calendar.*
(MTP) • [*not in*] (MS Morgan); *Thanksgiving Day.* Let all give humble,
hearty, and sincere thanks, now, but the turkeys. ['but the turkeys' *struck
through so as to remain legible, then deleted in earnest; then, interlined
above deletion:*] ˏbut the turkeys.ˏ [¶] [Print those words, but strike
line ~~through~~ through as in the copy] [¶] In the island of Fiji they do
not use turkeys, they use plumbers. It does not become you and me
to sneer at Fiji. (MS in CU-MARK); [¶] THANKSGIVING DAY. Let
all . . . use turkeys, . . . at Fiji.—*Pudd'nhead Wilson's Calendar.* (*Cent*);
*Thanksgiving Day.—Let all . . . use turkeys; . . . at Fiji.—Pudd'nhead
Wilson's Calendar.* (E) [TEXTUAL NOTE: *For this aphorism we revert to
the author's punctuation and styling as seen in the MS draft (CU-MARK,
Box 40, no. 5); the other witnesses, Cent and E, have been styled by editors
and printers*]

316.13   theatre (MS Morgan, E) • theater (*Cent*)

316.16   up stairs (MS Morgan) • up- | stairs (*Cent*); upstairs (E)

316.20   around (MS Morgan, *Cent*) • round (E)

316.22   out, (MS Morgan, *Cent*) • out (E)

316.28   a while (MS Morgan, *Cent*) • awhile (*Cent*, E)

317 *illus*   "KEEP STILL—I'S YO' MOTHER!" (*Cent*) • [*not in*] (MS Morgan)

318.3   said, (MS Morgan) • said (*Cent*, E)

318.4   it. (MS Morgan) • it! (*Cent*, E)

318.4   I'm (*Cent*, E) • I am (MS Morgan)

318.8   *bes'* (MS Morgan) • bes' (*Cent*, E)

318.9   so. (MS Morgan) • so! (*Cent*, E)

318.15   rebound, (*Cent*, E) • rebound (MS Morgan)

318.23   gwyne (MS Morgan, E) • gwine (*Cent*)

318.24   jes' (MS Morgan, E) • jes (*Cent*)

318.25   man, (MS Morgan, E) • man; (*Cent*)

318.26   could a (MS Morgan, E) • could 'a' (*Cent*)

318.26   a ben (MS Morgan, E) • 'a' be'n (*Cent*)

318.27   ben (MS Morgan, E) • be'n (*Cent*)

318.27   comfortable; (MS Morgan, E) • comfortable: (*Cent*)

318.27   good lookin' (MS Morgan, *Cent*) • good-lookin' (E)

318.28   agin (MS Morgan, *Cent*) • ag'in (E)

318.28   'mongst (*Cent*, E) • mongst (MS Morgan)

318.29   satisfied, (MS Morgan, E) • satisfied (*Cent*)

318.30   agin (MS Morgan) • ag'in' (*Cent*); ag'in (E)

318.31	mawnins (MS Morgan, E) • mawnin's (*Cent*)
318.32	many's de lashin' (MS Morgan) • many's de lashin's (*Cent*); lashins (E) [TEXTUAL NOTE: *E and Cent agree in the plural form, so it must have stood in TS2a; but it is incorrect and contrary to SLC's practice, so it is probably an error of the TS2 typist*]
318.32	caze (MTP) • becaze (MS Morgan); 'ca'se (*Cent*, E) [TEXTUAL NOTE: *E and Cent agree on the shorter form, showing that it was in revising TS2a that SLC altered MS Morgan's reading; the spelling has been altered to the manuscript's invariable* 'caze']
318.33	wuz (*Cent*, E) • 'uz (MS Morgan)
318.37	en (MS Morgan, *Cent*) • an' (E)
318.38	jist (MS Morgan, *Cent*) • jes' (E)
318.38	*no* (MS Morgan) • no (*Cent*, E)
318.38	mo'! (MS Morgan) • mo'. (*Cent*, E)
319.1	he (*Cent*, E) • [*not in*] (MS Morgan) [TEXTUAL NOTE: *In the text edited from PW-MS, this necessary word is added editorially; here, it is an emendation adopted from Cent*]
319.5	sombre (MS Morgan, E) • somber (*Cent*)
319.7	*was* (MS Morgan) • was (*Cent*, E)
319.9–10	But her flash of happiness was but (MS Morgan, E) • But her flash of happiness was only (*Cent*) [TEXTUAL NOTE: *E agrees with MS Morgan in the awkward double-use of* 'But . . . but', *which shows that this is what stood in TS2a and that the alteration to* 'but . . . only' *was done by a Century editor, or by SLC in proofs; judging from SLC's revising practice, removing assonances was more in a magazine editor's line than his own*]
319.12	again. (*Cent*, E) • again: (MS Morgan)
319.13	couldn't (MS Morgan, *Cent*) • could not (E)
319.13	weeks (*Cent*, E) • weeks, (MS Morgan)
319.14	lashin's (*Cent*) • lashins (MS Morgan, E)
319.14	down-hearted (MS Morgan, E) • downhearted (*Cent*)
319.15	noth'n (MS Morgan, E) • noth'n' (*Cent*)
319.19	workin', (MS Morgan) • workin' (*Cent*, E) [TEXTUAL NOTE: *The agreement of Cent and E shows the reading of TS2a; but MS Morgan's comma is an easily overlooked insertion right next to a deletion, and the TS2 typist apparently missed it*]
319.20	me— (MS Morgan, E) • me,— (*Cent*)
319.20	caze (MS Morgan) • 'ca'se (*Cent*, E)
319.21	eat— (MS Morgan, E) • eat,— (*Cent*)
319.22	stick (MS Morgan, E) • stick, (*Cent*)

319.22   broom-han'le (MS Morgan) • broom-handle (*Cent*, E)

319.24   *stan' it!* (MS Morgan) • stan' it. (*Cent*, E)

319.25   flat! (MS Morgan) • flat. (*Cent*, E)

319.27   plum (MS Morgan, E) • plumb (*Cent*)

319.27   gathered (*Cent*, E) • gethered (MS Morgan) [TEXTUAL NOTE: *If SLC made this revision to Roxy's speech, and it is not instead a banalization by the TS2 typist, it may be he decided that* 'gethered' *was* white *dialect; in* Huckleberry Finn *only white characters use this form*]

319.27   roun' (*Cent*) • 'roun' (MS Morgan, E)

319.29   *me* (MS Morgan) • me (*Cent*, E)

319.29   in (MS Morgan, *Cent*) • [*not in*] (E)

319.30   dat dey'd (MS Morgan) • dat, they'd (*Cent*); dat they'd (E)

319.32   gitt'n (MS Morgan, E) • gitt'n' (*Cent*)

319.32   towards (MS Morgan, *Cent*) • toward (E)

319.33   *got* (MS Morgan) • got (*Cent*, E)

319.36   caze (MS Morgan) • 'ca'se (*Cent*, E)

319.36   fum (MS Morgan, E) • f'om (*Cent*)

319.36   work mules (MS Morgan) • work-mules (*Cent*, E)

319.37   gwyne (MS Morgan, E) • gwine (*Cent*)

320.4   a spinnin' (MS Morgan) • a-spinnin' (*Cent*, E)

320.5   mo'; (MS Morgan) • mo', (*Cent*, E) [TEXTUAL NOTE: *The TS2 typist probably mistook MS Morgan's semicolon for a comma*]

320.6   gwyne (MS Morgan, E) • gwine (*Cent*)

320.7   mine (MS Morgan, *Cent*) • mind (E)

320.8   midnight, (MS Morgan, *Cent*) • midnight (E)

320.11   agin (MS Morgan) • ag'in' (*Cent*); ag'in (E)

320.11   den (MTP) • de (MS Morgan, *Cent,* E)

320.11   most (MS Morgan, E) • 'most (*Cent*)

320.12   Gran' Mogul (MS Morgan) • *Gran' Mogul* (*Cent*); "Gran' Mogul" (E)

320.12   chambermaid (*Cent*, E) • head chambermaid (MS Morgan)

320.14   a hammerin' (MS Morgan) • a-hammerin' (*Cent*, E)

320.14   engine room (MS Morgan) • engine-room (*Cent*, E)

320.16   boat en (MS Morgan) • boat and (*Cent*, E)

320.16   jes' (MS Morgan, E) • jes (*Cent*)

320.17   step 'board (MS Morgan) • step' 'board (*Cent*); step' board (E)

320.17   hot; (MS Morgan) • hot, (*Cent*, E)

320.18   fo'cas'l, (MS Morgan) • fo'cas'l', (*Cent*); fo'cas'l; (E)

320.19   caze (MS Morgan) • 'ca'se (*Cent*, E)

320.20   watch— (MS Morgan) • watch!— (*Cent*, E)

320.20–21 a noddin' (MS Morgan) • a-noddin' (*Cent*, E)

320.21   companionway (MS Morgan, *Cent*) • companion way (E)

320.21   'em (*Cent*) • em (MS Morgan, E)

320.21   en (MS Morgan, E) • 'en, (*Cent*)

320.22   myself (*Cent*, E) • myseff (MS Morgan)

320.22   wisht (MS Morgan, E) • wished (*Cent*)

320.23   *I* (MS Morgan) • I (*Cent*, E)

320.23   is! (MS Morgan) • is. (*Cent*, E)

320.24   biler (MS Morgan, E) • b'iler (*Cent*)

320.25   mos' (MS Morgan, E) • 'mos' (*Cent*)

320.26   *home* (MS Morgan) • home (*Cent*, E)

320.26   agin (MS Morgan, E) • ag'in (*Cent*)

320.26   *I* (MS Morgan) • I (*Cent*, E)

320.27   hear (MS Morgan) • heard (*Cent*, E) [TEXTUAL NOTE: *The shared reading of E and Cent is rejected; the fact that in the rest of this long passage Roxy speaks in the historical present tense makes it likelier that TS2's typist mistakenly typed MS Morgan's 'hear' as 'heard'*]

320.29   *dat* (MS Morgan) • dat (*Cent*, E)

320.29   agin (MS Morgan) • ag'in (*Cent*, E)

320.30   agin (MS Morgan) • ag'in (*Cent*, E)

320.30   agin (MS Morgan) • ag'in (*Cent*, E)

320.32   myself, (MS Morgan) • myself (*Cent*, E) [TEXTUAL NOTE: *MS Morgan's comma is surrounded by revisions and could easily be overlooked by the TS2 typist*]

320.32   all.' (*Cent*) • all. (MS Morgan); all." (E)

320.32   Mogul (MS Morgan) • *Mogul* (*Cent*); "Mogul" (E)

320.33   jes' (MS Morgan, E) • jes (*Cent*)

320.35   me, (MS Morgan, E) • me; (*Cent*)

320.35   *dem* (MS Morgan) • dem (*Cent*, E)

320.36   chambermaid (MS Morgan, *Cent*) • chambermaid, (E)

320.37   guard, (*Cent*, E) • guard (MS Morgan)

321.3   wuz (*Cent*, E) • was (MS Morgan)

321.3   den I (*Cent*, E) • I (MS Morgan)

321.3   house (MS Morgan, E) • house, (*Cent*)

321.3	away (MS Morgan, *Cent*) • away, (E)
321.4	down (MS Morgan, *Cent*) • down to (E)
321.4	caze (MS Morgan) • 'ca'se (*Cent*, E)
321.6	pass'n (MS Morgan, E) • pass'n' (*Cent*)
321.6	street (MS Morgan, *Cent*) • Street (E)
321.7	bills, (*Cent*, E) • bills (MS Morgan)
321.8	mos' (MS Morgan) • 'mos' (*Cent*); 'most (E)
321.12	now, (MS Morgan, E) • now: (*Cent*)
321.12	take. (MS Morgan) • take! (*Cent*, E)
321.14	Grand Mogul (MS Morgan) • *Grand Mogul* (*Cent*); "Grand Mogul" (E)
321.16	State (MS Morgan, *Cent*) • state (E)
321.18	*couldn't* (MS Morgan) • couldn't (*Cent*, E)
321.19	*here* (MS Morgan) • here (*Cent*, E)
321.22	*help* (MS Morgan) • help (*Cent*, E)
321.27	face, (*Cent*, E) • face (MS Morgan)
321.28	sharply (*Cent*, E) • sharply, (MS Morgan)
321.30	Dah (*Cent*, E) • Dah, (MS Morgan)
321.31	shirt! (*Cent*, E) • shirt. (MS Morgan)
321.31	ben (MS Morgan, E) • be'n (*Cent*)
321.33	Ye-s (MS Morgan) • Ye–s (*Cent*); Ye—s (E)
322.1	me. (MS Morgan) • me! (*Cent*, E)
322.4	wood-cut (MS Morgan) • woodcut (*Cent*, E) [TEXTUAL NOTE: *Probably an error of the TS2 typist*]
322.6	heading (*Cent*, E) • heading, (MS Morgan) [TEXTUAL NOTE: *Another easy-to-miss MS Morgan comma*]
322.6	*$100 Reward.* (MS Morgan) • $100 REWARD. (*Cent*); $100 REWARD. (E)
322.8	Fourth-street (MS Morgan, *Cent*) • Fourth Street (E)
322.11	bill. (MS Morgan) • bill! (*Cent*, E)
322.13	said, (MS Morgan, E) • said (*Cent*)
322.14	you, (MS Morgan, E) • you; (*Cent*)
322.17	*all* (*Cent*, E) • all (MS Morgan)
322.21	while, (MS Morgan, E) • while; (*Cent*)
322.24	*is* (MS Morgan) • is (*Cent*, E)
322.25	man, (MS Morgan, E) • man (*Cent*)
322.25	sk'yerd (*Cent*, E) • s'kyerd (MS Morgan)
322.25	scasely (MS Morgan, E) • sca'cely (*Cent*)

322.26	dollah (MS Morgan) • dollar (*Cent*, E)
322.26	ben (MS Morgan, E) • be'n (*Cent*)
322.30	noth'n; (MS Morgan) • noth'n', (*Cent*, E)
322.30	mos' (MS Morgan, E) • 'mos' (*Cent*)
322.31	roun', scasely (MS Morgan) • roun' sca'cely (*Cent*); roun' scasely (E)
322.31–32	ben a stannin' (MS Morgan, E) • be'n a-stannin' (*Cent*)
323.2	printed, (MS Morgan) • printed (*Cent*, E)
323.8	agin, sho' (MS Morgan, E) • ag'in, sho (*Cent*)
323.9	Now, (MS Morgan) • Now (*Cent*, E)
323.9	gwyne (MS Morgan, E) • gwine (*Cent*)
323.9	ast (*Cent*, E) • ask (MS Morgan) [TEXTUAL NOTE: *Both E and Cent, setting type independently from TS2a (or a copy thereof), read* 'ast', *so this must have been the reading of the typescript. SLC writes* 'ast' *in dialect passages in* Huckleberry Finn, Tom Sawyer Abroad, *and other works; but MS Morgan's only other instance of* 'ast' *was revised by him to* 'ask' *(143.15). Still, the Cent-E reading has been adopted as a possible authorial revision of the dialect*]
323.10	gwyne (MS Morgan, E) • gwine (*Cent*)
323.13	ben (MS Morgan, E) • be'n (*Cent*)
323.14	*him,* (*Cent*, E) • *him* (MS Morgan)
323.14	tar (MS Morgan, E) • t'ar (*Cent*)
323.14	he (MS Morgan, E) • de (*Cent*) [TEXTUAL NOTE: *From E we can see that MS Morgan's reading* 'he' *was faithfully typed in TS2, and left standing by SLC when he revised it as TS2a, from which E descends. The alteration to* 'de' *was therefore made at the Century Magazine, conceivably by SLC in proofs, but a compositorial error or editorial adjustment seems just as probable*]
323.24	a while (MS Morgan) • awhile (*Cent*, E)
323.25	*you* (MS Morgan) • you (*Cent*, E)
323.26	hide. (MS Morgan) • hide! (*Cent*, E)
323.26	*Would* (MS Morgan) • Would (*Cent*, E)
323.26	it? No— (*Cent*, E) • it! No!— (MS Morgan)
323.26	*dog* (MS Morgan) • dog (*Cent*, E)
323.27	pup'd (MS Morgan, *Cent*) • pupp'd (E)
323.27	I's (*Cent*, E) • I is (MS Morgan)
323.28	it!"—and (MS Morgan, *Cent*) • it!' And (E)
323.29	offer (MS Morgan) • effort (*Cent*, E) [TEXTUAL NOTE: *Since Cent and E concur in* 'made no effort to resent this', *it must reflect the reading of*

TS2a—but idiomatically one 'offers' *to resent an insult, and this may be
an error by the typist of TS2:* 'offer' *and* 'effort' *look similar, and* 'made
no effort' *attracts by virtue of familiarity*]

323.30	gwyne (MS Morgan, E) • gwine (*Cent*)
323.30	gwyne (MS Morgan, E) • gwine (*Cent*)
323.32	agin (MS Morgan, *Cent*) • ag'in (E)
323.36	gamblin' (*Cent*) • gamblin (MS Morgan); gambling (E)
323.36	debts, (MS Morgan, E) • debts (*Cent*)
323.38	agin (MS Morgan) • ag'in (*Cent*, E)
324.5	it. (MS Morgan) • you's a-goin'. (*Cent*); it! (E)
324.5	caze (MTP) • becaze (MS Morgan); 'ca'se (*Cent*); beca'se (E) [TEXTUAL NOTE: *The variation of Cent and E is best explained as SLC revising to* 'caze' *in Century proofs, which was then respelled according to Cent's norm; on this hypothesis E follows the earlier reading of TS2a*]
324.7	river, (*Cent*, E) • river (MS Morgan)
324.7	it. (MS Morgan) • it! (*Cent*, E)
324.8	rose, trembling (MS Morgan, *Cent*) • rose trembling, (E)
324.12	de (MS Morgan, *Cent*) • the (E)
324.12	honey—set (*Cent*, E) • honey. Set (MS Morgan)
324.12	down! (MS Morgan) • down. (*Cent*, E)
324.13	gwyne (MS Morgan, E) • gwine (*Cent*)
324.13	gwyne (MS Morgan, E) • gwine (*Cent*)
324.16	expression, (MS Morgan, *Cent*) • expression (E)
324.18	Gwyne (MS Morgan, E) • Gwine (*Cent*)
324.19	*tole* (MS Morgan) • tole (*Cent*, E)
324.20	dat (*Cent*, E) • dat, (MS Morgan)
324.20	Now (MS Morgan, *Cent*) • Now, (E)
324.21	kin (MS Morgan, *Cent*) • can (E)
324.21	gwyne (MS Morgan, E) • gwine (*Cent*)
324.24–25	sullenly— [¶] "Yes." (MS Morgan, *Cent*) • sullenly: 'Yes.' (E)
324.26	gits (MS Morgan, *Cent*) • gets (E)
324.26	self (*Cent*, E) • seff (MS Morgan)
324.28	tell (MS Morgan, *Cent*) • till (E)
324.30	umbereller (MS Morgan) • umbreller (*Cent*, E)
324.32	Becaze (MS Morgan) • Beca'se (*Cent*, E)
324.32	gwyne (MS Morgan, E) • gwine (*Cent*)

324.33	*it* (MS Morgan) • it (*Cent*, E)
324.34	gwyne (MS Morgan, E) • gwine (*Cent*)
324.36	gwyne (MS Morgan, E) • gwine (*Cent*)
324.38	*I* (MS Morgan) • I (*Cent*, E)
325.1	diffrent (MS Morgan) • diff'rent (*Cent*, E)
325.1	fum (MS Morgan) • fom (*Cent*, E)
325.1	yo'n. (MS Morgan) • yo'n! (*Cent*, E)
325.6	that (MS Morgan) • this (*Cent*, E)
325.8	home (*Cent*, E) • home, (MS Morgan)
325.10	*her* (MS Morgan) • her (*Cent*, E)
325.11	myself, (MS Morgan, E) • myself; (*Cent*)
325.11	rob (MS Morgan) • *rob* (*Cent*, E)
325.12	skinflint! (MS Morgan) • skinflint. (*Cent*, E)
326.2–3	[¶] Few things . . . *Calendar.* (*Cent*, E) • [*not in*] (MS Morgan)
326.4–6	It were not best that we should all think alike; it is difference of opinion that makes horse-races.—*Pudd'nhead Wilson's Calendar.* (*Cent*, E) • It would not be best for all to think alike. It is difference of opinion that makes horse-races.—*Pudd'nhead Wilson's Calendar.* (MS Morgan); [TEXTUAL NOTE: *In MS Morgan a version of this aphorism is inscribed (and deleted) at the head of chapter 12. Cent and E testify to the slightly revised form of SLC's reinscription in TS2a*]
326.7–10	Dawson's Landing . . . carried it. (*Cent*) • Dawson's Landing had . . . to Judge Driscoll. (MS Morgan [177.2–16])
326.8	waiting too (E) • [*not in*] (MS Morgan); waiting, too (*Cent*)
326.10	Judge Driscoll (*Cent*, E) • The Judge (MS Morgan)
326.11	added, (MS Morgan, E) • added (*Cent*)
326.30	things, (MS Morgan, E) • things; (*Cent*)
327.3	for (*Cent*, E) • of (MS Morgan)
327.8	all,— (MS Morgan) • all— (*Cent*, E)
327.13	song-birds; (MS Morgan) • song-birds, (*Cent*, E)
327.13–14	harem of cats (MS Morgan, E) • howling colony of cats (*Cent*) [TEXTUAL NOTE: *The Century Magazine did not proscribe all uses of 'harem', but as its use in MS Morgan alludes to the sexual promiscuity of cats, its replacement in Cent, although clearly written by SLC, has been treated as the result of censorship*]
327.15	filings, (*Cent*, E) • filings (MS Morgan)
327.16	Nature, (MS Morgan, *Cent*) • Nature— (E)
327.19	him. (MS Morgan) • him! (*Cent*, E)

327.21   will (*Cent*, E) • shall (MS Morgan)

327.22   leaving, (MS Morgan, *Cent*) • leaving (E)

327.22–23 said— [¶] "The (*Cent*, MS Morgan) • said: "The (E)

327.23   still (*Cent*, E) • [*not in*] (MS Morgan)

327.24   so, (MS Morgan, E) • so; (*Cent*)

327.24   out, (*Cent*, E) • out (MS Morgan)

327.25   the Twins (MTP) • Luigi (MS Morgan); the twins (*Cent*, E)

327.27   Dawson's, (*Cent*, E) • Dawson's (MS Morgan)

327.30   any one, (MS Morgan) • any one (*Cent*, E)

327.31   window-blinds (*Cent*, E) • window shades (MS Morgan)

327.31   lit (MS Morgan, E) • lighted (*Cent*) [TEXTUAL NOTE: *The Century editors seem to have banned the use of 'lit' as a transitive verb. An alteration from 'lit' to 'lighted' is also found in the Century's edited excerpt from* A Connecticut Yankee *(CY, 103.27)*]

327.32   hat (*Cent*, E) • hat, (MS Morgan)

327.33   it and laid it by. (E) • it. (MS Morgan); it, and laid it by. (*Cent*)

327.34   a burnt cork (MS Morgan) • burnt cork (*Cent*, E) [TEXTUAL NOTE: *MS Morgan's 'a' is a superscript insertion, written very small, and could easily have been missed by the TS2 typist*]

327.35   was, to (MS Morgan, *Cent*) • was to (E)

327.35   sitting room (MS Morgan) • sitting-room (*Cent*, E)

327.36   bedroom (E) • bed- | room (MS Morgan); bed-room (*Cent*)

327.38   little, (MS Morgan, *Cent*) • little (E)

328.1   say, (*Cent*, E) • say (MS Morgan)

328.3   hiding place (MS Morgan) • hiding-place (*Cent*, E)

328.5   halfway (MTP) • half way (MS Morgan); half- | way (*Cent*); half-way (E)

328.5   down, (*Cent*, E) • down (MS Morgan)

328.11   sofa; on (*Cent*, E) • sofa. On (MS Morgan)

328.12   old man's (*Cent*, E) • [*not in*] (MS Morgan) [TEXTUAL NOTE: *In MS Morgan, Judge Driscoll's cash-box had already been mentioned at this point, in a passage excised by SLC in revision (PW-MS, 167.16). This two-word insertion smoothes over the omission*]

328.13   bank notes (MS Morgan) • bank-notes (*Cent*, E)

328.18   sleep, (*Cent*, E) • sleep (MS Morgan)

328.19   thumping (MS Morgan, E) • thumping, (*Cent*)

328.21   prize (*Cent*, E) • prize, (MS Morgan)

328.21   seized (*Cent*, E) • siezed (MS Morgan)

328.23   home— (*Cent*, E) • home (MS Morgan)

328.24   his notes (MS Morgan, E) • the notes (*Cent*)

328.26   hand (MS Morgan, E) • hand, (*Cent*)

328.26   seized (*Cent*, E) • siezed (MS Morgan)

328.28   him. He (MS Morgan) • him. [¶] He (*Cent*, E) [TEXTUAL NOTE: *The typist of TS2 probably misinterpreted the first uncanceled line of MS Morgan page 549 ('He jumped . . .') as the beginning of a new paragraph*]

328.31   room (*Cent*, E) • room, (MS Morgan)

328.32   Twins (MS Morgan) • twins (*Cent*, E)

328.32   man. (MS Morgan, E) • man! (*Cent*) [TEXTUAL NOTE: *The reading of E shows that the period stood in TS2; the alteration to an exclamation point could therefore be either SLC's, in revising TS2a or on Century proofs, or the Century's in-house contribution*]

328.34   room-door (MS Morgan) • room door (*Cent*, E)

328.37   back stairs (MS Morgan, *Cent*) • back-stairs (E)

329.1   centred (MS Morgan, E) • centered (*Cent*)

329.1   now; his (MS Morgan, *Cent*) • now. His (E)

329.2   back yard (MS Morgan, *Cent*) • back-yard (E)

329.3   half-dressed (*Cent*, E) • half dressed (MS Morgan)

329.3   had joined (*Cent*, E) • were with (MS Morgan)

329.4   Twins (MS Morgan) • twins (*Cent*, E)

329.5   gate, (*Cent*, E) • gate (MS Morgan)

329.7   was (*Cent*, E) • was, (MS Morgan)

329.8–9   dress—they (MS Morgan, *Cent*) • dress; they (E)

329.10   lit (MS Morgan, E) • lighted (*Cent*) [TEXTUAL NOTE: *See PW-REV, Textual Apparatus, entry and textual note at 327.31*]

329.10   candle (*Cent*, E) • candle, (MS Morgan)

329.14   the most of (MS Morgan, E) • most of (*Cent*) [TEXTUAL NOTE: *'the most of' is frequent in SLC but has not been found in the Century Magazine*]

329.15   scattered the ashes, (*Cent*, E) • [*not in*] (MS Morgan)

329.17   road (*Cent*, E) • road, (MS Morgan)

329.18   down stream (MS Morgan, E) • down-stream (*Cent*)

329.21   St. Louis (*Cent*, E) • St Louis (MS Morgan)

329.22   himself, (MS Morgan, *Cent*) • himself: (E)

329.23   clew (MS Morgan) • clue (*Cent*, E)

329.24–25 mysteries, and people won't get done trying to guess out the secret of it for fifty years (*Cent*, E) • mysteries (MS Morgan)

329.28–30 "Judge . . . be lynched." [*not styled as extract*] (MS Morgan) • Judge . . . be lynched. [*styled as extract*] (*Cent*); 'Judge . . . be lynched.' [*not styled as extract*] (E)

329.29 Italian nobleman or barber, (E) • ex-freak called the Italian Twins, (MS Morgan); Italian nobleman or barber (*Cent*)

329.30 The assassin (*Cent*, E) • One of them is considered innocent, but the other one (MS Morgan)

329.31 "One of the (*Cent*, E) • "The (MS Morgan)

329.31 Twins!" (MS Morgan) • twins!" (*Cent*); twins!' (E)

329.31 soliloquised (MS Morgan, E) • soliloquized (*Cent*)

329.32 him (*Cent*, E) • them (MS Morgan)

329.34 back, (MS Morgan, *Cent*) • back (E)

329.37 aunt (MS Morgan) • Aunt (*Cent*, E)

330.1–2 "Have seen . . . I come." [*not styled as extract*] (MS Morgan) • Have seen . . . I come. [*styled as extract*] (*Cent*); 'Have seen . . . I come.' [*not styled as extract*] (E)

330.1 prostrated (MS Morgan, *Cent*) • prostrate (E)

330.3 [*one line space*] [¶] When (MS Morgan, *Cent*) • [*no line space*] [¶] When (E)

330.3 mourning (MS Morgan, *Cent*) • mourning, (E)

330.5 command (*Cent*, E) • command, (MS Morgan)

330.8 Twins and (MS Morgan) • twins and (*Cent*, E)

330.8 Twins away (MS Morgan) • twins away (*Cent*, E)

330.9 defence (MS Morgan, E) • defense (*Cent*)

330.12 finger-prints (*Cent*, E) • finger- | prints (MS Morgan)

330.13 knife handle (MTP) • knife-handle (MS Morgan, *Cent*, E)

330.13 Twins (MS Morgan) • twins (*Cent*, E)

330.15 Twins (MS Morgan) • twins (*Cent*, E)

330.18 girl (*Cent*, E) • girl, (MS Morgan)

330.19 matter; (MS Morgan, *Cent*) • matter, (E)

330.22 up stairs (MS Morgan) • up-stairs (*Cent*); upstairs (E)

330.25 it. (*Cent*, E) • it. The grand jury indicted Luigi for murder in the first degree and Angelo as accessory. The Twins were transferred from the city jail to the county prison to await trial. (MS Morgan)

330.26 the unfortunates (*Cent*, E) • them (MS Morgan)

330.27–30 The grand jury . . . to await trial. (*Cent*, E) • [*not in*] (MS Morgan) [TEXTUAL NOTE: *The text follows Cent but adopts two variants from the parallel passage in MS Morgan, at 181.28*]

330.28 degree (MS Morgan) • degree, (*Cent*, E)

330.29 Twins (MS Morgan) • twins (*Cent*, E)

330.31 knife handle, (MS Morgan) • knife-handle (*Cent*); knife-handle, (E)

330.32 Twins (MS Morgan) • twins (*Cent*, E)

331.4 answer, (MS Morgan, E) • answer; (*Cent*)

331.4 *wasn't* (MS Morgan) • wasn't (*Cent*, E)

331.7 knife handle (MS Morgan) • knife-handle (*Cent*, E)

331.8 glass-records (*Cent*, E) • glass records (MS Morgan)

331.9 past (MS Morgan, E) • last (*Cent*) [TEXTUAL NOTE: *The Century Magazine's style sheet disallowed 'past' in phrases such as 'the past two years', requiring 'last' (McKnight 1923, 408–9)*]

331.14 knife, (*Cent*, E) • knife (MS Morgan)

331.15 it (MS Morgan, *Cent*) • it, (E)

331.15 pretence (MS Morgan, E) • pretense (*Cent*)

331.16 Twins (MS Morgan) • twins (*Cent*, E)

331.16 Twins (MS Morgan) • twins (*Cent*, E)

331.18 said, (*Cent*, E) • said (MS Morgan)

331.18 so. (MS Morgan, E) • so! (*Cent*)

331.21 knew (*Cent*, E) • knew, (MS Morgan)

331.22 for, firstly (MS Morgan) • for first (*Cent*, E) [TEXTUAL NOTE: *The agreement of Cent and E confirms that 'first' is what stood in TS2a, where it may, however, have been the TS2 typist's error*]

331.23 *could* (MS Morgan) • could (*Cent*, E)

331.26 gone, (MS Morgan, *Cent*) • gone (E)

331.27 gone, (MS Morgan, *Cent*) • gone (E)

331.27–28 had really been revived, as was now discovered, (*Cent*, E) • *had* been revived, (MS Morgan)

331.29 talky, (*Cent*, E) • talky (MS Morgan)

331.29 St. Louis (*Cent*, E) • St Louis (MS Morgan)

331.34 Twins (MS Morgan) • twins (*Cent*, E)

331.36 *was* (MS Morgan) • was (*Cent*, E)

331.38 Twins (MS Morgan) • twins (*Cent*, E)

332.3 Twins (MS Morgan) • twins (*Cent*, E)

332.3 *with* (*Cent*, E) • with (MS Morgan)

332.9	knife handle (MS Morgan) • knife-handle (*Cent*, E)
332.13	house doors (MS Morgan, *Cent*) • house-doors (E)
332.14	visits (MS Morgan, *Cent*) • visits, (E)
332.26	"realized now, as (MS Morgan, E) • realized now, "as (*Cent*)
333.4	*any* (MS Morgan) • any (*Cent*, E)
333.4	*any* (MS Morgan) • any (*Cent*, E)
333.5	witnesses, (MS Morgan, *Cent*) • witnesses (E)
333.6	pencil, (MS Morgan, *Cent*) • pencil (E)
333.8	Twins (MS Morgan) • twins (*Cent*, E)
333.9	Aunt Patsy Cooper (*Cent*, E) • the two old aunties (MS Morgan)
333.10	life; (*Cent*, E) • life, (MS Morgan)
333.14	Twins (MS Morgan) • twins
333.14	didn't (MS Morgan, E) • did not (*Cent*)
333.16	court house (MS Morgan) • court-house (*Cent*, E)
333.17	around (MS Morgan, E) • around, (*Cent*)
333.20	Howard, (*Cent*, E) • Howard (MS Morgan)
333.21	Twins (MS Morgan) • twins (*Cent*, E)
333.21	one friend (*Cent*, E) • two friends (MS Morgan)
333.22	countenance, their poor old sorrowing landlady. She (*Cent*, E) • countenance. These (MS Morgan)
333.23	her friendliest. (*Cent*, E) • their friendliest. One was aunt Patsy Cooper, the other was aunt Betsy Hale. (MS Morgan)
333.24	on, (*Cent*, E) • on (MS Morgan)
333.27	Twins (MS Morgan) • twins (*Cent*, E)
333.28	temper (*Cent*, E) • fury (MS Morgan)
333.30	*her* (MS Morgan) • her (*Cent*, E)
333.31	those (MS Morgan) • these (*Cent*, E)
333.31	him, (*Cent*, E) • him (MS Morgan)
334.1	trial, (MS Morgan, *Cent*) • trial (E)
334.3	toss (*Cent*, E) • resolute toss (MS Morgan)
334.4	I's (MS Morgan, *Cent*) • I'se (E)
334.4	gwyne (MS Morgan, E) • gwine (*Cent*)
334.4	you! (MS Morgan) • you. (*Cent*, E)
334.6	evidence (MS Morgan, *Cent*) • evidence, (E)
334.9	presence (*Cent*, E) • silence (MS Morgan)
334.23	brief: (MS Morgan) • brief. (*Cent*, E)

334.24   budding career (*Cent*, E) • new reputation (MS Morgan)

334.27   Twins (MS Morgan) • twins (*Cent*, E)

334.30   court room (MS Morgan) • court-room (*Cent*, E)

334.33   defence (MS Morgan, E) • defense (*Cent*)

334.35   on (*Cent*, E) • in (MS Morgan)

334.35   added, significantly, (MTP) • added, significantly (MS Morgan); added significantly, (*Cent*, E)

334.38   defence (MS Morgan, E) • defense (*Cent*)

335.2   Murmurs (*Cent*, E) • Murmurs, (MS Morgan)

335.8   sitting room (MS Morgan) • sitting-room (*Cent*, E)

335.9   brother— (MS Morgan) • brother. (*Cent*, E)

335.12   Twins (MS Morgan) • twins (*Cent*, E)

335.17   blood-stains (MTP) • blood stains (MS Morgan, *Cent*, E)

335.18   followed, (MS Morgan, E) • followed (*Cent*)

335.21   proven (MS Morgan, E) • proved (*Cent*) [TEXTUAL NOTE: *The Century Magazine's style sheet required* 'proved' *(McKnight 1923, 408–9)*]

335.23   that (*Cent*, E) • [*not in*] (MS Morgan)

335.27   to, (*Cent*, E) • to (MS Morgan)

335.33   events (MS Morgan, *Cent*) • event (E)

335.35   old-lady friend (*Cent*, E) • two old-lady friends (MS Morgan)

335.37   Twins (MS Morgan) • twins (*Cent*, E)

335.37   Aunt Patsy (*Cent*, E) • the two old aunties (MS Morgan)

335.37   gay (*Cent*, E) • great and noble (MS Morgan)

335.38   pretence (MS Morgan, E) • pretense (*Cent*)

335.38   finishing. (*Cent*, E) • finishing, and went away crying. (MS Morgan)

336.1–31 [¶] Absolutely secure . . . now and then. (*Cent*, E) • [*not in*] (MS Morgan)

336.5   court room (MTP) • [*not in*] (MS Morgan); court-room (*Cent*); court-| room (E)

336.9   up, (E) • [*not in*] (MS Morgan); up (*Cent*)

336.10   certainly, (*Cent*) • [*not in*] (MS Morgan); certainly (E)

336.23   said, (*Cent*) • [*not in*] (MS Morgan); said: (E)

336.25   ask him (*Cent*) • [*not in*] (MS Morgan); ask him, (E)

336.25   guileless, (E) • guileless (*Cent*); [*not in*] (MS Morgan)

336.33   records (MS Morgan, *Cent*) • "records," (E)

337.4   have (*Cent*, E) • haven't (MS Morgan)

337.5   man, (MS Morgan, E) • man; (*Cent*)

337.6   child's-play (*Cent*, E) • child's play (MS Morgan)

337.7   sun-spot (MS Morgan, E) • sun- | spot (*Cent*)

337.9   always? (*Cent*, E) • always, just because you won once? (MS Morgan)

337.10 Wilson, (MS Morgan, *Cent*) • Wilson (E)

337.15 kicking; (MS Morgan, *Cent*) • kicking. (E)

337.16 the brunette one's (*Cent*, E) • their odious (MS Morgan)

337.18 mourners' (MS Morgan) • mourner's (*Cent*, E)

337.23 and (MS Morgan, *Cent*) • And (E)

337.26 usually"—and (MS Morgan, *Cent*) • usually.' And (E)

337.26 indifferently, (*Cent*, E) • indifferently (MS Morgan)

337.28 face, (MS Morgan, E) • face; (*Cent*)

337.30 Heavens, (MS Morgan, *Cent*) • Heavens! (E)

337.33 him (MS Morgan, *Cent*) • him, (E)

337.37 to-day; (MS Morgan, *Cent*) • to-day— (E)

338.1   Good night (MS Morgan) • Good-night (*Cent*, E)

338.5   are. (MS Morgan) • are! (*Cent*, E)

338.6   whisky (MS Morgan, E) • whisky, (*Cent*)

338.7   unintentionally (*Cent*, E) • [*not in*] (MS Morgan)

338.8–9 knife handle (MS Morgan) • knife-handle (*Cent*, E)

338.9   (for his trained eye), (*Cent*, E) • —for his trained eye— (MS Morgan)

338.10 was! nothing (MS Morgan) • was!—Nothing (*Cent*, E) [TEXTUAL NOTE: *In MS Morgan, SLC made a mark canceling a comma, which may have suggested a dash to the TS2 typist*]

338.16 record. "Now (MS Morgan) • record. [¶] "Now (*Cent*, E) [TEXTUAL NOTE: *These readings suggest that the TS2 typist, after transcribing an insertion on the verso of an MS Morgan leaf, began a new paragraph after 'record'—possibly mistaking the placement of SLC's inserted '¶', which is further on*]

338.20 all—hang it, (MS Morgan, *Cent*) • all. Hang it! (E)

338.21 hour (MS Morgan, *Cent*) • hour, (E)

338.24 use, (MS Morgan) • use; (*Cent*); use— (E)

338.28 out, (MS Morgan, *Cent*) • out (E)

338.31 away, (*Cent*, E) • away (MS Morgan)

338.32 recal (MS Morgan) • recall (*Cent*, E)

338.32   it; "what (MS Morgan, *Cent*) • it. 'What (E)

338.32   *was* (MS Morgan) • was (*Cent*, E)

338.32   dream?—it (MS Morgan, *Cent*) • dream? It (E)

338.35   seized (*Cent*, E) • siezed (MS Morgan)

338.37   *so* (MS Morgan) • so (*Cent*, E)

338.37   Heavens (*Cent*, E) • Great guns (MS Morgan) [TEXTUAL NOTE: *'Great guns' is too mild an expletive to prompt an editor to substitute 'Heavens', and the reading of E testifies that it stood in TS2a*]

338.38   it. (MS Morgan) • it! (*Cent*, E)

339.4–6   [¶] *April . . . Calendar.* (*Cent*, E) • [*not in*] (MS Morgan)

339.4   *1.* (MS in CU-MARK) • [*not in*] (MS Morgan); 1. (*Cent*); 1.— (E)

339.5   sixty-four (*Cent*) • [*not in*] (MS Morgan); sixty four (E)

339.7   purposes (*Cent*, E) • purposes, (MS Morgan)

339.8   high (*Cent*, E) • tremendous (MS Morgan)

339.12   pantagraph (MS Morgan, E) • pantograph (*Cent*)

339.12   pantagraph (MS Morgan, E) • pantograph (*Cent*)

339.14   sworls (MS Morgan, E) • whorls (*Cent*) [TEXTUAL NOTE: *The reading of E confirms that MS Morgan's 'sworls' was faithfully replicated in TS2 and was not revised there by SLC. A Century editor doubtless made the correction to 'whorls', a word also used by SLC in MS Morgan*]

339.17   times, (MS Morgan) • times (*Cent*, E) [TEXTUAL NOTE: *In MS Morgan after 'times,' there is a direction to turn the leaf 'OVER', under which distraction the TS2 typist may have lost the comma*]

339.22   feature, (MS Morgan, E) • feature; (*Cent*)

339.23   pantagraph (MS Morgan, E) • pantograph (*Cent*)

339.25   advanced, (MS Morgan, *Cent*) • advanced (E)

339.26   o'clock (MS Morgan) • o'clock, (*Cent*, E)

339.26   ready (MS Morgan, E) • was ready (*Cent*)

339.27   later, (MS Morgan) • later (*Cent*, E)

339.27–28 "records." [¶] Tom (*Cent*, E) • "records." Tom (MS Morgan)

339.28   records (MS Morgan) • records, (*Cent*); 'records,' (E)

339.30   case (*Cent*, E) • case, (MS Morgan)

340.5   lick. (MS Morgan) • lick! (*Cent*, E)

340.5   continued—"I (*Cent*, E) • continued— [¶] "I (MS Morgan)

340.6   testimony— (*Cent*, E) • testimony,— (MS Morgan)

340.6   better." (MS Morgan, E) • better. (*Cent*)

340.6   compelled (*Cent*, E) • roused immediate (MS Morgan)

340.6   and evoked (*Cent*, E) • and also evoked (MS Morgan)

340.7   detectible (MS Morgan, *Cent*) • detectable (E)

340.10   since, (*Cent*, E) • since (MS Morgan)

340.11   words. (*Cent*, E) • words." (MS Morgan)

340.12   court (MS Morgan, E) • Court (*Cent*)

340.13   say (*Cent*, E) • say, (MS Morgan)

340.14–16   *that the person whose hand left the blood-stained finger-prints upon the* *handle of the Indian knife is the person who committed the murder.* (MS Morgan) • that the person . . . murder. (*Cent*, E)

340.15   *finger-prints* (MTP) • *finger- | prints* (MS Morgan); finger- | prints (*Cent*); finger-prints (E)

340.17   added, (MS Morgan, E) • added (*Cent*)

340.18   "We grant that claim." (MS Morgan) • *"We grant that claim."* (*Cent*, E)

340.19   admission (*Cent*, E) • admission as this (MS Morgan)

340.21   judge (*Cent*) • Judge (MS Morgan, E)

340.24   said. (*Cent*, E) • said. The two old aunties seemed smitten with a col- lapse. (MS Morgan)

340.30   chain (*Cent*, E) • chain, (MS Morgan)

340.38   brothers (*Cent*, E) • [*not in*] (MS Morgan)

341.1   one of them (*Cent*, E) • they (MS Morgan)

341.1   Judge (*Cent*, E) • the late Judge (MS Morgan)

341.2   his (*Cent*, E) • their (MS Morgan)

341.3   secretly (*Cent*, E) • by night and take their enemy by surprise (MS Morgan)

341.4   Count Luigi (*Cent*, E) • themselves (MS Morgan)

341.4   his adversary (*Cent*, E) • him (MS Morgan)

341.13   not slander (MS Morgan, *Cent*) • slander not (E)

341.18   details (MS Morgan, *Cent*) • details, (E)

341.20   knife, (*Cent*, E) • knife (MS Morgan)

341.25   *secretly* (MS Morgan) • secretly (*Cent*, E)

341.27   not (MS Morgan) • *not* (*Cent*, E)

341.28   himself." (MS Morgan, E) • himself. (*Cent*)

341.29   "In (MS Morgan, E) • In (*Cent*)

341.31   pawn shop." (MS Morgan) • pawn-shop. (*Cent*); pawn-shop.' (E)

341.32   "I (MS Morgan, E) • I (*Cent*)

341.33   was (MS Morgan) • *was* (*Cent*, E)

341.34   *before* (MS Morgan) • before (*Cent*, E)

341.34   it." (MS Morgan, E) • it. (*Cent*)

341.35   court room (MS Morgan) • court-room (*Cent*, E)

341.36   "If (MS Morgan, E) • If (*Cent*)

342.1   [Another (MS Morgan) • Another (*Cent*); (Another (E)

342.3   "It (*Cent*) • 'It (MS Morgan, E)

342.4   hit."] (MTP) • hit.'] (MS Morgan); hit!" (*Cent*); hit!') (E)

342.7   table, (*Cent*, E) • table (MS Morgan)

342.10   course; (MS Morgan, E) • course;— (*Cent*)

342.11   seized (*Cent*, E) • siezed (MS Morgan)

342.16   mementoes (MS Morgan, E) • mementos (*Cent*)

342.18   faces, (*Cent*, E) • faces (MS Morgan)

342.20   records (MS Morgan, *Cent*) • 'records' (E)

342.25   physical (*Cent*, E) • [*not in*] (MS Morgan)

342.28   physiological (*Cent*, E) • [*not in*] (MS Morgan)

342.33   exist (*Cent*, E) • exist, (MS Morgan)

342.33   *this* (MS Morgan) • this (*Cent*, E)

342.34   globe." (MS Morgan) • globe! (*Cent*); globe!' (E)

342.38   fingers— (MS Morgan, E) • fingers,— (*Cent*)

342.38   eyesight— (MS Morgan, E) • eyesight,— (*Cent*)

343.1   dainty, (MS Morgan) • dainty (*Cent*, E) [TEXTUAL NOTE: *The comma is near an insertion caret and was overlooked by the TS2 typist*]

343.4   fingers." (MS Morgan) • fingers. (*Cent*); fingers.' (E)

343.6   ejaculations of (*Cent*, E) • ejaculations of, (MS Morgan)

343.7   *that* (MS Morgan) • that (*Cent*, E)

343.7   "The (MS Morgan) • The (*Cent*); 'The (E)

343.8   left." (MS Morgan) • left. (*Cent*); left.' (E)

343.9   "Taken (MS Morgan) • Taken (*Cent*); 'Taken (E)

343.9   neighbor's." (MS Morgan) • neighbor's. (*Cent*); neighbour's.' (E)

343.10   made (*Cent*, E) • made, (MS Morgan)

343.10   judge (MS Morgan, *Cent*) • Judge (E)

343.11   "The (MS Morgan) • The (*Cent*); 'The (E)

343.14   rule." (MS Morgan) • rule. (*Cent*); rule.' (E)

343.14   Twins' (MS Morgan) • twins' (*Cent*, E)

343.15   "You (MS Morgan) • You (*Cent*, E)

343.18   autograph! *That* (MS Morgan) • autograph. That (*Cent*, E)

343.20   stopped (*Cent*, E) • stopped, (MS Morgan)

343.28   level and passionless (MS Morgan, *Cent*) • level, passionless (E)

343.32   sign (MS Morgan, E) • sign, (*Cent*)

343.33   forth (MS Morgan, E) • forth, (*Cent*)

343.37   *"Order in the court!—sit down!"* (MS Morgan) • "Order in the court!—sit down!" (*Cent*, E)

344.8   day (MS Morgan, *Cent*) • day, (E)

344.11   finger-prints (E) • finger- | prints (MS Morgan, *Cent*)

344.14   fellow creatures (MS Morgan) • fellow-creatures (*Cent*, E)

344.15–16   it." [The interest of the audience was steadily deepening, now.] (MS Morgan) • it! [The . . . deepening, now.] (*Cent*); it!' (The . . . deepening now.) (E)

344.19   back, (MS Morgan) • back (*Cent*, E)

344.20   hair, (*Cent*, E) • hair (MS Morgan)

344.21   their (MS Morgan, E) • *their* (*Cent*)

344.25   million, (MS Morgan, *Cent*) • million (E)

344.26   guesswork, (MS Morgan) • guess-work (*Cent*, E)

344.29   them,— (MS Morgan) • them— (*Cent*, E)

344.29   tree, (MS Morgan, *Cent*) • tree (E)

345 *illus*   "AM I RIGHT?" (*Cent*) • [*not in*] (MS Morgan)

346.1–3   Robinson." . . . "This . . . Blake." . . . "This . . . juryman." . . . "This . . . sheriff." . . . "I (MS Morgan, E) • [*without quotation marks*] (*Cent*)

346.1–3   [Applause.] . . . [Applause.] . . . [Applause.] . . . [Applause.] (*Cent*, E) • [*in italics*] (MS Morgan)

346.7   standing, (MS Morgan) • standing (*Cent*, E)

346.8   sheriff, (*Cent*, E) • sheriff (MS Morgan)

346.10   Now (MS Morgan, E) • Now, (*Cent*)

346.11   children— (MS Morgan, *Cent*) • children, (E)

346.11   pantagraph (MS Morgan, E) • pantograph (*Cent*)

346.12   any one (MS Morgan, *Cent*) • anyone (E)

346.13–348.13   A [*or*] A's [*eight instances*]; B [*or*] B's [*nine instances*] (MS Morgan) • [*in italics*] (*Cent*, E)

346.13   finger-marks, (MS Morgan, *Cent*) • finger-marks (E)

346.14   months." (MS Morgan, E) • months. (*Cent*)

346.14   "They (MS Morgan, E) • They (*Cent*)

346.18   down, (MS Morgan, *Cent*) • down (E)

346.21   pantagraph copies (E) • things (MS Morgan); pantograph copies (*Cent*)

346.23   window panes (MS Morgan) • window- | panes (*Cent*); window-panes (E)

346.23   same." He (MS Morgan) • same." [¶] He (*Cent*, E) [TEXTUAL NOTE: *The sentence printed in E and Cent as a separate paragraph is, in MS Morgan, an afterthought squeezed into the space after* 'same.";' *this misled the TS2 typist into beginning a new paragraph*]

346.24   magnifying glass (MS Morgan) • magnifying-glass (*Cent*, E)

346.26   judge (*Cent*) • Judge (MS Morgan, E)

346.29   one (MS Morgan) • one, (*Cent*, E)

346.30   knife handle (MTP) • knife-handle (MS Morgan, *Cent*, E)

346.33   *"We find them to be exactly identical, your honor."* (MS Morgan) • "We … honor." (*Cent*, E)

346.37   knife handle (MS Morgan) • knife-handle (*Cent*, E)

347.1   jury: (MS Morgan, *Cent*) • jury. (E)

347.3   proceeded, (MS Morgan, *Cent*) • proceeded (E)

347.5–6   came— [¶] *"They* (MS Morgan, *Cent*) • came, 'They (E)

347.6   *resemble!* (MS Morgan) • *resemble,* (*Cent*, E)

347.6   thunder-crash (*Cent*, E) • crash (MS Morgan)

347.6   followed and (*Cent*, E) • followed, (MS Morgan)

347.7   but was quickly (*Cent*, E) • and the two old ladies flung themselves with hysterical gratitude at the Twins, but were promptly (MS Morgan)

347.8   again (*Cent*, E) • along with the rest of the assemblage (MS Morgan)

347.10   house's attention was become fixed once more (*Cent*) • house was become tranquil again (MS Morgan); house's attention was becoming fixed once more (E)

347.11   Twins (MS Morgan) • twins (*Cent*, E)

347.12   innocent—I (MS Morgan, *Cent*) • innocent. I (E)

347.12   them." (MS Morgan, E) • them. (*Cent*)

347.13   "We (MS Morgan, E) • We (*Cent*)

347.14   guilty." (MS Morgan, E) • guilty. (*Cent*)

347.15   sockets—yes (MS Morgan, *Cent*) • sockets. Yes (E)

347.15   *was* (MS Morgan) • was (*Cent*, E)

347.16   "We (MS Morgan, E) • We (*Cent*)

347.17   pantagraph (MS Morgan, E) • pantograph (*Cent*)

347.18   tally?" (MS Morgan, E) • tally? (*Cent*)

347.19–20 responded— [¶] "Perfectly." (MS Morgan, *Cent*) • responded, 'Perfectly.' (E)

347.21   pantagraph (MS Morgan, E) • pantograph (*Cent*)

347.24	No—they differ widely. (MS Morgan) • *No—they differ widely!* (*Cent*); No—they differ widely. (E)
347.25	pantagraphs (MS Morgan, E) • pantographs (*Cent*)
347.28	pantagraph (MS Morgan, E) • pantograph (*Cent*)
347.28	'B, eight months.' (MS Morgan) • *B,* eight months. (*Cent*, E)
347.30	By no means. (MS Morgan) • *By no means!* (*Cent*, E)
347.31	these (MS Morgan) • those (*Cent*, E)
347.33	*changed those children in the cradle* (MS Morgan) • changed those children in the cradle (*Cent*, E)
347.34	naturally; (MS Morgan, *Cent*) • naturally. (E)
347.34–38	was astonished . . . smiled privately. (*Cent*, E) • began to fan herself violently, although the fall weather was pleasant; it certainly was not uncomfortably warm, at least. (MS Morgan)
348.3	*and the person who did it is in this house.* (MS Morgan) • and the person who did it is in this house! (*Cent*, E) [TEXTUAL NOTE: *In MS Morgan this phrase is in drama-heightening italics. If, as other evidence suggests, TS2 neglected to reproduce the underscoring of MS Morgan, then in revising, SLC will have found this phrase in roman type and recreated the missing emphasis with an exclamation point rather than an underscore*]
348.4	Roxy's pulses stood still! (*Cent*, E) • Roxy collapsed and fell over against her next neighbor, but quickly recovered herself. (MS Morgan)
348.5	rose, (MS Morgan) • rose (*Cent*, E)
348.8	kitchen, (MS Morgan) • kitchen (*Cent*, E)
348.9–10	slave"—[Sensation—confusion of angry ejaculations]—"but (MTP) • slave"—[*Sensation—confusion of angry ejaculations*]—"but (MS Morgan); slave [Sensation— confusion of angry ejaculations]—but (*Cent*); slave'— (Sensation—confusion of angry ejaculations)—'but (E)
348.11	free!" [Burst of applause, checked by the officers.] "From (MTP) • free!" [*Burst of applause, checked by the officers.*] "From (MS Morgan); free! [Burst of applause, checked by the officers.] From (*Cent*); free!' (Burst of applause, checked by the officers.) 'From (E)
348.13	pantagraph, (MS Morgan), • pantograph (*Cent*); pantagraph (E)
348.14	knife handle (MS Morgan) • knife-handle (*Cent*, E)
348.15–16	answered— [¶] *"To* (MS Morgan, *Cent*) • answered, *'To* (E)
348.17–18	said, solemnly— [¶] "The (MS Morgan, *Cent*) • said solemnly, 'The (E)
348.18	Driscoll (*Cent*, E) • Driscoll, (MS Morgan)
348.19	sits in your midst! (MS Morgan) • sits in among you. (*Cent*); sits in your midst. (E) [TEXTUAL NOTE: *The agreement of MS Morgan and E testifies to the reading of TS2a before editing. The Cent reading, besides being*

a grammatical botch, was mandated by the magazine's house style, which
disallowed 'in our midst' *and required* 'among us' *(McKnight 1923,*
408–9]

348.20   slave— (MS Morgan, E) • slave,— (*Cent*)

348.20   Driscoll— (MS Morgan, E) • Driscoll,— (*Cent*)

348.25–26 words— [¶] "There (MS Morgan, *Cent*) • words: 'There (E)

348.31   handcuffed (MS Morgan, E) • hand- | cuffed (*Cent*)

349.2–6   [¶] It is often . . . *Calendar.* (*Cent*, E) • [*not in*] (MS Morgan)

349.4   *October* 12.—The Discovery.—It (MTP) • [*not in*] (MS Morgan);
        October 12, *the Discovery.* It (*Cent*); *October* 12.—*The Discovery.*—It (E)
        [TEXTUAL NOTE: *Our text follows E, whose spelling and styling here*
        looks more like SLC's; '12' *has been italicized to conform to his typical*
        manuscript usage]

349.7   day (MS Morgan, *Cent*) • day, (E)

349.11   golden, (MS Morgan, *Cent*) • golden (E)

349.11–12 His long fight against hard luck and prejudice was ended; he (*Cent*, E) •
        He (MS Morgan)

349.12   good. (*Cent*, E) • good, this time; nothing could ever shake his founda-
        tions again. (MS Morgan)

349.14   remorseful (*Cent*, E) • remorseful and shame-faced (MS Morgan)

349.15   *this* (MS Morgan) • this (*Cent*, E)

349.15   *us* (MS Morgan) • us (*Cent*, E)

349.15   have (MS Morgan, *Cent*) • has (E)

349.16   years! (MS Morgan) • years. (*Cent*, E)

349.16   friends (*Cent*, E) • boys (MS Morgan)

349.17   isn't (*Cent*, E) • ain't (MS Morgan)

349.17   elected! [*short rule*] [¶] The (MS Morgan) • elected." [*one line space*] [¶]
        The (*Cent*); elected.' || [¶] The (E)

349.19   Twins (MS Morgan) • twins (*Cent*, E)

349.19   romance, (MS Morgan, *Cent*) • romance (E)

349.19–21 with rehabilitated reputations. But they were weary of Western adven-
        ture, and straightway retired to Europe. (*Cent*, E) • they came . . . right,
        this time. (MS Morgan [199.14–200.17])

349.27   solace. (*Cent*, E) • solace. [¶] Aunt Patsy . . . of this kind. (MS Morgan
        [200.23–30])

350.4   up, (MS Morgan, E) • up; (*Cent*)

350.8   "nigger gallery" (*Cent*, E) • "nigger gallery (MS Morgan)

350.12   per cent (MS Morgan) • per cent. (*Cent*, E)

350.14   forward, (MS Morgan, *Cent*) • forward (E)

350.14–15   through an error for which *they* were in no way to blame (*Cent*, E) • [*not in*] (MS Morgan)

350.17   rightly (*Cent*, E) • [*not in*] (MS Morgan)

350.22   Driscoll, (MS Morgan, E) • Driscoll; (*Cent*)

350.23   erroneous inventory (*Cent*, E) • dishonest inventory which had suppressed his name (MS Morgan)

350.28   river. (MS Morgan, E) • river. [*centered on new line:*] THE END. (*Cent*) [TEXTUAL NOTE: *In MS Morgan the text of the story ends on page 632;* 'THE END.' *comes on a page following the aphorism on March weather (reproduced in facsimile, p. 208). This "March weather" page must have been transcribed in TS2, but it was discarded in the July 1893 revision of the text. It is not clear that SLC reinscribed and salvaged* 'THE END.' *in TS2a; it is absent in E, which is, at this point, the most immediate descendant of TS2a, while Cent's* 'THE END' *is boilerplate text, supplied for all the magazine's serials*]

TEXTUAL APPARATUS:

THOSE EXTRAORDINARY TWINS:

A POSTSCRIPT TO PUDD'NHEAD WILSON

Witnesses and extents. This table shows which source documents have been drawn on in constructing the text of each chapter of *Those Extraordinary Twins*. Mark Twain's local revisions, additions, and excisions are recorded in the entries which follow. The source documents, which are described on pp. 617–21, include MS Berg; MS Morgan (which in some places is TS1); Apf; A; James 1743; and SLC 1890.

Text	Source documents
Title	Contract with the American Publishing Company; Apf; A
[Prefatory remarks]	Apf; A
Chapter 1	MS Morgan chapters 6–7, derived from MS Berg chapters 1–2; Apf; A
Chapter 2	MS Morgan chapter 8, derived from MS Berg chapter 3; Apf; A
Chapter 3	MS Morgan chapter 9, derived from MS Berg chapter 4; Apf; A
Chapter 4	MS Morgan chapter 10 (derived from MS Berg chapter 6) and chapter 11 ('The visitor . . . moment, now,' PW-MS 66.23–28); Apf; A
Chapter 5	MS Morgan chapter 18; Apf; A
Chapter 6	MS Morgan chapter 22; Apf; A
Chapter 7	MS Morgan chapter 24; Apf; A; and, for the prescription (148.3–19), James 1743 and SLC 1890
Chapter 8	MS Morgan chapter 25; Apf; A
Chapter 9	MS Morgan chapter 26 ('During Monday . . . Mississippi Valley.', PW-MS 155.5–16) and chapter 27; Apf; A
Chapter 10	MS Morgan chapter 29 ('Dawson's Landing . . . distinctly damnable.', PW-MS 177.2–9); chapter 27 ('The new . . . Monday fortnight.', PW-MS 167.24–29); and chapter 32 ('city government had . . . objection to that.', PW-MS 199.16–200.12); Apf; A
Final Remarks	Apf; A

353.1–2   *Those Extraordinary Twins: A Postscript to* Pudd'nhead Wilson. (MTP) • THOSE EXTRAORDINARY TWINS. [*short single rule*] (Apf, A) [TEXTUAL NOTE: *The title adopted here is taken from the publication contract of August 1894, which quotes the title of the printer's copy submitted by Clemens to the American Publishing Company as* 'Those Extraordinary Twins—a postscript to Pudd'nhead Wilson.'; *see the Note on the Texts, pp. 611–13*]

353.3–355.24   [¶] A man who . . . no explanation. (Apf, A) • [*not in*] (MS Berg, MS Morgan)

353.14   *motif* (MTP) • [*not in*] (MS Berg, MS Morgan); motif (Apf, A)

354.19   love-match (MTP) • [*not in*] (MS Berg, MS Morgan); lovematch (Apf, A) [TEXTUAL NOTE: *Spelling adjusted to SLC's typical manuscript usage*]

354.32   side-tracked (MTP) • [*not in*] (MS Berg, MS Morgan); side- | tracked (Apf, A)

354.41   17 (MTP) • [*not in*] (MS Berg, MS Morgan); XVII. (Apf, A)

357.1–2   THE SUPPRESSED FARCE | *Chapter 1* (MTP) • [*not in*] (MS Berg, MS Morgan); THE SUPPRESSED FARCE. [*short single rule*] CHAPTER I. (Apf, A)

357.3–6   [¶] The conglomerate twins . . . hearing of it: (Apf, A) • [*not in*] (MS Berg, MS Morgan)

357.3   1 (MTP) • [*not in*] (MS Berg, MS Morgan); I. (Apf, A)

357.8   Honored Madam (MS Berg, MS Morgan/TS1) • HONORED MADAM (Apf, A)

357.11   journal—'" (MS Berg, MS Morgan/TS1) • journal——'" (Apf, A)

357.14   twins—'" (MS Berg, MS Morgan/TS1) • twins——'" (Apf, A)

357.15   Twins! How sweet! (Apf, A) • [*not in*] (MS Berg, MS Morgan)

357.16   are. (MS Berg, MS Morgan/TS1) • are! (Apf, A)

357.17   birth—'" (MS Berg, MS Morgan/TS1) • birth——'" (Apf, A)

357.18   *so* (MS Berg, MS Morgan/TS1) • so (Apf, A)

357.19   that. (MS Berg, MS Morgan/TS1) • that! (Apf, A)

357.20   —"'but (MTP) • —'but (MS Berg, MS Morgan/TS1); "—'but (Apf, A)

357.22   ma. (MS Berg, MS Morgan/TS1) • ma! (Apf, A)

357.24   so; (MS Berg, Apf, A) • so: (MS Morgan/TS1)

357.25   Cappello—'" (MS Berg, MS Morgan/TS1); • Cappello——'" (Apf, A)

357.27   names! (MS Berg, MS Morgan/TS1) • names. (Apf, A)

357.29   madam (Apf, A) • Madam (MS Berg, MS Morgan/TS1)

357.29   you. We (Apf, A) • you, for we (MS Berg, MS Morgan/TS1)

358.1   ma. (MS Berg, MS Morgan/TS1) • ma! (Apf, A)

358.2   them. (MS Berg, MS Morgan/TS1) • them! (Apf, A)

358.6   Well, (MS Berg, MS Morgan/TS1) • Well (Apf, A)

358.12   different, (MS Berg, MS Morgan/TS1) • different (Apf, A)

358.13   Maybe— (MS Berg, Apf, A) • May be— (MS Morgan/TS1)

358.20   Those (MS Berg, MS Morgan/TS1) • These (Apf, A)

358.22   it (Apf, A) • them to be, yourself, ma (MS Berg, MS Morgan/TS1)

358.23–24 [¶] [And . . . toward midnight.] (Apf, A) • [*not in*] (MS Berg, MS Morgan)

358.23   so on and so on (MTP) • [*not in*] (MS Berg, MS Morgan); so-on
          and so-on (Apf, A) [TEXTUAL NOTE: *In this A-only passage* 'so-on' *is
          emended to conform to SLC's usage in MS Morgan*]

358.25   [¶] At (Apf, A) • [*no* ¶] At (MS Berg, MS Morgan/TS1)

358.27   up stairs (MS Berg, MS Morgan/TS1) • up-stairs (Apf, A)

358.27   guest room (MS Berg, MS Morgan/TS1) • guest-room (Apf, A)

358.27–29 followed a stupefying apparition—a double-headed human creature
          with four arms, one body, and a single pair of legs! (Apf, A) • entered
          a human creature that had two heads, two necks, four arms, and one
          body, with a single pair of legs attached. (MS Berg, MS Morgan/TS1)

358.31   respond, (MS Berg, MS Morgan/TS1) • respond (Apf, A)

358.33   slave wench (MS Morgan/TS1) • slave girl (MS Berg); slave- | wench
          (Apf, A)

358.34   petrified (MS Berg, MS Morgan/TS1) • pertified (Apf, A)

358.34   tea things (MS Berg, MS Morgan/TS1) • tea-things (Apf, A)

359.1   new-comer (Apf, A) • new comer (MS Berg, MS Morgan/TS1)

359.2   dignity— (MS Berg, MS Morgan/TS1) • dignity: (Apf, A)

359.3   Madam and Miss (MS Berg, MS Morgan/TS1) • madam and miss (Apf, A)

359.4   Count Luigi (Apf, A) • Luigi (MS Berg, MS Morgan)

359.4   Cappello (MS Berg, MS Morgan/TS1) • Capello (Apf, A)

359.4   (the other head bowed,) (MS Berg) • —/the other head bowed,/— (MS
          Morgan/TS1); (the other head bowed) (Apf, A) [TEXTUAL NOTE: *See
          PW-MS, Textual Apparatus, entry and textual note at 38.13*]

359.4   Count (Apf, A) • [*not in*] (MS Berg, MS Morgan)

359.5   Angelo, (MS Berg, MS Morgan/TS1) • Angelo; (Apf, A)

359.6   unavoidable; (MS Berg, Apf) • unavoidable (MS Morgan/TS1); una-
          voidable, (A)

359.8   out— (MS Berg, MS Morgan/TS1) • out: (Apf, A)

359.11	in (MS Berg, MS Morgan/TS1) • into (Apf, A)
359.12	a sup (MS Berg, MS Morgan/TS1) • sup (Apf, A)
359.16	good-night (Apf, A) • good night (MS Berg, MS Morgan/TS1)
359.17	Rowena's small brothers (Apf, A) • the boys (MS Berg, MS Morgan/TS1)
359.21	heat, (MS Berg, MS Morgan/TS1) • heat (Apf, A)
359.23	lightnings (MS Berg, MS Morgan/TS1) • lightning (Apf, A)
359.24	thunder, (MS Berg, MS Morgan/TS1) • thunder; (Apf, A)
359.26	weird (Apf, A) • wierd (MS Berg, MS Morgan/TS1)
359.26	soft spoken (MS Berg, MS Morgan/TS1) • soft-spoken (Apf, A)
359.26	manner, (MS Berg, MS Morgan/TS1) • manner (Apf, A)
359.27	its (MS Berg, Apf, A) • it's (MS Morgan/TS1)
359.27	grewsome (MS Berg, MS Morgan/TS1) • gruesome (Apf, A)
359.28	meagre (MS Berg, MS Morgan/TS1) • meager (Apf, A)
359.29	voice— (MS Berg, MS Morgan/TS1) • voice: (Apf, A)
359.30	*look* (MS Berg, MS Morgan/TS1) • look (Apf, A)
359.30	phillipene (MS Berg, Apf, A) • phillipena (MS Morgan/TS1) [TEXTUAL NOTE: *In MS Berg the final letter could be read either as 'e' or 'a'; both spellings are viable. The typist of TS1 interpreted it as* 'phillipena', *and we would expect to find this form in its descendant A; but A reads* 'phillipene', *suggesting that in TS2b SLC revised it back to its original form*]
359.32	resentfully— (MS Berg, MS Morgan/TS1) • resentfully: (Apf, A)
359.33	*I* (MS Berg, MS Morgan/TS1) • I (Apf, A)
359.35	is—" (MS Berg, MS Morgan/TS1) • is——" (Apf, A)
359.37	good-hearted (MTP) • good hearted (MS Berg, MS Morgan/TS1); good- | hearted (Apf, A)
360.1	*its* (MTP) • *it's* (MS Berg, MS Morgan/TS1, Apf, A)
360.4–5	one; the one that was west of his brother when they stood in the door (Apf, A) • one (MS Berg, MS Morgan/TS1)
360.6	trouble (Apf, A) • trouble enough (MS Berg, MS Morgan/TS1)
360.12	complexion—" (MS Berg, MS Morgan/TS1) • complexion——" (Apf, A)
360.13	say. (MS Berg, MS Morgan/TS1) • say! (Apf, A)
360.16	*this* (MS Berg, MS Morgan/TS1) • this (Apf, A)
360.16	hands!— (MS Berg) • hands— (MS Morgan/TS1, Apf, A)
360.17	and—" (MS Berg, MS Morgan/TS1) • and——" (Apf, A)
360.18	*you* (MS Berg, MS Morgan/TS1) • you (Apf, A)
360.22	dizzy (MS Morgan/TS1, Apf, A) • dizz (MS Berg)
360.24	*I* (MS Berg, MS Morgan/TS1) • I (Apf, A)

360.24	shoulder—" (MS Berg, MS Morgan/TS1) • shoulder——" (Apf, A)
360.25	now! (MS Berg, MS Morgan/TS1) • now. (Apf, A)
360.28	They (MS Berg, MS Morgan/TS1) • *They* (Apf, A)
360.34	said— (MS Berg, MS Morgan/TS1) • said: (Apf, A)
361.1	seven,— (MS Berg, MS Morgan/TS1) • seven— (Apf, A)
361.1–2	one on the left—no, it was the one to the east of the other one (Apf, A) • left-hand one (MS Berg, MS Morgan/TS1)
361.3	called, (MS Berg, MS Morgan/TS1) • called (Apf, A)
361.7	Sho' (MTP) • Sho (MS Berg, MS Morgan/TS1, Apf, A)
361.11	said— (MS Berg, MS Morgan/TS1) • said: (Apf, A)
361.14	him. (MS Berg, MS Morgan/TS1) • him: (Apf, A)
361.15	Why (MS Berg, MS Morgan/TS1) • Why, (Apf, A)
361.16	grand. (MS Berg, MS Morgan/TS1) • grand! (Apf, A)
361.17	reproachfully— (MS Berg, MS Morgan/TS1) • reproachfully: (Apf, A)
361.18	if—" (MS Berg, MS Morgan/TS1) • if——" (Apf, A)
361.19	can (MS Berg, Apf, A) • can can (MS Morgan/TS1)
361.19	*I* (MS Morgan/TS1) • I (MS Berg, Apf, A)
361.22	Twins (MS Berg) • twins (MS Morgan/TS1, Apf, A)
361.23	partnership coat (MS Berg, MS Morgan/TS1) • partnership-coat (Apf, A)
361.24	tarantula, (MS Berg, MS Morgan/TS1) • tarantula; (Apf, A)
361.31	as (MS Berg, MS Morgan/TS1) • so (Apf, A)
361.37	bitterness— (MS Berg, MS Morgan/TS1) • bitterness: (Apf, A)
362.2	indifference— (MS Berg, MS Morgan/TS1) • indifference: (Apf, A)
362.3	*I* (MS Berg, MS Morgan/TS1) • I (Apf, A)
362.5	*you* (MS Berg, MS Morgan/TS1) • you (Apf, A)
362.12	cruelly (Apf, A) • bitterly (MS Berg, MS Morgan/TS1)
362.17	night shirt (MS Berg, MS Morgan/TS1) • night-shirt (Apf, A)
362.20	"Whole Duty of Man," (Apf, A) • Testament, (MS Berg); Whole Duty of Man, (MS Morgan/TS1)
362.21	became (MS Berg, Apf, A) • become (MS Morgan/TS1)
362.23	tobacco (MS Berg, MS Morgan/TS1) • tobacco, (Apf, A)
362.24	*so* (MS Berg, MS Morgan/TS1) • so (Apf, A)
362.25	that—" (MTP) • that— (MS Berg, MS Morgan/TS1); that——" (Apf, A)
362.27	*you* (MS Berg, MS Morgan/TS1) • you (Apf, A)
362.27	learn, (MS Berg, MS Morgan/TS1) • learn (Apf, A)
362.33	smoke, (MS Berg, MS Morgan/TS1) • smoke (Apf, A)

362.34   principles (MS Berg, MS Morgan/TS1) • *principles* (Apf, A)

362.36   bosh (Apf, A) • d-bosh (MS Berg, MS Morgan/TS1) [TEXTUAL NOTE: *MS Morgan's peculiar reading may have been altered by SLC in revision*]

363.1   "From Greenland's Icy Mountains" (Apf, A) • [*not in*] (MS Berg, MS Morgan)

363.5   whisky (MS Berg) • whiskey (MS Morgan/TS1, Apf, A)

364.9   breakfast room (MS Berg, MS Morgan/TS1) • breakfast-room (Apf, A)

364.9   Twins (MS Berg) • twins (MS Morgan/TS1, Apf, A)

364.11   said— (MS Berg, MS Morgan/TS1) • said: (Apf, A)

364.14   fine, (MS Berg) • fine (MS Morgan/TS1, Apf, A)

364.14   high-bred, (MS Berg) • high- | bred, (MS Morgan/TS1); high-bred (Apf, A)

364.15   *every* (MS Berg, MS Morgan/TS1) • every (Apf, A)

364.15   village— (MS Berg, MS Morgan/TS1) • village; (Apf, A)

364.20   *I* (MS Berg, MS Morgan/TS1) • I (Apf, A)

364.20   them, (MS Berg, MS Morgan/TS1) • them (Apf, A)

364.21   pause, (MS Berg, MS Morgan/TS1) • pause (Apf, A)

364.22   singing. (MS Berg, MS Morgan/TS1) • singing! (Apf, A)

364.24   *ever* (MS Berg, MS Morgan/TS1) • ever (Apf, A)

364.24   'Greenland's Icy Mountains' (Apf, A) • Greenland's Icy Mountains (MS Berg, MS Morgan/TS1)

364.27   'Old Bob Ridley' (Apf, A) • Old Bob Ridley (MS Berg, MS Morgan/TS1)

364.29   'Bob Ridley' (Apf, A) • Bob Ridley (MS Berg, MS Morgan/TS1)

364.33   thought—" (MS Berg, MS Morgan/TS1) • thought——" (Apf, A)

364.34   *They* (MS Berg, MS Morgan/TS1) • They (Apf, A)

365.2   unusual—" (MS Berg, MS Morgan/TS1) • unusual——" (Apf, A)

365.7   But (MS Berg, MS Morgan) • But, (Apf, A)

365.7   *I* (MS Berg, MS Morgan/TS1) • I (Apf, A)

365.7   right, (MS Berg, MS Morgan/TS1) • right (Apf, A)

365.8   *is* (MS Berg, MS Morgan/TS1) • is (Apf, A)

365.17   said— (MS Morgan/TS1) • said: (Apf, A)

365.18   coming. (MS Morgan/TS1) • coming! (Apf, A)

365.20   shoutingly (MS Berg, Apf, A) • shoutingley (MS Morgan/TS1)

365.21   breakfast room (MS Berg, MS Morgan/TS1) • breakfast-room (Apf, A)

365.22   pocket knives (MS Berg, MS Morgan/TS1) • pocket-knives (Apf, A)

365.25   comradeship (MS Berg, Apf, A) • comeradeship (MS Morgan/TS1)

365.26	its (MS Berg, Apf, A) • it's (MS Morgan/TS1)
365.28	beef steak (MS Berg, MS Morgan/TS1) • beefsteak (Apf, A)
365.28	hands (Apf, A) • arms (MS Berg, MS Morgan/TS1)
365.36	turned (Apf, A) • turning (MS Berg, MS Morgan/TS1)
366.5	break (Apf, A) • break in it (MS Berg, MS Morgan/TS1)
366.6	Twins (MTP) • twins (MS Berg, MS Morgan/TS1, Apf, A)
366.11	became (Apf, A) • had become (MS Berg, MS Morgan/TS1)
366.15	watching, and guessing, (MS Berg, MS Morgan/TS1) • watching and guessing (Apf, A)
366.16	*that* (MS Berg, MS Morgan/TS1) • that (Apf, A)
366.17–18	dark-complected (MS Berg) • dark complected (MS Morgan/TS1, Apf, A)
366.18	potato (Apf, A) • potatoe (MS Berg, MS Morgan/TS1)
366.18	*it* (MS Berg, MS Morgan/TS1) • it (Apf, A)
366.19	light-complected (MS Berg) • light complected (MS Morgan/TS1, Apf, A)
366.19	sure's (MS Berg, MS Morgan/TS1) • sure as (Apf, A)
366.19	said— (MS Berg, MS Morgan/TS1) • said: (Apf, A)
366.21	herself, (MS Berg, MS Morgan/TS1) • herself (Apf, A)
366.24	shan't (MS Berg, MS Morgan/TS1) • sha'n't (Apf, A)
366.25	Oh, (MS Berg, MS Morgan/TS1) • Oh (Apf, A)
366.27	did not (MS Berg) • didn't (MS Morgan/TS1, Apf, A)
366.28	Y-es (MS Berg, MS Morgan/TS1) • Y—es (Apf, A)
366.31	mustn't (MS Berg, Apf, A) • musn't (MS Morgan/TS1)
366.31	*he* (MS Berg, MS Morgan/TS1) • he (Apf, A)
366.32	potato (Apf, A) • potatoe (MS Berg, MS Morgan/TS1)
366.33	*he* (MS Berg, MS Morgan/TS1) • he (Apf, A)
366.33	So, (MS Berg, MS Morgan/TS1) • So (Apf, A)
366.35	Twins (MTP) • twins (MS Berg, MS Morgan/TS1, Apf, A)
366.35	laughed, (MS Berg, MS Morgan/TS1) • laughed (Apf, A)
366.35	said— (MS Berg, MS Morgan/TS1) • said: (Apf, A)
367.2	of (MS Berg, MS Morgan/TS1) • [*not in*] (Apf, A)
367.3	potato (Apf, A) • potatoe (MS Berg, MS Morgan/TS1)
367.6	these (MS Berg) • the (MS Morgan/TS1, Apf, A)
367.7	overcrowded (MS Berg, MS Morgan/TS1) • over-crowded (Apf, A)
367.7	table-room (Apf, A) • table- | room (MS Berg); table room (MS Morgan/TS1)
367.8	of the passengers (Apf, A) • [*not in*] (MS Berg, MS Morgan)

367.12   see, (MS Berg, MS Morgan/TS1) • see (Apf, A)

367.15   It's (MS Berg, MS Morgan/TS1) • It is (Apf, A)

367.16   enviously (MS Berg, MS Morgan/TS1) • enviously, (Apf, A)

367.18   its (MS Berg, Apf, A) • it's (MS Morgan/TS1)

367.19   fact, *has* (Apf, A) • fact it *has* (MS Berg, MS Morgan/TS1)

367.19   its (MS Berg, Apf, A) • it's (MS Morgan/TS1)

367.21   any more (MS Berg, Apf, A) • anymore (MS Morgan/TS1)

367.24   seat, (MS Berg, MS Morgan/TS1) • seat; (Apf, A)

367.26   practical, (MS Berg, MS Morgan/TS1) • practical (Apf, A)

367.29   ought—" (MS Berg, MS Morgan/TS1) • ought——" (Apf, A)

367.30   didn't! (MS Berg, MS Morgan/TS1) • didn't, (Apf, A)

367.32   'often.'" (Apf, A) • 'often'." (MS Berg); 'often'". (MS Morgan/TS1)

368.1–2   convinced without being converted (Apf, A) • convicted without being convinced (MS Berg, MS Morgan/TS1)

368.7   eyes, (MS Berg, MS Morgan) • eyes; (Apf, A)

368.10   theatre (MS Berg, MS Morgan/TS1) • theater (Apf, A)

368.16   aggressive, (MS Berg, MS Morgan/TS1) • aggressive; (Apf, A)

368.16   much (Apf, A) • [*not in*] (MS Berg, MS Morgan)

368.18   and—" (MS Berg, MS Morgan/TS1) • and——" (Apf, A)

368.20   he (MS Berg, Apf, A) • *he* (MS Morgan/TS1)

368.22   Well, (MS Berg, MS Morgan/TS1) • Why, (Apf, A) [TEXTUAL NOTE: *Transcribing from TS1, the TS2 typist's eye may have skipped to the 'Why' that introduces Aunt Betsy's previous utterance, two lines above*]

368.22   *never* (MS Berg, MS Morgan/TS1) • never (Apf, A)

368.22   life. (MS Berg, MS Morgan/TS1) • life! (Apf, A)

368.22   you! (MS Berg, MS Morgan/TS1) • you. (Apf, A)

368.27   hand! (MS Berg, MS Morgan/TS1) • hand, (Apf, A)

368.28   Twins (MTP) • twins (MS Berg, MS Morgan/TS1, Apf, A)

368.29   her: (Apf, A) • her, and said— (MS Berg, MS Morgan/TS1)

368.32   again, (MS Berg, MS Morgan/TS1) • again (Apf, A)

368.36   though (MS Berg, MS Morgan/TS1) • though, (Apf, A)

369.1   cordially (Apf, A) • with cordial effusion (MS Berg, MS Morgan/TS1)

369.7   its (MS Berg, Apf, A) • it's (MS Morgan/TS1)

369.12–13   said— [¶] "Et (MS Berg, MS Morgan/TS1) • said: "Et (Apf, A)

369.15   *good* (MS Berg, MS Morgan/TS1) • good (Apf, A)

369.16   *food* (MS Berg, MS Morgan/TS1) • food (Apf, A)

369.16   a et (MS Morgan/TS1) • eat (MS Berg); 'a et (Apf, A)

369.18   and—" [¶] (MTP) • and saved . . . our bread. (MS Berg, MS Morgan/
          TS1 [48.20–49.10]); and——" (Apf, A)

369.19–21 [¶] "Shucks! . . . till you're asked." (Apf, A) • [*not in*] (MS Berg, MS
          Morgan)

369.22–25 [Angelo goes on . . . semi-starvation.] [¶] "That (Apf, A) • That (MS
          Berg, MS Morgan/TS1)

369.26   black bread (MS Berg, MS Morgan/TS1) • black-bread (Apf, A)

369.26   time, (MS Berg, MS Morgan/TS1) • time; (Apf, A)

369.27   affair—" (MS Berg, MS Morgan/TS1) • affair——" (Apf, A)

369.28   Mister (MS Berg, MS Morgan/TS1) • *Mister* (Apf, A)

369.36   why—" (MS Berg, MS Morgan/TS1) • why——" (Apf, A)

370.1   But (MS Berg, MS Morgan/TS1) • But, (Apf, A)

370.5–371.10 "Rowena! . . . buggy— (Apf, A) • "And you've . . . and therefore (MS
          Berg, MS Morgan/TS1 [49.26–54.21])

371.3   Twins (MTP) • [*not in*] (MS Berg, MS Morgan); twins (Apf, A)

371.8   Twins (MTP) • [*not in*] (MS Berg, MS Morgan); twins (Apf, A)

371.16   malice, (MS Berg, MS Morgan/TS1) • malice (Apf, A)

371.17   Twins (MTP) • twins (MS Berg, MS Morgan/TS1, Apf, A)

371.18   about, (MS Berg, MS Morgan/TS1) • about; (Apf, A)

371.20   farmers' (MS Berg, Apf, A) • farmer's (MS Morgan/TS1)

371.23–28 [It was . . . Angelo.] [¶] They (Apf, A) • The Judge showed . . . and more.
          They (MS Berg, MS Morgan/TS1 [55.3–57.36])

371.24   freethinker (MTP) • [*not in*] (MS Berg, MS Morgan); Freethinker
          (Apf, A)

371.30   Twins (MS Berg) • twins (MS Morgan, Apf, A)

372.2   Freethinkers' (Apf, A) • freethinkers' (MS Berg, MS Morgan/TS1)

372.4   you, (MS Berg, MS Morgan/TS1) • you (Apf, A)

372.4   added, (MS Berg) • added (MS Morgan/TS1, Apf, A)

372.15   proportions, (MS Berg, MS Morgan/TS1) • proportions (Apf, A)

372.18   point, *i.e.,* (Apf, A) • point: (MS Berg, MS Morgan/TS1)

372.20   the (MS Berg, MS Morgan/TS1) • a (Apf, A)

372.21   offence (MS Berg, Apf, A) • offense (MS Morgan/TS1)

372.34   that! (MS Berg, MS Morgan/TS1) • that. (Apf, A)

372.34   point of view (MS Berg, MS Morgan/TS1) • point (Apf, A) [TEXTUAL
          NOTE: *An error of transmission seems likeliest here*]

372.37   the (MS Berg, MS Morgan/TS1) • a (Apf, A)

373.4   beauty, and, (MS Berg, MS Morgan/TS1) • beauty; and (Apf, A)

373.5   heart, (MS Berg, Apf, A) • heart (MS Morgan/TS1)

373.5   influence (MS Berg, MS Morgan/TS1) • influences (Apf, A)

373.12   had drank (MS Berg, MS Morgan/TS1) • had drunk (Apf, A) [TEX-
          TUAL NOTE: *For this form see* PW-MS, *Textual Apparatus, entry at 59.12*]

373.13   the (MS Berg) • and (MS Morgan/TS1, Apf, A)

373.13   cobwebby (MS Berg, Apf, A) • cob-webby (MS Morgan/TS1)

373.14   dissipation, (MS Berg, MS Morgan/TS1) • dissipation (Apf, A)

373.15   and (MS Berg) • [*not in*] (MS Morgan, Apf, A)

373.17   Judge's (Apf, A) • [*not in*] (MS Berg, MS Morgan)

373.17   laudations (MS Berg, Apf, A) • landations (MS Morgan/TS1)

373.18   congruous (MS Berg, MS Morgan/TS1) • congrous (Apf, A)

373.20   dinner, (MS Berg, MS Morgan/TS1) • dinner (Apf, A)

373.21   brother. Luigi (MS Berg, MS Morgan/TS1) • brother, Luigi, (Apf, A)

373.22   energy, (MS Berg, MS Morgan/TS1) • energy; (Apf, A)

374.2   Rowena (MS Berg, Apf, A) • It is a mistake to inflate the truth. Dress
          a fact in tights, not in an ulster.—*Pudd'nhead Wilson's Calendar.* [¶]
          Rowena (MS Morgan/TS1)

374.2   Joe and Henry (MTP) • the brothers (MS Berg, MS Morgan/TS1); Joe
          and Harry (Apf, A) [TEXTUAL NOTE: *A's 'Harry' could reflect the TS2
          typist's error, or SLC's revision on the typescript; revising in August 1894,
          two years after writing MS Morgan, he may well have forgotten what
          name he had given this character*]

374.4   Twins (MTP) • twins (MS Berg, MS Morgan/TS1, Apf, A)

374.4   Betsy (MS Berg, MS Morgan/TS1) • Betsey (Apf, A)

374.11   encouragingly— (MS Berg, MS Morgan/TS1) • encouragingly: (Apf, A)

374.13   anything, (MS Berg, MS Morgan/TS1) • anything (Apf, A)

374.15   said— (MS Berg, MS Morgan/TS1) • said: (Apf, A)

374.16   yourself. You (MS Berg, MS Morgan/TS1) • yourself; you (Apf, A)

374.19   yours, (MS Berg, MS Morgan/TS1) • yours (Apf, A)

374.20   with. (MS Berg, MS Morgan/TS1) • with! (Apf, A)

374.22   But, (MS Berg, MS Morgan/TS1) • But (Apf, A)

374.23   *isn't* (MS Berg, MS Morgan/TS1) • isn't (Apf, A)

374.26   said— (MS Berg, MS Morgan/TS1) • said: (Apf, A)

374.27   Why, (MS Berg, MS Morgan/TS1) • Why (Apf, A)

374.29   brother's. (MS Berg, MS Morgan/TS1) • brother's! (Apf, A)

375.3   well— (MS Berg, MS Morgan/TS1) • well; (Apf, A)

375.4	Teetotalers (MS Berg, MS Morgan/TS1) • teetotalers (Apf, A)
375.5	Anti-Teetotalers, (MS Berg, MS Morgan/TS1) • anti-teetotalers (Apf, A)
375.8	Babtist (MS Berg, MS Morgan/TS1) • Baptist (Apf, A)
375.8	Bible class (MS Berg, MS Morgan/TS1) • Bible-class (Apf, A)
375.9	market house (MS Berg, MS Morgan/TS1) • Market-house (Apf, A)
375.9	*they* (MS Berg, MS Morgan/TS1) • they (Apf, A)
375.9	mush-up (MS Berg, MS Morgan/TS1) • mush up (Apf, A)
375.19	down stairs (MS Berg, MS Morgan/TS1) • down-stairs (Apf, A)
375.21	legs (MS Berg) • legs, (MS Morgan/TS1, Apf, A)
375.22	first, (MS Berg, MS Morgan/TS1) • first (Apf, A)
375.22	case, (MS Berg, MS Morgan/TS1) • case (Apf, A)
375.24	week. (MS Berg, MS Morgan/TS1) • week! (Apf, A)
375.28	property right (MS Berg, MS Morgan/TS1) • property-right (Apf, A)
375.29	Well, (MS Berg, MS Morgan/TS1) • Well (Apf, A)
375.29	*do* (MS Berg, MS Morgan/TS1) • do (Apf, A)
375.31	Angelo, (MS Berg, MS Morgan/TS1) • Angelo (Apf, A)
375.35	never. (MS Berg, MS Morgan/TS1) • never! (Apf, A)
375.37–38	shade and fraction (MS Berg) • shade of a fraction (MS Morgan/TS1, Apf, A)
376.4–5	said— [¶] "So (MS Berg, MS Morgan/TS1) • said: "So (Apf, A)
376.6	regulated weekly (MS Berg, MS Morgan/TS1) • regulated (Apf, A)
376.7	the hundreds (MS Berg, MS Morgan/TS1) • hundreds (Apf, A)
376.10	*me* (MS Berg, MS Morgan/TS1) • me (Apf, A)
376.10	any more (MS Berg, Apf, A) • anymore (MS Morgan/TS1)
376.11	Jericho (MS Berg, Apf, A) • Jerico (MS Morgan/TS1)
376.11	warn't (MS Berg, MS Morgan/TS1) • wa'n't (Apf, A)
376.18	solemnity— (MS Berg, MS Morgan/TS1) • solemnity:" (Apf, A)
376.20	No (MS Berg, MS Morgan/TS1) • Now (Apf, A)
376.20	you're (MS Berg) • you've (MS Morgan/TS1, Apf, A)
376.22	parson (MS Berg, MS Morgan/TS1) • Parson (Apf, A)
376.23	will (MS Berg, MS Morgan/TS1) • would (Apf, A)
376.23	Well, (MS Berg, MS Morgan/TS1) • Well (Apf, A)
376.24	*borrow* (MS Berg, MS Morgan/TS1) • borrow (Apf, A)
376.27	now-a-days (MS Berg, MS Morgan/TS1) • nowdays (Apf, A)
376.30	*all* (MS Berg, MS Morgan/TS1) • all (Apf, A)
376.32	doesn't (MS Berg, MS Morgan/TS1) • does not (Apf, A)

376.33   a Sunday (MS Morgan/TS1) • a Monday (MS Berg); Sunday (Apf, A)

376.34   *such* (MS Berg, MS Morgan/TS1) • such (Apf, A)

376.35   uprising, (MS Berg, MS Morgan/TS1) • uprising (Apf, A)

376.36   walk!'" (MS Berg, MS Morgan/TS1) • walk'?" (Apf, A)

376.37   cretur (MS Berg, MS Morgan/TS1) • cretur' (Apf, A)

377.1   God (MS Berg, MS Morgan/TS1) • Lord (Apf, A)

377.3   ladies, (MS Berg, MS Morgan/TS1) • ladies (Apf, A)

377.4   softly— (MS Berg, MS Morgan/TS1) • softly: (Apf, A)

377.5   learnt (MS Berg, MS Morgan/TS1) • learned (Apf, A)

377.8   Twins (MS Berg) • twins (MS Morgan/TS1, Apf, A)

377.9   said— (MS Berg, MS Morgan/TS1) • said: (Apf, A)

377.17   up stairs (MS Berg, MS Morgan/TS1) • up-stairs (Apf, A)

377.21   sake!—" (MS Berg, MS Morgan/TS1) • sake!" (Apf, A)

377.24   *be* (MS Berg, MS Morgan/TS1) • be (Apf, A)

377.32   *that* (MS Berg, MS Morgan/TS1) • that (Apf, A)

377.33   its (MS Berg, Apf, A) • it's (MS Morgan/TS1)

377.37–38   we are no more twins than you are (MS Berg, MS Morgan/TS1) • *we are no more twins than you are* (Apf, A)

378.1   people (MS Berg, MS Morgan/TS1) • ladies (Apf, A)

378.1–2   paralyzed, petrified, one may almost say, and (MS Berg, MS Morgan/TS1) • paralyzed—petrified, one may almost say—and (Apf, A)

378.3   said, impressively— (MS Berg, MS Morgan/TS1) • said impressively: (Apf, A)

378.4   proofs (MS Berg) • proof (MS Morgan/TS1, Apf, A)

378.5   two, (MS Berg, MS Morgan/TS1) • two (Apf, A)

378.7   added, (MS Berg, MS Morgan/TS1) • added: (Apf, A)

378.8   *anywhere* (MS Berg) • *any*where (MS Morgan/TS1); anywhere (Apf, A)

378.11   *Anybody* (MS Berg, MS Morgan/TS1) • *Any*body (Apf, A)

378.14   O (MS Berg) • Oh (MS Morgan/TS1, Apf, A)

378.14   *dear* (MS Berg, MS Morgan/TS1) • dear (Apf, A)

378.16   just (MS Berg, MS Morgan/TS1) • [*not in*] (Apf, A)

378.20–21   "*That* swindle . . . with satisfaction. (MS Berg, MS Morgan/TS1) • Luigi muttered to himself with satisfaction: "That swindle has gone through without change of cars." (Apf, A) [TEXTUAL NOTE: *This alteration in A is of the clause-juggling type which, in the Century Magazine text, has been interpreted as editorial interference. The occurrence of two such alterations (here and at 396.26) in EXT, which did not pass through the*

Century's hands, raises the question whether such changes were not after all made by the author, on TS2; but many an editor might make such syntactical alterations, and the sense that they are uncharacteristic of SLC has been allowed to prevail]

378.22 old (MS Berg) • [*not in*] (MS Morgan, Apf, A)

378.23 tongues' (MS Berg, Apf, A) • tongue's (MS Morgan)

378.27 applied, (MS Morgan) • applied; (Apf, A)

378.29 A visitor (Apf, A) • [*centered:*] Chapter 11. [¶] Whenever you find ... *Calendar.* [¶] A visitor (MS Morgan [65.1–7])

378.29 Twins (MS Morgan) • twins (Apf, A)

378.32 question— (MS Morgan) • question: (Apf, A)

379.4 First rate (MS Morgan) • First-rate (Apf, A)

379.10 Oh, (MS Morgan) • Oh (Apf, A)

379.11 was (MS Morgan) • were (Apf, A)

379.15 Well, (MS Morgan) • Well (Apf, A)

379.20 manner— (MS Morgan) • manner: (Apf, A)

379.23 to-day (MS Morgan) • to- | day (Apf, A)

379.25 could a (MS Morgan) • could 'a' (Apf, A)

379.25 breakfast, (MS Morgan) • breakfast (Apf, A)

379.35 Twins (MS Morgan) • twins (Apf, A)

380.3–381.18 to invite ... earlier chapter.] (Apf, A) • on a special errand ... against thy neighbor.—*Pudd'nhead Wilson's Calendar.* (MS Morgan [66.28–107.4])

380.3 Bible class (MTP) • [*not in*] (MS Morgan); Bible-class (Apf, A)

380.5 Bible class (MTP) • [*not in*] (MS Morgan); Bible-class (Apf, A)

381.2 Twins (MTP) • [*not in*] (MS Morgan); twins (Apf, A)

381.6 endorse (MTP) • [*not in*] (MS Morgan); indorse (Apf, A)

381.12 Bible class (MTP) • [*not in*] (MS Morgan); Bible-class (Apf, A)

381.13 11 (MTP) • [*not in*] (MS Morgan); XI. (Apf, A)

381.19 news: (MS Morgan) • news; (Apf, A)

381.19 Pudd'nhead (Apf, A) • Punk'nhead (MS Morgan)

381.22 court (MS Morgan) • court, (Apf, A)

381.26 Twins (MS Morgan) • twins (Apf, A)

381.26 defence (MS Morgan) • defense (Apf, A)

381.29 Wilson— (MS Morgan) • Wilson: (Apf, A)

382.8 client, (MS Morgan) • client (Apf, A)

382.9 extraordinary (MS Morgan) • extraodinary (Apf, A)

382.11	could (MS Morgan) • can (Apf, A)
382.14	Harkness, (MS Morgan) • Harkness (Apf, A)
382.16	amongst (MS Morgan) • among (Apf, A)
382.24	Twins (MS Morgan) • twins (Apf, A)
382.32	said, sarcastically: (Apf, A) • said: (MS Morgan)
383.3	opinion—" (MS Morgan) • opinion——" (Apf, A)
383.4	question! (MS Morgan) • question. (Apf, A)
383.9	Twins (MS Morgan) • twins (Apf, A)
383.11	gentlemen (Apf, A) • gentleman (MS Morgan)
383.13	sir" (MS Morgan) • sir," (Apf, A)
383.20	so—" (MS Morgan) • so——" (Apf, A)
383.21	theorizing, (MS Morgan) • theorizing (Apf, A)
383.25	it! (MS Morgan) • it. (Apf, A)
383.29	man." (MS Morgan) • man.' (Apf, A)
383.35	casually, (MS Morgan) • casually (Apf, A)
383.36	simply, (MS Morgan) • simply: (Apf, A)
383.37	out, (MS Morgan) • out (Apf, A)
384.2	*they* (MS Morgan) • they (Apf, A)
384.5	brother; (MS Morgan) • brother, (Apf, A)
384.8	unprotected," [titter from the audience], (MS Morgan) • unprotected" (titter from the audience), (Apf, A)
384.13	Now, (MS Morgan) • Now (Apf, A)
384.13	*might* (MS Morgan) • might (Apf, A)
384.14	one (MS Morgan) • [*not in*] (Apf, A)
384.14	*didn't* (MS Morgan) • didn't (Apf, A)
384.15	humiliating (MS Morgan) • humilating (Apf, A)
384.16	possible?" (MS Morgan) • possible?' (Apf); possible? (A)
384.17	*I* (MS Morgan) • I (Apf, A)
384.18	that—" (MS Morgan) • that——" (Apf, A)
384.22	Twins (MS Morgan) • twins (Apf, A)
384.24	plaintiff. (MS Morgan) • plaintiff? (Apf, A)
384.32	it?" (MS Morgan, A) • it?' (Apf)
384.33	saw (MS Morgan) • *saw* (Apf, A)
385.7	said! (MS Morgan) • said. (Apf, A)
385.8–9	said— [¶] "Silence! (MS Morgan) • said: "Silence! (Apf, A)
385.15	Twins (MS Morgan) • twins (Apf, A)

385.17   *A Voice.* (MS Morgan) • A Voice: (Apf, A)

385.17–18   [Laughter. Silenced by the court.] [¶] *Another Voice.* (MTP) • [*Laughter. Silenced by the court.*] [¶] *Another Voice.* (MS Morgan); (Laughter. Silenced by the court.) Another Voice: (Apf, A)

385.18–19   [Laughter. Sharply rebuked by the court.] (MTP) • [*Laughter. Sharply rebuked by the court.*] (MS Morgan); (Laughter. Sharply rebuked by the court.) (Apf, A)

385.20   Now, (MS Morgan) • Now (Apf, A)

385.22   Twins (MTP) • twins (MS Morgan, Apf, A)

385.23   ifs or ands (MS Morgan) • if's and and's (Apf, A)

385.24   Twins, (MS Morgan) • twins (Apf, A)

385.34–35   word— [¶] "Ready (MS Morgan) • word: "Ready (Apf, A)

386.1   Now, (MS Morgan) • Now (Apf, A)

386.3   look— (MS Morgan) • look: (Apf, A)

386.4   man in the world (Apf, A) • man (MS Morgan)

386.24   Now—" (MS Morgan) • Now——" (Apf, A)

386.25   But (MS Morgan, Apf) • But, (A)

386.26   jury—" (MS Morgan) • jury——" (Apf, A)

386.33   and—" (MS Morgan) • and——" (Apf, A)

386.35   *not* (MS Morgan) • not (Apf, A)

386.35   the—" (MS Morgan) • the——" (Apf, A)

386.37   law. (MS Morgan) • laws. (Apf, A)

387.1–2   in— [¶] "But (MS Morgan) • in. "But (Apf); in: "But (A)

387.2   unprecedented. (MS Morgan) • unprecedented! (Apf, A)

387.6   where (MS Morgan) • *where* (Apf, A)

387.8   said, (MS Morgan) • said (Apf, A)

387.8–9   dignity— [¶] "I (MS Morgan) • dignity: "I (Apf, A)

387.9   acquainted (MS Morgan) • aquainted (Apf, A)

387.13   they—" (MS Morgan) • they——" (Apf, A)

387.14   But (MS Morgan) • But, (Apf, A)

387.14   Europe—" (MS Morgan) • Europe——" (Apf, A)

387.16   *has* (MS Morgan) • has (Apf, A)

387.17   for (MS Morgan) • for both (Apf, A)

387.18   [Great applause.] (MTP) • [*Great* Applause.] (MS Morgan); (Great applause.) (Apf, A)

387.23   [Applause.] (MS Morgan) • (Applause.) (Apf, A)

387.28   honor, (MS Morgan, A) • honor. (Apf)

387.38   oath—" (MS Morgan) • oath——" (Apf, A)

388.3   present; (MS Morgan) • present, (Apf, A)

388.4   Mr. (MS Morgan) • Mr (Apf, A)

388.11   apparent (MS Morgan) • apparant (Apf, A)

388.11   "*Your* (MS Morgan) • '*Your* (Apf, A)

388.12   impudence." (MS Morgan) • impudence!'" (Apf, A)

388.13   Now (MS Morgan) • *Now* (Apf, A)

388.28   thirteen (Apf, A) • seventeen (MS Morgan)

388.31   as a (MS Morgan, A) • to (Apf)

388.36   No, (MS Morgan, A) • No. (Apf)

389.8   the old favorites (Apf, A) • they (MS Morgan)

389.11   Twins (MS Morgan) • twins (Apf, A)

389.12   nod (MS Morgan) • nod, (Apf, A)

389.15   young man (Apf, A) • [*not in*] (MS Morgan)

389.15   desk?—why (MS Morgan) • desk? Why (Apf, A)

389.15   declare (MS Morgan) • declare, (Apf, A)

389.15–16   Jack Bunce (Apf, A) • Jake Bunce (MS Morgan) [TEXTUAL NOTE: *A's alteration is accepted because it appears SLC decided, while revising this text in August 1894, to create a semiprivate reference to his Hartford friend Jack Bunce; see the explanatory note at 389.15–16*]

389.16   —I (MS Morgan) • I (Apf, A)

389.16   jury?" "Why (MS Morgan) • jury? Why (Apf, A)

389.17   Price, (MS Morgan) • Price (Apf, A)

389.17   Turner (MS Morgan, A) • Tumer (Apf)

389.18   a thought—" (MS Morgan) • a' thought——" (Apf, A)

389.19   point (MS Morgan) • point, (Apf, A)

389.23   issue (MS Morgan) • issue, (Apf, A)

389.28   what (MS Morgan) • whatever (Apf, A)

389.30   fact (MS Morgan) • *fact* (Apf, A)

389.30   be (MS Morgan) • *be* (Apf, A)

389.32   *do* (MS Morgan) • do (Apf, A)

389.36   Hear it?— (MS Morgan) • *Hear* it? (Apf, A)

389.37   Why (MS Morgan) • Why, (Apf, A)

389.38   to—" (MS Morgan) • to——" (Apf, A)

390.1   Come-come (MS Morgan) • Come, come (Apf, A)

390.1   and—" (MS Morgan) • and——" (Apf, A)

390.3   I've—" (MS Morgan) • I've——" (Apf, A)

390.4   down. (MS Morgan) • down! (Apf, A)

390.5   Must (MS Morgan) • *Must* (Apf, A)

390.5   when—" (MS Morgan) • when——" (Apf, A)

390.6   laughter (MS Morgan) • laughter, (Apf, A)

390.8   continued (MS Morgan, A) • contiuued (Apf)

390.11   they told (MS Morgan) • *they* told (Apf, A)

390.12   Well, (MS Morgan, Apf) • Well (A)

390.12   they *told* (MS Morgan) • *they* told (Apf, A)

390.12   there; (MS Morgan) • there. (Apf, A)

390.14   up stairs (MS Morgan) • up-stairs (Apf, A)

390.18   he—" (MS Morgan) • he——" (Apf, A)

390.19   remembers, (MS Morgan) • remembers— (Apf, A)

390.23   always—" (MS Morgan) • always——" (Apf, A)

390.24   please go *on* (MS Morgan) • *please* go on (Apf, A)

390.25   Now (MS Morgan, A) • Now, (Apf)

390.25   she, (MS Morgan) • she (Apf, A)

390.26   me (MS Morgan) • *me* (Apf, A)

390.27   that—" (MS Morgan) • that——" (Apf, A)

390.28   more (MS Morgan) • more, (Apf, A)

390.30   know— (MS Morgan) • know—— (Apf, A)

390.34   it. (MS Morgan) • it! (Apf, A)

390.34–35 [Laughter—suppressed by the court.] (MTP) • [*Laughter—suppressed by the court.*] (MS Morgan); (Laughter, *suppressed by the court.*) (Apf, A)

391.3   Twins (MS Morgan) • twins (Apf, A)

391.6   besides,— (MS Morgan) • besides— (Apf, A)

391.6   All—" (MS Morgan) • All——" (Apf, A)

391.8   might, (MS Morgan) • might; (Apf, A)

391.9   laughter (MS Morgan) • laughter, (Apf, A)

391.10   last (MS Morgan) • last, (Apf, A)

391.11   said— (MS Morgan) • said: (Apf, A)

391.13   But (MS Morgan) • But, (Apf, A)

391.14   cross-exam—" (MS Morgan) • cross-exam——" (Apf, A)

391.16   out, (MS Morgan) • out (Apf, A)

391.17   know?" (MS Morgan) • know." (Apf, A)

391.20   till—" (MS Morgan) • till——" (Apf, A)

391.23   Twins (MS Morgan) • twins (Apf, A)

391.24   defence (MS Morgan) • defense (Apf, A)

391.25   the one (MS Morgan) • one (Apf, A)

391.28   them, (MS Morgan) • them; (Apf, A)

391.29   then (MS Morgan) • then, (Apf, A)

391.35   witnesses; (MS Morgan) • witnesses: (Apf, A)

392.3   court, (MS Morgan) • court (Apf, A)

392.4   Twins (MS Morgan) • twins (Apf, A)

392.7   judge (MTP) • Judge (MS Morgan, Apf, A)

392.8   roached (MS Morgan, A) • reached (Apf)

392.10   bench (MS Morgan) • bench, (Apf, A)

392.10   sacred (MS Morgan) • [*not in*] (Apf, A)

392.15   seized (Apf, A) • siezed (MS Morgan)

392.16   circumference (MS Morgan) • circumstance (Apf, A)

392.23   *but* (MS Morgan) • but (Apf, A)

392.25   gift— (MS Morgan) • gift, (Apf, A)

392.29   need! (MS Morgan, A) • need. (Apf)

392.30   [¶] "Prisoners (Apf, A) • [*no* ¶] Prisoners (MS Morgan)

392.30   up! (MS Morgan) • up. (Apf, A)

392.32   injustice (Apf, A) • unjustness (MS Morgan)

392.34   more. (MS Morgan, Apf) • more! (A)

392.35   court (MS Morgan) • Court (Apf, A)

392.36   Twins (MS Morgan) • twins (Apf, A)

392.37   aunties (Apf, A) • Aunties (MS Morgan)

393.1   crowds (MS Morgan) • crowd (Apf, A)

393.1   tavernwards (MTP) • tavern- | wards (MS Morgan); tavern-wards (Apf, A)

393.3   depreciation, (MS Morgan, A) • depreciation,. (Apf)

393.4–5 blown from the fields of (Apf, A) • wafted from (MS Morgan)

394.2–6 [A deputation . . . timid protest.] (MTP) • [*not in*] (MS Morgan); A deputation . . . timid protest. (Apf, A)

394.4   Twins (MTP) • [*not in*] (MS Morgan); twins (Apf, A)

394.7   [¶] It was late Saturday night—nearing eleven. (Apf, A) • [*not in*] (MS Morgan)

394.11   principal's (MS Morgan, A) • primpipal's (Apf)

394.15	approvingly (MS Morgan, A) • appovingly (Apf)
394.21	Twins (MS Morgan) • twins (Apf, A)
394.23	and— (MS Morgan) • and—— (Apf, A)
394.25	Why, (MS Morgan) • Why! (Apf, A)
394.26	extraordinary (MS Morgan) • extraodinary (Apf, A)
395.1	Twins (MS Morgan) • twins (Apf, A)
395.6	effectiveness (MS Morgan, A) • effectivencss (Apf)
395.14	One——two——three——fire!—— (MS Morgan) • One—two—three—fire!— (Apf, A)
395.19	*can't* (MS Morgan) • can't (Apf, A)
395.21	you're (MS Morgan) • *you're* (Apf, A)
395.21	*you* (MS Morgan) • you (Apf, A)
395.23	Angelo (Apf, A) • Angelo, (MS Morgan)
395.26	stood, (MS Morgan) • stood (Apf, A)
395.29–31	"Two—! [¶] "Three—! [¶] "Fire!—" (MS Morgan) • "Two—!" [¶] "Three—!" [¶] "Fire—!" (Apf, A)
395.37	time, (MS Morgan) • time (Apf, A)
395.37	fired; (MS Morgan) • fired, (Apf, A)
396.1	jumped, (MS Morgan, Apf) • jumped (A)
396.2	out (MS Morgan, A) • out, (Apf)
396.7	got nothing to do with it (Apf, A) • delegated his authority to another (MS Morgan)
396.9	officially (MS Morgan, A) • officially, (Apf)
396.13	Now (MS Morgan) • Now, (Apf, A)
396.18	more; he (MS Morgan, A) • more. He (Apf)
396.26	he might fairly be considered entitled to another trial himself (MS Morgan) • he himself might fairly be considered entitled to another trial (Apf, A)
396.29	*was* (MS Morgan) • was (Apf, A)
397.2	picture, (MS Morgan) • picture (Apf, A)
397.4	higher—in (Apf, A) • higher— || —in (MS Morgan)
397.5	Boom (MS Morgan) • *Boom* (Apf, A)
397.5	distance. (MS Morgan) • distance: (Apf, A)
397.12	*that* (MS Morgan) • that (Apf, A)
397.12	before,(MS Morgan) • before! (Apf, A)
397.15	Twins (MS Morgan) • twins (Apf, A)

397.23   that, (MS Morgan) • that (Apf, A)

397.23   *finish* (MS Morgan) • finish (Apf, A)

397.27   plaster (Apf, A) • plaister (MS Morgan)

398.2   legitimate, (MS Morgan) • legitimate (Apf, A)

398.5   whatsoever (MS Morgan) • whatever (Apf, A)

398.9   it (MS Morgan) • [*not in*] (Apf, A)

398.14–16   [It was now . . . the doctor feared.] (Apf, A); [*not in*] (MS Morgan)

399.2   house, (MS Morgan, A) • house (Apf)

399.4   Twins (MS Morgan) • twins (Apf, A)

399.4   sitting room (MS Morgan) • sitting-room (Apf, A)

399.6   but (MS Morgan) • and (Apf, A)

399.8   kind-hearted (MTP) • kind- | hearted (MS Morgan); kindhearted (Apf, A)

399.14   nothing, (MS Morgan) • nothing (Apf, A)

399.20   oesophagus (MTP) • aesophagus (MS Morgan, Apf, A)

399.21   *maxillaris superioris* (MS Morgan) • maxillaris superioris (Apf, A)

399.23   arteries (MS Morgan) • arteries, (Apf, A)

399.26   bi-cuspid (MS Morgan) • bicuspid (Apf, A)

399.26–27   *populo redax referendum rotulorum* (MS Morgan) • populo redax referendum rotulorum (Apf, A)

400.2   hope;" (MS Morgan, A) • hope"; (Apf)

400.4   Po' thing (MS Morgan, A) • Po'thing (Apf)

400.5   thoo (MS Morgan) • throo (Apf, A)

400.5   dat;" (MS Morgan, A) • dat"; (Apf)

400.7   babtizing's (MS Morgan) • baptizing's (Apf, A)

400.15   *can't* (MS Morgan) • can't (Apf, A)

400.16   word (MS Morgan) • word, (Apf, A)

400.16   of! (MS Morgan, A) • of. (Apf)

400.23   im—" (MS Morgan) • im——" (Apf, A)

400.24   Joe! (MS Morgan) • Joe. (Apf, A)

400.25   doctor (MS Morgan) • Doctor (Apf, A)

400.27   prescription— (MS Morgan) • prescription; (Apf, A)

400.27   fact (MS Morgan) • fact, (Apf, A)

400.30   congested lungs (MS Morgan) • lungs (Apf, A) [TEXTUAL NOTE: *It is tempting to follow A, with its medicine that removes everything* 'from warts all the way through to lungs'*; but* 'congested' *may have been omitted by a typist or compositor*]

401.31 Missouri, (MS Morgan) • Missouri; (Apf, A)

400.34 Dr. (Apf, A) • Dʳ˙ (MS Morgan)

400.36 family, (MS Morgan, A) • family (Apf)

401.1 Take (James 1743, MS Morgan-SLC 1890) • "Take (Apf, A)

401.1 Asarabacca (James 1743) • Afarabocca (MS Morgan-SLC 1890); afarabocca (Apf, A)

401.1 Henbane (James 1743, MS Morgan-SLC 1890) • henbane (Apf, A)

401.1 Carpobalsamum (James 1743, MS Morgan-SLC 1890) • corpobalsamum (Apf, A)

401.1 Drams (James 1743, MS Morgan-SLC 1890) • drams (Apf, A)

401.2 Cloves, Opium, Myrrh, Cyperus (James 1743, MS Morgan-SLC 1890) • cloves, opium, myrrh, cyperus (Apf, A)

401.2 Drams (James 1743, MS Morgan-SLC 1890) • drams (Apf, A)

401.2 Opobalsamum (James 1743, MS Morgan-SLC 1890) • opobalsamum (Apf, A)

401.3 Indian Leaf, Cinamon, Zedoary, Ginger (James 1743, MS Morgan-SLC 1890) • Indian leaf, cinnamon, zedoary, ginger (Apf, A)

401.3 Costus (James 1743) • Coftus (MS Morgan-SLC 1890); coftus (Apf, A)

401.3–4 Coral, Cassia, Euphorbium, Gum Tragacanth, Frankincense, Styrax Calamita (James 1743, MS Morgan-SLC 1890) • coral, cassia, euphorbium, gum tragacanth, frankincense, styrax calamita (Apf, A)

401.4 Celtic Nard, (James 1743) • Celtic, Nard, (MS Morgan-SLC 1890); celtic, nard, (Apf, A)

401.4–5 Spignel, Hartwort, Mustard, Saxifrage, Dill, Anise (James 1743, MS Morgan-SLC 1890) • spignel, hartwort, mustard, saxifrage, dill, anise (Apf, A)

401.5 Dram (James 1743, MS Morgan-SLC 1890) • dram (Apf, A)

401.5–6 Xylaloes, Rheum Ponticum (James 1743, MS Morgan-SLC 1890) • xylaloes, rheum ponticum (Apf, A)

401.6 Alipta Moschata (James 1743, MS Morgan-SLC 1890) • alipta, moschata (Apf); alipta moschata (A)

401.6–7 Castor, Spikenard, Galangals, Opoponax, Anacardium, Mastich (James 1743, MS Morgan-SLC 1890) • castor, spikenard, galangals, opoponax, anacardium, mastich (Apf, A)

401.7 Brimstone (MS Morgan-SLC 1890) • crude Sulphur (James 1743); brimstone (Apf, A)

401.7–8 Peony . . . Thyme (James 1743, MS Morgan-SLC 1890) • peony, eringo, pulp of dates, red and white hermodactyls, roses, thyme (Apf, A)

401.8 Acorus (James 1743) • Acorns (MS Morgan-SLC 1890); acorns (Apf, A)

401.8–10 Penyroyal . . . Xylobalsamum (James 1743, MS Morgan-SLC 1890) • pennyroyal, gentian, the bark of the root of mandrake, germander, valerian, bishop's weed, bay-berries, long and white pepper, xylobalsamum (Apf, A)

401.10 Carnabadium, (MS Morgan-SLC 1890) • Carnabadium (that is, according to the Commentator, Ethiopian Cummin) (James 1743); carnabadium, (Apf, A)

401.10–11 Macedonian Parsley-seeds (James 1743) • Macodonian, Parsley-seeds (MS Morgan-SLC 1890); macedonian, parsley-seeds (Apf, A)

401.11 Lovage, the Seeds of Rue (MS Morgan-SLC 1890, James 1743) • lovage, the seeds of rue (Apf, A)

401.11 Sinon, (MS Morgan-SLC 1890) • Sinon (a Sort of Wild Parsley, according to the Commentator) (James 1743); sinon, (Apf, A)

401.11 Dram (James 1743, MS Morgan-SLC 1890) • dram (Apf, A)

401.11 and a half (MS Morgan-SLC 1890, Apf, A) • and half (James 1743)

401.12–15 Gold, pure Silver . . . of Ivory (James 1743, MS Morgan-SLC 1890) • gold, pure silver, pearls not perforated, the blatta byzantina, the bone of the stag's heart, of each the quantity of fourteen grains of wheat; of sapphire, emerald and jasper stones, each one dram; of hazel-nut, two drams; of pellitory of Spain, shavings of ivory (Apf, A)

401.15 Calamus Odoratus (James 1743, MS Morgan-SLC 1890) • calamus, odoratus (Apf); calamus odoratus (A)

401.15–17 each the . . . sufficient Quantity (James 1743, MS Morgan-SLC 1890) • each the quantity of twenty-nine grains of wheat; of honey or sugar a sufficient quantity (Apf, A)

401.17 Boil down and skim off. (MTP) • [not in] (James 1743, MS Morgan); Boil down and skim off." (Apf, A)

401.19 hour— (MS Morgan) • hour—— (Apf, A)

401.20 —"While (MS Morgan) • "—while (Apf); —"while (A)

401.20 Luigi— (MS Morgan, A) • Luigi. (Apf)

401.21 —"and (MS Morgan, A) • "—and (Apf)

401.21 hot (MS Morgan) • hot, (Apf, A)

401.36 with, (MS Morgan, A) • with. (Apf)

401.39 *to-day* (MS Morgan) • to-day (Apf, A)

402.3 I (MS Morgan) • [not in] (Apf, A)

402.7	baptised (MS Morgan) • baptized (Apf, A)
402.8	O (MS Morgan) • Oh (Apf, A)
402.12	eyes (MS Morgan) • eyes, (Apf, A)
402.15	martyrdom (MS Morgan) • martydom (Apf, A)
402.21	lost! (MS Morgan) • lost. (Apf, A)
402.22	O (MS Morgan) • Oh (Apf, A)
402.26	*Looy* (MS Morgan) • Looy (Apf, A)
402.28	O (MS Morgan) • Oh (Apf, A)
402.28	of protecting (MS Morgan, A) • o fprotecting (Apf)
402.34	feet—" (MS Morgan) • feet——" (Apf, A)
402.37	damnation (MS Morgan) • Damnation (Apf, A)
402.37	it. (MS Morgan) • it! (Apf, A)
403.1	*Looy* (MS Morgan) • Looy (Apf, A)
403.1	fractious (Apf, A) • cantankerous (MS Morgan)
403.3	that (MS Morgan) • *that* (Apf, A)
403.4	postponed, (MS Morgan) • postponed (Apf, A)
403.4	ago; (MS Morgan) • ago, (Apf, A)
403.6	judgment (Apf, A) • judgement (MS Morgan)
403.7	there-there (MS Morgan) • there,—there (Apf, A)
403.8	you, Looy—I won't have it. (MS Morgan) • you—I won't have it! (Apf); you,—I won't have it! (A) [TEXTUAL NOTE: *In MS Morgan, 'Looy' is an interlined insertion and would have been easy for the TS2 copyist to miss*]
403.9	But (MS Morgan) • But, (Apf, A)
403.9	Patsy—" (MS Morgan) • Patsy——" (Apf, A)
403.11	But (MS Morgan) • But, (Apf, A)
403.11	*I'm* (MS Morgan) • I'm (Apf, A)
403.12	prescri—" (MS Morgan) • prescri——" (Apf, A)
403.13	Yes (MS Morgan) • Yes, (Apf, A)
403.14	finger (Apf, A) • finger; but turning her head to give an order, the finger wandered in reach of Luigi's mouth and he bit it. "Why, you impudent thing!" and she gave him a rap; but she was flattered, nevertheless, perceiving that it was a love-bite (MS Morgan) [TEXTUAL NOTE: *The biting of Aunt Patsy's 'wandering finger' by one of the conjoined twins might well be considered improper—the more so as it is called 'a love-bite'. A's omission may therefore be classed as censorship; but, unlike the case of the Century Magazine, no real evidence exists suggesting that ExT was censored at the American Publishing Company. It is best treated therefore as self-censorship, and not reversed*]

403.16	doctor (MS Morgan) • Doctor (Apf, A)
403.20	candle-light (MS Morgan) • candlelight (Apf, A)
403.22	baptised (MTP) • baptized (MS Morgan, Apf, A)
403.22	it (MS Morgan) • me (Apf, A)
403.23	said, "Why (MS Morgan) • said: [¶] "Why (Apf, A)
403.24	all. (MS Morgan) • all! (Apf, A)
403.24	lion! (MS Morgan) • lion. (Apf, A)
403.27	applauded, (MS Morgan) • applauded (Apf, A)
403.27	as (MS Morgan) • [*not in*] (Apf, A)
404.5	conscience (MS Morgan) • conscience' (Apf, A) [TEXTUAL NOTE: *See* PW-MS, *Textual Apparatus, entry and textual note at 151.5*]
404.7	Twins (MS Morgan) • twins (Apf, A)
404.9	Sunday school (MS Morgan) • Sunday-school (Apf, A)
404.13	wound (MS Morgan, A) • would (Apf)
404.13	resolute (MS Morgan, A) • resolate (Apf)
404.15	enthusiasm (MS Morgan) • enthusism (Apf, A)
404.19	and so • and so (MS Morgan); [*not in*] (Apf, A) [TEXTUAL NOTE: *In MS Morgan, SLC's ampersand borders on a bold ink deletion and could easily have been overlooked by a copyist*]
404.26	it was the time, (MS Morgan) • it, was the time (Apf, A)
404.26	forgotten (MS Morgan) • forgotten, (Apf, A)
404.27	ever (MS Morgan) • even (Apf, A)
405.8	think (MS Morgan, A) • tnink (Apf)
405.14	the (MS Morgan) • [*not in*] (Apf, A)
405.15	Twins (MS Morgan) • twins (Apf, A)
405.19	hours, (MS Morgan) • hours (Apf, A)
405.21	Aunt (MS Morgan, A) • Annt (Apf)
405.24	No-no (MS Morgan) • No—no (Apf, A)
405.26	he—" (MS Morgan) • he——" (Apf, A)
405.28	and—" (MS Morgan) • and——" (Apf, A)
405.29	*I*—" (MS Morgan) • I——" (Apf, A)
405.30	*Will* (MS Morgan) • Will (Apf, A)
405.30	quiet, (Apf, A) • quiet (MS Morgan)
405.33	I feel (Apf, A) • I tell you I feel (MS Morgan) [TEXTUAL NOTE: *This is the first of a series of authorial-looking alterations reflected in the text of A. As there is a definite authorial revision nearby (at 406.17–18), A's*

readings are accepted, except where they are removals of profanity or blasphemy]

405.34 *can't* (MS Morgan) • can't (Apf, A)

405.38 heaven (MS Morgan) • goodness (Apf, A)

406.3 off; (MS Morgan) • off, (Apf, A)

406.6 cold (Apf, A) • thundering cold (MS Morgan)

406.13 *this* (MS Morgan) • this (Apf, A)

406.16 infernal (MS Morgan) • infamous (Apf, A)

406.16 prescri—" (MS Morgan) • prescri——" (Apf, A)

406.17–18 "There, you're sneezing . . . dear." (Apf, A) • "Why, I'll . . . and a man.— *Pudd'nhead Wilson's Calendar.* (MS Morgan [153.15–155.4])

407.2 Twins (MS Morgan) • twins (Apf, A)

407.13 and hotter (MS Morgan, Apf) • [*not in*] (A)

407.14 presently (MS Morgan, Apf) • [*not in*] (A)

407.15 in it (MS Morgan, Apf) • [*not in*] (A)

407.16 which was (MS Morgan, Apf) • [*not in*] (A)

407.16 he (MS Morgan, Apf) • but he (A)

407.20 Teetotalers' Union (MS Morgan) • Teetotaller's Union, (Apf, A)

407.20 and its (MS Morgan, Apf) • its (A)

407.23 the Twins (MTP) • Twins (MS Morgan); the twins (Apf, A)

407.25 Angelo (MS Morgan, A) • Angeio (Apf)

407.25 horse-races (MTP) • horse races (MS Morgan, Apf, A)

407.26–27 his church (MS Morgan) • the church (Apf, A)

407.28 and did (MS Morgan, Apf) • doing (A)

407.28 get back (MS Morgan, Apf) • regain (A)

407.29 which (MS Morgan, Apf) • [*not in*] (A)

408.1 and it was (MS Morgan, Apf) • [*not in*] (A)

408.2 Twins (MS Morgan) • twins (Apf, A)

408.2 extravagant and (MS Morgan, Apf) • extravagant, (A)

408.5 canvass (MS Morgan) • canvas (Apf, A)

408.5 He led his brother a fearful dance. (Apf, A) • He began his . . . block of votes. (MS Morgan [164.29–165.6])

408.6 he (Apf, A) • Luigi (MS Morgan)

408.6 best (Apf, A) • greatest (MS Morgan)

408.7 Teetotalers' (MS Morgan) • Teetotaller's (Apf, A)

408.9 whisky (MS Morgan) • whiskey (Apf, A)

408.9–10 steadied ... his mind (Apf, A) • did not affect him in the least (MS Morgan)

408.11 Teetotalers (MS Morgan) • Teetotallers (Apf, A)

408.12 pretensions (MS Morgan) • protensions (Apf, A)

408.12 extra-temperance (MS Morgan) • extra | temperance (Apf, A)

408.15 hiccups (MS Morgan) • hiccoughs (Apf, A)

408.18 a ringing (MS Morgan, Apf) • an (A)

408.19 persons (Apf, A) • rowdies (MS Morgan)

408.21 a general burst of (MS Morgan, Apf) • [not in] (A)

408.24 even (MS Morgan, Apf) • [not in] (A)

408.25 had begged for (MS Morgan, Apf) • wanted (A)

408.25 But now (MS Morgan, Apf) • Now (A)

408.26 frankly (MS Morgan, Apf) • [not in] (A)

408.29 coldly (MS Morgan, A) • oldly (Apf)

408.31–32 [There was ... a previous note.] (Apf, A) • [not in] (MS Morgan)

409.10–11 His election was conceded, but he (Apf, A) • He (MS Morgan)

409.14–15 In due course ... the (Apf, A) • The (MS Morgan)

409.15 standstill (MTP) • standstill ever since election day (MS Morgan); stand-still (Apf, A)

409.21 up and up and up (MS Morgan) • up and up (Apf, A) [TEXTUAL NOTE: *More probably an editorial curtailment or compositorial oversight than an authorial revision*]

409.21 court to court (Apf, A) • court to court till it promised to reach the high court of the hereafter (MS Morgan)

409.25 officials (MS Morgan) • officals (Apf, A)

410.3 left (MS Morgan, A) • [not in] (Apf)

410.4 Yes (MS Morgan) • Yes, (Apf, A)

410.6–7 shouted— [¶] "That's the ticket!" (MS Morgan) • shouted, "That's the ticket." (Apf, A)

410.8–9 [¶] But others said— [¶] "No (MS Morgan) • [no ¶] But others said, "No (Apf, A)

410.13–14 they hanged Luigi ... Extraordinary Twins." (Apf, A) • the town ... the river. (MS Morgan [200.13–201.22])

411.5 *Final Remarks* (MTP) • FINAL REMARKS. (Apf, A)

411.12 it. This (Apf) • [not in] (MS Morgan); it; this (A)

411.23 *Mark Twain.* (MTP) • MARK TWAIN. (Apf); MARK TWAIN. (A)

WORD DIVISION IN THIS VOLUME

The following compound and dialect words that could be rendered either solid or with a hyphen are hyphenated at the end of a line in this volume. For purposes of exact quotation, each is listed here with its correct form.

9.10–11	hearthstone	221.15–16	hearthstone
12.31–32	care-free	227.20–21	finger-marks
14.20–21	finger-marks	245.19–20	year-worn
35.15–16	year-worn	251.12–13	sidewalks
68.7–8	respect-worthy	256.17–18	second-hand
71.28–29	freethinkers	285.2–3	death-stroke
77.4–5	newsboys	305.9–10	still-hunt
77.35–36	birth-place	315.3–4	brother-monkey
107.13–14	bone-bruising	323.26–27	low-downest
130.29–30	semi-consciousness	324.19–20	low-downest
141.9–10	nutcrackers	327.28–29	stair-foot
156.20–21	still-hunt	336.32–33	finger-prints
174.19–20	low-downest	340.4–5	back-down
175.12–13	low-downest	343.13–14	finger-balls
179.32–33	stair-foot	354.23–24	broken-hearted
185.2–3	hooraw	380.6–7	freethinking
187.1–2	finger-prints	381.27–28	bone-bruising
194.12–13	finger-balls		

REFERENCES

This list defines the abbreviations used in this volume and provides full bibliographic information for works cited by author's name and date or by a short title or abbreviation. The signs used for the sources of the text, and the abbreviations used for the texts in this volume, are also defined here.

———

A. *The Tragedy of Pudd'nhead Wilson and the Comedy Those Extraordinary Twins.* Hartford: American Publishing Company, 1894. See Description of Source Documents, pp. 617–21.

Alden, William L. 1894. "The Book Hunter." *Idler* 6 (August): 213–24.

Allen, William Francis, Charles Pickard Ware, and Lucy McKim Garrison. 1867. *Slave Songs of the United States.* New York: A. Simpson and Co.

American Art Association. 1925. *The Collection of the Late William F. Gable of Altoona, Pennsylvania.* Part 8. Sale of 16 April. New York: American Art Association.

Anderson, Jeffrey E. 2005. *Conjure in African American Society.* Baton Rouge: Louisiana State University Press.

Apf. Proof copies of A, in DLC and MH-H. See Description of Source Documents, pp. 617–21.

Armstrong, Regina. 1900. "The New Leaders in American Illustration. I. The Academicians: Loeb, Sterner, Clark and Christy." *Bookman* 10 (February): 548–55.

Austin, Henry, ed. 1896. *Gallery of Players from the Illustrated American, No. 9.* New York: The Illustrated American.

AutoMT1. 2010. *Autobiography of Mark Twain, Volume 1.* Edited by Harriet Elinor Smith, Benjamin Griffin, Victor Fischer, Michael B. Frank, Sharon K. Goetz, and Leslie Diane Myrick. The Mark Twain Papers. Berkeley and Los Angeles: University of California Press. Also online at *MTPO.*

AutoMT2. 2013. *Autobiography of Mark Twain, Volume 2*. Edited by Benjamin Griffin, Harriet Elinor Smith, Victor Fischer, Michael B. Frank, Sharon K. Goetz, and Leslie Diane Myrick. The Mark Twain Papers. Berkeley and Los Angeles: University of California Press. Also online at *MTPO*.

AutoMT3. 2015. *Autobiography of Mark Twain, Volume 3*. Edited by Benjamin Griffin and Harriet Elinor Smith with Victor Fischer, Michael B. Frank, Amanda Gagel, Sharon K. Goetz, Leslie Diane Myrick, and Christopher M. Ohge. The Mark Twain Papers. Oakland: University of California Press. Also online at *MTPO*.

BAL. 1957. *Bibliography of American Literature. Compiled by Jacob Blanck. Vol. 2: George W. Cable to Timothy Dwight*. New Haven, Conn.: Yale University Press.

Barnum, Phineas T. 1855. *The Life of P. T. Barnum, Written by Himself.* New York: Redfield.

Bartlett, John Russell. 1859. *Dictionary of Americanisms. A Glossary of Words and Phrases Usually Regarded as Peculiar to the United States*. 2d ed. Boston: Little, Brown and Co.

Baylen, Joseph O. 1964. "Mark Twain, W. T. Stead and 'The Tell-Tale Hands.'" *American Quarterly* 16 (Winter): 606–12.

Beard, Dan. 1939. *Hardly a Man Is Now Alive: The Autobiography of Dan Beard*. New York: Doubleday, Doran and Co.

Bellamy, Donnie D. 1973. "Free Blacks in Antebellum Missouri, 1820–1860." *Missouri Historical Review* 67 (January): 198–226.

Berger, Sidney E.

   1976. "Editorial Intrusion in *Pudd'nhead Wilson*." In "Bibliographical Notes," *Papers of the Bibliographical Society of America* 70, no. 2: 272–76.

   1978. "Determining Printer's Copy: The English Edition of Mark Twain's *Pudd'nhead Wilson*." In "Bibliographical Notes," *Papers of the Bibliographical Society of America* 72, no. 2: 250–56.

Berkelman, Robert. 1952. "Mrs. Grundy and Richard Watson Gilder." *American Quarterly* 4 (Spring): 66–72.

Bird, John. 2013. "The Mark Twain and Robert Ingersoll Connection: Freethought, Borrowed Thought, Stolen Thought." *Mark Twain Annual* 11: 42–61.

Blathwayt, Raymond. 1891. "Mark Twain on Humor." New York *World*, 31 May, 26.

Bok, Edward W.

   1891. "Literary Letter. 'Mark Twain' to Live Abroad for Two Years." Buffalo (N.Y.) *Courier*, 17 May, 9.

   1894. "Literary." Brooklyn *Standard Union*, 19 March, 5.

Bond, Adrienne. 1981. "Disorder and the Sentimental Model: A Look at *Pudd'nhead Wilson*." *Southern Literary Journal* 13 (Spring): 59–71.

Borough of Richmond Census. 1900. *Twelfth Census of the United States. Roll T623. New York: Borough of Richmond*. Photocopy in CU-MARK.

Boyesen, Hjalmar Hjorth. 1895. "Two Humorists." *Cosmopolitan* 18 (January): 378–79.

Brack, O M, Jr. 1972. "Mark Twain in Knee Pants: The Expurgation of *Tom Sawyer Abroad*." *Proof* 2: 145–51.

Brodwin, Stanley. 1973. "Blackness and the Adamic Myth in Mark Twain's *Pudd'nhead Wilson.*" *Texas Studies in Literature and Language* 15 (Spring): 167–76.

Brooks, Van Wyck. 1920. *The Ordeal of Mark Twain.* New York: E. P. Dutton and Co.

Brown, Sterling A.

1933. "Negro Characters as Seen by White Authors." *Journal of Negro Education* 2 (April): 179–203.

1937. *The Negro in American Fiction.* Washington, D.C.: The Associates in Negro Folk Education.

Budd, Louis J.

1987. "Mark Twain's Fingerprints in *Pudd'nhead Wilson.*" *Études Anglaises* 40 (October–December): 385–97.

1992. *Mark Twain: Collected Tales, Sketches, Speeches, & Essays, 1852–1890.* The Library of America. New York: Literary Classics of the United States.

1999. *Mark Twain: The Contemporary Reviews.* Cambridge, U.K.: Cambridge University Press.

Butcher, Philip. 1965. "Mark Twain Sells Roxy Down the River." *CLA Journal* 8 (March): 225–33.

Carnegie, Andrew.

1890. "How to Win Fortune. Andrew Carnegie Says It Can Be Done as Readily as Ever." New York *Tribune,* 13 April 1890, 18.

1910. "Tributes to Mark Twain." *North American Review* 191 (June): 827–28.

Carocci, Guido. 1906. *I dintorni di Firenze.* Volume 1. Rev. ed. Florence: Galletti e Cocci.

Cather, Willa. 1970. *The World and the Parish: Willa Cather's Articles and Reviews, 1895–1902.* Edited by William M. Curtin. 2 vols. Lincoln: University of Nebraska Press.

CC (Clara Langdon Clemens, later Gabrilowitsch and Samossoud). 1931. *My Father, Mark Twain.* New York: Harper and Brothers.

Cent. Pudd'nhead Wilson: A Tale, in the *Century Magazine,* December 1893–June 1894. SLC 1893c, 1894a–f. See Description of Source Documents, pp. 617–21.

Chellis, Barbara A. 1969. "Those Extraordinary Twins: Negroes and Whites." *American Quarterly* 21 (Spring): 100–112.

City of New York. 1911. Proceedings of the Board of Aldermen of the City of New York, from January 2 to March 28, 1911. Volume 1. [New York:] Published by the authority of the Board of Aldermen.

Cohen, Philip. 1982. "Aesthetic Anomalies in *Pudd'nhead Wilson.*" *Studies in American Fiction* 10 (Spring): 55–69.

Cole, Simon A. 2007. "Twins, Twain, Galton, and Gilman: Fingerprinting, Individualization, Brotherhood, and Race in *Pudd'nhead Wilson.*" *Configurations* 15 (Fall): 227–65.

Congressional Globe. 1859–60. *The Congressional Globe: Containing the Debates and Proceedings of the First Session of the Thirty-Sixth Congress. Also, of the Special Session of the Senate.* 4 parts. Washington, D.C.: John C. Rives.

Cooper Union. 1881. *The Twenty-Second Annual Report of the Trustees of the Cooper Union for the Advancement of Science and Art.* New York: M. Lowry and Co.

Cox, James M. 1966. *Mark Twain: The Fate of Humor.* Princeton, N.J.: Princeton University Press.

Craigie, Sir William A., and James R. Hulbert. 1936–44. *A Dictionary of American English on Historical Principles.* 4 vols. Chicago: University of Chicago Press.

CSmH. Henry E. Huntington Library, Art Collections and Botanical Gardens, San Marino, Calif.

CStbK. Karpeles Manuscript Library, Santa Barbara, Calif.

CtHM. Hartford Medical Society, Hartford, Conn.

CtHMTH. Mark Twain House and Museum, Hartford, Conn.

CtHSD. Stowe-Day Memorial Library and Historical Foundation, Hartford, Conn.

CtY-BR. Yale University, Beinecke Rare Book and Manuscript Library, New Haven, Conn.

CU-MARK. University of California, Mark Twain Papers, The Bancroft Library, Berkeley.

Cummings, Sherwood.

    1957. "Mark Twain's Social Darwinism." *Huntington Library Quarterly* 20 (February): 163–75.

    1996. "The Commanding Presence of Formerly Enslaved Mary Ann Cord in Mark Twain's Work." *Mark Twain Journal* 34 (Fall): 22–27.

CY. 1979. *A Connecticut Yankee in King Arthur's Court.* Edited by Bernard L. Stein, with an introduction by Henry Nash Smith. The Works of Mark Twain. Berkeley and Los Angeles: University of California Press.

DARE. 1985–2012. *Dictionary of American Regional English.* Edited by Frederic G. Cassidy and Joan Houston Hall. 6 vols. Cambridge, Mass.: Harvard University Press.

Darwin, Charles. 1884. *The Variation of Animals and Plants under Domestication.* 2d ed. 2 vols. New York: D. Appleton and Co.

De Vinne, Theodore L.

    1890. "The Printing of 'The Century.'" *Century Magazine* 41 (November): 87–99.

    1901. *Correct Composition: A Treatise on Spelling, Abbreviations, the Compounding and Division of Words, the Proper Use of Figures and Numerals, Italic and Capital Letters, Notes, etc. With Observations on Punctuation and Proof-Reading.* New York: Century Company.

    1926. *Manual of Printing Office Practice.* Reprint, with an introductory note by Douglas C. McMurtrie. New York: Ars Typographica.

DeVoto, Bernard. 1932. *Mark Twain's America.* Boston: Houghton Mifflin Company.

Dixon, Ella Hepworth. 1895. *The Story of a Modern Woman.* Leipzig: Bernhard Tauchnitz.

DLC. United States Library of Congress, Washington, D.C.

E. *Pudd'nhead Wilson: A Tale.* London: Chatto and Windus, 1894. See Description of Source Documents, pp. 617–21.

Ellis, Edward S. 1895. *Common Errors in Writing and Speaking: What They Are and How to Avoid Them.* New York: Hinds, Noble and Eldridge.

Ellsworth, William Webster. 1919. *A Golden Age of Authors: A Publisher's Recollection.* Boston: Houghton Mifflin Company.

ET&S2. 1981. *Early Tales & Sketches, Volume 2 (1864–1865).* Edited by Edgar Marquess Branch and Robert H. Hirst, with the assistance of Harriet Elinor Smith. The Works of Mark Twain. Berkeley and Los Angeles: University of California Press.

EXT. The text of *Those Extraordinary Twins: A Postscript to Pudd'nhead Wilson,* as presented in this edition, pp. 351–411.

FamSk. 2014. *A Family Sketch, and Other Private Writings by Mark Twain; Livy Clemens; Susy Clemens.* Edited by Benjamin Griffin. Oakland: University of California Press.

Faulds, Henry. 1880. "On the Skin-Furrows of the Hand." *Nature* 22 (28 October): 605.

Feinstein, George W. 1942. "Vestigia in *Pudd'nhead Wilson.*" *Twainian* 1 (May): 1–3.

Feldman, Lew David. 1956. *With a Bow to the Manuscript Society . . . Literary Manuscripts, Presentation First Editions, Association Items, Inscribed and/or "Signed by the Author."* Sale catalog, May. Jamaica, N.Y.: House of El Dieff.

Fenner, Thomas P., ed. 1876. *Cabin and Plantation Songs: As Sung by the Hampton Students.* New York: G. P. Putnam's Sons.

Fiedler, Leslie A.
   1955a. "'As Free as Any Cretur . . .' [I]." *New Republic* 133 (15 August): 17–18.
   1955b. "'As Free as Any Cretur . . .' II." *New Republic* 133 (22 August): 16–18.

Fishkin, Shelley Fisher.
   1990. "Race and Culture at the Century's End: A Social Context for *Pudd'nhead Wilson.*" *Essays in Arts and Sciences* 19 (May): 1–27.
   1991. "False Starts, Fragments and Fumbles: Mark Twain's Unpublished Writing on Race." *Essays in Arts and Sciences* 20 (October): 17–31.

Fletcher, Beaumont, pseud. 1895. "An American Drama: 'Pudd'nhead Wilson.'" *Godey's Magazine* 131 (July): 8–14.

FM. 1972. *Mark Twain's Fables of Man.* Edited by John S. Tuckey. Text established by Kenneth M. Sanderson and Bernard L. Stein. The Mark Twain Papers. Berkeley and Los Angeles: University of California Press.

Freitag, Florian. 2015. "The Treachery of (Local) Colour: Representations of Skin in Louisiana Local Colour Stories." In Caroline Rosenthal and Dirk Vanderbeke, eds., *Probing the Skin: Cultural Representations of Our Contact Zone,* 12–39. Newcastle upon Tyne: Cambridge Scholars Publishing.

Gair, Christopher. 2005. "Whitewashed Exteriors: Mark Twain's Imitation Whites." *Journal of American Studies* 39 (August): 187–205.

Galton, Francis. 1892. *Finger Prints.* London: Macmillan and Co.

Gevinson, Alan, ed. 1997. *Within Our Gates: Ethnicity in American Feature Films, 1911–1960*. American Film Institute Catalog. Berkeley: University of California Press.

Gillman, Susan, and Forrest G. Robinson, eds. 1990. *Mark Twain's* Pudd'nhead Wilson: *Race, Conflict, and Culture*. Durham, N.C.: Duke University Press.

Goble, Corban. 1997–98. "Mark Twain's Nemesis: The Paige Compositor." *Printing History* 18: 2–16.

Goldstein, Philip. 2017. "Reading *Pudd'nhead Wilson*: Criticism and Commentary from the Gilded Age to the Modern, Online Era." *Reception* 9: 4–22.

Gooder, Richard D. 1991. "Canon to the Left of Them." *Cambridge Quarterly* 20 (no. 4): 358–69.

Green, Edward C. 1978. "A Modern Appalachian Folk Healer." *Appalachian Journal* 6 (Autumn): 2–15.

Greg, W. W. 1950–51. "The Rationale of Copy-Text." *Studies in Bibliography* 3: 19–36.

Gribben, Alan. 2022. *Mark Twain's Literary Resources: A Reconstruction of His Library and Reading. Volume Two: Author-Title Annotated Catalog and Reader's Guide*. Montgomery, Ala.: NewSouth Books.

Hall, B. H. 1856. *A Collection of College Words and Customs*. Rev. and enl. Cambridge, Mass.: John Bartlett.

Hall, Frederick J. 1947. "Fred J. Hall Tells the Story of His Connection with Charles L. Webster & Co.," *Twainian* 6 (November–December): 1–3.

Hamberlin, Larry. 2011. *Tin Pan Opera: Operatic Novelty Songs in the Ragtime Era*. New York: Oxford University Press.

Hargrave, W. L. 1853. *Old Bob Ridley. Sung by Kunkel's Nightingale Opera Troupe*. New York: Firth, Pond and Co.

Harper, J. Henry. 1912. *The House of Harper: A Century of Publishing in Franklin Square*. New York: Harper and Brothers.

Hatton, Joseph. 1894. "Cigarette Papers." Newcastle (England) *Chronicle*, 8 December, 4.

HDAS. 1994–97. *Random House Historical Dictionary of American Slang*. 2 vols. New York: Random House.

HF 2003. 2003. *Adventures of Huckleberry Finn*. Edited by Victor Fischer and Lin Salamo, with the late Walter Blair. The Works of Mark Twain. Berkeley and Los Angeles: University of California Press. Also online at *MTPO*.

HHR. 1969. *Mark Twain's Correspondence with Henry Huttleston Rogers, 1893–1909*. Edited by Lewis Leary. The Mark Twain Papers. Berkeley and Los Angeles: University of California Press.

Higginson, Thomas Wentworth. 1870. *Army Life in a Black Regiment*. Boston: Fields, Osgood and Co.

Hopkins, Frank E. 1936. *The De Vinne and Marion Presses: A Chapter from the Autobiography of Frank E. Hopkins*. Meriden, Conn.: The Columbiad Club.

Houghton Library. 1953–54. Accession books, in MH-H. 1953–54, vol. 1. https://nrs.harvard.edu/urn-3:FHCL.HOUGH:32751223?n=546. Accessed 28 July 2021.

Howells, William Dean. 1910. *My Mark Twain: Reminiscences and Criticisms.* New York: Harper and Brothers.

Hutton, Laurence. 1905. *Talks in a Library with Laurence Hutton. Recorded by Isabel Moore.* New York: G. P. Putnam's Sons.

Inds. 1989. *Huck Finn and Tom Sawyer among the Indians, and Other Unfinished Stories.* Foreword and notes by Dahlia Armon and Walter Blair. The Mark Twain Library. Berkeley and Los Angeles: University of California Press. Also online at *MTPO.*

Ingersoll, Robert.

   1878. *The Gods, and Other Lectures.* Washington, D.C.: C. P. Farrell.

   1892. *Six Interviews with Robert G. Ingersoll on Six Sermons by the Rev. T. De Witt Talmage, D.D. To Which Is Added a Talmagian Catechism. Stenographically reported by I. Newton Baker.* New York: C. P. Farrell. [First published 1882.]

   1894. *About the Holy Bible. A Lecture.* New York: C. P. Farrell.

Ishihara, Tsuyoshi. 2014. "Mark Twain's Italian Villas." *Mark Twain Journal* 52 (Spring): 18–39.

James, Robert. 1743. *A Medicinal Dictionary; Including Physic, Surgery, Anatomy, Chymistry, and Botany, in All Their Branches Relative to Medicine.* Vol. 1. London: for T. Osborne, 1743.

JC. (Jean Lampton Clemens). 1891–94. European diary. MS, NElmC.

Jeffs, Osmund W. 1890. "Buried Toads," *Research* 2 (1 January): 151–52.

JLC. Jane Lampton Clemens.

John, Arthur. 1981. *The Best Years of the* Century: *Richard Watson Gilder,* Scribner's Monthly, *and the* Century Magazine, *1870–1909.* Urbana: University of Illinois Press.

Johnson, Merle.

   1910. *A Bibliography of the Works of Mark Twain, Samuel Langhorne Clemens.* New York: Harper and Brothers.

   1935. *A Bibliography of the Works of Mark Twain, Samuel Langhorne Clemens.* 2d ed., rev. and enl. New York: Harper and Brothers.

Johnson, Robert Underwood. 1923. *Remembered Yesterdays.* Boston: Little, Brown, and Co.

Jones, John Bush. 1977. "Victorian 'Readers' and Modern Editors: Attitudes and Accidentals Revisited." *Papers of the Bibliographical Society of America* 71 (First Quarter): 49–59.

Julian, John. 1957. *A Dictionary of Hymnology: Setting forth the Origin and History of Christian Hymns of All Ages and Nations.* 2 vols. New York: Dover.

Kennedy, Randall. 2022. *Nigger: The Strange Career of a Troublesome Word.* With a new introduction by the author. New York: Pantheon.

Kiely, Declan. 2016. "Paging Dr. Baldwin." http://www.themorgan.org/blog /paging-dr-baldwin. Accessed 17 November 2020.

Kinch, J. C. B. 1989. *Mark Twain's German Critical Reception, 1875–1986.* New York: Greenwood Press.

King, Grace. 1932. *Memories of a Southern Woman of Letters.* New York: Macmillan.

Kirkham, Samuel. 1835. *English Grammar in Familiar Lectures, Accompanied by a Compendium; Embracing a New Systematick Order of Parsing, a New System of Punctuation, Exercises in False Syntax, and a System of Philosophical Grammar in Notes; To Which Are Added an Appendix, and a Key to the Exercises: Designed for the Use of Schools and Private Learners.* 105th ed. Baltimore, Md.: John Plaskitt.

Kruse, Horst H. 1981. *Mark Twain and* Life on the Mississippi. Amherst: University of Massachusetts Press.

KyLoU. University of Louisville, Louisville, Ky.

L1. 1988. *Mark Twain's Letters, Volume 1: 1853–1866.* Edited by Edgar Marquess Branch, Michael B. Frank, and Kenneth M. Sanderson. The Mark Twain Papers. Berkeley and Los Angeles: University of California Press. Also online at *MTPO.*

L3. 1992. *Mark Twain's Letters, Volume 3: 1869.* Edited by Victor Fischer, Michael B. Frank, and Dahlia Armon. The Mark Twain Papers. Berkeley and Los Angeles: University of California Press. Also online at *MTPO.*

L6. 2002. *Mark Twain's Letters, Volume 6: 1874–1875.* Edited by Michael B. Frank and Harriet Elinor Smith. The Mark Twain Papers. Berkeley and Los Angeles: University of California Press. Also online at *MTPO.*

LaBrUHM. Louisiana State University, Hill Memorial Library, Special Collections, Baton Rouge, La.

Lawrence, Robert Means. 1898. *The Magic of the Horse-Shoe, with Other Folk-Lore Notes.* Boston: Houghton, Mifflin and Co.

Leavis, F. R. 1956. "Mark Twain's Neglected Classic: The Moral Astringency of 'Pudd'nhead Wilson.'" *Commentary* 21 (February): 128–36.

Legros, Lucien Alphonse, and John Cameron Grant. 1916. *Typographical Printing-Surfaces: The Technology and Mechanism of Their Production.* London: Longmans, Green and Co.

Letters 1876–1880. 2007. *Mark Twain's Letters, 1876–1880.* Edited by Victor Fischer, Michael B. Frank, and Harriet Elinor Smith, with Sharon K. Goetz, Benjamin Griffin, and Leslie Myrick. *Mark Twain Project Online.* Berkeley and Los Angeles: University of California Press.

Lewis, Henry. 1857. *Das Illustrirte Mississippithal, dargestellt in 80 nach der Natur aufgenommenen Ansichten vom Wasserfalle zu St. Anthony an bis zum Golf von Mexico.* Düsseldorf: Arnz und Comp., 1857.

LLMT. 1949. *The Love Letters of Mark Twain.* Edited by Dixon Wecter. New York: Harper and Brothers.

Mayo, Frank.
  1895a. "Mark Twain's Masterpiece Pudd'nhead Wilson." Typed play-script in NNMus.
  1895b. "'Pudd'nhead Wilson.'" *Harper's Weekly Magazine* 39 (22 June): 594.

McCoy, Sharon D. 2017. "'Fiction of Law and Custom': Personhood under Jurisdictional Law and Social Codes in *Adventures of Huckleberry Finn* and *The Tragedy of Pudd'nhead Wilson.*" *Mark Twain Annual* 15: 192–221.

McKeithan, Daniel Morley. 1961. *The Morgan Manuscript of Mark Twain's Pudd'nhead Wilson.* Essays and Studies on American Language and Literature. Uppsala, Sweden: A.-B. Lundequistska Bokhandeln.

McKnight, George H. 1923. *English Words and Their Background.* New York: D. Appleton and Co.

McWilliams, Wilson Carey. 1990. "*Pudd'nhead Wilson* on Democratic Governance." In Gillman and Robinson 1990, 177–89.

MEC. Mary E. (Mollie) Clemens.

MH-H. Harvard University, Houghton Library, Cambridge, Mass.

Miller, Joaquin. 1874. *Unwritten History: Life among the Modocs.* Hartford: American Publishing Company.

Missouri Statutes. 1845. *The Revised Statutes of the State of Missouri, Revised and Digested by the Thirteenth General Assembly.* St. Louis: Chambers and Knapp.

MoHM. Mark Twain Museum, Hannibal, Mo.

Moore, G. W. 1870. *Bones: His Anecdotes and Goaks.* London: C. H. Clarke.

Morris, Linda. 2007. *Gender Play in Mark Twain: Cross-Dressing and Transgression.* Columbia: University of Missouri Press.

Morris, Peter. 2006. *A Game of Inches: The Stories behind the Innovations that Shaped Baseball. The Game on the Field.* Chicago: Ivan R. Dee.

Morrison, Toni. 1993. "Toni Morrison: The Art of Fiction CXXXIV." *Paris Review,* no. 128 (Fall): 82–125.

Moss, Robert. 1998. "Tracing Mark Twain's Intentions: The Retreat from Issues of Race in *Pudd'nhead Wilson.*" *American Literary Realism* 30 (Winter): 43–55.

MS. Manuscript.

MS Berg. The Berg Manuscript. See Description of Source Documents, pp. 617–21.

MS Morgan. The Morgan Manuscript. See Description of Source Documents, pp. 617–21.

MSM. 1969. *Mark Twain's Mysterious Stranger Manuscripts.* Edited with an introduction by William M. Gibson. Berkeley and Los Angeles: University of California Press.

MSU Libraries. 2003. "McCulloch-Williams, Martha." Michigan State University Libraries. *Feeding America.* https://d.lib.msu.edu/content/biographies?author_name=McCulloch-Williams%2C+Martha%2C+approximately+1857-#. Accessed 25 January 2022.

MTB. 1912. *Mark Twain: A Biography.* By Albert Bigelow Paine. 3 vols. New York: Harper and Brothers. Volume numbers in citations refer to this edition; page numbers are the same in all editions.

MTBus. 1946. *Mark Twain, Business Man.* Edited by Samuel Charles Webster. Boston: Little, Brown and Co.

MTHL. 1960. *Mark Twain–Howells Letters.* Edited by Henry Nash Smith and William M. Gibson, with the assistance of Frederick Anderson. 2 vols. Cambridge, Mass.: Belknap Press of Harvard University Press.

MTL. 1917. *Mark Twain's Letters.* Arranged with comment by Albert Bigelow Paine. 2 vols. New York: Harper and Brothers.

MTLP. 1967. *Mark Twain's Letters to His Publishers, 1867–1894.* Edited by Hamlin Hill. The Mark Twain Papers. Berkeley and Los Angeles: University of California Press.

MTPO. Mark Twain Project Online. Edited by the Mark Twain Project. Berkeley and Los Angeles: University of California Press. [Launched 1 November 2007.] http://www.marktwainproject.org.

N&J2. 1975. *Mark Twain's Notebooks & Journals, Volume 2 (1877–1883).* Edited by Frederick Anderson, Lin Salamo, and Bernard Stein. The Mark Twain Papers. Berkeley and Los Angeles: University of California Press.

N&J3. 1979. *Mark Twain's Notebooks & Journals, Volume 3 (1883–1891).* Edited by Robert Pack Browning, Michael B. Frank, and Lin Salamo. The Mark Twain Papers. Berkeley and Los Angeles: University of California Press.

Nathan, Hans. 1962. *Dan Emmett and the Rise of Early Negro Minstrelsy.* Norman: University of Oklahoma Press.

NCH. Hamilton and Kirkland Colleges, Clinton, N.Y.

Nelson, S. A. 1907. *The Consolidated Stock Exchange of New York: Its History, Organization, Machinery and Methods.* New York: The A. B. Benesch Company.

NIC. Cornell University, Ithaca, N.Y.

Nickerson, Matthew. 2012. "How the Fourth Became a Day of Celebration Rather than a Day of Carnage." Chicago *Tribune,* 1 July, 25.

NjP. Princeton University, Princeton, N.J.

NN. New York Public Library, New York, N.Y.

NN-BGC. New York Public Library, Albert A. and Henry W. Berg Collection, New York, N.Y.

NN-L. New York Public Library, Research Library for the Performing Arts at Lincoln Center.

NNMus. Museum of the City of New York, N.Y.

NNPM. Pierpont Morgan Library, New York, N.Y.

NPV. Vassar College, Poughkeepsie, N.Y.

Ober, K. Patrick.

    2003. *Mark Twain and Medicine: "Any Mummery Will Cure."* Columbia: University of Missouri Press.

    2011. "Mark Twain's 'Watermelon Cure.'" *Journal of Alternative and Complementary Medicine* 17 (October): 877–80.

OC. Orion Clemens.

ODaU. University of Dayton, Roesch Library, Dayton, Ohio.

Odum, Howard W., and Guy B. Johnson. 1925. *The Negro and His Songs.* Chapel Hill: University of North Carolina Press.

OED. 2000– . *Oxford English Dictionary.* Oxford: Oxford University Press. https://www.oed.com.

OLC. Olivia (Livy) Langdon Clemens.

Orth, Michael. 1969. "Pudd'nhead Wilson Reconsidered or the Octoroon in the Villa Viviani." *Mark Twain Journal* 14 (Summer): 11–15.

OSC. Olivia Susan (Susy) Clemens.

P&P. 1979. *The Prince and the Pauper*. Edited by Victor Fischer and Lin Salamo, with the assistance of Mary Jane Jones. The Works of Mark Twain. Berkeley and Los Angeles: University of California Press.

PAM. Pamela A. (Clemens) Moffett.

Parker, Hershel.

1978. "Aesthetic Implications of Authorial Excisions: Examples from Nathaniel Hawthorne, Mark Twain, and Stephen Crane." In Jane Millgate, ed. *Editing Nineteenth-Century Fiction: Papers Given at the Thirteenth Annual Conference on Editorial Problems, University of Toronto, 4–5 November 1977*, 99–119. New York: Garland.

1981. "The Lowdown on *Pudd'nhead Wilson*: Jack-Leg Novelist, Unreadable Text, Sense-Making Critics, and Basic Issues in Aesthetics." *Resources for American Literary Study* 11 (Autumn): 215–40.

1984. *Flawed Texts and Verbal Icons: Literary Authority in American Fiction*. Chicago: Northwestern University Press.

1995. "The Auteur-Author Paradox: How Critics of the Cinema and the Novel Talk about Flawed or Even 'Mutilated' Texts." *Studies in the Novel* 27 (Fall): 413–26.

Parker, Hershel, and Henry Binder. 1978. "Exigencies of Composition and Publication: *Billy Budd, Sailor* and *Pudd'nhead Wilson*." *Nineteenth-Century Fiction* 33 (June): 131–43.

Pettit, Arthur G. 1974. *Mark Twain and the South*. Lexington: University Press of Kentucky.

Pfeffer, Miki, ed. 2019. *A New Orleans Author in Mark Twain's Court: Letters from Grace King's New England Sojourns*. Baton Rouge: Louisiana State University Press.

Platz, Paul Alwyn. 1916. "Ohio Censor Scissors Snip without Rhyme or Reason." *Motion Picture News* 13 (4 March): 1304.

PW-MS. The text of *Pudd'nhead Wilson: A Tale*, as presented in this edition, pp. 1–211.

PW-REV. The text of *Pudd'nhead Wilson: A Tale*, as presented in this edition, pp. 213–350.

Radbill, Samuel X., and Gloria R. Hamilton. 1960. "Measles in Fact and Fancy." *Bulletin of the History of Medicine* 34 (September–October): 430–42.

Railton, Stephen. 2012. "Performing *Pudd'nhead Wilson*." *Mark Twain in His Times*. University of Virginia Library Electronic Text Center. https://twain.lib .virginia.edu/wilson/pwplayhp.html. Accessed 31 July 2020.

Randolph, John. 1833. "Original Letter." Letter dated 2 December 1811. *National Gazette*, 31 May, 1.

Rasmussen, R. Kent. 2007. *Critical Companion to Mark Twain: A Literary Reference to His Life and Work*. 2 vols. New York: Facts on File.

RI 1993. 1993. *Roughing It.* Edited by Harriet Elinor Smith, Edgar Marquess Branch, Lin Salamo, and Robert Pack Browning. The Works of Mark Twain. Berkeley and Los Angeles: University of California Press. This edition supersedes the one published in 1972. Also online at *MTPO.*

Ribblesdale, Lord (Thomas Lister). 1897. *The Queen's Hounds: and, Stag-Hunting Recollections.* London: Longmans, Green, and Co.

Robertson, Wyndham, and R. A. Brock. 1887. *Pocahontas, alias Matoaka, and Her Descendants.* Richmond, Va.: J. W. Randolph and English.

Rodney, Robert M., ed. 1982. *Mark Twain International: A Bibliography and Interpretation of His Worldwide Popularity.* Westport, Conn.: Greenwood Press.

Rosenbach, A. S. W.

1917. *Books, Broadsides and Autograph Letters Relating to America.* Philadelphia: The Rosenbach Company.

1927. *Books and Bidders: The Adventures of a Bibliophile.* Boston: Little, Brown, and Co.

Rowlette, Robert. 1972. "Mark Twain, Sarah Grand, and *The Heavenly Twins.*" *Mark Twain Journal* 16 (Summer): 17–18.

Royal Archaeological Institute. 1892. "List of Members." *Archaeological Journal* 49: 447–54.

Royal, Derek Parker. 2002. "The Clinician as Enslaver: *Pudd'nhead Wilson* and the Rationalization of Identity." *Texas Studies in Literature and Language* 44 (Winter): 414–32.

RuM2. Russian State Archive of Literature and Art, Moscow, Russia.

S&B. 1967. *Mark Twain's Satires & Burlesques.* Edited by Franklin R. Rogers. The Mark Twain Papers. Berkeley and Los Angeles: University of California Press.

Schleiner, Louise. 1976. "Romance Motifs in Three Novels of Mark Twain." *Comparative Literature Studies* 13 (December): 330–47.

SLC (Samuel Langhorne Clemens).

1863. "Maguire's Opera House—Ingomar." Virginia City *Territorial Enterprise* (21 November) clipping, Scrapbook 2, p. 142, CU-MARK. Reprinted, in part, as "'Ingomar' Over the Mountains. The 'Argument'" in Budd 1992, 59–61.

1867. "The Holy Land Excursion. Letter from Mark Twain." [Number Twenty-five.] Letter dated 6 September. San Francisco *Alta California,* 21 November 1867, 1. Reprinted in *TIA,* 313–19.

1869a. *The Innocents Abroad; or, The New Pilgrims' Progress.* Hartford: American Publishing Company.

1869b. "Personal Habits of the Siamese Twins." *Packard's Monthly,* n.s. 1 (August): 249–50. Reprinted in Budd 1992, 296–99.

1876. *The Adventures of Tom Sawyer.* Hartford: American Publishing Company.

1883. *Life on the Mississippi.* Boston: James R. Osgood and Co.

1890. "A Majestic Literary Fossil." *Harper's New Monthly Magazine* 80 (February 1890): 439–44.

1892a. *The American Claimant.* New York: Charles L. Webster and Co.

1892b. *Merry Tales.* New York: Charles L. Webster and Co.

1892c. ["The Cholera Epidemic in Hamburg"]. MS of 7 leaves, dated 9 September, in CU-MARK.

1893. "Pudd'nhead Wilson. A Tale by Mark Twain." *Century Magazine* 47 (December): 233–40. [Chapters 1–3.]

1894a. "Pudd'nhead Wilson. A Tale by Mark Twain." *Century Magazine* 47 (January): 329–40. [Chapters 4–8.]

1894b. "Pudd'nhead Wilson. A Tale by Mark Twain." *Century Magazine* 47 (February): 549–57. [Chapters 9–11.]

1894c. "Pudd'nhead Wilson. A Tale by Mark Twain." *Century Magazine* 47 (March): 772–81. [Chapters 12–14.]

1894d. "Pudd'nhead Wilson. A Tale by Mark Twain." *Century Magazine* 47 (April): 817–22. [Chapters 15–17.]

1894e. "Pudd'nhead Wilson. A Tale by Mark Twain." *Century Magazine* 48 (May): 17–24. [Chapters 18–19.]

1894f. "Pudd'nhead Wilson. A Tale by Mark Twain." *Century Magazine* 48 (June): 232–40. [Chapters 20–21 and Conclusion.]

1897. *Following the Equator: A Journey Around the World.* Hartford: American Publishing Company.

1899a. *Pudd'nhead Wilson and Those Extraordinary Twins.* Uniform Edition of Mark Twain's Works. New York: Harper and Brothers.

1899b. *Pudd'nhead Wilson and Those Extraordinary Twins.* The Writings of Mark Twain: Autograph Edition. Hartford: American Publishing Company.

1955. *Pudd'nhead Wilson: A Tale by Mark Twain.* With an introduction by F. R. Leavis. Evergreen Books. New York: Grove Press. [Also published London: Zodiac Press.]

1968. *Pudd'nhead Wilson and Those Extraordinary Twins, by Mark Twain. A Facsimile of the First Edition.* With an introduction by Frederick Anderson. Chandler Facsimile Editions in American Literature. San Francisco: Chandler Publishing Company.

1980. *Pudd'nhead Wilson and Those Extraordinary Twins.* Edited by Sidney E. Berger. New York: W. W. Norton and Co.

1982. *The Adventures of Tom Sawyer . . . A Facsimile of the Author's Holograph Manuscript.* Introduction by Paul Baender. 2 vols. Frederick, Md.: University Publications of America; Washington, D.C.: Georgetown University Library.

1996. *The Tragedy of Pudd'nhead Wilson and the Comedy Those Extraordinary Twins.* With a preface by Shelley Fisher Fishkin, an introduction by Sherley Anne Williams, and an afterword by David Lionel Smith. The Oxford Mark Twain. New York: Oxford University Press.

2015. *Pudd'nhead Wilson* [and] *Those Extraordinary Twins.* Introduction by Werner Sollors. John Harvard Library. Cambridge, Mass.: Belknap Press of Harvard University Press.

2016. *Pudd'nhead Wilson and Those Extraordinary Twins.* Edited by Hsuan L. Hsu. Peterborough, Canada: Broadview.

Sloane, David E. E. 1971. "Censoring for 'The Century Magazine': R. W. Gilder to John Hay on 'The Bread-Winners,' 1882–1884." *American Literary Realism, 1870–1910*, 4 (Summer): 255–67.

Smith, Henry Nash. 1962. *Mark Twain: The Development of a Writer*. Cambridge, Mass.: Belknap Press of Harvard University Press.

Sollors, Werner.

    1999. *Neither Black nor White yet Both: Thematic Explorations of Interracial Literature*. Cambridge, Mass.: Harvard University Press.

    2002. "Was Roxy Black? Race as Stereotype in Mark Twain, Edward Windsor Kemble, and Paul Laurence Dunbar." In Jonathan Brennan, ed., *Mixed Race Literature*, 70–87. Stanford, Calif.: Stanford University Press.

Sotheby Parke Bernet.

    1974. *The William E. Stockhausen Collection of English and American Literature. Part 1*. Sale of 19 and 20 November. New York: Sotheby Parke Bernet.

    1976. *Catalogue of Valuable Printed Books, Autograph Letters and Historical Documents*. Sale of 23 and 24 February. London: Sotheby Parke Bernet.

Steward, Dick. 2000. *Duels and the Roots of Violence in Missouri*. Columbia: University of Missouri Press.

Sykes, Nancy. 1895. "The New York Stage." New Orleans *Times-Democrat*, 28 April, 20.

Szladits, Lola L. 1974. *Owen D. Young, Book Collector*. N.p.: The New York Public Library, Astor, Lenox and Tilden Foundations, and Readex Books.

Tanselle, G. Thomas. 1994. "Editing without a Copy-Text." *Studies in Bibliography* 47: 1–22.

Thomas, Brook. 1989. "Tragedies of Race, Training, Birth, and Communities of Competent Pudd'nheads." *American Literary History* 1 (Winter): 754–85.

TIA. 1958. *Traveling with the Innocents Abroad: Mark Twain's Original Reports from Europe and the Holy Land*. Edited by Daniel Morley McKeithan. Norman: University of Oklahoma Press.

Ticknor, Caroline. 1922. *Glimpses of Authors*. Boston: Houghton Mifflin.

Tooker, L. Frank. 1924. *The Joys and Tribulations of an Editor*. New York: The Century Company.

TS. Typescript.

TS1. Typescript 1. Typed copy of MS Berg, incorporated into MS Morgan. See Description of Source Documents, pp. 617–21.

TS2. Typescript 2. Typed copy of MS Morgan, revised by Mark Twain as TS2a and TS2b. See Description of Source Documents, pp. 617–21.

TS2a. Typescript 2a. Pages from TS2, revised. Not extant. See Description of Source Documents, pp. 617–21.

TS2b. Typescript 2b. TS2 pages excluded from TS2a, revised as *Those Extraordinary Twins*. Not extant. See Description of Source Documents, pp. 617–21.

TS 1980. 1980. *The Adventures of Tom Sawyer; Tom Sawyer Abroad; and Tom Sawyer, Detective*. Edited by John C. Gerber, Paul Baender, and Terry Firkins. The Works of Mark Twain. Berkeley and Los Angeles: University of California Press.

Turner, Arlin. 1968. "Mark Twain and the South: An Affair of Love and Anger." *Southern Review* n.s. 4 (Spring): 493–519.

TxFTC. Texas Christian University, Fort Worth, Tex.

TxU-Hu. Harry Ransom Humanities Research Center, University of Texas, Austin.

UkLW. Wellcome Library, London.

UkReU. University of Reading Library.

U.S. Special Census. 1888–95. *U.S. Special Census on Deaf Family Marriages and Hearing Relatives.* Photocopy in CU-MARK.

Van Nosdall, G. A. 1938. List 641, October. New York: G. A. Van Nosdall.

ViU. University of Virginia, Charlottesville.

Warren, Calvin Hills.
 1886. "Hop Picking. A Vagrant Art Student's Sketches in Western New York." Trenton (N.J.) *Sunday Advertiser*, 8 August, 2.
 1890. "An Old Post Road." *Frank Leslie's Monthly Magazine* 29 (January): 36–45.
 1905. "The Rabbits' Garden, Where Chickens Grew." Boston *Herald*, 12 March, Children's Section, 3.

Way, Frederick, Jr. 1983. *Way's Packet Directory, 1848–1983.* Athens: Ohio University Press.

Wecter, Dixon. 1952. *Sam Clemens of Hannibal.* Boston: Houghton and Mifflin.

Whitney, William Dwight, and Benjamin E. Smith, eds.
 1889–91. *The Century Dictionary: An Encyclopedic Lexicon of the English Language.* 6 vols. New York: The Century Company.
 1911. *The Century Dictionary and Cyclopedia.* Rev. and enl. 12 vols. New York: The Century Company.

Wigger, Anne P.
 1957a. "The Composition of Mark Twain's *Pudd'nhead Wilson and Those Extraordinary Twins:* Chronology and Development." *Modern Philology* 55 (November): 93–102.
 1957b. "The Source of Fingerprint Material in Mark Twain's *Pudd'nhead Wilson and Those Extraordinary Twins.*" *American Literature* 28 (January): 517–20.

Wiggins, Robert A. 1951. "The Original of Mark Twain's *Those Extraordinary Twins.*" *American Literature* 23 (November): 355–57.

Williams, Martha McCullough. 1894. "In Re 'Pudd'nhead Wilson.'" *Southern Magazine* 4 (February): 99–102.

WIM. 1973. *What Is Man? and Other Philosophical Writings.* Edited by Paul Baender. The Works of Mark Twain. Berkeley and Los Angeles: University of California Press.

Wright, Catharine Morris. 1979. *Lady of the Silver Skates: The Life and Correspondence of Mary Mapes Dodge, 1830–1905.* Jamestown, R.I.: Clingstone Press.

WWD. 1968. *Which Was the Dream? and Other Symbolic Writings of the Later Years.* Edited with an introduction by John S. Tuckey. Berkeley and Los Angeles: University of California Press.

Zanger, Jules. 1966. "The 'Tragic Octoroon' in Pre-Civil War Fiction." *American Quarterly* 18 (Spring): 63–70.

Zola, Émile. 1894. *Money*. Translated by Ernest A. Vizetelly. London: Chatto and Windus.

Zupitza, Julius. 1895. Review of *Pudd'nhead Wilson: A Tale* (Tauchnitz, 1895). *Archiv für das Studium der neueren Sprachen und Litteraturen* 94: 458–59.

Founded in 1893,
UNIVERSITY OF CALIFORNIA PRESS
publishes bold, progressive books and journals
on topics in the arts, humanities, social sciences,
and natural sciences—with a focus on social
justice issues—that inspire thought and action
among readers worldwide.

The UC PRESS FOUNDATION
raises funds to uphold the press's vital role
as an independent, nonprofit publisher, and
receives philanthropic support from a wide
range of individuals and institutions—and from
committed readers like you. To learn more, visit
ucpress.edu/supportus.